# THE SURVIVORS

## HEROIC EDITION

*V. L Dreyer*

# V. L. Dreyer

THE SURVIVORS
*The Survivors Book I: Summer*
*The Survivors Book II: Autumn*
*The Survivors Book III: Winter*
*The Survivors Book IV: Spring*
*The Survivors: Heroic Edition*

# Foreword

This series would never have been finished without the loyalty and dedication of my family. Without your eternal faith in me, Sandy's adventure would have forever remained untold.

To my family and friends, for reasons beyond counting.

To all of my fans from my early days as a graphic novelist, thank you as well. Your love and endless stream of inquisitive questions gave me the strength to carry on in the darkest hours, and opened my mind to all kinds of new possibilities.

To Holly, my editor, for her incredible patience and high degree of tolerance to my idiosyncrasies.

And most of all, to Alyssa, for being my Skylar. Where would I be without you? You pick me up when I'm feeling down, smack me down when my ego gets too big, and call me out on my grammar at every turn.

Thank you.

*The Survivors* series is set in New Zealand. In order to preserve the authenticity of the setting and the heroine's voice, this novel has been written in New Zealand English.

New Zealand English (NZE) is an off-shoot of British English, but the geographical isolation of the country has given rise to a quirky sub-dialect that is neither entirely British, nor Australian.

I have attempted to make this novel as easily accessible as possible for readers around the world by providing contextual explanations for most words. However, as the language variations are subtle and frequent, it is not always possible to do this.

A more in-depth article on the language used in this book is available on my website, where you also have the facility to ask me questions.

## http://www.vldreyer.com

# THE SURVIVORS

## BOOK I: SUMMER

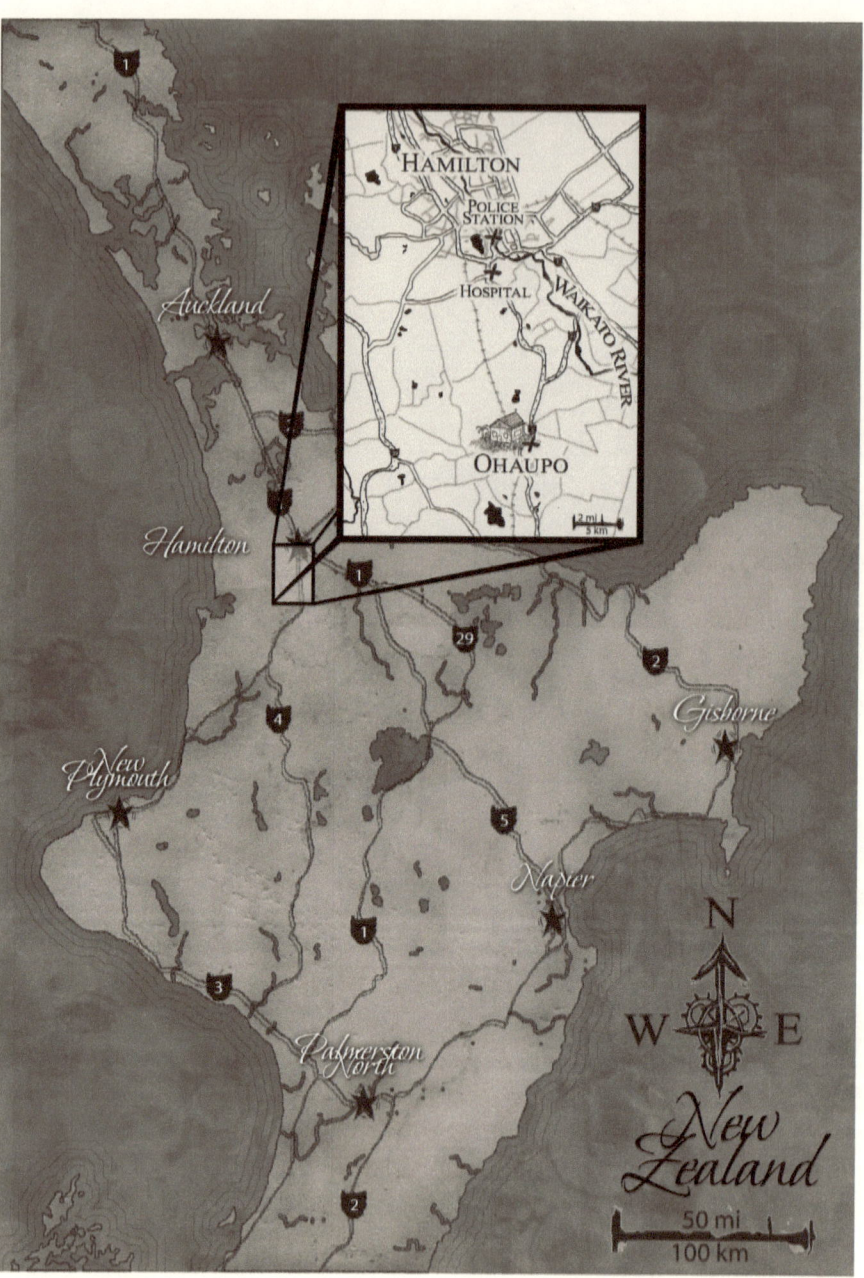

# Chapter One

It seemed like a cruel irony.

I'd survived the brutal end of civilization and watched our world fall from grace; I'd watched helplessly while all of my friends and family died one by one, or were reduced to the walking dead. I lived on and yet now, a decade later, my salvation lay behind a faded poster for a film called *Zombieland*.

Crouched between a dumpster and a stack of decaying boxes, I stared at the ruined poster, wondering at life's morbid sense of humour. I remembered that movie. It had been out for a few years at the point when the world ended, so it seemed strange to see it still hanging in the window, but places like this backwater little town did tend to be behind the times. I used to enjoy that kind of thing, back when I was a teenager and the world was still whole. The zombie fad had been so popular – there were copies of *The Walking Dead* in the window, too.

If only we'd known what was to come.

The virus that struck us down was nothing like any of those movies. There was to be no *Dawn of the Dead* for us, no *28 Days Later*. I was eternally grateful for that fact, actually; my reality was very different to the fantasies dreamed up by Hollywood, but mercifully less violent. The dangers in my life sprang from the living, not the undead.

There was one of them in the DVD store across the road from me. I could just see him past the tatty photograph of Jesse Eisenberg, shuffling back and forth between the shelves. He wandered tirelessly, trying to organise his stock with hands no longer capable of gripping.

Some of the undead were still dangerous, but most of them were slow and heart-wrenchingly pathetic, like the little old man in the store. I'd take him over a fast-moving, angry movie zombie any day, even if it did break my heart to look at him. The difference came down to which one was more likely to eat my brain. The real undead weren't interested in brains, which was fine by me. I liked my brain right where it was.

There was nothing left on the shelves now; the old man had knocked all the videos to the ground long ago, and then crushed them beneath his wandering feet. He was far gone after all these years, his flesh half-rotted and his eyes unseeing. Only instinct kept him moving in his relentless, unattainable quest for perfection.

A lot of the infected seemed to retain the basic memories of their lives, but only the things that they had repeated so often that the action ended up deeply ingrained within their subconscious. The core of their personalities seemed to linger as well, but it was just an echo of the person they'd once been. That made them unpredictable.

I had seen a great many different kinds of infected over the years, and their behaviour seemed to vary depending on the person they'd been before death. Mothers still rocked the withered husks of their dead babies. Soldiers gunned down non-existent foes until the chamber of their weapons ran dry. Most of the infected just went on about their un-lives, oblivious, like that old man in the store. Even though his conscious mind was long gone, he stayed in the place that he knew best, going through the same motions now as when he was alive.

The old man must have really loved that little store. Ten years was a very long time.

The virus had come from somewhere deep in Central Africa; a mutation of the deadly Ebola virus. They'd named the new strain the Goma ebolavirus, after the city

where the first cases were found. By the time they'd decided on a name, it had killed a hundred thousand people and infected millions more.

The media nicknamed it Ebola-X, and that version stuck. It had more of a ring to it.

In the beginning, diagnosis and research was slow. The doctors, nurses, and scientists studying the pathogen kept getting infected, no matter what they did to prevent it. Level four biohazard containment was not enough. Nothing was ever enough. It's funny how much a kid like me learned about biohazard containment in those first few years. Not so much "funny-ha-ha" as "funny-horrifying", though.

The thing that made Ebola-X so terrifying was its virulence. It spread so fast that no one could hope to contain it. It had infected half of the African continent before the rest of the world even realised that it was a threat.

It was vicious and untreatable. What it did to the human body was horrific and irreversible; like other strains of the Ebola virus, it liquefied healthy cells. Unlike its ancestors though, the thing it destroyed first was the delicate tissue of the brain. Within hours of infection, the temporal lobe began to disintegrate, taking with it speech, memory, and perception. The rest of the cerebrum followed soon after, leaving only basic motor function behind.

Eventually, the motor function went as well, but by that stage the body was usually starting to fall apart. Given enough time the virus destroyed the entire infected body, but it sometimes took years to get that far. Even a decade after the infection first hit us, there were still plenty of undead wandering aimlessly around the landscape.

Some of the victims died within hours, but others survived for many years after the infection erased their minds. It had been almost ten years since the first reported case arrived on New Zealand's shores, and nine and a half since they stopped telling us what the body count was. It was safe to say that most of the people that used to live here were dead.

I had seen a few other survivors over the years, but experience left me wary of strangers and I always gave them a wide berth. Resources were limited, and a lone female in a world without rules was easy prey. My sense of self-preservation told me to keep to myself, so I did.

For me, the worst part was that I didn't know if the infected were conscious or aware up until the end, or if they felt any pain. I had no way to ask them. It made me feel terrible to put them out of their misery but I had to do it; they were human beings, or at least they had been, and they deserved a little dignity. Somehow, killing them felt like an act of mercy.

Before the roar of the media shrank to a whisper, they told us that there was a small percentage of the population who had been born with a natural genetic abnormality which made us immune to the effects of the virus. The only thing separating me from that poor old man was one tiny twist of fate. I was still infected, but my immune system had the rare and precious ability to fight it off. I had no idea how long my immunity would last, though. The virus could mutate at any time, leaving me defenceless.

Einstein was wrong. God did play dice, and I was lucky enough to roll high this time.

The virus was aggressive and indiscriminate; it was in the water, the air, and was even carried by some of the animals. For the people who weren't as lucky as me, transmission was unavoidable. If you were near an infected and you were not immune, then you were going to die. It was just a matter of time.

Within a year of the first reported case, a billion people were gone.

There was no cure.

There was no antivirus.

There was no hope.

After so many deaths, there was no one left alive to study the virus and look for a cure, at least not as far as I was aware. Perhaps there was a bunker somewhere full of scientists working diligently to try and find a solution that would preserve humanity from extinction, but if there was, they hadn't invited me. No great surprise there; I was eighteen years old when the plague devastated my world, just a useless kid who hadn't even decided what she was going to do with her life. Now, I no longer had the choice. I was a survivor, and that was all I'd ever be.

The infected man in the store, he had been a person once, too. A good man, probably. An innocent man. In my imagination, it was his life's dream to retire to this little town and spend his twilight years running that tiny store.

I wondered if his wife was dead, too. His children. His grandchildren. Thinking about it made what I had to do so much harder.

I couldn't just leave him like this, though. It wouldn't be right. There was no way for me to know if he was in pain, but it sure as hell looked like he was suffering. No one would want to spend the rest of their existence shuffling around mindlessly until their legs finally fell off. As one of the lucky few that had won the genetic lottery, I felt like I had an obligation to free him from his torment and let him move on to whatever came next.

With silent care, I slipped my backpack from my shoulders and set it on the ground at my feet, then paused to check if anyone had seen the motion. Nothing else moved except me. Me, and my decomposing friend across the street.

I rose to my feet and crossed the cracked roadway in a dozen quick steps, drawing from my pocket the single most effective weapon in my arsenal: a small hand taser. In most cases, it was enough to put down the infected once and for all. Why was a non-lethal weapon lethal to the pseudo-dead? I had no idea, but what I did know is that it was quick, bloodless, and hopefully painless – that was what was important to me.

I thumbed the switch to the *on* position as I entered the store; the taser crackled to life in my hand, ready to discharge its high-voltage payload. The clerk did nothing. He just stood there, helpless, shuffling the one lone DVD case left on the shelf back and forth with a limp hand.

"Hey," I called softly, hoping to draw his attention. "You okay, buddy?"

Of course he wasn't, but I had to be sure in case the old man wasn't really undead. Sometimes a survivor just went completely off his nut. It happened occasionally in our short and brutal existence. The old man just stood there, staring off into space, oblivious. I let out a soft whistle, trying a different frequency to get his attention.

That time, it worked.

His head rose and turned to look at me with blind eyes, worn over by cataracts long before the virus compounded his problems. His brow knitted into a frown, and he opened his mouth as though to speak but no sound came out.

I cringed. He looked so much like my grandfather, who had died when I was a little girl. Even after all these years, I still remembered holding my Poppa's wrinkled old hand as he lay on his deathbed, gazing up at me with those sad, blind eyes. In retrospect, I could take comfort from the fact that Poppa didn't have to watch the world crumble into ruin, but that didn't ease the pain.

Slowly, cautiously, I circled around the old man. His head jerked side to side, seeking the sound that had drawn his attention.

Most of the infected weren't really dangerous. I'd yet to see a strain of the disease turn them into violent monsters, like the ones in the movies. They had been stripped of their awareness but they still resembled the people they'd been in life. A gentle person was still gentle; a violent one was still violent. The virus took away the laws of civility that had once helped them to fit into a neat and well-ordered society, but it didn't change who they were.

"It's okay, buddy. I'm just going to put you to sleep." I kept my voice low and calm; like animals, the pseudo-dead responded more to tone of voice than the words themselves. "I'll make the pain go away."

He didn't turn to face me, but just stood there shuffling his limbs listlessly. One of his hands moved absently in mid-air, shifting a non-existent video case towards a better imaginary location. Crushed plastic and cracked discs crunched ominously under my feet, like dry old bones picked clean and left brittle in the sun. The taser made a soft crackling sound when I pressed it to the nape of the old man's neck, and he collapsed like a sack of potatoes at my feet. I knelt beside him to check, but he was already gone. To Heaven, I hoped, or whatever came next. Anything was better than lingering in purgatory while your body rotted away around you.

I hung my head to reflect and to offer a silent prayer for the old man's soul. Although I had been raised as an atheist, spending so much time surrounded by violence and death made me wonder if there was something more. I hoped so. It hurt too much to think about so many good people just ceasing to be.

I'd been alone for a very long time. Even so, killing someone who looked like a person that I loved still affected me more deeply than I could express. I sometimes wondered if it would be easier to feel nothing at all, but at least the pain kept me grounded in reality. They weren't monsters, they were people. Just like me, just like my family, just like everyone else. The day I stopped feeling something towards them was the day that I became the monster.

Years ago, I had made myself a promise: if the day ever came when I stopped feeling grief and remorse for what I had to do to survive, then I would put my gun against my head and join my family in the hereafter.

# Chapter Two

*Ten Years Earlier*

Fresh from school and full of energy, I pulled open the front door, trotted inside, and flung my school bag into its usual corner by the door. It landed with a heavy 'thunk', full of books and all the other junk I had to bring home at the end of the school year.

"Mum, I'm home!"

My voice echoed down the hall as I headed for the kitchen in search of something cool to alleviate the summer heat. Although it was only mid-December, it was hotter than Hades and muggy to boot. The cheap polyester of my school uniform clung in all the wrong places, and did not breathe at all.

I yanked open the fridge, and relished the wave of cool air that smacked me in the face like a glorious arctic ice floe. When my mother didn't respond, I glanced over my shoulder and called her again. "Mum?"

After grabbing a can of lemonade from the top shelf, I shouldered the fridge closed and went off in search of my missing parental unit. I wasn't worried, but I wanted to talk to her and she was always home at this time of day to greet me. It was a family tradition for us to hang out for a couple of minutes after school and work, just to talk and catch up on the day. I was always bursting with gossip, and she was happy to listen. That's just how my mum was – she was a listener, and she was always there for me no matter what.

I stuck my head into the stairwell and called out to her again.

"Mu-um?" I paused, waiting impatiently for a response.

"She's not he-ere." The reply came in my father's voice. My curiosity was doubly-piqued now – Mum was out and Dad wasn't at work? My home environment was usually very organised and well-ordered; it was unusual for things to be out of place. Following the sound of his voice up the stairs, I made my way into his office.

"Why aren't you at work?" I asked, curious.

"Why aren't you at school?" he countered, frowning at me.

"Dad, it's after four." I laughed and shook my head. "School let out an hour ago."

His brow furrowed into a look of confusion. I glanced over his shoulder at the computer screen behind him, and caught a glimpse of some gruesome photographs on what looked to be a current affairs website.

As soon as he realised where I was looking, my father spun and switched off the monitor, then turned back to give me an awkward smile. "I guess I lost track of the time."

"Uh-huh. You know they talked about that thing in school, right? You don't have to hide the photos." I layered on the sarcasm, the way I always did.

Dad bolted from his chair and grabbed me by the shoulders, a movement so sudden that it startled me right out of my cavalier mood. "They did *what*?"

"T-they talked about the thing happening in Africa." I stared up at my father wide-eyed, shocked by his vehemence. "We got a big lecture about hygiene and stuff in the final assembly today. I don't get it. It's just another SARS, it'll blow over soon enough."

My confusion must have been written on my face, because his expression softened as he looked down at me. Finally, he released me and turned away, rubbing the bridge of his nose between finger and thumb; a familiar anxious habit of his.

5

"I don't think so, sweetheart. This is different." He glanced at me again; the look on his face was one I'd never seen before, and that scared me.

My heart skipped a beat. "Daddy?"

"Go get out of your uniform, Sandy. I'll make us some smoothies and then we'll talk. Okay?"

Dad always knew how to get my attention, and he knew I loved a good smoothie.

"Okay," I agreed, happy to put the morbid conversation aside. I left the office and crossed the hallway to my bedroom door, which stood ajar to reveal the mess within. The sight struck me as strange, because my mother usually picked up after me while I was at school. Perhaps the impending 'talk' I was about to get from my father was the one about how I was old enough to clean my own damn room.

Blast, I'd been trying to delay that one as long as possible.

The door closed with a soft click as I pushed it shut behind me. I sat myself down in front of my vanity and unlaced my shoes. When the laces came free, I kicked them off and leaned down to yank off my sticky socks as well. My clothing was sweaty and repulsive, so I stripped off my skirt and polo shirt and tossed them into the laundry basket by the door. Silently cursing the humidity, I stood flapping my arms like a demented duck for a few seconds to cool off. My mother often joked that you needed gills to survive an Auckland summer, and as far as I was concerned she was very, very right.

My household was just an ordinary, average Kiwi family. Mum, Dad, two kids and a fat old cat, living in a fairly nice house in an upper-middle class area of Auckland's North Shore. The house was big enough that my little sister and I each got our own rooms, but it wasn't huge. We went to good schools and our parents were always happy to help with our homework. We never went on amazing, globe-trotting holidays like some families did, but our grandparents were well-off enough to own a holiday house at the beach. My little sister and I were happy to spend our summers playing in the sun, swimming, and building sandcastles.

Dad was an accountant, and Mum had been an office manager until she'd fallen pregnant with me. After I was born, she decided to become a stay-at-home mum instead. We were financially stable but not rich, and we survived comfortably on Dad's income alone. I both loved and respected my parents beyond words.

When I cooled down enough to feel human again, I pulled on a pair of shorts and that baby-doll tee Dad hated because it showed a little sliver of my belly. I enjoyed teasing him about it, and saying that he was just jealous because he couldn't pull off the look. He always laughed, but I doubted he'd see the humour today.

My hairbrush sat waiting for me, so I grabbed it and turned to face the mirror. The face that looked back at me was pretty by anyone's standards, but I was a teenage girl so all I saw were the flaws: my breasts weren't big enough, my thighs were too fat, and there was a zit on the side of my nose that looked like Mount Vesuvius.

Of course, I knew full well that the flaws weren't half as bad as they seemed – Harry chided me all the time for being self-conscious. It was a girl thing, though. I figured I'd grow out of it when it was time.

I sighed heavily and pulled out the elastic band that held my tresses back in a practical schoolgirl ponytail. With a shake of my head, golden curls bounced down around my shoulders. Whatever else I thought of myself, I did love my hair. Dad always said that it was a gift from my mother. He was olive-skinned with black hair, while my sister and I looked like Mum: fair skinned and prone to freckles, with blue eyes and curly blonde hair. The down side was that fair skin meant I burned like a lobster if I spent too long in the sun. In the summertime, I turned into a mass of freckles instead of getting a tan. It was only mid-December, and I already had a plague of them dusting my nose.

I'd just finished my last day of high school, so I had the entire summer ahead of me, and then the rest of my life. Maybe I should get a job? Or should I go to university? I already knew that I didn't want to be either an accountant or a homemaker, like my parents. As usual, I relegated the decision to the 'too hard' basket, and moved on without really answering the question.

With my hair freshly brushed and hanging loose around my shoulders, I stood and padded barefoot down the stairs to join my father. He was in the kitchen as he'd promised, with the blender out on the bench, fruit everywhere, and glasses waiting for the impending delicious smoothie goodness. His back was to me as I entered, his attention intensely focused on slicing a banana into little, mushy pieces.

"Mum will kill you if you make a mess," I said as I slipped onto a stool at the end of the breakfast bar. My words made him jump. He shot a glare at me, but I just grinned and planted my elbows on the counter, resting my chin against my knuckles to watch him work. When he didn't say anything for a couple of minutes, I decided to break the silence. "Hey Daddy, can I borrow twenty bucks?"

"Eh?" He paused in his banana-murdering and shot me a confused look.

"My friends are going to the movies tonight to celebrate graduation. I wanna go with them." I paused for a breath, and then lathered it on a bit thicker. "Please, Daddy? I'll wash your car tomorrow. Mum's, too."

"I—" Dad hesitated, then looked back down at his fruit. "I don't think that's a good idea, sweetheart."

His answer surprised me. It was true that I could be a bit cheeky on occasion, but I was generally a good kid. I never stayed out late, never went boozing and hardly ever got myself into trouble. Dad knew that he could trust me, because I respected his trust in return.

They knew that Harry and I were intimately involved, but they also knew that they had raised me smart enough and worldly enough that I would never come home on drugs or pregnant. As far as my parents were concerned, teenagers would be teenagers regardless of what their parents wanted them to do, and smothering a teenager never worked out well. They wanted me to be comfortable enough to come to them with questions or if I ever needed help – and I was. They weren't just my parents, they were my friends.

That was what made his response so strange. That, and the fact that Dad had never turned down a chance to have someone wash his car before. The thing drew bird poop like a magnet, so offering to wash Dad's car was generally a guaranteed way to get whatever I wanted.

"Why not?" Confused, I tilted my head and sought clarity. "It's just Harry and Katie and a couple of others, you know all of them; you know their parents, too."

"Oh— that's not it, honey." He looked at me and smiled weakly. "I trust you, and I know your friends. It's just—" He finally paused and put down his knife, then turned to look at me fully with that same strange expression. "Sandy, I'm home today because they've quarantined the central business district."

"*What?*" I was just a kid, but even I knew what a big deal it was if they closed down the centre of Auckland City. It was the biggest financial hub in the entire country, where more than eighty thousand people lived and worked on any given day. I could not believe my ears.

"Well, a quarantine is when they—"

"I know what a quarantine is, Dad." I rolled my eyes. I swear, sometimes Dad still thought I was five. "I mean, why?"

"Oh." There was a pregnant pause, and then he sighed deeply. "The infection is here, sweetie. They said on the news last night that there is someone being held at Auckland Hospital that tested positive."

"Oh, shit."

"Hey, language. But— yes. This morning my supervisor called me, and told me no one was to come into work today. The next thing I knew, it was all over the news that the council had declared an emergency, and set up a quarantine zone around the hospital. The authorities just extended the zone to cover the entire central city and the surrounding suburbs. No one goes in – and no one leaves."

My brow furrowed. "No one *leaves*? But doesn't that mean the people stuck inside the zone are at risk of infection?"

"Yes." He grimaced and looked at me, and there was a flicker of something in his eyes that I barely recognised – fear. "The authorities have been talking about it all day on the news. They say the risk of exposure to anyone inside the zone is pretty much guaranteed, but if they let anyone out there's a risk to everyone else in Auckland – maybe even the entire country. Anyone that's inside that zone, stays in that zone."

"But what about my friends?" I stared at my father wide-eyed. "They all live in the city. I haven't heard from them since we left school. When did they extend the quarantine? Do you think they might be inside the zone?"

Before Dad could answer, the front door opened and Mum shuffled in, struggling to juggle a couple of very full grocery bags, with my eight-year-old sister, Skylar, whining for attention behind her.

"Mum!" I squeaked in alarm and jumped up to go help her with the bags. I snatched a couple from her hands before she could drop them, then almost did so myself. "Whoa, these are heavy. What have you been buying? Rocks?"

Mum looked up, and shot me an uncomfortable smile. "Canned food and bottled water. A lot of it."

"Geez, is the apocalypse coming or something?" I asked. My parents exchanged a glance.

"I was just about to tell her," Dad said, and then looked back at me. "Sandy, they're going to lock down the whole city soon. They haven't told the public yet, but you remember how your uncle Rick works for the council? He saw the plans on someone's desk to extend the quarantine zone. So you, me, Mum and Skylar, we're going to go for a bit of a road trip. We're going to get out of Auckland tonight, and try and get as far away as we possibly can. We'll go to Palmerston North and visit Grandma, and see where it goes from there."

I looked at him for a long time, and then I switched over to stare at Mum instead. I could see in both their eyes that they were deadly serious, and that they were scared. Really, really scared. As much as I wanted to ask about my friends, the look in their eyes made me think better about pushing for an answer.

Then I looked down at little Skylar, and saw that she wasn't oblivious to the mood in the room either. She sensed the fear Mum and Dad were trying to hide, and clung anxiously to our mother's hand. With no other safe recourse but a healthy dose of sarcasm to try and lift everyone's spirits, I looked over at Mum and quirked an eyebrow.

"Uh, Mum? If we're leaving again in a few hours, then why did you bother lugging all that stuff inside?"

My mother blinked owlishly at me, then looked down at the bags scattered around her feet as though seeing them for the first time. As I turned towards the stairs, I heard her muttering a muffled curse, and the sound of my father's laughter. At the foot of the stairs, I turned back and shot an impish grin at him.

"So, can I swear *now*?"

# Chapter Three

I never imagined one day I would be dragging around the corpse of a rotten old man. I thought I'd be something special by now: a doctor or a lawyer, maybe a scientist or an astronaut. Maybe someone's wife. Maybe someone's mother.

I never thought that I would be a survivor.

The things you learned as a survivor were hard and brutal life lessons, like how to ignore the smell of decay. How to kill when you had to. How to ignore the feelings of guilt, and the incessant gnawing of depression around the edges of your psyche. I was not very good at any of those things, but I had no choice.

"I'm sorry," I whispered to the old man as I dragged him out of his beloved store. He had a nametag on. His name was Benny. Knowing that made it so much harder to ignore the pain; it made him even more human in my eyes. He wasn't meat, he was a person, just like I was, just like my family had been. A good, loving person who sure as hell didn't deserve the bum fate that life had given him.

And he didn't deserve to spend the rest of eternity rotting between a dumpster and a stack of mouldy cardboard boxes.

I stood and looked down at the worn old face, etched with age and diseased torment. He wasn't there anymore, I reminded myself. He hadn't been there for a long time. He wasn't a nice old man named Benny anymore, he was just meat, rotting meat that was going to attract rats if I left him too close to where I was sleeping.

If there was one thing our new civilization did have in droves, it was rats. At least they seemed to be immune.

There was one good thing about Ebola-X, though. Once the infected organism was dead, the virus often went into overdrive and consumed the rest of the remains fast. In those cases, within a few weeks not even the bones were left behind. Not always, though. Sometimes the virus burned itself out before the remains were entirely gone. There were skeletons everywhere; seven billion people didn't just vanish into thin air without a trace.

I often wondered what would happen once the last of the infected finally fell, and their remains dissolved into eternity. What would happen to the disease? Would it just die out, or would it mutate to survive? Would it find a way around my immunity so that it could consume me, too? Or would it go the way of the dinosaurs and become nothing but a terrible memory, leaving a bleached bare world for me and my descendants to reconstruct over the next hundred generations?

More hard questions. I was just too tired to think about it today.

With one last look at the old man, I grabbed my backpack from where I'd left it and turned my back to him. But a twinge of guilt plucked at my heart and made me hesitate. I glanced back over my shoulder; his blind, old eyes stared blankly up at the clear blue sky, focused on nothing. Could I live with myself if I just left him there, in the open, to be eaten by the birds and rats? I tried to tell myself that I had to, or I'd end up digging a grave for every corpse I saw. Being the world's most prolific gravedigger wasn't quite the legacy I planned on leaving for my children.

Still...

It was a haphazard grave at best, but I grabbed a few of the grimy cardboard boxes and gently piled them atop the old man's corpse to cover him up with as much respect as I could manage in the circumstances. Although it wouldn't really keep the rats at bay, at least it would keep the birds from taking his eyes. That bothered me a lot. I guess it was a phobia.

With my civic duty done, I tried to put poor old Benny out of my mind and turned my attention back to setting myself up a nice little base of operations. At least, that was what I hoped to achieve. The store looked promising from afar: a stand-alone building at the end of town separated from the nearest other buildings by a decent sized car park on the right, a road on the left, and a narrow walkway behind that separated it from an old motel in the rear. It looked like there was a loft above the store, probably where the owner used to live. If I was lucky, there might even still be power.

The power grid had been spotty for a number of years, though the fact that it was still on at all was amazing. I had heard rumours of a selfless group of survivors working in one of the big power stations, trying to keep the electricity flowing for as long as possible. Whether that was true or not, I didn't know.

When had I arrived in town early this morning, there was a single street lamp glowing brightly in the semi-darkness, like a beacon of hope drawing me in with its wordless promises. Perhaps this place would offer a respite from the trauma I had suffered in the south. Maybe I could stay a while, and be safe and comfortable. I hadn't felt either of those things in a very long time. So far, there were no signs that indicated anyone else lived in this area. A tui had sung on the power lines overhead as I'd tiptoed past the sign that welcomed me to the township of Ohaupo, and its song was a familiar memory from my childhood.

The township was a tiny, quiet place, a blip on the map somewhere between Hamilton and Te Awamutu. At first glance, there wasn't much here – a small group of shops clustered around the main street, a handful of homes and a motel, and a few farmsteads further out. It was the kind of place that a snobby Aucklander should turn her nose up at and drive right on through.

But I was no snobby Aucklander anymore. To me, this little hamlet set in the flat green pastureland of the Waikato was a relief to both the eyes and the soul. Most of the survivors congregated in the shells of the old cities, picking out a living from amongst the ruins torn apart by ten years of storms and earthquakes and flooding. I'd learned a long time ago that tiny townships like this one often provided a bounty of supplies, if I was lucky enough to be the first one to land there.

It seemed like I'd been lucky for once. The only sign of life was Benny, the tui, and a couple of cheeky magpies that chided me as I crept down the barren streets near their nests. There didn't even seem to be all that many rats. Like the survivors, the pests tended to be more attracted to city life.

I left Benny to his eternal sleep and returned to the shattered remains of his livelihood to see what I could salvage from the wreck. If the place proved to be liveable, then I would go back and move his corpse farther away, but there was just no point in wasting my energy unless I knew the place was going to be worth the effort.

I crept back inside in a low, stealthy crouch-walk, my body as conditioned as a soldier's by years of having to survive on my own against all the odds. The main room of the store was a mess. Shattered discs formed a hazardous carpet that crunched underfoot as I checked between the shelves for any signs of danger. I found nothing, only dust and discarded merchandise. Content that I wasn't going to be jumped from the shadows, I picked my way to the front counter to investigate what lay behind it.

I paused to take stock of the contents of the refrigerators, then glanced at a narrow doorway to my right. My heart sank when I noticed the lock, still intact and shiny even after all these years. Refusing to give in to disappointment, I looked down and around, and used my booted foot to shove aside piles of cracked plastic until finally the glint of steel caught my eye. Correction, several different glints of steel. Jackpot.

Careful not to cut myself on the mutilated shards, I pried the key ring out from beneath the rubble and held it up to the light. To my eternal relief, all the keys looked more or less intact. I crossed to the door and tried a couple in the lock until one of them turned. The door popped open to reveal a small office, decorated with a couple of desks, some computer equipment, a filing cabinet and large framed painting of brightly-coloured lilies hanging on the wall.

Then the stench hit me and sent me reeling back, gagging. Afraid that I was about to find another corpse, I dropped my backpack outside the door and yanked a small cloth mask out of one of the cavernous pockets of my cargo pants. This wasn't the first time I'd had to deal with stench. In a world where almost everyone was dead, you had to find ways to keep the odour at bay. My method was a strip of cloth soaked in the strongest perfume that I could find.

I dove into the stinking gloom and looked around. Thankfully, I didn't find another body, just one little glass jar sitting open beside an old computer. It was a very, very rancid jar, that had presumably once contained some kind of pickle. Now, after a decade's worth of decomposition, the olfactory nightmare had sprouted fungus almost ten centimetres high. Something about that struck me as amusing, and made me smile. Maybe I should keep it and try to harvest penicillin from it.

I didn't, of course. The smell was just too horrifying. Instead, I yanked open a window and dropped the doom-pickle into the long grass below.

Beyond the office, I spotted a second doorway. I went over to open it and found a set of stairs leading up into semi-darkness. From one of my many pockets, I drew out a torch and clicked it on, then scampered up the stairs as quietly as I could. One of them creaked ominously underfoot, making me flinch. As unlikely as it was that anyone was alive up there, you never knew. I hadn't survived this long by being careless.

At the top of the stairs, another door opened onto a small, dusty landing, decorated by ancient furniture and lit from above by a little rectangular skylight. Another piece of art hung on the wall; this time, it was a painting of a beautiful landscape, a quaint little village bustling with life. I stopped and stared. It took me a minute to recognise that it was a painting of Ohaupo township, the way it had been before the plague came and turned this lovely place into a ghost town.

God, how that brought back memories.

# *Chapter Four*

*Ten Years Earlier*

The drive south felt like it was taking forever, with a nervous eight year old in the back constantly begging for attention. Where were we going? How much longer would it be? Why weren't we going home? It seemed like Skylar had a million questions.

She was driving me crazy, but I was worried about her too. She was my baby sister, after all. I was ten when Skylar had been born, an unexpected burden on a family that had been perfect just the way it was. My parents had only planned on having one child, and I remembered listening to them argue when they found out that Mum was pregnant again. A second child interfered with all their plans for the future, their financial stability, and their hopes for my education.

I had been too young to understand the problem; I was intrigued by the idea of having a baby to play with. The arguments continued right up until the day that Skylar was born, but once they saw her little face, they couldn't help but fall in love with her. The burden of a new baby became a blessing.

Just not right now.

"Skye, please shush." Mum was eternally patient when it comes to her kids, but even she was getting frustrated. The stench of fear in the car was so thick that you could cut it with a knife. The three of us were jammed into Mum's tiny hatchback, while Dad followed behind in his bigger sedan. Her logic didn't make any sense to me, but for some reason Mum insisted that we travel with her, while Dad carried the supplies and the cat in his car. I realised that she was feeling extra protective, and that her maternal instinct had gone into overdrive the moment that her babies were threatened.

I was upset, and Mum knew it. My parents had insisted that I not contact anyone, not even my best friend Katie, or Harry, my boyfriend. I wasn't even allowed to check if they were okay, and it was driving me crazy. Normally I was willing to accept that Mum and Dad knew best, but in this case I thought it was completely unreasonable. They'd even had the nerve to take away my cell phone, and that lack of trust pushed me over the edge from upset into annoyed.

"But Mum, I need to pee!" Skye whined from the back seat, clutching herself dramatically as though that would make her plea look more genuine and urgent.

"Just hold on a couple of minutes longer, there's a petrol station right up the road." Mum's voice carried an element of frustration, but she struggled to stay calm and reasonable. "You don't want to pee in the bushes like Mushkin, do you?"

Mushkin was our elderly tabby, who had a bit of a bladder problem.

"Mushkin doesn't pee in the bushes," Skye said matter-of-factly. "He pees on the little rug by the door."

"He does *what* now?!" Mum exclaimed. "Damn, I was wondering where that smell was coming from, but I could never find the source."

"Language, Mother," I said dryly.

My mother shot me a dark look, but it didn't last for long.

"Honey, I need you to help me. Please?" This time, her tone was one of earnest appeal. She sounded exhausted, but concern for my friends made me tense and angry.

Although I knew it was petty, I decided that the silent treatment was in order and said nothing.

"Sandy, please?" she pleaded. "I can't do this by myself. I know you're angry at me, but we'll talk about everything later, I promise. We'll work everything out, but we shouldn't discuss it in front of Skye."

Mum was trying to appeal to my good-natured side. It worked. I was not made of stone, even when I was annoyed at her. I sighed and looked at her.

"Fine, but I'm holding you to that promise. What do you need?" I asked gruffly, doing my best to maintain my show of being the injured party.

"Send a text to your father. Tell him we need to stop at the next town for a rest," she answered. With one hand on the steering wheel, she fumbled in her purse for my phone and then offered it back to me.

I hesitated, staring at it as if it might explode in my hand. "But I thought you didn't trust me?"

The wounded look that she gave me made me immediately regret saying it.

"I do trust you, honey," she said. "There are just some things that we need to keep to ourselves. Promise me you won't text, call, email, or Facebook anyone without my permission, okay?"

"What about Twitter?"

"No, no twitting either."

"'Tweeting', Mum. The verb is 'tweeting'."

"Well, whatever it is, none of that. Promise me." She suddenly reached over to grab my hand; her palm was sweaty and tense. That broke the last of my resistance. I couldn't stay mad when she was trying so hard to be brave for our sake. I had been trying to gloss over the seriousness of the situation to make it seem less scary, but I was not oblivious to it. There was only so long that I could deny reality before I would have to accept it and deal with it, even if I didn't want to.

"Okay. Okay, okay, I promise. I won't contact anyone." I summoned a weak smile to reassure her, then switched on my phone and thumbed through a text to my father.

Once it was sent, I resumed staring out the window. A green government-issue road sign rolled past, announcing that we were about to enter some little town called Ohaupo, a tiny place that was nothing more than a blip on the map.

\*\*\*

*Present Day*

I stared at the painting, remembering the way I'd felt when I first came here at the age of eighteen. I had been passing through on my way to somewhere else, but my first impression of the place was that it looked dull, like one of those little country towns where old people went to die. Back then, it had been alive and full of people. Well, not full in the Auckland sense of the word, but there were people nevertheless.

It looked like they were all gone now. They were either dead, lingering in the purgatory of undeath, or had left for other places. There was a thick layer of dust on the little decorative table directly beneath the painting, and the tiny china figures were faded and dirty.

*Faded and dirty, kind of like Mum, Dad, and little Skylar*, I thought. The idea brought tears to my eyes. I hadn't seen any of them in so long. It hurt just to think about them.

I shoved that thought back into the little corner of my mind that kept me awake at night, and tried to focus on the task at hand. There were only a couple of hours of daylight left, and it was best for me to use them wisely.

At the end of the hallway stood yet another door, this one hanging slightly ajar. An angular beam of afternoon sunlight shone through the crack, making the dust stirred up by my footsteps sparkle like fairy dust. I opened the door with one hand, the other resting on my taser, just in case.

I needn't have bothered. Nothing stirred within.

The place was undisturbed, a time capsule dating back to a whole other era. The landing opened into a small living room, with an antique couch and a plump armchair sitting in front of a box television that was probably older than me.

Dust coated everything, shimmering in the rays of afternoon sunshine that filtered through net curtains. Behind the television, large windows overlooked the street below, framed by thick curtains in an old damask print that gave the room a special kind of rustic charm. Shelves covered in knick-knacks decorated the walls, and an old, framed black and white photograph of a happy couple on their wedding day took centre stage directly above the television.

Beside the photograph was a small urn. I stepped closer and stared at it, then reached out to brush away the dust that blurred the inscription. It bore a woman's name and a short verse.

Margaret.

Beloved wife, beloved mother.

Rest forever in Heaven.

I stood back to consider it, feeling an unexpected rush of relief. It hurt to think of an innocent little old lady going through what Benny had to suffer – or worse, having to watch him go through it. But she had been dead long before he became infected. She was already at peace, and never had to know what would happen to her home and her world. That thought gave me some sense of peace, as well.

Perhaps later on, I would bury them together. It seemed like the right thing to do.

# Chapter Five

I sneezed violently.

*Mum would be so proud,* I thought dryly as I rubbed my nose. God knows I never did this much dusting at home. Still, if I wanted to make this little loft into my new home then it would have to be clean. It was hard enough to find food and water without a crusty layer of dust getting all over everything.

An hour earlier, I had finished my inspection of the little apartment, and found that there really wasn't much to it. A tiny kitchen opened up off the living room, with a stove, a fridge, and a decent-sized pantry. At the far end of the living room, a door led into a small bedroom with an attached en suite. It was just right for one person, maybe two if they didn't mind getting a bit cosy. For me all on my lonesome, it was perfect.

The bad news was that the dust was just as thick everywhere else as it was in the living room, and the kitchen was a disaster area of a whole other stripe. The good news was that when I tried a light switch, I discovered the place was still attached to the power grid, and the grid was miraculously still going. Thank you mysterious power station heroes, whomever you may be.

I was going to have to invest a substantial amount of time in getting the place clean, but it was water-tight, wired, and very secure. There was no sign of rats or roach infestations, which was a blessing. I hated rats. While I was immune to Ebola-X, that immunity did not extend to all the other diseases that could be brought by pests – and if something were to happen to me, where would I go for treatment? Being a survivor meant being self-sufficient, but it also meant being a bit of a neat freak. It was better to stay healthy to begin with than to have to try and pull myself back together after a nasty bout of the flu – or worse.

As soon as I had finished my inspection and judged the place fit to be my new domicile, I went back down to retrieve my backpack so that I could leave it somewhere safe while I cleaned. No time like the present; the sooner I got started, the sooner I'd be finished.

I discovered a small vacuum cleaner hidden in the back of the linen cupboard, but my inner survivalist was loathe to give away my position over something as minor as a little dust. Our world was a silent place now, without the drone of traffic and human voices; the noise of a vacuum cleaner would carry over half the township. As far as I was concerned, there was no reason to assume that I was safe and alone just because I hadn't seen anyone yet. After the pain that I'd been through, I chose to err on the side of caution.

Luckily for me, it seemed that Benny had been a rather fastidious fellow in his former life, and kept the place well stocked with cleaning supplies before his untimely infection. In no time at all, I had the windows open to let the apartment air out and I'd tossed the worst of the dust right back outside where it belonged. In some places, the dust was so thick I didn't even need to use a dustpan; I just picked it up with my fingers and it all came up in one big wad of filth.

The spiders were another story. They were a little territorial. Thankfully, any arachnophobia that I might have once suffered from was a distant memory.

"Sorry, mate, but this is my house now," I told one particularly large daddy longlegs as I swept him off the ceiling with my broom, and shook him out the window.

Good thing that spiders were also immune. Could you imagine a zombie tarantula?

That thought made me chuckle, even in the face of so much horror. I figured that you had to keep up your sense of humour, or you'd go crazy. But I suppose when you'd spent the better part of the last ten years alone, it didn't really matter if other people thought you were crazy, did it? All kinds of things stopped mattering when you no longer had society watching and judging you, and from what I'd seen it seemed to be different for every person.

For some survivors, personal hygiene was one of the first things to go, but I still considered it vitally important. Perhaps it was because I'm female, and girls are just more sensitive to that kind of thing. I hate that unspecified itchy feeling when your skin is all filthy and sweaty, and I loathed being able to smell myself. Most of the male survivors I'd met didn't seem to care. I could only guess that they couldn't smell their own stench the way I could.

Yet another reason to avoid them, as if I needed any more after what had happened the last time I'd seen another living human being.

I let the broom head drop to the floor, and stood back to admire my handiwork. Not perfect, but it was a start. There was still the matter of the bed, though. The last person who'd slept in that bed was Benny, and that had been years ago. I hated to think what kind of foulness lingered in those stale sheets. They'd have to go.

I crossed to the bedroom with determination, and set about stripping off all of the bedding. Sheets, duvet, and pillows alike, I flung them into a pile on the floor. When I reached the mattress, I was relieved to discover that it was still in excellent condition, with no signs of fungus or pests aside from a tiny bit of mildew on the underside. A wee spot of mould wasn't enough to deter me from sleeping in it, not after I'd spent the last couple of years living in the back of an old shipping container. It gave me the shivers just thinking about sleeping in a real bed again.

I gathered up the old linens and dumped them in a pile in the living room so that I could deal with them another day. As filthy as they were, a survivor threw nothing away if there was any chance it could be saved. Waste not, want not. After the end of the world, you became the ultimate recycler.

From the linen cupboard, I fetched the spare set of bedding. Despite the years, the sheets were relatively clean. I unfolded them and flapped them out the window, giving them a damn good shake to get rid of any excess dust.

There would be time to wash all the bedding out another day, but not tonight. I was working against the clock, with not much time left before the sun set. Knowing that the power was still on did relieve the tension of impending darkness, but I preferred not to rely too heavily on something that could abandon me at any moment. It was not terribly surprising that we suffered a lot of blackouts in this day and age.

When the new bedding finally passed my critical inspection, I returned to the bedroom. There, I flicked the bottom sheet over the mattress and quickly mitred and knotted the corners the way my mother had taught me when I was a little girl. A pang of longing and loneliness twisted my heart, but I fought it off. If I gave in to despair, I might as well have killed myself right then and gotten it over with. Mum wouldn't have wanted that.

Besides, I still had to deal with the kitchen, and I wasn't looking forward to that at all.

*** 

By the time I finished sanitising the kitchen, I decided it was appropriate to coin a whole new word to describe it. 'Epigross' seemed appropriate, or perhaps 'grodetacular' was better. Too bad that Oxford probably wasn't taking submissions anymore.

The kitchen held all kinds of smells in unexpected places, and none of them were good. Most of them came from the fridge, which I was sad to discover had burned out years ago. Given enough time I could probably have fixed it but there was no real need to do so. What would I refrigerate? Everything I ate came in cans or packets, or was fresh out of the ground. I settled for scraping out the contents and giving the fridge a quick wash, then I left it alone.

The pantry was in no better state, and everything that was in there soon went into a rubbish sack as well. Sadly, my good friend Benny was not the kind of fellow that kept a stash of canned food in case of emergency. Rather selfish of him, if you ask me. I did come away with a couple of tins of baked beans and minted peas. Not an amazing haul, but decent enough. Combined with what I'd brought with me, it would be enough to keep me going another couple of days – long enough to explore this pretty little town and map out the available resources. What was important was that it meant I wouldn't have to eat cat food or bugs for dinner tonight. Been there, done that. Not fun.

When the pantry was clean, I put my tins back in and lined them up in an obsessively neat little row with their faded labels facing forward. Tidy little soldiers, all standing at attention, ready to be devoured at my leisure. By the time I was done, I was starting to lose the daylight.

"Time to batten down the hatches," I murmured to myself as I glanced out the window at the setting sun. While I had artificial light if I wanted it, I didn't want to go advertising my position to every Tom, Dick, and Harry in the local area. Don't poke the bear.

*Bear? What bear?* I crinkled my nose; I was starting to go a bit peculiar, and apparently my head was full of delightfully inappropriate clichés.

I shook my head and decided to let that one go. I'd worry about my mental health later, along with my many, many other problems. Such as figuring out if the plumbing in my new home still worked. Oh, how I longed for a hot shower. That would have been just lovely.

Taser in one hand and keys in another, I trotted back downstairs and peered cautiously out at the office through a crack in the door. Nothing stirred.

Then I crept into the main room of the store, and inspected that just as thoroughly before proceeding. Still nothing.

I stuck my head outside, and looked up and down the street. Once again, I found no signs of life except a pair of magpies chatting about how silly I was for being so paranoid.

You think that's paranoid, maggies? Just watch me.

Still not satisfied, I slipped outside and circled the store in a low crouch, peering into bushes and over obstructions to make sure beyond a shadow of a doubt that I really was entirely alone. One full circuit completed, I turned right back around and went the other way, checking that my footprints were the only ones visible.

Satisfied at last, I returned to the front door of the shop and paused to examine the debris in the doorway, making sure everything was exactly as I'd left it. It was.

I was safe and alone.

Part of me wondered if that was a good thing or a bad thing, but the part of me that remembered the pain of violence most vividly reassured me that it was definitely a good thing. In this messed-up world, there was no one that I could trust, no one that I could love – no one that would put my safety above their own. I was alone in every sense of the word.

With a sweep of my foot, I cleared away as much of the debris from the doorway as I could, then shoved the outer door closed and turned the lock. I didn't have much faith in the door's strength, given that the glass was badly cracked, but it would do. At least if someone – or something – tried to come through it, I'd have plenty of warning… and the taser wasn't the only weapon in my possession.

Retracing my steps, I went back behind the counter and paused to examine the old refrigerator that had once housed drinks for sale to the public. I didn't trust the various kinds of soft drinks and juices, but there were a number of bottles of water inside that were still sealed.

I gathered up an armful and took them with me as I retreated back into my new home, closing windows and locking doors behind me. First, the office was locked up, then the door to the stairs, and then the door at the top of the stairs as well. Apparently, Benny was as paranoid as I was, or at least liked the security of having several locked doors between him and the rest of the world. I wasn't sure what Benny's excuse was, but who could really blame me? I had barely survived my last encounter with other people, and the experience had left me scarred both mentally and physically.

Once I was finally safely confined to my new home, I lined up my water bottles on the kitchen bench – more neat little soldiers destined to sacrifice themselves to fill my belly. I broke the seal on one and sniffed at the contents, then tasted it cautiously. Nothing but fresh, clean water. A little tainted by the plastic over the years, but it wouldn't kill me – at least, not anytime soon. 'Have a drink!' the bottle encouraged, with its happy little cartoon mascot dancing for my amusement.

"Don't mind if I do", I said to myself, and swigged from the bottle as I meandered through my little flat, to close up the windows that I'd opened earlier to let in the afternoon breeze. It was getting cooler, I realised as I studied the setting sun. Clouds were rolling in from the west, obscuring the sunset. It had been fine all day, but it looked like this evening there would be rain.

Not that I cared. I was safe and sound, inside an elevated building well away from the risks of city life. It could rain all it liked. I didn't mind at all.

*** 

I discovered that the bathroom fixtures still worked, but hot water was a lost cause until I had time to look at the tank. A cold shower was better than no shower though, so I stripped down hastily and stepped beneath the icy flow, determined to get clean before the sun slipped away completely. With the aid of a bar of soap I found under the sink, I sloughed away the day's grime from my skin, and enjoyed the feeling of relief that cleanliness brought.

A few minutes later, I stepped out and dried myself on a towel liberated from the faithful linen cupboard, feeling like a whole new woman. Right up until I caught a glimpse of myself in the mirror, and realised that new woman looked like a *crazy woman.*

My hair was a mess, unbrushed for days and yanked back into a messy braid. I still wore it long in memory of my mother, but apparently I didn't groom it nearly as much as I should. I usually didn't have time for that kind of thing, but for some reason, today I felt the need. I dug around in one of the medicine cabinets until I found a comb, and set about taming my bird's nest as I wandered out of the room with the towel wrapped around my naked body.

Boy did it hurt to get all those knots out, but it felt good regardless. Who did I think I was going to impress, anyway? Just me and the magpies, I guess. But it didn't matter – this was for me, not anyone else.

As the sun dipped below the horizon, I paused my grooming to close the curtains, making sure that the thick fabric joined perfectly in the middle to block the light. There were no windows in my bedroom or in my bathroom, but the light might still shine through to the living room if I wasn't careful.

I decided to err on the side of caution once more, so I closed myself into my new bedroom with only a single small lamp above the bed to give me light. That was enough for me to finish combing my hair, then have a basic meal of cold baked beans straight from the tin.

Once I finished eating, I set the tin aside and snuggled down beneath the relatively clean sheets, enjoying the softness of the mattress beneath me. It felt so good after months of sleeping on cold concrete padded with dirty, scavenged rags in a pathetic attempt at bedding.

I was exhausted, and fell fast asleep a moment after my head hit the pillow.

# Chapter Six

I awoke to the familiar sound of heavy rain on the roof above my head. I blinked, then squeezed my eyes closed again, focusing on that sweet noise. It brought back images of summers spent on the beach and winters with family close by. It rained all year round in New Zealand, and the end of human civilization had not changed our climate at all.

I often wondered what effect it'd had on the climates of other countries. We were lucky, down here in little Aotearoa. We possessed no nuclear reactors, no major military installations. Nothing that could break down and poison what was left of our tiny little island nation beyond all repair. Our power stations were either fossil fuel, hydroelectric, or thermal, all relatively clean energy sources compared to nuclear.

I wondered what it was like in Europe, Asia, and America. Had their nuclear reactors failed and spewed toxic poisons into their skies? Did their few survivors live under the perpetual cloud of nuclear winter?

Was there even anyone left alive over there? I had no way to know. Communications were basically gone. There were only a few limited ways for survivors to communicate with one another and they were spotty at best. The mobile phone networks still functioned in some places, but they were useless without knowing the number of the person you were trying to reach. Radio was the only way left to bridge the oceans that separated us from our nearest neighbours, and I had never gained access to one of those. In some ways, that kind of isolation kept us safe.

If only it had been enough to keep us safe from the plague itself.

\*\*\*

*Ten Years Earlier*

Skylar leaned against me as we sat in the kitchen, drinking milk and eating the cookies Grandma baked for us that morning. We'd been banished to the kitchen while the adults huddled around the television in the next room, watching the news. Mum made me promise to keep Skylar away so she wouldn't see what was happening in the world outside. She was just a little girl, but she was bright for her age and knew that something was going on.

"What're you drawing, Skye?" I asked, trying to keep her attention focused on happy thoughts. She glanced up from her colouring with a mouth full of cookies, and gave me a bright smile.

"Zombies," she answered cheerfully, spraying me with crumbs.

"Zombies?" I stared at her, surprised; that was the last thing I'd expected her to say.

"Yup." She nodded and went back to her colouring like it was the most normal thing in the world.

"Why are you drawing zombies?" I asked her. "Zombies are yucky."

"Cause they're coming," she answered simply. With delicate little fingers, she selected a bright red crayon from the box. I watched as she applied the red crayon to her artwork, scribbling over the figures that looked like members of our family. The sheer volume of crimson that she used bothered me immensely; I was suddenly overwhelmed by the need to talk to my mother. I stood carefully, so as not to disrupt my sister's artistic endeavours, but she barely noticed. She was thoroughly engrossed in destroying her own creation.

Now I was *really* bothered.

With barefoot stealth, I crept down the hallway that separated Grandma's kitchen from her lounge, and quietly pushed open the door to sneak a peek. A noise that sounded like a muffled sob jolted me; I shoved the door open the rest of the way to see what was going on. I found my mother with her face pressed against my father's chest, while Grandma clung to their hands. None of them seemed to notice me.

On the television, people screamed and surged against police cordons, the low volume of the TV muffling their cries. It was a riot. A full blown riot. In the background, I could see the shopping centre where Katie and I had spent so many afternoons hanging out together and doing nothing, as teenagers were wont to do.

Then suddenly, there she was: my best friend in the whole wide world. Her tear-stained face was split in a scream as she strained against the cordon with the others. Begging to be let out of the quarantine zone. Begging for a chance to live.

My breath caught in my throat, and it was my turn to muffle a cry when I saw that familiar face in distress. Dad heard me, of course. It was too late to protect me now, so he just beckoned me closer and invited me to join the huddle on the couch.

"Is that why you wouldn't let me call them?" I whispered as I sandwiched myself in between my parents, afraid to hear the answer. Mum clung to me, unable to reply. It was Dad who answered, though his voice trembled as he did so.

"Yes. They were already in the zone, Sandy. It was too late for them," he said, hugging us both tightly. "Your mother and I knew you wouldn't let them go without a fight, so we had no choice but to protect you from the truth. I'm so sorry." He looked at me, his eyes full of so much pain and fear that I couldn't be angry at him. "Now, the entire city is quarantined. All of Auckland. No one can leave. The infection is spreading too fast. They can't stop it. Thank God we got out in time."

"I don't think we've gone far enough, Dad," I said, though in my doe-eyed teenaged wisdom, I had no idea how right I was yet. "It's only been a week. We need to... go further away. Get away from people. Get away from the towns."

"No, we'll be fine right here. We're five hundred kilometres away; we'll be safe for sure," Dad insisted stubbornly. My grandmother knew better though, and interrupted him with her own wisdom.

"Don't be stupid, Roger," she said, interrupting him. "She's right. This isn't the flu we're talking about here. It's come all the way from Africa. It will reach Palmerston North." Her wrinkled face furrowed. "We'll go to the beach house. I'm not sure anywhere is safe, but at least it's isolated. Maybe that will give us a chance."

Dad started to protest, but he was voted down by all the women in his life. We knew in our hearts that nowhere would be far enough to save us, but still we had to try.

Then from behind us came a soft little voice, a voice that filled me with dread.

"I told you," Skylar said, clutching her favourite doll. "It's too late. They're already coming."

\*\*\*

*Present Day*

By the time the sun rose, the rain had stopped and the clouds drifted away on a stiff summer breeze. The day dawned with a flawless blue sky, adorned with the lightest dusting of high puffy clouds around the ring of the horizon.

Another beautiful day in my dead world.

As I often did, I found myself wondering what the date was, but I had given up trying to keep track a long, long time ago. It was at least December, maybe January; perhaps it was Christmas Day? I had no way of knowing. The date is one of the many things that stopped mattering when society vanished from the earth.

I mean, what difference did it make if it was December or January? The only difference to me was how far away winter was, and I would figure that one out when the birds started flying north. In this part of the country, we suffered from no real weather extremes. There was no snow in winter, and the temperature rarely climbed above thirty degrees Celsius in the summertime.

Without the climate to dictate my actions, the days blended together into an endless cycle of day and night. Time only mattered in the abstract, and in the most literal sense. When it was dark, I slept. In the mornings and afternoons, I worked. At midday, I rested until the heat of the day passed. I had a vague sense of the weeks, months, and years drifting by and my body gradually getting older, but no real sense of scale.

I wasn't even sure when my birthday was any more. I just counted myself a year older with each summer that passed, but sometimes I had trouble remembering what I was up to. I thought I was about twenty-eight.

I stretched languidly in bed, enjoying a moment of peace while I could, then I rolled myself out of bed and padded into my little en suite to indulge in another cold shower. Ten minutes later, feeling pleasantly clean, I dressed and devoured a quick breakfast of minted peas and bottled water before I set off about my day.

*I'm going to need to find some kind of protein soon*, I thought to myself as I disposed of my trash; I could feel my muscle-mass waning by the day. I put the thought aside for now, and just kept my hopes high that I would find some canned meat during my day's exploration. If I didn't, then I would have to consider hunting and killing something – and that was something that I despised. I had killed before and I probably would kill again, but I was not *a* killer.

Feeling safe with the security the loft provided me, I left my backpack behind and took only the necessities I needed for salvage. I could move faster without the burden of my pack, and with the keys to the store safely deposited in one of my cavernous pockets I felt confident that no one would be able to steal my few precious belongings.

In some ways, I was like a skinny blonde turtle. Everything I owned had to fit in my backpack and be light enough for me to carry when I travelled on foot. Even though I was relatively young, fit, and strong, I was bound by my natural limitations; there was only so much I could carry and still be able to walk and fight effectively. Whenever I decided to add something to my pack, I had to justify its weight. If it wasn't worth it, then I had to leave it behind.

My necessities were few but practical. Like every teenager, I had owned a slick-looking smartphone, but now there was no one for me to call, and it could be days or even weeks between opportunities to charge it. When I'd figured that out, I had discarded the thing in favour of an old GPS unit with a long battery life. The software was ten years out of date, but without city councils changing street names and building new subdivisions, things weren't exactly changing very fast. I did wonder how much longer the satellites would continue to function, but for now they still seemed to be working just fine.

Like everything else I owned, the GPS had proved its worth many times over the years, but today it would stay at home. I didn't need a map to show me around this tiny little township. I'd already seen most of the town on my way in, so now I was just going to go back and investigate it in more detail.

Like most other survivors, I lived by scrounging supplies from the ruins of old towns like this one. While I had water aplenty in my new home, my food supplies were running low. Still, water was more important than food and I had lots of it, both safely bottled drinking water and running water from the tap. I didn't really trust the tap water for drinking unless I boiled it thoroughly, but at least I could use it to wash in or to flush the toilet. That kind of extravagance was a luxury that a lot of us didn't have anymore.

Food was a problem, though. For the past several years, I had lived in the ruins of the town of Te Awamutu, about twenty kilometres to the south. I was the only person there, because the place was a total disaster-zone. At some point between the fall of humanity and my arrival, a terrible earthquake had reduced the entire town to rubble. There was enough there for a clever survivor to live off for a while, but not indefinitely. Eventually, I had exhausted the supplies I could get at without seeking help from others, so I was forced to come north in search of food.

Compared to Te Awamutu, Ohaupo was in nearly perfect condition. Although there were signs of storm damage everywhere, the buildings all appeared to be more or less structurally sound. There were a lot of shattered windows and downed fences, but most of the buildings still had their roofs, and their doors and porches were intact.

I hoped that meant that I would be able to find plenty of food stashed around the town. At the moment, I was down to a half-dozen tins of unknown quality, one of which was cat food. I was saving that for when I had no other choice. Eating cat food was one step above eating bugs, and I had no intention of doing either of those things any time soon.

Of course, if I wanted to keep avoiding it, I would have to find other options fast.

The tiny shopping centre was the logical place to start, and also the closest; it was only about half a kilometre down the road. The buildings stood sad and vacant, adorned by faded Old West-style signs that marked what they had once been used for in the simplest of terms. 'Cafe', one proclaimed vibrantly; 'Bar', said the one next door; 'Function', advised the third.

*That's a little vague,* I thought, peering suspiciously at the ambiguously-named function building.

Of course, 'Fish'N'Chips' stood out, in its bright blue and white TipTop colours, now so faded that it looked far less appetizing than it had long ago. I decided to skip that one; abandoned takeaway joints were a haven for rats and cockroaches. There was rarely anything worth salvaging in them anymore.

Across the road, another small storefront attracted my eye, one that was simply labelled 'Ohaupo Store'. The front window was smashed, the faded Lotto logo barely visible through the spider-webbed glass, and the old magazine racks that framed the doorway were tattered beyond all recognition. Old spray paint proclaimed a mixture of biblical end-of-days prophecy and faded swear words. Still, despite the damage, I drew my taser and approached the doorway with silent-footed caution.

The door swung in the wind, squeaking rhythmically with each gust. I paused and drew a deep breath of the clean, cool air, made pleasant by last night's rain, then ducked through the doorway into the waiting stench. Crouching just inside the entrance, I waited until my eyes adjusted to the dark, breathing shallowly through my mouth to keep the inevitable stink at bay.

The place appeared to have been ransacked.

Not surprising. In the riots during the final days of civilization, many places had been devastated by the panicked populace as they tried to flee the cities, or by the undead who simply didn't know any better. Most of those people were dead now, or they were like me: picking a living from the ruins of the old world.

Regardless of the destruction, I snuck deeper inside with my taser at the ready. Most of the time there was still something left in these old, trashed general stores. You just had to know where to look.

Glass crunched underfoot as I crept along the end of the aisles to check for unwelcome guests of any stripe. The only sign of life was a nest of mice behind the counter, full of angry babies that hissed at me when I passed.

Behind the counter, I spotted a closed door. I moved closer to examine it, and found that it was made of solid steel with a modern lock. It was still intact despite dents that spoke of repeated attempts to burst it open. I tried the handle and found it firmly locked. A quick hunt turned up no keys nearby; I would have to return later with the proper tools to try and figure out a way inside.

I was always up for a challenge – particularly since there was probably a storeroom back there with stock that didn't fit on the shelves, a virtual goldmine for someone like me. As it was still sealed, the chances were extremely good that no one else had gotten in there yet. I added the location to my mental map and moved on.

Picking over what was left on the store's shelves did not yield quite the bounty that I'd hoped for. Most of the tinned goods were long gone, and the dried goods were well past the point of being remotely edible. Piles of decay sat in what had once been displays of fresh vegetables, and rancid-smelling slivers of glass were all that remained of the preserves.

Even the cash register had been cracked open, and the drawer hung half-out of its socket, sad and empty. A tiny mouse stuck its head out of one and squeaked in horror, then fled back into its sanctuary.

That's not to say the store was useless, though. In the back of the store, I found a small stash of hardware that no one had thought to steal during the riots. I came away with half-a-dozen knives, two metal can openers, and a few small hand tools, items that were useful and precious now that there was no longer a shop on every corner.

I stuffed my treasures into a plastic bag liberated from behind the counter, and left the store behind.

***

By midday, I had picked over most of the other stores in the district as well, and come away with enough food and bottled water to last me for a few weeks, with some careful rationing.

Even more exciting, I found a small automotive workshop fully equipped with machinery, and a few cars that I thought I could salvage with enough time and determination. Not that I planned to go anywhere, but if I needed to get out of town in a hurry, then having a functioning vehicle made it so much easier. Plus, with a vehicle I would be able to visit the outlying farms more easily, and see what treasures waited for me there.

I was feeling rather buoyant and pleased with my morning's work. The pantry was filling up nicely and I had even found a few treats along the way. I was practically salivating at the thought of the large tin of peaches I'd found in the back room of the cafe. They were long past their 'best before' date, but a girl could still hope.

As a reward for a morning's hard work, I decided to stop for lunch and crack open the peaches. To my delight, I found that they were still good. They tasted a little metallic, but I couldn't complain; it was rare to find fruit that was still edible in the towns these days. I did hope to find a local orchard that might have some fruit growing wild, but it would be a few days before I was prepared to go that far out of town.

In the meantime... ah, I could practically taste the vitamin C. De-lish!

Peaches in one hand and fork in the other, I wandered back down the stairs. In front of the store was a battered bench, left for people passing by to sit and rest their feet; now it was my turn. Like everything else, the bench had seen better days, but in my imagination I could picture this as Benny's favourite place to sit and watch the evenings go by. It was mine now, and I gave silent thanks to the poor old fellow for his foresight.

All in all, I was feeling pretty relaxed by that stage. I had almost finished securing the town and seen none of the tell-tale signs of danger, so I let my guard down for a moment, to enjoy the warmth of the sun and the simple human pleasure of eating.

Needless to say, the ambush took me completely by surprise. With no warning at all, a tiny kitten suddenly leapt out of the overgrowth, and up onto the seat beside me.

"Mew?" the kitten queried, its little face canted at a curious angle as it watched me eat.

Some ambush. Beware the fuzzy terror.

Still, the kitten's arrival was completely unexpected, and its fearlessness struck me as peculiar. I immediately worried that it might be diseased, but it showed no signs of any illness that I was familiar with. Rabies had been eliminated from my country decades before Ebola-X decimated us, and this tiny cat showed none of the symptoms either of those diseases. Its wasn't frothing, its eyes were alert, and... well, it was quite vocal. The walking dead are not.

"Mew?" it cried again, inching closer to me on cautious paws, not quite confident enough to touch me but too inquisitive to back away. Likewise, I was too curious to shoo it off, but too wary to try to touch it.

I put another slice of delicious peach in my mouth and chewed thoughtfully, which drew yet another demanding cry from the kitten. I held the tin down low enough for it to smell the contents, and it immediately lost interest.

"Yeah. You don't eat peaches, kitty," I told it dryly, and resumed eating them myself.

Thusly rebuked, the kitten sat down and started grooming its little paws with intense concentration, pretending that it didn't see me at all. My heart softened. It seemed hungry, with the way it was crying at me, and it was so young – no more than six weeks old. Maybe its mother was dead, like mine?

"Damn it. What am I, made of stone?" I muttered. "Stay here, kitty."

With a long-suffering sigh, I rose and headed upstairs to find that dreaded can of cat food. Well, at least if I fed it to the kitten then I wouldn't have to stomach it myself. My morning's exploration had turned up plenty of supplies, so I could spare one can for a hungry kitten.

Even after all those years alone, I still had compassion. I'd decided a long time ago that the day I lost that was the day I wouldn't be a human being any more.

I returned upstairs to find the can right where I'd left it – hidden at the back of the pantry, where I wouldn't have to think about it unless things got desperate. I cracked open the pop-top lid, scooped a couple of spoonfuls of the foul-smelling pseudo-meat into a bowl liberated from Benny's cupboards, then carried it back downstairs.

In the doorway, I stopped and looked around.

The kitten was gone.

# Chapter Seven

I found myself surprisingly disappointed by the kitten's disappearance. As much as I tried to ignore it, I longed for some kind of companionship, anything to help keep the loneliness at bay. I was tempted to call for the little cat, but I didn't want to risk giving away my position in case there were larger creatures around. With few other options, I set the bowl down on the ground beneath the bench and left it there. There was still much of the town left to explore, and perhaps while I was gone the kitten would return.

There were only two stores left on the main drag for me to investigate – a little antique store, and the simply-named 'Function' building. I wasn't expecting much from either, but instinct said to check anyway. At least then I'd sleep easier at night, because I would know the buildings were safe. Lacking any particular inspiration, I flipped a mental coin and headed for the antique store.

As it turned out, 'antique' was a fancy name for 'second hand'. The store had survived the riots surprisingly well, mostly due to the fact it stocked very little of conventional value. The lock on the door had been forced open and the contents of a few shelves strewn across the floor, but mostly it was just dusty and quiet. A quick look told me that there was nothing of great value to me, but I still felt drawn inside.

The shelves that were still standing contained things that fascinated my inner child. Along one high shelf was a row of tiny porcelain tea sets in miniature, with little teapots, sugar bowls, teacups, and saucers all to perfect scale, and resplendent with beautiful, hand-painted patterns. Unlike just about everything else, porcelain survived the years without fading; the painted flowers were still just as bright and vibrant as the day they felt the artist's brush.

I found that fascinating. Even after all this time, there were still some things made by human hands that stood the test of time. But it wasn't the cheap, mass produced things from my generation; it was the old, beautifully hand-crafted items of yesteryear that had survived the best.

Some morbid part of me hoped that if the human race survived long enough to flourish again, in a thousand years archaeologists would come to dig through these ruins and find these beautiful little things. Maybe that way, our distant descendants could look back on our civilization with some sense of pride, instead of with shame.

I picked up one tiny teapot and turned it over between my fingers, half-expecting it to crumble to powder at my touch. It didn't. It just sparkled prettily, its glossy paint still just as flawless as the day it had been made. I wanted to put it in my pocket and take it with me, but I knew it would not survive the rigors of my journey and it felt like a sin to destroy something so beautiful. With gentle reverence, I set it back down with its little teacups and moved on.

There were a great many things in this store that served no real purpose, or whose function I could simply not name. They were things that had once been so important to society, but their purpose had been forgotten long before I was born. Now that the generation who remembered them was gone, there was no one left to understand them.

But there were some things I understood, like the beautiful doll house beside the counter. Oh, I remembered longing for something just like it when I was a little girl, a doll house so perfect in every detail. I bent down to peer inside, and in the living room

I found a family of little figurines, humanised bunny rabbits – a mother, a father, and two little girls. They were dressed in human clothes, old-fashioned but perfect in their own way.

In my memory, I heard Skylar's sweet little voice cry out with delight. Suddenly, I remembered that once, long ago, we had stood in this very store together, admiring that doll house.

A pang of grief socked me in the gut, and I stood sharply to leave. I was halfway to the door before a sense of longing overwhelmed me, and forced me to turn back and look at that little family again. They were so perfect, happy, and sweet.

I felt such a sense of abandonment at the thought of leaving them behind that I just couldn't bear it. Those little dolls reminded me of my own lost family. I could justify it if I thought about it. There was no harm in one tangible keepsake to remember them by. They weighed next to nothing.

So I took my little family, and I put them in my pocket.

Tears blurred my eyes as I left the antique store behind, putting as much distance between it and myself as I could. There was one last port of call for today, that vaguely-named 'Function' building. I assumed it was used by the community for events, possibly even as a multi-purpose church or chapel, but beyond that I really didn't know what to expect.

Following my usual protocol, I kept my weapon in hand while I slipped open the door and moved into the building. I hovered in a half-crouch while my eyes adjusted; when they did, I found myself in a short hallway with a double-door in the centre and a single door on each wall flanking it.

I tried the left and right doors first and found them both unlocked, revealing small, basic offices beyond. The religious paraphernalia told me that they had probably been used by the preachers who gathered their flocks here, and that there was little of use to me. I was just about to close the door to the second office, when something out of the ordinary caught my eye: in a clear plastic bag on the desk was a quantity of tiny prescription bottles. A very large quantity.

Overcome by morbid curiosity, I crossed the room to the bag and pulled out a couple of the little bottles, and then turned them over to read the faded labels. Trilam, Riopnol, Hypnovel, and Laroxyl? I was no pharmacist, but I did have a lot of time to read. I knew what those tablets were: sleeping pills and antidepressants. Strong ones. Every single one of those little prescription bottles was empty.

Suddenly, I had a very bad feeling about this. The claws of dread tangled in my gut as I returned the bottles to their bag and retraced my steps to the hallway. There, I hesitated in front of that last set of double-doors. I wasn't entirely sure I wanted to open that door, but I needed to know for sure.

I'd seen a lot of death in the last ten years. What were a couple more bodies? My hand shook on the door handle as I turned it, but I swallowed hard and pushed it open anyway.

A moment later, I slammed it closed again and burst into tears.

\*\*\*

*Ten Years Earlier*

This was not how I'd pictured spending my first New Years as a legal adult. I wasn't the kind of girl who would go out drinking and dancing on tables and flinging my knickers at anything with a penis, but anything would have been better than spending the night crammed in a car with a panicked mother and stressed-out grandmother. Not my idea of fun.

Mum was in a panic because Skylar, ever the adoring Daddy's Girl, had insisted on travelling in Dad's car. When Mum had tried to force the issue, my sister threw such a tantrum that I was afraid she would wake the dead.

Now the problem had multiplied. We'd lost sight of Dad's car an hour earlier, and none of us were able to get a cell phone signal to try and call him.

We pulled into the driveway of Grandma's holiday home on the coast, but the sedan was nowhere to be seen. The holiday house was miles from anywhere, totally isolated from the rest of civilization. It had taken most of the night to get there; by the time we arrived, the sun was rising over the ocean to the east.

As soon as we stopped, I leaped out and climbed up onto the roof of the car to look for Dad. I stretched up on tiptoes and shaded my eyes with one hand, staring long and hard into the gloom behind us, but there was no sign of him.

"Do you see anything?" Mum asked, her voice shaking. The fact that she let me stand on her car without kicking up a fuss told me just how upset she really was. I shook my head, and looked away so that I wouldn't have to see the tears well up in her eyes. As fast as I could without breaking an ankle, I hopped down and wrapped my arms around her, holding her tight as she cried helplessly.

"Oh God, Roger," she sobbed, shaking convulsively in my arms. "I have to go back for him. I-I have to—"

"No, you can't." I tried to keep my voice even, but I could hear it shaking despite my best efforts. "They're going to come here looking for us soon, and if you're not here then Dad will panic. They'll make it, I promise they will."

Grandma's cool hand landed upon my shoulder, and I looked at her over my mother's head, staring deep into her eyes. I gently released my distressed mother into her care, and she led her off towards the house.

"Come along, sweetheart. You're very tired, let's get you to bed. I'm sure they'll be here by the time you wake up," she cooed, leaving me to tend to Mushkin and the supplies we carried in Mum's tiny hatchback. Silently, I prayed that Dad and little Skylar would arrive soon, so that my beloved family could be whole again.

But they never did.

*\*\**

*Present Day*

I sat in the sun on my bench with my head between my knees, gasping for breath. Tears rolled freely down my cheeks, but I didn't have the willpower to wipe them away. You would think that after this long, my heart would be hardened to this kind of thing, but it wasn't. I was still a person, still a human being.

Just like they had been. There were at least a hundred of them, all crammed into that hall together. A decade later, their skeletons lay in the positions in which they'd died. Clinging to one another, curled up in as though in sleep.

So many bodies… so very many bodies – and the smell… oh God, the smell. I couldn't get it out of my head.

I muffled a sob and wiped my nose on my sleeve. Not the most elegant thing to do, but as I was having a bit of a breakdown and there was no one else around to see me so it didn't really matter. There was only so much one can person could handle before it became *too* much.

There were so many of them: men, women, and children alike all crammed into that dusty hall. They probably hadn't even been infected. Maybe a couple were, but not many. The skeletons were still there, bleached by the humid air over the years, their clothing preserved from the elements. If they had carried the infection, then there would be no bones left, or at least not nearly as many.

They might have lived!

My mind rebelled at the idea. Some of them could have been immune, but they hadn't dared to take the risk. They'd chosen to die together, huddled in a dark building for all of eternity. Husbands and wives, friends and neighbours, and even parents and children.

The parents – how could they do that? How could they murder their own babies?

But it was to spare them the horror of becoming like poor, poor Benny. I could understand that. I couldn't bear knowing my children might end up like that.

But they might have lived!

*If I don't find some way to calm myself down, I am going to lose my peaches.* That thought made me laugh, but it was a hysterical kind of laugh that did nothing to stop the sobs from wracking my body. It had been awhile since I'd had a full blown break down, so I suppose I was entitled to one.

I'd seen suicides before, but never so many all at once. A lot of people had chosen to take their own lives rather than let the disease run its course. My own mother had, as had my grandmother. But I'd never seen so many in one place before. I was completely overwhelmed.

"Mew?" A soft head bonked against my hand; I looked up and found myself staring down into a pair of huge golden eyes, set into a fluffy little tabby face. The kitten had returned. How did the animals always know?

\*\*\*

*Ten Years Earlier*

Mushkin purred contentedly in my lap, oblivious to the shaking of my hands as tears rolled silently down my cheeks. No, oblivious wasn't the right word. He wasn't oblivious. As soon as I'd started crying, he'd climbed up into my lap and started purring, rubbing his soft head against my hands until I patted him. He knew something was wrong. He always did.

Mum was the first of us to get sick. It had started a week ago, with a fever. When Dad and Skylar failed to arrive, it was like all the strength had drained right out of her and with it had gone her will to live. She wouldn't let me out of her sight, she was so terrified that she might lose me as well.

It had ended up being just the three of us huddled around the television while the latest updates were read out by an exhausted and frightened news anchorman.

"That man needs a shave," Grandma had commented dryly as we sat together, with her usual irreverent sense of humour. My parents had always joked that I inherited my sense of humour from her, and they were probably right. At that moment though, even I hadn't felt like jokes. I was watching my mother more than the television. Once I'd became aware of how pale she was, I'd started getting anxious.

"Mum, are you all right?" I'd asked, reaching over to take her hand. She had turned and looked at me with dark, sunken eyes, and then shrugged.

"I don't feel very well." Her voice was husky, and her skin felt hot and clammy to the touch.

29

"Well, off to bed with you, then," Grandma had said, hiding her emotions behind a mask of strength like she always did, and then she bundled Mum off to rest.

That was a week earlier. The fever hadn't broken, and Mum was starting to have trouble speaking. Grandma had banished me from the room while she tended to my poor mother, so I was curled up on the couch watching yet another news report. This one was about the immune. They'd discovered that some people were resistant to the disease, and they hoped that immunity would give the scientists enough information to protect the rest of us.

The anchorman still hadn't shaved.

It was then that I realised that I hadn't seen any other people on the news in days. I wondered if they were all sick. Was this anchorman the only one left? That thought scared me, so I hugged Mushkin tight and buried my face in his rumbling warmth. Maybe if I wished hard enough, Mum would be okay, and Dad would arrive with Skylar in tow. We'd be safe and happy forever.

Grandma's cool hand landed on my shoulder and interrupted my wistful delusion. When I looked up and saw her expression, dread clamped its ice-cold talons around my heart.

"You need to go say goodbye to her," Grandma told me softly. All the humour was gone from her voice, but somehow she stayed strong. Her daughter lay dying and yet she managed to keep her wits together. It didn't occur to me until much later that Grandma felt like she had to stay strong for my sake.

I picked Mushkin up, and headed for the bedroom where my mother had spent the final week of her life. I made no attempt to wipe the tears from my cheeks. There was no point; I knew I'd be crying again soon enough.

I also knew that I was about to lose my mother forever, and that there was nothing in the world I could do to stop it.

Mum lay limp in her bed, propped up on as many pillows as we were able to scavenge from around the house. Her skin was so pale she looked like a porcelain doll. There was a clammy sheen of sweat on her brow that never seemed to go away.

I wondered briefly why Grandma would let me near her when she was so sick, then I realised that it was already too late for us both. If my mother had the disease, then we'd both been fatally exposed already. It was only a matter of time.

I sat down beside her and reached out, taking her clammy hand in mine. I gave it a gentle squeeze; she opened her eyes and looked up at me helplessly. Although she tried to speak, when she opened her mouth nothing came out.

"She can't talk anymore," Grandma explained softly, her expression unreadable. I was about to lose my mother, but she was about to lose her only daughter. I could not imagine how she felt.

I made no attempt to stop the tears rolling down my cheeks as I leaned over to stroke my dying mother's forehead. I couldn't think of what to say. Everything seemed inadequate. How do you say goodbye to the one person you love more than anyone else in the world? Lacking any other option, I just told her the simple truth.

"I love you, Mum."

The only response she gave me was a tiny smile and a gentle squeeze of my hand. She was too far gone to reply, but she still understood. Then suddenly, Grandma was bundling me out of the room, though I fought to stay longer.

"Please," I implored her, feeling completely helpless, "at least let me stay with her until the end."

Grandma caught my shoulders as I tried to get by her and held me firmly. "You can't, sweetheart. I made her a promise when she could still speak; now I have to keep it. Take Mushkin outside, I'll join you soon." She turned me around and ushered me out the door. Defeated, I took my fat old cat out and sat down on the doorstep to wait.

A few minutes later, a single gunshot shattered the silence. My head jerked up in surprise. Not long afterwards, Grandma stepped out beside me, her face a mask of grief. There was a small handgun clutched between her frail fingers. I looked up at her in horror, and she looked at me with more emotion than I'd ever seen on her face before.

"She made me promise." Grandma's voice was choked up, grief and guilt warring on her face. She sat down beside me on the stoop, staring down at the gun in her hand.

Then she looked at me. I realised with a jolt that her skin was clammy, and now that same sheen of sweat shone upon her brow as well.

"Sandy, I need you to make me a promise."

***

The promise had been the same one that my mother swore her to. When the disease took them to the point where they became helpless, they chose a quick and painless death over waiting for the inevitable.

My grandmother and I buried the body of my mother in the back yard. A week later, I buried my grandmother alone. Then it was waiting, waiting for weeks, waiting for the fever to claim me as well. All alone, just me and my cat, living on the supplies we'd brought with us from Auckland and what was already in the house.

Eventually, they ran out and I started to get hungry.

After a month passed, I realised that if I wasn't sick now then I wasn't going to get sick. I was one of the immune – alive but all alone. I needed to leave, to find food somewhere, but without my parents to guide me I couldn't even think of where to begin. I was absolutely terrified, but I was so hungry I could think of no other option. My choice was either to lay down and die with my family, or find to some way to survive.

I chose to live.

I took Mum's car and drove away, with Mushkin curled up on the seat beside me. For the first year or so, he was my loyal companion and followed me everywhere. But he was already old by the time the plague hit. One night, we curled up to sleep together, and he just never woke up.

After he died, I really was all alone.

***

The kitten was aggressive with its affection and demanding but it helped me to centre myself, to bring me back to the present and to focus on what needed to be done. I patted it gently, letting its soft fur bring back pleasant memories from childhood, happy memories of nights spent curled up with my beloved Mushkin, safe and warm in bed.

Eventually, I calmed down enough to function. It took a while, but the kitten's sweet-faced inquisitiveness helped. Whenever I started to slip away, she nudged me with her little head and brought me back to the present. Finally, after I'd cried my way through utter despair and out the other side, I felt strong enough to get up. I would have to do something about that damn 'Function' building, or else I would not be able to sleep tonight.

There was an unspoken code amongst survivors. A way to both respect the dead, and warn others away from something they really didn't want to see. I'd come across a few marked sites during my years on my own, and I knew what the black mark meant without anyone ever having to tell me. With that in mind, I set off in search of tools.

I found what I needed stashed away in the workshop I discovered earlier. While I

31

was gathering things, an idea began to grow in the back of my mind. I had initially planned to bury Benny and his beloved wife together, but it seemed more appropriate for them to spend their eternity with the community that they'd loved.

A coil of rope slung over my shoulder and a can of spray paint in my pocket, I returned home to fetch Benny and Margaret. It was not a pleasant trip, dragging a decaying corpse a few hundred metres along the street in the bright summer sun. He was already starting to fall apart, but I managed to keep him intact long enough to get him into the function centre.

I left Benny in the lobby. I couldn't bring myself to open the inner doors and take him all the way inside. I reassured myself that Benny would be happy just being close to his friends. It felt right. I straightened up his rotting limbs with as much respect as I could, set the jar of his wife's ashes into his wrinkled old hands, and placed his wedding photo on his chest, then I stood back and looked down at him.

"Rest in peace, Benny," I whispered.

Leaving them to their eternal sleep, I backed out of the function centre one last time, pulling the outer doors closed behind me. I slipped the coil of rope from my shoulder, and then I wound it around the door bars and pulled it tight, knotting it a few times until I was satisfied.

A few knots wouldn't be enough to stop a determined survivor, but it would keep anything inside from getting out, which was really the point. I rattled the doors to check that my knots were tight, and then fished my can of spray paint out of my pocket.

It took a bit of shaking to get the thing going, but when I did, I painted a large, black X across the doors, the universal sign that meant 'you really don't want to see what's in here, buddy'. I went over it a few more times, making it as bold as possible, then below it I added three simple letters: R I P.

I don't think I could have been any clearer than that.

# Chapter Eight

The kitten padded after me as I spent the rest of the day keeping myself busy. Occasionally, would she vanish, only to reappear a few minutes later in the most unexpected of places. After a quick cold scrub to get the stink of death off my hands, I hunted down the hot water cylinder of my new home to see if I could figure out what was wrong with it.

I was no electrician, but I had learned enough over the years to be self-sufficient. My father had taught me the basics of automotive engineering when I was a teenager, and I'd picked up a bit at school as well. The rest was really just logic, combined with large amounts of trial and error.

It didn't take me long to figure out that the heating coil was blown. I could replace it, but I would have to find another one in order to do so. There were quite a few homes scattered around the outlying reaches of town. With any luck, one of them might have a spare.

Another problem for another day.

On the plus side, at least now that I knew where all the bodies were, I was less worried about stumbling over a corpse in an unexpected place. You never quite got over the horror of tripping over a dead person when you didn't expect it, particularly if the corpse belonged to a child.

I eased myself out of the cupboard where the hot water cylinder lived and stood up, and then I moved to the window to check on the weather. There were clouds rolling in from the west again, thicker and darker than the ones the night before, warning me of foul weather yet to come. I opened the window and stuck my head outside, drawing in a deep breath through my mouth and nose. Sure enough, the tell-tale taste of a storm was on the air. Probably best to stay indoors then, rather than out in the open.

There were still a few hours left before dark, and at least a couple before the storm arrived, so I decided to use them wisely. I returned to the automotive workshop, to see if I could salvage one of the cars.

They were a pack of rust-buckets after so many years without maintenance, but not entirely without hope. There were even a couple of different choices. There was a sedan up on the hoist, and another out in the yard, a hatchback parked by the gate, and a four wheel drive under shelter. I chose the four wheel drive, for practicality, comfort, and the fact that it was old enough that it probably had a lead acid battery that I could refurbish. Plus, after the end of the world you couldn't really trust the roads to be well-maintained.

I found the keys in the office, discarded amongst piles of records that probably once meant something to someone, but not to me. I didn't care who the owner of the vehicle was. If they were still alive, they would probably have taken it already. No one had claimed it, so that made it mine.

It was a good machine, a double-cab Hilux with a canopy over the back; solid and well-built. One thing I'd learned is that Japanese cars really were made to last, and the parts were common and easy to find. After a quick peek through the windows to check for corpses and rats, I unlocked the driver's door and climbed behind the wheel. The interior was still in good condition, less dusty than most due to being safely sealed for almost a decade. The smell was a little off, but that could be fixed with a bit of airing out. Resting one hand upon the wheel, I put my foot on the brake, slipped the keys into the ignition and turned.

Nothing.

Ah well, you didn't get something for nothing in the scavenger's life. I tried the key again, listening closely for telltale sounds that would let me know what was wrong. Again, there was nothing.

I concluded that the battery was flat, and hauled myself back out of the driver's seat. Not a surprise at all. Car batteries only lasted a few months at most when not in use, and after a while they turned into glorified paper weights. That wasn't enough to turn me away, though. A few years after the plague, I'd met and befriended a survivalist who had taught me how to bring a car battery back to life, amongst other valuable titbits. We'd only known one another for six weeks before he'd vanished, but I used what he'd taught me nearly every day, and it had kept me alive. I popped the bonnet and propped it up with its little metal arm, then leaned in to get a closer look. A few cobwebs, but not much in the way of rust. That was a good sign.

I didn't bother trying to find another vehicle to jump start the battery. After ten years, I knew that it wouldn't be that easy. Still, the battery was the old lead acid kind, and I knew how to revive one of those. I grabbed a wrench from a toolkit nearby and disconnected the battery, then set about the rigorous task of doing just that. Luckily, I found all the tools and materials I needed in the workshop and storage sheds nearby and I was familiar enough with the process that I had it down to a science.

Once I was finished, I hooked the refurbished battery up to a mobile charging unit and left there. It would take all night to charge up, so I filled in the time with general maintenance. I checked the fluids, and found that there was still a full tank of petrol that looked fine and smelt fine, but the oil was congealed and dirty. That was probably one of the reasons that its old owner had brought it in for maintenance all those years ago.

Ah, well. No time like the present, right?

*** 

By the time I was finished draining the old oil and cleaning the components that needed it, the storm was getting close. As I hauled myself out from beneath the Hilux and wiped the grease from my hands, I spotted the kitten watching me from a workbench nearby. Her little head was canted curiously as she regarded me, as if she were trying in vain to figure out what I was about. I offered her a hand, but she turned her nose up and danced away from me, playing hard to get.

"Have it your way, then," I told her, and walked over to a sink nearby instead. With some difficulty, I cranked open the rusted tap to wash my hands. There was some old, harsh soap nearby, crusted up over the years, but still useful enough for scrubbing the grease from my skin.

*Craaaacka-boom*, the sky agreed.

Startled, the kitten inflated like an angry puffer-fish and vanished down behind the workbench.

"Pussy," I called after her. Then the rain started, an explosive downpour that set off a deafening cacophony on the roof above my head.

Hm. Perhaps the kitten was right.

Even though there was still more than an hour until sunset, the clouds obscured the sun and left me in near-darkness – a situation that I'd never really much cared for. I always preferred to be somewhere safe, secure, and easily defensible when darkness fell; danger often lingered in the shadows.

The workshop was more or less waterproof, so I left the battery charging and decided to return home for the evening. There was an old oilskin coat hanging by the doorway, which I liberated and shook free of spiders, then draped over my head. I was going to get drenched one way or another, but the token gesture made me feel a little better.

Out into the weather I went, huddled beneath my oilskin as I darted from shelter to shelter, keeping close to the edge of the buildings so that I could avoid the rain as much as possible. Despite my best efforts, I was soaked by the time I finally burst through the door of the old video store. I dropped the coat somewhere in the dark interior and shoved the door closed behind me, muttering profanities under my breath.

Mum would've been so furious if she'd heard, but I was a grown up now and could swear as much as I damn well liked. Still, I cringed and apologised to her memory inside my head, like I always did.

Sorry, Mum.

I shuffled through the sea of plastic shards and retreated upstairs, locking each door behind me. I'd left an upstairs window open that morning to let in some fresh air; now, one of the curtains was sopping wet, and there was a puddle on the floor.

I hurried over to close the window before it became a flood, and then retreated to the bathroom, shedding clothing along the way.

*My boots will be wet for days,* I thought morosely, wishing I that I owned a spare pair. I didn't even have a change of clothes. I did have a few spare pairs of underwear, but that was really about it. Clothing was yet another thing to add to the weight I had to carry around on my back from place to place. Unfortunately, you couldn't eat clothing so when it came to a choice between clothes and food, it was the clothes that got left behind.

I removed my taser and the other contents of my cargo pants from their pockets and dried them carefully on a towel, then set them in a neat, organised row on the dresser. Each one of them could mean the difference between life and death one day, so each of them was assigned a specific place.

Off went my underwear and bra, flung over my shoulder into the bathroom and replaced a moment later by a spare set of knickers and an undershirt from my backpack. It wasn't really cold despite the weather, so I just stayed that way. There was no real need for modesty beyond a little personal grace, since there was no one around to see me.

Left with little to do to pass the time, I returned to the living room and stared out the window at the raging storm – and found myself face to face with a bedraggled, miserable-looking tabby.

*"Mew?"* she mouthed, the sound muted by the glass, as she perched haphazardly on the windowsill waiting to be let in.

"Well, aren't you a determined little thing?" I smiled to myself and cracked open the window just enough for the kitten to squeeze through. In a blaze of fur she was inside, just as soaked to the bone as I was. By the time I'd closed the window again, she had claimed the couch as her own and settled in to groom determinedly.

"How the hell did you even get up here?" I watched the kitten with amusement, but of course, she didn't answer. The logical conclusion was that she climbed up, but no one ever said my imagination was a logical place. In my head, she'd bounced up like a cartoon character, and that was how she got her new name: Tigger.

\*\*\*

The storm raged outside as I tinkered with the television, curious to see if I could get any life out of it. Not that there were any shows worth watching anymore, but there was still the news.

As I had discovered in the months and years following the outbreak, that poor, unshaven man my grandmother had criticised was one of the immune, like me. Every evening at six o'clock sharp, he came on and spoke for an hour about whatever he felt anyone wanted to hear about. The six o'clock news was an old tradition, and he seemed determined to keep it going for as long as he was alive. I appreciated his stoicism, and I respected it. It was nice to have one thing left in life that I could rely on.

Plus, he was kind of cute.

Over the years, he had been the only form of male companionship I felt I could trust in any way, so I had developed a bit of a crush on him. Of course, I mocked myself mercilessly for it since I knew full well the anchorman didn't even know I existed.

I wondered what would happen when he died.

I had no idea where he broadcasted from. Would someone find his old studio and take over? Or would yesterday's traditions die right along with him? It was something that I didn't like to think about, but death was inevitable.

I often wondered how he got his news. In the past, he'd mentioned that people could call his studio and gave a cell phone number and a radio frequency, so I guessed it just came from other survivors. I had no news to give, so I'd never tried it. In my little world, keeping away from other people was the only way to stay safe.

There was a soft click as I reconnected a loose wire, then the tell-tale hiss of snow. I wriggled out from behind the television and sat down in front of it, fiddling with the tuning and scanning channels until finally I found the one I wanted.

The anchorman's solemn face filled the screen, a week's worth of whiskers fuzzing his jaw as he spoke into the camera. He was a handsome fellow, in his early forties with dark hair and bright blue eyes that somehow always looked so sad. His shirts were always crumpled, his hair looked like he'd probably cut it himself in a mirror, and his chin was perpetually overgrown. In some strange way, he always seemed to embody the way I felt at the end of the day – rumpled and worn, and far older than my years.

Something about that was comforting.

"...Repeating our top story, survivors in the Greymouth region are encouraged to relocate at the earliest possible time to another location, as supplies have run out. A bus departs tomorrow morning at dawn from the town hall for Nelson, and all survivors are encouraged to take it..." His voice was a morose drone, repetitive yet strangely restful. I relocated from the floor to the armchair, and curled up to watch.

It was morbidly fascinating, watching the news after the end of the world. There was never any good news. Everyone was dead except for a handful of us. The anchorman was our only form of communication aside from actual word of mouth or the occasional two-way radio. Still, the sound of another human voice was pleasant and welcome, even if it was from someone as obviously depressed as our anchorman. I leaned my head on my hands and closed my eyes, letting the sound of his voice soothe me.

Eventually, it lulled me into sleep.

\*\*\*

I awoke to the sound of static and birdsong the next morning, still curled up in the armchair like a sleepy child. Unlike all the times that I'd fallen asleep on the couch as a child, this time there was no Mum or Dad to carry me off to bed, so I'd spent the night where I was.

I sat up and uncurled, my joints protesting at the discomfort of having slept in such a peculiar position, yet I felt physically replenished. Outside my window, a tui sang a love song to its mate. The kitten sat on the window sill, observing the songbird with intense interest, oblivious to my awkward stretching. Once my limbs were awake enough to cooperate, I moved over to the window to look out as well.

The sky looked grumpy and overcast, but it was not raining at the moment. That seemed appropriate, since I felt a little grumpy myself. The thought of spending the day in wet boots did nothing to help my mood. My clothing was still damp, and clung unpleasantly as I pulled it on, but what other choice did I have? I cheered myself with the thought that perhaps, if I got the car going, I could visit some of those outer homesteads; maybe find some clean, dry clothing and spare shoes. That would be nice. I wouldn't be able to take them with me when I eventually left this town, but having them for now would be a treat.

At least breakfast was readily available, which always made me feel better. Tigger joined me, and ate some more of the cat food from a bowl on the kitchen floor, while I indulged in another can of baked beans. Oh, what I wouldn't have given for some real beans. I'd just about forgotten what they tasted like. Maybe one of the homesteads would have some of those, too.

Maybe they'd have chickens. Chickens, even wild ones, meant eggs that could be stolen. My new home came with a working stove and cooking equipment. Perhaps tomorrow morning I would have a real omelette for breakfast. Now, that idea really cheered me up. All of a sudden, my capricious mood was gone and I was raring to go.

I packed my essentials back into their pockets and laced on my wet boots, then padded off to check on my Hilux. The air smelt fresh and clean, and it was pleasantly cool after the heat of the last few days. Although the sky was still low and threatening overhead, it was nice enough outside and the thought of fresh food spurred me on.

When I arrived at the garage, I ducked in through the side door and checked the room for uninvited occupants; again, I found nothing out of the ordinary. The battery was showing fully charged now, so I reinstalled it in the engine and closed the bonnet. Fighting down a wave of excitement, I climbed back into the driver's seat and tried the ignition again.

The utility roared to life. It didn't sound terribly happy, but it was functional. Functional was what I needed. Keeping it going long term would probably be impossible, but it worked for now and that was enough. I disengaged the engine and tried it again, and got the same response. Content that it was going to work for at least one more day, I hopped back out and scampered over to the big roller doors that blocked my exit.

They screeched in protest as I hauled them up, and then screeched again when I closed them behind me. I didn't mind. I was suddenly in possession of the freedom of wheels, and that pleased me immensely.

Just let the other survivors find me now, I thought. I'll run them over and they can be damned!

# Chapter Nine

My first week in Ohaupo passed peacefully, with my days spent exploring the outlying countryside, and my nights spent tinkering and sleeping. It wasn't a good life or even a satisfying life, but at least it was a life. I was, more or less, content.

Several of the farms did have chickens, and a number of them had vegetable gardens as well. Like the chickens, the gardens had gone wild but that didn't bother me one bit. Wild or tame, fresh food was delicious and it made me feel a good deal happier than I had for a long time. After a few days on fresh vegetables and protein-rich eggs I felt healthier again, well-fed and ready to take on the world – or at least, my tiny corner of it.

The Hilux thrummed contentedly beneath me as I drove out to one of the few homesteads left to explore, hoping this one would yield more treasures to add to my growing stash. I had yet to find a functioning element for my hot water cylinder, and I still longed for a nice, hot shower.

I pulled the Hilux up the winding driveway to the homestead, carefully negotiating the rugged potholes and overgrown limbs hanging from the trees that framed the path. The house was a large one, someone's retirement mansion after many years of hard work, but just like all the others it was run-down and abandoned. Nature had reclaimed much of what was hers over the years.

Rose vines crept across the entire front of the house, covering it in a complicated lattice of foliage. Even at a distance, I could see fat, happy bumble bees darting from bloom to bloom, glutting themselves on sweet nectar.

I parked my truck, climbed out with my taser at the ready, and approached the old home to see what I could find. The smell was unexpected: it was an overwhelming mix of sweet, cloying scents from the dozen different kinds of flowers that warred for sunlight. I swept my gaze around, alert for danger, but detected nothing more hostile than the bees.

The gardens were a beautiful sight. I took a moment to enjoy the loveliness that spread out around me, then I turned and picked my way up what remained of the front walkway. Along the way, I bent to pluck a particularly perfect bloom from its stem and lifted it to my nose to savour the scent. After so much death and decay, the flower smelt like heaven on a stem.

With cautious fingers, I stripped away the thorns from said stem and then tucked the flower behind my ear. It was a silly little thing, but the woman in me longed to keep that beautiful scent close to me for a while longer. It reminded me of my grandmother. I thought of her wistfully, remembering the beautiful flowers she had once grown around her home in Palmerston North. Maybe one day I'd go back and plant roses upon her grave. She'd like that.

I ducked beneath an overhanging vine and climbed up the front stairs to the porch. The front door was unlocked, so let myself in; I doubted there was anyone home to complain. A quick glance around the dusty interior told me that I was correct – no one had been home for a very long time.

The front door opened into a spacious dining room, resplendent in hard woods and rose-print fabrics. The floor and fittings were all varnished oak, which had survived the years almost untouched. All it would take was a touch of polish to bring out their shine and have it looking like new again.

A dinner set waited in a wooden hutch to my left, the kind of good porcelain crockery that stood up well to the years. Much like the miniature set I'd found in the antique store, these were resplendent in rose prints with a hint of gold around the edge of each plate. The good china, waiting for the family to come home for Christmas.

They'll be waiting a while, I thought wistfully.

To the right of that was a set of wide glass doors that led out to an overgrown veranda. Wall hangings and paintings that spoke of better times decorated the walls, mounted with good, solid wooden frames rather than the plastic junk that had become more common in the later years. A table with enough chairs for six people sat in the centre of the room, and off to one side an archway led towards a kitchen. To my right, a long flight of stairs led upwards into shadow.

Foliage blocked most of the sunlight coming through the windows, but it was only dim inside rather than truly dark. I could see what I needed to see. I paused to ponder, thinking how beautiful the place must have been in its prime, when it was clean and cared for and the garden was groomed.

I could imagine a Christmas tree in the far corner, ready to welcome the grandkids on Christmas morning. They were probably all dead now, along with their parents and their grandparents.

That thought was sobering and brought me back to the present. There was nothing I could do for those people now, except kill them if I saw them shuffling about vacant-eyed at the end of their half-life. For their sake as much as mine I needed to survive, so that one day my descendants could live like this again.

I went for the kitchen first, as I always did. Ignoring the smell from the long-dead fridge, I made a beeline for the spacious double-door pantry. It was well stocked with all the necessities of life, though most of them well past their best-before date. On the lowest shelf was a veritable treasure trove of canned goods, just waiting to be plundered.

I grabbed an old rubbish bag from a higher shelf, and knelt down to gather up my bounty, pausing to examine each can before I put it into the bag. There was no point lugging something back that was guaranteed to be rotten on the inside, after all. I learned long ago what survived the years, what didn't, and which things were hit-or-miss.

Then, suddenly, I spotted something at the back of the pantry that made my heart skip a beat.

You knew you were a survivor when the most excitement you'd had in months revolved around finding a single, unopened can of Campbell's Creamy Mushroom Soup in the back of a dead person's larder, wedged behind a huge bag of rotten potatoes. I pulled it free and held it up, drawing a deep breath to try and contain my excitement.

This flavour had been my favourite in my old life. It brought back memories of snacks shared with my mother in winter, sitting around the table at the end of the school day. Talking, sharing funny stories, and enjoying soup together. It was so corny that we could have written scripts for commercials. Back in the days when commercials still mattered, and Mum was alive, that is.

I knew as well as anyone that canned soups were very much in the hit-or-miss category after this long. Chances were good that the can contained a congealed mass of black goo by now, completely unrecognisable as any form of food product. But, for the sake of my memories, I would try anyway.

I reverently added the soup to my sack of booty and finished clearing out the rest of the cans. To my distaste, I discovered that amongst them was a large amount of cat food. Great, just what I needed. More cat food. Tigger would be happy. Me, not so much. At least I could reassure myself that I had a decent firewall of other food between me and the dreaded cat food.

Once I was done with the cans, I looked around. A neat row of decorative storage tins painted in pretty colours drew my attention next. Carefully prying them open one by one, I found milk powder, rolled oats, and several kinds of pasta, most of which still looked edible courtesy of careful storage a decade ago. I added them – tins and all – to my sack, along with a couple of bags of white rice that I found tucked away in the back. White rice lasted forever if the pests didn't get at it. I practically lived on the stuff when I had access to cooking facilities. It went without saying that I was sick of eating it, but at least it was food. It wasn't exciting, but it kept the hunger pangs at bay.

Sweeping my gaze upwards, I examined the top shelves and found little of interest.

Wait… no, what's that? That tin up there, the one painted with the Christmas decorations? I reached up on tiptoes and pulled the tin down, to stare at it suspiciously.

Fruitcake. It had to be.

I remember the old urban legend that fruitcake was so full of preservatives that it would never go stale, so I couldn't help but be curious.

I cracked the tin open and peered inside, then promptly closed it again and returned it to the top shelf. Myth successfully debunked: fruitcake did *not* last forever. Frankly, I was a little relieved. If it had still been good, then I'd have been morally obligated to eat it at some point. The thought of eating decade-old fruitcake was less than appetizing.

The memory of my grandmother's Christmas fruitcake twisted my gut; no other fruitcake compared. Hers was actually edible – and quite tasty, in fact. The last time I'd eaten it was the Christmas just a few weeks before she died.

Shaking off the wave of sadness, I bundled my loot up on my shoulder and carried it out to where my Hilux waited faithfully. It was a heavy burden, but one of the perks of being a survivor was that you were never in need of a gym membership. If you sat around doing nothing, you died. Simple. Staying alive kept you fit.

I grumbled a few choice words under my breath as I unfastened the back canopy of my utility and hauled the heavy bag up onto the deck. I left the truck unlocked in a rare moment of carelessness and headed back inside. My reasoning was simple; who on earth was going to steal my supplies all the way out here? The nearest human being was many kilometres away.

I mounted the stairs to search the first floor, where I found myself in a dusty land of yesteryear. Old photographs faded with age decorated the walls, and there were a number of empty rooms that seemed to exist for decoration rather than any real purpose. Through one doorway, I saw a sitting room. Through another, a sewing room. A third was a hobby room, where a huge model train set took centre stage, rusting away amidst its carefully detailed landscapes.

Things were in good condition aside from the usual layer of dust, but I left most of it where it was. I took only some spare linens and a couple of pieces of clothing that looked to be around my size, and the rest of it I confined to the inventory map in my head.

In the world beyond the decline of man, you never quite knew what might come in handy one day. Whenever I saw something that I might need, I made a mental note of it in case I needed to find it in the future. It was the survivalist's mental encyclopaedia: useful only after the expiration of human civilization.

It was also handy to know where things were if you ever needed to find something to trade with other survivors. Be it physical items or just information, it all had value. You could never have too much knowledge.

That thought froze me in my tracks as I was passing back by the sitting room door, and the bookshelves that I had ignored on the way through. Books were heavy and you couldn't eat them, so I generally left them behind when I was out on salvage missions. This time though, I had a safe berth to return to, a good supply of food, and time on my hands. It would be foolish not to use the time wisely, so I stepped through the doorway and went over to look at the shelves.

Nothing struck me as particularly interesting. The shelves were mostly filled with cookbooks intended for use with ingredients I could no longer get, old magazines advertising businesses long since dead, and books on trains. Oh so very many books on trains.

I was about to leave when something finally caught my eye. Tucked in between the magazines was a small, worn paperback, a tatty copy of some silly romance novel I'd never heard of. All things considered, it seemed like an appropriate way to waste my time, indulging in fantasies that would never be.

I tucked the book into my pocket and went on my way.

*** 

Further exploration of the property revealed more chickens, an old dairy cow grazing in a huge paddock behind the house, and – to my delight – a small orchard. I armed myself with plastic bags, and spent much of the afternoon out amongst the trees, gathering up as much windfall as I could.

There were peaches, plums, apples and pears, a veritable feast of ripe, tasty nutrients. Needless to say, it was the peaches that drew me most. I plucked a soft, golden peach from a low-hanging bough and held it to my nose, drawing in a deep breath of the ripe scent.

It was too much for me to bear.

I took a huge bite and closed my eyes to savour the sweet, sweet taste on my tongue. Oh, how long it had been since I'd eaten a *fresh* peach! I devoured it in moments, juice running stickily down my chin, then snatched up another, and another. Finally, my sense of self-preservation kicked in. It took a hell of a lot of willpower to hold myself back from feasting until I exploded, but the last thing I needed was a tummy ache to go with all my other problems.

I drew a deep breath to steady myself, and knelt to gather up as many peaches as I could fit into my bags. There were so many on the ground I didn't need to pick any more from the tree itself. So many that finding ones not yet eaten by the birds and bugs was no trouble at all. It was unlikely that I would be able to eat them before they went bad, but there was no point letting them go to waste, right?

I was in the process of lugging the heavy bags back to my Hilux when I was distracted by something even more tempting than a fresh peach. Who knew that was even possible? I stopped for a moment to rest my aching biceps when I caught a whiff of a scent on the breeze. It was a familiar scent, a wonderful scent, a scent that took me back to childhood all over again.

The scent of strawberry bushes.

It was kind of a miracle that my nose was still so sensitive, but apparently it was. I could smell them, quite clearly from however far away, even over the overwhelming scent of the flowers. So many lovely strawberries, and so close.

I passed the Hilux en route to the patch, and deposited my bags of precious fruit on the front passenger seat. Then I scampered off in search of strawberries, as excited as a child. Every so often, I paused to sniff the cool breeze, following my nose to what turned out to be a very pretty little vegetable garden tucked away behind the house.

It was full of weeds and half of the plants had gone to seed, but I didn't care. I smelled strawberries and I had to have them. Careless in my footing, I scampered through the overgrowth until I found the strawberry patch.

That would be a moment that I would come to regret, very, very soon. Busy as I was stuffing my face with sweet, overripe strawberries, I wasn't paying attention to where I put my feet. I didn't notice the old board hidden amongst the bushes until it was too late.

More importantly, I didn't notice the nail.

At first, I didn't feel the wound; just was a strange sensation, like a prick, followed by a weird, invasive cold. I tried to step backwards to see what had bitten me, but my right foot wouldn't move. It was trapped, impaled through the arch on a six inch housing nail that was hidden amongst the weeds.

A flash of panic struck me right about the same time the pain did; I threw back my head and screamed. Even in agony, I possessed enough presence of mind not to give in to the urge to fall on my backside to try to take the pressure off the wound. God knew what else was hidden in the undergrowth, and it would be very hard for me to get back up again with my foot trapped the way it was.

*Trapped on a nail. A dirty, filthy nail. A sharp and probably rusty nail,* I thought with gritted teeth. I fought the urge to scream again as I shifted my weight carefully into a better position to lever my foot free. There was no one I could call, no one to come and help me. I was alone. I had to do this myself.

The nail ground against the bones in my foot as I jerked it free. I couldn't hold back the scream any longer. The pain was overwhelming. I half-limped, half-crawled out of the vegetable garden and got as far as the garden path before I collapsed, panting, in too much agony to go any further. I sat heavily on the paving stones and dragged myself further into the clear so that I could see my foot.

Or see through my foot, I thought.

Okay, I was being dramatic. I couldn't see *through* my foot. The tension of my muscles held the wound closed, but... man, it really, really hurt. Through tear-filled eyes, I struggled to focus on the wound as I wrestled to get my boot off. The pain was so intense I bit my lip to try and keep myself from screaming myself hoarse.

My boots had done me well for a number of years, but the soles were worn thin from all the walking I'd done; they had offered little protection or resistance. The nail had gone straight through the sole, into my foot.

There's not as much blood as I expected, I considered absently as I wrestled with the bootlaces. Why isn't it bleeding more? And when did it get so hard to undo a double-bow?

My fingers were trembling, slick with sweat and what little blood there was. It took twice as long as it should have to get the laces undone, and it felt like an eternity. I could feel the hot surge of my pulse in the wound, though the blood only oozed sluggishly.

"Oh, Christ!" I gasped as I finally pulled off my boot, and then stripped off the sock to lay the wound bare. It didn't look so bad, but the pain was nearly unbearable. Any number of terrible images flashed through my head.

Infection. Blood poisoning. Tetanus.

Oh God, when was my last tetanus shot? Before the plague, I thought. Panic rose in my chest. Oh my God. Oh my God. What do I do?

I didn't really know. I'd learned a little about first aid over the years, which was a necessity for surviving on your own, but I'd never been seriously injured before.

"Stop the blood flow," I hissed between clenched teeth, giving orders to my shaking hands. With one, I bundled up the sock and pressed it against the entry wound, while my other hand fumbled with one of the pockets of my cargo pants in search of the small emergency kit I carried out of habit. Awkwardly, using one hand and my teeth, I got the kit open and peered at the contents.

There was antiseptic, which I was quick to pour on the wound, but beyond that I felt lost. I had nothing to prevent a worse infection. People died from blood poisoning, from tetanus, from any number of ailments.

I had to find antibiotics.

I owned nothing more powerful than an over-the-counter dose of painkillers, and I knew there was nothing better to be found in this little township. I needed a pharmacy – or better yet a hospital. Although there would be no one there to help me, at least I could find the medication and administer it myself.

I hated needles, but I hated dying more. I refused to die. It was not my time and I was not ready.

I would have to go. Leave my little safe haven and go someplace else. I'd seen some hospitals in my travels to the south, but they were many, many miles away. Te Awamutu was picked clean, and I couldn't go further south without running the risk of encountering the very men I'd fled north to escape. So my only option was to go further north, to the city of Hamilton. There were bound to be survivors there, too, but what choice did I have?

I wasn't just afraid. I was fucking terrified.

# Chapter Ten

I thought that I'd known pain and what it felt like to be totally helpless, but none of my past experiences compared to what I felt as I dragged myself to my feet and hobbled back to my Hilux, nearly crippled with agony.

Tears ran freely down my cheeks, but at least the bleeding was stemmed for now. It was a pretty knock-up job, to be frank, but it functioned adequately. I used my sock for gauze and bound it up tight with the one pathetic bandage in my first aid kit. It wasn't enough, but I had to keep going.

Unfortunately, I wasn't one of those badass soldiers that can stitch up their own wounds and be fit for battle ten minutes later. I was just an ordinary human being stuck in extraordinary circumstances, and right now all I wanted to do was curl up in a ball and cry until the pain went away.

It felt like a kilometre, though it was really only a couple of hundred metres. It felt like it took an hour, though it was really only about ten minutes. Eventually, though, I made it back to my truck. Leaning heavily against the Hilux's flank, I fumbled open the driver's door with a hand that trembled uncontrollably, and suddenly I was glad that I'd left the vehicle unlocked. Keys in the ignition, too. Good thing no one was about or I'd really be in a pickle.

Even in my damaged state, I took a second to check the rear of the cab, to make sure no one was hiding back there waiting to take me by surprise. I was in no position to do anything about it if there was, but paranoia was a hard habit to break.

Getting into the car proved easier said than done, even with two good hands and one good foot. Everything I did seemed to knock the injury around and send white-hot stabs of pain all the way up my leg. I swore inelegantly every single time, then apologised to my mother's memory right after. Under the circumstances, I was sure that Mum would have understood, but that wasn't the point. I apologised for my sake, not hers. Trying to keep my mother's memory alive helped to keep me grounded and somewhat civilized.

I braced myself on the handhold on the roof and literally hauled myself the last few centimetres into the cab. Shoving my butt as far back in the seat as was possible, I grabbed a hold of the fabric of my cargo pants for leverage. My leg didn't seem to want to bend right now, so I hauled it in with my hands.

Then I realised suddenly that there was another problem: it was my right foot that was injured. My driving foot.

"Aw, Christ." I gritted my teeth, trying the pedals with my bad foot. Nope, not going to happen. I could barely move it, not until the swelling went down anyway. I was going to have to learn to drive with my left foot.

"Just what I need," I groaned to myself. "Bleeding, in pain, and a menace on the roads. I better put a seatbelt on. Would that even make a difference right now?"

I thought about it for a second, then buckled the belt anyway. Safety first. Didn't want to go getting myself killed, after all; I was fairly certain the other survivors would do it for me if I gave them half a chance. Still, I had no other choice but to expose myself, or suffer a terrible death by infection.

Thinking about that sent a cold shiver down my spine, so I focused on figuring out how to drive with the wrong foot. It was hard, like learning to drive all over again, but better that than thinking about what had happened the last few times I'd encountered other survivors. I knew from experience just how bad desperate people could be.

At least I'd learned as a result that I never wanted to be like them. Ever.

***

By some miracle, I made it back to Ohaupo without hitting a tree or rolling into a ditch. There, I met with a dilemma. Did I return to my haven and get my things before I left, knowing that if I took them there was a chance I would have them all stolen by the survivors in Hamilton and be left with nothing? Or did I go on without them, and risk being stuck in a situation where I needed them but would have to make do without?

One thing was for sure: I needed my GPS, and I needed my gun. That meant figuring out how to tackle stairs on one good foot.

I managed to make it out of the truck and into the store without falling on my face, which I considered a small victory in itself. The store was another story; I was forced to shuffle awkwardly amidst the plastic shards in an attempt to avoid injuring myself any further.

Of course, like a diligent survivor I had covered my tracks each time I'd come through the shop floor, so now there was no clear path for me to follow. I ended up with a collection of nasty scratches by the time I made it to the office, but none significant enough to worry me any more than the bloody great hole I already had. I didn't have the strength to close the door behind me, but that didn't seem to matter. Everything was as I'd left it. There was no one about but me.

And Tigger, apparently. She appeared behind me as I was crawling up the stairs on hands and knees, watching me with a curiously-tilted head. I could practically hear her thoughts. What on earth is that silly human doing? Oh, she's bleeding? Goodness gracious, I better go beg for food, post-haste. You know, in case she forgets that I'm a stomach with legs.

Sure enough, as soon as I made it to the top and struggled to my feet, she came bounding up after me and almost tripped me over.

"You know, you're supposed to be a wild cat. You're not meant to be this friendly," I told her, to which she replied with a heart-felt mew. I guessed she was born and bred in the area so she'd never learned the wild cat lessons to fear big, scary humans. I was a big, scary human that administered food, which made me perfectly okay in her book.

Even in my injured state, the need to nurture rose in me. I dragged myself into the kitchen to fill the kitten's food dish, giving her the last of a tin I'd opened that morning just for her. I'd been feeding the kitten regularly over the last week and she'd gradually become tamer, but she was still playing hard to get and wouldn't let me touch her again.

Now I felt like that was a good thing; I didn't know if I was going to survive this trip, so I didn't want her to be too dependent on me. My reasoning for feeding her to begin with was that she was too young to be hunting on her own, but she was bigger now and I felt a little more confident she would be fine without me.

Truth was, she'd probably have been fine without me from the beginning, but a part of me wanted something, anything, to care about in this dead world. No, not wanted. Needed. Even without physical contact, little Tigger helped to alleviate the loneliness. My eyes blurred, and I brushed the tears away impatiently. No time for that now.

"I'll be back if I survive, I promise," I told the little kitten, who ignored me with great vigour. She was far too busy gobbling down her dinner to notice me. I left her to it and I hobbled out of the kitchen to the bedroom, looking for my pack. There was a better first aid kit in there, and I needed to clean that wound before I went anywhere.

Needless to say, that was a painful experience. By the time I was done, Tigger had fled from the sound of my gasps and cries. Personally, I was just amazed that I managed to stay conscious. It was a close call at times, when the pain got so bad that that I started to see stars and got light-headed, but somehow I made it.

Hell, if that's how much it hurt to clean the wound and wrap it in proper gauze and a bandage, I didn't know how all those fictional soldiers were supposed to have been able to do their own stitches. I probably did need stitches, come to think of it, but I'd pass out for sure if I tried to do it myself. No time for that. The wound was still bleeding sluggishly, but the tension of the muscles in my foot staunched the worst of it.

"God, this hurts like a giant flying inflatable bejebus," I groaned, closing my eyes to try and block out the pain somehow. "Drugs. I need drugs. I think I have some in here somewhere."

I dug into my pack, and down in the bottom I found a box of painkillers so old that the brand name had faded away. As I popped back a couple and washed the bitter tablets down with water, I hoped that they'd still have the desired effect. They were the cheap non-prescription kind that I had found in a ransacked store years ago, back when the brand was still visible.

"I really hope this stuff doesn't go off – or go toxic," I muttered to myself. "Well, I guess I'm about to find out."

I didn't have any time to waste on thinking about it, so I put the thought aside and focused on what I needed to do. My boot was gone. I'd left it back at the farmstead, and there was no time to go back and fetch it. Luckily, a few days earlier I'd found a pair of athletic shoes in my size. They'd probably do a better job with my injury, anyway; they were old and worn by time, but the soles were soft and thick, and they'd help me keep moving for a little while longer.

I stripped off my other boot and tossed it aside, since it was useless without its mate. The only thing worse than wet boots was mismatched boots. I was having enough trouble walking without my balance being off due to uneven weight distribution from ill-matched shoes.

Scooting along the bed on my behind with my bad foot awkwardly elevated, I stuck my nose over the edge to search for my new-shoes and a clean pair of socks; the old set were kind of a mess now. The wound hurt terribly as I carefully pulled on the new footwear, a hot, rhythmic throb in time with my pulse, but once there was pressure on it I was surprised to find that the pain diminished a bit.

Maybe I've done the bandages up too tight, I pondered with a brief flash of morbid amusement. Ah, well. Not complaining unless my toes drop off.

Mission accomplished, I flopped backwards onto my bed and allowed myself a couple of minutes to rest and recover. I closed my eyes and drew long, deep breaths, trying to visualise the pain flowing away. Whether it was the meditation or the medication, the pain did seem to lessen a little.

In all honesty, it was probably just the fact that I wasn't trying to hobble around that eased the pain.

What was the incubation period for tetanus, anyway? I tried to think back to high school health class, but I couldn't remember. I did remember a time when Katie had cut herself at camp, though. They'd rushed her off for a series of injections straight away. How much time did I have?

That thought stirred me out of a doze. It was getting dark. Could I stand to wait until morning? Normally, I refused to go anywhere after sunset – it just wasn't safe. Unfortunately, right now my choices were kind of limited.

"Just go now. Get it over with," I told myself, easing my aching body back up into a sitting position. There was plenty of food in the car, and if I locked this place up nice and tight it would be fine without me. I estimated that Hamilton was about an hour away by car, less if I drove like a maniac, so in theory I could be back before dawn. I would sleep when I got home.

Filled with sudden determination, I grabbed my backpack and began sorting out the items I would take with me. The first aid kit, of course, in case I needed to change my bandages. My GPS, since I wasn't familiar with Hamilton. A couple of emergency pairs of socks and underwear – you know, just in case. My sewing kit, for the same reason. My taser.

And last but not least, the box containing the one thing I hated looking at most in the world, and the one I couldn't discard. The thing that brought back so many terrible memories.

The last gift from my grandmother.

The very thing that had taken her life, at my hand.

I opened the box and looked at it, checking that the nine millimetre Smith & Wesson handgun was still in its place. It was, nestled alongside a couple of boxes of spare bullets that I had collected over the years.

With a shaking hand, I removed the gun from its place and checked over all the moving parts, making sure nothing was rusted or stuck. It seemed to be fine. Trying not to think about how it had felt when I'd put the barrel against my beloved grandmother's head and pulled the trigger, I slipped it back into its box and closed the lid.

I'd only fired it a few times since then. Each time, it had been at another survivor rather than at the walking dead. Well, no. That was a lie. I had tried to shoot one of the infected once, but all that did was cripple the poor thing. They no longer felt pain, and the only part of the brain left was their brain stem, which was a small target and difficult to reach. The taser worked better on infected, and since it was rechargeable it just made more sense. The gun was a weapon of last resort.

I added the gun and its ammunition to the small pile of items I would take with me. The food in the car was more than I'd need; enough to feed me for a couple of weeks at least. Still, I was in no condition to remove it so it would have to come with me. Even if I didn't eat it all, I could potentially use it to trade.

I paused for a moment and thought. I should take money as well. To most survivors, cash was about as useless as monopoly money – our currency was essentials, like food, water, and personal effects. Still, there were a few people out there that clung to the old ways. To most, my bags of fruit were far more valuable than money, but knowing my luck I'd find the medicine I needed in the hands of the one person left who still wanted hard currency.

Most of the time, I didn't bother to carry cash since it was basically just dead weight, but I did carry a few hundred dollar bills in case of emergencies. I fetched them out and stared at them, not entirely convinced that they would be enough for what I needed. Life-saving supplies did not come cheap.

I closed my eyes, and thought back over the layout of the town. Suddenly, I realised that in my exploration of this very building, I hadn't seen a safe. There must have been one. Someone paranoid enough to put four locked doors between himself and the outside world would not have left his cash sitting around in an unsecured lock box.

"If I were a paranoid old man, where would I put the safe?" I asked myself. My head was spinning and it was getting hard to think, but verbalising my ideas seemed to help. "The office would be the logical place, wouldn't it?"

The reasoning made sense to me, so I decided that I would check on my way out. I wasn't sure I would be able to make it back up the stairs again, so it was better to plan my movements carefully. I repacked my bag, dumping out everything non-essential, and then triple-checked that each of my tools was in its proper place.

In my head, I went through a mental checklist like I'd done a thousand times before. I removed each item in order and examined it, then returned it to its pocket. It was a ritual more than anything, and helped me ensure I always had everything I needed and never wasted weight on anything I didn't.

Something small and soft poked my hand midway through my checks. I blinked and reached further into the pocket, then pulled out that little family of toy bunnies I'd found the week before. One by one I set them on my palm and stared at them. In my head, they weren't just bunnies; they were a representation of the family I'd lost so long ago.

The smallest one, in her tiny pink dress – oh, how she reminded me of my baby sister. The bunnies had been there ten years ago, when we'd first passed through this little town. Sitting together in their little dollhouse, waiting for the right person to come along and buy them. Mum had left me in charge of Skylar while she stopped into the local grocery store for some more supplies, and Skye had dragged me over to stare at the precious things on display in the antique store's front window.

How clear her young voice was in my memory, full of wonder and delight. She begged me to buy her those bunnies, along with just about everything else in that store. When I told her I couldn't, she cried and cried as though her little heart would break – right up until Mum had found us and given her an ice cream treat instead.

I'd been here before. So, why couldn't I remember the face of the cashier behind the counter? That bothered me; the cashier had been a human being, just like me, just like everyone else. Had she died in that horrible hall along with all the others? Or did she still wander the earth, waiting for the end to come?

I closed my hand around the tiny, velvet-soft forms, and set them on the dresser as I rose. My tiny family, always perfect, always happy, never lost and all alone. I would leave them here, where they were safe. I took one last long look before I walked away, and shuffled awkwardly into the kitchen. There, I added a couple of water bottles to my pack and slung it over my shoulders. That would have to do. I couldn't carry much more in my current condition, and it would be a stupid idea to try.

It took me a while to get back down the stairs again, mostly because I ended up having to scoot down on my butt. Ah, how that brought back memories of playing silly games with my little sister, though our games were never in life-or-death situations.

Thinking of little Skylar made me so sad. Again, I wondered what had happened to her. She'd been such a sweet little girl, so innocent, all fairies and princesses and unicorns at the tender age of eight. I hoped her death had been quick and painless. She didn't deserve to suffer. I couldn't bear to think of her suffering. I sighed, and resigned myself to never knowing for sure.

At the bottom of the stairs I hauled myself back to my feet with the aid of the door frame, and looked around the little office. I saw no sign of a safe or anything that resembled one. The room was so small that I should have seen it straight away, unless it was hidden somewhere.

…Hidden somewhere?

With a sudden flash of cognition, I remembered the painting on the wall, the one I'd instinctively felt was out of place in the room. I hobbled over to examine it more closely. Sure enough, behind the painting was a recess in the wall. Within it was a small safe. To my relief, there was no combination or numerical pad, just a keyhole. That made life easy, since Benny's keys were in my pocket. I tried them, one after another, until one of them clicked. The safe swung open.

"Easiest burglary ever," I mumbled. Hey, my foot might have been busted, but my sarcasm-bone was still intact.

There wasn't a lot of cash in the safe, but there was some. The plastic notes were sticky but showed no sign of fading or decay. The Reserve Bank made things to last. I took the small stack of bills, probably about five hundred dollars in tens and twenties, and stowed it in my pack. Some was better than none.

It struck me as kind of funny how my dad used to gripe at us kids about how money didn't grow on trees. It sure did now. Everywhere you turned was free cash, and it was all worth a grand total of nothing. You couldn't even burn the stuff for warmth, since it was all made of plastic.

There was a box of coins in the safe as well, probably the float Benny used for his cash register, but the weight outweighed the value. You could find coins everywhere and they were only really useful if you had a vending machine and you were too lazy to pop the lock with a crowbar.

"Well, that's it," I told myself. "No more excuses, time to go."

Man, I was not looking forward to this little adventure, but I had no choice. Go and maybe die horribly, or stay and definitely die horribly? I had to go, for Mum's sake, for Dad and little Skylar. They wouldn't want me dying of any kind of infection, not after I'd been lucky enough to survive Ebola-X. I was the only one left to carry on their memory and keep their bloodline alive. I was the only one left to remember how much they had been loved.

I shouldered my pack and hauled myself up straight, doing my best to ignore the renewed pain in my foot. I locked the door to the stairs, and then backed out of the office and locked that door as well.

*Where's Tigger?* I wondered, peering about. The last time I'd seen her had been at dinner, so I hoped that I hadn't locked her inside. Then I spotted her, curled up fast asleep on the still-warm bonnet of my Hilux.

I indulged myself in a weak smile and hobbled over to shoo the kitten off. She ignored me. Losing patience, I went to pick her up and shift her myself, but she hissed and swatted at my hand.

"Have it your way, kid," I grumbled, snatching my hand away before she could draw blood. "But you're not going to like what happens next."

I checked the cab again, then opened the door, threw my backpack into the rear and hauled myself in. The keys slipped into the ignition and the engine roared to life. Sure enough, the kitten inflated like a hedgehog and practically levitated off the bonnet in a mad dash for the safety of the overgrowth. I immediately felt guilty for giving her a scare, but reassured myself that it was for the best. I needed to go now and she was being stubborn.

I was also glad she was nowhere nearby when I awkwardly pulled the truck away from the curb and hit the road. It would have just about killed me if I'd run the poor little fuzzy over.

I was such a sucker for cats.

# Chapter Eleven

The trip to Hamilton was unpleasantly long, but uneventful.

I was not a huge fan of travelling, but at least when I was driving I didn't get carsick. Still, given a choice I would probably have just settled down in one place and stayed there forever, or at least until the supplies ran out.

I had planned to do that in Ohaupo, but now I didn't know what I was going to do. It was my hope that I would be able to return, but my gut was all twisted up with a sense of foreboding. I chided myself with the fact that I was probably just worrying over nothing, like I usually did. I was the kind of person who was over-prepared for every situation, the one who churned themselves into a tight little knot of anxiety thinking about everything that could possibly go wrong, even the scenarios that were completely impossible. Hopefully, this would be just another time when I'd gotten myself all worked up over nothing.

The road cut a swath across the broad, flat green land, dotted with cows and sheep that grazed on, oblivious to the loss of their farmers. Most domesticated animals had flourished in the wake of the outbreak, their numbers unchecked. New Zealand had no predators to speak of, or at least nothing that could have taken down a full grown cow.

I had heard on the news that a few lions had been spotted near Wellington Zoo a few years back, but I doubted they would get this far north. And if they had, I imagined those cows out there would have been looking a hell of a lot more worried. There were pigs, of course, but they were blessedly rare, and mostly stuck to heavily forested areas.

Right now, the cows seemed to be more bothered by the growl of my engine than any risk of predation. Bovine heads came up as I passed, watching me with long-lashed eyes. To them, I was a noisy, alien menace that disrupted their contented, cud-chewing world, and they were glad to see me gone.

I flipped on my headlights as the sun slipped below the horizon and plunged the world into darkness. This far from any kind of significant township, there was no light aside from the stars. Once, there had been street lamps lighting the way at regular intervals, but at some point in the past the wind had claimed their lives. Now, they lay scattered along the roadsides like fallen supermodels after someone greased the runway.

I found myself absently wondering how strong the wind must have been to rip those street lamps out. There were still some standing in Ohaupo, so it seemed like a localised kind of destruction; perhaps a tornado had ripped through here. With no one around to fix things, once stuff fell over it just stayed where it landed.

The deepening gloom forced me to slow down. If would get messy fast if I hit one of those fallen street lamps at high speed – or if a cow decided to sleep on the road. It had probably been years since they last saw a car. They would have no idea they were supposed to stay off the road.

I decided to err on the side of caution, and eased the Hilux down to a more sedate pace. I flicked the headlights on to high beam and leaned forward over the wheel, focusing intently on the road ahead. The asphalt was in terrible condition, with long cracks running in all directions; grass grew through the cracks, making it hard to tell where the tar seal ended and the verge began. Debris of all kinds littered the way, and often I was forced to slow or swerve to avoid something that might damage the car.

A green-and-white sign flashed by: Cambridge exit, two kilometres. Right lane only.

There were lanes? I saw nothing. The years had stripped away the road-markings, leaving it a simple ribbon of dark grey. What were the old rules again? Keep left? Keep right? It didn't even matter anymore. The chance of meeting someone else on this dark, deserted highway in the back end of nowhere was one in a million. Maybe more.

Cambridge exit, one kilometre.

The signs were made of a reflective material that glowed like a neon sign in the beam of my headlights, even after ten years of wear. Did I want that turn-off? I didn't think so, but I grabbed my GPS off the dashboard and consulted it anyway. No, I needed to keep on going. There was nothing in Cambridge I wanted right now. The supplies I needed *might* have been there, but I didn't have time to risk it.

I was headed straight for the biggest hospital in the area, the one located on the southern fringe of Hamilton city. I wanted to spend as little time as possible within the city itself, and since I was coming from the south that hospital was the one that made the most sense.

The dread in my gut turned my stomach like I'd eaten rotten eggs.

\*\*\*

It was almost midnight by the time I reached the outskirts of the city. Fatigue was starting to catch up to me, and I found myself struggling to keep my eyes open.

The first thing I noticed was that there were signs of devastation everywhere; the riots had hit this place hard. Road signs had been torn down or defaced, and the cracked white paint flashed by like old bones in the light of my headlights.

Real bones lit up as I passed by as well, some full skeletons still dressed in the clothes they'd died in, some just random limbs or skulls bleached bare by the scorching heat of the long summer days. Many people had died here. I wondered how many were suicides and how many were murders; how many innocent people had been killed in the riots that the police had not been able to contain?

I slowed to a crawl as I negotiated the city streets, scanning the shadows for any signs of life, death, or anything in between. I saw nothing, but I didn't trust my own limited vision in the darkness. The street lights in this part of the city appeared to be out, or the power grid was having a fit. Aside from the occasional flash of a crumpled street sign when my lights grazed it and the distant glow from other parts of the city, it was too dark to make much sense of anything I saw.

It made me feel so exposed. If anyone was looking, they would see me long before I saw them, unless they were stupid enough to walk right in front of the truck.

I checked my GPS, and found myself close to one of the old entrances to the hospital grounds. I pulled over and stared into the darkness, but I couldn't see anything. I fished my torch from its pocket and clicked it on, then shone it out the window at the roadside. A high metal fence topped with spikes barred the gap between the footpath and the car park beyond. There was no way I was getting past that in my current condition – at least, not without a blow torch.

I drove forward slowly, searching for a break in the fence or some kind of entrance that I stood a chance of negotiating. A few metres further on, I caught sight of something that looked a little like a guardhouse, and inched the truck closer to get a better look.

Suddenly, light flared up and blinded me for a second. When the initial glare faded and my vision adjusted, I found the street lamps were back on, along with spotlights around the car park and hospital grounds; I just happened to be unfortunate enough to have one of those spotlights pointed straight at me.

*Just a blackout*, I concluded with relief. Maybe things weren't as bad as I thought. With the lights on, the place seemed less scary all of a sudden. I could even see light shining through a couple of the windows of the hospital itself. Maybe things would be all right after all.

Yes, there were skeletons all over the place, but there were skeletons everywhere in this day and age. I could handle skeletons… in small doses. I'd gotten used to them over the years. Human remains were impossible to avoid. They were still gross and upsetting, though.

I took the time to look around my newly-lit world in more detail. The grounds surrounding the hospital were a mess, littered with all manner of refuse – everything from old newspapers to the decomposed remains of human beings. A banner flapped in the breeze amid a forest of road cones; the plastic hazard tape that stretched between them was limp and faded with age.

*Hey, road cones – they might be useful someday.* My mental inventory updated, but aside from sarcastic jokes and witch hunting, I was unable to imagine any real use for the things. But, who knew? Maybe something would come up.

A strong gust of wind caught the banner and pulled it straight for a moment, long enough for me to read the biohazard quarantine warning. The words were marred by brown-black stains that were most likely blood, or perhaps paint. I had suspected as much – the hospitals were the first places the infection broke out, for the obvious reasons. Where else would you go when you were sick and terrified? You went to hospital, hoping for salvation and a miracle, like you saw on all those TV medical dramas.

Unfortunately, there was no miracle for the infected. Most of those poor people had gone to hospital to die.

Of course, that fact also meant that the hospitals usually had the highest concentrations of undead loitering within. Although most of them had once been hospital staff and tried to be helpful, a zombie with a syringe was still a zombie with a syringe. I would keep my taser close at hand.

As I turned into the car park, the fallen barrier arm crunched beneath my tyres; I wondered briefly what happened to it, but there was no way to be sure. Perhaps it had been smashed in the riots, or torn down in the storms, but for whatever reason the arm that once held back unauthorised traffic now lay shattered on the ground.

A doorway loomed before me, its doors hanging open like a gaping, toothless maw. The hallway beyond was pitch black aside the distant flickering of a fluorescent light bulb well past its prime. Deeper within, I could see a steadier glow, but this entrance was dark and foreboding. I pulled the Hilux to a halt directly in front of the door and stared as far down the hallway.

Nothing moved as far as I could tell, but the flickering light bulb made it hard to be sure. I considered my options, pondering whether it was worth driving around looking for another entrance or whether I should go with what I had. I decided to just roll with it and move as fast as possible.

I put the truck in park, and fetched my pack from the back seat. From within, I drew out the box that contained my gun, feeling its unhappy weight in my hand. I hated the thing, but it was a necessary evil. With careful fingers, I slid out the magazine and checked the contents, then slid it back into place with a solid click. I was ready.

Setting the gun on the dashboard, I checked the shadows one more time before I struggled my way out of the cab, my foot stiff and swollen. As I put my backpack on and slipped the gun into the pocket closest to my hand, I hoped that it wasn't the first stage of infection setting in. Another reason to move my ass, just in case.

I locked the truck and took the keys with me this time. The truck was my best means of a quick escape, so there was no way I was risking its security. Even though I couldn't see anyone, there might have been any number of people watching from one of the dozens of dark windows all around me. Biding their time. Watching, waiting.

Creepy.

I moved as swiftly and carefully as I could to the entrance of the hospital, tolerating terrible pain in an effort to hide my limp. When I reached it, I turned and stared behind me, searching the deepest dark recesses all around, before finally turning to confront the terrible shadows within. I drew my torch from one pocket and clicked it on, my other hand fumbling to fetch my gun as I stepped forward into the darkness.

And promptly tripped, almost falling on my face before I could even get inside. That was a promising start.

I swung the torch down and dropped a mental curse or two: there was an old black pushchair blocking the doorway at a level just below the line of my torch. It was rusted and dirty but small, so I just gave it a gentle nudge with my shin to push it out of the way. Its rusted wheels gave way and it tumbled sideways, scattering the tiny bones of its former occupant across the floor.

A baby. There had been a baby in there.

Bile rose in my throat and I fought down the urge to cry. Poor little baby. There was no way for me to have known. I hadn't meant to send its little corpse flying. Silently whispering apologies and prayers, I stepped around the scattered bones and forced myself to look away. I must keep moving, find the medicine, get somewhere safe again. If I let myself break down every time I saw a dead child, I would never achieve any of that.

The hospital was deathly silent. Not even the drone of the wind reached this far inside. It was creepy, like an old horror movie. A weird, chemical smell overlaid the ever-present stench of decay. I never had cared for hospitals. Too many movies as a kid, I guess. They both gave me nightmares, and now I had to live the nightmare. Great fun.

I shone my torch side to side, and finally spotted a sign that hadn't been completely defaced during the riots: Maternity Ward.

I'm in Maternity? I thought, swearing under my breath. Oh Christ, that's just what I need.

If I found a zombie baby, I was going to turn myself right back around and go die of tetanus in my truck. On the scale of horrification, zombie baby beat death by tetanus any day.

As I snuck further inside, I spotted doorways flanking the hall, each of them just as dark and ominous as the hallway itself.

I wondered if the power was still out to this part of the building, or if a surge at some point in the past had burst all the bulbs. There seemed to be light further up, so it was reasonable to assume that it must just be this part. Ten years was a long time to leave the lights on.

Sweeping my torch from side to side, I checked the first room for hostiles, then the second, and moved methodically down the hall. No bad guys. No zombie babies either, thank goodness.

I was wound up tighter than a starlet's Spanx by the time I got to the T-intersection at the end of the hall, my brain set to a hair-trigger. I moved under the flickering light, half-expecting to be attacked the moment I stepped into the light, but nothing happened.

The closer I got to the corner, the brighter the light grew, though 'bright' was a relative term. The hallway was lit only by old, dull emergency lights that bathed the corridor in a dirty, artificial glow.

I raised my gun as I slowly approached the junction, keeping close to the left wall. Although I moved with the natural stealth of a survivalist, my uneven footsteps sounded loud enough to wake the dead, and my breath was deafening to my own ears. I was almost afraid to breathe at all. In truth, they were barely audible, but I felt like a rampaging elephant.

Keeping near the left wall meant I could scan down the right arm of the junction before exposing myself on the left. I saw nothing. As smoothly as I could, I slid around the corner to stare along the left arm, again seeing nothing. Instinct made me stop to assess the distances between myself and the next junction in either direction, to take stock of the rooms I needed to risk passing in order to continue. The hallways were short in both directions, branching after a half-dozen metres into more corners, more risk, more places for enemies to hide.

I made a snap decision: I didn't want to stay exposed for too long, so I chose the left hallway and hobbled around the corner with my gun tucked in close in front of me. There was a room just down the passageway; I limped towards it to see what was inside. The lights were on, so I clicked off my torch and held the gun carefully with both hands. Of course, it didn't occur to me until much later that with my shuffling gait, my gaunt frame, my tatty clothes, and my tangled hair, I probably looked more undead than alive from behind.

My foot was starting to really hurt as the painkillers wore off, and my heart was hammering in my chest at a mile a minute. The sense of urgency I felt was growing more and more overpowering, leaving me feeling increasingly panicked and vulnerable.

*This is a terrible idea*, I thought, mentally cursing myself for being such an idiot. *Why didn't I wait until morning?*

I limped into the side room, looking for supplies, any kind of supplies that might help with my injury. There was a locked cabinet on the far side that contained a promising array of little bottles, jars, and prescription boxes. I shuffled towards it and stared at the contents, trying to make out what was inside before I decided whether it was worth the risk of breaking the glass.

Something shattered beneath a heavy boot right behind me, and I froze. Reflected in the glass cabinet, a dark shadow loomed in the doorway. A second later, my self-defence instincts kicked in and I spun to face the incoming threat. Or at least I tried to, but my damn foot gave out in the process and I ended up in a heap on the floor.

That fall saved my life.

The shotgun blast shattered the window right above my head as I fell, showering me in shards of glass and hot shrapnel. I screamed and covered my eyes with my forearm to protect myself, fully expecting a second shot to tear me apart at any second. I would say that my life flashed before my eyes, but it didn't; I just found myself wondering if it would hurt to die. Would I see Mum again? Dad? Skylar? Were they waiting for me? Or would I just... cease to exist?

The second shot never came.

"My god, you're alive!" a deep voice gasped, then a strong hand latched around my forearm and hauled me to my feet before I could react. "Are you crazy? What are you doing here at this time of night? I almost shot you – you could have been killed!"

The survivor was tall, dressed in worn, dark blue combat armour, the upper half of his face concealed by a helmet and night vision goggles that gave him a terrifying, alien look.

I didn't even stop to think. I just reacted.

Now, I was a scrawny thing. While I was pretty tall for a girl, malnutrition had robbed my frame of any body fat that I'd once possessed. I was maybe fifty kilograms soaking wet, but every gram I had was muscle, driven by a mind that long ago learned the only good defence was a swift and brutal offense.

Long story short: I don't hit like a girl.

I clocked him square in the jaw with every bit of my physical strength, and the man's head snapped back. He stumbled away from me, tripping over an old chair and almost falling. Weighed down by his armour and the combat shotgun, it took him a second to right himself.

That was enough for me.

I snatched my gun and my torch from where they'd fallen, and then I was off like a... slow-moving, half-gimped shot. It wasn't very fast, but it was as fast as I could go.

I was terrified, my heart pounding in my chest and adrenaline tingling through my extremities. Every time I tried to pick up to a run, my foot sent a stab of pain all the way up my leg that was so bad the limb almost gave out on me, so I was forced to be satisfied with a shambling trot.

I was out the door before the man could recover, and headed deeper into the hospital, frantically searching for someplace to hide. I needed to get away from him – him and his terrible shotgun. Every moment of my past experience told me the only thing that could come from an armed man was pain, humiliation, and death.

Sweat beaded on my brow. It felt like I was moving in slow motion, swimming through treacle, except that instead of treacle it was pain and a gammy bloody foot. I was never going to make it in time, I realised with painful clarity. I had hit him hard, but not hard enough. I could hear him stumble out into the hall just as I was about to round the nearest corner, and heard him scream at me.

"No, don't go that way, they'll kill you – get back! Get back!"

I shot a look behind me and found that he wasn't even aiming at me, just frantically running after me with a panic-stricken look on what little I could see of his face. My fear turned to confusion.

Then, I heard the growl.

It was a deep, low rumble from a dark doorway not far from where I was. The fear surged back up again. I wasn't his target, I realised with dreadful certainty. There was something else here, something terrible.

And now it was after me.

The thing emerged from the shadows with a disturbingly sinuous grace, moving on all fours with its head held low, its bloodshot eyes fixed on me. Its frame looked human, like any other one of the infected – but the infected did not move like *that*.

I froze like a deer in the headlights. This thing, it was outside any of my experiences, something I'd never seen before. Every ounce of my being screamed at me to flee, and yet I couldn't get my muscles to obey.

The creature squatted, regarding me. It seemed to be considering me, its horrible eyes roaming up and down my body – the stare was almost sexual in its intensity. I felt nauseated, but too terrified to move. There was blood all over it, from head to toe, and its clothing was shredded and almost unidentifiable. Then suddenly, it straightened up and I recognised the deep blue scrubs of a nurse.

Christ, I was going to get killed and eaten by an undead nurse. Not quite how I pictured my death.

At the same moment the armed man caught up with me, the creature sprang. The stranger's bulk struck me hard and shoved me clear. A fraction of a second later, he swung his shotgun around to bear. The muzzle flash blinded me as I fell, my torch and gun once more clattering away. When my vision cleared, I saw the creature lying in a crumpled heap not two feet away from me.

It was still moving.

Even with its face caved in and the liquefied remains of its cerebellum leaking out of the terrible cavity that had once been the front of its skull, it was still struggling to get up. Still trying to get me. Human fingers bent into ragged-nailed talons clawed in my direction; I muffled a shriek and scooted out of its reach. The scattershot had done a real number on the creature. Half its head was gone and shrapnel burns covered the entire upper half of its body. I was fairly certain that I could see the bloody remains of its brain stem, shattered by the shell. That should have done it. That should have killed it. It should *not* still be moving.

"How the hell is it still moving?" I whispered, as much to myself as to the other survivor, but he still heard me and gave me the answer.

"It's a mutation. We don't know how it's happening, but this is the fifth one we've seen this month – the second in a week. We think the virus is evolving." His voice was harsh, like he'd been running for a few hours without stopping to catch his breath.

As I scooted farther away from the horrible thing, the stranger put himself between me and the creature again, in a protective move that surprised me. With a glance over his shoulder, he spoke softly to me.

"Stay back. There's only one thing that we know for sure kills them."

There was a bottle in his hand, a red metal flask about the size of a drink bottle. He unwound the cap and emptied the contents of the flask over the crawling undead. From the smell, I realised immediately it was either kerosene or lighter fluid.

He returned the empty flask to one of his pockets and pulled a box of matches from another. I noticed his hands shook when he struck the match and dropped it onto the bloody creature, but he didn't hesitate. The fire caught and spread instantly. He hopped back just in time to avoid being burned, then turned to look at me.

I was a few metres away by then, trying in vain to put distance between myself and danger. To my frustration, my body still didn't want to respond. He moved closer, cautiously offering me a hand to help me up. I shoved it away, afraid to let him touch me. A surge of adrenaline hit suddenly, and gave me the strength to get up on my own, and as soon as I was up I started backing away. I needed to use the wall to support my weight, which made my retreat inelegant, but it also made my fear quite obvious.

In my mind, I was remembering all the terrible, painful, violent things that men had done to me, and forced me to do to them. Even though he had helped me and seemed to want to help me again, my instincts were reluctant to forget the terrible things that human beings were capable of doing to one another – and to me.

He hesitated as he watched me scoot away, uncertainty etched on what little I could see of his face. Finally, he reached up and slid his night vision goggles up onto his head, letting me see the rest of him. He was handsome in an angular sort of way, and his eyes made me hesitate. They were gentle and full of concern for me despite my resistance.

"Hey, it's all right." His gruff voice was soft, as if I was a wild animal that he could tame with gentle tones. "I just want to help you. Survivors have to help each other, right?"

"Not in my experience," I snapped back, my voice almost as harsh as his. It had been a long time since I'd held a conversation with anything that actually understood what I was saying.

His expression changed, from concern to sadness, and he closed his eyes for a moment. When they opened, he reached up to his chest, and pointed to a faded logo.

"Miss, I'm a police officer," he said, drawing my eye to the faded word printed above his left pectoral. "I didn't mean to shoot at you, I swear on my life. I'm sorry. I thought you were one of them. I came here to hunt the mutants."

Then he looked down, suddenly noticing my gun at his feet. He gave me a quizzical look, then stooped down and picked it up. I tensed, expecting to be shot with my own gun, but he didn't. He just turned the weapon around, and offered it back to me hilt first without a word. A peace offering. A gesture of trust.

I snatched the gun away and turned it on him, pointing the weapon straight at his handsome face – but I didn't pull the trigger. He held up his hands, obviously trying to show me that his intentions were good. Although one of those hands did hold a shotgun, the gun was pointed about as far from my direction as it possibly could be.

Behind him, the fire cracked. The undead thing was still writhing. Oh god, it was still alive. My panic was fading, leaving me shaking from tension and sick to my stomach. The smell of burning flesh and hair in an enclosed space was nauseating. The survivor followed my eye to the writhing corpse, then swiftly stepped to his left to block my view.

"Don't look, please. You look like you've seen enough terrible things to last a lifetime," he said softly, his gruff voice barely audible over the crackle of flames. With slow, measured movements, he extended a hand towards me. This time, it was in the form of a handshake.

"I'm Michael," he said. "Constable Michael Chan. I'm part of a group of survivors that live around here." He glanced at my foot, obviously aware of my injury, then looked back up and offered me a wry half-smile. "One of my friends is a doctor."

I stared at his hand like it was a serpent that was going to bite me. The sound of hands striking flesh – my flesh – echoed in my memory, bringing with it the remembrance of pain. Then I looked up at his face, and saw only concern in his kind eyes. My gut did a flip-flop. There was a certain honesty about that face that my instinct said wasn't faked.

I lowered my gun, feeling uncertain and confused, unsure of what to do. He waited, his hand extended, an open invitation of— what? Friendship? I didn't understand friendship anymore. But, he was a police officer, sworn to protect and serve. He knew a doctor. I needed a doctor, so badly. And the way he was looking at me, that sweet, earnest concern.

Finally, my intuition as a human being overcame my learned paranoia as a survivor. I reached out to take his hand. A moment before our fingers would have touched, a blood-curdling shriek echoed through the empty corridors. It was swiftly joined by a second, then a third.

All of a sudden, Michael wasn't so scary after all. Not compared to whatever was making those terrible sounds.

He spun and stared down the corridor beyond the burning corpse, his face suddenly intense. Careful steps brought him back towards me, and this time I didn't flee. I had to admit, after hearing those sounds, I really wanted a nice, big meat shield between me and whatever was making them. I didn't care if I was being self-interested.

But then I damn near jumped out of my skin when he turned and shoved his shotgun into my hands.

"I'm going to pick you up." His voice was calm and even. "And then we're going to run for our lives. Please refrain from hitting me or shooting me until we're out of here."

Despite the warning, I still squeaked in surprise when he scooped me up into his arms, and fumbled to keep hold of the pair of guns. My torch was gone now, rolled away when he'd bowled me over to save me from the undead.

Another one screeched, this one closer.

*Forget the torch. Forget the scary man. Fucking run!* My instincts screamed at me. Apparently his did as well, because Michael took off with me in his arms, heading back the way we both came. I clung to him, surprised to find myself considering him the lesser of two evils at this particular moment.

The screeches were drawing closer and closer, like the baying of wolves. They were closing in on us, following our scent. Hunting us.

Just as we arrived back at the T-junction, another shriek joined the fray – this one was directly in front of us, from the direction Michael must have come, the opposite leg of the junction from the direction I'd chosen.

"Wait," I cried, self-preservation overriding my fear of him. Right now, my only hope for survival rested in the arms of a strange man who claimed to have once been an officer of the law. I was not ready to die. I shot out an arm, pointing to the right, through the Maternity Ward. "Go that way! There's an exit, and I have a car waiting."

I didn't have to tell him twice. He was off like a shot down the dark corridor. I found myself praying that nothing had snuck in behind me after I'd cleared that corridor a few minutes earlier. The shrieks were coming more and more frequently, drawing closer and closer, making my ears ring with their volume and ferocity.

Suddenly we were outside, the bright spotlights that bathed the car park startling after the dark corridor. My truck was where I left it, like a beacon of hope that we might yet survive this night.

"The keys?" Michael was gasping, out of breath from his frantic run while bearing my weight, but he made no effort to put me down even as I fumbled to get the car keys from my pocket. He held me close, protectively, bracing me against the door until I found the right key and shoved it in the lock. Central locking did the rest.

Unexpectedly, he yanked me away from the driver's door, and somehow managed to juggle my weight long enough to open the rear cab. I felt a flash of panic at the strength of his hands, but all he did was lift me in gently and sit me in the back seat. With a moment of understanding, I realised that he intended to drive and that he'd seen all the supplies piled on my passenger seat; the back seat was just the quickest and safest option for us both. Despite my inner paranoia screaming in protest, I thrust the keys into his waiting hand. He slammed the door as soon as I was safely inside, and then dove behind the wheel. The engine roared to life, and he threw the car into reverse.

As the car swung around, the headlights flashed up the corridor, briefly lighting the figures that were loping towards us. They were horrible, hunched, their strides uneven. There were four or five, and they were coming fast.

"Michael!" I cried, their demeanour shooting pure, animal terror into my heart. I'd never seen undead move like that. It was like something out of one of those goddamn zombie movies I'd watched as a kid.

"I see them. Put your seatbelt on." His voice was still calm somehow, and I fumbled to obey. As soon as he heard the click of my belt sliding into place, he put his foot down.

The Hilux leapt forward, careening out the gate I had snuck through so carefully before; the combination of speed and weight crushed that fallen barrier arm into splinters beneath us. He swung the car to the right and deeper into the city, gaining speed at a dangerous rate. I clung to the hand hold on the roof above me, suddenly more afraid of his driving than of the zombies.

Luckily, he seemed to know the streets and their obstacles well, and we miraculously survived our high-speed dash. As we drove I saw the flash of murky water to our right. I stared at it, trying to piece together what I saw with what I remembered from looking at my map, but my brain was too tired to co-operate.

"I'm taking a circuitous route to lose them," Michael said, as though reading my mind. "Our base is only a few kilometres from the hospital grounds. I'd hate to lead those things back home."

"They can track?" I asked, surprised. Being able to hunt was a sign of intelligence, and that seemed unlikely from what I'd seen of the creatures in the past.

"We're not really sure," he replied, "but I'm not taking any risks with the lives of my friends. I hope you understand."

I did understand. I took the moment to catch my breath instead and fell into silence, staring out the window as I considered his possible motives. He seemed so genuine, so honest. Those were things you couldn't really fake. Could you?

I'd been alone for so long that I had lost my knack for reading people. Feeling overheated despite the cool evening air, I rubbed a hand across my forehead and slumped back in my seat. Then a thought struck me, and I sat up a little straighter.

"You knew they were there," I said, watching what I could see of his body to gauge his reaction. "You came here all alone, at night, to a place where you knew those things were living. Why?"

Even I understood what it meant when I saw the way his hands tightened on the steering wheel; I could imagine his knuckles going white inside his gloves. I knew what that kind of tension meant.

"They killed one of my... friends. Two days ago." His voice was so low I could barely make it out over the sound of the engine. My sympathy bloomed into understanding. "We've only seen them attack during the day, so I hoped to catch them unaware at night. I won't let them take anyone else. I can't. For her sake. I'll kill them all, if I have to."

"You were close," I surmised, curiosity getting the better of me. It surprised me that I was interested in this stranger's motives at all, but what better way to understand someone than to learn about what drove them to kill?

"Yes," he said, his voice deep and husky. I wondered if there were tears in his eyes, but I couldn't see from where I sat. "She was my niece. My brother's little girl. She was only twelve." I heard him swallow and could imagine him trying to centre himself, just like I would do in his place.

My heart softened when I heard the pain in his voice. I knew that pain so well; I felt it every day. Every time I saw a child's toy or a little pair of shoes, I thought of my baby sister.

For him, the pain was still so raw, so recent. I understood that, too.

In spite of myself, I found myself reaching out to touch his shoulder. I don't know if he could feel it through the body armour, but it didn't matter. He was motivated by revenge and a powerful need to protect what little was left. I could understand that. More importantly, I could respect that.

I sat back in my seat after a brief moment of contact, pondering what had happened over the last few hours. With the back of one hand, I wiped my forehead and found that I was sweating despite the cool night air. Strange. A minute ago I'd felt like I was boiling alive, and now I was freezing. A wave of sparkles danced in front of my eyes, which left me feeling a little light-headed. I'd put the strange feeling down to adrenaline at first, but now that I was calm I wasn't so sure.

I laid my cheek against the glass of the window beside me, letting its coolness draw some of the heat from my cheeks. My mind wandered, and I found myself bouncing from one thought to the other without connection as I stared off out the window.

Today had not been a good day for me.

\*\*\*

By the time we reached our final destination, I was feeling dizzy and disoriented, and was having trouble focusing both my thoughts and my eyes. I felt the engine stop, and then Michael was saying something, but I couldn't quite understand his words. If he was talking to me, then why was he so far away?

My eyes were closed but I wasn't asleep, just too dizzy to focus on the road anymore. I cracked my lids open and saw his concerned face peering back at me in the half-light. I managed a weak smile, then laid my head back down against the window again. It felt so nice and cool.

I heard a door slam. A moment later, the window I was leaning against moved and I felt myself slipping towards the ground. Strong arms caught me, and a cool hand pressed against my forehead and cheeks. I wondered at it, but it didn't seem to matter so much anymore. I was so tired. All I wanted to do was sleep.

I felt myself being disentangled from my seatbelt, then gathered up and held close to someone, but I wasn't sure who it was anymore and it didn't seem to matter. I heard worried voices, but when I tried to open my eyes it felt like the lids were weighted down with bricks. No, lead. No, bricks made of lead. Bricks of lead tied to my feet.

So tired...

# Chapter Twelve

Eventually, the fever broke.

One minute I was lost in the land of nonsense dreams of times long gone, happy times spent with family and friends. The next, my eyes were opening and I felt lucid and alert for the first time in what seemed like forever. I blinked slowly as my vision cleared, then reached up to rub the crust from the corners of my eyes and lips.

Every part of me ached. How long had I slept? I rolled myself up into a sitting position, shaking my head to clear away the cobwebs. As I sat up, the thin blanket slipped down to my waist, and I realised with a flash of shock that I had been stripped to my knickers and undershirt.

My cheeks coloured, first in fear and embarrassment, and then in anger as my memory came crashing back.

How *dare* he? After all his talk about trust, after the way he'd gone on about wanting to help me, he'd betrayed me just the same? A sense of overwhelming outrage shot through my breast, sending spasms of energy to the furthest reaches of my limbs. I shot a glance around the room, intent on escape, looking for anything I could use as a weapon to defend myself.

There, on the table by the door: a gun!

...and a taser. A familiar-looking taser. My taser. Actually, that gun was pretty familiar too, come to think of it. Next to the weapons, my other belongings sat stacked with care. My clothing was washed and folded, with my shoes placed neatly atop the stack. They'd even gone so far as to clean my shoes for me while I slept.

My anger evaporated, and a cocktail of confusion and guilt replaced it as I came to understand what had transpired while I was unconscious. There was a bucket of water on the floor beside my bed, with a pile of wet rags near it. I vaguely remembered the strange feelings as I drifted away in the car, and now realised that I had been sick. A fever. They'd only removed my clothing to keep me cool, to try and keep the fever at bay.

They'd left my things untouched, aside from washing my clothing, and left me untouched as well. I knew the feeling of violation very well, and I did not feel it now. I shifted my foot and found the pain was muted, and the wound was dressed in clean bandages. There was even a tiny purple flower sitting on the table beside my bed, in a makeshift vase made out of a shot-glass.

*A flower? That's strange*, I thought as I stared at it. I was so focused on the bloom that I didn't notice the door crack open, nor the little face peer through. My attention snapped to the doorway when the child peeking at me giggled, but she shut the door before I could get a good look at her.

Someone was out there and they knew I was awake. Animal instinct kicked in.

I swung my legs out of bed and examined my foot, finding it stiff but relatively functional. I resisted the urge to tear the bandages off and douse the wound in bleach; the bandages were far neater than anything I could have done myself, so I could only hope the wound had been thoroughly disinfected. Feeling woozy from fever and possibly painkillers, I managed to get out of bed and limp the three steps to my clothing before the door burst open again. Michael hurried in, followed closely by a stocky older gentleman and a small girl of six or seven years of age.

I was still so weak and disoriented from my recent illness that when Michael swept me off my feet and tucked me right back into bed again, I didn't have a chance to protest. Probably a good thing, for his sake; there was a huge green-black bruise along his jaw from where I'd hit him, and it was only just starting to fade. Something else for me to feel guilty about, when he'd been so nice to me. Add it to the list.

Suddenly, everyone was talking at once and I was having trouble keeping up. I didn't know how to respond to so many questions, coming from all angles. It was like a verbal barrage and I didn't know how to counter-attack. After so long alone, it was hard enough to follow one line of conversation, let alone two or more.

Amazingly, it was the little girl who saved me.

"Shhh," she hissed, silencing the adults with a sharp gesture. She pointed at me with one little finger, and with wisdom beyond her years got right to the heart of the matter. "She has been alone outside, probably for a very long time. Talk one at a time so she can understand you."

I couldn't help but smile at the precocious child, and she smiled back at me. She leaned in close and whispered to me. "I picked you a flower. I hope you like it."

Aww. Well, that explained that.

"Sorry," I apologised automatically. "But she's right. It's been a few years. Longer, I think." My voice was dry and croaky from thirst, but it gave validity to my claim. Michael smiled, looking a little embarrassed, and the older gentleman frowned deeply.

"How are you feelin—" Michael started to ask, but the older man cut him off with a gesture.

"You hush, young man. Who is the doctor here? I am. I go first, and you may talk to her afterwards." He scowled at Michael, who held his hands up in self-defence. The doctor then turned penetrating hazel eyes back to me, and eyed me over the scratched lenses of his spectacles. "As for you – I am going to touch you, as I must examine you. Please refrain from hitting me. The boy says you pack quite a punch."

The gentleman had a strange accent that I couldn't quite place. His demeanour, though less than friendly, spoke of a professional candour that put me relatively at ease. I nodded my consent, and braced myself for the unfamiliar sensation of human touch.

To my own amazement, I managed to refrain from panicking, as the examination was blessedly short. He leaned over me to check my temperature with the back of his hand, and then felt behind my ears with calloused old fingers. He checked my pulse, peered into my eyes, ears, and the back of my throat, then finally ended up asking me the exact same thing Michael had tried to. "How are you feeling?"

"Sore," I admitted, absently rubbing one of my shoulders. It felt like I'd slept on it for a long time, long enough that my arm had gone to sleep, and now it was tingling as the circulation returned. "A bit stiff. Really thirsty, too. How long was I out?"

"Three days. It was touch and go for a while there; you were very ill," the old man answered, and his expression softened just the tiniest bit. He opened one of the drawers beside the bed to show me the contents. Inside, a couple of bottles of water were flanked by several precious items of personal hygiene – toothpaste, a toothbrush, a bar of soap, and a few other things.

Things that had once been life's necessities, but were now rare and valuable. I was surprised to see them; putting them in the drawer beside my bed was obviously an offer for me to use them. It was generous beyond belief. I was suspicious, of course.

I looked at him uncertainly then looked at the water, afraid to reach for it in case it was a trap. With a disapproving click of his tongue, the man snatched a bottle out and put it right in my hand. He even opened the lid for me, then made impatient hurrying gestures until I drank deeply and quenched my intense thirst. I immediately felt better as the cool water poured down my dry throat. I supposed running a fever did that to a body.

"Where did you come from?" he demanded while I was still swallowing the last sip of my water.

I peered at him questioningly. "Originally or most recently?"

"Most recently, of course," he snapped, as if I were silly just for asking. The older fellow was a bit grumpy, I decided, but he was a doctor and that counted for a lot. Behind him, I saw Michael hide a chuckle behind a cough, and pretend to be fascinated by something on the floor. He looked amused, but I was so isolated that I couldn't figure out what he found so funny.

"South. I've been travelling around the south for the last few years. Most recently in a rural area about twenty kilometres south of here," I answered, although I was wary of the question. My distrust ran deep, but I didn't have the courage to ask why he wanted to know.

"Rural?" he repeated my answer, and I nodded. "Mm. Did you see any horses? Or pigs?"

"No, just sheep, some chickens, and a few cows," I replied. The pieces were coming together; his line of questioning suddenly made sense. He was trying to work out my chances of exposure to tetanus and other infections. "A lot of the fences were down, though. There could have been horses in the past, I can't be sure." I paused to consider. "I wasn't attacked though, so I doubt there are any pigs left in the area."

"Attacked?" the doctor echoed, his brow furrowing. Behind him, Michael looked equally confused.

"Attacked by the pigs?" I repeated, peering at them. Were we speaking different languages here?

"Why would pigs attack you?" the doctor asked, looking bewildered.

"Because of the infection?" I was incredulous, but the looks on their faces said they didn't have a clue what I was talking about. "Do you guys live under a rock or something? Pigs can catch the infection. It makes them crazy and violent. Kind of like…" I trailed off when something clicked. Michael stared at me, wide-eyed with understanding, and I stared back.

"Great." Michael squeezed his eyes closed and rubbed his forehead with his fingertips. "Psychotic zombie-pigs. They're really a thing now. Please tell me you're kidding?"

I shook my head, and he groaned.

The doctor sat down heavily in an old wooden chair beside my bed, and pinched the bridge of his nose with his fingers. "Ah, just what we need. Perhaps that is how the mutation happened."

"I think I remember reading that humans and pigs are genetically similar," I said, suddenly feeling sick in the pit of my stomach. I'd only encountered a pig once in my travels, and it had been so riddled with infection that it had screamed a horrible sound and charged right for me. Like any sane person, I'd panicked and fled. The only reason I'd survived was because both of the animal's back legs had been so badly mutilated that it couldn't keep up with me.

The men looked horrified when I shared the story with them, and I shot a worried glance at the little girl, but she seemed totally disinterested in the grown-up talk. I wondered briefly how traumatic her short life must have been, but given her age it was the only life she had ever known.

"What about survivors?" the doctor asked, very deliberately changing the subject. "Have you seen any other survivors? Why did you come north?" The questions came quick and fast, forcing me to take a second to process them before I replied.

"No, no other survivors where I was most recently. I-I usually stay away from people," I said, twisting the edge of my bed sheet nervously between my fingers. "I came north because I lacked the medical supplies or expertise to treat the infection I was bound to get from that." I gestured at my foot. "I stood on a nail in an orchard. I knew there was a hospital here, so I was hoping to find some antibiotics."

"An orchard? That explains the fruit," Michael said, smiling at me. Despite the smile, I felt my stomach lurch. He must have read the concern in my expression, because his smile faded quickly. A look of uncertainty flitted across his face, as though he wasn't sure how I would react. "I didn't want to leave it in your truck to rot. I put it in our cold storage for you."

"You didn't eat it?" This time I was genuinely surprised, and pleasantly so. I had expected from the moment I awoke in a strange place that I would have been robbed of all my supplies and left with nothing.

"Of course not!" he exclaimed; both the constable and the doctor looked mortified at the very thought. "We are *not* thieves. What kind of people do you think we are?"

I looked at my hands, feeling a sudden rush of heat in my face and neck as embarrassment and guilt curdled in my belly. Again I'd misunderstood, applying the template of past cruelties against good people who didn't deserve it, and now I had upset my benefactors. I felt like crying, but that wouldn't really help anything. Everything was just so confusing.

"I-I'm sorry," I apologised softly, not sure what else to say.

A small body alighted on the bed beside me, and a pair of skinny little arms wrapped around me. I glanced sideways and discovered the little girl looking up at me with huge, doe-brown eyes. She translated my unspoken thoughts to her elders, then gave me a tiny smile. "She thought that we were going to hurt her and take her food."

Tears blurred my vision and I hurried to brush them away, afraid to show weakness. How could this child know me so well, and yet the grown adults didn't get it at all? I felt so confused, so out of place. The child wasn't the traumatised one, I realised suddenly. I was. I was so broken that I needed a seven-year-old to translate my reactions to rational adults.

I finally looked up, and found the old doctor looking worried and Michael standing nearby looking confused and upset. He was the first to speak, his gruff voice a little grainier than usual. "We would never do that to you, or to anyone else. We're good people. I would rather starve than steal from you."

He sounded like he really meant it, too. I lowered my head, feeling ashamed of myself for judging them before I knew anything about them. Seeing the hurt on his face stung like a snake bite, even though I didn't quite understand why I cared at all. I guessed it was because I am still human, and human beings are innately social creatures. Even me. *Especially* me.

"We must do your next injection, and then you should rest." Looking embarrassed, the doctor hurried to change the subject again. He leaned over to grab a small leather satchel that was beside my bed and fussed around inside it.

If it was a tetanus shot then I agreed wholeheartedly, but now I was feeling shy and reclusive, too ashamed to say a word. The little girl was still hugging me, watching my face intently. I understood that she was trying to comfort me, and I felt no urge to push her away. She was so small, unthreatening, and sweet. Even my somewhat overzealous self-defence mechanism didn't kick in over her touch. While the doctor was preparing his medication, she tried to distract me with her childish cheer.

"My name is Madeline," she said, leaning up against me. "What's yours?"

"Sandy," I replied, feeling awkward and uncertain. "Um, thank you for the flower."

"You're welcome." She beamed brightly, and then pointed at the old man. "That's my granddaddy." Her finger shifted to Michael. "That's Mister Officer Chan. He looks after me and Granddaddy; and Mummy too, before she died."

"Maddy-monkey, come down from there and leave the young lady be," the doctor scolded gently, busy filling a syringe from a small, official-looking medicine vial.

"It's okay," I said, suddenly feeling protective. "She's fine. She reminds me of my sister." I looked at the girl and added softly, "My sister was about your age when I last saw her."

"Is your sister dead, like Mummy?" she asked.

I flinched. Oh, from the mouth of babes. There was no point denying it, since this child clearly understood death better than most.

"Probably," I said, nodding sadly. "I didn't see her die, but the last time I saw her she was driving away with my daddy and I never saw either of them again."

"Aw. I would have liked to play with her." Madeline looked crestfallen.

"All right, enough of that. Injection time," the doctor advised, shuffling closer to me with a syringe in one hand and a cotton swab soaked in cleaning alcohol in the other. I tensed up at the sight of the needle, which drew a disapproving sound from him. "Hold still now. This will only take a moment. Unless you *want* to get tetanus, of course?"

He did have a point. I nodded my consent, and looked away.

I felt the fluff of the swab on my arm as the site was being cleaned, then the prick of the needle followed by that creepy sensation of something being injected into my body. As much as I hated that feeling, I held still like a good girl. One little prick was a hell of a lot better than getting lockjaw. Like he promised, it only took a second and then he was pressing a clean rag over the tiny wound to staunch any bleeding.

"There, all done," the doctor said. Despite his stern face, his voice was soothing. I took the rag from him as soon as he would let me, and kept pressure on the wound.

"You were a real doctor, weren't you?" I asked. It sounded like a stupid question after I'd asked it, but he seemed to understand.

"Yes, I was a general practitioner," he replied. "I'm sure there's an office around here somewhere that still has my name on the door. I also studied pharmacology, which has come in rather handy these days. I make most of our medication, when I can find the resources." He paused when he noticed me staring at him expectantly. "My name is Dr Cross, but you may call me Stewart. We are rather informal around here."

"Thanks," I replied, with a sudden surge of sarcastic humour. "You're a bit young for me to be calling you 'Granddaddy'."

Madeline giggled, Michael laughed, and even Dr Cross cracked a smile, the first one since we'd met. I felt a little better after that, a little more accepted. Maybe they would forgive me for assuming they were thieves and murderers.

At least, I hoped so.

# Chapter Thirteen

The other survivors interrogated me for a few minutes longer, and then left me in peace with instructions to rest. I couldn't fall back to sleep so I just lay there staring at the bare concrete walls for about an hour, trying to figure out where I was. The place looked like a bunker, but I couldn't think of a reason for Hamilton to have a bunker. Hamilton was small by city standards, with only a couple of hundred thousand residents in its prime. It was mostly a farming hub for the lush Waikato region, and all the businesses required to support that industry. Why on earth would it have a bunker?

The more I lay there and thought about it, the more I realised that I wasn't going to get an answer without asking – and the more I started to realise that I was going to need a lavatory soon. That was an uncomfortable feeling. Someone must have been dealing with my biological needs while I was unconscious, but I was in no way ready to trust anyone with that while I was awake.

Stuff doctor's orders, it was time to get up.

I shoved the blanket back and swung my feet to the floor, then stretched my arms up over my head to get the blood-flow going again. Despite the fact that I hadn't really slept, I felt pretty good, or at least better than when I first woke up. Who knew daydreaming was good for the body *and* the soul?

I rose carefully to my feet, keeping my weight on the heel of my injured foot. Although that made walking awkward, Dr Cross had warned me repeatedly not to go tearing my stitches. Still, I was restless and it was time to move. They had implied that there were other people here, which meant more potential risks that I needed to assess. I also kind of felt the need to apologise to Michael for bruising his jaw.

While I was dressing, I decided in a rare moment of trust to leave my other belongings where they were. If these people had wanted to rob me, then they would have done it while I was unconscious. They'd chosen not to, so I could not imagine that they would suddenly change their minds. It would just make no sense at all.

Once I was properly clothed, I opened the door and stuck my head out into the hall. I found myself in a long concrete corridor, lit by fluorescent bulbs that cast the passages in a dull artificial glow. Occasionally one flickered, reminding me of the hospital – I shivered at the thought. Still, people lived here, so there must be a lavatory somewhere. One problem at a time.

I picked a direction at random, and headed off along the corridor, limping slowly to avoid putting undue strain on my foot. There was a doorway up ahead on my left, which turned out to be another small room with a cot much like mine. Judging by the scattered toys and the mountain of pink clothing, I assumed that it must have been Madeline's room. A second cot, neater than the first, lay against the opposite wall. Although I couldn't be as sure, I guessed that was likely to be the doctor's bed. Neither of them were there, so I moved on.

The next doorway along was on the right. When I looked inside I found a small kitchen area, with a table, chairs and a couple of tatty couches. It had probably been a break room for the people working in this building forever ago, but right now it was empty.

There were a few more rooms on the left which appeared to be storage rooms.

They were packed with goods appropriated from around the city, everything from food and clothing to old computers and cell phones. There were a couple of large refrigerators which I imagined must be the 'cold storage' that Michael mentioned, and a few big metal drums that I assumed contained fuel, water, or possibly rice. No wonder they didn't feel the need to steal from others; their larder was full, and they would not have to go hungry any time soon.

Beyond the storage rooms was a dead end, so I headed back the way I'd come to try another direction. The place was quite extensive, and solidly built. I could understand why they had chosen this as their base of operations. It wasn't pretty, but it sure felt safe.

I passed more rooms: a couple had been converted into bedrooms, a few were obviously just for storage, and some seemed to serve no purpose at all. A noise from one of the rooms farther down the hall drew my attention, and I slipped up to the doorway to see who was inside.

I found Michael Chan sitting on a narrow, metal-framed cot, whittling away at a wooden plank with a chisel. There were a few other pieces of wood scattered around him, along with a hammer, screwdriver, nails, and other tools. As someone who had always been interested in handcrafts, I noticed he wasn't very good at woodworking, but at least he was trying. Effort always counted for something.

His head was down so he didn't notice me at first, which finally gave me the opportunity to really study him. He was tall, probably a good three inches taller than me, which would put him at a little over six foot, and he was built quite large, with broad shoulders and muscular arms that told me he spent a lot of time engaged in physical activity.

Unusually large for someone of Chinese ancestry. I pondered that thought, and although I was curious, I didn't know him at all and couldn't really guess at his origins. Right now, he was dressed in civilian clothes. Jeans, boots, and a t-shirt that was a little too small for his powerful frame.

I found that I didn't mind. After all these years and so much abuse, it was strange to admit that I found him rather handsome. Well, he was handsome. Almost beautiful, in that sculpted way Asian men could sometimes be. He possessed a strong jaw, angular cheekbones and a fine, straight nose, with short black hair combed straight back from his forehead. It was still his eyes that fascinated me, though. They were dark brown, fathomlessly deep and yet so kind and gentle.

I was off in my own little world, getting myself all addled with conflicting thoughts and emotions, when he suddenly sensed my presence. His head shot up, startled. For a moment I thought he was going to leap to his feet and defend himself, but then he seemed to recognise me, and relaxed.

"You're supposed to be resting." His gruff voice was somehow both scolding and caring simultaneously. It finally occurred to me that the gruffness wasn't from hostility, but rather the result of an old accent that my ear just wasn't used to hearing.

"I did rest," I said, then I lifted a brow pointedly. "But nature's calling, and no one told me where the loo is."

"Oh." His laughter was a friendly sound; I decided that I liked it. He set aside his woodworking and rose. I retreated as he approached the doorway, but he made no attempt to touch me. "I'll show you the way. This place is pretty big."

He headed off and I fell in behind him, resting one hand on the wall as I walked to help keep my weight off my foot.

"I would offer to carry you again, but I'm afraid you'll hurt me," he joked, keeping his pace slow enough that I had no trouble keeping up.

"I can walk," I retorted with mock indignation. "Just not very well."

He chuckled and turned a corner, and I hurried to keep up with him. The lavatory turned out to be a large, military-style bathroom, with a row of toilet stalls along the back, a wall of lockers and benches down the middle, and a half-dozen shower stalls to our right.

The shower stalls had originally been open-faced, but the group had hung colourful shower curtains in front of each to provide some degree of privacy – a fact for which I was grateful. I inspected the room thoughtfully, before making my way towards the toilets. Halfway there, I noticed something that made me gasp. "You have toilet paper? Real toilet paper?"

"And hot water, too," he replied, his dark eyes sparkling with mirth.

"Really? Hot water?" I could hardly believe it. After how hard I'd worked trying to get the tank working back at Ohaupo, hot water was being handed to me on a platter. "Can I—?"

"Knock yourself out." He moved over and opened one of the lockers with a dramatic flourish, revealing that it was being used as a makeshift linen cupboard. Neat stacks of towels in an assortment of cheerful colours filled it, along with various personal hygiene items.

"How do you guys have so much *stuff*?" I blurted. Given how hard I had struggled just to survive, seeing such a stockpile was mind-boggling.

"Well, I've been using this as a base since the outbreak happened," Michael replied, shrugging sheepishly. "This is the underground portion of the police precinct. I was serving here and just sort of stayed here. There were hardly any other folks in this area to begin with, so I've had time to collect stuff. There isn't a lot of competition."

"The others weren't here with you from the start?" I asked, tilting my head to look up at him.

"No. It was just me and Sophie – my niece – for three or four years before I found the Doc and his family," he replied. "Doc's from around here, but his son's family were down in Otago. He went all the way down there looking for them, only to find out his son was already dead. He found his daughter-in-law was still alive, though, and that she had a little baby with her.

"They managed to get back to Hamilton, and I found them one day while they were scavenging in the ruins." He smiled shyly and shot me a sideways glance. "I couldn't very well leave them out there, so I brought them back here where it's safe and warm. We've acquired a few other stragglers since then, and, well, here we are."

"Huh." I looked down at my feet thoughtfully. I guess I was the latest straggler. That was food for thought.

After a moment of silence, Michael waved and made to leave. "You do your thing. Just call if you need me. Sound travels down here, so chances are good that I'll hear you – or someone else will, and they'll come help you."

Then he was gone, leaving me alone in that big bathroom. I stood there pondering for a couple of moments before I realised that I was wasting precious shower time.

I quickly ducked into a stall to relieve myself, before turning my attention to enjoying the longest, hottest shower of my adult life.

*** 

They had soap. They had shampoo and conditioner. They even had razor blades. Shaving wasn't exactly something you had time to do when you were surviving in the ruins of a shattered civilization, but I did it every chance I got. I hated the feeling of hairy legs almost as much as I hated being sweaty. It might have been a bit pedantic, but I liked to feel clean.

The hot water was amazing. I practically roasted myself washing and shaving every part of my body that I could reach. It was a difficult prospect with doctor's orders to keep the bandages dry, and in the end I just gave up. A hot shower trumped clean bandages any day of the year.

After three shampoos and a conditioning, my hair felt cleaner than it had in a very long time. Oh, the sweet, glorious smell of shampoo, I'd almost forgotten how wonderful it was.

I must have spent at least half an hour in there, getting nice and clean, but when I finally convinced myself it was time to get out I felt absolutely wonderful. The world seemed like a brighter place. I was so clean, so very clean. Pruney, but clean.

I dried myself off and dressed in the clothing I'd been wearing previously, and then braided my hair to keep it out of my face while it dried. Sodden towel in hand, I looked around for an appropriate depository for soiled articles but couldn't find one, so I took it with me as I left the bathing hall.

I made my way back in the direction I suspected the kitchen was, and heard voices speaking softly in a room nearby. Curious, I inched closer until I could hear what they were saying.

"She's emotionally scarred, son. I'm not sure it's good for the others to have someone like her around here. Look what she did to your face."

The voice sounded like Dr Cross, and 'son' turned out to be Michael.

"Of course she's emotionally scarred," Michael replied, sounding tense. "Put yourself in her shoes and think about what she's been through. You and I have always had someone with us to keep us real, but she's a pretty, young woman all on her own. I'm not at all surprised that she hit me; I must have scared the hell out of her, the poor thing."

"What if she's dangerous, or crazed?" the doctor protested. "You don't know anything about her. She's clearly a loner, and that says things about her mental state. What if *she's* a thief? What if she's a serial killer and playing on our pity?"

Michael's deep voice was firm and commanding as it rose to my defence. "The only thing it says about her mental state is that she's been through a lot of pain, Doc. You saw her face when we were talking. Even Maddy could see it. She honestly thought we were going to rob her or kill her – or worse. Just think about what it must have been like to live like that for so long."

I heard footsteps, but they weren't coming closer; it sounded like he was pacing.

"We can't just abandon her." It was Michael's voice again, low and solemn. "If she wants to go, that's one thing. But forcing her out would be wrong – it's both immoral and unethical. Frankly, Doc, I'm a little disappointed that you would even suggest it. She's a human being, just like all the rest of us, and she's traumatised. She needs us."

My heart leapt into my throat. Dr Cross wanted to throw me out? It felt like someone dumped a bucket of ice water over my head. I wasn't surprised though, really. I probably wouldn't want me around either.

There was silence in the room, while out in the hall I slumped against the wall. Tears ran down my cheeks, and I wiped them away with a corner of my towel.

"Ah, what is it with you and picking up strays?" Doc said, and then I heard him sigh heavily. "I suppose you're right. She does deserve a chance. But I must insist that if she becomes any kind of threat to Madeline, you evict her immediately or we will leave. You understand, of course."

The sound of footsteps came again as the men parted ways, heading in opposite directions. I didn't know where the doctor went, but it was Michael who emerged from the doorway where I was eavesdropping. He turned to head in the direction of the bathroom, then froze when he saw me right there, in tears.

"If your friend doesn't want me here, then I'll go," I said softly and sniffled, not wanting to blow my nose on their nice towel. With as much dignity as I could muster, I shoved myself away from the wall and drew myself up to my full height. Then I gave the handsome young man a long, hard look, trying my best to pretend I hadn't been crying like a baby a second before. "It's okay, I understand. This is your home, not mine. I wouldn't feel right staying here if it made you and your friends fight."

I gave him the faintest of smiles, then turned and limped my blubbery mess off in the direction I was at least slightly certain my room was. The truth of the matter is that I wasn't comfortable with the situation at all and I wasn't sure how to react. The whole thing was overwhelming, and my automatic response to the unknown was to retreat.

Behind me, Michael swore under his breath. The sound of his footfalls behind me sped up, so I picked up the pace to try and outdistance him. Injured and vulnerable as I was, he caught up with me easily; his big hands captured my shoulders from behind.

I tensed, instinctively expecting that I was about to be beaten or violated. Even though I'd already come to understand that Michael was a gentle man by nature, my instincts were so warped that I was ready to defend myself in a heartbeat. But one thing held me back: no matter how hard I fought, violence wouldn't fix the terrible emptiness I felt at the thought of being alone all over again. I had tasted the simple joy of human acceptance, and I longed for it – but the last thing I wanted was to tear apart other people's relationships in the process.

Michael didn't hurt me, of course. He just held me gently, close enough to him that I could feel his body warmth on my back, but not quite close enough to touch.

"The doc's just a cranky old man, and he's always picking a fight over something." Michael's voice was hard at first, but it softened as he spoke. The last words were almost a whisper, and I sensed something in them that I didn't quite understand. "Don't pay any attention to him. *I* want you to stay."

I couldn't think of an answer.

He turned me around to face him, as gently as if I were a porcelain doll. I stared up at him silently, and saw the look of concern on his face.

"Nobody should have to be alone unless they want to be," he said, his voice calm and reassuring. "You don't want to be alone, do you?"

The tears sprang back unbidden. Although I tried to blink them away, the lump in my throat made it impossible. The pressure of spending all those years alone was just too much for me to bear. My head ached and I felt like it might burst at any second. I looked away and tried to think of an appropriately sassy response, but all I could think of was little Tigger, the kitten who had been my only companion in many years.

Did I really want to be that alone again? It hurt just to think about it. These people were so nice that it brought me back to another place and time. A time when I was young, before I needed to be afraid of everyone. Back to being with my family, safe and loved.

Did I really want to go back to the endless silence, where the only kind of conversation I could have was with myself? No, I really, really didn't.

I shook my head and closed my eyes against the onslaught of pain. Michael seemed to understand my turmoil. He put his arms around me and drew me up against his broad chest, holding me so tenderly it was like he was afraid he might break me if he squeezed too hard. I tensed up again, before I realised that he was just hugging me in an attempt to comfort me. I hadn't been hugged since Grandma died. I barely even recognised what it was.

It felt… nice.

Lacking the experience to know what to do, I just stood there pathetically, my face pressed up against his chest. The tears flowed freely, and he held me as I cried. The longer he held me, the weaker my defences grew and the more the wordless emotion poured out of me. But even when my shoulders shook and I struggled to muffle the convulsive sobs that fought their way out, he was there for me, like a pillar of strength to hold me up while I was weak.

Something in me had burst. Over the years, I'd built up an emotional dam to survive. That dam had been full to bursting for a very long time, and every day it was a battle to keep it under control. Something about the warmth of human contact made it impossible to keep forgetting and keep suppressing, and so I wept. I wept for all the things I'd lost, for all the things I'd never have, and for all the lives that had been snuffed out in futility all around me. For the unbearable pain I'd suffered in silence all these years, with no kind of vent or release to keep me sane.

I had no sense of how much time passed before I regained control of my emotions, but when I did I felt exhausted, drained, and sore all over again. I leaned against him for almost a minute longer while I caught my breath, then I finally broke the embrace. He let me go, but kept his hands resting on my shoulders, his face full of kindly concern. Not a word of judgement, no questions, he just waited, giving me as much time as I needed until I was ready to talk to him.

"Bleh." My first word was not an elegant one. "I think I'm dehydrated now." I buried my face in the towel and scrubbed away salty tears with the dampest corner I could find. Michael blinked owlishly at my comment, and then cracked a smile.

"We better get you something to drink, then." His voice was soft and husky in a way that sent shivers down my spine. Without asking permission this time, he slid his arm around my shoulders and led me off toward the kitchen – and I let him. I was not in the mood to fight.

I let him seat me at the table and watched listlessly as he poured two glasses of cool water from the fridge. He set one down in front of me and seated himself across the table, sipping deliberately from his glass. I mostly just played with mine, more interested in figuring out the weird feelings that careened through my gut than drinking water.

It was a good five minutes before he finally broke the silence. When he reached out to me, it was with the dry, sarcastic brand of humour that I always resorted to; apparently he'd already noticed that, and turned my own verbal weapon back against me. He was trying to get a rise out of me, any kind of rise, so that he could assess the extent of my psychological damage – and I knew it.

"Are you moping?"

"Yeah," I answered without missing a beat, then heaved a dramatic sigh. "Apparently my brain is broken. I feel stupid and rude and– and–" I looked up at him, finally seeking out his kind eyes. "And I'm sorry I hit you."

"You do pack a mean right hook." He smiled and rubbed his jaw sheepishly. "Don't even worry about it. I understand. Big, scary guy sneaks up behind you in a dark, terrifying hospital, and almost shoots you in the butt? I'd have punched me, too."

"I didn't break your jaw, did I?" I asked, feeling an unexpected flash of concern.

"No, I don't think so," he replied. "Doc says it might be a little cracked, but it'll heal just fine."

I stared at the bruise, noticing the fine stubble on his chin for the first time. It was nice, just a half day's growth but it made him a little less perfect, a little more human. Just the right touch of scruffiness. I wondered if the bruise made it hurt to shave, but I decided not to ask. Instead, I looked down again with another soft sigh.

"You've been so patient with me. I'm really sorry, for everything," I said. I felt ashamed of myself and didn't quite know how to express it. "I'm just, you know..."

"I know. You're broken," he said, reaching across the table to rest his hand over mine. "It's okay. You've been through a lot. We'll talk about it, gradually, when you're ready. I'll help you get better."

"You mean that?" I asked softly, feeling hope for the first time in what felt like forever.

"Damn right, I do. We're friends now, okay? You and me. And Doc and Maddy, too. And the others once you get a chance to meet them. We're all friends, and we're here to support one another. Right?"

"Yeah," I agreed readily, though I barely remembered what it was like to have a friend. There had been a lot of friends in my early life, before the outbreak, but now I was in uncertain territory.

"Besides," he added, "if we ditched one another just because we were a little broken, this place would be completely empty."

I couldn't help but laugh. It was the first laugh I'd had in a while, too. The sound of it made him smile.

***

We just talked for a while about nothing in particular, about cartoons we'd watched as children and the places where we'd grown up. The conversation stuck to cheerful things. Skillful manipulation on his part, but I wasn't complaining. I needed it, to just talk about good times and forget all the bad ones.

He even broke out the food to keep me distracted, and we ate reheated spaghetti-from-a-can together while we chatted.

"Call me crazy, but I think the little sausages are the best part," he said, stabbing one of the tinned sausages with his fork.

"Yeah, I agree," I replied. "I always begged my mum to get the kind with the sausages in it when I was little. She always said 'no, no, it's not good for you, they're more expensive, blah blah'; but then she'd end up buying them anyway."

I had to admit, Michael was really good at keeping a conversation positive. Usually when I thought about my mother, I suffered a terrible pang of grief; this time, all I felt was the wistfulness of remembering a happy memory. With an impish grin, he waved the little sausage at me, and then popped it in his mouth. I stuck my tongue out childishly in return, and found my own sausage to eat.

"Mich-ael?" a female voice called from some distance away, drawing our attention away from our lunches. A few seconds later, the voice called again. "Mi-ike?"

Michael grunted in annoyance. "She knows I hate being called that."

"I understand," I said, twirling spaghetti on my fork. "I don't like it when people use my full name."

"What, Sandra?" he asked.

"That's actually not it," I replied.

"Then what is it?" he enquired, looking curious.

"I'm not telling," I said, waving my fork at him in mock threat. "If I tell you, then you'll be tempted to use it, and if you use it then I'll have to give you a shiner to match your jaw."

"Oh no, anything but that." He feigned terror briefly, then stood up and stretched. "I better go see what they want. They were out scavenging, so they probably found something big and want me to help them move it. You want to come meet them?"

"In a minute," I said, gesturing for him to go ahead without me. "I want to finish my food while it's hot; I'm pretty hungry. Don't worry, I'll find you. You're kind of loud."

"I am not loud!" This time he was the one faking indignation, but it didn't last for long. His scowl melted into a grin, and he gave me a wink before he left the room.

I took my time finishing off my lunch, not entirely sure how I felt about meeting yet more potentially dangerous survivors. In spite of everything, I really felt like I could trust the three I'd met so far, but adding more strangers to the mix felt like I was pushing my luck somehow.

Still, Michael would probably bring them to me if I didn't go to them. I popped the last bite of spaghetti in my mouth and stood up to take my bowl and utensils to the sink. I rinsed them and left them to dry, then headed off in the direction my new friend had gone.

It didn't take me long to find them. He wasn't really all that loud, but voices did carry in these cold, concrete halls. I found him deep in conversation with a pair of young people – a man and a woman – over some item of salvage they wanted to bring back to base.

The male was a fairly short fellow in his early twenties, skinny as a rake with a shock of red hair and a plague of freckles across every inch of visible skin. By contrast, the woman was blonde and pretty, no older than eighteen or nineteen, with pale skin that showed just a touch of sunburn across the nose. Her hair was clipped at a practical shoulder length, and fell in tight natural curls that reminded me of my mother. I also noticed that she was heavily pregnant.

"Hey," I called softly to announce myself, and the trio looked up from the map they were studying.

"Oh, hey, you must be Sandy. Michael was telling us about you. I'm Ryan." The redhead approached with a hand extended, and I managed to shake it without freaking out. I thought that was a pretty major achievement in Project: Tame Sandy – I hadn't even freaked out and attacked anyone yet.

"Hi." My reply was a bit awkward but was functional, then I looked over at the young woman and froze when I realised that she was staring at me intently, looking puzzled.

"Sandy..." she repeated my name, as though trying it on for size, her brow furrowed. "Sandy... McDermott?"

"Yes?" Something was going on here. How did she know my last name? I hadn't told anyone that. My brain shifted into overdrive. Then, something clicked and all the pieces fell into place.

The age, the hair, the complexion. This young woman was the spitting image of my mother from her old wedding photos. But, it couldn't be. It just couldn't be. Could it?

"Oh, my God. Skylar?"

# Chapter Fourteen

There was a lot of squealing and bouncing and hugging as Skylar and I reunited. The men watched with bewildered expressions, clueless as to why we'd both suddenly gone mad – but we didn't care. We clung together making inarticulate noises, but too impossibly happy to form a rational thought.

After a whole decade, hundreds of kilometres of wandering, and against all odds, I had found my little sister alive and well. I could hardly believe it. I'd spent ten years mourning for her, and all that time she was still alive. It seemed like a wonderful dream and I was afraid to think about it too much in case I woke up. We were so noisy that we even attracted the doctor and his granddaughter from wherever they had been. With everyone gathered around, I finally managed to gasp down enough breath to explain the reason for our joy.

"This is my sister," I told them. "My little, baby sister. Though not a baby anymore, by the looks of it." I eyeballed her pregnant belly and gave her a playful nudge, which made her giggle. Then the reality of the situation finally struck home and dampened my levity. "I thought you were dead, Skye. Where the hell did you go? Why didn't you meet us at the beach house?"

"I couldn't," Skylar said, clinging to me like a limpet. I didn't mind – I was just as determined to cling back. "We got a flat tyre halfway there, so we tried to walk but we got lost. Dad found an empty farmhouse for us to sleep in, but I think he was already infected. He put me to bed one night, and when I woke up he was gone.

"Ryan's family owned the house. He was away at a school camp when the infection hit and had to walk home. When he got there, he found me hiding in his house and his family was all gone. He's been looking after me ever since."

"I wish I'd known," I said. Overcome by a surge of emotion, I squeezed my little sister so hard that she squealed in protest. "All these years, I thought you were dead. If I'd known, I would have come looking for you."

"I know. If I'd known you were alive, I would have done the same," she replied. Suddenly, she shoved me back and stared at me with huge, hope-filled eyes. "Is Mum alive, then? Grandma?"

My heart sank, knowing that I was going to have to break her heart all over again. I just shook my head. "We made it to the beach house, but they got the infection anyway. I'm so sorry."

I hugged her tight and gave her a minute to absorb the information. She looked pretty crushed, but took the news well. I understood how she felt. I'd already mourned for Dad so much over the years that finally hearing for sure that he was dead didn't hurt nearly as much as I thought it would. That wound had scabbed over and turned into an old scar years ago.

"Well, at least I've got you again." Skye squinted up at me, as though trying to figure out if I was the real thing. "Though, I do remember you being taller."

I shook my head and gave her a smile. "Nah, you were just shorter."

Suddenly, little Madeline decided that she'd heard enough of our nonsense. She stomped over and poked me unceremoniously in the bottom. I squeaked in surprise and looked down at her.

"Miss Skylar can't be your sister," she told me in no uncertain terms. "Your sister is my age. You told me so." The little girl stomped petulantly, drawing a chuckle from the adults in the room. I stood awkwardly for a moment, not entirely sure how to respond to that. The childlike answer seemed like the best response, so I went with that.

"Well, she was your age when I last saw her, but she grew up. But, look." I poked Skylar's pregnant belly. "She's making a new baby for you to play with. That counts."

"But the baby won't be my age either," Madeline complained, pouting.

"She will be when she's your age," I said cryptically but with confidence, as though it made perfect sense.

"Ohhh." Maddy's eyes lit up as if she suddenly understood. "Well, I guess that's okay then. She can be your sister."

"Thanks for, uh, giving me permission to be related to my sister," I said, shooting an amused glance at the other adults in the room. Oblivious, Maddy skipped off and vanished down the corridor in search of something fun to do.

Awesome. Apparently I spoke fluent seven-year-old now. I should add that to my resume.

"That kid is so cute." Skye giggled and leaned up against me. Even as an adult she was still a little shorter than me, but in some strange way that pleased me. At least she was still my little sister.

All grown up. Still alive. I marvelled at the fact. I could hardly believe it. After a decade, a whole decade, somehow we had both survived and found each other.

It was a miracle.

***

We didn't have much time to get reacquainted. As it turned out, Ryan and Skye had been off scouting for resources and had found a cache that had been opened up by the storm a few nights earlier. An old tree had come down in the wind, taking out the wall of a building in the process.

Once it had been a big general goods store, but the front of the building had collapsed years ago, trapping all the stock inside it. When the tree fell, it had exposed the stock room and all the merchandise that was hidden safely within. It was like a time capsule of retail greed and it was ours for the taking.

The good news, Ryan and Skylar told us, was that a lot of the stuff still looked viable – clothing, shoes, home wares, and much more. The bad news was that we would have to be quick. The tree had taken out half the roof when it collapsed, so the stock was exposed to the elements.

"It's going to take us a lot of trips to get all that stuff back here," Ryan said, peering down at the map spread on the table while he explained the situation. "We could probably scavenge some shopping trolleys, but it's about two kilometres each way."

"We're going to need every able body," Skye said, then she shot me a pointed look. "You're on babysitting detail."

"Hey, I can help," I protested, feeling stung.

"With that?" Michael cut in, pointing at my foot. "Oh no, you stay here." With one big hand, he reached out and gave my shoulder a gentle squeeze to soften the blow of what he had to say next. "With that injury, you're more of a liability than an asset in the field. You know that. Plus, someone has to stay here to protect Maddy."

My shoulders slumped. I didn't like it, but I knew they were right. I was a liability until I healed. Still, I wanted to help in some way. This was my *sister*, for crying out loud. Her presence in this group changed everything.

"Take my truck," I offered on impulse. "It still has half a tank of gas and it needs to be taken for a drive to keep the battery charged anyway. It should get you back and forth a few times."

"You have a truck?" Skye stared at me, wide-eyed. I squinted at Michael, who shrugged sheepishly.

"I forgot to mention it," he admitted. "I parked it in the garage with all the others, but none of them work and we don't know how to fix them, so we never really go in there."

"Huh." There were other vehicles? And these survivors didn't know how to repair them? I stored that piece of information away for later use. "Anyway, yeah, I resurrected an old ute. The back is pretty spacious."

"Thank you, Sandy. We appreciate the offer," Michael said, giving me that kind smile of his. "That'll help things go much more quickly."

I felt an unexpected flush of pride at his praise, but I just smiled back and nodded.

"All right, so we've got a plan." Michael turned to the others and took command with an ease that just seemed natural. "Sandy stays with Maddy, everyone else is with me. Has anyone seen Dog?" He looked around at the others, but they all shook their heads.

"He was off scouting this morning, like us," Skye said with a shrug. "I imagine he'll be back before dark."

"Hm, okay." Michael glanced over at me again. "If you see a skinny kid come waltzing in with a big black Labrador, don't panic. He's one of us. He's also deaf, so don't be offended if he doesn't hear you yelling at him. I'll leave a note for him on the fridge in case he gets back before we do."

I nodded my understanding.

"Right." Michael clapped his hands, drawing everyone's attention back to him. "Go get your gear, guys. Ryan, come and help me get Sandy's stuff out of the car before we go." He looked at me. "You don't mind if we put it in your room, do you?"

I hesitated. They seemed perfectly happy to let me be selfish with my supplies, but for the first time in a very long time I felt like being generous.

"No, just add it to your stores," I said, shyly tucking a strand of hair back behind my ear. "You've all been so kind to me – I don't mind sharing."

Michael looked both surprised and pleased at my decision. He nodded his understanding, then clapped Ryan on the shoulder and vanished off down a corridor. The doctor left to gather his things, leaving me alone with Skylar. She beckoned for me to follow her, which I did. Together we made our way through the cold, concrete passages towards her room.

We walked in companionable silence, each of us hampered in our own way by our medical conditions: me by my foot, her by her swollen belly. Judging by the size of it, she must have been at least seven months along, maybe even eight. She looked about ready to burst, and yet she was still going, still game to help with the search. I was impressed by her stubbornness and determination. That was a survivor's attitude.

"So, who's the dad?" I asked eventually, curious even though I was pretty sure I could guess.

"Ryan, of course." Skylar grinned broadly and glanced over at me, her big blue eyes sparkling. "He's such a sweet guy, the way he's been taking care of me all these years. He was twelve when he found me, and I was eight, so we grew up together. A couple of years ago, we both kind of realised we were adults, things got a bit more serious, and, well—" She trailed off and rubbed a hand over her belly, smiling contentedly. "He's asked me to marry him, but we haven't found a living priest yet."

"I'm sure there's one around somewhere, we'll just have to find him." I gave her another mischievous little nudge – and tried to ignore the way relief flooded through me when she named her Ryan as the father.

For some bizarre reason, I had been a little afraid that Michael was the father. It was a basic, animal kind of jealousy, but it worried me because it meant there was some kind of attraction there, and I didn't know how to feel about that. I hadn't been with a man in a long, long time. At least... not willingly.

But when he gave me that quirky little half-smile of his, it made my gut do a backflip. Whether I liked it or not, there was something there, and his behaviour said that it was mutual.

"Hopefully." Skylar's voice interrupted my thoughts, and suddenly I felt the warmth of a small hand slipping into mine, just like when we were kids. "It doesn't really matter anymore. All that matters is the way we feel about each other, right?"

"Right," I agreed, squeezing her hand. "Aren't you worried, though? About the immunity?"

"What do you mean?" she asked, her smile fading.

"Well, I guess you were too young," I said thoughtfully, staring down at my feet as we walked. "Before the internet went down, I found articles online from scientists that were studying the immunity. They said that they'd discovered the gene that makes us immune is a recessive gene—"

"What does that mean?" Skye stopped walking and grabbed my arms, a panicked look crossing her face. "Is my baby in danger?"

"I-I don't know!" I grabbed her in return and hugged her close, hating to be the bearer of bad news. "I just remember reading that they said there's no guarantee our immunity will be passed on to our children."

Skylar's lean frame shook in my arms. For a moment I was scared that she was crying, but when she pulled back and looked up at me I saw that her eyes were dry and her face set in a mask of determination.

"But there's a chance, right?" she said, and it wasn't a question – it was a demand. "There's still a chance my baby will be immune? I mean, Maddy was born after the outbreak, so there must be a chance."

"There's always a chance," I replied. She looked so resolute, and I had no evidence one way or another. It was the only answer I could think of.

I braced myself, expecting an explosion of some kind. Tears, shouting, blaming, something – but none of that came. She merely accepted my word with a curt nod and resumed walking. The only sign of whatever she might have been feeling was that one small hand rose to protectively rub her belly.

I had no idea what to say after that, so I just stayed silent, feeling uncomfortable and confused. If I had been in her position, I would have been freaking the hell out and crawling up the walls.

Then it occurred to me that perhaps she was just tougher all around than I was. This was the only life she'd ever known, a life of death and struggle. Even if she lost her baby, she would still have Ryan to help her through it. That kind of emotional support was something that I'd never had.

That was the difference between us, what made her so strong while I was so fragile. I felt a little bit of envy creep into my thoughts, but it was dashed by a cold flash of realisation: that meant I was the high-strung sister, didn't it?

\*\*\*

Skye and the others got their stuff together and departed within ten minutes, leaving me alone in their bunker. As I limped along the corridors looking for little Madeline, I pondered over all the changes that had happened in my life in a few short days. It had only been a few hours since I'd awoken from my fever, and yet they trusted me enough to leave me alone with their most precious possession: Maddy.

In return, I felt a sense of trust towards each of them that I hadn't felt since I lost my family. Skye's presence helped with that, of course, but that wasn't all. I felt a sense of trust towards Michael and the doctor that almost bordered on affection, despite the conversation I'd eavesdropped on.

Michael's talk had reassured me and set my mind at ease. He had helped me to understand that this group worked together, like an extended family. They weren't just a group of random castaways that had come together for mutual survival. I was surprised by how much they cared about one another. Each member was trusted just as much as any other. That was a rare thing in the world that we lived in since the plague. Most of the gangs I had seen were just that: gangs, with one charismatic leader surrounded by a group of minions. They were not family. In most cases, they were hardly even friends. The gangs were held together by one thing, and that was fear.

Despite the doctor's initial misgivings, they'd accepted me as one of their own. I felt both honoured and bewildered by that, but I'd already come to value it more than words could express. I had no desire to lose that trust, or do anything to violate it. The behavioural conditions the doctor had put on me just made sense, and after everything I'd seen and suffered, I agreed with them. They were the very same conditions I would have put on him, if I had been in his position. As upset as I was in the minutes after hearing it, once I'd thought it through I realised that I understood his reasoning. I could respect that.

I was a little surprised that he'd agreed to let me babysit Madeline. The revelation about my relationship with Skylar seemed to have changed his opinion of the threat I presented, since it kind of made me family too. It bound me to their group dynamic, and to their communal moral code. If I wanted to stay with my sister then I had to follow their rules, and we all knew it.

I found Maddy in her room, playing with a couple of rag dolls. She didn't even look up when I entered the room, nor when I sat myself down on her bed with my back against the wall and crossed my legs comfortably. Whatever little game she had invented for herself was far more interesting than me.

Watching the little girl play, I thought back to when Skye and I were growing up together. I'd been ten when she was born, old enough to be fascinated by the new baby but young enough to not really understand her limitations. Mum had given me a thorough scolding when she caught me filling the newborn's crib up with every Barbie doll I owned. I had been the only child up to that point, and the only grandchild as well, so I had a *lot* of Barbies. The memory made me smile. I was only trying to share.

Madeline looked up at me at last, her head tilted curiously to one side. "What are you grinning for?"

"Nothing. Just thinking," I said. "I like your dollies."

"Thanks." Maddy beamed and held up her dolls one by one as she named them for me. "This one is Granddaddy, this one is Mummy, and this one is Mister Michael."

The Michael doll had a piece of old Velcro for hair, and was so overstuffed in the chest that it took all of my willpower to keep myself from laughing out loud.

"Yeah? What about that one?" I asked, pointing to a fourth doll that sat lonely in a corner, excluded from her games.

Maddy reached over and picked it up, frowning down at the doll. "It was Sophie. But Sophie died. Playing with her makes me feel sad."

My heart just about broke. I watched her set the doll back down, propped against the leg of the bed.

"I'm sorry to hear that. Was Sophie your friend?" I asked gently, hoping to gain a little insight into the group so that I could be careful of the subject in future.

"Yes. We used to play together lots and lots." Maddy looked even more upset now, and I suddenly realised I'd crossed a line. Michael had lost his niece, but Maddy had lost her only friend. I hurried to change the subject.

"Hey, I have an idea. Do you want to help me make something?" I asked, praying she'd take the bait.

She did.

"What kind of something?" Maddy enquired, looking up at me curiously.

"I was going to make everyone a big bowl of fruit salad to share for dessert," I replied. "I could use a hand."

Generosity wasn't an emotion that I felt often, but when I did, it hit me like a sledgehammer to the face. Besides, there was no reason to let all of that fruit go to waste, when there were plenty of hungry mouths that could use the vitamins.

"Fruit salad, like from the cans?" she asked, looking up at me with big brown eyes. "Granddad lets me have that sometimes."

"No." I shook my head, then stood and offered the little girl my hand. "I mean a real fruit salad, made from fresh fruit."

"Fruit from a tree?" Madeline's eyes went huge. She bounced up to her feet and took my hand, following obediently as I led her from the room.

"That's right, real fruit from a real tree," I replied. "It even has skin on it."

"Fruit doesn't have skin," she said incredulously.

"Yes it does," I explained. "They take the skin off before they put it in the can."

"But, why does a fruit have skin?" she demanded.

Okay, she had me there.

"Uh... I don't know," I admitted with a shrug. "To protect the soft, squishy inside bits, I guess. That's why *you* have skin. I'll show you and prove it. I brought some fruit with me, but Mister Michael put it into cold storage so we'll have to go find it."

"Okay," she agreed happily, and together we went off in search of fruit.

Our first stop was the storage room with the big commercial refrigerators. I opened them one by one, until at last I found my bags of fruit. They were untouched and unopened, just the way I'd left them when I put them in the truck three days before.

I grabbed them and hobbled off towards the kitchen with Madeline hot on my heels. When I set the bags down on the table in the kitchen, she was quick to hop up on a chair and look inside them.

"What's this?" she asked, holding up a glossy red fruit and staring at it in confusion.

"That is an apple," I replied. I felt so useful for having knowledge that someone else didn't have, even if she was a child. "It's delicious. You can eat it if you like, but make sure you wash it first."

She sniffed it and examined it thoroughly, then hopped off the chair and scampered over to the sink to do as I instructed. While she was busy, I opened each of the bags and began sorting out the fruit that was the ripest and needed to be eaten swiftly, from that which would last a while longer. A few pieces were overripe and would need to be thrown out, so I set them aside. Ah, such a waste, but that was life. Nothing lasts forever.

"This is amazing!"

I glanced over my shoulder at the girlish squeal behind me, to find that Maddy had taken her first bite of a real apple. She devoured it in record time, then raced over and went to grab another one.

I caught her hand to stop her, and gave her a playful grin. "Don't eat too many, you'll get sick. Plus, we've got to save some for dessert."

She pouted, but obediently retracted her hand.

*What a good kid*, I thought. Although I was not the most maternal person by nature, I still reached over and gave her a pat on the head.

"Okay, now I need a big bowl, a real big bowl. Is there one here?" I asked. Her eyes lit up and she nodded rapidly, glossy black tresses flying all around her face, then she scampered off to fetch a big plastic bowl from one of the low cupboards. She came rushing back a moment later and held the bowl up to me triumphantly.

"Perfect," I said as I took the bowl from her little hands and put it on the table. "So what we're going to do, is we're going to wash all this fruit, cut it up, and put it in the bowl all mixed together. That's a fruit salad."

"Ooohh." She sounded genuinely amazed, and my heart melted a bit. I'd honestly forgotten how adorable little kids could be.

"Yeah, it's very yummy," I said. I picked up a few pieces of fruit and offered them to her. "I'll do the cutting, but my foot hurts so I should sit down as much as possible. Can you wash the fruit for me?"

Madeline nodded enthusiastically, and snatched the fruit from my hands. She scampered over to the sink and started washing it with a determined thoroughness. While she was busy, I rose to find a knife in one of the drawers and a chopping board in a cupboard, then returned to the table. I wasn't kidding about my foot hurting. All the walking I'd been doing recently was starting to make it ache something terrible.

Still, it felt good to be doing something useful for others; I felt helpful, productive and a little bit domesticated. I'd even go so far as to say it made me feel like a good person.

I hadn't felt like that in a long, long time.

# Chapter Fifteen

Maddy and I had finished our project and returned to her bedroom to play with her dolls when the ruckus started.

My head shot up. I was on my feet a moment later, immediately alert for danger. My hand instinctively went to the pockets of my cargos, but my taser was not close at hand, but Maddy didn't seem concerned at all.

"Granddaddy's back, Granddaddy's back!" She leapt to her feet, chanting gleefully, and skipped out of the room before I could stop her. Concerned she might be mistaken, I hurried after her as fast as I could, but she was small and nimble and was gone before I even made it to the door.

Oh great. I'd lost my charge on my first day of babysitting duty. For all I knew there was a hoard of mutated infected coming this way right now. Thankfully, I was wrong.

"Out the way, Maddy-monkey!"

The voice was deep and commandingly male. It took me a second to realise that it was Michael's voice, and that he just sounded a little different when he was out of breath. He rounded the corner a moment later, burdened by a huge box of god-knows-what but looking flushed and excited regardless. Madeline was bouncing around him trying to see what was in the box, full to the brim with energy in that way only a small child can be.

I grabbed the little girl as she passed by and gently restrained her to keep her out of the way as the loot-procession moved past us. It took them a couple of trips to bring in all of the goodies they found, with the men carrying the heavier items and insisting that Skylar only carry lighter objects. As much as their chivalry seemed to piss Skylar off, it gave me a bit of a warm feeling to see the men being gentlemanly in this day and age.

She stopped beside me after one trip to catch her breath and greet Madeline, and while we were talking she mentioned that they'd found a lot of useful things in the store alongside the general home wares. They found camping equipment, tools, gardening utensils, and even seeds that they suspected would probably still be viable. Although there was no space to grow them here, they'd brought them all anyway since they might prove vital in the future.

I agreed, of course. You never knew what you'd need one day. Even if we never used the seeds, a rake could be a handy weapon in a pickle. Besides, every one of us was aware in our own way that we couldn't keep living off the skeleton of a dead society forever. Eventually, we would need to fend for ourselves and become self-sufficient.

They wouldn't let me do much to help with the unpacking due to my injury, so I settled for keeping Madeline distracted and out from underfoot. For whatever reason, she was extremely excited and possessed more energy than all of us adults combined. As I followed her around, I found myself wondering how my mother had managed to do this for all those years. No wonder she'd always looked so tired.

In the end, I distracted the little girl by getting her to help me make dinner. There wasn't much that we could do that was terribly creative, but we did our best with the resources at hand. By combining canned meat with tinned Italian-style tomatoes, we managed to craft a fair approximation of spaghetti bolognese. The packets of dried pasta that we found in the storage room were a little bit floppy, but once they were cooked they tasted just fine.

When the exhausted survivors finally finished their task and filed into the kitchen, Maddy sat them down around the table and handed out plates and utensils like a pint-sized maître d'. She took the job so seriously that everyone was smiling by the time the food was ready. When I served up the food, it was met with exclamations of surprise and delight. As I found out later, no one really bothered to try and make something that resembled real food anymore.

I never did either, so I understood. I just felt like impressing my newfound family in some small way. To them, I probably looked like a puppy desperately wanting a pat on the head, but nobody said anything.

After dessert, which was a treat for everyone, they thanked me one by one and trundled off to bed. The doctor and Maddy went one way, Skylar and Ryan another, but Michael stayed behind to help me clean up.

"Thank you for doing that," he said as he stacked the dirty dishes in the sink, while I was busy clearing the leftover food off the table. I glanced at him and found him smiling at me. "I haven't eaten like that in a long time. You're a good cook."

A hot flush crept into my cheeks and I looked away, embarrassed. "My mother would disagree with you. She kept trying to teach me to cook, and then getting frustrated with me and chasing me out of the kitchen." The warmth faded away as my thoughts drifted back to my family, and I found myself staring down at the table thoughtfully. "I miss her."

That was the first time I'd admitted that fact to another human being since my grandmother died. It was kind of cathartic, to tell someone the truth about how I felt. I didn't quite know why I felt like I could talk to Michael so freely, but something told me that he would understand.

"I know." His voice was soft and thoughtful, barely audible over the sound of the sink filling with water. "I miss my mother, too. All of my family. Especially Sophie."

Even though I was still out of practice at reading expressions and tones of voice, it sounded like the first time he had admitted that to anyone as well.

Perhaps it was. He'd taken it upon himself to act as the de facto leader of this group, which meant he had to be the strong one, the one who always stayed positive for the sake of everyone else. Admitting that he could be hurt was difficult for him. Even with my rusty social skills, I sensed a great need in him that had gone ignored for far too long.

"Do you want to talk about it?" I offered tentatively, uncertain how my offer would be taken.

He shook his head, and stared intently at the filling sink as though it was the most important thing in the world. "Not really." After a long moment, his shoulders slumped and he looked back at me. "But I guess I should talk to someone."

There was so much pain in those kind eyes that I wanted to run over and comfort him right then and there. But I didn't. I couldn't. I froze with indecision. While I hesitated, he opened up and told me the story of his pain.

***

All of his life, Michael had known he wanted to be an officer of the law.

As a child, he had been that one kid who showed up to fancy dress parties in a police officer's uniform every time – with the exception of a brief stint when he was six, when he'd decided that he wanted to be an astronaut instead. His infatuation with outer space had lasted all of a couple of weeks before he lost interest and went back to his original dream.

He grew up in an affluent suburb of east Auckland with his parents and his older brother, Paul. His mother was born and raised in Beijing, while his father was of mixed race, a union of European and Asian bloodlines who had been born and raised in New Zealand. They'd met while his father was in Beijing on business, fallen in love, and married. Michael had been three and his brother six when the family returned to New Zealand in search of a brighter future for their children.

The children were raised bilingual and multicultural from an early age. Michael's mother was intensely ambitious when it came to her children's futures, the way Chinese mothers sometimes were. She insisted that they learn multiple languages and instruments, and always demanded that they do well in school.

His father had been much more relaxed and was perfectly content to let Michael do whatever he wanted, but it was his mother who was the dominant parent in their union and it was her will that ruled the nest. Michael's childhood was one of school and endless tutoring, with very little time for friends or fun.

For years, his mother had tried to convince him to become an architect or an accountant or a doctor, but Michael stayed resolute. He watched Paul grow up and go off to university to study economics, but Michael didn't care about money or prestige. All he wanted to do with his life was to protect and serve.

By the time he finished high school, Michael was fluent in four more languages in addition to the English and Mandarin that they spoke at home. He was an excellent student with top grades, head prefect, and a prominent member of the athletics team. He could play the flute and the cello with reasonable competence, and showed a genuine talent for the violin. Although he had few friends, all of his teachers agreed that he was a diligent, intelligent, and affable young man with a bright future ahead of him.

In spite of all of that, Michael never doubted for a second which career he would choose once he graduated. He could have been anything, but the only thing he wanted was to be a police officer. Every ounce of effort he put into his studies was just another means to push himself a little bit closer to that goal. The same day that he graduated from high school, he applied to the Royal New Zealand Police College and was accepted. Six months later, he graduated with honours and was offered a position in Hamilton.

He took the position and moved south. In spite of the move and the clashes with his wilful mother, he was a good son and loved his family. He returned to Auckland often to visit them, and made sure to always be there for important family events. He was there for his brother's graduation and wedding, and there for every Christmas. He was there when his only niece, Sophie, was born, and he was there for her first birthday.

When the plague first started to spread, the constables were kept well informed. He told me about the dread he'd felt in the pit of his stomach when he heard the news that the infection had reached New Zealand's shores. He'd spent what felt like forever trying to phone his mother, father, brother, and sister-in-law, trying desperately to reach anyone in his family.

There was no answer; the phone lines were always engaged. No one answered his emails or his text messages. It was like they were simply gone.

Then the riots started and he was too busy to think about his family anymore. Day and night, he was out trying to calm the panicked populace of his adopted home, only to see them fall ill one by one. The only person he could rely on was his partner, an older police officer that he'd been paired with to help him learn the ropes.

But then his partner got sick.

By the time Michael fought through the crowds to get him to the hospital, he'd lost the ability to speak and his eyes were glazed over. The nurses swept him away without a word, leaving Michael to do his job alone.

By that stage, the riots were starting to fade. People were just too sick to put up a fight anymore. Michael did his best to make them as comfortable as possible, but there was nothing he could do to help them. Exhausted and helpless, the young police officer spent every day and every night out in the city helping anyone that he could, while waiting for instructions from his superiors on what to do.

The orders never came.

At last, he returned to the police station only to find it completely abandoned. Everyone was gone, from the administration staff to the senior sergeant. For the longest time, he sat alone in the break room – the very room we were in now – as he tried to figure out what to do.

Like all of us, he'd heard through the media that there were some people with a natural immunity to the disease, but he'd never considered that he would be one of them. He never imagined that he would be left all alone with no one to guide him. He was just twenty-two years old, from a sheltered background and a career where he was still used to having someone to boss him around and tell him what to do.

Now there was no one.

He looked me in the eye when he admitted that he'd been terrified. I knew he was ashamed to admit it, but I just nodded. I understood. I had been, too.

"I abandoned my post," he told me flatly, without breaking eye contact. "I took my squad car and went north, along the motorway towards Auckland. The only thing I could think about was finding out what happened to my family."

He explained that halfway there he came across overturned trucks blocking the entire span of the motorway, forcing him to abandon his car and travel the rest of the way home on foot. It was more than twenty kilometres, but he walked and walked until finally, he reached the house where he'd grown up.

The house was empty, the door thrown wide and partially broken off its hinges. He saw signs of looting, but no blood and no clue that told him where his parents were. There were no messages, no notes, and the computer was gone so he couldn't see if there were any half-written emails that they'd never had the chance to finish. He told me how he used the last of the battery power in his cell phone to try and ring theirs, but again there was no answer.

He waited for hours to see if his parents would return. He sat in his favourite armchair, the one he'd spent so many hours in doing homework, just staring at the door. Hoping, praying.

His parents never came. No one did. Finally, he forced himself to make a decision on his own. He needed to find out what happened to his brother.

It was close to sunset when he reached Paul's house. The door was unlocked so he let himself in, and called out his brother and sister-in-law's names at the top of his voice. There was no answer. On the wall near the door, the telephone hung off the hook; the endless dial tone was a low, sad sound. He picked it up and set it back in the cradle, not sure what else he could do.

Then, he heard the baby crying from upstairs.

He raced up as fast as he could go, taking the stairs two or three at a time, to find his tiny niece sitting in her crib. She was exhausted, filthy, and starving from being trapped there for so long without food or water; her bed had become a cage.

When she saw him, the two-year-old cried his name and reached for him frantically with tiny, grasping hands. He scooped her up and carried her back down the stairs to her high chair. Although he had no children of his own, paternal instincts kicked in and soon the toddler was fed and changed.

She was terrified though, he told me. Terrified of being abandoned again. Any time he put her down, she started crying. Any time he left her line of sight, she screamed. He was desperate to leave before he went crazy, but he couldn't leave the baby behind. It just wasn't an option.

While he was gathering the little girl's things in preparation for their departure, something out in the back yard caught his eye. He told me how he went outside with the baby huddled in his arms, and found his brother and sister-in-law standing there in the semi-darkness on the lawn.

They were completely unresponsive, and stared off into space with cold, glazed eyes. They didn't even blink when he and Sophie called out to them, nor did their eyes focus when he moved into their line of sight and waved to them.

They were already gone.

Sophie was too young to understand. She cried and cried when he took her away; she didn't understand why they were leaving Mummy and Daddy behind. She didn't know what he knew, that once the infection took their speech away there was no turning back. That wasn't his brother anymore, it wasn't little Sophie's mummy and daddy. But how could he possibly explain that to a two-year-old?

Fuelled by terror and a fierce need to protect the one family member he had left, he took the tiny child and carried her south. He walked non-stop through the night, pausing only to eat, drink, and feed Sophie, and then he picked her up again and walked some more. Eventually, Sophie fell into an exhausted sleep in his arms, but still he walked on. He'd never walked so far in his life, and by the time he reached safety it felt like his legs were about to drop off.

With no other option and no one to give him a better idea, Michael took his precious cargo back to the only safe place he could think of – his home away from home in the crew quarters beneath the Hamilton police station.

There, he raised her like his own daughter, and taught her all the hard lessons he had to learn to survive in the world after humanity was gone. He watched her grow, taught her to read and write, played with her, and told her stories about her daddy from his own childhood.

He was always honest with her and never babied her. He took her with him when he was scavenging because experience was the only way that she would learn. Sophie had been a sweet and intelligent child who learned quickly, and soon became as useful as any of the adults who later joined the group.

\*\*\*

"If only I hadn't been so lenient." He finally turned to look at me, his eyes filled with so much sadness that my heart dropped into my stomach. "If only I'd insisted that she stay home where it's safe. I only turned my back for a second.

"I didn't notice that she'd run off. We were out poking around, and I guess she saw something that caught her eye. I have no idea what it was, and now I'll never know. I heard her scream, but by the time I got to her it was too late. The infected had already torn her throat out and it was— hitting her. She was still alive, but only just. I managed to get it off her, but she was bleeding out and I knew she was dying. I tried to get her home, but she didn't make it."

Michael drew a deep, rough breath and put a hand over his face, like he didn't want me to see his emotion. But I knew and I understood. It was a fresh wound, still raw. It had only been a few days since he'd watched the little girl he loved like a daughter die a horrible, painful death. Even after so long alone, I still felt all the human emotions, like sympathy, remorse, and grief. In that moment when he needed me most,

I put aside my fear of other survivors completely. I wrapped my arms around him and just held him, not saying a word while he grieved for the poor child snatched away long before her time.

With each of us distracted in a different way, it wasn't until much later that any of us realised that we'd forgotten one important thing: night had fallen, and the kid named Dog still hadn't come home.

It was an oversight that we'd all come to regret.

# Chapter Sixteen

I slept poorly that night, tossing and turning in my bed as my mind went over and over Michael's story. For the longest time, there had only been one story in my head, and that was my own. I'd never even considered the terrible things that other survivors had gone through, and now my psyche was in distress.

In my nightmares, it was me making that long, long trek between the cities, frightened and alone except for a little girl begging and begging and begging to see her mummy again.

*Please, please,* she pleaded in my dream, twisting her little hands in the fabric of my uniform. Her face was a blur, since my subconscious didn't have a face to give her. Sometimes, she was Skylar. Other times, she was a stranger.

I want my mummy…

I awoke in a cold sweat, unsure whether it was the nightmare that had interrupted my sleep, or a sound I'd heard. Years of living on my own had left me a very light sleeper. I felt like I might have heard something, but I couldn't be certain. I lay awake in the dark, straining my ears for anything out of the ordinary, but I heard only silence. I brushed it off as a figment of my imagination, then rolled over and closed my eyes.

Then I heard it, clear as a bell: a whispery voice begging for help, but struggling to form the words. I came awake instantly and was out of bed a second later, dressed in nothing but a grey nightshirt. There was a wet cough beyond the door and a faint scraping sound.

I froze, listening intently.

The noises were so soft that I could barely hear them. I was the closest, so it seemed unlikely that anyone else would hear them at all. It was up to me to investigate.

I fumbled for my taser in the dark before I switched on the light. My room was as I'd left it. The noise was definitely coming from outside. I thought I could hear someone crying, and then there was another sodden cough. Whatever was out there, it couldn't possibly be a threat. It sounded pathetic, injured. Harmless.

I didn't feel reassured. My back was up, so to speak, and I was ready for a fight.

Then my sleep-addled thoughts darted to something that someone said the day before. Michael had mentioned another person, a deaf boy that was staying with them. I thought back to the previous night, and realised I hadn't seen anyone matching that description come back to the bunker. I was paranoid, but I wasn't stupid; I swiftly put two and two together.

Taser in hand, in case whoever or whatever had injured the boy was still nearby, I threw open the door and stepped out into the murky hall.

A moment later, the weapon slipped from my fingers and clattered to the ground. My hands flew up to my mouth in horror.

There was so much blood. So much blood.

"Dr Cross!" I turned and raced down the corridor with no thought of my foot at all, panic and adrenaline dulling the pain. When I reached the doctor's door, I beat on it with my fists and screamed his name until it opened.

"What? What is it?" The doctor looked sleepy and confused. I couldn't get the words to come out the way I wanted, so I just grabbed him by the wrist and dragged him back to where the wounded survivor lay in a puddle of blood. I'd seen enough death in my lifetime to know how much blood was in the human body. I could hardly believe that poor boy was still breathing.

The kid lifted his head and looked at us pitifully with his one remaining eye; the other had been torn from his head along with half his scalp. Flesh hung in tattered strips off the bone around the empty socket.

"Help..." Blood dribbled from his lips as he struggled to speak, but then he coughed again. It was a terrible spasm that racked his entire body with pain, and blood sprayed from his mouth across the floor.

"Oh, sweet mother Mary." Dr Cross dropped to his knees beside the young man, ignoring the blood that soaked his pyjamas. I heard a cry behind me, and turned to see that Skylar and Ryan had joined us. The doctor looked at us and started issuing orders.

"Skylar, fetch my medical kit, now." He words were a command and Skye jumped to obey them. "Ryan, go check all the outside doors are closed. And you—" He pointed at me. "—go fetch Michael!"

I nodded and raced off, limping as fast as my body would let me. The leader of the group slept in a different part of the building, so he was unlikely to have heard the racket we were making – or so I assumed. As it turned out, I'd underestimated exactly how loud I'd been screaming. As I rounded the corner into the corridor that led to Michael's room, I found myself face to face with a broad, bare chest. I crashed into it before I could slow down, and almost bowled him off his feet.

He managed to brace himself just in time and caught me before I could fall. "I heard something..."

I was out of breath from the run and the panic, and struggled to form coherent words. I only managed to get out one: "Dog."

It was enough. Michael looked in the direction that I pointed, immediately understanding what I meant. He set me back on my feet and raced off, with me in hot pursuit. Every second was precious, while a human life was bleeding out on the floor.

I was the last to return to the group besides Ryan, who was still off checking on our security. During the short time I'd been gone, Dr Cross had acquired a bundle of towels and was trying frantically to stem the blood flowing from the young man's terrible, terrible wounds.

The face wasn't the worst of it, I realised with horror. Poor Dog's torso was a mess of deep cuts, with chunks of flesh missing completely in a number of places. His left hand was gone, severed at the wrist and pumping blood from the ragged stump. The doctor had managed to staunch it with a tourniquet, but I feared it was already too late.

"Help me get him into his bed," Doc said to Michael, who hurried over to obey. He knelt to carefully lift the youth in his arms, obviously trying not to jostle his injuries, but that seemed like an impossible task. The boy looked so small and fragile compared to Michael's lean bulk that in my imagination he weighed next to nothing. With half of his face missing, I couldn't even guess at his age. Silently, I hoped I would have the chance to ask him one day.

Dog cried piteously, his one remaining hand grasping at Michael's shoulder. He was in excruciating pain and fighting for his life, I realised. Terrified. Alone. Trapped in a dark, silent world. His one remaining eye darted about but blood hindered his vision, and I could see the muscles inside the empty socket twitching convulsively to match. The sight was almost enough to make me throw up.

The poor boy. I'd never really wished death on another human being in my life, but right now I found myself praying he would die soon just so that he wouldn't have to suffer any more. It seemed impossible for us to save him. I couldn't bear to watch his torment, but I couldn't just run away and hide. Nobody should ever have to die alone.

Suddenly, the boy's good eye cleared and found Michael's face; recognition flashed across what was left of his. "Muh… Muh…"

He stumbled over his words, obviously trying to say his friend's name, but he couldn't get it out. Tears gathered in his eye and he began signing frantically with his one remaining hand, trying to express with his own language what he couldn't do with the spoken word.

"I've got you, buddy. You're home, we've got you." Michael tried to reassure him as he carried him to his bed and gently lay him down on the sheets. I wondered if the boy could even see him clearly enough to read his lips. The moment he was safely down, the doctor shoved Michael away and went to work trying to save the poor kid's life before he bled to death.

Skylar and I huddled by the door, watching with mute despair. Skye handed Michael a clean towel when he came over to join us. He accepted it without a word, and used it to wipe Dog's blood off his hands, shoulders, and chest.

Once he was as clean as he could be, Michael tossed the towel out into the hall and looked around to check on the rest of his group. He took one look at me then put an arm around me and pulled me up against his side. My expression must have been transparent as glass – I was pretty upset. Okay, really, really upset. I felt no desire to protest, strike him, or shove him off. I just hugged him back in silence, shaking like a leaf from the adrenaline and horror of it all.

I'd seen wounds before, terrible wounds, even wounds that I'd inflicted – but I'd never felt so helpless.

Ryan returned, out of breath from his run.

"The doors are all locked. I don't think anything followed him in," he announced breathlessly, joining us in our huddle. He took Skylar's hand to comfort her, and looked around at the rest of us. "There's blood everywhere. Is he…?"

"He's alive, but I don't know how much longer he'll last," Skye said, her voice grim.

I half-expected the doctor to yell at us and tell us not to give up hope, but he was too busy to even notice us. This was not some TV drama where the patient always makes a miraculous recovery by the end of the episode. Our reality was so much more brutal.

A life hung by the slenderest of threads.

With a flash of guilt, I realised that it had come down to me, one choice made in a heartbeat. If I'd slept a little bit deeper, then we would have awoken come morning to find nothing but a corpse in a puddle of blood. It might have even been Madeline that found him. Somehow, that thought was even more horrifying than anything else.

I'd almost missed the sound of the poor boy's struggles. I'd almost decided to just roll over and go back to sleep. Tears welled up in my eyes and I brushed them away hurriedly, trying to reassure myself that there was nothing more I could have done. But try as I might, I couldn't quite shake the unreasonable feeling that somehow, this was my fault.

The four of us stood dumbly for ten minutes before Skye excused herself to go check on Madeline, and Ryan left to go start the job of cleaning up the blood before it congealed. Michael offered to help him, but Ryan declined. Someone needed to stay with the Doc in case he needed anything.

He was right, of course, so we stayed. One stitch at a time, the doctor wove torn flesh back together where possible, or bound it as best as he could where it was not, until the youth was a mass of bandages with just one eye and a patch of soft brown skin visible. The eye was closed in blessed, drug-induced sleep. Thankfully, Dr Cross stockpiled anaesthetics. Just looking at those injuries made me feel nauseated – I could only imagine how poor Dog felt. It seemed like it was only sheer willpower that had kept him alive for so long.

At last, exhausted, Dr Cross sat back and looked at us. His face was a mask of regret. "That's the best I can do, but he's lost a lot of blood. He needs a blood transfusion, but even with one I'm not sure he'll live."

"But there's a chance he'll survive?" Michael asked, his voice sharp and hard.

Dr Cross shrugged. "There's always a chance. It's just not a very good one."

Michael nodded curtly and slipped his arm out from around me. He moved past me, further into the room, and dragged a chair close to the bed so that he could sit down. He offered his arm to the doctor without a word, who stared back at him in confusion. "What are you—"

"I'm O-negative, the universal donor. *Do it.*" Michael's voice was a hiss; startled, the doctor nodded and started setting up his equipment for a transfusion.

Great, more needles. I already felt queasy, but at the same time I didn't want to leave Michael to suffer alone. That seemed so wrong. Although my moral code might have been a little askew, I still had one. Michael was my friend, and he was doing something very brave. He deserved my support. Lacking any other option that was remotely useful, I sat down on the floor beside his chair and rested my head against his leg.

He looked surprised by the gesture, and stared down at me thoughtfully. I felt a gentle hand stroke my hair as we both tried to ignore the needle being inserted into his arm. Even though no words passed between us, there was a silent understanding: I was offering comfort, and he was accepting it. I took his hand in mine and put my cheek against it, giving him what support I could from simple closeness and human warmth.

I was socially retarded, but I wasn't without instincts. There were risks associated with what he was doing, but I understood why he *had* to do it. His friend's life was at stake. If there was even the slimmest chance that he could help, then any risk was worth it. If he didn't, how would he live with himself afterwards? I closed my eyes and tried to ignore the metallic scent of blood, just waiting for it to be over.

***

When the transfusion was done, I helped Michael back to his room. He was pale and shaky from blood loss and did not complain when I tucked him back into bed with doctor's orders to stay put. Feeling unexpectedly protective, I brought him some fruit and water a few minutes later, and waited with him while he ate.

When he finally closed his eyes to rest, I closed the door softly and padded back out into the hallway with barefoot stealth, to check on the doctor and Dog.

The doctor looked exhausted, and was intensely focused on his patient. I suspected that he would get so wrapped up in his patient he'd forget about himself, so I brought him some food and water as well. It took a fair amount of bullying to get him to take food with his patient struggling for life. Eventually, I managed to convince him that Dog stood no chance at all if his doctor fainted from hunger when he needed him most. When I was sure I could trust him to take care of his own needs as well, I departed and went off to check on the others.

Maddy was still sleeping, innocent as the child she was, so I left her in peace. I found Ryan and Skylar hard at work mopping up blood, so I joined them instead. Three sets of hands would make the work go faster, and there was an awful lot of blood. We worked in silence for some time, until Skye finally got up to go take the soiled towels off to be washed, leaving me alone with Ryan.

His head came up and he watched her until she was out of earshot. When she was gone, he turned to me with a worried look on his face. "Skye told me what you said to her yesterday, about the immunity."

My heart sank, but I nodded. "I only know what I've read. I don't know if there's more to it, or maybe they were wrong."

"We don't want to risk it," he said, his voice quiet and reserved. "We're going to leave, go south, try and find a little farm somewhere. We want our baby to be born as far away from danger as possible."

This time my heart went the exact opposite direction and leapt up into my throat. "You're leaving? Have you– have you told Michael yet?"

"Not yet. We only decided last night." Ryan looked down at the puddle he was mopping, a myriad of emotions playing across his face. "We're not really a hundred per cent sure what we're going to do. From what you've said, there's a whole bunch of other dangers out there. And now these– things, these mutants, killing us one by one."

"You're just thinking about your baby's safety. I understand," I said. I felt sick at the thought of losing my sister after I'd only just found her, but equally sick about leaving sweet Michael and little Maddy behind. And the doctor, too. I was still a little uncertain around him, but I understood why he'd said those awful things about me and I was in the process of forgiving him. "Maybe we should all go. It would be safer in numbers."

Ryan looked at me with a mixture of hope and despair. "Do you think they would?"

"I don't know. But like you said, it's not safe here anymore." I tossed a bloody towel out of the way, then I looked at his earnest young face and offered him a faint smile. "We'll talk about it with Michael when he recovers. I know a place we could go, for a while at least."

"Really?" he said, his expression brightening.

"Yeah, there's this town south of here that I spent some time in," I explained. It felt strange to willingly share my haven with others, but it also felt like the right thing to do. "It's as safe as any other place I've seen down there. It could probably be even safer if we put a little effort in to fortifying it."

He nodded, and hope brought a smile to his freckled face. I offered a silent prayer that I wasn't leading the lad to his death, or worse.

Only time would tell.

***

In spite of everyone's best efforts, the kid named Dog died two days later, surrounded by the group of people he'd come to call his family. Just before he passed, he managed to tell Michael what happened to him with awkward, one-handed sign language.

"He was with his dog when they attacked him," Michael translated for us, signing back to the boy to confirm he understood what he was being told. The boy nodded stiffly, his one good eye almost glazed over. "Several infected knocked him down, and they were eating him when his dog attacked them. His dog fought for him while he ran away, and then he came home as fast as he could."

*Eating him?* I felt sick at the thought and leaned against Skylar for support. Judging by how pale she was, she was caught up on the same word as well.

Dog's hand was trembling as he signed, making it hard for Michael to understand him.

"What?" Michael looked confused and upset, signing to the youth and speaking out loud for our sake. "Of course you'll go to Heaven one day, son, but not yet."

Dog smiled weakly at him and shook his head, then signed one more sentence before he rested his head back on his pillow and closed his eye. With one last deep, rattling breath, he left our mortal world of suffering to explore whatever lay beyond.

We all knew instinctively that he was gone, even before the doctor leaned over to check his pulse. Skye burst into tears and hugged me, while I stood dumbstruck, not sure how to feel. I hadn't known him at all, and now he was one more person that I would never have the opportunity to meet. I felt a sense of grief and loss for the friendship we would never be able to share.

I would never have the opportunity to ask him how old he was. Never have the chance to ask how he got his name. We would never get to share those moments of laughter and camaraderie or any of the other things I'd longed for over the years.

I looked at Michael, and found him staring at that young face, that seemed so very small against the pillows.

"What did he say?" I asked, even though I was afraid to hear the answer.

Michael looked at me, his expression unreadable. At first, he didn't quite seem to understand the question. It took a second before comprehension sunk in, and then he closed his eyes and smiled weakly.

"He said he was going to go see Sophie again," Michael said, his voice shaking. "He promised to tell her how much we all loved her."

Somehow, Michael managed to stay strong, but I didn't. That was enough for me. I melted down in tears, and cried for what felt like a very long time.

***

We buried them side by side, in Soldiers Memorial Park. It seemed like an appropriate place to entomb survivors who had spent their whole lives fighting an impossible enemy against insurmountable odds, and it was a beautiful green place where lovely willow trees overhung the river. A nice place to spend the rest of eternity.

Wildflowers had already begun to grow atop Sophie's grave. As the men lay Dog into a hole beside her, I marvelled at how swiftly nature reclaimed us when we are gone. I knelt and picked a particularly beautiful flower that grew at my feet, and wondered briefly what species it was. I didn't know, but it was pretty. I stepped close to the grave and I dropped it atop the corpse before they began to shovel the dirt onto him. Perhaps the flower's seeds would sprout and cover the grave with its children.

The sun felt far too bright to be putting someone so young into the earth. I had found out his age after all, from Michael and the others. He was only twenty-three.

I blinked back tears as I retreated to where Skylar stood holding Madeline, who watched blankly as the men laboured to shift the dirt back into the hole. She looked up at me, and a bright smile lit up her face.

"Don't worry, Miss Sandy," she said, reaching out to take my hand. "Mummy and Sophie will take good care of him."

I smiled weakly back at her, uncertain what I believed. Once I had been like her, innocent and full of absolute trust. Now, I wasn't so sure.

In the golden sunshine that filtered through the leaves, we watched the men working, the sweat glistening on their backs. It was the heat of summer and even under the shade of the trees, it was swelteringly hot. Although I hadn't been outside in days, I already longed to retreat back to the cool, dark bunker that had become home so quickly.

But I couldn't. There were important things that needed to be discussed and time was of the essence. I waited until they patted down the last shovelful of earth, and everyone got their chance to say goodbye. On the way back to the car, I drew Michael aside with a gentle touch on the arm.

When the others were out of earshot, I told him about my conversation with Ryan two days before and about the fear the young couple held for their baby. That, combined with the threat from these new mutated infected, made me feel a sense of urgency to get out of the area, but I desperately wanted to convince him to join us. I couldn't fathom the thought of leaving him behind.

"If two of us are going, then we should all go. She's my sister so I have to, but she's going to need the doctor when she gives birth, and we all rely on you for leadership." I paused for breath as the words tumbled out, worried by his peculiar expression. "We need to get out of here, get away from those things before they kill us all. You know what I mean, right?"

He nodded slowly as he mulled over what I said, his expression distant. When he finally spoke, his answer was not the one I was hoping for. "You're right. You should go somewhere safer. I'll remain here, and kill as many of those new things as I can."

"What? No!" I must have exclaimed louder than I meant to – I saw a couple of faces turn towards us, watching curiously. Ignoring them, I reached out and grabbed his hand. "You have to come with us as well."

"Why?" he asked bitterly. "You don't need me. I haven't done a very good job at protecting any of you so far." Somehow, he seemed to look like a lost little boy despite his stiff posture. Gazing up at him, I realised that he felt responsible for the deaths of those closest to him. My heart did a somersault in my chest.

"Don't be silly," I said, squeezing his hand firmly. "We do need you, and you have done a very good job of protecting us. Bad things happen sometimes – it's not your fault. We need you, Michael, now more than ever." Caught in a sudden, confusing surge of emotion, I brought his hand to my chest and wrapped my fingers around it. "*I* need you."

He stared at me, bewildered, until finally the pieces seemed to click together in his head. Then he looked away, towards the car full of people whose lives depended on him.

Finally, he took a deep breath and nodded once.

Just like that, the decision was made. We would leave the only home he'd known for more than a decade, and we'd do it together. They were putting their faith in my knowledge as they set out into the unknown. I just hoped that I had enough knowledge to keep us all alive.

# Chapter Seventeen

Having a plan of action helped to keep everyone from falling apart in the wake of Dog's death. When we returned to the bunker, Michael called a meeting to discuss the options for our departure. It was agreed by universal consensus that Ohaupo was the place to go, since it was the only place any of us had been to recently that was still secure and reasonably well supplied, with ready access to farmland.

What to do with the supplies in the bunker was an issue. The only functional vehicle we had was my utility, and if we crammed everyone into it then there would be no room left for anything else. We needed to find more vehicles. As the only member of the group with any mechanical knowledge, however rudimentary it was, that task fell to me. The others began organising what needed to be taken with us, and packing it into anything they could find that would make it easier to move.

There was also a new rule in the group: nobody went anywhere alone, or unarmed. Since the only weapons we had were my pistol and taser and Michael's shotgun, the new rule meant only two of us could leave the bunker at any one time. After what happened to Dog and Sophie, it seemed like a reasonable precaution. No one complained.

I spent the first morning after Dog's death in the bunker's underground garage, examining the vehicles the others had deemed unsalvageable. Since they had no idea what they were looking at, I'd decided to take a look at the wrecks myself before I wrote them off. I discovered that the majority of the vehicles were either completely useless or only good for parts, but there were a couple I thought I could fix up with a bit of effort. One in particular caught my eye – a large prisoner transport, with barred windows and double-doors in the back that locked from either the inside or the out.

I was lying on the ground beneath the transport van when Michael came looking for me around midday. I saw his boots walk past, and then he stopped and looked around before cautiously calling my name. "Sandy?"

"Down here."

The sound of my voice from an unexpected direction made him jump. He looked around, confused, before finally noticing my feet sticking out from beneath the transport. With a soft grunt, he eased himself down to ground level to peer at me.

"What on earth are you doing down here?" he asked.

"Salvaging," I replied with a playful smile.

He raised a brow. "And?"

"Well, I have good news," I replied. "A few of the spark plugs needed to be replaced and some of the cables were perished, but I've managed to salvage replacement parts from one of the other trucks. I think once I've finished refurbishing and charging the battery, this one will be good to go."

I finished up what I was doing and eased myself out from under the van. Michael offered me a hand up and I took it, glad for the assistance. Once I was back on my feet, I grabbed a rag I'd left nearby and used it to wipe the grease off my hands.

"That is good news," he agreed, examining the solid-looking van with an approving eye. Like me, he knew at a glance that we could fit a lot of good supplies in the back of a vehicle that size. His eyes shifted back to me, and he gave me a quirky smile. "You missed a spot."

"Ehh?"

"Right here." He reached over, and wiped a spot of grease off the tip of my nose. I felt my cheeks burn at the contact, but he pretended not to notice.

"Oh, thanks," I said, feigning disinterest as best I could. "Didn't see it. Remind me to enjoy another hot shower before we leave."

"No hot water where we're going?" he asked.

"Not unless we can find a heating coil before we go," I said, shaking my head. "I turned that township upside down looking for one before I hurt myself, but they were all blown."

"Hmmm," he rumbled thoughtfully, staring off into space. "Actually, I think I know a place. A plumbing supply store. I found it a few years ago, but I didn't need anything at the time so I left it untouched."

"Add that to the list of things we need to do before we go." I heaved a long sigh, and then shot a sideways glance at him. "What about weapons? Any hunting stores here? I'm not familiar with the area."

"Nothing in the way of guns, if that's what you're asking." Michael grimaced and shook his head. "There used to be, but they were looted or burned out in the riots, and someone cleared out the gun lockers down here before I had a chance to look." He paused for a moment, then flicked an uncomfortable glance at me. "I got my shotgun off a corpse, in the early days right after the riots. We've found a few others since then but they were all too rusted to be any good to us."

"Damn. Well, at least you've got spare ammunition," I said. I decided that it was politic to change the conversation at that point – Michael looked a little uncomfortable talking about weapons, and I couldn't blame him. It was a cultural thing. We Kiwis always had been peaceful little birds. "So, what are you doing here, anyway?"

"I came to call you to lunch, madam." He put on his best charming smile and sketched a mocking half-bow. "We need to make sure you put on some more weight before we go."

The playful wit and the quick, appraising glance he gave my physique made me flush all over again. Suddenly I felt awkward and uncomfortable. I wasn't sure how to deal with such obvious flirtation, so I settled for my usual defence mechanism: sarcasm.

"What, are you saying I'm too thin?" I said, putting on an offended face. "I'll have you know that the emaciated look is totally en vogue at the moment."

Thankfully, he took my comment the way it was intended and laughed. Without being invited, he slipped an arm around my waist, and I let him. Despite my nerves around other people, there was just something about him that put me completely at ease.

"Ah, mademoiselle," he said in a very fake French accent. "I am afraid that your fash-ions are somewhat, how you say, out of date?"

I smiled, my embarrassment alleviated by the levity. In the week I'd spent in the bunker enjoying good food and minimal exercise, I'd gained a decent amount of healthy weight – a fact which he clearly hadn't missed, either. As we walked, I caught him glancing down at me on occasion, studying me with interest.

"What?" I asked at last, curious and slightly unsettled by his glances.

"Just thinking that you're filling out rather nicely," he answered softly. The humour was gone now and replaced by that gentle kindness that I'd come to appreciate. And… something else. I would say that got me blushing, but my cheeks were already on fire. Aside from sunburn, that was the biggest disadvantage of being as fair as I was – the slightest blush was painfully obvious.

"Are you calling me fat?" I retorted; I didn't know how else to react, so I fell back into humour. He, however, did not.

"No." His voice was a whisper, and his arm tightened around my waist. I tensed, but his strength was tempered with gentleness. Suddenly, he stopped walking and caught my chin, to turn my face up towards his. "Never."

I sensed that there was so much more to the word than just the obvious. He didn't have to say it; I saw it in those dark, fathomless eyes.

He would never hurt me.

He would never let anyone else hurt me.

He would never leave me all alone, unless I asked him to.

His face was so close to mine that I could smell his scent, feel his breath on my skin. Even so, the kiss caught me by surprise. The wild part of me panicked, terrified and desperate to get away, but for once it was held in check by the rational, intelligent part of me.

That was the part of me that longed to be close to someone, to be cared about again. That was the part that was so fascinated by my growing attraction to the man who had almost killed me and then saved my life within the span of a few minutes. That was the part of me that wanted this kiss so badly.

My eyes closed as his lips tasted mine, softly, as though expecting at any moment that I would panic and flee. He was right, of course. He understood me so well already. If it had been anyone else, then I would never have let that kiss happen. I would have fought him for all I was worth.

Not with this man, though. I'd come to understand him in the short time we'd known each other, too. I understood that he had nothing but the best of intentions for me, and that when he kissed me it was because he meant it.

I drew a sharp breath when our lips parted, my heart racing, my mind surging with a mix of fear and longing. When my eyes finally opened, I found him looking down at me with a bemused smile on his face. I felt a stab of concern. "What?"

"I just had a silly thought." He looked a touch embarrassed as he trailed gentle fingers along the length of my jaw. "Like, maybe I should thank you for not hitting me."

I stared at him.

"You hit like a truck!" he exclaimed.

"Um— you're welcome." My brain was in a million places all at once, and I couldn't quite process his humour. Sensing my need for time, Michael let the conversation lapse into silence and led me the rest of the way to the kitchen. Just before we arrived his arm slid away and I found myself experiencing a sense of loss that I hadn't expected, a feeling that left me even more confused.

"Why is my sister the colour of a tomato?" Skylar's voice cut through my confusion like a knife. She eyeballed me and Michael both, like she sensed something was going on, but Michael only shrugged and let me keep my privacy.

I felt a flood of relief at his discretion. Of course, Skye would be the first person I talked to if I decided I wanted to talk, but I needed the time to figure out how I felt before I said anything to anyone.

I eased myself into a chair to take the weight off my injured foot, mumbling something non-committal about not feeling well. With a knowing smirk, my sister set a bowl in front of me, and put a fork in my hand.

The group dynamic had changed since my arrival. They had gone from each making and eating their own food to sharing group meals at every opportunity, cooked by whoever felt like being adventurous that day. Frankly, most of us were terrible cooks, me included. But eating together, sharing stories and camaraderie, it brought all of us a little bit closer together. Not to mention, all of us agreed eating off crockery tasted better than eating out of a can.

It also helped us to learn more about one another, and it gave Skylar and me the chance to get closer. She had been just a sweet little child when I last saw her, and now she was a spunky teenager with a bun in the oven.

I had discovered that I liked her a lot as a person. Despite looking like she was about to pop at any second, she was a bundle of energy and rarely complained about anything. It felt like her belly was almost as big as she was, and yet she was up and about from the crack of dawn, doing laundry or organising supplies or poking around in the kitchen. If something needed doing, you could count on Skylar to think of it before you did and be halfway through doing it by the time you got there.

That morning, I'd woken to the sound of joyful squeals, and emerged bleary-eyed from my room to find her chasing a delighted Madeline up and down the corridors with gleeful abandon. When she paused to catch her breath, she explained that she'd caught the child moping, and a good game of chase seemed like the easiest way to keep her spirits high.

Though I hadn't quite accepted the thought of being someone's aunt, I really hoped her baby would be okay. From the way she was with Maddy, I knew she'd be a fantastic mum, just like ours was for us.

Although she readily admitted that Ryan saved her and kept her alive all these years, it was quite obvious that she was the one who wore the pants in their relationship. He doted on her like an adoring puppy and was perfectly happy to follow her instructions in any circumstance. More than once, I'd seen her handing out orders and him trundling off about her bidding with a dopey smile on his face, perfectly content with his lot in life. It was kind of adorable.

The doctor was a different story. I'd learned that he was kind of a loner by nature and preferred to spend his free time reading quietly in his room. Although his face was set in a permanent scowl, I'd come to realise it wasn't because of some deep-seated anger at the world — it was because he was short-sighted. He had glasses, but the prescription was ten years out of date and the lenses were scratched all to hell.

That knowledge came as something of a relief, since he had intimidated me when I first met him. It was nice to know that most of the time, if he was glaring at me it was not because he was mad at me, it was because he couldn't see me properly. We'd come to a grudging understanding over the last week, and while I wouldn't call our relationship anything warmer than cordial, we had found a mutual respect for one another.

Now, Madeline was truly an enigma. I'd come to the realisation after spending some time with her that, although she was just a child, she was intelligent to the point of being brilliant. As much as we all instinctively wanted to protect her from the world, she always seemed to know what was going on around her. She flip-flopped between periods of childish play and moments of intense, adult clarity that never ceased to surprise me. Sometimes I wondered if she could actually read minds.

Although she got bored swiftly with adult conversations, I often found her watching me doing things that should not interest a seven-year-old at all. Earlier that morning, she'd spent nearly an hour watching me work on an engine, asking me questions about everything. Some of those questions had been too technical for me to answer.

Right now, she looked like any other child as she shovelled her food down so fast that her grandfather needed to scold her and warn her that she'd choke. Ryan was off in his own world that completely revolved around Skylar, and Skylar was talking to me.

"So, how's it going?" she prompted while she spooned her culinary creation into a bowl for Michael. He took it gratefully, and settled himself into the chair beside me as though it were the most natural thing in the world. I tried to ignore him and focused on my sister.

"It's good," I said. "I found a couple of salvageable engines, though only one vehicle large enough for what we need. You had all the stuff I needed to restore the battery in your stores, so with any luck it'll be good to go tomorrow morning."

"When did you learn to fix a car anyway?" Skye peered at me askance as she served up her own lunch, and then sat down opposite me.

"Well, in Year Twelve I decided to do a practical class, and automotive engineering was the only one I could get into without a ton of prerequisite classes," I said. I didn't really want to explain that Dad had gotten me interested in cars in the first place, so I chose an answer that didn't dredge up old pain. "Who would have thought it would end up being the only useful thing I learned in school?"

"Handy. I wish I'd gotten the chance to go to high school." Her eyes drifted out of focus, and one hand absently rubbed her swollen middle. I knew what she was thinking without her having to say a word: she wished her child would have that chance, as well.

"You weren't missing much," I said, trying to distract her with humour. It worked... sort of.

"Oh, really now?" she said, laughing. "What about Robert? And Bryce? And Harry? Oooo..." One by one, she named all my high school boyfriends, then playfully made kissy fish lips at me. Michael shot a look at me with raised eyebrows, and I felt the heat rush back into my cheeks. Suddenly, I wished I could just crawl under the table and die.

"How the hell do you even remember their names?" I demanded, fighting the urge to run away and hide. Or maybe kick my sister to the moon. Yes, that seemed like an appropriate response. "I barely remember them at all."

"Well." This time, it was her turn to look embarrassed.

My anger faded, replaced by curiosity. "Well?"

She blew out a sharp breath, and then finally admitted, "I named my Ken dolls after them, all right?"

"You did what?" I was flabbergasted. Why on earth would she name her dolls after my high school boyfriends?

"Well, I named my Barbie after you," she said, hanging her head as though she were admitting something humiliating. "It seemed like a good idea at the time, okay?"

I stared at her while I processed that information. She'd named her doll after *me*? She loved that doll. It went everywhere with her, to day care when she was tiny and later on to primary school as well. I remembered Mum having to pry it out of her hands when it was bedtime. If Mum failed to tuck the doll into its bed at night, she would kick up such a fuss. One time she got so loud that the neighbours complained, thinking someone was being murdered in our house.

"Aww." My brow furrowed and I fought an unreasonable urge to cry. "That's so sweet, Skye. I never knew."

"Well, don't go telling everyone now," she shot back, tilting her chin up in a petulant manner that reminded me of our mother when she was teasing Dad. "They'll start thinking I have a heart or something."

I immediately forgave her for embarrassing me in front of Michael. How could I possibly be mad over something like that? Overcome by a flash of almost unbearable affection towards the young woman that had once been my baby sister, I reached over and squeezed her hand. She didn't say anything, but she gave my hand a squeeze back.

She understood.

# Chapter Eighteen

Shortly after lunch, Michael and I took Skylar to examine the prisoner transport I had managed to salvage.

"This is good," Skye murmured thoughtfully to herself as she circled the van, examining it from all angles. "Very good, but I think we need another one."

I looked at Michael, who nodded thoughtfully. "She's right. From what you've said, the supplies down south are limited. We should take as much with us as we can."

"Particularly medical supplies," I agreed. "There's almost nothing down there. That's why I had to come north to begin with."

"There are a lot of things we need to take." Skye sighed, bracing a hand against the small of her back to stretch her spine. "We need more vans."

"How many of us know how to drive?" I glanced back and forth between them, uncertain.

"You, me, and the doctor," Michael answered, ignoring the irritated sound Skylar made. "Skye and Ryan say that they know how, but I'd prefer not to trust them behind the wheel of a heavy vehicle until we've had a chance to give them a few lessons."

"We may not have a choice," I said, gesturing to my foot. "I can't really drive with this, and we need to take as much as we can carry."

Michael grunted and Skylar beamed. I raised a brow, but neither of them explained what was going on between them, so I just had to guess it was some kind of inside joke.

"Okay, so we need to find one more. A van or a light truck, something along those lines then." I looked around the garage at the other vehicles and shook my head. "We'll need to look outside. Everything we have here is either too small to be any use, or too far gone to fix."

Michael stared at me, his exasperation fading into a deep frown. Concern etched itself across his handsome face. "Are you sure you can handle a trip outside? You're still wounded."

I felt a surge of warmth at his concern. It was nice to know that someone cared.

"You can't keep me locked up in here forever," I said. Feeling a little bold all of a sudden, I gave him a fearless grin and limped off towards my room. "Besides, you'll be with me if anything goes wrong. Go get your kit on, officer. Time's a'wasting."

Behind me, Skylar snickered.

\*\*\*

I found it kind of funny how in one short week, I'd adapted to a life where I no longer had to carry everything I owned on my back like a tortoise. It wasn't all that long ago I'd been so paranoid my taser everywhere with me, even for something as simple as a dash to the ladies' room. I'd grown comfortable in this bunker though, and I no longer felt the need to have my hand on a weapon at all times. Those things I had once considered vital necessities now sat in my room, in a neat row upon the table by the door.

I stood looking at them for a minute, thinking things over. I was a creature of habit, but it was interesting how quickly those habits had changed. One by one, I checked that my necessities were all in working order and packed them into the pockets of my fatigues, until all that was left was the gun.

I stared at the weapon, wishing that I didn't have to take it with me, but I knew in my heart I did. If that horrible weapon was the only thing standing between me and death, then Mum and Grandma would forgive me for using it. It wasn't the gun's fault. It was only a tool. It was the disease that had taken them away from me, and now I had Skylar to protect, not to mention my unborn niece or nephew.

"It's not going to bite you, you know."

Michael's voice almost made me jump out of my skin. I spun around to face him, startled half out of my wits. He was leaning casually against the doorframe, watching me with his eyebrows raised, but he didn't move from the spot until I calmed down. I shoved the gun in my pocket and buried the wave of embarrassment I felt at my overreaction. He knew I was... quirky, what was one more piece of evidence? Just as I was about to say something snippy, he distracted me with something completely unexpected.

"I made you a present," he said.

"Eh?" I paused, surprised again but in a whole other way. "What? Why?"

"To help you while your foot heals," he said. He reached out the door and grabbed something that was out of my line of sight, and then thrust the haphazardly-constructed wooden object at me. It took me a moment to realise that it was supposed to be a crutch. So *that* was what I'd caught him working. The gesture was sweet and unexpected.

"Oh, thank you," I said. What I didn't want to say out loud was that I was a little afraid to put my weight on it. It wasn't well made. My Year Seven woodwork teacher would have called it shoddy at best. Still, I tested it and it held up well enough, so I gave him a grateful smile. He looked so pleased that I liked his gift I couldn't quite remember why I had been preparing to get defensive a minute earlier.

"You'll heal faster if you keep your weight off your foot," he said with a shrug, and beckoned for me to follow him.

We returned to the garage to gather up the basic tools we'd need for the trip, with me trailing behind while I practiced my crutch-walking. Although the petrol was running low, we agreed that taking the Hilux made more sense than going on foot. We needed to find some more fuel for our trip south anyway, so by taking the truck we could do both at once.

Michael helped me into the passenger seat, then climbed in behind the wheel. The engine spluttered when he turned it over, but it started on the second try; the noise worried me, but I pushed my concern aside for now. He turned the truck around and drove it up the ramp that lead to the automated parking garage doors. They clanked open after he leaned out the window and swiped a card against the lock, and then off we went.

The sunlight seemed so bright after being indoors that I had to shield my eyes. For a moment, I thought I saw movement out of the corner of my eye, but by the time my vision adjusted there was no sign of anything out of the ordinary. Michael didn't seem to have noticed anything, so I dismissed it as a figment of my imagination.

We drove for a while, slowly dodging around debris of a hundred different kinds. I watched where we were going with my GPS in hand, but Michael didn't need any guidance from me. After ten years in this city, he knew the ruins like the back of his hand. Still, I felt the need to keep busy, to keep my hands and mind distracted.

Being alone with Michael had me twisted all up in knots. Without something to distract me, that kiss was all I could think about. There was just something hypnotic about his boyish charm, and I found it hard not to think about how close he was. About the taste of his lips on mine, the scent of his skin, the feel of his hands that were so strong and yet so gentle.

I shook my head and rubbed a hand over my eye, pretending to be distracted by an errant bug. To my relief, he didn't seem to notice that anything was amiss.

When had my hormones gotten so out of control? A week ago, I would have – and had – sooner slugged him than kissed him. It had been so long since I'd felt any kind of attraction to another human being, that it made me so uncomfortable that I couldn't think of anything to say. Thankfully, he didn't seem bothered by the silence.

Still, I was relieved when we arrived at our destination. He eased the car off the road into the forecourt of a long-abandoned petrol station, and I was glad for the distraction.

The place was desolate, the forecourt cracked and overgrown with weeds as nature battled to reclaim what was hers. The pumps stood like lonesome soldiers of some forgotten war, their faces shattered by the riots a decade ago. I was out of the car by the time Michael switched off the engine, hobbling my way over the uneven ground towards the glass shell that protected the petrol station's attached convenience store.

The spider-web of cracks in the glass made it difficult to see inside – more remnants of the riots, I assumed. Somehow, no one had managed to get through the door or any of the surrounding windows. That was unusual, since service stations used to stock all kinds of food, alcohol, cash, and car maintenance items in addition to fuel. In my experience, they were usually the first places to get ransacked.

And then I saw something that made me realise why the rioters had left this place untouched.

Through the fractal lens of shattered glass, I saw a hunched figure standing behind the counter, still clad in the decaying remains of a forecourt attendant's uniform. He didn't move. He didn't pace. He didn't fidget. He just stood there, a perfect statue of eternal plebeian servitude.

Michael came up behind me, and immediately saw what I was looking at. "What do we do?"

His voice was a whisper, but he needn't have bothered; the creature was completely unaware of our presence. I shot him a look, amused that for once I knew how to proceed and he didn't.

"We do this," I said, raising my makeshift crutch. With a sharp thrust, I used the foot of the crutch to smash out the night service window near the cashier's left arm, sending shattered glass flying everywhere. The cashier didn't move, even when shards of glass tinkled across the service counter and the floor around his feet. He was way beyond caring. Content that he was unlikely to attack me, I reached through the hole and released the security lock. It disengaged with a rusty click.

With my free hand on my taser, I tucked my crutch back under my arm and led the way into the building. Although the goods were untouched, there was little that would be any use to us now. Most of the food here had been fresh, sandwiches and baked goods. The stench of decay hung heavily in the air. The only things of use were a few cans stacked on one shelf, but it was the stuff in the auto-care section that caught my eye.

"Take as much of that as you can carry," I said, pointing towards a display of precious motor oil near the counter. "Motor oil lasts pretty much forever, so long as it's kept sealed and doesn't have any of the additives that make it separate. Take it all; I'll sort it out when we get back home."

He hurried to obey, while I hobbled around to take care of the unfortunate cashier. Much as I had done for dear old Benny, I dispatched the poor fellow with a quick jolt to the back of the neck. He collapsed with a disturbingly wet thud, as if he was already liquefied on the inside and the only thing that kept him in human shape at all was his skin.

"Off you go to the big service station in the sky, mate," I said. I was no good at eulogies, but I offered him a quick farewell anyway. "Sleep well."

Michael stared at the corpse for a moment, then looked at me and nodded silently.

Between his strength and my experience, we stripped the building of useful resources and disengaged the lock on the petrol pumps. Luckily for us, no water had leaked in, so the petrol was still good. I invested a moment in teaching Michael how to determine whether or not petrol was still viable by smell, then we set about filling up the Hilux and the barrels we'd brought along with us.

"The other trick is to make sure you use metal containers, like these ones. Plastic leeches over time and taints the gas," I explained as we were working. After we capped off the last of them, I looked at Michael. "That should keep us going for a while."

"Yes," he agreed. "Most of the people around here were more interested in mobbing the pharmacies and hospitals than the petrol stations." He frowned deeply, and the expression on his face said that he remembered the riots first hand.

His tone made me consider how lucky I'd been, in a manner of speaking. By the time I'd returned to civilization, the riots were long over – everyone was already infected. For some reason, that thought disturbed me more than usual today.

"Let's go check out that plumbing supply store while we're here." I made the suggestion as much to distract myself as from any real desire to go. I had a funny feeling in my gut, like something bad was about to happen and I didn't know what. As we climbed back into the truck, I found myself watching the bushes intently, like I expected something to come screaming out of them at any second.

Nothing did.

*Yet*, my brain added perversely. I muttered a low curse under my breath.

"You have a potty mouth." Michael shot an amused sideways glance at me.

"And you have ridiculously acute hearing," I said, vaguely annoyed for reasons that I couldn't quite put my finger on. Urge to brood... rising...

Thankfully, he took the hint and left me to my sour mood, focusing all his attention on finding the thing that most closely resembled a roadway. In some places, it was hard to tell. Nature was determined to reclaim this city, and the roads were overgrown and wild. A drive that would have taken five minutes before the outbreak took twenty now, but at least it was an uneventful twenty minutes. Finally, we pulled up outside a shop that looked remarkably intact, aside from needing a bit of a clean and a fresh coat of paint.

"I guess no one wanted to loot a plumbing supply store," I commented dryly. "If only they knew that plumbing supplies would be more valuable than gold one day."

"Hey, look back there." Michael pointed, distracting me. I followed his finger to a workshop next door. There, an old seven-seater minivan waited patiently for the service that would never come.

"That's perfect," I said, easing myself out of the truck. "See if you can find the keys; I'll go get what we need from the store."

Michael hesitated, torn by indecision about whether to follow me or do as I asked. I was already halfway to the store by the time he made up his mind and headed off to look for the keys. In retrospect, I should have known better than to split up. I mean, in horror movies, someone always got killed when they did that. So, guess who got the kudos for the stupidest idea of the day? That's right, it was me.

The store had seen better days, but aside from a thick layer of dust things were mostly just the same as they had been left years ago. Tarnished brass display fixtures hung on the wall, above models of sinks and shower units. The place was small and cramped, which forced me to pick my way carefully towards the stockroom in the back.

The door was locked. Undeterred, I lowered myself to my knees and drew a small set of lock picks from one of my pockets. This lock was one of those old, simple ones, and I would have no problem opening it. After a few minutes, it made a satisfying click and I knew I was in. I levered myself back to my feet and switched the set of lock picks for my taser.

The door swung open to reveal a room hazy with dust, abandoned to its fate long ago. A quick sweeping glance reassured me there was nothing more threatening than rat droppings and the odd cockroach inside. Despite the dust, whoever used to be in charge of this stockroom had kept it well-organised, and I found what I needed without difficulty. There were a number of spare elements there as well, so I grabbed as many as I could carry.

I had no intention of coming back to this place any time soon. Still, you never knew. With that thought in mind, I pulled the door closed behind me as I left, until I heard the lock click back into place.

Then, leaning heavily on my crutch with my free arm full of supplies, I hobbled back to the truck. It took some awkward juggling to get the rear cab's door open but somehow I managed it, and when I did I set my treasure down on the back seat.

As I was shutting the door, I realised something: it shouldn't have taken that long to find the keys or to give up and come looking for me. Where was Michael?

I froze, head tilted, listening for the tell-tale sound of his footfalls, or the soft hiss of his breath against the silence of our empty world. I heard nothing. That worried me.

I managed to take a single footfall towards the garage before the blast of a shotgun discharge shattered the mid-afternoon silence.

"Oh, fuck." Sorry, Mum. I picked up the pace, using my crutch like a pole to vault myself over fallen debris. "Michael? Michael!"

My answer was a blood-curdling, inhuman scream.

I rounded a corner into the alley that ran behind the building, and found my friend pinned to the ground beneath the weight of a female undead, frantically trying to protect his face from her ragged fingernails. He had the shotgun held crosswise, using it to keep her at bay, but while he was protecting himself there was no way for him to go on the offensive.

"Sandy!" He saw me and called my name, his breath coming in ragged gasps as he battled to keep the undead off him; her ragged nails were mere centimetres from those kind eyes that I adored. "Sandy, run. *Run!*"

I ignored him. In three strides I crossed the gap between us, screaming at the undead creature until her head jerked up to stare at me. She howled a bloodthirsty wail, mouth wide to reveal bloody jaws.

"No, fuck *you!*" I screamed right back at her as I swung the crutch with all my might, using it like an impromptu cricket bat.

The undead flew backwards and crashed into a low wall a few feet away, but even with her skull caved in and most of her face gone, she was still trying to get up. I was on her before she could right herself, and jabbed the crossbar of my crutch down into her throat to pin her to the ground. The taser was out of my pocket and crackled to life within a heartbeat, ready to deliver its high-voltage payload.

And deliver it did, when I crammed it down into the bloody socket where the creature's face used to be. Electrical current surged through the its body, and made her limbs jerk convulsively as she lost control of her nervous system.

My chest heaved with exertion as I stumbled back, only to be caught by Michael's strong hands. Like me, he was panting, struggling to catch his breath. Adrenaline had our hearts going at a mile a minute, and it took a second for me to notice that he was covered in blood.

"Is that yours?" I gasped, pointing at the stains. He shook his head and pointed wordlessly at the jerking corpse; I nearly fainted with relief. Then the still-living carcass distracted me. I stared at it, not quite believing what I was seeing. It was still trying to get up. "Oh Christ, those aren't death throes, are they?"

Michael shook his head, rendered speechless by his brush with death. It came down to me, then, while he was still recovering.

"Watch her. If she manages to get up, shoot her." I righted my crutch so I could use it for its intended purpose again. It was slippery with blood and other fluids that I'd rather not have thought about, but there was only one thing on my mind and it wasn't grey matter.

I returned to the abandoned garage, and it didn't take me long to find what I needed: a bottle of methylated spirits, left behind by the former occupants. I imagined they had used it to clean equipment, but I had a much simpler use for it: an impromptu cremation.

I snatched up the bottle and hobbled back to the rear of the building, where I found Michael guarding the flailing infected with focused intensity. When he saw me coming he lowered his shotgun and hurried to meet me. He took the spirits and undid the cap, then upended the bottle over the writhing corpse.

Oh God, it was trying to howl, but all that came out of its shattered face was an infuriated gurgling. Its tongue flailed through the bloody mass that had once been a pair of jaws, disembodied and horrifying. My gorge rose.

Thankfully, Michael had his nerve back and took care of the gruesome task for me. Once it was burning, we left the corpse behind us and hurried back to the front of the building, to put as much distance between us and the stench of death as we possibly could.

Back at the Hilux, Michael rounded on me with anger on his face. "I told you to run – why didn't you run? You could have been killed!"

I'd never seen him angry before, but I was too riled up on adrenaline to care. My back was up and I was still in fight or flight mode. Social graces were completely out the window.

"And I said *fuck you!*" I shouted at him.

"No you didn't – you said that to her!" he yelled back, jabbing a finger in the creature's direction.

"Whatever– I don't even– Shut up!" My patience was gone, and my pulse pounded deafeningly in my ears. There was only one thing on my mind, and I needed to sate it before I went mad.

The crutch clattered to the ground when I lunged at him, taking him completely by surprise. He tripped, and then I had him pinned with his back up against the car before he knew what hit him. The kiss was hot and hungry, passionate, fuelled by our recent brush with death. It was a completely different kind of kiss to the tender taste he'd sampled earlier in the day. It was animalistic. I'd almost lost him before I even had the chance to get to know him, and I was furious about it.

Not at him, though. I was furious at myself.

It was my stupidity that almost cost this sweet, kind man his life. My moronic need to show him how strong and independent I was. It was so idiotic. I felt like a fool.

Our lips parted after a moment that seemed to last forever. I shoved myself back away from him, now out of breath for a completely different reason. He stared at me, both of us still riled up but our anger was fading into… something else.

Perhaps he understood me a little bit better now, after seeing me fight to protect him. Even if I lacked the means to eloquently express my attraction out loud, he seemed to understand that I couldn't have abandoned him just because he ordered it. Like him, I would do anything to protect someone that I cared about – even if it cost me my life.

All of a sudden, it felt like we had far more in common than we'd initially realised.

***

It would have been impossible to coax any life out of the minivan without spending some time working the battery, so we hooked it up to Hilux's tow bar and dragged it back home the old-fashioned way. As the gate rumbled closed behind me, I breathed a sigh of relief at being back in our nice, safe, secure bunker again.

The relief didn't last for long. Shortly after we disembarked, we both stopped and stared at each other, uncertain of what we were hearing. There was a sound echoing around the bunker, a terrible sound, and it was coming from inside the building.

It took us a few moments to figure out that it was the sound of a little girl screaming in terror.

We both took off running simultaneously, though with my foot almost crippled Michael soon drew out in front of me. The farther into the belly of the bunker we went, the worse the noises became. Madeline's muffled screams were interspersed with those bloodcurdling yowls that were steadily becoming all too familiar to us, punctuated by the intermittent wet crash of flesh on wood.

There was another screech, followed by the sound of wood splintering, and Maddy screamed again. The sound was followed by an older female voice issuing orders that we couldn't quite make out: Skylar.

Michael rounded the corner ahead of me, his shotgun loaded and aimed from the hip. The discharge roared in the narrow corridors and made my ears ring, but I didn't care about the discomfort or the pain in my foot. All that mattered right now was Maddy and my little sister.

The door the undead was beating on was a bloody mass of splinters. The creature was so focused on getting at the helpless morsels inside that it had torn pieces out of its own flesh as it was trying to get through.

Michael charged it, unloading the shotgun again and again, until the barrel ran dry and he was forced to stop and reload. The creature had been taken completely by surprise by his vicious assault, and now it was on the ground with its head and shoulders churned to a bloody mess by hot shards of metal. His attention was completely focused on it, so I turned mine towards our family. Through the door, I could hear Maddy crying and the sound of someone in pain.

"We're here – is everyone all right?" I shouted, leaving Michael to vent his temper on the creature.

"Sandy? Oh, thank God." It was Skylar's voice, and I felt a surge of relief. There was the sound of moving furniture, then the door flew open and Skye was suddenly in my arms, hugging me tight around the neck. I hugged her back and did a quick headcount, finding everyone alive and accounted for.

Alive, but not necessarily well.

Ryan was groaning on the bed, bleeding badly from several nasty cuts across his chest and left arm. The fact that they were not yet stitched and bandaged told me all I needed to know: Skye and the doctor had barricaded everyone inside the room, and they'd dedicated all of their strength to keeping that terrible thing out.

There wasn't much left of it now. I released Skye and turned my attention to Michael. I moved up behind the former police officer and grabbed his forearm before he could unleash another shot into the bloody mound of flesh. His eyes darted towards me, wild and full of bizarre, mindless berserker rage. I somehow instinctively knew that the emotion wasn't directed at me, but rather that something snapped inside his mind.

I stared back at him, keeping my gaze level and unflinching, and my voice soft and soothing. "You're wasting ammunition."

He blinked, then looked at the body. It had been shredded by a dozen blasts of buckshot, its body reduced to a few twitching limbs, its torso all but liquefied. He nodded dumbly and handed his shotgun to me, then began the gory process of picking up the writhing limbs from the puddle of body parts.

Now there was a sight that I prayed I would never have to see again. I could only be thankful that the face on that corpse didn't belong to someone that I cared about.

I followed him as he moved the corpse outside, and guarded the door with vigilance while he piled the pieces together and poured accelerant over them. When the pile was alight, we returned to the bunker.

The others were taking care of one another, and Michael was clearly in shock. He didn't say a word to anyone, not even me. I was the one that locked the door behind us, and I was the one that took him by the hand and led him to the bathrooms. I was the one who stripped the blood-splattered clothing off us both, and I was the one that guided him into a hot shower.

He just stood there, like a statue, while I soaped his muscular frame, making the kind of soft, soothing sounds that I didn't know I had in me. Still, I understood in some intuitive way that a part of him was shell-shocked beyond comprehension for a while, so I bathed away the blood that soaked us both and then bundled him up in a towel and guided him to his bed.

He didn't seem to notice my presence at all. He obeyed my every touch without showing a response. I sat beside him until he fell asleep, gently stroking his hair the way that a mother might. Finally, exhaustion won out over the shock, and his eyes closed.

My clothes were far too repulsive to put back on, so I was dressed only in a towel wrapped around my midsection when I went off in search of the others. I found Skye and Madeline in the kitchen, huddled together. Maddy was sobbing uncontrollably, but Skye was aware enough to look up when I entered the room.

"Michael?" she asked softly, as though afraid to hear the answer.

"He's asleep," I said. "I think, you know... Sophie..." Skye nodded. I didn't have to explain further. "What about Ryan? What happened?"

"It attacked us in the storage room, while we were packing." She suppressed a shiver as she explained the story. "Ryan tried to protect me, and got a bit torn up. I managed to get it off him and shut it in the room while we ran, but it got out.

"We barricaded ourselves in the doctor's room, and then you two arrived." Tears welled up in her eyes but she blinked them back, showing a remarkable degree of personal strength. "I don't know what we would have done if you hadn't gotten here when you did."

"Don't think about that." I put my hand on her shoulder and gave it a gentle squeeze. "We arrived in time, that's all that matters. Is Ryan going to be okay?"

To my relief, she nodded. "He bled a bit but not nearly as bad as Dog; Doc says he'll be fine, but it'll take some time to heal."

"Then I guess it comes down to the McDermott sisters to save the day again." I leaned down to give both her and Madeline a hug. Her smile was weak but determined. Feeling a flash of affection towards her, I brushed the hair back from her forehead, and planted a light kiss there. "What's most important is that everyone survived the day. But, the first rule from now on is that no one goes outside until we're ready to leave."

"Amen to that," she agreed wholeheartedly.

# Chapter Nineteen

I spent most of that night awake, patrolling the corridors with shotgun in hand while the others slept intermittently. Occasionally I'd see one of them up and about, anxiously roaming the halls unable, but I was simply too keyed up to sleep. I did try for a bit, but I ended up getting up again, feeling this overwhelming need to protect the people I'd claimed as mine. My friends. My family. Mine, mine, mine. The infected would take them over my cold, dead body.

It was hard to tell how many hours that passed in the dimly-lit corridors of the bunker, but with unrelenting determination I checked each and every single room in that warren for anything that even remotely resembled a threat. I might have been in my nightshirt, but by God I would bring hell upon anyone or anything that threatened my family.

A week earlier, I wouldn't have even considered walking around half-dressed when there was a chance people might see me, but something had changed since then. They'd all seen my legs before, on the night of Dog's ill-fated return, so modesty seemed like such a waste of energy in the face of impending doom.

As far as I could tell, it was the darkest part of the night; that time right before the dawn when the body should be in its deepest sleep. I padded along the hallways with barefoot stealth, the cold concrete numbing any pain I may have felt in my wounded foot. I was indulging a compulsion, a need. There was no logic in it. Not tonight.

One by one, I checked on my family. Ryan, stitched and bandaged, lay asleep on the breast of his would-be wife, who had finally settled into a fitful doze herself. In the next room, the doctor slept upright in bed, propped against the wall with his little granddaughter snuggled against his tummy. Safe. Serene. Oblivious to the world. Good.

I moved on to the last of them, the farthest one away and the one who gave me the most confusing feelings of all. I silently opened his door and found him awake, sitting on the edge of his bed with his head in his hands. For a moment I thought he might have been crying, but then I realised he was just trying to organise his thoughts.

I lowered the shotgun and cleared my throat softly, alerting him to my presence. His head came up, and he stared at me blankly for a minute before recognition dawned.

"I'm sorry..." he murmured, lowering his head back into his hands. "I don't know what came over me."

"I do," I said. I slipped into the room, closed the door, then I put the shotgun down and sat down beside him. "It was shock, Michael. It happens to us all."

He looked at me, his eyes unreadable and his expression solemn. "I'm supposed to be tougher than that. The leader. I-I froze..."

"You're an officer of the law, not a soldier," I pointed out softly. "You're not meant to be a battle-hardened warrior. That's not your role. Your role is the protector, the community leader who exists to keep us safe. What you did was exactly what you were meant to do." I put my arms around him and drew him against me, trying my best to ignore his nakedness. "You protected us."

He slumped against me, and I found myself supporting most of his weight. His voice was just a whisper when he spoke. "I did a piss-poor job of it, yet again."

"No, you didn't." I stroked his cheek, feeling the roughness of his stubble against the curve of my neck as he leaned against me. It sent a shiver down my spine. "If it had just been me all alone, they probably would have died – and I would have joined them."

He sighed, his breath hot against my skin, but no words accompanied it this time.

"It's okay, you know." I stroked my fingers through his hair, trying to reassure him. "There's only so long you can possibly be strong. Something has to give eventually."

"But I have to be strong," he said, his voice weak, and his face so close I could almost feel the brush of his lips against my skin when he spoke. "For all of us, I have to be strong."

I drew away from him, and cupped my hand beneath his chin until his eyes rose to meet mine. They were so sad right now, so hopeless. I'd always wondered what people meant when they talked about puppy-dog eyes, and now I understood.

"You don't have to be strong when you're with me," I whispered, and then kissed him softly.

At first he didn't respond, but after a moment his hands slid around my waist and drew me gently up against him. His lips parted and the tip of his tongue flicked out, tasting me tentatively, perhaps afraid I might bite him.

I didn't, of course. That familiar hot prickle crept up the sides of my throat and brought heat into my cheeks as his head tilted to draw me deeper into the kiss. Oh God, I'd forgotten what it felt like, to really kiss a man, a man that I cared about and wanted to get closer to. It felt so good, so right, like I could fall into that kiss and just live in there forever.

I felt a gentle hand upon my thigh, creeping up beneath my night shirt to trace the line of my underwear. Our lips parted, and his head dipped lower, to the side of my neck to press soft kisses against the sensitive skin there. My heart raced and my breath came faster, responding to his touch. Part of me was terrified and wanted to run, but it was only a very small part; the rest of me wanted that touch so badly that it almost hurt.

Those strong hands lay me back on the bed while his lips explored my throat, my collarbone and down to leave a trail of kisses across my skin. The buttons of my nightshirt came open as though by magic, exposing my skin to the cool air. I shivered, but the cold had nothing to do with it.

His kisses drifted lower, into the crevice of my breasts. There he lingered, breathing deeply for the longest moment before he drew back just enough to look at my face. His dark eyes searched mine, seeking my thoughts, my needs, before they drifted down across the curve of my bosom.

The softest sound escaped him, a sound I recognised as one of deep longing and need that had been held in check for far too long. His tongue flicked out and danced across the sensitive apex of my left breast. The feel of it made me gasp out loud, and his breath was so warm on my skin that it left me quivering. He was so handsome, so strong, so… everything that I needed.

His lips touched my navel, and kissed a soft trail down further and further. I wondered briefly where my knickers had gone, then realised that somehow he'd managed to slip them off me without my even noticing.

Oh, but his lips were going even lower now, and I found myself not caring anymore. He was so very gentle, careful not to even scrape my skin with the stubble of his chin. Oh, and his tongue... what was it doing down there? My mind was so addled by arousal that I could barely keep track of what was going on anymore.

I couldn't remember ever being so turned on before, not even with Harry, who had been my first and last lover. It had been so long since then, a long time since I wanted anyone to touch me, but I wanted him now. I wanted him so badly. More than anything I'd ever wanted in my life.

But then, while I was weak and at my most vulnerable, the memories came crashing down on me like a bucket of ice water. The flash of hot pain, of violation, of humiliation. Violence, so much violence. I cried out again, but this time it was a sound of blind, animal terror, and then I forced poor Michael away from me, terrified beyond words of a phantom that only I could see.

The knives cutting my skin, the burns, and the harsh sound of laughter as the men gloated over my beaten frame. In my memory, a fist struck me and I fell, crying, begging, alone and terrified. Oh God, I was so afraid.

An uncontrollable sob wracked my body. I was on my feet without thinking, fleeing from him, fleeing from his bedroom, fleeing to anywhere where the spectre couldn't find me. I left him staring after me, confused, aroused, and hurt. I could hear him calling my name but I couldn't respond. He didn't understand why I was rejecting him in the moment when he, too, was at his most vulnerable. He couldn't possibly understand. I didn't understand.

They laughed and laughed, mocking me with their horrible, naked bodies.

*Do you want it, little slut?* they gurgled drunkenly in my memory, their faces blurred by time into the ghosts of a past that could not be forgotten. All I remembered was their terrible tattoos and their corpulent, repulsive bodies. And the pain, so much pain.

*No, no,* I begged, *please, anything but that.* But they didn't listen. It hurt, it hurt so much. They made it hurt, because it gave them pleasure to watch me suffer.

I ran, or at least hobbled, as far and as fast as I could, and soon I found myself back in the locker room. Feeling unclean beyond words, I stripped off my nightshirt and flung myself beneath a blast of hot water. The water hid the tears. The warmth between my thighs mocked me, teased me, and made me question myself and everything about me. Everything about everything. Why hadn't I fought harder? Why hadn't I killed myself when I had the chance? Why did I now want to do something that had caused me so much pain before? How could I ever want to be with a man again? How could I even consider making love to one? He would hurt me; they always wanted to hurt me.

It's my fault, my battered psyche told me. I brought it on myself. I'm a bad person.

I'm dirty, unclean. No one will ever love me again.

I hate myself.

My shoulders shook convulsively as I slumped against the wall, pressing my face to the rough concrete. The strength faded out of me and I slid down the wall, to curl up into a wet, shivering ball in the corner of the shower stall.

I was still there when Michael finally found me, huddled beneath the water that did nothing to wash away the feeling of terrible sin. I had cried all my tears and there was nothing left to spare, but I was off in a world where everything was terrible, bloody and violent. A world where I was the victim, and yet somehow I thought it was my fault. Where was a psychologist when you needed one?

"Sandy?"

His voice was so soft and gentle that it cut through my nightmare, but I didn't have the strength to reply. I heard the shower curtain twitch, then the water turned off and strong hands bundled me into a big, soft towel. The animal part of my brain screamed and flailed and told me to flee, but I was too exhausted to even move.

Wrapped up and dripping, he carried me to a nearby bench and cuddled me into his lap. His touch was so soft and his voice so soothing that it finally began to calm me down again. I shivered and turned my face against his chest, where I found him dressed in crisp blue fabric. My eyes flickered open and I saw that he was fully clothed, dressed in his police uniform. I'd never seen him wearing that before.

It was a wise choice of attire. The uniform soothed me in some way I didn't quite understand. I'd been raised to trust that uniform, and that trust persisted into my adult years.

*That's why he's wearing it now,* I realised numbly. For me. To show me who he really was, and why I didn't need to fear him. The uniform embodied everything about him, and everything that I trusted.

"It's okay," he whispered soft, soothing nonsense in my ear, and stroked my hair in a way that oddly mirrored what I'd done for him not so long ago. In spite of everything, I snuggled closer, finding comfort in his warmth.

He was still aroused, I realised suddenly – I could feel him hard against my hip. But through cloth, it was so much less threatening, less real. A flash of affection overrode my panic, followed by guilt for making him suffer. I could only imagine the discomfort of going from a state of intense arousal to where we were now. Yet, he was trying so hard.

"I'm sorry," I said, my voice hoarse from crying. "I'm so sorry. I just... I just... I-I..."

"Sandy." He tilted my chin up to make me look at him. "I know. They trained me to recognise the signs of..." He hesitated for a moment, reluctant to say the word, and I felt his arms tighten protectively around me. "...abuse."

I made a sound that wasn't really a word at all, but more of a whimper. He'd figured out what I couldn't put into words. He did understand.

With gentle fingers, he stroked my cheek and down along my jaw, then kissed me again, just quickly and tenderly. The kiss ended almost as swiftly as it began, and didn't give panic a chance to resurface.

"I want you, Sandy," he whispered, "and I want you to be my lover. I've never had a lover before..." His words trailed off, and he broke eye contact. "...but I've waited a lifetime, I can wait a few more days, a few more weeks. A few more years if I have to. Until you're ready. Until then, just know that I'll always be here for you. I'll never let anyone hurt you again. I swear to you, on my life."

I had no idea what to say, so I just stared at him – but it was okay, because he knew that I understood.

"When you're ready," he added softly, as he gathered me up to carry me back to my own bed, "you just tell me, and I'll be waiting for you."

*** 

I slept late that morning, later than I'd done in years. When finally I awoke, groggy and confused, I found myself with strong arms wrapped around me and the warmth of a human body pressed against my back.

Then, it all came crashing back to me.

I slumped against the pillow and let the comfort of his arms soothe me. After we'd finished speaking, he had carried me back to my bed and tucked me in, then he'd gotten up to leave. Suddenly terrified of being alone, I'd panicked. I'd grabbed his hand and begged him to stay.

Please, please don't leave me...

He'd stayed. He'd snuggled into bed beside me, keeping his trousers on to make himself as unthreatening as possible. I appreciated the effort, considering that I was naked as a jaybird and had been too exhausted to get dressed at the time.

It was okay. True to his word, his touch stayed innocent. He lay behind me with his arms wrapped around my waist and his face snuggled against the back of my neck. I shifted slightly but he didn't move, still fast asleep.

I lay there for a while, just thinking. Wondering what I'd gotten myself into.

*He's never been with a woman before*, I thought, and found myself mulling over that point in my head. Was it really such a surprise, though? He had been twenty-two years old when the world ended, and he'd grown up in a carefully monitored environment of study and personal development. He had been a good guy – still was a good guy – and too wrapped up in his studies and his ambition to waste time on girlfriends and frivolous relationships. The concept of one day having a wife and children had been a very distant thought on that day ten years ago when our world changed forever.

I wondered if he regretted those lost opportunities now, when the only chance he had at love was with an underweight blonde with severe psychological issues. He didn't really have many other options. The only other females about were Skye, who was enamoured with someone else, and Madeline, who was seven.

*Don't think like that*, I scolded myself when I realised what I was doing. There were still plenty of other women left in the world, and he'd chosen me. I smacked my self-doubt across its dirty little face, and shoved it back into the deepest recesses of my brain where it belonged. I refused to let it control me and ruin what I might be able to develop with this kind man in the future.

With one of my demons successfully conquered – for now – my thoughts drifted back to Michael again. I felt a little disappointed at myself for wondering if he was the father of Skye's baby. In retrospect, it seemed so obvious. He was just the kind of man who was protective by nature and respectful to everyone, particularly women. He would have protected her regardless of whose baby it was. My brief bout of jealousy had been completely misplaced.

I shifted a little in his arms, feeling wrung out and exhausted from the night's adventure. My body had responded to him with such intensity that I still felt the dampness of past arousal between my thighs. It had faded now to a dull discomfort, like an itch that had gone unscratched.

Was the discomfort much worse for him? I had explored my sexuality in high school as most young people did, and I understood in a distant sort of way just how uncomfortable it was for a healthy young man to go unsatisfied. Poor Michael had gone for more than ten years without satisfaction – and then there was me, getting him all riled up like a dirty temptress and leaving him in the lurch.

Okay, now I felt bad. He'd been so sweet to me, and in return I'd put him through such hell that he really didn't deserve. Somehow, it made it even worse that he'd been so nice about it. As much as he tried to be strong for the others, he had let me in to see the vulnerable young man inside him. Now I felt like I'd kicked a puppy.

I lay there, pondering ways to make it up to him, until I finally came to a decision. There were ways that I could thank him for his kindness and let him experience blessed relief without putting myself back into panic mode. It would take a good deal of courage on my part, and some obedience on his, but I felt like I could do it for his sake. The attraction that I felt towards him was so intense and so genuine that I wanted to overcome my demons somehow, and that would only come with effort.

It was being vulnerable that made me freak out, I realised. Being sprawled on my back with a man atop me, no control about what was going to happen to me. If I took back my control then I should be fine. I sensed that Michael would probably let me. I rolled over within the circle of his arms and turned towards him, gazing down at his handsome face, so peaceful in sleep.

*Oh, but I shouldn't wake him*, my inner voice crooned, but I smacked it aside as the voice of cowardice. He'd be perfectly happy with being woken up this way.

I drew a deep breath and let it out slowly. We were so close together that my breath stirred his eyelashes. The stubble on his chin had grown overnight, I noticed with a detached fascination. I'd forgotten how swiftly a man's beard grew.

With one gentle hand, I slid my fingertips down across his belly to trace the contours of his abdomen. It rose and fell slowly in time with his breath, and I found myself marvelling at the warmth that radiated from his skin. Something else that I'd forgotten. My fingers found the waistband of his trousers, and carefully undid the top button. The zipper slid down, and I discovered that in his hurry to catch me the night before, he had neglected to find his underwear. No wonder he'd been so insistent about keeping his pants on when he climbed into my bed.

I suppressed a smile at the thought, and slid my hand down the front of his trousers. In spite of myself, I felt my own breath begin to quicken when I felt his body respond to my touch. So did his, for that matter. His brow furrowed and he stirred against me before his eyelids cracked open. A second later he was fully awake, lying stiff in bed beside me.

"What are you doing?" His voice was a harsh whisper; I silenced him with a finger across his lips.

"Shh..."

With a firm but gentle hand, I pressed him onto his back. He obeyed reluctantly, and his eyes went wide when the blankets fell away to reveal what I'd been doing to him in his sleep.

"But—" He tried to protest, but I shushed him again.

"Just lie still and follow orders, officer," I said, putting on my best playful tone to mask my own nervousness. Making a great show of confidence, I slipped a leg over him to straddle his thighs, my bottom resting upon his knees. "We're going to play a game. I want you to pretend that I'm your sergeant, and you're my good, obedient constable."

"Ah..." There was a flush of colour creeping up the sides of his throat and I felt a surge of pride at his reaction. "...but... my sergeant was an ugly old man."

Way to ruin the mood, Mike.

"Okay, well pretend I'm your sergeant, if your sergeant was a sexy twenty-something girl," I said, giving him my best approximation of a sultry pout.

He laughed and nodded his consent. "Ah, okay. Y-yes, ma'am."

Then he shot me a salute. With me pinning him to the bed, his pants unzipped and naked above the waist, it struck me as the funniest thing I'd ever seen. It took all of my willpower not to burst out laughing and completely destroy the mood once and for all.

"Much better," I play-acted, letting my confidence grow with time. He was letting me play, even if it made him uncomfortable, and that reassured me. He seemed to understand that I needed this to bolster my own personal confidence, and he was willing to let me try. "Now, you have been such a good and understanding person, that I feel I must reward you for your loyalty. Sadly, I'm all out of medals, so we'll have to find something else that'll do for a reward."

"Ehhh?" He just looked totally bewildered now.

"Okay, I'm not good at this game," I admitted. "Just shut up and enjoy yourself, would you? I'm a little rusty, so try to make encouraging noises or something."

He looked down at his crotch, then looked back at me. It was a confused look, like he couldn't quite figure out what I was about, but he still seemed inclined to let me do as I pleased to him. That was what I needed.

I leaned down and planted a playful kiss upon his stomach. I felt his deep intake of breath as he realised with shock what I planned to do

As it turned out, I wasn't as rusty as I thought.

\*\*\*

Later, we lay contentedly in one another's arms, his eyes closed and arms wrapped around me possessively. Though he tried to say something, all that came out were whispered half-words that meant nothing.

It was fine, though. I knew what he meant.

Frankly, I just felt better for no longer being that crazy bitch that runs off screaming and flailing because a cute guy kissed her. Not that he would ever dream if calling me that, but that was how I'd been thinking of myself. Sometimes the worst critic was the one inside your own head, and I hated that feeling. I hated knowing that I was judging a good man against the template of other people's wrongdoing. Worst of all, I hated knowing that I had hurt him. He'd made it clear that he didn't judge me for that, but his opinion of me was still secondary to my own. I had to follow my instincts, and do what felt right to me, and my conscience.

I let him have a couple of minutes to rest and recover before I cleared my throat and gave him a gentle nudge. "Time to get up, sleepy-head. Day's a'wasting."

He grunted and opened one eye to give me a glare. It didn't last long, though. It faded as I smiled back at him playfully, then melted into a look of contented relaxation. He started to lay his head back down, but I wasn't having any of it – and neither was he, since I took the blanket with me when I extracted myself from the warmth of his embrace.

I heard grumbling behind me as I dressed in some of the spare clothing I'd acquired since my arrival. My normal clothing would probably be almost dry by now, but getting it would mean prancing through the hallways butt-naked, and I wasn't *that* self-confident. Jeans and a t-shirt would do. Not my usual attire, but functional and, more importantly, clean. As I pulled the shirt over my head, I felt strong hands sneak around my waist.

"What's this, then?" Michael whispered in my ear, his lips so close enough that I could feel his breath.

"What's what?" I turned my head just a little, to look up into his eyes.

He said nothing in return, just smiled knowingly. One of his hands crept up beneath my shirt, across my belly, until his fingertips grazed the curve of my breast. I felt myself flush at the touch and suddenly I understood the question. He grinned at my embarrassment – or was it the fact that I didn't pull away?

"Oh, that, um… You clearly have no idea how hard it is to find a decent bra in this day and age," I admitted when I finally managed to gather the wits to reply. "I only have *one*, and I left it in the bathroom last night."

It was true. Good lingerie was hard enough to find before the end of the world; afterwards, it was nearly impossible. Since it was made of such light fabrics, it doesn't last long to start with, and when you lost one it took forever to find a replacement.

"Oh." He seemed a little disappointed at that answer, and his hands drifted back down to rest on my hips. "Here was me, getting all excited and you were just being practical."

I turned within the circle of his embrace and slipped my arms around his waist in a moment of uncharacteristic boldness. "Well, at least you can comfort yourself with the fact that you're the only one that knows?"

His expression brightened. "That… is true."

Amused, I pressed a quick kiss to his lips, then released him and took his hand instead. "Come on, the others will probably be frantic with worry since we didn't show up to breakfast."

"Hu-uh?" He looked dazed and still a wee bit sleepy. "What time is it?"

"Almost midday, I think."

"Ah, cripes," he exclaimed. "They've probably sent out search parties by now."

Suddenly wide awake, Michael took the lead. He opened the door and led me out, leaving me to admire just how nice he looked in his uniform. While I was dressing, he'd put his shirt back on and straightened himself up. Now, he looked like a real police officer at last. I was a sucker for a man in uniform.

"I should go find the doctor," I admitted reluctantly, loathe to let go of his hand. "I need my bandages changed. They're soaking wet."

"Yeah," he said, just as reluctantly. "I should find Skye and see how she's getting on with the packing all by herself."

We looked at one another and a flash of understanding passed between us. Neither of us particularly wanted to leave the other, and yet we had to. The look was long and charged with tension, but finally I released his hand.

"I'll see you soon?" I tried not to sound too hopeful, but failed miserably.

"Count on it," he replied, then turned with a wave and headed away from me.

*I hate to see you leave, but love to watch you go*, I thought, my demented brain dredging up yet another stupidly clichéd old quote from the deepest recesses of my memory. I shook my head to distract myself, and then limped off in search of the doctor.

***

It didn't take long to find him. He was a creature of habit as well, and I already knew his patterns. After a thorough scolding taking so long to come and see him, he sat me down and pulled my foot into his lap to strip off the soggy bandages.

"Again, you get these wet." He sighed, a sound of long-suffering annoyance. "How many times must I tell you to keep them dry?"

"I know, I know; I'm sorry. I had a momentary lapse of judgement." My explanation was weak, but I didn't feel like telling him the truth. I liked it better when what was developing between Michael and I was our little secret.

"Mm-hm," the doctor murmured, staring at me over the rim of his spectacles. "'Feeling ill' again, were we?"

Oh great. He even made the air-quotes with his fingers. I could feel my cheeks turning red all over again.

"That's what I thought." His lips narrowed to a disapproving little line, then he turned his attention back to my bandages. He dried and cleaned the wound, replaced the gauze, and bound it all back up again in a clean bandage. "Do try to keep this one dry, won't you?"

"I'll try. Sorry, doctor," I replied, feeling a bit like a scolded child. He grunted, clearly not believing me, and hauled himself back to his feet with an audible creaking of joints. I rose as well and made to leave, but he stopped me with a gesture.

"I've prepared these for you in case you start 'feeling ill' again," he said, shoving a scrappy cardboard box into my hands. "I insist that you begin taking these immediately. One first thing in the morning, every morning, and do not miss a day."

"What?" I looked down, and then realised with a flash of distress what the box contained. "Oh."

Birth control medication.

"I don't care what you and the boy get up to," he said, his voice snappish and abrupt. "I know you're both young and full of energy and feel the need to go throwing yourselves around, but the last thing we need right now is for another one of our able bodies to be burdened with a pregnancy. And for the love of God, don't waste them – the ingredients for these are getting very hard to come by."

I wanted to curl up in a corner and die.

"One, every day, at the same time," he repeated himself and held up a finger, like he didn't expect me to understand what he was saying without it. "And do not miss a day."

"Doc, I don't even... you know, get a 'monthly' anymore," I said hesitantly. "I don't think I can get pregnant, even if we were... you know. Not that we are."

Technically.

"Not yet, no. You've been too malnourished." He adjusted his glasses and hiked them back up on his nose. "Your body probably wouldn't have the strength to support a foetus to full term just yet, but there's always a chance – and there's also the matter of miscarriages. Just take the pills. Better safe than sorry."

I nodded and fled from him, red as a beetroot.

He was right, of course – that was, if I ever got over my issues long enough to do anything that would put me at risk of getting pregnant. I didn't want a child right now, I was in no position to care for one – and I definitely didn't want to have to go through another painful miscarriage.

I deposited the box in my room and hobbled off towards the garaging area, intent on distracting myself with work. I got about halfway there before something else caught my attention: the sound of raised voices coming from the direction of Michael's room.

"Tell me!" It was Skylar, and she sounded angry.

"No! It's none of your business." The second voice was Michael's, and he sounded... peculiar. I rounded a corner and found myself confronted with a bizarre scene. Skye had Michael cornered and was poking him threateningly in the chest with her index finger. Michael looked confused and a little bit afraid. Despite being five inches shorter than me, with a tiny frame that made her belly look like a bowling ball by comparison, my sister was kind of terrifying when she was pissed off.

"You *will* tell me." Skye's voice was low and threatening. "Or else I'll have to—"

"Look, there she is; ask her yourself!" Michael pointed at me, distracting her. The second her attention wavered from him, he was off like a shot, fleeing down a corridor away from us.

"Sandy!" Skye was on me in a heartbeat. She grabbed me by the shoulders, then she was shaking me until I was afraid my head would pop off. "Where have you been? I was worried sick."

"Jesus, Skye." I squeaked and wriggled out of her grasp, then backed away, holding up my hands defensively. "I just slept in."

"But your door was locked so I thought you were out, but I couldn't find you anywhere. I couldn't find Michael until a minute ago, either, and the car was still in the garage, and... and... and..."

This time, I grabbed her and gave her a solid shake.

"Calm. Down," I told her in no uncertain terms. She bristled, but I didn't give her a chance to protest. "I was just in bed. I had a late night and I was tired. I locked the door because I don't like people barging in on me unannounced."

Yes, that was the reason. Not because I had a half-naked man in my bed. No, not at all.

"You could have just knocked if you were so worried," I added. "I probably would have been annoyed at being woken up, but at least you would have had an answer."

"Knocked?" Skylar echoed, looking confused.

"You know, tapped on the door until I responded?" I replied, uncertain whether she was being deliberately dense or really didn't know what I was talking about.

"Oh..." She paused for a second, thinking that one over. "I always thought that was just something the doctor yelled at me when I opened his door."

I felt the overwhelming urge to facepalm. Oh, right. She had been eight when the world ended. Eight-year-olds don't knock. "You haven't been living here much longer than I have, have you?"

"About six months," she said with a shrug, then suddenly seemed to remember that she was at my throat for a reason. "Wait, but if you were asleep, then where was Michael? I looked all over for him. He wouldn't go outside alone…" She trailed off as the pieces began to fall into place, staring at me.

I avoided eye-contact, trying very hard to prevent myself from turning red again and giving us away.

"Sandy," Skye said, her eyes narrowed. "Look at me."

I looked anywhere but at her, fighting the urge to flee that rose in my chest.

"Look at me!"

I cleared my throat and pretended to be fascinated by my feet, while silently plotting my escape route.

"Sandrine McDermott, did you sleep with Michael?"

Oh crap, she was on to us. Time to go.

"Hey, get back here!" she squealed as I dashed off as fast as I could go. Go, go, race of the cripples.

Luckily for me, I was quicker in spite of my injury, what with her belly being so swollen that she could barely waddle at a fast pace. When I was out of her line of sight, I ducked into one of the many rooms in the underground maze, and dropped down behind an old desk to hide. I heard her footsteps patter past, and then sighed softly in relief.

"Your sister scares me."

I almost jumped out of my skin; I hadn't noticed that Michael was hunkered down close by until he spoke. He looked back at me with the most embarrassed expression I'd ever seen.

"Hey, you abandoned me," I complained, though in truth I didn't really blame him. "I'm so mad at you."

He shrugged helplessly. "She was accusing me of everything from eating you to stealing your soul. I had no choice. At least she won't kill *you*. Me, I'm not so sure about."

I made a show of thinking it over for a second, then I nodded. "Yeah, you're probably right. Okay, I forgive you."

Michael helped me up, his hand lingering in mine even after we were back on our feet. He turned my hand over, as though studying it, then brought it to his lips and kissed the tips of my fingers. "Good. I'm not sure I could bear you being angry with me."

I smiled at him and stepped in close, to press a soft kiss against his cheek. "Yeah, me either. Let's go get some work done before Skylar finds us."

Hand in hand, we left our hiding spot and went off about our business.

# Chapter Twenty

Michael and I snuck around like thieves for two whole days while our group prepared to leave its home, stealing what moments of privacy that we could. Skylar became something of a menace and demanded the latest gossip at every turn, but eventually she began to grudgingly accept that neither of us were interested in sharing the details of our tryst.

During the process of stripping the bunker of everything that we could carry, I came across a set of walkie-talkies. They were good, solid things, heavyweight with rechargeable batteries. When I showed them to Michael, he told me that they were police issue. He recalled that he'd found them in the bunker when he first moved in, and put them into storage in case he needed them some day.

*We need them now*, I reasoned and put them on their chargers. The next morning, they crackled to life, and a few minutes later I had them working. As we were preparing for our departure, I assigned one to each person, and explained how to use them.

"If anything goes wrong, if we get separated, if you get lost or attacked, call the rest of us," I included in my instructions. "Don't hesitate. Even if you see something but you're not a hundred per cent sure what it is, call us. It's better safe than sorry."

Yes, I blamed myself for Ryan's injuries, though I hadn't admitted it to anyone. I kept my shame a secret, bottled up deep inside where the only person that it could hurt was me. But it was a lesson learned, a lesson that I was determined to make sure none of us would ever have to repeat.

As the sun rose on the third day, the six of us gathered one last time in the parking garage. The trucks were all packed and our scant personal possessions had been crammed in amongst the supplies. We looked around one last time, making sure everything was switched off and locked, and said goodbye to the place that had been our home. For me, it had only been so for ten days; for Michael, it had been home for a third of his lifetime. For Maddy, it was the only home she'd ever known. Despite that, she was practically bouncing off the walls with excitement, ready for an adventure. The rest of us were quiet, determined, and focused, ready to fight our way free if we had to.

Michael issued orders and assigned each of us to a vehicle. Madeline and Skylar were placed in the minivan in the middle of the convoy so that we could protect them easily. They were the two most vulnerable members of our group, and we wanted to have them somewhere safe. I half-expected an outburst of rebellion from Skylar, but it never came. She was simply delighted that she was going to be allowed to drive.

Ryan and the doctor would bring up the rear in the bulky prisoner transport, with the doctor behind the wheel. Despite his injuries, Ryan was alert and capable with the hand not swathed in bandages. Although he couldn't drive in his condition, he could keep a lookout and fight if he needed to. With my blessing, Michael armed him with my handgun and cleared a space in the back of the van for him to sit in, so that he could watch the road behind us for danger. Although he looked disappointed at being separated from Skylar, Ryan acquiesced without protest on the understanding that he was still protecting her.

Michael and I would lead the convoy in the Hilux, as both the most capable fighters in the group and the only ones that knew where we were going. My foot was almost healed but we didn't want to risk it, so Michael took the wheel.

Before he climbed in, he handed me his shotgun. He'd already briefed me on how to use the weapon, how to reload the shells and how to fix it if it misfired, so I felt confident that I could defend us if necessary. Ryan and I flanked the roller door while everyone else went to their places, waiting with weapons in hand and ready in case anything went wrong.

The garage reverberated with the sound of three engines starting at once. I swelled with pride that not one of them stumbled and died. A job well done. No time to pat myself on the back, though. It was time to go.

I looked at Ryan and he nodded to indicate that he was ready. With the shotgun tucked in the crook of my arm, I reached over and swiped the key card against the lock. The door began to rise, with a rusty clanking that felt loud enough to wake the dead – or at least alert them to our presence.

Side by side, Ryan and I approached the opening door, our weapons aimed at the entrance. Bright morning sunlight crept through the gap as the door rose, sneaking across the floor to attack our feet before it gradually illuminated the rest of our bodies. It was just after dawn and the sun was already intense. A wall of heat washed over us in stark contrast to the cool darkness that we were used to. It was time.

I led the way, my footing cautious but the limp almost gone. In a militaristic crouch-walk, I stalked the entrance at an angle, clearing the right side before I rounded to the left. Just as we had practiced, Ryan covered my back as I stared about for any sign that we had been detected. After ten seconds, he moved up to join me, back to back, and added his eyes to my search grid.

Nothing moved. With fluid footsteps despite our injuries, we slid further out into the daylight, far enough to check every bush, every crevice that might hold some horrible dead thing. The only corpses we saw were the kind that didn't move.

The door whined in protest as its tiny automated brain decided that it was time to close. I returned to the entrance to swipe my card again, and waved the all-clear signal to the others waiting in the garage below.

Michael led the charge, surging up the ramp with a heavy foot on the accelerator, kicking up a breeze that stirred my hair as he passed. He cleared the entrance in a few seconds, and came to a halt a short way down the street to wait for the rest of the convoy to assemble.

I gestured to Skylar to come next and she did – eventually. It took her a few tries, and in the process she somehow managed to bunny-hop an automatic engine. It took all of my willpower to fight down the urge to laugh. Instead, I gave her the thumbs-up sign in encouragement and waved her on out the door.

The doctor came last in the prisoner transport, which groaned and struggled to clear the ramp with its heavy burden. For a moment I worried it wouldn't make it, but then it was over the lip and out into the street beyond.

I cast one last glance around the garage as the door rumbled closed again, and silently said goodbye to all the dead cars that I would never have a chance to bring back to life. Then the door shut with a heavy clank, and it was all gone to me. There was no need to lock the door; it was keyed to the card in my hand. Without the card, no one was getting in. Although we were leaving, we had agreed that everything we left behind was still ours. We left it all stored safely, on the off chance we might have to come back for something.

All of us hoped that we would never have to.

I returned to Ryan, who was watching for trouble while the rest of us moved out, and gestured to him that it was time to move. He nodded and fell in beside me as I escorted him to the rear of the prisoner transport, and there I helped him up into the nook we'd left clear for him.

"Don't forget to lock the door from the inside," I reminded him as he settled in. He gave me a lopsided smile in return.

"I remember, sis."

Sis? When did that happen?

"Pft, you don't get to call me that until you marry my sister," I said with a playfully indignant scoff.

"Working on it." He grinned brightly, then slammed the door and locked it securely.

I was the last one left exposed, and I did not like that feeling. With great effort, I fought down a spurt of panic and hurried to the passenger door of the Hilux. A second later, I was inside and pulled the door closed behind me. The locks clunked as Michael engaged them, and only then did I feel secure. I pulled on my seatbelt, then grabbed my walkie-talkie off my belt. "Everyone lock up tight. Don't open for anyone you don't know."

What I got in return was a series of silly answers and fake military jargon. Even Michael picked up his radio and added a "Roger-roger, Cap'n!" in a nasally falsetto, garnering laughter from the others.

I rolled my eyes and clicked the microphone off. One by one, we pulled away from the bunker, and left our home behind us.

***

The sun rose higher in the sky, and brought with it the stinging heat of midsummer. The trip was torturously slow considering the short distance we needed to travel. The roads were in even worse condition than I remembered, and the heavier vehicles struggled in many places. Our Hilux had no issues with the terrain, thankfully. Its big tyres carried us easily over the roughest ground, but the others were not so lucky.

It took us almost an hour to reach the southern edge of the city. I breathed a sigh of relief when we finally cleared the outskirts and found the shattered concrete ribbon of highway that wound its way out through the pasturelands towards our destination.

I was just beginning to relax when the radio crackled to life, and nearly gave me a heart attack.

"I see something, I see something!" Maddy was screaming and sounded terrified. "I see something *moving*!"

There was a muffled sound, and then Skylar's voice came on. "Please disregard that emergency broadcast. Madeline has just seen her first cow."

"What's a 'cow'?" We heard the little girl's voice in the background. Skylar heaved a long-suffering sigh, and then the line crackled off. Michael and I glanced at one another, and then burst out laughing. It felt so good to have someone to share a laugh with.

***

A slender tree had fallen across the road since I'd come north, effectively blocking the path. It wasn't a big one, but there was no way the vans would get past it unless we found some way to move it.

The Hilux rolled to a stop, and Michael grabbed his radio. "We've got a blockage. Everyone stay where you are."

"What kind of blockage?" Skylar asked.

"Just a tree down, nothing dangerous." He unfastened his seatbelt, then clipped the radio onto his belt and climbed out. I followed him, shotgun at the ready as I scanned the horizon.

"Calm down, Sandy," Michael said. "It's only a tree."

"Not necessarily," I replied, shaking my head. "I've seen raiders use something very similar as a trap for travellers. You'll forgive me, but there is a reason I'm this paranoid."

He had nothing to say to that, and just silently acknowledged that he was out of his element. With my weapon held at the ready, I soft-stepped towards the tree, and angled around the fallen trunk until I could see the base. The sure way to know if it was a trap or natural deadfall was to figure out whether the trunk had been cut.

The stump was shattered, rotten, eaten through by insects. I immediately relaxed and called over my shoulder to Michael. "It's okay, it's just deadfall. It's probably not a trap, but keep your guard up anyway."

"*Probably* not a trap?"

"You never know," I replied. "People can be opportunistic."

"This is a very depressing conversation." Michael sighed as he drew up behind me, to help me examine the tree for the best way to get rid of it.

"Welcome to the world outside your nice, safe bunker, sweetheart. It's depressing out here," I answered dryly, prodding at the deadfall with my boot. "It's rotten through and all soggy. We should be able to cut it easily enough and move it in sections."

"What about towing it out of the way with the four-wheel drive?" he asked, looking at me for guidance. I shook my head.

"Maybe in chunks, but if we try to do that with the whole trunk it'll just crack. Look." I shoved at the trunk with my foot, and showed him how the bark was spongy and moved beneath my foot. Squish, squish, squish.

"All right. I'll go find an axe," he said simply, deferring to my judgement without a word of complaint, and headed off towards the rear of the convoy.

I pulled my own radio off my belt and clicked it on. "Guys, Michael's coming to get the axe. Does anyone know where we put it?"

"I've got it," Ryan said, his voice crackling through the radio.

"You hear that?" I called after Michael, and he waved to acknowledge that he had.

A few minutes later, he was back with the doctor and Ryan beside him. Between the three of them, they made short work of the rotten tree while I patrolled the perimeter of our little caravan on the lookout for trouble. I stopped to chat briefly with my sister and Madeline while they waited, but I didn't linger for long.

As I was returning to the front of the queue to check on our progress, something in the distance caught my attention. I stretched up as tall as I could and I shielded my eyes against the sun. Something was moving, and moving with far more vigour than a cow or a sheep.

"Guys," I said. The low, urgent tone of my voice got their attention immediately. "Did any of you bring binoculars?"

Without a word, Michael drew a pair out of his vest and handed them to me. They were small with a low magnification, but they were enough. I focused on the movement in the distance, and then swore softly.

"We have a pig incoming," I told them softly, keeping my voice low and calm to disguise my concern. Then, something else caught my eye, another flash of movement. Smaller and quicker – and running for its life. My whole body tensed. "It's chasing a person!"

"A living person?" Michael asked, straining to see what I was seeing, which was a solitary survivor fleeing from three hundred and fifty kilograms of rampaging, infected pork.

"Definitely alive," I said. "For the moment."

The others looked at me for guidance, but I wasn't sure what to tell them. If I had been on my own, I wouldn't have stood a chance so I would have had to leave the man to his fate.

But between the four of us…

I looked amongst them, and saw faces that ranged from determination to fear. It was Michael that made the decision for us, though, in that soft, deep, commanding voice he used when he'd made up his mind about something. "We can't just leave him to die."

We all nodded, and I battled a mixture of relief and terror. We were going to fight a pig. A massive, undead, rampaging wild boar. This was madness. Still, someone needed to organise us now that the decision was made, and they were all looking at me.

"Doctor Cross, I would appreciate if you stayed with the girls," I said. I glanced at him, and saw his relief. "You're our last line of defence in case the worst happens." He nodded his agreement and moved off, leaving me with Michael and Ryan.

I pointed at the gun in Ryan's hand. "That little peashooter won't do anything more than piss it off. If it gets close to you, use the axe."

He nodded. I turned and handed the shotgun to Michael. He took it, his brow furrowing into a look of concern. "What about you?"

"I'm bait," I answered with a giddy kind of confidence that was based more on bravado than real courage, then I pulled out my taser. "Remember, these things charge. They're much stronger and faster than they look, but they can't turn quickly. Stay light on your feet." Suddenly, I was feeling almost buoyant, charged full of adrenaline – ready to do the impossible.

The survivor saw us and turned, pelting towards us as fast as his legs would carry him. The paddocks were uneven and full of hidden obstacles. I silently prayed he wouldn't lose his footing. If he fell, the creature would be on him in a heartbeat.

The taser cracked to life in my hand. I strode forward, and felt the two men fall into place on either side of me with their weapons at the ready.

"Be prepared to scatter," I told them softly, calmly. "We should be able to confuse it. These things are nasty, but they aren't smart."

The stranger was shouting and waving at us. I waved back and gestured for him to keep coming. He was close enough now that I could see the sweat glistening on skin the colour of milky coffee. I wondered how long he'd been running for, because he looked close to collapse.

The pig was hot on his heels, its head down and snorting furiously. Then it saw us, and it squealed a terrible sound. The running figure was forgotten as it turned its attention onto us.

"Wait for it," I said, keeping my voice low to keep them calm.

The creature stopped and stared at us, making the kind of noises that would echo in my nightmares forever. Low, deep squeals, sounds that no pig should ever make. It stomped its hoof, slowly swinging its head from side to side.

The horrid thing was already half decomposed, with innards hanging out in places and patches of muscle that lay bare beneath tattered skin. Its spinal column stuck out, white and naked against rotted flesh. I focused on that, and flexed my fingers on the taser.

Then, suddenly, it charged.

The three of us scattered in a neat three-pronged formation, just as we'd planned. The men with the guns put distance between themselves and the pig, while I cut it so fine that I could smell the pig's terrible stink as it barrelled past me. I struck without hesitation, and jabbed my taser at the exposed bone of its spine. Electricity surged along the biological conduits intended for an entirely different kind of current, and the creature screamed.

It was slow to turn towards me, hindered by my attack. As I retreated, Ryan darted in and struck at it with the axe, swinging the weapon overhead with all the strength in his one good hand. He struck in the same place that I had, aiming for the exposed bone, but he missed and the axe bounced off.

The shotgun roared a moment after Ryan retreated, peppering the beast's side with hot shrapnel. It screamed again, a terrible, blood-curdling sound. It was turning on the spot, almost spinning in place, struggling to decide which of us to charge first.

It chose Michael.

The pig took him by surprise and bowled him over, knocking the breath out of him. It was on him in a second, and he barely had the chance to get the gun up in time to defend himself. It bit down on the shaft of the gun, which did little damage to the weapon itself but it prevented him from firing and forced him to twist himself awkwardly to keep out from beneath trampling hooves.

Ryan and I leapt forward and went on the offensive. I struck it behind the ear with my taser, while Ryan hacked away at its spine. Finally, one of his blows slid between the vertebrae and severed its spinal cord.

The pig's hind-quarters collapsed, distracting it for the few seconds that Michael needed to yank his gun around into position to fire.

The shell exploded in the pig's mouth, and penetrated the soft membrane at the back of its throat. Shrapnel exploded within it and sent hot shards scattering about, dicing what was left of its brain.

The pig died unceremoniously, and this time its death was permanent.

It took our combined strength to drag Michael out from beneath the corpse before it collapsed, but we got him free just in time. I was relieved to find he was uninjured aside from some bruises and the ringing in his ears from the shotgun blast so close. He shook his head to clear it as we hauled him to his feet, then we looked down at the pig with a mixture of amusement and confusion.

Then Michael looked up and grinned at us both. "Bacon, anyone?"

***

It felt amazing to laugh together, all of us feeling the rush of victory. We made our way back to our convoy together, slapping each other on the back and administering high fives all around.

When we arrived, we found the stranger leaning against one of our vans, talking to Skylar and Dr Cross. As we drew closer we could hear his words.

"—sickness. They sent a couple of us out looking for a treatment. Then the fucking pig—"

"What are the symptoms?" Dr Cross interrupted him, adjusting his glasses absently. His face was already set in the scowl he wore when he was thinking about something intensely.

"Diarrhoea mostly, you know, real nasty diarrhoea. Vomiting. Some of them have a fever." The kid glanced back over his shoulder and his expression brightened when he saw us closing in. "Hey! Oh man, I owe you fullas my life. I don't know what I woulda done if you hadn't been here."

"Glad to help, mate," Michael said, approaching the stranger with an extended hand. The youth grabbed it and shook it enthusiastically, reaching out with the other to clap him on the shoulder.

"I can't believe that fucking pig, man," he said. "I heard about them on the news but never seen one before. It bowled me right off my bike. Hell, you folks are heroes!"

"Hell's the word for it; that was one scary bundle of demon-pork," Michael agreed, then he glanced back at me and gave me one of those smiles that made my heart race. "Luckily for all of us, we have an expert along."

I felt my cheeks burn, but I hung back and sidestepped behind Ryan. My inner paranoia warned me away from the stranger-danger, but the others seemed relaxed and the stranger looked friendly, so I wasn't in too much of a panic.

"An expert? Damn. We're real lucky." The stranger shook his head and ran a hand back through his tight black curls. "Bro, I'm still freaked out."

"You and me both," Ryan commented dryly, then shot a curious look at me when he realised that I was hiding behind him. "Let's not do that again anytime soon."

"Agreed." The stranger nodded, then extended his hand to Ryan as well. "Hey, I'm Hemi."

"Ryan." The redheaded youth awkwardly shook the offered hand with his one good one, and then he proceeded to introduce the rest of us.

"So what are you doing out here?" Michael asked curiously. "You were saying something about a sickness?"

"He was telling me that his *whanau* live near here, and that a lot of them have been getting sick recently," the doctor piped up with the information he knew.

Hemi nodded exuberantly. "Yeah, man. Real nasty sick in the stomach. Puking and crapping all over the place."

Now there was a pleasant thought.

"Did you get sick, young man?" the doctor asked.

"Nah, I'm good," he said. "That's why I volunteered to go looking for medicine."

"I'm relieved to hear that." I peered at the youth with natural suspicion, but he didn't seem to mind.

He just laughed and nodded. "Me too, man. Me too."

"So, you guys have a community?" Skylar suddenly joined the conversation, her curiosity getting the better of her.

"Yeah, there's about a dozen of us. We built us a *pa* southwest of here." He used the Maori word for a fortified town, but it was a word that most of us were familiar with from the time before the plague. Then he looked around at us and gave us a lopsided smile. "We can trade, if you have medicine. We've got cows and sheep, so we can trade beef, milk, or lamb. Or wool, if any of you guys are knitters. Maybe other things, depends what you want."

"Weapons?" Yes, that was me. Surprise, surprise. I felt exposed, like we needed more to protect ourselves.

"Guns?" Hemi repeated, then he shook his head. "Nah, sorry. We only have one old rifle and we use it for hunting. A few knives, but nothing good for fighting with."

Damn. Couldn't blame a girl for trying.

"It's okay," Michael said. "If we can help you, we will. You can return the favour later. It's more important to get your people feeling better."

Hemi's eyebrows shot up, and he gave Michael a long, sideways look. So did I for that matter. We had the opportunity for trade, and he was willing to just give away our advantage?

As though reading my mind, Michael looked back at me and gave me one of his sweet smiles. I melted a little bit, and smiled back; his smiles were so addictive.

"That's generous man, real generous." Hemi bobbed his head thoughtfully as he mulled it over, then he flashed another one of his lopsided grins. "Not a lot of trust left in this world, but I ain't gonna say no when the *whanau* need help, you know? Appreciate it. We owe you one."

Michael nodded, and gestured for the doctor to do his thing.

While Dr Cross spoke to the young man in great detail about all kinds of colours and consistencies I didn't want to think about, Michael drew me aside. Together, we walked to the front of the convoy, and put the Hilux between ourselves and the others.

Once we were alone, he took my hand in his and drew me in close to him. The kiss was quick and feather-light, for fear of sneaking Skylars hunting us down.

"You were amazing out there." His voice was a breathless murmur as he wrapped his arm around my waist to draw me up against his lean frame.

"Me?" I said, bewildered by the compliment. "You were the one that killed it."

"No, *we* killed it, with teamwork. " He slipped his other arm around my shoulders, and his fingers softly caressed the back of my neck. "But you... you were magnificent. So confident and graceful. I didn't know you had it in you."

"Oh."

His lips were on the side of my neck now, planting tender kisses across my skin. A little nuzzle, and then I felt the softest nibble on my earlobe – it sent a lightning bolt right through me. My back came to rest against the truck's door, pinned by his strong hands.

"Ah, M-michael..." I tried to protest, but my heart wasn't in it. His breath was hot and heavy across my skin, and I could feel the swell of his rising arousal despite his body armour. "W-what about—"

"Shh..." He silenced me with a kiss. "They can't see us back here. What they don't know—"

"What we don't know, huh?"

Uh-oh.

Skylar stood a few meters away, her arms folded across her chest and a look of smug satisfaction on her face.

"I knew it!" She jabbed an accusatory finger at us, then turned on a heel and skipped off.

Michael groaned, and reluctantly released me. "Can't we get a moment's privacy around here? God."

"Of course not." I sighed and straightened my clothing. "This is what happens when six people live in close proximity for too long. No one has any privacy."

"Well, I sure hope we can find our own space in this new town. What I wouldn't give to have you all to myself for a while." He paused and gave me a long, thoughtful look that made me tingle all over.

"Oh, really?" I lifted my brows, half-teasing and half-curious. "And what would you do with me if you had me?"

"Well," he said, his voice dropping to a low, throaty purr. "I would have to spend some time exploring you. Cataloguing your most sensitive spots." He reached a hand up and stroked a curl of hair away from my cheek. "Or at least, the ones you'll let me touch."

"Hmm," I mumbled and turned my head to nuzzle at his palm. "We should *definitely* try and find our own space, then."

He shot me a wicked grin, and then took my hand to lead me back towards the others.

***

It took some time for the doctor to work out the medication required, and the prescriptions for the number of sick people Hemi described. As he worked, we learned more about the group that Hemi came from.

He told us that his *whanau* consisted of about a dozen Maori survivors from across the region, who had banded together gradually over the course of the last ten years with a communal need to survive and keep their old traditions alive. They'd built their village on the edge of one of the local lakes a few years earlier, and had lived there in relative seclusion ever since. After speaking with Hemi for a while, the doctor reached the conclusion that human occupation had inevitably tainted their water source.

"Make sure you boil any water that you're going to drink or are going to use to cook or clean something that you're going to eat," Dr Cross said, handing out information and medication with his usual efficiency. "Be sure to get the sick people to drink as much clean water as you can; they'll be quite dehydrated by now."

Hemi nodded happily, and examined the little box full of prescription bottles. "And everyone who's sick gets one of these, three times per day with a big glass of water. Got it. Thanks, Doc." On a sudden impulse, the youth snatched up the doctor's hand and shook it vigorously.

"You're quite welcome, young man." The doctor looked flustered but pleased by Hemi's gratitude. As grumpy as he appeared to be, he did always seem to get a thrill from helping a patient. Medicine really was his calling in life.

"Hey, where are you folks heading to?" Hemi looked back and forth between us, his dark eyes sparkling with youthful exuberance. "The *ariki* will want to come visit you. *Homai o homai*, eh? A gift for a gift."

Michael hesitated for a moment, and then made the decision for the rest of us.

"Ohaupo. We're planning to settle there," he replied. He sounded a little unsure of himself, but Hemi didn't seem to mind.

"Oh, eh? Sweet as, I'll let her know." He grinned, and there was nothing but genuine friendliness on his young face. "We'll come visit you, bro; bring you some presents."

Something about the youth put me at ease. In spite of my learned paranoia, I found myself liking him. He was no older than my sister, and there was a real openness to his character that made him instantly likeable. A thought came to me suddenly, and then I reached out to touch Michael's arm. He turned and looked at me, surprised, since I'd mostly stayed quiet throughout the conversation. "Tell him about the mutants."

Michael immediately understood what I meant. Even if this tribe did turn out to be hostile in the end, it would be cruel not to warn them about a potential threat that might spread into the local area.

Michael summed up our encounters with the mutated infected in as few words as possible, glossing over the painful details of the deaths of his friends. Despite his brevity, he got the point across quite efficiently. By the time he finished, the kid's smile was gone.

"No wonder you folks were after weapons," he said, looking back and forth between us, wide-eyed. "Had me worried for a second, but now I get it. Man, that's scary. I better get home fast, tell the boss. She'll decide what we do."

"Be careful," Michael said. "We haven't seen anything this far south aside from the pig, but there's no way to be sure."

"Yeah. Stay safe, bro." The kid nodded respectfully to Michael, and then to the rest of us in turn. He looked up at the sun to get his bearings, and then with a wave he was off at a long, loping jog towards the south-west. We watched him go, then turned and looked at one another.

"We should probably get moving before it gets too hot," I said, running my hand over my brow. The others nodded their agreement.

Suddenly, Michael chuckled. I looked at him quizzically, not quite sure what the joke was at first. He signed and rolled his eyes heavenwards.

"We never did finish moving that tree."

***

It didn't take us long to finish removing the deadfall. In no time at all, we were back on the road, picking our way slowly towards the township of Ohaupo. It was just after midday and the sun was high overhead, burning down on us with merciless intensity.

"Ugh." I groaned and plucked my singlet away from my sweaty tummy. Even with the windows rolled down, the humidity was getting unbearable. "I never thought I'd be fantasising about a *cold* shower."

"Mmngh," Michael agreed unintelligibly, half way through taking a long drink from his water bottle. He swallowed and sighed heavily, then offered the rest of the bottle to me.

I took it without thinking and drank deeply, even though it was warm and tasted a little brackish. After the last few drops rolled down my throat, I sighed as well and plunked my elbow on the edge of the window. Suddenly, a thought struck me, and it was so silly that it made me giggle.

Michael glanced at me, bemused. "What are you chortling at?"

"Just a thought." I pulled a face and shook the empty drink bottle at him. "Is sharing your water with another survivor the post-apocalyptic equivalent of sharing your juice box with the cute girl you like in kindergarten?"

"What?" he asked, chuckling and shaking his head. "Where did *that* thought come from?"

"I honestly don't know. Maybe it's heatstroke?" I shrugged and shot a sideways look at him. "Are you going to push me over so you can sneak a look up my skirt now?"

"Why, of course not." Michael feigned offense at the very suggestion, then his eyes narrowed, and a wickedly flirtatious grin danced across his lips. "If I wanted to get a look up your skirt, I'd just ask politely… and maybe kiss you on that spot on your neck that makes you go all gooey."

He had a point. When he kissed me *there*, I was putty in his hands.

I was about to say something cheeky back when he interrupted, his tone going from one of playful flirtation to one of pure excitement. "Hey, hey look!"

Ahead of us, the details of a tiny township were beginning to emerge from the heat mirage. I sat up straight and scanned through the haze until I spotted familiar landmarks.

"Yes, this is it." It was hard to contain my excitement as I confirmed his suspicions, and then I fished my radio off my belt to inform the others about the good news. "Attention all passengers, please be advised we will be reaching our destination in a few minutes. Please ensure your seatbelt is fastened, and your tray table is in a secure, upright position."

A chorus of cheers echoed from the others. No one was any happier about travelling in the heat than I was. I dropped the radio in my lap, and flopped back in my seat with a sigh of relief. "Thank goodness that's over."

# Chapter Twenty-One

We toured slowly through the town of Ohaupo. Michael followed my directions as I pointed the way through the township, until at last we eased to a halt in front of my familiar old video store.

"I've claimed that flat up above the store," I said, pointing it out to Michael proudly. He looked, and then gave me an odd sideways glance. I laughed at his expression. "It's nicer than it looks, I swear."

"Hrm. I don't know, Sandy." He looked worried, and I knew that feeling well – it was the feeling of being exposed and vulnerable. "Everything seems so... open. It doesn't feel very secure."

"We can't live in a bunker forever, honey. We'll turn into mushrooms." I gave him an impish grin, and leaned over to reassuringly rub his thigh. "Don't worry, there are ways to make this place secure, too. I've explored pretty much the entire town and only found one infected, plus I know exactly where we can stay."

"Only one infected?" His brow furrowed. "Surely there must have been more people living here than that."

"Yeah, about that." I paused and looked at him again. "Don't go into that function building we passed."

"Oh." He paused for a long moment to think that over, and then looked at me again. "Group suicide?"

I nodded, and he grimaced.

"As loathe as I am to destroy perfectly good shelter, we may want to consider burning the whole building down," I said, struggling to suppress the chill that rolled down my spine. "There are a lot of bodies in there. A *lot*."

He just nodded and looked grim as he put the Hilux into park and killed the engine. We climbed out and went back to check on the others. One by one, they disembarked and stood around, smelling the air. A cool breeze blew, and it smelt fresh and clean after the cloying stink of decay that hung over Hamilton.

"Where do we go?" Skylar asked, absently plucking her sticky t-shirt away from her neck. Even in the shade, it was humid.

"Well, I was staying above the video store, but it backs onto a small motel," I said, looking back and forth between them. "There's a half-dozen rooms upstairs that are clean, dry, and zombie-free. You have to go through a staircase in the lobby to get to them, so you've got a natural choke point to defend."

"Sounds good," Michael agreed, gesturing for me to take point. "Let's go take a look."

We gave everyone a moment to lock up their respective vehicles, and then I led the way. Madeline, fresh from a nap in the car, skipped ahead of us singing happily to herself, despite our best efforts to keep her from running off. The rest of us moved as a group, weapons relaxed but ready in case they were needed. We picked our way across the cracked pavement past my store, and took the side road to the left. The entrance to the motel was an old glass door that was webbed with cracks, yet still solid. The hinges protested as I shoved it open and led the way into the dusty interior.

The lobby was nothing to write home about, just an open space no bigger than the average living room. It was decorated with a faded reception desk and a couple of overstuffed couches off to one side. On one side of the desk, an archway led out to an overgrown courtyard. On the other side, stairs led up into brilliant sunshine. Magazines ten years out of date decomposed on the coffee table.

"We should be able to bolt this from the inside, but it'll take a little lubricant on the hinges," I said, gesturing to the front door, then I led the way inside.

A bunch of keys sat on the front desk, exactly where I'd left them two weeks before. I picked them up and headed upstairs. The staircase let out onto an open-air landing; the motel was shaped like an old Roman villa, built in a square with a courtyard in the centre. Half a dozen doors flanked the upper landing, each with a number on it that had once meant something to someone. I'd gone through them all in my initial exploration and at the time I'd just mentally catalogued their contents. Now, I used that knowledge to point out the ones that were immediately liveable to the others, separating them from the rooms that would need work to become habitable.

Each room was a self-contained unit, with a bathroom and basic kitchen, while there was a larger kitchen on the bottom level that had once served as a small restaurant. Much like the rest of the building, the downstairs kitchen was filthy and it would take all our combined efforts to get it in functioning order again.

Still, after they had looked around for a while, the others agreed that this old motel would work well as our new home.

***

The next few days were spent hard at work, turning our little motel into a fortress. We scavenged enough boards from the other buildings nearby to cover up all the downstairs windows and the fire exit at the rear, which left the front door as the only way in or out of the complex. As I'd predicted, with a little maintenance the front door closed and locked easily, and we slept soundly at night.

Each of the others chose their own rooms. Ryan and Skylar claimed the honeymoon suite, amidst exclamations of delight at the sheer size of the bed and the bright morning sunshine that the room got. The doctor took a two-bedroom suite on the opposite side of the building, so that Madeline could have her own room. He was thrilled by the idea of being able to close off her mess when he didn't want to look at it anymore, and I couldn't say I blamed him.

Michael, on the other hand, chose a small room right on the corner of the building that had once been the owner's personal office. The sole reason for his choice was that the room had a window less than two meters from the upper floor of the video store where I preferred to stay. His window lined up almost exactly with the one on the tiny landing of my loft, close enough that we could almost touch if we leaned out.

The two of us spent some time together, constructing a walkway between the two buildings. It was really just a couple of planks for a floor and ropes for handrails, but it was strong enough to support our weight when we wanted to duck back and forth to visit one another. Which we did, often.

Michael swiftly came to appreciate my affection for the little loft, particularly the soft double bed. After the narrow, rock-hard cots that we'd been sleeping on in the bunker, it felt like sleeping on a cloud.

On the third morning after our arrival, I awoke to the sound of birds chirping and Michael snoring contentedly beside me. I rolled over and looked at him, and found him sprawled on his back with his arms and legs flung in all directions. He looked so peaceful that I couldn't bear to wake him.

I rose and slid out of bed, careful not to disturb the blankets draped over him. Stretching languidly, I moved out to the living area to open the curtains, and let the bright morning sun wash over my naked body. It felt so good to be able to walk around freely without the fear of running into a curious seven-year-old. I liked kids, but sometimes it was nice to be able to be an adult without little eyes peeping in.

Feeling relaxed and refreshed, I wandered contentedly around my living space, opening the windows one by one to let in the morning breeze. True to his word, Michael had been using his time alone with me very well. Although I still couldn't quite conquer my fears completely, we'd learned so much about our own limits through experimentation and play. Every day, he was helping me to hate myself a little bit less.

I sighed and looked down at myself, considering the curve of my breasts, my stomach and legs. It had been years since I'd had proper female curves. With a healthy, regular diet and exercise, my body was gradually leaving starvation mode. I was starting to feel healthy and fit again, and it felt good. I had breasts again. That fact made me happy, and made Michael even happier. I hadn't even realised how much I'd missed having a proper bust line until there was someone in my life that I wanted to share it with.

My foot had been healing cleanly, and last night the doctor had finally announced that I no longer needed to keep the bandages on. It still ached, and it was pink and tender, but the stitches were out and I was more or less functional again. I stretched the foot out in front me to examine the scar, like a silly, naked ballerina. It wasn't pretty, but my foot was working again and that was all that mattered to me.

Full of energy after a good night's sleep, I danced back through the bedroom to the en suite, and flicked on the shower. It had taken some doing, but with time, determination, and lots of bad language, I'd managed to get the hot water cylinder working again. Skye insisted I do hers as well, so once I knew the trick to it I ended up fixing everyone's.

I didn't mind at all. The work kept my mind active and my days busy, and Michael kept my nights… interesting, and exciting. My lips quirked into a smile as I slipped beneath the hot water and let it cascade over my face and down my body like a hot caress. I closed my eyes and ran my hands back through my hair, enjoying the feel of hot water cleansing me.

All of a sudden, there were sneaking fingers blocking the falling water as hands crept around from behind to cup my breasts. I opened my eyes and looked back over my shoulder, to find my lover grinning impishly back at me.

*My lover*, I thought possessively, and spun beneath the water to face him. Driven by the heat of the water and my own surging emotions, I wrapped my arms around his neck and drew him down into a kiss.

Mine, mine, mine.

Though I supposed if you wanted to be technical, we weren't lovers yet. Over the last few days, we'd done everything but the final act of consummation. Little by little, he was coaxing out my inner harlot, that saucy young thing I had been in my youth before harsh reality had torn it away. And yet, no matter how much I wanted to, I couldn't quite bring myself to take that final step.

God, how much I wanted to, though. I longed for it, I thought about it constantly and even dreamed about it, but every time I tried to gather the courage, the spectres lunged out of their hiding place and chased me back. Michael had been so patient with me, and he never tried to put any pressure on me to do anything I was uncomfortable with. Over the time we'd spent together, my trust in him had grown, to the point that I could feel it turning into something deeper.

It scared me a little bit, but at the same time it was exciting and new. If there was one thing in this world that I knew for sure, it was that I wanted to be with him one day, when the time was right and we were both ready. In the meantime, he was helping me to repair the damage that bad men had done to me over the years.

His hand caught the small of my back, and drew my belly up hard against his as he kissed me deeply. The heat of the water had always been something that made my desires stir – and now I had the fantasy man to go along with the steamy shower. I wanted to have him so badly, to be pinned to the wall and ravished in that hot, hot shower, and yet… I couldn't. Not yet.

*Soon?* a part of me begged, writhing in unsatisfied torment.

*Soon!* the rational part of me demanded, the part that loathed being a victim.

But the part of me that was the victim wasn't so sure just yet. It didn't know what it wanted, and it was so afraid.

***

Half an hour later, the hot water finally ran out. Exhausted, flushed, and not nearly as clean as we probably should have been, we finally managed to pry our hands off one another long enough to get dressed.

Everyone else had already figured out what was going on between us by now. There were no secrets in a community this small. Still, there was an unspoken agreement between Michael and me, that we would keep our business as private as possible. It was driving Skylar crazy. After ten years of only having one person with her, someone whose business she already knew intimately, she was gossip-starved and desperate to talk about something new. Still, sisters or not, I liked having something that was mine and mine alone. Michael seemed to be a private person by nature, and I respected that. Neither of us were willing to indulge Skye's need for gossip just yet.

When Michael and I finally made our way into the communal kitchen to join the others for breakfast, hand in hand, Skylar gave us a knowing look but didn't say a word. As we settled down at the breakfast table, she sauntered over to give us both the hairy eyeball.

"I'm making omelettes," she said. "You two okay with that?"

"Oh, you found the chickens?" I replied, grinning at the thought of savoury, nutritious food.

"Yup!" she replied, looking proud of herself. "I found a vegetable garden, too, so I've got tomatoes and parsley as well. I hope no one's allergic?"

We all shook our heads and she grinned brightly, then waddled back to her stove to get cooking.

"Shame we don't have some toast and Marmite to go with it," I reminisced dreamily.

"And don't forget the bacon." Michael's comment was laced with dry humour; we all laughed.

"So, we were talking earlier," Ryan piped up as the levity faded. "We've got this jungle happening in the central courtyard right now, but if we cleared out all the weeds and bushes, then we could plant our own vegetable garden in there."

Skye added her input to the conversation, as she cracked eggs into a huge bowl. "That way even if something happens and we have to lock this place down, we'll still have a secure source of fresh food."

"That's a good idea," Michael said, nodding slowly.

"Yeah," I agreed. "We could transfer some of the adult plants from the gardens outside. That way we should have food before winter. I think I saw some hydroponics equipment out at one of the farms, too."

"We could clear out one of the downstairs rooms for that," Ryan said, sounding excited now. "If we bring back that equipment, we can grow all kinds of things."

I looked around at the faces that had become so familiar to me in such a short period of time, and felt an unexpected surge of affection towards them all. Then I noticed a strange little smile on Dr Cross' face, and shot him a curious look. "What are you grinning at, Doc?"

"Oh, nothing," he said, chuckling softly. "I was just thinking that you young folks sound as excited as my late wife when she first saw the big gardens behind our first house. She loved to garden." The doctor sighed, and absently raised a hand to stroke Madeline's hair. Maddy, of course, was off in her own little world, playing with her dolls, and didn't even seem to notice.

"Oh, good," I said, grinning playfully. "Hopefully you can tell us how to not kill things, then. I'm pretty sure no one in this room has ever planted a vegetable garden before."

Embarrassed chuckles from the others around the room answered that question – apparently, my guess was bang on the money.

"Ah, I see." The doctor shoved his glasses up his nose, but for once the smile lingered on his face. It was nice to see him happy for a change. "I've been volunteered as the king of the vegetable patch. I shall try my best to teach you youngsters what you need to know."

"After breakfast," Ryan said, and everyone else agreed. Skylar's savoury concoction was just about done, and to our deprived noses it smelled like the most delicious thing ever made in the entire history of the world.

We waited impatiently while she finished cooking, our grumbling bellies whining in protest about how long it took to cook. Once it was served, the food was devoured with delighted gusto; more than one of us suffered a burnt tongue in our haste, but it was well worth it. I couldn't remember a breakfast I'd enjoyed more.

"You're getting good at this, Skye," I told her after I finished my last bite, while settling back in my chair to digest. "I think you've inherited Mum's culinary skills."

"Thanks." She beamed, glowing from the praise. "I'm really enjoying it, actually. Cooking, I mean. I found some cook books while I was exploring the other day, and looking through the pictures has got me feeling so inspired."

I smiled at her enthusiasm and nodded. "Well, if we can find the ingredients, I'm sure no one would mind if you experimented a bit and tried out some of the recipes."

A chorus of grunts came from the menfolk that we both took to be agreement.

"I'd love to, but there are so many words in there that I don't know," Skylar admitted. "I'll have to get someone to help me read the recipes."

I stared at her, but it took a second for what she'd just said to actually sink in. When it did, my eyes widened in surprise. "You can't read?"

"I can, sort of," she replied, looking taken aback by the accusation, and a little offended. "But not very well. I was eight, Sandy. Eight! I only got to go to school for a few years, so I didn't get to learn much. I haven't had very much practice since then so I'm just not a good reader."

Her tone stung; it was so full of bitterness, something I hadn't heard from her before.

"I didn't mean it like that, sis." Suddenly on the defensive, I held my hands up in front of me as though to ward off a physical attack. "I just mean, you know. I hadn't thought about it. Don't worry about it though, we'll teach you."

"Yes, we absolutely will." Dr Cross' voice cut in, surprising us since he usually spent our mealtimes in silence. "You shall join Madeline's lessons immediately. So much of human history is now only available in the written form; it is critical that each of us understand it so that we can keep our language and our history alive. The written word is the only reliable way that we can preserve our history for our children, and our children's children."

Skye was speechless for once in her life and sat staring into space for a while, with her hand rubbing protectively over her swollen belly. I could see that the doctor's words had reached her – particularly the very last of them. Finally, she nodded. "Okay. If nothing else, then I'll learn for the baby's sake."

"And don't forget the cookbooks," Ryan chipped in helpfully. Someone kicked his ankle under the table, and he yelped. I wasn't sure if it was Skylar or one of the men, but either way everyone laughed.

***

The day grew hotter and hotter as the sun climbed higher in the sky. I paused in my work to wipe the sweat from my brow with the back of my hand, and then peered upwards.

*It must be February*, I thought absently as I considered the heat mirage that radiated off the ground and the roof of our building. February was the hottest month of the year, and with all the time I spent outside I had a good sense of the rise and fall of the seasons even if I didn't know the exact dates. This was by far the hottest day that I'd felt all year.

With a group effort, we had managed to clear the biggest weeds from the garden before the sun climbed high enough to reach the courtyard. The men had strained and strained to pull them out; some of those weeds had grown into small trees over the years. Eventually, we won the battle, and then we combined our forces to lug the unwanted greenery away.

Digging out the smaller weeds was going to take time, though. I was on my hands and knees in the dirt with a trowel, digging them out one by one. I twisted out one rampantly overgrown dandelion and flung it over my shoulder without looking, in the general direction of the pile on the concrete behind me.

"Hey!" a voice yelped. I glanced back and saw Michael brushing dirt off his trousers from where the plant had hit him. He kicked the weed into the pile, and then joined me in the dirt. "Geez, attacking me with weeds now? What did I do?"

I smiled and tilted the wide brim of my hat back to look at him. "You were clearly trying to sneak up on me, so it was self-defence."

With a grin, he grabbed one of the little gardening forks we'd scavenged from around town, and set about helping me to gouge out the verdant weeds. My gaze lingered on him a moment longer, admiring the way his broad shoulders glistened with sweat in the sunshine. He'd ditched his shirt at some stage and was clad only in dirty jeans. It was a pleasant sight – until I realised that his pale skin was starting to turn red.

"You're getting sunburnt," I warned him. The combination of his ethnicity and the length of time he'd spent living underground made him even more vulnerable to the sun than I was, but at least I was smart enough to wear a hat.

"I know." He sighed and absently rubbed a hand down his arm, then shrugged and gave me a sideways look. I noticed the bridge of his nose was red as well, as was his forehead and upper cheeks.

"Get inside, you. You're getting roasted," I scolded him and shook a dirty finger at him. "We've got enough things trying to kill us without adding melanoma to the list."

He mumbled something inarticulate and yanked out a weed. I leaned over and snatched it from his hand, then tossed it aside. "Oh no, you don't. Inside, right now."

He gave me a sulk that made my innards quiver, but I wasn't going to let him injure himself for the sake of pride. In the time I'd known him, I'd learned that the biggest danger to Michael Chan's health was not zombies or food poisoning, but his own stubbornness. I knew that he considered our safety and health far above his own, and tended to ignore his own condition until it was almost too late.

I hauled myself to my feet and dusted my knees off with my hands, then stripped off my dirty gardening gloves. I dumped them at my feet, put one hand on my hip and offered the other to him. Loathe to admit his own weakness, he stared at my hand for a second, and then pointedly looked away.

"Ahem?" I wiggled my fingers deliberately, until finally his shoulders slumped in surrender. With a long sigh, he took my hand and let me help him to his feet, then he trailed along behind me as I led him into the shade.

"I'm fine, really." He was still protesting when we found the doctor in the midst of organising one of the storage rooms. The doctor took one look at him, and then started scolding him like a naughty child. Michael promptly put on his whipped puppy expression, but neither of us were having any of it. Between the two of us, we bundled him off to one of the bathrooms and bullied him into a cold shower.

"But I'm fine!" he spluttered beneath the chilly flow, sending cold droplets flying in all directions.

"You feel like it now, but you won't in an hour," I said, giving him a stern look that told him I would brook no arguments from him. "Trust me."

"I'm afraid your lady friend is quite right, young man," the doctor agreed. "It may not look or feel so bad right now, but the damage is already done. You're inside for the rest of the day, doctor's orders."

Michael visually deflated and slumped in against the shower's wall. "But what am I supposed to do inside all day?"

"Clear out one of the rooms for the hydroponics." I sighed and pulled off my hat. "I'm going to go this afternoon when it cools down a bit, and see what I can scrounge up. Right now, I don't think any of us should be out there. It has to be thirty-two degrees in the sun."

"Mmn." The doctor made an inarticulate noise of agreement. "Go fetch them in, Ms McDermott. I'll keep an eye on our good constable here."

"But I'm fine!" Michael protested weakly, but he'd given up the fight.

"Sure you are, lobster-man." I chuckled, and reached over to trail a fingertip over his wet shoulder. The water felt so cool and nice I almost wanted to join him. "You seem to forget you've been living in a basement for the last ten years. Your skin has forgotten what the sun is."

Michael mumbled something inarticulate in return. The doctor caught my eye and rolled his, as if to comment on Michael's foolishness. I smiled at him and then left them to it, content to know that my sweetheart was in good hands.

Luckily, the others were not half as stubborn as Michael was; they were already filtering in out of the sun on their own. When I caught up to Skye and Ryan, they were heading for the kitchen. Ryan plodded along contentedly behind my sister, his arms burdened by an old plastic washing basket filled to bursting full of freshly-picked lettuces, tomatoes, cucumbers, and green beans.

Skylar waddled ahead of him with her arms wrapped around an enormous watermelon, her gait awkward but determined. The melon was almost as big as her belly, so I hurried over to help her with it – or at least I tried to, but she refused to relinquish her prize.

"No, I've got this," she said, shooing me away, and vanished into the kitchen.

Ryan gave me an amused look and lifted a shoulder in a shrug. "Yeah, I tried that too. There's no helping her when she's got it in her head to do something."

I chuckled and nodded – I understood that stubbornness very well. It was a family trait. "What about you? You sure you should be lifting that with your arm?"

The youth looked down at his arm, which was still swathed in bandages, and then shrugged.

"Probably not, but I'm not letting *her* do it." He grinned and tilted his chin in the direction Skylar had gone. "It's all good, though. We're almost there." Then he adjusted his burden and followed Skylar into the kitchen, with me trailing along in their wake.

"Salad for lunch?" I queried, reaching over to snatch a juicy tomato from the basket when Ryan set it down on the table. I held it to my nose and inhaled deeply, enjoying the garden-fresh scent. There was nothing quite like the smell of a freshly-picked tomato.

"A'yup, and watermelon," Skylar said proudly as she rolled the massive melon along the bench and up onto the chopping board.

"That thing is huge, Skye. Think I should get the axe?" I was only half kidding. The thing really was ridiculously enormous. She actually paused to consider that option too, before shaking her head firmly.

"Nah, I don't want anything that touched that gross pig anywhere near my watermelon. Ry, come hold this while I get the knife."

"Oh god, I'm going to get killed, aren't I?" Ryan joked as he trundled over to do her bidding.

I couldn't help but join in the laughter. "Well, I'll leave you two to it, then. Have either of you seen Maddy?"

"Not recently," Skylar said with a shrug, unconcerned. In the three days that we'd been in the area, we had yet to see a single thing that even remotely resembled a threat. "She followed us towards the garden, but scampered off while we were picking veggies. I figured she must have gotten bored and come home."

"Sweet as, I'll go find her," I replied. "Doc says it's time to come in out of the sun." I waved to them both and headed out. My first port of call was to head upstairs and check her room, but when I got there the room was empty.

"Made-line?" I called as I wandered through our little fortress, sticking my head into each room to check for her. After a few minutes, I came to the conclusion that she wasn't inside. Although I felt a brief stab of concern, I fought it back down and convinced myself that wherever she was, she was probably just fine.

*She'll just be off playing somewhere,* I decided as I headed back downstairs to fetch my hat. The sun was so intense that I didn't really want to go back out into it, but I had my orders. As I crossed the threshold from the lobby to the street outside, the heat hit me like a wall. I lifted a hand to shade my eyes as I peered up and down the street, and called the girl's name again. No answer.

If I were a kid, where would I go?

I thought about it for a minute, and ran over the options the town had to offer that would interest a seven-year-old. There weren't many places to play here, except–

With a flash of cognition, I snapped my fingers and jogged off in the direction of the old primary school not too far from our base of operations. If I remembered correctly, the place had an extensive but overgrown playground in the yard. If I were a bored child, that was definitely where I'd go.

I ducked down a weed-choked walkway that ran between two houses, a pathway that had once been used by children as a shortcut to their school. The homes had big, old trees in the yard, with branches that hung so low that I had to duck beneath them as they tried to snatch away my hat, but the shade was a welcome respite from the intensity of the midsummer sun. At the far end of the corridor, I emerged from beneath the trees and stood squinting in the bright daylight.

Sure enough, there was a little figure playing on the swings. As I drew closer, I could hear her chattering away to someone or something I couldn't see. Since there was no reply, I assumed she was just talking to her dolls.

"Hey, Maddy," I called to her as I crossed the overgrown field, following the trail of crushed grass she'd left behind her towards the swings. She turned around to look at me. After a second she waved happily, and beckoned me over.

"Miss Sandy, look, look what I found. Look!" she squealed gleefully and pointed to a climbing frame nearby. I followed her finger with my eye and looked up.

Lo and behold, who was sitting up there but my little friend Tigger. She'd grown a lot in the two weeks I'd been gone and now lay basking contentedly in the sunshine.

"Well, look at that," I said, pleased to see the little housecat was fine. I may have been a little bit worried about her while I was away, so it was a relief to see she'd stayed happy and healthy in my absence.

"It's so cute!" Maddy twisted on her swing, looking bright-eyed and excited. Suddenly she spun the swing around to face me, and stared up at me with enormous eyes. "What is it?"

"It's called a kitten," I said, struggling not to laugh; it wasn't her fault that she'd grown up in a world without pets. I reminded myself just how limited her experiences were, and expanded on my answer for her benefit. "A kitten is a baby domestic cat."

"Oh, like Puss In Boots?" she asked. Her eyes were so wide I was almost afraid they'd pop right out of her head.

"Sort of, except real cats walk on four legs." It was starting to get really hard not to laugh, her expression was just too cute. "I named this one Tigger when I was living here before. Like from Winnie the Pooh?"

"Ohh. Tigger like a tiger, because he's got stripes?" She looked delighted by my childlike logic, and hopped off her swing. "Tiggers-Tiggers-Tiggers are wonderful things, their heads are made of rubber and their tails are made of springs!" She chant the old rhyme gleefully and bounced around the yard.

"Yes, yes they are. And Maddy-monkeys need to come inside for lunch," I told her with a grin, offering her my hand. She bounced over to take it, and together we walked – and bounced – back towards our little fortress.

Behind us, Tigger stretched and rolled onto her back to watch us go. Just as we were about to leave her line of sight, she hopped up and scampered after us, to follow us back home.

*∗∗

Lunch was a noisy affair that day, full of boisterous joy and happy mess. Madeline had never eaten watermelon before, and she was quick to announce it was her new 'favouritest food ever', to the amusement of the adults.

Since I lacked Madeline's sweet tooth, the salad was the bigger treat for me. Skylar had even added some hard boiled eggs for protein, just the way Mum used to when we were little. I ate several helpings before I was satisfied, and then sat back in my chair to watch the others stuff themselves.

There's going to be a few sick tummies tonight, I thought to myself with amusement.

The only one not joining in on the feast was Michael, who sat beside me in silence, picking quietly at his food without much interest. I watched him for a minute before I finally decided to check on him.

"Are you okay?" I asked softly, and reached over to stroke his knee in case my question was lost in the din.

The others didn't notice, but he did and shrugged absently. I looked at him closely and noticed that the sunburn was getting darker as the burn settled deeper into his skin. I resisted the automatic 'I-told-you-so'; just as we had predicted, he hadn't realised how bad the burn was until hours after the damage was already done. Now, he was in pain.

I knew that pain well, and I understood it. I rose to fetch another bottle of cool water for him from the fridge. Without a word, he took it and drank deeply, then gave me a weak smile. "Thank you."

"Of course." I rubbed his knee softly, sympathy twisting my gut. Sunburn could be a terrible thing.

Finally, the doctor noticed the conversation and joined in. "I made him some aloe vera gel, if you want to help him put on another dose." He fished a jar out of his pocket, and offered it to me across the table. I accepted it with a nod and then looked at Michael, who rose from his chair without a word.

He followed me out of the kitchen and plodded up the stairs behind me to his room. There, I sat him down in an old wooden chair beneath the window. He slumped into it with his chin resting on the back rung, staring miserably out the window.

"Ah, you poor thing," I murmured as I knelt on the floor behind him to study his burns. He was in too much pain to have put on a shirt.

"Doc says it'll take days to get better." He flinched as he folded his arms under his chin to give me better access to his burned back. He heaved a long sigh and mumbled plaintively. "Make it better?"

"You know that I would if I could." I opened the jar of cream to examine the contents. The gel smelt strange and pungent, but I scooped out a generous helping anyway and lathered it across his broad back. His sigh of relief just about broke my heart, and he immediately relaxed beneath my touch.

With gentle fingers, I spread the gel over his shoulders and upper biceps, then up the back of his neck. Even the tips of his ears were burned, so I added a dollop on each and gently rubbed it in.

"You should lie down for a nap," I suggested as I tended to him, to which he grunted inarticulately and didn't answer. "I mean it. You'll feel better, and it'll keep you out of the sun."

He looked back at me with those sad puppy eyes. He'd already learned I was vulnerable to those silent, appealing looks, but I was building up a resistance to it. Unrelenting, I helped him to his feet and guided him to his bed. I lay him down on his tummy and leaned over him to fluff his pillow. A hand tried to sneak up beneath my top while I was bent over him, but for once I pulled away.

"Sleep," I told him firmly as I disentangled myself. He sighed sadly.

"I should have listened to you," he said, his voice muffled by the pillows.

"Everyone has to learn their own lessons," I replied, gently running my hand over the back of his head. "Sleep, honey. I'll bring you some dinner later on and you'll feel better tomorrow."

"Thank you," he mumbled, closing his eyes. I left the jar of gel beside his bed and I slipped out of the room, closing the door behind me.

When I turned to walk away, I almost ran straight into the doctor, who was waiting outside. I backpedalled to avoid running him down, then stopped and stared. There was a very strange look on his face.

"Ms McDermott, might we speak?" His voice was low, almost a whisper. He shot a glance back over his shoulder to make sure we weren't being observed.

"Of course," I replied. I was a little bewildered, but followed as he turned and lead the way back towards his room. When we arrived, he closed the door behind us, and then he stuck his head into Maddy's room to check if she was there. Evidently she wasn't, because he returned a moment later with a deep frown on his face.

"Ms McDermott – Sandy – I need to ask you for a favour," he said, sounding strangely nervous. "It's regarding your sister."

Suddenly, I felt a cold chill run through me. "Skylar? Is she all right? Is the baby—"

"She's fine at the moment, but I am concerned about her," he said, cutting me off. "She is at a very delicate stage of her pregnancy, when she should be taking it easy, but as you know she resists all attempts to convince her to rest. I have tried to speak to her about it, but she brushes it off and ignores me."

"You want me to talk to her?" I said, cringing internally. "I can try, but I don't know what good it'll do. We've only known one another as adults for two weeks."

"But you are sisters, and blood runs thicker than water," he said. "She loves you. I hope that she will listen to you, or else…"

"…She could lose the baby?" I whispered, horrified by the thought.

The doctor shrugged. "That is one possibility; more likely she will injure herself. But, we are in a dangerous and unsanitary environment, and she neglects to acknowledge that she is particularly vulnerable right now. If she were to cut herself and get an infection, like you did, it could complicate the pregnancy. Given our limited access to medical technology, complications of any kind drastically increase the chance that she could lose the baby – or her own life."

I grimaced, feeling a surge of mixed emotions. Part of me was worried, while part of me filled with cold anger. What was it with the people in my life deliberately putting themselves at risk?

"I'll talk to her right now," I said. The doctor nodded, but his concern did not seem to lessen. I felt like time was of the essence, so I let myself out of his room and hurried off, looking for any sign of my sister.

I spotted her downstairs doing exactly what she probably shouldn't be: Lugging a heavy box from one room to another. Ryan was trailing along behind her, protesting, but she was too stubborn to let him take it. The anger welled up to overwhelm my caution, and I raced down to intercept them.

I took the stairs two at a time, and then sprang around the corner to take them both by surprise. Without giving her a moment's notice, I snatched the heavy box from Skylar's grip and shoved it into Ryan's hands instead.

"Hey!" Skylar exclaimed in alarm, but I wasn't having any of it. I grabbed her by the arm and dragged her off towards the nearest room, without giving her time to protest or pull away.

She sure tried, though, but I wouldn't let her. I dragged her into one of the storage rooms and slammed the door behind us, then grabbed her by the shoulders and gave her a hard shake.

"What the hell is wrong with you?" she protested at the rough treatment and tried to shove me off. Despite all her determination, I proved to be physically stronger than her and managed to keep her restrained.

"You need to stop it." My voice hard and threatening. It was the kind of tone that I'd never used on my baby sister in my entire life. I could see her getting angry but I refused to let her go. "You are almost nine months pregnant, Skylar McDermott. You need to slow down and start taking care of yourself."

"Oh, so the doctor's been whining at you too, has he?" she snapped and again tried to shove me away, but she just couldn't shake me.

"Stop being so fucking stupid, Skye. You are going to *kill that baby.*" I was practically snarling now, so angry that it took all of my willpower to fight down the urge to slap her. My choice of words did a better job of it than my fist ever could have, though, and her eyes widened in shock. When I suddenly released my grip on her shoulders, she was so stunned that she stayed exactly where I'd put her.

I jabbed a finger at her. "I know that you think you're invulnerable, but you're not. You're human, and subject to human weaknesses. So is that baby," I redirected my finger at her midsection, "and she has more than enough to worry about without her own mother trying to *murder her* with stubbornness. Frankly, I would very much like the chance to meet my niece or nephew one day, so knock it off right now or I will lock you in your room until you go into labour. Got it?"

She stared at me with huge eyes, shocked beyond words by my harshness. I wasn't generally the most threatening person. Frankly, I was a skinny little doll-faced slip of nothing – but I was Skye's big sister and she'd never seen me angry before. Judging by the look on her face, it scared the hell out of her.

Finally, she gathered her wits enough to nod quickly. I narrowed my eyes at her, and she seemed to understand instinctively that meant I would not brook any more of her headstrong behaviour if it put her baby at risk. She couldn't hold my gaze; her eyes dropped, and a hand rose protectively to her tummy. I suddenly realised there were tears gathering in her eyes, and I felt a mixture of victory for making her see sense, and guilt for making my little sister cry.

"I don't want my baby to die," she whispered.

"I know, Skye. I know." I softened my tone to comfort her. "That's why you have to slow down, for your baby's sake. Your body is more fragile than you know."

My anger had done its job, and now that it was no longer required it began to drain away. I reached for her and drew her into a hug made awkward by the very baby we were trying to protect, sandwiched in between us. She hugged me back, and I felt tears soaking into my shoulder.

"I'm just so scared." Her voice was watery and muffled against my shoulder. "I don't want my baby to get the infection. I feel like I can't do enough to keep her safe."

"I know." I hugged her close and stroked her hair, as if she were a little girl all over again. As much as I knew that she needed the shock to protect her growing baby, I hated to cause her distress. I was comforting myself with the gesture just as much as her, and trying to reassure myself that it was in the name of the greater good.

After all, what were sisters for, if not giving you a kick in the pants when you were being an idiot, and borrowing your favourite sweater with no intention of ever returning it?

# Chapter Twenty-Two

The fire crackled, roaring up into the night sky, while we stood around with hoses at the ready in case the flames decided to spread.

I watched with mixed feelings as the blaze consumed the ambiguously named 'Function' building, along with the dozens of bodies housed within. We'd decided that this was best way to keep the area safe for Skye's incoming baby, and to keep the risk of infection to a minimum. The makeshift graveyard would become a crematorium.

There were four of us there: Michael, Ryan, the doctor and me. Skylar had decided to stay at home with Madeline. Since our talk almost a week ago, Skye had finally accepted her condition and started to spend most of her time indoors cooking or focusing on her studies, or in the courtyard tending to our little garden. Tonight, she had actually volunteered to stay home, complaining of a persistent headache. I was relieved by her decision; the nearer she got to full term, the more I worried about her.

*Goodbye, Benny*, I thought to myself as I watched the flames rage. I really hoped that there was a Heaven, and that his sweet Margie was waiting for him there.

That thought made me sad. I hoped there was something more, anything more, than just this world of suffering that we knew. Somehow, Michael heard my sigh over the crackle of flames and he reached out to put his arm around me. I'd told him everything over the course of the last week or so, even about old Benny and his wife.

Well, no. Not quite everything. There were still some things that I held back, even from him. Things that had happened to me over the years that I didn't want to think about, let alone talk about. I couldn't even bear to say the word out loud. It was such a terrible, terrible word.

The worst four letters of the English language.

I leaned against his side, watching as the fire we'd set so carefully consumed the function hall, and the café and bar next to it. The buildings were separated from the other ones nearby by some distance, but we still practiced great caution in our act of arson. We'd waited until the heat-wave passed and rain came, which it finally had that morning. The ground was dry again by the time we started the blaze, but the morning's rain reduced the brittleness of the plants and the buildings nearby and lessened the chance that our fire would spread.

Regardless, we'd hosed down the nearest buildings before we planted accelerant in the bar and café. Then, we waited until we saw more clouds on the horizon, promising another shower on the way. It came just before sundown, when the air was still and humid. We judged the time just right for our bonfire to begin.

The fire had caught quickly and burned with a furious intensity that had worried us at first. None of us were professional arsonists, but we all remembered the warning signs about the summer fire danger from our younger days.

The flames had raged unabated for hours, and now there was hardly anything left – just the most basic framework and the roof. Suddenly the roof caved in with a terrible noise and an explosion of sparks, reducing the buildings to flaming rubble. A few smouldering ashes drifted towards nearby buildings, but we doused them before they could land.

Something cold and wet struck me on the top of the head as we retreated back to a safe distance again. I looked up, and another raindrop splattered me right between the eyes. The next thing I knew, it was coming down in a torrent and we were caught in the deluge. After the intense heat of the past week, none of us really seemed to mind.

The flames burned so hot that it took another hour before they died down completely. When they did, they left behind only ashes and a few shards of human bone where there had once been a building. A building where so many people had taken their own lives. I let sadness wash over me in the darkness as the flames retreated. The rain turned everything to a hot, muddy soup, which would probably bake to a crust in the sun when the storm passed. We would return another day and bury the ashes and bits of bone deep within the earth, but for now it was time for my bedraggled group of survivors to go home.

We gathered up our things, and trudged off to wash away the stench of smoke and retire to our beds.

***

It was still raining the next morning. I came awake slowly to the sound of rain on the roof, my face buried in the back of Michael's neck. My breath ruffled his short hair as I heaved a sigh, and I felt him stir.

"G'morning," I greeted him, and he murmured a sleepy reply. Lost in a pleasant doze, we snuggled together listening to the sound of the rain on the roof for a good, long while, before a different, alien sound finally brought us both awake. It was the sound of a small engine moving down the road outside our building.

I opened my eyes reluctantly and rose, to pull on a t-shirt and underwear. Content with being halfway-decent, I wandered out into the living room to investigate the unfamiliar noise. Hemi waved up at me when he spotted me peeking through the curtains, and I waved back. He was soaked to the bone from the rain, but his smile was broad as he greeted me.

"*Kia ora!*" he called when I opened the window and leaned out. "We've come to visit, brought you some *kai*. Where are your friends?"

"Probably still sleeping," I called back, amused. "It's the crack of dawn, and we didn't realise you were coming. Give us a minute and we'll be downstairs."

"Sweet as." He gave me his funny, lopsided grin, and settled down on his farm bike to wait.

I pulled back from the window and returned to our bedroom, where Michael was stretching languidly in bed. It took all of my willpower not to get distracted admiring the tan he'd acquired over the last week. "Your friend Hemi is here to visit. Put some pants on, you nudist."

He grinned at me and rolled out of bed to do just that. A few minutes later, when both of us were properly dressed, we trundled downstairs to greet our visitors. Although I was always concerned about our security, we left most of our weapons behind. I kept my taser in my pocket just in case, but no guns. I had to admit that I felt a little naked confronting another survivor relatively unarmed, but Michael was unconcerned.

By the time we walked out the front door, Hemi was off his bike and waiting for us. A woman had joined him, and the two stood comfortably in the rain exchanging light banter in their native tongue.

When we emerged, Hemi grinned brightly and approached us both with a hand extended. "G'day, mate – sorry to wake you."

"*Kia ora*, mate. *Haere mai,*" Michael greeted the young man like they'd been friends all their lives, with a warm handshake and a broad smile. I hung back and watched them, amused and secretly impressed by Michael's social graces. Not only did he speak sign language, but he spoke decent Maori as well. I knew the basics from back in school, but I could never quite tell the contexts apart. He didn't seem to have any problem with it at all.

Suddenly, I realised the woman was watching me, and I tensed up as I was assessed. I felt oddly uncomfortable, uncertain whether I was being considered as a potential friend, enemy, or rival.

The strange woman was unabashedly beautiful, with creamy brown skin and long, dark hair that fell in waves down her back. Her lips were full and sensual, the lower one stained by a *moko*, a Maori tribal tattoo, that curled down across her chin. Although she looked older than I was, her skin was smooth and unflawed by age, and there was no trace of grey in her hair.

But it was her eyes that struck me most. Although dark and framed by long lashes, they spoke a whole other language to the rest of her body. There was a confidence in them, a quiet strength and a hypnotic personal magnetism; she held my gaze unflinchingly, and I was caught by her charisma.

I wasn't afraid to admit that I felt a little bit intimidated. Those beautiful eyes held such deep intelligence that I felt small by comparison. I found myself trapped by her charm, hypnotised, afraid to make eye-contact but equally afraid to look away.

In the end, it was she that broke the staring contest, not I. She looked away when Hemi started to introduce her to Michael, leaving me feeling shy and uncertain as I lurked in the background.

"This is my mum, the boss-lady." Hemi had his usual impish grin on, and the strange woman smiled in return. The expression softened her beauty, and I felt my tension ease a little.

"*Kia ora.*" She accepted Michael's outstretched hand with grace. "My name is Anahera. I lead what little is left of the Waikato *iwi*." Then she looked straight at me, and gave me a smile that made my heart race. "And what is your name, my dear? You are very quiet."

"Sandy. Sandy McDermott." I felt a surge of panic as all eyes turned towards me, and barely managed to get my name out before anxiety overwhelmed me. I looked to Michael for rescue; he understood immediately that my self-confidence was low and stepped in on my behalf.

"She's a bit cautious around strangers." He glanced at me to make sure it was okay to tell them; I nodded, silently giving him permission. "She's had a few bad experiences."

Anahera nodded her understanding, and then she approached me with a grace that was almost feline. When she was close enough, she went to take my hand and I allowed her to gently draw me in, to press the tip of her nose to mine. Having a stranger so close to me made me tense up, but I knew it was only a *hongi* – a greeting – and that she meant me no harm.

"It is good to meet you, Sandy McDermott," she said softly as we parted. "Hemi says I have you to thank for the fact that I still have a son."

My cheeks started to burn, but I managed an unsteady smile. "It was a group effort. Michael made the killing blow."

"She's also modest," he commented dryly as he wandered over to put a protective arm around me. "We're just glad we could help."

"And you did, more than you know," she replied. "Between your doctor's medicine and his expertise, you may have saved my entire *whanau*. I feel that we owe you a debt that can never be repaid." Anahera bowed her head in respect, and said a few words in her native tongue that I didn't understand.

Michael seemed to, though. He smiled and bowed his head in return. "You honour us with your presence, *ariki*."

"Bah," she said, flapping a hand. "That title does not fit me. I am no chieftain, I'm just the only one of us left with any ability to organise these slackers into some kind of community. Before the plague, I was a teacher."

A teacher, huh? I thought to myself. With cleavage like that, it's a wonder that her students got anything done...

Oh crap. Was I jealous?

I suddenly felt ashamed of myself, and lowered my gaze while Michael led our guests to the entrance of our motel and invited them in out of the rain.

"My brothers will be here shortly with your gifts," Anahera added. Just inside the entrance, she stopped to admire the building. "Ah. I see you have built a *pa* of your own here. Well done."

She nodded her approval, and stepped out into the rain to examine our little vegetable garden. The moisture didn't seem to bother her, and I found myself distracted, admiring her curvaceous figure with some confusion. She was so beautiful, I found watching her fascinating.

Then came a flash of panic when I realised that Michael would be just as attracted to her natural magnetism as I was. I looked up at him, and found him... looking right back at me. He smiled and touched my chin, lifting it up just a little for the softest of kisses while no one was looking.

I couldn't believe it. Someone so beautiful right in front of him, and he only had eyes for me? Even *I* wanted to stare at her all day, and I wasn't even inclined that way. Either I was the luckiest woman alive, or my new lover was crazy.

*You know what? I think I'm okay with that,* I decided after a moment of careful consideration.

"Are these strawberry seedlings I see here?" Anahera called to us, attracting our attention to where she was pointing. When we nodded, she made a sound of delight. "You have many plants we don't have. Would you be willing to trade seeds some time?"

"Share and share alike, my friend," Michael said, all boyish charm and diplomacy. "We know of a patch run wild not far from here, and we're happy for you to help yourselves so long as you leave some for us."

"You are rare, generous souls." Anahera's smile was so radiant that it made my stomach do a flip-flop. "I am pleased to have you as our neighbours. Too many have become wrapped up in themselves in these self-absorbed days, and forget that community is what will keep the human spirit alive."

I felt an odd mix of emotions: a swell of pride at her praise, coupled with a sense of guilt that I would have handled things so much differently if I were the leader of our group. She was right, and I was one of those selfish ones. Without Michael's sweet soul to temper me, I was just another greedy survivor clutching her precious scraps. I didn't like that feeling.

"I agree completely," Michael said, oblivious to my internal conflict. "Come and meet the rest of our group."

Although Michael led the way, he kept his arm looped around my waist in a manner that was both protective and a little bit possessive. I couldn't help but wonder if he had seen me looking at Anahera, and was feeling just as jealous as I had been a few minutes ago. There was no chance to ask him or reassure him now, though. A moment later, we entered the kitchen where the others were sitting around the table discussing breakfast.

Introductions were made, with Anahera showing delight over the littlest members of our company. She greeted Maddy like an adult, and spoke softly to her until the child beamed and nodded happily. Then her attention turned to Skylar, who blushed and smiled shyly when the older woman crooned over her belly; she looked both confused and pleased by the attention at the same time.

"When are you due, dear one?" Anahera asked. "It must be soon, surely?"

Skylar nodded and rubbed a hand over her belly as though to soothe her unborn child. "In about a month, a little less. Very soon."

"Ah, it must be terribly uncomfortable in this heat," Anahera said sympathetically. She reached over and hovered a hand above Skye's belly, then shot the young woman a quizzical look. Skylar nodded her permission, and Anahera gently rested her hand upon her tummy. "I remember being pregnant with my youngest son at this time of year. It was terrible. I spent half my time soaking in a cold bath just to keep the swelling in my ankles at bay."

Skye smiled at the understanding, and rubbed the side of her belly. "I do that sometimes, too. Well a cold shower, anyway. She kicks more when it's too hot, and the cold water calms her down."

"Ah, feel her kicking now!" Anahera laughed, and it was the sweetest sound I'd ever heard. "I think she knows we're talking about her."

Skylar's smile faded, though, replaced by an intense concern. "I'm sorry to ask, ma'am, but… have any women in your community had babies since the outbreak?"

Anahera drew back and stared intently at my sister, clearly sensing there was a reason behind the question. "No. I am the only woman in my community, and I will not take another man since the plague took my husband." Her head shifted a little, tilting to one side. "Why do you ask, dear?"

Skye looked at me for help, obviously a little uncertain what to say. Despite my instinctive reticence, I stepped in to the rescue. "There was some research that I read, which said that immunity is not necessarily passed from mother to child. We're worried that her baby might get infected."

Anahera's expression changed to one of concern. "I am afraid I have no information to give you, but I pray that does not happen."

The conversation was interrupted at that point by the sound of quad bikes outside. Of course, I felt anxious that we were about to be attacked, but no one else looked worried. Anahera quickly informed us that it was just her tribe-mates arriving with their gifts for us.

Anahera and Michael led the way back outside, with the rest of us trailing along in a rag-tag group strung out behind them. I brought up the rear, and was the last one to step back out into the moody weather. By the time I left the building, the leaders of our two groups had descended on the quad bikes and were chatting about something I couldn't quite hear.

I lingered near the doorway, feeling mildly uncomfortable. More strangers to worry about, more potential dangers. My inner recluse was not happy. While the others splintered off to investigate the newcomers, I stood quietly in the doorway, watching Michael. Even at a distance, I found his presence reassuring. A humid breeze caught my hair and tugged a few loose tendrils across my face. I reached up to pluck them out of my eyes, and tuck them back behind my ear—

—and then I froze, as a cold sensation shot right through me from the back of my throat to the tip of my toes.

There were three quad bike riders standing in a gaggle off to one side, obviously members of Anahera's tribe. They stood in a group watching the leaders chat, shoulders slouched and hands in pockets. They were oblivious to me.

I wished I could say the same. Two of the three faces were unfamiliar to me.

The third one was not.

The shaking began as a faint trembling in my hands when recognition hit me. Then came the panic in icy, surging waves that rippled through my body from head to toe, and made my body shake harder and harder, until I thought that I could hear the sound of my bones rattling in their joints.

Skylar said something to me but I couldn't hear what she was saying over the rush of noise in my own eardrums. I took a step back, and then another, but my back hit the wall beside the door and I couldn't quite assemble my thoughts enough to turn around.

I knew that horrible face, with its flat, oft-broken nose.

I knew the tattoos that wound across his brow like a wicked serpent.

I knew that corpulent body, the one that hid thick muscle deep beneath its fat.

Oh God.

Skylar was looking at me and I knew that she was concerned, but I couldn't understand what she was saying. I couldn't breathe.

Oh God. Oh God.

It was the spectre from my nightmares, my tormentor, the one that writhed and hit. I heard the sound of flesh striking flesh, and I felt the pain all over again.

He was here. The demon was here, in my home.

I'd prayed so hard that I would never see him again.

I felt hands on me and then I felt myself being dragged inside until I could no longer see the demon. Once he was gone from my sight, I collapsed both literally and figuratively. The hands caught me as I fell, and supported me.

"Sandy? What's wrong?" I heard my sister's voice, but it sounded like it was coming from a million miles away. Stars danced around the edge of my vision, and I felt like I was falling, falling, falling...

The next thing I knew, I was lying down with a semi-circle of concerned faces hovering around me: Skylar, Ryan, and Madeline. They were familiar faces, friendly faces, and yet I couldn't put aside the uncontrollable, animal panic. I couldn't speak, couldn't control my limbs. I suddenly realised that I was crying, but I was too afraid to make a sound.

"Maddy, go get your granddad," I heard Skylar say.

The little girl shook her head. "No... we should get Mister Michael."

"What? She needs a doctor, not her boyfriend." Skylar leapt to her feet to go fetch the doctor herself, but Maddy sprang up as well and grabbed her hand to hold her back.

"You don't understand; the bad man is here." The little girl stared at her, then repeated the words with an intensity that should never have come from a child's lips. "*The bad man is here.*"

Skylar stared at her, not quite comprehending what she was saying for what felt like forever. Finally, something seemed to come together in her mind. Her eyes widened in shock.

"*The* bad man?" She hesitated for a moment then made a snap decision. "I'll go get Michael."

All this time I felt like I was paralysed, watching a play unfold before me. It was less than a minute before Skylar returned, but it felt like an eternity. Michael was with her, my kind, sweet Michael, and his concerned face joined the circle that floated above me.

"Jesus... Sandy? Sandy, what's wrong?" His gentle fingers caressed my cheek, and came away wet with my tears. It took all of my willpower to raise my hand just a little bit, but it was trembling so badly I couldn't coordinate it enough to touch his hand.

"The bad man is here," Maddy repeated softly for Michael's benefit. Like Skylar, he just stared at her, confused for a second before understanding appeared on his face.

Then, driven by some sixth sense, he reached for me and gathered my shivering body up against his broad chest, to cradle me close against him.

His warmth was like a pillar of light to my ice-cold mind, the tonic that I needed to coax my frozen muscles back to life. A convulsion shook my entire body as I wrapped my arms around his waist, and buried my face in his chest.

"Sandy, sweetheart." His voice was a gruff whisper, and he stroked my hair tenderly. "Talk to me. Tell me, which one of them did it? Which one of them hurt you?"

The sobs wracking my body left me mute and inarticulate, but Maddy knew.

"It was the one with the bad drawings on his face," she said, staring at Michael like he would know what that meant.

"Bad drawings? Do you mean the tattoos?" he asked, but she was only a little girl and didn't know what that meant.

"What's happening?" A new voice entered the fray, one that I recognised as Anahera. There was a gasp, and then another body joined the circle around me. "Is she all right?"

Michael's voice was like ice, so cold it practically froze the hot summer air. "Are you aware that one of your brothers is a rapist?"

There it was. The R-word. The worst four letters of the English language, and spoken from the lips of the man I cared about. I muffled a sob against his chest.

"What?" Anahera's voice was soft but it carried so much dangerous intensity that for a moment I felt a wave of irrational alarm. They were going to hurt me, going to hurt my sister, hurt my unborn niece, hurt my Michael.

No, no!

But I couldn't see her face. I didn't see the anger, the unbridled fury that bubbled up from deep within her. I didn't know that it wasn't targeted at me. Oh, but I could hear her voice, the hiss of her breath through clenched teeth. "Which one of them did it?"

"T-the one with the full face moko..." I said, struggling to summon the willpower to name my abuser because I couldn't bear the thought of little Madeline having to say the words again.

There was a sound like a growl from the beautiful woman, an animal thing of wild and primal fury, and then she was up on her feet and gone. Suddenly I was afraid for her, afraid for my family, and my instinct was to fight. I struggled against the palsy that held me, unintentionally fighting against Michael's grip as well – but he understood. His strong hands helped me to my feet and kept me upright until I could stand on my own. I shook off the dizziness and headed to the door, with my family hot on my heels.

As I made it to the doorway with the others in a gaggle behind me, I could hear the sound of raised voices arguing back and forth in the Maori tongue. Then I heard the distinctive sound of a fist striking flesh, and I was afraid Anahera was being attacked.

As it turned out, I needn't have worried for her. It was her fist that I heard, and the target of her ire was the very one that was causing my distress. He was screaming at her, spitting curses around a mouth full of bloody teeth, but he was held back by the three other men of his tribe. His leader struck him, again and again with astounding viciousness, until her knuckles ran red with his blood.

He didn't look so terrifying now, not when he slumped semi-conscious in the arms of his captors, and his own leader kicked him so hard that I saw teeth fly. Then, panting heavily with exertion, she gestured to her companions and they dropped their captive in the dirt. She saw me, trembling amongst my family, and she turned to face me.

"He would not deny it," she spat the words like they tasted bad, as enraged as a wild cat. "All these years he's lied to us, told us that his only crimes were petty thefts." She jerked a finger at the slumped man, and her brothers hauled him back to his knees. "This is the one, dear heart? You are sure? He is the one that hurt you?"

I could only nod; there was no way I would ever forget that horrible face.

"Wait." There was a voice behind me, and then Michael walked past me with the strangest look on his face. "I didn't realise it before, but I think I know this man as well. It's been a long time."

"From where?" Anahera asked softly as she stared at him, her eyes narrowed dangerously in the grips of an irrational berserker rage.

Michael circled the prisoner and stared at him from all angles, his brow knitted deeply in thought. "I know his face. I just… need a moment to remember."

Silence descended over both groups. I stood back drawing deep breaths, trying to keep the shaking in my limbs under control. I worried for my sweetheart, but I was afraid to move closer. I wasn't sure whether I would faint again if I did, or whether I would attack like a pack animal and tear that terrible man apart.

Suddenly, Michael drew a sharp breath and straightened up.

"I remember now." He looked at me for a long moment, and then his dark eyes returned to Anahera. "He was a wanted man, but the riots hit before we could catch him. I'm sorry to say that Sandy wasn't his first victim."

"What did he do?" Anahera's voice was like ice. I could see her twitching, barely in control of her anger. Michael stared at her, almost as though afraid of telling her the truth – or perhaps he was afraid of what he would do to the man himself if he said the words out loud.

"He's a paedophile. A baby killer. He abducted a pair of little girls." Michael closed his eyes and swallowed hard. "Twins. It was all over the news when they went missing. They were… five or six." I felt my stomach drop to my knees. I remembered seeing those sweet-faced children on television. It was one of the last things we saw before the plague became everyone's news. Michael's voice was heavy with sadness as he continued. "He… violated them, strangled them, and then threw them into the Waikato River.

"My colleagues found them," Michael said, his face a grim mask. "One of the girls was already dead, but the other one was still alive. She lived long enough to name her killer, but then she died in hospital. He was her uncle. They distributed pictures of him to everyone in the precinct, and it was all hands on deck looking for him. I don't think I could ever forget those tattoos."

In the silence that followed, tears sprang unbidden into my eyes again. I remembered those little girls. It had been weeks between when they went missing and when they were found. Someone had kidnapped them and tortured them for a long, long time.

Just like me.

It was the softest little noise that broke the silence, but it wasn't a sob or a cry – it was a growl. I looked up and saw Anahera shaking with pent-up fury, her gaze focused on the half-conscious man held up by her brethren. They dropped him unceremoniously in the dirt and stepped back, as though sensing something terrible was to come.

"You–" Her voice was a husky whisper as she rounded on the man, her feet planted wide apart, her hands clenched to fists. "–are not *my brother!*"

The last part wasn't spoken, it was screamed. She punctuated the sentence with a kick so brutal that it sent the tattooed man rolling through the dirt.

Screaming in wordless fury, she chased after the crumpled form and stomped on him again; I heard the tell-tale sound of ribs snapping. Her voice was so loud, so charged with pure rage that it startled birds out of the trees nearby and sent them fluttering away in distress.

At last, exhausted, she stepped back and took a deep breath to calm herself, then turned and looked straight at me.

"He's your *brother*?" I asked, horrified by the idea.

"No, not by birth," she replied. "I consider all the men of my group to be my brothers, in the sense that common interests bind us into a form of adopted kinship. But this one betrayed me and everything that we stand for. He is a murderer. There are no judges anymore. No juries. In *my* tribe, the only just punishment that I see is death." Her voice was dangerously soft, her eyes unreadable. "But, you are the last living person that he sinned against, dear one. His punishment is yours to decide."

"Mine?" The statement didn't quite sink in straight away. She wanted me to decide the fate, the ultimate punishment for the man who had held me captive for days; brutalised me again and again until I was so traumatised that even years later I felt crippling fear every time I met a stranger. This was the man who had left me so emotionally damaged that I struggled to trust even good people, people who were kind to me and showed me generosity far beyond what I deserved. This was the man that had broken my psyche so badly that I was afraid to make love to the man I adored. This was the man who destroyed those beautiful little girls, and most likely many others since then.

It was his fault, and his fate was mine to decide.

But, did I want the blood of another human being on my hands? I had killed before to save myself, but only in the heat of the moment and never in cold blood. That was how I'd escaped from him, three years earlier. He'd gone somewhere and left his lazy, drunk accomplice to use me as he pleased. He'd been careless; now he was dead.

Did I want the ringleader dead as well?

Yes, I did – but also no. Not like that.

"I don't want him to die." My voice was so low and breathless that it forced Anahera to draw closer to hear my words. "He doesn't deserve a quick death. I–" I could hardly believe I was saying this. "I don't know. I think he deserves to suffer, like he made me suffer all of these years. Like he made those little girls suffer. I just want him to understand what he's done to us."

"What do you want me to do to him, dear heart?" she asked softly, her anger diluted by the pain she saw reflected in my eyes.

I shook my head and fought as tears gathered in my eyes. "I don't know. I don't want to know. Just… make him understand. Make it so he'll never want to hurt another girl ever again. Please?"

Anahera watched me quietly for the longest minute, and then she nodded. "I think I understand. You do not wish to cause another person pain, but you must so that others like you never have to feel it. I will do for you what your kind soul cannot."

I nodded, speechless, my face frozen in an attitude of distress. This woman, this teacher-turned-leader – she knew my innermost thoughts.

There was a soft sound of steel on leather, and then a long, curved knife appeared in her hand. "Go inside and rest, dear. This man will never hurt you or any other person ever again."

Michael gathered me to him and hurried me away, but not before I saw the other group pick up the fallen man and drag him off. They took him far away from our home before they began his punishment, but it wasn't far enough.

Even as Michael was tucking me into his bed where I felt safe and protected, I could hear the prisoner screaming.

# Chapter Twenty-Three

The sound of the man's torment haunted my dreams, but in spite of that I slept deeper and longer than I had in years. The spectre no longer haunted me, mocking me, hurting me; the spectre was gone. It was no longer an immortal, inhuman thing, but a physical being that I could fight off and destroy if I needed to.

I wasn't afraid anymore.

It was dark when I awoke, and the room was faintly lit by moonlight through the open window beside the bed. I could hear the sound of breathing in the dark, soft and even, but didn't feel the warmth of a familiar body beside me. I rolled over and saw the faint outline of the man I'd come to care about so much, sitting in his chair by the window. The faintest glint of steel told me that his shotgun rested in his lap. He was protecting me.

"Michael?" I whispered his name in the shadows.

He snapped awake at the sound of my voice; I heard his sharp intake of breath, and saw his outline moving. "Sandy? You're awake?"

"Yeah." I yawned softly and snuggled down in the soft blankets. "Why are you all the way over there?"

"You need some space right now." His voice was soft, but he still rose from his chair to sit on the edge of the bed instead. Close enough for me to reach out and touch him, which I did.

"I'm… okay, I think," I said. I sought out his hand in the dark, and when I found it I twined my fingers through his. "Are they gone?"

"Yes, hours ago." He shifted a little bit and drew my fingers up to his lips to press a soft kiss against them. "They left their gifts and went, and they took him with them. The woman, Anahera, said that they were going to take him as far away from here as they could before they let him go."

"What did they do to him?" I asked. I wasn't really sure that I wanted to know the answer, but morbid curiosity drove me to ask anyway.

"I'm not sure," he replied, but I felt him tense up and knew that he was lying. I decided to let it pass. Would knowing really help me to heal? No, it wouldn't. My imagination could fill in the blanks.

I sighed and sat up, to lean against my sweetheart's broad back. "I wish I knew how to feel right now. Part of me wishes I'd just let her kill him."

"I know," he said, and then heaved a sigh himself. "To tell you the truth, I almost did it myself. If Anahera hadn't been there, then I might have… might have…" He trailed off, and I felt his body tense up again.

"I know," I whispered, sliding my arms around his waist. There was no need for him to finish the sentence. I knew what he was thinking. Still, there were so many questions left unanswered, about everything. "Michael?"

"Hm?" He glanced over his shoulder at me.

"Why do you think he did it?" I asked. "Not just to me, but to the others. God knows how many women and children he's murdered over the years."

Again there was silence, but this time it was while he thought it over. Finally, he spoke again, hesitant and uncertain. "I think that he just didn't care. I've seen men like him before, men that think women just exist to please them. They have no respect for the sanctity of human lives." I heard a deep intake of breath, let out as a sharp exhalation a moment later. "People like that don't deserve to live."

I pondered that response and weighed my conflicting emotions against one another. He was right, of course. Some people were just born evil, and no amount of nurturing or punishment would break them of the habits that nature had bred into their psyches. As much as I'd have liked to put some logic to my former tormentor's decisions, there simply wasn't any. I was just unlucky. He'd seen me all alone, and that was enough. If not for a moment of luck weeks later, that would have signed my death warrant.

I lay my head against my policeman's back and closed my eyes as I sifted through my muddled feelings. On the one hand, I felt terrible for being the source of someone else's misery. On the other, he deserved it. Those little girls hadn't deserved their fate, but they certainly deserved justice. I was sure there were others out there like me, whether they were alive or dead.

But now I'd had my justice. That feeling brought with it a sense of peace. What was there to be afraid of, if that man was no longer a threat? I smiled to myself and snuggled closer to Michael, enjoying the warmth of his skin beneath my cheek. In my lowest moment, he'd not only stayed true to me, but he'd helped me to get that justice.

While Anahera had been the judge, jury, and executioner, Michael was my officer of the law. My protector. My hero.

"Michael?" I whispered his name again, a flush of warmth rising in my cheeks. It'd been such a long time coming, but at last I truly felt safe.

There was a faint sound of movement as he turned towards me, and then his big hands drew me up against his chest. I snuggled in against him happily, feeling content and relaxed.

"I think I'm ready," I whispered the words softly in the darkness, trailing my fingers across his stomach. I could feel the heat of his skin beneath the light t-shirt he was wearing, and I longed to strip it away and have him all to myself.

One of his hands cupped my chin and tilted it upwards and his lips met mine in the darkness. He kissed me slowly and tenderly for what felt like forever, before finally drawing back to give me a quirky smile that I could only half see. "No, you're not."

That was not the answer I expected.

"What? Yes, I am!" I protested in confusion.

"No, you're not, and neither am I." Although it was dark, I could see and feel his tension, and it was not a kind of tension I recognised. I didn't like the way it felt. Still, his hands were gentle as he ran his fingers through my long hair. "Sandy, if we were to do this now, it wouldn't be about you and me. It would be about him, and revenge."

I froze, not sure what to say to that.

He did, though. His voice dropped low as he cupped my face in his hands. "I don't want that. I want to wait until it's perfect and we're both ready for it. I want it to be about us, just us, no one else. This isn't just about sex to me, you know that. This is about the fact that I love you, Sandy McDermott – and I want you to love me back."

"Y-you... what?" Did he just say what I thought he said? It took me totally by surprise in a moment when I was already off balance.

But Michael, he just smiled enigmatically and silenced me with a kiss.

\*\*\*

The thought that someone loved me galvanised me for days. Although we didn't speak about it again, I found myself in a rare good mood that nothing seemed to be able to shake. My foot had finally healed enough that I could walk around without pain, my family was safe and gradually settling into a comfortable routine, and I had a sweet, kind man that loved me.

Loved me. Loved *me*. In spite all of my flaws, he loved me.

I wasn't angry at him for rejecting my proposal that night, because in reality he was right. If we had made love, it wouldn't have been as special when the wound was still so raw. Amongst other reasons, it would be his first time ever and he deserved more than a wild fuck fuelled by hatred and revenge. I wanted our first time together to be special, too.

I often thought of the man whose name I had never learned over the days that followed. Eventually, my feelings of guilt faded, replaced by a strong sense of relief. Although he was still alive out there somewhere, he had lost his demonic countenance within my mind and my nightmares. It seemed apt that Anahera was the weapon of his punishment – another woman, the avenging angel for his victims. I hoped his other victims could feel the sense of relief that I felt now, if they were still alive. If not, then I hoped they rested easier for knowing they had been avenged.

I wondered if perhaps I would have to face him alone someday, if he might come after me. For the first time, I was no longer afraid of that thought. He was no longer a faceless, mocking beast that writhed and hurt me in my memory. That memory had been overwritten by one where he was just another human being, just as weak and pathetic as the rest of us. The difference was that he had chosen to act out and try to make himself look strong by taking advantage of those who were weaker than him, something that I would never do. That made him nothing more than the worst kind of bully.

If it ever came to a point where I had to kill that man, I decided that I'd think of Anahera and try to be strong like her. My initial admiration of her had grown into something more like hero-worship, although I knew as well as anyone that it was ridiculous to worship someone who was just as human as I am. She was just as flawed on the inside, and yet she showed so many traits that I coveted – her emotional fortitude was just one of them. I truly hoped that one day, I would grow to be like her.

Beauty tempered by intelligence. Ruthlessness tempered by compassion. Strength tempered by gentleness. She was everything I wanted to be. She reminded me of my grandmother, my namesake and the woman who had inspired so much of my early life before I lost her to the plague. I thought having a new, living role-model would be good for me in the long term. I could only hope that having her to look up to would help me grow as a person. Was there anything else that anyone could ever really ask for?

In the days that followed, my group was well-fed but not entirely content. We spent most of our time tending to our little garden as a safeguard against winter's inevitable arrival, but there was a thread of disharmony that ran through every conversation. Not everyone was happy about the punishment that Anahera had handed out on our behalf. Even I, the most socially inept of us, sensed the discontent amongst the group and it made me feel uncomfortable.

On the third day, Michael found me sitting alone in the kitchen in the middle of the afternoon, brooding over a cup of black coffee.

"Why the long face, honey?" he asked. I almost jumped out of my skin when his voice broke the silence, and promptly spilled hot coffee all over myself and the table.

"Ah, shit." Sorry, Mum. "Ow. Michael! Don't sneak up on me like that," I complained, as I leapt up to go run my hand under a cold tap. I heard him chuckling behind me, and then one strong arm slid around my waist from behind.

"Sorry," he murmured softly in my ear, then planted a kiss upon my cheek. "So, why the long face? Are you sulking again?

I paused for a long moment and thought over my answer, then I let out a deep sigh and shrugged. "I've been thinking about him."

Michael nodded. I didn't have to explain which 'him' I meant. "He's long gone, honey. You don't have to worry about him anymore."

"It's not that." I switched the tap off and turned around to face him, though I couldn't quite meet his eye. "It's... I don't know if we've done the right thing, Michael. How do we know what's right and wrong? It used to be that we had people specially trained to do this for us, but now what do we do? If the law falls into the hands of the people that it's supposed to be protecting... I'm not sure I like where I can imagine that taking us."

Michael went silent as he thought over what I was saying, and then he nodded again. "We do need some form of justice, but not just lynch-mob justice."

"Exactly," I said. I put my arms around his waist and leaned against him, but for once his strength couldn't banish the troubled thoughts from my mind. Eventually, I sighed again, and looked up at him. "What do we do?"

Michael stared off into space for a few seconds, lost in thought. "I have an idea, but I think it should be a group decision. Let's get everyone together."

"Okay," I said, nodding my agreement. We separated then, and went off to round up our friends.

Twenty minutes later, we had our entire group – all six of us, including Madeline – gathered together in the kitchen around the table. As our leader, Michael stood at the head of the table while everyone settled into their places.

"Thank you for coming," he said in that soft, deep voice of his, the one that always carried a note of strength and command. "As you all know, we recently had to deal with an issue that has left many of us feeling troubled. I think that we need to address the matter, and set up rules for the future. As Sandy once pointed out to me, the world outside our nice little bunker is not a safe place. We already have our own code of conduct, but we need to establish some method for dealing with things when they get out of hand."

"You mean, what do we do if someone *else* tries to rape our women and murder our children?" Skylar asked, her face pale and tense. Out of all of us, she had been the one most vocal in her discontent. "We should have killed him. The just thing to do would have been to kill him!"

"You don't know that," the doctor interrupted, and waggled a finger at Skye like a disapproving school teacher. "Who are we to decide if a man lives or dies? If we start murdering people wantonly, then we become no better than they are. Who are we to play God with the lives of others?"

"But now he knows where we live," she argued back vehemently. "What if he decides that he wants to come after us for revenge? What happens then? What about Sandy – or me and Maddy? We're just his type!"

"Enough." Michael held up his hands for silence, and then looked each and every one of us in the eye. When he got to me, he gave me a soft, reassuring smile. He could see that I was tense and nervous, but his smile made me feel better. "What's done is done. We can't change that. We're going to be alert and careful in case something does happen, but what I've gathered you here for is to work out a way to prevent this kind of disharmony from happening in future."

"You said you had an idea?" I said softly, to prevent further argument from breaking out.

"I do," he replied with a nod. "I suggest that we use a system not unlike the one that we had before the plague, to ensure that justice is had for all. If a crime is committed, then we appoint one person to act as an adjudicator and consider the evidence. If the person is found guilty, then all of us vote on the punishment. The adjudicator would be the person who has the least emotional investment in the crime that occurred. That way, everyone has a chance to have their say, but we're not driven purely by emotion."

"Who suggests the punishments?" I asked, genuinely curious. It was an interesting idea, but I shouldn't have been surprised. Michael *was* our paragon of justice, after all.

"The victim, if they want to," he answered, "or if they're not comfortable then the adjudicator can. It's unlikely that any of us could be completely impartial towards someone that hurt one of our friends, but I think that's as close as we're going to get."

"That... does seem fair." Skylar had calmed down enough to look interested in the discussion, and beside her Ryan nodded thoughtfully.

Michael and I looked towards the Doc, and he nodded as well. "I also agree with your proposal. I feel it is important that we do everything we can to avoid descending back into barbarism."

"I think it's a good idea." The little voice that spoke up was the last one that we expected: Madeline. We all turned and looked at the girl, who stared back at us with huge, solemn eyes. "There are bad men out there. Lots and lots of bad men. Some bad ladies, too. We should be careful. We don't want to become bad like them. Do we?"

None of us quite knew what to say to that, but it settled the issue once and for all. By universal consensus, we had created our own internal judicial system. I think that we all felt better for having that, even if we hoped that we'd never have to use it.

# Chapter Twenty-Four

A few days later, I found myself wandering through our motel looking for my sister, feeling relaxed and content for the first time in what felt like forever.

I drifted past the hydroponics room, but instead of Skylar I found the doctor focused on the tiny seedlings while he instructed his granddaughter in their care. They were oblivious to me, but I stood and watched for a moment anyway. A surge of affection rose in me. Although we share no blood ties, they were becoming like family to me. Mutual survival bonded you in a way I'd never understood before. Now that I did, I felt strangely complete.

I left them without alerting them to my passing and moved on.

A few minutes later, I peeked into the communal lounge, where I found Ryan and Michael lost in conversation over some point of maleness that was completely irrelevant to me. Again, I retreated without being seen, and left them to their bonding as I moved on in search of Skylar.

When at last I found my little sister, she was where I least expected her to be: in her own room, curled up in bed, looking pale and unhappy. She wasn't asleep though, and when I stepped into the room she looked up at me with sad eyes.

"Hey, you," I said. Suddenly concerned, I forgot all about the reason I had been looking for her, and crossed the room to seat myself on the edge of her bed.

"Hey." She gave me a pathetic look, and nuzzled miserably at her pillow.

"What's wrong?" I asked, reaching out to brush a strand of hair off her cheek.

"I feel like crap," she replied. "My head's been hurting for days and I feel like throwing up all the time."

"Have you told Doctor Cross?" I asked, concern twisting like a knife in my gut.

She shook her head. "I don't want to worry anyone…"

"I'm sure you'll be fine." I tried my best to sound reassuring, then leaned down to plant a kiss on her forehead, just like Mum used to do when we were little. "Let me get Doctor Cross anyway, just in case."

She nodded silently, and that was permission enough for me. I patted her head one last time, then rose and went off in search of the doctor. He was exactly where I'd last seen him, so it didn't take much effort. When I told him what she'd said to me, he nodded thoughtfully.

"Pregnancy comes with many aches and pains and mysterious illnesses all the way through, particularly towards the end," he said in that self-assured way of his, the doctor's voice that says everything would be just fine. "I'll go check on her anyway."

"Thank you, doctor." I gave him a smile to mask my own worry, and watched him leave to check on her. Maddy skipped along after him, singing to herself, and left me alone with my internal anxiety.

'I don't want to worry anyone.'

Something about the way she'd said that bothered me immensely. Skye was never one to mince words when she was feeling slighted or unhappy about something. Why would she suddenly change her mind completely?

Unless… unless she knew in her gut that it was something serious.

I shook my head to dismiss the thought. If it had been something serious, then the doctor would have picked up on it before. He'd been watching Skye like a hawk through the last few weeks of her pregnancy. It seemed unlikely that something serious would miss his attention so completely. She was probably just feeling hot and bothered in the humidity, like the rest of us.

I decided that a present was in order, to cheer up both the parties involved, so off I went to get my things. Once I had my taser and my radio safely in my pockets, I set off on a scavenger hunt to find the perfect gift for my little sister.

In my head, I ran through the list of appropriate things that I'd seen over the last few weeks. Something for the baby would be best, but the question was what? There was a home not far away that had once housed a young family. I remembered that there had been toys and children's books scattered all over the living room. That seemed like a logical place to start. I broke into a jog and headed off towards the building in question, feeling a surge of simple joy over the fact that I could run again.

It was a quaint little house, surrounded by small gardens and what was left of a white picket fence. Once, it had been someone's dream home. Now, the paint was cracked and peeling, baked by ten years' worth of sun with no maintenance, and the garden was a jungle just like all the others. The gate shrieked in protest when I opened it and then I picked my way along the remains of the garden path towards the front door.

I had left it unlocked when I'd last visited, and everything was exactly the same as it had been weeks earlier. To my left, a tiny kitchen and dining room stood beneath a thick layer of dust. To my right, an archway led to a small living room, with cheap, overstuffed couches in front of the television. Toys still scattered the floor.

I bent to examine the toys, searching for something suitable, but none of them seemed quite right to cheer Skye up today. Perhaps when the baby was old enough to play then I could come back for them, but for now they stayed where they were.

A narrow staircase led to the second floor. I scampered up it, feeling light-footed and agile. Doorways flanked the hall leading to a couple of bedrooms. The first one I opened had obviously once belonged to a young girl. Dolls lay discarded where they fell, stuffed animals lined the bed; everything was pink and pretty, all ballerinas and fairies and princesses. It looked just like Skye's room before the outbreak. For once in my life, that thought made me want to laugh instead of cry.

The second room I cracked open was more promising: it was the baby's room. It was hard not to think about the fact that both of those innocent children were dead now, but I tried to ignore that as I crossed the room to peer into the crib.

A little pink blanket lay folded across the foot of the bassinet. I reached out and touched it, marvelling at its softness. Upon it sat a little matching teddy bear, waiting to receive the newest addition to the family, the one that would never come.

*It will now,* I thought, and that cheered me up. These were just perfect. I gathered up the teddy and the blanket, and gave both of them a gentle shake to rid them of the dust, then I hurried out of the little house and headed back towards my home.

A few minutes later I bounded up the stairs towards Skylar's room with my prizes clutched to my chest – only to find a small group of people standing outside the door. Everyone was there, except for the doctor and Skye. Concern returned like a sledgehammer, and this time it socked me full in the jaw. I hurried over to join them, my gifts forgotten.

"What's happening?" I whispered and tried to push through them to get a better view. No one had an answer for me.

Panic swelled up in full force, so I squeezed my relatively small frame between the men and burst into my sister's room. I found the doctor bent over her, so intently focused that he didn't notice my arrival until I was right beside him. Skylar lay unconscious on the blankets, her skin so pale and waxy that there was no way that it could be normal.

"She appears to have contracted an infection." Dr Cross' soft voice broke the silence as he checked a small thermometer resting in my sister's mouth. Even I could see that the fever burned painfully high.

"But how?" I demanded, tears leaping unbidden into my eyes. "We've been so careful to keep her safe."

"Pregnant women are just more susceptible to infection than any other normal, healthy adult," he replied, his frown more intense than usual. The last time I'd seen his scowl etched that deeply was when he was tending to poor Dog. That expression did nothing to reassure me. "It may have been something she ate. Sadly, we do not have the facilities to run blood tests to figure out exactly what it is. I am giving her the strongest broad-spectrum antibiotic she can have in her condition, and we'll just have to hope that it's enough."

I felt an arm creep around me and realised Michael had joined me. His support was very, very welcome. As soon as I felt him there, my strength drained away. I sagged against him and let him lead me away from the bed so that we weren't in the way. There was only one chair in the room, so he sat and drew me into his lap, then held me close while we waited.

Darkness fell, and Skylar still didn't wake up.

\*\*\*

Late that night, I was dozing when a scream jerked me awake; a terrible, bloody scream of unbearable pain. I was up a second later with Michael right behind me, and we hurried to the bedside where I found the doctor struggling to hold my sister down. She was writhing in agony, and I realised with horror that there was a terrible red stain spreading below the waist of her nightshirt and inching across the blankets beneath her.

"Help me," the doctor begged us for aid, and we both leapt in to try and hold my frantic sister. She was oblivious to us all, and her body seemed to hold an unnatural amount of strength. A third set of hands joined us; I glanced up, and saw Ryan's ghost-pale face join us while we struggled to control her convulsions.

Suddenly the doctor was holding a syringe, which he injected it into Skylar's pale, sweating arm. It took a minute before she relaxed as the painkillers took effect, but even once the convulsions stopped she was whimpering and her eyes rolled in her head. It was a terrifying sight. All the while, the blood was spreading.

"She's going to lose the baby," I whispered, clinging to Michael for support through the shock and horror of that realisation. The doctor blew out a short breath, and a look of regret pinched his brow.

"Yes," he admitted. His shoulders slumped, and he looked at me with the kind of expression that made me want to run and hide rather than hear what he was going to say. "And I'm not sure I'm going to be able to save her, either."

I felt like I'd been punched in the face, or the gut, or maybe both. I had found my baby sister, alive after all these years, and I was going to lose her again after just a few short weeks? It seemed impossibly cruel and so terribly unfair.

"No... no, no, no, please – you have to save her!" I begged. The words tumbled out of me without control, pleading, as if sheer force of will could save her life.

"I have no intention of giving up, Ms McDermott, but you need to understand there is a strong possibility that she may not make it." The doctor shook his head regretfully, then seemed to steel himself. "Please leave the room; I will call you if I need you."

Although the doctor's voice was soft it felt like he'd yelled at me. Michael had to drag me bodily from the room. I fought to stay even though I knew there was nothing that I could do, driven by primitive instincts that had no real name. Eventually I gave up and sank into Michael's arms, my emotions surging with such force that I couldn't figure out which one of them to respond to first.

It was all a matter of time, and hope. I had no choice but to put all my faith in Dr Cross' skills, pray that they would be enough.

***

It was breakfast time but no one felt like eating. My sister's screams were raw and primal. Every time one of us relaxed, another scream would come and put us all back on edge.

I had managed to doze for a few minutes with my head lolling against Michael's shoulder, but it wasn't enough to actually rest. I felt wrung out and exhausted, emotionally drained and tense to the point of snapping.

At one point, Ryan rushed out from the sick room and summoned Michael for his skills as a blood donor, leaving me alone with little Madeline.

She had no wisdom for me today.

A short time later, Michael returned looking pale and woozy, but he refused to go to bed. He sat beside me and wrapped his arms around me again, letting me bury my face against his chest.

Even his warmth couldn't hide the terrible sound of my baby sister in agony. My sweet little baby sister. I loved her so much that it was unbearable.

Eventually, the screams trailed off to a distant, pathetic sobbing, then they stopped altogether. A few minutes later, an exhausted Dr Cross emerged from the sick room and found us huddled together. We looked at him expectantly, but he just shook his head.

"I have done all I can." His voice was hoarse and regretful, and he wouldn't make eye-contact with me. "Only time will tell now."

The memory of an identical statement made just before Dog's death flashed through my mind. I was up before Michael could stop me and dashed past the doctor, back into my sister's room.

Ryan sat on the edge of their bed, cradling something wrapped in the soft pink blanket I'd intended as a gift for my sister. As I drew closer, I realised that it was the baby. It was dead.

The baby's skin was a terrible shade of blue-purple, and its tiny face was contorted and stiff. Tears ran down Ryan's cheeks as he looked down at the tiny child in his arms, the terrible litany of loss written across his freckled face.

"We were going to name her Kylie, after her grandmother," he said softly when he saw me, cuddling his firstborn daughter, dead before he had the chance to know her. "Kylie Sandrine Knowles-McDermott. That was going to be her name. She was going to have beautiful blue eyes like her mama, and my freckles, and we were going to teach her to sing and read and play games with us. We were–" His voice broke, and he trailed off into sobbing, the tiny body clutched against his chest.

I didn't know what to say. There was nothing I could say that would make this better. The baby was dead, and with her all their hopes and dreams for a family together.

Behind him, my sister lay unconscious, her breathing shallow and uneven. Her skin was waxy, and so very pale I felt like what little hope I had left would never be enough to save her.

The tears gathered in my eyes and I let them fall unhindered as I knelt beside her bed. In my mind's eye, she was still that sweet-faced little girl I adored. She would always be my baby sister.

My one living relative.

My best friend.

I took her cold, clammy hand and pressed it to my cheek, praying that somehow, someway, she might hear my words and fight a little harder. "Please, Skye. Please. Don't leave me."

# THE SURVIVORS

## BOOK II: AUTUMN

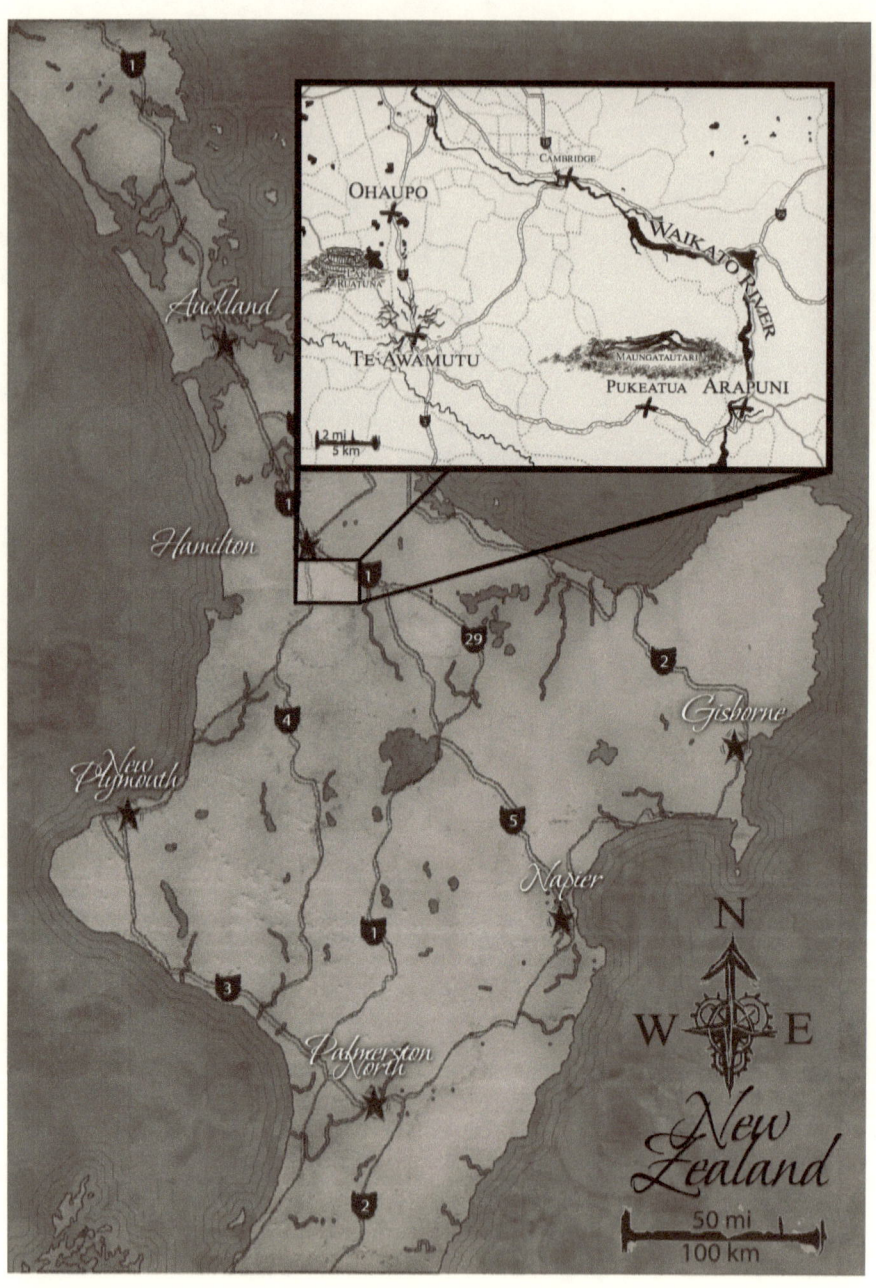

# Chapter One

I had been through a lot of bad days in my twenty-eight years of life. Terrible, painful days. The kind of days that no human being should ever have to go through. But today felt like the worst.

Even the sky wept as we lay her in her grave. Despite the rain, the ground had been baked hard by the long, hot summer. It was like digging through rock. It was a struggle to dig her grave deep enough to protect her body from the elements, and from pests. We had no choice, though. We couldn't just leave her to rot in the sun and be eaten by rats. She was family.

When we finally deemed the grave deep enough, the sweating men climbed out of the hole. All except one: Ryan Knowles. Our friend. He was only twenty-two, but he had been so ready to be a father. Now, it was like someone had stripped the life right out of him. His face was expressionless as he reached up for the tiny body. The light was gone from his eyes.

Skylar looked reluctant to surrender her baby's body to the earth. She was even younger than Ryan was, just eighteen years old and barely more than a child herself – but like her fiancé, she had been so ready for that baby. She had so much love to give. Now, she wouldn't have the chance. She could still have another baby in the future, but I understood the look in her eyes on some instinctive level, both as a woman and as her sister. No other child could ever replace her firstborn, lost to a miscarriage.

She held the tiny body for a moment longer, then leaned down to place her daughter in Ryan's outstretched arms.

He took the child and looked at her stiff little face, his jaw clenched in silent tension. He didn't say anything, but my imagination filled in the blanks about what he was probably thinking. That face should have smiled and cried, laughed and loved along with the rest of us, but now she would never have that chance. In a heartbeat, her innocent life had been snatched away from us. We'd been excited to welcome her into our little family; now, all our hopes for her had been dashed. Her life had been taken from us before she had a chance to learn how much we loved her.

Ryan leaned down and kissed the baby's forehead, then he placed her in the little box we'd found for her. We had buried other members of our family before, but it felt wrong to just put her into the dirt. She was so tiny, helpless and fragile that even in death, we wanted to protect her.

I knelt beside my sister on the edge of the grave and put my arm around her for support. She'd cried so much over the last few days that her tears had run dry; now she just stared into the hole in the ground, looking wrung-out and heartbroken.

Her baby. Her firstborn child. Gone, just like that.

Skylar trembled beneath my touch, but she didn't seem to have the strength to cry anymore. A part of her was in that hole, her flesh and blood. A piece of her had died along with her baby. We'd already lost so much; losing one more piece was devastating to us all.

All we had was each other, just the six of us against the world. There used to be more people in the group, but they'd lost little Sophie just before I arrived, and Dog not long after. We should have been nine by now, but we were only six. Six people living in the ruins of a civilization that had collapsed a decade ago beneath the weight of a deadly plague. Six people in a country that used to house more than five million, before Ebola X had decimated the entire human race.

Humankind was on the verge of extinction. It wasn't just one tiny baby that we were burying, but a part of the future. Now that there were so few of us, every life was integral to the survival of our entire species. Forget the whales and the tigers; now homo sapiens were on the critically endangered list.

It seemed to take forever for that hole to fill. The rain fell steadily and plastered our hair to our heads, like a constant reminder from Mother Nature about the burden of grief that lay upon us. Even those of us who didn't share a blood relationship with the baby felt a bond with her. They suffered just as much as we did.

I looked at Michael, the man who had once been a police officer and was now my lover and my friend, and I found his face solemn and stern. I knew him well enough to understand that he blamed himself for the baby's death, even though there was nothing that he could have done to predict Skylar's fever. Beside him, Stewart Cross, our doctor, looked just as grim – I suspected that he felt the same way.

I didn't blame either of them. No one had suspected that Skylar's headache had been the symptom of an infection that would have the strength to take her baby's life, and almost take hers as well. There was no way we could have known. Surviving after the fall of mankind meant that we only had access to rudimentary medical supplies, so we didn't have the means to test for listeria poisoning. The doctor had figured it out just in time to save Skylar, but by then it had been too late for the baby.

The poor baby. She should have had her whole life ahead of her. She didn't deserve such an undignified end.

Grief surged within me, and I closed my eyes to try and fight it off. Like my sister, I'd already cried so much that I wasn't sure I could cry any more. Beside me, Skye clung to a tiny pink teddy bear that I'd scavenged for her as a gift. My intention had been to cheer her up when she wasn't feeling well, but now it could only serve to comfort her in her time of mourning.

We watched as the last of the soil went back onto the grave, and the men gently smoothed it and patted it down. It was a mud pie. We'd buried my only niece in a mud pie. A tangled web of emotions surged within me. I wanted to laugh and cry and scream at the top of my lungs until my throat was raw. I'd barely had enough time to accept that I was going to be someone's auntie, and now she was gone.

Michael held his hand out for the wooden grave marker I was holding, his face set in an expression that looked just as wrung-out and exhausted as I felt. I handed it to him without a word; he took it and drove it as deep into the dirt as he could, to make sure that the wind wouldn't knock it askew.

*Kylie Knowles-McDermott*
*We loved you before we knew you.*

I read the marker again even though I'd read it a dozen times before, struggling to fight back the surge of emotion that threatened to overwhelm me. It was true, so true. The loss of that baby made me feel like someone had ripped a hole in my heart.

Michael came and sat beside me once his work was done, while the doctor stood with his head bowed beside the tiny grave. None of us could bring ourselves to say anything, so we stood and sat silently, each of us wrapped up in our own grieving process. We were so focused on ourselves that none of us noticed when Ryan left, and no one saw where he went.

\*\*\*

The storm turned violent, forcing us to leave the graveside and seek shelter. We were wet and bedraggled by the time we filtered back into the old motel we'd refurbished and converted into our home, but we were all too wrung out to complain. Skylar disentangled her hand from mine and headed off towards her room. The doctor took his little granddaughter, Madeline, off towards theirs.

Michael stayed with me, though he was silent and solemn. We stood hand-in-hand on the upper walkway that overlooked our garden, and watched the sky roiling overhead. A cold wind blew past us; I snuggled against his side, comforted by his warmth and stalwart strength.

Lightning split the heavens. We smelt the tingle of static discharge in the air. The thunder came a few seconds later, a deafening rumble that seemed to reverberate around and around until it shook us to our very cores.

Michael nuzzled his face against the curve of my neck, seeking some way to comfort me. I knew without words that it upset him to see me in pain. Although we had only known each other for a short time, I'd come to depend on him so much. I touched his cheek, and he kissed mine in return, while the cold wind swirled around us.

"I feel so helpless," I admitted softly, not sure what else to say. There was nothing I could do, for my sister or her child.

"Let's go inside." He hugged me gently, his deep voice barely audible over the storm. "A hot drink will make us feel better."

It wouldn't, but I gave him credit for trying. I nodded and let him lead me down the stairs to the ground floor. We went through the lobby and back out into the cold, passing by the garden that we had planted together. I glanced at it, wondering if our precious little plants would survive the weather.

And what about Skylar? Would she be strong enough to weather the emotional storm she was going through? I worried about her constantly, but no matter how hard I tried I was helpless to protect her. She was my only sister, the one person I had left from the days before the disease came. Our mother and father had died years ago, and we had been separated then. Now, a decade later, a miraculous freak of fate had brought us back together. The thought of losing her again was more than I could bear.

Michael and I retreated into our communal kitchen, and there we found Skylar sitting at the table as though reading my thoughts. There was a note in her hands: a scrap of damp paper that looked like it came from a notebook. I stared at it. What was she doing with a scrap of paper?

She looked up at us as we entered, her expression haunted.

"I found this on my bed," she said, her voice barely more than a whisper, then she looked at me with huge eyes and held the note out towards me. Although her rudimentary reading level was more than enough to handle a simple note, now was not the time for me to push her to read it herself. I took the note from her and sat down opposite her, while Michael went off to make our drinks. I had to read the note three times before it made sense to me.

I looked up and stared at my poor sister, with dread twisting in my stomach. The last thing I wanted to do was break her heart again, but I had no choice. I read the note out loud to her, fighting my own raging emotions to try and keep my voice steady for her sake.

*Dear Skylar,*
*I can't stay here right now. I don't know where I'll go but it can't be here. I don't know if I'll come back. Maybe one day. I'm sorry.*
*Ryan.*

When I finished reading, my eyes shot up to my baby sister. Her expression would have been unreadable to the uninitiated, but I could see the emotional collapse that took place behind her eyes. Although her face stayed neutral, I saw her falling apart like a house of cards on the inside. Ryan had been the one constant in her life for ten years. He had been her companion, her lover, and her pillar of light and support for more than half of her life. Just like that, her baby was dead, and her fiancé had left her as well.

"It's my fault." Her voice was shockingly harsh in the silence. "I did it. I killed my baby, just like you said I would. I didn't mean to. I don't know what I did, but it's my fault."

"No!" I exclaimed. "You heard what the doctor said: it was food poisoning. It's no one's fault, least of all yours."

I tried to grab her hand, but she pulled away from me. She wouldn't make eye contact, and she wouldn't answer. Trepidation washed over me like a rising tide when she rose and left the room, but Michael held me back when I tried to follow her.

"Leave her, Sandy," he whispered. "She needs time."

I turned on him, tears blurring my vision. "But– what if–"

"Hush." He swept me in close against his broad chest, and drew me back into the security and warmth of his arms. "When she needs us, she'll let us know. This is your sister we're talking about, remember?"

I didn't have an answer to that. He was right. My little sister was stronger than all of us put together. I just had to hope that it would be enough to get her through.

So, we left her alone, and sat together drinking tea and listening to the storm raging outside while I struggled to cope with the internal storm that raged within me. Ryan's departure had brought us down to five: two experienced fighters, an elderly man, a child, and Skye. His departure not only cost Skylar her mate, but it cost the entire group one of its few able-bodied defenders. I wasn't sure how we were going to survive.

# Chapter Two

The pallor of death hung over our household like a palpable force in the days that followed. We decided by universal consensus to put Skylar on suicide watch, just in case. She was so quiet that it shook me to the very core, and if it hadn't been for Michael's gentle strength, I probably would have fallen apart as well.

As far as we could tell, the grief and self-loathing seemed to have been too much for Skylar's young mind. She shut down completely and retreated deep within herself to somewhere the rest of us couldn't reach her. Although we stopped in and checked on her regularly, she had nothing to say to any of us; if I asked her a question, all she did was nod or shake her head. My little sister was usually so verbose and argumentative that seeing her like that was a real shock to the system.

Her depression was infectious. At night, I curled up in bed beside Michael and cried myself to sleep, and every morning I awoke feeling exhausted. Neither of us could summon any interest in the love-play that had filled our evenings not so long ago. We were just too tired, and it seemed inappropriate somehow.

It wasn't all bad, though. More than once, I had gone to check on Skye and found Madeline sitting beside her. The child possessed intuition far beyond her years, and seemed to have taken a great interest in helping Skylar to get through her grief. Once, I even caught them playing together. It was a sight that filled me with hope. There was something about Maddy that seemed to be able to reach people in a way that no one else could.

As the week passed, I gradually began to recover. There was only so much grief that one person could bear before she either killed herself or clambered back out of the deep, dark hole and got on with her life. With Michael's unwavering support, I eventually dug myself free. It was not in my nature to sit around and mope, so he encouraged me to find active things to do.

To keep myself occupied, I decided to improve our fortifications. I'd managed to install a ladder up to the roof, but the weather had been intermittently foul all week and hampered my plans to build a railing around the edge. The general idea was to provide a safe area where we could position a watcher, to keep an eye out for danger or visitors.

On the seventh day after the baby died, I climbed up to sit on the roof of the motel and watch the sun rise. The morning was clear, but I sensed more rain to come. I'd spent a good deal of time living off the land over the years, and had developed a keen nose for the natural world as a result. Still, even knowing that the rain was coming back, the sunrise was beautiful. The deep clouds along the horizon glowed pink when the dawn's rays struck them, and sent creeping tendrils of rose and gold across the arc of the sky.

The sound of someone climbing the ladder behind me attracted my attention, but I wasn't concerned. The ladder could only be accessed from inside the motel, which meant that the climber had to be one of my companions. Sure enough, it was.

"I was wondering where you went," Michael said as he clambered up onto the roof.

I glanced back over my shoulder and watched him pick his way cautiously across the slanted tiles towards toward me. "Yeah, I didn't feel like sleeping in today."

He sat down beside me, then jerked in surprise when he suddenly discovered that the roof was wet. I hid a smile behind my hand and struggled not to laugh.

"Ah, damn – these jeans were clean." He shot me a mock glare, but I could see in his eyes that there was no real anger behind it. "You could have warned me."

"Oh, it's just a little water. They're still technically clean."

He smiled at my joke, even if it wasn't really a very good one. My gaze lingered on him, studying the contours of his profile in light of dawn. I'd heard that sunrise was referred to as the photographer's golden hour, and I could see why. The gentle light softened the hard angles of his face and made him look almost angelic. Emotion surged up within my chest, an overwhelming wave of affection towards the man that had worked so hard to save both my life, and my humanity.

"Michael," I whispered his name and reached over to take his hand.

His gaze shifted to me, a faint smile on his lips and a quizzical look in his eyes. "Yes?"

Ah, he was such a good man. Such a sweet, kind, wonderful man. What on earth had I done to deserve someone like him? I snuggled against him and reached up to trail my fingers along his jaw. For once, there was no stubble there; he must have shaved just before he came looking for me. I found myself just the tiniest bit disappointed. I had grown fond of him with a touch of scruff. I'd grown fond of him in a lot of ways, really.

He watched me with those dark eyes of his, as if he was trying to figure out what I was about. I smiled cryptically up at him, and his brow furrowed. "Are you feeling okay, Sandy?"

I couldn't help but giggle. I was feeling a little giddy, actually. A little girlish. A little silly. I hadn't felt that way about someone in a very long time.

"I feel a bit peculiar, actually," I said, then quickly finished my sentence before he started worrying about me. "Like maybe I might be in love. I think I am, actually. I think I'm in love with you, Michael Chan. I'm not sure if I should offer you congratulations or condolences."

He stared back at me while my words sank in, so many different emotions flickering across his face that I couldn't keep track of them all. Finally, just when I was about to start getting concerned, the tiniest, sweetest little smile crept across his face, and he hugged me tight.

"Congratulations, definitely." His voice was even huskier than usual and hardly more than a whisper. One gentle hand caressed my jawline, and then he planted a tender kiss on my lips. It lingered for just a moment before he drew back to speak again. "I love you, too. And… thank you."

"Eh? For what?" This time he had me confused.

"Well." Suddenly, he seemed very interested in looking anywhere but at me. "When I told you how I felt last week, and you didn't say it back… I was worried. I thought perhaps I'd misunderstood your intentions, and that I was the only one who felt like that. I thought that maybe you didn't…"

He trailed off, and my heart just about broke looking up at him. In a sudden flash of overwhelming emotion, I threw my arms around his broad shoulders and hugged him as tight as I could.

"Oh, no." I squeezed his firm body with every ounce of my strength. "No, no, no. I just needed time. You know how I am."

He laughed and squeezed me back; the sound of his laughter made me feel a surge of happiness that I hadn't experienced since before Skylar's illness. With it, came a feeling of hope. With Michael at my side, it felt like somehow everything *had* to work out in the end.

\*\*\*

166

After we finished our sappy moment, Michael volunteered to help with my project while the weather was still fine. I was glad for the assistance, not just because that it would get the work done faster, but also because it gave me an excuse to spend time with him. That, and he had twice my physical strength, which was handy in construction projects. A girl had to be practical in our day and age.

With his help, we managed to get a railing up around half of the south-eastern side of the roof before the weather started to close in again. I barely heard the distant rumble of thunder over the sound of my own hammering, but Michael did.

"Storm's coming back," he informed me as I wriggled out from beneath the construction we were erecting. He helped me to my feet, and together we watched the clouds gathering in the distance.

"Looks like a bad one," I said. He nodded his agreement. A strong gust of wind blew, almost knocking me off my feet. All of a sudden, I was glad that I'd put a few extra nails into the new railing.

"We should get everything that's not nailed down inside," Michael suggested.

"Yeah, and let's do it fast," I agreed immediately. After ten years on my own, I'd learned to read the weather like a book, and this one had the smell of trouble all over it. It was late summer heading into autumn; while we often got storms at that time of year, this one felt different.

We both hurried to gather up our tools and the left-over wood, and raced back down the ladder to the relative safety of ground level.

There, we found the doctor had anticipated our next step and was in the process of covering up our little garden with a frame I'd made for just that purpose. We tossed our tools into the safety of one of the downstairs storage rooms, and then ran over to help him. We had the garden battened down and protected by the time the first of the rain started to splatter down around us. Thunder rumbled ominously, getting closer with each passing moment.

Michael froze and looked over his shoulder towards the lobby. "Wait, what was that noise?"

"What noise?" I followed his gaze, but didn't see anything.

"I could have sworn I heard engines," he mumbled, half to himself. He headed off towards the front door to check, so I followed him. The wind caught the door as soon as he opened it, forcing him to put his weight behind it to get it to open all the way.

I shoved my hair back out of my face as the wind tried to blind me with it, and peered off into the distance. "I still don't hear anything."

A blur of tabby fur bounded past us as Tigger took the opportunity to escape from the incoming storm. She danced between our feet, and then vanished into the depths of the motel.

"I'm sure I heard something." Michael frowned, leaning heavily against the door to keep it open.

"I really don't—" Then I paused and tilted my head, straining to listen. "No, wait, you're right – I hear it too. That sounds like farm bikes."

Sure enough, it was. A pair of figures on little motorcycles skidded around the corner a heartbeat later, struggling to keep their balance against the surging winds. I waved to them and beckoned them towards us as soon as I recognised the riders as friends: Anahera and Hemi, members of the Maori group that lived not far away. They came to a stop a half-dozen meters from the entrance. I hurried out of the safety of the building to help Anahera with her bike. The leader of the Maori tribe was bundled against the weather in a heavy anorak with the hood pulled up over her head, but the wind was so strong it tugged her glossy black curls in every direction. I fell in beside her and helped her wheel her bike into the safety of our lobby, with her son close behind us. Once we were all safely inside, Michael eased the door closed and bolted it shut behind us.

"We may have underestimated the weather," Anahera said, sounding out of breath as we rolled her bike over to a corner and leaned it against the wall. Once it was safely stowed, she leaned back and heaved a sigh, plucking a few long strands of hair out of her eyes.

"No kidding," I answered dryly. Like a good little hostess, I offered her a hand to help her get out of her coat, which she accepted.

"I hope you don't mind that we arrived unannounced." She shot an apologetic glance towards me. "We hoped to consult with your doctor on something, and if we waited then it would only get worse."

"The doctor?" I frowned at her, feeling a stab of concern. Although we had only met once before, I considered Anahera and her son to be our friends. She'd shown herself to be a good, loyal person and had helped me at my lowest point; I felt a sense of gratitude toward her that I wasn't sure I could ever repay. "Of course, Anahera. You're always welcome here. What's wrong?"

"Ah, my boy has gone and gotten himself hurt." Anahera sighed and shot a look at her son, drawing my attention to the young man; for the first time, I noticed he was moving strangely, favouring his left side.

"Aw, mum! It's not like I did it on purpose," Hemi protested, but his mother wasn't having any of it. She stomped over to him and yanked up the hem of his shirt to show us the blood-soaked bandages beneath.

"Ouch." Michael grimaced at the sight of the blood. "What did you do, lad?"

"Someone took a pot-shot at me from the bush while I was out possum hunting. Tane and Iorangi chased him off, but we didn't get a good look at the bastard." He flicked a sheepish-looking glance at his mother. "Sorry, Mum."

"It's fine, dear. I understand." Anahera patted his arm, then turned and looked at the two of us. "I suspect it was an air rifle rather than the real thing, but it got him at a bad angle. We don't have the tools to get the pellet out without doing more harm than good."

"I'll go find the doctor," Michael said, then shot a glance at me to make sure I was okay with being left alone. I nodded and gave him a reassuring smile; he smiled back and hurried off, leaving me to tend to our guests.

"Let's get you somewhere comfortable." I beckoned them both to follow me and led them off toward the room next to the kitchen, which we'd converted into our communal living room. The rain pelted down on the courtyard as we passed, and a gust of wind rattled the windows and doors so hard that it made all of us flinch.

We reached the living area safely, despite the weather's best attempts to fling things at us. Once we were back indoors, I hung Anahera's coat over the back of a chair and cleared a pile of assorted junk off one of the couches so that Hemi could lie down. He protested weakly as his mother stripped him of his jacket and shirt, but by the time Michael arrived with the doctor in tow, we had his bandages laid bare.

"Hey, Doc," Hemi greeted him with a lopsided smile.

"'Hey', indeed. Let's get these bandages off and have a look at you." Doctor Cross frowned deeply at the youth and settled down in his chair beside the couch. Michael and I took that as our cue to leave. We filtered back outside, with Anahera trailing behind us.

"You want a cuppa?" I offered, gesturing towards our kitchen.

"After being out in the storm, I certainly wouldn't say no," she answered agreeably, running her fingers back through her damp hair. I nodded and led the way to the kitchen, where I set about making tea while Anahera and Michael sat at the table.

"How's your sister?" Anahera asked me in her usual pleasant way.

I froze for a second, halfway through setting a pot of water on the stove to heat up, then I turned slowly and stared at her. The last time she or any of her tribe had visited us was before the sickness, when Skylar had been heavily pregnant but more or less happy.

Actually, come to think of it, the last time I'd personally seen her was when she was beating the living shit out of the man who had brutally raped me years ago. Needless to say, there was a damn good reason that I was fond of her.

Anahera wasn't stupid. She knew from the look on my face that something was wrong. Her brow furrowed. When I didn't answer, she looked at Michael instead. He drew a deep breath and looked down at his hands. There was no nice way to say what had to be said.

"She lost the baby," he said, so quietly that I could barely hear his voice. I didn't have to, I already knew. Anahera, however, went wide-eyed and her hands flew up to her mouth.

"Oh, no… how?" she whispered, tears gathering in her beautiful eyes.

"Skye got sick," I spoke up at last, to help break the bad news. "Really, really sick. We think that she got listeria poisoning from something she ate."

"Is she…?"

"She's alive, thank goodness." Michael frowned and shook his head. "But the doctor couldn't save her child."

"Oh, the poor dear." Anahera heaved a long sigh and closed her eyes. "She must be devastated. How long ago did it happen?"

"About a week ago." I sighed as well – and then jumped in surprise when a gust of wind rattled a boarded-up window beside me ominously. No one had it in them to laugh at my jumpiness today, not even me.

"May I speak with her?" Anahera looked from Michael to me, as though seeking permission from us.

"You can try. She hasn't been very talkative recently, but…" I looked at her thoughtfully. "Perhaps she would respond better to someone who is a mother."

What I meant but didn't say, was that my sister might respond better to a mother who had already lost most of her children, and understood the pain of losing a child better than any of us could. I didn't need to say it though; Anahera seemed to know exactly what I meant.

"I'll go see her now." She rose from her seat, just as an almighty bolt of lightning flashed outside. The lights flickered and then went out, leaving us in semi-darkness. I grunted in annoyance and reached over to switch off the stove.

"So much for tea," I muttered, and then I pointed Anahera in the right direction. "Upstairs, second door on the left. She'll be in her room, where she always is."

Anahera nodded and left without another word. I looked at Michael and he looked back at me, then lifted a brow that I could barely see in the dark kitchen.

"You know, this would be a great chance to go spend some quality time together, if we weren't all so depressed." He flashed me an impish grin, just in time for his face to be illuminated by another flash of lightning. The humour got a smile from me.

"Well, it is good snuggling weather," I agreed, shifting the pot of water to a safer spot. The rain was so thunderous that it masked the sound of his footsteps coming up behind me, so when his arms wrapped around me he took me by surprise.

"Let's go have a snuggle, then," he suggested, nuzzling the side of my neck. The nuzzle was followed by a nibble, then a kiss, and I was putty in his hands.

"Sure, why not?" I smiled to myself as he kissed his way up and down the curve of my neck. "Snuggles are, um... very good for the soul. I think I could use a healthy dose of snuggles."

"I think we could all use a healthy dose of snuggles," Michael answered, then he gave me a smile, took my hand, and led me out of the kitchen.

***

We settled for his bedroom, where we had a bit of privacy but also could keep an eye out for trouble along the upstairs landing. The wind howled around our little fortress, yanking our hair aggressively as we made our way up the stairs and headed for his room. Well, it yanked at mine, since my hair was long; it barely ruffled his.

"You know, I've been meaning to ask." I looked at him as he stripped off his t-shirt and flopped down on his bed. "How on earth do you keep your hair so neatly trimmed without the benefit of a barber? I can barely keep mine brushed."

"A mirror, a pair of nail scissors and a hell of a lot of patience." His grin was so playful that I couldn't figure out if he was telling the truth or joshing with me. Luckily, my curiosity flew right out the window when he stretched out languidly, in just such a way as to make his taut muscles ripple beneath newly-tanned skin. After that, I completely forgot whatever I was thinking before, enraptured by his teasing.

It never failed to impress me just how quickly he'd learned to push my buttons, considering that he'd never had a girlfriend before. Not that either of us had used the boyfriend-girlfriend words just yet. Between the two of us, we had the emotional maturity of a fourteen year old boy – and that was only if you added us both together and rounded up generously. We'd get there, though. We were learning and growing together every day, and that was what mattered.

He grinned and patted his stomach invitingly. He knew I couldn't resist, so I didn't even try. The breath exploded out of him as I leapt on him in a mock tackle, and we both went head over heels in a mass of tickling silliness. A few minutes and a couple of muffled squeals later, we finally remembered that we were supposed to be adults. Michael flopped on his back with an arm tucked under his head, and I snuggled up against his belly to enjoy the warmth of his skin.

Even though he was out of breath from our play, I could hardly hear his panting over the roar of the wind. It was getting stronger by the second. I rolled onto my belly to rest my chin on his firm stomach, and watched the storm rage beyond the open door.

A disembodied branch crashed into the wall beside his door. It wasn't a big one, but it hit hard enough that the sound of its impact made us both jump.

"Geez, it sounds like it's turning into a cyclone out there." Michael frowned, absently rubbing his chin. "Good thing we brought all that junk in."

"It's going to take hours to clean up this mess tomorrow." I sighed heavily, rubbing my cheek against his stomach. "I hope Ryan isn't out in this."

"I hope he is," Michael spat the sentence with a vehemence that startled me. He was a gentle man by nature, and I rarely saw him angry. For him to wish suffering on someone was unexpected. My brows rose, and I lifted my head to regard him quizzically. He didn't make eye contact with me, but he looked pretty steamed up.

"Aren't I the one that's supposed to be furious at him?" I eased myself up to plant a tender kiss on his throat, right in the spot that I had learned through trial and error was his most vulnerable.

A sharp exhalation of breath was my reward, followed by the feeling of a strong arm sneaking around my waist. "I'm surprised that you aren't."

"Oh, I am." I nuzzled and nibbled at that tender spot, until his head tilted back to give me better access. "I haven't forgiven him, but I understand that he had to go."

"Mnngh…" He murmured inarticulately as I kissed a trail down the side of his throat and across his collarbone. "He abandoned the love of his life when she needed him most. I'll never forgive him for that."

"If there were more men like you in the world, then there would be a lot more happy women," I told him, and then promptly distracted him with a play-bite, right on the nipple.

Michael yelped and stared at me with wide eyes, covering his 'wound' with his hand. "What was that for?"

"For being you." I grinned up at him, and then leaned down to plant a playful kiss on his stomach. Anticipation made his breath catch in his throat, but for now the kiss was all he got. That, and a snuggle when I nestled back up against his side. "I've got to mark you as mine somehow. Unfortunately, people aren't cats; no matter how much I rub my face all over you, it just doesn't work."

That got a laugh from him. "No, it probably wouldn't, but you're more than welcome to try."

I gasped and feigned injury. "You're just trying to get me to rub you in all the interesting places. I see what you're up to, sir."

He gave me such a wicked grin that I broke down giggling. The wind took the opportunity to yowl mournfully and rattle our windows, sending an ice-cold gust tearing through our little nest. I shivered and cuddled closer to him. It was so dark I could hardly see him in the gloom, but just knowing he was there was enough for me.

"I wonder what the others are up to," I considered aloud, and felt more than saw Michael shrug beneath me.

"Honestly, I'm not entirely sure what *we're* up to, let alone the others."

With a laugh and a poke in the side, I rolled onto my back to stare at the murky ceiling above us. "We're snuggling, remember?"

"Ah, of course." His smile softened to one of affection, and I felt his fingers stroking my hair. I relaxed and closed my eyes, enjoying the sense of closeness.

"You know, in retrospect I'm really glad I didn't shoot you." I sighed and reached up to capture his fingers in my own.

"I'm glad I missed."

I stretched out languidly, listening to the sounds of the storm raging all around us. All the window panes were rattling, and I heard something creaking ominously. A moment later, the sound of glass breaking downstairs made me jump, but Michael restrained me from rushing off to investigate.

"It'll just be one of the downstairs windows," he soothed, drawing my fingers up to his lips for a reassuring kiss. "They're boarded up on the inside, don't worry."

"It could be one of those mutant zombies taking advantage of the storm," I protested, but he dismissed the notion with a shake of his head.

"Even the mutant zombies aren't stupid enough to be outside in this weather. They'd just end up cartwheeling down the street." His voice was so dry, and the image was so amusing that I couldn't help but smile.

"You're always so calm and collected; I don't know how you do it." I sighed heavily. A thought struck me then; I turned to look at him quizzically in the semi-darkness. "You did bring your uniform with you when we moved here, right?"

"Of course." He peered down at me, perplexed. "Why?"

I smiled to myself – he really had no idea about the power that uniform had over me. I gave him a long, sideways look, and then I hid my face against his tummy before he could see me blushing. "Oh, no reason."

Why no, I didn't plan to make him wear it when we finally got over our... hurdle. Call me a sucker for a man in uniform, but it looked fantastic on him. Of all the cops

I'd seen in my life, none wore it better. Michael grunted inarticulately, like he didn't quite believe me. He always seemed to know when I was up to no good. Cop instincts or something, I guessed.

Oh, but what about the…?

I sat bolt upright like a meerkat, and made him jump in surprise. "I don't suppose you kept the hat as well, did you?"

"Uh, I think so. It's probably in there." He pointed to a corner of his room, where a couple of bags were still waiting to be unpacked. Part of me wanted to scold him for waiting all this time to get settled in, but part of me understood completely – you never quite knew when you were going to need to pull up roots and run. We had settled in nicely, but there was no guarantee that we could stay in our motel forever.

Hell, there was no guarantee either of us would live out the week. Life was fickle, and far too short to spend the entire time being serious.

I sprang over him and dived into the corner, to root around inside his bags in search of the hat. Although I heard him protesting, he made no attempt to actually stop me from digging through his belongings. It was only fair, after all – he'd gone through mine on several occasions, looking for something. We were close enough that he knew I was no threat to his possessions, just like I understood that he was no threat to mine.

Socks and shorts went flying as I turned his bag upside down, until I finally found what I was looking for, right at the very bottom.

"Victory is mine!" I yanked out one slightly crushed, navy blue police officer's cap. I dusted it off, popped it back into shape and plonked it on my head. There was a muffled snort behind me. I turned and gave him a look of wide-eyed mock innocence. "What?"

"What on earth has gotten into you, Sandy McDermott?" he asked. I bounced back over to join him in bed.

"Me? Oh, I'm just feeling a bit playful, is all." I gave him a grin, to which he responded by snatching the hat off my head and placing it upon his own.

"You're just trying to cheer me up, aren't you?" He peered at me from beneath the brim of his cap, his smile fading away.

I heaved a sigh and flopped back down with my head on his chest. "Pretty much, yes. Trying to cheer myself up, too. It's been such a miserable week."

"I know." He ran his fingers through my hair, stroking a few golden-blonde strands back away from my face. One finger hooked under my chin and tilted my face up towards his so that he could look me in the eye. "It's been a rough couple of months for everyone."

"It's been a rough decade." I broke eye contact and looked away. "I need a vacation from being miserable before I go crazy."

"You and me both." He nodded his agreement and wrapped an arm around my waist to draw me closer against him. Then he kissed me, softly and tenderly; suddenly, it seemed like everything was going to be fine after all. The kiss lingered for long minutes as we both tried to lose our worries in one another. It was a moment of warmth and comfort, the kind of moment shared between two people who had suffered so much and only had one another to fall back on.

We were so wrapped up in one another that we didn't hear the footfalls of someone approaching, nor did we notice the presence in the doorway until Anahera cleared her throat pointedly and knocked on the door frame. Startled, we jerked away from one another and stared at her.

"Sorry to interrupt." She was obviously trying very hard not to laugh at the expressions on our faces. We looked at one another, half-naked with hands in all kinds of interesting places, then promptly started frantically disentangling ourselves. By the time we were straightened up, both of us were blushing furiously, and Anahera could barely keep a straight face.

"Um, sorry." I felt the need to apologise as I straightened my t-shirt, but she just shook her head.

"Don't be, dear. I was your age not that long ago; I remember what it's like to be in love." Her smile faded, and I felt a stab of guilt when I remembered how she had lost her husband to the plague. "Just make the most of him while you can. And you–" She pointed at Michael. "–take good care of her as well. Or else."

Michael flashed his cheeky smile and saluted her, which looked a little ridiculous considering he was still dressed in his policeman's cap.

"Don't just stand out there in the wind, you'll get hit by something." He gestured towards the chair in the corner of room with a flourish, inviting her inside. Somehow, he even managed to sound nonchalant about it. "Come in, sit down. How's Hemi?"

Anahera accepted the invitation and stepped inside, closing the door behind her to keep out the wind. It was getting loud outside, so I thought nothing of the gesture; with the door open we could hardly hear ourselves think.

"He's fine, thank you," she answered as she settled in the chair by the window, adjusting her clothing about her to get comfortable. "The good doctor has removed the pellet, and given him some antibiotics to ensure it doesn't get infected." Her lips twisted into an appreciative smile. "It seems we owe you gifts once again."

"Oh, there's no need for that." Michael shook his head and gave her a smile in return. "Friends help friends, that's all that matters. I'm sure you'd do the same for us if we needed help."

"Absolutely," she agreed amicably, then shifted her gaze to me. "I spoke with your sister."

My heart leapt into my throat. "How is she?"

"She's in a great deal of pain, but she is healing." Anahera sighed heavily. "It will take time and support, and the love of the people around her. She told me that her man left her as well, and I fear that has only compounded her grief."

I felt an arm creep around me and turned to look at Michael; the expression on his face was one of deep anger. Anahera seemed to notice it as well, but she said nothing.

"I don't know how to help her," I admitted, turning my attention back to our visitor. "I've forgotten how to be a sister. We were separated for a long time, and only found one another recently."

Anahera nodded understandingly. "This is a strange world we live in, but I think there is more to your bond than just time spent together as adults. Just knowing that you're here for her is enough."

"How do you know?" I looked down at my hands, feeling helplessness hit me in the gut all over again. "I don't know what she needs."

"I know because she told me as much," Anahera said. I looked up to find her regarding me with an expression that spoke of fondness. "She told me that if it weren't for you, she would have nothing left to live for."

"Oh." I looked back down and leaned against Michael for support. "But I haven't even done anything."

"You don't need to, dear. You're her sister. That's all that matters." I could hear the smile in her voice without looking up, and found it reassuring somehow.

"Is there anything we can do to help her through the grieving process?" Michael asked.

"Perhaps." I heard her shift in her seat, and glanced up to find her staring out the window at the raging storm. "I was going to suggest that some time away from the place where her baby died might help her. Of course, it is difficult to find somewhere safe in this world, so I thought some of you might like to come and visit my group for a few days. After the storm passes, that is."

"That sounds like an interesting idea." Michael gave me a squeeze. I looked up at him, staring deep into those kind eyes of his. "What do you think, Sandy? Shall we go for a visit?"

I stayed silent for a moment to consider the question, then looked back at Anahera, regarding her profile thoughtfully as she watched the weather.

My first instinct would have been to say no, to stay safely holed up in our little fortress with the people I knew I could trust, but I knew that feeling stemmed from cowardice. Anahera was a good person, as was her son Hemi. I liked them both and felt that I could trust them, especially after I had seen the way Anahera reacted to finding out one of her brethren had been preying on women and girls for years before he'd joined her tribe.

She had evicted him from her tribe without hesitation, mutilated him and thrown him out into the wilds as punishment for his crime. I didn't have to go through a lengthy trial, recount my ordeal in great detail, and suffer through the horror of being judged by a jury. Nobody had tried to tell me that I'd been asking for it because of my gender or my state of dress, and nobody tried to pass it off as a misunderstanding. She had listened to me and confronted him, and when he was found guilty, her punishment had been swift.

In a way, I felt like I had gotten more justice from Anahera than I would have gotten in a court of law. I trusted her. With that thought in mind, I nodded my consent and we began to make plans for the nearest thing to a vacation that any of us had taken in a very long time.

# Chapter Three

The storm raged for almost a day, tearing branches from trees and uprooting any plants and fixtures that were not lucky enough to be protected from the winds. Every so often, we'd hear the sound of something breaking or being thrown around, but we were safe within our precious haven.

No one even considered sending Anahera and Hemi back out into the storm. It just wasn't an option. Their chances of making it home safely on those little farm bikes would be slim to non-existent. Luckily, our hotel had plenty of spare bedrooms and furniture that had survived the years, so we set them up with beds and insisted they stay the night. I wasn't terribly surprised that neither of them protested.

Without power, lunch and dinner were solemn events. I did my best to cheer everyone up by assembling a salad with canned meat for protein, but I lacked my sister's flair for creative cooking.

Skye didn't leave her room the entire day. At mealtimes, I braved the weather to bring her food, but she barely even looked at me. Each time I checked on her, she was just sitting on her bed, staring out her window at the raging storm, clutching that tiny pink teddy bear. She ate the food I left for her, but never made any comments.

Night seemed to fall earlier than normal that evening, because the sun was obscured by the roiling clouds. I left the others to finish cleaning up the kitchen by candlelight, and went back upstairs to bring Skylar a little lantern for her room. For some reason, the thought of leaving her brooding in the dark made me feel sick to my stomach.

She was still sitting in exactly the same spot when I arrived, her eyes a million miles away. When I set the lantern down and turned it on, she stirred a little, as though coming out of a dream. Her head turned towards me. I looked back at her, and found her watching me with eyes that were sunken and hollow from grief. My heart lurched at the sight of the sorrow etched on her face.

I sat down beside her and wrapped my arm around her slender frame; she felt tiny and fragile now that the weight of her pregnancy had begun to fade. She'd always been slender and small-boned, but now it felt like I could break her if I gripped her too firmly. I wondered if that was how Michael felt, all those times when he held me as gently as if I were a porcelain doll. Now, I understood the feeling.

"Anahera invited us to stay with her clan for a couple of days." I found myself talking to her automatically, even if she was away with the fairies. "So we're going for a trip once the storm is over. Just for a little while. Anahera says it'll be good for us to get away for a bit. I think she's right. What do you think?" I wasn't expecting an answer, so when I got one it just about gave me a heart attack.

"I think… I'd like that." Skye shifted and snuggled up against me. "She's nice."

"Yeah, she is," I agreed, fighting to contain the flood of relief that poured through me from the simple fact that my little sister was talking to me again. "She's downstairs with Hemi and the others. We were thinking of playing a game to pass the time. Why don't you come and play with us?"

"A game?" She stirred and looked up at me with those big blue eyes, set into a face that looked so hauntingly similar to my mother's that it made my gut twist. "What kind of game?"

"Well, I found a few different ones while I was out exploring the other day. We could play a card game, if you want?" I suggested. She wrinkled her nose and shook her head.

"No, card games are boring." She pulled a face, but apparently I had her attention now. Sometimes I had to remind myself that she was only eighteen. Our relationship had become a bit peculiar. To me, she'd gone from being an adorable eight-year-old to being a grown, very capable young woman without me having a chance to watch the change happen naturally. I was still struggling to work out how to cope with that. Sometimes I didn't know whether to treat her like an adult or a child. Luckily, she seemed to understand how jarring the transition was for me, and was generally patient with me.

"What about a board game?" I suggested. "I found Cluedo, Monopoly, and Scrabble. Take your pick."

"Oh, I remember Monopoly." Her eyes lit up. "We used to play that with Mum and Dad."

"Yeah, that's right. I don't remember the rules, but I'm sure we can figure it out." I gave her a squeeze and held her close until she finally smiled and nodded.

That was all the permission I needed. I grabbed her hand and dragged her off for an evening of frivolity before she could lose herself in depression again.

The others joined us in the common room, and helped us to set up the board. None of us really remembered how to play and the instructions were faded with age, but between us we managed to figure out enough to get the game going. The pieces were dirty and tarnished, and the old paper money was wrinkled, but no one really minded. Although I offered to play with my sister as a team, she rejected the help with a stubborn determination that made my heart swell with joy. That was the Skylar I knew. Her personality was coming back at last.

We played long into the night by lantern light. Eventually the doctor retired and took Madeline off to her bed, leaving five of us to battle it out. I fell quickly to my sister's brutal wiles, and Michael and Anahera soon joined me in bankruptcy.

Defeated, we sat back to watch the two youngest members of our groups battle it out, their faces masks of intense concentration. Then it all came tumbling down, when one unlucky roll of the dice made Hemi's little race car land on Mayfair. It was stacked high with Skye's motels, so that was the end of him.

"I can't believe it. Beaten by a girl," Hemi complained jokingly.

"And I'd beat you again, too," she retorted, leaning over to smack his arm.

"Hey now! You're not allowed to hit me," Hemi protested, holding his hands up in mock defence. "That's not fair, since I'm not allowed to hit you back."

"Seems perfectly fair to me." Skye grinned wickedly at him. "You think I'm *only* a girl. I'll show you!"

A crack of thunder so loud that it made the windows rattle punctuated Skylar's sentence, and made us all jump. We exchanged looks, and then melted into communal laughter at our own expense.

"Okay, children; off to bed," Anahera commanded once the levity subsided, making shooing motions at Skylar and her son. I expected protests, but neither of them said a word. They stood obediently and departed, still teasing one another as they went out the door.

I watched them go, then turned and looked at Anahera with a raised eyebrow. "You know, if I tried that I'd probably just get jeered at. What's your secret?"

"My secret?" She laughed and shook her head. "I'm old enough to be both their mothers. Mum will always be Mum."

I heard Michael chuckle behind me, then felt a hand run across my shoulders. "Hear that? You're just too young to be the boss."

"Hey!" I pouted at him. "You're only four years older than me. That means you're too young to be the boss, too."

"You're both youngsters." Anahera peered at us with a peculiar little half-smile on her face. "Therefore, I am the boss."

"This entire conversation is silly," I announced, sliding down off the couch to start picking up the game pieces and putting them away. There was a soft grunt as Michael slid down beside me to help, while Anahera watched on from her armchair.

"Yes, it is," she agreed thoughtfully, absently crossing her long legs. "A little levity is good for everyone, though. I am glad you convinced Skylar to join us. This was a wonderful idea."

I glanced up at her, and she smiled at me, a smile so beautiful that it made my heart do a somersault in my chest. There was just something about that woman that was so strong and so charismatic that her praise made me feel like a puppy who'd gotten a treat. I smiled back, shyly, and looked back down at the strewn game pieces.

"Thanks. I'm just glad that she agreed. I was really worrying about her." I absently reached out to touch Michael's hand as it happened to pass by me while gathering up motels. He hesitated, then gave my hand a squeeze, understanding my need for contact.

"We were all worried about her," he said quietly in that deep, grainy voice of his, then shot a glance towards Anahera. "There were a few days where we thought that she might…"

He trailed off and looked at me, leaving me to finish the sentence. I did, but only with great reluctance. "…kill herself."

"Ah," Anahera said. She thought about it for a second, then shook her head. "I don't think you need to worry about that. Your sister is a very strong and determined young woman. She just needs time to sort through her grief and find her own strength again. The two of you are much alike in that manner."

"Me?" I looked up again, bewildered. "You must be kidding. I'm the biggest wimp in the universe, just ask Michael."

"Wimp? Hardly." Michael laughed. He grabbed my shoulder and gave me a light shake. "You just have a warped sense of your own self-worth, sweetheart."

"He's right," Anahera agreed, amusement flickering across her face. "How long were you alone out there? A decade, was it? You went through terrible things all by yourself, with no one to support you, no one to fall back on, and no one to keep you grounded. And yet, here you are, alive and well, and forming bonds with other people. You have had to learn how to have friends and how to trust all over again, and you're doing very well at it from what I can see."

I felt my cheeks grow hot with embarrassment, but when I opened my mouth to protest Michael cut me off.

"Oh no, I know what you're going to say," he scolded gently, sliding an arm around my shoulders. "Don't you even think about it. She's bang on the money, and you know it."

Tears sprang into my eyes. Suddenly, I found myself fascinated by the tiny game pieces in my hands, unable to meet their eyes. "I don't feel like I'm doing very well."

"You are." Anahera joined us on the floor, and reached over to take the game pieces from my hand. She set them aside, and then wrapped her hands around mine. "Darling, I know that you struggle. I saw the way you looked at me when we first met, and I know that look. You have been trapped for a very long time in a prison fate made for you, and now you're learning to cope with the world outside that prison." She reached over and cupped my chin in her hand, forcing me to meet her gaze. "You are doing very well, and I want you to remember that. Promise me."

I wasn't sure what to say to that so I mumbled something inarticulate. She smiled and shook her head but let it pass. She eased herself back into her chair, leaving me to resume picking up the scattered toys.

Michael was never one to leave me to sulk when he knew I was feeling a bit down, so he distracted me with a playful pinch on the bottom. I squealed in surprise and leapt away from him, then laughed and gave him an equally playful slap across the shoulder in return.

"Ow! I was just about to point out that it's been weeks since you hit me, too. So much for that," he teased. I flung a tiny metal shoe at him in retaliation. He yelped as it bounced off his arm and tumbled away, then went scrambling after it. When he found it, he flung it right back at me. It missed me and hit Anahera in the shin instead.

"Hey now, you two," she scolded us with amusement, leaning down to grab the fallen toy and toss it into the box with the others. "I thought you were supposed to be the responsible ones?"

"Me?" I snorted indignantly and flapped a hand. "God, no. He's the responsible one. Did he tell you he used to be a police officer?"

"He did mention it, yes." She gave Michael a long, pointed look. This time, it was Michael's turn to look flustered by her scrutiny.

"I was a constable, yeah," he admitted. "I guess that's why I feel like I'm responsible for protecting these troublemakers. Or arresting them, I haven't decided which yet." He shot an impish grin at me, and I laughed.

"Yeah, right," I scoffed. "If you arrested me, where would you put me?"

"Oh, I have some ideas..." he teased right back, and then gave me a wink that made me start blushing all over again.

Anahera watched with amusement, clearly enjoying the sight of our youthful exuberance. Then, out of the blue, she hit us with a question that stunned us both. "So, when are you two getting married?"

I stared at her, and then glanced at Michael to find him looking just as dumbstruck.

"Er... well, but we've only known each other for about six weeks..." he stumbled awkwardly, absently rubbing at the back of his neck. As I watched, I saw a flush of colour rise in his cheeks and the side of his throat, mirroring the rush of heat I felt in my own face.

"Life is short and brutal in this day and age," Anahera said with a shrug. "You two are clearly besotted with one another. God only knows how much time you'll have together. You should make the most of it while you can."

"But, we haven't even... you know, done 'it'," I stumbled, feeling completely out of my element; I'd never discussed my personal issues with anyone besides Michael.

Anahera's brows shot up. "Really now? I never would have guessed." She paused to think about it, then a flicker of understanding passed through her eyes. "Ah, but I suppose I should have. Alas, that is something I cannot advise on."

"It's okay." I looked down at my feet, pretending to be fascinated by anything that didn't involve making eye-contact with anyone. I heard rather than saw when Anahera stood up and stretched, in a rustling of cloth and denim.

"I'm sure the two of you will resolve that matter in your own time, when you're ready," she said in a gentle, maternal tone. "For now, I believe I shall retire. Assuming the storm passes by morning, we have a journey ahead of us."

Then she was gone, stepping around our mess to leave Michael and me both feeling awkward and trying very hard not to look at one another. After the door clicked closed behind her, it left the room nearly silent. The only sound was the shuffling of paper and the clicking of metal and plastic pieces, barely audible over the raging storm outside.

Once we put the last of the pieces away, I slid the lid back onto the box and shoved it into a corner where it was out of the way. Finally, I glanced up and found Michael watching me with a look of pure confusion on his face. Our eyes met for a fraction of a second before he looked away, studying his hands with great interest. Neither of us knew what to say.

Finally, he broke the silence. "Do you... think she's right?"

"No, I don't think so." I drew a deep breath and let it out as a sigh. Marriage? Good God, I barely knew the man. "It's way too soon. I mean, yes I love you, but... I think we need to give it time. We have no idea where this might go. Marriage is a huge commitment, and we have no idea what will happen once the hormones wear off."

"Yeah..." he trailed off, staring thoughtfully down at the ground. Suddenly, he looked up at me with the strangest look on his face. "But the possibility is still open for the future, right?"

My heart just about broke at the expression on his face. I smiled and shuffled over to cuddle up against him. "Definitely still open, when the time is right."

His expression relaxed, and his arms slid around me to hold me close. "Okay. Good. You know, one day. Just in case."

"Right." I hid a smile against his broad chest. Sometimes he could be such a little boy. Sweet, but completely transparent and utterly without guile. It was all part of his charm, though. Thirty-two years old and built like a brick shithouse, but so emotionally inexperienced that I could see right through him. At least I had the experiences of my rambunctious youth to fall back on. As far as I could tell, he'd never even kissed another woman unless you included his mother.

As though reading my mind, I felt strong fingers cup my chin again and then his lips closed over mine. He had learned a lot in the time since we'd met, and apparently he was determined to show me just how much. I definitely wasn't complaining. Practice makes perfect – and we were getting a lot of practice.

# Chapter Four

We spent a noisy night huddled in our room, hiding from the storm's wrath. Every so often something would bang, or crash, or rattle and wake us up, so by the time morning came none of us felt like we'd gotten much sleep.

The sunrise was a beautiful thing, though. The world took on a rosy pallet that cast tendrils of colour across the arc of the heavens. Clouds still marred the sky, but the sunrise turned them from grey to pink, and made them seem impossibly beautiful.

I awoke nestled in Michael's arms, like I did every morning, except this time the dawn light had painted our room in lovely colours. I stretched and rolled over, studying Michael's profile in the vivid dawn light. He looked so peaceful when he was sleeping, so young and vulnerable. A surge of hot emotion welled up in my belly; I found myself struggling to stay in control.

I lay my head back down on the pillow beside him, watching him sleep. With one hand, I reached up and trailed a finger along his jaw, feeling the fascinating roughness of his stubble beneath my fingertip. He grimaced in his sleep, wrinkled up his face and mumbled something I couldn't hear, then let out a deep breath and relaxed again. Something deep inside me quivered.

*Soon*, I promised it, and this time I really meant it. For all the pain I'd suffered, no matter how broken my psyche was, I really did love that man with an intensity that almost hurt. We lay together in sleep, nude and yet innocent, comfortable with one another in a way that I'd never experienced before.

I slipped a hand beneath the blankets and trailed my fingers down his chest. His skin was so smooth, with a light dusting of dark curls in just the right places. My fingers drifted lower, tracing the line of hair that adorned his belly just below the navel. Thoughtful and inquisitive, I followed it lower…

I suddenly realised that he was aroused, and the discovery sent a flash of heat tingling through my limbs. Was he dreaming about me? I often dreamed of him, of all the wonderful things we would one day do together. Equally often, I woke confused and excited, with my most basic animal instincts at war against learned behaviour.

Oh, but he wasn't asleep anymore. His dark eyes were open just a sliver, watching my face. He shifted and drew me closer, burying his face in the curve of my neck.

"Taking advantage of me in my sleep again?" he murmured, his voice so soft and deep that it sent a shiver down my spine. Suddenly, his arms tightened and he had me on my back, belly to belly, chest to chest. His lips closed on mine, a hot, deep kiss that told me so much more than he meant it to. I understood intuitively that yes, he had been dreaming about me.

I had no chance to answer his accusation; my breath was stolen away by the passion of that kiss. He had me pinned, his hands roving across my body, and yet I felt no fear of him. My policeman, my lover. He would never hurt me. I could feel his body pressed against me, but true to his word, he resisted every one of his natural impulses and held himself back until I could tell him I was ready for him.

His lips left mine and drifted lower, seeking out that sensitive spot just below the corner of my jaw. Nibbling, kissing, driving me wild. Oh, I was so ready for him.

I struggled to draw the breath to tell him that, but just as I did, I opened my eyes–

–and found myself face to face with the most enormous, horrifying insect I'd ever seen in my life, squatting on the pillow right beside my head with its talons waving threateningly in the air. The breath I had drawn to surrender myself to him completely turned into a bloodcurdling scream. Poor Michael just about levitated off of me and ended up on the floor, while I fled to the far end of the bed and had myself a nice little heart attack in the corner.

The weta – a huge native insect that resembled nothing so much as the offspring of a gigantic cricket and the Devil himself – was not impressed.

Michael shoved himself up off the floor in a tangle of blankets, trying to figure out what had me so horrified. He spotted the enormous insect immediately, and then flopped right back onto the floor laughing himself silly at my expense.

"That is so not funny!" I was almost in tears, huddled up at the end of the bed. Then it hit me all of a sudden. It was just a bug. I'd seen them a hundred times before. It wasn't really dangerous, despite its horrifying appearance. The worst it could do was draw a little blood. Okay, it was slightly funny.

I burst out laughing, the romantic mood completely gone. I hurled one of our non-bug-covered pillows at Michael. It hit him square in the face, but it was only a pillow so all it did was make him laugh harder.

With great difficulty, he pried himself out of his tangle of blankets and snatched up his hat from where we'd left it the day before. Naked as a jaybird and armed only with a hat, he captured the offending insect, then yanked open the window and flung the creature outside. I joined him at the window just in time to see the huge bug hit the ground below and roll a couple of times. A second later, it was up and off at a run, uninjured but horribly offended by our rude behaviour. Michael looked at me and I looked back, both of us still struggling to control the urge to laugh.

"Fear not, madam! Captain Bugcatcher is here to protect you," he announced, flailing a playful salute.

I'd had about as much as I could stand, and that crossed the line. I dissolved into hysterics and collapsed back into bed, laughing until tears rolled down my cheeks and my stomach hurt. It was clearly not going to be a morning for love-making, but at least we both got a good laugh out of it.

*** 

Later, dressed and finally back under control, we descended the stairs to the kitchen. There, we found Anahera, Hemi, the doctor and Maddy sitting around the table, while Skylar stirred something savoury-smelling on top of a bench-top gas cooker.

"Power's still off?" I queried, fighting down a wave of relief at the sight of my baby sister back in the kitchen. Not only did that mean she was feeling better, but she was the best cook we had. All our bellies welcomed the sight of her with a spatula in hand.

"Yes," Anahera answered, then she turned and gave us a strange look. "Glad you could join us. When we heard all that screaming, we were concerned someone was getting murdered."

"All that... oh." I stared at her, unsure what to say. Although I could feel the heat rising in my cheeks, I couldn't fight the uncontrollable urge to start laughing all over again. Luckily, Michael found the willpower to answer while I was still in stitches, with an enormous grin on his face.

"She woke up to the biggest weta I've ever seen, on her pillow," he explained, using his hands to indicate the size of the beast. "It scared the hell out of us both. I guess it must have come inside on one of those branches that got blown about yesterday. Fear not, good citizens! The demon has now been evicted from the building."

He promptly struck a heroic pose, and soon everyone was laughing right along with me – except for little Madeline, who sat regarding us with eyes that said she thought we were all crazy.

Breakfast was a cheerful affair in comparison to the solemn meals we'd shared the day before. The storm had passed, and although the wind still whined around our building, it left us feeling like we'd survived a disaster.

After we'd finished eating our scrambled eggs, we went outside to inspect the damage done by the storm. Our little garden had survived mostly intact thanks to our forethought, but the outside of the building was a disaster zone. The remains of one large tree lay uprooted across the road, and down the street we could see another, smaller tree leaning up against the side of the building next to it at a drunken angle, its roots partially dislodged from the earth.

Leaves and debris were strewn everywhere, including large shards of broken glass that threatened our feet as we picked our way around the motel to inspect it. Our building had survived mostly intact, and I was amazed to see my haphazard construction on the roof was still standing strong. It'd take a bit of effort to clean it up, but only a couple of boards were missing completely.

A few of the other buildings in town had suffered far worse than ours. Michael nudged me and pointed at a portion of a roof that lay slumped across an overgrown lawn a short distance down the road, reducing the jungle to a crushed mess.

"Glad none of us were under that," I whispered to him. He nodded, but I saw the look on his face. He was thinking the same thing I was: Ryan may have been out in that weather last night. As angry as he was at Skylar's former fiancé for abandoning her, no one deserved the full force of nature's wrath.

I reassured myself with the thought that he'd survived just as many storms as I had over the years. He would know the warning signs, know when to go find shelter, and what kind of buildings would be sturdy enough to survive the weather. New Zealand was an island, and we were all Aotearoa's children. Our country had been subjected to many different kinds of storms over the years, not to mention the geological activity, floods and even tidal waves. You couldn't go anywhere without seeing some kind of natural damage.

Years ago, I'd honestly thought that my number was up. I had been travelling near the centre of the island when an earthquake struck that was ten times more violent than anything I'd felt before. I had fallen to the ground and hadn't been able to get back up for what felt like forever; in the distance, a massive plume of ash had shot up into the sky.

To my eternal relief, I later discovered that it had only been Mount Taranaki venting its red-hot disinterest at the world, as it did on a semi-regular basis. The eruption had caused little damage beyond light ash fall. Nature was a fickle mistress, and she scolded us often; we'd all survived it before.

*He's probably fine*, I reassured myself, then took Michael's hand and led him back towards the others.

\*\*\*

Anahera and her son stayed long enough to help us repair some of the damage to our home. Our motel was low, squat, and solid; the work mostly involved clearing debris, so that it wouldn't endanger us in the future.

The wind blew in brief but violent gusts as we worked, yet it only took a few hours to clear up the worst of the mess. There was nothing we could do about the tree that blocked the road without putting all our people at risk, so we decided to just leave it where it was. At least it meant convenient firewood nearby, or a makeshift barricade in a pickle.

Surprise, surprise. The barricade idea was mine. It's not that I'm paranoid, per se. I just like to be prepared for every contingency. That was the same thing that I told Anahera when we were debating whether or not to bring our weapons on our trip west to visit her home.

"It's not that I don't trust you or your people," I explained to the group as we stood around the kitchen, making plans, "but there are a lot of dangers between here and your place that we should be able to defend ourselves against."

"I don't think it's necessary," Michael protested. "We're only going for a short vacation, and it's just a few hours walk away."

"Hemi was only a few hours from home when the pig found him," I pointed out. The youth grunted in agreement.

"She's right, man," Hemi said, then pointed at his bandaged side. "Don't forget about the bugger that's out there taking pot shots at us, too."

The others looked undecided, but it was Anahera who broke the tie.

"I agree with Sandy. You should bring your weapons along." She looked at me and smiled. "However, I appreciate you making the effort to ask my permission before you made the decision. Thank you."

"Of course," I stammered; her praise always left me feeling a little flustered. "You don't bring a shotgun to a mate's house without asking first. That's just bad manners."

"Your mother clearly raised you well." Anahera's smile broadened.

"Well, it's settled then," Michael finally agreed reluctantly. "Everyone go get your things, we'll leave in fifteen minutes."

Those of us who were going filtered out to collect our packs, and left the doctor to chat with our guests. He'd decided to stay behind with Madeline rather than come with us, protesting that our gardens still needed care and someone should protect our home base. I assumed that he just didn't like being out of his element, but I hadn't said anything. If Michael hadn't been so determined to go and Skye wasn't so clearly in need of an adventure, then I would have stayed home as well.

Home. It felt funny using that word, particularly to describe a run-down old motel and a tatty former video store. Michael slipped his hand into mine as we walked back towards his room, and I was forced to quickly reassess that thought. Maybe it wasn't so strange after all. Home is where the heart is, and mine was here.

He opened the window to our walkway between the buildings and offered me a hand up, which I accepted. I slipped out onto the damp planks, testing their stability carefully, then I crossed the alley to the top floor of my old video store to gather my things. Michael stayed behind, to pack his own bags.

My backpack lay in a distant corner of my bedroom, slumped sadly against the wall like an abandoned toy. Unlike Michael, I'd taken the time to clean out the drawers in my room, and replaced all the former occupant's belongings with my own. I didn't have much in the way of personal possessions, but I had acquired a few and it felt nice to have them organised in my drawers.

During my original expedition through the area, I'd spent a good deal of time exploring the town and scavenging anything that looked like it might fit me. When I had returned from Hamilton with my new friends in tow, my prizes still waited where I left them. Over the course of the last few weeks, I tried everything on and sorted the ones that fitted from the ones that didn't. My sister benefited from anything too small for me, and everything else went into storage. You never knew what you'd need to use for trading one day.

I pulled my drawers open one by one and added enough clean clothing to my backpack to last me three days. Our plan was to stay for a couple of days then head back home, so I doubted that I would need any more than that. If our plans changed, so be it. It wouldn't be the first time I'd had to go a bit longer than preferable without a change of clothing.

I had started to relax my usual dress code recently, too. During the decade I spent on my own, I'd usually worn military surplus, which was abundantly available if you knew where to look. It wasn't pretty, but it was hardy, long-wearing and easy to clean. Settling into life with my group had made me reassess my priorities. I found myself wearing casual civilian clothing more and more. It was mostly jeans and t-shirts, but I did have a few nice outfits that I'd hidden away to surprise Michael with one day. It amused me to imagine the look of shock on his face if he ever saw me wearing a dress.

I pondered that fact as I changed into my travel clothes: my old cargo fatigues, paired with a dusky grey tank top. Would I even know how to get dolled up anymore? I had gotten a wee bit of experience between puberty and when the plague hit, but a decade had passed since then. Michael had one up on me there. All he had to do was put on his police uniform, and suddenly he was the sexiest man alive. What did I have? Not much of anything, really.

With a hefty sigh, I sorted through the neat row of items sitting on top of my dresser. My GPS went into one pocket, my taser into another, my first aid kit into a third, and my gun went into my backpack. That should be enough for a couple of days in friendly territory, if I didn't give in to my natural urge towards caution.

What's the worst that could happen? I told myself as I picked up my pack and headed back to the window on the landing. Lake Ruatuna's two hours away at most, over open farmland. If something happens, we'll just come home.

Famous last words, my inner cynic contradicted, but I decided to ignore it. Michael scolded me regularly for being too pessimistic, so I had made it my personal mission to try and stay positive, for his sake. Positive, but realistic. I wasn't about to let a cheerful disposition get all of us killed.

I eased myself out the window onto the walkway, and closed the window behind me. Although it wasn't locked from inside, someone would have to get through the motel to reach it. That seemed pretty unlikely. I crossed the space between my window and Michael's and ducked back into his room. just in time to be confronted by a very nice pair of tight, manly buttocks.

"Well, hello there," I teased as I hopped off the window sill onto the bed below.

Michael shot a glance over his shoulder at me. "Oh, you're back. That was fast."

"I pack efficiently. Call it a skill." I gave him a smile, then flicked a pointed look down over his body. "Why are you naked?"

"What?" He glanced at me again, and then looked down. "Oh, right. I got distracted. Have you seen my vest?"

I flung myself down on my belly and reached under the bed, to pull out a dark blue body armour chest piece. "This one?"

"That's it!" He brightened as soon as he saw it, then came over and took it from me with a smile. "What would I do without you?"

"Lose things, apparently," I answered dryly. "You put it under there last week. Did you forget already?"

"I'm just not quite used to being here yet," he admitted sheepishly, turning his back to me as he got dressed. As sad as I was to see that delicious bottom covered up, we weren't going to go anywhere without pants. "I lived in that bunker for a very long time. I'm so used to everything always being in the same place, and now it's not."

"You'll get used to it," I said, lazing on my belly to watch him pulling on his boxer-briefs and jeans.

"I know, I know; it just takes time to adapt." He gave me that sweet smile of his, then tugged a close-fitting white t-shirt over his head. Once he'd straightened his clothes, he wandered over to plop down on the bed beside me. I felt the warmth of a hand on the small of my back, followed by inquisitive fingers slipping up beneath the hem of my top. "You understand that better than anyone."

"I guess I do," I agreed, rolling onto my back to look up at him. His hand slid over my skin, until it came to rest on my belly. He stared down at me thoughtfully, trailing gentle fingers over the smooth curve of my stomach, as though considering moving them higher. If he did, the chances of us setting off on time were slim to none.

He let out a long, deep sigh and reluctantly removed his hand from beneath my clothing. Self-control could be difficult at times, even for the best of us, but he was a good man and tried so hard. I felt a sudden rush of affection towards him and popped upright to plant a kiss on his cheek.

Michael's brows shot up at the gesture. Suddenly, before I knew what was happening, he caught me in a playful embrace and bore me down onto the bed. I found myself pinned down by strong, gentle hands, and could only squeal helplessly while he planted kisses on my belly. He released me a few seconds later, but it was so sudden and unexpected that it got me laughing all over again.

"You're so weird," I scolded him, giggling; he just grinned right back at me and went about strapping on his vest. It was only then that I realised he'd been looking for it because he intended to wear it for our trip. My levity oozed away. "Wait, you didn't want to bring the guns, but you're going to wear that?"

"I thought about what you said downstairs," he admitted, tugging a strap tighter against his skin, "and I realised that you were right. I don't think Anahera's *whanau* mean us any harm, but anything could happen. We should try to be prepared."

"I've trained you well, my pet," I teased him. While he was busy, I wriggled back over to close the window above his bed, so the rain and insects couldn't get in while we were away. "We'll make a proper survivalist out of you yet."

"I hope not," he answered dryly, then he reached over to poke my bottom while he could reach it easily. "Positivity!"

"Hey, hey, what's with the poking?" I spun around and poked him right back. "I keep telling you, there's a difference between negativity and realism."

"Ah, but there must be a balance, grasshopper," he told me sagely.

"So you're the Yin to my Yang, Officer Chan?" I asked, moving back to the edge of the bed to sit beside him.

"Something like that, except it's the other way around. Yin represents the feminine and yang the masculine." He gave me a quirky sideways smile, and started putting his socks and boots on while we were talking.

"No, I'm pretty sure I meant exactly what I said," I countered dryly. A little too dryly, apparently; it took him a second to cotton on to what I'd said. When he finally put two and two together, he shot me an amused glance.

"Really now? I'm pretty sure that *I'm* the one with the—"

"Maybe so, but which one of us hits like a truck?" I waved a fist at him playfully.

"Okay, you win that point," he conceded, laughing.

Dressed at last, Michael rose to his feet and stretched languidly. Although the action was quite innocent, it distracted me from our conversation; I watched with interest, admiring his physique. He really was a remarkable man: mentally, physically, and emotionally. Suddenly, I felt a little inadequate by comparison.

Michael glanced over his shoulder at me, as though sensing instinctively that something was amiss. "What's the matter, sweetheart? You're being quiet. It worries me when you're quiet."

"It worries you?" I couldn't help but laugh at that comment. "I'm quiet by nature; why would that worry you?"

"No, you're not," he said, reaching out to take my hand. With that wonderful, gentle strength of his, he drew me up to my feet and wrapped one arm around my waist to hold me up against him. "You're quite gregarious by nature, love. The only time you're quiet is when you're scared, angry, or sleeping. Or when you're thinking, but I can usually tell when you're doing that because of the smoke coming out of your ears."

"Smoke!" I put on an offended expression. "I'll have you know I was thinking just a moment ago, mister. You're so mean to me. Just because I'm blonde doesn't mean I'm dumb!"

"You know that I love your hair, and that I don't think you're dumb at all," he said, his humour fading. With his free hand, he slipped a finger beneath my chin and tilted my face up towards his. "Penny for your thoughts, then?"

Oh, compliments. I still wasn't used to those. Not that I wanted him to stop, but I had no idea how to respond. Feeling the heat rising in my cheeks all over again, I paused for a second to formulate my answer before I replied. "Well... I was thinking about you, actually."

"Me?" He raised a brow, looking curious.

"Yeah, it's just that..." I broke eye-contact and looked away, when a wave of shyness reared its ugly head. It had been a long time since I'd talked to a boy about my feelings. Hell, it'd been a long time since I had a boy to have feelings about.

No, not a boy, I corrected myself. A man. A wonderful, sweet, loving man who deserved to know he was doing a good job.

"You're just so perfect, Michael," I admitted, staring at some point beyond his right shoulder as I tried to organise my thoughts. "You're so kind and generous, and you always know just the right thing to say. I just... sometimes I feel like I don't deserve you. I try to tell myself that you must see something in me, but you're just so amazing that I feel like I'm nobody compared to you."

His expression softened, and his arm tightened around me protectively. "Oh, Sandy..."

"I know!" I groaned and rolled my head back, ashamed of myself for feeling that way at all. "I know that it's ridiculous, and that it just sounds whiny and pathetic. I'm a shame to empowered women everywhere. You probably just think I'm fishing for compliments, but I'm really not. I just... don't know how to—"

"Shh." He silenced me with a quick kiss, then hugged me. "You don't have to explain it to me, sweetheart. I feel the exact same way every time I'm with you."

"...What?" I stared at him, stunned. "You feel inadequate beside *me*?"

"Sometimes, yes," he admitted. "I wish that I had half the strength I see in you. Every time I think about what you've been through and survived all on your own, it makes me feel sick for you, proud of you, and envious of your resilience all at the same time." His strong arms tightened around me, not enough to hurt but enough to make me feel safe and secure, while his words made me feel so vulnerable. "It makes me want to be more than I am, for your sake."

I wasn't sure what to say to that. My emotions were a mess at the best of times, and when I felt weak and exposed it only got harder to stay in control. Part of me wanted to laugh, part of me wanted to cry, and part of me wanted to rip his clothes off and have my merry way with him right then and there. Unfortunately, the 'cry' part won. Tears sprang unbidden into my eyes. I buried my face in his chest to hide them as I thought over what he'd said.

Never one to let me mope unmolested, Michael used the opportunity to unleash his wicked sense of humour. He leaned down and put his lips right against my ear to whisper, "Plus, you're fucking gorgeous." Then, he grabbed my bottom in both hands and gave it a vigorous squeeze.

The gesture took me completely by surprise; I squealed like a stuck pig. A second later, I laughed and shoved myself out of his embrace, rubbing my poor, abused bottom. Then his words struck me, and I felt like a teenage girl with her first crush all over again.

"You really think I'm pretty...?"

He'd said it before, but it still felt strange. I'm aware of my physical properties, of course – every person judges his- or herself in front of a mirror at least once in their lifetime – but hearing the words from the lips of someone you adored was a whole other story. It made me feel all twisted up inside, a Gordian knot of tangled emotions.

"No," he chided, which shattered my daydream and took me by surprise, but a second later he smiled and clarified his words. "I do believe I said 'fucking gorgeous'. There's a difference."

"Oh." Man, he was really good at rendering me speechless. Not sure what else to say, I settled for being polite. Mama may have raised a crazy girl, but she didn't raise a rude one. "Thank you, I think."

"You think? Hah!" Michael grabbed both of our bags and draped an arm around my shoulders. "Come on, the others will be waiting."

Unable to resist the allure of his boyish charm, I let myself be led away. Sure enough, the others were waiting in the foyer, ready to depart. Skye took one look at us as we made our way down the stairs and rolled her eyes. "Oh God, Sandy's mutating into a tomato again. What'd you do this time, Michael?"

"He didn't do anything," I said in Michael's defence. By the time we reached them, my emotions had started to settle down, shifting from a turbulent ocean of conflicting pride and self-consciousness into a buoyant sort of happiness. "He was just giving me a pep talk, that's all."

"Sure, he was." Skylar gave me a disbelieving look, but let it drop. Instead, she handed me a small jar, full of what looked like mayonnaise. "Here. The doctor made us some sunscreen. We probably won't need it today, but bring it anyway. You know, just in case." She shot Michael a long, pointed look. The filthy look that he gave her in return made me smile. The relationship between my sister and my lover was an endless source of amusement to me. It was like an antagonistic brother/sister relationship, which was kind of appropriate, considering the circumstances.

"I'll make sure to put some on if the sun comes out," I promised, cutting them both off before the banter could turn into an actual argument. "We should go. I'm not sure how long the weather's going to hold off."

Noises of agreement met my comment, and the group of us finally pulled ourselves together enough to leave. Anahera and Hemi took the lead, wheeling their light farm bikes so the rest of us could keep pace. Skylar walked with them, looking bright and full of energy for the first time since she'd lost her baby. There was a spring in her step, and she quickly fell into conversation with our new friends.

Michael and I lagged behind. At some point he took my hand – or perhaps I took his, I'm not really sure. It just sort of happened, like it was the most natural thing in the world. We walked together in companionable silence, until a thought popped into my head that I felt the need to express.

"Sandrine."

"What?" He looked at me, one brow raised.

"My full first name. It's Sandrine," I explained. It was a trust thing; I didn't usually tell people my full first name, because it was too painful to hear it spoken out loud. Still, I trusted Michael. He deserved to know.

"Oh." He went silent while he thought that over, staring off into the distance.

"It was my grandmother's name," I elaborated for him, trying to explain why I felt so strongly about it. "I was named after her, but when I was little everyone called me Sandy so there wouldn't be any confusion. She... died."

"And now it hurts to hear her name," he finished for me.

I nodded, looking down at the long grass in front of my feet. "She made me promise, that when she got too sick to speak... she didn't want to become one of the wandering dead. My gun belonged to her, but she gave it to me. I had to... t-to..." I swallowed hard, struggling to get the words out.

Michael shook his head and gave my hand a gentle squeeze. "You don't have to say it, sweetheart. I understand. You had to kill her, because you loved her. Now every time you hear your own name, it reminds you of what you had to do."

Damn, he was good.

I nodded again, fighting back a wave of misery that threatened to bring tears to my eyes. Sweet and intuitive as always, Michael let me have some time to recover from the emotional onslaught.

"I already knew your full name," he finally admitted. Perplexed, I looked up at him, and he gave me a faint smile. "Your sister. She didn't tell me directly, but I overheard her when she was chasing us, back in the bunker."

"Oh, of course. I forgot about that." It made sense, now that I thought about it. Skylar had spit the dummy over something, and I had scampered away and hidden. Somehow, I'd ended up hiding right beside Michael. Of course he had heard. "Well, geez. Way to ruin it. That was supposed to be how I was going to show you I finally trust you with my big secret."

"It still works," he answered softly, his smile growing. "You telling me means way more than overhearing your sister screaming at you. You don't have to worry, though. I won't use it unless you ask me to. I couldn't bear to do anything that upsets you."

"Thank you." I smiled back, relieved that he was so understanding. That he'd known all along and hadn't said a word, even in jest, meant more to me than words could possibly express.

We walked in contented silence for a long time after that.

# Chapter Five

Although it wasn't far as the crow flies, the journey took longer than it would have in the old days, even on foot. Ten years ago, you could have driven from Ohaupo to Lake Ngaroto in fifteen minutes, but Anahera told me that the roads were unreliable and overgrown. As we walked westwards, I started to see evidence of what she meant.

The farther we got from Ohaupo, the more wild and unpredictable the route became. Once, the area had been flat, green pastureland dotted by picturesque farm houses, but nature had gone mad in the decade since human supervision ended. The grass stood waist-high in places, and the debris from a hundred storms hindered us at every turn. It forced us to go slowly and carefully, particularly those of us with the bikes – a punctured tyre could turn a useful tool into trash.

Eventually, the grass gave way to young native bush. That came as a relief, since it was easier to negotiate the thin undergrowth than the long grass. That's not to say it was easy going, though; heavy ferns and bushes grabbed at our feet, forcing us to take a twisting path between the trees.

For whatever reason, the herds of feral farm animals seemed to have avoided these parts, letting the plants grow lush and verdant since there was nothing to keep them in check. Birds sang in the trees overhead, fell silent as we passed beneath them, then resumed their songs only once we were out of sight. The familiar, distinctive warble of a territorial tui made me smile.

"Keep an eye out for rabbit," Hemi said, keeping a wary eye on the ground near his feet. "Sometimes they get infected."

I'd seen them before, so the warning came as no great surprise to me, but Michael looked positively horrified. "Zombie bunnies? That's a thing?"

"Yeah." Hemi shrugged helplessly. "Not always, though. Just sometimes. I guess it depends on the bunny."

"Are they violent?" Michael asked. His expression was one of such distress that I felt an overwhelming urge to comfort him, despite the ridiculousness of it all.

"Nah." Hemi paused, then shot us a thoughtful look. "Well, not usually. Sometimes. We usually shoot them if we see them, just in case."

"The poor little things." Michael looked crestfallen. Suddenly, he realised we were all staring at him, and his expression turned defensive. "What? I like bunnies. They're cute. There's nothing wrong with a grown man liking bunnies."

"Whatever you say, honey." I patted his hand, amused. Who was I to judge? I liked bunnies, too. Just not zombie bunnies. Being the shining beacon of diplomacy that she was, Anahera discreetly distracted us.

"The path should be just over there," she said, pointing through the trees. I couldn't see anything, but our guides seemed confident that they knew where they were going. Sure enough, a few minutes later sunlight broke through the canopy and we emerged into a clearing.

My foot struck something solid as I stepped forward. I looked down, and saw railway sleepers nestled beneath the short grass. A glance in either direction confirmed my suspicion: the path continued along a tunnel framed by lush trees, the boughs arching high overhead but not encroaching on the path. Even after all these years, the old railway line was still a solid means of travel. Long after the trains had turned to rust, we could use the scars they left upon the landscape as a walkway. Our boots crunched across gravel as we travelled southwards, but the grass struggled to take root in it.

We travelled much faster once we were inside that emerald corridor. As we walked, I looked around and saw the tell-tale signs of human occupation emblazoned on the local plant life. The tracks left by human feet and small tyres grew in frequency the farther south we went, marking the routes that Anahera and her tribe travelled the most.

An hour later, we left the tracks and followed a narrow path that branched off to the west. This one showed even more obvious signs of human interest in the region; the trees had been cut back and the scrub cleared, to keep the passageway clear. After following the slender green corridor for a few minutes, the trees began to thin out. The sounds of civilization reached us before we saw it: a dog barked, accompanied by the distant murmur of voices raised in good-natured chatter, occasionally broken by the sound of laughter.

We rounded a bend and came to a halt as the camp opened up before us. Raw wooden palisades built atop earthen ramparts formed a wall, built up to a height of at least two metres. In front of the walls, a carefully-planned line of trenches and platforms marked the hillside, forming an impressively formidable defensive position.

Even I recognised the ingenuity of the design. If an enemy force wanted to get close to this village, they would have to negotiate the trenches and platforms to reach the walls, which would slow them down significantly. The heavy gates stood open at the moment, and a ramp had been lowered over the defences to welcome the travellers home.

Within the compound, I saw a mixture of old, pre-plague buildings, and newer, rough-hewn structures made from local materials. Rising high above the walls, an observation platform of carved logs stood silhouetted against the midday sun. I looked around and realised the land had been cleared for more than a hundred metres in any direction, so neither friend nor foe could approach without being spotted.

And spotted we were. The sentry shouted something I couldn't hear and waved broadly at us. Anahera and Hemi waved back.

"More than two hundred years ago, my ancestors fought the largest land battle in New Zealand's history on this very spot," Anahera told us, pride glinting in her eye. She swept her arm out towards the village, and bowed. "This may not compare to the mighty *pā* of my ancestors, but I am proud to call this spot home. *Haere mai*, my friends – welcome."

"Thank you," Michael said, his deep voice almost a rumble. "We appreciate being invited."

"You shared your home and your hearth with us; it is only fair that we return the favour." Anahera smiled, and beckoned for us to follow her. "I hope you will forgive us for skipping the formalities. As much as I try to keep my people's traditions alive, I have little patience for ceremony."

I was a little relieved to hear that. You could fit the amount I knew about traditional Maori welcoming ceremonies on the back of a 10 cent piece, and I hated the idea of doing something wrong and upsetting my new friends.

People had begun to gather near the entrance by the time we reached the ramp, a half-dozen men of all ages, shapes and sizes. A couple had lighter skin than the rest, indicating that they had other ethnicities mixed in with their Maori blood, but they didn't seem bothered by or excluded because of that fact. Anahera led us towards them, and as we drew closer I could hear the sound of excited chatter amongst them.

"You're the first women besides me that my boys have seen in quite a while, so be gentle on them." Anahera shot us a wink, and then turned her attention to making introductions.

It took some time for us to learn everyone's names, but they made us feel so welcome that the time flew by. I was relieved to discover that all of them were fluently bilingual, and excited to see new faces. Michael stayed close to me, to help keep me calm with his presence alone. Although I did feel a little uncomfortable at first, Anahera's brothers were perfect gentlemen. In no time at all, their friendliness and manners put me at ease.

Skylar seemed to enjoy the attention immensely. While I was content to let Michael do the talking for both of us, she went off on her own, and seemed happy to chatter to anyone that she could find. There was a natural effervescence to her personality that was finally getting the chance to bubble up to the surface; surrounded by so many friendly faces, she was in her element.

Once introductions were over, we were invited into the tiny fortress for lunch. I discovered to my amusement that the central building of the complex was actually an old yacht club. They had converted it and made it their own, decorating it with intricate carvings cut into the building's wooden framework. There were monsters and gods, men and women, all poised in the distinctively stylized poses traditional to Maori culture. I was fascinated. Handicrafts had been one of my interests since childhood, and the carvings had a professional look to them that surprised me.

"This place is amazing," I whispered to Michael as we were led off to the room they'd converted into a dining hall.

Despite my attempt to be discreet, Anahera overheard and shot me a smile. "Thank you, dear. I'm glad you approve."

I flushed with embarrassment, but there was no sign of sarcasm in her tone. "It is. I mean, these carvings – they're so detailed. Did you do them?"

"Me?" She laughed, and the sound of it reassured me. "Oh, if only I had that kind of skill! No, Ropata is our carver." A stocky man in his early forties looked up from where he had been busy sorting out something lunch-related, but Anahera just gave him a wave and a smile. "He apprenticed as a carpenter in his youth, then went on to learn a variety of other types of woodworking – including *whakairo rakau*, our traditional carving. It's possible that he may be the only master carver left alive."

"I'm glad that someone survived to keep the art going," I answered, pausing to admire a particularly elegant carving around the doorway. "It must be handy to have a proper carpenter in your group, too. I can build something simple and functional, but nothing like this. This is beautiful."

"It is," Anahera agreed. She touched my arm to draw my attention away from the carvings, then led us to the long wooden table that filled the centre of the room. Instead of chairs, benches flanked its sides. As the guests of honour, she sat us right in the middle, with Michael and me together on one side, Skylar and herself opposite us.

Once we were settled, her comrades came in bearing steaming hot food on a mismatched assortment of platters. The smell of it made my mouth water even though most of the scents were unfamiliar to me. When one of the men set a platter near me, I suddenly realised why.

"Is that fish? Real, fresh fish?" I exclaimed, delighted. I was a poor hunter and even worse at fishing, so it had been years since I'd had any kind of fish except the canned kind. Killing animals for food wasn't in my nature, but I was perfectly happy to eat things that other people had killed for me. No sense in letting a living thing's life go to waste.

"Fresh from our lake. Don't worry, we make a point of fishing far from any of the contaminated parts now." Anahera smiled at us, and then leaned over to point out the different kinds of food as they were brought in. "That's catfish, and this is eel. That one over there is wild duck…"

The list went on. My eyes just about popped out of my head at the bounty before us. There was even freshly-baked bread, made with potato in the Maori way. I didn't care that it wasn't the kind of bread I'd grown up on. It was bread, and I hadn't eaten bread in almost a decade.

I'm not afraid to admit that I gorged myself like a pig, because Michael and Skylar did the same. Our new friends laughed and joked with us, pleased by our enthusiasm for their efforts. For once in my life, I didn't mind being laughed at. The meal was without a doubt the best one of my adult life. Even when I was so full I thought I might pop, I still found room for just one more slice of delicious *rewena* bread, just one more piece of *kumara*, just one more…

It was never just one more.

Eventually, my stomach just couldn't take any more abuse, so I had to stop. With a deep groan of satisfaction, I leaned back on my bench to try and find a position where my tummy didn't ache quite so much, but every angle hurt.

The others, including Michael and Skylar, were still busy stuffing their faces with gusto, but I couldn't possibly eat another nibble. I'd become a bit of a light-weight in the eating game over the years; after spending the better part of a decade on a starvation diet, my stomach had shrunk.

Eventually, Anahera noticed my uncomfortable condition. She hopped off her bench to help me up, and then escorted me down a corridor to somewhere I could rest. It turned out to be a small, makeshift dormitory, little more than a storage room with a couple of old double mattresses on the ground. I wasn't too bothered. I'd slept in far worse places over the years. It was clean and dry, and there were fresh linens on the mattresses.

Anahera helped me to lie down, and then left me to digest in peace. I rolled onto my back and flopped out across the mattress with a groan.

*Too full, hurts to breathe,* I whined mentally but couldn't work up the willpower to say anything out loud. Not that it mattered, there was no one there to hear it. *Too full. No care. Must sleep.*

My eyes closed and I drifted into a contented doze, soothed by the distant sounds of happiness from the dining hall. I had no idea how long I napped, but eventually I heard the shuffling of feet nearby, then someone flopped heavily onto the mattress beside me. Ever the cautious one, I opened one eye to inspect the new arrival.

Michael. Friend. Safe.

I grunted an inarticulate greeting, and he replied with a groan. Ah, clearly he was suffering the same as me. Good.

*Resume sleep mode now,* my brain told me in no uncertain terms. I acquiesced without a fight. My eyes drifted closed, and before I could form another coherent thought I was fast asleep.

\*\*\*

I awoke to the sound of Michael snoring beside me, the only sound in the silence. I rolled over and stretched, then looked around curiously to try and figure out what time it was. I decided that it was still daylight, based off the glow that filtered in between the haphazard curtains strung across the nearby window. A beam of light fell across us, bright enough that I could pinpoint the time at somewhere in the mid-afternoon.

Michael was sprawled on his back with one arm draped over me. He was in such a deep sleep that he didn't even stir when I extracted myself from under his arm and sat up. After so many years of living on a survival diet, where every mouthful was carefully rationed in case it was your last, the chance to actually feast was something neither of our bodies quite understood. It was like ten years of Christmases had hit us all at once. We'd both managed to overload our senses, as well as our poor, distended bellies.

I was feeling better after my sleep, though. It had been ages since I'd eaten that much in one sitting, and all of a sudden I was bouncing with energy and ready to take on the world. So I left Michael sleeping, and went off to explore on my own – and to find a lavatory in quick order.

Luckily for me, I discovered the door next door to mine was the toilet block, so I was able to relieve myself without any issues. Infinitely more relaxed as a result, I went off to wander the halls, sticking my head into various rooms to see what was happening and where.

I found a few people hard at work in rooms nearby, but no one I knew well or felt any inclination to disturb. I left them in peace and moved on. Eventually, I found myself in a large room on the lake side of the building, where several small boats rested. Although I had grown up in an island nation, I knew a grand total of nothing about boats. I saw oars nearby so I presumed the boats were canoes, but that was my best guess. The only thing I was sure of was that there was a gap in the row, so one of the boats was missing or in use.

Beyond the boats, a large concertina door stood half open, which let in a square of daylight and gave me a glimpse of the lake beyond. I moved closer to look outside. The day was still overcast, and it was raining lightly. Beyond the door, a patch of trimmed grass separated the building from the edge of the lake, where a small dock had been built out into the water. Someone sat on the end of the dock with a fishing rod. I could see dark hair pulled back in a braid and a feminine figure, so I assumed it was Anahera.

A distant squeal drew my attention out over the lake. Shielding my eyes with my hand, I stared out across the water at a small boat in the distance, and realised that I could see blonde hair. Although I couldn't see a face at that distance, it had to be Skylar. Curious, I stepped out into the drizzle and picked my way across the damp grass towards the dock. The day was warm despite the weather; the rain was nothing more than a pleasant coolness to counteract the heat.

My feet made a hollow sound as I stepped from slippery wet grass onto wood, which made the person on the end of the dock look up. Sure enough, it was Anahera. She smiled when she saw me and beckoned for me to join her, so I did.

Water soaked through the seat of my cargo pants as I settled on the edge of the dock beside her, but I didn't mind. It was still late summer, so getting wet wasn't an inconvenience. It brought back memories of childhood: like every child, I'd spent many a summer afternoon dressed in my bathing suit, dashing back and forth through the sprinklers in our garden.

"What are they doing out there?" I asked curiously, canting my head in the direction of the distant boat.

"Hemi's teaching your sister to fish," Anahera answered, absently adjusting the slack of her own line. "They bite more when it rains, so now is the best time for it. Fishing generally isn't that noisy, though."

As if to punctuate her sentence, Skylar squealed again. We both grinned.

"She is a little loud," I agreed. On a whim, I shuffled my bottom back away from the edge, and started removing my shoes and socks.

"Just a little," Anahera agreed good-naturedly.

When my shoes and socks were off, I rolled up my pants and slipped my feet into the cool water. It was nice, just hanging out, doing nothing. Like being a teenager before the plague. Even Anahera wasn't trying very hard to catch a fish; I quickly figured out that she was just doing it to relax, rather than to be productive.

Occasionally we chatted, mostly about fishing or the bounty of food the local area had to offer, but primarily we just sat in companionable silence. Skye squealed, laughed, and jumped around, keeping us both entertained with her antics. I was just happy to see her enjoying herself. After everything she'd been through, she deserved a moment of joy. Part of me worried that she'd fall out of the boat or hurt herself, but I wasn't really concerned.

*She can take care of herself – and if she gets herself in trouble, Hemi will take care of her*, I reassured myself. I was certain he would. They were of a like age and had swiftly become friends. Then, a thought occurred to me. I shot a sideways glance at Anahera. "Does Hemi have a crush on Skye?"

Anahera laughed and nodded, then gave me a long look in return. "I think he has a crush on both of you, actually. But, Skylar is his age and you're clearly enamoured with Michael, so she seems like the logical focus of his ardour."

"That's adorable." I grinned to myself and peered out across the lake. "I'm glad to hear it. After Ryan left her, I wasn't sure how well she was going to hold together. They were together for a long time."

"Hah!" Anahera barked a laugh and shook her head. "I think you underestimate how resilient your sister is. There is a great deal of strength hidden within her. Just give her a bit of time to recover. She'll be fine."

"I really hope you're right." I heaved a sigh, and eased myself back to lie on the dock, folding my arms beneath my head. The rain felt wonderfully cool as it fell on my face. For a moment, life felt perfect.

# Chapter Six

We spent our afternoon doing absolutely nothing remotely constructive, and it felt great. Michael eventually emerged to join us, and the three of us talked about all kinds of unimportant things as we relaxed on the dock, watching Skye learn to fish.

When the shadows started to grow longer, Hemi and Skylar paddled their boat back to shore. Skye leapt out of the boat as soon as it was tied off, anxious to show off her catch. She looked so proud that my inner big sister forced me to lavish endless praise on her.

We trailed along behind the teenagers as they carried their fish off to be prepared for dinner, but when Hemi dragged her off to instruct her on how to scale, gut and fillet their catch, we decided to be elsewhere. Of course, by 'we', I mean 'me'. I have a weak stomach when it comes to hurting lesser animals. That was one of my biggest flaws, and probably the reason I'd ended up so malnourished over the years. I just couldn't bear the thought of killing an animal for the sole intention of eating it.

Anahera led us out to the front of the building, to show us where her men were preparing the *hangi* pit for dinner. Although both of us knew the concept, it was fascinating to see the underground oven being prepared. The men laughed as they juggled red hot rocks into the bottom of the pit, and then laid the cloth-wrapped food on top of it.

A second before they were about to fill in the hole to let the food cook, Hemi and Skye came tearing out of the building with their arms full of fish fillets, yelling for the others to wait. The men digging the hangi added the fish to the hole, then filled it in and left it all to cook in the heat.

Later on, when the food was cooked, they dug the hole up again and carried the food inside to the dining room. We all helped to unwrap it and serve it, so that we could learn more about the traditions our Maori neighbours employed in their efforts to preserve their own culture.

Dinner itself was a jovial affair, just like lunch had been, full of boisterous laughter and play. Since we were still full from lunch, my group only ate a little to avoid gorging ourselves unconscious again – but Skylar insisted that everyone had to try her fish. I wasn't lying when I told her it was delicious.

After dinner, we volunteered to help with the cleaning up. As it turned out, washing dishes was exactly the same in both our cultures. Skylar and I took that task while Michael went off to help the men with the heavier end-of-day tasks, leaving us alone together.

I was up to my elbows in hot, soapy water, when Skye suddenly spoke up. "Hey, Sandy? Can I ask you something?"

"Of course. What's up, little sis?" I answered, handing her a freshly-scrubbed plate to dry, then I turned back to grab another.

"What did Mum look like?"

I dropped the dish I'd just picked up, splashing soapy water all over myself. That was a question I hadn't been expecting. I glanced over my shoulder at her, wiping foam off my clothing. "What do you mean?"

"I mean… well, I…" She sighed and lowered her head, staring down at her feet. "I don't remember what she looked like, Sandy. I remember her name, I remember her voice, I even remember what she smelled like and what it felt like to cuddle her. But when I try to think about her, I can't remember what her face looked like. When I dream about her, her face is just… kind of a blur."

"Oh…" Wow, that was an unexpectedly deep question to have to answer while doing the dishes. I chewed my lip while I thought over the answer, and finally decided to go with the most obvious one. "She looked like you, Skye. Just like you."

"Like me?" Skylar echoed, looking bewildered.

"Yeah, just like you," I answered. Her brow furrowed in confusion, so I set aside the dishes to explain further. "When I was little, I used to like looking at Mum and Dad's wedding photos. She was eighteen or nineteen when they got married, so she was right around your age. When I first saw you as an adult, back at the bunker, I just about had a heart attack because you look just like her in those old pictures. The only difference is that her hair was longer, and you have a few more freckles."

Skye stared down at the ground, her young face set in such a look of confusion that I felt the need to hug her – so I did. I grabbed her and squeezed her hard, and she hugged me back.

"Any time you want to see your mum again, all you have to do is look in the mirror," I said softly.

"Thank you, sis," she whispered back, and then gave me one last hug before the topic was dropped, and we resumed washing dishes.

The three of us had to share a room that night, as it turned out that the room with the mattresses was the only spare bedroom our neighbours had. The permanent members of the group each had their own hut built in the space between the yacht club building and the outer wall, made by their own hands and decorated to their tastes, but they rarely had guests.

Skye teased us mercilessly as we settled into our beds, warning Michael and me that there would be big trouble if we got up to hanky-panky with her in the room. She was so silly about the whole thing that all three of us ended up laughing uncontrollably, with tears streaming down our cheeks.

Eventually, though, exhaustion claimed us all, and we each drifted off into a deep slumber.

*** 

I woke in the middle of the night, jerked out of pleasant dreams by a terrible, gut-wrenching sound: someone was screaming. I sat bolt upright in bed, straining to hear what they were saying, but I couldn't make out the words over a weird crackling sound that was so loud it made it hard to think.

Wait… a crackling sound?

My eyes widened as I came awake enough to put two and two together. I leapt out of bed and ran to the window. My foot hit Skylar's sleeping form along the way and almost tripped me, but adrenaline helped me to keep my balance. With no consideration for the delicacy of the curtains, I yanked them open and stared outside, at a yard turned hellish by the surging heat of flames.

"Fire!" I screamed the word as I leapt back over to my companions, and dragged them from their beds despite their sleepy protests. The fire was huge, and it was close. The smell of smoke was already drifting into our room. My survival instincts kicked in straight away. Before anyone else was fully awake, I had them pulling on clothing and arming themselves. Without a thought for myself, I shoved my taser into Skylar's pocket while she was still struggling to get dressed, and then shoved her baggage into her hands.

196

Michael had his pants on but was struggling with his shirt. Time was running out. It was starting to get hotter, and a haze of smoke had started to fill the room. I stuffed the rest of our belongings into our packs, and dragged the baggage with us as we raced for the door.

The smoke was even thicker out in the hallway and left us coughing as we struggled to find an exit. It seemed to be coming from the front of the building, so I led the way towards the rear instead. We burst into the boat room and ran the last few metres to the concertina doors, which had been closed for the night. We struggled with the latch in the semi-darkness, but finally we managed to get it open, and tumbled outside into the darkness.

The air was clearer on the lakefront – at last, we could breathe. Gulping down a lungful of clean, cool air, I dropped our belongings on the damp grass and turned to stare at the burning compound.

The fire was huge. I could see shadowy figures on the other side of the building racing back and forth, struggling to put out the flames, and realised that it must be Anahera's clan. That was a relief. Perhaps we weren't under attack after all. Perhaps it was just terrible misfortune.

That thought lasted for about two seconds. There was a strange sound behind me, followed by a muffled cry from Michael. He hit the ground just as I was turning to see what had happened, his hand clutched over one side of his chest. Blood was leaking through his fingers; it took a second before I came to the horrifying realisation that he'd been shot.

I dropped to my knees beside him, just as Skylar started screaming. There was too much happening, I was too confused; I couldn't see past the fact that Michael was bleeding on the ground. I didn't realise at the time that Skye was trying to warn me, that she'd seen the figures appearing out of the smoke behind me. Michael was in pain, and that was all I could think about.

Then, something hit me in the back of the head, and I blacked out.

***

I came to slowly this time; my brain felt muddled and confused. It took a few long seconds for memory to return, but when it did the sick feeling of dread settled into my belly. Only then did I start to feel my own pain.

The ground was hard beneath my shoulder and sharp rocks cut into my bare skin. I struggled to get up and found my hands were bound cruelly behind my back, with ropes that were so tight my fingers were starting to go numb. I opened my eyes, and my head swam. I discovered that I was lying naked on the ground, stripped of all my clothing.

A small fire burned in the clearing, and a shadow sat in front of it with its back towards me. It was a few minutes before dawn, and the sun was just starting to peek up over the horizon, heralding the start of another day.

*Perhaps my last day*, I thought perversely, but for once I didn't scold myself for my pessimism. I seemed to be in a pretty bad predicament. My heart hammered in my throat from the force of the adrenaline surging through my veins.

As if reading my mind, the man by the fire turned towards me and I got a look at his face. My stomach dropped to my knees. I knew those tattoos, that blunt, oft-broken nose. The rotten teeth, and scars – and most of all, I knew that terrible smile when he was thinking about hurting me. That smile was on his face right now.

"You're awake. Good. I was starting to get bored," he growled as he rose to his feet, his corpulent body swaying – I could smell alcohol, and realised that he was drunk. I wondered if that was good for me, or bad for me. Probably bad.

"Awfully kind of you, really," he slurred. "All this time, I was thinking that I'd have to come and get you later, once I got my revenge on that bitch at the village. And then what do my boys tell me? Two little blonde sluts showed up this very day, just waiting for us to come and visit? Perfect." He leapt on me suddenly, and grabbed my chin roughly with one enormous hand.

"You brought this on yourself, you little whore," he hissed. I could feel his spittle on my face. His breath was rank, like something had crawled into his mouth and died; the stink of it made me feel nauseated. "You escaped once. You killed my boy. You could have left it at that, but you didn't. Now I'm going to make you suffer so much you'll wish we'd killed you the first time."

He shoved me back down and kicked me hard, sending me rolling away in the dirt. It was only then I realised that my feet were untied. It was a small thing, but enough to give me hope.

*Don't be afraid*, I told myself silently. *He wants you to be afraid. That's the part he likes best.* My entire body was shaking, either from the cold or fear, but I fought to keep myself under control. I wouldn't say anything, and I wouldn't scream. I would not give him the satisfaction. There was always hope, until you were dead.

When I righted myself, I realised he'd moved away from me and that he was bent over examining something. Then he straightened up, and I saw the glint of steel in his hand – a knife.

Great. Just what I needed.

"That bitch friend of yours cut off my cock, and you're going to pay for that," he told me as he closed on me. I inched away from him warily, my eyes on the knife. "All of you are going to pay. Even that sweet little piece of ass you brought with you. Shame I can't tap that anymore – my boys will have to have all the fun with her. You're mine, though. Since I can't fuck you any more, we'll just have to make our own fun."

Hot pain surged across my breast as he lashed out with the knife. I felt blood flow, but my thoughts were on Skylar rather than myself. Jesus, Skye. I couldn't let them hurt her. I had to do something. He lashed out again and again; I felt the knife bite in, but this time I responded. I kicked out with all my strength at his left knee, and heard a satisfying crack when my blow hit home. The brute yelled and fell back away from me. For a moment, I felt a surge of victory in my chest, but I swiftly realised that wouldn't be enough.

"You bitch. You *bitch*. I was going to play with you a bit before I destroyed you, but maybe I'll just destroy you first and then play with you after!" he yelled at me, hobbling back to the tool kit I could only just see at the edge of my vision. Then he was coming back towards me, with a screw driver and a pair of pliers; a surge of horror lurched through me like a shot of pure ice.

He must have seen it on my face, because he grinned that terrible grin at me. "Yeah, that's right, you little bitch. I'm going to hurt you like you've never been hurt before. I'm going to cut out your fucking tongue, and then tear out every one of your fucking teeth." He gestured at me threateningly with the pliers. "But first... Oh, first, I'm going to cut out those pretty eyes of yours. Let's see how feisty you are when you can't see the pain coming!"

*Oh, Jesus. He's sick. Crazy!* Panic overwhelmed me and I fought to get up. He kicked me again and sent me rolling, laughing all the while as I scrambled away and tried to flee. Despite the injury to his knee, he caught up with me before I could get up, and pinned me to the ground with one foot – then he lashed out with the knife.

I managed to jerk my face away at the last second; the tip of the blade skidded across my cheekbone instead of taking out my eye as he'd intended. The pain was so intense that I screamed despite my conviction. I couldn't help it. I was going to die – no, worse! Oh God, this was so much worse! But there was no way that I was going without a fight.

I twisted with all my strength and managed to make him lose his balance for a moment; he slipped off of me, dropping the knife into the dirt. I kicked out with as much force as I could, again and again. I felt my blows striking flesh, but all that did was make him laugh. He was stronger than me by a factor of two. The only thing that gave me hope was that by the time he managed to get me pinned down beneath his weight, the knife and the other weapons were gone. Dropped somewhere in the undergrowth, I imagined. It was only a tiny hope, and it wouldn't last for long.

I screamed again when he hit me, a closed fist right across the face with such force that it slammed my head into the ground. His weight was right on top of me, crushing my arms beneath me. I couldn't move, I couldn't reach him with my feet. No matter how hard I tried, I couldn't get him off me. Hope faded as he hit me again, and again. Each blow drew a cry of pain from my battered body, and sent stars dancing across my vision.

I'm going to die. I'm going to die and there's nothing I can do about it. Oh God, but what about Skye? No, no, no – you can't have my sister!

I struggled with all my might, but there was nothing that I could do, and he just laughed at me. He slapped me across the face with an open hand, then drew his fist back to unload another blow.

The blow never came. It was interrupted by the sound of someone else screaming. But this wasn't a scream of pain. It was a scream of rage.

The bastard's head jerked up and he stared at the other side of the clearing. I was too battered to see what he saw, though. My head was spinning from the violence, and blood blurred my vision. But I did hear the roar of a shotgun blast, and I did see the man's head dissolve in a bloody shower of hot shrapnel and carnage. With the last of my strength, I dragged myself out from beneath the corpse before it could crush me, and only then did I see who my rescuer was.

It was Skylar. My baby sister. She strode across the clearing like an avenging angel, her eyes wild, her hair a golden halo around her face in the pre-dawn gloom, the shotgun nestled at her hip ready to deliver more deadly payload should it be required.

It wasn't. Unlike the walking dead, that man was only human. A terrible, evil human, but a human nonetheless. He was dead before she got close enough to check. I, on the other hand, was bloody, broken, but very much alive.

Skylar kicked the body hard, rolling the sack of dead meat away from me, then she came back and knelt down beside me to inspect my condition. Although black and blue from bruises, and bleeding from a half-dozen cuts, I was conscious. She helped me sit up, and used the very same knife that he had planned to blind me with to cut the bonds around my wrists.

My first instinct was to hug her. She hugged me back gently, and then helped me to my feet. A few seconds later, Michael joined us in the clearing and rushed over to help me as well. His chest was bound up in a makeshift bandage, but I could see the blood seeping through it already.

"How...?" I managed to gasp, though my mouth had the metallic taste of blood in it. My lips were cut, but I didn't seem to have lost any teeth.

"Your taser," Skylar explained as the two of them helped me back towards the relative safety of the lakeside fort. "After they knocked you and Michael out, two big men grabbed me and carried me off. They started arguing about which of them was going to rape me first, so I told them that I was still bleeding from my miscarriage and they both got mad.

"They dropped me and started yelling at each other. While they were distracted, I got out your taser and hid it behind my back. When they came back, I hit them with it. They were so surprised that I managed to get them both before they realised what was happening."

"You knocked them both out?" I gasped, amazed at my little sister's tenacity.

"Yeah." She nodded, hugging my battered frame gently. "Then I ran back to the camp and woke up Michael, and we went looking for you."

"I'm so glad you did," I told her, my voice hoarse from screaming and pain. "He was... going to... get his revenge on me by taking my eyes."

Tears welled up, but I didn't bother to wipe them away as they fell. It was too much effort, and I felt exhausted and wrung out. I was safe, I had survived, and even though I had screamed, I hadn't submitted. Michael swore under his breath. I knew instinctively that he felt like he'd failed to protect me, but I didn't have the strength to tell him it wasn't his fault.

Speaking was too hard for all of us, so the rest of the trip back was in silence. When we finally made our way out into the clearing beside the lakefront, the fire had been extinguished, and we found our Maori friends huddled around our belongings trying frantically to figure out what had happened to us.

Someone spotted us and shouted; the next thing we knew, we were enveloped in a friendly mob. Someone got a blanket around me to protect my modesty, then Michael and I were guided off to one of the huts that had survived the fire.

We were put to bed side by side, and our wounds were tended as best they could. Outside, I heard Anahera issuing orders. From what little I could understand of her bilingual shouting, I realised that she planned to take us home as soon as it was safe to move us. She was also sending people out to deal with the brutes my sister had left in the forest.

Beside me, I could hear Michael's uneven breath, and I worried for him more than I did for myself. It was only a small bullet, probably from an air rifle like the wound Hemi had come to us with, but it was in his chest and it could do serious damage.

I squeezed my eyes closed and leaned against him, praying that my love would be okay.

# Chapter Seven

By midday, we were on our way back home, each of us on the back of a quad bike with one of our friends driving. Although fuel was precious, Anahera insisted. She wouldn't let us walk all that way in our condition, not after what had happened to us while we were guests in her home. She felt responsible. I understood, but I felt no reason to blame her. It wasn't her fault.

With the bikes to carry us over the uneven terrain quickly, it only took a couple of hours for us to reach our old motel. Hemi and Skylar arrived first. They leapt off their bike and ran to go find the doctor, while the rest of us travelled more sedately so as not to jostle our injuries. Anahera parked her bike beside the door and helped me off, while behind us Ropata did the same for Michael.

Once the adrenaline had worn off, it left me in terrible pain. My wrists were black with bruises and it hurt so much to breathe that I wondered if I might have a broken rib. My sides and back were covered in grazes from where I'd been kicked across the dirt, and I needed a bath something terrible to get the dirt out of my wounds.

The doctor took one look at me and agreed. Skye and Anahera bundled me off to the shower, bathed me, and cleaned my wounds. The water was cold since the power was still off, but that helped to numb the pain.

I didn't even mind being bathed by two women all that much. After what I'd been through, being naked in front of friends didn't feel like the end of the world any more. At least they could reach my back for me – I was so stiff that I could barely move my arms.

Once I was bathed and dried, I was led back to Michael's room, where he lay recovering from makeshift surgery. The doctor knew me too well, and reassured me about his condition before I could even ask.

"He'll be fine," Dr Cross told me in no uncertain terms. "His ribs stopped the projectile, and I've removed it now. Aside from that and a minor concussion, he's going to be right as rain. Now, come here and let me look at you."

Given the extent of my injuries, I had to stay naked while he examined me. That was a more uncomfortable experience than the shower because of his gender, but he was also my doctor. I reminded myself of that every time he needed to fish a piece of gravel or a twig from a wound in an intimate place. I just closed my eyes and bore up to it, reminding myself that I was lucky I still *had* eyes to close. I owed Skylar big time for that.

A couple of the cuts were so deep that they required stitches, including the one on my face. Dr Cross warned me that I would probably have a scar from it, but I couldn't have cared less. All that mattered to me was that I could still see. I'd come so close to losing the privilege forever. I'd come so close to losing my life.

My ribs were examined by gentle touches, but the news from there was good – I probably had a couple of fractures, but no actual breaks. None of my injuries were life-threatening. Every inch of me hurt, but I still took that diagnosis with a smile. The way I saw it, it could have been so much worse. Despite the pain, I felt buoyant, even joyous.

Once my wounds were washed and dressed where appropriate, he gave me painkillers and put me to bed with firm instructions to rest. For once in my life, I felt no inclination to defy the doctor's orders. Frankly, I felt like a couple of miles of bad road, and all my body wanted to do was sleep.

I snuggled up against Michael's good side, resting my head on the half of his chest that wasn't covered in bandages. I felt an arm slip carefully around me, and the closeness was very comforting.

I slept fitfully through most of the afternoon and into the evening. Often, I woke up and just lay there with my eyes closed, thinking over everything that had happened. When I thought back to my brief captivity, I realised that I felt... nothing. No fear, no anger, no hatred, despite how close I'd come to losing several body parts that were very precious to me. All I felt was relief that it was over, and that everyone had gotten home safely.

At the time, yes, I had been afraid. I had panicked. But, more importantly, I realised now that I'd put up a damn good fight. I had screamed, but I hadn't surrendered. Although I hadn't realised it at the time, my screaming had helped my rescuers to locate me. Screaming saved my life.

Thinking over it logically, I came to the decision that I'd done very well, considering the circumstances. My entire attitude had changed. If this had happened six weeks earlier, I probably would have ended up a blubbering mess and not had the strength to fight back.

These survivors, my friends, had changed me. No, that wasn't right – they'd shown me that I wanted to change myself. I wanted to be stronger, for their sakes as well as my own, and when the chips were down I had been stronger. I was growing, as a person and as a woman. Skylar and Anahera both gave me good role models to look up to after being alone for so long. I was proud of them, and proud of myself. I felt like my mother and my grandmother would have been proud of me, too.

Realising that I'd managed to hold my own in an emergency brought with it a sense of pride, and a sense of personal achievement. I had done nothing to be ashamed of. Even though I hadn't told anyone the details of my ordeal yet, I felt like I could without any kind of shame. Considering how humiliated I'd felt for years after my first encounter with that man and his cronies, that was a vast improvement.

All of a sudden, I realised that I felt good about myself, for the first time in a very long time. More than just that, I came to another conclusion, one that I had to discuss with someone very important to me. I opened my eyes and discovered that it was dark, but I could hear the sound of uneven breathing that told me he wasn't asleep.

"Michael?" I whispered.

"Mhm?" he mumbled, shifting a little beneath me. The moon was full and our curtains were wide open; a shaft of moonlight fell across his face, so I could see his dark eyes watching me.

"I've been thinking," I told him softly, reaching up with one hand to trail my fingers along his jaw. His stubble was longer than usual, rougher, but I didn't mind. We'd both been through an ordeal. I couldn't blame him for being lax in his personal grooming.

"Yes?" He closed his eyes, leaning in to my touch.

*God, he is handsome,* I thought to myself, studying him in the moonlight.

"We almost lost each other today," I whispered, shifting closer against him so I could press my cheek against his. Understanding my need for closeness, he tightened his grip around me and held me gently against his side. "We live in a world where so much is outside of our control. There's so much danger. We could both die tomorrow. It's never going to be perfect; the only thing in this life that's perfect is the way we feel about one another."

He started to say something, but I interrupted him with a kiss. I wasn't interested in hearing protests or complaints, not this time. We loved each other, and that was all that mattered – I knew he wanted me just as much as I wanted him. We had both been delaying the inevitable out of fear. So I kissed him, deeply and tenderly, to give him something else to think about besides his own nerves. I felt his body respond to it.

When our lips parted, I gazed down at him and saw a mixture of confusion and longing on his face. I understood the feeling well. I'd felt it so often in the recent weeks. Every time I looked at him, in fact – except for right now. For the first time in a very long time, I felt a kind of clarity. My desires and my needs were crystal clear. I knew exactly what I wanted.

"Michael, I don't want to lose you without ever having the chance to show you how much I love you," I told him in no uncertain terms. "I want to make love to you, right now, however imperfect the circumstances may be."

"But… your injuries…" he protested. I snuggled closer against him, my lips seeking out the curve of his throat. He was right, it hurt to kiss him with my split lips, but I didn't care.

"So be gentle. You're very good at that," I whispered huskily, my breath hot against the side of his neck. He loved being kissed there, and I felt him shiver in response.

"Are you sure?" Even though I already had him aroused and I knew he wanted me, he still showed such restraint for fear of hurting me. I knew it, and I loved him all the more for it. Drawing back just enough to look down at him, I gave him an adoring smile.

Then a kiss, and another, and another. A series of hot, quick, playful kisses. He responded instinctively, and I felt gentle hands upon my body. I rolled onto my back and he went with me, supporting his weight on his hands to keep from hurting me. With increasing enthusiasm, he returned my kisses and I felt his body pressing down against mine. His skin was so warm, his belly firm and taut, and his manhood…

Only then did I break the kiss long enough to reply, when I was trapped beneath his strong frame and knew for certain that he was just as ready as I was.

"I've never been so sure of anything in my life," I told him, and it was true. After all this time, after how gentle, sweet, and endlessly kind he had been to me, I wanted nothing more than to make love to my policeman at long last. To return his kindness with pleasure, and to show him how much I'd grown – because of him.

And so we did. Tangled together in bed, with our wounded bodies bandaged and bloodied but our minds finally at peace, we made love beneath the moonlight. I was oblivious to the pain as we fell into a world of our own pleasure, all things forgotten except for my love for the man in my arms.

It felt like that pleasure would last forever, and it was like nothing I could ever remember feeling before. So gentle, so expressive, so… right. I heard myself cry out, but I didn't care; I heard his voice whispering my name, and that was all that mattered in the world. This world was our world, and ours alone. Nothing else mattered here, except for the two of us.

After what felt like forever, we collapsed exhausted and replete in one another's arms, our bodies slick with sweat and our breath racing. He kissed me tenderly one last time as I snuggled up against him, before we both drifted off to sleep.

This time, we both slept deeply.

# Chapter Eight

I had often wondered in my youth what people meant when they spoke about true love being the only real source of satisfaction, about unrelenting passion and desire so strong it addled all of your senses. My early experimentation with boys in high school had done nothing to prepare me for what I experienced with Michael that night. When I awoke late the next morning, I felt lazy and satisfied in a way I'd never known before, and felt no desire to move from the position I had slept in. I couldn't even be bothered to open my eyes, lest the wonderful feeling dissipate in the light of day.

It didn't occur to me that Michael might have woken up before I did until I felt gentle fingers stroke my temple, sweeping a lock of my hair away from my face. I opened my eyes and found him propped up on one elbow, watching me with a smile of pure contentment on his face.

"Good morning," he whispered, leaning down to kiss me. My response was muffled by his lips and it wasn't necessary anyway. He knew how I felt better than I did. It felt like he always had. Words were just unnecessary between us; our bodies and our hearts spoke louder than words ever could.

Ignoring the stiffness of my joints, I drew him down atop me once more, and this time he came willingly. All his reluctance was gone when we made love for a second time, in the light of the golden morning sun. I felt such joy that I never wanted to let him go. I'd finally found a place where I felt safe, happy, and welcome, and it was right there with him.

Ever the gentleman, Michael refused to put his own pleasure above mine at any stage. He held himself back with a resilience that amazed me, and focused on pleasuring me instead. His lips touched my throat, my collarbone, and my breast, while gentle hands explored what he could of my flesh around the bandages and wounds. Only once I was satisfied did he let himself join me, and then he finally collapsed with his head upon my uninjured breast, his breath coming in harsh gasps that sent chills across my skin.

Eventually, Michael rolled onto his back and drew me atop him, so that I could lie comfortably in his embrace. Despite our exhaustion, neither of us felt the urge to sleep again. We'd rested for almost a full day now, and were starting to get restless. I heaved a long sigh and stretched languidly, only to get distracted when I felt curious fingers creeping across my belly.

I opened one eye, and I found him grinning at me. The look on his face made me laugh. He looked like the cat that had finally gotten the cream. The fact that he'd been willing to be so patient with me made it feel so much better in the long run.

"Insatiable, huh?" I teased him right back, trailing a few exploratory fingers in interesting places of my own. My touch drew a deep-throated growl from him, but I knew him well enough to know he was only playing.

Unfortunately, our play was interrupted by a knock on the door. We had just enough time to separate and feign innocence before the door swung open, and Skylar entered with a couple of plates of something that smelt so good it made my mouth water.

"Breakfast, you two." She gave us a knowing look, and set the plates down on the small table beside Michael's bed. As she was turning to leave, she added, "The doctor will be up to check on you both shortly."

We exchanged looks at her warning. I cringed, since I knew that we were about to get a lecture for messing up our dressings so badly. As far as I was concerned, it was more than worth it, and if I was any judge of expressions then Michael felt exactly the same way. Still, the doctor had a way of making us feel like naughty children over the smallest misdeed.

Breakfast ended up being more interesting than usual. We had to fight to keep our hands off each other and our food going in the right place, but we got there in the end. I wasn't terribly hungry, but as always Michael cajoled me into eating, and my resistance to his demands was at an all-time low. Besides, I knew he was right. My body needed food to heal, and it had a lot of mending to do.

By the time the doctor arrived to check on us, we'd finished eating. We were just relaxing side by side, chatting casually like nothing had happened. He took one look at us and seemed to know better, but for once he said nothing. Even though we were both braced for a scolding, he didn't say a word – he just changed our bandages, inspected our injuries, then left us in peace.

Michael and I exchanged a confused look, but no answers were forthcoming. I was glad to go without my daily scolding, and content to leave well enough alone. Michael was more reluctant to let it go, until I distracted him to the point that he didn't care anymore.

***

Hours later, we languished abed trying very hard to rest, but I was too restless to relax.

"I want to get up," I complained, absently rubbing at one of my bandages.

"You're supposed to be resting," Michael scolded, and gently grabbed my hand. "Stop scratching. If you scratch it, it'll never heal."

"But it itches," I whined like a spoilt two-year-old, wriggling to try and escape his grasp. Of course, he wasn't having any of that and held me tightly until I finally gave up and relented with a heavy sigh. "Okay, okay, I won't scratch – but I still want to get up."

"Bored of me already?" he said, feigning injury with such conviction that my heart leapt up into my throat.

"No! It's just that I... I..." Then I saw the smile twitching at the corners of his lips, and realised he wasn't serious at all. "You're just pulling my leg, aren't you? Damn it! You had me going!" I snatched up one of our pillows and flung it at him.

He laughed merrily at my antics, then picked up the pillow and deposited it back where it belonged. "Of course I am. I'm bored, too. We've wasted an entire day."

"So, let's get up then. I'm sure there's something productive we can do that won't put too much strain on our injuries." I leapt out of bed before he could stop me, despite my aching muscles. I needed to move, to stretch and to get my biological engine going before it froze up completely, and there were only so many times I could use Michael for that before he ran out of steam.

"Like what?" he asked curiously, easing himself out of bed with much greater care than me. While he was stretching, I went over to my gear to find clothing. Luckily for me, the others had left my belongings in the room when they escorted me up here, so I didn't have to go far to find what I needed.

"I have no idea." I shrugged. I pulled on my clothing, fighting the urge to curse at the pain. It was a necessary evil, though; I couldn't exactly go prancing around naked. Michael probably wouldn't have minded, but everyone else would. "I suppose we could work on the roof?"

"Nah." Michael shook his head, his back to me while he dressed as well. "Climbing ladders isn't a good idea in our condition. We'll tear our stitches."

"Ugh, you sound like the doctor," I complained, plopping back down on the edge of the bed to put my socks and shoes on. In the middle of the task, I paused to stare at the horrible pink scar in the middle of my right foot.

That scar was the legacy of the injury that had brought me to this group of survivors. Although it was a memory of terrible pain, it had brought me something wonderful in the end: a family, and a lover. Two things I so desperately needed in my life. Now, I couldn't imagine my life without them.

Michael caught me staring at the scar. He knelt down on the floor in front of me, captured my foot in his big, gentle hands, and planted a kiss on the top of it.

"Someone has to make sure you take care of yourself, Little Miss Reckless," he said, surrendering my foot back into my own care. In spite of everything we'd been through together, that little gesture made me blush.

"Says Mister Hero," I retorted, poking a finger in the direction of his wounded shoulder. "The man who took a bullet for me."

"Well, I didn't really take it for you," he said, suddenly looking embarrassed. "I mean, I would have in a heartbeat, but I didn't see the shooter before he got me."

I immediately regretted my choice of words when I saw that embarrassment on his face. I reached out to stroke his cheek, instinctively seeking to reassure him. "I know, sweetie. I didn't mean it like that. It was just a little joke."

"I know." He closed his eyes and leaned into my touch. With a sigh, he lay his head down on my thigh, letting me run my hands through his short hair and over the contours of his face.

For some reason, the moment felt even more intimate than the time we'd spent in bed together. I admired him thoughtfully, letting the contact warm and relax me. A surge of emotion brought tears to my eyes unexpectedly, and I found myself wondering at the feelings that this man could make me experience. It was new and intense. I'd never felt anything like it for anyone else. I wondered if it was the decade alone in the wilderness that made my feelings so extreme, or if it was possible that he was 'The One'. I had so little experience to compare it to. From what my mother used to tell me, it could happen unexpectedly. Sometimes, you just knew that it was meant to be.

*Only time will tell*, I told myself, turning my attention back to the task at hand.

"Well, there is a place," I said, running my fingers over his nailbrush hair. "In the township. I found a door, but it was too solid to break through on my own. Perhaps between the two of us, we can figure out a way to open it."

"A mystery door?" He lifted his head out of my lap and looked up at me, curiosity twinkling in his dark eyes. "Where?"

"In the old general store, at the back. The rioters tried to get in, but couldn't get past the locks." He sat back on his haunches to give me room to finish putting on my shoes and socks, then I rose to my feet. Michael joined me a moment later. Together we made our way out onto the landing and down the stairs to where we stored our equipment. "I was going to go back and try to pick the lock, but I never got around to it."

"You can pick locks?" His brows shot up, and he peered at me askance.

"Sometimes." I shrugged noncommittally. "I'm okay at opening the older-style locks, but this one was pretty modern. I'm not terribly confident about my chances."

"Hmm." He rubbed his scruffy chin absently, as we crossed the courtyard and entered the storage room. "Why don't we just take off the door?"

"Take off the door? What do you mean?" I shot a curious look at him.

"If the door is on the right way, then we might be able to force the bolts out of the hinges, and lift the whole thing off," he explained. We paused so he could show me what he meant on the storage room door.

I made a thoughtful sound and nodded slowly. "That might work. I don't remember which way the hinge was on. Let's bring a crowbar anyway – we'll probably need it, one way or another."

Okay," he agreed. With a plan in mind, the two of us dove into the boxes of goods we kept stored in case of emergencies, until we found a tool kit and a large crowbar. Armed with those, I led the way out of our motel and held the door open for Michael. Of course, he insisted on being the one to carry the heavy stuff despite the wound in his chest, so I just let him. It wasn't worth the fight, and my muscles were sore enough that I wasn't sure I was up to it any more than he was.

We traipsed down the road towards the town centre, stepping carefully over the debris deposited by the storm a few days before. Every now and then I spotted something potentially hazardous, like broken glass or a downed sign post, and marked it to be cleaned up. A few minutes later, we arrived at the little shopping centre that dominated the centre of town, though Ohaupo was so small that "town" was kind of an overstatement. Since we'd destroyed the function centre complex, there were only a half-dozen shops left, including my tiny video store.

Michael peered around us with interest as we walked, as though seeing everything for the first time. We rarely came this way without a purpose, so he'd only seen it a handful of times in daylight. I, on the other hand, had turned the place upside down over the weeks since my arrival, and knew it as well as any inhabitant.

"Hold your breath," I warned as we approached the creaking doorway of the old general store – and with good reason. The stink of decomposition didn't get any better for being aired out. And even though I'd been in there before, I was never one to ignore personal safety. I had my taser in hand as I stepped through the doorway into the reeking darkness beyond, and kept it armed until I had cleared the building.

Nothing stirred, not even the baby mice that I'd seen last time I was there. That was interesting. Perhaps Tigger had eaten them. I heard gagging behind me, and turned to watch poor Michael with amusement.

"And I thought I had a weak stomach," I teased. He shot me a dark look in return.

"It just… takes a second to get used to it, is all…" He gulped down a lungful of the stinking air, then straightened himself up and put on his best manly airs. I hid a smile and led him deeper into the building.

We passed row after row of dirty shelves covered in rotten produce and shattered glass, picking our way towards the back counter. There, the mysterious door stood waiting for us, as implacable as a gargoyle guarding its treasures. At least, I hoped it was guarding treasures. Otherwise, all the effort we were going to have to put in would be for nothing.

"Huh. That's a tough door for the back room of a little corner store," Michael pondered out loud, rapping his knuckles against the old metal.

"Yeah, that's what got me curious. I mean, it seems like a lot of security for relatively nothing," I agreed, edging around the door to get a good look at it. "At least the hinges are on this side. I think we should be able to get these off."

"I assume that you already checked if there was a back door, or a window?" He glanced at me, then looked back at the door.

"Of course." I nodded and gave him a smile. "What kind of scavenger do you take me for?"

"Well, you never know. Let's get to it then, eh?" He grinned back at me, handed me the crowbar, and set the tool kit down on the countertop nearby. "Feel like making a bet on what's in there?"

"I don't have a clue. Probably money or something equally useless, knowing my luck." I pulled a sour face, but Michael laughed.

"Hey, hey, hey – positivity!" he scolded me lightly, while fishing around in search of a screwdriver big enough to survive the abuse we were about to unleash on it.

"I know, I know." I sighed and gestured towards the hinges. "Have we got any lubricants in there? These are rusted solid; it's going to be a bitch to get them loose."

"Language!" Michael teased me playfully.

"Sorry, Mum," I answered dryly.

He gave me a peculiar look, but I was too amused to explain. Did it make me weird to have spent so much time alone that I had inside jokes with myself? Yeah, probably. Oh well.

Michael shook his head and shot me a lopsided smile, then tossed a can of industrial lubricant to me with a gentle, underhand throw. I caught it easily and popped the top, then covered my face with the neck of my tank top to protect me from the fumes as I lathered the hinges with grease. When I was done, I stepped aside and Michael attacked the hinges with his screw driver, while I smeared lubricant over the locking mechanism as well.

It took all of Michael's strength and a great deal of cursing from both of us before the bolt began to slide up out of the hinge with a blood-curdling, rusty screech. I ducked beneath his muscular arm and sprayed the bolt with more grease. It came up easier after that. After a few minutes of work, the first bolt came loose and we moved on to the next one.

The top bolt was even more difficult than the first one had been, since it required him to clamber up on an old crate to get the angle he needed, but eventually we got it out as well. By the time we got to the bottom hinge, we had our technique down; the last bolt came out easily compared to the first two.

Once we were done, we cast aside the loose bolts and stepped back to admire our handiwork. Now, the door was only held up by the tension of the lock itself, and a decade's worth of rust.

"Honestly, who on earth thought metal doors were a good idea? Really, that's just selfish, if you ask me," I commented. My usual technique for solving any problem involved attacking it with a liberal dose of sarcasm, and this situation was no different. I grabbed the crowbar, then jammed it into the gap between the hinges and the wall. Michael added his strength to mine and we pulled as hard as we could, but all we got was a metallic whine that set my teeth on edge.

"No good," Michael muttered. We released the tension and stood back again.

"The lock's in too tight, I think." I bent down for a second to peer at it closely, then straightened up and went over to the toolkit. "Give me a second, I have an idea. Ah, here we go." I pulled out the tools I had been looking for, and showed them to him: a hammer and chisel.

"How will those help?" Michael peered at the tools dubiously. "It's metal."

"The door is metal, and the hasp is metal," I answered, then reached over and tapped the door frame. "But this is just wood. I suspect if I dig deep enough, we should be able to rip the whole locking mechanism out of the wall."

"Ahh..." he breathed in understanding and nodded his approval. I set about destroying the structural integrity of that frame with a vengeance. Michael slipped up behind me to brace the door closed while I worked, just in case it happened to come loose. With careful, practiced strokes, I reduced the old wood to splinters, taking care not to risk injuring either myself or my lover in the process.

In due time, I uncovered the base of the hasp buried deep within the wooden frame. My chisel struck it with a resounding clang, which let me know that I'd dug deep enough to reach my goal. I widened the hole carefully until we could see the entire mechanism, then I set the hammer and chisel aside.

"That should be enough," I announced, and looked back at him. "Now we just need to break the screws on the other side. It's brute force time."

Michael nodded his agreement. With another terrible clang, he drove the head of the crowbar into the gap between the hasp and the wall, and I added my strength to his.

"Brace yourself," he warned, though it was pretty much unnecessary. Both of us knew all about the terrible infections we could catch if we were to fall and cut ourselves in a filthy place like this.

"So much for taking it easy, huh?" I commented. Michael chuckled and nodded his agreement. He planted his feet wide and leaned his weight against the crowbar; once again I pulled with him. The door groaned in protest, but I could feel it moving. We released after a moment, and he shifted the bar to a slightly different point.

"And again," he instructed. I joined him, pulling with all my strength. The door was definitely moving now; I could see it arching and I heard the whine of old metal protesting that it had been left untended for far too long. Then, with a violent cracking sound, the left side of the door came free, with what was left of the hasp still clinging to a shattered segment of the door frame.

Suction kept the door from falling in on us, though. Michael braced himself against it to keep it in place while I took the bar and loosened it around the edges. It creaked and whinged as I chipped away at a decade's worth of rust until, with one last shriek, the entire door came away from the frame.

I lent my strength to help him shift the heavy door to one side, leaving both of us breathless but feeling victorious.

"How's that for teamwork?" he gloated. He grabbed me and gave me a quick kiss, then we turned our attention towards finally discovering what our prize actually was.

I was the first one through the doorway, so when I skidded to a halt without warning, Michael just about bowled me over. Then he saw what I saw and we both froze with shock.

When we finally regained our senses, Michael reached up to scratch his scruffy chin. "You know, all of a sudden I feel this overwhelming urge to arrest someone."

# Chapter Nine

"Hell, yes!" I laughed with glee, and broke out my best impression of the Snoopy Dance.

"This shouldn't be here," Michael mumbled to himself, his expression one of intense concern. "This really, really shouldn't be here."

"It shouldn't, but it is," I pointed out happily, bouncing around him like an over-excited toddler on a sugar rush. "And whoever used to own it must be dead, so now it's ours!" There was still a locked grill between me and our findings, but I didn't mind. We had all the time in the world to figure out how to get into that cage, and I was pretty sure I knew exactly where I could find just the right tools for the job.

"You're entirely too happy about this." Michael shot a stern glance at me, then he grabbed my hand and drew me into a protective embrace. "You do realise how dangerous this is, right?"

"Take a second to consider who you're talking to, then ask that question again," I answered dryly, and gave him a long look in return. A faint flash of annoyance rose in my breast at his tone of voice, but I shoved it back down. He was just trying to protect me, and everyone that we held dear. "Of course, I know. I know better than anyone – but I also know exactly how useful this will be for keeping our family safe."

Michael looked at the cage and heaved a long sigh. "I suppose you're right, but I worry. There's military-grade hardware in there, Sandy. Just imagine what could have happened if those thugs that attacked us had been armed with one of those instead of a couple of air rifles. We'd probably all be dead."

He had a point, and that calmed me down. I stared at the cage, where a half-dozen semi-automatic assault rifles of various makes glinted ominously in the half-light, flanked by an assortment of handguns. As much as I had longed for a real gun to defend myself with, he was right – any weapon could be used against its owner.

"We should still take them," I said, then looked back at him. "We can't leave them here now. Let's hide them instead, somewhere that only we can get at them. If those mutants come south, they could save our lives one day."

Michael nodded thoughtfully, his dark eyes distant as he mulled over the idea. Finally, he nodded again, more firmly this time. "Okay. That makes sense. Like you said, we can't just leave them here – anyone could grab them."

"Go fetch the others to help us carry things back," I instructed, reaching over to give his hand a gentle squeeze. "Bring boxes or crates, anything that we can hide stuff in so no one knows what we've found except our group."

"What are you going to do?" He raised a brow and looked at me.

I gave him an impish smile, and flexed my fingers dramatically. "I'm going to get that cage open."

***

I'm nothing if not efficient. By the time Michael returned with the doctor and Skylar in tow, I'd just about finished with my task. The cage was held closed by a small padlock, so I had simply taken a pair of bolt cutters to it. Problem solved. The lock hit the ground with a heavy clang just moments before my family arrived to join me.

"My goodness!" the doctor exclaimed, adjusting his scratched spectacles to get a better look at our find. "I thought you were kidding, but I see you were very serious."

"Wow." Skylar stared at the guns with enormous eyes. "That's a lot of guns."

"No kidding," I agreed, shooting her an amused look. "Do me a favour and check out the rest of this place while we're getting this ready to shift?"

"Sure," Skye agreed readily. She turned and vanished through a doorway nearby, while Michael and I began carefully lifting down each weapon and inspecting it. I wasn't exactly an expert on guns, but I'd learned through trial and error how to disassemble and clean a handgun, and I definitely knew how to shoot one.

Michael seemed to know what he was doing better than any of us. He took each gun I handed to him and lifted it to his eye, carefully sighting down along the barrel. One by one, he inspected them, then either nodded or shook his head when he handed it back to me. Those he judged salvageable, I carefully packed into a crate they'd brought for that purpose. Those that were not, I set aside to be stripped down for parts. Everything would be useful, one way or another.

When we were done with the rifles, we moved on to the handguns, then to the boxes of ammunition stacked in neat columns beneath the weapon display. That was the most dangerous part, but we were lucky. Everything had been safely stored all those years ago, so nothing exploded in our hands.

"Sandy, come and look at this," Skye called through the doorway. I exchanged a glance with the others, then handed the box of ammunition I was inspecting to Michael and went off to see what my sister had found.

The doorway opened up into a tiny, single-room flat, with a decrepit old bed against one wall, and a kitchenette against the other. The entire living quarters was probably no larger than the stockroom where the guns were kept. My sister was bent over staring at something on a dusty old desk at the foot of the bed, but she looked up as I approached.

"This is a radio, right? One of those old-school things they used before cell phones?" She reached out to brush some dust from it, a look of intense curiosity on her face.

"I think so." I shrugged helplessly. "I couldn't tell you for sure, though – you know how I was about communication before I met up with you guys."

Skye heaved a long-suffering sigh, then called over her shoulder towards the door. "Doc? Michael? Do either of you know anything about radios?"

"Indeed, I do." The doctor responded to her cry for help, and came trundling over to peer at the object of our interest, absently adjusting his spectacles. "Well, now. If I am not mistaken, that's a shortwave ham radio kit."

"Ham radio," I echoed, rubbing my bruised wrist absently. "I remember that term. That was amateur radio, the two-way kind – right?"

"Indeed," the doctor agreed, then suddenly lashed out and smacked the back of my hand lightly. "Stop scratching!"

I yelped and danced out of his reach, while my lovely little sister laughed at my misfortune. The sound of my cry attracted Michael's attention, and he stuck his head into the room as well.

"What's going on in here?" he demanded.

"The doctor's beating me," I whined, retreating to the relative protection of his embrace – or at least, I tried to, but he knew me better than that.

"Well, stop scratching then," he teased me mercilessly, and left me pouting to go examine our find. "A radio? That'll be useful. Look, it's even hand-cranked – no batteries required. Good find. Skye, can you gather up all the pieces and take it back with us? Look around and see if you can find any spare components, too."

"Okay," Skylar answered agreeably and set about doing just that, while the men filtered back out to the guns. As soon as their backs were turned, she promptly stuck her tongue out at me and whispered, "Who's finding the cool stuff now?"

If I were a puppy, I'd have had my sad face on for a second there – sometimes sisters were *not* the coolest thing in the world. Then Michael called my name, and I forgot all about pretending to be the injured party as I hurried back out to join him.

***

It took us a while and a good amount of muscle power to get all of our new toys back to base. When the guns were in their crate it proved to be too heavy for one person to lift, so we each took a side and man-handled it back the way we'd come. A few more trips later, we finally had everything safely hidden in one of the downstairs storage rooms, beneath a mound of old clothing and behind a couple of huge sacks of rice.

There was some argument about what we should do with the guns now that we had them. Skylar argued that if we had them then we should use them, while the doctor joined the rest of us on the cautious side of the fence.

In the end, it was decided that we would train everyone to use them but only in the case of an actual emergency. Skye wasn't happy, of course, but she grudgingly accepted our more experienced judgement. She was too young to understand the concept that violence begets violence, but she did understand that we would make ourselves targets if we waved around something so valuable.

The radio was a whole other story. Radios had not been that common before the plague hit; by that stage, they were already outdated and had been replaced by the internet and mobile phones. Now, ten years later, our wonderful modern technology had more or less failed us, which turned a radio into something precious.

Skylar had found an instruction manual squirrelled away in the closet of the person who had once owned the ham radio. She was intensely fascinated by the idea of communicating with people outside of our own group, and roped all of us into helping with her project. We took turns assisting her with setting the radio up and learning to work it, which also gave us an opportunity to help her improve her reading as well.

We spent the next week or so keeping to ourselves. Michael and I divided our time between learning to use our new weapons, resting our injuries, and exploring the bounds of our new romance. Needless to say, we spent a lot of time in bed. And in the shower. And in any other interesting place we could get away with. Call it an experimental phase.

I'd missed out on that phase in my early twenties. Now that I was almost thirty, I felt like I deserved it – we both did.

Skye spent most of her time hunched over her radio, scanning the frequencies for any signs of life. Despite her reading difficulties, she picked up the basics of ham radio swiftly. After the first few hurdles, she only came to us for help on a rare occasion. However, she discovered that there just wasn't much to be heard on the airwaves anymore. I encouraged her to keep trying. After all, anyone on the other end was just another human being. They had to eat, sleep and forage for survival just like the rest of us, so they were unlikely to be sitting there all day waiting for her to contact them.

It was getting late in the season. Summer was almost over, and autumn well and truly on its way. The wind blew cold on occasion, but the sunshine was still warm. Over the course of the week, the weather cleared up. On one sunny morning, Michael and I lay contentedly on the roof, basking in the sun while we could. We'd finished assembling the railing around the edge, and had even added a small shelter at one end, in case we decided to position a guard up there one day. All in all, it was a ratty piece of work but it was functional.

I heaved a long sigh and folded my hands beneath my head, letting the warm tiles soothe me. The sky was a beautiful shade of azure adorned with delicate, fluffy clouds, and the sun shone down with just the right degree of heat – enough to warm, but not to burn. The breeze was crisp but not chilly, cooling us when the sun got a bit much, but not enough to make us shiver. Our bellies were full, our home was secure, and our family was safe. All in all, it was a perfect day as far as I was concerned.

Beside me, Michael made a contented sound and stretched out languidly, then turned his head and looked at me. "We should probably be doing something constructive."

"Nah." I flapped a hand to brush away the idea. "We've done plenty of constructive things. We deserve a rest."

"I like the way you think," he agreed amiably. Apparently, he was in too good a mood to fight over something as inconsequential as being useful. It was a beautiful day, too beautiful to waste on work. Winter would be here all too soon, and then we'd be trapped inside, dreaming about days like today.

So we loitered for a while, sunbathing, as useless as a pair of statues. I wasn't sure how much time passed, and I really didn't care. One of the few benefits of watching civilization fail was that we stopped having to count the time.

The days flowed in an endless stream, with no calendars to tell us what date it was. I didn't know what day of the week it was, or even what month. I guessed from the weather that it was around the middle of March, but more than that was a mystery. We had a vague idea of the year from counting the summers that had passed since we last saw our loved ones, but it really didn't matter anymore.

The days of counting the minutes between work or school and home were no more. Gone was the daily grind. The watchful eye of society, that had once told me where to be and when, had gone to sleep forever. None of it mattered now. These were our days, and only we dictated how we spent our time.

Once the necessities of survival were taken care of, nobody could complain if we spent our days wisely or not. No one cared if we spent hours lost in books, exploring or even indulging in casual love-making, because there was no society left to judge us.

There was a strange kind of freedom that came with losing everyone and everything that used to matter. Without the shackles of social and moral guidance, each person had only his or her will to guide her actions. I used to hate having no goal or purpose; now that I had others to enjoy it with, the freedom had actually begun to be enjoyable.

I'd always been the type of person that went out of my way to keep myself busy. If I had nothing to do, then I usually ended up getting bored and inventing tasks for myself. I'd done it so often over the years that it had become second nature. Skylar once commented that I was the most proactive person she'd ever seen, but the truth was that I had just gotten really good at keeping myself busy, to avoid having to confront the reality of my world. When you spend a decade alone, you get very good at that. Now, my new family was teaching me the joys of laziness, and I found the process to be quite pleasurable.

The sun was still only halfway to its midday apex when the sound of a distant engine stirred me from my doze. For a moment, I thought the sound was in my head, but when I opened my eyes to check I spotted a small figure bouncing along the trail from the west on the back of a farm bike.

I nudged Michael. He grunted in displeasure at being woken, but his annoyed expression faded into curiosity when he heard the engine as well.

"Trouble?" he wondered out loud, and glanced at me.

"Nah." I shook my head and stretched, feeling no great sense of urgency. "Looks like Hemi. He's probably just coming to chat up Skye."

Michael chuckled and flopped back down on the warm tiles, draping an arm over his eyes. "Ah, puppy love."

"If that's puppy love, what do we have, then?" I laughed, stretching up a little taller to wave at the kid on the motorcycle.

"Well, clearly we have an extremely mature relationship based on mutual friendship and respect," he answered dryly. His joke made me laugh even louder; the only time 'maturity' belonged in the same sentence as our names was with a thick slathering of sarcasm on top.

Our playful jousting was cut short when Hemi cruised into range, his little motorcycle bouncing under the weight of a heavy basket on the back. The bike swerved as it came to a halt, but Hemi knew what he was doing; he'd been riding that thing since childhood. The young man shielded his eyes against the sun and peered up at us curiously.

"*Haere mai*," I called down, and waved to him. Although I didn't speak as much Maori as Michael did, I knew a few phrases, and considered it respectful to use them where I could. Our neighbours seemed to appreciate the effort, even if they spoke English as fluently as I did.

Hemi grinned and waved back at me. "Kia ora, mate! What are you doing up there, eh?"

"Sunbathing," I called back. "What are you doing down there?"

"Mum sent me to check on you guys." He grinned even wider and jerked a thumb back over his shoulder. "Plus, we were hoping to do some trading. You game?"

"Sure. I'll be right down," I agreed. I leaned over to nudge Michael and see if he was awake. He grunted and flapped a hand at me, so I let him be. I was happy enough to talk to Hemi on my own. In my mind, the kid had already moved from the 'stranger danger' category into the 'can be trusted… more or less' category. That was a big leap for someone was naturally paranoid as I am. There was also the fact that I was three inches taller than him, which probably helped my confidence.

I crawled across the roof and swung myself onto the ladder, then scampered down to the ground with light-footed ease. I had always been fit and agile, but over the last few weeks I'd spent more time running up and down ladders than the rest of my life combined.

When I hit the ground, I took off at a trot across the courtyard. Hemi had barely finished parking his bike by the time I stepped out the front door, and he was in the middle of trying to wrestle the basket off his bike without dropping both. I hurried over to help.

"Thanks, mate," he acknowledged with a grateful smile. I took the basket's weight, and braced it against my knee so he could get the straps undone. The youth shot me another one of his impish grins while he was working, and looked me up and down. "You're looking better."

"I'm feeling better," I agreed, watching him worrying the straps to free the basket. "Definitely going to have a scar, though. Alas, my beauty is forever flawed."

"Somehow, I don't think Michael cares," Hemi teased. We both laughed at the joke.

Once the basket was free, he took its weight and carried it inside, with me in the lead to hold the doors open for him.

"How are the repairs going?" I asked as we made our way into the kitchen, where I helped him to lift the basket up onto the table. I'd learned from the others that the tribe had survived the fire physically unscathed, aside from a little smoke inhalation and a few light burns, but the damage to the buildings was extensive.

Hemi blew out a sharp breath and shook his head. "Not well, eh. A lot of our supplies got damaged. We've got plenty of food, but we're running low on construction materials – lumber, nails, tools, that kind of thing. I mean, we got plenty of trees so we can get lumber no problem, but it's hard to cut them down when all our saws are melted."

"Damn, that's rough. I guess that's why you're here, huh?" I gestured to the basket. Hemi nodded and gave me a wry smile.

"We need as many hands as we can get for the repairs, so it's easier to trade than scavenge. You guys are the closest," he admitted readily, then heaved a deep sigh. "Mum thinks that Lee's boys did it on purpose. They lit the fire where they knew it would cause us the most grief, to destroy all the stuff we can't replace. Bastards."

"Yeah, I wouldn't be surprised." I heaved a matching sigh and gestured for him to sit down. "You know, I didn't even know that guy's name until you just said it? We'll help, of course. You want a drink before we get started?"

Hemi nodded, so I fetched him one of the bottles of purified water we kept stocked up on at all times. He took it gratefully, popped the lid and took a swallow before continuing. "Thanks. We're happy to trade food for tools. I brought as much as I could carry, but we'll bring more over time. Even if we can just borrow some tools until we find our own to replace them, that would really save our hides."

"Don't worry, mate. I've got you covered," I reassured him as I settled down in a chair across the table from him. "I've got this place all mapped out so I know exactly where we can find what you need. Did your mum give you a list?"

"Yeah." Hemi fished a crumpled scrap of paper out of his pocket and handed it to me. I read over it quickly and nodded, confident I could find what they needed in short order.

"This is all basic stuff, no worries. You give me a couple of hours and I'll have what you need, okay?"

Hemi nodded enthusiastically. "Yeah, man – sweet as."

"I'll move faster on my own, so you can stay here," I told him as I rose back to my feet. I caught his glance towards the door, and hurried to hide my smile behind my hand. "Go on, then. She's probably in the common room."

"Cheers, mate!" Hemi waved, then rushed off with unseemly haste, leaving me chuckling to myself.

The kid was transparent as glass, but I wasn't complaining. Hemi was a nice boy, and Skye could use a nice boy to help her forget the one that had abandoned her. If there was one thing that Michael had taught me, it was that having someone to love you was a very important part of the human condition. It didn't matter whether it was the love of a friend, the love of a sweetheart, or the love of family – it was important just to be loved.

# *Chapter Ten*

I don't know how Michael managed to find me, but he did. Apparently, that man either had a hell of a nose for his lady, or he was a way better tracker than I gave him credit for. I was bottoms up in the back of a dusty garage at the time, rooting around for a saw that I was sure I'd seen six weeks before.

He managed to take me completely by surprise; I damn near jumped out of my skin when I emerged from the garage with my prize, and came face to face with an unexpected human figure in the doorway. It took me a second to realise that he was just standing there, with a grumpy look on his face.

"Why the long face, sour-puss?" I enquired, picking my way across the overgrown yard to retrieve my sack of miscellaneous goodies from where I'd left it.

"I got pooped on," he answered dourly.

"Eh, what?" I turned and stared at him over my shoulder, then I suddenly realised that he'd changed shirts since I last saw him. "Oh, did a bird get you, sweetie? I'm sorry to hear that."

"That was my favourite shirt, too." He gave me the kind of pout that made me go weak at the knees, then wandered over to help me with my sack of treasures.

"It's just a little poo, it'll come out in the wash," I reassured him with a sympathetic pat on the shoulder, though it was very hard to keep a straight face. "Well, since you're here, you can help. Anahera's group are in need of tools and stuff to help them rebuild. I've already got most of it, but there's a few more things I need to grab."

"I'm always happy to help. Lead on, my love." His grumpy look faded away completely, and he gave me one of his sweet, lopsided smiles. When I leaned down to pick up the sack, he stopped me with a gentle touch so that he could take it instead. "Don't worry, I've got that. What am I good for if I let you carry all the heavy stuff?"

"Well, if you insist. Thank you, honey." I leaned up to press a kiss against his lips, then turned and led the way towards the last stash we needed. Although my inner feminist might have protested that I didn't need a big, strapping man to help me, she was swiftly silenced by the part of me that was just happy to have him close to me. I didn't need Michael's help, I wanted it. That was the difference. I wanted it, because I wanted his company. After spending ten years on my own, who could really blame me?

We walked together in companionable silence, the tromping of our boots across the overgrown fields the only sound that interrupted the birdsong all around us. The singing stopped when we passed beneath the boughs of a tree, but it started again the moment that we moved on. The sound of it made me smile, but it also made me think.

"I wonder if we'll ever really be able to salvage what we used to have," I pondered out loud. "Do you think one day, in ten or twenty generations, we'll have towns again? Cities?"

"I don't know," Michael said, his deep voice close behind me. "I hope so. I hope that we'll have the chance to learn from our mistakes."

"Which mistake is that?" I asked, shooting a grin over my shoulder. "'Don't take Mother Nature for granted, because she's a vindictive bitch?'"

He chuckled and nodded. "That, and don't take the people you love for granted, either."

"I think that's the most important thing," I agreed, pausing for a moment to step carefully over a few fallen fence posts as we crossed the dividing line between properties. "You never know when you'll lose them. In retrospect, I guess I was one of the lucky ones. At least I had the chance to say goodbye."

"I'd give anything for that chance," he said softly, his voice huskier than usual. I glanced back again, concerned I might have upset him, but instead of tears I saw a wistful sort of sadness in his eyes. When he realised I was looking at him, he glanced up and offered a sheepish smile. I returned his smile, and led the way across an overgrown field that had once been someone's back yard.

With no one to trim it, the grass had grown thick and lush. It was waist-high now and difficult to wade through, but at least the mud had dried up. Come winter, the place would practically turn into a swamp. I silently prayed that I would not need to come through there during the wet season. Mud and I were not close friends.

I ducked beneath a lopsided clothesline and slogged the rest of the way across the yard towards the little shed at the back of the property. It was a small thing, no more than a couple of meters wide and about the same deep, but I had found a treasure trove of tools inside the last time I'd explored the area. The door swung on rusted hinges, squeaking faintly in protest with every gust of wind.

"I thought I closed that," I mumbled to myself, but I shrugged it off – there were doors askew and windows broken all over the place thanks to the storm.

I shoved the door open the rest of the way and quickly checked that there was nothing inside, then made my way into the gloom. Everything was as I left had it. I gathered what I needed without any problems, then picked my way back out to join Michael. I found him looking perturbed, staring down at the ground near his feet with a strange expression on his face.

"What is it?" I asked.

"Blood, I think." He didn't sound entirely certain. When I got closer, I could see why. The patch he'd spotted was old, dry and brown; it was hard to tell if it had been blood or just mud. Whatever it had been, it was large and spread over a sizable area. The grass had been crushed flat in the area, but no trace remained of whatever might have died there except for the blood – if it was blood.

"That's creepy, but it looks old. At least a couple of weeks." I shook my head and then looked up at him. "Whatever did that must be long gone by now. Let's go home."

"Agreed." Michael nodded, then he took my hand and together we left the scene and returned to our motel.

\*\*\*

We made it home without any issues. I led the way back inside, and headed to the kitchen where Hemi's basket still waited patiently. Michael frowned when he saw it and shot me a look.

"Are you really going to make them give us stuff in exchange for things they need?" he asked, his tone of voice disapproving. I bristled instinctively. I hated it when he used that tone of voice on me.

"I'm not going to 'make' them do anything, but that is how trade works," I said, dumping my armful of goods down on the table beside the basket. "We have something they want, they have something we want, and so we swap. It was their idea to offer a trade, and they've always been willing to trade fairly."

He didn't have an answer to that. When I glanced at him again I saw a strange expression on his face. Once more, I was forced to acknowledge that he was new to the world outside his safe little bunker. I reached out to him, to place my hand upon his arm.

"This is how it works out here, sweetie." I softened my tone and rubbed his arm gently. "Trade and barter. We're lucky that Anahera and her group are honourable, but not everyone is like that. Many people will take whatever you offer them and run, then come back with a bunch of friends who 'need help' as well. They'll take everything you have and leave you with nothing." I ran my hand all the way up his arm to caress the side of his neck, gazing up at him. "If everyone were as generous as you, this world would be a much nicer place – but they're not."

He sighed and looked down, silently acceding the point to me. "It's just… it feels wrong, taking things from people in need. Particularly our friends."

"It's not wrong," I reassured him, trailing my fingers up over his cheek. "They offered us things they have in plenty – they're not going to suffer for losing them. That's how trade works. You save up things you find that other people might need, and when you need something, you barter with stuff you can afford to lose. It's also a little bit about pride, too. Some people don't like accepting charity. They'd rather have a fair trade, or work for what they're given. Trust me, I've been doing this for a long time."

I smiled up at him. He smiled back, nodding his agreement. "I defer to your experience, my love."

"Good." I stepped back so he could set his burden down, and then I started arranging the assorted tools we'd collected on the table beside the basket. "While we're on the subject though, I think we should give one of our walkie-talkies to Hemi to take back with him. It's a long way to run to check on one another, and it would be nice to have some way to connect with our neighbours if we need them, or they need us."

"That makes sense to me," he agreed. "Good thinking, Batman."

I started to reply, but before I could I suddenly found myself swept up in his arms, being cuddled vigorously, and kissed all up and down the side of my neck. The gesture took me so much by surprise that he had me well and truly caught before I had any chance of escaping it. I squeaked in surprise and wriggled in his arms, but I have to admit that I didn't fight very hard.

Of course, it was right at that moment that Hemi came tearing into the room with his arms flailing like a demented windmill, frantically calling our names. He skidded to a halt when he caught us mid-canoodle, staring at us wide-eyed. Michael released me so suddenly that I almost fell over.

"Gah! I don't need to see that!" Hemi yelped, covering his eyes with his hands. Once I recovered from the shock, I laughed merrily.

"Then don't come running in unannounced," I teased him. "'That' is fun, so we're doing it every chance we get."

Poor Hemi made a pathetic whining noise like an injured puppy, but he was a good-natured youth and was soon laughing right along with us. When the levity faded, he suddenly seemed to remember why he'd been looking for us to begin with.

"Oh, oh, I almost forgot. Skye told me to find you guys. She got a signal – come on!" Hemi beckoned to us excitedly then rushed from the room. Michael and I exchanged a look, and then took off after him.

That signal could mean more survivors, or it could mean nothing. There was only one way to find out.

\*\*\*

The three of us huddled behind Skylar as she struggled to tune in the signal. We could hear the sound of a voice speaking, but it was too faint to make out the words.

"The reception might be better upstairs," I suggested. "There might be something blocking the signal down here."

Skye nodded, leaping to our feet. With our combined efforts, we carried the radio upstairs, along with the little card table and chair she'd acquired to sit it on. Along the way, the doctor stuck his head out to see what we were doing. Soon he and Madeline joined our entourage as well. A few minutes later, all six of us were huddled around the little radio while Skye searched for the signal she'd heard earlier.

This time when she found it, it came through clearly enough for us to understand the words. The signal strength wasn't great, but it was enough.

"—any able-bodied survivors in the Waikato region. Urgent assistance is required. Attention any able-bodied survivors, please respond…"

"He sounds exhausted," I said, glancing at the ring of faces around me.

"Can you answer him?" Michael asked.

"I think so. Let me try." Skye stared at the radio thoughtfully for a moment, then she fussed with it a bit and spoke awkwardly into the small microphone. "Hello? Can you hear me?"

"Affirmative, we can hear you!" The reply came almost immediately, and the voice sounded very relieved. "Oh, thank God. We were starting to think there was no one out there."

"Sorry, we only just detected your signal. It's very faint," Skye replied, then glanced over her shoulder at us. "Where are you located, mate? What's wrong?"

"Arapuni Power Station," the voice replied, then there was a pause. The silence dragged on for so long that we thought we'd lost them, but then they returned. This time, the voice was female. "Please, we need assistance. We've been doing our best to keep the station going, but a tree came down in the last storm and it's blocked the intakes. We had to shut the power station down and we can't clear it alone."

"So that's why the power's still off." I looked up again and caught Michael's eye. He nodded silently, acknowledging what I was thinking. We'd all wondered why the grid hadn't come back online yet.

"Well, if we ever want to have another hot shower again, we should see if we can help them," Skye said. There were nods of agreement all around – even from Hemi. Michael hurried out to go find our maps, while Skye spoke into the microphone again. "What kind of help do you need?"

"Muscle-power, mostly," the voice replied. "We have all the equipment we need, but we just don't have enough hands. It's just me and my husband here." There was another short pause, and then the woman's voice dropped down low. "We could use medical supplies, if you have any to spare."

There was a fuss in the background and we heard the male voice protesting, but the female ignored him. "My husband broke his arm trying to clear the block. I trained as a nurse, so I've set the break, but we have no painkillers or antibiotics of any kind. I'm concerned about infection."

Skye looked at me for instruction, as de facto leader in Michael's absence. I thought it over for all of half a second before I gave her a nod and gestured to the doctor, who also agreed immediately. Skye clicked the microphone on again, and spoke into it once more. "We have a doctor with us. I'm going to put him on to talk to you, so he can work out if we can help you."

We could all hear the voice thanking us profusely as Skye stepped back, and Dr Cross took her place. Michael returned a moment later, so we filled him in on the conversation he'd missed as we spread out the maps and located the point in question.

"Here. The power station will be close to Arapuni township," I said, my finger falling on a point about 50 kilometres from our current position. "It's a long way, but if we want power back then we have to help. Plus, it's the right thing to do."

Michael smiled at that comment and nodded his agreement. "You're right. They're alone and injured, we can't just leave them."

"And they've been providing us with a service all of these years," I added. "We owe them a lot for that. It seems like a fair trade to me."

"I think Mum will want to help, too," Hemi added, leaning over to inspect the map with us.

"Can you spare the manpower right now?" I shot a worried look at him, but he just shrugged.

"We have to, I think. Like you said, we owe these people a lot, and we want the power back on as much as you do." He flashed us a grin, showing straight, white teeth that contrasted vividly against his smooth brown skin. "Lord knows I need a shower."

"Yeah, you really do," Skye teased him playfully, then squealed gleefully and ducked out of reach when he made a mock charge in her direction.

"Keep it down, you two – Doc's trying to listen," I scolded playfully, amused by their antics. To my surprise, they actually obeyed, though that might have been because Skylar ducked behind me to use me as a human shield.

"I'll go get Hemi sorted with a radio and his tools, so he can head home and speak to Anahera," Michael volunteered, then glanced to me. "Take care of the planning for us? You know the area best."

"I'm on it." I sketched a salute, which made him smile. He nodded to me and quickly kissed my cheek, then took Hemi and left us to our planning. The doctor was just finishing up with his questions when I approached. He glanced at me and gestured for me to take over. I settled in the chair and drew a deep breath to bolster my confidence. Skye quickly showed me the button to press to make it work, and I did so.

"Hi, I'm Sandy," I introduced myself. "I need to ask you some questions about the terrain en route to your location. Are you able to answer?"

"Hello. My name is Rebecca Merrit and my husband's name is Jim," The female voice replied. "We haven't moved from here in a while, but we'll do our best to answer your questions. Which direction will you be coming from?"

"The west," I said. "Our base of operations is in Ohaupo."

"Ohaupo? That was my home town. How's the place holding up?"

"Not well," I told her honestly; there was no sense in lying. "You really don't want to know what it was like when we got here."

"Oh… I'm sorry to hear that, but I'm not surprised." She paused for a long moment, then pointedly changed the subject. "How many people do you have with you?"

"Five, but that's including children, so we'll only be bringing two adults." I heard Skylar start to protest, but I ignored her. "There's also about a dozen people living on one of the lakes a little further west, too, but I'm not sure how many they'll be able to send yet – they've just had a fire."

"Only two… well, seven hands are better than three. We'll take any help we can get. We've been broadcasting as often as we can all week and you're the first people we've heard a reply from."

"Your signal is very faint," I explained. "We barely heard you at all – we just happened to get lucky. What's the terrain like between here and Arapuni? I've been to the south and the east a bit, and it was pretty wild out there. I have maps and a GPS unit, but I'm sure I don't need to tell you how out of date they are."

"Definitely wild this way, too," the woman agreed. "We have tried to keep the roads clear, but there's only so much two people can do. Keeping the station running takes most of our time. You'll need to take the south road through Te Awamutu. The northern route was blocked a few years back by a rock fall."

"Got it." I followed the route on the map with my finger. "What's the condition of the river? I can't tell from this map."

"It runs through a gorge at Arapuni, and flattens out to the north and south," she explained. "Stick to the road though, and cross at the bridge by the catchment dam. The bush is extremely dense on your side of the river. I don't recommend trying to ford the river if you can avoid it. The current is deceptively strong."

"Noted." I traced the curve of the river to the bridge and tapped it absently with one fingernail. That bridge meant a long detour to the south, but we'd have to do it – I had no intention of getting myself drowned. "What about the infected in your region? Are they a threat?"

"Infected humans? No. We've put most of them out of their misery already. This is pig country, though, so be careful."

"Ugh, I hate pigs." I sighed and made a mental note to go armed.

"Yeah, me too. They're no good at negotiating steep inclines, though, so at least the terrain works to your advantage." She sounded sympathetic. I filed that bit of information away for future reference. "When you're on the east side of the river, follow the road north. The station is on the centre island, where the river splits. Do you see it?"

"I see it. How do we cross?"

"When you're heading north towards the town centre, keep an eye out for an old walkway that branches off towards the west. I'll mark it for you so you can't miss it. The path will lead you to a swing bridge, and then just follow the path south again."

"So, kind of like a spiral." I considered the map thoughtfully. That was a lot of extra travel, but we didn't have much choice. "Are you okay for supplies? Food, water, clothing?"

"We're fine for the basics, thank you. Arapuni township was well-stocked, and we're pretty much on our own down here. We can feed your people while you're here, too." There was silence for a moment, and then the man's voice returned. "If you've got any vodka, though, I'd kill for a drink."

I couldn't help but laugh, and heard the others chuckling behind me. "I'll see what I can do. It'll take us a couple of days to reach you, so stay safe."

"You too, lass. Mind the pigs. And… thank you."

# Chapter Eleven

As soon as I was off the radio, Skylar was on me like a dog on a bone.

"Why can't I go? I'm an adult. I'm useful. I could help!" She smacked me in the arm with one petite fist. "Don't treat me like a baby!"

The doctor took one look at the potential fight brewing and made himself scarce. He muttered something about needing to put the prescriptions together and hurried out of the room. I just rolled my eyes, then turned my full attention on Skylar.

"I have never once treated you like a baby, Skye. I consider you a grown adult, and a strong, capable member of this group," I told her calmly. That answer seemed to surprise her, which gave me a momentary respite to justify my decision. "In fact, that's why I want you to stay. If we took you as well, we'd be stripping all the defenders away from our home and leaving it completely undefended.

"I need you to stay here because I know I can trust you to take care of our home, and Madeline. Doc's getting on in years, and you know that he just about wets himself if someone asks him to fight. If something happens, I want someone here that I know can hold her own. I also need you to manage communications, and you're especially good at that."

Skylar stared at me, her brow furrowed in confusion.

I sighed, and translated into layman's terms. "I need you to talk to other survivors on behalf of the group."

Her expression brightened. "Oh, you mean like Hemi's tribe?"

"Precisely," I said, nodding. "Michael's giving him one of our walkie-talkies, but by the time he gets home we're probably going to be out of range. If they decide to come and help as well, you're going to need to pass the directions on to them. You were listening, right?"

"I remember every word." Skye nodded enthusiastically, her anger forgotten and her eyes twinkling. I knew then that I'd sold her on the idea. Hey, apparently I was getting back into the big sister groove after all, or maybe I'd picked up one or two of Michael's leadership skills..

"Good." I put a hand on her shoulder and gave it a gentle squeeze. "If they decide to go, tell them everything. They're cool, so if they need to borrow anything, then let them, so long as it doesn't put us in danger. I trust you to use your best judgement. Even more importantly, I need you to keep track of things around here, and reassure me you guys are okay – you know how worried I get. I'll call you on the first evening after we arrive, at sunset."

"Okay, I can do that." She nodded again and embraced me quickly, then stepped back and looked up at me. "Sorry I doubted you, sis."

"It's okay." I smiled down at her and gave her a wink. "I'd have thought the same thing in your position. The only reason I selected Michael and me to go is because he's the physically strongest of us, and I have the most mechanical knowledge. You're better at managing people than I am, and you're a good shot as well, so it just seems logical that you hold down the home front."

"Makes sense," Skye agreed, her short blonde curls bobbing as she nodded vigorously. "You can count on me."

Suddenly looking very pleased with herself, Skye spun on her heel and bounced out of the room. I watched her go, shook my head in amusement, and headed off about my own business. My task, as the group's makeshift mechanic, was to make sure our even more makeshift mechanicals were in functioning order before we went anywhere.

I popped into the kitchen to fetch the keys to the Hilux off their shelf, then headed for the door. During my routine check-ups on the vehicles, the utility's engine had been starting to get less and less reliable. Something was wrong with it, but I couldn't work out exactly what it was or how to fix it. It came as no great surprise to me, though. The poor old truck was probably about as old as I was; it was kind of a miracle that we'd gotten this much use out of it.

When I stepped outside, I saw Michael and Hemi working together to load the basket back onto the little farm bike. I waved at them. They waved back, but they seemed to have everything under control so I left them to it and headed down the road towards the old mechanic's workshop. The workshop was clean, dry and spacious, and had all the tools I needed on hand, so it had seemed like a logical place to keep our cars.

The minivan sat abandoned in the yard, waiting to be disassembled for parts. It had died the long death barely two days after we'd arrived in Ohaupo, and no amount of coaxing or cursing had convinced it to return from the other side of the grave. Our prison transport was faring much better than either of the others, for the simple reason that it'd been stored underground for the last decade. Unfortunately, it was ill-suited for our current mission.

I knew the condition of the roads near Te Awamutu, and we'd need a four-wheel drive to get through. My Hilux was the best vehicle for the job, but the problem was that whenever I started her up, she made a bizarre sound, like the cough of a dying walrus. I hadn't found the source of the problem yet, but I knew that was not a good noise for a car to be making.

The temperature changed as I stepped out of the sun and into the cool, dark shadow of the garage. For a moment, I regretted the need to leave the sunshine, but then my internal temperature adjusted and I forgot all about my brief discomfort. I went over to the car and pulled open the driver's door, then stuck the keys in the ignition and turned. The Hilux whined and coughed pathetically, complaining about the need to work.

It took three tries before the ignition finally caught. The engine spluttered to life, but it only did so reluctantly and with an assortment of very unhappy noises. Intent on trying to figure out what was the matter, I went around to the front of the machine and popped up the bonnet. The Hilux was a lifeline for us. It was the only way we had to get from point A to point B without having to travel on foot. I was concerned that losing it would cut off our freedom to move. There were a few other vehicles lying abandoned on the outlying farms that I could probably repair if I had to, but fixing them up would cost valuable time that we didn't really have.

"What's wrong with it?" a familiar, deep voice asked. I glanced over my shoulder and saw Michael's broad frame outlined in the doorway.

"I think it needs a new starter motor, or maybe an alternator," I answered, returning my attention to the engine. "The problem is that I have no idea how to replace one of those, and we don't really have time for me to figure it out."

"I guess we'll have to risk it. If something happens, we'll ditch it and come back for it later," Michael suggested. I sighed, not much liking the option, but it was the only one we had.

"We better pack wisely, then," I said, straightening up and planting my hands on my hips. Then a second pair of hands joined mine, and I felt a strong, warm body pressing up against my back.

"Mhm… very wisely," he agreed, nuzzling his face in against the curve of my neck. His hands slipped around my waist, sliding up beneath my top to explore my belly; I suddenly realised that I could feel the evidence of where his thoughts had gone pressed up against my back.

"Really, Officer Chan?" I teased him. "Here? Isn't public nudity a criminal offense?"

"It's only an offense if you have a public to offend," he answered, grunting something that resembled a chuckle. His lips were so close against my ear that I could barely make out what he was saying – but for once in his life, his law-abiding nature didn't seem to be at the forefront of his thoughts.

Before I knew it, our clothing had somehow miraculously disappeared, and we were up against the side of the Hilux breaking as many laws as we could think of.

***

Later, once our rampant libidos had been sated and we could focus on the task at hand, I drove the Hilux around to the motel and parked it out the front while we organised our gear. Since we knew that we might have to ditch the truck at a moment's notice and continue on foot, we packed lightly.

One spare change of clothes, plus socks and underwear for a week. Four days' worth of food and water, GPS unit, maps and a first-aid kit. Camp stove and cooking equipment. Sleeping bags and jackets for night time. Walkie-talkies. Weapons.

Michael and I decided that it was in our best interest to take one of the new weapons with us, since we were going in to pig country. Neither of us had any desire to take on a pig without the proper protection. I took Michael's shotgun, since it was a weapon that I was familiar and comfortable with, and Michael armed himself with one of the M16s.

We added spare ammunition to the pile, on the justification that it was better to be safe than sorry when it came to infected wildlife. Michael volunteered to take the weight, and I was grateful for it. While I was athletic, I had to acknowledge his superior physical strength. It wasn't his success or my failure. It was just a fact of nature. He was biologically hardwired for it.

I found it interesting to observe that one of the side-effects of having to live in the ruins of a dead civilization was that in some ways feminism had died along with it, while in other ways it had grown stronger than ever. Now, every hand was equally important to the survival of the group as a whole, because the strengths of one person balanced out the weaknesses of another. We'd finally achieved equality, but it was through acknowledging and accepting our differences instead of trying to ignore them. The gender dynamic of the human species seemed to have evolved.

Anahera's tribe was a prime example. In her previous life she'd been a primary school teacher, but now that experience gave her the skills to lead. She wasn't the strongest, oldest, or the most skilled of her group, but no one seemed to doubt her leadership, or suggest that someone else should be in charge. She ordered her men to jump, and they jumped – not because she had breasts, or because she scared them, but because they knew that they could rely on her to keep them all alive.

I had noticed with a detached fascination that the same thing seemed to have begun to evolve amongst the members of my own group. Although Michael had been the de facto leader when I met them, more and more often my group-mates were looking to me for advice, information or guidance – even Michael. No… *especially* Michael.

I rather liked the feeling, knowing people looked up to me. Despite having spent the last ten years as a loner, Michael had been right when he pointed out that I was a social butterfly by nature. The only reason I had become an introvert to begin with was as a defence mechanism to protect me from the terrible situations that I'd found myself in over the years. Fear was a cocoon, to protect the fragile butterfly inside me from the dangers of the outside world.

Michael had once called me gregarious, and at the time I'd denied it. As time passed and I had a chance to mull it over, I'd come to understand what he meant – and more importantly, to realise that he was right. Necessity had forced me to bottle up that aspect of my personality, and bury it so far down in my psyche that I'd forgotten about it. As I spent more and more time more time around good people, I began to remember the parts of me that I'd hidden away: I liked people. I liked being around people. I liked talking and helping, loving and being loved.

That was a trait that had made me vulnerable, and that vulnerability had made me an easy victim for the predators of the world, so I'd hidden it away deep inside where it couldn't hurt me anymore. Now, being around friends and family that cared about me had helped me to dig that trait back up from the deepest recesses of my mind. Not only had I gained a family, but I had also regained a piece of myself.

Once, when we'd lain together in the dark enjoying the easy companionship of being together, Michael had told me how much he enjoyed watching me evolve before his very eyes. He had said it was like watching a butterfly finally emerging from her chrysalis after so many years of waiting.

I had smiled to myself in the dark, thinking that was probably about the most romantic thing anyone had ever said to me, then I'd promptly accused him of calling me a caterpillar. We'd both laughed.

Although it had been less than two months since I had joined the group, I'd come to greatly value the opinions of my little family. I really enjoyed knowing that they looked up to me, and that they respected me for my experience. I was pleased by the thought that they missed me when I went away, and were happy to see me when I came home again.

I guess everyone likes to feel wanted and needed. It's human nature. Even after everything that had happened to me, I was still no different at the core.

# Chapter Twelve

It was early afternoon by the time we were ready to depart. Rather than wait for the next morning, we decided to set off immediately and make the most of the hours we had left until sunset. The days were still long at this time of the year, so I estimated we could probably get as far as Te Awamutu before dark.

Skylar, the doctor, and Maddy stood together in a huddle by the door while Michael and I loaded our backpacks into the rear cab of the Hilux. Once we were done, the doctor came over to give us the medicine, and Skylar brought a bottle of something she'd found in our stores.

"I don't know what this is, but I think it's alcohol." She peered at the label and read it out slowly. "Rum... rum? Is that booze?"

"Yes." I laughed as I took the bottle from her, and wrapped it up in my spare clothing to keep it safe. "Well done, your reading is getting much better."

"Thanks." Skye beamed proudly, and then she enveloped me in a hug that lingered just a little longer than it should. "Take care of yourself, sis."

"I will. We'll be back before you know it." I hugged her back, understanding without words that she was worried about us and trying very hard not to show it. I felt the same way, so I held her tight for a minute, then hugged Maddy and the doctor as well.

They waved to us as we headed away from the motel, and I found myself wondering if we'd ever see them again. I felt guilty for lying to my sister when I had told her the reasons I wanted her to stay. While every word I'd said had been true, I'd lied to her by omission. I had failed to tell her the biggest reason I didn't want her along was because I feared that we were walking into a trap. I couldn't stop Michael from coming if I tied him up to the nearest lamppost, but at least if I died then I would die knowing I'd kept my baby sister safe. There would be someone left to carry on my family line, and there would be someone left to remember me.

I took the wheel for the first leg of the journey, since I'd come along the southern road on foot not that long ago. Our plan was to take the same route for a while, then swing east at Te Awamutu. With any luck, that would keep us well clear of the dangerous gang territory further south.

For over a year, I'd used Te Awamutu as a refuge from those gangs. At some point before my arrival, a localized earthquake had devastated the little city, and reduced its buildings to hazardous piles of rubble, shards of glass and twisted steel. Most of the water sources were tainted, and there was little to interest the other survivors when easier sources of sustenance were just a few days away. I was no ordinary survivor.

When I had arrived in that little town, I'd felt just like one of those shattered buildings. I had just escaped from captivity, after being tormented, tortured, and brutally raped over the course of days, maybe even weeks. I had been so wrapped up in my own misery that I'd lost track of the time.

I had limped into that town a broken woman, my clothing in tatters, my hair matted, and my body covered in filth and blood. Most of the blood was mine, but some of it had belonged to the man I'd killed to escape.

My survival had been a matter of sheer luck. The man with the tattooed face, Lee, had left camp with most of his friends, leaving just one man behind to guard me. They'd thought I was too far gone to fight back. I remembered that the guard had been drunk. He'd tried to force himself on me again, but had fallen asleep before he could get it up. I remember the rank stench of his breath as he snored in my face, as clear as day.

They had underestimated my desire to live, and it cost that man his life. I knew where they'd tossed my belongings when they caught me, and the drunk had loosened my bonds when he'd decided to use me. I found my bag, and in it was my gun. The drunk had stirred awake just long enough to see his own death coming. I shot him right between the eyes, with no hesitation and no mercy. God knows they hadn't shown me any.

Then I took my things and I ran, as far and as fast as I could. I ran for days, until my water ran out and my feet were so blistered I could barely walk. But I was clever enough to cover my tracks, and when I reached Te Awamutu I knew I'd found somewhere I could hide. I'd searched carefully amongst the ruins until I found one water source that was still clean. I made my home near it, inside an old shipping container.

Living in the ruins of Te Awamutu had been a humbling and depressing experience, one that reminded me of the destruction of the beautiful city of Christchurch in similar circumstances, almost a decade earlier. Except back then, there had been people. People to recover and rebuild. Te Awamutu had been a ghost town. There was no one there to care for her, or return her to the way she had been.

It was an appropriate place for the shattered soul I had been to cower and lick her wounds. Now, I was going to return, with the man I loved at my side. I had mixed feelings about returning to that place in my life.

"You're scowling," Michael commented softly. I glanced at him, and discovered that he was watching me. He was relaxing in the passenger seat with one arm resting on the edge of the open window, content to let me negotiate the uneven roads in peace. At least, he had been. Now after many long minutes of silence, he was studying me. I suddenly felt uncomfortable.

"I'm just... focused." I tried to brush it away rather than have to explain, but Michael wasn't having any of it.

"No, you're not. I know that face." He absently brushed away an insect that had buzzed inside the cab, and then gave me a faint smile. "Tell me what's bothering you."

My shoulders slumped; I was so transparent, I couldn't even get away with harmless white lies. "It's just... I lived down this way for a while, before I came north. It wasn't a good time of my life. I'm not ready to talk about it yet. I'm sorry, Michael."

I gave him an imploring look, a look that silently said 'if you love me, you'll leave it at that'. Apparently, he did love me. He gave me a long, hard stare, then he just nodded and went back to watching the scenery roll by.

The road directly south of Ohaupo was familiar to me; I'd walked this way once, and then driven around the area a few times to reach the outlying farms. The roads were fractured and overgrown but not blocked, so we made good time to start with. As we left the township, the narrow rural roads widened into a thick strip of dusky grey that wound off into the horizon, the road markings worn away by time and the weather.

Land that had once been all picturesque little farmsteads set amongst tidy green fields had grown into wild, overgrown pastures interspersed with destroyed buildings, fallen fences and the occasional patch of young native bush. Nature's reclamation process was brutal and unforgiving, but it was beautiful in its own way.

I kept our place slow but steady as the road surface grew gradually more erratic. A flash of water through the trees to our left drew our eye momentarily, marking the passing of another lake. Michael shifted the map around and identified it, to keep track of our progress.

A few minutes later, we came across an overturned milk tanker blocking the road, its contents long since evaporated away. I'd walked around it on the way north so I knew that it was coming and had planned my route in advance. When we reached it, I nudged the Hilux far to the left and eased it gently around the wreck. One tyre clipped the ditch on the side of the road and spun for a moment in the gravel, then it caught and we were off again.

Eventually, the road began to narrow, turning into a slender ribbon of cracked asphalt. The bush flanking the road grew thicker and thicker, but it was still young and wasn't tall enough to block out the sun yet. The roots were well on their way to destroying the road itself, though. Grass already peeked up through the cracks. In another ten or twenty years, there would be nothing left of this old highway.

"The storm really made a mess here," Michael said thoughtfully, staring out the window. I made a sound of agreement, but I had to keep my attention focused on the road to avoid the very debris that he was talking about. When I had walked northwards, it'd only been a mild inconvenience, but now there were large branches and mounds of leaves scattered all across the road. Our tyres ground over something that I failed to spot in time and made the entire vehicle shudder, but I had chosen the Hilux for a reason. I gunned the powerful engine until I felt us clear the obstruction, and then we were back on our way.

The road began a long, slow curve to the left and the trees began to thin. A few minutes later, they trailed off into an assortment of low, scrubby bushes that allowed us to see the first signs of the devastation. I glanced at Michael, and caught him staring in mute fascination at a low farmhouse to the left of the road. The tremors had hit it with enough force that the little homestead had collapsed like a house of cards.

Suddenly, the truck hit a deep rut in the road. Beside me, Michael grunted in surprise and grabbed the dashboard to keep himself from being flung out of his seat.

"Put your seatbelt on, honey," I warned him. "It's only gets worse from here."

"What happened to this place?" he asked, hurrying to obey my instruction. I belted up as well, then gently nudged the truck forward. Again, we grated over deep furrows in the roadway. The entire truck bounced and shook. Michael leaned out the window and stared at the ground, and I heard his sharp intake of breath.

I knew what he was seeing, I'd walked over it on my way north. The road had ended up rippled like the surface of a pond that had been snap-frozen in the middle of a windy day. In some places, the pressure had been too much for the old tar seal to bear, and it had left behind jagged ridges and ruts. The truck struggled to get over some of them, even with its four-wheel drive.

"Earthquakes. Brace yourself," I explained, and took my own advice as we went over a particularly rough ridge. Beside me, I heard Michael yelp. I shot a worried glance at him as we cleared the lip. He was clinging on with both hands now, a look that was equal parts nervousness and steely determination on his face. "There was at least one big one, possibly more than one, and a bunch of aftershocks I'm betting."

"Jesus. And you lived down here?"

"Yep," I winked at him, then turned my attention back to the road. "Keep holding on. It's only just begun."

\*\*\*

By the time we reached the outskirts of Te Awamutu, we'd found a whole new meaning for that old saying about five miles of bad road. The Hilux was making even more unhappy noises than usual, and we were in no better condition. The tension of having to brace ourselves for hours against the constant juddering, the sudden drops and peaks, and the occasional ominous screeches was stressful in the extreme.

We passed from farmland into the rural equivalent of suburbia, but the devastation was so wholesale that it was painful to look at. Nothing had been left standing. What the earthquake had failed to flatten had been razed by fire in the aftermath of the quakes, or by storms over the subsequent years.

The frame of a gutted house stood stark against the setting sun, like the carcass of a long-dead monster, its bones blackened by the raging flames of yesteryear. The fire had burned out of control and spread death through the forest for kilometres to the east. Even years later, it hadn't fully recovered. Only a few sprouts of grass and a couple of saplings had managed to sprout from the barren earth. That would be our highway.

"We're going off-road," I warned Michael. I felt him tense up beside me as I eased the wheel to the left and took us down off the edge of the roadway. The wheels crunched as we rolled across the ashen wasteland and slowly headed towards the east. Strangely, it was a smoother ride across the sooty ground than over the broken asphalt, and most of the small obstructions were so badly burnt that they dissolved beneath the Hilux's tyres.

"Didn't you say that she said to stick to the road?" Michael protested. I shook my head.

"Impossible. They obviously haven't been here since before the quake," I explained, leaning high in the driver's seat to eyeball the uneven ground before us. "You think it's bad here? You haven't seen anything like the centre of town. If we cut across here, we should hit one of the back roads soon, and we'll use them to skirt around the edge of town."

"Planning to get us killed already?" he teased, obviously trying to relieve the tension. I gave him a smile as a reward, even if I didn't really feel it. This place was full of memories, and none of them were good.

The ground was spongy with decayed plant matter, but it held out beneath the truck's weight. By the time the sun started to set in earnest, we'd cleared the other side and found a narrow, winding back-country road, one that was little more than a single-lane track. The bush started to get thicker again, to the point where it covered our path with long shadows that made it difficult to see.

There was a low, deep crunch when the asphalt ended, and we found ourselves on a gravel road barely visible through the long grass. In front of us, the trail climbed up a gentle hill, and at the top I could see a clearing. I gently touched the accelerator to ease us up the incline, wary of damaging the truck on something I couldn't see.

As if reading my mind, we hit something with a heavy clunk. I froze for a second, then leaned out the window to check what it was. An old electric fence – electric no more – lay crushed beneath our wheels.

"Oops." I gave Michael a sheepish grin.

He laughed and patted my knee reassuringly. "Oh well, too late now. Keep going."

I nodded and put my foot down again. We cleared the obstruction and climbed the rise slowly. Although it was only a slight incline, the view as we came over the crest was stunning. The hill was just high enough for us to see the landscape for miles in all directions, and it gave us a commanding view of the land we had yet to traverse.

"This seems like a good place to stop for the night," Michael suggested, pointing ahead of us. "In there?"

At the crest of the hill, our path branched off towards a high metal fence that still stood proudly, guarding a large house that had been turned to kindling in one of the quakes. I saw what attracted him immediately. It was a defensible position that we would be able to fortify easily. I nodded and eased the truck closer.

With his gun at the ready, Michael hopped out of the passenger seat and moved to the gate, scanning the area for anything remotely hostile. Once he was done, he turned and gave me a thumbs-up, then he opened the gate so that I could drive through. Once we were safely inside the ring of high metal fencing, he shut the gate and I backed the Hilux up until its tail rested against it, effectively preventing anyone – or anything – from entering without permission.

I put the truck in park, killed the engine, and climbed out to join him with my shotgun at the ready. Between the two of us, we stalked the interior of the compound, guarding one another's backs as we circled the old house to ensure nothing was hiding behind it. Everything seemed safe from a distance, but neither of us were willing to take chances with the life of the person we loved; we'd only just found one another, and I certainly had no intention of putting that love in jeopardy.

The long grass hid few secrets from our watchful eyes. The only things that stirred were the birds in the trees, singing and fluttering from branch to branch as they put themselves to bed. I agreed with that notion; after a long day of travel, I was ready to rest. Although the bare earth might have been softer, Michael and I unrolled our sleeping bags side by side on the cracked concrete of the old homestead's driveway, because it felt safer than sleeping in the long grass.

"We could sleep in the back of the truck, if you want. It'd probably be more comfortable," I suggested as we sat down on our sleeping bags, and began setting up the gear to cook our dinner. The little gas cooker felt like such a luxury when resources were running low, and there were so few people around capable of making things to replace them. We'd found it in a cache before we left Hamilton. If it hadn't been for that, then we would have had to gather dry wood and build a fire the old fashioned way.

"Nah." Michael shook his head. "I think it'll be more comfortable out here. I've always enjoyed the thought of sleeping beneath the stars."

"I think you've been living in a bunker for too long, honey," I told him with amusement.

He gave me one of his quirky smiles and shrugged. "Maybe. I used to like camping in the old days, too."

"I guess it's all fun and games when your life doesn't depend on it," I answered, thinking back to my own childhood. I'd felt the same way. To distract myself, I rooted around in my backpack and fished out the food I had planned for our dinner. In addition to a few other things, I pulled out that old can of mushroom soup that I'd scavenged so many weeks ago. I still hadn't worked up the courage to open it and find out if was edible, but tonight was the night. If it was still good, then it seemed appropriate to share it with someone that I loved.

"Hey, I remember this stuff." Michael reached over and took the can from my hands, turning it over to examine the familiar branding on the label. "Where in the world did you find that?"

"In someone's larder," I answered, leaning over to take it back. "I've been hanging on to it for a while. You up for a gamble, honey?"

He gave me a smile and leaned over to brush a strand of hair off my cheek. "I took a gamble on you, didn't I?"

"You have a point. Okay, cross your fingers – and hold your breath." I took my own advice as I reached for the pop-tag that opened the tin; I knew as well as anyone that when canned soups decided to go rancid, they did so in a spectacular fashion. After weeks of anticipation, I was almost afraid to end the wait, but it was time. I squeezed my eyes shut as I thumbed open the tag. There was a creak as the lid rolled back and then… nothing.

I opened my eyes and stared down into the can, astounded to discover that the food was actually still edible. After all the build-up, I'd been expecting a congealed black mess.

"Hey, looks like we win," Michael commented, eyeing the contents of the can. Then he leaned over and planted a kiss on the side of my neck, along with a little playful little nuzzle. "Are you planning to share that with me?"

"'Course not," I teased, putting on an offended face just to mess him. "What kind of girl do you think I am, sharing my food with creepy old men? Go get your own, this is mine!"

I wasn't being serious and he knew it, but he made a show of whining like a neglected puppy and trying to steal my soup away. By the time we were done playing, I found myself giggling like a schoolgirl and feeling surprisingly refreshed. After spending hours travelling through the devastated countryside, his good humour helped to elevate my mood.

"Okay, okay, you can have some. Now, give me the pot, you silly man," I scolded playfully. Grinning, he fished the little steel cooking pot in question out of his pack and put it in my hand. I dumped the contents of my precious can into it and set it over the gas cooker to warm up. While it was heating, I added some more water to thin it, then a packet of dried noodles and some smoked fish to turn the soup from a light snack into a proper dinner.

"Now, this is food I approve of," Michael commented, leaning over my shoulder to watch me curiously while I was cooking.

"But there's no vegetables," I complained.

"Caveman need no vegetables, only meat." He made a few silly grunts, then caught me around the waist and pulled me up close against him. "Meat and pretty lady. Pretty lady looks tasty."

I squealed in surprise when he unleashed a teasing love-bite on my neck, followed by a string of kisses and even a little light tickling. When he was done, we both collapsed in a panting, laughing heap, exhausted but happy just to be in one another's company.

Once the food was cooked, we ate together, enjoying the delicious savoury taste of mushroom and fish, then we curled up to sleep in one another's arms.

It may not have been the most comfortable camping trip, but having Michael there with me made it a hell of a lot more pleasant than the last time I'd slept beneath the stars. Before I knew it, I was fast asleep, nestled cosily in the crook of my sweetheart's arm.

## Chapter Thirteen

I awoke to the savoury scent of eggs cooking in the pre-dawn gloom. Disorientated by waking up in a strange place, it took a second before my brain warmed enough to connect the sounds and scents to reality

"Good morning." Michael looked at me over his shoulder, his ever-present smile resting comfortably on his lips. "Did you sleep well?"

"Well enough, I guess – but I miss my bed," I said, stretching to get the stiffness out of my joints. After six short weeks, my body had decided that it didn't care for sleeping on the ground any more. Or maybe I was just getting old.

"Your bed, or my bed?" Michael teased, leaning over to give me a quick good-morning kiss.

I returned it happily, and then gave him a grin of my own. "Your bed is my bed; I claimed it. Communal beds, that's how we roll."

He chuckled and went back to scrambling eggs. "That's true. I don't know how I'd sleep without you snoring away beside me."

"What?" I froze, staring at him. "I don't snore, do I?"

Michael looked away and didn't answer, which instantly made me suspicious. He turned even further as I crept around to get a look at his face, trying in vain to hide his smile.

"Ah-hah, I knew it!" I exclaimed, hopping up to my feet. "Pulling my leg again, you big meanie? You can't talk. You snore worse than I ever will."

"Eh?" He shot me a started look. "I do not!"

"Yes, you do – but only when you sleep on your back," I informed him cheerfully, and then I skipped off to the bushes to relieve myself, leaving him to mull over that new revelation.

By the time I returned, breakfast was ready and waiting for me. We settled down together to eat straight out of the pot, leaning against one another for warmth in the early-morning chill. We were both ravenous, and devoured our scrambled eggs in record time.

The sun had only just begun creeping over the horizon by the time we were done, casting golden threads of light and long, angular shadows across the landscape all around us. Michael went off to take his turn in the bushes while I cleaned up our breakfast utensils and packed our cooking equipment back into our bags. He returned in time to help me roll up our sleeping bags, and then we were off on our voyage once more. Or rather, we would have been... if the Hilux hadn't died in its sleep.

I turned the key in the ignition. The engine spluttered and whined, making sad, sad noises. I tried pumping my foot on the accelerator to give it a little more juice, but all it did was whimper and click unhappily. Michael stood outside the driver's window, waiting for me to move the truck so we could get out, but the truck refused to play ball.

"Well, this is a fine time to cark it." I climbed out from behind the wheel, and jogged around to the front. I lifted the bonnet up and set it on its little arm, then leaned over the engine and peered at it. "Honey, can you please try to start it?"

"Sure, one second." Michael put his gun down on the roof, then leaned in and tried the ignition again. Nothing.

"It's dead, Jim," he quipped morosely, shooting me a sad look. It had been so long that I couldn't remember where the quote even came from.

I examined the engine for a few minutes longer, then heaved a long sigh and leaned back to stretch my spine. "I think it's the starter motor. There's nothing I can do unless we can find a replacement. Let's just go, I'll keep an eye out for spare parts along the way. Maybe we can get it going again on the way back."

"And here I was, hoping to give my poor feet a rest," Michael complained, but he was still smiling. I had figured out weeks ago that he was just a glass-half-full kind of guy; I think that was part of the attraction. He was quite literally the polar opposite of me, so we stuck together like magnets.

I also suspected that personality trait had helped him to keep it together in the wake of his beloved niece's death. It'd been almost two months since he held her in his arms as she died, but he seemed to be coping well with the grief. Occasionally, he lapsed into a dark mood, but they were rare and I could usually coax him out of them.

My other suspicion was that our relationship helped him to cope as well, since it gave him something new and exciting to cling to instead – and it also meant that he had someone to help him through the grieving process. Sometimes I wondered if our relationship had begun because we both needed someone to cling to, and I worried that when we had both finished healing I'd lose him.

Well, if there was one thing Michael had taught me, it was not to let my self-doubt get me down. Whenever thoughts like that crept up, I slapped them away and contented myself with the fact that I enjoyed what I had at the moment. If something happened in the future, at least I would have these wonderful memories for the rest of my life.

"Well, I suppose you have to maintain your girlish figure somehow," I teased him as I wandered around to take the keys out of the ignition. I stared at them for a second, then tossed them on the driver's seat and slammed the door closed. No point adding extra weight to my burden when there was no guarantee I'd get the truck working again.

When I turned back, I caught Michael watching me with an amused smirk. I blinked in surprise and asked, "What?"

"Sandy..." He seemed on the verge of bursting out laughing, but I couldn't quite figure out why.

"What is it?" I demanded, starting to get frustrated. He knew that I hated being laughed at, even if I knew it was only in jest.

"How are we getting out?" He gestured towards the gate, which we'd pinned closed with the Hilux the night before.

Suddenly, I felt foolish, and I ended up laughing at myself. "I didn't even think about that."

"And here you thought that I was the pretty one, and you were the smart one," he teased; this time, I was equally amused. Somehow, that sweet, silly man always seemed to make every situation funny.

"Nuh-uh. I'm the pretty one and you're the strong one. Get around the other side and push," I ordered playfully, then I yanked open the driver's door, took the handbrake off and set the car in neutral. Between the two of us, we managed to roll the truck forward just enough for us to be able to squeeze out of the gate.

Once we were free, we stripped everything useful from the car, shouldered our packs, and set off on foot towards the rising sun.

\*\*\*

Saying that it was a long walk was the understatement of the century, but two fit people on foot could travel almost as fast as two in a four-wheel drive in our day and age. It was actually easier to negotiate the uneven landscape without a car – but that didn't mean it was fun.

The sun climbed slowly in the sky as we made our way eastwards. Eventually, clouds began to gather, but they were light and fluffy, not rain clouds. Just enough to keep the sun out of our eyes, for which we were grateful. We stuck to the remains of the old roads for most of the journey, occasionally cutting diagonally across fields when it was necessary to keep us moving in the right direction.

After an hour, we found ourselves skirting around the edge of the outermost suburb of Te Awamutu, avoiding the worst of the destruction. East of the town, we reached the main road towards Arapuni. We followed it until midday.

By the time our rumbling stomachs advised us it was about time to stop for lunch, the sun had burned away the last of the clouds and beat down on us with an intensity that was almost painful. Michael shielded his eyes against the sun and stared at the road ahead of us, then he looked back at me.

"We should stop soon, and wait until the heat of the day passes," he suggested.

"Agreed." I nodded. "My foot isn't too happy right now. This is the most walking I've done since it healed."

"Over there?" Michael pointed towards a huge oak tree that grew close by the roadside. Together, we made our way over to the cool, welcoming shade, and flopped down side by side.

"I may be a little out of shape," I admitted, unlacing my shoes and easing them off to examine my feet. The right one was swollen and sore, so I massaged it between finger and thumb to ease the tension in the scar tissue. Michael made a sympathetic noise and reached over to take my foot in his strong hands.

"Poor little foot," he rumbled softly, rubbing it gently to ease away the aches and pains. "So abused. Your mistress is so mean to you." Then he leaned down and planted a kiss on my big toe, which took me completely by surprise.

I yelped and pulled my foot away, staring at him with wide eyes. "What on earth are you doing? I've been walking all day in sweaty socks, you crazy man."

"Do you honestly think I'm concerned by how you smell when you're a little sweaty?" He raised a brow at me, then grabbed my foot again and resumed massaging it. His nimble fingers kneaded away the tension more effectively than I could do myself, so I let him have it. "You do realise that I've kissed you in far sweatier places, right?"

"That wasn't *sweat*, per se," I sniped back.

He grinned wickedly at me. "Hmmm… true. Perhaps I should find another way to distract you from your sore foot."

I felt a surge of warmth in my belly at the look of lust he shot my way; all of a sudden, I found myself giving serious thought to the possibilities. Even though there was no possible chance of being caught in the act, there was still something inherently naughty about a tryst beneath the open sky. It was… appealing, and more than a little arousing. Not that I had any intention of telling him that; the chase was half the fun.

"Oh, you mean lunch?" I retorted playfully, giving him my most innocent look.

"No, that's not what I had in mind at all," he rumbled back in that deep voice of his, the one that sent chills all up and down my spine. I'd swiftly learned what it meant when he used that husky tone on me, but I still loved to hear it. It made me quiver all over.

"Oh, really now?" I said, enjoying the rising tension in the air. It crackled between us like static electricity; every touch of his hand sent tingles through me.

"Mmhm," he answered inarticulately. He pressed his lips against the inside of my ankle, then he drifted higher, trailing kisses along the inside of my leg. Even with us both fully clothed, my breath began to quicken in anticipation. By the time he reached my stomach, he had me all a'quiver.

"Out here in the open? And I thought you were such a good boy," I commented as his kisses drifted higher; I could hear the huskiness in my own voice, and I felt his body respond to it. He lifted my tank top up painfully slowly, inch by inch, rolling it back to expose a little more skin with each kiss.

"It's your fault," he murmured breathlessly as he finally lifted my top enough to expose my bra. He slipped his thumbs beneath the band and raised it up as far as my chin, exposing my skin to the warm breeze. I gasped as his head dipped down to taste me, and I felt my back arch but could do nothing to stop it.

"Ooh... My fault? How is it my fault?" I was having trouble following the conversation, and yet the conversation was half the fun. The heat in my belly was so intense, I could barely breathe, barely focus.

I felt him unzip my trousers and ease them down off my hips, and then those same fingers were teasing me, with just enough pressure to drive me mad. I couldn't bear it any longer. The chase was over – I had to have him.

His lips found that sensitive spot on my neck while I was still struggling to get his trousers off, and his breath was hot across my ear. "Because you're irresistible, Sandy McDermott. You're irresistible, and I love you."

That was the last coherent thought either one of us had, before we tumbled head-first into the world of voyeuristic pleasure.

\*\*\*

An hour later, we lay together watching the fluffy clouds roll by, satisfied, exhausted, and energised all at the same time by our brief lunchtime tryst. Michael lay on his back with his hands folded behind his head, perfectly happy to let me doze with my head lolling on his firm belly. I felt safe and comfortable, knowing he was watching over me while I napped.

Eventually, hunger won out over the desire to sleep. I sat up and stretched lazily, absently wondering where my clothing had gone. Then I felt eyes upon me, and glanced over to find him watching me with great interest.

"Don't get any ideas," I teased him. "We'll end up stuck here all day."

"I know, I know." He heaved a long-suffering sigh. As I hopped up to retrieve my trousers from where they'd landed in our frantic haste, I almost missed the slow, self-satisfied smile that crept across his face. "That was fun though, wasn't it? Who knew public indecency was such an enjoyable crime?"

"I imagine all those people you arrested knew, right up until the time you slapped them in cuffs," I retorted, stepping over his prone body to retrieve my tank top from where it adorned a nearby bush. As I passed, I felt playful fingers creep up my leg but I was out of reach before they could achieve anything.

"Well, they should have invited me," he laughed merrily, watching me while I hunted around for my missing undergarments.

"They probably just like being in handcuffs. I hear that's a fetish." I was only kidding of course, but the noise Michael made was somewhere between a low growl and a purr; a sound of intense, animal interest. I turned to him in surprise, and raised my brows. "You? Really? You don't strike me as the kind of man that would like to cuff a girl up and give her a feel."

"What?" He looked equally startled for a moment, and then laughed and shook his head. "No, no, not like that. The other way around."

"Oh?" I peered at him with interest, equal parts curious and fascinated by the revelation. "Horny young police officer goes to arrest the sexy she-villain, only to get captured in the line of duty? That sounds like the theme of a dirty movie."

"Something like that," he said looking embarrassed, as if he were admitting to a dark secret.

"I'll have to remember that." I gave him a wicked, flirtatious smile. Just at that moment, the wind caught something stuck in the tree above us and set it flapping. The movement attracted my eye. I glanced up, and then gasped in astonishment. "How did my bra get up there?"

"I plead not guilty," Michael answered cheerfully. As if to contradict his statement, a particularly strong gust caught the garment and tugged it free, dropping it right on his face. He was laughing so hard by the time I reached him that he made no attempt to keep it from me.

With a victorious whoop, I pulled on my bra and tank top, and then went back to searching for my underpants. It took me a second to realise that Michael was still laughing. I glanced back at him and spotted him holding up my poor knickers teasingly.

"You thief!" I accused playfully, leaping on him in an attempt to capture the metaphorical flag, but he laughed even harder as he held them out of my reach. We tumbled together in the grass, both laughing and shouting like silly children, oblivious to how foolish we would have looked to anyone else. Sometimes, the fact that we were almost entirely alone in the world was a good thing.

After a few moments of play-wrestling, I finally got my underwear back and managed to get dressed. It took some coaxing to get Michael to do the same, though; after being cooped up in that basement surrounded by small children for so long, he was enjoying the freedom of his own nudity a little too much.

I wouldn't have minded, if not for the fact that we would need to get moving or we'd never reach the dam. Eventually, the promise of lunch coaxed him back into decency. It was a little bribery on my part, but it worked.

"What have you got now?" he asked curiously, leaning over my shoulder to watch while I sliced and assembled our meal.

"Sandwiches," I told him proudly. It really shouldn't have been so exciting, but it was. After ten years without bread, I relished the thought and the texture of something so simple. The idea had come to me just before we left, so I had found an old Tupperware container in one of our cupboards and packed it full of the fixings of a good sandwich: tomatoes, lettuce, smoked fish and the delicious rewena bread our Maori neighbours baked.

Anahera understood my longing for bread like nobody else, and had sent along a freshly-baked batch when Hemi came to trade with us. Who would have thought that something as simple as bread would become more exciting than cake?

I sliced the bread thickly and carefully arranged the other fixings upon it, with Michael watching over my shoulder the entire time. As soon as he had figured out what I was doing, he was riveted by the idea. Although Michael had been born in China, he'd grown up in New Zealand and that made him just as much a Kiwi as I was when it came to our tastes in food. Ten years of living on rice was a bit much for anyone, so he longed for bread just as much as I did.

The fresh produce wouldn't last forever outside in the heat though, so we had to eat it before it went to waste. I filled the sandwiches full to bursting, then I carefully picked one up and handed it to him, and took the other one for myself.

We enjoyed our old-fashioned lunch immensely, far more than either of us would have liked another boring meal from a can. Although Michael never complained, I knew he must be as frustrated as I was with having to live that way. The introduction of a steady supply of fresh food into our diet had brightened both of our moods almost as much as the new romance blooming between us. It brought back memories of decades past, and made us feel… human again.

After lunch, we waited until the heat died down before we slathered on a fresh coat of sunscreen, picked up our backpacks, and moved off. The wind picked up just after midday, bringing pleasant gusts to cool us, which made the walk much more pleasant. My foot felt a little better for the rest, but I longed to soak it in the cool waters of the Waikato to take the swelling down. It already felt like we'd been walking forever, and we were unlikely to reach Arapuni before sundown. I wondered if we would find somewhere safe to rest before nightfall.

In contrast to what Rebecca had said about the bush being dense in this part of the country, the land directly east of Te Awamutu was flat and pleasant with only a few trees sprinkled along the route. The roadway was narrow and cracked, flanked on either side by gorse bushes that kept all other plant life from encroaching too closely on the road itself. Aside from the long grass that stuck up through the cracks in the asphalt, the walk was relatively easy. Still, the road was so well-preserved that I regretted losing the Hilux – we would have made good time in those conditions.

Beyond the gorse, long grass waved placidly in the wind. We watched it for any sign of trouble, but held our weapons relaxed with the safeties on. If something as large and dangerous as a pig approached us, then we would be sure to see it coming long before it got close enough to concern us.

The road took a bend, and we followed as it wound its way into a small patch of woodlands. A flash of neon yellow amongst the trees caught my eye. I nudged Michael and pointed it out. His expression turned grim when he spotted it, but he nodded and walked on regardless. What I'd seen was an old sign post warning non-existent drivers of the school up ahead.

I had no doubt that we shared the same thought: we both dreaded the thought of finding an infected child.

The trees began to clear as we reached another bend. We looked, and saw the overgrown remains of a primary school nestled within the curve of the road. The playground was rusted and bent by a decade's worth of weather, but what made me freeze and grab Michael's hand was the sight of a small human figure sitting on the swings.

He saw her at the same time I did. I looked at him. He looked back, and I saw my own indecision reflected on his face. I knew that we shared similar feelings about the infected. Despite our experiences with the mutated ones, the regular infected were objects of pity, to be put out of their misery whenever possible.

"We can't just leave her there," I whispered, shifting my shotgun into the crook of my left arm. With my right hand, I drew my taser out of my pocket, and then I looked at him again. He nodded his agreement and adjusted the weight of the rifle in his hands. I understood the precaution. Our encounters with the violent, mutated infected in Hamilton had left us both tense and on edge.

With stealthy footsteps, we crept closer to the young girl on the swings. We were wary, but we'd both done it before. This time, though, something was different. Just as we were closing on the lone figure, I grabbed Michael's arm to halt him and paused, listening intently. He glanced at me in surprise, then seemed to realise what I was hearing: the girl on the swings was singing quietly to herself.

We exchanged looks of shock as we both reached the same conclusion. Either that little girl was some kind of infected that neither of us had seen before, or she was actually alive. Michael grabbed my arm and pulled me back out of earshot.

"Are there any groups of survivors in this area?" he whispered urgently.

"I don't know. I haven't heard of any, but things change." I shook my head slowly, unable to tear my gaze away from the young girl. She had her back to us and hadn't noticed us yet. I couldn't guess her age without seeing her face. I couldn't even identify the language she was singing in.

"Maybe she's on her own," Michael said, and then he looked at me as though seeking my advice. I stared back at him, turning the thought over in my head, trying to decide the best way to proceed. Eventually, I came to a decision.

"I'm going to talk to her. Stay here," I said. I offered him my shotgun, which he took from my hand with a frown of obvious concern.

"Are you sure?" he asked. "I'm happy to do it, if you want me to."

"No, I'm less threatening." I shook my head firmly, my mind made up. "Goodness knows what she's been through. I don't want to scare her. You just cover me, okay?"

Michael nodded slowly, but I could see the worry in his eyes. He knew better than anyone else in the world that my past experiences made me skittish around strangers, but this was different. This wasn't a big, strapping man, it was a young girl. I could handle a young girl. At least, I hoped I could.

Armed only with the taser hidden in my pocket, I circled around the edge of the playing field until I moved into her field of vision. She didn't seem to see me at first; her attention was focused on something nestled in her lap. Once I was fully in front of her, I slowly walked towards her, making no attempt at stealth and no sudden movements. As I drew closer, I could hear her singing again. The words were nonsensical to me, but it didn't take long for me to figure out that she was singing in a foreign language that I didn't recognise.

The girl was young and small, fragile from malnutrition, with long, tangled dark brown hair that hung almost to her knees. She was so thin it took me a while to pinpoint her age at around thirteen or fourteen; her rag-clad body showed a few of the earliest stages of puberty, but not much. In her lap, she nursed what appeared to be a very threadbare teddy bear. At least, that's what I hoped it was. All I could really see was light brown fur.

I did a quick calculation in my head and worked out that she must have been three or four when the virus hit. A surge of sympathy hit me along with the realisation that she would have been hardly more than a toddler when she was left on her own. I wondered if her parents had been immune, or if she'd been completely alone since she was a little child, and somehow miraculously survived all these years without any adults to help her. I wondered if she spoke English, or if she just remembered a song her mother had sung to her as a baby. There was only one way to find out.

"Hello," I said softly, halting about five metres from the swings. The girl looked up sharply, her otter-brown eyes huge against skin the colour of milk chocolate. I recognised her ethnicity as someone who originated from India, but I couldn't even begin to guess which province.

The girl didn't say anything, just sat there looking totally shocked by my unexpected presence. She didn't seem to be frightened so much as bewildered, which made sense since she probably hadn't seen another human face in a very, very long time.

It occurred to me that she might only speak Hindi. Maybe her parents had never had a chance to teach her English – or maybe she'd just forgotten over the years. I raised a hand and waved a harmless greeting, then repeated myself. "Hello."

The girl looked at my hand, then looked at my face, then looked down at her own hands. Slowly, as if uncertain what to do, she raised her hand and waved back at me. The confusion on her face tugged at my heartstrings; her eyes were so big that she looked like a little girl, despite being in her early teens.

In an effort to make myself smaller and less intimidating, I eased my backpack off my shoulders and set it down, then sat down on the ground a few metres away from her.

"Can you understand me?" I asked, speaking gently so as not to frighten her, but slowly and clearly.

The girl stared at me while the question sank in. It was a look I understood better than most; after a decade of isolation, it was hard to think in terms of questions and answers. Conversations were no longer second nature. At last, she nodded hesitantly and found a question of her own. "Are you... real?"

The question confused me a little, but I took it in my stride. "Yes, I'm real. My name is Sandy. What is your name?"

Her brow wrinkled. For a moment it seemed like I'd lost her, but I just waited and gave her time, not rushing her for an answer.

"Priyanka," she said at last. All of a sudden, she was off the swing and kneeling on the ground in front of me, almost close enough to touch. Those enormous eyes studied me through her tangle of dark hair, somehow seeming entirely too large for her little face. "Sometimes I see Mama and Baba in my dreams. Are you a dream?"

"No, I am real and you are awake." I shook my head slowly and extended a hand towards her, palm up, to show her that I was real and she could touch me. To my surprise, she did. The girl grabbed my hand and turned it over, staring at it as though it was the first she'd ever seen besides her own. Up close, I could see that she was a filthy little thing, but I ignored it. Under the grime and the smell was a little girl, and she was all alone.

"Real..." She touched my hand with covetous fingers, then laid her hand over mine and compared them, looking fascinated by the contrast between her dark skin and my fair skin. Eventually she looked up at my face again, and I saw that her eyes were rimmed by tears. "Thought all people gone. Thought I was only one."

"No, there are still some people out there," I told her, turning my hand over slowly so that I could hold hers. It was so tiny and bird-like compared to mine that I was almost afraid to break it. To my surprise, she not only let me hold her hand but seemed happy for it; she ducked her head down and sniffed at my hand. I felt a spot of moisture on my skin and couldn't tell whether a tear had fallen on me or if she'd licked me for some reason, but either way I managed to keep myself from flinching.

It was a child-like fascination, inquisitive, young. With no adults to care for her, she'd never had the chance to learn anything more. Her education had stopped as a toddler. Even Skylar's education had included the company of other human beings.

"I want," she whispered, nuzzling against my hand like a little child. "I want. I want. No go, please. No go."

My heart just about broke when I realised her cheeks were wet with tears. I found myself stroking her tangled hair without even thinking about it, letting her work through her emotions at her leisure. In my mind, all I could see was a cherub-faced child, toddling the countryside all alone, confused, frightened and hungry. Without anyone to care for her, it was a miracle that she'd survived.

Over her head, I saw Michael approaching with a look of concern on his face, but he relaxed when I gave him a reassuring smile. I tilted my head towards a patch of grass beside me. He understood that I meant it was safe for him to join us, so he did. He settled cross-legged a little way away and hid the weapons behind his back. The sound of his bulk settling on the grass attracted the girl's attention, though she still clung to my hand as though afraid to let me go.

"This is Michael. He's a friend," I told her, and then looked at him. "Her name is Priyanka. I'm pretty sure she's alone out here."

"Michael." The girl repeated his name, stumbling over the pronunciation a little. Wide-eyed, she looked back and forth between us, then down at her own dusky-skinned little hands. "Different?"

"Our mamas and babas come from different places," I explained, using her own language to help her understand. Her speech was obviously stunted due to limited exposure to other people, but there was no reason to assume she was unintelligent. "People look different in other places. Michael is also a boy, while I am a girl, like you."

"Ah-hah." She made a universal sound of understanding and leaned back on her haunches to examine us both. The movement let me get a good look at the object she'd been cradling; I was relieved to see the fur did belong to a ratty old teddy bear, as opposed to something less savoury. It was so ancient its fur had worn bare in patches, and the stitches around its throat had come loose to reveal the dull grey stuffing within.

Seeking a way to bond with the girl, I pointed at the teddy bear. "Would you like me to fix him? His head is about to come off."

The dirty little girl looked down at her teddy bear uncertainly, then back up to me. "Fix?"

"I can sew his head back on for you. Make him all better. See, his insides are coming out?" I leaned in closer to point out the damage, but made no attempt to take the bear from her in case she misinterpreted the action as a threat. She seemed to understand, though.

"Make better, please," she said, holding her precious bear out to me. I smiled at her manners, and gently took the teddy from her outstretched hands. Priyanka inched closer to watch while I opened my backpack and dug out the tiny sewing kit I always kept with me during long journeys. It was one of those things that had proven itself well worth the minimal weight over the years. Things always tended to break at the least convenient moments.

I caught Michael watching with interest as I deftly threaded a needle and began sewing up the gaping wound in the bear's neck with small, neat stitches. Being a survivor made you self-sufficient; I'd learned the patience required for tidy sewing through trial and error. Fast, sloppy stitches would only come loose again, and force you to do the work all over again.

The girl's eyes widened as the wound shrank, as if I were showing her an amazing magic trick. I suppose to someone with the life experience of a three-year-old, it was. There were a lot of things she'd been denied beyond just the obvious.

The learning that took place in those early formative years was so much more in depth than just reading, writing and arithmetic, and she had missed out on all of it. I felt pity for her, and sympathy – it would be hard to learn those lessons later in life, but I hoped that she'd be willing to try.

She showed patience beyond her years as she watched me work. I suppose she felt the passage of time much like I had when I was out on my own; the rise and fall of the sun only provided a vague sense of when to eat and when to sleep, but time was more or less meaningless.

Eventually, I closed off the last stitch and bit the thread short, then offered the newly-repaired bear back to the girl. She took it reverently, as if she had just witnessed a miracle, and turned it slowly within her hands. Then all of a sudden, she smiled and hugged the bear to her chest. "All better. Fix."

"All better," I agreed, feeling a flush of pride at the joy I'd brought to her with something so small. I guessed that bear must have been with her for a while, but I doubted she would be able to explain its origins. I tried a simpler question instead. "Where do you live, Priyanka?"

The young girl looked at me thoughtfully, and then stared around herself as though seeking an answer. Finally, she shrugged and hugged her teddy again. I took her silence to mean she lived wherever she could.

"Where did you sleep last night?" I asked, trying another tactic. That one she could answer more easily; she pointed at the playground, towards a small, sheltered enclosure at the head of the rusty old slide. I nodded my understanding and asked another question. "What do you eat?"

She looked down at her feet and shrugged again, absently plucking at the long blades of grass around her. I felt a stab of sympathy, intuiting that expression meant that she ate whatever she could find. Judging by her small size, it wasn't a lot.

I exchanged a glance with Michael, and he gave me a nod. There was an understanding between us, a survivor's code: we couldn't leave this poor girl on her own any more than Michael could have thrown me out when he found me.

"Would you like something to eat?" I asked her, leaning forward to look her in the eye. Her expression changed so swiftly that I couldn't decipher the emotions. I saw fear, longing, hope, and so many others all twisting together. Her response was another shrug.

I saw right through her mask of nonchalance. She was just a little girl, and she was half-starved. I reached into my backpack again, pulled out the small lump of rewena bread left over from our lunch, and held it out to her.

She stared at it as though afraid that it might be a trick, and then looked up at me with confusion on her grubby little face. I smiled at her reassuringly and broke a tiny piece off the bread, which I put it in my mouth to show her that it was edible. It didn't take a psychoanalyst to know that she wanted it but was just afraid to take it.

When I offered it to her again, she snatched it from my hand. She seemed poised on the verge of flight, about to leap up and scurry away with her prize like a frightened animal – but something held her back. She looked back and forth between us, uncertain. We sat there patiently with smiles on our faces, watching her indecision.

Eventually, she figured out that we weren't going to take her bread away from her. She sniffed it, licked at it, and then took an enormous bite. The texture of the food enticed her in, and soon the small hunk was devoured. Once it was all gone she licked the crumbs off her dirty fingers, and looked around anxiously for more.

That was the last of our bread so there was none to be had, but Michael followed my lead and gave her an apple from his pack instead. She only hesitated for a moment this time before snatching that from his hand, and devouring it with glee. She wasted nothing, and even ate the core. When she was done she flopped back on the grass with a satisfied sigh.

"Thanks you, thanks you," she whispered, just about breaking my heart all over again with her sweet expression of gratitude. Whoever had been the 'mama' and 'baba' of this young lady, they had done a good job teaching their little one manners.

"You're welcome, Priyanka," I said gently.

"Would you like a drink? Water?" Michael spoke up for the first time, holding up one of our smaller water bottles for her to see. His deep voice seemed to startle her, and it took her a moment to translate his words in her head. When she made sense of them, her expression brightened and she nodded vigorously. He took the lid off the bottle and handed it to her. She drank gratefully.

Michael and I exchanged glances as the girl drank. On his face, I saw the same concern I felt mirrored back at me. We both knew we had to take the girl with us, if she was willing to go. The doctor would scold us for collecting more strays, but we had no choice. No decent human being could leave another in a situation like that and not feel guilty.

"Priyanka." I leaned forward to catch her eye. She stopped drinking, and stared up at me. "Michael and I have to go soon. We have a very long trip to go on, to meet with some friends. If you would like to, you can come as well. Would you like to come with us?"

That may have been the stupidest question of all time. She had no intention of letting either of us out of her sight any time soon.

# *Chapter Fourteen*

Despite her fragile build, Priyanka didn't slow us down at all. Since she had no belongings besides her teddy bear, we were back on the road within minutes of her decision to join us. She skipped along beside us as we walked, singing happily to herself in Hindi. Or at least, I presumed it was Hindi. For once, Michael had no insight to offer despite his usual adeptness as a translator.

A couple of times, Priya's dancing took her so far ahead of us that we almost lost sight of her. Each time, she suddenly panicked when she realised that we weren't close by, spun around, and came tearing back to us as though afraid we would leave her behind.

We wouldn't, of course, but I understood that desperate, irrational fear; I had felt it myself on more than one occasion since I joined Michael's group. Sometimes she latched onto my arm and clung to me like a limpet, but even then I couldn't bring myself to be annoyed with her. Human beings are innately social creatures, and the fear of rejection is almost as strong as the fear of death. Sometimes, it's even stronger.

Each time she attached herself to me, I stroked her hair and spoke softly to her until she calmed down again, like you would with a frightened puppy. Her fits of clinginess never lasted for long. Once the latest one had passed and she'd scampered off about her play, I glanced at Michael and found him watching me with amusement.

"What?" I asked, shooting him a smile in return. His expression turned into a grin.

"I think that girl likes you," he replied, slipping an arm casually around my waist. "I have the sneaking suspicion we won't be able to have any more romantic interludes on this trip."

"Oh, I'm sure we'll think of something," I replied, reaching up to pat his cheek affectionately. He leaned down to plant a tender kiss on my lips. I closed my eyes for a moment to enjoy the closeness. When I opened them again, I found that Priya had returned, and was watching us closely with her head canted at a curious angle.

Well, this was going to be an uncomfortable conversation. How to you explain the birds and the bees to someone with the social experience of a three-year-old?

"You kissies," she commented in her childlike manner, looking fascinated by the discovery.

"Sandy is my girlfriend," Michael explained, heroically leaping to the rescue. "Like your mama and baba."

"Oh." The young girl bobbed her head in understanding and smiled broadly. "You have baby?"

"No, not yet. It's not safe for babies," Michael answered, shaking his head. "Maybe one day, when it's safer."

Priyanka seemed satisfied with that and contentedly skipped off to resume her play. I, on the other hand, found myself all a'fluster. Ever observant, Michael was quick to notice my expression.

"What's wrong, honey?" he asked, gently drawing me closer against his side as we walked. "You're blushing."

"You called me your girlfriend," I answered, stunned and incredulous.

"Aren't you my girlfriend?" He frowned at me, an uncertain look in his eye.

I felt a stab of panic and rushed to reassure him. "No! I mean, yes– I mean, I didn't mean it like that. I mean, you've never called me that before. It just took me by surprise." I was even more flustered now; my emotions darted all over the place, but as always Michael seemed to understand.

"Do you want me to stop?" he asked, but this time a smile danced across his lips instead of a frown.

"Nah." I resorted to humour to cover my embarrassment. "I think it's okay. Hell, you can do it more often, if you want. That might be awesome. I'm not so sure about the babies thing, though."

"I am," he answered, his expression softening as he looked down at me. "I mean, not right now – but one day, I definitely want to have a child of my own. I think I could be a good father. Don't you?"

"God yes, you'd be the best father in the world," I blurted with all the elegance of a rhinoceros in a tutu. "It's me that I'm worried about. I've just, you know, never even thought about it. Two months ago, I couldn't imagine letting anyone touch me, let alone starting a family with someone."

"I know, sweetheart – and there's the worry about the immunity. But one day, when it's safe, then we can think about it." He grinned suddenly and gave me a playful nudge. "You have to admit, we'd make some pretty cute babies together."

I had to laugh at that, and nodded my agreement. "Yeah, so long as they look like you. Chinese babies are the cutest things since kittens in tuxedos."

"Well, if I remember my high school biology right, the eyelid thing is a dominant trait, so there's a good chance they would." His grin turned impish, and he reached over to grab my plaited hair, giving it a playful tug. "It's a shame blonde is recessive. Could you imagine a little girl with your hair and my eyes?"

"Now that's a frightening thought." I laughed even harder at the mental image he conjured up; throw in a big frilly dress, and Maddy would have some competition for the cutest kid on the block. "It could happen, though. Your dad might have passed on a recessive gene to you."

"That's true. Granddad was a Kiwi mutt, like you," he teased. I knew it was all in fun, so I took no offense and teased him right back.

"Hey, I'll have you know that I'm only *half* Kiwi mutt. My daddy was pure Scottish stock, but he moved here when he was two." I flicked back a strand of hair loosened by his playfulness, and gave him a smile. "I'm an actual McDermott. We have a plaid and everything."

"I can think of a hundred other things I'd rather see you in than a kilt," he gave me a flirtatious wink, but with curious young eyes intensely interested in everything we did, our flirting stayed firmly in the realm of decency for once.

*\*\*\**

The landscape we passed through gradually changed over the course of the afternoon. Wide, flat expanses of pastoral land that had once grazed farm animals gave way to fields that had been used to grow crops. As we moved further eastwards, we began to pass by enormous cornfields, gone wild over the years. They stretched as far to the south as the eye could see, their tall stalks swaying gracefully in the breeze.

Michael and I watched the cornfields warily, our weapons at the ready; the perpetual movement and incessant rustling made us nervous, because it could hide the approach of any number of enemies. Priyanka showed no such concern, though. She darted away from us and vanished into the long stalks with a squeal of delight.

I glanced at Michael and shrugged. "I guess now we know how she's survived all these years on her own."

"I guess we do," he agreed.

"We should bring some corn back with us; we could make our own bread out of it. Maybe we could even grow it." I glanced over at him to see what he thought. He nodded slowly, turning the idea over in his head.

Whatever his answer may have been, it was interrupted by Priyanka's return. She scampered back to us at full tilt, her bare feet flashing across the grass. With a prodigious leap to clear the long grass on the verge, she darted back across the tarmac and proudly presented each of us with an ear of corn.

We thanked her, then resumed walking eastwards. Priya and I stripped the husks off our corn, so that we could nibble on it as we travelled. Just as I was about to tuck in to mine, I cast a glance sideways and caught Michael staring at his cob, looking totally perplexed.

"What's the matter?" I queried, amused by the look on his face.

He shot me a helpless look, and shrugged. "I'm a city boy. I've never... opened one of these before."

"Give it here." I chuckled, shoved my cob into my pocket, then reached over to take his. With practiced expertise, I showed him how to snap off the stem and peel back the leaves, revealing the golden sweetness within. "I've eaten a lot of this stuff over the years. It just takes a bit of practice. And... there you go, just like that."

"Huh. Just like that. That was easier than I thought." Michael took the cob, sniffed at it, and then took a bite. He nodded thoughtfully as he chewed, considering the texture.

"Tastes a lot better than the canned stuff, doesn't it?" I asked jovially, pulling my cob back out of my pocket.

"Definitely," he agreed. "Better than cooked, as well. I believe we may be obligated to bring back as much as we can carry."

"Shame it's so far away, or we could just come back here and pick as much as we need at our leisure," I commented thoughtfully.

"If only the roads were functional." He sighed and nodded.

"Where's a bureaucrat when you need one?" I joked, drawing a chuckle from my companion.

Priyanka laughed too, but not because she understood the joke. She laughed because she was happy to hear the sound of people around her after so long alone.

\*\*\*

Eventually, the fields gave way to long, rolling hills; the further east we travelled, the steeper they became. The forest grew denser as we walked, and the road began a long, slow climb towards the heavens.

My hamstrings protested as we ascended the hill, but none of us said anything out loud. Priyanka seemed less bothered than Michael and me, but her energetic bouncing did slow to a plodding walk. I worried about her bare feet on the uneven roadway, but she didn't seem concerned at all. I could only guess that after ten years without shoes, her feet were probably a lot tougher than mine.

"Have you walked this way before?" I asked her, breathless but curious. The girl looked around herself a bit, then she looked up at me and shook her head.

"Is new place to me. Has you walked?" she asked me in return, equally curious.

I shook my head as well and pointed behind us, to the west. "No. We come from very far in that direction."

"Why we go this way?" she enquired with child-like inquisitiveness. I could tell at a glance that she wasn't complaining, she was just interested in knowing our reasoning. Curiosity was a trait I encouraged in everyone, so I answered her as best I could.

"There are some people that live over there, far on the other side of these hills," I explained. "They called to us for help. We're going to help them."

She made a noise of understanding, but further conversation was interrupted as we crested the hill. Directly ahead of us, the roadway vanished over the edge of a ragged cliff. Once, years ago, a rest area beside the road had commanded a magnificent view of the valleys all around, but sometime in the past the cliff face had collapsed. Now, only jagged edges remained.

The three of us inched closer to the end of the road to peer over the edge; beneath us, a small truck lay smashed upon the rocks. My guess was that its weight had caused the collapse, but that knowledge didn't help us at all.

"We'll need to go around." I pointed to the right of the road, where the verge climbed sharply into a shoulder-height cliff. Beyond the verge, the hill top was dense with forest, but the only other choice was to climb down and up the other side of the break in the road. Although the cliff was only a few metres high, it was starting to get dark, and climbing at dusk seemed like a very bad idea.

Michael nodded without a word and went to the verge, where he cupped his hands to boost me up. I placed my foot in his hands and a hand on his shoulder, and then I was up and over the ledge easily. The two of us helped Priyanka up, and then Michael vaulted up after us.

The bush on the hilltop was dense, dark and threatening; I felt a sense of foreboding just looking at it. Instinctively, I brought my shotgun around in front of me and slipped off the safety.

"Priya, you stay between me and Michael, okay?" I glanced at her as I gave the order. She tilted her head curiously, not quite seeming to understand, but she did as she was told as we moved off.

I led the way, scanning the woodlands around us as we walked. I could hear the faint rustle of small wild things all around us, but in the shadows beneath the canopy I could see very little. Keeping the verge within sight to our left, I picked my way carefully amongst the trees. Leaves brushed at my cheeks and tugged at my hair, forcing me to shove them away impatiently. Although we were far more exposed out on the road, at least I could see any threats coming; in the dense undergrowth, things could sneak up on us much more easily.

The impending twilight was another concern. We were in the middle of nowhere, and the last building we'd seen was several kilometres behind us. Finding a place to stop for the night was becoming more urgent. Although we both carried torches, it was unsafe to keep travelling after dark. The batteries wouldn't last forever, and this far from anywhere, the only other light we had was starlight.

"I think I see the road," Michael whispered; I understood that he felt the need for stealth, like I did. I looked where he pointed, and spotted the flash of grey through the trees.

I nodded and led the way forward. A dozen metres further on, I stepped around a particularly dense bush – and almost fell over the edge of a low cliff. Michael grabbed me and pulled me back, then he held me reassuringly for a moment while I recovered my wits. Two metres below us, the roadway resumed its course.

"Over there," I gasped, my heart racing from my brief encounter with potential injury or even death. A little further to the east, the cliff between the forest's edge and the road was lower and more manageable.

The three of us hurried to the lower spot and scrambled down the bank, back to the roadway. By the time we were able to resume our eastward march, the sun had drifted lower and sunset was beginning in earnest. I glanced back over my shoulder and shielded my eyes from the sun's glare. I estimated that we had about an hour left before we'd be walking in total darkness.

"We should hurry," I told the others. They both nodded in agreement. Even little Priyanka seemed to understand the dangers of being out after dark. For most of the day we'd wandered along at a leisurely pace, but now we all felt a sense of urgency. None of us wanted to be left exposed at night.

*** 

I had always found it kind of amazing how much ground a human being could cover on foot when he or she put her mind to it. As a child and a teenager, I would never have imagined that I'd be out walking the roads instead of driving, and as such I never stopped to think how long it would take to travel those routes without the benefit of a car.

Dusk cast long shadows all around us as we descended the eastern side of the hill into the valley beyond. The low angle of the sun rendered the landscape in shades of grey and made it harder and harder to see. The trees around us were tall, making the world beneath their boughs seem darker and more threatening.

"I think I see something." Michael was the first of us to speak up. At first I worried, but the tone of his voice was one of relief, not fear. My shotgun held at the ready, I stepped forward to try and locate what he'd seen. There it was, nestled amongst the trees – an old white mailbox. I couldn't see the house though, because the trees were too thick.

"I think we're going to have to risk it," I said. Michael nodded in agreement. He took the lead this time, and we sandwiched Priyanka between us as we picked our way in the direction a driveway had once gone.

With the sun almost down and darkness descending across our wild little world, we could hardly see beneath the trees. We clicked on our torches to light the way, but the tiny beams of light they produced barely penetrated the gloom. I strained my ears but I couldn't hear any threats, just the sound of the birds chattering as they went to sleep, and the sound of our own footfalls.

Between one step and the next, Michael's tread changed in timbre. I recognised the sound of gravel crunching beneath his boots. Ten years ago, I would never have noticed the difference in the sound, but now it sounded like a clarion call to me.

"I see a house." Michael's voice was soft as a whisper, but I heard it clearly in the relative quiet around us. It was so dark that I couldn't see his broad back in front of me anymore, only the sweep of his torch as it swung back and forth.

"Lead on," I whispered back, as much to reassure him that we were still following as for any real need to give him instruction.

Our little convoy picked its way across the old, grass-hewn gravel that had once been someone's driveway. Again I found myself worrying about Priyanka's feet, but she didn't protest at all. The flash of Michael's torch beam cut across timber, and again I heard the sound of his boots change; he was climbing wooden stairs, and then walking across a porch.

As loathe as I was to turn my own torch away from the dark forest behind us, we had to focus in front to make it safely up the stairs. I felt a hand touch my arm gently as I cleared the top step: Michael, reassuring me of his protective presence.

"Watch the door while I clear the house," I instructed. I felt more than saw him nod, then his torch beam cut away from us to scan the edge of the forest.

I found the front door not far away, and when I tried the handle it was unlocked. I could hear Priya's breathing behind me as I stepped inside and scanned the interior of the house by torchlight. The place wasn't large, just a small, cosy home that had seen better days. To the right of the doorway I saw a living room with a couple of fat couches and a fireplace. To the left was a dining room and kitchen.

Directly in front of me was a long corridor that led towards the rear of the house, where I imagined bedrooms must be located.

"Stay with Michael," I told Priyanka, then I crept deeper into the house to check each of the rooms carefully. Nothing stirred in the living room, kitchen, or dining room. I picked my way carefully along the hallway towards the rear of the building. One at a time, I opened doors and checked for hostiles, but I found nothing more threatening than an army of dust bunnies.

At the far end of the hallway, a back door opened into darkness. I closed it quickly and locked it, then I hurried back to the front of the building. I found Michael still standing guard, and Priya hovering uncertainly between him and the doorway.

"We're clear. Get in here so we can lock the door," I whispered to him. Michael fell back on my word, his torch still sweeping the dark forest. The moment they were both inside, I closed the door and locked it. Suddenly, we all felt safer.

I heard Michael heave a sigh of relief, and I grunted wordlessly in agreement. A strange, dark house in the middle of nowhere was not my favourite place to be, but at least we weren't out in the open any longer.

"We've got a fireplace. That should give us some light." I padded across the thick, dusty carpet and knelt down in front of it to see if I could get it going. "Honey, there's a back door at the end of the hall. I've locked it, but I'd feel a lot safer if we could figure out some way to block it, just in case."

"I'm on it," he answered, his deep voice disembodied in the shadows. "Priyanka, come help me? I'll need someone to hold the light."

"Okies," the girl agreed amiably, and I heard their footsteps retreat towards the rear of the house. Soon, there were sounds of things being dragged around, but I ignored them and I focused on getting the fire started.

A stack of old wood still sat nearby, with all the fixings to get it going. After so many years indoors, it couldn't have been any drier; the fire started easily and stayed burning with minimal effort. It didn't give us a lot of light, but it was enough. By the time they returned, I had the fire burning cheerfully in the fireplace.

"We found some blankets," Michael told me, dumping them in a pile in the middle of the living room. "I'll bring out one of the mattresses as well. We should be able to sleep comfortably."

I nodded my approval, and he hurried off. Priyanka stayed with me this time, settling down on the floor beside me to watch me poke at the flames. Without the breeze to blow away her funk, the smell of her hit me more strongly than ever.

"You need a bath," I told her gently. She tilted her head and looked up at me, clearly not understanding. "A bath – you know, a wash? You're dirty."

I pantomimed scrubbing myself until she finally understood, but she misunderstood my intentions. Tears welled up in her eyes and she looked at me like I'd just kicked her. "I am bad?"

"What? No, no – you're a good girl." I swiftly struggled to alleviate her fears. "You just need a bath, so you won't get sick. I'll help you tomorrow, when the sun is up."

"Oh…" The girl absently scratched at herself and looked down. "The dirty is bad, not I am bad?"

"That's right." I reached over and stroked her hair; her expression relaxed at the touch, reassured. "The dirty is bad, it can make you sick. We'll give you a bath, make you clean. Then you won't get sick – and won't be itchy either."

"Itchy," Priya agreed readily, scratching at her arm. Up close, I could see a couple of little sores on her arm, and understood just how desperate for a bath she was. And clothing, for that matter – hers were just rags, so tattered that I couldn't even figure out what they'd originally looked like. She could use a haircut, too. Her hair was so long that she probably hadn't had one since before the plague struck.

"You poor little thing." I sighed as she cuddled up against me, staring up at me with those big, sad eyes of hers. "I promise, you'll feel much better after a bath. No more itchy."

"No more itchy," she echoed. Further conversation was interrupted as Michael returned, carrying with him a mattress pilfered from a single bed. He shoved it up against the wall beneath the windows and piled the blankets on top of it.

"Bathroom seems to be functioning, if either of you want to 'go'," he told us helpfully, glancing back at us as he went about turning the couch and the mattress into functioning beds.

It had been a while, so I did need to relieve myself. I guessed that Priya probably did as well, so I took her by the hand and led her off down the hall, where we took turns using the lavatory. I was relieved to discover that she was toilet-trained. At least that was one less thing for me to worry about.

Afterwards, I showed her how to wash her hands with soap and explained in simple terms how important it was to do so. She was a ready student and didn't argue, apparently content in the knowledge that grown-ups knew best. If only she knew that we were all just making it up as we went along, too.

Illuminated by the narrow beam of my torch, we made our way back to our little campsite in the living room. Michael had put dinner on while we were away, and the savoury smell of fish cooking lured us to join him. The three of us sat in a circle around our cook stove until it was ready, then he divided it up into a bowl for each of us and handed it out.

Priya didn't even bother with a spoon. She just dove right in face-first, to our amusement. Now wasn't the time to try and teach her manners, so we just left her to it while the two of us ate at a more sedate pace and talked quietly about the day's adventures.

"We should probably keep a night watch," I suggested. "We didn't really have a chance to secure this place before we bunked down, so it would make sense."

"I defer to your experience," he agreed, popping a spoonful of fish and rice into his mouth. Once he'd swallowed it, he added, "I'll take the second watch, if you want. That's always the harder one."

"It's sweet of you to offer." I smiled up at him gratefully, since he was right. Waking up in the middle of the night and trying to stay alert was always harder on the body. "I won't say no."

"I didn't think you would." He gave me a playful wink. We finished our meal in companionable silence.

By the time we adults had finished eating, Priyanka was fast asleep. She just curled up on the floor like a sleepy kitten, without a blanket or a pillow. Between the two of us, we moved her to the couch and wrapped her in warm blankets to keep her comfortable, then we settled down on the mattress on the floor.

Michael snuggled up against me with his head in my lap, while I sat upright resting my back against the end of the couch. I ran my fingers absently over his short hair as he fell asleep, feeling a strange sort of contentment wash over me. Although it felt weird to be sitting guard while others slept around me, I felt a strong desire to protect them. Sleep would not come to me while I sat watch, keeping my family safe.

After a while, I got bored with my own thoughts, and dug into my pack for the book I'd stolen weeks before. I'm still not sure what had driven me to bring it along but I had, so I made use of it. Angling the book so the flickering light from the fireplace fell across the dusty pages, I lost myself in a world of foolish fantasy romances and long-dead places.

Every so often, a noise would disrupt my peaceful world. Something outside would creak, a gust of wind would disturb the trees, or an owl would hoot. Every time, it got my heart racing all over again, only to end with me chiding myself for being so jumpy. Once, I heard something that sounded like a footstep, but it faded before I could determine exactly what I'd heard.

At around midnight, I felt Michael stir against me. As though awoken by some internal alarm clock, he stretched and yawned, then looked up at me with those fathomlessly dark eyes of his. "Any trouble?"

"Nothing I'm worried about," I reassured him as we swapped places; he sat up, while I snuggled down beneath the blankets, looking forward to my half-a-night's sleep. Despite the odd noises, I felt content knowing that Michael was watching over me. He would never allow any harm to come to me while I was vulnerable, and that made me feel comfortable and relaxed.

I nuzzled my face against his firm thigh and closed my eyes. Before I had time to ponder another thought, I was fast asleep.

# Chapter Fifteen

I slept deeply that night. My dreams were full of knights, princesses, and beautiful young girls with dark eyes and long, Rapunzel hair. I awoke just after dawn, feeling warm and comfortable – until I realised that the firm thigh I'd been using as a pillow was rigid with tension. I looked up, and saw Michael's jaw was clenched and his face was set in a mask of intense concentration.

"What's wrong?" I whispered, jerked fully awake by the look on his face. He started at the sound of my voice, then let out a deep breath, as though he'd been so tense that he'd forgotten to breathe.

"There's something outside," he whispered back. "I've heard it walking around out there for the last few hours. It hasn't tried to get in, though. Seemed safer to wait until dawn before we go see what it is."

"Good thinking," I agreed, easing myself up into a sitting position. "Let's go find out, then."

Both of us had slept fully clothed that night. With Priyanka in the room, it felt inappropriate to disrobe – and neither of us liked to let our guard down in unknown territory. As reluctant as I was to leave the warm nest I shared with my beloved, necessity required it. We extracted ourselves from bed and found our weapons in the semi-darkness, then we headed for the front door.

I peeked through the curtains that hung over the nearest window and saw nothing. Room by room, we checked each window to see if we could get some idea of what was out there, but we saw and heard nothing.

Michael was ahead of me as we crept down the corridor towards the back. Suddenly, he froze and jerked a hand up to silence any questions I might have had. He tilted his head to one side, silently communicating that I needed to stop and listen. I did so. From the other side of the barricade, we could quite clearly hear the shuffling of feet. I opened my mouth to say something, but an unexpected sound interrupted my train of thought: a faint whine.

We stared at each other in surprise, not quite sure what we were hearing.

"Was that a dog?" I whispered. Michael hesitated and then nodded, probably for lack of any better explanation. For reasons that I couldn't guess at, domestic canines had been a rare sight since the plague hit, but they weren't completely unheard of.

As if to answer our question, a low, pitiful howl came from the other side of the door, followed by more whining and whimpering. We both stared at the door, and I saw my own indecision mirrored in Michael's face.

"If it's hurt, then we should help it," he said, echoing my thoughts. "But, it also might just attack us on sight."

"There's only one way to be sure," I answered, shooting a glance at him. "We have to go look. I think we should go out the front and walk around, rather than move the blockade. That way we can always run back in and lock the door."

"Sounds like a plan," he agreed with a firm nod. Together, we returned to the front end of the house. Priyanka still slept soundly on the couch, so we left her there and we headed out the front door with our weapons at the ready. I led the way down the front steps and swung around the house in a wide arc, treading lightly across the grass-hewn gravel. Now that we were in daylight, I could see that the little bungalow sat in a small, overgrown clearing amidst the trees; to the rear of the building, I saw a large, open shed that backed up to the house. It seemed like a safe assumption that whatever had been making the noise was hiding inside.

Michael fell in beside me as we tiptoed around the edge of the building. I swung out wide to try and get a look inside the shed before we exposed ourselves in danger, but the long shadows of sunrise made it hard to see. I could only just barely make out the outline of the creature hiding within. What I did see was that it was leaning hard against the back door, and I heard it whining pathetically.

It didn't seemed to have noticed us even though I was standing silhouetted against the morning light. I glanced at Michael, then looked back at the animal and let out a whistle. Its head came up immediately, ears pricked, then it struggled to its feet with some difficulty. With slow, hesitant steps, it limped towards me, swinging its head slowly from side to side.

When it stepped out into the light, I realised that it wasn't sick, just elderly. I'm an animal person by nature, so the sight melted my heart. Michael seemed to feel the same way. He handed me his gun and knelt down, making soft clicking noises and calling the dog until it turned its head towards him.

"Come here, buddy. Come on," he called, snapping his fingers to attract the dog's attention. It came towards him slowly, swinging its head back and forth as if trying to isolate the sound of his voice. A few steps closer, it paused and sniffed the air, then whined again and inched closer with its tail wagging shyly.

Michael held out his hand and let the dog sniff it, which it did. The creature's breath made wuffling noises between whines, and then it licked his hand. Michael took that as an invitation and reached over to rub the old dog's ears, making comforting noises to keep it calm. As soon as he did, the dog's tail started wagging frantically.

"Doggie?" Priyanka asked from behind me, just about scaring me out of my wits. I glanced back to find her hiding behind me, staring at the creature with wide eyes. Her gaze shifted up to me, her expression one of apprehension. "Doggie will bite?"

"No, I don't think he'll bite you unless you're mean to him." I extended an arm out to her. Priyanka ducked beneath it gratefully, and cuddled up against my side.

Together, we watched Michael talking to the elderly canine, ruffling its ears and making comforting sounds. The dog's tail wagged so hard I could practically hear the old joints creaking, but it seemed thrilled to feel a human's touch.

"You know, the doctor's going to kill us if we bring home two strays," I commented dryly.

Michael laughed and nodded, keeping his voice low to avoid scaring his new friend. "But he doesn't have a choice in the matter; he was my first stray and he knows it."

"I am stray?" Priyanka asked, looking bewildered by the comment.

"You were a stray," I corrected her gently, giving her a sideways hug. "But you're not any more. Now, you're our friend."

"Oh... stray means not friend?" Her brows furrowed in obvious confusion.

"Not quite. In this situation, a stray is just a friend you haven't met yet," I tried to explain, using simple terms that her limited vocabulary could understand. "It's a new person, or a stranger."

"Oh." Understanding dawned in the girl's eyes. "Doggie is stray, but can be friend if no bite?"

"Yes, that's right," I agreed. It was close enough until we could expand her vocabulary. Looking pleased at her new-found knowledge, Priya disentangled herself from me and crept over Michael and the dog. She knelt down beside them, staring at the creature.

While Michael took over her education and showed her how to let the dog sniff her hand, I stood guard. I divided my time between watching Michael's paternal instincts coming out, and keeping my eyes peeled for danger.

I had to admit, I was secretly impressed by his adeptness. The years he'd spent raising Sophie, his niece, paid off. Even though I had no interest in having children of my own just yet, some part of me found his skill with youngsters extremely attractive. Despite being so physically large with a deep, powerful voice, neither the child nor the animal seemed to be frightened of him at all.

Eventually, I drifted off into my own thoughts while the others played, staring into the bush surrounding the clearing. Suddenly, a squeal of delight attracted my attention. I glanced back and saw Priyanka hugging the dog around the neck while it licked her face, tail wagging frantically. Michael laughed merrily, and even I found myself unable to resist a smile.

The age of technological and capitalist pleasures was long gone. Now, it was the simple joy of a child's laughter, of fresh food and clean water, and the companionship of lovers, friends, and family that brought happiness into our lives. As much as I missed my parents, I felt like we might actually be better off for it in a broader sense. The downfall of our species brought us back to our roots, to what we were meant to be before the Promethean lure of the modern age had turned us into something else completely.

"Doggie need bath," Priya told me as she disentangled herself from the old sheepdog and hopped up to her feet. "We have bath now?"

"You first," I told her, holding out my hand. The young girl raced over to take it and skipped along beside me as I led her back to the front of the house. Behind us, I heard Michael coaxing the old dog along as well. Soon, the four of us were safely back inside.

***

Bath-time proved to be a noisy and rambunctious affair that ended with water and soap suds all over the old bathroom. By the time I'd peeled Priya out of her filthy rags and gotten her into a tub full of cold water, I'd come to the awful discovery that she was infested with all manner of parasites. Her rags had to go, as did her long, matted hair.

I half-expected a fight, but when I told her that I was going to cut off her hair she seemed more fascinated than upset. As it turned out, she hadn't realised that hair could be cut; her parents had never given her a trim. She waited obediently while I hunted around for a pair of old scissors, then attacked her mane with gentle determination. Lock by lock, her tangled tresses fell away into a pile on the bathroom floor, until all that was left was a short, manageable crop.

"Gone?" she cried happily as she ran her fingers through her newly-cut hair, looking delighted by the funny feeling of short hair beneath her fingers.

"That's right, all gone. It'll grow back, but we must keep the yucky bugs out," I told her, and then promptly dunked her back under the water. She popped back up again a moment later, spluttering and laughing, then she splashed me playfully in retaliation.

"Yuck, bugs!" she repeated, poking at a patch of floating dirt that had come off her skin. "Yuck, yuck. No more bugs?"

"No more bugs," I agreed, amused. She was a bright kid, and her English was improving with every sentence. "Close your eyes tight, okay? I'm going to put soap in your hair to kill the yucky bugs."

"Okies," she agreed readily, squeezing her eyes closed. I found a few unopened bottles of children's shampoos and anti-nit treatments stashed away in a cupboard, and since the bottles were still sealed I judged that they were likely fine. With a twist, I opened one and then applied a liberal amount to her head.

The pleasant scent of shampoo filled the room as I rubbed it into her scalp. The smell and the feeling of my fingers massaging her scalp drew happy noises from her. When I told her to dunk her head, she obeyed. We rinsed the shampoo off, then applied another treatment just in case.

Once she was done, I drained the bath and put her under a cold shower to wash away the last of the dirt, then bundled her up in a big towel. Shivering and dripping, she followed me happily from room to room as I searched for new clothing that would fit her.

At first, we had no luck; the three bedrooms we found appeared to belong to parents, and a pair of teenagers – one boy, and one girl. Unfortunately, Priyanka was a tiny thing for her age, so their clothing was much too large for her. But in the back of the girl's wardrobe, we struck a goldmine: a box full of old clothing that had been packed away when it no longer fitted, but no one had ever gotten around to throwing out.

Priyanka looked delighted by the bright colours and happy patterns. It took some doing to teach her how to wear underwear and which way the other garments went on, but she was a clever little thing and learned readily. With my help, we got her dressed and picked out some spare garments for her to bring along with us.

In the corner of the room I spotted a faded pink backpack, someone's old school bag tossed aside on that day long ago when the world changed forever. I picked it up, and discovered that it was still crammed with faded school books and homework that would never be graded. Although I felt a momentary pang of sadness for the young woman who had owned that bag, Priya needed it now. I emptied it out, and carefully folded Priyanka's new clothing into the bottom of it.

"This for mine?" she asked while I was packing her bag. She snatched it up as soon as I was done, and hugged it to her chest.

"You mean, 'is this for me?'" I corrected, and then nodded. "Yes, sweetie, that's for you now. The girl who used to live here doesn't need it anymore, so you can have it."

"She dead?" Priyanka asked thoughtfully, looking around the bedroom as though seeking some trace of the person who had once lived there. "She had pretty things. I like pretty things, too. She like me, I think."

"Would you like one of the pretty things to take with you?" I asked, lifting a hand to rest on her shoulder. It seemed like a good time to teach her a few valuable lessons, and to make her happy at the same time. "She's gone now, so you can take something if you'd like. Just remember, you never take things from living people without asking. And if you want to take something from here, you have to carry everything that you pick yourself. Okay?"

"Okies. I want pretty thing. I carry," Priyanka agreed readily. She scampered away from me and went over to the girl's bureau, where she began poking around amongst the various bits of girly nonsense. I decided that she was going to be busy for a while, so I left her to it. I headed back to the bathroom to gather up all the anti-nit treatments that were left, and added them to my pack. Priya would probably need another treatment in a few weeks, and my fastidious nature left me intensely aware of the fact that both Michael and I had been in physical contact with her several times. It was getting later by the minute so there was no time to treat our hair now, but I planned to make sure we both got a dunking as soon as possible, just to be safe.

Once the bottles were safely stowed away, I went off to check on Michael. I found him sitting on the kitchen floor with his arm draped over his new canine companion; the dog had its muzzle buried in a bowl of dog food. Michael looked up when I entered the room and gave me a shy smile.

"I found some dog food in the kitchen," he told me. "There's some stuff for us as well. I figured, you know, that you wouldn't mind if we brought the dog along, so long as we're not feeding him out of our own supplies." To my surprise, Michael actually looked a little embarrassed, like he thought I would actually say no to the idea of bringing the dog with us.

"Of course, I don't mind if we take him along." I knelt on the floor beside him, and leaned over to kiss his cheek. "Did you honestly think I'd mind? My only concern is that he might be sick, or might not be able to keep up with us."

"Well, I wasn't sure," he admitted, putting his free arm around my waist to draw me up against his side, then his lips captured mine for a quick, tender kiss. In the heat of the moment, any resentment I might have felt was brushed aside by the overwhelming adoration I felt for that kind, strong man. I couldn't possibly be angry with him for making that assumption, and I didn't want to be.

When our lips parted, I chose the moment to tease him, just as mercilessly as he routinely poked fun at me. "Well, okay, you can keep him – but you do have to give him a bath."

Michael's eyes widened as he struggled to figure out how serious I was. As if to punctuate my statement, a fat flea leapt off the old dog's fur and landed the floor tiles beside us. I was quick enough to crush it with my fingernail, then I gave him a pointed look.

"I bathed Priyanka, you have to bathe the dog. There's flea soap under the sink in the bathroom."

"But… but, I…" he stammered, staring down at the dog with uncertainty. "I don't know how to bathe a dog."

"Doggie needs a ba-ath," Priya called from the far end of the house, catching us both by surprise. A second later, we melted into laughter.

"Okay, okay. Doggie needs a bath," Michael agreed, once the levity had subsided. "There must be instructions on the bottle, I'm sure." The elderly canine had just finished up his last mouthful of food, so Michael stood and called him until the animal padded out of the room after him.

With everyone else busy, I turned my attention to the important task of breakfast. It was an hour past sunrise, and we weren't on the road yet; if we didn't reach our destination soon then my sister was bound to start worrying. Although I had warned her I wasn't sure how far the Hilux would take us, on foot it should only have taken three days at most. In theory, we should have been there before sunset – but that estimate hadn't included being distracted by lost children and stray dogs.

I was sitting in the lounge stirring a pot of canned spaghetti on our little camp stove when Priyanka came looking for me. She was so stealthy in her bare feet that I didn't even notice her arrival until she knelt down beside me.

"What is this?" she demanded, thrusting a small, sparkling trinket into my hand as soon as I turned to look at her. I took it without thinking – she didn't really give me a choice – and examined it thoroughly before I answered.

"This is a bracelet, a charm bracelet. I used to have one just like this when I was your age. It goes like this." I reached out and took her hand, then showed her how to put the bracelet on. It was made of silver and semi-precious stones, but it had aged well. There was only a little bit of tarnish, since it had been kept in a dry, relatively clean environment over the years.

"Bracelet?" Priyanka drew her hand back and shook her wrist, watching the light dance off the sparkling stones. "I remember… Mama wore bracelet. Many lots of bracelet. Went 'rustle rustle' when she cuddled me when I was little."

The thought didn't seem to upset her, but it did appear to interest her. In my mind's eye, I saw her as a chubby little toddler being picked up by a woman wearing stacks of bangles. I found myself wondering, and curiosity got the better of me, as it often did.

"What did your mama look like, Priyanka?" I asked carefully, cautious of dredging up painful memories.

"Pretty." Priya's eyes lost their focus as she thought back, seeking an answer to my question. "Mama was very pretty. She hands same colour as my hands." She held her hands out towards me, as though I might have forgotten what she looked like. "Hair like my hair. Long, long. No bugs, though." The girl pulled a face. I laughed.

"Your hair will grow long again, and this time we'll keep it clean so no bugs get in," I told her with a smile. "Promise."

"Good." She nodded vigorous approval, and then resumed her tale. "Mama like to wore the pretty colours, always pretty colours. Pretty like this." She pointed to a patch of colour on her newly-salvaged clothing. "I no know the name for this."

"Pink," I supplied helpfully.

"Pink?" she repeated, looking up at me with those huge, soulful eyes of hers; I nodded and she smiled. "Pink. Mama wore this colour often. And the colour like the sky, and sometimes the colour like the grass. She wore long, pretty dresses with patterns on them. Not like the dresses in we look at here, other kind of dress. Had a... a thing."

She mimed something, indicating a flap of cloth worn over the shoulder; it took a minute for me to interpret what she meant and dredge the word out of my memory.

"A sari?" I supplied, a little uncertain if I was giving her the right answer, but she nodded vigorously.

"Sari, yes," she echoed, looking happy with that definition. "Very pretty sari. She wore pretty sari that was pink with shiny on it, and very many bracelets. I remember Mama giving me many hugs, and letting me play with her bracelets. She read to me many, many books, all the time. Teach me many things. Mama love me, and me love Mama."

"I think that you are much like your mama, Priyanka," I told her. "You are also very pretty, and you're a good girl."

She visibly swelled with pride at my praise, too young to have developed any sense of modesty yet. I liked that about kids. No false pretences. No pretending one thing when they thought another. They were honest.

"I go look at more pretty-pretties," she announced, springing up to her feet with a pleased look on her face.

"Breakfast will be ready soon," I called after her, but she'd already vanished down the corridor. Shaking my head in amusement, I returned my attention to cooking.

A few minutes later, the sound of splashing and unhappy noises, both human and canine, caught my attention. Priyanka came dashing back into the room, laughing her head off.

"What are they doing?" I asked, trying to push aside my instinctive panic-response. How much damage could an old sheepdog possibly do? Priyanka's gleeful response answered my question in quick order.

"Doggie give Michael bath!" She chortled merrily, and mimed shaking water off herself like a dog would. Then, she suddenly seemed to remember she had come looking for me for a reason, and plunked down on the ground beside me. She pointed at my feet, then held up a pair of sneakers that appeared at a glance to only be a tiny bit too large for her. "Look-look! I found like what Sandy has."

"Hey, that's great. They're called 'shoes'," I explained, reaching over to take the object from her. They were dirty and well-worn, of course, but that didn't matter to us at all. To a survivor, anything that was new to you was as good as being brand new. "Good for walking in so the stones don't cut your feet. See these nice, thick soles? These are good, they'll protect you very well. Now, we just need to find you some socks."

"Socks? Sssssocks. That word is funny." She giggled gleefully, repeating it a few more times for good measure. "What is socks?"

"Underwear for your feet," I explained simply, rolling up the leg of my fatigues to show her mine. "They stop your shoes from getting stinky."

Priyanka stared dubiously at the shoes in her hands. "Shoes already stinky."

"Then they'll stop your feet from getting stinky," I answered with a laugh. "You want some breakfast, Priya?"

"Breakfast? Food?" She leaned over to examine my concoction, and her eyes widened. "What is? Is funny colour."

"It's called spaghetti. Yes, it's food." I gave her a smile and picked up a bowl, filling it with the fragrant orange sauce. "You'll probably like it. Kids always seem to love spaghetti. Now, this is hot so don't try to eat it with your fingers, okay? Do you know how to use a fork?"

Priyanka took the bowl from my hands and stared down at it dubiously, apparently unsure what to make of the substance I was trying to tell her was food. I couldn't blame her; the stuff was so full of food colourings it sure didn't look all that edible, but the smell of hot canned spaghetti could still make my mouth water even after all these years.

She looked up at me and shook her head, bewildered. I gave her a smile and a pat on the head in return, then leapt right on into teaching her how to use a fork and spoon. It was a messy business and took some doing, but by the time Michael finally joined us, our little foundling was well on her way to being competent with utensils.

I made a point of not looking when Michael plopped down beside me, because I was really struggling to hide my amusement. I could tell from the scent and the sound of his movements that he was soaked to the bone. Without a word, I dished up his breakfast and handed it to him, and we sat in a ring around the stove, eating our food.

Or at least, we did – right up until the dog padded out into the living room, and shook himself off, spraying water droplets in all directions.

# Chapter Sixteen

A few hours later, we were back on the road, and I found myself pondering the strange turn of events that had doubled the size of our little party in less than a day. Michael and I walked together in the rear, while Priyanka skipped along in front with the dog prancing around her legs. The two of them had become firm friends, and spent most of the morning playing together.

"Penny for your thoughts?" Michael asked. I felt a strong hand slip around mine. When I looked over, I found him watching me. He smiled, and I felt a flush of heat in my belly. I looked away, absently tucking a strand of hair behind my ear with my free hand.

"Oh, you know." I stole a glance back and found his smile was a little wider than before. "I was just thinking that it's kind of amazing the dog can keep up so easily. I noticed that his eyesight isn't great, so I was a little concerned that he'd slow us down. He really isn't, though."

"It is pretty impressive." Michael's gaze shifted to follow the old sheepdog bounding ahead of us. "Kind of makes you feel like we humans got the bum end of the stick when it comes to sensory input, doesn't it?"

"You're not kidding," I agreed. "I remember when that bastard, Lee, was telling me that he was going to put my eyes out. The only thing I could think of was just how helpless I'd be if he blinded me. I don't think I could bear it."

"You'd still have me," he quickly reassured me, giving my hand a gentle squeeze. "If anything like that happened, I'd protect you and take care of you."

"I know you would, but what if something happened to you and there was no one else around?" I gestured towards the happy dog, who was leaping around Priyanka without a care in the world. "He can find food and avoid danger with just his nose and his ears. I can barely tell when my socks need changing."

"Well, I can tell when your socks need changing," he teased playfully. I responded by giving him a smack on the shoulder, to which he reciprocated with his best impression of a dying walrus. The peculiar sound startled both the girl and the dog. They both froze and stared at us in perfect unison, and the looks on their faces were so priceless that Michael and I burst out laughing.

"Grown-ups are silly," Priyanka told her canine companion solemnly. The dog barked his agreement, then bounded off again with his tail wagging frantically. The girl squealed in glee and chased after him, apparently forgetting all about us again.

***

It was around midday when we reached the township of Pukeatua, a blip on the map that was even smaller than our little Ohaupo. The place was so tiny that it barely even warranted a name.

At first, I didn't even realise that we'd arrived. All I noticed was that the trees thinned out a bit, and then suddenly a clearing opened up in front of us. A handful of road signs sprang from the overgrown verge like a crop of ugly mushrooms as we climbed a low rise, then we crested the hill and saw the ruins of the town sprawled out below us.

Of course, using the word 'town' to describe a place like Pukeatua was taking some liberal usage of the noun; there were maybe a half-dozen houses within sight, in various states of disrepair. There was something off about the place, though. Something that instinctively put my nerves on edge. I cradled my shotgun close against me as we moved further down the road. As if sensing my disquiet, my companions fell silent behind me.

I picked my way carefully past the debris strewn across the road, trying to put my finger on what was bothering me. There had to be a reason. My instincts were a little over-aggressive at times, but they were well-honed. I'd spent years living in the bush, always alone. I knew the sights, sounds, and smells of New Zealand like a wild animal.

And then it struck me. It was quiet. Too quiet. Although the bush thinned out around the town, there were still plenty of trees – but no birds were singing. I held up my hand to halt the others, scanning the road and buildings ahead of us for anything out of the ordinary. I spotted a few dark, ominous shadows dotting the asphalt, like puddles of dried blood. In the distance, I could see spray paint on the side of a building. It was too far away to tell if it was a gang sign, but that was warning enough for me.

"There's something very wrong here," I whispered. "We should leave, now."

Then the dog began to growl, low and deep in his throat.

I had the safety off my shotgun in a second, and dropped into a defensive crouch. Michael flanked me as I took a couple of cautious steps backwards, his expression one of focused intensity that mirrored my own. However, his instincts were honed for urban combat, while I possessed a completely different set of skills.

The footfall sounded like an elephant's tread against the quiet world around us. I spun around, but it was too late; the stranger had one massive hand around little Priya's throat, and in the other he held a very large, very sharp machete. Priya cried out in surprise as she was swept up against the huge man's body like a human shield. She struggled, but he was three times her size – at least four inches over six feet tall, all rippling muscle, and outfitted in full army battledress.

"Let her go," Michael said, trying to negotiate even though we both had our weapons trained on the massive soldier. "We're just passing through, we mean no harm."

"No harm? Heh…" The man's voice was a deep-throated rumble, but it was totally different to the familiar purr of my lover's voice. His voice was pure threat, and it sent the alarm bells in my head ringing like crazy. "You should have listened to your woman, chink, and left while you still had the chance."

I saw Michael bristle at the use of the slur, but I cut him off before he could respond.

"There are two of us, and one of you," I pointed out coldly, calmly; I felt the surge of adrenaline pumping through my veins. Usually it brought fear, but not this time. I had learned something over the last few months, and improved myself. This time, the adrenaline brought with it a detached kind of clarity. "We're well-armed and well-trained. If you hurt her, we'll kill you before you can draw your sidearm."

"Well, aren't you a feisty one?" The stranger showed teeth, but it wasn't a smile. "I have no problem with you. You can leave if you prefer. These two, though... a fucking chink and a curry-muncher? Their kind brought this plague on us. I'll kill them all!"

My eyes did not leave the stranger, but at the edge of my vision, I could see Priya's terrified eyes staring at me, enormous and confused. She didn't understand what was going on, and she was too afraid to fight anymore. I sensed more than saw Michael's readiness, but we were trapped, with that innocent little girl caught between us.

"You're an idiot if you believe that," I told the man coolly. Reasoning with a madman was impossible, and yet I had no choice. "The plague came from monkeys, not people. Any five-year-old knows that."

"Fucking lies, spread by that nigger president in America!" the man roared, his face turning red with fury. For half a second he was distracted, and I saw his grip on Priya loosen.

That half a second was all I had, so I used it. I sprang forward and lashed out, using the butt of my shotgun as a club. The blow struck home with the resounding crunch of bone fracturing; his roar of rage turned to one of pain.

He lashed out blindly with the machete, but I twisted away and caught Priyanka by a fold of her clothing to yank her from the madman's grasp. The hot flash of pain exploded across my ribs, but I barely felt it – my only concern was for Priya. I would worry about my own health once she was safe.

I shoved her away, and felt her fall somewhere behind me, but I didn't have time to find out where; I'd pissed the racist soldier off right royally, and it was right at that moment that I realised he wasn't alone. Although they were hidden out of sight, the intensity of life-or-death fighting put my senses on edge. I could faintly hear the sound of human breathing in the clumps of trees on either side of the road. We only had moments before they would enter the fray, and then we'd be outnumbered.

The behemoth sprang at me, but I was waiting for him. I leapt back out of the range of his machete, and unleashed a brutal kick to the groin while he was off balance. Although he was huge and presumably strong, his size was a disadvantage against someone as comparatively small and nimble as me – particularly since I fought dirty.

The man crumpled to his knees, all the breath gone from him. As he tumbled forward, I jerked my own knee up and caught him in the forehead. He went down hard, like Goliath to my David. I didn't take any time to celebrate my victory, though; we were in intense, immediate danger, and I knew instinctively that that Michael hadn't realised it yet.

"Follow me," I ordered breathlessly as I raced past him. I grabbed Priyanka's hand, and sprinted into the nearest patch of bush without a second of hesitation. A man was waiting there with a weapon drawn, but I took him by surprise. I shoulder-charged him before he could fire, bowling him to the ground, then I leapt over him and kept on running.

I heard heavy footfalls behind me, and a quick glance back confirmed that Michael and the dog were right on my tail. The canine may not have understood the exact nature of the threat, but it had decided to follow us anyway. Michael, on the other hand, just knew me well enough to trust my instincts without question at a time like this. Reassured that he was still safe, I turned my attention back to guiding our flight, deeper into the bush.

My ears were tuned for danger, and I heard all the sounds that happened around me: the heavy breathing of my companions, the crash of my own feet as I cleared a path through the heavy brush, even the alarm sounds of the birds in the trees all around us. Over that, I could hear the furious shouting of our pursuers as they chased us. The behemoth's deep voice rang out above the others like a herald of doom, ordering them to find us and kill us without mercy. Then, suddenly, I heard another sound. It was much closer at hand, and ominously familiar.

In the bushes to our right, I could hear low, deep squeals, punctuated by the thud of flesh striking flesh. Those squeals were the kind of sound that would forever haunt my nightmares, but this time they brought a flash of inspiration. I skidded to a halt and thrust Priya's tiny hand out to Michael, who took it without thinking. He started to say something but I interrupted him. There was no time for questions, no time for thinking – it was time to act.

"I have an idea," I told him, then I pointed him in the direction we had been going. "Stick to the forest. Keep heading east until you reach the river, then follow it south to the bridge. I'll meet you there."

"But—"

"Just go, now!"

He tried to protest but I waved him away. Although I could see the tension in his handsome face, he nodded grimly. A quick kiss and then he was off, vanishing into the undergrowth. I was left alone, between a pair of vicious enemy factions.

The hellish squealing drew me back to the ferns. I peeked through, and saw what I expected to see: two infected pigs were fighting one another, locked in a bloody battle for supremacy. They didn't notice me at first, but that was going to change. I cocked my shotgun, then aimed it from the hip and peppered both their hideous bodies with hot shrapnel.

The shotgun's retort rang in my ears, and sent birds scattering from the trees overhead. I'd given away my position, but that was part of the plan. The two horrid monsters instantly lost interest in one another and turned on me, but the underbrush was too thick for them to charge properly. When I turned and ran, they barrelled after me at top speed, but I was light on my feet and much more nimble than they were amongst the trees.

The creatures were single-minded in their intensity, but they couldn't quite catch me. Although my heart hammered in my chest from the knowledge that a single misstep would spell my doom, I somehow kept myself calm. The adrenaline fuelled me, and again I felt that strange kind of clarity of purpose, the drive to succeed at all costs. It was powerful, and it was addictive. Feeling cool and collected in spite of the danger, I drew ahead of the pigs a little bit, just enough to give me an advantage, but not quite enough to lose them. For my plan to work, the pigs had to stay close. Very, very close.

Suddenly, I saw a human figure amongst the trees. Although he was shadowed by the forest, his size gave him away as the madman who wanted us dead for no better reason than our ethnicities. I sprinted straight at him, my feet crushing the ferns that flourished in the lightless land beneath the canopy.

The sound of my footfalls alerted him before I reached to him. I tried to dodge past him, but he was quicker than I estimated despite his size. He made a grab for me and managed to get hold of a handful of my clothing, preventing my escape. I felt a momentary flash of panic, but the act of grabbing me spun him around, so he couldn't see his death incoming.

"Oh, so you changed your mind, did you?" he growled and shook me roughly, unconcerned by the weapon in my hands. "You know, I was going to let you stay with me and my boys once I killed your friends, show you what a real man looks like. Pretty, white girl like you? Could have had some fun, you and me – but now I think I'll just kill you as well."

"I hate to tell you, but I've already got a real man," I answered him breathlessly, feeling a surge of victory despite the danger I was in. "So this seems way more appropriate. A swine like you deserves nothing better."

My dark smile must have alerted him that something was amiss. He glanced back over his shoulder just as the huge boar burst through the underbrush, and bowled him over from behind. His grip on me faltered, and I was ready for it. I twisted away just in time, and ducked behind a tree out of the sight of the incoming beasts.

For all his size, the man was only human, while the infected boar was the largest I'd ever seen. It bore him effortlessly to the ground, and then it was on him, attacking viciously. Hidden from sight, I heard rather than saw when the sow joined in the attack, but I could barely hear their squeals over the man's screams.

Suddenly, I felt nauseated about what I'd done. I reminded myself that it was for the sake of my lover and our innocent young charge. That man would have killed them both for no better reason than the colour of their skin. If those bloodstains were anything to go by, we had not been the first victims of his gang. He deserved a horrible fate.

While the pigs were both completely focused on their attack, I ducked out of my hiding spot and ran as fast as my legs could carry me. Even though I'd been the instrument of that man's well-deserved destruction, I could not bear to watch the creatures kill and eat another human being.

His screams rang through the forest behind me as I fled to the east, putting as much distance between myself and the grisly scene as I could.

# Chapter Seventeen

I ran like a madman, ducking and dodging through the undergrowth despite the constant risk of personal injury. A few minutes later, I found the road again, far to the east of the little town. I froze and stared all around, listening to the sounds of the wilderness until I was certain that I was alone. Sticking to the road would be dangerous, but I could travel faster if I took that route. It only took a second to decide, and then I was off again.

I ran as hard as I could for as long as I could along that cracked grey ribbon, until my breath seared in my lungs and my heart started making a serious effort to bust its way out of my ribcage. The late summer sun beat down on me mercilessly, and sweat carved rivulets through the sunscreen protecting my skin.

Eventually, I had to slow down to a walk. By that stage I judged that I had probably put three or four kilometres between me and my enemies. I didn't stop, though. I couldn't stop until I knew Michael and Priya were safe. I was alone, but I was well-armed and in my element. My concern was for them, not me.

On my own, I moved much more quickly than I had when I was with the others. Weeks of good food had begun to restore my body to a decent state of health; I felt better than I had in as long as I could remember. My foot had adjusted to the rigors of travel once the muscles had time to warm up and stretch, too. Although it ached, it was an ache that I understood and could safely ignore. I knew it wasn't an injury anymore, just a mild discomfort.

When my lungs had recovered, I eased myself back up to a trot. After a few hundred metres, I slowed to a walk to recover, pacing myself for the long haul.

Water was a concern. Michael had most of our supply in his backpack, and the small bottle I kept in my pocket to sip as we walked was almost empty. I took a swig from the bottle anyway, since there was no point conserving it. If worse came to worst, I could always boil river water. Right now, I was parched and sweating. My body needed water to keep going.

The trees hung low over both sides of the road, granting me a temporary respite from the heat. I paused for a moment to listen, but I heard nothing that indicated a threat. The birds still sang contentedly in the trees, and the wind rustled the branches. Everything seemed safe and calm, with nothing to indicate any danger nearby.

I continued on, guiding myself up to a loping trot for another few hundred metres. As I ran, I found myself thinking that something good had come out of the attack: running for our lives had put us back on track to reach the power station before nightfall.

The thought made me smile. Perhaps Michael's positive attitude was starting to rub off on me after all. I decided that it was best not to think about the other things that had happened; the sun was shining too brightly for me to dwell on morbid thoughts. Instead, I focused on keeping myself alert for danger. I had no idea how many members of the neo-Nazi gang were in the area, so I chose my path carefully in case they decided to track me. Each footfall connected only with solid tarmac; I crushed no blades of grass with my weight, and avoided any patches of gravel that might leave a footprint behind.

It was strange to think that I had learned so much about tracking over the years. I'd begun life as a city girl, raised in pleasant suburbia without a care in the world. But when the plague had come, I found myself on my own and often under attack. I had learned the way of our new wilds, and fast. That was how I'd survived all these years.

I was no genius but I wasn't stupid. Logic dictated that a footprint didn't leave itself, that a healthy leaf or flower bud didn't break without reason. I'd learned to look for those signs, and to listen to the world around me for the telltale markers of something that didn't belong. After spending so much time on high alert, that sense had become second nature to me. For a while, in Hamilton and later Ohaupo, my sense of the world had begun to fade away – but the moment I returned to the familiar places I used to call home, that sense came back to me in force.

Everything I knew I'd learned the hard way, because I had been lucky enough to survive my mistakes. I learned which wild berries I could eat by watching the birds. In the early days, roaming the bush starving and alone, I ate a berry from a tree. It had made me so violently ill that I had been unable to move for hours. While I'd lain in the leaf-litter, recovering, I had noticed that the birds flitting around in the canopy above me avoided the fruit from that particular tree. Instead, they favoured the product of another tree. When my stomach recovered, I tried a few of those berries instead, and discovered that they were safe for me to eat.

I could survive in the bush if I had to, and I wasn't afraid to retreat to the wild places if the urban regions became too dangerous for me. However, I generally still preferred the urban life. It was easier to find food and water, and it was more likely for the amenities to still be functioning in town than it was in rural areas.

But, the bush was safer. There, I could hide and live wild. I had learned to listen to Mother Nature and to trust her, even when she was in one of her more capricious moods. The sights, sounds, and smells were familiar to me, and I generally knew how to respond to them. I could only imagine that was how Priya had survived all these years, too. Trial and error, and learning to trust nature to provide a solution. When it came down to it, we were all Mother Nature's children. Some of us had just forgotten that.

My mind drifted at random as I travelled east, running a few hundred metres then walking a few hundred. As a teenager, I'd read a book that had recommended that method as the most efficient way for a human on foot to travel without exhausting themselves. That knowledge had served me well over the years. My nostrils flared wide with each breath, drawing air deep into my lungs to power the efficient hydraulics of my body.

It was during one such breath in that I caught a scent on the breeze that was out of place. The wind blew from the east, and it carried with it the acrid smell of gunpowder, and coppery scent of blood. Ahead of me, the road bent slightly and sank down behind a small hill. I slowed to a walk and brought my shotgun up in case I needed it.

As I crept towards the bend, I eased myself into a low crouch-walk, my senses extended and alert. The birds still sang on, aside from the few directly above me. My small size, soft footfalls, and the dark green camouflage print of my clothing meant that I bothered them much less than a grown man thundering through the brush – or worse, a pig.

Of course, there might be someone hiding nearby that was as savvy in the rules of bush-law as I was, but I would not know until I sensed him. Regardless of the risk, I followed the road rather than moving into the underbrush, and stepped carefully around the bend until the source of the smell came into view. A human body lay in the middle of the road ahead of me, blood pooling on the tar seal beneath it.

The corpse was so fresh that the blood had barely begun to congeal in the hot sun. I stared at the brush nearby for a long minute until I was sure there was nobody watching, then I crept closer to the body to get a better look.

It was a man, sprawled on his back with dead eyes staring blankly at the sky. He was clad in battle dress, just as the massive soldier had been, but wore no body armour. That mistake had cost him his life: his chest was riddled with bloody wounds. I judged by their location and the way his body lay that he'd died nearly instantly, in a hail of high-powered bullets.

A fold of his clothing half-concealed something. Curious and analytical, I prodded the corpse with my boot to clear the cloth away. It revealed an empty holster on his hip, big enough to hold an automatic pistol and a couple of spare clips. The holster was empty now, and a quick glance around revealed no sign of the weapon or the ammunition.

I did see shell casings though, small ones, probably from a 9mm gun like the one that this man had carried. In my mind, I turned the physical evidence over and replayed the scene a few different ways until I had a clear picture of what must have occurred.

The dead man had fired first, I guessed; he must have done, as the wounds in his chest were from a heavier weapon. For there to be shells from his weapon on the ground, he must have opened fire before the person with the heavy weapon shot him. The corpse was facing east, and I recognised the wounds in his chest as entry rather than exit wounds.

The scenario crystallized in my head: this man had been following someone heading east. He had approached them from behind and opened fire, and they had in turn killed him in self-defence and taken his weapon. Michael. It had to be.

I had told him to stick to the forest, but it didn't surprise me that he had gotten lost along the way. His sense of direction in the wilds was still developing, which was why I was our guide. I was just relieved that by some dumb luck he'd found the road instead of wandering off in the wrong direction. Even he could follow a road. As far as I could tell, he was going in the right direction.

I left the corpse, not caring if the man was the victim of pests or animals this time. He was nothing to me, someone that wanted to hurt me and my family. He deserved no respect in death.

A dozen metres further down the road, my boot struck something small and sent it tumbling across the asphalt with a metallic chime. I paused to look, and discovered the shell casings from the heavier weapon scattered across the ground. Although I couldn't be sure, I was fairly certain that they'd come from Michael's rifle.

Unfortunately, I also spotted something that worried me. Sprinkled amongst the fallen shells were a few droplets of dark crimson, that were rapidly turning brown in the heat: blood. One of my companions was injured. Which one, I couldn't tell. Spurred on by concern, I picked up to a run and headed eastwards as fast as my tired legs could carry me. It was more than an hour past noon now, almost two, and my friends would be worried sick about me.

I was relieved to see the blood trailed off after only a few metres, meaning it had been staunched rather than left to bleed. That reassured me, but still I felt the overwhelming need to return to them as soon as possible. I longed to feel Michael's arms around me, holding me safe and warm. Then there was Priyanka and her elderly pet; the girl had a smile that could light up the room, and I feared either she or the helpless animal might be the ones hurt.

I could not abide that thought, and it made me feel better about what I'd done to protect them. The guilt would come later, when I had time to brood – but for now I was busy, my thoughts and actions dictated by necessity. There was no time for recriminations or regrets until after I knew my companions were safe.

\*\*\*

An hour later, I was drawing close to the end of my reserves of strength. My legs trembled with every step, but my resolve held strong. I was almost there, I could sense it. I'd covered many more kilometres, and I could feel the land beneath me beginning to slope gently downwards. The bush grew denser and denser, until I was travelling through dark shade despite it being the heat of the afternoon. The changes in the landscape around me told me the river must be nearby.

As I began to pad around a long, gentle curve in the road, I was startled by the sound of a human voice shouting. Another shouted back, but I couldn't make out their words. Then there were gunshots, rapid and piercing, from several different kinds of weapons. I skidded to a halt as self-preservation kicked in. Until I could see them, I couldn't be sure who was shooting at whom. It could be friends, it could be foes. It could be both.

The shotgun held close against my chest, I pressed myself into the shadows of the undergrowth and crept around the bend at a wide angle. The paved plateau in front of the bridge opened up below me, providing a wide area of open ground that would leave me exposed if I moved much further. There were two bodies there, sprawled out and still twitching, no more than a minute dead.

I glanced around cautiously and saw nothing besides the two of them. My heart hammered in my chest as I emerged from the shadows and snuck towards them to see if I could determine what had happened. Both of the bodies were male, both in battle dress and at a glance I could see that both of them had been killed by a hail of high-calibre bullets.

It was only then that I sensed eyes upon me. I spun towards the bridge, with my shotgun raised automatically to defend myself. I found myself looking at a familiar face on the other side of a longer barrel: Michael.

Both of us were still in fight or flight mode, so it took a second for what we were seeing to sink in. When it did, we both lowered our weapons and rushed to one another. His longer strides covered the ground more swiftly than my exhausted ones, and he caught me before I made it a half-dozen steps.

Strong arms enveloped me and held me close. I buried my face in his sweating chest, luxuriating in the heat and the scent of his body. A few months ago, I would never have imagined that I could find the odour of a sweaty man to be pleasant, let alone intoxicating – yet now, I did. It was fresh and healthy, and it belonged to the man that I loved with all my heart. I clung to him, overwhelmed by sensations of affection and relief so strong it made everything I'd done seem so worthwhile.

After a minute, I drew back and kissed him, quickly and repeatedly, indulging a need to express my affections as physically as possible. He understood and held me close, returning my shower of kisses with his own until I calmed down.

"I was afraid I'd never see you again," he whispered to me, his arms still wrapped around my waist. His voice was huskier than usual and I detected deep emotion in it that made my heart lurch.

"I know, but... I had to. You know I had to," I whispered back. He nodded, silently telling me that he understood. He always understood. It was the same reckless abandon that had driven him into a violent rage when one of the undead had cornered members of our family, weeks ago. Unlike him, I had not been driven into shock in the wake of my actions, though. I had stayed calm and rational throughout. It felt like it had happened to someone else.

"They're fine. I've got them hiding under the bridge," he told me softly, anticipating my question before I could ask. I nodded and glanced at the corpses for a moment, then I suddenly remembered the blood I'd seen on the ground.

I shoved myself back and stared at him, inspecting his body from head to toe. Sure enough, there was a crude bandage wrapped around his bicep, and another around his left wrist. He didn't bother to put up a fight when I took his hand, and dragged him off towards the shelter of the bridge to get him cleaned up.

"I saw the first body, way back, and I saw your blood on the ground. I've been so worried about you," I admitted as we retreated down the bank and ducked into the dark recess beneath the bridge's span.

Very little plant life grew down there, since it never saw any sunlight. When my eyes adjusted, I spotted Priya sitting on a patch of hard concrete, her knees drawn up to her chest and arms wrapped around them. Her eyes were closed and young face was a picture of misery, but the dog spotted us straight away and alerted her to our presence by letting out a happy yip.

The moment she saw me, her eyes widened. A second later, she had her arms around my waist and was clinging to me like she was afraid that I'd left her forever. Even though I was anxious to see to Michael's wounds, I understood her vulnerability and made no effort to detach her. Instead, I led both of them back over to sit on that patch of concrete, the three of us all huddled in a row in the shadows.

Priya leaned against me crying quietly while I stripped away Michael's makeshift bandages. I inspected the wounds, cleaned them, and then redressed them with proper, sterile dressings from my first aid kit. Although it caused him pain, he clenched his jaw and bore up well to the discomfort. I knew that he trusted me to only have the best of intentions for him, and he knew I would only cause him pain if it was for good reason.

For my part, I was relieved to discover the injuries were only flesh wounds, and none of them would cause him any real trouble unless they got infected. Of course, with someone as attentive as me to be his nurse, there was no way he was getting infected any time soon. At least, I hoped not. I'd had enough of infections to last a lifetime.

Hell, we had barely recovered from the last time we ended up in bandages. That was the last thing we needed. Michael still had a tiny red pucker mark of half-healed tissue on his ribs from when he'd been shot with that air rifle ten days earlier. He still had to cover it, but it was past the danger stage.

Michael had the presence of mind not to ask what had happened. Even if he had, I wouldn't have told him with young, innocent ears sitting right there beside us. A vague reassurance from me that our racist friend wasn't going to trouble us any further was good enough for both of them.

After the wounds were cleaned, the four of us just sat catching our breath for a while. Priyanka finally stopped crying and clung to me in silence, while Michael stared off thoughtfully into space. I sat in the middle, turning over in my mind the strange situation I found myself in this time. I felt so protective of that young girl even though I'd only just met her, and I could see in Michael's face that he felt the same way.

Was it animal instinct that drove us to protect the young, even when she wasn't our child? It was a strange feeling, but it made sense to me. In little Priya, I saw someone who had an entire life ahead of her, one that was so full of promise and potential. Although she'd come from someone else's womb, in that young child I saw the future of my species. We were on the verge of extinction, and yet she gave me hope.

She, and all the other children like her. Madeline, Priya, any children that Michael and I might have one day. They were our future. Without them, there was no tomorrow for humankind.

I didn't realise that I was squeezing Michael's hand until I noticed him looking at me with concern. I gave him a sheepish smile and relaxed my death-grip, but he seemed to understand. He put his arm around me instead and drew me up against him. I contentedly nestled against his side and closed my eyes.

Suddenly, the dog let out a yip and sat bolt upright. Startled, the rest of us looked at him and then at each other, trying to work out what the dog knew that we didn't. I started to say something, but Michael held up a hand to silence me; a moment later, I heard the sound as well. There was an engine coming our way. No, several engines.

"Stay here," I whispered to the others, extracting myself from between their bodies. I crept noiselessly out from beneath the bridge and inched up the bank beside it, keeping myself hidden deep within the long grass. Despite my instructions, I felt the warmth of a large body beside me and knew that Michael had followed me. Side by side, we lay in hiding, waiting for the source of the noise to come into sight.

From the west, along the very same road we'd come down less than an hour before, came a small group of quad- and farm-bikes. The lead bike stopped when the rider spotted the corpses lying in the road, and the others came to a halt in a gaggle behind him. After some discussion, the rider of the first bike hopped off and hurried over to the corpses to examine them.

As he drew closer, I recognised him, and heaved a deep sigh of relief. Shoving myself up out of my hiding spot, I waved to the startled rider until he realised who I was and waved back.

"Kia ora, mate!" Hemi shouted. "Fancy seeing you here."

# Chapter Eighteen

It took some explaining to get Hemi up to date on the situation that had led to us being in possession of a number of corpses, an elderly sheepdog, and a small, buzz-cut-wearing teenage girl. Luckily for us, Hemi was good-natured and patient. He listened with interest to our tale, and expressed relief over our survival.

Priyanka needed some time to adjust to the presence of more people in our group. When the others first arrived, she was too frightened to come out of her hidey hole under the bridge. Eventually, curiosity won out over caution. I felt her tiny presence manifest behind me. When I looked down, I found her staring at the newcomers with enormous eyes.

By the time we finished talking, she was standing beside me instead of hiding behind my back, though she still clung to my hand. I glanced down at her occasionally, and each time I found her watching Hemi or one of the other men with intense fascination. I decided that was most likely to do with their physical appearances. Although they were still different to her, they looked much more similar than Michael or myself.

"Priya, this is my friend Hemi. Say 'hello' to Hemi," I told her, trying to introduce her to the young man. The girl stared at me, then ducked her head shyly and hid behind me again. I exchanged a glance with the others and shrugged. "Sorry, she's had a bit of a scary day. She'll come back out of her shell when she's ready."

"Sweet as, man." Hemi grinned cheerfully. He gave the girl a playful wave when he caught her peeking at him again. She stared back at him, her mouth agape and eyes almost as wide as saucers. Everyone chuckled.

There were four men besides Hemi in the group, and all of them were familiar to me from the time we'd spent with the tribe. I was pleased to see that Ropata, the carpenter, was with them, since his skills would no doubt prove invaluable in the task waiting for us.

Tane and Iorangi were there as well. The two men were brothers, who stood tall and imposing, but I'd learned that they were just big teddy bears full of good-humour and fun. Tane was around my age, and wore his hair in long, distinctive dreadlocks. Iorangi was a few years younger, but taller than his brother by several inches.

The last member of the group was a slender, wiry man in his mid-thirties. I knew his name was Richard, but that was about all I knew. We'd only spoken twice before, but he seemed like a nice enough guy. He was just quiet, and usually kept to himself.

Once the explanations were over, we set out on foot to find a better place to sit down and have lunch together. The bridge followed the rim of the catchment dam for the power station down river, but it was bisected in the middle by a small island which was home to an overgrown picnic area. It seemed like a good place to rest for a bit, since it gave us a clear view in all directions in case there were any more neo-Nazis coming after us.

After we had eaten, we gathered our belongings and moved on. The road continued in a long curve, but this time it didn't just span water – it crossed the top of the Arapuni dam itself. That was by far more terrifying than the first half of the crossing had been. The river pooled placidly to our left, while on our right the only thing that separated us from a drop of more than a hundred meters was a tattered mesh fence. When we made it safely to the eastern side of the river, I let out a deep breath to calm my frazzled nerves. I'm not a huge fan of heights.

"Oi, Sandy – we'll give you a ride, eh?" Hemi called to me. I glanced back and watched his group wheel their bikes the rest of the way onto solid ground.

"Sure. We'll cover more ground that way," I agreed. I looked down at Priyanka, who still clung to my hand like a limpet. "We're going to go for a ride, okay? Go sit behind Hemi and hold on tight."

Priya's eyes just about bugged right out of her head. She shook her head frantically and ducked behind me. "Don't wanna."

"C'mon, it'll be okay," I reassured her. "I'll be right there, too. We're going to go fast. You don't want to get left behind, do you?"

Priya stared at me in horror, then looked back at Hemi.

"Go on, sweetie," I said, leading her towards the bike. "It's okay. I'll be right here. Hemi won't hurt you, he's my friend. He's a good boy."

"Good boy?" Priya echoed softly, though she still looked dubious.

"Yeah, good boy." I nodded firmly, and guided her up to sit behind him. "Put your arms around his waist and hold on tight, okay?"

"O-okies," she said, and did as she was told. I smiled and ran my hand over her head, then went to find my own ride. Michael did likewise, calling the dog after him.

Although we were forced to travel relatively slowly so the elderly canine could keep up with us, we made much better time over the last leg of the journey than we could have hoped to do on foot. The nimble little bikes bounded over the tattered tarmac without complaint, their light weight and good suspension keeping us safe from harm.

Seated on the back of Tane's quad bike with my arms wrapped around his waist, I watched the scenery pass in a blaze. Every so often I got smacked in the face by a dreadlock and had to shove it out the way, but I took it with good humour. The last leg out of trip passed swiftly and painlessly compared to the first couple of days.

Within just a few minutes – about ten or fifteen, I estimated – we were bouncing our way out of the countryside and back into relative civilization. Abandoned buildings sprang up out of the overgrown lawns and gardens on the right, while the left side of the road was lined by heavy bush.

Remembering the instructions Rebecca Merrit had conveyed to us, I kept an eye out for something obvious to mark our path. She hadn't been specific on what she'd be using, though. I could see Michael looking around too, and in the end he spotted it before I did. He shouted and waved, which brought our little column to a halt.

A moment later, I saw what had caught his eye – a bright yellow high-visibility vest tied to a tree, flapping languidly in the breeze. As she'd promised, it really couldn't have been any more obvious. As soon as Tane stopped our bike, I leapt off and hurried over to examine the flapping cloth, with Michael and Hemi hot on my heels.

"I think there's a walkway back here." I reached out and moved aside a branch, revealing a deep, cavernous gloom beneath the trees. It had the look of a tunnel, trimmed back to be easy to traverse on foot, but the branches hung too low for the bikes to pass safely.

"We'll go find somewhere to hide the bikes, and then we'll follow you, eh?" Hemi glanced at me for confirmation. I nodded, so he hurried off. Priya scampered over to join us, looking refreshed and high-spirited after her exciting ride on the back of a quad bike, with the dog close behind her.

With Michael and me in the lead, and Priya behind us, we set off down the dark pathway to see what lay beyond. The passage was so narrow and dark that it felt like travelling through a cave. Behind me, I heard Michael muttering as low-hanging branches tugged at his hair, and even I had to duck on occasion to avoid getting a twig in the eye.

Every so often, a metal pole divided the path into bike lanes; we could feel concrete under the leaf litter beneath our feet. Once, this had been a public walkway and cycle track, for tourists wanting to visit the power station. Now, it was something else entirely. The wilds had reclaimed it. Walking that track was a strange experience but somehow comforting, kind of like being back in nature's womb.

Eventually, I saw filtered sunlight dancing across the end of the path, startlingly bright after the tunnel's gloom. I stepped out into the sunlight, raising a hand to shield my eyes – and drew a sharp breath of surprise.

"Oh, lordy," Michael rumbled as he drew up beside me, staring at the bridge. The walkway terminated in a small, open area that bordered the edge of the Arapuni gorge. A hundred metres below us, the river rumbled over rapids. The bridge that spanned the gap was little more than rails and netting with a narrow walkway down the middle.

I picked my stomach up from about my knees, and took a long, deep breath. "At least the bridge is still intact. No holes… I'm not sure I could handle holes."

"I feel like I should make a joke about that," Michael answered, "but I can't think of one right now." He looked at me, his dark eyes unreadable. "Do you want me to go first?"

"No… no, I've got this." I'm not entirely sure if I was trying to reassure him, or myself. Regardless, I swallowed hard and stepped out onto the bridge, expecting it to bounce and sway beneath my weight. To my relief, it didn't.

As terrifyingly exposed as it felt, the bridge had clearly been designed with public safety in mind. The entire length of the crossing was lined by a mesh fence nearly twice my height; if I wanted to fall off, I would have to put some serious effort into it. Unfortunately, I could still see through the mesh, so knowing that I was safe didn't help with the vertigo.

As I stepped out further onto the narrow walkway I felt the bridge swing languidly in the wind, but it didn't bounce or jostle the way many rope bridges did. This one was steel and chain rather than wood and rope. Even the panels that made up the footpath had metal peeking out through the wooden veneer. I let out a sharp breath and tried to relax, reassuring myself that I wasn't going to fall.

When I heard the others filter out onto the bridge behind me, I paused to turn and check on them. Michael was assisting a nervous-looking Priyanka with gentle words, holding her hand as he led her out onto the span. It was only then, when we were fully committed to the bridge, that we heard a voice call out to us.

"Hold it right there!" It was a male voice, and it was shouting. "Do not come one step closer, or I will drop you."

I froze. Those words told me that the speaker was armed, and meant business. Although it was completely against all of my basic instincts, I managed to release my death-grip on the handrails and slowly raise my hands above my head in the universal sign of surrender. Closer to the start of the bridge, I saw Michael do the same whilst discreetly inserting his bulk between the gunman and our young charge.

"That's right. Now, turn around slowly. No sudden moves." The instructions were obviously for me, so I did as I was told. It was difficult to move slowly when every one of my instincts was screaming to get the hell off that bridge and back onto solid land. "Identify yourselves and tell me why the hell I shouldn't shoot you."

"We were invited here," I called back, mentally cringing at how out-of-breath I sounded. My heart was racing more and more the longer I stayed up there. I could feel panic gripping at the edge of my psyche, running icy talons up the back of my neck. "Rebecca Merrit invited us. Check with her, she'll tell you. She said that you needed help, so here we are. My name is Sandy."

My answer was silence.

I realised suddenly that I was trembling all over, whether from adrenaline or basic animal terror; felt like the chasm was drawing me over the edge even though I wasn't moving. My breathing had accelerated to the point that I was panting, and I felt the tickle of sweat gathering on my forehead. If I didn't get off that bridge soon—

"Why are you armed?" the voice demanded suddenly, interrupting my internal monologue.

"You told us it was pig country," I answered, with a stab of annoyance. They had asked us for help, and yet we were the ones getting interrogated? "By the way, you failed to mention that Pukeatua is neo-Nazi territory. We almost got shot getting here. Come on, Jim – let us off this damn bridge. We've brought rum."

"Rum? But I asked for vodka," the man complained, but my words had the desired effect. He stepped out of the brush where he'd been hiding, a long hunting rifle nestled in the crook of his bandaged arm. "Well, come on then. Hurry up, we don't have all day."

Gun or no gun, I couldn't get myself off that bridge fast enough. As soon as my feet hit solid ground, I nearly collapsed with relief. A second later, Michael and Priyanka joined me, and the three of us clung together for a moment to recover. The dog bounded along after us, showing no sign of being any the worse for wear for his adventure.

"I really don't like heights," I admitted, letting Michael's comforting bulk steady me until I felt better. Then I turned and looked at the portly man that had briefly held us hostage, studying him. He was an older fellow that I estimated to be in his late fifties, but it was hard to tell. A ring of scrabby reddish-blonde curls stuck out over his ears, but other than that he was completely bald. He had the heavy summer tan, rough skin, and beer gut of the typical Kiwi bloke, but there was a degree of intensity about his eyes that the average bloke didn't have.

"You said it was just going to be two of you," he accused. "You didn't say anything about a kid or a dog."

"We found them along the way," I explained. "We couldn't very well leave them behind. However, you'll be happy to know we managed to convince five of our big, strapping friends to join us and help clear up your problem."

"Five?" The man's eyes widened. "Cripes, that's more than we expected. We didn't even know there were that many people left in the Waikato."

"You'd be surprised," I answered sympathetically, relaxing now that I was out of harm's way. Sure, he was carrying a gun, but so was I. Neither of us were aiming at one another. "My group consists of five people, six if you count Priyanka here, plus our friends have a group of eleven."

"Bloody hell." Jim itched at his balding pate with his good hand. "Had no idea. Figured there was maybe a half-a-dozen folks still around, but no more than that."

"You kept the power going all these years for a half-dozen people?" I asked, incredulous and a bit stupefied.

"Well, I've been working here since I was a pup. Keeping this power station going is all I know. I ain't got no family, so when the plague took my mates I just stayed here, kept doing what I've always done." The man absently rubbed his jaw and lifted his good shoulder in a shrug. "Then I found Rebecca in town. She'd had a bit of trouble with a few lads further south, so we decided to get married to keep her out of trouble. Seemed like a good idea at the time."

I chuckled and shook my head. "I'm going to tell her you said that."

"Hah." Jim grunted a laugh as well. "The old bat already knows. Bloody nag, never lets me get a moment's rest." Despite the aggression in his words, his tone was affectionate.

A shout from the other side of the bridge drew our attention. I turned and saw Hemi and his crew gathered on the far side. With a wave, I beckoned for them to join us despite the wary look on Jim's face.

He relaxed once introductions were made. For some reason, knowing someone's name made them seem infinitely less hostile. Besides, we were a generally good-natured crew, and we came bearing booze. When Jim finally consented to lead us off towards the power station, there was a fair amount of joking and heckling going on between us, which seemed to put him at ease.

Michael and I followed Jim, with the rowdy group of lads, Priya and our dog strung out in a pack behind us. I glanced back to check on my small charge, and found her staring adoringly up at Hemi. Amused, I shook my head and smiled to myself. Oh, how quickly her opinion of him had changed.

Suddenly, an arm snuck around my waist, and took me by surprise. I shot a curious glance at Michael and found him chatting away with our host despite the possessive grip. Though he was still smiling and joking, I could see a strange tightness around his eyes that confused me. It took a few seconds for me to realise that it was nervous jealousy.

That was an emotion I had only seen from him once before, when we'd first met Hemi's enigmatic mother. Although I had no sexual interest in women, I found her fascinating to the point of being hypnotic, and Michael had seemed irked by that fact.

Now, I realised it was the fact that, aside from Priya, we were completely surrounded by men. I could only imagine he felt some basic animal need to exert his ownership over me, as the only adult female in the group. I didn't really mind, per se, but it was a strange feeling and left me a little uncomfortable. The thought of being claimed like a piece of meat was not a happy one, but I knew Michael didn't think of me that way. It was an instinctual thing, and I would probably have felt the same way if we'd been surrounded by a pack of women, and Michael had been the only virile man in sight. Hell, that made me nervous just thinking about it.

All of a sudden, I felt an overwhelming need to reassure him that he had my full attention, and I simply wasn't interested in anyone else. I placed an arm around his waist and leaned against him comfortably, but I didn't say anything. I didn't have to. That was enough.

As it turned out, access to the power station was not for the faint of heart. Jim led us down the steepest flight of stairs I'd ever seen in my life, a concrete pathway etched directly into the side of the gorge. Through a mesh of overgrown branches, the river valley opened up below us; it was a sight of unparalleled beauty that took my breath away even more than the steep descent did.

The river was the colour of carved greenstone, still running high after the recent storms. It wound between steep hillsides lined with thick bush. I found myself amazed by the fact that the trees and ferns had managed to survive clinging to the slopes, but not only had they survived, they'd flourished. The closer to the riverside that we got, the louder the rush of water became. By the time we reached the landing, it was loud enough that it was getting hard to hear anyone's voice.

If this is how loud it is when the station is off, how do they get any sleep when it's running?

I glanced around the massive concrete platform curiously; the power station was enormous, possibly the single largest human-made structure I'd seen in my life. A relatively narrow concrete walkway ran around the edge of the monolithic structure;

although it seemed slender compared to the size of the station, it was easily wide enough to drive two trucks down side-by-side.

There were no trucks, of course. I saw no sign of a road or access-way to the lower portion of the station, so there was no way to get them down there.

To our left, a concrete wall rose ten or fifteen metres above my head, perhaps more. It was hard to get a sense of scale on a building so impossibly large, particularly when a significant portion of it was buried within the rock wall of the gorge. Enormous windows glinted in the sun, but they were up too high for me to be able to see inside.

Jim opened a door and led us in. I found myself feeling a little like Alice in Wonderland, stepping through a door that looked so tiny compared to the monstrous wall it was set into. We entered a hallway that was of a more normal scale, and were shown about a dense network of old offices that had been converted into living space. The thick concrete drowned out the rush of the water, so it was relatively quiet inside.

"Rebecca?" Jim bellowed his wife's name suddenly, startling me with the volume of his voice inside an enclosed space. "Where the hell are you, woman?"

"In here," a female voice replied through a partially-open doorway. Jim shoved the door the rest of the way open and strode in, muttering to himself beneath his breath.

"Visitors," Jim grunted noncommittally, then promptly left the lot of us in his wife's care and stomped off about whatever business he thought was so much more important than us.

"Welcome, and sorry about my husband," Rebecca greeted us, glowering in the direction her antisocial spouse had gone. Introductions were made, and explanations for the unexpected presence of our new companions.

Unlike her husband, Rebecca Merrit didn't seem bothered. I found myself taking an instant liking to her as she led us through the warren of old offices and storage rooms beneath the power station, assigning us sleeping quarters.

"I'm afraid we don't have enough beds for everyone," she admitted, looking apologetic. "We weren't quite expecting this many people. I've only made up two, but we can probably drag a few more out of storage tomorrow. It's a little hard, what with Jim's arm."

"It's fine," I answered, and gave her a smile. "I think we're all used to sleeping on the ground from time to time. So long as we don't wake up covered in dew, anywhere you can spare is just fine."

"That much I can definitely do," she agreed, smiling back at me.

She was at least a decade younger than her husband, fit and spry with no trace of grey in her long, brunette hair. Although her hair was pulled back in a practical ponytail and she was wearing men's clothing, she was slim, vivacious, and full of life – the complete opposite of her portly, grim-faced husband. The comparison amused me, though I thought it impolitic to mention it to either of them.

"Now, I'm assuming you boys don't mind letting the ladies have the good beds?" she asked, shooting a pointed look at the men trailing along behind us. They'd obviously been well trained by Anahera, so her question was met with noises of consent.

She showed me and Michael to one room, and Priya to another across the hall from us, then left us there to get settled in. The 'good bed' was nothing more than a narrow cot with a thin mattress, but neither of us minded. We'd shared a similar sized bed back in Hamilton. We didn't mind getting cosy for a few nights.

Priyanka, on the other hand, was thrilled at having a room to sleep in with a real bed. "Mine room, for me!" she told us with great glee, bouncing back and forth between the chambers. As relieved as I was to see her happy again, I found myself wondering about the issue of privacy.

"We should figure out how to lock the door," I commented dryly, shooting Michael a pointed sideways look. He instantly took my meaning and laughed merrily.

As though to prove my point, Priya promptly stuck her head in the room to find out what we were giggling about. I burst into laughter as well. Poor little Priyanka just stared at us, bewildered, like all the adults in her life had suddenly gone mad.

There were some things in life that I just wasn't ready to explain to a cloistered thirteen-year-old yet. It was safe to assume someone would have to have The Talk with her at some stage, but today was not the day.

# Chapter Nineteen

By the time everyone had settled into their rooms and changed out of their grubby travelling clothes, there were only a few hours left until sunset. We left Jim with his prescription of booze and painkillers, and headed out to inspect the work that needed to be done.

Hemi, Michael and I followed Rebecca, with Hemi taking the leadership role for his group in his mother's absence. It seemed like a natural progression; despite his youth, Hemi appeared to have inherited his mother's organisational abilities, and at least a little of her charisma.

Rebecca led us out of the building, and along a walkway around the edge of the power station. Eventually, we made our way down another narrow set of concrete stairs onto a smaller ledge that ran just above the water line. About half way between one end of the station and the other, Rebecca stopped and pointed at the concrete beneath our feet.

"These are the intake vents." Rebecca knelt down on the concrete and leaned forward. I joined her, and stared where she pointed. "There's a grille over them that normally stops things from getting into the vents, but the storm knocked a big tree over. Somehow, the tree went right through the grille. It's lodged in the intake down there."

The water was clear as glass near the surface, but it lost its translucence just below the surface due to the turbulence of the recent heavy rain. I couldn't see much, just a few branches and a handful of leaves.

"How big a tree are we talking?" I glanced at her, curious.

"Big." Rebecca sat back on her haunches and heaved a long-suffering sigh. "It's an old oak tree, used to grow over the river down by the dam. We found the stump; it looks like it got split by lightning. Even with eight able-bodied people, I have no idea how we're going to get it out."

"You said you had equipment?" I asked. "What kind of equipment?"

"All kinds of equipment, but unless you know how to scuba dive it's not going to do much good."

I looked at Michael and he looked back at me. Sure enough, he nodded. I found myself fighting a smile. "We may just have someone that can help with that."

"What?" Rebecca stared at me, and then looked around at the others. It took a moment before she cottoned on to the fact that she was missing a joke. "You're kidding me, right?"

"Not at all. Michael was a cop," I explained to her. "He's trained in all kinds of different things."

"Actually, I learnt to scuba dive while I was in high school," he interjected helpfully, and flashed me that silly grin of his.

"Or he's just an overachiever. Something like that." I shot him a mock-glare for contradicting me, but that just made his grin widen.

"Well." Rebecca absently rubbed the back of her neck, staring thoughtfully down at the murky water. "I guess that does change things, doesn't it?" A flicker of hope passed through her eyes, and brought a smile to her face. "I guess we have a chance after all."

"Let's hope so," Michael spoke up, then he glanced around at the rest of us. "We'll need to get down there and have a look before we formulate our plan of attack. None of us have any experience with hydroelectric power stations besides you. Which of us can swim?"

Hemi grinned at him. "Man, my boys live on the edge of a lake and take our kai from the water. What do you think?"

"I'll take that as a yes." Michael winked, and then glanced at me. I simply nodded; I didn't swim very often, but I could if I had to. He nodded back, then looked up at the sky to judge the time. "We probably have enough time to take a quick look. Is your equipment ready?"

"One set is," Rebecca answered, easing herself back to her feet nimbly. "I'll go fetch it."

"I'll help," Hemi volunteered cheerfully. The pair of them scampered off, leaving Michael and me alone.

I watched them go, then looked up at him and playfully raised a brow. "So, if you're going swimming, does that mean you're going to take your clothes off?" I teased impishly.

Michael just grinned at me and waggled his eyebrows.

***

By the time Rebecca and Hemi returned with the scuba gear, Michael had stripped down to his boxer-briefs and given his clothes to me for safekeeping. I folded them up neatly and put them aside, and promptly initiated an in-depth conversation on the weather. No, really. For reasons that I couldn't quite determine, I had started finding it hard to concentrate the moment that he'd undressed, which seemed to amuse him greatly.

"It definitely smells like rain," I commented, shading my eyes against the setting sun.

"You keep saying that, but I don't smell anything." Michael looked at me curiously. "How can it smell like weather?"

"I don't know how to explain it, but I can definitely smell it." I did my best to explain what my instincts were telling me, but he didn't seem to fully understand. "If you draw in a deep breath through your nose and mouth, you can feel a coolness and moisture on the air."

"I can't smell anything." I heard him sigh sadly, and shot a quick, worried glance his way – except that when I did, I caught him smirking and realised that he had deliberately drawn my eye.

"Damn it!" I complained, swiftly covering my eyes. "That's not nice. You know how to play me like a fiddle."

"I think a flute would be a more appropriate instrument, don't you?" he teased mercilessly, then reached out and grabbed me around the waist to pull me into a playful kiss. Suddenly, it was very, very hard to concentrate on the task at hand.

Someone scoffed in mock-disgust. Startled, I squeaked and leapt out of his arms, leaving him looking incredibly amused. With a flash of completely irrational embarrassment and a touch of annoyance, I blushed furiously and stalked off a short distance to cool down while Rebecca and Hemi helped Michael into the diving gear.

"The current is quite strong," I heard Rebecca warning him, "so be careful. The turbines are all off so you can't get sucked into any machinery, but you could get stuck down there."

"I'll be careful," Michael rumbled. The imminent danger distracted me from my strange mood; although I was feeling out of sorts, he was still my Michael and I loved him, so I returned to the group to offer my support.

They hadn't bothered with a wetsuit since the water would be warm, and he wasn't going to be down there for long. Residual moisture left on the tank and mask sent water droplets rolling down his skin like a gentle caress. I tried not to see them, but the more I tried to look away the harder it was to focus. One droplet survived long enough to trek all the way down across his hard belly, to moisten the rim of his shorts; try as I might not to see it, my eyes followed it all the way down.

Thankfully, no one was looking at me as the heat rose in my cheeks again, which was a blessing in disguise. My sister taunted me mercilessly about the blushing thing. My skin was so fair that I turned as red as a tomato at the drop of a hat. Suddenly, I was very glad that she'd stayed at home.

"If you need us to haul you out, tug the rope sharply three times." Oblivious to my distress, Rebecca continued her instructions as she fastened a secure line onto Michael's weight belt with a heavy-duty clasp, and fed out enough line for him to be able to move freely.

He nodded and slipped the mask over his face, settling the mouthpiece within his lips. My heart skipped a beat as he stepped backwards into the water, but he popped up again a moment later and flashed us a thumbs-up sign. Rebecca tossed him a waterproof torch, and then he was gone into the depths.

We were left to feed out the safety line as he needed it, but other than that all we could do was wait. I sat down on the edge of the concrete platform to wait, and slipped off my shoes so I could dip my feet in the river and let the cool water take down the swelling.

I watched the trail of bubbles diminish as Michael moved beneath us; I could imagine his powerful strokes as he swam, even if I couldn't see him. With no other option, I pushed my anxiety aside and tried to relax. Michael was a competent swimmer and seemed to have an impressive assortment of skills. He'd be just fine.

All kinds of different skills. I trailed a toe in the water as I mulled over the idea. You might even call them talents. He's… a very talented man…

"Are you still blushing?" Rebecca's comment made me jump. When I glanced up, I saw both her and Hemi watching me with amused expressions.

"No," I retorted sharply and looked away, suddenly embarrassed beyond words.

"Uh-huh." Rebecca did not sound convinced. I could practically hear her rolling her eyes. My embarrassment deepened, and anger rose within me. Michael shouldn't have put me into that position. He knew very well I was shy and cautious around strangers, though he had made it his life's mission to draw me out of my shell.

Embarrassing me in public was certainly not the way. He must have seen them coming and decided to assert his position of ownership over me right when they could see it. It was the only logical conclusion. For once in his life, I felt like he had made a very serious judgemental error. I glared at the water and kicked it absently, gritting my teeth in brooding silence.

I heard the other two wander away a short distance, and then a whispered conversation between them that ended in muffled laughter. I felt sure that I was being gossiped about, and I didn't like that feeling at all. Sulking, I stared off into the water, willing my boyfriend to return so that I could kick his shapely backside all up and down the river for leaving me in this state.

My annoyance grew in leaps and bounds the longer I was left to think about it. Then Worry reared its ugly head, and smacked Annoyance aside. To say that my emotions were at war would be a misstatement; it was more like a vicious barroom brawl going on inside my head. My conflicting emotions were locked in a catfight for dominance.

Concern won for the time being, but I wasn't sure how long that would last. As annoyed as I might be, I loved Michael more than I had any means to express. I worried about him all the time. Even though he was technically still close to me, it felt like he was a million miles away, in a whole other world. I estimated it had been about ten minutes, maybe fifteen. I leaned forward, staring down into the murky water, willing myself to be able to see more than a few feet down.

Something moved, a shadow in the depths. I leaned out further, straining to make out what it was, but I couldn't see it clearly. Then, suddenly, something cold and slippery fastened onto my ankle and pulled; before I could even scream, I was yanked bodily into the cold river. My head went under, then I popped up spluttering and fighting the current.

Michael grabbed me around the waist to keep my head above the surface. It took a second before I realised that he was the one who had pulled me into the water, then I let out an inarticulate shout and smacked his shoulder.

He just laughed playfully and helped me back to the river's edge, where strong hands grabbed me and hauled me back out of the soup. As soon as we were back on dry land, I planted my hands on my sodden hips, and fixed Michael with a dark glower.

"Dammit, Michael; that water is cold, you know," I complained, soaked from head to toe. The breeze chilled me and left me shivering.

"I know, but you made me wash the dog so it's only fair," he answered cheerfully, as he shed his mask and stripped off the tank and weight belt, leaving himself clad only in a pair of distractingly wet shorts.

And with witnesses, too. Annoyance sprang back on the offensive and bitch-slapped Worry with her purse.

Thankfully, Michael knew when to quit. He must have seen something in my face that told him enough was enough, because he settled down and put his serious face back on. Rebecca handed him a towel, but rather than use it on himself he put it around me and rubbed my shoulders to dry me off. The gesture relaxed me a little, but I was still feeling cantankerous and had to bite my tongue to keep from saying something smarmy.

"Let's head back inside," he suggested, glancing at the others. "Once we've dried off and changed, we'll gather the troops and formulate a plan of attack."

They took the hint. Relieving us of the scuba gear, the two of them hurried off, leaving Michael and me to follow at a more sedate pace. Sensing something was amiss, Michael gathered his clothes under one arm and put the other around me, but I was stiff and unresponsive as the fight continued inside my head. I felt him watching me but I didn't make eye contact. Instead, I glared down at the ground by our feet.

He waited until the others were gone to point out the obvious. "You're mad at me."

I grunted wordlessly; I had no idea how to verbalize what I was feeling.

"Hey," he whispered, trying to catch my chin and tilt it up as he so often did, but for once I resisted him. "Please don't be mad, honey. I was just playing around. I thought you liked the water."

I could hear the hurt in his voice, and that softened my annoyance. He was as new to this as I was, I reminded myself. He had no way to know what would hurt me unless I found some way to articulate it.

"It wasn't the dunking; I was already angry by then," I told him. My voice came out harsher than I intended it to. When I finally looked up at him I could see the pain in his eyes.

"What did I do?" His voice was confused and pleading. For the first time in our relationship, he didn't understand me, but even though I'd hurt him with my sharp tone he was still trying. Guilt suddenly reared her ugly head, and shanked Annoyance right in the kidney. I looked down again, but this time it was for a whole other reason.

"It's just... I... I don't know how to say it." I sighed heavily and closed my eyes; I felt his strong hands on my shoulders, rubbing me gently through the towel.

"Please try?" he whispered, drawing me up against him. "If I've done something that hurts or offends you, give me the chance to make it up to you. You know that I would never, ever deliberately hurt you."

My shoulders sagged as I felt his warm, comforting bulk press up against me, holding me close. He was right, I did know that. I knew it wasn't his fault. He couldn't understand unless I explained it. He was a sweet, kind man, and he didn't deserve the cold shoulder.

"I-I... I don't like it when the others laugh at me, at us. When you get me all, you know, blushing and stuff, and then they're there and they laugh. I feel so embarrassed." Tears stung at my eyes; it all felt so ridiculous, but I couldn't help how it made me feel. "Rebecca laughed at me after you made me blush before. I was so humiliated."

"Oh, sweetheart, I'm so sorry." He brushed away my tears with one hand, and leaned down to plant a kiss on my forehead. "I didn't mean to. I guess I'm just... out of practice on how to behave in public."

"I think we all are," I agreed, snuggling up against him. His skin felt simultaneously warm and cool where the wind had chilled it, and closeness always felt so wonderful.

"What can I do to make it better? Or not do, so it doesn't happen again?" He sounded anxious, far younger than his thirty-two years of age. Like me, his emotional growth had been truncated by the disaster that had devastated our planet. At the age of twenty-two, his world had ended, and he had no romantic experience to fall back on except what he was learning from me. "Would it be better if I didn't touch you in front of others?"

"No," I hurried to reassure him. "I don't mind if you touch me. I like that. It's just, sometimes when you tease me... you know how easy it is for you to get me worked up. I'm vulnerable when I'm worked up. You're the only person I trust to see me that vulnerable."

I heard a soft intake of breath; when I glanced up at him, I finally saw understanding dawn in his eyes. He nodded and offered me a tiny smile. It was then I knew that I had reached him. He hugged me gently and I hugged him back, snuggling my face up against his broad chest as a pleasant sense of tranquillity drifted through me.

We had officially survived our first fight, if you could call that little tussle a fight. At least this time, no one ended up with a cracked jaw. I felt him nuzzle me, the rough stubble of his chin brushing my cheek as he put his lips beside my ear. His voice was a whisper, cool enough to chill my wet skin but warm enough that I only shivered in the pleasant way. "Are we okay, then?"

"We're okay," I whispered back, brushing my wet hair out of the way so that I could kiss him and show him that I still loved him. I felt him relax as our lips met; his hands were so gentle, it felt like nothing in the world could ever make him want to deliberately hurt me.

All of a sudden, the troubles of our lives seemed so far away, and the only thing in the world that mattered was the man in my arms.

*** 

Michael and I retreated back to our room hand-in-hand. I felt buoyant, so much better than I had a few minutes before. Despite how recently I'd been in a sulk, I now felt happy and content. More importantly, I finally understood what people meant when they talked about the make-up period after a fight.

I definitely looked forward to spending some pleasant alone-time with him later on in the evening. Hell, I would have dragged him off to bed right then and there, except for a promise I had made to my sister. It was almost sundown, and I'd sworn to contact her on the first evening after we arrived.

When we reached our room, we found a few more towels waiting for us, as well as an old plastic drying rack for our wet clothes. Michael set up the frame, while I peeled off my sodden garments and flung them into a pile on the floor. By the time I was down to my underwear, I realised that I was being watched.

"What?" I shot Michael a look over my shoulder, and narrowed my eyes at him as though I were on the verge of taking offense. This time I wasn't, but two could play at the teasing game.

The poor man looked so tormented that I couldn't keep the ruse up for long. A smile snuck its way past my mask of indignation, at which point he suddenly realised that I was pulling his leg. His expression brightened immediately, and with it returned his wicked sense of humour.

"Hey, it's not my fault that I like watching you take your clothes off," he retorted, folding his arms across his broad chest. Suddenly, his smile turned impish, and he made an encouraging gesture with one hand. "Oh, don't stop there. The rest of your clothing is soaked as well."

I felt the heat rise in my cheeks at his flirtation, but since we were alone I didn't mind at all. While his cheeky humour had gotten me so upset before, now it struck just the right chord with my increasingly playful mood. I found myself giving serious consideration to whether we had time for a little indulgence before sunset.

Michael snuck up behind me while I was still frozen with indecision, and the feel of his chest against my back made the choice for me. Skylar could wait a few more minutes.

"Here, let me help," he murmured, his lips right behind my ear; I felt nimble fingers unfastening my bra and then a chill as he peeled the wet garment away to expose my skin to the air. A shiver ran right through me, but it was the good kind of shiver; goose bumps rose across my breast.

"Why thank you, sir. How terribly helpful of you," I purred back. I hadn't even realised that I was capable of making that kind of sound until I met him, and it never failed to startle me. Thankfully, Michael distracted me by slipping his hands around my body, his fingers exploring my moist skin.

One drifted down across my belly, drawing me back against his chest, while the other snuck up to cup my breast. His fingertips tickled me in all the right places, and his lips graced the curve of my neck with tender kisses and nibbles. I felt myself responding instinctively to his touch; all thoughts of my sister were gone, lost in the overwhelming, animal desire to mate.

Before I rightly knew what was happening, the flimsy, wet cloth that separated our bodies had been stripped away, leaving us naked in one another's arms. Lost to the moment, I was more than happy to let Michael guide me up against a nearby wall, and take me from behind.

Although we coupled like wild things, never for a moment did that gentleness fade from his hands or his disposition. Never once did I feel any kind of fear, only pleasure so intense I couldn't hope to contain it. I turned my head, seeking his lips with my own; he understood and kissed me with a heat that drove any rational thought right out of my mind.

Each time we made love, I found myself shocked by the intensity of the feelings he stirred in me. Each time, it seemed so impossible that what we had felt before could improve, and yet each time he left me breathless and astounded. I marvelled at just how intense and wonderful it felt.

Although it had been a decade ago and I may have simply forgotten, I had no memory of ever reaching climax through the awkward fumbling of my teenage boyfriends. This was new, and this was special. I vaguely remembered faking it for the sake of their egos; with Michael, I had never once felt the desire to fake anything. He could bring me to the edge of orgasm with the merest touch of his lips or his fingertips.

I wondered if perhaps it bespoke more of my feelings for him than of his abilities as a lover, but I decided it didn't matter. That's not to say that he wasn't gifted, because he was, but I vaguely recalled someone once telling me that the pleasures of sex were always more intense when backed by the emotions of intimacy and love. That certainly seemed to be true.

Our lips parted and I felt the strength drain right out of me, but he caught me before I could slip away. I felt myself bundled up and carried off to bed, where I just relaxed contentedly in the warmth of companionship as I recovered from our brief but potent tryst.

When I regained my senses, I found myself draped across Michael's lap comfortably, while he sat on the bed with his back against the wall. There was a sheen of sweat on his tanned skin, and for some reason I found it fascinating. I couldn't resist the urge to reach out and trace a finger across his chest and down his toned belly.

One of his eyes flickered open at my touch, watching my finger's progress. I looked up and gave him a smile, and he smiled contentedly in return.

"If that's make-up sex, then we should fight more often," he said in that deep, husky voice of his. As always, it sent a chill down my spine, but his words made me laugh.

"How about if we skip the fighting and just go straight to the make-up sex every time?" I suggested.

"Good thinking. I like it," he agreed with a languid grin, running his fingertips through my wet hair. I closed my eyes and sighed contentedly, only to have my impending doze interrupted in advance. "Hey, don't go to sleep; you have to call your sister."

I grunted at Michael's reminder, then opened my eyes and fixed him with my best effort at the sad puppy eyes. "Don't wanna."

Apparently, he was much better at it than I was. When I tried it on him, he only laughed. "If you don't, by this time tomorrow we'll have her on the doorstep freaking out."

He did have a point. Knowing Skylar, she'd probably do exactly that.

"I'm up, I'm up." I sighed heavily and straightened up, perching myself coyly on his knee. "But, if I have to get up then so do you."

His sigh echoed mine as he slowly sat up as well. One big hand ran up the length of my thigh, and then shifted up to cup my cheek. I turned my head willingly as he guided me into another kiss – a tender one this time, soft and affectionate, the kind of kiss I wished that I could curl up in and live inside forever. Alas, it was not to be.

All too swiftly, he broke the kiss and gazed down at me, absently stroking the curve of my jaw with his calloused thumb. "I know, my love. I have to go rally the troops. This will just have to do until bedtime."

"Bedtime isn't very far away. I'm sure we'll manage." I smiled up at him, feeling a surge of hot emotion through my chest as I gazed up into his handsome face.

"Oh, we'll manage," he agreed, "but tonight…"

His words trailed off with an entirely different kind of heat, one that made my belly go all quivery at the mere sound of it. I bit my lip and looked down for a moment, then flicked my gaze back up to regard him. "Is that a promise?"

"No," he answered with his usual razor wit and wicked grin. "It's a threat. Now, put your clothes back on and go call your sister."

I gave him a pout of course, even though he was right. The sun was just dipping below the horizon, and I had promised to call.

# Chapter Twenty

It took a while to track down Rebecca and get her permission to use their radio to contact home, but once I found her she agreed right away. She led me to the radio and briefly showed me how to use it, then hurried off to gather everyone else for dinner.

I tuned the radio carefully to make sure it was fully in the band, then pressed the submit button and spoke into the microphone. "Arapuni Dam to Skylar McDermott, come in Skylar."

There was no answer. I waited a few moments then tried again, tweaking the tuner a little to the left and the right. Again, no reply. I frowned and twiddled the buttons, trying to boost the signal without really knowing for sure what I was doing. Thankfully, I got lucky; on the third try, I received a reply.

"We receive you, Arapuni; this is Skylar. Who is speaking?"

I smiled with relief and sat back for a moment to let my concern flow away before I replied. "It's me, sis. We arrived safely a few hours ago."

"Sandy! Thank God, I was worried." Skylar's reply was crackly, but the signal was strong, "How are you? How was the trip?"

"We had a few hiccups, but we got there in the end. You're not even going to believe what happened, though," I answered, and then I took a deep breath and launched into the story. I told her about losing the Hilux but gaining a little girl and a pet, and about the ambush at Pukeatua. I glossed over the more gruesome details, though. There was no need for anyone to know those but me. I told her about meeting up with Hemi's tribe, and about the situation at the power station.

"Wow, you did have an adventure. I'm glad everyone's okay," she answered quietly, but then there was a pause. A distinctive kind of pause told me something was wrong at home. "There's… something weird going on around here…"

"Weird?" I echoed, furrowing my brow in concern. "What kind of weird? Good-weird? Bad-weird? Weird-weird?"

"Weird-weird," she answered, sounding a bit uncertain. "It's Maddy. The last two nights since you guys left, she's been having nightmares. She keeps waking up in the middle of the night, screaming that her bed is on fire. The doctor says it's just a phase, but I don't know. Maddy's…"

"…special." I finished the sentence for her, understanding exactly what she meant. Although she was only seven years old, Madeline Cross had shown intuition well beyond her years on a number of occasions. I'm usually the biggest sceptic on the planet, but Maddy had proven that she was anything but an ordinary child.

"Yeah. I don't know, sis. I feel like maybe we should listen to her. What do I do?" It wasn't often that my sister sounded lost, but right now she did. I thought about it for a moment before I answered.

"Well, it's better to be safe than sorry," I said decisively, and then I started issuing orders. "There's a bunch of fire-fighting stuff in one of the downstairs storage rooms. If I remember correctly, there should be three or four small fire extinguishers and half-a-dozen hoses in different sizes. What I want you to do is put one of the little fire extinguishers in your room, one in the doctor's room, and one in the kitchen under the sink.

"Then I want you to take the hoses and spread them out as well. Put one in each bathroom and one in the kitchen. Make sure everyone has one of those little plastic adaptors on their tap so the hose fits, and check the hoses all work.

"Lastly, I want you to take the biggest hose and hide it under the porch of the house across the street. You know, the one with the fallen-down tree in the yard? If there are any spare fire extinguishers, put them there as well. Okay?"

"Okay," Skye agreed, sounding relieved that someone was taking her concerns seriously. "I think we should move the you-know-whats, too. Just in case."

"The... oh, right, the you-know-whats." It took a second to click that she was talking about the guns. "Yes, absolutely. Put them in the downstairs room of my apartment. I left you the keys. There's a little office at the bottom of the stairs that can be locked from both directions." I thought for a second. "Come to think of it, put some spare food and water in there, too. Enough to last all of us three days. Some spare torches and batteries, and one of the first aid kits – you know, emergency supplies."

"Good idea, sis. I'm going to go do that right now, before it gets too dark." Skye heaved a heavy sigh. "Talk to you at sunset tomorrow?"

"Yeah." I paused for a moment, searching for the right way to phrase what was on my mind. "Before you go, though... how are you, little sis? Are you holding up okay?"

There was silence on the other end of the line for a while. When she spoke again, her voice was subdued but determined. "I'm coping. I'll be okay, I just need time. I've been spending a lot of time playing with Maddy, to keep myself distracted."

"I'm glad to hear it," I answered. It wasn't a lie, either; I worried about her, but she was stronger than I gave her credit for. She'd always be my baby sister, even now that she was grown up. That was my problem though, not hers. The last thing she needed was me hounding her to express her feelings. "If you ever need to talk, just let me know."

"Thanks, sis. I better go before it gets dark. Good luck with your tree."

We signed off then, but I sat for a few minutes longer staring into space as I thought over what she'd said. I found myself way more concerned than I probably should have been under ordinary circumstances – but Maddy was special. It was more logical to think that she was just a little kid having nightmares, but as I'd told Skye, I felt that it was better to be safe than sorry.

Besides, the precautions were all logical and reasonable. Anything could happen. It made sense to be prepared. Scout's motto and all that. Once I calmed my nerves, I focused on the task at hand. The sooner we got that stupid tree out, the sooner we could go home and keep an eye on things personally.

I rose from my seat and went looking for the others, following the sound of their noise through the maze of passages. After living in the bunker, it was familiar and comforting to hear the echo of human voices through cold, concrete tunnels, even if the tunnels themselves were new to me.

When I found the other survivors, they were gathered in a noisy mob around a small office-turned-dining-room. There wasn't enough seating for everyone, so Rebecca had put on a buffet instead. My friends stood around or sat on the floor, eating and talking to our hosts. The food was nothing to write home about, but it was hot and filling. After ten years living as scavengers, most of us weren't all that picky anymore.

I slunk through the mob and filled up a plate of my own, then wandered over to join Michael. He was sitting on the floor in a corner with Priyanka and the dog, talking to the girl while they ate. They both glanced up at my approach; I was both amused and flattered to see their eyes light up, though for completely different reasons.

"Hey guys," I greeted them, as I settled down on the floor beside Michael. Priyanka waved happily and showed me the utensil in her hand.

"Look look! I am forking," she told me proudly. Michael snorted with laughter and almost choked on his mouthful of food.

"You mean, 'I am using a fork'," he corrected her gently once he managed to swallow his food, his eyes shining with good-natured fun.

"Ooh." She stared at him for a moment, and then beamed at me again. "Look, I am using a fork!"

"What a good girl you are. Well done," I praised her, reaching over to give her an affectionate pat on the head. She positively glowed at the commendation. My heart would have melted, if it hadn't already been a big, soppy puddle of goo for that kid. She was so sweet that I had no kind of resistance against her charm. She even made me feel a bit maternal, which was unusual for me in all kinds of different ways.

"How's everyone at home doing?" Michael asked.

I glanced at him and shrugged. "Maddy's been having nightmares about fires, so Skye was pretty freaked out. I've got her out right now fireproofing the motel, just in case."

"You think it's a premonition?" Michael looked as dubious as I felt.

"No, of course not – but there's no harm in being prepared. I mean, look what happened to Anahera's tribe." I shrugged absently, shovelling a fork-full of food into my mouth. After swallowing I added, "Having a plan in place in case of fire is a good idea."

"Yeah, that's true. It's not like we can call the fire department anymore." Michael nodded slowly and leaned back against the wall. "Well, I suppose I should go get this meeting started."

"Probably a good idea, before they get into the rum," I agreed with a smile, then I leaned over to touch his hand reassuringly. "Good luck."

"Thanks." He sighed heavily and levered his powerful frame up off the ground. He returned his plate to the receptacle that waited for soiled dishes, then he clapped his hands loudly and yelled over the noise. "Okay, guys. Shut up for a minute."

To my surprise, the din settled down and all eyes turned to him straight away. Michael took the opportunity while he had it, and went over to stand in front of an old whiteboard that still hung on the wall from the days when this room had been used for business. He picked up a marker that was miraculously still working, and began sketching on the whiteboard as he spoke.

"I think everyone knows why we're here, but just in case anyone's unclear, there is a tree stuck beneath the power station," he explained as he illustrated the situation underwater. "I went down a few hours ago and had a look. It's wedged in the first intake, which is basically a big rotating fan. To get it out, we're going to need to get down there and cut off all the branches, then winch it out.

"Rebecca says they have enough scuba gear here for three people, so I'm going to need volunteers to learn to dive." He paused and glanced around. Hands came up from most of the people in the room. "Okay, good. Hemi and Iorangi, you're in; the rest of you will need to be on the river bank to clear the debris we bring to you. I may swap you out later, depending on how it goes.

"Sandy and Richard." He shifted to look at me, and gave me a faint smile. Someone in the room wolf-whistled, but they were silenced by jeering before I could figure out who it was. When the room quieted down again, Michael continued. "I have a special project for you two. Jim tells me there's a small boat kept in a shed a little way down river. It's designed for this and has a winch on the back, so we're going to need it. I want you to find it and figure out how to get it going."

I nodded reassuringly, even though I knew nothing about boats. Over the years, I'd learned enough to jerry-rig most mechanical things back to life for a little while, so I had confidence I could at least get the engine going. Richard could deal with the 'boat' part of the equation.

"I'm sure all of you want to get home as soon as possible," he continued, to grunts of agreement from around the room, "so we'll get started at first light. Don't stay up too late. I will be waking you up at the crack of dawn regardless of how tired or hungover you are."

He flashed an impish grin at the crowd, who laughed and jeered as he finished up. Once it quieted down, he moved back over to where I sat and offered me a hand up. I had finished eating while he was talking, so I took it and eased myself up to my feet.

"You know, I was wondering about something." I glanced at him curiously as I put my plate in the basket. "I just realised while you were talking that the lights down here are still on. How are the lights on when the power grid is offline?"

"I was talking to Rebecca about that earlier, actually." He threaded an arm around my waist casually. "She told me they have a solar-powered generator in case of emergencies."

"Oh." My mood brightened immediately. "So... hot showers?"

"Yes ma'am." He shot me a sideways look, his voice soft enough that only I could hear it over the renewed noise in the room. "It's almost time for bed anyway, so why don't you tuck Priya in, I'll take the dog out, and then we can see where it goes from there."

"I like this plan," I agreed readily, giving him a sideways squeeze before I detached myself from his embrace. I looked at Priyanka, and discovered that she'd finished eating and was watching the two of us with a puzzled look on her face. The moment she realised I was paying attention to her again, her expression brightened. "Bedtime, sweetie. Come on."

"Okies," she answered happily, bounding to her feet. I took her hand and showed her where to put her plate and utensils, then led her out of the room. We wound our way through the passages to one of the communal lavatories so that she could relieve herself, before I took her back to her little sleeping chamber.

There, I helped her to change into a nightie I'd salvaged for her and put in her backpack, gently explaining the difference between night clothes and day clothes. As always, she was a quick study. I was still sitting on the edge of her bed, talking to her, when Michael returned from taking the dog out.

I hadn't even realised he was there until I happened to glance up and noticed him standing in the doorway with his arms crossed, smiling affectionately at the two of us. Suddenly feeling shy, I smiled back and absently tucked a strand of hair behind my ear.

"Doggie sleep with me?" Priya asked suddenly, looking back and forth between us.

I glanced at Michael, who shrugged. There seemed to be no good reason to deny her request, so I acquiesced. "Sure, sweetie. Call him to you. Say 'come, doggie' and clap your hands so he can hear you."

"Come, doggie!" she promptly cried, clapping her hands enthusiastically. The dog's ears pricked up. After she called a couple more times, he padded away from Michael's side and went over to the edge of the bed, sniffing curiously.

"Now, say 'up, doggie' so he knows he has to jump up," I instructed. Priya mimicked me obediently. After a few false starts and a little help from the humans, the elderly canine managed to get up on the end of the bed. "There you go. Now, you go to sleep and he'll go to sleep as well."

"Okies," Priyanka answered agreeably. I leaned down and gave her a gentle hug, then she lay down and snuggled herself up under the covers. Michael and I said our goodnights to her and backed out of the room, closing the door behind us.

Then we looked at one another, and I found myself grinning. "So, what was that about a hot shower?"

*\*\*\**

Hours later, I awoke to darkness, my back snuggled comfortably against Michael's firm, warm chest, his arms wrapped like a blanket around me. I could hear the sound of his breathing, slow and even on the back of my neck. Nature was calling, but I didn't really want to get up. I closed my eyes and tried to go back to sleep, but the pressure in my bladder was too uncomfortable. As much as I wanted to stay in bed, I couldn't.

With no other choice, I carefully extracted myself from beneath my sleeping lover's arm, taking my time to avoid waking him. Although the room was pitch black, I'd left a torch beside the bed in case of circumstances like this. I fumbled in the dark and found it, then tiptoed towards the door.

The lights were all off in the hallway outside our room. I had no idea what time it was, except that it was night. Still, a need was a need, so I clicked the torch on and I crept along the corridor towards the nearest bathroom.

A few minutes later, I was on my way back to my room when I accidentally took a wrong turn and ended up in an unfamiliar corridor. Just as I was about to turn myself around and retreat back to an area that I knew, a strange sound reached me and made me hesitate. It was coming from around a bend in the corridor.

Always alert for trouble, I followed the sound until I reached the corner. When I peeked around, I saw a shaft of light cutting through the darkness. The sounds were coming from that doorway. They were strange, animal sounds, grunts and curses, and the sound of flesh striking flesh.

Then there was a woman's cry, strange and strangled, that struck a chord of concern through my heart. I clicked off my torch and hurried forward, my bare feet silent on the cold concrete floor.

With as much stealth as I could, I crept up to the partially open door and snuck a look through. The sight that greeted me was the last thing that I expected. I was so stunned that I stopped and stared for a long second before I retreated and headed back towards my room. There was no one in that room that needed my help... but they might if Jim figured out what was going on.

Not only was his wife cheating on him, but she was doing it in spectacular fashion. I couldn't even imagine taking on two men at a time, let alone big, strapping lads like Tane and Iorangi. Her muffled cries and the look of devilish enjoyment on her face echoed in my head as I fled, trying to put the scene behind me.

I felt a little nauseated by the time I got back to my room. I hadn't seen anything that intense since the one time Harry had convinced me to watch a pornographic video with him. Now, I was left feeling dirty. As I burrowed back into bed and hid safely under Michael's arm, I tried to remind myself that it wasn't my fault. I hadn't encouraged her to cheat on her husband, and I'd only gone to look because I was afraid someone was being hurt.

Even snuggled under the warm, comforting bulk of my sweetheart's body, it took me a long time to get back to sleep after that.

*\*\*\**

When morning came, I woke up feeling guilty and slightly soiled. Normally, my dreams were a happy place, filled with friends, family and the warm, sensual moments that I shared with Michael. After what I had seen the night before, my sleep had been troubled, filled with vague, shadowy human forms playing 'the beast of two backs'.

Well, the beast of three backs, technically. That made it so much worse. In spite of my effort to suppress the outward signs of my disquiet, I shuddered at the thought.

"What's the matter, sweetheart?" Michael asked quietly, just about scaring me out of my skin.

"Nothing," I said quickly, but he knew me too well to let me get away with that.

"Really? I felt you shiver just then. It's not cold, so that means you're brooding." He propped himself up on an elbow and leaned over me to switch on the light, so that he could study my face. "Ah-hah, just as I thought. You look like you kicked a bunny. What did you do?"

"I didn't do anything," I answered glumly; there was no point in lying to Michael when he could read me like a book, "but I saw something last night. I don't know what to do about it."

"What did you see?" he asked, gently capturing a strand of my hair and plucking it out of my face. I cringed, because telling him meant I had to think about it again when I was trying very hard to block it out.

"I got up in the middle of the night to go to the bathroom." I sighed, finding it hard to meet his eye. "On the way back, I got a little lost. I ended up in another part of the building. I saw... I, um..."

"Out with it," he demanded when I hesitated a few seconds too long. My shoulders slumped.

"I saw Mrs Merrit shagging Iorangi and Tane. Now I don't know what to do." I buried my face in the pillow to try and hide my anxiety, but it was a pointless endeavour.

"Wow, that is a pickle." I could hear the disapproving tone in Michael's voice, but I knew it wasn't aimed at me. "We should probably tell Jim— wait, Iorangi *and* Tane?"

"At the same time." I lifted my head and turned to look at him. If I had to suffer, then so did he. It wasn't that they're unattractive people, but there was something so slimy about the whole situation. Even if it weren't for the infidelity aspect, Rebecca Merrit was at least fifteen years older than the younger of the two brothers – that made her old enough to be his mother. An underage teenage mother, but still. The cheating aspect was worse though, and made me feel really sick. "Christ, what do we tell him? Do we tell him? Is it our business?"

"It's our business now," Michael answered grimly, his expression set in a look I hadn't seen before. "If I cheated on you, you'd want someone to tell you, right?"

The logical side of my brain knew he was just using that as an example, but the irrational, emotional half heard those words and promptly went nutty as a drunk wombat.

"Yes!" I exclaimed. "I mean, no, I mean—oh my God but you'd never do that, right? I'm not sure I could handle it if you—"

"Whoa, whoa, calm down." Michael held his hands up in self-defence, a panic-stricken look crossing his face. "Where did that even come from? You know I'd never play around on you."

"I know, but I don't know – anything could happen. You might start to hate me one day, and then you might cheat on me and then... and then..." And then I burst into tears. The worst part was that I could actually see myself going nuts, and I knew it was completely and utterly without reason. It was like the rational part of me was looking down from above, watching my emotional side go into total overload, without being able to do anything about it.

Poor Michael looked about the same way. His expression was one of utter bewilderment as he struggled in vain to comfort me. Neither of us could quite work out what was going on, until it suddenly hit me. My fit of inexplicable rage the day before, followed by the intense desire to screw his brains out, and now this? There was only one possible explanation.

As suddenly as they had started, the tears stopped. I stared at Michael with wide-eyes, not quite sure how to react. "Oh, my God. Honey, I think I'm premenstrual."

"...What?" He just looked even more bewildered.

"Oh, um... hormonal. I think I'm hormonal." Well, this was an awkward conversation to have with my boyfriend, but he did have a vested interest in that region of my body. "Like, seriously hormonal. As in, I think I'm going to get, um, 'that time of the month' soon."

"Oh." He stared at me for a long second before realisation dawned in his eyes. "*Oh.* You mean..."

"Yeah. I mean that." As soon as I had a name for what was bothering me, I felt much better. Embarrassed, I summoned a weak smile for him and I wiped my eyes. "I'm sorry, I haven't had one in years, so I guess I'm a little unbalanced. I think my body kind of forgot it was female for a while there."

"Thank God, you had me panicking." Michael looked so relieved that for a second I thought he was going to faint. "It's okay, no harm done. That just means that you're recovering and getting healthier again. That's good news." He smiled at me and gave me a hug, which instantly made me feel better.

"I'm so glad you understand." I snuggled up against him, feeling relief like a palpable force. While I wasn't looking forward to dealing with ol' Aunt Flo again, at least I knew it was in the name of the greater good. "Actually, I'm glad I understand, too. It's been so long that I had no idea what was going on at first, but now it all makes sense. You know I'm not usually this irrational. I think it's just been so long that things are a little haywire inside me."

"It does make sense, and it's a good thing. I want you to be healthy." I felt tender fingers running through my hair, and then Michael gently pushed me back to look me in the eye. "In the meantime, I know what will make you feel better."

"For once, I'm sad to say I'm not quite in the mood." I gave him a wry smile.

"What?" He blinked owlishly. "Oh! Oh, no, not that. I mean that I have a present for you."

"A present?" This time it was my turn to look surprised. I thought about it for a second, then tilted my head curiously. "Is it food?" The moment the words were out of my mouth, I suddenly felt stupid. "Wow, I really am premenstrual."

"No, it's not food. It's a real present." Michael laughed and tickled my ribs, drawing a girlish giggle from me. Then he slid out of bed and rose to his feet, padding barefoot over to where our bags sat in a corner. He knelt beside his backpack and dug around in the pockets until he drew out a couple of small, shiny objects that I couldn't quite make out from afar.

"What is that?" I asked, curiosity getting the better of me, but he closed his fist around the shinies before I could get a good look.

"Well, I had an idea. Something Anahera said got me thinking." Michael returned and stood in front of me, dressed only in the boxer-briefs that he usually slept in, and the bandages over his wounds. Gazing down into my eyes, his expression turned serious. "Life is short and brutal. We really have no idea how long we're going to have together. Either one of us could die tomorrow. If that happens, I want the world to know how much I love you."

My breath caught in my throat as he eased himself down onto one knee on the ground in front of me. He opened his hand to show me his gift: a pair of rings. One was simple and delicate, made for a woman's finger. The other was a thicker band, clearly designed for a man. Each ring was threaded onto a delicate silver chain. I stared at them for a moment, and then looked back up at his face. "But I thought..."

"I know. But, I also know that I want you to be my wife one day. No one says we have to get engaged one day and married the next. If we get engaged today then we can wait as long as we want to make that final step." A smile touched his lips, just a faint ghost. "There's more to what we have than just lust, and I think you know it as much as I do. You are my Yin. I want everyone to know it – and most of all, I want you to know it. Marry me, Sandy."

Tears blurred my vision as he spoke, making the rings in his hand seem to dance and sparkle. His logic made sense – and he was right. What I felt for him was so much deeper than lust, deeper than anything I had ever thought I was capable of feeling for another human being.

"I don't know what to say," I whispered, feeling truly stumped for one of the few times in my life.

"Then just say yes. We'll work out the details later." He smiled adoringly at me as he held the rings. I sniffed and tried to blink back my tears so that I could see him clearly, but the harder I tried to keep from crying the more determined they were to come.

"I... I..." Part of me was mad at him for getting me all emotional all over again, but a bigger part of me was so thrilled by the idea. It felt so right. He was The One. Somehow, my instincts had told me that from day one, even if I had ignored them. Now, things had changed. I bit my lip for a moment longer, then drew a deep breath and nodded. "...Yes. Yes, I will marry you. Thank you."

"'Thank you'? I wasn't expecting that." He laughed gently and reached up to place the delicate silver chain that supported my ring around my neck. As he leaned back, he trailed his thumb along the curve of my jaw. "No, sweetheart. Thank you. I don't quite know how I know, but my gut tells me this is meant to be."

"Mine too," I agreed, fussily wiping the tears from my eyes. "It feels strange, though. I mean, marriage is kind of an archaic ritual now, isn't it?"

"It is, yes. But I think marriage now will be different to what it was ten years ago. Everything is different." His thumb followed my hands, brushing away a tear that I hadn't gotten to yet. "All the rules that defined our society are irrelevant now. Now, we make our own rules. No one but you and I can tell us what our marriage is supposed to be."

"That's true." The thought cheered me up. "First rule – I'm not wearing a big, stupid white dress. But there will be food, lots and lots of food. And lots of snuggles, too."

Michael laughed merrily, and eased himself up to sit on the bed beside me. With strong, gentle hands, he dragged me into his lap and cuddled me close, a situation that I was more than happy with given the circumstances. Only once I was comfortably seated on his firm thighs did he take a moment to slip his own chain around his neck.

I found myself watching with interest as the ring it carried settled against his tanned skin. On an impulse, I leaned over and pressed a kiss against his collarbone right beside it. A surge of simple joy passed through me, and I smiled in spite of myself as he arms closed gently around me.

"This does feel right," I said, snuggling up contentedly in his arms. "I... I want you to know that I only have eyes for you, Michael. I saw how nervous you were yesterday around all those other men."

"Oh, you noticed that?" I heard him sigh heavily, and felt his fingers running through my hair. "I'm sorry, I was hoping you didn't notice. I did feel a little, I don't know... jealous, I guess. I caught Tane looking at you when you didn't see, and I've caught Hemi at it a few times too."

"There do seem to be a lot more male survivors than female. It's bound to cause trouble one day, particularly with the likes of Mrs Merrit around." I grimaced and tried not to think about the reason why there were more men still alive than women, but unfortunately I knew it well. I was one of the lucky ones, but many were not as fortunate. Without laws to protect us, women like me were vulnerable.

For a moment, we were both silent as we thought over that grim fact. An idea had been forming in the back of my mind, an unexpected idea but one that certainly had merit. It was too early to say anything to anyone, but the more I turned the idea over in my head the more interesting it became.

"We should probably go get this tree sorted," Michael said, breaking the thoughtful silence. I sighed, but he was right. One step at a time.

***

By the time the sun cleared the hills, I was fed, dressed and out in the bush, picking my way carefully through the thick, verdant ferns. Richard and Jim followed in my footsteps, letting me break the trail for them. Jim's arm was bound up in a sling, and Richard had insisted on carrying our gear, so it came down to me to lead. I decided that was the way I preferred it.

"Should be up there a ways," Jim huffed, out of breath from our walk. It had been an awkward trek for all of us, because we were following the line of the river through the heavy bush. The ground beneath our feet was slanted down towards the water's edge, so each step required careful balance. Every so often, a spot that appeared to be solid would turn out to be a mesh of twigs and leaf-litter that gave way underfoot, so I had to choose my path with care. Just to make matters worse, the ground was wet and slippery beneath us; as I'd predicted, it had rained overnight.

"When was the last time you came up here?" I asked, almost as out of breath as Jim.

"Few years back," he answered, "but we didn't need it at the time, so we let it be."

"Fair enough. Done that a bit myself," I agreed amiably, trying very hard not to think about the bad news I might have to break to him at some stage. Michael and I agreed that we would try to gently probe him for information when we could, to get a feel for how he'd react. The last thing we wanted to do was put either of them in danger, even if we didn't like what Rebecca had done. We were both keeping an eye out for the right time to do it privately and gently, and if the opportunity arose then whichever one of us was there would take it.

Jim mumbled something unintelligible in response, which I took to mean he wasn't interested in casual conversation. I was fine with that; it was hard enough to focus on where I was putting my feet.

Michael and I had also decided to keep our engagement a secret for the time being. I wore my ring on its chain around my neck, hidden beneath my clothing, but Michael had reluctantly taken his off since he was going to be spending most of his day underwater. It was in my pocket now, nestled safely within the most secure compartment I had.

I suppose, in theory, carrying the rings went against my normal ethics. They were technically dead weight that added to our burdens while contributing nothing, but for once in my life I was okay with that. Even in my most perverse moment, I couldn't bring myself to resent the tiny added weight of an engagement ring from my beloved around my throat. I couldn't even feel it, but knowing it was there made me feel like I was connected to him even when we were separated. When I thought about it that way, it was worth a hundred times its meagre weight in emotional value.

Hiding a secretive smile, I ducked beneath an overhanging branch and scrambled up a shallow ledge that was slippery with leaf mould. The debris was so thick that I didn't even realise the ledge was made of concrete until I was standing on it.

"I think we've got something," I called over my shoulder to the men. With great care, I negotiated the ledge to the far side, and found that it dropped sharply down to the river. A narrow channel of filthy, clogged water ran into the hillside, terminating in a dark, ominous cavern. The ledge turned to a walkway barely wide enough for one person as it wound into the cave's mouth alongside the water.

Eternally vigilant, I brought my shotgun up and slipped the safety off as I made my way down the stairs towards the entrance. I moved with a smooth, practiced step, stealthy yet efficient. When I reached the entrance, I paused to listen, sniffing the air while I waited for my eyes to adjust.

The only sound was the soft tone of water against wood and concrete, but the scent was much more complicated. I could not only smell the forest and the dirt, but also the faint odour of rusted metal, fuel, and decaying flesh. When my eyes adjusted to the dark, I could make out the faint outline of something bobbing in the water below us, which eventually resolved itself into a small boat.

The cave itself was shallow, only just deep enough for the boat, with a slender walkway around the edge. A frayed old rope creaked morosely with the rise and fall of the water, keeping the boat tethered to its mooring. Between the boat and the open river, an old grill gate stood half open, too crusted with rust to go anywhere without significant force.

"We're clear," I called to the men waiting on the walkway above me. I heard their footsteps crunching over the leaf litter, then changing timbre as they descended to join me.

"Hm. We're going to need to get that gate open," Jim pondered, absently rubbing his chin.

"There's a lot of debris in the water, too," I agreed, clicking the safety back on my shotgun. Since Jim couldn't do much more than stand watch, I handed him the weapon and beckoned for Richard to follow me. Together, we moved to the edge of the walkway and knelt down to inspect the junk floating in the water. It was a tangled mess of branches, old trash, and even a few animal bodies. At least, I really hoped they were animal bodies.

"See if you can clear some of this while I take a look at the boat, huh?" I glanced towards Richard. He nodded quietly and set our gear down on a ledge near the boat. While he was busy hunting around for something to scoop the trash out of the water with, I turned my attention to the little bucket of rust that I was loathe to call anything remotely resembling a vehicle. Frankly, I was amazed that it was still afloat.

With great care, I moved around to the side of the dock closest to where it was moored, and lowered myself down to sit on the edge of the concrete. Tentatively, I poked the bottom of the boat with my foot, half expecting it to sink at the lightest touch. To my surprise, it didn't. In fact, the 'rust' came off all over my boot, leaving me a little bit filthy and more than a little confused.

I poked the boat with a wary finger and came away even dirtier; what had first appeared to be rust was actually a thick layer of slime. I wasn't sure if that was a good thing or a bad thing, but under the slime, the little aluminium runabout appeared to be quite solid.

Settling back on my haunches, I considered the evidence I saw and came to the conclusion that the boat must have gotten swamped at some stage in the last decade, probably during a heavy storm or something. With no one to bail it out, the water just sat there until it evaporated, leaving behind a layer of all the crusty things that infested river water during a flood. I judged that it must have happened recently, or perhaps even repeatedly – the gunk was still wet.

Luckily, we had anticipated a certain degree of filth and come equipped. Jim carried a light backpack full of cleaning rags and a few other small things, which he handed to me without a word. I took it, fished out a grotty old towel, and set about the unpleasant task of de-sliming our boat.

Needless to say, it wasn't my favourite task of the year, but at least I wasn't fishing corpses out of the river like Richard had to. I could hear him gagging while I was wiping away the gunk, but he didn't curse or complain at all. I had to admit that I was impressed by his stoicism; in his place, I would have been bitching up a storm.

It took some time to return all of the slime to the water from whence it came, but at last the task was done. I sat back to admire my handiwork. Beneath the slime, the little boat was in surprisingly good condition. It was a small thing, probably only about four metres from bow to stern, with an inboard engine that powered not only the boat's propulsion, but also a pair of light chain winches.

I inched towards the aft to examine the winches, and found that while they wouldn't be strong enough to tear the gates off Fort Knox, they should be more than adequate for what we needed. The chains were rusted, but not so badly that they'd be useless. The steel clasps on the ends screeched faintly with disuse at first, but they still worked.

"Hey Jim. Can you bring me a screwdriver, mate?" I asked, casting a glance back over my shoulder. "Medium-sized, Phillips head."

Jim grunted and went off to do my bidding, while I turned my attention to the housing that protected the motor. It appeared to be watertight, and the last person who'd used the boat had locked that box up tight. The caution of some long-dead mechanic would be our salvation.

It took a bit of lubricant and a great deal of cursing to convince the screws to let me in, but when I finally lifted the lid I was pleased to find the motor in very good condition. The seal had held for all those years, through all those storms, leaving the important mechanical components no worse for wear than any other boat that had been kept in storage for a decade.

That is to say, it wasn't perfect, but it would do for a start.

***

By mid-afternoon, courtesy of some fresh petrol and a new battery, the little boat finally roared to life. Although the noise of the sputtering engine was deafening in the closed space, it felt like the prettiest sound I'd ever heard. Feeling pleased with myself, I reassembled the engine housing and sat myself down in the rear of the boat.

Richard handed the toolkit down to me, then he helped Jim into the boat as well. The rocking motion as the older man walked over and sat down made me tense up, but he didn't seem concerned. While Richard untied the slimy rope that held our craft against the docks, Jim took the wheel in his one good hand and looked over the controls.

Richard had managed to clear away the worst of the debris, and wedged the water-gate open far enough for us to get out. Now, the only thing between us and the freedom of the open river was figuring out how to drive a boat.

The men seemed to know what they were doing, or were at least good at faking it. They fought for a minute before Jim finally relinquished the wheel to Richard and came to sit opposite me in the aft. He was huffing and grumbling so much I had to fight hard to hide my amusement.

There was no time to laugh, though. A few moments later, Richard put the boat into whatever passed for 'in gear' in a floating craft, and we leapt away from the dock. I yelped in surprise and grabbed the edge, half-expecting to hit something at high speed and burst into flames.

Luckily for all of us, he figured out what he was doing before that came to pass. With a little more care this time, he nudged the boat out of the cavern and eased us out into the open river. A pleasant breeze hit us, bringing with it fresh, pleasant scents. It was raining again, just a light drizzle, enough to refresh but not enough to drench.

The wind caught a few strands of my hair that had escaped from my braid, and sent them dancing around my face as we slowly picked up speed. In spite of my initial caution about the unfamiliar sensation of boat travel, I found myself enjoying it. Like riding on the back of a quad bike, it got my heart pumping and adrenaline flooding through my veins.

Unfortunately, thinking about the quad bike brought back memories of Tane, and what I'd seen the night before. I stole a furtive glance at Jim and found him staring off into space, oblivious to my concerns. It seemed so cruel. After all the sacrifices he had made to keep the electricity on all these years, he'd been betrayed by his own wife. I had to talk to him, but not now. Later, in private. No need to humiliate him in front of Richard.

Trying to distract myself before a dark mood could settle in, I watched the trees flash by along the edge of the water, then looked back to admire the ripples we left behind in our wake. It was kind of mind-boggling to think about the fact that it had been ten whole years since any human crafts had troubled the placid waters of the Waikato River. I hoped ours would not be the last.

The more that I thought about it, the more the idea gestating in the back of my mind made sense. The human species – my species – was on the verge of extinction. The only possible way for us to survive was for someone to intervene in the survivor culture that had sprung up over the last decade.

Someone needed to take a hand in the future of humanity. God knows we'd done the same for many other species over the years. I thought about the zoos, where scientists had strived so hard to preserve the most vulnerable animals against their inevitable extinction. Now, it was our turn. Someone had to do it, or there was no guarantee that my kind would live to see another generation.

When I watched Michael with Priya, something stirred inside me that had lain dormant for a very long time. I was shocked to realise that I did want children one day. When the time came, I knew I could rely on him to be a wonderful father, just the way my own dad had been for me.

Although I had initially rebelled at the idea of having my own offspring, the truth was that perhaps they would help me to fill the hole in my heart that had been so empty since I lost my family a decade ago. But there was a problem. Several problems, in fact. Even if our children were born immune to Ebola-X, there was no guarantee that they'd be safe if we continued to live the way we were.

If I wanted to have my own child one day, then it was my duty to make sure that the world I brought her into was a place where she could grow up, be educated, and live amongst friends. That meant that something had to change, and it had to change within my lifetime.

As our little boat rounded a bend in the river and the massive power station came back into view, I came to a decision. I've never been the kind of person who relies on others to do things for her. It's against my nature.

If I wanted this world to be better, for my children and my children's children, then I would have to change it myself.

# Chapter Twenty-One

A cheer erupted from the gaggle of survivors on the river bank as the power station roared to life.

It had taken a week for us to clear the obstruction from the turbines, but at long last we had succeeded. A few hours before, we'd hauled the last of the debris down-river and disposed of it where it would no longer pose a danger to anyone. Now, we stood watching as our victory came together at last.

For the last week, I'd struggled to try and get Jim alone for a moment, but it seemed like there was always someone around to get in the way. Although it was frustrating, my temper had calmed down when my hormones settled back into their normal routine. I had patience again, so I bided my time, waiting for the right opportunity.

On the day after we had found the boat, a sharp stab of pain in my lower abdomen had advised me that I'd guessed correctly: my emotional outbursts had been a symptom of an impending visit from Aunt Flo. Although the discomfort – both physical and emotional – made it much harder to work up the urge to lug around bits of tree, necessity had driven me to keep on trucking. The worst of it had passed now, and the cramps had subsided to a dull ache.

Michael had proven himself to be a real keeper during that week, too. Even though I had been in no mood for sex, he'd been so sweet and understanding that it made me want to cry. He was always on hand to administer kind words, back-rubs, and cuddles when I needed them most. Best of all, he knew without me having to say anything that my condition meant I was often unhappy and in pain; he had made it his duty to be a pillar of comfort and sympathy throughout, and that made it so much easier to deal with.

He was with me now, standing with one arm looped casually around my waist as we watched the power station begin sucking water in through its enormous turbines. Everything seemed to be going fine, but we still observed with avid interest as the station went through its start-up routine. Eventually, it settled into a low, deep thrum that sent vibrations through the ground beneath us and all the way up our legs.

"Big noise," Priyanka whispered theatrically, looking nervous as she hovered nearby. I smiled reassuringly at her and reached over to ruffle her hair, which brought a bright smile to her face. After a solid week in our company, the girl had begun to truly blossom into the lovely young lady she was going to become.

Watching her grow more relaxed and social had been one of the most pleasing experiences I'd felt in a very long time. Although her speech was still a little stunted, she improved every day. She was constantly cheerful and busy; it seemed like she was always rushing about, helping anyone that expressed a need, which was an attitude that quickly endeared her to everyone.

She was no longer afraid of Hemi and the others. Quite the opposite, in fact. I often caught sight of her following one person or another around, looking fascinated by everything that they did. Despite that, she never seemed to get underfoot. There was just something about her sweet-faced innocence and earnest desire to help in that made even the staunchest of us happy to have her around. Looking down at her young face, all I could think was that she deserved so much more than to live out her life as a solitary survivor.

"Well, I guess that's our work here done," Michael rumbled, holding me close against his side.

I nodded thoughtfully and glanced up at him. "It'll be nice to go home. Skye sounded pretty stressed when I spoke to her last night. Maddy's still freaking out pretty badly."

"Agreed. I hope they're okay." He sighed softly and reached up to trail a finger around the curve of my neck, tracing the chain that held my ring. It had taken some time for me to get used to the idea of getting married, but once I'd warmed to the idea... well, let's just say that I had only taken my ring off to bathe. When I looked up at him and saw the flash of silver around his throat, I knew that he felt the same way. On a sudden impulse, I leaned up and pressed my lips to his. Surprised, Michael hesitated for a moment before returning my affections.

Priyanka giggled gleefully, as she often did when we expressed our feelings for one another in front of her.

"Kissie-kissie," she teased, but there was no malice in it so I took no offense. Instead, I teased her right back.

"You just wait, little miss." I waggled a finger at her. "One day you'll meet a boy that you fall in love with. Then, you'll kissie-kissie him, and I'll laugh at you."

"No!" she cried, looking mortified. "Boys, yuck yuck. Boys have bugs."

"Boys do not have bugs!" I laughed, surprised and amused by her outburst. "Who told you that?"

Priyanka looked at Michael with enormous eyes, but said nothing. He stared back at her, looking sheepish. I looked back and forth between them for a moment, then fixed Michael with a pointed stare. It only took a second before he started looking guilty. "I just didn't want to see anyone taking advantage of her."

"So you told her boys have bugs?" I said dryly, fighting the urge to laugh my head off. "That's some solution, honey. Good thinking."

"Hey, give me a break!" Michael put on his best whipped-puppy expression. "I haven't had to deal with a girl going through puberty before – but I know what I was thinking about at her age."

"True." I sighed heavily, and gave him a long, thoughtful look. "I think we've got some time yet, but one of us should probably give her The Talk at some stage."

"Hey, don't look at me," Michael protested. "When I tried, she ended up thinking that boys have bugs."

"Fine, fine, I'll take care of it." I snorted mockingly, but I wasn't angry at him at all. He was right. I had more experience with teenage girls than he did, since I'd been one. Sure, that felt like it had been a lifetime ago, but I still remembered the hot surge of hormones that had driven me towards anything that remotely resembled a male. That gave me a moment's pause, then I looked back at Michael. "On second thoughts, let's ask Doc to do it. I'm sure he'll be able to traumatise her enough that she'll never want to touch a man, ever."

"Now that sounds like a plan," Michael said with a good-natured laugh.

"In the meantime – do you see what I see?" I asked, raising my eyebrows pointedly.

He blinked, then looked around curiously. "That depends. What do you see?"

"I see Rebecca over there, along with everyone else, so it occurs to me that means Jim must be on his own inside. I should go check on him." I shot another pointed look at Michael, who smiled grimly and withdrew his arm from around my waist.

"Good luck," he said. I nodded and touched his hand, then turned and walked away from my little family. Priyanka tried to follow me, but Michael distracted her with something I didn't quite catch before I was out of earshot. The sound of voices faded behind me as I made my way away from the group, and picked my way carefully up the stairs that led back into the depths of the power station.

The door closed heavily behind me, blocking out the sound of the churning turbines, but not the vibrations. I could still feel the tremor beneath my feet as I made my way through the tunnels, and found the set of stairs that led up into the engine room itself.

There, a single figure stood hunched over a control panel, monitoring a mind-boggling array of dials and doohickies. I had no idea how he knew what he was doing, but he seemed to. Jim was so focused that he didn't even seem to notice my approach until I cleared my throat loudly. Only then did he glance up, with a look of annoyance at being interrupted.

"What? Can't you see I'm busy here?" He glared at me. The dirty look gave me a moment's pause, but I braced myself against it.

"Jim, I need to talk to you about something and I wanted to get you alone to do it," I answered calmly, keeping my tone of voice as even as possible despite my annoyance at his attitude. "This is the first time I've managed to all week."

"Christ, what's so important that you have to tell me now, of all times?" He grumbled a few choice words and turned his attention back to the panel in front of him.

"Jim, I just want to know… about you and Rebecca." As Michael and I had agreed, I chose my words carefully. I didn't want to get Rebecca in trouble – or worse, put her in danger. "I don't know what kind of relationship the two of you have. If she got involved with another man, would you be angry?"

"What?" He froze for a second and stared at me. "That's all? You came all this way and interrupted my work to ask me that? I wouldn't care. I already gave her permission to shag whoever she likes."

"You… I… what?" I stared at him, shocked. "So you already know?"

"Of course I bloody well did!" he snapped. "She asked my permission when your boys arrived, and I agreed. Christ, you think she'd do something like that without my permission?" As though suddenly realising just how much distress I'd been in for the last week, he turned and looked at me. "You were really that worried?"

"Yes," I answered, feeling more and more confused by the second. "I mean, I thought…"

"Aw, Christ." Jim absently scratched at his balding pate and eyed me uncertainly. "Erm… how do I put this? Rebecca is my friend. We've been friends for a very long time, but we're not friends 'like that'. About a year or so after the plague, she was living in Arapuni township while I ran the station. She used to bring me food and stuff, but then some boys from the south started coming by and bothering her. She was getting really scared for her safety, so I convinced her to move in here and be my 'wife', so that I could protect her. It's never been any more than that, though. She ain't my type."

"She's not your type?" I stared at him, bewildered by what I was hearing. "I don't understand. She's a nice lady, and I'm sure she's pretty attractive, if you're that way inclined. What's not to like about… wait…" My eyes widened in surprise when realisation struck me. "Do you mean…?"

"Aye, lass. I'm gay." Jim looked amused by my freshly-caught-fish expression. I could only guess that he got that a lot when he told people.

"But, you don't—"

"I know, I know. I don't look gay, and I don't act gay. I'm homosexual, not a bloody ponce. I'm just a regular Kiwi bloke who happens to prefer other blokes. There's a difference." He glared at me for a moment, right up until I started feeling like a total idiot. It must have shown on my face, because an amused smile suddenly flickered across his lips. "Stereotyping is rarely right on the money, kid. You should know that."

"Damn... I'm sorry, mate." I looked down at my feet, rubbing the back of my neck. "I had some trouble with the blokes down south as well, so I've spent most of the last decade alone. I don't really know how to read people anymore."

"Don't worry about it, lass. You meant well." He brushed my shame aside with a vague gesture. "Just be glad your boyfriend isn't my way inclined, or I'd give you a race for your money."

I smiled shyly, sensing the joke behind his words despite his deadpan expression.

"Fiancé, actually," I corrected him, reaching up to draw my necklace out from beneath my clothing to show him the ring. "He proposed a few days ago."

To my surprise, Jim looked genuinely pleased. "That's good to hear. You two make a nice couple. You'll work well together, I think."

"I think so, too. He's the only other person that I told about Rebecca, Tane and Iorangi. We didn't want to embarrass you, but I guess it doesn't matter now." I sighed, feeling relieved all of a sudden. "I'm so glad it turns out there was a perfectly reasonable explanation for it. To be honest, it's been tearing me up inside all week thinking that she might have been betraying you with my friends."

"Two of them, huh?" Jim chuckled, a dark sort of chuckle that set my teeth on edge, but he didn't seem to notice. "That little slut. Well, I suppose a girl's gotta do what a girl's gotta do."

"I guess she was a little pent up?" I suggested with as much humour as I could, even though the comment made my inner feminist a little uncomfortable. I'd learned that Jim was a special kind of fish, and that it was best not to take his comments seriously.

"Must be. Now, you get out of here, I have work to do," Jim grumbled and made shooing gestures at me.

"Okay, okay, I'm going," I answered as I retreated towards the door. "Thanks for not killing me."

"It's fine, lass. Thanks for giving a shit," he replied. A moment later I was out the door, and left him in peace. That also left me alone with my thoughts, which were a very confusing place. How on earth was I going to explain this to Michael?

***

It turned out to be easier than I was expecting.

By the time I tracked Michael down, he was back in our room packing our bags in preparation for our departure. It was still fairly early in the day and we were all anxious to get home to our families, so it seemed wise to set off as soon as possible. I plunked myself down on our bed and repeated word-for-word exactly what Jim had told me. Michael stayed quiet the entire time I relayed the conversation, and it wasn't until after I was done that he said anything.

"Well, I suppose that's a relief then," he said uncertainly, absently scratching the stubble on his chin that he hadn't gotten around to shaving away.

"Yeah, I guess so. It kind of feels like we got all worked up over nothing now, doesn't it?" I smiled and leaned over to give his scruff a little scritch of my own. Michael gave me an amused glance in return, but didn't complain.

"That's a good thing though, isn't it?" he asked, looking up at me curiously. "I'd rather get worked up and have it turn out to be nothing than break up someone's marriage. Wouldn't you?"

"That's true," I agreed simply, and then slid down off the bed to sit beside him on the floor. "I'm relieved, too. Now we can just go home, and worry about whatever the hell is wrong with Madeline instead."

"She's a kid. Kids have nightmares. Don't worry about it." Michael put his arm around my shoulders and drew me close, planting a reassuring kiss on my cheek. "Once we introduce her to Priyanka, they'll be the best of friends and she'll forget all about fires and scary things. She's just lonely and bored."

"That reminds me, actually." I sighed heavily and reached over to grab my bag so that I could stack my things back into it. "We need to look for some replacement parts for the Hilux on the way back."

"Gotcha covered, sweetheart." Michael smiled and gave me a quick snuggle, catching me by surprise. "I told Hemi and his boys about it the other day. They're going to take us into town to look for parts, and then they'll give us a lift back to the truck. I think he still kind of feels like he owes us for something."

"Well, that'll be handy," I agreed, then glanced up at him curiously. "Will your dog be able to keep up for that long, though?"

"Hemi reckons he can get Alfred up on the front of one of the bikes," he answered cheerfully.

"Alfred?" I laughed in surprise. "You named the poor pooch Alfred?"

"Damn straight, I did." His smile widened into a full grin. "It'll take a little practice, but he should be fine. You know how dogs are about the wind."

I chuckled at the image his words conjured up. "That's true. We should get ourselves some quad bikes." Suddenly, my smile faded. The moment to reveal the first stage of my plan to Michael had arrived without any warning at all. I wasn't prepared, but I decided to plunge ahead anyway. "Actually, I've been pondering something and I want to run it by you. I think that we should talk to Anahera about combining our groups."

Michael blinked like a possum caught in the headlights. "Why?"

"Well, I…" How did I explain this to him? It was a thought that I could barely wrap my head around myself. "Michael, we need to do something for our futures. Not just us personally, but *all* of us. The entire human species. We're not going to be able to survive picking over the bones of this old corpse of a world indefinitely. We need to find somewhere, settle down, and start gathering people. As many people as we can. It needs to be somewhere defensible, so we can grow crops and raise animals. We'll need every hand we can get.

"It's the only way we'll ever be safe, and the only way our children will have the opportunity to live in the kind of world that our parents took for granted. We need to build a sanctuary, and fill it with as many good people as we can find. There's safety in numbers, and if we can build a permanent settlement then we'll have a chance to eventually grow our numbers."

"You want to build a city?" Michael stared at me, stunned. It took me a second to process what he'd said, before the words actually sank in.

"I hadn't thought of it quite like that, but… yes, I think so." I nodded thoughtfully. "Not build from scratch, though. At least, not to start with. We need to get the first wave of people together before we can think about that, so we'll need to find somewhere safe and secure to house them, somewhere we can grow food and become self-sufficient.

"Once we have a large enough number of people, we won't have to worry about gangs or anything like that anymore, and we can focus on repairing what Ebola-X did to us and planning for the future. Combining our group with Anahera's would give us a solid base to start with. That would give us sixteen people, which is a large enough group that most of the gangs would steer clear of us."

"And once we've got a safe place," Michael said thoughtfully, picking up where I left off, "and enough numbers to protect everyone, then we get word out. We'd attract people from all over, particularly the women and children who are vulnerable out there on their own – like you were."

"Yes, exactly," I nodded, relieved that he understood my idea.

"This is ambitious, Sandy." he looked at me uncertainly. "It'll take a long time, a lot of hard work, and it's dangerous. Are you sure you're up to it?"

"I've got you to help me, right? With you and all the others, I think we can make this dream a reality." I paused for a second, and then shook my head. "No, I *know* that we can make it a reality. We have to. The only other option is to watch our friends and family gradually slide towards barbarism. Think about it, honey. Humanity is the only species that has ever actively attempted to save another species from extinction. It's time that we did it for ourselves."

"That's... really profound." Michael drew a deep breath and let it out slowly, closing his eyes. "I think you're right, though. I think we can do it. Like you said, we have to do it. For Priyanka and Madeline."

"For all the children," I agreed softly, reaching over to take his hand, "including ours, when the time is right."

He looked at me, and it was like a light had come on behind his eyes. Watching that understanding dawn in his expression made all the effort worthwhile. I knew then that I had him, and that he would stand by my side to the end. A slow smile crept across his face, then he drew me into an embrace and held me close. "New New Zealand?"

"What?" I blinked owlishly, before I realised he was offering a name for the city we planned to build. "Oh, no. That's terrible, honey."

"I know," he answered, lifting his head up so that I could see his grin.

"Mocking me already? Sheesh." I made an indignant noise and tilted my chin up defiantly. "You just wait, we'll both be hailed as heroes one day. There will be statues of us in the town square, and school children will have to memorise every detail about our lives."

"Not *every* detail, I hope. Some of those details are pretty X-rated," Michael laughed merrily and dragged me into a kiss. My cheeky answer to that was muffled by his lips, just to prove his point.

# Chapter Twenty-Two

"Oi, Sandy!"

At that moment, I was bottoms-up under the dusty bonnet of an ancient ute, so my answer came out muffled. "What?"

"Sandy? Where the hell are you?" The voice drew closer, close enough that I could identify that it belonged to Hemi.

"In here," I called back. Unfortunately, drawing the breath to yell meant I inhaled a good deal of dust, and ended up sneezing. By the time the fit passed, he'd found me.

"Hey, careful there." The youth grinned impishly at me. "You'll sprain something."

"*You'll* sprain something when I get you." I shook my fist at him teasingly. "Anyway, what are you shouting about? I'm a little busy here."

"I was just coming to tell you we found a truck you might be able to scavenge." Hemi leaned around me to get a look at the old ute. I was half way through disconnecting the starter motor to replace the one that I suspected had died in the Hilux. "You already find what you need?"

"It's all good. I have no way to test this one, so we're better off taking a couple of spares." I beckoned him closer, and ducked back under the bonnet. "Come help me with this one, I could use an extra set of hands."

Hemi came over to help me out. Together, we managed to get the component free and wrapped it up in an old towel to keep the grease from getting everywhere. I put it in my backpack and shouldered it, then we headed out to go see the car he'd found.

When we arrived, I discovered a gaggle of bewildered-looking blokes standing around another old utility, with its hood raised. They were alternately scratching their heads and shooting sneaky glances at one another as they tried to figure out what they were looking at, without giving away that they were completely clueless on all things car-related.

Amused, I shouldered my way through the crowd and leaned over to inspect the engine myself. The starter motor looked fine, so I enlisted the help of a couple of strong hands to extract it. Once the component was out, I wrapped it up and added it to my pack as well, then shooed the guys back towards their bikes.

Ten minutes later, we were on the road at last. The wind streamed through my hair as I clung on to Ropata's waist, enjoying that feeling of freedom. With the bikes at our disposal, I estimated we could be back to the Hilux by midday. Assuming things went well with the repairs, we could be home by just after sunset.

I was looking forward to sleeping in my own bed again, so much so that I could almost feel the soft pillows beneath my cheek already. Although home was wherever Michael was, there was a pleasant familiarity about our old loft that I adored.

The outskirts of Arapuni passed by in a blaze with our quad bike bouncing over the dips and cracks in the road. I heard a yelp from the dog and glanced back to check on him, but he seemed perfectly happy to perch in front of Hemi, panting in the wind.

We slowed as we approached the narrow roadway that passed atop the dam, but I had no time to worry. Before I quite realised where we were, we were across the far side and making our way up the slope on the far side of the river. The corpses of the men Michael had killed in self-defence still lay where they'd fallen the week before.

Now, their blood had crusted over and dried, washed and baked by alternating periods of rain and hot sun.

We passed them without stopping, and angled our way up onto the long, flat expanse of road between Arapuni and the ruins of Pukeatua. The sun crept slowly higher in the sky as the kilometres fell behind us.

The sky was clear, a beautiful, breathtakingly-infinite arc of blue dusted with fluffy clouds, but the wind was cool and carried with it the bluster of early autumn. As we passed by, I suddenly realised that the forests on either side of the road had begun to take on their golden-orange coats. Another summer had passed us by, leaving me to wonder what we would do come winter.

Should we wait for spring before we began our venture? Or should we set out immediately to seek a site for our new city? As much as it saddened me, I knew that Ohaupo would not serve for my grand scheme. What we needed was somewhere larger, a bigger town or a small city. More importantly, we needed to get further away from Hamilton.

I had a gut feeling that we would see those abominations again, the living, hunting dead. I felt like we were living on a time limit. If they were determined enough, they would find us in Ohaupo, and then we would have to fight again. The future of our children – born or unborn – rested in our hands, and we couldn't risk that anywhere less than perfect.

South seemed like a logical direction to go. I already knew the areas to avoid, so we could focus on the regions that were unknown. Though, if we could convince Anahera to join us, our combined force would be enough to give any of the gangs pause. The largest I had seen was five or six people; a potentially deadly threat to a lone female armed only with a taser and a small pistol, but not much of a problem to a dozen trained, determined, and well-equipped fighters.

And if I had my way, that's exactly what we'd have in a few days' time.

\*\*\*

The rain came around mid-morning.

Plump, black clouds rolled in from the west to pelt us with fat droplets that left us shivering and cold. We didn't stop, though it did force us to slow down a bit for everyone's safety. I ended up hiding my face against Ropata's broad back to keep the water from stinging my eyes. The asphalt hissed beneath us and kicked up a spray that made it hazardous for the bikes following us.

Suddenly, there was a clunk and the rain became lighter. I opened my eyes and looked up to discover that we were driving beneath trees, picking our way through the undergrowth at a more sedate pace. The canopy above us filtered the heavy rain into a light mist. It took me a moment to realise that we'd gone off-road, to avoid the same break in the asphalt that had hindered us on the trip eastwards.

The bike bounced nimbly over tree roots and through clumps of ferns, leaving a trail behind us that felt like it was a mile wide. None of the riders seemed to care, and it made some sense. We'd passed Pukeatua about an hour before and seen no sign of the neo-Nazi threat, so they had no reason to assume there were other dangers lurking about.

I was warier, of course – but I always am, suspicion is in my nature. While we rode, I watched the deep shadows of the underbrush for any sign of trouble, but I saw nothing. Ropata and I were in the lead with the others strung out behind us. Eventually, we left the bush and thundered back onto the tarmac again, where we paused to wait for the other riders to catch up.

I sat up straight and looked back, counting heads as the other bikes emerged from the brush until I was satisfied everyone was safe and sound. I waved to Michael and Priyanka reassuringly, and then we were off again, following the curve of the road towards Te Awamutu.

***

The rain passed after a while, though we had to keep our pace relatively sedate on the wet roads. It was a little after midday by the time we reached the outskirts of Te Awamutu. I leaned past Ropata and pointed the way towards where our truck waited for us; a few minutes later, the quad bike crunched to a halt on the gravel at the top of the hill, beside the high steel fence that had served as our little fortress on that first night. By the time the other bikes joined us, I had already hopped off and squeezed through the half-open gate to check on my Hilux.

Everything was as I had left it, even the keys sitting on the driver's seat. No-one had passed by in our absence; our footprints were the only ones visible in the long grass. While I popped the hood and leaned over the engine to start work, I heard the others parking their bikes and fanning out to relieve themselves and organise lunch.

Before we'd left, Rebecca and Jim had thanked us profusely for our help, and given us enough supplies to see us back home safely. To my surprise, neither of them had suggested that they wanted us to stay, or would like to come with us.

At first, I had found that a little strange, but after taking some time to think about, I'd come to realise that Arapuni Power Station was their home. They felt safe and secure there, even if they were alone together. They always had one another, not as lovers but as friends. When it came down to it, companionship and friendship was so much more important than sex anyway. They were comfortable together, and once we left they would continue being comfortable with one another, even if they had enjoyed our visit while it lasted.

Priyanka scampered over to join me while the guys were busy getting lunch ready. She hopped up on the front bumper to get a better vantage point and stood staring intently into the depths of the engine for some time, mimicking me. Eventually, she glanced over at me for guidance. "What we looking at?"

"What *are* we looking at," I corrected gently. "We're looking at an engine. This engine will make the car drive for us, but right now it's broken. We're going to fix it." I looked at her and gave her a smile. "Do you want to help?"

"I will help." Priyanka nodded solemnly, always ready to assist even if she had no idea what she was doing. I couldn't help but be amused by her serious, intense expression, but it was an opportunity to teach her a useful life skill so I snatched it up.

In simple terms, I explained to her what the engine did and named each of the major components for her. She was a quick study, and repeated the names that I gave her with confidence. After each one, I gave her a brief explanation of what it did. When we reached the starter motor, I went into more detail and told her how I knew that it was broken.

"Is broken because engine no go broom-broom?" she repeated once I was done, simplifying what I'd told her into her stunted English.

"Exactly. So, we're going to take the broken one out, and put a new one in." I opened my pack and removed one of the components, to show her what it looked like.

"Ooh. New one not broken?" She reached out to touch the component, and then sniffed at the grease that came off on her finger.

"I hope this one is not broken – but we'll find out when we put it in. Come over here, I'll show you." I beckoned for her to follow me, and together we bent over the engine and worked to replace the component. Although her inquisitive little fingers sometimes got in the way, it felt important to teach her everything that I could, so I stayed calm and patient, explaining each step as we were doing it.

Eventually, we got the new starter motor in and stood back to admire our handiwork. At some stage, Michael had wandered over to observe what was going on, but I hadn't realised he was there until I felt a gentle hand touch the small of my back. I jumped in surprise and glanced at him. He smiled in return.

"How is it?" he asked softly, in that deep, sultry rumble he reserved just for me.

"We're about to find out," I answered, absently reaching up to tuck a strand of hair back behind my ear. I froze half way through the gesture when I realised that I was unconsciously flirting with him yet again. Suddenly embarrassed, I glanced away. "Um... would you mind turning the key for me, please?"

"Of course," he answered, barely able to hide the amusement in his voice at my momentary shyness. But, more importantly, he understood me well enough not to mention it. He just gave my back a gentle rub, then moved around to the driver's door and slid in behind the wheel. The engine spluttered for a moment when he turned the keys, but then it roared to life with a deep, throaty growl.

Priyanka squealed in surprise at the loud noise and clapped her hands over her ears. For a second, she looked so utterly terrified that I thought she was going to make a run for it, but she held her ground. She stared at me wide-eyed until I smiled and reached over to ruffle her short hair, the way I often did. She seemed to like it when I did that, and equated it with being praised.

"It's okay, sweetie," I told her, then waited until she took her hands off her ears before I explained further. "That noise just means it's not broken anymore. We fixed it."

"We fixed it? No more broken?" Priya stared suspiciously at the rumbling truck for a long moment while she processed that information. Suddenly, her expression brightened. "Fixed, no more broken. Yay! We fixed it. I helped?" She looked at me with those big, soulful eyes of hers. I couldn't even hope to resist them.

"Absolutely. You're a good helper." I ruffled her hair again and gave her a little hug. "Get your bag, we're going to go for a drive in the car now. Going to go home."

"Go home to where Sandy comes from?" she asked quizzically.

"Yep," I told her gently. "We're going to go back to my home. We have some new friends for you to meet. There's even a nice little girl there that you can play with. She's a bit younger than you, but I think you'll like her."

Priya's expression lit up like a Christmas tree. She nodded rapidly and scampered off to fetch her things. While she was gone, I picked up my backpack and headed over to join Michael. He was just climbing into the truck, but he paused to take my bag and placed it in the passenger's side footwell.

"I'll drive first, so you can eat," he offered, pointing me towards where Hemi and the others were cleaning up the remains of their lunch. I noticed at a glance that they'd set something aside for Priya and me, which made me smile.

"That's sweet of you. Thanks, honey." I looked back at him and reached out to touch his hand. "Are they going to go their own way home?"

"Nah, they're going to escort us back to our place and stay the night with us, then go home in the morning," Michael answered, closing his hand around my fingers gently. "It'll be after dark by the time we get there. It's too dangerous for them to be driving along that track of theirs in the pitch black."

"Good point. At least the Hilux has proper headlights," I agreed, absently stroking his big fingers. For some reason, the contrast between us never failed to fascinate me in my more introspective moments. I loved every aspect of his body and his mind, no matter how different it was – but it was the differences between us that really intrigued me.

In the six weeks since we'd left our bunker home in Hamilton, his fair skin had turned dark with a smooth tan. On the other hand, I was still pale but had turned into a mass of freckles during the heat of summer, as I usually did. His hair was still jet black, while mine had bleached even blonder in the sun. We couldn't have looked any more different unless one of us turned green – but that was okay, because I loved him for who he was, not what he was. He could have turned into a giant flying spaghetti monster, and I'd probably still love him.

Priyanka scampered back to us with her backpack, the dog bounding along at her heels. Michael and I parted then, to guide our respective charges to their seats in the rear cab of the old truck. I opened the door and helped Priya climb in, then showed her how to fasten her seatbelt.

"What's this for?" she asked curiously, tugging at the strap as I adjusted it over her shoulder.

"This is a seatbelt. It keeps you safe in case the road gets rough. Make sure you leave it on, but if there's an emergency and you have to take it off, just push this button here." I pointed to the appropriate place, and then gave her a smile and put her bag in her lap. "The doggie doesn't fit in a seatbelt, so you need to make sure he doesn't jump around for me, okay?"

"Okies," Priyanka agreed obediently. She unzipped her backpack and pulled out her old teddy, so that she could cuddle it. On a sudden, overwhelmingly maternal impulse, I leaned over and kissed her forehead, then closed the door and climbed into the front passenger's seat. By the time I was settled, Michael had managed to coax the dog into the back, and opened the window a crack so that he could smell the interesting things we were passing.

Hemi came over to give Priya and me our lunches. The food was nothing exciting, but it was hot and edible so I took it without complaint.

"We'll be right behind you, eh?" Hemi leaned against the sill of my window and looked at us.

"Sweet as," I nodded agreeably. "You know you're always welcome at our place. Not sure where we're going to put you, but we'll figure something out."

"Man, so long as we're not sleeping in the rain, it's all good." Hemi grinned vibrantly, then shoved himself back and went off to gather up his men.

In no time flat, we were back on the road again. We led in the Hilux, since the lads on the bikes had more mobility than we did. We had to pick a path that the truck could handle, so it made sense for them to follow us instead of the other way around.

To my amusement, Priya squealed in mixed delight and terror every time we went over a bump or rolled down a slope. I glanced back at her every so often to check on her, and found her clutching her teddy and staring out the window at the passing scenery with enormous eyes.

The dog, for his part, mostly just slept. Priya's enthusiasm seemed to have exhausted him, which I could understand. She was young and full of energy, while he was elderly and tired. I was pleased to notice that she didn't do anything to wake the dog, and he didn't seem bothered by her noises.

As the hours and kilometres rolled by, I found myself yawning as well. Michael didn't need me to guide him; he remembered the route we'd taken when we had come through before. Despite the jolts that the broken tarmac sent through our vehicle, I lay my head against Michael's firm shoulder and closed my eyes.

# Chapter Twenty-Three

It was dark when someone shook me awake.

I opened my eyes, feeling disorientated and groggy, but before I was even fully alert I knew that something was wrong. Michael's shoulder was tense, and I could see him staring intently into the distance.

"What is it?" I whispered, following his gaze. Before he could respond, I saw exactly what had him tense: the horizon was glowing a hellish kind of red. "Oh, God. Please tell me that's just the sunset."

"The sun went down ages ago," he whispered back, his voice taut as a bowstring. "That's not the sunset. That's something else. I don't know what that is."

"It's a fire. A very big fire," I answered with dread certainty, then I stuck my head out the window and yelled Hemi's name.

"We see it!" he shouted back over the noise of the engines. "Pick up the pace; we're right behind you."

I didn't need to convey the message, Michael had heard him as well. He gave me just long enough to brace myself before he put his foot down, and the Hilux leapt forward. Priya squealed in fright at the sudden increase in speed; a quick glance back showed that she was clinging to my seat, holding on for dear life. Then the smell of smoke hit me, and distracted me completely.

"Oh my God, it's big. It's really big," I exclaimed, leaning forward in my seat to try and get a look. We were still a couple of kilometres from Ohaupo, but I could already taste the falling ash on the wind. The truck lurched over a break in the road, almost throwing my head into the dashboard, but I didn't care. My home was on fire. My sister could be in there. It was all that I could do to sit still as we careened faster and faster through the broken streets.

Suddenly, we were passing familiar buildings on the outskirts of town. I knew before we even rounded the corner onto our street that it was our motel burning. Michael slammed on the brakes and threw the truck into park, then we were both out the door. Side by side, we sprinted the last few metres to the front of the building that had been our home, which was now illuminated by a terrible wreathe of flames.

The fire had consumed the front corner of the building above the kitchen, and burnt all along the roof. Fat raindrops began to fall all around us, but it would be too little, too late. I looked at Michael and saw him frozen in shock. I felt the same way, but I had to shake it off.

*My sister. My sister might be in there. Oh God, Skye!* I stared at the building, struggling to work out the way to respond.

Suddenly, a memory flashed through my mind. If Skylar had followed my instructions, then there would be hoses and fire-fighting equipment in a nearby building. I turned and ran towards the building, ducking beneath a low-hanging something. In the hellish semi-darkness, I couldn't even tell what it was. Behind me, I heard an explosion as a window blew out, and had to fight down the urge to be sick.

Hold on, Skye – I'm coming!

I vaulted over a half-collapsed fence and dodged around a shattered tree that lay at an odd angle against the side of the house, heading for the porch. I could only pray that

Skylar had done as I'd instructed, for her own sake. With my path only lit by the crackling glow of flames, I didn't see the hose sprawled across the ground until I stood on it and slipped. I fell hard, the breath knocked out of me, but I was so focused that I was struggling back to my feet before I even realised that I'd fallen. That was when I heard the muffled sobs of a child crying.

"Maddy? Maddy, is that you?" I whispered into the dark space beneath the porch. "Maddy-monkey, it's Sandy. Are you okay, sweetheart?"

"Miss Sandy?" A little voice answered from the shadows. A moment later, a tiny body flung itself into my arms, sobbing out of control. "Granddaddy's in the fire! Please, please, save Granddaddy. I tried to get the hose to put the fire out, but it's too heavy."

My heart leapt into my throat. "Where's Granddaddy? Is he in his room? Where's Skye?"

"The man took her. Granddaddy's in the garden. The big boy hit him and he fell down, then they hit Miss Skylar and she fell down too." Maddy sobbed in my arms as I struggled to make sense of what she was saying. "Then the man and the boy screamed and yelled, and they picked up Miss Skylar and ran away. But Granddaddy's in there and he's too big for me to lift so I tried to get the hose but—"

"It's okay, sweetie," I interrupted her, hugging her tight. I heard footsteps and familiar male voices, and then a torch beam illuminated us.

"There's a hose here, and some fire extinguishers!" I heard Hemi's voice as they rushed past us, snatching up the fire fighting equipment from under the porch.

"There's a fire hydrant fitting over there, the hose should fit on that," I called over the noise, pointing in the direction of the old blue symbols painted on the pavement to mark the fixture. Hemi shouted something I couldn't hear and ran off in that direction, lugging the hose along between him and a couple of his comrades; I couldn't tell which ones.

Ignoring the pain in my knees and elbows from where I had fallen a moment earlier, I gathered Madeline up in my arms and carried the sobbing child back to our truck. There, I found Priyanka hovering nearby, looking terrified.

"Priya," I called her name breathlessly, pulling her gaze away from the fire. "I need your help, honey. This is Maddy. I need you to take care of her for me, okay? Stay with the truck if you can, but if you see anyone you don't know I want you to take her, run away, and hide. Do you understand?"

"Okies," Priya whispered, though she was obviously very frightened. I set Maddy back on her feet beside the older girl. As soon as she realised that Madeline was younger than she was, something protective came out in my little foundling. She took Maddy's hand without any further instruction, and led the little girl to hide in the gloom behind the truck, where they were out of sight.

Once the children were safe, I turned back to stare at the fire. I could see the silhouettes of my friends rushing back and forth, and heard the hiss of fire extinguishers and hoses running, but the smoke was thick and black. I remembered from my school days that smoke killed faster than fire ever did. If the doctor was unconscious in there, then we had to get him out before it was too late.

The motel's thick glass doors hung open, with only the faintest trickle of smoke oozing out of the ground floor. I hesitated for a second, then reached into the front seat of the truck and pulled out my backpack. I snatched out a singlet and a bottle of water, soaking the fabric thoroughly before I tied it over my nose and mouth.

"What are you doing?" Michael's voice startled me; I hadn't realised that he was there until he spoke. I glanced back and found him watching me with concern, his face and arms already smudged with soot.

"Doc's in there," I told him. "I'm going to get him out before it's too late, so either help me or get out of my way."

He didn't even bother to reply. In a single smooth movement, he slid his t-shirt up over his head and pulled it off, then grabbed the bottle of water from my hands. He followed me as I turned and ran back towards the burning building, my feet splashing through the puddles left by the rain and Hemi's attempts to fight the fire.

I heard Hemi shouting at us as we ducked through the open door, but I didn't stop to see what he was saying. Every single one of my senses was screaming at me, warning me that what I was doing was dangerous – potentially even lethal – but if I didn't do it then someone was guaranteed to die. Michael was a footstep behind me, forced to run in a half-crouch to keep his head clear of the smoke; his bulk was a hindrance in a situation like that.

There were no flames in the foyer, but the smoke hung thick and heavy in the air. I burst out into the central courtyard, where I could see that the flames had originated from the kitchen and crept up the inside of the building to engulf Skylar's bedroom and the roof above. The back end of the building was still untouched, but the smoke had saturated the area, filling the building in a deadly, billowing black miasma.

Careful to keep my head clear of the smoke as much as possible, I hurried across the garden. I could feel my feet crushing our precious baby plants, but I didn't care. The plants could be replaced; our friend couldn't.

"Where is he?" Michael's shout sounded like it came from miles away, even though he was right behind me. The noise of the flames was deafening, overwhelming all of my senses.

"Maddy said he was here. She said he was in the garden!" I shouted back, staring around frantically. Our doctor was not a small man, he shouldn't have been that hard to find. "I don't see him. You check the hydroponics room; I'll check the storage room."

I heard a vague grunt of agreement, and footsteps retreating behind me as I hurried in the direction of the room where we kept our spare supplies. The smoke was particularly thick in the doorway, and it took me a second to spot the human figure on the ground in the flickering half-light. I screamed for Michael as I dropped to my knees beside him. Stewart was half-conscious, but he moved weakly when he realised I was there.

"Turn it off." He coughed pathetically, and pointed at the wall. I suddenly realised that he had been trying to reach the main switchboard for the power, on the wall above our supplies. Understanding came a moment later; now that the power had come back on, it had the potential to keep feeding the fire far beyond our control. I leapt up and flicked the rows of switches into the off position as fast as I could.

By the time I was done, Michael had found us, and was already gathering the doctor over his shoulder in a fireman's carry. The doctor was struggling though, frantically trying to tell me something.

"Gas!" he grated, his voice so hoarse I could barely make out what he was saying. "Use that!"

Suddenly I realised that he was pointing at something, something half-hidden beneath the stacks of goods. I followed his finger and realised he was pointing at a huge fire extinguisher, one of the strange ones used for fighting special kinds of fire. I couldn't remember which kind, but I trusted him to know. Whether he was delirious or not, the doctor was a brilliant man. I took the hint, grabbed the extinguisher, then rushed after Michael as he hurried to get the doctor to safety.

In the courtyard, we parted ways. He headed for the exit, while I went for the kitchen. Yanking the safety clip out of the nozzle, I closed to within a few metres of the edge of the flame and pulled the trigger. A spray of thick powder exploded from the tip of the hose, and struck low at the base of the nearest flames. They retreated a few centimetres, and I advanced a few centimetres, focusing my efforts on one step at a time.

I could vaguely see the stove through the inferno, and wondered if that was the source of the fire. It was too hot to tell, though. Everything was melting. Sweat dripped down my skin, and occasionally I had to dance away to avoid getting burned.

Suddenly, a hand grabbed me from behind and pulled me back. I found the extinguisher snatched from my hand by a pair of strong, dark-haired youths, their faces wrapped in cloth just as mine was. It took a second for me to realise that it was Tane and his brother, who had come to take over from me. Iorangi gave me a shove towards the exit and shouted something that I couldn't make out, but I didn't need to hear it. The gesture was enough.

They'd stripped me of my means to do any good anyway, so I ran for the exit. The smoke had started to thin out, just a little bit enough to be significant. Beyond the exit, I saw Hemi bracing himself against the power of the fire hose he had aimed at our roof. I rushed to help him, but he shooed me away.

"We've got this. Go find your sister!" he yelled over the endless blast of water and the roar of the flames.

I had nothing to say to that.

I turned and ran back towards the Hilux, where I could see shadowy figures crouched around one another on the ground. As I got closer, I could see the two little girls and Michael kneeling beside the doctor, who was struggling to talk around a terrible, hacking cough. He was gesturing towards the north, but by the time I reached them he had lost the ability to speak.

It didn't seem to matter, Michael had heard enough. As soon as he heard me coming, he rose to his feet and turned to me to relay the tale. "He said that two men came wanting to trade this evening. They came from the north, and said they wanted to trade for food, but it was late so Doc tried to send them away.

"One of them panicked and hit him; he's not sure which one. He fell down and passed out for a minute, and when he woke up he heard Skye screaming at the men. Then there was a terrible crash and everyone started yelling. He managed to get into the garden before he passed out. Maddy said she saw the men carry Skylar away."

"So wherever she is, she's alive," I said, my voice husky from the smoke and exertion.

"Yes," he answered, but I could see the look in his eyes, and knew he was as concerned as I was. With good reason. These men could be anyone. They had set fire to our home and kidnapped my sister. They were dangerous. I felt my hands clench up, and I knew that the only way I'd be able to relax was when Skye was safely back home where I could protect her.

"Get your gun. We're going to get her back," I told Michael. My voice came out strangely, ice cold even though the anger I felt was red hot. Without waiting for his response, I discarded my makeshift mask, and dove into the Hilux to find the shotgun. Michael was a second behind me, grabbing his assault rifle out of the back seat. He let out a sharp whistle to call his dog to heel, and then he was a step behind me was I raced off towards the north.

"What are we going to do when we find them?" Michael's voice was urgent and concerned. "We don't know how many there are, or how well armed they are. They could have us outnumbered."

"First, we find them," I answered breathlessly, flicking my hair back out of my face, "and when we do, we'll improvise."

There was a grunt that told me he didn't quite care for my plan, but he had no choice. I was going whether he liked it or not, so his only option was whether or not he was going to help me. Adrenaline thrummed through my veins as I picked up the pace, my path illuminated by the glow of the fire, and the moon overhead. It was almost full, and its silvery glow cast our world in a strange mixture of black, white, and flame-orange.

Behind me, I heard Michael's feet on the asphalt and the panting of his dog beside him. In just a few minutes, we had passed the run-down old shops that flanked the northern edge of town, and were out in the wild countryside. The noise and smoke from the fire diminished until the only sounds I heard were our own footsteps and harsh breathing. How far had the strangers come? I could only guess – but to my surprise, the dog told us.

Just as we were passing a stand of dense bush, Alfred skidded to a stop and froze, sniffing the air sharply. Michael halted a second later, and the sound of his change in pace alerted me that something was out of place. By the time I returned to them, Michael was kneeling beside the dog and talking to him in the half-gibberish talk that humans instinctively used when talking to animals.

Taking the hint, I slipped the safety off my shotgun and approached the edge of the forest, examining it as best I could in the dim light of the moon. Even with my very human senses, I could see that there was an obvious trail leading deeper into the gloom. Several people had come this way; it was too dark to tell how many or how recently.

Suddenly, a voice pierced the darkness, a female voice raised in a blood-curdling shriek. It wasn't the sound of my sister in pain, though; it was the sound of an unknown woman screaming in fury. She was too far away for me to make out her words, but her anger gave us a fix on their location. I glanced at Michael and nodded; he returned the gesture, then fell in beside me as we crept deeper into the gloom.

Our stealth was unnecessary. The woman was still screaming, yelling abuse at someone that we couldn't see. As we rounded a bend in the narrow pathway, we could see the distant flicker of a camp fire, illuminating a small clearing amongst the trees. I held up a hand to halt Michael, then beckoned for him to follow me as I melted into the shadows beside the path. Together, we inched forward until we crouched between the ferns. Carefully, we parted the fronds so that we could see the scene unfolding in the clearing without being detected.

The woman was starvation thin and furious, with a shock of frizzy brunette hair and weather-worn skin that made it difficult to estimate her age. I couldn't make out the details of her face in the semi-darkness, but it was obvious the target of her ire was a man. She smacked him hard and yelled at him incoherently, then turned away holding her head in her hands.

"You were only supposed to trade!" she wailed, tugging at her hair. The man she'd struck cringed, and backed away. He was tall, but just as skinny as she was, with olive skin and dark hair; his face bore an expression of guilt. A teenage boy stood behind him, looking terrified.

I glanced across the clearing and saw three younger children of different ages huddled together, all looking equally frightened. Between the children and the adults lay a body slumped unconscious on the grass. Even from afar, I recognised the form as Skylar's. Her curly blonde hair fanned out across the grass, but she didn't seem to be restrained in any way.

"I swear, I didn't mean for this to happen," the man protested, holding his hands up in defence.

"I sent you up there to trade for food," the woman yelled, rounding on her husband with fury, "not to set their home on fire and steal their women!"

"It was an accident!" The man backed away, as though fearing another blow. "We panicked when they said no. We just wanted to grab something and run, but she surprised us and the gas cooker she was using got knocked over. What was I supposed to do? Leave her to burn to death?"

"It's my fault," the teenager spoke up suddenly, looking for all the world like he was about to cry. "I hit the old man. I... I was just so hungry, when he said no... I'm sorry, Mum..."

"Old man?" The woman spun around to face the teenager. "There was an old man? And you left him in there?"

"We couldn't find him." The man jumped to the teenager's defence, though the woman looked so weak from starvation that she probably couldn't have hurt either of them even if she'd wanted to. "We tried, but the smoke was getting too thick and he wasn't where we'd left him."

I glanced to my left at Michael, and saw an expression on his face that looked just the way I felt. This was not what we had expected. These people were not vicious, heartless marauders, but a starving family that had been looking for food. Whether we believed that it was an accident or not, it made sense. Then, suddenly, the dog began to growl.

The fight in the clearing continued unabated, and none of them seemed to have heard the growl. I glanced at Alfred and then at Michael, lifting a brow to ask the silent question. Michael shrugged, but I could just barely see the tension in his shoulders. The dog had heard or smelt something that it didn't like. When I reached out to touch the canine, I found his back was up and he was ready for a fight.

A second later, we heard the shriek.

It was a terrible, blood-curdling screech that froze me to the core, and halted the argument in a heartbeat. It was a noise both Michael and I had heard before, and we both knew very well what it meant. This was a moment that we had dreaded, but now it was here. The predatory dead had come south.

In a split second, we were presented with a choice. We could either grab my sister and run, leaving these people as a human sacrifice to buy us time, or we could try to save the very same people that had almost burnt our home to the ground. None of them had anything that even remotely resembled a weapon. They were completely helpless.

I glanced at the three tiny children, the youngest no older than four. The look on those little faces made the decision for me. If I wanted to save my species, it had to begin with the very thing that makes us human: our ability to cooperate and work together.

Michael was right beside me as I surged to my feet and lunged into the clearing, just as a second and third screech reverberated all around us. The teenager shouted in surprise when he saw us coming, but the noise only attracted the creatures to him. I saw a flicker of movement in the bushes on the opposite side of the clearing; a moment later, I levelled my shotgun and fired from the hip into the brush. A terrible howl told me that the buckshot had struck home.

"Get the kids behind us," I ordered sharply, catching the woman's eye. Without hesitation, she grabbed her son and husband, dragging them over to protect the children. I leapt over my sister's prone form and crouched on the far side of her, staring into the bushes, waiting for the creatures to come.

They didn't come. In fact, they did something far worse. They stayed hidden, screeching their horrifying noises, without exposing themselves. It was too dark for us to spot them in the undergrowth, unless we got lucky. They could flank us from any direction and our only warning would be if they howled.

"We need to retreat before they get behind us," I told the family. "Grab anything you can't live without – and I expect one of you to carry my sister if you want to live out the night. Do you understand?"

There was a chorus of agreement, followed by a flurry of activity. The people had almost nothing except a couple of small bags of things for the children. I heard a grunt as someone lifted Skye up, but I didn't dare to look away from the forest's edge.

"Michael," I called, waiting until I heard his response before I issued another command. "I want you to lead off. I'll cover the rear. Take them back to town. We'll work things out there."

There was another noise of agreement, and then I heard the sound of his footsteps retreating. I waited until I heard the others hurry off as well, then I back-pedalled after them, keeping an eye on the trees all around us and my ears alert for danger. As soon as I was out of the clearing, I turned and ran as hard as I could.

I caught up with the group a few moments later. With the children slowing them down, they had barely reached the road. There was another shriek, but it was further away now, which gave me a brief flash of hope. In the glow of the moonlight, I dimly saw the man carrying my sister just in front of me, casting fearful glances over his shoulder. I saw the woman stoop and pick up the smallest child. Michael shouldered his rifle and gathered up the next youngest.

We ran as hard as we could, with me in the rear to make sure no one got lost. The sound of harsh breathing and footsteps pounding over the asphalt drowned out everything else. For all our differences, there was one thing that united us, and it was the pure, animal terror of the beast we couldn't see, waiting to devour us if we stopped for a moment to catch our breath. Even the children seemed to understand that to lag behind was to die a horrible death.

Somehow, we made it back to the township. The screeches had faded further and further away, moving off in another direction. By some freak of fate, we had been spared to fight another day. Eventually, we drew to a ragged halt near the Hilux, where the raging fire lit our faces in a devilish glow.

Only then did I have a second to think about what we'd done, and who we had just saved. A heartbeat later, I made up my mind about what to do. The next step to going beyond survival was to find a way to forgive those who had wronged against us. Now was the time to practice what I hoped to one day preach.

"Put the little ones in the truck where we can protect them," I told Michael. He nodded and hurried to obey, opening the door to the rear cab so he could place the little child he was carrying safely inside. The woman hesitated for a moment, and then passed the toddler to him as well. Soon, all five children, including Priyanka and Maddy, were safely inside.

I looked at the man who carried my unconscious sister, and tilted my head towards the truck. Understanding my gesture, he carried her over and placed her gently in the passenger seat, and then stood back, looking at me with uncertainty. All of them were looking at me, I realised suddenly: the two strangers, their teenage son, Michael, Doc, and even the dog. They were waiting for me to say something, to make some monumental decision that would somehow make everything okay.

I drew a deep breath and fumbled with my thoughts for a moment, then looked at the strangers and carefully set an expression on my face that was both firm and kind at the same time. At least, I hoped it was; this whole leadership thing was kind of new to me.

"I don't think I need to tell you what you've done to us here," I gestured behind me, to the building wreathed in flame. Frantic figures ran back and forth, silhouetted against the fire: Hemi and his team, hard at work trying to extinguish the damage these strangers had done. The man and the teenager looked down, guilt clearly written across their faces. The woman glared at them, then looked back at me.

"They weren't meant to do that," she explained, obviously trying hard to keep her anger under control. "I only sent them to trade for food."

"I know. We heard everything." I shook my head and gave her the faintest of smiles. "Accidents happen, unfortunately. This was an accident. As such, I'm willing to offer you a choice. You can either leave now and take your chances on the road, or we can work out an alternative."

"What kind of alternative?" The woman's expression flickered; the firelight playing across her features made it hard to work out exactly what she was thinking. I took another deep breath and plunged ahead anyway.

"We need friends, miss. I think we both do. Friendship and trust are the only way we can prevent things like this from happening again." I pointed to the car full of children, their little faces ghostly pale as they stared at us through the windows. "It's the only way that we can protect them from the terrible things in the darkness. My alternative is this: stay with us and help us put this right, and then we can look towards the future together – for our children."

The strangers stared at me, looking shocked beyond words by the generosity of my offer. At first, they had no response, so I smiled and sweetened the deal a little. "We have food here, and a real doctor. This man beside me was a police officer, and still lives by the ethos to protect and serve. We are good people, and we're happy to share what we have with other good people, so long as those people are willing to help us in return."

"Help you to do what?" the woman asked softly, her expression flickering between hope and concern.

"To rebuild. To recreate what we lost." I reached out towards her and placed a gentle hand upon her shoulder. "For the sake of the next generation, we have to look to the future and stop living in the ruins of yesterday's world. We have to plan for tomorrow, and work towards a common goal. We have to find something to hope for.

"We've all spent the last ten years scavenging, but if we want to survive another decade, then we have to invest in our future together." I squeezed her shoulder and smiled at her, looking her straight in the eye. "My name is Sandrine McDermott, and I say that merely surviving is no longer enough."

# THE SURVIVORS

## BOOK III: WINTER

# Chapter One

"On the count of three. One, two, three – Lift!" I shouted. Right on command, we strained with every ounce of strength that we had, and the girder moved. First one inch, then another, then suddenly it came free completely. We shuffled the beam awkwardly out of the ruins of our motel, into the street beyond, and dumped it unceremoniously on the asphalt. Ash billowed up when it struck the ground, enveloping my filthy group in yet more dirt. It was starting to feel like I would never be clean again.

I ran my hand over my blackened brow and shot a glance towards the Hilux to check on the children. They were sleeping now, cuddled together like five exhausted puppies in the back seat of the truck. In the front seats, two of the adults from my original group sat recovering from their night's ordeal, given an exemption from the physical labour due to their injuries.

The doctor was fast asleep, but Skylar was not. She was wide awake, watching anxiously as we struggled to save as much as we could from the remains of our former home. When I looked her way, she caught my eye and waved tentatively. I smiled and waved back, then turned my attention back to the task at hand.

Despite everyone's best efforts, the western half of the motel had been reduced to blackened rubble by the fire that had raged through the night. We'd managed to save the rest of our home, though, including the storage rooms where we kept the majority of our supplies. The burned-out areas were still too hot to get inside safely, so we were on a retrieval mission while we waited for them to cool down. Everyone desperately needed food.

Although we were really too busy to get to know one another, I had learned the names of our newest members: Zain and Elira Yousefi. The names of their children were still a mystery to me, but there was too much work that needed to be done for me to worry about that right away. I brushed my hands off on my filthy cargo pants, and beckoned for Elira to follow me over to the truck.

By the time we arrived, Skye's door was open and she was halfway out. She didn't get far, though – a second after she stood up, she put a hand up to her head and plopped right back down in her seat again.

"I told you to stay put," I scolded her gently, though there was no anger behind my words. Skylar was my sister, my one living relative, and I loved her so much it hurt.

"I'm just a little concussed, I'm fine," she protested, trying to stand again. This time I caught her and sat her back down myself.

"Don't worry, you can help in a minute. This is Elira," I said, gesturing to the woman behind me, "Elira, this is my sister, Skylar."

"Please, call me Elly." Elira bobbed her head in a half-bow. Despite the fact that her family were responsible for accidentally starting the fire, I had come to like her in the few hours I'd known her. She was a soft-spoken, no-nonsense woman in her mid-thirties, with wild brown hair and a faint Middle Eastern accent. "My husband and I came to this country with the intention of becoming Kiwis. I prefer to use a Kiwi name. I am very sorry about what my foolish husband and son did to you, Skylar. They panicked."

"Yeah... I'm sorry we had to meet like that, too," Skye replied, absently rubbing the bruise on her forehead.

"You'll make it worse if you rub it too much," I scolded her softly, reaching up to capture her wrist and pull her hand away from the bruise. Skye gave me a long-suffering look, but I just smiled back at her. On a sudden, spontaneous impulse, I pulled her into a hug. "Sis, I need you to help Elly get some food into these kids, please – it looks like they haven't eaten in days. There's a camp stove in one of the bags in the back. Can you two get it started? I'll bring you some food as soon as we find something that looks edible."

"Okay," Skye agreed readily. We looked at Elly, who also nodded her agreement.

"I cannot thank you enough for accepting us after what we put you through," Elly added, reaching out to take my hand. I glanced at her and found her studying me with eyes that shone with gratitude. "I thought there was no kindness left in this old world."

"Just remember what I said," I told her softly, giving her hand a gentle squeeze.

"Yes. For the children, we must work together." She cast a glance at her sleeping progeny, and then she looked back at me and sighed heavily. "I would do anything to give them a chance at a better life."

"And we will," I assured her. "Just remember that, so we can keep up the strength and determination to protect them – through the good times and the bad."

I'd never been much of a public speaker, but over the last week or so I had found myself with the right words to say in the most unexpected moments. I guessed that my new-found eloquence was a side-effect of finding a goal that I really cared about: the idea of building a city, and bringing together the last survivors of the plague to try and craft a better future for all of us.

As I left Elly and Skylar and returned to the burned shell of our former home, I found myself wondering at the changes I'd begun to notice in my own personality. I glanced around at the others, all working hard to salvage what they could from the ruins, and suddenly realised that they were all following my commands. It was bewildering to think that after ten years living as a recluse, I was becoming a leader.

Someone had to, though. Michael had been the leader of the small group of survivors I joined over the summer, but he readily admitted that he hated being in command. He led because he had to, but he was happy to let that responsibility go to someone else, someone he trusted implicitly. I still wasn't sure how I felt about the way I'd just sort of fallen into the role, but at least I knew I could rely on myself to do the right thing for everyone.

Michael stood watch half-way between the building and the truck, looking tense and anxious. I knew that he longed to be helping more directly, but I needed him to stand guard in case the mutants returned while we were unaware. I went over to check on him on my way back. He glanced at me when he heard my footfalls, and gave me a faint smile. "No sign of trouble."

"That's strange. I didn't think they were intelligent enough to know when to pick their battles," I replied. I leaned up to kiss my fiancé softly, trailing my fingers across his cheek. We were both equally filthy, but even through the layer of ash I could taste the sweetness of his kiss. It reassured me and bolstered me up, even in the face of exhaustion.

"I'm a bit worried about Anahera's tribe," he admitted. I shot him a curious look, before suddenly understanding dawned.

"Oh, my God – you're right!" I gasped. A sudden stab of panic struck me right in the chest, and stole away my breath. "I didn't even think about them. They're alone and defenceless. They don't even have any weapons. What if the mutants circled around and went to their camp instead?"

Michael shot me a worried look. "We should check in, and warn them."

"I agree." I pulled my walkie-talkie off my belt, switched it on, and quickly tuned the radio to the frequency that we had established for communicating with our neighbours. As soon as the radio was in band, we heard a voice screaming.

"Hello? Hello? Is anyone out there? Christ, we need help! Where is everyone?"

The voice was female, and although it was a struggle to make out her words, I could hear panic in her voice. Behind her, we heard the crash of flesh on wood, and the screams and groans of people in pain. Then, a shriek. A deathly, blood-curdling shriek that sent a shiver down my spine like a bolt of ice. I shot a wide-eyed look at Michael. Bile rose in the back of my throat, but I fought it back down and took a deep breath to try and calm myself. I had to keep a clear head if we were going to help our friends at all.

"Michael, I need you to go get the guns," I said quietly, pointing him towards the old video store that adjoined the motel. "When Maddy started having nightmares, I got Skye to move all the weapons into the downstairs office. It should be locked up. I want you to get them, and make sure everyone that's strong enough to use one is armed and trained to use at least one of those guns."

"I thought we were going to hide them?" he asked, staring at me uncertainly. I just shook my head.

"We've got a simple choice here. Either we take the risk that one of them might turn against us later, or we watch our friends die now. I know which one I pick." I fished a bunch of keys out of my pocket and offered them to him. He nodded once, took the keys, and hurried off. While he was gone, I turned my attention to the radio. "Anahera, it's Sandy – can you hear me?"

"Sandy! Oh, Sandy, thank God, I was starting to lose hope." Anahera's voice was shaking; I couldn't tell if it was from fear, adrenaline, or both. "We need help, desperately. Creatures attacked us a few hours ago and they've got us trapped. They killed two of my boys; there's only four of us left and one is seriously wounded. Can you help us?"

"We're on our way," I replied, trying my best to keep my voice calm and reassuring. "How many creatures have you seen?"

"I saw four but I think there's more," she answered breathlessly. "I can't be certain."

"Just hang on, and stay put. Do not open that door until you hear my voice. We're coming to get you," I told her resolutely. "Do you understand? We're coming to get you, Ana."

"I understand. Please... please, hurry."

"We will," I answered. "We'll be there soon. Just stay safe."

I clicked the radio off and put it back on my belt, then I looked at the people milling around. Several of them were looking at me. They weren't stupid, they knew something was up. Although it went against every one of my instincts, I had to get their attention all at once. I drew a long, deep breath, and pushed my instincts aside.

"Everyone, urgent meeting," I shouted at the top of my lungs. "Drop whatever you're doing and assemble in front of the truck!"

I repeated myself a couple more times, then I raced over to the truck as well. There, I found Skylar and Elly watching me with trepidation. I forestalled their questions with a gesture, and vaulted up to stand on the bonnet of the car so that I could be clearly seen by everyone in the group.

Within a few minutes, all the adults had gathered around and stood looking up at me, waiting to hear what I had to say. I looked down at them, feeling a strange mix of pride and fear, but I did what I had to do without hesitation.

"As of right now, everyone is being issued with a gun," I told them, loudly enough that no one could pretend they hadn't heard later on. "I expect you to learn to use it, but to only use it in self-defence. These guns officially belong to me, and if anyone is caught using their weapon against another member of this group, or even threatening someone with it, they will lose the privilege indefinitely.

"There is a lethal enemy in the area, and I need all of you to help me protect our innocents. Can I rely on you?" I looked down at Zain and Elly. They both nodded, though Zain's expression was harder to read than his wife's. "Good, because there is a complication."

This time I looked at Hemi, who stood with his brethren gathered around him. "As we speak, your home is under siege. I'm sorry to be the one to tell you that two of your friends are dead. I have a plan to save the rest of them, but I'm going to need everyone's help."

"Just tell us what we have to do, and we'll do it," Zain said suddenly, his voice clear as a bell in the silence that followed my announcement. I glanced at him, and saw the same unreadable expression on his face as before, but there was something in his eyes that I understood. I nodded to him, and then I looked at Hemi and his friends, who stood in mute shock.

"Hemi, Tane, and Iorangi." I looked at each of them as I named them. "We're going to go rescue everyone that's still alive. Time is of the essence, so we'll take your quad bikes. Michael will issue each of you with an assault rifle and teach you how to use it. Make sure you all have a water bottle. We're not going to have time to eat, so we'll just have to go hungry until we get back. Go meet Michael in the video store; I'll join you once I'm done here."

Hemi stared at me for a second, and then grabbed his friends and rushed off. Once they were gone, I looked down at the people that remained.

"Each of you will be given a small handgun, something light and easy to use," I explained. "We'll work on getting you cleared to use the bigger guns later. Skye and Doc, you're in charge of protecting the children. I want you to feed them and move them into my loft as soon as possible. It'll be a tight fit, but at least we can defend it easily until we decide what we're going to do next.

"Everyone else, I want you on salvage duty. Gather everything you can out of the ruins and move it into the bottom level of the video store – Skye will show you where. If you finish before we get back, just get inside and stay there. We don't know what these creatures will do next. If you must go outside, then take someone with you. No one goes out alone.

"I'm leaving Alfred here, and he knows what those things smell like. If he starts to growl, listen to him." I paused and glanced around again. "Does everyone understand?"

Grunts and soft-spoken words of agreement met my orders. I nodded once more and hopped down off the bonnet of the truck. As I started towards the video store, Skylar fell into step beside me. Once we were out of earshot of the others, she turned a pleading look on me. "Can't you stay here? I'm scared. I don't want you to go."

It was a tone I'd never heard from my strong-willed baby sister. I glanced at her, and found her watching me with eyes that seemed way too big for her face.

Assuming she was afraid of our newcomers, I reached out and slid a reassuring arm around her shoulders. "It's okay, they won't hurt you. They didn't mean to hurt you last time. You'll have Doc right here, plus Ropata and Richard as well – you know you're safe with them."

"What?" She blinked at me owlishly. "No, I mean, I'm scared for *you*. You're going into battle. You might get hurt – or worse. I don't want you to end up like Sophie and Dog."

"Oh." I blinked right back at her, processing her words. "I have to go, Skye. Anahera's in danger, and she's my friend. If I can do anything to help her, then I'm obligated to do it. I wouldn't be able to live with myself if I just left her to die."

"I know," Skylar lamented, scuffing her toe on the dirty asphalt. "But I still don't want you to go."

"Are you just being a big baby?" I teased, trying to use humour to lighten her mood. "And after all the effort you've put into trying to convince me that you're a grown up now."

My reward was a cheeky smile and a nudge in the side. "I am grown up. All grown-ups worry about their big sisters. You're the only family I've got now."

"Well, if I have any say in the matter, then that's going to change." I wrapped my arms around her and drew her into a tight hug. "These people are going to be our family now. All of them. I need you to be a big sister to those little kids, and I need you to be strong for me. I trust you to keep things organised while I'm gone."

"I will." Skylar hugged me back and then released me. "Just… stay safe, okay?"

I sketched a playful salute, then I pulled away from her and hurried the last few steps to the entrance of the video store. The stench of smoke was thick on the air, but aside from a layer of soot on the front door and the window sills, the building had survived unscathed. I shoved aside a few broken movie cases and made my way behind the counter, where I found Michael instructing the chosen few on the use of automatic weaponry.

He glanced up when I entered and smiled at me; even in the tension of the moment, his smile made my heart race. The others looked at me, and each of them gave me a nod. Hemi's face was a grim mask, and his friends looked no better.

I joined their ranks and gave the young man's shoulder a reassuring squeeze. "We'll get to her in time, Hemi. I promise."

"No matter how fast we get there, it'll be too late for the guys that are already dead." Hemi looked miserable, and his shoulders sagged beneath my touch.

"Then we'll just have to make sure no one else joins them, right?" I gave him a gentle shake, and looked at the ring of faces around me. One by one, they nodded their agreement. Sensing that morale was at an all-time low, I looked each of them in the eye to try and assess their state of mind.

Michael looked as determined as I felt. He met my eye squarely, his jaw set in the look I'd come to know so well. His smile was reassuring. The others were not so confident. Tane's face mirrored Hemi's; they looked sad and completely bereft of hope, and neither of them would meet my eye.

Iorangi was another story altogether. When our eyes met, I saw hot rage surging behind his impassive mask. He was angry, really, really angry. I drew a deep breath to steady myself, and then set about the difficult task of rallying my troops.

"Guys, I need you to be here with me," I said softly, sympathetically, reaching out to my friends to try and give them hope. "Anahera is relying on us. We can still save her and the others, but we need to work as a team. It's the only way we'll have a chance. Can I rely on you?"

Unsurprisingly, Michael was the most vocal of the group and supported me without hesitation. Iorangi joined in a moment later, though I could see on his face he was motivated more by revenge for his fallen friends than any real hope of success. His older brother glanced up at me when I spoke, his gaze lingering thoughtfully on my face, but something about my words did seem to stir him. A few seconds after the others, his voice joined in, leaving only Hemi quiet and withdrawn.

"Hey." I shifted my attention to the young man, and put my hands on his shoulders. "I need you, too, man. Your mum needs you."

"Damn, Sandy. I don't know if I can do this." Hemi's voice was laced with despair. "I'm no fighter, man. I'll just get in the way, and then Mum will die."

"Don't talk like that," I protested. "Your friends believe in you – I believe in you. I know you can do this." I was studying him closely enough that I could see he wasn't entirely convinced, so I decided to switch tack. "Do you remember when we first met?"

"Yeah, of course," he said, nodding. "That pig, man. How could I forget?"

"Right, the pig. And do you remember what you said to us afterwards?" I didn't wait for him to respond, but supplied him with the answer. "You said that you didn't know what you would have done if we hadn't arrived when we did. You called us heroes. Do you remember that?"

"Well, not the exact words, but yeah, I remember." He was staring at me now, trying to figure out where I was going. I didn't keep him waiting long.

"This is your chance to learn what it takes to be a hero," I elaborated. "None of us are soldiers. We fight because we have to, to preserve what's ours. That's how heroes are born. We're going to teach you, and we're going to save your mum at the same time." I tugged him into a quick hug, then pushed him back and looked at him again. "Can you do this for us? For her?"

This time, there was fire burning in his eyes. "Yeah, okay. Yeah. I can do this." He looked around at the others and saw conviction written across every face. That seemed to bolster him up even more. At last, he puffed up his chest and looked me right in the eye. "Hell, yeah. I can do this. Let's go!"

"Good lad." I grinned at him and gave his shoulders a squeeze, then I released him and looked at the others. My little pocket-sized, rag-tag army. There were only five of us, but we had determination and courage on our side.

It would be enough. It had to be enough.

# Chapter Two

The quad bike's engine thrummed beneath me as we bounced along the overgrown path towards Lake Ruatuna. Even though it was the first time that Michael or I had driven one of the little bikes, we were rattling along at breakneck pace, exercising just enough caution to keep ourselves from getting killed.

I spent half the time standing up in the saddle, bracing myself with my knees as we passed over uneven ground. Through the bike's suspension, I could feel the change in texture as we moved from the bush into the emerald tunnel lined with old railway sleepers. We were getting closer. A branch reached out and tried to grab my hair, but I ducked beneath it at the very last moment. I gained a few scratches on my cheeks from accidents early on, but I was a quick study – the vengeful trees with their grabbing claws wouldn't get me again. They were certainly trying, though.

It was the height of midday, yet the world we were travelling through was all shadows, ferns, and dappled light. We were jumpy and on high-alert, fully expecting one of the creatures to leap out at us at any moment, but nothing had so far. If they were in the area, then their attention was elsewhere.

I held up one hand to signal the others to halt, and then eased off the throttle and let my bike cruise to a stop. Ahead of us, the side passage that led towards the village opened up, dark, ominous, and too narrow to ride through safely.

"We'll leave the bikes here and go the rest of the way on foot," I said, looking back at the others. "I want to be able to make a quick getaway if we have to."

A chorus of determined noises answered me. No one questioned my orders; they just accepted them. It was a feeling that left me both proud and confused. Even Michael deferred to my judgement; he seemed relieved that someone else had taken on the burden of leadership. Our footsteps rustled in the grass as we dismounted and wheeled our bikes around so that they were facing the right direction for when the time came to flee.

While the others were preparing for combat, I pulled out my walkie-talkie. I quickly checked in with Skylar to let her know that we'd arrived safely, and then I switched the band over to Anahera's channel.

"Anahera, are you still there? Come in, Anahera."

It was the longest twenty seconds of my life before someone picked up on the other end – but the person who answered wasn't Anahera.

"Sandy?" The voice was male, and it sounded terrified. It took me a second to recognise him.

"Wiremu? Is that you?" I asked, keeping my voice as calm as possible in hopes that it would rub off on the others. Behind me, I could feel the men gathering to listen. "Is everyone all right?"

"No." The man was struggling to keep his fear under control, but I could tell his heart was racing a mile a minute from the way he was panting into the radio. "Anahera fainted. From blood loss, I think. I don't know what to do. The things are still out there. I can hear them growling."

I swore under my breath.

"She said someone was injured – she didn't say that it was her." I looked back at the boys behind me, my face a grim mask. I clicked the send button down and spoke into the radio again. "We're not far away now, and we're coming to get you. Where are you?"

"W-we're in the pantry." The man laughed, but there was a hysterical edge to it. Behind him, I heard the faint sound of a thud and an inhuman scream. His laugh turned into a gasp. "Aw, Christ. They won't give up. Sweet mother, we're going to--"

"Stop." It was not a request, it was an order. "You're not going to die. We're coming to get you right now, and we'll be there in a few minutes. I need you to be ready to move the moment we get there. If I remember correctly, you guys have a couple of old knapsacks in there, don't you?"

There was a pause, and in the background I heard Wiremu shifting around. "Yeah, there's some here. You want me to fill them up with food?"

"Yes," I answered simply. "You probably aren't going to be able to come back again, so grab everything you can carry that won't weigh you down too much. Fill the knapsacks up, put them on, and be ready to run the second that you hear my voice. Okay?"

"O-okay." He stumbled over the word, sounding so frantic and terrified that it made my heart lurch. "Please, please hurry; I'm not sure how much longer the door will hold."

"We're coming right now." I tried to be firm and reassuring to hide the shaking in my own voice. "Just hold on a few more minutes."

There was a wordless grunt of agreement from the man on the other end. With no more time to waste on talking, I clicked the radio off and tucked it onto my belt. I looked back, and found myself ringed by four very determined faces, each clutching his weapon as though his life depended on it.

I nodded to them and unslung the shotgun off my back. In a swift, well-practiced motion, I slipped off the safety and loaded a shell into the chamber. A chorus of soft metallic clicks told me that the others were ready as well, so I didn't delay any further. I spun around and charged down the narrow green corridor at a run.

My heart hammered in my chest, but there was something cathartic about finally being in action instead of just worrying about it. I'd always been the kind of person that chose diplomacy over brute force unless I had no other choice, but now I felt surprisingly calm and rational. I was ready for this. We were ready for this. We could do it. I thought the pep talk had been to rally the troops, but apparently it had worked just as well on me.

My feet crunched over the leaf litter as we charged through the passageway, then out into the fields beyond. What greeted me was a scene of carnage. The last time I'd visited that little fortress, it had been a pleasant, picturesque sight, surrounded by fields full of animals grazing peacefully. Now, every single one of those poor farm animals lay dead and dismembered, torn to pieces. I snatched a deep breath to calm myself and ran on, trying to ignore the smell of death hanging on the air.

I leapt over a mound of entrails that I chose not to try and identify, and powered my way up the hill towards the fortress itself. The doors hung open, still damaged from the recent fire; just inside the entrance, we found the first human corpse. There wasn't much left, just a tattered heap of skin and bones with half a face attached. The organs were all gone and the puddle of blood spread in all directions; there was no way the man could have survived.

Another body lay not far beyond the first, and it was in an equal state of disarray. His face was completely gone, but I recognised him from the tattered remains of his favourite old plaid shirt.

Honi. His name had been Honi. I'd known him. I'd counted him as a friend.

I swallowed and tried not to look at Honi's corpse, but it was hard. Every death was a step closer to the permanent annihilation of our species. A death was no longer just a sad event worthy of mourning – it was an absolute tragedy for all of humankind. What was even harder was the knowledge that yet another one of my friends was dead and gone. I had so few left that each of them was precious to me.

If we didn't hurry, then more friends would end up like that. We could not allow that to happen. I shot a quick look around us, then sprinted across the clearing towards the nearest wall. The compound our Maori friends had built over the years was a maze, but it wasn't a big one. I knew the layout well enough.

The pa had been built up around an old yacht club, which was one of the few buildings that had survived the fire relatively unscathed. It was scorched with soot even weeks later, but it was still intact. The door hung ajar and I could see into the hallway beyond. Without hesitation, I threw myself down that narrow passageway, half-expecting to get attacked at any moment. Nothing sprang at me, but the moment I was inside I could hear the low, guttural growls and thuds of a creature on the offensive.

A creature. Just one. That was worrying. Anahera said they'd been attacked by at least four – where were the others?

I could feel Michael's protective bulk at my back as I crept forward, keeping myself low to the ground to present as small a target as possible. My ears were alert for every sound, but the only thing I could hear above the sound of our breathing was the uneven thump of flesh on wood.

Suddenly, the creature howled in rage and there was a louder thump than before, followed by an ominous cracking sound. I heard guttural human cries behind it, muffled but terrified. The thing had almost finished breaking through the door.

My shoes crunched across the debris that littered the floor as I followed the noise towards the kitchen. It took all of my willpower to move slowly and cautiously, and not give in to the urge to run. We passed a doorway. I swung my weapon around to scan the empty room, found nothing, and moved on.

The kitchen was the next door on the left. I took a long, deep breath to steady my racing heart, and then silently gestured Hemi and the brothers to watch the halls around us for trouble. Michael was a step behind me as I slipped around the corner and into the kitchen, my protective knight that refused to let me out of his sight.

The creature had its back to us, and was distracted by its desire to break through the door and get at the helpless prey within. It yowled in rage and reached up high, its fingers leaving bloody trails on the warped door. Michael lifted his gun and prepared to fire, but I held up my hand to forestall him. It took a second before understanding dawned on his face: the door wasn't all that thick. If we fired at the creature from behind, then chances were good that we'd also hit the people huddled inside the pantry.

He nodded and looked to me for guidance. I took a moment to consider my options, then decided that the one I least wanted to do was unfortunately the best. With a gesture to Michael to keep him from following me, I stepped forward to do the unthinkable. I walked towards the howling undead.

It didn't seem to notice me. At least, not at first. I managed to get within three feet of it without being seen, and then I circled around it to the left and carefully lined up my shot. Just as I was preparing to fire, it finally realised I was there and turned to stare at me with wild, bloodshot eyes. A horrifying shriek escaped from its bloody jaws.

That blood probably belonged to one of my friends, I realised with a detached certainty. But in that moment of danger, something happened that I still wasn't used to. Clarity. I didn't even flinch at the sound. I just pulled the trigger, and a blast of buckshot delivered at point blank range reduced the creature's head to a pulverised mass of flesh. I fired again, and a second shell sent the writhing mass tumbling away. It wasn't dead, and it wouldn't be unless we set it on fire, but that didn't matter. It couldn't do us any substantial harm without a head.

Cold, calm, and collected, I fired one last time, reducing the creature's legs to splinters of bone and flesh. "And stay down."

When I glanced back, I caught Michael staring at me with surprise on his face, but I didn't have time to ask what was wrong. I could hear the sound of human voices shouting from the other side of the door, begging for help, even praying. They were the most important thing, and everything else could come later.

"It's us," I called through the door, tapping on it with my knuckles. "Open up; we need to get out of here before those things come back."

"Praise the Lord!" someone cried. I wasn't sure which one it was, but it didn't really matter. It was a sentiment shared by everyone. I heard the sound of heavy objects being moved, and then the door was flung open from within. The group looked wrung out and exhausted from their ordeal, but they were ready to move in a few seconds. Anahera was still unconscious, so two of the men lifted her between them and carried her towards the door.

"You have no idea how glad we are to see you," Wiremu said, sounding terrified and exhausted.

"Oh, I have some idea," I answered dryly, then I glanced back at Michael and the others. "We need to get out of here, and I don't think we're going to be able to come back. If you have room in your gear, grab any spare food you can carry and let's get out of here."

He nodded and hastily grabbed whatever extra supplies he could out of the pantry. I quickly shoved a few things into my empty backpack, but not enough to hinder my ability to flee. Within less than a minute, we were all ready to go.

A blood-curdling screech and a human shout from the doorway warned me that we'd finished just in time. A few seconds later, I heard the sound of high-powered bullets being fired in an enclosed space. By the time I reached the door, the creature was down and twitching.

"Just one?" I shot Hemi a worried look. He nodded and lowered his rifle. "There should be at least two more. Where are the rest of them?"

"Somewhere else," Michael replied. "Would you rather they were here?"

"Definitely – then we could take care of them and not have to worry anymore," I answered dryly, shaking my head. "It doesn't matter. Let's just get out of here before the damn things find us again. Tane, Iorangi, cover the rear. Hemi, you stay in the middle with your friends. Make sure nothing gets near them, and no one falls behind. Michael, you're with me."

A chorus of grunts acknowledged my orders. As I moved off in the lead, I heard my friends falling into formation behind me. We had to move at a slightly more sedate pace than before, but we still made good time. Nothing jumped us along the way; while I should have been glad for that fact, under the circumstances, it just made me even more nervous.

"Everyone, keep your eyes peeled," I shouted over the sound of our running feet and harsh breathing. "I smell a trap, and it stinks worse than week-dead fish."

More grunts. No one seemed to have the willpower to answer me at that moment, but it wasn't necessary. They heard me, and that was all that mattered. A few seconds later, we burst out into the courtyard, and raced past the bodies of the fallen on our way out the door. Someone cried out again at the sight of the dead men, but I couldn't tell who it was.

No matter how much we might have wanted to stay and bury the dead, there was simply no time. We passed them and hurried down the ramp outside the complex, heading for the forest. A moment later, I was running through cool shadow, but this time it wasn't a relief. This time, it definitely felt like the darkness only concealed death.

Nothing happened, though, and that was the worst part. We made it to the far side safely, and tumbled out into the clearing where the bikes waited, but there was no sign of where the mutant undead had gone. The tension was just about killing me, but an old saying kept ringing in my mind: 'Don't look a gift horse in the mouth.'

"Michael, I want you up front with Anahera," I instructed, pointing him towards one of the big quad bikes. "Take the lead, and don't stop for anything. Your task is to get her home safely so Doc can fix her up. Got it?"

"Got it," Michael agreed, hurrying over to his bike. The others helped him to load the unconscious woman in front of him, and then he was off.

"Everyone else, double up. I'll cover the rear and make sure nothing follows us." I made a quick gesture for them to fall in, and they jumped to obey. In less than a minute, they were ready to go. I shooed them off, then hopped on my own little bike and headed after them, keeping an eye peeled for trouble.

The scenery flashed past on either side of me in a river of verdant green, but the ground beneath me was rough. I stood up in the seat and braced myself against the uneven trail, my bike bouncing and juddering over railway sleepers hidden under the thick grass. Within a few minutes, we'd successfully traversed the long tunnel of the old train line, and I saw my companions up ahead turning off to make their way into the brush beyond. I glanced back over my shoulder to check the trees behind us, but I saw nothing.

Unfortunately, that also meant that I didn't see whatever was hidden under the grass in front of me. I faintly heard a thud, and then I found myself flying head-over-heels. I had enough presence of mind to try to tuck and roll, but it wasn't enough. I landed messily. My forehead struck something hard, and I blacked out.

# Chapter Three

When I came to, the only sounds I could hear were the peaceful tones of nature: the trill of birds in the trees, the wind in the leaves, and the faint, low growl of a predator stalking nearby.

Wait. A predator?

My eyes snapped open to a sight that I had never wanted to see. Squatting beside me was one of the mutants, blood still dripping from its jowls. It was just sitting there, watching me, covetously stroking my belly with its horrid fingers. For reasons that only it knew, it hadn't attacked me yet.

My gut twisted in disgust. Even though my body ached from the fall, every one of my instincts screamed at me in unison to get away from that horrible dead thing before it changed its mind and decided to hurt instead of pet. I rolled away and came up to my feet in a fighter's crouch, fully expecting the thing to attack me at any second.

It didn't, though. It just sat there, staring at me, looking almost… contented.

And then realisation struck me. It was drenched in blood; it had killed recently, and already eaten its fill. It was playing with me, like a cat plays with a mouse even though it's not hungry. It would kill me for fun if it decided that I no longer amused it.

"Screw you, buddy," I told it quietly, side-stepping around the languid undead in search of a weapon. Where was my shotgun? It wasn't on my back, so it must have fallen off when I'd taken my tumble. The grass was so long that I wouldn't see it until I stepped on the damn thing. With no other choice, I snatched up an old branch that lay on the ground at my feet, and armed myself with that while I hunted for my gun.

The mutant didn't seem to care much. It was perfectly content to sit there, watching me, as if amused by my fighting spirit. I can't say that I felt the same way, but at least that gave me time. A little bit of time. How much time? A few seconds, a few minutes?

I spotted my little dirt bike sprawled in the long grass and circled around towards it, careful not to turn my back on the mutant. One glance was enough to tell me that it had been damaged beyond repair by the crash; the entire front half was all bent out of shape. A glint of steel beneath it gave me hope, though. I shoved the bike aside, to find my shotgun beneath it.

Not a moment too soon, either. Just as I dropped the branch and darted down to grab the gun, I heard a low, deep growl in the bushes behind me. Instinct kicked in; I flicked off the safety, spun, and fired from the hip. Shrapnel tore through the creature that had been creeping up behind me and sent it tumbling off into the grass. I swung back to finish off the lazy mutant that had been watching me, only to find that it had vanished while I was distracted.

I swore beneath my breath, but there was no time to stop and look for it now. None of us had any idea how many of the things existed, or if the mutated plague was spreading. There could have been dozens, even hundreds. They could be anywhere. I was not about to stick around and find out. I spun on a heel and raced off into the brush as fast as my legs could take me.

My feet crunched over the leaf litter as I dove into the shadows amongst the trees, and ran for home. So long as I didn't lose my way, I could be there in a couple of hours. It wasn't far, as the crow flies. I wasn't a crow so I couldn't go in a straight line, but I was well-adept at racing through the wild, overgrown world that New Zealand had become in the decade since her population had vanished.

There was a problem, though. My head throbbed in time with the pounding of my feet. I'd spent enough time alone to have a good sense of my own body, its limitations, and its needs. Right now, it wasn't happy with me. I estimated that I'd probably sustained a mild concussion, and running was the last thing I should be doing.

Although I'm no doctor, I spent a lot of time reading and I was aware enough to recognise the symptoms. My limbs weren't responding quite the way they should, and my vision was a little blurred around the edges. I was alert, though, and fully awake, which were both good signs so soon after being knocked unconscious. Judging by the angle of the light filtering through the trees, I'd been unconscious no more than half an hour; it was still early afternoon, and the sunbeams came almost straight down from above.

"Just keep running," I told myself softly, using the sound of my own voice to keep me going. "It's not far. Just a little bit more. Michael will be worried about you. Just keep running, okay? Okay. Good girl."

The undergrowth was old and thick, but I knew the pathways, and I knew all of Mother Nature's tricks. I knew which trees would have tangling roots that would try to grab my feet. I knew which bushes hid thorns, and which ones were safe to cut through. They were lessons I'd learned the hard way, but they were ones that I would never forget.

Eventually, I reached the edge of the trees, where I slowed to a jog. The sun seemed entirely too bright as I stepped out of the comfortable shade and into the fields beyond. Waist-length grass swayed placidly in the breeze, but it felt like every movement was hiding an enemy. I didn't like that feeling, not one bit. I felt exposed, and a little befuddled. The light stung my eyes and made my head hurt.

"Just... keep going. Walk for a bit, but keep going," I said softly, trying to keep my spirits up. "It's not far. Where are our tracks? I should be able to find them, then I can follow them home." I nodded to myself and set off with renewed determination, using my instincts like a homing pigeon to guide my way back to where my family was waiting for me.

I made it a few hundred paces before my vision began to blur again, and my balance faltered. Whether I liked it or not, I was going down for a bit, so I chose to sit rather than fall. I plopped down on my backside in the grass, and dug my water bottle out of my backpack. The water helped; it cooled my throat as it flowed down, and left me feeling refreshed.

"Okay... okay. You need to keep moving," I ordered myself softly. "Up we get. Come on, Sandy."

Getting up again was harder than sitting down, but I made it. I tried to run, but all I managed was an unsteady trot. That was an unsustainable method of travel, so I settled for walking. I knew better than most that a person could walk further than she could run, particularly when that person was dumb enough to go getting herself a concussion.

"Shut up, Self Doubt," I scolded my inner demon irritably, and squeezed my eyes closed for a second to try and steady myself. When I opened them, the world was spinning. "Whoa. Okay, that's not a good sign. I'm also talking to myself. Some people say that's not healthy, but you know what?" I paused again, and took a sip of my water, then continued where I left off. "Most of those people are dead. So, stuff it. Just keep going, Sandy. You can do it."

Normally, I wasn't one to hold conversations with myself. Ten years of hiding from danger had driven that trait right out of me. However, there were some times when you needed to. I remembered that you were supposed to talk to people with concussions, to keep them awake. There was no one to talk to me now, except for myself. I was used to being self-reliant, so that was nothing unusual to me.

I plodded along carefully, paying close attention to every twinge and complaint that my body had to offer so that I could keep track of how functional I was. It was getting harder to move, to the point where I was putting one foot carefully in front of another to keep my balance steady. It wasn't the easiest task in the world when my body was in such a disagreeable mood, but it seemed to work.

As I walked, I sipped my water to keep myself refreshed. If I estimated my timing right, Michael and the others should reach home very soon, and when they did they were bound to notice that I was missing. A few minutes later, the radio on my belt crackled to life.

"Sandy?" Michael's voice was crackly and distant, but clear enough that I could make him out. "Sandy, where the hell are you? Please respond."

I picked the radio up, and answered him. "I'm here. I had an accident, but I'm okay. Mostly okay. I'll be home in a couple of hours."

"Jesus, you just about gave me a heart attack," he answered; his relief was so audible that I could detect it in his voice even through the walkie-talkie. "Wait – what do you mean by 'mostly okay'?"

"I took a bit of a tumble," I admitted, absently rubbing my eyes. When had the sun gotten so bright? It hurt just to look around. "I've got a mild concussion, but I should be fine. Add it to the list, right? Seems like you're the only one that doesn't have a head injury right now."

"Head injuries are no laughing matter," he scolded me, concern thick in his voice. "You stay right where you are; I'm coming to get you."

"No, don't waste the fuel," I protested. "I'll be fine. Just focus on getting the others comfortable. I should be home before suns—"

A blood-curdling screech cut me off mid-sentence, and my words died in my throat. The sound was less than a kilometre away.

"Yeah, I heard that," Michael's voice crackled from the radio in my hand. "I'm coming to get you, and that's final."

"Yeah," I agreed, nervously scanning the treeline far behind me. "Yeah. Yeah, okay. Um. I'm going to try the running thing again now. Wish me luck."

He didn't bother to respond. There was no need, and no time. I shoved the radio back onto my belt, and took off at a sloppy, wobbling trot. My body didn't want to respond the way it should, but a spurt of adrenaline kept me going.

Behind me, I heard a handful of inquisitive growls, carried on the soft breeze. I couldn't tell which direction they were travelling in, and the long grass made it impossible to spot them unless they stood up straight. The mutated undead were an unknown element, though. I didn't have enough information to try and predict what they'd do. My only choice was to keep going, and hope that Michael arrived before they caught up with me.

The grass rustled and swayed around me; the movement made my head swim. At least I was travelling mostly eastwards, so the sun was at my back; the intensity of the sunlight hurt, but at least it wasn't constantly in my eyes, blinding me. That was a small blessing, but a blessing nevertheless.

The sound of my own breathing rattling in my ears felt deafening, like it would lead the undead right to me. I tried to breathe quietly, but that just made me even dizzier. My footsteps sounded like an elephant crashing through the brush.

The fact that I could hear anything at all over my own noises was a miracle, but I did. I heard the growls closing in on me. Every so often one of them would start to get further away, then another one would shriek and draw it back into the hunt. There was definitely more than one, and I had no doubt that they were following me. Stalking me. I was wounded prey, and they were after me.

"I'm not prey," I told myself softly, shifting my shotgun around into a defensive position. There was a soft click as I eased the safety off again. I had a handful of spare shells in my pocket for easy access, so I pulled them out and carefully reloaded them by touch as I jogged eastwards. The combat shotgun held eight shells, which was usually more than enough. Would it be enough now? How many were after me?

"There's at least two," I murmured. There was no point in trying to be stealthy when I couldn't move quietly. If talking to myself helped me stay grounded, then so be it. "At least two, maybe more. I think there's more. I gotta conserve my ammunition. I think I should hit the road soon. That's good. Clear line of sight. Yeah. I am not prey."

I took a deep breath and spurred myself on, forcing myself to pick up the pace even though all my body wanted to do was lie down and go to sleep. I couldn't do that. Sleeping meant death. I was too damn stubborn to die. My family needed me. Michael needed me. The future of my species needed me.

For some reason I couldn't define, that thought steadied me and helped me to keep going well beyond the point of collapse. Adrenaline and determination meshed together into some kind of bizarre hybrid emotion that erected itself like a wall between my conscious thoughts and the desperate, panicked animal instincts that pressured me to just drop everything and run for my life.

"I'm running, but I'm not running away," I told myself firmly. "I'm running, but I'll fight you. I'll fight you all, if I have to. I am no one's prey!"

As if understanding my words, a blood-curdling screech behind me drew my attention. I spun and dropped into a crouch, aiming my shotgun from the shoulder so that I could sight along the barrel. Every shot had to count now. There would be no firing until I had a clear target. I drew a deep breath and held it, so that I could hear the sounds all around me as clearly as possible.

There, to the right!

A twig broke beneath a humanoid foot. I swivelled around and stared into the long grass, watching, waiting. They were like a school of piranhas, circling me before they closed in for the kill. As frustrating as it was, I knew that following them into the grass would be suicide; eventually, when they were ready, they'd come for me. They had no brains, so surely they had no patience either. But, as the seconds stretched out into minutes, I started to wonder. They were there, but they weren't showing themselves. Were they waiting for me to pass out? Or were they just waiting for my guard to drop?

Whatever they were doing, I wasn't about to sit there and wait until they decided to kill me. I did have a brain, and it told me that every second I was away from the safety of cover as one that I'd end up regretting – if I lived to regret it at all. I took a deep breath, then I launched myself back to my feet and raced off towards the east again.

In the process, I almost bowled over the creature that had been working its way around to take me from behind. I screamed in surprise, swung my shotgun around, and frantically fired at it before it had a chance to recover from my unexpected movement. I would love to say that my success was based on skill and awareness, but in this case it was just pure luck. If I'd waited a few seconds longer, then the thing would have had me.

My heart hammered in my throat as I leapt over the buckshot-riddled pseudo-corpse and ran for my life, and this time it was fear that kept my head steady. Pure, animal terror. The creature had been so close that I could still smell its stink, still feel the unnatural chill that radiated from its body.

"Oh, Lord. Screw this. Screw this!" I gasped as I fled, using the words as a mantra to keep me going. "Screw this shit right out of the goddamn water!"

Behind me, the creatures lost their pretence of stealth and began shrieking in what sounded so very much like rage – but it couldn't be, they didn't have emotions. They didn't have thoughts or feelings or anything that made us human. They were hollow shells that did nothing but kill, kill, kill. And if I stopped, they'd kill me, too.

I found the old roadway quite by accident. As Anahera had warned me weeks earlier, it was in terrible condition, a shattered grey ribbon broken into uneven strips, with grass sticking up through the cracks. Still, it was relatively flat and straight, and that would give me a chance. I dashed out onto the tar seal and pulled my radio off my belt as I sprinted along as fast as I could go.

"Michael?" I called into the receiver. "Michael, I'm following the old east-west road. They've found me. Please, please hurry." I risked a quick glance over my shoulder, and saw half-a-dozen dark shapes emerging from the long grass behind me. "Oh, God! There's so many of them. I see… at least six—no, seven. Please, please hurry!"

There was no answer, but I didn't expect there to be one. He was too busy driving to answer. I could only hope that he'd at least heard. With no other choice but to rely on myself for now, I shoved my radio back onto my belt and ran as hard and as fast as I could.

Every so often, I glanced back and saw the creatures chasing after me, but they didn't seem to be gaining any ground. The problem was, I couldn't keep that pace up forever, not with my head the way it was. Right at that moment, I was fuelled by nothing but panic, and as powerful as that was it wouldn't keep me upright forever. Stars began to dance around the edge of my vision, warning me that a faint was incoming sometime soon if I didn't stop for a rest.

But the moment I stopped, they'd be on me, and I'd be dead.

Even with my particularly good sense of direction, I had lost track of how far it was to home. It could be a kilometre, or it could be ten. I couldn't outrun them, so I'd just have to outsmart them.

"Okay," I panted. "Okay, think smart. What can you do that they can't? Um… aside from thinking. Love? No, that's useless. Christ, come on, Sandy." I paused for a moment to jump over a particularly wide crack in the road, then lifted my head and scanned the horizon for any signs of Michael. Nothing.

"Wait, no. Not nothing," I exclaimed. "Yes! Inspiration!" With an unladylike whoop, I channelled what little reserves of strength I had left into one last burst of speed, and raced towards the buildings in the distance. Even with my vision wobbling and my head throbbing in time with my racing feet, I could see that one of those buildings was a barn, with a pair of doors up high that indicated there was a hayloft above it.

The kind of hayloft that would have a ladder. A ladder that would require human coordination to climb. If my undead friends couldn't operate a door handle, then it seemed unlikely that they'd be able to climb.

Seconds later, I raced across the overgrown courtyard in front of the barn, and plunged into the pleasant darkness within. I felt instant relief, after being out in the sun's glare, like plunging into a cool swimming pool on a hot summer's day. My pupils must have already been dilated from the concussion, because it only took a second for my vision to adjust to the gloom; the first thing I spotted was a ladder leading up towards the loft, and safety.

I shoved my shotgun back on its shoulder strap and darted forward, dodging around a few rusted farming implements and pieces of equipment. Right behind me, I could hear the creatures screaming. Their prey was out of sight, but they were closing on me fast.

I threw myself at the ladder and raced up as fast as I could go, but not quite fast enough. I was one rung away from safety when I felt an icy-cold grip close around my ankle. I kicked out and felt my foot connect with something solid, but I couldn't see what I'd hit. It didn't matter; it was enough for me to pull free. A few seconds later, I was at the top of the ladder, and safely out of reach.

"Thank God," I gasped breathlessly as I threw myself onto the dusty platform of the hayloft. If there had been any hay up there before, it had long ago turned to mulch, then to dirt, and eventually to dust without enough access to sunlight and rain for the grass seeds lying dormant within it to grow. Frankly, I didn't care how dirty it was. I didn't care if there were slaters, spiders, or even wetas making their home up there. Anything was better than the mutants.

As if reading my mind, one of the creatures below me let out a blood-curdling screech, which was quickly answered by a second and a third. Enough light filtered in through the open doors for me to see them circling around beneath me, like sharks waiting for their prey to come back within reach.

A sudden flash of anger clouded my judgement. Before I realised what I was doing, I had my shotgun back in my hand, and trained on one of those circling creatures. The shot rang out in the silence like a clarion call, and sent birds shrieking up into the clear blue sky from their nests nearby. One of the undead collapsed in a mound of blackened blood, its limbs writhing and flailing grotesquely around its shredded torso.

"I am *not* prey," I growled, taking aim at a second undead. Before I could fire, it retreated out of my line of sight and left me seething in impotent rage. I lowered my gun and gritted my teeth, then took a deep breath to calm my tension.

"I've been prey before, but I won't be prey again," I said softly to myself once the blind anger started to drain away. "Never again. Not for you. Not for him. Not for anyone. I am no one's prey."

\*\*\*

I sat for a while in that dirty hayloft to catch my breath, and let my spinning head recover. Just as I'd predicted, the creatures didn't seem to be able to climb up after me, nor could they jump high enough to put me at risk. I could still hear them growling and circling around below me, but it was a frustrated sort of noise that told me that they couldn't get at me.

Once I had my breath back, I inched back over to the edge to see if I could remove the ladder and haul it up after me. Unfortunately, it was firmly bolted to the deck, so it wasn't going anywhere.

"Well, shit – there goes that idea," I muttered to myself, then paused. "Sorry, Mum. I'm sure you'd understand. There has to be something else, though. Something I can use."

I drew a deep breath to steady myself, and hauled myself back to my feet. Now that I was relatively safe, the adrenaline was starting to drain away, and with it went the frantic burst of energy that had kept me going through the pain and the dizziness. I quickly searched through the equipment that had been stored in the loft, but came away with nothing more useful than an old shovel. Still, if I ran out of ammunition, I might need it.

I could feel my strength beginning to wane by the second, so I went over to the loft doors and tried to open them while I still could. They squealed in protest on ancient, rusted hinges, but with enough brute force I managed to let in the afternoon sun.

"Christ, that's bright," I mumbled, easing myself down to sit on the edge of the loft with my legs hanging over the edge. I wasn't a fan of heights, but I was too dazed to care. When I went to pluck my radio off my belt again, I found my fingers trembling uncontrollably. It took three tries before I managed to successfully line my fingers up with the receiver and press the button. "Michael? Michael, if you can hear me, please stop for a second. I need to talk to you. Please?"

The wait was only a few seconds in reality, but it felt like it took forever. Eventually, the radio crackled in my hand, and then I heard his deep, reassuring voice in my ear.

"I'm here, sweetheart. Are you okay?"

"I'm... I'm not doing so hot, to be honest," I admitted. "But I am kind of safe for now. I found the road, and I managed to get to a barn. I'm up in a hayloft, out of their reach. Apparently they can't climb, so that's pretty awesome. Downside is that I'm trapped up here. I have some food, but my water's almost gone. I managed to shoot one, but there are six more down there. I don't think they can get up here, but... I don't know."

"I'm almost there. You just need to keep it together a little bit longer, okay? Now, tell me exactly where you are."

"Yeah... yeah, okay. Yeah." I paused and blinked up at the sun, trying to get my bearings. "I'm a little bit north of the road that runs westward out of Ohaupo. There's a house. It used to be painted blue, but it's faded now. So, you know, faded blue. It has a collapsed roof in the front. There's a barn about a hundred meters further back. That's where I am. There are mutants in the barn, though. Be careful. I don't think I... I—" Tears welled up in my eyes. I knew I was rambling, but that was the concussion kicking in. "I don't think I could handle it if anything happened to you. I love you. I love you so much."

"Nothing's going to happen to me," he told me in that deep, husky voice that sent shivers down my spine every time. "I am coming for you, do you hear me? Just stay strong a little bit longer. I love you, too, and I won't let anything happen to you. Not again. Okay?"

"Okay," I agreed softly; the weakness I could hear in my own voice was alarming, but I was too exhausted to care. I switched the radio off and clipped it back onto my belt, then lay my head against the old wood and settled in to wait.

*** 

I had no real sense of time passing as I waited, drifting in and out of consciousness. Every so often, one of the mutants below me would snarl or yowl and bring me awake again, but I couldn't see what they were doing. I could hear them circling below me, like a school of piranhas, just waiting for me to come down so that they could devour me.

"Leave me alone," I mumbled sleepily, closing my eyes. Maybe if I wished hard enough, they'd go away, and I could just go home. That'd be nice. I missed home. I missed Michael.

"Sandy? Are you still with me?"

"What?" I blinked owlishly, startled by the unexpected voice. It took a few seconds for my addled brain to comprehend that it was actually coming from my radio. I picked the radio up and pressed the receiver. "Hey, I'm here. Please tell me you're nearby."

"I am. I see you. Look towards the road."

I lifted my head and stared into the distance. My eyes didn't want to focus properly, but I could just make out the figure on the big quad bike, waving at me. Relief rushed through me as I raised my hand and waved back.

"Thank God. I don't feel good, and the barn is full of mutants. What do I do?"

"I'm going to give them something else to worry about," he answered, his voice deep and commanding even through the radio. With a direct line of sight to him, the connection was as clear as a bell. I could almost feel his arms around me... right up until he threw a spanner in the works. "You just get ready to jump."

"Wait, what? Jump?" I shot a glance down at the ground below me. "Are you crazy? That's gotta be like three, maybe four meters."

"Don't jump now, silly," he answered dryly. "Just get ready. I'll tell you when to jump."

"I'm not sure I like this plan, but... okay," I agreed grudgingly. "Be careful."

While he was doing whatever he had to do, I quickly unloaded my shotgun and shoved the spare rounds back into my pocket, then strapped the gun to my back. If I was going to have to fall that far, then having the gun loaded was a terrible idea, even with the mutants swarming below. Besides, Michael said that he had a plan.

Once I was ready, I inched close to the edge of the platform and watched him getting ready. I couldn't see the details, but I could see him doing something with an object in his lap. Suddenly, he looked up and waved at me, then I faintly heard the sound of his bike revving up.

A few seconds later, he turned the bike around and tore across the overgrown fields that separated the barn from the road. As he drew closer, I realised that I could see his M-16 resting across his lap, ready for action at a moment's notice – and there was something else, something that I couldn't quite make out.

He came on hard and fast, at an angle that kept him out of the direct line of sight of the things inside the barn. At the very last moment, he took a hard turn to the left and came to a halt directly below me. Shrieks of what sounded like either hunger or rage filled the air. Michael didn't even hesitate. He threw the thing he'd been holding into the dark recess of the barn, and then lifted his gun and opened fire.

The sound of bullets filled the air with their terrible tattoo, and I smelt the stink of gunpowder on the air. Then, I realised that I could smell something else, something familiar. It took a second for me to realise that it was gasoline. Just as that realisation struck me, an explosion ripped through the back end of the barn below me, and the smell of gasoline was replaced by one of burning.

Michael shoved his gun back on its shoulder strap, and looked right at me. "Jump!"

"But--" I started to protest, but the rapidly spreading fire drowned out my words.

"Just do it!" he shouted over the noise. "You trust me, don't you?"

A second explosion shook the barn, and very nearly made me lose my seating on the edge of the hayloft. There was no choice. I had to do it. I had to trust him. I took a deep breath to steady myself, then shoved myself off the ledge. For a second, I felt the sickening sensation of falling, but it barely lasted long enough for me to start panicking. A moment later, I felt strong arms catch me and suddenly I was enveloped in warmth.

"You're okay, I've got you," Michael whispered in my ear as he sat me down on the seat in front of him. I started to say something, but a third explosion left my head ringing and my mind unable to focus; whatever I had been intending to say vanished like water through a sieve.

It didn't matter, though. Michael had me. He helped me get comfortable on the seat in front of him, and reached around me to grab the handlebars. I heard the bike rev up, and then we were off at high speed, heading for home. The motion made my stomach reel in protest, but I couldn't bring myself to care. Relief was a tangible force inside me, so overwhelming that all I wanted to do was wrap my arms around Michael's waist and bury my face in his chest.

So, I did. There comes a time in every person's life when they need someone else's help to survive. This moment was mine.

*That's what having a family is for, isn't it?* The bike was too loud for me to bounce my thoughts off Michael, so I didn't even try to speak. It had taken some time for me to acknowledge it, but they were there for me in my darkest moments, to help, protect, save, and love me. How had I survived for so long without that safety net of social acceptance?

*Hard questions. Shut up and rest, brain,* I scolded myself, then I closed my eyes and let myself relax.

# Chapter Four

At some point during the trip back home, I fainted. Even if I'd been aware of it happening, I probably wouldn't have been able to do anything about it. As far as my body was concerned, enough was enough; it was time to rest.

When I started to come to again, I could no longer hear the sound of the bike, just someone moving around nearby. I opened my eyes slowly, then immediately regretted it. The world around me spun like an out-of-control roller coaster. Someone must have heard my groan, because I felt a hand alight softly on my shoulder.

"Don't try to sit up," Doctor Cross said quietly. Curiosity overwhelmed my urge to avoid the dizzying sensation, so I opened my eyes again and carefully looked around.

I was lying in my own bed, in the loft above the DVD store, but the place looked like it had been converted into a triage unit. Supplies, primarily medical in nature, were stacked up along the walls, and beside me lay Anahera. She was still unconscious.

"Is everyone all right?" I asked, my voice coming out far huskier than I intended. The doctor nodded, and put a glass of water against my lips. I drank gratefully, then lay my head back on the pillow and looked up at him.

"More or less, yes," he elaborated. "I haven't seen this many concussions in one room since the time my son dragged me off to watch a roller derby match. Everyone is alive, though."

"And they'll be all right?" I repeated, glancing towards the enigmatic woman that lay beside me. "What about Anahera? Is it serious?"

"She's the only one I'm concerned about at the moment," Doc admitted. "Everyone else is going to be fine. Only time will tell for her, though. The human head is a delicate object, and she sustained quite a severe injury."

"I need to get up, doc," I told him, shooting him a pointed look. "How long do I have to wait until it's safe to do so?"

"Until you feel better," he gave me a stern frown in return. "Your sister has everything under control. Stop worrying and rest."

"Ugh. Don't wanna." I sighed heavily and closed my eyes. "You know, I'm actually kind of surprised that Maddy didn't warn me that this was going to happen. She was pretty spot-on about the fire."

My answer was silence. After a few seconds, I opened my eyes and looked up at him. Eventually, he glanced at me and shrugged. "I don't know what to make of Madeline's... premonitions, to be frank. I am a man of science. I believe what I can see, touch, and feel."

"I know exactly what you mean," I replied sympathetically. "If you'd suggested I'd be taking guidance from a psychic kid six months ago, I would have laughed at you. Well, there isn't much we can do about it now, is there? Tell me what happened while I was away, Doc."

"That much I can do." The portly gentleman hiked his scratched glasses a little higher up his nose, and sat down on the bed beside me. "Things went as well as can be expected in your absence. The Yousefis have done nothing to violate our trust, and have been working hard to make up for what they did."

"Good." I nodded, gesturing for him to continue. "How are we for supplies?"

"Better than we initially thought." He gave me a rare smile. "I might even venture to say that we have been very, very lucky, considering the circumstances. The fire started in the kitchen, and consumed most of Skylar's room. We've been able to clear enough debris to get inside, but it's still fairly hot. The storage rooms have survived mostly intact. With the exception of what was in the refrigerator, our food supplies should be fine – though, everything may taste like barbeque for the next few weeks."

"We're going to need to find a new food supply before then." I paused and did a quick head-count, then grimaced. "We've got twenty mouths to feed, including Anahera's men. There isn't enough here to last more than a fortnight, and that's if we ration it to the mouthful."

"You plan to keep them, then?" Doc stared at me, his expression thoughtful. "Somehow, I'm not surprised."

"What's that supposed to mean?" I asked, giving him a quizzical look.

"Well, you and the boy do have a habit of picking up strays." Suddenly, the old man chuckled and shook his head. "Just where are you planning to put them all, Ms McDermott? We didn't have enough room for them before the fire. It'll be near-impossible to house them all now."

"I don't know," I admitted. "I just know that we need to find somewhere safe and secure. I want to build a city, Doc. These people are the future of humankind; we need to find somewhere safe enough to put down roots, and plan for the next generation."

"Bold, idealistic, and slightly naïve," he summarized dryly. "Sounds like just what we need."

"Hey, if you have a better plan to save us from extinction, I'm all ears." I stuck out my tongue and blew a raspberry at him. Despite the childish gesture, he actually paused to think about it for a second.

"I don't," he replied thoughtfully. "Frankly, it's a valiant plan. I have no idea if we can achieve it, but we do need to try." His affirmation surprised me. I shot him a startled look, and caught him smiling. Before I could say anything else, he put his hand on my shoulder. "Go to sleep, Sandy – or is it Sandrine now? You'll need your strength if you're going to lead us to this idealistic new world of yours."

"But I don't wanna sleep," I protested without really meaning it. "You're so mean. Hate you, Doc."

"No, you don't." He chuckled softly as he turned away, and walked back towards the door. "If you hated me, then you would have left me to die in that inferno instead of risking your life to rescue me."

I had nothing to say to that.

***

I slept for another few hours, until my head finally started to feel right again. Although my body ached from the tumble I'd taken, I had been through worse and was more than capable of dealing with a little bit of pain.

When I woke again, the room was murky with the shadows of twilight. There were no windows in my little bedroom, but I had come to know it well over the time I'd lived there. Darkness was falling, but it hadn't fallen yet.

I sat up slowly, careful not to set my head spinning again, but the rest had done its job. I felt much better. Even when I switched on the light, my body didn't protest too much. Thinking about my own condition made me worry about my friends, though; I glanced back at Anahera, and heaved a deep sigh.

"Get better, mate. I need you," I told her. She didn't reply, of course. Still, she was alive. That was more than I could say for a lot of my other friends – and hers, too. I blew out a soft breath, and murmured thoughtfully, "There are going to be a lot of people grieving tonight. I should get out there."

I turned away from her, and eased myself out of bed. I'd been stripped down to my underwear, but my filthy clothing and shoes weren't far away. A few months before, I would have freaked out over that, but now I didn't even bat an eyelash. I grabbed a clean t-shirt and a pair of jeans out of my dresser and pulled them on, then made my way out into the living room.

The sight that greeted me was unexpectedly heart-warming. The five children in our group – Maddy, Priya, and the three younger Yousefi boys – sat in a circle on the living room floor with Tigger, the kitten that had adopted me earlier that summer.

"Mama!" Priya squealed in delight when she saw me. A second later, she was latched around my waist, hugging me fiercely.

"Mama?" I peered down at her, curious. "When did that happen?"

"I decided," she answered firmly, and gave me one of her radiant smiles. "My old mama is gone, so you're my new mama now." Suddenly, a look of anxiety crossed her face. "Is okay, yes? You mama, Michael baba?"

That look melted any protests I might have had about my new status. I just smiled, and hugged her back.

"Sure, Priya. I'll be your mama," I agreed, then looked up at the other children. "What are you guys doing?"

"Babysitting!" Priya said proudly, pointing at the little group. "The pretty lady said I'm old enough to look after the little ones."

"Well, you seem to be doing a good job of it," I praised her gently, and looked up at the circle of little faces again. The three boys were shy and wary, but it was Madeline's expression that took me by surprise. She looked sullen, her attention intensely focused on the kitten. "Maddy? Are you okay?"

The little girl just shrugged and said nothing. She didn't even look at me. I looked at Priya for answers instead, since she seemed to be the only one interested in talking to me.

"Maddy is sad-sads, because of the fire," Priya explained in a dramatic stage whisper. "I think she be okay, but is sads now and does not want to talk."

"Ah. A bit of shock, then." I nodded and looked back at the little girl. "Maddy, I wanted to thank you for telling us about your dreams. I don't know how you did it, but you may have saved everyone's lives. You're a good girl, and you've done well."

A flicker of something that I couldn't identify passed through her eyes. She nodded and gave me a faint smile. "Thank you for believing me, Miss Sandy."

"I always believe you, Maddy," I said softly, prying myself out of Priyanka's grip so that I could go over and kneel down beside her. "You're special, Maddy. I don't know how it happened, or what kind of special you are, but you're definitely special. I remember how you helped me when I first met your family, and now this? You're one of the most special people I've ever met."

"I—" She hesitated, staring up at me with huge brown eyes. Suddenly, they filled with tears. "I'm sorry, Miss Sandy. I didn't mean to make the fire happen."

"What?" I blinked, startled. "You didn't start the fire, honey. Zain did, by accident. You weren't even there."

"But I started it by dreaming about it," she said. Suddenly, she burst into tears. "I'm sorry! I didn't mean to. Please don't be angry with me."

"Whoa!" Flabbergasted by the sudden outburst, I grabbed her and pulled her into a hug. "Shh, honey, it's okay. You didn't make the fire happen. It's not your fault. Promise."

"B-but I dreamed it before it happened," the little girl blubbered, clinging to me as though her life depended on it. "If I hadn't dreamed it then it wouldn't have happened."

"Okay, I'm no expert on these things, but I know that it's not your fault." I gently held her back away from me, and wiped the tears off her cheeks. "Sweetie, you did not cause the fire. The fire was going to happen anyway. You just… sensed that the fire was going to happen, and you warned us. You saved lives by giving us the advanced warning to prepare. You did not cause the fire."

"I didn't?" She sniffled loudly and looked up at me, her little face stained with tears.

"No, you didn't," I told her firmly, and gave her a smile. "You saw what was going to happen and told us about it. The fire was caused by a gas stove falling over. You weren't even in the room when that happened, so it couldn't be your fault. Could it?"

"Well… no, I guess not," she agreed, then took a deep breath and rubbed her hands across her cheeks to wipe the tears away. "I was so scared, Miss Sandy. I thought Granddaddy was doing to die."

"Nobody's going to die on my watch," I reassured her, and gave her another quick hug. "Everyone's okay because of you, Maddy. You saved them. Look, even Tigger knows that you're a hero."

Maddy looked down at the purring bundle of fluff in her lap, and shot a dubious look at me.

"No, really," I said, grinning at her. "She won't even let me pat her, but she's letting you hold her. That's special right there, isn't it?"

Maddy looked down at the kitten, then picked her up and gave her a cuddle. Tigger barely even stirred, but the sight made me smile. It might take some time to get over the shock, but I decided that she was going to be fine.

"Okay, kids," I announced, easing myself back to my feet. "I need to go see what the others are up to. You be good for Priya and stay inside where it's safe."

"Okies!" Priya agreed cheerfully. I waved and headed out of the apartment. As I made my way down the stairs, I heard voices speaking on the other side of the door. I tried the handle and found the inner door locked, so I knocked instead.

The voices on the other side stopped for a moment, then I heard my sister. "Priya, is that you again? I told you to stay upstairs."

"It's me, sis," I called back. "Let me out."

"Oh, hey! Just a second." I heard the sound of a key turning in the lock and the door opened. Skye yanked me into a quick hug, then pulled me into the office where she and Elly had been speaking. "Man, am I ever glad to see you up and about again. I've been so worried."

"Sorry about that," I answered sheepishly. "I'm feeling a bit better now. How's your head doing?"

"Better. Doc says that it wasn't too bad, all things considered." Skye chuckled and shook her head. "Look at us. We're like concussion twins or something."

"I'm pretty sure that's not actually a thing, but I know what you mean." I grinned at her, then looked back and forth between the two women. "So, how are we situated? It's about to get dark, and those things could get here any moment if they decide to come back this way."

"There's no sign of them at the moment, but we've got Michael and his boys on guard duty anyway," Skye explained, then she grabbed my hand and led me out of the office. When she opened the door, I was surprised to see that the lower level of the old store had been cleaned up, and all the old trash removed. In its place, supplies had been stored in neat piles.

"Wow, you guys have been hard at work," I commented, impressed. "This has to be just about everything we had in the motel. Good job."

"Almost," she agreed, nodding. "We still have a bit more to retrieve, but we should be finished tomorrow morning. We've also sent Zain and Ropata out in the Hilux to look for cars and trailers that we can salvage. If we're going to be leaving, then we'll need transport."

"Do they know what they're looking for?" I asked curiously, shooting a glance at Elly. To my surprise, she laughed.

"I would hope so," she said dryly. "I do not know about the other man, but my husband was an automotive engineer for twelve years before the plague, if you include his apprenticeship. We were only travelling on foot because we ran out of petrol, and couldn't find any more. Skylar says that you have fuel, so there is no problem."

"You mean we actually have someone who knows what they're doing now?" I stared at them wide-eyed for a second, then let out a whoop of delight. "Finally! I don't know how to tell you guys this, but I've just been faking it the whole time."

"Faking it, huh?" Skylar gave me a long, sideways look, followed up by a wicked smile. "That's the only thing you've been faking though, right?"

"Eh?" I stared at her, my joviality replaced by confusion. "What do you mean by that?"

"I mean, you're not faking it for Michael, are you?" she answered in a gleeful, sing-song voice, then danced over and threaded her arm through mine. "So, when were you planning to tell me, huh? I'm your sister; it's not nice to keep secrets from your sister."

"Whoa, suddenly this conversation has gone into uncomfortable places!" I exclaimed, holding up my free hand in self-defence. "What the hell are you talking about, Skye? You already know about me and Michael."

"Yeah, but you didn't tell me about… this!" She snatched the chain that held my engagement ring out from beneath my shirt before I could hope to stop her. "We had to undress you while you were unconscious. Did you think you could keep that hidden forever?"

"Oh, that." Embarrassed, I tugged the ring back out of her grip and shoved it back under my shirt. "I was going to tell you eventually, but we've been a little busy, you know? It only happened a week ago, while we were away, and it's not a full-on engagement. Just sort of a… promise. Michael gave it to me so I'd have something to show for our relationship if anything ever happened to him."

"Awww, how sweet," Skye crooned. Behind her, Elly giggled girlishly, a sound that seemed far too young to be coming from a face that looked twice my age. The years had not been kind to her, but her eyes were alert and intelligent despite her weather-worn skin. I gave her a faint smile, and pointedly changed the subject.

"So, you guys already figured out that we're going to be leaving," I said, glancing back and forth between them. "That's good. It's going to be dangerous, but it'll be safer if we stick together."

"I don't think we have much of a choice, to be honest," Skye answered, her demeanour changing from playful to serious. "Those things have already killed six people, and from Michael's stoic silence I gather that they almost got a seventh today. You've mentioned gangs in the south, but we can deal with those. These things are just… monsters."

"I'm concerned that the mutated virus may be spreading," I admitted, shooting a glance back over my shoulder towards the heavily-barricaded front door. "There were so many of them out there. At least nine, by my count."

"Yeah," Skye agreed, nodding thoughtfully. "I doubt you're the only one thinking that, either. Speaking of which, we better get everyone inside. It's starting to get dark. Elly, can you grab the bullhorn?"

"Bullhorn? We have a bullhorn?" I asked curiously, but Skye just gave me a grin and said nothing.

Instead, she reached into her pocket and pulled out one of our walkie-talkies, and spoke into it. "Home-time, guys. Everyone start heading back to base."

A chorus of agreement came back to her from the holders of the other radios. When Elly returned with the bullhorn, she stuck her head out the door and repeated the message loudly enough for anyone without a radio to hear. Within a few minutes, the other survivors began to return.

The first to return were the men who had been involved in the salvage operation at the old motel, covered in soot and looking exhausted. I was a little surprised to see Anahera's men among them at first glance, but after a moment of thought I realised that it made perfect sense. One of the many things that had changed since the fall of the human empire was the average person's attitude towards group effort.

Back when we could rely on a steady food source and a roof over our heads, it was okay to be fully focused on your individual wants and needs, or those of your direct family. Now, it had become second nature to do your part for everyone in the group, regardless of how you were feeling. Helping the group was helping yourself. If you didn't work, you didn't eat. They'd been through a lot of trauma and were grieving for their lost friends, but they were still willing to work for their supper. I understood that, and I respected it.

As they filtered through the door, I took a moment to greet them. I could see the deep sadness in their eyes, but also relief and gratitude. All of them had a smile for me, even if it was a little weak. One by one, we sent them upstairs to the loft.

"It's going to get pretty crowded up there tonight," I commented. Just at that moment, Doc arrived with a huge armful of sooty blankets and pillows. The three of us rushed over to help him.

"Yeah," Skye agreed as we unfolded the blankets, and shook them out the door to get the worst of the soot off them. "We've retrieved as much bedding as we can, but it's still going to be a bit uncomfortable for everyone. Better safe than sorry, though."

"Well, we're going to need to have some people on night watch, anyway," I answered, glancing around the little building for inspiration. "I'm thinking two watching upstairs, two downstairs. We don't want those things sneaking up on us while we're sleeping."

"Now, that is an awful thought," Elly commented quietly; I glanced at her just in time to see her shudder. "It frightens me to think how close they came to taking my children from me."

"I won't let them," I said firmly. "I'll protect your kids to the death, if I have to. I'll protect all of the kids, one way or another."

"Well, aren't you Little Miss Determined now?" Skye teased impishly, and gave me a nudge in the side. I stuck my tongue out at her and gave her a shove back.

"Someone's got to be." I folded the blanket I'd been shaking over my arm, and turned to look her in the eye. "We may be all that's left of humanity in this country right now. Even if we aren't, we have a duty to try to protect ourselves, and to grow this group so that the next generation can have a decent chance. We owe them that much, don't we?"

"True." Skye sighed heavily, the humour draining out of her face. "I barely remember what it was like before the plague came. I just remember everything being... so clean. And smiling people everywhere. It would be nice to have that again." Suddenly, she glanced up and gave me a cheeky wink. "I also miss chocolate. Chocolate was awesome."

All of us laughed at that.

# Chapter Five

By the time full darkness fell, everyone had returned safely from whatever mission they'd been about. The last people to return were Michael and his crew, who had taken responsibility for keeping the rest of us safe. Not really a huge surprise.

I won't lie and pretend that I was all dignified or coy about seeing him again. The second he came through the door, I threw myself into his arms and smothered him in kisses, much to the amusement of everyone around us. And you know what? I didn't care. I didn't care at all. After the kind of day that we'd had, we had both earned a moment of weakness.

Once we had finished reuniting, we closed, locked, and barricaded the front door with the heaviest things we could find, then we filtered upstairs into the crowded loft.

"Elly and I will take care of dinner," Skye volunteered, heading off to the kitchen. That left the rest of us standing awkwardly in a small living room, crammed with way more people than it was ever meant to hold.

"You know, I really hope the floor doesn't collapse or something," I joked lightly, nudging Michael in the side.

He smiled faintly in response to my joke, but his expression stayed serious. "We should probably do something about getting people bathed, though. It smells like a frat house in here."

"Good point." I nodded and cleared my throat loudly, putting an end to the quiet conversations taking place around the room. One by one, they all turned and looked at me expectantly. "All right, everyone. Michael says you stink. Bathroom's through that door there, on the left. I'd like the kids to go first, since they have to go to bed earlier than the rest of us – Doc, Zain, can you please take care that?" I glanced at them. They both nodded, and stood to round up their respective progeny. "Thanks, guys. As for the rest of us… well, there isn't going to be enough hot water for everyone to have a warm shower. Sorry. No fist-fights, okay?"

There were some groans from the younger men, but there was really nothing that any of us could do to alleviate the situation so there were few real complaints. A cold shower was better than no shower, and most of us were used to going without modern conveniences when we had to. The conversations resumed, but with so many people crammed into a single room it was hard to follow any of them. Michael was clearly in one of his dark moods, and that always bothered me.

Ever since the death of his niece, there were times when he went into a strange, black place that was so out of keeping with his personality that it made me worry. I hated to watch him brood, so I gently reached out and touched his arm. When he looked at me quizzically, I tilted my head towards the door, silently telling him I wanted to talk to him without alerting the others that anything was amiss.

He followed me out onto the landing without a word, and closed the door softly behind him. Before I could say anything, he grabbed me and drew me into a fierce hug. The gesture was unexpected and took me by surprise, but not for long. Michael was not one to stay silent; he was a deeply expressive man, who tended to take things to extremes. Whether he was laughing or crying, he never hid himself from me.

"Hey, it's okay," I whispered, wrapping my arms around his broad shoulders. "I'm fine. Everything is fine. You made it in time."

Michael drew back and looked down at me, then let out a low, deep sigh. "I know – but I almost didn't. I've been kicking myself that I didn't notice when you fell behind. I could have lost you, and never known what happened."

"Better to never know than watch me get torn apart, right?" I answered with my usual dry sarcasm, but the look that he gave me immediately made me regret my choice of words. It was a look of total horror. It took a moment for me to put together what I'd said with what he had seen when Sophie died. "Oh my God, I didn't mean it like that! I'm sorry, honey. I-I didn't mean--"

"It's okay," he answered, cutting me off mid-stammer. "I know, it was supposed to be a joke. I'm just… having trouble with this whole situation. I feel so helpless."

"You saved my life once again," I reassured him, gently reaching up to grab his shoulders. "Again and again, you're there for me. Honey, you're the strongest man I know. Please don't doubt yourself like this, because I don't. I have absolute confidence in you. I trust you. You know better than anyone how hard it is for me to say that."

He nodded, his expression softening. "Yeah, I do. It means so much to me to hear you say that. But, still… it's hard to feel in control when you have no idea where the enemy is going to strike from next."

"I know what you mean." I sighed heavily, turning away to stare out the little window at the dark sky, and the ashen ruins of our former home. "I haven't felt like I'm truly in control of my own destiny in a long time. Hopefully, this voyage south will change that. No more waiting."

"It's going to be a hard trip," he said quietly. I felt his warm body come up behind me, and his arms slid around my waist. "For everyone, but especially for the little ones. Do we even know where we're going?"

"No, not really." I shrugged and leaned back against him, drawing comfort from his strength. "I figure that we head for Wellington, and see where the winds take us. We'll stop by that corn field along the way and stock up on food. That'll keep us going for a while."

"I've never been to Wellington," he said, resting his chin comfortably on my shoulder. I shot him a glance, and saw his dark eyes were distant, focused on nothing.

"I have – well, I've been in the area." I nuzzled his cheek and then closed my eyes to think. "It's been a long time. If we stick to the areas that used to be farmland, then we should have an easier time foraging along the road."

"We could find boats, and take the river south," Michael suggested.

I opened my eyes and gave him a curious look, then shrugged. "Maybe. They can't follow our tracks if we're on the river, but the river would only take us part of the way and then we'd be stuck scavenging for trucks in an unfamiliar location. We're heading through Arapuni, so we can check while we're there. I don't want to leave without offering Rebecca and Jim the chance to join us."

"It can't hurt to ask." Michael smiled at me, and gave me a gentle hug. "You know, I can hardly believe how much you've changed since we met."

"For the better, I hope?" I laughed and nudged him in the side.

He chuckled back and nodded. "Of course. I fell in love with you just the way you were, but this person that you're becoming… I love her, too. You're metamorphosing before my very eyes, from someone that was impressive to begin with, into someone truly amazing. Words can't express how glad I am that we met."

"And to think, if it hadn't been for these undead, then we'd never have found each other." I grinned at him, turning within the circle of his arms so that I could drape my own across his shoulders again. "Think we should thank them?"

"Hm, let me think about that." He tilted his head, pretending to think about it, then grinned at me. "Nah, I think we should just keep shooting them."

"Good plan," I agreed, leaning up to plant a kiss on his lips. When we parted, I glanced over his shoulder at the room beyond. "We should probably assign people to the night watch. I was saying to Skye that I think we should have two groups of two, one downstairs watching the door, one upstairs keeping an eye on the sleepers, just in case."

"Sounds good," he agreed amiably. "First shift from bedtime until just after midnight, then second shift from then until sunrise?"

"Yeah." I nodded my agreement. "I think we should try and divide it up between the newcomers and the old – both so they can get to know one another, and so we can keep an eye on them."

"I'll take care of it." Michael smiled down at me, then leaned down and planted a kiss against my forehead. "You worry about organising the journey."

"I don't mind taking a watch," I started to protest, but he just shook his head.

"You're one of the walking wounded today, sweetheart," he rumbled in that soft, deep voice of his. "I want you to rest. I'll be watching over you, so you know you'll be safe."

"Sometimes I think you're way too nice to me." I sighed, lifting a hand to trace the contours of his cheek.

"Do you want me to stop being nice to you?" he asked, raising one eyebrow inquisitively.

"Nah." I laughed, then leaned up and planted another quick kiss against his lips. "To be honest, I've almost forgotten what my life was like before I had you in it. Which is a good thing, because my life was pretty awful before I met you."

"I understand." He drew me back into a hug, and wrapped his arms around me. "Everything happened so quickly, but it feels so right. I've never felt as sure about anything as I feel certain that you and I are meant to be together. I only wish that you'd had a chance to meet Sophie."

"Me too," I murmured, snuggling in against his warmth. "You're just the kind of guy to take home to meet the parents, if you remember that old saying. I think my folks would have loved having you for a son-in-law."

"My dad would have liked you, but I have this sneaking suspicion that you and my mother would have fought like cats." He pulled back and looked down at me, a playful twinkle in his eyes. "I suppose that would have been funny to watch, though. From very, very far away."

"Hey!" I laughed and gave him a playful shove. "You never know, we might have gotten on so well that we'd spend all our time plotting ways to make your life miserable."

Michael groaned. "Don't even joke about that. That's so not funny."

"Yes, it is." I gave him an impish grin, and wriggled my way free of his grip. "Anyway, we should get back to work. You take care of the defences for the night, and I'll sort out our travel plans."

"Yes, ma'am!" He gave me a mock salute, then moved past me and headed back into the living room where the others were waiting.

I followed a few paces behind him, but while he started talking to the group, I headed into the kitchen. There, I found Skye and Elly hard at work, preparing something that remotely resembled food. Most of our fresh food had been destroyed by the fire, but the years had taught all of us how to be resourceful.

"Heyas," Skye greeted when she noticed me. "Dinner's still a wee while away yet. We'll let you know when it's ready."

"Oh, I'm not here about that." I moved the rest of the way inside, and closed the sliding door that separated the kitchen and living room, to cut off the noise the men were making. "I needed to talk to you, actually. Both of you."

"Oh?" Skye shot me a look, her brows raised curiously. "What's up, sis?"

"A couple of things, actually. One at a time, though." I paused for a moment to gather my thoughts, glancing at the stack of supplies wedged into the corner of the room. "You know we're going south as soon as possible. I want you guys to take care of provisioning. You have my permission to rope in anyone else you need, but I need someone who's in charge to keep things from getting messy. If you're cool with it, I'd like to put you in charge, and have Elly serve as your second-in-command."

"Yeah, sounds fine," Skye agreed, waving a wooden spoon at me. "We're already doing that anyway, so make it official. What else?"

"I need to know if you managed to salvage the radio," I asked bluntly; there was no point beating around the bush where my sister was concerned.

To my surprise, she hesitated. "Um... sort of."

"Sort of?" I raised a brow.

"Well, it's a little melted," she admitted, sounding sheepish. "I can't make it work, but you might be able to. I think it's just the shell that's melted, but something inside must have come loose from the heat. I mean, it's not totally melted."

I muffled a chuckle behind a cough. "Ah, right. Radio's melted. Got it."

"Just a little melted!" she protested. "It's probably still good. I mean, I hope so. It's in with the supplies downstairs."

"I'll take a look at it tomorrow," I answered dryly. "How much bedding did you manage to collect?"

"Not enough for everyone," she said with a shrug. "Some people are going to have to share. I guess we'll just have to get used to getting a little cuddly if we're going to stay together."

"Not for long." I gave her a smile and a wink. "We'll look for some more as we head south. I'm sure we'll find more than we need."

"True." Skye heaved a sigh and stretched. "Is that all? I'm knackered; I just want to get dinner done and curl up to sleep."

"Yeah. Thanks, sis." I waved to her and ducked out of the kitchen again, then went off to begin the arduous task of assigning bedding. I found a mound of it downstairs, and dragged it all up to hand it out. Sure enough, there wasn't enough to go around, but the group was pretty relaxed about being paired off with cuddle-buddies for the night. By the time dinner was served, half the men were laughing and teasing one another, and then they were distracted by food.

I deemed that a good thing, considering that so many of them had lost close friends that day. The longer I could keep them distracted and smiling, the better it would be for everyone. When dinner was served, I sat down quietly on the floor between Skylar and Michael, and ate my serving without a word, lost in my own thoughts.

It was going to be a long night, and an even longer few months as we headed south, but it had to be done. We couldn't just stay here and wait to see what the mutants decided to do next. As hard as it was to accept that it was better to flee than to stand and fight, I knew in my gut that I'd made the right choice for everyone. It wasn't the easy choice, but it was the right choice.

# Chapter Six

It took us three days to prepare to leave Ohaupo – three very tense days, and very long nights. Every night, the guards reported hearing strange sounds outside our building, but by dawn there was no sign of anything there. It was unnerving, to say the least. We were all tense and on edge, and it grated on everyone's nerves. People were snappish, and more than once I found myself having to step in to diffuse a potential explosion.

On the fourth morning, I woke early with my head nestled on Michael's belly, to the familiar sound of Priya's soft snores beside me. My concussion had healed fine, as had Skylar's, but Anahera was still unconscious.

I lifted my head, careful to avoid disturbing the people around me, and discovered that I was the first one awake in the pre-dawn gloom. It took me exactly three seconds to decide that made it the perfect time to get up and have a quick shower, before we had twenty people all clamouring for the bathroom at once.

As gently as I could, I extracted myself from my cuddle-pile and snuck towards the bathroom, tiptoeing around the sleeping forms of my friends. It was a nerve-wracking trip, but somehow I made it without waking anyone – or so I thought. When I glanced back over my shoulder at the last moment, I realised that Michael had somehow snuck up behind me. He gave me a playful grin and held a finger up to his lips, then grabbed my hand and dragged me into the bathroom.

There were very few moments of privacy with that many people living in such close proximity. Since the bathroom door had a lock, and the shower was one of our favourite spots anyway, it seemed logical. We were quick and stealthy, but it was enough. A brief moment of stolen passion was enough to leave me feeling happy and revitalized.

By the time we were finished, bathed, and dressed, the others were starting to wake up around us. Michael and I went into the kitchen to get breakfast started; one by one, the others dragged themselves out of bed and toddled off to the bathroom to relieve themselves, yawning broadly.

By the time a bleary-eyed Skylar wandered into the kitchen, breakfast was ready.

"What's going on?" she asked sleepily. "I thought you guys hated cooking?"

"Well, we need an early start this morning if we want to make it to a secure spot by sunset, so we figured we should get breakfast cooking as soon as possible," I answered, offering her a plate. "My scrambled eggs may not be as good as yours, but they're still food. Eat up."

She started to say something, but all that came out was a sleepy mumble, then she grabbed the plate and wandered back into the living room. I shot an amused glance at Michael, and opened my mouth to crack a joke, but before I could say anything the sound of a voice raised in alarm interrupted me.

Michael's expression turned to one of concern, mirroring my own feelings. The shouting was coming from the upstairs lobby. If something had figured out a way to get inside, then we were all in danger. I turned and ran out into the living room, with him hot on my heels.

A second later, I burst through the door onto the landing, where I found Tane leaning against the windowsill, staring intently down into the courtyard of our old motel. He glanced back when he heard us, and pointed down into the yard.

"I saw someone down there," he explained quickly. "I didn't get a good enough look to know if it was a survivor or one of the undead, though. I just saw a silhouette moving."

"Let's go find out, then," I answered resolutely. I led the way down the stairs to the lower level. At the bottom of the stairs, I banged on the door until it opened, and Hemi's startled-looking face peeked up at me.

"What's the ruckus, Sandy?" he asked, looking tense and wary.

"There's someone – or something – in the motel," I explained, gently shoving my way past him into the office at the base of the stairs. I grabbed my shotgun from its shelf, and led the way towards the exit. Iorangi was standing guard beside it; he took one look at my face, then hastily unlocked the door and pulled away the blockade to let us out. "Thanks. You two stay here. I don't want anything to sneak in while the door's open."

"We've got it covered," Hemi replied. "If you need us, shout."

"Good man. Don't worry, we will." I nodded grimly, and beckoned for Michael and Tane to follow me. I heard their footfalls behind me as I raced down the street towards the corner, and headed for the front door of the old motel. There, I paused and listened for a moment, but I heard nothing.

I felt a soft touch on my shoulder, then Michael leaned past me to point at the sooty ground near the door. A fresh boot-print marred the ash, clear as day, the edges not yet blurred by the breeze or rain. I crouched down and stared at it, then nodded and rose back to my feet. It might have been left by one of the undead, but it was just as likely to have been left by a living person.

Ahead of me, I spotted another boot print on the blackened concrete, then a third and a fourth. They were spaced wide, but an even distance apart. That settled it for me – the infected had an uneven, loping gait, and the prints were too regular for that. Our visitor was a person, and he or she had been running.

I glanced back at the two men following me and touched a finger to my lips for silence. They both nodded in agreement. Lowering my shotgun into a defensive position, I followed the tracks across the soot-stained lobby and out into the courtyard, then followed them up the stairs towards the second level. As quietly as I could, I slipped the safety off my shotgun and brought it up to my shoulder, aiming carefully along the length of the barrel. Without knowing if the new arrival was friend or foe, I chose to err on the side of caution.

The footprints continued along the upper landing, to the door of the room that had been Skylar's. They overlapped one another a bit there, as though the person had paused to look around, then they headed into the room itself. I eased myself down into a crouch-walk as I approached the door, and slid around the corner, ready to fire in a heartbeat.

Then, I lowered my shotgun and stared in surprise. "Ryan?"

The befreckled youth almost jumped out of his skin at the sound of my voice. He'd been standing with his back to the door, staring at the blackened remains of Skye's bed, and clearly hadn't heard me come in.

"Sandy!" he exclaimed. "Jesus, what happened here? Is Skye all right?"

I let out a deep sigh of relief, and eased myself back up to my feet. "She's fine. You gave us a hell of a fright, kid. Where have you been?"

"Just… you know, around." He lifted a shoulder in a vague shrug, and stared down at his feet. "I couldn't face it – I couldn't face her – and I had to run away for a while. Clear my head."

"You have a hell of a nerve to come back here," Michael growled over my shoulder; the tone of his voice almost scared *me* out of my skin, because it was one I'd never heard him use before. "You left her when she needed you most. You're the worst kind of coward. How dare you come back here, after what you did?"

Ryan flinched visibly and took a step back away from us. "Look, I-I did what I had to do, you know? I couldn't stay here. I needed to—"

"You ran off and left her!" Michael stepped around me, his face a mask of fury. "She almost died giving birth to your child, and you *left her*! I've half a mind to—"

"Stop it!" I shouted, leaping in to put myself between the two men. I turned to Michael and softened my tone, giving him an appealing look. "Michael, stop. This isn't you. Remember what we talked about? About forgiveness? He's just a kid. Everyone makes mistakes when they're young. Everyone deserves a second chance."

Michael stared down at me, his expression a hostile mask – right up until I lifted my hand, and rested it on his chest, right above the spot where his ring was hidden on its chain around his throat. Then, a flicker of something softer passed through his eyes. He nodded, and looked away.

I breathed a second sigh of relief and returned my attention to Ryan. "We need to get back inside. We're leaving Ohaupo today. Come on."

"If Skye's half as angry at me as I deserve, then I'm probably safer out here," the young man answered nervously, shifting from one foot to the other as though anxious to flee.

"I have no idea how angry she is." I shrugged and turned away, heading for the door. "She won't talk about it. You're just going to have to find out the hard way."

Behind me, I heard Ryan sigh.

***

By the time we made it back upstairs, breakfast was a charred disaster. I found Skye half way through rescuing as much of it as she could. When I told her who was waiting for her, she dropped her spatula with a clatter, and stared at me in white-faced shock for nearly a minute.

I couldn't blame her. When Ryan had vanished nearly a month before, none of us had really expected him to return.

"He came back?" she whispered. "Why? Why would he come back now?"

"I don't know, but he's waiting out in the lobby if you want to ask him," I answered gently. "You don't have to, though, if you don't want to. I can tell him to go away."

"No, there's no need for that." She shook her head slowly, bit her lip, and looked down at the ground. "I'll go talk to him. Maybe it'll be okay. I mean, maybe."

"Don't let him push you into anything you don't want, okay?" I said, reaching out to my baby sister with a gentleness that I reserved only for her. She nodded and hugged me quickly, then went out to meet her estranged fiancé with a brave face.

Elly and Michael stood nearby, watching the exchange with very different expressions on their faces. Once my sister had left, I gave Elly a long-suffering smile, and Michael a hug. He hugged me back in silence, then detached himself and went off to gather up his belongings.

"There is a lot of tension in this group," Elly observed as she dished up the last of the food for those that hadn't eaten yet. "I hope this will not cause problems later on."

"I have no idea if it will or not," I admitted, accepting the plate that she offered to me. "I guess we'll just have to find out along the road. We can't stay here, so this isn't going to delay our departure."

"Well, eat up, then." Elly smiled at me and gestured towards my plate. "My husband has gone off to fetch the cars that he's repaired for us, and wanted me to tell you that he'll be back soon. Once he returns, we'll need to go."

"Yeah, we will." I stuck a fork into my breakfast and shovelled some into my mouth, and tried not to think about how it was going to feel to leave my little home behind. It hadn't been mine for very long, but I had more happy memories in Ohaupo than anywhere else in the last ten years.

As loathe as I was to admit it, I was going to miss that little town. At least this time, I was leaving with a sense of hope in my chest, instead of despair.

***

"All right, here we go. And... up!"

I watched from the side-lines as the men struggled to lift the heavy barrels of fuel up onto the back of one of the new utility vehicles that Zain had managed to scavenge from the outlying farmsteads. The addition of a qualified, experienced mechanic to our team had done a world of good. I would be the first person to admit that I was pretty much just guessing, and had no idea what I was actually doing.

Under Zain's touch, my Hilux was purring like a kitten, and he'd managed to find three more tough, reliable utes to add to our small fleet. Yeah, I was a little jealous of his skills, but I was mostly just relieved. Having cars gave us freedom, and having a real mechanic meant that we could pick and choose rather than going with the ones that I thought I might be able to fix up through trial and error.

Two of the trucks had been relegated for cargo, and the other two for a mixture of cargo and passengers. Now, the women stood guard while the men put their strength to good use, loading everything that we could carry onto the back of the trucks.

"We should be ready to go by mid-morning," I commented, glancing up at the sky. "I don't trust those clouds; I think we'll have rain soon."

"Not much we can do about it," Skye answered, following my gaze up to the darkening heavens. "Let's just hope we find shelter by nightfall."

"We won't – we're sleeping under the stars tonight." I gave her a sideways grin and nudged her in the side. "Good thing we have tarps, right?"

Skye smiled, but didn't say anything. My grin faded away when I realised that she wasn't going to rise to the bait, but I didn't want to call her out on it. She'd been quiet and sullen since Ryan's return, but I didn't really want to push her too hard until she'd had time to recover from the shock. At least she hadn't retreated into herself like when he'd first left, and keeping her active seemed to help her take her mind off it.

"I think that's the last of it," Michael said as he came up to us, dusting off his hands. "Let's go grab your things from upstairs, honey."

"All right," I agreed, leading the way back into our little store. It looked so sad and empty without its layer of trash and junk, familiar objects that I'd gotten used to. For a while, it had been home.

As if sensing my bleak thoughts, I felt Michael's hand fall on my shoulder and I was drawn into a gentle hug. "It's okay, Sandy. We'll find somewhere else. And this time, it really will be ours, won't it?"

"Yeah," I agreed softly. I gave him a weak smile, then went back upstairs to the loft. We had chosen to leave the furniture behind, but we were taking all the blankets and pillows with us, along with the food, cutlery, cookware, and everything else that we had a use for. That had already gone into the trucks, and it left my beloved loft looking strangely barren.

Michael hugged me tight, right at the moment when tears threatened to break through my emotional reserves. With great difficulty, I fought them back and kept myself strong, for myself as much as for him. I knew he wouldn't judge me for crying. The children were already downstairs, waiting safely in one of the new trucks, along with Alfred. Of course, thinking about the dog made me think of my kitten.

"Has anyone seen Tigger this morning?" I asked, suddenly concerned.

"Maddy's got her, don't worry," Michael answered gently, leaning down to press a kiss against my cheek. "When she sat down and put her seatbelt on, Tigger jumped right into her lap, curled up, and went to sleep. I think she's coming whether we like it or not."

"Oh." I took a deep breath, trying to force myself to relax. "That's good, I guess. I mean, I'm sure she'd be fine without us, but… I don't like the idea of abandoning her forever. I'm fond of her."

"I know you are." Michael chuckled softly. He slid his arm around my waist and guided me through the living room, into the bedroom where we'd spent so much of our early relationship getting to know one another. The bed had been stripped, all the medical supplies moved to the trucks, and Anahera had been carried out to the back of the Hilux. The only things left were my personal belongings – my backpack, my salvaged clothing, and the few tiny personal items that I'd collected along the way.

I disentangled myself from Michael's embrace, and went over to finish packing. My backpack was already full, but I had collected a few small suitcases for my spare clothing. No point letting it go to waste. One by one, I emptied the drawers out, and packed the neatly folded garments into the cases waiting for them, then did them up and gave them to Michael to carry downstairs.

Eventually, all that was left was me, my backpack, and my travel items. One by one, I packed my taser, GPS, and medical kit into the pockets of my cargo pants, and put on my backpack. On top of the dresser, a single incongruity stared back at me: the little group of Sylvanian Families bunnies that I'd collected months ago, before I even knew that my sister was still alive.

They were dead weight. Taking them with me would be a waste of space. There had been times when that alone would have been enough for me to leave them behind, but my whole attitude towards life had changed since then. Now, sentiment mattered. It mattered more than anything else in the world. That little family represented my own lost family, and now that I'd found my sister it seemed more important than ever to keep the memory of our parents alive. It took me no time at all to make the decision to bring them along.

Michael had never asked about the bunnies, even though he'd seen them on numerous occasions. He was an intuitive man, so he had probably already guessed what they meant to me. Skylar, on the other hand, shot me a curious glance when I came out the door with the little toys in my hand.

"What are those?" she asked. "I saw them when I was going to the bathroom, but never got around to asking."

"You were probably too young to remember." I smiled at her, then took her hand and put the little family of bunnies in it. "When the plague first arrived in New Zealand, our family travelled through Ohaupo on our way south and we stopped here for a while. You saw these in the old antique store, and begged me to buy them for you. I couldn't, and that made you cry.

"So, consider this my gift to you, baby sis. I couldn't give them to you when you were eight, but I can give them to you now. Hang onto them and keep them safe. One day, one of us will have kids to play with them."

Skylar stared at me with the stunned-mullet expression that she sometimes got when I pulled a real curve ball on her, but I didn't have anything else to say. I just patted her shoulder, and guided her towards her place in the convoy, then went to say my last goodbyes to my store. The door stood open and empty, revealing a room beyond that was dark and shadowy but cleaner than it had ever been before.

"Ah, Benny, if only you could see this place now," I commented to myself. I went through and locked the inner doors one last time, then set the key ring down on the counter. There was no point taking them with me. Unlike when we'd left Hamilton, this time we were leaving nothing behind that we might want to come back for, except our memories. Lots and lots of memories. Thankfully, memories were portable, and they only weighed as much as we let them.

With that thought in mind, I turned my back on my little store, and headed out to the waiting convoy.

# Chapter Seven

The rain came around lunchtime. We stopped for a few minutes to shovel down a cold meal, then piled back into the cars, onto the bikes, and resumed travelling. By the time we were on the move again, the rain was pelting down with such force that the fat droplets had our windscreen wipers working overtime.

"Are you sure Hemi and his lads will be all right out there on those little bikes of theirs?" Michael asked suddenly, hunched over the wheel as he struggled to make out the road in front of us. He and I led the convoy in our Hilux, with everyone else strung out behind us along the road south towards Te Awamutu.

"Well, I suggested that they come in until the rain passes, but he said they'd be fine." I glanced at him and shrugged. "They know where we are if they change their minds."

"It's going to be a miserable night tonight." He glanced back at me and smiled wryly. "I'm guessing that you plan for us to stop at the same place we spent the night last time?"

"Yeah. It's not dry, but at least it's secure." I returned his smile, and shifted my attention back to trying to fix the radio in my lap. "Like I told Skye, at least we have tarps. We'll rig something up. Gotta be a bit inventive in this day and age, right?"

"True that," Michael agreed dryly. "I think we're about to enter the earthqu—"

Just as he was saying the words, we hit the first break in the tarmac. Years earlier, a terrible earthquake had flattened the city of Te Awamutu, and left the road rippled like a concrete ocean. The jolt took him by surprise, but I'd been watching our position on the GPS so I was braced for it.

I grabbed my walkie-talkie off my belt, and held it up to my lips. "Guys, we're entering Te Awamutu. The ground here is really rough, but your trucks should be able to take it. Go into four wheel drive mode, just in case. Hemi, if you and your boys have any trouble, sing out and we'll put you in one of the trucks."

"We're fine!" Hemi snapped back from somewhere down the line. "It's just a little rollercoaster, like Rainbow's End. We'll – WHOA – we'll be fine!"

"Stubborn, that's what you are," I teased him, then clicked the radio off and looked at Michael. "You wanna take bets on how long it'll be before someone throws up?"

"No bet." He laughed and shook his head. "Honestly, I'm amazed we've made it this far without one of the kids complaining that they need to pee."

"Don't jinx it," I answered dryly.

"What... is that noise?" a voice asked weakly from the back seat. I looked back over my shoulder, and I found Anahera's bewildered face peering back at me. "Sandy? Sandy, is that you?"

"You're awake!" I gasped, surprised and thrilled at the same time. "Thank God. You worried us half to death, Ana. How are you feeling?"

"Terrible," she answered bluntly, slowly lifting a hand to touch her bandaged head. "Where... where am I?"

"You're in a car, heading south with us," I told her. Sympathetic to her discomfort, I grabbed my own water bottle, took the lid off, and held it out to her. "Here, drink this. You've been unconscious for four days."

"Four days?" Her eyes flew wide in surprise. She tried to lean forward, but we'd strapped her in nice and tight to keep her from bouncing around too much while she was unconscious. "Where's Hemi? Where's my son? And Wiremu, Nikora, and Petera? Last I saw them, we were in the pantry, and death was pounding on the door."

"They're all fine," I reassured her. "They're here, in different parts of the convoy. We rescued the four of you from the pantry and brought you home with us, but it was too dangerous to take you back to your camp. Those things are everywhere, so we've all joined together and we're heading south. All of your tribe are with us, except for the ones that… we couldn't get to in time. I'm sorry, Anahera. We saved everyone we could."

"I know," she said softly, sadly. "I know that you would have done everything in your power to save my family. I am grateful that you saved as many as you did." She suddenly seemed to remember the bottle of water I was still holding, and reached out to take it from me. Although her grip was weak, she drank deeply and it seemed to refresh her. When she finished drinking, she handed the bottle back to me, looking a bit more relaxed.

"We did," I agreed. "And we're going to keep doing everything we can to protect your clan, if you agree. I want to combine our groups. If you want to take your men and leave, we'll understand, but—"

"There's no need to explain, Sandy," she interrupted me, a gentle smile touching her lips. "I understand. I was going to suggest the same at our next meeting, anyway. It is a shame that we were not able to gather our things before we left, but our lives are more important than our possessions."

"Yeah." I nodded, screwing the cap back onto my bottle. "There are plenty of things out here for the taking, but we can't replace you, or Hemi, or any of the others. The mutants are spreading, and leaving death in their wake."

"They are." She closed her eyes, her expression turning grim. "I underestimated the threat they posed. Now, I wish we'd taken your warning more seriously."

"Don't blame yourself." I reached back, and rested my hand over top of hers. "We're only just realising what they're capable of. "That's why we're going south. We're going to go as far as we can, and hopefully outrun them."

"What about the others, though?" She opened her eyes, and stared at me intently.

I blinked and stared back at her. "What others?"

"The other survivors," she answered. Suddenly, she grabbed my hand. "There are others out here, though we rarely see them. We must find some way to warn them, or they are lambs to the slaughter. Even the bad ones do not deserve to be eaten."

"I'm all for warning them, but how can we contact them?" I shrugged helplessly. "We had a shortwave radio, but we searched for days and only ever found the folks at the power station, which is where we're heading now."

Anahera went silent for a long moment, then looked me in the eye again. "Avalon. We must go to Avalon."

"…Excuse me?" I stared at her, wondering if she'd been hit on the head a little too hard. Of course, Anahera wasn't one to mince words. She flapped a hand, and quickly clarified what she meant.

"We must go to the suburb of Avalon, in Lower Hutt," she explained. "There, we'll find the Anchorman. He is the only means we have to disseminate information across the entire country."

"The Anchorman? You know where he is?" I asked, surprised.

"The who?" Michael asked, shooting a confused look at us.

"The Anchorman," I repeated. "He's the guy that runs the six o'clock news. He's been running it ever since the plague."

"Oh, that guy. Yeah, I think you mentioned him once." His expression turned sheepish. "Sorry, I never watched much television."

"Nothing to apologise for," Anahera said, waving the apology away. She smiled faintly to herself, her eyes drifting out of focus. "He's an old friend. His name is Simon. Simon Wentworth. We knew one another a lifetime ago, back in university, and we used to keep in touch. We haven't spoken recently, but I know that he was working at Avalon Studios around the time when the end came. My bet is that he's still there."

"Okay, so we want to go to Avalon – now there's something I never thought I'd say seriously." I eased myself back into my seat, picked up my GPS, and thumbed in the location. "That's a long, long way south. Almost as far as Wellington."

"It'll get us far away from the mutants, which seems like a very good idea if you ask me," Michael commented dryly.

"No argument here." I chuckled softly, and leaned over to pat his thigh. "We can follow the State Highways south to Lake Taupo, and then try to cut across the Desert Road from there, but I'm not sure what kind of condition it's in. Last time I was down that way, Mount Tongariro was still erupting."

"Ah, the guilty lovers," Anahera murmured thoughtfully from the back seat. "Yes, let us go visit them. It seems appropriate, though you do not have a husband to betray with your lover."

"I have no idea what you're talking about now," I admitted, glancing over my shoulder at her.

"It is an old legend amongst my people." She smiled at me dreamily, then turned her head and stared off out the window again. "In Maori folklore, different aspects of the natural world are embodied with spirits, just like people. The volcanoes, Ruapehu and Taranaki, were once husband and wife, but while Taranaki was out hunting one day, Ruapehu betrayed him with her fiery lover, Tongariro. Taranaki caught them in the act and fled westwards towards the sea, where he rests to this day, glaring at the traitorous lovers from afar. Ruapehu regrets her infidelity, and sometimes she sighs with longing for him. Tongariro smoulders with jealous anger, for he knows that he can never truly own her heart."

I listened curiously as she told her tale; I knew as much as anyone that the Maori people had legends to explain every aspect of the natural world, but I'd never had the chance to learn that particular one. When she finished the story, I sat quietly for a moment, and then looked at her again. "Were they real people? Ruapehu, Taranaki, and Tongariro? Were the mountains named after them?"

"I don't think so." Anahera laughed and shook her head. "Every tribe has their own variations of the legends. Another one states that there were once seven mountains around Lake Taupo, all male except for the lovely Pihanga. The men fought over her, throwing molten rock high into the air and shaking the ground with their war-dances. In the end, Tongariro won the battle, and with it Pihanga's hand." Suddenly, she grinned. "In that legend, Ruapehu is a male, one of the many vying for Pihanga's love."

"I can't tell if those stories are romantic, or if it's disturbing that no one can agree if Ruapehu is a male or female mountain," I commented, amused. "I mean, surely you could just lift up its skirts and check, right?"

Anahera chuckled at that. "My dear, if you can figure out a way to lift up a mountain's skirt and check its gender, then good luck to you."

***

We reached the campsite overlooking the ruins of Te Awamutu just as the sun was starting to set. The rain was still pelting down, and it drenched me to the bone the moment I hopped out of the Hilux. Ignoring the cold, I raced around to open the gate for Michael. It was the same spot that we'd camped at on our way to Arapuni a couple of weeks earlier, and everything was just as we'd left it. The only difference was that this time, we were leaving for good.

I waited by the gate while each of the trucks drove through, then the outriders on their little motorcycles. Once everyone was safely inside, I heaved the rusty gate closed, and sealed it with a length of heavy chain and an old padlock that we'd brought with us from Ohaupo.

As I wound the chain tight between the bars of the fence, I heard Michael shouting orders. By the time I was done, the trucks had been parked in a ring around our campsite, like a circle of wagons. I paused to admire the simple utility of the action: not only would the trucks serve to protect us from the enemy, but they'd guard us from the wind and rain as well. It amazed me to think about how the tricks used by our ancestors in the early days of colonization had come back into use, hundreds of years later. I didn't have long to think about it, though; there was too much work to be done for me to stand around wool-gathering.

There wasn't enough space in the trucks to bring individual tents for everyone, even if we had enough, which we didn't. Instead, we'd brought along a single huge canvas awning, large enough to shelter us all from the rain. I hurried over to help Michael, who was struggling to lift the heavy pole on his side of the awning. One by one, the other three corners of the awning went up, and we rushed around securing the ground ties to keep it steady.

Michael smiled at me, and leaned down to give me a quick kiss. "Orders, captain?"

"I thought you were taking command tonight?" I asked, raising a brow.

"Only when you're busy," he answered, a touch of embarrassment flitting across his face. "I prefer to leave it in your capable hands. I never wanted to be in charge. I'd rather be able to focus on just keeping everyone safe."

"Fair enough." I gave him a quick hug, to reassure him that I didn't think any lesser of him for surrendering his leadership position, then I pulled back and did as he asked. "We need a watch for the night. I want four people on guard at all times, one to watch each side. Two rotations, like normal, but give priority to those that won't be driving tomorrow, since they can sleep in the car. Also, I want you to get Priya and that Yousefi boy, what's his name?"

"Matt?" Michael supplied.

"Right." I nodded. "I want Priya and Matt to take a watch. They're old enough to start learning how to contribute."

"Good call," Michael agreed. "It'll make them feel more included, too. I'll spare Doc the watch, though – I think he needs his sleep."

"Yeah, spare the wounded." I grinned suddenly and reached up to pat his cheek. "But not me. I'll take a watch. I'm feeling fine."

"If you insist." Michael chuckled, kissed me again, and went off about his business. I allowed myself a moment to savour the taste of his lips, then I went off about mine as well. Thinking about Priya and Matt gave me an idea, another little task to make all the kids feel more included. It seemed odd to put them to work to welcome them, but it was a strange world that we lived in.

I found the two oldest children sitting right where we'd left them on arrival, waiting obediently in the truck with the animals and the younger kids. They looked at me in surprise when I opened the door beside them.

"Hey guys, I need help with something," I told them. "You want a job to do?"

"Yes!" Priya agreed immediately, followed a moment later by Maddy. The Yousefi boys were more reserved; the younger three regarded me silently with large, solemn eyes, but Matt, the eldest, nodded hesitantly.

"Awesome. Now, I'm going to split you into two groups. Matt, Priya, and--" I hesitated for a moment, then looked at the second oldest boy, a scrawny kid of about eleven. "What's your name?"

"Javed," he answered shyly.

I smiled at him and nodded. "Javed. Cool. Okay, Matt, Priya, and Javed, I want the three of you to go over to that old house over there and see if you can find some dry firewood." I turned and pointed past our campsite, at the ruins of the homestead that had once occupied the rear half of the enclosure. "Be careful not to cut yourselves, okay? Bring back whatever you find, and put it somewhere that the rain won't make it wet."

"Okies," Priya agreed happily, practically leaping out of the car. She raced off towards the ruins, leaving the boys staring after her. They exchanged a look, then climbed out and raced after her. Once they were gone, I turned and looked at the three remaining kids.

"You guys are a bit young to go digging around in there, but I have a job for you, too," I explained. Maddy smiled and nodded, but the two younger boys just stared at me. Suddenly, I realised that they were frightened of me – possibly of all of us. It had been a rough few days for all of them, and I was a stranger. "Aw, hey, don't be scared, sweeties. I won't hurt you."

Maddy's smile widened. "I'm glad you noticed, Miss Sandy. They're very scared."

"I haven't been around kids very much, but I'm learning," I admitted sheepishly. "You hear that? My name is Sandy. That's not a scary name, is it?"

The youngest child just stared blankly, but the older boy was around Maddy's age, old enough to understand what I was trying to say. He shook his head slowly. I smiled at him in return.

"It's not a scary name, because I'm not a scary person." I hesitated for a moment, and decided to channel my inner child a bit. "I'm only scary when the bad monsters come and try to eat you, and then I'm scary to them. I go 'grrr!' and chase the bad monsters away! Remember?"

The boy smiled a little bit and he nodded again. Beside him, Maddy giggled.

"Miss Sandy is very nice, I promise," she added in my defence, then pointed at the boys. "The big one is Barry, and the little one is Ommie. Don't worry, Miss Sandy – they're my friends, so we'll help."

"That's great." Relieved, I reached over and patted the top of the little girl's head. "Thanks, Maddy. What I want you guys to do is start spreading plastic sheets on the ground. No one wants to sleep on the wet ground. The plastic sheets should be in the back of this truck."

"Okay!" Maddy agreed cheerfully. She picked Tigger up out of her lap and set the kitten on the seat beside her, then hopped up and scurried off. Sure enough, the two boys climbed out and followed after her. Once they were gone, I left Tigger to sleep and went off in search of my sister.

I found her few minutes later, sitting on the tailgate of one of the trucks, staring intently at the tip of her left index finger. Curious, I went over to her to see what had her so fascinated. Just as I was getting close, I heard her issue a deep, soulful sigh.

"What's the matter, baby sis?" I asked, suddenly concerned. There hadn't been much time to talk recently, so I had no idea how she was handling the emotional fallout from her painful miscarriage a little over a month before.

"Huh?" She glanced up suddenly, but relaxed when she recognised me. "Oh, hey Sandy. I cut my finger this morning, and it's annoying me. It's not deep or anything, and it's not bleeding, but there's this little flap of skin. It keeps catching on everything, and it's driving me crazy."

I blinked in surprise, then laughed. I just couldn't help it. After everything she'd been through, what made her sound sad was a little flap of skin?

"Gnaw it off," I suggested. "That's what I do. It looks gross, but at least it'll stop catching on stuff."

"You reckon?" She stared at her finger dubiously, then shrugged and lifted her finger to her mouth to do as I suggested. While she was at it, I went over and sat down on the tailgate beside her. It was rare for us to have a moment alone, so I decided it was as good a time as any to check on her well-being.

"How are you doing, Skye?" I asked softly, watching her carefully to gauge her reaction. "With the baby thing, I mean. We've hardly had time to talk at all."

She paused in her nibbling and stared at me for a moment, then shrugged and glanced away. "I'm... coping. It sucks, and it hurts – both physically, and in my heart – but there's no way for us to go back and change the past. At least we learned a lesson from it – listeria poisoning is bad, and now we know how to avoid it. So, when you and Michael have a baby, you won't have to go through that."

"What makes you think that Michael and I are having a baby?" I asked, startled by the notion. We'd talked about it in passing, sure, but mostly just as a joke.

"I've seen the way you look at him, sis," she said with a tender smile. "You love him. You really, really love him. The two of you should have a baby together, because all babies deserve a mother and father that love each other that much."

I stared at her for a moment, then turned away, feeling the heat rising in my cheeks. She wasn't wrong, but that was what made it so difficult to accept. Michael was so ready to be a dad, but I was not ready to be a mother.

"Maybe one day, but not today," I answered. Suddenly, I desperately wanted to change the subject. "So, anyway. I've got the kids finding some firewood. Can I trust you to take care of preparing dinner?"

"Of course," she agreed, rising to her feet. "I'll go see what I can rustle up."

"Thanks, little sis." I gave her a grateful smile. She returned it, and scampered off about her business, leaving me to ponder hard questions on my own.

# Chapter Eight

The night passed more or less uneventfully. Every now and then, one of the watchers called out that they'd spotted something, and once I even thought I heard a growl, but when the sun finally rose there was no sign of danger. If the mutants had followed us, they'd retreated by morning.

We were back on the move as swiftly as possible, following the same road eastwards that we'd used previously. Once we left the earthquake zone, the going was smooth and easy. I napped in the passenger seat of the Hilux for most of the morning, leaving Michael to concentrate on driving. We stopped briefly at the cornfield to bolster our supplies, then we were back on the road again.

Shortly before noon, I felt the Hilux roll to a stop. I dragged myself out of the warm, comfortable embrace of sleep, to find that we'd already reached the point at the base of the hills where the road started to climb up into cliffs and narrow ravines.

"We can't follow the road up there," Michael said, looking at me for guidance. "Remember, there was that break we had to climb around?"

"I remember." I nodded thoughtfully. "We're just going to have to go around the base of the cliff. It's not going to be fun, but at least the rain's cleared up for now."

A few minutes later, I stood with my group spread out around me, enjoying a moment of sunshine while I could. When the last of them fell into place, I cleared my throat and addressed them.

"All right, guys, we're going off-road for a while," I said. "Unfortunately, there's a bloody great hole in the road up ahead, so we're going to have to take the long way. I need every strong hand that isn't behind the wheel of a car or the handles of a bike out in front, clearing away any obstructions. This is pig country, so everyone stay on high alert. Don't let your guard down. Now, I need two people to ride ahead and scout for the best route. Volunteers?"

The hands of everyone that knew how to ride the bikes – and several who didn't – shot up. I didn't even try to fight my grin. It felt like the bigger our group got, the more people wanted to volunteer to help. They probably just wanted to impress one another, but I didn't mind. It pleased me to see people willing to participate.

"Okay, Skye and Richard," I called, pointing to each of them in turn. "I need you two to find the path of least resistance and guide us to it. Be extra careful, and if you see, hear, or smell anything out of the ordinary, come back. Got it?"

Skylar blinked in obvious surprise. "Really? You want me to go?"

"You put your hand up," I pointed out. "Do you want to go or not?"

"Well, yes, but I didn't expect you to pick me," she answered. "You never pick me."

"It's just logistics, sis," I answered, chuckling. "You two are small, agile, and can move quickly, plus I know you can handle yourselves in a fight. Sending you two means I have the stronger lads here to help with the heavy lifting. No offense, Richard."

"None taken," he answered, grinning broadly. Richard was a slender, soft-spoken man, and while he was stronger than he looked, he didn't possess the brute strength of his kinsmen. I smiled back at him, silently acknowledging his understanding.

Skye cocked her head to one side thoughtfully, then suddenly she grinned as well. "Okay, cool! I like this logic. C'mon, Richard. You'll need to show me how to ride."

"Take the quad bikes, they're easier on rough terrain," I called after her.

Once they were off, I turned my attention back to the rest of the group. My group, I realised with a sudden flash of pride. My friends. My family. My... minions? The thought almost made me laugh out loud. Instead, I distracted myself with more logistics.

"Okay," I clapped my hands and started handing out roles. "Zain, I want you to lead in the Hilux. You know these trucks better than anyone, so make sure you sing out if we try to take them somewhere they can't handle. Doc, you're in the second truck with the youngest kids. Ana, are you good to drive?"

"Yes, I should be able to," she answered, nodding.

"Good." I smiled at her, trying to be reassuring. She wasn't quite back to her usual bubbly self yet, but she was definitely on the mend. "Please take the third truck. Elly, bring up the rear. Matt, Priyanka, I want you on watch duty. Do you know what that means?"

"Means we watch," Priya answered immediately, playfully pulling her eyelids back with her fingertips. "We watch for pigs, for bad mens, all bad things. Yes?"

"Perfect." I nodded and grinned at her. "If you see anything bad, or even something you're not sure about, you shout as loud as you can. Okay?"

"Okies!" Priya agreed immediately. "We watch good. No bads get past us!"

"Very good," I acknowledged, pleased by both her enthusiasm and her quick uptake. I looked at Matt, and gave him a smile as well. "Do you understand what you need to do, too?"

"Yes ma'am," the youth answered quietly. "Watch duty. Anything out of the ordinary, we'll shout."

"Good man," I answered. "Don't hesitate, even if you're not sure. Take Alfie with you. I don't want you two taking any risks, got it?"

Both of the teenagers nodded their understanding. I looked at the rest of the faces in the crowd, and gave them a grin.

"All right, guys," I announced. "Everyone else is with me. Let's get to it!"

*** 

A few hours later, a cool wind told me that the rain was about to return, and this time it came as a relief. Most of the brush was thin enough for the trucks to just drive through, there were still occasional mounds of deadfall and loose rocks blocking the path. It was hard, heavy labour, and I ended up drenched with sweat in no time at all.

I felt a raindrop land on my shoulder and glanced up at the sky. Dark clouds were rolling in, but they weren't truly threatening. It wasn't a storm, just rain. A few droplets fell on my face, and made me smile.

"What are you grinning at?" Skylar asked.

I jumped at the unexpected sound of her voice, and spun around. "Damn, don't scare me like that. No one told me you were back."

"We just got here," Skye replied. "So, what are you grinning about?"

"Oh, just the rain," I admitted with a shrug. "I like the rain. It's peaceful. Soothing. Washes away all our sins, and leaves the world clean and sparkling."

"It's also wet and cold," Skye pointed out. "Anyway, I need to show you something so we can figure out what to do."

"Okay," I agreed. "Is it far? Should I get a bike?"

"Nah, not far. We can take mine. Richard's back there, talking to Ropata." Skye turned and led the way off into the bush. I grabbed my shotgun and hurried after her. We climbed onto the back of her quad bike, and then we were off.

It only took a few minutes to reach our destination. Skye eased our bike to a stop and pointed ahead of us, but the gesture was unnecessary. I spotted the problem immediately: a shallow stream cut across our path, winding between earthen banks at least a foot high.

"Well, that is a problem," I said, easing myself off the back of the bike so I could take a better look. Skye joined me a few seconds later. "If I remember rightly, we crossed a little to the north on our way home from Arapuni, in the deeper forest. The trucks can't go that way."

"Yeah. We already checked, and this is the only way that isn't blocked by trees," Skye replied, shaking her head. "Unless we want to backtrack for ages, we have to find a way across. Can we build a bridge, do you think?"

"Nah, I don't think we need to," I answered thoughtfully. "We'll just flatten the banks. It'll take a bit of digging, but it shouldn't be too bad." I pulled my walkie-talkie off my belt, and spoke into it. "Michael?"

There was a momentary delay, then his deep voice came on, husky and out of breath. "Yes?"

"Can you please send Richard back this way with shovels?" I asked. "He should be somewhere near you."

"I see him," Michael said. "No problem, I'll pass on the orders. Stay safe."

"Always." I hung up, and put my radio back on my belt. When I glanced back at Skylar, I caught her trying very hard not to laugh. I raised a brow, and gave her a look. "What are you giggling at, little sis?"

"Oh, just you and Michael," she answered dryly. "You're so formal when you know people are watching, but as soon as you think no one's looking, the lovebirds come out."

"Gah, this again?" I threw my hands up in mock irritation. "You're such a gossip fiend."

"Totally am," Skye agreed cheerfully. "What can I say? You're an easy target."

"Don't make me kick your butt, you cheeky miss," I told her, but she must have seen on my face that I was only joking. She just laughed.

"As if!" She planted her hands on her hips, and rolled her eyes dramatically. "I'm your baby sister. You couldn't hurt me if you tried."

"True." I paused for a second, studying her thoughtfully. "Speaking of which, how are you dealing with Ryan being back?"

"I dunno," she admitted with a shrug. "We've… talked, but it's not like it used to be. I'm not sure it'll ever be like it used to be. He's changed so much that I'm not sure he's still the same person I was engaged to."

"Did he tell you where he went while he was away?" I asked, genuinely curious to hear the answer. To my surprise, Skye hesitated.

"He…" She glanced down at the ground, and her expression changed to something I'd never seen before. "He tried to kill himself, Sandy."

"What?" I exclaimed, stunned by the revelation. "Seriously?"

"Seriously," she said softly, nodding. "Have you noticed that he's always wearing long sleeved shirts now, even though it's not that cold? It's to hide the bandages. He didn't want me to know, but I made him show me. He tried to cut his wrists." Suddenly, there were tears in her eyes, and she was struggling to keep them under control. "He couldn't find a knife, so he tried to use a saw blade. A saw blade!"

"Oh, my God," I whispered, my hands flying up to cover my mouth without any conscious thought on my part. "But he survived?"

Skylar nodded miserably, wiping tears from her eyes. "He said that he passed out in a puddle of his own blood, expecting to never wake up. But he did. He said that he didn't cut deep enough, and he was too scared of the pain to try again."

"Jesus. I think I saw his blood." I plopped down to sit on a fallen log, the strength draining right out of me. "Michael and I did. Just before we left for the power station. We couldn't figure out what happened, so we just… left it. It was a couple of weeks old, so we figured whatever left the blood was long gone."

"It was, sort of," Skye said, wiping away the last tear. "He said he went to one of the farthest outlying farms for a while, and just stayed there. He saw Zain come by when he was out looking for our new trucks, but he stayed out of sight until they left. When he realised that Zain was going back to Ohaupo, he got worried and came to check on us." Skye heaved a long, deep sigh that was painful just to listen to. "I kind of wish he'd stayed gone, but it's hard to stay mad because I understand how he felt."

"Aw, sis," I whispered, shoving myself back to my feet. I went over and put my arms around her, drawing her into a tight hug. "I wish I could make this better for you."

"You can't," she said softly, snuggling up against me. "No one can. I miss Kylie so much, I just… I want to take care of someone's baby, even if it's not mine." She pushed herself back and looked up at me. "Are you sure you won't have a baby with Michael? I'll look after her for you, if that's what you're worried about."

"I can't, honey," I answered, gently stroking her hair back away from her forehead. "Not yet, anyway. Not until it's safe. This journey could take us a couple of months, and I'm pretty sure it would suck to be travelling while pregnant. Right?"

"Yeah," she agreed reluctantly. "But once we find a place to call home, will you consider it?"

"I… I don't know," I admitted. "I'm kind of scared of the idea. I don't know if I could be the kind of mother that you'd be. I mean, I'm pretty crazy, right?"

"You are not crazy!" she yelled suddenly, then she shoved herself back away from me and slapped me hard on the shoulder. "Don't talk about yourself like that. Don't you *dare* talk about yourself like that!"

"Whoa!" Startled, I jumped back away from her, rubbing my bruised arm. "What the hell, sis?"

"That is not you talking," she answered, stalking up to me to wag a finger in my face like a disapproving school ma'am. "That is Lee talking, and he is dead. You are not allowed to let him control you anymore. Do you understand me?"

"No, I really don't," I admitted. "What are you talking about?"

"This is not you, sis," she repeated, suddenly turning gentle, yet somehow stern at the same time. "The Sandrine McDermott that I remember was a beautiful, confident, intelligent, friendly girl. I remember her. I looked up to her. Maybe I don't know everything that happened to you over the years, but every time you open your mouth and something self-deprecating falls out, it's like I'm hearing someone else's voice coming out of you."

I felt myself flush and glanced away, helplessly trying to derail the conversation with dry humour. "Self-deprecating, huh? That's a big word. You been reading the dictionary?"

"Shut up," Skye told me in no uncertain terms. Suddenly, she grabbed me and shook me hard. The action stunned me so much that I didn't even think about fighting back. "You did this for me once, so now it's my turn to do it for you. Stop trying to sabotage yourself, Sandy. You don't even realise that you're doing it.

"Every time you say something like that, something that puts you down, you're letting someone else's opinion take control of you. Those words are his words, and the way that he controlled you when you were his. You're not his anymore. You beat him. You are your own woman again. You need to learn to stop letting him control how you feel about yourself."

I started to say something, but whatever I was thinking of saying just sort of died in my throat. I wanted to deny it, I wanted to tell her that my words were always my own, but some part of me knew that wasn't true. Suddenly, I realised that the voice of self-doubt that I'd been warring with for so long, it wasn't my voice at all. It was his. It had been his for a long time.

Before I quite knew what was happening to me, I felt my emotional dam breaking down, and the screaming, thrashing, irrational, uncontrollable pain that had been building up behind it broke free. Skylar caught me a moment before I would have collapsed, and held me in her arms while I wept.

# Chapter Nine

My fit passed by the time the others joined us, leaving me feeling wrung-out but strangely refreshed. They found us sitting side by side on a log, both of us soaking wet; thankfully, the rain hid the fact that I'd been crying. Michael would no doubt have known at a glance, but he wasn't with them, so I had a brief respite in which to recover.

Richard brought his quad bike to a stop a couple of meters away from us, with Ryan and Nikora close behind him. I shot a glance at my sister to gauge her reaction, but her face was an expressionless mask. She just nodded for me to go ahead, so I rose to my feet and went to meet them.

"Hey, guys," I said by way of greeting. "We need to flatten these banks out so that the trucks can get over them. Skye, Richard, you two keep watch; we can take care of this. When the convoy reaches us, we'll stop for lunch."

"Sounds good," Skye agreed, nodding. She and Richard took up their weapons and went to watch the perimeter, while I took my crew and got to work. I've never been one to dither about when there was something that needed to be done, so I grabbed the nearest shovel and hopped down into the stream. It was only a shallow thing, a slender trickle of water no deeper than my boots. I bent down to examine the banks for a few seconds, then I gestured to Ryan and Nikora.

"Let's shift the dirt over there," I said, pointing a few meters beyond the stream. Ryan nodded silently, but Nikora hesitated.

"Why don't we just fill in the stream?" he asked, shooting me a peculiar look. "Wouldn't that be easier?"

"Easier, yes, but it would damage the ecosystem," I explained. "I'd rather not do that, just to save us a couple of minutes. My ancestors did enough damage to this beautiful land; I want to do whatever I can to preserve her. Don't you?"

The young man looked like he was going to protest for a second, but he stopped before the words left his mouth. He paused and thought about it, nodding slowly.

"True," he admitted quietly. "But it's not just your ancestors to blame. Mine are, too. I think all of us are."

"Exactly." I smiled at him, gesturing broadly towards the natural world around us. "It's down to us now. You, me, and the rest of our tribe. Our choices are the only ones left that can scar Mother Nature's beauty. We have the choice of whether to act responsibly, or irresponsibly."

"Too right." Nikora grinned suddenly, and picked up his shovel. "You're good at this, chica. No wonder they put you in charge."

"I'm only in charge because no one else wants to be," I answered. "I guess Mother Nature is just lucky that I care enough to think about that kind of thing. Come on, let's get started; the convoy will reach us soon."

The two men nodded, and hopped down to join me in the stream. Soon, we were hard at work demolishing the bank, but the rain washed away the sweat as fast as it formed. Every so often, I heard the crackle of the radio on my belt when someone called in to report something, but there was nothing out of the ordinary.

In due time, the convoy reached us just as we'd planned. Skylar shouted a greeting and waved. I stood up straight, running the back of my hand over my forehead to clear the rain from my eyes, and watched as the convoy moved in to park. They had everything under control without me, which left me and my small team to finish up our task in peace.

Soon, the others were settled in and the smell of cooking food tickled my nose. I heard footsteps behind me, and glanced up just in time to catch Michael's sweet smile. He grabbed me around the waist and kissed me quickly, then shoved me back with a good-natured laugh.

"You're wet, muddy, and sweaty, but still somehow manage to be gorgeous," he teased. "I don't know how you do it."

"Thanks for that, honey. You sure know how to make a girl feel pretty," I responded with my usual dry sense of humour, then I leaned up on tiptoes to give him a kiss in return. I caught Ryan looking at us oddly, but he turned away as soon as our eyes met.

"Kissie, kissie, kissie!" Priya's voice rang out, drawing my attention away from Ryan. She flung her arms around us both, and hugged us fiercely. "Kissie for me?"

"Always." I laughed, leaning down to plant a kiss on the top of her head, then I hugged her tight.

Priya giggled happily and wriggled within my embrace, then she pulled back and looked up at me. "Can I help, Mama?"

"We're pretty much done here," I answered. "You go find Matt, stay on guard duty. You keep the big bads away from the little kids, okay?"

"Okies!" Priya agreed happily. She disentangled herself from us and scampered off just as suddenly as she'd arrived. I looked up at Michael, and found him looking perplexed.

"What?" I asked, raising a brow.

"Mama?" he echoed. "When did that happen?"

"I have no idea," I admitted with a shrug. "Apparently, she just decided. I'm her mama now, and you're her papa. I didn't want to discourage her from bonding with people, so I figured I'd just roll with it."

"Well, that's sweet," he said quietly, a slow smile creeping across his face. "That kid is so far beyond being merely 'resilient' that we need to make up a whole new word just to describe her."

"Let's just stick with 'special', and not in the sarcastic sense of the word." I grinned at him, and gave his arm a playful punch. "Or how about 'inspiring'?"

"Oh, I like that," he agreed. "Let's go with inspiring. That makes her a perfect foster daughter for you, after all."

"If you keep talking like that, you're going to make me throw up." I laughed, shoving him playfully back towards the convoy. "Shoo, Officer Sexy. Go help with lunch. We'll be with you in a minute."

"You got it, boss!" He flailed a dramatic salute and jogged away, leaving me chuckling in his wake. I went to resume the last of the work needed to cross the stream, only to find Nikora watching me with open amusement.

"Hey, now. Don't you look at me in that tone of voice!" I planted my hands on my hips and fixed him with a mock glare. He laughed and started to say something, but his words died on his tongue as a shout rang out from the column. A moment later, the terrible sound of a weapon being discharged shattered the forest's tranquillity.

I leapt out of the stream and was off at a run before my conscious mind even fully realised that there was a threat. There was a scream and the sound of people shouting, followed by more gunfire. Then, there was a squeal. A blood-curdling squeal. A squeal that I knew very well.

"Pig!" I yelled at the top of my lungs. "Grab your weapons, and find cover! They need space to charge, and they can't climb. If you can get on top of the trucks or up a tree, then do it!"

"Sandy!" Elly screamed my name. Suddenly, she leapt out and grabbed my arm, her expression one of total panic. "It grabbed Ommie!"

"What?" I gasped, frantically searching for the beast; I could still hear it, but I couldn't see it. "Where is it?"

"It went that way!" she cried, pointing past the trucks towards the far end of the convoy. "Please, you have to help him!"

"Stay back, leave this to me," I told her, fighting down the bile that rose in the back of my throat. The thought of what an infected boar could do to a little child... I couldn't bear to think about it. I left her, and ran as hard as I could towards the back of the convoy, following the squeals. The gunfire had stopped now, but the pig's noises were interspersed with heavy thunks and human grunts.

Then, I heard something I never thought I'd have to hear: a young girl's voice raised in anger. "Dumb pig! Look at me!"

Just at that moment, I rounded the last truck in the convoy, and came face to face with a scene right out of my worst nightmares. A few meters in front of me, Ommie's bloody little body lay crumpled in the dirt. Maddy was crouched beside him, tense and alert, her attention fully focused on the battle. A dozen meters further away, Priya and Matt were locked in battle with a large, angry sow.

"No, I said look at me!" Priya demanded, rushing in to strike the beast as hard as she could with a branch. She raced away when it turned towards her, nimbly dodging its bloody teeth. Then Matt leapt forward, struck it from behind, and shouted something to draw its attention back to him. They weren't doing much damage, but they'd managed to lure the beast away from Ommie.

Elly cried out inarticulately and rushed past me, dropping to her knees beside Maddy. I froze for a second, my brain unable to process all the information at once. Then, Priya spotted me. She called out to me, and that made the decision for me. I couldn't do much good for Ommie, but I could still help Priya and Matt.

I left Elly to care for her fallen child and raced past her. The teenagers were doing exactly what they should be doing, but they were just kids. They wouldn't be able to keep it up forever. I crashed through a patch of ferns and leapt over a tangle of fallen branches, all while clutching the shovel in my hands. My shotgun was strapped across my back, but I didn't want to waste the precious seconds required to arm it.

Four more steps, and then I was there. The pig's back was to me. It didn't see me coming. I might not have been as strong as Michael or one of the other men, but I was well-practiced at making my blows felt; my shovel came crashing down on the back of the pig's neck, hard enough to make it stumble and drop to its knees.

Before it could recover, I lifted the shovel high above my head, and brought it down again with every ounce of strength in my body. It struck edge-on, channelling the force into a narrow area, and it had the desired effect. I felt bone crunch and break. I didn't stop, though. I kept hitting it, again and again, until it finally stopped moving.

"Someone go get the accelerant. We have to be certain." I heard a voice behind me, and turned to see Michael coming up to my side, his gun trained on the fallen pig. He gestured to the men standing beside him, and jerked his head towards the nearest vehicle. "I put some lighter fluid in the glove compartment of each car."

I jerked my shovel out of the pig's flesh and stepped back, letting Michael take command of the situation. Priya and Matt came to stand beside me. We watched in silence until the pig was ablaze; only then did I finally remember the important thing I'd forgotten in the adrenaline rush.

"Oh God – Ommie," I whispered, then I turned and raced back to the convoy. There, I found a group of people standing clustered together, whispering amongst themselves. I shoved my way through the wall of bodies, anxiety twisting a knot in my gut. "Please, please tell me that he's still alive."

"He is," Doc answered. "It looks bad, but it's mostly flesh wounds. I'll put in a few stitches and give him a shot to protect him from infections. He should be right as rain in a couple of days."

He glanced up at me, then looked back down at the little boy, who was nestled in his mother's arms. Suddenly, Zain shoved his way through the crowd and dropped to his knees beside her; he wrapped his arms around his wife and child, and hugged them both fiercely. His eyes shone with tears of relief, and I felt a knot of emotion gathering in my own throat in response. When I looked around, I saw that I wasn't the only one affected by the sight.

"Thank Allah." Elly sighed heavily, hugging her child's battered body. "Someone truly is watching over us this day."

The little boy stirred in her arms. His eyes fluttered open and looked up at her. "Mama? Papa?"

"We're here, Omid," Elly said, with the kind of tenderness that only a parent could have. "It's all right, my baby. You're safe."

"Is he okies?" Priya whispered to me. I just nodded and put my arm around her.

"Yeah, he's okay," I answered. "Thanks to you, Priya. You and Matt."

"No," Priya said quietly. I glanced at her, and saw a strange expression on her face, one that I didn't recognise. "Thanks to Maddy."

"What do you mean?" I asked, equal parts curious and surprised.

"Maddy knew," Priya said, turning to look up at me with huge eyes. "Maddy *knew*. She said to me last night that a pig was going to come, and we had to save Ommie or he would die. She told me what we had to do. She made me practice with her, and told me which stick to pick up and keep with me. I thought she was just... strange, but she knew, Mama. How? How she knew?"

"I don't know, honey, but I'm glad she knew." I tightened my grip around her shoulders, pulling her into a hug. "You did the right thing by listening to her."

"The little girl is a prophet?" Suddenly, Zain's voice interjected. I glanced at him, and found him and Elly watching us with wide eyes. "Madeline?"

"I don't know," I admitted, searching for her in the crowd, but now she was nowhere to be seen. I gave up and looked back at Zain. "Maddy has a gift. We don't know exactly what kind of gift, but whatever it is, it's saving lives."

"It's given us much more than that," Elly said, her tone carrying equal quantities of determination and awe. "That child has given us a miracle. You were the one that said to us that we must find our own hope, to save the children. If Madeline is a prophet, then she is the one that can lead us to a new future."

Suddenly, I heard a child laugh. Maddy squeezed through the wall of people and plopped down on the ground beside them, with her hand resting on Elly's arm.

"That's not my job, Missus Yousefi," Madeline told her. She smiled broadly, an expression that made her little face seem almost angelic. "That's Miss Sandy's job. She's going to save the children – *all* of the children, even me." Suddenly, she turned and looked at me, her eyes twinkling. "Isn't that right, Miss Sandy?"

Madeline had a way about her that never failed to take me by surprise. It took me a second to recover, but once I did, I simply nodded my agreement. Maddy beamed for a moment, then her expression turned serious.

"We need to go now," she told us all. "There are more pigs. If we wait too long, then they'll come here as well."

"I don't know about you lot, but that's enough warning for me." I straightened up, and gestured broadly to the people gathered around me. "Sorry, guys. Lunch is going to have to wait. Let's clear the forest, and see where we stand after that."

A chorus of wordless grunts met my instructions, and the crowd dispersed back to their assigned tasks. I waited until Ommie had been transferred to one of the trucks, then returned to the vanguard where I belonged.

# Chapter Ten

We made it to the edge of the forest safely. A shout from the scouts greeted me as I stepped out of the foliage and back onto solid tarmac. I waved to Skylar, then plucked my radio off my belt and relayed the news back to the rest of the convoy.

Within a few minutes, all the vehicles were lined back up and waiting to go. I did a quick headcount to make sure that no one got left behind, including the animals. Once I was sure that everyone was where they were supposed to be, I climbed back into the passenger seat of the Hilux and we were off. Michael was back behind the wheel again, but this time the only company we had was Alfred in the back. I shot a glance at Michael, and studied the contours of his face in the midday sun.

"You're staring at me," he pointed out without looking at me. "What's up?"

"Nothing," I answered. "I'm just thinking about Ryan and Skylar. Or more specifically, Ryan and Hemi. When Ryan figures out how Hemi feels about Skylar, it's going to be trouble. I can feel it in my bones."

"Ah." Michael nodded thoughtfully, then shot me a quick glance and gave me a smile. "There isn't much we can do about it, so try not to worry. Their relationships aren't our problem."

"It's not them I'm concerned about, it's the structural integrity of the group," I replied, sitting back in my seat and folding my arms across my chest. "Still, like you said, there isn't much we can do about it now. I'm going to try and take a nap. Wake me if you need me."

"Of course." Michael turned his attention back towards the road and fell silent. I shifted around in my seat until I was as comfortable as I could be, then closed my eyes and relaxed. At first, my mind was too busy for me to sleep, but eventually the sound of the rain, the hum of the engine, and the boredom of the road lulled me off to sleep.

\*\*\*

I snapped awake suddenly, instantly alert but uncertain what had woken me.

"What is it?" I demanded. "What's going on, what's wrong?"

"Nothing at all," Michael answered. I glanced at him, and found him peering at me curiously. "Everything is absolutely fine. We just passed Pukeatua, and we should reach Arapuni in another hour."

"Oh." I paused for thought, suddenly feeling a little bit stupid. "That's good. Sorry, it seems like whenever I sleep in the car, I wake up to bad things happening."

"You do have some particularly bad luck in that regard," he agreed, an amused smile dancing across his lips. "But, not this time. Everything's fine. Let me guess: you were having the shoe dream again, weren't you? You always wake up stressed out after the shoe dream."

"Argh, I never should have told you about that," I groaned, covering my face with my hand. "Yes, I was having the shoe dream again."

"It's okay, honey," he said, his tone deep and soothing. "Tell me about it. What was it this time?"

"Well, I guess there's no point trying to hide it." I sighed heavily, and shot him a long, sideways glance. "Sparkly purple pumps. They were awful and magnificent at the same time, but I didn't have enough money to buy them."

"So, what did you do?" Michael asked. His expression was one of eternal patience, even in the face of my stupid recurring dreams.

"Same thing I always do," I admitted. "I stole them. I ran out of the shop wearing these stupid purple stilettos, but then they turned into roller skates. I was skating down the street, wearing sparkly purple pumps. And then the police were chasing me, and—" I stopped mid-sentence and stared at him, suddenly embarrassed.

"—and I was the police officer, wasn't I?" Michael finished for me.

"Yes, but after you arrested me, you started taking your clothes off." I looked away, feigning interest in the foliage on the side of the road. "And you can guess where it went from there."

"Your recurring shoe nightmare turned into a sex dream?" Michael asked incredulously. "You really are a worry, Sandy."

"I know!" I groaned and covered my eyes again. "I don't even know what it is. I'm not obsessed with shoes or anything. I mean, they're all over the place! They're right there for the taking. If I wanted sparkly purple pumps, I could grab some out of any store, and no one would care. So, why does my subconscious turn me into some kind of kleptomaniac shoe fiend all the time?"

"I suspect it has something to do with issues of possession," Michael answered, his voice turning serious. "You mentioned your philosophy, about everything you possess having to be carried on your back from place to place. I think some part of you hates that, and desperately wants to own something pretty and completely frivolous. That's not such a bad thing, Sandy. In fact, once we find a place to settle, I'm going to bring you lots of pretty, frivolous things. I bet that will put an end to your nightmares."

"You think?" I looked at him, far more curious than I had any right to be. "I mean, I don't need any of that stuff. It's not practical. In fact, it's the opposite of practical. We probably shouldn't waste any time on it."

"Just because we live in a post-apocalyptic world doesn't mean that you can't have nice things, honey," he told me firmly, reaching over to take my hand. He gave it a squeeze and smiled at me. "You want to take a turn driving, to distract yourself?"

"Sure," I agreed. "Let's change over all the drivers for the rest of the way. I'm sure the morning drivers could use a rest."

"No kidding," he commented dryly. "Watching you nap was putting me to sleep."

"Well, that doesn't sound very safe at all." I laughed; somehow, Michael always knew just the right things to say to cheer me up when I was feeling down, no matter what the reason was. He just gave me that dopey grin I loved so much, and eased the Hilux over to the side of the road. By the time I'd conveyed the order to switch drivers, he had already climbed out, and come around to open the passenger door for me.

I felt strong arms around me before I even realised that he was there. He undid my seatbelt, guided me out, and wrapped me up in a hug. It was just a brief hug, but it was enough to make my heart race.

"How is it that you always make me feel like a teenager again?" I asked. "In the good way, I mean. Not the grumpy, hormonal, puberty-is-kicking-my-ass way."

He just laughed, of course. "Are you blaming me because you feel good? Again?"

"No!" I exclaimed, shoving myself out of his grip. I planted a quick kiss on his cheek, and raced around to the driver's side. "It is your fault, though."

"I am more than happy to accept the blame for that," he said cheerfully. While I was buckling up and getting myself ready, he reached over and picked up my radio. "Everyone ready to go again?"

"We've been ready for a while, but you were too busy groping our illustrious leader to notice." Skylar's voice crackled through the radio, laced with a heavy dose of sarcasm. My automatic response was to turn red as a beetroot, but thankfully no one was there to see it.

Well, no one except Michael. And he loved it, because it really was entirely his fault.

\*\*\*

As it turned out, Michael hadn't been kidding about his desire to indulge in a nap. Within a couple of minutes, he nodded off to sleep with his head resting against the glass. I shot a quick glance at him and smiled to myself, then returned my attention back to the not-so-arduous task of driving.

The roads east of Pukeatua were in decent enough condition, compared to some of the other ground we'd covered. We were still in pig country, though, so I kept myself alert for trouble in all its forms. Of course, thinking about pigs turned my mood sour. To lighten it, I distracted myself by trying to think up ways to improve my group's overall chances of success. Eventually, an idea began to form in the back of my head. I picked up the radio and spoke into it.

"Doc, you there?"

A few seconds later, Doctor Cross' voice came on the line. "I'm here. What can I do for you, Ms McDermott?"

"I want to discuss something," I replied. "First, though – how's Ommie?"

"Young Master Omid is doing very well, thank you," the doctor replied. His voice was even and calm, and immediately relaxed my nerves.

"Oh, good." I sighed heavily, and made no attempt to conceal my relief. "Is he awake?"

"Very much so," Doc answered. "In fact, he seems to be more loquacious than he was before the accident. The children were trying to play I Spy earlier, but it somewhat failed due to the fact that Omid isn't terribly good at spelling yet. So, Madeline has taken it upon herself to improve his reading, and she's teaching Priyanka as well. At this rate, I won't even need to hold lessons myself anymore."

I couldn't help but laugh at that. "That's great news. I don't suppose you've had a chance to assess the other Yousefi kids yet? "

"I have, actually," he said. "Mrs Yousefi tells me that she's been teaching them as much as she can along the road, and she's done an excellent job of it. All four of them are fluent in both English and Farsi, and they have a grasp of mathematics and science well beyond their years. She's quite the teacher, if I do say so myself."

"And I have told you to call me 'Elly', Doctor," a third voice intervened, crackling through the radio in my hand. "But, I thank you for the compliment nevertheless."

"Hey, Elly," I greeted her. "I thought you were with the kids?"

"There wasn't enough room," she answered. "I opted to let the good doctor ride with the children, since he can take better care of Ommie at the moment. Besides, it has given me an opportunity to get to know your friend Anahera."

"Ahhh." I nodded my understanding, even though none of them could see it. "I bet you two are getting along like a house on fire. You're cut from the same cloth."

"I like to think that we are, yes," Elly answered.

"Good." I paused for a moment, then took a deep breath and continued. "Speaking of Anahera, is she there?"

There was a moment of silence, then the voice changed to Anahera's. "Yes, Sandrine; I'm here. How can I help?"

"I've got a project for you and Doc," I replied. "We need to start thinking about ways to improve the survivability of our group, and I think the best way we can do that is through education. I don't just mean the kids, either – I want you to go through the entire group, and work out who has skills they're willing to teach. Pair them up with people that want to learn."

"You mean the way you've been picking Zain's brain when you think no one's watching?" Doc asked dryly, his voice carrying a note of deadpan humour.

"We had been trying to avoid making a big deal out of it, but yes, exactly like that," I agreed just as dryly, more amused than annoyed that he'd let the cat out of the bag. Why shouldn't I be the first to do what I was asking the others to? "Talk to people, see what they're interested in. I want everyone to have important basic skills like self-defence, cooking, first aid, driving, and how to start a fire, but we also need to start planning for the long-term survivability of more complex skills. I mean, what would we do if we lost you tomorrow, Doc?"

"To use your own terminology, you'd be pretty much screwed," he replied dryly. "I'm happy to help, of course."

"As am I," Anahera added. "We'll take care of it, don't worry. But, while we're speaking, there is something urgent we need to discuss. I feel it's critically important that we find some way to warn the other people in the Waikato as soon as possible."

"Isn't that why we're going to Avalon Studios?" I asked, uncertain what her point was.

"Well, yes," she answered dryly, "but it'll take us weeks to get there, perhaps even months, and by that stage the entire population of the Waikato may very well have been wiped out. We can't allow that."

"All right," I acknowledged, nodding thoughtfully. "You have a fair point. What's your suggestion?"

"At this stage, I don't know." There was a long sigh on the other end. "But we need to do something. It is our duty to try and save as many as we can, even if all we do is warn them to be away as soon as possible."

"Okay, so we keep our eye out," I said. "If anyone has any ideas or sees anything useful, sing out. Otherwise, we're going to have to keep going and hope for the best. We're almost at Arapuni. Once we get there, I want to find us somewhere secure to bed down for the night. If I remember right, there's a big, empty warehouse somewhere in the north of the town. We should be able to get all the trucks in there and lock the door."

"But we still have a few hours of daylight left," Michael spoke up suddenly in the seat beside me.

I shot a startled glance at him. Everyone else had heard the comment while I was speaking, so I answered them all. "Yes, but we're going to try and convince Rebecca and Jim to join us. If they agree, then they'll need time to get ready. I want you guys to spend the time foraging. Look for clothing and footwear, specifically. We need to get some stuff for Anahera and her blokes, otherwise they're going to be stuck wearing the same thing until their body odour leads the mutants right to us."

A chorus of guffaws and chuckles punctuated my joke. I grinned to myself and put the radio down, then I shot a glance at Michael. "I thought you were sleeping?"

"And I thought you were driving," he countered, grinning right back at me. "I slept for a bit, but you woke me up. My little social butterfly."

"Oh God, that again?" I groaned and rolled my eyes heavenwards. "If I have to be the boss, then I have to act like the boss, and that includes pretending that I know what I'm doing."

"Well, you certainly do a good job of it." Michael leaned over, and pressed a kiss against the curve of my neck, which sent a shiver all the way down my spine. "Have I told you how sexy it is when you get all commanding?"

"No, and I'm not sure that you should right now," I answered, shooting him an alarmed look. "Do you really want to distract me while I'm driving?"

"Maybe not," he answered with a chuckle, easing himself back into his own personal space. "Sorry. We haven't been getting much private time lately, and ever since you freed the genie…"

"That's what we're calling it now?" I teased, giving him a wicked grin. "That does seem kind of appropriate, considering what happens if I rub it just right."

Michael froze, staring at me, then he burst out laughing so hard that he couldn't speak for several minutes. By the time he got himself back under control, we'd crossed the top of Arapuni dam, and turned north towards the power station, and the township.

"Phew," he gasped when he finally started to sober up. "Thanks, I needed that."

"You're more than welcome," I answered brightly. "Now, if you're done, I need you to do something."

"Anything," he agreed immediately.

"Good." I gave him an appreciative smile, then focused back on the road. "I want you to take Hemi, and go bring Rebecca and Jim to talk to us."

"Oh, so you give us the dangerous mission, while you guys slack off scavenging?" He made an indignant sound, but when I glanced at him, I could see on his face that he was only kidding.

"Hah! You're not getting out of scavenging duty that easily, mister," I told him dryly. "I just think it's best if you two go since you're familiar, and I don't want to cross that damn bridge again."

"Fair enough." He laughed and nodded his agreement. "Of course, honey. Wish me luck."

"Good luck," I replied with a knowing grin. "You're gonna need it."

Michael just sighed dramatically, and rolled his eyes heavenwards.

# Chapter Eleven

It took us less than an hour to find what we were looking for. My mental encyclopaedia was not infallible, but it was generally pretty good. Once our vehicles were safely stowed inside the warehouse, Michael and Hemi departed and I gathered the remaining people around me to hand out duty assignments.

"Okay, guys," I called, vaulting up to stand on the Hilux's bonnet again, so that everyone could see me. "Doc, Anahera, I'd like you on babysitting detail, please. The rest of you, I want you to break up into pairs and head out into the town. We need clothing, footwear, petrol, and any toiletries you can find. Also keep an eye out for fishing gear. If you can find any, that'll help us supplement our food supply as we travel. Skye, can you think of anything else we need?"

"We could use a couple more sharp knives, and another can opener or two," she called back. "And more propane to power the stoves." She paused and glanced at Doc. "Oh, what was it you asked me about the other day?"

"Citrus," Doc supplied, adjusting his spectacles. "Any kind of citrus. I'm slightly concerned about everyone's vitamin C levels with winter coming on, and want to make sure we're getting enough in our diets. Lemons, oranges, grapefruit, anything you can find."

"Speaking of winter," I added once he was done. "Keep an eye out for clean blankets, sleeping bags, and tents. It's not going to be fun being out in the weather without a few conveniences. If you find something and aren't sure if we need it, bring it back anyway. Better safe than sorry. Everyone good?" A chorus of agreement met the question. I smiled and nodded. "Right, let's get to it, then!"

A spontaneous cheer went up from the crowd, for reasons that I couldn't define. It pleased me, though, knowing that people were more or less content with my leadership. One by one, my companions paired off, picked up their weapons, and headed out into the streets of Arapuni. Soon, the only people left were me, Skylar, and the folks that were staying with the youngest kids.

I shot a glance at Anahera and Doc, and gave them a reassuring grin. "I hope you two don't mind being left behind."

"Oh, not at all," Doc answered dryly. "My back is too old to go out there lugging goodness-knows-what around, anyway. I'm more than happy to leave that for you young folk."

Anahera chuckled softly and nodded her agreement. "While I would be more than happy to help, I appreciate that you must consider me as one of the walking wounded today. I shall turn my efforts towards taming these little monsters instead. The good doctor and I can begin training them in the vitals."

Madeline laughed merrily, and the Yousefi boys gave us grins so naughty that the rest of us laughed as well.

"Come on, Skye," I clapped my sister on the shoulder when the levity subsided. "Let's go see what we can find."

Just as I was turning away, a young voice cried out to me. "Wait!"

I turned back, to find Javed rushing after us.

"I want to come," he told me, his face a mixture of anxiety and excitement. "Please?"

"Oh? We're just going foraging." I raised my brows, genuinely curious. It was the first time that any of the boys had shown an interest in the activity around them, including Matt. While the eldest Yousefi boy did as he was told, he never looked pleased about it.

"I know." Javed took a deep breath, and puffed out his chest; it took all of my willpower not to melt into laughter at the sight. "But I'm almost an adult! I want to help. May I please help?"

My barely-hidden amusement vanished in the face of his earnestness. "Well, of course you can, if you want to. Stay close to us, though. Don't go out of our sight, okay? If you see something you want to investigate, tell us."

He grinned, and nodded in agreement. "Yes, ma'am!"

"Well, all righty then." I laughed and led the way out the door and back into the muted sunlight. Heavy clouds still obscured the sky, but the rain had passed for the moment. I glanced back, and watched as Anahera slid the door closed behind us, locking herself and the others safely inside.

"I saw a house back that way that looked pretty much intact," Skylar suggested, pointing deeper into town. "Shall we go check it out?"

"Sounds good." I unslung my shotgun, and moved it around to rest in the crook of my arm. "Lead on, little sis."

Just as he'd promised, Javed stuck to me like glue the entire way. When we reached the front door, he watched with interest as I picked the lock. I beckoned him closer so that I could show him what I was doing. He was a quick study; within a matter of minutes, the door swung open to let us into the dusty interior.

"Why was the door still locked?" Skye asked, coughing and waving her hand in front of her face to chase away the dust. "Surely those two down at the power station scouted this place."

"They have an entire town to themselves," I answered with a shrug. "I guess they just never needed to. Or maybe they did, but locked it up when they left. Check the pantry, we'll know soon enough."

Skye nodded and passed through a doorway into a dusty dining room. I headed towards the back of the house, to check out the other rooms. I felt Javed close behind me as I made my way across the faded carpet, but neither of us said anything. Ever-cautious, I eased myself into a defensive crouch and slowly opened the first door that I came across.

Nothing leapt out at me, except for a few ancient dust bunnies. I waved them away and took a quick look around the room. It wasn't much, just an old storage room, with a bunch of boxes along one wall, and a few pieces of furniture beneath drop-cloths that had long since become obsolete. I heaved a sigh and eased myself back up straight.

"Javed, can you please take a look through those boxes and see if there's anything useful?" I asked, gesturing towards the crates under the window. The boy nodded and hurried off, leaving me to investigate the rest of the house on my own.

At the far end of the hall, I found three closed doors. The first opened into a linen cupboard, and the second into a small bathroom. By the time I reached the third door, my nerves were on edge. Something wasn't right. It wasn't something I could see, though. It was something I could smell. I smelt the pungent odour of decaying meat.

I took a deep breath and braced myself, one hand on the door handle and the other on my gun. Instinct and experience told me that whatever I found wasn't going to be pretty. Still, better I see it than Javed or Skye. I silently counted to three, and then I swung the door open.

The wall of stench that hit me almost made me retch. In retrospect, I was glad that we hadn't taken the time to stop for lunch, so there was no chance of me losing it all over the floor.

"Jesus, what is that?" Skye demanded. I jumped, and shot a startled look over my shoulder.

"Just… stay out of here," I ordered quietly. "I mean it. Please?"

"Yeah, I'm not fighting you on this one." She wrinkled up her nose and vanished into the bathroom instead. I sighed softly and turned back to the opened doorway, staring into the gloom within.

It wouldn't be the first time that either of us had seen a dead body, and it wouldn't be the last. Still, it didn't feel right to subject my little sister to yet another dose of horror when she'd already been through so much, and I definitely wanted to protect Javed. As much as I loathed what I had to do, I put my feelings aside and stepped into the room.

The lights flickered when I touched the greasy switch, but after a moment they steadied. I almost wished they hadn't, as if that could protect me from the sight of two corpses snuggled in bed together, their flesh almost entirely rotted away. Shrivelled eyeballs stared at me blankly from beneath eyelids that had pulled back due to the natural mummification of age.

I wanted to take another deep breath, but that would only make the stench of putrefaction worse. I pulled my faithful cloth out of my pocket, and tied it over my mouth and nose. The perfume had begun to fade away, but it was enough to at least keep the stench at bay for a couple of minutes while I searched the room.

A few strands of grey hair lay on the pillows, which told me that the couple had been elderly when they died. I stepped around the bed with as much respect as I could, and went over to rifle through their drawers and the wardrobe in the corner. All I came away with was a couple of woollen jerseys that were in fairly decent condition, and a dozen pairs of socks. Everything else was beyond salvaging.

"Sorry," I whispered to the couple as I made my way back to the door, then closed it up tight behind me. Sure, I could have searched more thoroughly and maybe come away with something else, but… it felt wrong. I wanted to leave the elderly couple to their eternal slumber in peace. Still, some part of me thought that they'd like to know that their belongings would help to prolong the human race well beyond their own expiration date.

I found Skylar in the bathroom, digging through a medicine cabinet and tossing assorted jars, bottles, and boxes into the sink beneath it. She glanced up at me, and jerked her head towards a small stack waiting on the floor by the door.

"I've got a few bars of soap, and a tube of toothpaste that's still sealed, plus some assorted medicine for Doc to look through," she told me. "Nothing much in the kitchen besides a few cans of spaghetti. What did you find?"

"Just a couple of jumpers, a few pairs of socks, and some dead people," I answered, tossing my findings down on top of hers. I unslung my backpack and set it down at my feet, then began folding things and stuffing them into the bottom for easy carrying.

"Oh." Skye paused and stared at me, then she shuddered. "Yeah, okay. No wonder you didn't want me going in there."

"Sorry. I know you hate being treated like a baby, but there are some things that I don't want to subject anyone to if I can avoid it." I heaved a long, long sigh, and tried to distract myself with packing the toiletries into my bag. But when I picked up the toothpaste, I paused for a second to look at the label. "Uh, Skye? This isn't toothpaste. It's haemorrhoid cream."

"What?" Skye turned and stared at me, her expression one of total bewilderment. "What's haemorrhoid cream? And how do you spell that?"

"I have no idea how you spell it," I admitted, "but it's cream that's supposed to help when your butt starts bleeding."

"Oh!" she exclaimed. "I had that when I was pregnant. It sucks. I didn't know there was a treatment for it."

"It's probably long past its use-by date, but we'll take it back to Doc anyway." I tossed the box into my backpack, and carried it over to her. "Here, put whatever you want to take back in here. I'm going to go check on Javed."

"Sure," she agreed cheerfully. I patted her on the shoulder and left the room.

I found Javed exactly where I'd left him, except now it looked like a small tornado had gone through the storage room. The boxes had been torn open, and their contents lay scattered across the floor. In the middle of the room, Javed sat cross-legged, staring fixated at something on the ground in front of him.

I stepped carefully over a mound of old photographs, and came up behind him. "Hey, kiddo. What have you got there?"

The youth jumped, and shot a startled look back over his shoulder. Once he recognised me, he relaxed and held something up for my inspection. "I don't know. What is this?"

"It's a train," I answered, kneeling down beside him to get a better look at it. "Not a real one, of course. It's a toy train. I bet it used to belong to a little boy just like you, back before the plague."

"A toy?" he asked softly. "My brother uses that word sometimes. What does it mean?"

My heart just about broke at the look on his face. I eased myself down to sit beside him, and reached out to take the train from him. "A toy is a plaything for kids. Sometimes they're for learning, but mostly they're just for fun. This one is a model train. You see this word here? That's the stamp of the people that made it."

Javed took the train back, and turned it over to inspect the undercarriage. He wrinkled his face up, and slowly read the letters out loud. "Märklin Trains… where's Märklin?"

"It's not a where, it's a what," I explained. "That's the name of the people that made this train, and probably the rest of the train set, too. It's from a place called Germany, which is a country a very, very long way away." I paused, and glanced down at the carriages scattered on the floor. "My dad used to collect these, back when he was still alive."

"Oh." Javed went quiet for a moment, then he gave me a long, thoughtful look. "I'm sorry your dad is dead."

"It's not your fault," I said, reaching out to squeeze his shoulder. "I still have my sister. Just make sure that you take care of your mum and dad while you can, okay?"

"Yeah," he agreed softly. He frowned to himself, then looked at me again. "Some people say it's our fault the plague came. My mum said they were lying, but I don't know. Is it our fault?"

"No," I told him firmly, shaking my head. "It's not your fault. It's not anyone's fault. The plague would have come here one way or another, that's the nature of a plague. You and your family are innocent."

"But then why are my mum and dad alive, and yours are dead?" the little boy asked, looking so crestfallen that for a second I thought he was going to cry. "Maddy told me that her parents died, and Priyanka's, and everyone's, but mine are still alive. Why? Why do I get a family, but no one else does? It's not fair."

"Hey, hey, it's okay." I reached out and put my arms around him, to draw him into a hug. He resisted at first, but once the tears finally broke through he slumped against me. "It's *not* your fault, Javed. It's just pure chance. Some people have this immunity, and some people don't. You were just lucky enough to have two parents who are immune, which is why you guys are immune."

"Then why did my sister die?" the boy demanded, rubbing his cheeks as though to banish the tears, but they were insistent. "God punished us for bringing the plague."

"Your sister?" I froze and stared at him. "You had a sister?"

"Yeah—well, sort of." He sighed deeply and shrugged. "When Mum had Ommie, there were two babies inside her – twins, I think it's called. One boy and one girl. Ommie came out first, but when our sister came, she... she wasn't right. She didn't cry. Mum and Dad told me that she was born dead, but she wasn't. I saw her. She was alive, but there was something wrong with her. Mum cried for days and days, then she made us pack up and move on. When we left, she didn't bring our sister with us."

"Oh, God," I breathed, shocked by the story. "So it's true... Oh, my God, it's true..."

"What's true?" he asked innocently, looking up at me.

"Nothing." I took a deep breath to steady myself, and wiped my eyes with the back of my hand. "God isn't punishing you, Javed. It's not your fault that this happened. Promise. I'll tell you what, I'll make you the same deal that I made Priya. If you want, you can bring the train with us, but if we end up walking, then you'll have to either carry it yourself or leave it behind. How does that sound?"

"I can have it?" He stared at me wide-eyed, all thoughts of dead families forgotten. "This train? I'm allowed to have a toy?"

"I don't see why not." I summoned a smile for him, doing my best to shove aside the disturbing topic as well. "I do have to put in a clause for your mother's sake, though. You have to share it with your brothers, okay?"

"Okay!" Javed's expression lit up. Suddenly, he leapt to his feet and rushed around gathering up the pieces of the train set so that he could shove them back into the box they'd come from. I smiled as I watched him, right up until I heard Skylar whoop in delight from the back of the house. Her words were some of my favourite words ever, words that would never lose their potency even after a decade of living in the ruins of our old world.

"Yes! Yes! I found toilet paper!"

"Woohoo!" I cheered, throwing my hands up in the air. Javed shot a bewildered glance at me, but didn't seem to care either way. "Well, I guess that's a girl thing, then."

"What is?" Skye asked, trundling into the room with my backpack over her shoulder, and the sealed package of toilet paper under her arm. It was so old that the plastic wrapping had faded to clear, but the paper itself looked fine.

"The toilet paper thing," I explained, gesturing at Javed. "Kid's more interested in his train set."

"Oh!" She laughed merrily. "Yeah, definitely a girl thing. Boys can be so gross sometimes."

"They sure can." I chuckled as well, and gave her a quizzical look. "Are we all done here, then?"

"I think so," she answered. She shrugged off my backpack and handed it to me, and I put it on my shoulders. By the time we were done, Javed had joined us, watching expectantly with the faded train set clutched against his chest.

"Let's head off, then," I suggested. I took point and led the way down the hall, out of the front door, and across the overgrown lawn towards the street. Along the way, I paused to check the mailbox; I'd found more than a few little treasures in them over the years. Sure, it was mostly just stacks of old bills and irrelevant junk mail, but every now and then you struck gold. As it turned out, today it was the latter.

"Hey, what have you got?" Skye asked curiously as I pulled the package out of the mailbox.

"Not sure, but it can't hurt to look," I answered. I turned the package over, and examined the label to try and work out who the sender was, but it was illegible. Skye and Javed came up behind me to watch as I tore open the package.

"Honey?" Skylar shot a bewildered glance at me. "Why would someone have mailed these people honey?"

"It was a thing, back in the day," I answered, excitement rising in my breast to replace the darker thoughts. "Mail-order honey. That means this'll be the good quality stuff. Oh man, Doc's going to be thrilled."

"It'll be nasty after all this time, won't it?" Skye asked, looking at me with interest. "The stuff's just like… sugar and bee spit."

"Actually, honey is one of the few foods that never expire," I explained. As I spoke, I crouched down and set the box at my feet, so I could examine the contents without the risk of dropping it. Inside, four sealed jars of perfect, translucent sweetness sparkled up at me. It was a sight that made me smile. "A few years after the plague hit, I met this guy down south. Up until then, I'd been surviving on trial and error, but that guy was ex-military and a survivalist. He knew a bunch of stuff. He taught me about honey."

"Oh, yeah?" Skye grinned and wiggled her eyebrows. "He taught you about honey, huh?"

I shot her a dark look. "It wasn't like that. We were just friends. He was a lot older than me, and treated me like a daughter, or at least a sister. Anyway, honey lasts forever if it's stored in an air-tight container without any impurities. There are a couple of other foods with an indefinite shelf-life, but honey is the only one that you can eat without cooking. It's a godsend when you're starving and desperate. It's also one of the most powerful all-purpose medicines that the natural world has to offer, so this stuff is going straight into Doc's medicinal stores."

"Oh." Skye stood back, watching as I closed the box and picked it up, then she and Javed both followed as I resumed our trek back to our bunker. She was silent for a few minutes, then she shot me a curious look. "So, what happened to him? You made it sound like you've been entirely alone for the last ten years. You haven't mentioned any friends before."

"There have been a few times when I had companions for a while," I admitted. "But it never ended well. I've been alone for the vast majority of the time. I spent about six weeks with him, but one day he just vanished. There were some gangs starting to develop in the area at that time, so it was getting dangerous for us. He'd taught me that if he didn't come home, I was to go to ground. So, that's what I did. I never saw him again."

"Well, that sucks." Skylar sighed heavily, folding her arms across her chest. "Sorry. Didn't mean to stir up bad memories."

"It's okay." I glanced over at her, and gave her a smile. "He's not a bad memory. In fact, he's one of the few good memories I have from that period. At the time we met, I was having trouble finding enough to eat. He taught me a lot of little things that have helped me to survive over the years, and now I get to teach them to the kids. Right, Javed?"

"Yup!" the boy agreed, even though it was clear he wasn't paying the least bit of attention to either of us. Skye and I laughed.

"Mama!" A voice in the distance called out. I paused and turned to look. A few seconds later, the voice called out again. "Mama, I heared you. Where are you?"

"Over here, Priya," I called back.

There was a rustling sound, then Priyanka appeared on the other side of a tangle of overgrown shrubs, with Matt right behind her. "Mama, we found the stinky stuff that's food for the cars! You come see, please?"

"Sure, sweetie," I agreed. I turned to Skylar, and offered her the box of honey. "Make sure this gets to Doc safely?"

"'Course." She took the jar and tucked it under her arm. "I can take your backpack, too."

"Thanks." I slipped the pack off, and handed it to her with a smile. "I'll see you guys soon."

"Stay safe," she said by way of farewell, then with a wave, she and Javed were off. It wasn't far back to the warehouse and Skye had her gun with her, so there was no valid reason to worry about them. I hurried over to meet up with Priyanka and Matt.

As soon as I found a way around the jungle that had once been someone's hedge, Priya threw her arms around my waist and hugged me. Then, she grabbed my hand and dragged me off without a word. We passed down a street and ducked through an alleyway that terminated beside an old gas station.

At some point in the past, someone had cracked open the underground tanks and started to syphon out the contents, but they'd stopped half way through the task. A large barrel, half-filled, sat on the forecourt with a length of hose still leading back to the tanks, but now both were gathering cobwebs. I detached myself from Priya and went over to inspect the barrel, but before I got within a few meters I knew that the petrol was unusable.

"Sorry, Priya. This stuff is stagnant," I told her gently. Taking the opportunity to educate them both, I lifted a finger to touch the tip of her nose. "Do you smell that?"

"Yeah. Smells like bads." She glanced over at the tanks. "Car food is bads?"

"Unfortunately." I sighed and put my arm around her. "Petrol – the stuff that the cars eat – can last for years and years if it's stored in underground tanks, or in metal containers, but if even a little bit of water gets in then it'll... let's just say that it'll go bad. Just like how people can't eat bad food, if we try to make the cars eat bad petrol it'll make them sick."

"Oh." Priya's expression sagged, but she didn't have much time to mope. A second later, Matt drew a sharp breath.

"Someone's coming," he whispered, taking a nervous step back. I turned to look, just as the shouting started.

"Oi!" Jim yelled, already red in the face and angry. "Just because we asked you buggers for help one time doesn't give you the right to come traipsing all over our land whenever you feel like it!"

"Hold up, mate." I raised my hands in a placating gesture. "We're here for a good reason. Just hear us out, okay?"

"Jim, stop being an ass." Rebecca emerged from between two buildings, followed by Michael and Hemi.

"Shut up, woman!" Jim snapped irritably. "You're not my mother."

"Maybe not, but I know where you sleep," she answered sweetly, coming up behind her 'husband' to place a hand on his arm. Unlike his, her expression was friendly, and she smiled at me. "Hello, Sandy. Nice to see you again."

"You too," I greeted her, lowering my hands. "I'm sorry to show up unannounced. There have been a few changes in our group, and our radio is out of order."

"I assumed as much." Rebecca glanced past me, at the open petrol tank. "That was us. We tried to salvage the fuel a few years ago, but water got into the underground tanks. We have another reservoir up the road, but this one's useless."

"I gathered as much from the smell." I shot another look at the worthless fuel and shrugged. "Not much we can do about it now. Anyway, we came here to talk to you two. We're all leaving the Waikato, and we wanted to invite you to come along with us."

"What?" Rebecca reared back, her eyes wide. "Why are you leaving? I thought you were happy in Ohaupo."

"We were, but… something's changed." I glanced up at Michael, and he gave me an encouraging smile. I returned it and looked back at Rebecca and Jim. "Guys, you remember the things in Hamilton, right? The killer mutant zombies?"

"Hard to forget about those," she answered, her expression turning grim. "Why?"

"They've come south," I answered bluntly. Her eyes flew wide, but I continued before she could say anything. "They attacked us at Ohaupo. We managed to escape without any casualties, but Anahera's tribe wasn't so lucky. While we were busy cleaning up at Ohaupo, they swung around to the west and attacked the hill fort at Lake Ruatuna. There were only four survivors."

"Oh, my God!" Rebecca clamped her hands over her mouth. Jim muttered a few curses under his breath, and put his one good arm around her shoulders.

"So, you think they're coming here next?" he demanded, his voice an odd mixture of anger and resignation. "If they do, it's because you led them here. You know that, right?"

"I know," I admitted. "But we had no radio. If we just went straight south, we might have led them away from you, but maybe not. They might have found you anyway, and they'd have taken you by surprise. You wouldn't have stood a chance." I took a deep breath, and let it out slowly. "Guys, I don't think you realise how much we appreciate what you've done over the years. By keeping the station going, you've helped us to keep in touch with our own humanity, and our link to civilization. Plus, hot showers. I can never thank you enough for the hot showers.

"But it's over now. It's time to move on. All of us. We've gathered up all the people that we know, and we're heading south. We're going to Wellington, and we're going to try something new there: we're going to build a city."

"A city?" Rebecca asked, her expression flickering through a variety of emotions all at once. "You're going to build a city? Seriously?"

"Yep." I smiled at her and nodded. "First, we're going to Avalon, a suburb in Lower Hutt, to find the Anchorman. Then, we're going to find the perfect site to build a new city. It's time. The mutant attacks were the catalyst, but this had to happen eventually. We can't keep just surviving, gnawing away at the bones of a dead civilization forever. We need to create our own civilization."

I shifted my gaze to Jim, and smiled at him as well. "It's going to be a place where everyone is welcome, so long as they're willing to contribute. We don't care about your race, creed, origin story, or sexuality, so long as you can share in our vision. Civilization has fallen, but it's fallen before. Humanity has survived before. We can rebuild. We can begin again.

"These people with me, they're the settlers that are going to found this new civilization, the bones on which the world is going to be rebuilt. There are twenty-two of us at the moment, but if you agree to join us, then there will be twenty-four. Our odds of success would be that little bit better. We need you, Jim, Rebecca. We also want you, as our friends.

"Please come with us, if not for our sake, then for yours."

There was a long silence in the wake of my impromptu speech. Rebecca and Jim just stood there, staring at me. Over their heads, I saw Michael and Hemi watching with interest. Eventually, Jim heaved a sigh and looked at his wife. "Up to you, woman."

Rebecca just smiled. "With an invitation like that, how could we possibly refuse?"

# Chapter Twelve

There was perhaps an hour of sunlight left by the time we made it back to the warehouse where we planned to bunk down for the night. Rebecca strode along beside me, content to chatter away about nothing of any real importance, but I could feel Jim's silent thunder at my back the entire way. Although he'd agreed to join us, there was always something off about his attitude that never failed to put me on edge.

A shout of greeting met us as we rounded a corner into the street outside the warehouse. I glanced up, and spotted a couple of the kids waving to us from a window on the second floor. I smiled and waved back, then turned my attention back to Rebecca.

"So, what should we bring?" Rebecca asked. Despite how sudden the proposal had been, she seemed excited by the prospect of going out in search of a new home. Her enthusiasm was infectious, and the only one not affected was her gloomy spouse.

"We'll have to travel light," I answered. "There are twenty-four of us now, and we've only got four cars. In terms of clothing and personal effects, I'd ask you to limit it to what you can carry on your person. So, try to keep it to one bag or backpack. Wear your favourite outfit, and bring your second favourite as a change of clothes, plus as many socks and undies as you can fit in your bag. We need to keep as much room as we can for vitals."

"We have a car," she piped up. "Would that help?"

"Maybe," I said. "What kind of car?"

"My little ladybug." She looked at Jim. "What's the proper name, dear?"

"Sports utility vehicle," he supplied for her.

"That's it!" She smiled, turning back to me. "I bought a brand new SUV just before the plague hit. Jim's been keeping her in running order for me. Her name is Sophie, and she's lipstick red. Can't miss her."

"Sophie?" I froze in my tracks, and shot a startled glance back at Michael. His expression mutated in an instant, from a genuine smile to one that was very much forced.

Rebecca looked back and forth between us, clearly sensing that something was going on. "What? What's wrong?"

"I had a niece named Sophie," he said flatly, his expression unreadable.

I reached out and touched his arm, drawing his attention to me. "That just means that it's fated, right? Meant to be?"

Michael stared at me for a long moment, then finally his expression softened. He nodded and gave me a faint smile. "I guess so."

I let out a breath that I hadn't quite realised I was holding until that moment, and put my arm around him. He hugged me in return. Somehow, through some sixth sense that I'd established purely for the purpose of reading my lover's mercurial moods, I could tell that he was okay once the shock had worn off.

"So, anyway," I cut in, directing the topic back to safe territory for the sake of his sanity. "Yes, it would be great if you could bring your car along. You have plenty of food, right?"

"Oh yeah." Rebecca nodded and laughed. "We have more food than we can eat right now. I'm not sure how much of it is still good, but I'll do an inventory when we get home, and then we can work out what's best to bring."

"Sounds good," I agreed. "You also mentioned at one stage that you have a generator. Is it transportable?"

"No, the solar generator is tied into the power station, like the radio," she said, shaking her head. "But I think we have a portable propane generator in storage. You want me to bring that?"

"Yes, and any gas you have as well," I answered. "We have a couple of propane camp stoves, and it's handy to have them since we're going into unknown territory. Do you want me to lend you a couple of the boys for the night, to help with the heavy lifting?"

"That would be appreciated," Rebecca said. She jerked a thumb at Jim and rolled her eyes. "His arm isn't healed yet, and I don't want to give him an excuse to strain it trying to show how manly he is."

Jim shot her a black look, but said nothing.

"It's all good." I smiled at her, amused by the playful banter. "You two head off whenever you're ready. I'll send the boys to meet you when I find them."

"Yes, ma'am!" Rebecca gave me a mock salute and grinned at the folks standing around me. "You know, I think I like having this lady in charge. She knows how to get things done."

I just laughed and shook my head. "I'm only in charge because no one else wants to do it."

Michael let out an indignant snort. "She's just trying to be modest. She's in charge because she's damn good at leading, and she actually has a vision, which is more than I can say for the rest of us."

It was my turn to shoot Michael a dark look as my cheeks started to burn. "I'm sure everyone would be just fine without me."

"Lass, don't put yourself down." To my surprise, it was Jim that spoke up in my defence. "You've managed to get together twenty-four very different people, and give them hope that there's something better out there for all of us. That's no small feat." Suddenly looking embarrassed, he issued an inarticulate grunt and walked away from the group.

Rebecca stared after him until he was out of sight, then laughed and shrugged. "Well, I guess that's that, then. I better catch up before he gets himself killed. Do me a favour, and send those sexy Maori brothers, huh?"

"I'll think about it." I laughed, and made a shooing gesture. "Go on. It's not safe to be out alone at the moment."

"You got it, boss-lady!" Rebecca saluted again, and rushed off. I watched until she was out of sight, then turned to look at my companions. Matt and Priyanka had already vanished, bored by the grown-up chatter, but Michael and Hemi stood watching me with open amusement.

"Are you actually going to send Tane and Iorangi?" Michael asked, fighting to keep a grin off his face.

"No," I answered, feigning a haughty tone. "I'm going to send Iorangi and Richard."

"Eh?" Michael raised a brow, his expression shifting to one of genuine curiosity. "Iorangi I get, but why Richard?"

Suddenly, realisation dawned in Hemi's eyes, and he burst out laughing. "She's playing match-maker! Very clever, Sandy. Very clever."

I grinned at him and nodded. Michael stared at us blankly, looking bewildered. "Matchmaker? Between who?"

"Richard and Jim, of course," I answered.

Michael's eyes widened in shock. "Richard's gay?"

"He's either gay or bisexual," I replied, nodding firmly. "It took me a while to figure it out why he always looks so out of place. He's so quiet and shy, my bet is that he wouldn't know what to say. Jim is the complete opposite. He's discreet, but not shy. If he figures Richard out and there's any kind of spark there, then I'm pretty sure Jim will take the lead. I feel like Richard needs that." I glanced at Michael, and gave him a smile. "Someone strong, to help him feel stronger, himself."

Michael looked surprised but not scandalised, and that pleased me. He'd never struck me as the kind of person that would be homophobic, and my instinct proved to be correct. "Wow, I had no idea. You're right, he does always look sort of lonely and uncomfortable. Let's hope your scheme works, honey."

"It will if it's meant to," I answered with a shrug. "You can't force love where there isn't a spark, and I wouldn't dream of trying. I just hope that there is a spark. Everyone deserves some happiness, right?"

Hemi cleared his throat, and shot an uncomfortable glance at me. "Actually, while we're on the subject... Sandy, could I speak to you alone for a second?"

"Of course." I smiled at him, then looked at Michael. "Can you go check on the foraging teams, please? If anyone's found fishing gear, send them down to the docks to see if they can catch us some dinner. I want them back here before dark, though."

"Sure," Michael agreed immediately. He kissed me quickly, then vanished into the warehouse.

I turned back to Hemi, and gestured for him to follow me. Side by side, we wandered far enough away to give us a little bit of privacy. "Okay. What's up, bud?"

"Aw, mate, it's your sister," Hemi admitted, shooting a helpless look at me. Suddenly, he seemed to fall apart on the inside, like a house of cards. "I think she likes me, but I don't know, I can't tell. I like her, though. I mean, I *really* like her. As more than a friend, you know? I thought I stood a chance, but now that Ryan guy is back... I just don't know any more. What do I do, Sandy?"

"You tell her," I answered, fighting the urge to laugh. I stopped walking and turned to face him fully. "You know as well as I do that the only person who makes decisions for Skylar is herself. I don't know if she likes you as more than a friend, but I know she respects people that tell her the truth. I'm not exactly the best person to give you romantic advice, but I'd say the best thing you can do is be honest with her."

"Honest... right." He nodded slowly, processing the information – then, suddenly, his expression changed to one of open panic. "But what if she says no? What if she isn't interested? What if she laughs at me?"

"I'm pretty sure she won't laugh at you." I gave him my gentlest smile, and reached out to rest my hands reassuringly on his shoulders. "But if she says no, so be it. You're still friends, and that's the most important thing, right? I know it feels terrifying, but even if she says no it's not the end of the world. Just relax and tell her how you feel. You won't know for sure until you do."

"True." Hemi took a long, deep breath, and let it out slowly. "Yeah. Yeah. Too right. Okay. I'm going to go do it right now, just get it out the way, and we'll see how it goes. Yeah! Thanks, Sandy!"

"Any time, kiddo." I released my grip on his shoulders and stood back. Hemi scampered past me and raced back to the warehouse, leaving me alone in his wake.

I loitered for a couple of minutes, just enjoying the sound of birdsong, and the clean smell of the breeze. Unlike many of the bigger cities, Arapuni wasn't full of the stench of decay. I suspected that Rebecca had spent some time cleaning up the bodies, with the exception of the two that she'd missed. She seemed a lot like me, in that regard.

Once I judged that enough time had passed, I headed back to the warehouse. I rapped on the door with my knuckles, and waited until I heard the rusted bolt slide back. The door opened, and the doctor waved me inside.

"Hey, Doc," I greeted. "What's our status?"

Doctor Cross closed the door behind me, and bolted it firmly. "Everyone's reported in to drop off various things, then the good constable came and took most of them down to the docks to fish for supper. The children are upstairs with Anahera and Skylar having a cooking lesson, and I'm working on an updated inventory."

"Great." I smiled at him and nodded my approval. "I'm going to go look in on them, then I'll be off to help the fishers."

"Understood." The doctor adjusted his spectacles, and pointed towards the stairs. "Up there, second door on the left."

"Thanks." I nodded in acknowledgement and headed off. Before I could get more than a dozen steps, he called out to stop me.

"Oh, Ms McDermott?" I paused and looked at him. To my surprise, our perpetually-grumpy doctor was actually smiling. "Excellent find with the honey. Well done."

"No problem at all, Doc," I answered with a grin. "I'm going to teach everyone to keep an eye out for it. It's nature's super-food, after all."

"That it is." He chuckled quietly, and waved me away. I left him in peace and headed up the stairs to the second floor of the building. The noise of the children would have led me right to them, even if he hadn't given me directions; the sound of Maddy's delighted squeals made me smile. I opened the door, and peeked inside.

What I saw was a scene right out of a holiday postcard. Anahera stood at the stove, stirring something in a pot and speaking patiently to the children gathered around her. Even little Ommie was there, swathed in bandages but wide-awake and alert. They glanced up when I entered the room, and I found myself the recipient of many smiles and waves.

"Well, what's going on here, then?" I asked curiously.

"We're learning how to make flour out of white rice, aren't we children?" Anahera looked down at her young charges and gave them one of those smiles that made my stomach do backflips. I was obviously not the only one drawn in by her natural charisma; the kids all nodded happily and shouted excited nonsense.

"Well, that sounds great!" I answered, as cheerfully as possible. "Are you guys having a good time?"

"Yes!" Maddy shouted at the top of her lungs. The volume made me cringe, but it was a good kind of cringe. There was nothing quite like the happy noise of children at play, and they were definitely happy.

"Good." I grinned and looked back at Anahera, my eyebrows raised in silent inquiry. She looked at me knowingly, winked, and pointed in a general 'down-the-hall' sort of way. I nodded, and withdrew. Somehow, she knew that I was hoping to check on my sister, and had supplied the information I needed without words.

I crept down the hallway on stealthy feet, carefully checking each room for any sign of life. There was nothing to be seen in most of them: just a lot of dust, old furniture, and faded paperwork. But then, I reached the door at the end of the hall, which stood ever-so-slightly ajar. With as much subtlety as I could, I snuck up to the door and peeked through.

Inside, Hemi and Skylar were wrapped up in a kiss of such intensity that neither of them noticed me snooping. I just grinned to myself and withdrew, leaving them in peace. My little sister was more than okay, and that meant my interest in the matter was at an end. She was quite capable of handling her own blossoming relationship.

I jogged back down the stairs, just in time to catch Michael coming inside with an armload of fabric, Alfred bounding along hot on his heels.

"Just put it over there, boy," Doctor Cross instructed with a long-suffering sigh, then he vanished through a doorway, back to whatever he had been doing before the interruption.

I fixed Michael with a disapproving look. "Aren't you supposed to be fishing with the others? And while we're on the subject, where's your forage buddy, Constable Chan? You know you're not supposed to go out alone."

"There weren't enough rods for me to help out, so I decided to find something else to do. Don't worry, I had Alfred with me." Michael grinned cheekily. He went over and dumped his armload of clothing where Doc had instructed, then came back to give me a kiss of greeting. "I take it everything is okay with Hemi?"

"It's fine," I answered, shoving my instinctive worry back down. Michael was anything but stupid, and he knew that I'd kill him if he put himself at risk. "He just needed a bit of advice, is all."

"Ah." Michael nodded and gave me a curious look. "Did he tell her, then?"

"Apparently." I grinned brightly and gave him a wink in return. "You know, I feel like I'm all up in everyone's business today. I'm not sure how to react to that."

"Well, so long as you're not interfering where it's not wanted, I imagine that it's fine." Michael shrugged, sliding his arm around my waist. "Part of it is your newfound sense of responsibility, I think. You want everyone to be happy."

"You reckon?" I leaned up against him, studying the contours of his face in the artificial light. "I'm not just being a busybody, then?"

"Maybe a little bit, but you mean well," he answered dryly. Sliding his finger up beneath my chin, he tilted my face up and planted a quick, tender kiss on my lips. Then, he drew back and smiled at me. "If we want our species to survive, then the children have to come from somewhere, right?"

"I suppose, if you ignore the fact that I'm trying to set up two gay guys," I pointed out dryly.

"It doesn't matter," he said, shrugging. "Love is love. They're just as entitled to find love as straight people are. Just because their love can't produce offspring doesn't mean they're any different to you or I."

"That's how I see it," I agreed, leaning up against his broad chest. His touch relaxed me, as it always did. I closed my eyes, and relished in his warmth and tenderness.

He seemed to sense my need, as he often did, and held me quietly for a couple of minutes. Eventually, he drew back and looked down at me. "I got you a present."

"Oh?" I looked up at him, curious. His dark eyes were twinkling, and there was a mischievous smile dancing across his lips. "Oh, I know that look. What have you done?"

"Why do you always assume I've done something wrong?" Michael exclaimed, his brows knitting together. "I just found something, and I want to give it to you. Is that a bad thing, Miss Negativity?"

"And I was just teasing you, Mister Takes-Everything-Literally," I answered, playfully nudging him in the ribs.

"Oh!" He laughed, his expression immediately brightening. "Sorry. You're so deadpan that I can't always tell when you're kidding. "

"I know." I grinned at him and gave him a wink. "So, what'd you find?"

"Hold that thought two seconds," he ordered, holding up a finger to stay my curiosity. He disentangled himself from my embrace and hurried back over to the mound of clothing he'd brought in a few minutes earlier. He grabbed something black and glossy from the bottom of the pile, and held it up for me to see. "Tada!"

"Whoa, is that leather?" I enquired, closing the gap between us to get a better look at the trench coat.

"Yep!" he answered. "Genuine leather, treated to be waterproof according to the label. I went back to the hunting and fishing store the guys found to see if there was anything else of use to us. If there were any guns in there then they're long gone, but I found a few of these up the back. This one looks just about your size, and it'll last you a lifetime." He turned the trench around so that I could slide it on, if I wanted to.

I hesitated, though. He was right, it would last me a lifetime. And with winter coming, I was going to need it. But… could I accept something like that knowing that there were other people in need? Reluctantly, I shook my head and took a step back.

"Honey, I appreciate the thought, but I can't take that," I said quietly. "Give it to Priya, or one of the other kids. They need it more than I do."

Michael's expression darkened. Without warning, he reached out and grabbed my arm, though his grip wasn't hard enough to hurt.

"Oh no you don't," he scolded. "I found this, Sandy. Scavenger's law says that I have first right of control over where it goes, and who gets it. You taught me that, and I brought this coat back for *you*, not anyone else."

"But—" I started to protest, but he interrupted me.

"No way. I'm not letting you do this to yourself." Michael heaved a long sigh, and released his grip on my arm. "Just take it, Sandy. Winter is coming, and you're going to need this to keep you warm and dry. Knowing you, you're going to be out in the thick of it all the way south, and the last thing we need is for our leader to freeze to death. The only thing resembling cold weather gear you have is that little army surplus jacket of yours, and that's summer weight."

My automatic response was to keep protesting until I got my way, but something about his expression silenced me. He was so determined, so intensely focused on winning this one particular battle that I couldn't turn it down in good conscience. I looked down at my feet and nodded once.

"Okay. Okay, I'll take it," I agreed reluctantly. "But you better have found something for the kids in there. You know they come first to me."

"I know they do." Michael's expression softened into a smile. He reached out and put the coat around my shoulders, using it to draw me into a warm, leather-scented hug. "But that's exactly why someone has to put you first. You're not immune to the 'flu, you know. What good are you to anyone if you catch a sniffle?"

"Oh, thanks. Much appreciated." I shoved him back and feigned a dirty look. "Some boyfriend you are."

"Fiancé," he corrected, returning my look with a playful grin. "And don't you forget it."

"I'm pretty sure I couldn't, even if I wanted to," I answered teasingly. On a sudden, overwhelming impulse, I leaned up and planted a kiss on his lips. When we separated, I smiled at him. "Thank you. Now, we really should get back to work."

"Yeah," he agreed. "Sounds like the others are coming back from fishing, anyway."

Right on cue, someone banged on the door beside us, making me jump. I laughed and nodded to him. Without me even having to ask, Michael went off to sort out the night's watch, while I went to organise the group going to help at the power station.

Then Skylar appeared, manifesting out of the chaos like a goddess come to tame the throngs, and soon everything was under control.

# Chapter Thirteen

"Looks like we pissed off the weather gods," I commented thoughtfully to myself.

The night had passed uneventfully, but when the sun rose it revealed a day that was dark and dreary. The rain had already settled in, and it clearly had no intention of letting up any time soon. I stood in the doorway, watching the weather and absently fingering my radio, waiting for the call from Rebecca that would let us know it was time to leave.

"Indeed. Tāwhirimātea has sent his children to hinder us once again," a voice said softly behind me. I glanced back, and found Anahera standing there, watching the rain over my shoulder. She handed me a bowl of leftover fish stew from the night before. I accepted it silently, and eased to one side so that she could join me in the doorway.

I ate quietly for a couple of minutes, enjoying a moment of peace while I could get it. I'd spent most of the night brooding on what Javed had told me the day before, and my mood was almost as bleak as the clouds outside. Eventually, the silence started to bother me a little. I glanced at Anahera, and asked simply, "Tell me about him?"

"About who?" She looked back at me, surprised.

"About Tāwhiri—what was it?"

"Tāwhirimātea," she supplied, a smile growing on her face. "You're interested in my people's legends?"

"Of course I am," I answered with a shrug. "There's no one else left to keep the tales alive, except for us."

"No, I suppose there isn't," she agreed. Her dark eyes flicked away from me, back to the rain. "How much do you know about our tales regarding the creation of the world?"

"I know a little bit," I replied. "They taught us in school about how the Earth Mother and Sky Father used to be joined together, until their children forced them apart. I also know the origin story of New Zealand. Māui, the demi-god, went fishing and caught a giant stingray which became the North Island. His canoe became the South."

"Ah, yes, an old favourite!" Anahera laughed merrily and shook her head. "Tāwhirimātea, or Tāwhiri for short, was one of the sons of Ranginui, the Sky Father, and Papatūānuku, the Earth Mother. When his brothers were trying to separate them, Tāwhiri fought to keep them together. He argued that they were happy together, so why drive them apart?

"In the end, Tāwhiri lost and his parents were driven apart. He was so angry that he sent his children – the winds, the rain, the snow, and the storms – to attack his brothers endlessly. Unfortunately, we frail mortals are trapped in the middle of that never-ending war."

"Wow," I murmured thoughtfully to myself, staring out at the dark clouds. A few splatters of rain made it past the overhang of the roof and struck me in the chest and stomach, but my new coat reached all the way to my knees, and kept me well and truly dry. "I can't help but wonder if any of it's real. Do you think it is?"

"Yes and no," Anahera admitted with a shrug. "Who are we to say what lives beyond this world that we see? Who knows whether my gods are real, or yours, or Elira's, or anyone else's. We won't know until we die, and even then I'm not entirely convinced that we'll ever be sure."

"I don't have a god," I replied. "You assumed I'm Christian?"

"No judgement was intended." Anahera smiled back at me, reaching out to touch my arm. "I just took a guess. If I was wrong, please don't take offense."

"It's okay. I'm not offended." I shrugged and returned my gaze to the pelting rain. "I guess I just don't know what I believe. Part of me feels like no kind god would ever force us to go through this kind of pain, but another part of me wonders if it's not for the best in the long term."

"Oh?" Even without seeing her face, I could hear the curiosity in her voice. "What do you mean?"

"Well, you remember what it was like," I said, gesturing at the world around us. "We took everything for granted. It was just assumed that you'd grow up, go to school, get married, have a family. We were so busy following the steps that society laid out for us that we never stopped to appreciate the tiny, every-day miracles of the world. I don't know about you, but I notice it now. I hold my breath and marvel at the way the rising sun creeps across the ground every morning. I close my eyes and listen to the sound of the rain on the roof. I marvel at the tiny miracle that can turn a seed into a plant that bears us food. We've all seen so much death, but we're alive." I paused and looked at her. "Life is a gift. I can see that now. I don't think I would have before."

"You are very philosophical for so early in the morning," Anahera answered dryly. Her dark eyes studied me thoughtfully in the gloom. "Sandy, what's wrong?"

I shrugged and glanced away, focusing on the falling rain. "It's something Javed said to me yesterday. Do you remember when we first met, we asked you if any members of your tribe had given birth since the plague?"

"Of course," she replied. "You were concerned about whether or not the immunity would be passed from mother to child."

"It turns out that we were right to worry," I said quietly, hugging myself against a chill that came from the inside more than the out. "Javed told me that Ommie had a twin sister, but when she was born she didn't cry. That she was alive, but... wrong. From birth." I glanced at her just in time to see the understanding dawning in her eyes. "You know what that means."

"The child was born infected?" Anahera whispered, a horrified look crossing her face, the kind of look that mirrored the way I'd been feeling since Javed told me. "But the other children..."

"Exactly. Javed was born just before the plague, but Barry, Ommie, and Maddy were born afterwards." I swallowed hard, and closed my eyes. "I don't know what to do, Ana. This changes everything."

"No, it doesn't." Her voice turned firm, and I felt her hand land on my shoulder. I opened my eyes, and saw a look of determination on her face. "We still have to have children, or our species is guaranteed to die out. At least now we know the risk is real, so we can plan for it. If it happens, it will be terrible but it won't be a surprise. It's better to know there is a risk and face it bravely than to have it come without warning and devastate us all."

I had no answer. Nothing seemed adequate. Anahera took the empty bowl from my hand, then she turned away from me. "I must go help Elly and Skylar with the children. Try not to spend too much time brooding on it. We'll find a way to get through this together."

I just nodded silently. Once she was gone, I turned my attention back to watching the wild weather and pondering this cruel new twist of fate.

\*\*\*

I stayed on watch as the sun slowly climbed higher in the sky. Every so often, someone came over to check in with me and let me know the progress of our preparations to leave, but they had things well under control. Hearing Skylar shouting like a drill sergeant never failed to make me smile, despite my dark mood. It was nearly an hour after sunrise before the walkie-talkie in my hand finally crackled to life, and Rebecca's familiar voice cut through my reverie.

"Testing... testing... hello? Is this working?"

"It is," I answered. "Good morning, sleepy head. I was starting to think I was going to have to come over and wake you myself."

"We weren't sleeping," she snapped indignantly. "It takes time to pack up your entire life, you know!"

"I know, Rebecca," I replied, adjusting my tone appropriately. "I was just teasing you."

"Teasing? Oh. Oh!" The radio crackled for a moment, which I could only presume was the result of her taking a deep breath and letting it out across the microphone without realising what she was doing. "Sorry. It's been a long time since I've been teased. I guess I forgot."

"Don't worry, I've totally been there," I answered, smiling to myself. I understood better than most. "You'll get used to it. Just give it time. Anyway, how's it going?"

"We're just about ready, but we had a question." There was a long pause, then she asked, "Sandy, what do we do about the power station?"

"What do you mean?" I asked, confused.

"I mean... do we shut it down? Do we leave it running?" She went silent for a few seconds, then Jim's voice came over the radio. "Theoretically, the power station could run itself... well, indefinitely. Most of it is automated. It's only when the unexpected happens that it needs human intervention – like the tree."

"Oh, I'm with you." I paused to think about it, processing the pluses and minuses of each scenario out loud. "If we leave the station running, there is a chance that something could damage it. But we have no intention of coming back, and if we leave it running then that would potentially give us the ability to access its power as we travel south, which could save our precious resources. I think we should leave it running. What do you guys think?"

"I think you're right," Rebecca said. "We haven't really had to do much to keep it running all this time. We just clean out the pipes occasionally, and keep an eye on the warning lights."

"Okay, leave it running," I decided, nodding thoughtfully to myself. "How much longer do you guys need before you're ready to go?"

"Give us half an hour to finish up down here," she answered. "We'll meet you at the warehouse when we're ready to go."

"Good." I straightened up, absently adjusting the unfamiliar folds of my coat around me. "We're pretty much ready to move out now, so we're just waiting on you. Let us know if you need extra help."

"Thanks, but I think we're good," she replied. "We'll see you soon."

The radio went dead in my hand. I tucked it back into its pocket in the lining of my coat, then buttoned it back up over my midsection. My stomach felt a little upset and it bothered me, but I was used to nausea. I had experienced it on a regular basis as a result of my odd, irregular diet.

"Sandy?"

As if reading my mind, I suddenly heard Anahera calling my name. She paused and looked me up and down, tilting her head to one side.

"Are you all right, dear?" she asked. "You look pale. Well, paler than usual."

"Oh, it's the fish," I answered with a strained chuckle. "I'm not used to having fish for breakfast. I'll be fine."

"Oh!" A smile lit up her face, one that was so friendly and understanding that it immediately made me feel better. "I'm sorry, I didn't think about that. I suppose your folks aren't used to having fish for every meal."

"I'm not used to having fish at all, to be honest. I'm terrible at fishing," I admitted sheepishly. "We'll get used to it. Anyway, was there something you wanted?"

"Yes, actually." Anahera sighed and came over towards me. She sat down on the edge of a nearby table and looked at me thoughtfully. "I want to go through Tokoroa."

I froze for a second, staring back at her. "Tokoroa was gang territory, last time I checked. I was planning to go around it. Why do you want to go there?"

"There's a radio station there," she said quietly, watching my face as though trying to divine my thoughts. "Like we discussed, the other people in this region deserve some kind of warning. I did a bit of research last night, and found out that Tokoroa's station is the nearest one that we're likely to pass before we leave the Waikato."

I swore softly beneath my breath and turned away from her, staring out the door at the driving rain. She said nothing, just sat watching me and giving me the time I needed to think over the decision. I knew there was really only one choice that I could make, but I didn't like it.

Unfortunately, she was right. Even the gangs included women and children, and not all of the men were terrible people. They certainly didn't deserve to die a bloody, brutal, painful death.

"Fine," I agreed grudgingly. "We'll go through Tokoroa."

***

Even with all the delays, we were back on the road before the sun had climbed high enough to peek over the trees. Michael and I led in the Hilux, with him behind the wheel and me hunched over our maps, plotting our route south.

"We'll need to swing east at the next junction," I told him, tracing the line of the road on the map. "Turn left."

"Okay," he replied simply.

While he was busy watching the road through the deluge, I pulled out my radio and called back to the convoy. "Rebecca and Jim, I need you for a second."

"We're here," Rebecca's voice answered within a few seconds. "What's up, boss?"

"Oh lord, don't start with that again," I protested with a dramatic groan. "I just need to know what we can expect on the roads today. How far east of Arapuni have you travelled?"

"Not far," she admitted. "A few kilometres at most. We really had no reason to go that way."

"Damn," I grumbled. "I don't suppose there's any chance you guys went down Old Taupo Road, is there?"

"No," she replied. "Not since before the plague. Sorry, mate."

"It's all good," I said. "We're just going to have to chance it, and hope for the best."

"Well, if it helps, the roads we saw were in pretty decent condition," she supplied, along with the verbal equivalent of a shrug. "Beyond that... I dunno, sorry."

"Thanks anyway. We'll let you know if we see any problems." I clicked off the radio and set it down on the dashboard in front of me, within easy reach should I need it. "Well, at least it doesn't seem to be a quake zone."

Michael grunted wordless agreement. The rain was coming down thick and fast, making it hard for him to see, so I fell silent and let him concentrate. Rebecca was certainly right about the condition of the roads for the first few kilometres; they were in practically perfect condition. We passed by a few old farmsteads, set amidst overgrown pastures and small patches of native bush.

A few minutes later, we reached a large intersection, with branches pointing out like the spokes of a wheel. Michael slowed down and glanced at me for directions.

"Right," I told him. "Turn right, and keep following that road until I say otherwise."

He nodded, and guided us around the corner, while I picked up my radio to convey the instructions to the rest of the convoy in case they were unable to see us through the gloom. I could barely see a dozen feet in front of the windshield, so I rolled down my window a crack… then I burst out laughing.

"What are you laughing at?" Michael asked.

"Corn," I answered, amused. "More corn. Always corn."

"Food is food," Michael answered. "Think we should stop and top up our supplies?"

"Nah, we're good for the moment." I shook my head, and planted my elbow on the window sill to watch the passing corn fields for any sign of danger. Or anything else, really, but there was nothing to be seen. The corn went on forever, or so it felt. Suddenly, a flash of white plastic interrupted the monotony, but it was only old bales of sodden hay, wrapped in tattered plastic sheets. Nothing of any interest to us. Then, more corn.

I heaved a monumental sigh, and gave Michael a look. "I spy with my little eye, something beginning with…"

"Is it corn?" Michael asked dryly, clearly sensing my mood was drifting into the silly.

"No way!" I feigned surprise. "How did you guess so fast?"

"I'm just lucky like that," he said with a grin. "Man, it's starting to feel like one day the entire Waikato is going to be conquered by an army of cornfields."

"Better cornfields than mutants and zombie pigs," I replied. "At least we can eat corn."

"Well, there's no logical reason to assume that we can't eat zombie pigs," he commented. "I mean, have you ever tried?"

"No!" I exclaimed, horrified by the mere suggestion. "You would have to be a special kind of crazy to actually consider doing that. They're all… rotten and stuff. Gross."

"Yes," he said slowly, as though talking to a child. "I didn't say they were appetizing. I was just suggesting that it's entirely possible that they're edible. Appetizing and edible are two different things."

I opened my mouth to argue, but at the same moment it suddenly clicked that he was trying to bait me. "Hang on just one corn-picking minute… are you just trying to get out of ever being put on kitchen duty again?"

"Of course not!" He made a dismissive gesture with one hand, but it was just a little bit too dramatic to be real. "I'm just saying, don't knock it 'til you've tried it, right? Like Brussels sprouts."

"That's it, now you're doing the dishes every night for the rest of forever," I teased right back, folding my arms across my chest.

"You have no sense of humour at all." He started to say something else, but something out in the rain caught his attention. His eyes flew wide and he slammed on the brakes so suddenly that I was jerked half out of my seat. If we hadn't been travelling at a snail's pace because of the rain, it could have done serious damage. Luckily for me, it just ruffled my feathers.

"What?" I exclaimed, shoving myself back into my seat. "What is it?"

"There's someone out there," he answered, his voice barely above a whisper. "Or something. I can't tell."

"Stop the convoy," I told him, my irritation at the sudden halt vanishing in the blink of an eye. "I'll check it out."

"Sandy, no," Michael protested, grabbing my hand. "Not by yourself."

"I have my gun right beside me, and I'm already dressed for the rain." I gently extracted my hand from his, and pulled the hood of my coat up over my head. "I won't leave your line of sight. Join me as soon as the convoy is safe."

He might have had a few more words to say, but I didn't hear them. In a single, well-practiced motion, I was out the door and in a fighter's crouch, with my shotgun aimed into the mists. I wondered briefly whether the weapon was safe to use in the rain, but there wasn't time to ask. If it was an enemy up ahead, I had to be sure.

The rain was so heavy that it had me drenched in a few seconds flat, but the leather kept my skin mostly dry. As silently as I could, I crept around to the driver's side of the Hilux, and stared at the road in front of us. There was something there, something moving with slow, jerky motions, but the details were obscured by the haze.

Suddenly, the door beside me opened and Michael leapt out, wrapped in a newly-salvaged leather jacket of his own. His lacked a hood, though, which forced him to squint to keep the water out of his eyes.

"What is it?" he asked, so quietly that his voice was almost a whisper.

"I don't know," I admitted softly. I lifted a hand and gestured for him to accompany me, but I didn't wait to see if he followed me. I didn't have to. If there was one person I knew, it was Michael. He'd always be at my side when I needed him, and that was why I trusted him.

I sensed him half a step behind me as we crept forward, weapons at the ready. Slowly but surely, a humanoid figure started to resolve out of the haze. It was moving southwards in a slow, halting gait. I knew without having to see its face that it was probably one of the infected, but I always erred on the side of caution. There was no undo button if you chose to shoot first and ask questions later.

I held up my hand and made a gesture instructing Michael to hold his position, and then I crept forward and began to circle around the creature. For a few seconds I walked beside it, following a parallel course while keeping myself well out of its reach. Eventually, I drew out in front of it, turning as I moved until I was very nearly walking backwards.

Suddenly, it turned and looked at me. Its mouth gaped, and it let out a terrible, blood-curdling, familiar screech. I jumped back, my finger on the trigger, fully expecting it to leap at me the way the mutants usually did.

Nothing happened. It just stared at me, completely expressionless, and kept on shuffling southwards. I glanced at Michael, but he didn't have an answer any more than I did. Once the creature passed me, it seemed to lose interest in me completely.

Curious, I took a few steps backwards, to bring myself back into its field of vision. Again, it looked at me, issued one of those horrid, skin-crawling screeches, then kept on walking as though nothing had happened.

"What the hell is that?" A breathless voice asked behind me. I glanced back, and saw that Skylar had joined us, along with most of the fighters of the group. "It sounds like a mutant."

"It sounds like one, but it isn't attacking," I answered, just as confused as she sounded. "I don't understand."

"How can it shriek like a mutant but not be one?" Michael asked what we were all thinking. "Why isn't it attacking us? Where's it going?"

"Maybe it's going south for the winter?" I suggested, trying to squeeze a little bit of humour out of a situation that wasn't funny at all.

"It's a proto-mutant," Skylar said suddenly. I glanced at her, and saw her staring back at me with wide eyes. "Like, something halfway between the mutants we know and the normal infected. It's turning into a mutant." She paused and stared at it for a second, then looked back at me. "What's it wearing? Is that a uniform?"

"I think so, yeah," I answered. I hurried back over, and slowly stepped back into the creature's line of sight. Again, it shrieked at me, but made no attempt to attack me, which gave me the time I needed to get a good look at it. "Looks like a nurse, or maybe a cleaner, I'm not sure. I think I see an ID tag. I'm going to try and grab it. Cover me."

A series of grunts, and the sound of bodies moving and guns being cocked was the reply to my request. I nodded once, then I leapt forward and tried to grab the tag hanging around the thing's neck. My first attempt failed, but it didn't even seem to care. I made a second grab, and this time my fingers closed around the cold, wet plastic. The safety clasp holding the lanyard in place popped open when I gave it a good, hard tug, and with that the prize was mine.

"It's so faded, I can barely read it," I said as I returned to my group. "That logo is familiar, though. Do you guys recognise it?"

"Yes," Michael answered, shading his eyes to keep the rain out of them as he studied the tag in my hand. "It's the logo of the hospital where we met. That thing is from Hamilton. How the hell did it get this far south?"

"It seems pretty determined to go wherever it's going," I commented, watching the thing shuffling away from us. Suddenly, realisation dawned on me. "Oh, God. It's not just a proto-mutant. It's a plague-bearer."

"What?" Skye exclaimed, turning to stare at me. "You think it's going south to spread the mutated virus? Can that happen? That the infected be re-infected?"

"I don't know, and I sure as hell don't want to find out." I spun around and pointed at her. "Go back to the convoy and get as much accelerant as we need to get this thing burning. We have to destroy it right now!"

Skylar nodded and ran off, leaving Michael and the others staring at me.

"Sandy, what are you thinking?" Michael asked, running his hand back through his wet hair to smooth it away from his face.

"I'm thinking..." I paused, turning the idea over in my head. The more I thought about it, the worse it got. "Michael, how many people worked at that hospital before the plague? And how many patients were there?"

"I don't know," he said. "Hundreds, at least. Probably thousands. I mean, where do people go when they get sick? They go to a hospital. It felt like half the city was there towards the end."

"So, where did all those people go?" I asked rhetorically, turning to look him square in the eye. He stared back at me, not quite seeming to understand. "Okay, think about it. Let's assume that there were at least a thousand people there. We know that sometimes the virus burns fast and devours everything, but we also know that sometimes it burns slower and takes longer to totally destroy the infected, right?"

"Right..." he echoed.

"So," I continued, "if we presume that half those poor folks have burned out by now, that leaves five hundred people that should have been in that hospital when we met. How many did we see?"

"Only four or five," he said, his eyes slowly widening. "My God... where did all those people go?"

"Out into the countryside," I answered morbidly. "Spreading the mutated infection between them and the regular undead that are still on their feet. If I remember my high school biology right, a virus breeds by consuming a host's cells, which in turn kills the cells and makes them unsuitable for the virus to keep breeding in. The visible decay that we see happens because of that cell death. So, if Ebola X is still living and breeding in these infected after so long, it must have figured out a way to keep reproducing inside dead cells, without destroying them completely."

"Right..." he repeated again, though I could see I was starting to lose him.

"Michael, this is it," I said, grabbing his arm. "This is why the mutants are happening. Somehow – I don't know how – the virus has been breeding inside dead cells to save itself from dying out. That means it can keep breeding indefinitely inside the same host. It's been doing that for ten years. If we estimate that a single virus produces a million offspring every few hours, what happens when we multiply that by a decade? What happens over the course of thousands and thousands of generations?"

Suddenly, the light bulb seemed to go on behind his eyes. "Evolution."

"Evolution," I agreed, my expression grim. "I think I get it now. I think I finally understand. There isn't just one strain of the virus, not like we thought. There are hundreds of ever-so-slightly different strains, because of the population evolution happening inside each host. We can group them into three primary categories, though – the fast-burning virus, the slow-burning virus, and the new mutation." I counted them off on my fingers, my brow furrowed in thought. "At first, we only had the two strains, fast-burning and slow-burning. Natural selection has most likely killed off the fast-burning strain by now. But, the slow-burning strain survived, because it evolved a way to breed without destroying its host. And then the slow-burning strain kept breeding over and over again, until it started to turn into the new mutation.

"With Ebola X being airborne, when the new strain emerged it could easily spread amongst the available hosts. So, we can assume it evolved in the hospital, where there was – or should have been – that big concentration of people. The infected would have no real immunity, so if the new mutation was dominant then it would spread like wildfire..."

"...and infect all of those docile infected with the new mutation?" Michael summarised for me, a look of horror spreading across his face. "So, if this plague-bearer finds another population of infected..."

"...then it's going to spread the new virus to them, and then they'll turn into mutated infected as well," I answered softly.

"We have to destroy that thing. Right now!" His voice rose to a shout, and he raced past me with his weapon at the ready.

"No!" I cried, dashing after him. "Don't waste ammunition! We have precious little as it is, and for all we know the same thing may have happened in Wellington or Palmerston North or anywhere else that there's a dense concentration of infected."

Michael froze with his gun already raised halfway to the firing position. He looked at me, then looked back at the infected. "You want to use your Taser on that thing?"

"Why not?" I shrugged, reaching up to rest my arm on his bicep. "It's reusable, and it works. We need to use renewable energy sources whenever we can, or we're going to end up with nothing left but a sense of regret and an empty chamber."

"Well, that seems a bit dramatic," he said dryly. With a heavy sigh, he lowered his weapon and nodded to me. "Do you want me to do it?"

"No, I've got this," I answered. Just as I was handing him my shotgun, Skylar came running back with a flask in her hands. She watched me pull out my Taser and flick it on, her eyes widening.

"Is that safe to use in this rain?" she asked. "I thought water was conductive?"

"These were made to be safe in all kinds of weather." I made a reassuring gesture with my free hand, and gave everyone a quick smile before I turned to deal with the unpleasant duty at hand. The infected was totally oblivious to me as I crept up behind it, trying to get close enough to use my Taser as a stun gun. Sure, I could have used the shot, but I only had one cartridge and I couldn't exactly run to the store and grab another one.

I drew a deep breath as I closed the last few feet, and reached out to press the Taser to the base of the creature's neck. It stumbled, but righted itself and kept on walking. A second blast of current brought it down, twitching. Before I could say a word, Michael was past me with the accelerant and a lighter.

With the rain pelting down and the wind howling around us, it took all of our combined efforts to get the creature burning to our satisfaction. When the fire was finally hot enough that it wasn't likely to go out on its own, we stood back and watched intently. No one complained about the cold or the wet. None of us wanted to leave until we were sure that plague-bearer was well and truly destroyed.

# Chapter Fourteen

The morning encounter left us wary and on edge for the rest of the day. I found myself feeling far too anxious to simply sit passively, so I hauled myself halfway out the window to watch the endless cornfields with a degree of alertness that bordered on paranoia. The cold made my teeth rattle and my butt went numb, but at least I felt better for doing something useful.

Eventually, a line of dark trees started to grow along the edge of the horizon, getting closer and closer with each passing second. I watched it warily, but to my relief our turn-off arrived before we plunged into darkness.

"Turn left in a hundred metres," I called down through the open window. With the rain pounding down on me, I barely heard Michael's grunt of acknowledgement. We reached the corner and turned onto another overgrown strip of roadway, almost identical to the last. A few minutes later, the cornfields ended abruptly, only to be replaced by waist-high grass dotted with dark specks in the distance. I lifted my hand to shade my eyes and stared intently at them, trying to work out what the specks were.

"Sandy," Michael said suddenly. I glanced at him, and realised that he was holding out his binoculars to me. I took them with a sheepish smile, and looked at the specks again. A second later, I relaxed.

"Just cows," I told him. Some things hadn't changed since the fall of mankind, and cows were one of them. They were still the same placid, even-tempered beasts they'd always been. The only difference now was that they were free-range animals, and the entire country was their ranch.

"Good." I heard Michael let out a deep breath, and when I looked at him again I saw that he was smiling. "You should probably come in, though."

"Why?" I asked curiously, lifting the binoculars back to my eyes so that I could scan the rest of the horizon for danger.

"I saw a flash of lightning when you were looking the other way," he answered. "It's still pretty far away, but I don't want my favourite girl getting electrocuted."

"Your favourite girl, huh?" I echoed in my most playful voice. I eased myself back down into the cab, and grabbed a towel out of the back seat to dry myself off.

"You say that like you didn't already know it," he answered dryly, shooting one of his silly grins in my direction.

I laughed and shook my head. "Oh, I know it. I just can't quite believe it."

"Well, believe it." He reached over and took my hand with his free one. "This is happening, Sandy. What we have, it's real and it's special. I've never felt like this about anyone before." He sighed, returning his hand to the steering wheel. "You know, there's something I've never told you."

"Oh?" I raised a brow, instantly cautious. "Are you secretly a serial killer? A failed superhero? A mime stripper?"

"No!" he exclaimed, laughing merrily. "Wait... a mime stripper? That's not even a thing!"

"Well, you better tell me what it is, then," I answered, folding my arms across my chest. "I've had a lot of time to think about this, you know."

"It's nothing like that, I swear," he said, struggling to get his laughter back under control. "I just... I didn't want to say anything until I was sure, you know?"

"You've already told me that you want to marry me and have babies with me," I pointed out. "What else could there possibly be that you were afraid to say to me?"

"Well, it's... a bit strange," he admitted, his expression suddenly turning serious. "Maddy told me I was going to meet you. A year ago."

"What?" I froze, startled. Of all the things he could have said, that was the last thing I had expected to hear.

"Yeah." He sighed softly and shrugged. "I didn't believe her at the time... let me start from the beginning. Maddy's special, you and I both know that. She wasn't always like that. I mean, she's always been a bit odd, but she started developing that strange intuitiveness the summer before last. At first I just assumed that it was because she's a kid. Sophie said strange things at her age, so I thought it was normal. But some of the things that she started saying were... not normal. For any little kid."

"What happened?" I prompted gently, watching his face to try and judge his thoughts from his expression. He hesitated, and then he shot me a look of such sadness and longing that my heart dropped right to my knees.

"I was so lonely, Sandy," he said quietly. "I mean, we talked about it when we first met, but there's no way for me to verbally express it. Even with Sophie, and the others... it wasn't the same. I was so lonely that it hurt. It physically ached inside me. Did you ever feel like that?"

"Yes," I admitted, lowering my gaze. "In the first couple of years, before the... the bad stuff happened. I cried myself to sleep more than once."

"Me too," he replied. I felt his big hand land on mine again, and his fingertips gently rubbed my skin. The touch reassured me; I took his hand in both of mine, and held it while he spoke. "I'm man enough to admit that I've cried over it more than once. We were so young when all this happened. I had never even considered that I'd lose my opportunity to have a family. I just sort of assumed that it'd happen naturally, you know? I figured I'd focus on my career for a while, then when the time was right, I'd meet the perfect woman. She'd be smart, beautiful, funny, and she'd love me as much as I loved her. I had the same vague dreams as everyone else: we'd travel the world together, then one day settle down and start a family.

"One day, I'm in my apartment daydreaming about the future. A week later, almost everyone I've ever known is dead, and my chance for a family is gone forever."

He paused and took a deep breath; I squeezed his hand, feeling the intensity of his emotion through his palm. Suddenly, he looked at me and I could see the terrible pain in his eyes. A moment later, he returned his gaze to the road, and he resumed speaking.

"I never got over that," he admitted. "I accepted the situation for what it was, but I could never get past the pain. It just got worse and worse every day, but I learned to hide it and focused on nurturing Sophie. She was all I had. And don't get me wrong, I loved her more than life itself and put my everything into raising her – but it was never the same as the life I'd dreamed of."

"I know," I whispered, leaning up against him to comfort him in some small way. Even though I was damp and smelt like wet leather, Michael smiled at the contact.

"I wish you could have met her, Sandy," he murmured. His eyes were focused on the road, but his expression said that his thoughts were a million miles away. "She would have loved you, and I think you would have loved her, too. She was a brilliant kid. Obsessed with books, and always smiling and laughing. I think she kept all of us sane, until..."

"I know," I repeated gently, hugging him as best I could without disrupting his driving. "I know that I would have loved her. From the sound of it, she's just like her uncle."

Michael gave me one of his quirky, lopsided smiles. "I suppose she was, in a way. The laughter kept us going." He sighed, looking back out the windscreen at the pouring rain. "But not always. You know how I am. Sometimes I drop."

"You're a Pisces, sweetie." I leaned up and planted a kiss on his cheek. "Pisces are always moody and mercurial."

This time, the glance he gave me was one of amusement. "Oh, are we just? And how do you know that, missy?"

"Sophie wasn't the only one who had a lot of time to read," I answered dryly. "I am a stubborn Capricorn, which is clearly why I'm the boss of you. So there."

"Oh, I see." Michael gave me a dubious, but amused look. "Well, then. I won't contest that. I like it when you're the boss of me."

"I know you do," I teased, playfully running my fingers along the top of his thigh. "Anyway, what were you saying about Maddy?"

"Huh?" He glanced down, momentarily distracted by my touch. "Oh, right, Maddy. Yeah, I was in my room in a dark mood, just lying in bed, staring at the ceiling. Moping, basically. Out of the blue, Maddy came marching into my room with a purpose. She sat down on the edge of my bed, looked me right in the eye, and said, 'Don't worry, Mister Michael. You won't have to be lonely for much longer.'"

"Really?" I sat up straight and looked at him. "She said that? A year ago?"

"And that's not all," he said. "When I asked her what she meant, she just smiled mysteriously, and said 'Your wife is waiting for you. She just doesn't know it yet.'"

"You're kidding me!" I exclaimed, startled. "You have to be making that up."

"I'm not, I swear. Cross my heart." He grinned and glanced at me again. "At the time, I figured she was just talking nonsense, so I forgot all about it. And then this crazy blonde walks into my life, punches me in the face, and suddenly I'm head-over-heels in love. I wasn't a hundred percent sure until you put that ring around your neck, but now I am. You're the one that Maddy saw in her vision. My future wife."

"Well, that's sweet, bewildering, and a little concerning all at the same time," I said, fighting a wave of conflicting emotions. "I mean, if we're, I don't know… fated to be together… well, what about free will? Don't I get any say in the matter? "

"No, and neither do I." Suddenly, he smiled at me. "Either one of us could walk away from this any time we wanted. Do you want to walk away?"

"No," I answered without a second of hesitation. "Do you?"

"Not a chance," he answered just as swiftly. "And that's why we're destined to be together. Because we *want* to be together."

"Oh." I paused to consider his point, and as I considered it I felt myself relaxing. My automatic fight-or-flight instinct switched off, and was replaced by human logic. "Okay. I think I'm good with that."

"Good, because I'd be really upset if you changed your mind now," he said with a laugh. There was a pause, then the subjected changed as swiftly as it had begun. "Hey, I see houses up ahead. Should we stop to look for supplies?"

"No," I said, shaking my head firmly. "This land is claimed. We don't scavenge here, and we don't stop for anything unless we have to. We need to find that radio tower and get out of here before we're noticed. I'm hoping this weather will work in our favour, and we can be far enough south by nightfall to relax."

"I think we may be out of luck in that regard," Michael said softly. I looked where he was pointing, just in time to catch sight of a human figure disappearing behind a house.

I swore under my breath, and picked up my walkie-talkie. "Guys, we've been spotted. I want you to move in close together, and lock the doors if you're inside one of the cars. Don't stop for anything unless we stop, or I tell you to."

Michael waited until I finished relaying the instructions to the rest of the convoy, then he gave me a worried look. "Are these people really that dangerous?"

"I don't know," I admitted, "which means we should presume they're dangerous until we find out otherwise. Gangs are... well, they are gangs. Every one of them is different, depending on the nature of the members and the leader. Also remember that to them, we're a rival gang travelling through their territory, which means that we're automatically a danger to them. They may shoot first and ask questions later."

"If they have weapons," Michael pointed out. "I mean, this is still New Zealand. Guns are rare, and ones that still work are rarer still."

"True," I agreed quietly. "Let's just hope that works in our favour. For now, keep following this street."

Michael just nodded and fell silent, apparently sensing that I was in no mood to be reassured. He was right. My run-ins with gangs over the years had been frequent and mostly unpleasant, and I didn't really want to have another one. Suddenly, I realised that I was clutching my shotgun with a death-grip, and my knuckles were turning white. I forced myself to take a deep breath, and relaxed my grip.

At least this time I had some control over the outcome of what felt like an inevitable conflict. I had people to watch my back. Not just one person, either. Now, I had twenty-three people, one feline, and an elderly sheepdog on my side. I couldn't exactly rely on the kids or animals in a fight, but I trusted most of the adults. The thought made me smile; how far I'd come, that I could use the t-word so freely.

"Something up ahead," Michael said suddenly. "I see a car."

I stuck my head out the window, and looked through the binoculars. There was an intersection coming up, where a car waited patiently at the stop sign. After a few seconds, I shook my head. "That car isn't going anywhere. No driver. You're getting as paranoid as me, honey."

"Better safe than sorry," he said sheepishly. We drove past the abandoned car and continued deeper into the city. Well, town. It was certainly bigger than Ohaupo and Arapuni, but not by much.

The trees on the roadside began to get thicker, interspersed with an odd mixture of vegetation. Shrubs and flower beds that had once been well-loved and tame had gone wild without the gardeners to care for them. Now, they encroached on the road and were engaged in a brutal, silent battle with the larger trees for dominance and sunlight.

Every few meters, there was a gap in the foliage and a flash of colour beyond that told me that we'd entered suburbia. Faded weatherboards, broken fences, and the odd piece of discarded refuse paid testament to the people that had once called this place home. They were gone now – or were they? A brief movement caught my eye, but by the time I focused on it, it had vanished.

"We're being watched," I concluded, trying to keep from sounding too morose; the last thing we needed was for me to make everyone else nervous. Nervous people made mistakes. Luckily for me, Michael wasn't the kind of man that disturbed easily. He just nodded silently, and accepted my warning for what it was.

A few minutes later, the roads began to widen and the foliage thinned out, letting me finally get a clear look at the buildings. Most of them were in fairly decent condition, but there was one thing that immediately leapt to my attention.

"Is that graffiti over there?" Michael asked suddenly.

"Stop reading my mind," I scolded, though there was no genuine irritation in it. "Yes, that's gang sign. Like cats pissing on the furniture to mark their territory."

"That's a lovely thought," he answered dryly. "Should we start worrying about your cat doing that?"

"Of course no," I said, putting on a mock-haughty tone. "I'll have you know that Tigger is a lady. She'd never do such an improper thing."

"Oh, I see!" Michael responded by putting on a haughty tone of his own. "Very good, then. Carry on." He returned to his normal tone of voice to ask a question. "Do you know what they mean?"

I lifted the binoculars to my eyes and studied the markings for a moment before it started to make sense to me. "'Aua le sau i totonu'. Looks like the Samoans. That sign looks pretty old, though. The paint is chipped and faded." I studied the various words painted on the buildings nearby for a few minutes, then lowered the binoculars and looked back at him. "If the Samoans are still here, that's potentially good for us. I've had dealings with them before. While they don't trust outsiders, they're unlikely to attack us unless we provoke them."

"I'm sensing a 'but' coming on," Michael commented, his brow furrowing in concern. I nodded grimly and set the binoculars down in my lap.

"But the sign is really old, and I'm not seeing any fresh tags," I replied. "The Samoans are usually quite diligent about keeping their territory markers up-to-date. It's unlikely that they'd let their tags fade that much."

"Unless they've been displaced," Michael said, finishing the thought for me.

"Or wiped out." I shook my head and shrugged helplessly, then I grabbed my GPS off the dashboard and checked our position against it. "Take this right, and keep following the road. We should be coming up to a level crossing in a minute."

"Follow the road? That may be easier said than done," Michael commented dryly.

I glanced up, and promptly swore beneath my breath. I heaved a long-suffering sigh, grabbed my walkie-talkie, and spoke into it, "So, I know you guys are just dying for some exercise. Who feels like wrestling a train?"

An assortment of groans and complaints came across the connection. I waited until the noise died down, then continued, "Yeah, yeah, whine all you want, but it's the fastest way to get where we want to go. Little kids and animals stay in the car with the doors locked. Teenagers and walking wounded, you're on guard duty. Watch the rear and sides. I want every able-bodied adult up at the front of the convoy. It's time to get wet. Sorry."

There were more groans, but I ignored them. Michael and I exchanged a smile as we climbed out and locked the doors behind us. I put my shotgun over my shoulder on its carry strap, and made my way over to examine the train.

"How on earth are we supposed to move that?" Michael asked, his voice raised to carry over the sound of the rain. "That thing has to weigh tons, and the wheels are rusted solid."

"We don't have to move the locomotive," I replied. "If we uncouple the last carriage, then that should give us enough space to get through. Cover me for a second while I take a closer look."

"Okay," Michael agreed, though I could tell from his voice that he was dubious about the integrity of my plan. I heard his footsteps behind me as I headed up to the train, and squeezed myself into the narrow gap between the last two carriages.

The coupling looked like a road map written in a foreign language. Still, I was pretty much used to working out all things mechanical based on pure logic. After a minute or so, I figured out which lever would raise the pin that was keeping the carriages together. I grabbed the lever and pulled, but it was rusted firmly into place. A glance back over my shoulder told me that the others had gathered behind me, waiting patiently for instructions.

"Hemi, can you please go find Skylar?" I asked. "I need a can of CRC, a hammer and chisel, and a crowbar. She should know where the tools are."

"Got it!" Hemi sketched a salute and raced off. I turned to look at the others.

"Okay, the plan here is that we're just going to get the last car loose," I explained. "Then, we muscle it about three meters down the rails. We should be able to squeeze through, no problem. I'm going to need a couple of you strong blokes over here to open this lever. Volunteers?"

Just about everyone stepped forward to volunteer, much to my amusement. I just grinned and beckoned Tane and Iorangi to my side. Just as they joined me, Hemi reappeared with the tools we needed. It took a few minutes of coaxing and a few teeth-grating shrieks, but eventually the lever began to move.

"That's it, we've got it!" I cried victoriously, waving the crowbar to the waiting group. "Okay, everyone. Pick a side, and find something to grab."

Eager to follow my own instructions, I raced up to the far end of the carriage and braced my shoulder against an ancient hand railing. I felt a warm body join me, and looked back to see Michael right behind me, his strong hands flexing on the railing above my head. He glanced down at me, smiled, and nodded his encouragement.

"On the count of three," I cried, loudly enough for everyone to hear me. "One, two, three – push!"

On command, I threw my weight against the train carriage's bulk. My feet slipped in the gravel for a second, then one of them struck a sleeper, giving me something to brace against. Michael growled deep in his throat, a noise of determination more than frustration. I felt him straining along with me, using every ounce of his strength to move the stubborn cab.

For ten long years, it had stayed in exactly the same place, waiting for an engineer that would never return. For ten years, it had endured the elements, exposed, slowly turning to rust. That much rusted metal didn't move easily – but, eventually, it did move.

At first, it was only a centimetre. Then another. Then five centimetres. Ten. Twenty.

"We're doing it!" I cried breathlessly. "How far are we?"

"About half way!" someone called back; I wasn't sure who.

"Keep going," I gasped, throwing my weight against the railing with renewed enthusiasm. "We can do this. It's coming a little easier."

And it was. The farther we managed to move it, the more those rusted wheels began to loosen up on the railings. Stars began to dance around the edge of my vision but I ignored them. I was intensely focused on the task, and oblivious to everything except that one more millimetre. Just a tiny, tiny bit more…

"That's it!" the voice cried from the end of the line. "That's enough, we can get through."

A collective cheer went up from the people around me. Overwhelmed by a sense of team victory, I shoved myself upright again – then promptly stumbled and fell against Michael's side.

He caught me before I could hit the ground, and turned a worried look on me. "Honey? You all right?"

"Yeah, I'm fine," I lied, waving away his concern. "Just over-extended myself, that's all."

"Okay…" he said softly, but his expression said that he didn't believe me. He gently helped me back to my feet and released me. I smiled at him and went to take a step back towards the others, except that my body didn't want to obey. Before I quite realised what had happened to me, my feet had once more gone out from under me and I was on my way down.

Michael caught me again, but this time he didn't let me go. Despite my protests, he scooped me up and carried me back towards the convoy, past a row of faces that turned to watch with concern.

"Put me down!" I demanded, thumping a fist ineffectively against his broad shoulder. "I just need to sit down for a second, I'm totally fine."

"You have a broad definition of 'fine' and we both know it," he answered, his voice deep, firm, and commanding. It was a tone that I rarely heard from him since I'd taken command, but it was one that brooked no nonsense. Before I could even think about forming a counter-argument, he'd carried me back to the car where Doctor Cross was standing guard over the children.

"What did she do this time?" the doctor asked. Without waiting for an explanation, Doc shoved his gun back into its makeshift holster, and stomped over to examine me.

"Hey, I don't injure myself that often," I complained, but I didn't even bother trying to fend off the examination. Doc was stronger than he looked, and I knew better than to resist his ministrations. "I just got a little light-headed after we finished moving the train. I keep telling him I'll be fine, but you know how much he worries about me."

"And with good reason." Doc stood back and gave me a sharp look, one that instantly made me feel like a naughty child caught with her hand in the cookie jar. "Ms McDermott, need I remind you *yet again* that you suffered a concussion not even a week ago? You are one of the walking wounded, and you know that you're not supposed to be exerting yourself."

"I needed to," I answered sharply; it always made me a little bit cross when he used that tone with me, and now was no different. "It was all hands on deck. We needed everyone."

"Did you let them try without you first? Are you sure that they needed you?" he countered, his eyes narrowed to slivers behind the scratched lenses of his glasses.

"Well, no," I admitted, then swiftly rose to defend myself, "but I didn't want to. A leader should always be willing to do anything that she asks her followers to do. It wouldn't be right for me to ask them to muck in, and not do it myself."

"And yet you were perfectly happy to assign the other walking wounded, myself included, to guard duty," he pointed out. His voice softened suddenly, and his expression turned almost fatherly. "Ms McDermott – Sandy – the most important thing about being a leader is learning your own limitations, and knowing how to follow your own rules. I know that you want to contribute so that the others don't think that you're using your position to slack off, and I understand that. I really do. But, it simply isn't necessary."

I started to protest, but he cut me off with a wave of his hand.

"You're human just like the rest of us, and your unique set of circumstances make you particularly vulnerable. Accept it. You're not invulnerable." He adjusted his glass, and gave me a stern frown. "She's fine, just give her a few minutes to sit down."

Then, before I could say anything else, he marched away to tend to whatever other business was demanding his attention. I blinked in surprise, and looked at Michael.

"What is it with everyone giving me lectures lately?" I asked dryly, both amused and a little annoyed by it. "Skylar, Anahera, Doc, you… it seems like everyone wants to tell me how to do my job."

"You're still learning," Michael said gently, slipping his arms beneath me to lift me up in his arms, as easily as a father lifting a child. "Everyone is, I think. But you're the one that has to learn the most in the shortest period of time, because people are relying on you. Don't worry, they're not lecturing you because of any kind of failure. They're lecturing you because they see so much potential in you."

"Oh." I paused to consider that as he carried me back towards the car. The explanation assuaged most of my annoyance, and left me thoughtful. "Well, that does make some sense."

"I should hope so," he answered, shooting a look at me. When we reached the car, he gently set me back on my feet and braced me against the Hilux's side panel with his body. "Do you notice the commonalities amongst the people that have been trying to educate you?"

"You lost me with the big words," I answered teasingly.

The joke earned a smile from him, and encouraged him to finish his thought. "They're either leaders themselves, or people of uncommon ability or experience. I hate blowing my own trumpet like that, but it's true. Anahera and I both led our groups for a long time, so we have experience with what you're learning now. Doc has the most life experience of any of us, and he's also the student of human nature. He's been studying people like us longer than we've been alive. And as for your sister, well – she has a deeper insight into your nature than any of us, even me. She's been studying, emulating, and loving you her entire life. That makes her an expert in... well, you."

"So, what you're saying," I summarized, "is that I shouldn't think about it like a kid getting a spanking, but more like university lectures?"

Michael laughed and nodded. "Yes, but you're definitely getting a spanking later on. In private."

"Oh my," I intoned dryly, wiggling a brow at him in a playfully suggestive manner. He grinned and gave me a kiss, then reached past me to open the passenger's door.

"In you go walking wounded," he ordered, guiding me back into my seat. For once in my life, I did as I was told. He even went so far as to buckle me in, then kissed my forehead. "You stay here and guard the car while I make sure everyone's safely loaded."

"Okay," I agreed reluctantly. Just as he was walking away, a flash of anxiety twisted my gut. "Make sure you do a headcount! Don't leave Tigger behind!"

"We won't," he replied, waving over his shoulder.

Relieved, I sat back and indulged myself in a long, deep sigh. If there was one thing I could rely on in life, it was Michael taking care of the people I loved. I tilted my head back and closed my eyes, forcing myself to relax. The sound of the rain was always something that brought me comfort, even when I was soaking wet and cold. During the bleak years I'd spent living in the back of that shipping container in Te Awamutu, the rain had always eased my terrors, chased away the demons, and lulled me to sleep.

The vertigo slowly began to fade, leaving me feeling better. I opened my eyes and blinked slowly – then I froze, staring at a distant junkyard. Through the haze, I thought I could see human figures watching us. I fumbled for Michael's binoculars, but by the time I found them, the figures were gone.

The driver's door opened, and Michael climbed in. He was soaked to the bone, rivulets of water oozing off his leather jacket, and his short hair was plastered to his head. Despite that, he still had a smile for me. In the back seat, Alfred lifted his head and yelped a greeting to his master, tail wagging frantically.

"All heads are accounted for and firmly attached to their necks," Michael told me playfully, reaching back to rub Alfred's ears.

I took the opportunity to steal a quick kiss, then I pointed towards the shipping yard a few hundred meters beyond our current position. "I think there are people over there, but I couldn't tell how many. Let's be careful."

"We could go a different way," Michael suggested, turning back to face front. He slammed his door, pulled his seatbelt on, and started the car, but waited while I pondered the suggestion.

"No," I decided, shaking my head. "It's not worth the extra risk. At least we've seen the lay of the land here, so we know more or less what to expect."

Michael nodded, put the truck in drive, and took his foot off the brake, letting us roll forward slowly until we felt the tyres bump across the train tracks. On the other side, a wide, open space yawned in front of us, flanked on one side by thick trees, and the other by warehouses and shipping yards. I picked up the binoculars again and studied the yards carefully, but if anyone lurked there I couldn't see them.

Michael kept our pace slow and cautious as we advanced. I heard the faint growl of an engine, and caught sight of a quad bike rider in my side mirror. A second later, another rider appeared on Michael's side, flanking us. I recognised the riders as ours, but they were so bundled up against the weather that I couldn't tell exactly who they were. One of them glanced at me and waved, but he looked away before I could reciprocate.

"Eight eyes are better than four," Michael explained. "I asked them to ride with us and help us keep watch for trouble. The others are spread out along the column, doing the same."

"Good call," I agreed softly, my natural caution slowly bubbling away beneath the surface and making me uncomfortable. It was only mid-afternoon, but it was darker than it should have been because of the weather. The treeline beside me was full of dancing shadows, which made it hard to determine if there were enemies about.

"Intersection," Michael said. "Direction?"

"Keep going," I replied. "We should start seeing more warehouses and stuff soon."

"Is that... a cannon over there?" Michael asked, sounding both excited and bewildered.

"Yes," I answered, laughing. "The map says that's the old Returned Services Association's hall. Pity that won't help us deal with our mutant problem, right?"

"Yeah, no kidding," he agreed with his usual playful grin. A moment later, he chuckled and pointed at one of the shop fronts up ahead of us. Three ride-on lawnmowers sat nestled amongst a grass verge so overgrown that we could barely make them out. "That strikes me as kind of ironic. Need a mower?"

"Nah, I'm good," I answered dryly. "Besides, good luck getting them to start after they've been sitting out in the rain for ten years. We should be coming up to a roundabout soon. Go straight through it."

"You mean that thing?" Michael asked, pointing to an enormous green dome that sprang up in the middle of the road, verdant with wildflowers and bushes. "It looks like a big green mushroom."

I couldn't help but laugh at the comparison. "It really does. I don't much like the look of those trees on the other side, though."

"They're just trees," he said, his tone turning gentle and reassuring. "Don't worry, it'll be fine."

A few seconds later, our convoy plunged into semi-darkness beneath the thick boughs. What had once been a row of shade trees planted in a neat median strip had become a jungle, just like the rest of the human world. Just as suddenly as it had begun, the trees parted into an area that had been a shopping centre. The glass fronts of the buildings had been shattered and broken away, and gang sign painted over every flat surface.

"Left," I instructed. "We're almost there. Just keep going straight through the next few intersections."

Michael nodded silently and obeyed. With careful determination, he guided the truck around a few cars that partially blocked the road. We found what we were looking for just a few minutes later: a low, glass-fronted building with an assortment of broadcast aerials on the roof. The windows were just as cracked and broken as everything else, but there was no sign of current occupation.

I grabbed my radio, and thumbed the receiver. "We're here. Form a circle in front of the building, bikes in the middle. Get some people up on top of the trucks to stand watch. Skye, Zain, Jim, and anyone else who knows anything about mechanical stuff or radios, you're with me."

As soon as Michael had brought the Hilux to a stop, I hopped out with my shotgun at the ready and scanned the surroundings for any signs of danger. I saw and heard nothing, just the occasional warble of birdsong and the pounding of the rain on the roof of the truck beside me.

"Stay out here and organise the watch," I instructed when Michael joined me. He nodded and went off to direct traffic, while I inspected the building that had brought us all that way. The moody weather meant that it was dark inside, too dark for me to be able to make out much beyond the ragged glass around the window frames. I reached inside my jacket and grabbed my torch, tucking it inside my sleeve to keep it from getting wet.

The golden beam probed the darkness and drove back the shadows, revealing a small room that had once been a lobby. Debris of a hundred different sorts littered the floor and gathered in the corners; I stepped over the window frame and made my way deeper, my feet crunching across a mixture of leaf litter and trash blown in over the course of a thousand windy days. Tiny, sparkling gems of broken safety glass glittered when my torchlight brushed past them, giving everything a strange, otherworldly feeling.

I heard quiet footfalls behind me, then Skylar's voice whispered, "We're here. Where do we go?"

"Cover me while I check the building is safe," I answered quietly. The response was a chorus of metallic clicks as my companions slipped the safeties off their weapons. I did the same, and led the way down the corridor towards the back of the building.

On either side of the hallway, doors hung open like shadowy, gaping maws. I checked each one, and found a couple of offices, a couple of sound studios, a small lunchroom, and a pair of single-stall lavatories beside an exit that let out into an empty car park.

"I guess the folks that worked here all went home to die," I commented, closing the door to the car park and locking it from the inside.

"Well, aren't you morbid today?" Skye answered, her voice dry and sarcastic. I grunted inarticulately in response, focusing on a more important question: was the power working in Tokoroa?

A light switch caught the beam of my torch. I gently slid past my sister and friends, and pressed it with my thumb. Light flared up, but it was dull and flickering, barely enough to see. I ran my gaze across the ceiling, and discovered that most of the bulbs had been shattered: only two were still intact. Whether that was deliberate or not was a mystery that I couldn't solve.

"Well, at least we've got power," I said, trying to make myself sound cheerful for the sake of my companions. I glanced at them to check who I had with me, and found Jim, Zain, and Ropata following me, in addition to my sister. I nodded and smiled at them. "I saw two sound studios. Let's split up and examine them, see if we can get one of them working."

They nodded obediently. Zain and Ropata headed off towards the studio on the right, leaving me, Jim, and Skye to look at the other one. I found a light switch just inside the door, and this one yielded better results than the one out in the lobby. Unfortunately, what it lit up was a bank of buttons, switches, and dials that looked about as complex as the control panel of a battleship to my inexperienced eye.

"Wow, I have no idea what to do here," I admitted, then I shot a look of appeal at the other two. "Help?"

"Don't worry, I know exactly what to do," Skye answered cheerfully.

Surprised, I lifted my brows and looked at her. "Yeah?"

"Yep!" She grinned suddenly and gave me a playful wink. "We find the manual. Then, we read it."

"Damn, I was hoping to be way out of town by sunset," I said, shaking my head. "Oh well. Nothing we can do about it. Anahera will never let me hear the end of it if we don't at least try."

"It's the right thing to do," Skye reassured me.

To my surprise, Jim also grunted and nodded his agreement. "We may not have liked having to leave our homes, but at least your warning gave us the option to choose. Better that than die unprepared."

"True." The thought cheered me up enough that the smile I gave them wasn't entirely forced. "All right, let's find this manual. You guys look in here, and I'll go check those offices we saw. Let's hope they kept a printed copy on hand, because we can't exactly Google it anymore."

Skye laughed and nodded. "I'll call you if we find anything."

I gave her a thumbs-up sign and left the room. Before I made it halfway to my destination, a shout from outside caught my attention. Startled, I raced back to the front of the building and dove out into the rain, just in time to see Michael standing at the head of a nearby alleyway, waving and yelling at someone I couldn't see. Beside him, Alfred was barking and wagging his tail, apparently oblivious to his master's distress.

"Hey! Come back!" he yelled, then shot a frantic look around. I could tell at a glance that he wanted to run after whoever had gone down that alleyway, and was straining to hold himself back.

I was at his side before he even realised I was coming. "What happened?"

Poor Michael almost jumped out of his skin, but as soon as he recognised me he grabbed my arm with a panic-stricken look on his face. "It's Priyanka!"

"What about her?" I demanded, my stomach dropping to my knees. "Is she okay?"

"She just ran off," he explained, out of breath from shouting. "I have no idea why. She just shouted something and then ran down that alley like all the hounds of hell were after her."

I swore under my breath. "We have to go find her. Come on!"

I heard his footsteps behind me as I raced down the alleyway. Alfred let out a happy yelp and bounded along after us. The old dog clearly presumed it was a game and was more than happy to play along. The alley swung sharply to the left, and emptied out into a vast parking lot that ran behind the shopping centre. On the far side, I could see Priya sprinting away from us as fast as she could go, her little pink running shoes splashing through the puddles.

"Priya!" I yelled as I ran after her. When that didn't reach her, I drew an even deeper breath, and screamed her name as loud as I possibly could. "*Priya!*"

The girl skidded to a halt, and shot a quizzical look back over her shoulder. As soon as she realised that we were following her, her entire face seemed to light up.

"Mama!" she called back, pointing at the row of houses on the other side of the car park. "Mama, there's a girl! I saw her!"

I didn't bother to waste the breath on answering her until we'd closed the gap between us. When we finally got close enough to speak normally, I slowed down to a walk, and then a stop.

"Honey, you can't run off like that," I scolded her gently. "Do you know how much you scared us?"

"Scared?" She blinked up at me, her big, expressive eyes full of confusion. "Why scared?"

I took a deep breath to calm my racing heart. "It's dangerous here. We have to go back, where it's safe."

"No!" Priya stomped her foot with sudden, unexpected vehemence and planted her hands on her hips; she'd never declined any instruction before, so the gesture took me completely by surprise. "I want to find the girl. I want to help her, like you helped me."

"She's probably not alone out here," I explained, gently placing my hands on her shoulders. "There might be bad people, people that want to hurt you."

"Then they'll hurt her, too," she answered stubbornly. "I want to find her and make sure she no hurt. Is dangerous, Mama. You said so."

"I…" I started to try and answer her, but then I realised exactly what she was doing. She was mimicking us, and copying our behaviour. While it was dangerous for all of us, what she wanted to do was ethically right. I sighed heavily and nodded. "Okay, we'll look for a couple of minutes. But we're going to be very careful, okay? Do you have your gun?"

"Yes!" She nodded and patted her pocket. "I have, like Baba taught me."

"Okay." I shot a quizzical look at Michael. "How good is Alfred at tracking?"

"Pretty good," he answered. "I think he was a working dog, back in the day." Michael knelt down, and ruffled the dog's ears. "Alfie? Alfie, fetch! Go fetch!"

The dog let out a delighted yelp, and sprinted off in the direction Michael pointed. The three of us took off after him a second later, and followed when he jumped over a low fence and into an overgrown yard. There, the old sheepdog paused to sniff the ground thoroughly, then he lifted his head and barked. In response to his bark, we heard a child's voice cry out in fear.

"Here!" Priyanka shouted, pointing at an old porch. She dropped to her knees in the mud without regard for her clothing, and peered into the darkness beneath it. "Girl! Come out, girl. Come out. We help you. We nice."

"Go away!" the girl cried back, her words choked by a sob. "I don't want your help. Leave me alone!"

"Whoa, Priya. Back off," I instructed gently. "You're scaring her. Come over here, so we can talk to her without frightening her."

"Me not scary," Priya answered indignantly. "Me nice!"

"You mean 'I'm not scary'. But, just trust me and come here." I smiled at her, and beckoned her over. "Come on."

Priya seemed on the verge of protesting, but she paused to think about it. Then she let out a huffing sound, and pushed herself back to her feet. "Yes, Mama."

"Mama?" the little voice under the porch echoed the word. Suddenly, I found myself being watched by a pair of large, delicately-slanted eyes, through a tangle of wild black hair. The girl froze, staring at us with a look of terror on her face, clearly torn between warring emotions.

"Yes, that's me." I reached up and put my hood back to reveal my face. The rain plastered my hair down against the sides of my head and oozed down the back of my neck, but I considered it a worthwhile sacrifice. "Hi there, sweetie. What's your name?"

The girl inched back a bit, hiding within the shadows under the porch. A quick glance around told me that there was only one way in or out, so she was stuck there unless she wanted to risk running past us to get away. To try and show her that I wasn't a danger to her, I put my shotgun back over my shoulder, and held my empty hands up for her to see.

"It's okay," I said softly. "We're not going to hurt you. My name is Sandy. Do you have a name?"

"Of course, I have a name!" This time, it was her turn to sound indignant. In spite of the tension of the situation, I laughed.

"Sorry. That was a dumb question, I guess," I admitted. "What I meant is, will you tell me your name?"

There was a moment of silence, then the girl let out a long sigh. "Fine. My name is Jasmine. Will you go away now?"

"Not just yet. Maybe later," I said dryly, impressed by the girl's spunk. "It's nice to meet you, Jasmine. How old are you?"

"I'm twelve," she snapped, though her voice trembled in such a way that it gave away her fear, even if she didn't want it to. "I'm old enough to fight you! If you think I'm going to let you take me away, then you're crazy!"

"Take you away?" I shot a glance at Michael, and found him looking as alarmed as I felt. "No one's going to take you away. We're just passing through on our way south, and stopped to see if we could make the radio work. Priya saw you, and wanted to make sure that you were okay." I slowly lowered myself down to crouch, so that I could see her huddled under the porch and she could see me. "Are you all alone?"

"No!" she snapped, inching back further into the shadows. "I have friends. Lots of friends. Big friends! They'll fight you if you try to take me to him! I don't want to get married!"

"Married?" My jaw dropped in surprise, and it took me a second to piece my wits back together. Then, understanding struck and a dark cloud of anger began to descend across my mind. "Jasmine, is someone around here hurting your friends?"

There was silence again, and this time it dragged out even longer. Then, I heard a soft, tell-tale sniffing sound that told me the girl was crying. My heart dropped to my knees.

"Jasmine?" I asked again, as gently as I could. "Honey, who did they take?"

"My sister," the girl whispered, barely loud enough for me to hear her voice. "Lily. We were just playing, like we always do, and he surprised us. He grabbed her, and said that she was a pretty little flower, just ready to be plucked, and that she was his wife now. Then he threw her in his truck and drove away."

I took a deep breath to try and calm myself, but it didn't do much good. Rage seethed within my chest, driven by my own experiences combined with outrage that anyone would do such a thing to a child. "When did that happen?"

"This morning," Jasmine said miserably. "One of my friends went to go look for her, but he hasn't come back."

"Did you know the man?" I asked. "Do you have any idea where he lives?"

"We've seen him sometimes," she answered. "He comes to town and takes things, but he looks scary so we stay away. We call him 'the farmer', because he always smells like dirt. He comes from outside of town. From that direction." She pointed towards the south.

I nodded and eased myself back to my feet. One look at Michael's face told me that he felt the same way I did. Jasmine took the opportunity to scramble out from under the porch and run away, but none of us made any attempt to stop her. There was no point, and no need. She had the choice to be free, and she made it. Her sister didn't have the same option.

"Well, I don't think we have any choice in this matter," I said. "We have to go save that girl."

Michael just nodded solemnly.

# Chapter Fifteen

The others were in a state of near-panic by the time we made it back to the radio station. The second that we stepped out of the alley, a cry went up and we were enveloped in a friendly mob. Once the initial excitement passed, I gathered everyone in around me and quickly explained the situation to them.

"I need two people to come with us to rescue the girl," I said, my voice raised enough to be heard over the general noise of rain and upset people. "Tane, Iorangi, you game?"

The brothers nodded vigorously and shouted their agreement; I could see the outrage etched on their faces even from afar.

"Good." I nodded, and looked at the others. "Everyone else, stay here and focus on getting the radio going. I suspect we're going to have to stay the night whether we want to or not, so scout out the local buildings and find one that we can secure. We also need to get some food into people before too long."

"We'll take care of it," Anahera said. Beside her, Skylar and Elly nodded silent agreement. "You just go. Save that little girl, before it's too late."

I gave them an appreciative smile, but wasted no more time on words. With a gesture to my companions, I raced over to where the bikes were waiting for us, and leapt onto one. Michael was a heartbeat behind me, and the brothers just behind him. There was a collective roar as we all started up our bikes, and then we were off.

I led the way towards the main road south, since I was the only one that had studied the map in great detail. Within minutes, we were bouncing along the uneven tarmac through a small shopping district that swiftly devolved into suburbia and even more swiftly transformed into farmland. Young native bush sprang up on either side of the road, fern fronds waving in the stiffening breeze.

Suddenly, a flash of lightning illuminated the world, followed by a deep-throated roar of thunder. A moment later the rain redoubled, as if someone had overturned a bucket in the sky. The full force of the storm had taken its time reaching us, but now it had arrived, it was vicious. The noise was so deafening that I barely heard one of my companions shouting an alert.

I carefully eased my bike to a halt, and looked back at the others strung out behind me. At the rear, Tane was yelling and pointing frantically into the bush, but he was too far away for me to make out what he was saying. Michael looked at me and tilted his head towards him; I simply nodded my understanding. Together, we wheeled our bikes around and drove back to the brothers.

"I think there's a pathway through there," Tane called as soon as we were close enough, pointing into the dense bush on the side of the road.

"I think you're right," I yelled back, shielding my eyes from the stinging rain. "I see tyre tracks in the mud, and the branches have been cut back recently. Come on!"

We should have dismounted and travelled on foot, but my gut told me that time was of the essence. There was no time for caution. I opened the throttle all the way, and guided my bike into the gloom. All of our bikes had headlights, but the bouncing, uneven light made me feel even more reckless. Still, what choice did we have? At least the boughs of the trees kept the rain more or less at bay.

The path swung around a particularly large tree, and I followed it. It wasn't until I was fully committed to the manoeuvre that I spotted the human figure hiding in the brush beside the path. I slammed on the brakes so hard that my bike went into a spin, and came to rest facing back the direction we'd come. The beam of my headlights cut through the gloom, and illuminated the crouched figure; before the others even realised what was happening, I had my shotgun out and trained on the bushes.

"I see you!" I shouted; even under the trees, the storm was loud. "Come out with your hands above your head."

"Don't shoot!" The voice that responded was male, deep and hoarse. He stood up slowly, one hand raised and the other shielding his face from the glare of my headlights. "I don't want any trouble. I just want the little girl back. She's part of my group."

I lowered my shotgun, and took a deep breath. "You're Jasmine's friend, then?"

"Jasmine?" The man sounded startled. I squinted to try and make out the details of his face while he was speaking, but I couldn't see them. "Yes, Jasmine is her sister. Please, I just want Lily back. We don't have a lot, but we'll give you anything you want."

Suddenly, it struck me that he thought we were a gang, and somehow responsible for what had happened. I shoved my shotgun back over my shoulder, and shook my head.

"We have nothing to do with the guy that grabbed Lily," I explained, deliberately softening my tone. "We were coming through town from the north-west, and caught Jasmine spying on us. She told us what happened. We're here to free Lily, too."

"Free her?" Now, he sounded bewildered. "Why would you want to do that?"

"Because she's a person, and every person has the right to choose her own destiny," I answered firmly and resolutely. "I'm not going to let someone force a young girl into marriage. Hell, I'm not going to let someone force anyone into marriage."

"Amen to that," he agreed, slowly lowering his hands to his sides. "I'm not armed. I was going to negotiate to get her back. What's your plan?"

"First, we find her," I said. "Then, we figure it out from there."

"Leave those bikes here and follow me, then," the stranger said. "It took me all day to find them, but I think this is the right place."

"Show us," I said. I switched off the bike, dismounted, and pocketed the keys. Around me, the others did the same. As soon as they were ready, the stranger beckoned for us to follow him and led the way through the damp, shadowy bush towards the east.

As we travelled, I realised that there was something familiar about him, but without seeing his face I couldn't put my finger on it. There was something about the set of his shoulders, his voice, or perhaps the way he walked. He had a pronounced limp, but I couldn't recall anyone that I'd known who had the same. Then we rounded a corner, the house came into view, and all considerations were forgotten except for Lily's welfare.

"Stop," I whispered, my voice barely audible over the storm. "Stay here for a minute while I scout around."

I only just saw their nods of agreement in the semi-darkness, but it was enough. Leaving my friends behind, I slid out of the bush and across the worn driveway towards the homestead in a military-style crouch-walk.

The house was nothing special, just another one of the basic, prefabricated boxes that had been popular in the late seventies. The weatherboards were faded and dirty, and the driveway pocked with potholes. I had to step carefully to avoid breaking an ankle, but there was just enough light for me to keep myself safe.

I crept down the right side of the building, and found myself in a narrow alleyway between the house and a vegetable garden framed by old-fashioned wooden fences. I paused beneath a window where the curtains didn't quite meet properly, and eased myself up to take a peek inside. What I saw made my belly curdle with rage.

A young girl lay on a filthy mattress, her hands bound cruelly behind her back. Although her hair covered part of her face, it only took me a second to realise that she wasn't just Jasmine's sister – she was Jasmine's twin.

A twelve-year-old-girl. That man planned to force a twelve-year-old-girl to marry him. Not on my watch.

I took a deep breath to cool my surging temper, and reached up to carefully test the window. It was firmly latched from the inside. Lily appeared to be either sleeping or unconscious, and didn't respond when I tapped softly on the window pane. I would have to find another way in.

Easing myself back down into my comfortable crouch-walk, I stepped softly up to the corner of the building and peeked around it. A beat-up old truck sat under a carport nearby, and farther away I could see an open-faced barn. There were no people around, as far as I could tell. A few chickens clucked in a henhouse nearby, but nothing else stirred.

I paused to consider the evidence around me. It seemed unlikely that the farm could support more than one or two people at the most without extensive scavenging, and there was only a single pair of dirty gumboots by the back door. I saw nothing that indicated anyone else lived there, which meant we most likely only had one enemy to worry about. My hopes soared for a moment, but I fought them back down to avoid letting them colour my reasoning.

I resumed scouting, checking each window and door that I could reach. They were all locked from the inside, but the back door was so flimsy that I felt sure we could break the latch without any trouble. Then, through a side window, I finally spotted the villain himself. It wasn't much to see: just a fat old man with a balding pate, slouched in an armchair in front of a TV playing a rerun of an old sitcom off DVD. The man had a beer in one hand and the remote in the other, but his eyes were closed and his chin was resting on his flabby chest. As far as I could tell, he was asleep.

I slipped back down and continued scouting, but I saw no sign of anyone else on the property. Once I was satisfied I had the lay of the land, I crept back to the bushes where my friends were waiting for me. As soon as they saw me approaching, I heard the stranger's voice.

"Is she okay?" he asked urgently, his voice trembling. It didn't take a psychologist to tell that he was nervous.

"It's hard to be sure, but she seems uninjured," I answered. "She's sleeping in a back bedroom... and she's still dressed. That's a good sign."

"Thank God," he whispered, his shoulders slumping. "I'm not sure I could bear to lose another one."

Sympathy blossomed in my chest. I couldn't see his face, but I knew that tone. It was the same tone that Michael used when he was talking about Sophie, the little girl he'd loved like a daughter.

"Don't worry, mate," I said, reaching out to squeeze his shoulder. "We'll get her back. I have a plan."

The man nodded silently in the dark, and gestured for me to continue. I turned, and pointed towards the house as I outlined my plan for the others.

"The house is just your basic prefab – rectangular, one door in the front, one door in the back. The back door leads right into the living room. The farmer is sleeping on the couch. Michael, Tane, Iorangi – I want you to go in the back. Give us sixty seconds to get in place, then storm that door. It's old and thin, you should have no trouble busting it open. Don't kill him, though. Just make sure he doesn't run or grab a weapon. While you're covering him, we'll sneak in the front door and grab Lily."

"Geez, you should have been on the Armed Offenders Squad," Michael commented dryly from the gloom behind me.

I laughed and shook my head. "Get out of here, you three. Remember, don't kill him. That's not who we are."

He nodded and then the three of them were off, mimicking the stealth I'd used earlier to the best of their ability. I beckoned the stranger to follow me, and led him towards the front door instead. A bolt of lightning lit up the sky, illuminating the world for a moment, and then the roll of thunder masked our footfalls in its wake.

I knelt at the front door and pulled out my lockpicks. The lock was as old as the house; it took me barely a minute to open it, even working by touch. Just as the last tumbler was sliding into place, I heard the sound of wood shattering, followed by deep-throated male shouts.

I threw open the door and hurried inside, ducking down the corridor that I guessed had to lead to the girl's room. The door at the end of the hall was locked, but it was so flimsy that this time I didn't even bother to pick it. I just threw my shoulder against it with all of my might. A second later, I felt the stranger's mass hit it beside me. The door buckled. One more good, co-ordinated charge from both of us was enough to shatter the lock. The door burst open, and we tumbled into the room.

I fell and landed on something soft: the mattress. I leapt up as though I'd touched a red-hot element, feeling a twisted kind of horror that I couldn't name. Beside me, I saw the stranger roll up to his feet as well, but he obviously felt no such disgust. His entire focus was on the girl. He grabbed her gently and rolled her over, struggling to untie her hands.

"Lily!" he demanded urgently. "Lily, wake up!"

I spotted a light switch on the wall beside me and flicked it on, then immediately wished I hadn't. In the semi-darkness, it had looked like the dark shadows on the bed were just mud, but under proper lighting I realised that it was a mixture of dirt and blood. The girl's cheeks were a mass of bruises, and her hair was matted. Fresh blood shone against her porcelain-pale skin, and made her look like a broken doll.

I heard the stranger swearing at the sight, but I was too stunned and angry to say anything at all. A cold, dark sense of purpose twisted my gut, and drove me out of the room, following the sound of voices raised in anger. My companions had the florid-faced farmer cornered, but even confronted by three men with guns he was still shouting.

As soon as he saw me, the farmer turned his wrath in my direction. "Oi! Are you the leader of these ruffians? Get out of my house! How dare you come storming in here like you own the place? I'm a taxpayer, and I—"

His words were cut off abruptly, when my fist connected with his jaw. The farmer stumbled backwards, knocking his television off its stand and sending both of them tumbling across the floor. By the time he recovered enough to realise what had happened, I had my shotgun off my back and aimed right at his face.

"Let me make one thing clear," I told him, my voice soft but cold as ice. "The thing that makes us human is our ability to make choices, and you have made a very, very bad one. If you ever take away someone else's right to choose again, then I will have you held accountable before a tribunal of law. We don't have jails anymore, so you better believe that our justice will not be gentle – but it will be just. You're lucky that we don't have time to deal with you right now, so consider this your lucky night – but if you *ever* touch anyone else without their permission again, then I will personally bring so much wrath down on your sorry head that you'll wish you'd died in the plague. Do you understand?"

The man just stared at me, open-mouthed, blood leaking from his split lip. I narrowed my eyes and tightened my grip on the shotgun, but I didn't have to use it.

The gesture alone was enough for him. He nodded frantically, shoving himself as far back away from me as he could, terror written across his face.

I nodded once and left the room without another word. This time, no shouting followed me. No sounds. Nothing but silence, and the distant sound of begging.

"Lily? Please, honey, come on, wake up... It's okay, *Onīsan* is here…"

I re-entered the bedroom to find our hooded stranger kneeling on the mattress, cradling Lily's battered body in his arms. He'd managed to free her hands and feet, but the girl was still unconscious. It took all of my willpower to work up the courage to kneel down beside him on that awful mattress, which brought back so many painful memories. As soon as I did, the stink of alcohol struck me. I hadn't smelt it before, so I knew it wasn't coming from the man; it had to be coming from the girl. Then, I spotted something even worse, lying on the mattress beside her.

"He's drugged her," I surmised, picking up the little white prescription vial. "Sleeping pills, and alcohol by the smell of it. Our best bet is to try and get as much of it out of her system as possible. It's not going to be pretty, but we need to make her vomit."

The man just nodded. With surprising confidence, he turned the young girl onto her belly and stuck his finger down her throat. Her entire body convulsed. The man held her until she finally threw up the entire contents of her stomach all over the floor. The stench of it was terrible, a combination of far too much alcohol, and half-digested sleeping tablets. As soon as she stopped convulsing, the girl curled up in a ball and started sobbing piteously.

The man just sat beside her, gently holding her through it all. "It's okay, honey. You're safe. I'm here."

"Onīsan?" she sobbed, her voice slurred. "I want to go home."

"I know, Lil. I know." The man looked up at me suddenly, and the light finally hit his features. "Thank you so much. These kids mean everything to me."

I had no response. He'd gained a lot of scars and one of his eyes was milky and blind, but I would have recognised his face anywhere.

"…Gavin?"

# Chapter Sixteen

The man blinked his one good eye in obvious surprise. "You know me?"

I didn't have any words to express how I felt. I just reached up and folded my hood back, revealing my own face for the first time. It took a few seconds before recognition dawned, and his mouth fell open.

"Sandy!" he cried. Before I quite knew what had hit me, I felt a strong arm clamp around my shoulders and I was pulled into a hug. "I thought you were dead, kid."

"I thought you were dead, too," I admitted, my shock finally passing enough for me to figure out how to use my words again. I shoved myself back out of his embrace, and gave him a long look. "You've seen better days, old man. We'll have plenty of time to catch up later, but for now let's focus on getting Lily home."

Gavin nodded his agreement, and looked back down at the battered young body nestled in the crook of his arm. "How about it, little sister? You ready to go home?"

The girl nodded weakly and gave him a smile. I took one look out the window at the driving rain, and then I shrugged off my coat and held it out to him.

"Here," I said. "Wrap her up in this. It won't keep her entirely dry, but at least it'll keep her warm."

Gavin hesitated for a second, but Lily's needs outweighed any concerns either of us might have had about me. He took the garment and gently wound it around her frail body, pulling the hood forward to protect her face. I took a deep breath, and used the moment to broach the subject of what to do with the farmer.

"Gavin," I said, resting my hand on his shoulder. "The man who did this to her, he's still alive. You probably heard that we don't kill indiscriminately. However, we do have a code of justice. I've already put the fear of God into him on your behalf, but if you want to, we can bring him back with us and have him put to trial before a judicator--"

"No," Gavin answered sharply, shaking his head. "I don't want to put Lily through that. Right now, the only thing that matters is getting her home safely."

I nodded silently and rose to my feet. Gavin picked up the child's leather-wrapped form, and followed me back to the front door. We found Michael and the others waiting for us there.

"Where's the farmer?" I asked, shooting a wary look back towards the living room.

"Curled up in the foetal position, crying like a baby," Michael answered dryly. "I think you scared him, honey."

"Honey?" Gavin shot a startled look at me, his brows raised. "You have changed."

"I had to," I answered with a shrug. "Gavin, this is Michael, my fiancé. The bloke with the dreads is Tane, and the one with the tattoos is Iorangi. Guys, this is Gavin. He's… an old friend."

"Oh?" This time, it was Michael giving me the surprised look. "I wasn't aware that you had any old friends."

"Neither was I, until about five minutes ago," I admitted sheepishly. "Looks like reports of his demise have been greatly exaggerated."

"I wouldn't say 'greatly'," Gavin said. "It was pretty close for a while."

I gave him a curious look, but it wasn't really the time or place to ask. Instead, I pushed my curiosity aside and turned my attention back to what mattered.

415

"We need to get Lily back to Doctor Cross," I said. "I don't think she's been... violated, but she's been beaten and drugged. I want him to make sure she's going to be okay. Michael, she's not entirely conscious so I want you to ride double with her. Gavin, you can ride with me."

"Much appreciated," Gavin replied dryly. "It's a long walk back."

"In this storm, it's going to be a long drive, too." I shook my head and gave him a wry smile. "Come on. If we leave now, we should make it back before sunset."

All four men nodded their agreement. Michael started to unzip his jacket with obvious intentions of giving it to me, but I didn't give him a chance. I'd already made up my mind about getting wet, so I wasn't about to let him take on that particular burden this time. Out into the driving rain I went, leading the way across the compacted gravel towards the edge of the bush beyond.

The rain hit me like a waterfall, soaking me to the bone within seconds, but I refused to let it bother me. Some days, it felt like I was never going to be dry again. By the time I made it to the shelter of the trees, I was absolutely drenched. I paused to wait for the others, hugging the thin fabric of my old army surplus jacket close around my shoulders to preserve what little warmth I had. Michael was on me a second later, with a dark look on his face.

"You didn't have to get wet," he protested, obviously annoyed with my stubbornness. "I would have given you my jacket."

"I'm already wet," I said with a shrug. "No point both of us getting drowned."

"Sometimes I really don't know what I'm going to do with you," he answered, sounding exasperated. I just grinned at him, and reached out to touch his hand in the cavernous gloom. Before either of us could say anything else, the others caught up with us and our brief moment of privacy was gone.

We arrived back at our bikes a few minutes later, wet and muddy but intact. Gavin and I helped Lily up in front of Michael, so that he could catch her if she started to slip. The girl was only half-conscious and trembling convulsively; even though he was a stranger, she huddled into Michael for warmth, her eyes glazed and distant.

I put my hand on Gavin's shoulder in some small attempt to reassure him. He just nodded faintly, and gestured for me to lead the way. I did, and soon we were on our way back to Tokoroa, bouncing along, with me in the lead, and Gavin's arms around my waist.

Once we burst back out onto the road, I found myself having to contend with stinging rain; I made a mental note to find some goggles for our riders to wear in bad weather, and squinted at the road in an effort to try and see where we were going.

Maybe helmets, too. Suddenly, helmets seemed like a very good idea. The last thing I wanted was to lose one of the last remnants of my species to a farm bike accident.

The wind howled around us, wailing like the mournful ghosts of the billions of souls lost to the plague. Lightning illuminated the sky in a blinding flash. The sun had begun to go down by the time we made it back to town, and it was so dark that I barely saw our turnoff in time. At the very last moment, I spotted a light glowing out of the corner of my eye, and that turned out to be the beam of a torch.

I hurled the bike around the corner with such reckless disregard that Gavin shouted in alarm, but we made it intact. Some part of my brain warned me against that kind of behaviour, but my conscious mind didn't care. I only had one concern, and that was the little girl nestled in my lover's embrace. Another stray. Another child, a forgotten throw-away left behind when civilization abandoned her. At least this one wasn't entirely alone, like my poor little Priyanka had been.

By the time I brought the bike to a stop in front of the radio station, there was a crowd of people waiting for us. They shouted greetings and questions, waving frantically at us from beneath their makeshift rain-gear. Behind me, I heard Gavin's sharp intake of breath.

"There are so many people," he said softly, just loud enough for me to hear. "Sandy, did you join a gang?"

"I did at one stage, but that's another story," I replied. "This isn't a gang. The group you see before you are going to be the founding members of the first city our country has seen in far too long. We just need to make it far enough south to lay the foundations."

"Good God," he murmured, easing himself off the back of the bike so that I could get up as well. "Sounds like we're going to have a lot to talk about."

"And you're going to have a lot of names to try and remember," I teased. I killed the bike's engine, and went over to meet my friends. It was just at that moment that I realised something was missing. "Guys, where are the cars?"

"We moved them around the corner," Skylar explained. She rushed over and threw her arms around me, hugging me close. Then she shoved me back roughly and gave me a disgusted look. "Ugh, you're sopping wet!"

"And now you are, too," I replied with a playful grin. "You're welcome."

She snorted in mock annoyance, but then she suddenly seemed to remember why we'd gone away to begin with. "Did you find her?"

"Yes," I said, looking back over my shoulder at the other riders, who were just coming to a stop beside my bike. Gavin rushed over to help with his young charge, his discomfort apparently forgotten for the moment. I looked back at Skye, and gave her a sad smile. "She's in bad shape, though. Where's Doc?"

"He's around the corner, too," she answered, jerking a thumb over her shoulder. "There's a big, abandoned office building behind the radio station. It's not much, but it has a kitchen and toilets, and it's dry. I left him, Anahera, and the kids setting up beds, but they should be about done by now."

"Can you take us to him?" I asked. She nodded and beckoned for me to follow her. I passed the gesture along to Michael and Gavin, and soon the four of us were hurrying through the driving rain, leaving the bikes to be tended to by the rest of the group.

Skylar ducked through a wild garden that had probably once been a courtyard, and down a pathway between two buildings. We came out next to a glass door that was, miraculously, still intact. Skye rapped her knuckles on the metal frame, and we waited.

A minute later, we saw Doc's face appear on the other side of the glass, ghostly pale in the dim light. He nodded, unlocked the door, and let us in. Everything seemed fine, right up until the moment that he saw Gavin, and realised that he was a stranger. He took a step backwards, blocking the hallway leading deeper into the building.

"And who is this?" he demanded warily, jerking his chin at Gavin.

"This is Gavin. He's an old friend of mine," I replied, glancing back over my shoulder at him. "Gavin, this is our doctor, Stewart Cross."

The doctor's brows knitted, and Skylar turned to look at me in surprise. Her eyes widened so suddenly that I realised she hadn't figured out that Gavin wasn't one of our own until that moment. With his hood up and the rain in her eyes, it wasn't all that surprising.

"Please elaborate, Ms McDermott," the doctor demanded, his brows knitting into a frown. "Do we know him well enough to let him near the children?"

"Don't worry, it's fine," I replied. "Gavin's good people. He helped me a lot when the plague first hit – I probably wouldn't have survived without him. I think it's fair to say I know him well enough to vouch for him."

"Wait, is this the honey guy?" Skye asked, curiosity flickering across her face. "I thought you said he was dead?"

"I thought he was dead, but he wasn't," I admitted with a shrug. "Just like I thought you were dead, but you weren't. Apparently, I'm just really bad at keeping track of the people I care about." I made an abrupt gesture with one hand to derail the conversation, and directed it towards the more urgent topic. "Anyway – Doc, we need you. Lily's hurt."

My words seemed to touch just the right nerve. Doc dropped his gaze to the leather-wrapped bundle in Gavin's arms. He glanced briefly at me, then looked at the girl again. Whatever else he might have been feeling, his healer's instincts clearly took precedence; he nodded once, and gestured for us to follow him.

"We found a cache of mattresses stashed away upstairs," he explained as he led us through the hallways. "There's some old food and clothing, too. Looks like someone used to live here, but they're long gone."

I glanced at Gavin, and he nodded. "There used to be a gang here, so it was probably theirs. As far as I can tell, someone came in and wiped them all out. One of the kids survived but he won't talk about it. Won't talk about much of anything, to be frank."

"How many people do you have with you?" I asked him as we climbed the stairs up to the second floor.

"Four," he replied, with just the faintest of smiles. "All kids. I've got the twins, Solomon – that's the kid who survived from the gangs – and another girl named Melody." He heaved a long sigh, his one good eye focused on the stairs at his feet. "After I lost you, I felt so guilty that I made it my duty to protect the kids. All of the kids. Whether they like it or not."

I couldn't help but laugh at that. "Sounds like they didn't want to be protected."

"No, not at all," he admitted. "They hate it, but they've accepted me hanging around because I'm good at finding them food. Melody and the twins were together for a long time, possibly since the beginning. When I first found them, they were like a pack of wild cats."

"Put her down on the mattress there," the doctor instructed, interrupting our discussion. Gavin did as he was told, then we went into the next room with the others, to let the doctor work in peace. The room turned out to be a kitchen, and Anahera was in there stirring something in a giant cooking pot. I took a moment to introduce both her and Skylar to Gavin formally.

"You lot go sit down," Anahera ordered once introductions were finished. "I'll bring you some dinner. You must be freezing."

"Yeah." I nodded my agreement, and went over to a nearby table with my dripping companions. Once we were comfortable, I gave Gavin a curious look. "You were saying the girls were like wild cats?"

"Yeah. It was so over the top that in retrospect, it's pretty funny," Gavin said, shaking his head slowly. "If Melody lets you meet her, then you'll get it."

"If she *lets* me meet her?" I echoed, amused. "Oh dear, now you have to tell me. What happened?"

Gavin laughed and nodded. "Yeah, all right. I was travelling through... I don't remember where, one of the towns on the east coast. You know how cautious I am, but I'm not as capable as I used to be before I lost my eye. These three little hellcats managed to ambush me. This would have been about three years ago, mind."

"Wait. Let me get this straight." I paused and did some quick maths. "You were ambushed by a pair of nine-year-olds, and – how old was Melody at the time?"

"About fifteen," he supplied, a mixture of embarrassment and amusement written on his scarred face. "Yes, I was ambushed by a fifteen-year-old girl and a couple of nine-year-olds. And they won."

"They won?" I echoed, surprised. "Are you serious?"

"I'm ashamed to admit it, but yes." Gavin shrugged and glanced down. "I'm not the man I used to be, Sandy. The reason I vanished was because I was grabbed by a bunch of gang-bangers, led by this big bloke with a bald head and the evilest eyes I've ever seen on another human being. They accused me of hunting in their territory."

"Oh, God," I whispered, my good mood suddenly vanishing. "So they're the ones that... did that? To your eye, I mean?"

"Yeah." He sighed heavily and nodded. "They broke both my legs, cut me up like a side of meat. The only thing that spared me was luck. One of their scouts spotted something that was apparently more interesting than me, and called them off. I managed to drag myself away and hide, but they didn't come back." Suddenly, he reached out and grabbed my hand, a look of absolute panic crossing his face. "I was so afraid that they'd spotted you. I looked for you for weeks, once I could walk again, but I never found you – or the gang."

Sympathy welled up in my breast. I reached out to place my hand over his, trying in some small way to reassure him. "I was fine. Well... I was fine at the time. I was captured by a gang later on, but that was years later. As you can see, I escaped."

"But not without scars," he said softly, reaching up to touch the pink mark on my cheek that had been left by Lee's knife, a few weeks earlier. "Though, this one here looks fresh. What have you been up to, girl?"

"It's a long story," I admitted. "But it actually sounds a little bit familiar. Tell me, the man with the evil eyes – was he a big guy, with a beer gut and tattoos all over his face?"

"Yes," Gavin said, surprise flickering across his face. "A real big bastard, with a full facial *tā moko*." He paused and shot a sheepish glance at Anahera, who also wore the Maori tattoos he was describing upon her chin. "No offense intended, ma'am."

She smiled and nodded. "None taken."

Gavin glanced back at me, and gave me a quizzical look. "Why do you ask? Have you seen him?"

"You could say that." I glanced over at Skylar, and held her gaze for a second, then I looked back at him. "I'd rather not talk about what he did to me, so let's just stick with the good news. He's dead. Skye killed him."

Gavin's expression flickered through an assortment of emotions in rapid succession, which eventually settled at relief. He nodded once, and looked down at his hands. "I'm glad. I looked for them when I was trying to find you, but all I found were... bodies. Mostly the bodies of girls."

"That's why we're doing what we're doing," I answered, gently squeezing his hand. "I've got a lot more scars that you can't see right now, but I survived them. I consider it my duty to help protect other young girls, so that they don't have to go through the same pain."

"Me too," he agreed. "After I lost you, I wasn't sure if I could forgive myself. I've spent all these years seeking redemption by helping other kids." Suddenly, his one good eye flicked to Michael, and his grip on my hand tightened. "You better take good care of her or else I'll have to kick your ass."

Michael blinked in surprise, then he laughed. "If I don't take good care of her, then I'll *let* you kick my ass."

"Good man." Gavin nodded firmly, and gave Michael a faint, lopsided smile. His gaze returned to me, and he turned the conversation back towards more pleasant things. "So, I was telling you about meeting Melody, wasn't I?"

"Yeah, you were saying something about getting kicked around by three little girls," I said, giving him a teasing grin. "How did that happen?"

"They came in from my blind spot, the clever little minxes." Gavin sighed and sat back in his seat, finally releasing my hand. "I should also mention that my hearing's been screwed up in that ear since the attack, so I didn't even hear them coming. One second, I thought I was alone. The next, I was flat on my back, with these three wild-eyed, filthy kids holding knives to my throat.

"They tried to rob me, as you can probably expect. I didn't have much for them to take, but I did have a few things that I'd made before I left my roost the night before. Particularly, honey rice cakes. I knew from looking at them that those kids had been on their own for a while, so I just gave them the cakes. You should have seen their eyes bug out. They inhaled them, and then demanded more. I told them I didn't have any, but that if they wanted I could show them how to make them. They've been following me around ever since."

"Ah, the way to a kid's heart is through her stomach." I laughed, and everyone else laughed right along with me.

"Speaking of which," Anahera cut in, setting a bowl of hot soup down in front of me.

I took it gratefully, and smiled at her. "Thank you."

"Of course, dear." She just smiled back, and set bowls down in front of the others. Once spoons were handed out, the conversation halted while we all tucked in. I hadn't eaten since that morning, so even plain fare was better than going hungry.

Just as I was wolfing down the last mouthful, Doctor Cross appeared in the doorway, holding my coat in his hands. I set my spoon down, and looked at him expectantly.

"Well, I have good news and I have bad news," he told us, absently handing the coat back to me. "The good news is that she'll live, and she wasn't sexually abused. The bad news is that she's going to be very sick for a while, until her body recovers from the beating he gave her. She has some internal injuries, but nothing that requires surgery. I would like to keep an eye on her for a few days, if we can."

Gavin looked at me, frowning. "Can you stay for a few days?"

I paused to think about it, and slowly shook my head. "We shouldn't. It's not safe. The reason we're on the road is because there's a mutation of the virus slowly spreading south, and it's turning the human infected into... well, it's making them like pigs. We've already lost way too many people. I can't risk losing any more." I paused, and looked at him. "You and the kids are welcome to come with us, though."

"I don't know how they'll feel about that," he admitted. "I'd be lying if I said I was in control of them. We just travel together, nothing more. I suppose I could ask them if they want to go."

"I'd appreciate it," I said, nodding. "They don't have to stay with us forever, just until Lily's feeling better."

Gavin nodded and slowly rose from his chair. "I'll go find them. Jasmine's going to be panicking about her sister, anyway. I should try to put her mind at ease."

I shot a glance at the others, then looked back at Gavin. "Can I send an escort with you? I'd hate for something to happen to you."

"No, I'll be fine," he said, shaking his head. "It's not far back to the place we're currently staying at. If they want to come and see Lily, then we'll be in a group. If not, I'll come back in the morning."

"Okay." I took a deep breath, and let it out as a long sigh. "If you're sure. Just be careful, okay? It's not safe out there."

"I'm always careful," he replied. "You just watch out for yourself, and keep an eye on Lily for me."

"Of course," I agreed. He nodded once, patted my shoulder, and then he was gone. The doctor followed him out, presumably to go back to tending his young patient. I turned and looked at the others. "Well, that was unexpected."

"The mysterious honey-man reappears, bringing with him a pack of wild kids," Skylar joked. "Sounds like trouble just waiting to happen."

"Oh, probably." I shrugged and gave her a smile. "Still, at least Lily's okay, and I'm pretty sure that guy on the farm won't try anything like that again any time soon."

"Did you kill him, then?" Skye asked curiously.

"No," I answered, shaking my head. "We're trying to avoid doing that, remember? I just scared the hell out of him, and made him realise that there are still rules in place."

"Oh." Skye actually sounded a little bit disappointed. She shrugged and stood up. "Oh well, not our problem. I'm going to go check on the kids. Don't go anywhere."

"Yes, boss," I agreed, giving her a smile. I watched until she left the room, then glanced at the others. To my surprise, I found Anahera watching her as well, her eyes narrowed. Once Skylar was out of earshot, she came over and sat down at the table near Michael and me.

"There is something I should probably tell you," she said, her voice low and discreet.

"What, about Skye?" I asked, uncertain how to interpret her expression. "Has she done something?"

"I don't know," Anahera said thoughtfully. "I have no idea what the implications are. I just want to make you aware of it. After you were attacked by Lee at our camp, I sent my boys out to catch the two men that grabbed Skylar. Do you remember that?"

"I remember enough, yes," I answered with a nod. "I mean, I was in pretty bad shape, but I know you sent people out to capture them. I never found out what happened after that."

"No, I never had an opportunity to tell you privately, until now." Anahera sighed, sitting back in her chair. "My men found them dead. Both of their throats had been slit."

"What?" Startled, I looked over at Michael and saw that he was just as surprised as I was.

"She said that she hit them with your taser, then ran back to find me so that we could save you," Michael said. "You think that she killed them?"

"I suspect so, yes," Anahera said, nodding. "My men said that the bodies did show odd burn marks that I presume are the kind left by a taser, but their throats had been cut afterwards. My men estimate that they were unconscious at the time, lying face down."

"Wow," I murmured, unsure what to make of the revelation. My baby sister just didn't seem like the kind that would cut a man's throat in cold blood, even when her life was on the line. But then, how well did I really know her? We hadn't seen each other in ten years. A person can change a lot between the ages of eight and eighteen, particularly in a world as brutal and unforgiving as ours.

I glanced at Michael, and saw the same kind of uncertainty reflected on his face. He'd known her longer than I, but only by a few months. I wasn't sure what to say, and he certainly didn't seem any more confident. I felt a hand touch my shoulder, and glanced over to find Anahera watching me with sympathy.

"I told you because I wanted you to know, not because I expect you to do anything about it," she said gently. "These are unpleasant times, and sometimes we must do unpleasant things in the name of the greater good. If your friend's story is true, then it is likely those men have done things just as terrible as Lee had. I would have done the same thing, in her situation."

I let out a long breath that I hadn't realised I'd been holding, and nodded slowly. "Yeah. You're right. It's just... I don't know how to feel about it."

"I understand." She smiled at us, and gently squeezed my shoulder. "Don't worry, Sandy. Just take your time to think over it, and your feelings will sort themselves out."

I nodded and gave her a grateful smile. Just at that moment, Skylar came rushing back into the room, forestalling any further discussion about her.

"Hey, guys?" she called, her tone urgent. "Have any of you seen Priya?"

"Not since before we left," I answered, shaking my head.

"Well, we have a slight problem, then." Skye glanced back over her shoulder, then looked at me. "She's gone."

# *Chapter Seventeen*

"What do you mean, she's gone?" I demanded, leaping up to my feet. "Where did she go?"

"I have no idea," Skye said with a shrug. "I put her to bed with the other kids about an hour ago, but she's not there anymore. I checked all the bathrooms in the building, but I can't find her anywhere."

I muttered a few choice words beneath my breath, and slammed my fist down on the table in an attempt to vent my distress physically. "She must have gone off looking for those kids again. I'm going to kill her."

"Calm down, honey," Michael said, in his most soothing voice. He put his hands on my shoulders, and turned me to face him. "She took care of herself for ten years before we found her. She can take care of herself for an hour or two."

"But what if she doesn't come back?" I asked, my gut twisting itself into all kinds of unpleasant shapes. "What if she decides to go with them instead of us?"

Michael just smiled, and drew me into a hug. "I doubt that she will. She loves you. She knows where we are; when she's ready to come home, she will."

"This is what it feels like to be a parent, Sandy," Anahera said sympathetically. "Every time your child leaves your sight, you worry that they won't come home. Usually, they do. Sometimes, they don't."

"I don't like this feeling," I admitted. "I'm torn between losing my marbles and bawling until she comes home, or storming off in search of her. Someone decide for me."

All of them laughed at that. Suddenly, I found myself in the middle of a group hug, with both Anahera and Skylar adding their arms to Michael's.

"How about we take the first watch?" Michael suggested. "That way, you can keep an eye out for her. I know you have trouble sleeping when you're worried."

"Good plan," I agreed immediately, relieved to have the decision taken away from me for a change. Although I was usually perfectly comfortable with being in command, there were some moments when I wanted the choice removed so that I couldn't blame myself if it was the wrong decision. I sighed heavily, and extracted myself from the web of arms. "We should start shutting up shop. Who's been fed so far?"

"Just you lot and the children," Anahera replied. She went over to stir her cook pot, which still simmered on the stove. "Dinner's ready, though. Time to feed the rest of the monsters. Someone needs to go call them in."

"Michael and I will go," I volunteered, then I glanced at Skye. "Can you see if you can get some food down Lily? I imagine she's probably starving, but her stomach will be a bit sensitive."

Skye nodded her agreement. "I'll try her on some broth, and if that doesn't work then I'll figure something else out."

"Thank you." I smiled and touched my sister's arm. "Be gentle, though. That kid's had a rough time."

"Of course." Skye put her hand over mine, and squeezed it gently. "Don't worry, I'll take good care of her. Besides, if I don't then I'm pretty sure honey-guy will kick my butt."

"Actually…" I paused for a moment, turning her words over in my head. "Get a bit of that honey off Doc, and mix it in with some warm water. That'll give her some vital calories, and she's probably more likely to drink it. It should also help her immune system, and hopefully help with the pain."

"Okies!" Skye agreed brightly, then she punched my arm lightly. It took me a second to realise that she was mimicking Priya's favourite phrase, just to tease me. I laughed in response, and gave her a playful shove. Skye took it as a running start, and dashed out of the room giggling like a schoolgirl.

Once she was gone, I glanced at the others and shrugged. "Sometimes, I worry about her. But, you were right, Ana. She's tougher than I ever gave her credit for."

"Of course I'm right," she answered dryly. "I'm Mum, remember? Mum is always right."

"Not always," I said. "But mums do tend to have more life experience than their kids give them credit for." I sighed heavily, and looked at Michael. Suddenly aching for a moment of closeness, I reached out and threaded my fingers through his. "Come on. Let's go herd the monsters."

Michael just smiled and nodded, apparently sensing my needs the way he so often did. I gave him a shy smile in return, then waved goodbye to Anahera and led him out of the kitchen. Happy with silent companionship, we made our way back to the door we'd come in through. There, I spotted a group of wet, bedraggled folks standing on the other side of the glass, hugging themselves and bouncing from foot to foot to keep the cold at bay.

"Why are they standing out there?" I asked, confused.

Suddenly, Michael laughed. "Gavin locked the door on the way out, didn't he?"

"Oh." I paused for a second, then burst out laughing as well. "Oh! Of course!"

I raced over to the door and undid the latch that locked it from the inside. The group turned around, and I immediately recognised them as Hemi, Ryan, and a bunch of the other blokes. As soon as I pulled open the door, they all bundled inside.

"Aw mate, am I glad to see you," Hemi greeted us; I could almost hear his teeth chattering. "We knocked and knocked, but no one heard us."

"Sorry," I apologised, feeling more than a little bit guilty. "We didn't hear you. You go on up and talk to your mum; she's got some nice, hot soup to warm you up."

"Brilliant." The young man grinned, showing the straight, white teeth that he'd inherited from his mother. He turned to leave, then suddenly seemed to remember something and turned back to us. "Oh, Mike. Your dog's still sitting in the truck. We tried to get him to come in, but he just wanted to sit there."

"We'll go get him," Michael replied. He took the car keys from Hemi's outstretched hand, and tilted his head in my direction. "What about Sandy's kitten?"

"She went inside with Maddy, I think." Hemi shrugged, glancing around at the others. They all looked just as uncertain.

"It's all good, I'll find her later." I smiled and waved them off. "Go on, before you catch a cold."

"Speaking of which – put your coat on before you go out there," Hemi told me. "There's a southerly rolling in, and it started getting cold as soon as the sun went down."

"Thanks." I nodded and did just that, unfolding my coat from over my arm and pulling it around my shoulders. I was still sopping wet, but at least the coat would keep the wind at bay. By the time I finished doing up the buttons, they were gone and I was alone with Michael again. I gave him a long, sideways look, followed by a playful grin. "I thought you hated being called 'Mike'?"

"I do," he said with a shrug. "But, you know me. I'm a fish. I just go with the flow."

I laughed and nodded. He put his arm around me, a gesture that was so simple and natural that it made both of us smile – but the second that the wind hit us, I was really, really glad it was there.

"Cripes, he wasn't kidding!" I gasped, snuggling in against Michael's side. What had been a dreary day had turned into a truly miserable night, and the driving rain had a bite to it that chilled me to the core. "Brrr! Let's go get everyone in before this gets much worse. Where'd they park the truck?"

"They said around the corner, so I'm guessing..." Michael trailed off, peering around in the gloom. Suddenly, his expression brightened. "Oh, it's right over there!"

"Convenient." I put my arm around his waist so that I could tuck my hand in the pocket of his coat, and guided him off towards the truck. Alfie saw us coming before either of us noticed him, and let out a happy yelp of greeting.

"Hey, buddy," Michael greeted his canine friend, juggling the keys with his free hand until he managed to get the door unlocked. As soon as it was open, Alfie jumped out and bounded around him, barking happily. Michael laughed, and reached down to ruffle the dog's ears. "That's a good boy. You didn't poop in the Hilux, did you?"

Alfie let out a high-pitched yelp that sounded for all the world like a vehement denial. We both laughed and looked at one another.

"Well, that's one monster," I said, tugging my hood down to protect my eyes from the stinging rain. "Who else are we missing?"

"It's getting hard to keep track, isn't it?" Michael paused to think about it, then rattled off a list of names. "Just the Yousefis, the Merrits, and Richard, I think."

"They're probably still working on the radio," I surmised. Michael nodded his agreement, and we set off together.

We found the back door to the radio station still locked, so we ducked through the overgrown courtyard to the street front. Sure enough, there was light glowing through the remains of the front window. As soon as we crossed the threshold, we found ourselves face-to-face with two very alert guards: Elly and Rebecca, both armed, both rational and calm. As soon as they recognised us, they smiled and lowered their weapons.

"Time to call it a night?" Elly asked, slipping her gun back into its holster. "I hope Anahera and Skye do not mind that I was not there to help with dinner. I worry about leaving Zain alone."

"I'm sure she understands," I answered. "Yes, it's time to turn in. Ana's got some hot soup waiting for you. Grab the blokes and head inside; we'll be back tomorrow to work on this."

"Good." Elly paused, and glanced back over her shoulder. "I fear that success is coming slowly. None of them really know what they're doing."

Suddenly, a new voice entered the conversation, from the gloom behind us. "Then count yourselves lucky that I'm around."

I almost jumped out of my skin, and had my weapon halfway to the firing position before I recognised the voice. "Damn, Gavin. You scared me half to death."

"Sorry." He stepped into the light, though his hood was pulled so far forward that I could barely see his face. "Old habits, you know?"

"Better than most." I smiled, then turned back to introduce him to the others. "Gavin, this is Elly and Rebecca. That's Zain just coming out of the office up the back – oh, and there's Richard and Jim. Guys, this is Gavin. He's an old friend. Please don't shoot him."

"She's kidding, Jazz," Gavin said, glancing back at the shadows behind him. "No one's shooting anyone."

I followed his line of sight, and could just barely make out a human outline hiding amongst the bushes. If I hadn't known where to look, I never would have seen her.

"Hello again, Jasmine," I said gently, making my voice as soft as possible. "We found your sister. She's a bit beaten up, but she's okay. Would you like me to take you to her?"

I heard a faint rustling sound, but beyond that there was no answer. Gavin heaved a sigh and looked at me. "That was a yes. She's feeling a bit non-verbal at the moment."

"So I noticed," I answered dryly, but I gave the girl another smile anyway. "I can't say I blame her. There are a lot of bad things out there that want to hurt girls like us, aren't there Jasmine?"

This time, I heard a faint reply from her dark hiding spot, a single word of agreement: "Yeah."

"It's okay, I totally get it." I pushed my gun as far back over my shoulder as it would go, and held my hands up to show her that they were empty. "I have no intention of hurting you, and I won't let anyone else lay a finger on you, either."

"These folks are okay, Jazzy," Gavin added, holding his arms out to the girl. "Come on. They've got a doctor looking after her right now, and I'll make sure you're safe."

There was a long minute of silence, then the girl dashed out of the bushes, and fled into Gavin's arms. She hid her face against his chest and peeked warily at me over his arm. Gavin just hugged her, and made gentle, paternal sounds of comfort.

To my surprise, I found tears gathering in my eyes. I glanced at Michael, and realised that he was no less affected by the sight. He glanced at me, and his hand silently tightened around mine. I knew in some guttural, instinctive way that he longed to have that kind of bond with a child again. What we had together was one thing, but the love between father and child was a whole other experience. He'd had it with Sophie, and we had something similar growing with Priyanka, but would it ever be the same as having a child that was truly ours?

Suddenly, I realised that everyone was watching me. I took a deep breath and brushed away the tears that threatened to bring my emotional dam crashing down. Now was not the time for that, so I pushed my feelings down and focused on the present.

"Okay, let's head back," I said, gesturing to the members of my group. "You guys go first. We'll bring Jasmine and Gavin up once you're settled in. We don't want to scare her."

The others nodded and filed out past us, heading back to the office block. We waited while they filed away, and in the meantime I looked at Gavin.

"I don't suppose you've seen my foster daughter, have you?" I asked, cuddling in against Michael's side for warmth. "She's an Indian girl, a little older than the twins."

"Wearing bright pink, with a buzz cut?" he asked. I nodded. "Yeah, she somehow managed to follow me home. She stayed behind with Melody and Solomon. Melody seems to have taken a shine to her, so don't worry about anything bad happening to her. Anyone that messes with Melody is just asking for trouble."

"You know, I actually can't wait to meet this girl." I grinned and beckoned for them to follow me. "Come on. The others should have cleared off by now, so let's get out of the cold. I'm sure Lily wants to see Jazz, too."

Gavin nodded his agreement. He released Jasmine from his embrace and made as though to follow me, but Jasmine didn't. She straightened up, threw her shoulders back, and gave me a dark look. "You're not allowed to call me that."

I lifted an eyebrow, a little surprised by her vehemence. Somehow, I sensed that my response to her defiance would count for a lot more than it would in any normal conversation. It was something I understood, though. Names were power, and they could also bring pain if used incorrectly.

I just nodded to her simply, accepting her choice without protest. "Well, I'll just have to try and earn the privilege, won't I?"

The girl jerked back a little, surprise written across her young face. I just gave her a smile, then I turned and walked away, with Michael at my side. A few seconds later, I heard footsteps following me, but I didn't look back until we reached the door to the office building. There, I found Skylar waiting for us, looking anxious.

"Jasmine," I said pointedly, glancing back at the girl. "This is my sister, Skylar. She's been looking after your sister since we got her back."

"Actually, about that," Skylar interrupted, hugging her cardigan around her to combat the wind. "There's another problem."

"Oh, God." I heaved a long-suffering sigh. "What is it this time?"

"Well, Lily's awake," Skye answered, backing up a few paces so that I could herd my group inside. Michael and Gavin went willingly, but Jasmine skidded to a halt, glaring at Skylar from beneath her messy tangle of hair. Skye stared back at her, obviously surprised. "Oh, they're twins." She glanced at me and opened her mouth to say something else, but her comment was interrupted by a screech from upstairs, followed by the sound of shattering pottery. Skylar flinched, and gave me a helpless look. "And that's the problem. She's freaking out, but she's still pretty out of it and doesn't seem to understand what we're saying."

I muttered a few choice words beneath my breath and looked at our guests. "Well, guys, it sounds like Lily needs you. This way!"

I hurried past my sister and raced up the stairs, taking them two and three at a time. At the top, I glanced back and found Jasmine just a couple of steps behind me, with Gavin right behind her. As soon as they'd caught up, I rushed off again, hurrying down the maze of passages towards Lily's screams. The sound of them put me on edge, even though I knew instinctively that they were screams of rage and fear, rather than pain. Somehow, that was no better.

I rounded the last corner at full speed, and almost bowled Doctor Cross right off his feet. He shot me a shocked look, and I gave him one in return; his glasses were missing, and a set of vivid red welts tarnished his cheek from where someone had obviously tried to take his eyes out with her fingernails.

"Sandy!" he gasped, in an obvious mix of relief and surprise. "Help me! I'm not sure how long I can keep this door shut."

"Is it the infection?" I asked urgently, suddenly terrified that the worst had happened. Had the virus mutated enough to infect the immune? If so, then we were all screwed.

"No, no, nothing like that," Doc replied. "It's some kind of reaction to the cocktail of drugs and booze that man gave her—" Suddenly, he let out a terribly unmanly shriek. "Look out! She's behind you!"

"Huh?" I jumped and looked back, only to find Jasmine and Gavin skidding to a halt right behind me. "Oh, no. That's Jasmine, her twin sister."

"What's wrong with my sister?" Jasmine demanded, her little hands balled into fists at her side. "Let her out!"

"We're going to, I promise," I said, struggling to keep my voice calm and even. "Jasmine, she needs your help. The man that took her – the farmer – he drugged her. We're trying to help her, but she's angry and afraid. Can you calm her down?"

Jasmine gave me another dark look, and put her hands on her hips. "Open. The door. Now."

I glanced back at Doc and nodded. He swallowed hard, then released the door handle and jumped back with a degree of dexterity that I'd never seen from him before.

A second later, the door popped open, and Lily exploded out, shrieking in a language that I didn't understand.

Jasmine leapt on her sister without a moment of hesitation, sending both of them tumbling back into the room. I heard the doctor protesting behind me, but there was nothing that either of us could do. The twins wrestled for a few minutes, until finally Jasmine got on top of her sister and managed to pin her to the ground.

"She doesn't recognise me," Jasmine shouted to us. "Why? What did he do to her?"

"It's the drugs," Doc called back to her. "She's... she's drunk, for lack of a better word. Just hold her for a moment; I'll give her something to make her sleep. And for the love of God, be gentle! The poor child has internal injuries."

Jasmine grunted something that sounded like a wordless agreement, but she was obviously having trouble holding her sister down. Lily thrashed beneath her, kicking and screaming with all her might, and even trying to bite her sister. I watched for a moment, then made a snap decision.

"Gavin, grab her legs," I instructed, and then I dove into the fray. I threw myself to my knees near the youngster's head, and pinned it still to keep her from injuring either herself or her sister. "Hold her, but be gentle! I don't want her to hurt Jasmine."

Jasmine looked up at me, her face just a few inches from mine as we awkwardly pinned her writhing sister to the ground. For the first time, there was something in her gaze besides hatred, something that might have even been respect. She gave me a faint nod, then she focused her attention on keeping Lily down. The doctor rushed up to us a few seconds later, with a syringe in his hand.

"Forgive me, child," he said quietly, though it wasn't clear which of the twins he was talking to. I saw Jasmine stiffen up, but she let him administer the dose of sedative to her sister. Lily screamed at the pinch of the needle and tried to fight even harder, but there was nothing she could do against two grown adults and her own sister.

"It's okay, sweetheart," I whispered soothingly as the sedative started taking effect. Once she stopped fighting us, I released her and gently smoothed her tangled hair back out of her face. "It's okay... no one's going to hurt you anymore. I won't let them. Shhh... you just go to sleep, and when you wake up you'll feel much better. I promise."

Lily stared up at me with eyes so dark and fathomless that it felt like I could fall into them and drown. Her mouth opened and closed a few times, but no words came out. Eventually, her eyelids drifted closed and she fell into a deep sleep.

I sighed heavily and sat back. "Are you sure the sedative is safe, Doc? We don't know what drugs are in her system already."

"I have no way to know," he admitted. "I didn't want to use this on her, but she really gave us no choice. I have no intention of leaving her alone until I know that she's going to be all right, though. "

"Good," I agreed, nodding. "If you need someone to assist you, I'll find someo—"

"Why?" Suddenly, Jasmine spoke up and interrupted me, her tone sharp and accusative. "Why are you trying to help us? We didn't ask for your help."

I looked at her, and gave her the faintest of smiles. "You didn't have to ask. Jasmine, I'm going to tell you a story. It's not very nice, but it's the truth and I think it will help you understand why I wanted to save your sister. Come over here, let's get out of the way so that the doctor and Gavin can get her back into bed."

I eased myself to my feet, and offered her a hand to help her up. She ignored my hand, but did as she was told. We moved out of the way, and watched while Lily was tended. I felt an arm slide around my waist from the other side, and knew without looking that Michael and Skye had joined us.

"Two summers ago, I was travelling alone when I was taken by a man kind of like the farmer," I said softly. I felt Michael's arm tighten around me, and silently appreciated the support. "I was just minding my own business, like you two were, when he saw me and decided that he was going to… make me his wife, to put it kindly."

I looked down at Jasmine and saw her watching me, her expression unreadable. I gave her a sad smile and looked away. "You shouldn't even have to know what that means at your age, but I think you do. I managed to escape, but only because I was very, very lucky. Since then, I've made a vow never to let anyone take away the rights of another human being, even if it costs me my life fighting to save them. I'd help anyone who needed it, but I admit that I have a particular empathy for young women like you, because I know from first-hand experience how hard it is for us to survive in this world. That's why you didn't have to ask for help, Jasmine. I'd give it to you willingly, because it's the right thing to do."

Silence descended on the room when I finished speaking. I closed my eyes, and savoured in the strange feeling of pride that washed over me. I'd made the decision to take up the cause to protect humankind on a whim, but today was the day that I'd finally been able to prove my conviction – not just to those around me, but to myself. It was no longer just words to appeal to the group. Now, it was reality, and I was living it.

Eventually, Jasmine sighed heavily. I looked at her, and found her staring down at her feet with great interest. A few seconds later, she glanced up and gave me a shy smile. "On second thoughts, I think you are allowed to call me 'Jazz' after all."

# Chapter Eighteen

It was a long, noisy, and anxious night. Jasmine and Gavin stayed glued to Lily's bedside; eventually, we decided to drag a few extra mattresses in so that they and the doctor could sleep in shifts. One by one, the others came to peek at the newcomers, but Jasmine wouldn't let anyone get close to her sister except for me and Doctor Cross. In the end, we brought them some dinner, then closed the door and let them be.

Before bed, I gathered the members of the group that weren't otherwise occupied in the kitchen, and spread out a couple of big maps on the table so everyone could see them.

"We need to decide on our route south," I told them, pointing to the large lake in the centre of the map. "Lake Taupo is just south of here, but before then we need to pick whether we want to follow the highway along the western shore, or the east."

"What's the difference?" Skylar asked, shooting me a curious look.

"The eastern route will take us through Taupo city, while the western won't," I explained, tracing the two routes with my fingertip. "I haven't been through Taupo since before the plague, but from what I've heard it's a hub of gang activity."

"It is," Anahera confirmed, nodding slowly. "The location is perfect. The lake has several feeder rivers to the south, which provide a constant supply of fresh water, not to mention the fish, ducks, and other game in the area. There's always someone living there. I sent a trading convoy there once, but they never came back."

"What happened to them?" I asked. Anahera just shrugged.

"We have no way of knowing," she admitted. "They just vanished. It's possible they ran into that pack of racists you met heading to Arapuni, or perhaps they ran afoul of some other gang. Maybe it was a pig. It could have been anything, really."

"But we know that they were heading for Taupo." I stood back and sighed, rubbing my fingers over the bridge of my nose. "That's not good. From what I remember, the western route is just scrubland, with no towns or buildings to speak of, but it's been a while. God knows what kind of condition it's in."

"So, whichever route we pick is a gamble." Anahera looked at me and tilted her head inquisitively. "May I suggest we take the western route, just to be safe?"

"Suggestion noted. All right, let's vote." I straightened up and looked at the others. "All in favour of the eastern route, raise your hand." I paused and waited. No one moved. "Okay, and in favour of the western route?" Hands popped up all over the room. I nodded, and leaned over to fold the maps back up again. "Western route, it is. Head to bed, everyone. We've got another long day ahead of us tomorrow."

Most of the group drifted out to go find their berths for the night, but Ryan lingered behind. I shot a curious look at him, but he averted his eyes and pretended to be very interested in a smudge on the paintwork until the last person had left the room. Only then did he finally glance in my direction, his expression unreadable.

"Can we... talk for a second?" he asked softly, his voice barely audible.

"Of course," I replied, equal parts wary and confused. He'd been quiet since he rejoined the group, so quiet that sometimes I forgot he was there at all. Given what he'd been through, his silence didn't surprise me. What did surprise me is that he'd pick me to chat with.

Ryan drew a deep breath, and slowly lowered himself down to sit in a chair.

"Thanks. I don't really have anyone else to talk to. I mean, there's Skye, but it's not the same. And the others..."

"I know," I said, seating myself at the table beside him. Although I had every right to be angry at him, all I felt when I looked at him was pity. "Sometimes it can be really hard to earn forgiveness. You don't need me to lecture you about what you did wrong, though. You already know that, better than anyone. So, what did you want to talk about?"

Ryan fell silent, his gaze focused on a speck of nothing in the middle distance. I'd never seen anyone looking quite so forlorn, not even my sister on the day she had to bury her firstborn. His hands tightened into fists, but I knew on some instinctive level that his tension was not a threat to me.

Suddenly, he looked at me and I saw the full force of his despair reflected in his eyes. "What do I do now?"

I frowned at him, not entirely sure how to interpret his request. "What do you mean?"

"I mean..." he hesitated and glanced away again, his eyes drifting back out of focus. "It's always been her and me. Ryan and Skye. Just the two of us against the world. Then, it was the two of us and the baby. I knew what to do. Now it's all gone. My friends don't want to know me, Skye hates me, and my baby's dead. I don't know what to do anymore."

"She doesn't hate you," I told him gently, reaching out to rest my hand over the back of his fist. He tensed up for a moment, then slowly relaxed when he realised that my intentions were innocent. He glanced at me, and I gave him a faint smile in return. "No one hates you, Ry. They just don't understand. They will, eventually, but they need time. If it makes you feel any better, I understand why you left."

"You do?" His expression changed to one of surprise, then I saw the faintest flicker of hope pass through his eyes. "I thought no one did. I mean, Michael..."

"Yeah, I know what he said." I sighed softly and gave his hand a squeeze. "Sometimes, when you're faced with something so devastating that your conscious mind isn't capable of processing it, your animal instincts kick in. It was fight or flight. You didn't have a choice. There was no one that you could fight, so you chose to flee. It could have happened to anyone."

"He called me a coward," Ryan repeated, darkness falling back across his face like a veil. "He's right. I am a coward. I ran away. He wouldn't run away. If it had been you, then he would have stayed."

"Maybe, but you're not him and you don't have to be," I told him firmly. "You're different people, and you are entitled to react to a tragedy in the way that best helps you to cope with your grief." I paused and glanced down at his wrists, still hidden beneath his long, black sleeves. As gently as I could, I laid my hand over the hidden injuries, and gave him a look of pure sympathy. "No one can know what they would do in the face of that much pain, and no one should have to find out. Skye told me what you tried to do, Ry. I hate to think about you suffering like that all by yourself. I know that at heart, you're a good man. Do you think it would help if we put aside a little time each day, just to hang out and talk?"

The young man fell silent for a few seconds, then he nodded slowly. "I think... I think it might. I don't know, Sandy. But maybe, yeah. Maybe talking would help." He managed a weak smile, and stood up slowly. "I should go. I'm on the late watch, so I have to be up at midnight. Thanks for listening."

"Any time," I answered. I rose to my feet, and pulled him into a quick hug. "You're not in this alone, mate. We'll get through it. Promise."

He didn't seem sure what to do with the hug at first, but eventually he relaxed and hugged me back. When we separated, there was a faint but genuine smile on his face.

Suddenly looking embarrassed, he ducked out of the room before I could say another word, leaving me to stare after him thoughtfully.

A few minutes later, Michael stuck his head into the room and called my name inquisitively. "Sandy?"

"Yeah, I'm coming," I replied, shaking off my bout of melancholy to focus on the evening's tasks.

***

Michael and I took the first watch. With all the downstairs doors firmly locked from the inside and Alfred's nose on the task, we felt secure enough to cut the watch down to just two at a time. We set up a guard post and barricade at the top of the only staircase up to our area, and watched it with vigilance.

One by one, the others stopped by to say goodnight before they turned in, until the only people left awake were the two of us. Outside, the wind howled and moaned, but inside there was only silence and the occasional sound of snoring. I lingered in the doorway to the main sleeping room for a few moments, enjoying the strange feeling of pride that came with it.

Those people were more than just my friends, now. They were my charges. They looked to me for guidance and protection. They trusted me to watch over them while they slept. It was a good feeling, and I liked it. I withdrew and went off to finish my patrol, then I returned to the barricade where Michael waited.

He glanced up as I sat down beside him and smiled at me. With that gentle strength that I loved so much, he drew me beneath the blanket wrapped around his shoulders, into the warmth. The scent of his body was familiar and comforting, and it stirred something inside me the way no other man ever had. I smiled back and leaned up to give him a kiss, then we settled in to silently watch and wait for midnight.

Eventually, midnight came and our replacements arrived to relieve us. We retreated to one of the beds left warm by their absence, and snuggled down to sleep. Even as I was drifting off, I was acutely aware of one fact: Priya still hadn't come home.

***

I woke late the next morning, lulled into a deeper sleep than usual by the incessant pounding of the rain. When my eyes finally opened, I realised that it was well past sunrise, and that everyone else was already up and about.

Maddy was the only one to notice that I was awake. She waved vigorously, then went right back to what she was doing. She was sitting in a circle with the three younger Yousefi boys, pawing over a couple of grimy children's books.

I tried to sit up, but as soon as I moved I felt a sharp, stabbing pain in my hip. Startled and still muddled with sleep, it took a second for me to realise that the source was Tigger, who was sitting primly on my hip, washing one of her paws. I tried to move again, and she dug her claws in deeper in protest.

"Ow," I complained. "Would you knock it off, please? I need to get up."

Tigger gave me the filthiest look in return, but she stood up and stretched dramatically. Then, she finally jumped off and trotted over to Madeline, her tail held high.

Despite the pain, the sight brought a smile to my face. I eased myself out of bed and indulged in a long, luxurious stretch of my own. Every inch of me was still damp and sticky, but there was nothing I could do about it. The rain was still coming down with force, so I was unlikely to dry off any time soon.

432

I put on my coat and shoes, and padded down the hallway to the ladies room. On the way back, I stopped in to the doctor's sick room to check on things. Doctor Cross was out like a light, lying fast asleep amid a tangle of blankets. Lily was still unconscious, and Gavin sat on the floor beside her bed with his head lowered, as still as a stone gargoyle.

I cleared my throat softly, to see if he was actually awake. He looked up, and held one finger to his lips to indicate silence. I watched from the doorway as he eased himself quietly to his feet and snuck over to me.

"Where's Jasmine?" I asked in a whisper, tilting my head towards the room. "I thought she wasn't going to leave her sister's side?"

"She wanted to go home and get some things," he replied, absently running his fingertips over the door to muffle the sound as he pulled it closed behind us. "She'll be back in a bit."

"Ah." I nodded my understanding. "What about Lily? How is she?"

"The doctor thinks that she'll be fine." He smiled again, an expression of such open relief that it warmed my heart. "Thank God. Did I ever tell you that I lost my wife and my little girl to the plague?"

"I think you mentioned it once, but you didn't seem to want to talk about it," I replied. On a whim, I reached out to touch the back of his hand and offer him some small iota of comfort from my presence. "I figured it must have been something like that."

"She died on her sixth birthday." He heaved a deep sigh, staring down at my hand as though seeing it for the first time. "She was my life. My wife had a medical condition, and the doctors told us that it was unlikely she'd survive to carry the baby to term. She was so determined to try, even if it might kill her. The day our baby was born, I honestly couldn't tell you which one was more beautiful: her, or my wife."

"I'm so sorry, Gavin," I said sympathetically, squeezing his hand gently. "You don't have to talk about it, if you don't want to. I understand."

"I know." He glanced up and gave me a smile. "But I want you to really, fully understand. I don't want anyone thinking that I'm just some old creep that likes keeping little girls around. It's just… I see these kids, and I see my daughter. I couldn't save her, but maybe if I save enough of them then I'll figure out how to forgive myself."

I let out a long, deep sigh, and pulled him into a hug. "It won't help if I tell you that it wasn't your fault, will it?"

"Of course not." He chuckled faintly and shook his head, but he accepted the hug without protest. "I know that. Intellectually, I know that. Emotionally… that's different."

"Yeah, I know exactly what you mean." I drew back, but left a hand resting on his shoulder. "Maybe this will help. If it weren't for the things you taught me, I probably wouldn't be alive today. You helped to save at least one person."

"True," he said, his expression brightening. "I honestly can't tell you how happy I am to see you, Sandy. I mean, I know I've said it, but the words can't express how overjoyed I am that you survived. I've seen some bloody nasty things done to women and children and been unable to stop it, but… you're right. That does help. Thank you."

"No, thank you," I replied, giving him a light-hearted nudge in the ribs to soften the seriousness of the conversation. "You gave me knowledge that saved my life; I haven't done anything to deserve thanks."

"Careful, those never healed quite right." He grunted dramatically, rubbing his ribs. "Yes, you have. You saved Lily, remember? That and what you did for Jasmine more than repays anything I did for you, and puts me firmly in your debt."

"Huh?" Confused, I blinked owlishly at him. "I didn't do anything for Jasmine. I mean, aside from saving her sister, but I would have done that anyway."

"It's way more than that," he replied, shaking his head. "You've given her something that I can't. You've given her a role-model. She's never seen a grown woman that's smart, capable, and a leader before. You impressed her in a way that I never could. I mean, do you know where she is right now?"

"You said she went to go get some things?" I answered, shrugging.

"I did, but to be specific, she's gone to *pack* her things." He grinned suddenly, and grabbed my arm. "She wants us to go with you, Sandy. I've never seen her this excited about something before. She told me that she wants all of us to follow you, so that she can learn to be like you when she grows up." He paused, and gave me a long look. "If you'll have us, that is."

"Well, that's a silly question," I said with a laugh. "I plan to build a city, Gav – I'm going to need as many people as I can get. And if those kids really want to join us, then they're welcome. All that we ask is that they contribute to the group in some way, and… you know, not try to claw Doc's eyes out again."

Gavin joined in laughing, nodding his head. "That wasn't normal! Lily's the shy, gentle one. She would never have done that under normal circumstances."

"Then they're both welcome, and I hope that the other kids will come along as well." I glanced back over my shoulder, in the direction of the makeshift bedroom where our children were busy teaching themselves to read. "Everyone's welcome, so long as they agree to abide by our rules."

"What rules are those?" he asked, looking at me expectantly.

"Simple ones, really." I glanced back at him, and smiled. "Don't kill, hurt, or threaten another member of this group unless it is in self-defence. No one has the right to abuse anyone else, verbally, physically, or sexually. Don't steal from us, or from each other. Treat other people the way you want to be treated. Breaches of the rules will be decided before a quorum chosen from within the group, as will the punishments."

"I see you've put some thought into it," Gavin replied. He went quiet for a moment while he considered what I'd said, then nodded slowly. "Sounds good to me. We should go get your radio message out, so that we can move on before it gets too dangerous here. I, for one, have no desire to meet one of your mutated infected."

"Hey, they're not *my* mutated infected," I protested, only half joking. "They're everyone's problem."

"I know." He gave me a weak smile. "Sorry, that was meant to be a joke. I remember you having quite the sense of humour."

"And you never were any good at telling jokes." I grinned at him in return, and clapped my hand on his shoulders. "All right, then. Do you want to wake up Doc?"

"No, no need," he replied, shaking his head. "Lily's fine. Doctor Cross told me that she passed the danger point in the middle of the night, and now she's just sleeping it off."

"Good. Poor kid doesn't deserve that kind of treatment." I stepped past him, and led the way towards the exit. Along the way, I found Michael sitting on the floor in one of the side rooms with a bunch of assorted weapon pieces spread out on old towels all around him. I stopped and leaned against the door frame, watching him work. Gavin joined me a second later, but neither of us said anything.

It took a few seconds before Michael noticed us. When he did, he glanced up and gave me a smile. "Morning, sunshine. Just cleaning the guns; they don't like being wet for too long. The shotgun's already done, if you want it."

"What, you're not going to tease me for sleeping so late?" I commented dryly, folding my arms across my chest.

Michael laughed and shook his head. "Now, would I do a thing like that?"

"Of course," I replied with some amusement. "That's why I agreed to marry you, isn't it?"

"Oh yeah. How could I forget?" Michael grinned that silly grin of his, and picked up the shotgun resting beside his knee. He held it up to me, and I took it. I quickly checked that it was loaded and the safety was firmly in place, then I put the strap over my shoulder and adjusted it across my back.

"Thank you for cleaning it for me," I said, turning serious again. "I should have remembered to do that myself, but after yesterday's excitement..."

Michael just held up a hand, and shook his head. "You don't have to apologise to me, sweetheart. That's what husbands are for, remember? We're partners. We watch each other's backs. We help each other up if we fall down. We may not be married yet, but that's what I want to be for you: your partner, through the good times and the bad."

I felt a flush of heat rise in my cheeks, and suddenly I was both pleased and embarrassed. I gave him a shy smile, then glanced away and quickly changed the subject. "We're heading down to work on the radio. Do you want to come?"

Michael paused to consider it. I glanced up just in time to see him shake his head. "Nah, I better stay here and finish up. I need to get these back to the troops as soon as possible. It's still pretty nasty out there, so most of them are holed up in one of the rooms downstairs, playing cards."

"Okay," I agreed. "I've got my radio on me. Call if you need anything."

"Will do." Michael sketched a salute, and then he glanced past me at Gavin. "Keep an eye on her, old man. I'll hold you responsible if anything eats her."

His sense of humour might have been a little rusty, but Gavin clearly understood the light-hearted comment for what it was. It was hard not to, when Michael was grinning like a fool. Gavin gave him a mock salute in return. "Sure, I'll keep an eye on her... but only one. I've only got one to spare."

"Okay, that one was actually pretty good," I said with a laugh. "I'm going to have to make you two spend some quality time together, so Michael's sense of humour rubs off on you."

Both of them laughed at that. I grinned and waved to Michael, then led Gavin out of the room. Once we were out of earshot, Gavin glanced at me and smiled. "He's a good man, your fiancé."

"I know," I said. "To be honest, I don't think there's another man alive who could have done what he did. I was a total wreck when we met. I didn't think it was possible for me to fall in love again, but he proved me wrong. I don't know what I'd do without him."

"Let's hope that you never have to find out," Gavin said softly. I just nodded my agreement, and led us onwards. We made our way past the barricade, down the stairs, and into the lobby where I found Nikora and Wiremu on duty beside the door.

"Morning, Nick, Will," I greeted them, using their preferred nicknames. "How's it going?"

"Pretty shite, but it could be worse. At least we're not out in that." Nikora grinned good-naturedly, and jerked his thumb over his shoulder at the door. "You two for in or out?"

"Out, unfortunately," I replied, pulling my hood up over my head. I shoved my hair under the leather as best I could, and peered past them at the gloomy weather. "I guess winter finally caught up with us."

"Well, we were about due for it," Will commented, heaving a long, dramatic sigh. "Ah, well. So the Lord deems it, so it must be. Let's just hope it doesn't start snowing."

"Amen to that," I agreed. Nick unlocked the door and held it open for me. I nodded my thanks and stepped out, only to be hit in the face by a blast of frigid wind. Behind me, I heard Gavin gasp and mutter a curse under his breath, to which I could only grunt wordless agreement. I pulled my collar up and hurried off towards the radio station as fast as I could, ducking from one patch of shelter to the next.

No matter how hard I tried, I still ended up soaked by the time I reached the front door. I hopped over the broken frame, and ducked into the shelter within. Elly was alone on watch this time, huddled up inside a thick woollen blanket for warmth. She nodded to me, but said nothing.

"Morning," I greeted her. "No Rebecca today?"

"No, she has come down with a cold," Elly replied. She sniffed and rubbed her nose, then gave me a pathetic look. "She is not alone, but I would rather be here watching over Zain than anywhere else."

"Aw, no one told me you guys were sick." I frowned at her and put my hands on my hips. "You should have said something. We found a bunch of jars of honey in Arapuni, so the doctor could have mixed you up something to make you feel better."

"I know, but I did not wish to wake him." Elly gave me a pathetic attempt at a smile, and made a shooing gesture. "You stay away. I do not want you to get sick as well."

"Okay, but you're on light duties until you feel better," I instructed gently. "And if anyone has a problem with that, tell them to bring it up with me."

Elly nodded quietly, and huddled under her blanket again. I took her silence to mean that her throat was probably hurting, so I didn't press her to keep talking. I just gave her a sympathetic smile, and headed down the hallway towards the back of the building. Both of the studios were empty, but the sound of voices arguing led me to the old lunchroom where I found my more technically-minded companions sitting around the table, looking frustrated.

"This is ridiculous," Jim complained, pounding his good fist on the table. "I'm not a sound engineer. None of us are. How on earth are we supposed to work this out?"

"He's right." Zain sighed deeply. He was holding a thick book, which he dropped on the table with a heavy thud. "This manual may as well be written in Greek, for all the good it does us."

Suddenly, Anahera appeared from behind the partition that separated the kitchenette from the tables, with mugs of steaming hot black coffee in her hands. She set one mug down in front of each of the men at the table.

"Calmness, my friends. We'll work this out together." She glanced up and gave me a warm smile. "Good morning. Would you care for some coffee? I also have some leftover food back here, if you'd like some."

"I can't tell if that's my stomach rumbling or the thunder, but I'd love some of both, please," I said. She nodded and went back to the kitchenette, while I shifted my attention to my unhappy engineers. "As for the radio… well, it turns out that we have someone right here that can help. Gavin?"

"I was a communications officer in the army for ten years," he explained, right on cue. "Radios were my life blood, until I resigned my commission to start a family. These commercial stations are a little different to the ones I'm used to, but I should have no trouble getting it going. You blokes willing to give me a hand?"

Zain and Jim exchanged startled looks, but Richard and Ropata smiled. All of them rose to their feet and nodded their agreement.

I glanced at Gavin, and raised a brow. "Well, looks like you've got your assistants. Don't you want to wait until after breakfast, though?"

"No, I don't usually eat in the morning, and I'd rather get this sorted." Gavin gestured to his newfound comrades, and then the five of them vanished into the hallway.

A second later, Anahera returned with a steaming cup in one hand, and a plate of scrambled eggs in the other. The eggs were cold, but I took them gratefully anyway. I sat down in one of the recently-vacated seats, and sipped my coffee. Anahera seated herself opposite me, watching me thoughtfully.

"You know, I don't think we've ever had the chance to speak alone," she murmured, trailing her fingers across the hot surface of her own mug.

I paused with a forkful of eggs half way to my mouth, and gave her a curious look. "Well, there was that one time on the docks at your old place."

"Ah, yes. I'd forgotten about that." She sighed and glanced down at her drink, as though seeking to divine something from the dark brew. "It's still hard to believe that I'll never see my home again."

"I know." I put my fork down, and reached across the table to touch her hand sympathetically. "I just wish that we'd thought to warn you earlier. I don't think I've told you how much I regret that."

"You don't have to." She smiled faintly, and placed her free hand over top of mine. "I understand you, Sandrine McDermott. I see much pain in your eyes, yet so much determination. It was a mistake that anyone could have made in a time of such stress. I hold nothing against you."

"Thank you." I smiled back at her, and gently withdrew my hand so that I could resume eating. Cold or not, the moment that I felt that food on my tongue, I was ravenous. I had almost finished before I realised that Anahera was watching me closely. I paused, and looked at her quizzically. "What is it?"

"Nothing, my dear. You just seem to be feeling better this morning, and that pleases me." She gave me one of those enigmatic smiles of hers that always made me feel like she knew something I didn't. "Would you like another helping? I wasn't sure how many we were going to be feeding, so I made more than necessary."

"I won't say no," I replied, setting my fork down on the empty plate. "Doc keeps hounding me to put some more weight on."

"As well he should. You are still much too thin." Anahera took my plate and stood up, her expression one of maternal kindness. "Don't worry about it too much. Now that we're living together I'm sure I'll be able to fatten you up."

"Don't fatten me up too much, or Michael will cancel the wedding," I said with a laugh, even though I knew it wasn't true. Hell, Michael seemed to like me even better when I gained a few more curves.

"Wedding?" Anahera popped back around the partition and stared at me, wide-eyed. "You two are engaged now?"

"Oh." I froze, suddenly realising that she was probably the one person that didn't know. "Oh, yeah. I guess I forgot to tell you. After the talk you gave us, we decided to get tentatively engaged, and just let things progress as they will. We've swapped rings, but it's nothing set in stone."

"Oh, Sandy, that's wonderful news." Before I quite knew what had happened, she'd pulled me out of my chair and swept me up into a hug. "Congratulations! I am thrilled for both of you."

"I thought you might be." Laughing, I hugged her back. "Sorry. I told you about everything else but I guess I forgot about that. It's been a busy few weeks, you know?"

"No, I completely understand." Anahera pushed me back and smiled radiantly at me. Just as suddenly as she'd grabbed me, she let me go. A second later, I found myself back in my chair with another helping of eggs in front of me. "Now, eat up and tell me all about it."

# Chapter Nineteen

Anahera and I talked for almost an hour over our coffee. At one stage, I got up to check on the men, but they were deeply engrossed in what they were doing and informed me that another set of hands would just get in the way. We went back to the kitchen and talked some more, until I accidentally disclosed that Elly was feeling ill.

Unsurprisingly, Anahera wasn't about to let her suffer. She hurried off to find the fixings for hot, honeyed tea, leaving me on my own. I washed my dish and mug out of habit, and returned them to the cupboard that they'd been borrowed from, then I went out to check on Elly. She was still awake and alert but miserable, and waved me away when I tried to enquire about her welfare.

With nothing better to do to pass the time, I decided to check out the local shops and see if there was anything left that had survived the riots. I ducked across the road, only to discover that the buildings over there were a perfect cross-section of things that were utterly useless to us now: several banks, a few offices advertising law services or politicians, and a post office. The only place that might be remotely useful was a small optometrist's office on the corner. Thinking of Doc's scratched lenses, I made a mental note to bring him over and check it out before we left town. In the meantime, I headed eastwards along the road, back towards the shopping centre.

My instinct told me that if there was anything useful left here, then that was where I'd find it. Part of me felt guilty for defying my own orders and going off on my own, but I was confident in my ability to defend myself should the need arise. I slipped my shotgun off my shoulder, just in case, and eased the safety off.

I ducked across a silent intersection, picking my way between a half-dozen cars in various states of disrepair, to the footpath on the other side. There, through the twisting vines of an overgrown plant, I spotted the familiar logo of a chain brand pharmacy. As soon as I got close to the door, my heart sank. The pharmacy had been ransacked.

"Since when did you get so spoiled that you care about that?" I muttered to myself, suddenly amused. I lifted my shotgun to my shoulder, and carefully stepped into the carnage within.

As soon as I crossed the threshold, I realised that 'carnage' was not an overstatement. Pieces that had once belonged to other human beings lay scattered across the floor, now reduced to nothing but bones and scraps of flesh. I took a deep breath and swallowed hard, struggling to keep my breakfast down. It wasn't hard to piece together the scene from the way the bodies lay; they'd come in frantically looking for medicine, and never left. I guessed they had been fighting one another for what little was available – not that any of it would help them.

I stepped carefully over the remains of someone's torso, and picked my way towards the back counter. The moment I got there, I realised that the hunt was going to be useless. I could see shattered vials and half-crumbled pills scattered across the floor like a carpet of melting candy. Someone had already been there, and thrown whatever they didn't want into a heap on the floor. Sorting it out would be impossible, even with the doctor's expertise. I withdrew, and focused my attention on searching the shelves instead.

A quick search of the usual places turned up a few packs of cloth bandages that had slipped under a shelf, but little else of value. I tucked the bandages into the inside pocket of my coat, and ducked back out into the rain.

Next door, I found a Salvation Army store that had been covered in graffiti but otherwise left alone. The door was still firmly shut and locked; the butt of my shotgun made quick work of the glass window pane. The noise made me flinch, but nothing stirred either inside or out. I waited for a second, just to be sure that I wasn't going to be ambushed, then I stepped over the broken glass into the store itself.

It took a moment for my eyes to adjust, but once they did I was pleasantly surprised to discover that the store was mostly intact. There were no stinking corpses, and I saw very little in the way of mould. Our world was full of discarded clothing, but I was painfully aware of the fact that the resources available to us were finite. Cloth didn't expire like food, but it did rot, tear, and fall apart with wear and exposure to the elements. Our generation might be able to pick and choose for a while, but the next would not survive so easily.

I paused in front of a rack full of children's clothing. The tiny garments attracted me, in some way that I couldn't quite name. I reached out and trailed my fingers over a baby-sized romper, marvelling at the softness of it. The texture brought back memories of holding Skylar when she was an infant. So soft and fragile, a tiny doll that smelt like baby powder and milk. She'd been so completely helpless, and reliant on us for everything...

Suddenly, I felt nauseated. I barely made it back outside before the heaving began, with such force that it knocked me to my knees on the cold pavement. My entire body convulsed, but to my relief nothing actually came up. Just dry heaves, enough to make me feel miserable without actually wasting any food.

When the heaves finally passed, I lifted my head and wiped my mouth with the back of my hand. It was only then that I realised I was being watched from the bushes across the street. The shotgun trembled in my hands as I lifted it, but I did my best to hide the weakness as much as I could.

"Who's there?" I demanded. My voice was hoarse, but it was still strong and confident. That was what I needed.

There was a long moment of silence, then a familiar voice called a greeting. "Is me, Mama. Priyanka."

"Priya!" I gasped in a mixture of relief and anxiety. "Oh, honey, you worried me so much when you vanished last night. Are you okay?"

"I fine, Mama. No worries about me," she called back. I saw her head pop up, easily visible under its bright pink raincoat, but she didn't immediately come to me. Instead, she looked down into the bushes and seemed to be holding a soft-spoken conversation with someone that I couldn't see.

I swiftly put two and two together. "Is that Melody with you? Or is it Jasmine?"

"Both, Mama, and Solo too," Priya called back. Someone hidden near her protested, but she just gave them a glare and made a curt gesture. This time, she spoke loud enough for me to make out what she was saying. "You shoosh! That is my mama you talking about, you not say like that. I love Mama."

My eyes blurred with tears all of a sudden, and I felt a rush of warmth at her words. Though it took strength that I wasn't entirely sure I had, I levered myself up to my feet and put my shotgun back over my shoulder.

"I love you too, honey," I called back. "Tell your friends that they can take as much time as they need. I understand how they feel. It's hard to trust."

Priya glanced at me, but before she could say anything, a second youngster popped up beside her. It took a few seconds before I realised that it was Jasmine, all wrapped up in a dark green oilskin raincoat. Jasmine said something that I couldn't quite make out, then shoved her way out of the bushes and crossed the road towards me. I just waited, watching her approach without making any sudden moves that might frighten her.

My caution was unwarranted. Jasmine came at me with stalwart determination, and didn't stop until she was standing right in front of me. She crossed her arms over her chest, and regarded me curiously. "Are you okay?"

"Huh?" I blinked in surprise; that wasn't quite what I expected.

"Are you okay?" she repeated, as if she were speaking to a slow child. "We saw you being sick."

"Oh!" Realisation hit like a sledgehammer, and left me feeling stupid. Of course, they were worried about illness. They'd seen all of their families die of the plague. "Yeah, I'm fine. I had a concussion a few days ago – a hard bump on the head – and sometimes that makes your body do dumb things like want to throw up for no reason."

"Oh. Okay." Jasmine nodded her understanding, then turned and looked at the bushes across the street. "You can come out. It's safe."

"She better not be infectious," a third voice called. There was a momentary argument between the third voice and Priya, but it ended when Priya made a rude noise and stomped out of the bushes. She came over and gave me a hug. I hugged her back, and planted a kiss on the top of her head, to which she responded with a much happier noise.

"I'm not sick," I called back, trying to clarify the situation for them. "I had an injury to my head, and it hasn't healed fully yet. That happens sometimes when you have a bump on the noggin. You're Melody, right? Gavin was telling me about you."

Finally, Melody stood up, along with a slender youth that I presumed must have been Solomon. I couldn't make out many of the details of their features from afar; just like the rest of us, they were wrapped up in raincoats to keep the storm at bay. Melody glanced around warily, then finally she crossed the road towards me. I caught a glimpse of fair skin tanned golden-brown and ash-blonde hair, but that was about it. She stopped a few feet away from me, studying me with an expression that was an odd balance of hostile neutrality.

"So, you're the one that saved Lily?" she demanded, her voice carrying an edge of violence that made me equally wary of her motives.

"I wasn't alone, but yes. I saved Lily." I straightened up to my full height and gave her a long, frosty look. Although I had no intention of acting in a hostile manner towards her, she clearly needed something a bit tougher than my usual mannerisms. Tougher was something that I understood. "Our doctor has taken care of her all night. She's going to be fine."

"Good." Though she was almost a hand span shorter than me, Melody did not look intimidated in the least. She folded her arms and met my eye with unwavering confidence. "As soon as she's well enough to walk, I want you to send her home."

"She's free to go any time she chooses, so long as she's sober enough to make the trek safely." I shrugged, but didn't break eye-contact. I sensed in some instinctive way that there was a contest happening, and the first of us to look away would be the loser. "My people stay with me because they choose to, Melody. Because I offer them protection, and all I ask in return is their best efforts to help the group survive. No one in my company is a prisoner."

The girl's gaze wavered. Finally, she blinked and looked at Jasmine. The two exchanged a few whispered words, then she looked at me with great interest. "Why are you going south?"

"Because there are monsters coming from the ruins of Hamilton," I told her bluntly, making no attempt to sugarcoat the truth. "They've already killed our friends, and members of our group. One of them was a girl, the same age as Jasmine and Lily. The monsters tore out her throat, and she bled to death in her uncle's arms. I have no intention of staying around to let them kill anyone else."

"Monsters?" Jasmine gasped and looked at Melody with wide eyes. Solomon looked back and forth between them nervously, hugging himself. Suddenly, all three of them looked at Priyanka, who just nodded.

"Bad monsters. Bitey. Screamy. Maddy told me." Priya cuddled up against me, and hid her face against my shoulder. "Mama protect us. Take us far, far away from the bad monsters."

"Have you guys ever seen a pig?" I asked, looking back and forth between the three young faces in front of me. Jasmine and Solomon shook their heads, but Melody nodded hesitantly.

"Only once," she said, her voice dropping to a quiet, almost reverent tone. "It chased me for half a day before I managed to lose it."

"Well, these new monsters, they're like that... except they look like people." I hugged Priya's wet little body against me, stroking the back of her hooded head. "They have arms and legs, and they can run as fast as you or I if they want to. They hunt in packs, and if they catch you they'll rip you to shreds." I glanced up and caught Melody's eye. "I outran a whole pack of them to get back to my family so I could lead them away from danger, and I'd do it again in a heartbeat."

"Is true," Priya echoed, backing up my story. "Mama ran and ran, so far and so fast! And Mama saved me and Baba from the bad mans that wanted to make us dead, too. Mama is very brave." She tilted her head back and looked up at me with those enormous eyes of hers. "Mama teach me to be like her, yes?"

"I don't think I have to teach you anything, little miss." I grinned and gave her a playful squeeze. "Did you tell your friends about the time that *you* fought a pig?"

The three youngsters gasped in surprise. Priya shook her head, looking a little embarrassed. "No... not yet. Too busy."

"Well, why don't you go tell them about it?" I suggested, gently releasing her from my grasp. "I need to go get a few people to come and see what we can retrieve out of this store, before the rain gets in and ruins everything." I shifted my gaze to Melody and the others, and gave them a smile that was a little bit playful and a little bit friendly. "As for you lot... we're leaving town as soon as we're done at the radio station. If you want to join us, then you're welcome to."

None of them said anything, so I turned and walked away. It was a risk, but a calculated one. Michael was right about Priya; she'd survived for ten years without me, and she'd clearly managed to forge some kind of bond with the little pack of ragamuffins. The likelihood that her friends would hurt her was slim, and even if they tried... well, I'd already learned that she could hold her own. It was hard for me to detach myself emotionally, but intellectually I knew it was for the best.

I made it almost twenty metres back towards our base of operations before I heard running footsteps coming up behind me.

"Hey, wait up!"

I turned back, and saw the four teens running after me, their feet splashing wildly through the puddles. A few metres away, they skidded to a halt. The other three looked at Melody, who in turn looked at me.

"We'll help," she said simply.

"With what?" I enquired, lifting an eyebrow.

"With the shop," she replied, gesturing back towards the Salvation Army store. "If we're going to come with you, then we need to contribute somehow. That's how it works, right?"

It took a moment before her meaning sunk in, but once it did I felt a slow smile creeping across my face. I nodded. "Yep, that's right. Are you sure about this, though? Tokoroa is your home."

"It's not our home," Melody said sharply, shaking her head. "Our home is wherever our group is, and my group wants to go with yours." She paused for a second, and gave me the tiniest of smiles. "And I want to go with you. Just for a while, though. I mean, if anything happens and we decide that we don't like it, then we're gone."

"Like I said, any member of my group is free to go at any time." I shrugged and gave her a smile. "While you're with my group, you're going to need to follow my commands. I won't ask you to do anything that I wouldn't do myself, ever. But, I need to know that I can rely on you to do what I tell you to the best of your abilities. Can you do that?"

Melody lowered her head and thought it over for a moment, then she nodded the affirmative. "Yeah. Yeah, we can do that. I can't promise we'll like it, but we'll do it."

"Good." I grinned at her, and beckoned for the group to follow me. "Come on, then! We've got lots of work to do, and not much time to do it in."

\*\*\*

By midday, we'd cleared out most of the Salvation Army store, and brought anything that was salvageable back to the office block where our own little army waited for us. There would be no salvation for any of us except that which we made ourselves, but we were certainly grateful for the stuff.

Introductions were made between our newcomers and the rest of the group. To my surprise, it was Jasmine that meshed with the rest of the group most swiftly; Melody was wary and standoffish, and Solomon was so quiet that I wondered if he was mute.

It was Priyanka that really came into her own, though. She spent the entire morning darting back and forth between the new members and the old, and I could practically see her carefully weaving a web of understanding between them like an artisan creating a complex tapestry. I was grateful for it, too; I spent most of the morning feeling mildly queasy, and it only started to pass by lunchtime.

Everyone gathered in the little kitchen for lunch. There weren't enough seats, so we stood or sat around chatting while we ate. Priya sat with her new friends in a tight circle, talking softly amongst themselves. I stood by Michael, discreetly watching them and keeping to myself.

"Thank you."

The voice was so sudden and unexpected that it made me jump. I glanced over, and realised that Gavin had snuck up beside us undetected.

"For what?" I asked, genuinely surprised by the gratitude.

"For taking us in," he said quietly. His eye swivelled to the children, and he gestured towards them with a tilt of his chin. "For having the patience to take them in. I know it's not easy."

"It's not meant to be easy," I answered, slowly shaking my head. "It's meant to be bloody hard. I knew that when I took this mission on. You don't decide to rebuild a broken world and expect anything to be easy. We are going to have to fight tooth and nail for every little thing, just like we have for the last ten years. But, do you know what the difference is?"

"Yes." He gave me a lopsided smile, and nodded. "Now we get to do it together."

"Exactly." I made a broad gesture towards the people all around us. "And every one of these souls is going to fight at our side. With teamwork and effort, we can achieve anything."

"Speaking of which," he said, changing the subject. "The radio station is up and running. We just need to record a message to put on infinite loop. I think you should be the one to record it."

"Oh yeah, that's not terrifying at all. My voice on record for all eternity, broadcasting into the ether." I heaved a dramatic sigh, then put my plate down on the table with the others. "Let's go get this done, then."

He nodded and led the way to the door, with Michael and me following him. For reasons unknown, several of the others decided to join us. By the time we'd reached the radio station and Gavin had helped me get settled into the recording booth, our entire group was crowded around outside the open door, jostling one another to make sure they could hear me. Every single one of them. The only person missing was Doctor Cross, who refused to leave Lily's side.

It was an unfamiliar feeling, knowing that there were so many pairs of eyes focused on my every move, and ears hanging on my word. I should have been used to it by now, but I didn't think I ever would be. It was strange and alien, but it was also a powerful feeling. With that thought in mind, I took a deep breath and nodded to Gavin. He patted my shoulder reassuringly, and pressed the button that set the big microphone in front of me recording.

"Survivors of New Zealand, heed my call," I said slowly, clearly, and with as much confidence as I could project. "The virus has mutated. As I speak, there are new infected spreading across the Waikato region. They came from Hamilton, but they are not stopping there.

"I implore you to leave your homes and head south. I repeat, head south. If you are currently north of Hamilton, exercise extreme caution when you're travelling through the Waikato. Assume that you'll never be able to return, and pack accordingly. Bring as much food and water as you can, along with anything that you hold dear.

"The mutants are pack hunters, and are recognisable by their distinctive howl. Carry a weapon at all times. If you are attacked, aim for the legs and cripple it. Then, you must set it alight, otherwise it will keep attacking you. Usual methods are ineffective. Fire is the only sure way to destroy them.

"My name is Sandrine McDermott. I am the leader of a large group. There is safety in numbers, so we will welcome anyone who comes to us in peace. We will be leaving from Tokoroa and heading south along State Highway 32 past the western shore of Lake Taupo, and then we will follow State Highway 1 south from Turangi. If you wish to join us, meet us along this route.

"If you're thinking of ambushing us, then I strongly advise against it. We are well-armed, well-trained, and we will defend ourselves.

"If you are uncertain whether to join us or not, then know this: our group has formed with one purpose, and that is friendship. We have numerous women and children with us, and every member of my group will fight to the death to protect any other member. We have no interest in power or material gain, only in helping our friends to stay happy and healthy.

"This message was set four days after the first full moon of winter, and will play on an indefinite loop. For further updates, please scan the nearby frequencies."

I glanced at Gavin and indicated for him to stop the recording. He did so, then he stood back and gave me a long, thoughtful look. Behind him, I heard faint murmuring from the others, then something happened that I didn't expect. Someone started clapping. I couldn't see who it was, but it spread like wildfire through the group. Before I quite knew what was happening, anything else I might have said was drowned out in a sea of applause.

# Chapter Twenty

We left Tokoroa at the crack of dawn the next morning, or what passed for it when the sky was perpetually clouded with rain. Before we moved off, I paused to do a headcount and check everyone's name off against a list that I'd written for myself the night before. There were so many people with us now that it was the only way I could keep track.

Michael and I led the way, to no one's great surprise. At some point during the journey, it had just sort of been assumed that was our position and that we were the trailblazers for the rest of the group. In the back seat, Melody and Solomon sat staring out the windows, leaving Priyanka to natter away happily between them. She'd already adapted to life on the road, but it would take the newcomers time to get used to it.

A few hours into the journey, I caught Michael watching me and shot him a curious look. "What?"

"You're scowling again," he pointed out. "What's on your mind now?"

"Oh." I indulged myself in a long, deep sigh, then I shrugged helplessly. "I'm worried about gas, to be frank. I estimate we've only got eight, maybe nine days of fuel left. We've been incredibly lucky so far in terms of fuel, but I don't think it's going to last. Hell, even with Zain working on the trucks every night, we can't guarantee that they'll last forever, either."

"So if that happens, we get out and walk," he suggested with a shrug.

"Even the little kids? The wounded? Doc?" I replied, staring thoughtfully at the road in front of me as I guided the Hilux forward. "No… we need to start thinking about ways to conserve fuel. Or better yet, alternatives to petrol. It's not so bad up here, but petrol was starting to get scarce last time I was down south."

"Hmm…" Michael sat back, and went silent for a couple of minutes while he thought it over. Suddenly, he glanced at me again. "What about propane?"

"What about it?" I asked, confused.

"Well, propane doesn't expire, right?" he answered, his brow furrowed in thought. "And I remember there being a big conservationist movement before the plague, dedicated to converting cars from petrol and diesel to natural gas. Could we do the same thing?"

This time, it was my turn to stop and think about it. I hadn't even considered the possibility. I picked up my radio with my free hand, and thumbed the receiver. "Zain? Come in Zain?"

A few seconds later, I received a reply. "I'm here. What is it?"

I glanced at Michael, then looked back out at the road in front of us. "Is it possible to convert a car to run on natural gas? Propane?"

"It's theoretically possible to convert a car to run on just about any fuel, with the right tools and parts," he replied. "Why do you ask?"

"Because I want you to start looking for the right tools and parts whenever you can," I answered. "Our supply of petrol is running low, and I'm sure I don't need to tell you how hard it's getting to find more."

There was silence for a few seconds, then his voice came back on the line. "I can't guarantee anything, but I'll try. We'll need to search every workshop and auto parts store that we pass. Alternately, we may want to consider going back to basics."

"What do you mean?" I asked.

"Horses," he replied. "Or even cows, if we can train them to pull a cart. Draft animals."

"Well, what was good enough for our ancestors is good enough for us," I commented, nodding thoughtfully. "All right, let's keep both of these ideas in mind. If anyone else has any suggestions, please bring them to me, even if they're far-fetched."

"We should build a rocket car!" Skylar suggested brightly. I sighed and rolled my eyes heavenwards.

"Not quite that far-fetched," I said dryly. "Put your thinking caps on, guys. We'll talk later."

***

That day passed without incident as we followed the road southwards, and so did the ones after that. For five days, we followed the winding path southwards, through landscape that gradually changed around us with every kilometre. The rolling hills of the Waikato became steeper and less forgiving, but we managed to find a path even when the road was impassable. It wasn't until an hour before sunset on the sixth day that we encountered a real problem. I slammed on the brakes and stared at the road in front of me, uncertain how to react to what I was seeing. Michael glanced up from his book, and uttered a few choice words under his breath.

"How in the world are we going to get through there?" he asked, leaning forward to stare into the dense brush blocking what had once been the road. "Do we need to backtrack?"

"If we backtrack, we'll lose days," I said, shaking my head. "No, let's at least give this a chance. Call the others to a halt and have them start setting up a base camp here. We need to get out and scout the area before it gets dark."

Michael grunted a non-verbal agreement and grabbed the radio to do just that. While he was busy, I put the Hilux in park and pulled up my hood to protect me from the incessant rain.

"What about us?" Melody asked from the back seat, her sharp voice cutting through my thoughts like a hot knife.

I glanced back at her, studying her face in the gloom. "You want to help me scout?"

"Why not?" Melody shrugged, obviously trying to look nonchalant to disguise her tension. "We've been on our own for years without you; I'm pretty sure we can handle ourselves."

"Your age has nothing to do with it." I winked at her, and jerked a thumb towards the window. "I'm just surprised that you'd volunteer to get wet. If you guys want to come along, you're more than welcome."

"Oh." There was a long pause, then she nodded firmly. "Well, we're coming."

"Okay." I glanced at Michael, who had paused in his conversation to look at me. "I'm taking these guys with me; you stay here and help with setting up camp."

"You got it." He leaned over and planted a kiss on my cheek, then resumed his conversation.

I threw open my door and slid out from behind the wheel. The ground beneath me felt moist and squishy; an odd combination of thick mud and spongy leaf-litter layered the old tar seal. I tested it a couple of times with my foot before I committed my full weight to it; it was a bit slippery, but it didn't give out when I stood on it. By the time I was ready, Melody, Solomon, and Priya had bundled themselves up and joined me.

"I don't much care for this weather," I said, pausing to look up at the sky. "It's raining too much. If it doesn't stop soon, then we may have to worry about flooding."

"I think we've still got a bit of leeway," Melody answered, following my gaze up to the clouds. "But, you're right. It smells dangerous."

"Exactly." We both stood silently for a few moments to consider the possibilities, then I sighed and shook my head. "Let's try to find somewhere elevated for them to pitch camp first of all. I'd hate to sleep in this mud."

"That way," Melody said, pointing westwards. "The land slopes up a little. Let's check beyond those bushes."

"Good call." I nodded my approval, then I reached back to grab my shotgun from its resting place and slammed the door behind me. "I'll take the lead. Melody, you watch my left flank. Priya, watch the right. Solomon, you keep an eye on our rear. Got it?"

"Yes, Mama," Priya agreed brightly.

I glanced at her, and saw that she already had her little pistol in hand, and was holding it exactly the way Michael had shown her. After her encounter with the pig, I felt confident that she could handle it. I shifted my gaze to Solomon, who just nodded silently. That was about as much as I was likely to get out of him, so I took it at face value. Shifting my shotgun into the offensive position, I eased myself down into a crouch and led the way into the brush.

Thorns grabbed at my sleeves as I forced my way between the bushes, but the leather kept them from biting my skin. With careful use of my forearm, I pushed my way through, and came out the other side into long, wild grasses. The landscape had begun to change from the Waikato region's lush greenery into the tough, mountainous foliage of the central plateau; I'd seen it a thousand times before, but I could see that the kids were less confident in unfamiliar territory.

"Up here," I said, guiding my charges deeper into the brush. A few pathetic trees clung to the slope, but the grass was tough and demanding, and sucked away what little nutrients they might have been able to find. Past the trees, a small clearing opened up, framed by more bushes and grass but otherwise clear; the ground was firm beneath my feet, and I felt stone under the leaf litter.

"There's a stream over there," Melody said, pointing to our left.

"Good," I replied. "That'll help us keep our water reserves going. Priya, you and Solomon head back to the convoy. Tell Michael to send people up here to cut back the brush, so we can set up camp here."

"Okies!" Priya agreed on behalf of both of them. Without another word, she turned and scampered away, Solomon hot on her heels.

I lowered my shotgun, and looked at Melody. This was the first chance we'd had to be alone together, so it seemed like a good chance to get a feel for exactly how much she knew. "Tell me what you see here."

The girl looked at me, her sea-green eyes unreadable. "What?"

"I need to know how much you know," I explained bluntly. "So, humour me. Look around, and tell me what you see."

Melody went quiet then, but her expression changed from defensive to thoughtful. When she finally spoke again, her voice was soft and even. "I see a steady supply of fresh water, with a good, solid wall of foliage that should block the wind from most directions. It's an elevated position, so it should be easily defensible. I can hear the birds singing in those trees over there, so there aren't any predators around. If there were, they wouldn't be singing."

"Good." I nodded my approval. "What else?"

Melody paused again, then pointed towards northern edge of the clearing. "Those rocks should also give us some more shelter. They look stable enough to climb on, so if we can get up there we should be able to scout the road ahead."

"Perfect." I smiled at her, and nodded towards the rocks. "Do you want to lead the way?"

She set off without a word, leaving me to follow along behind her. I did so, after taking a moment to return my shotgun to its normal place across my back. The afternoon chorus was loud enough that we'd know long in advance if anything was coming our way.

A few bold fantails danced across the trail as we slipped back into the brush, completely unafraid of our intrusion. The sight of them made me smile; I remembered a time when fantails had been endangered, thanks to humans destroying their habitat. If there was one good thing about the end of mankind, it was the fact that the rest of nature's children had a chance to flourish again.

Melody led me around the outside of the clearing until we reached the rock face. On closer examination, I saw that it was compiled of a single enormous boulder, surrounded by a dozen smaller ones of assorted sizes. She hopped up onto the lowest one, and nimbly climbed from one to the other until she reached the top of biggest. A second later, I joined her. We stood carefully, side by side, and stared towards the south.

"I can barely see the road," Melody admitted. "The bushes have managed to grow on the concrete. We can probably cut them back, I guess..." For the first time, she paused and looked at me uncertainly.

"We can," I said with as much confidence as I could muster. "It's not going to be easy, but we can do it."

"What are you going to do?" Melody asked. The question surprised me, and forced me to stop and think.

"I'm going to put it to the vote tonight," I said at last. "We have two choices. We can either backtrack and head south through Taupo, or we can cut our way through here. It's a decision that's going to affect everyone, so everyone should have their chance to have a say. In the meantime, let's go circle the camp and make sure there's nothing to worry about."

Melody nodded her agreement, and followed me back down to ground level. By the time we'd finished inspecting the surrounding area thoroughly enough to feel safe, Michael and the others had cut a path through the scrub from the road up to our campsite. He already had people standing guard, so Melody and I joined in with the setup instead.

By the time night fell, we had our camp ready. There were a couple of individual tents now, but most of us still slept under the roof of the giant tarpaulin. It wasn't all that comfortable, but it was good enough. I was tired and anxious to get to bed, but too stubborn to take a break when there was work to be done.

Rebecca and Elly were still recovering, so we decided to err on the side of caution. We put them straight to bed in one of the tents, with as many extra blankets as we could spare. With her primary helper out of the running, poor Skye was rushed off her feet trying to get dinner ready. I volunteered my own services to help her, and Melody's as well. She didn't complain. Priya soon joined us, and the extra hands were welcome.

Dinner was simple, but nutritious and filling. Once they'd eaten, we sent the younger kids off to bed, and gathered everyone else around the fire to discuss the matter of the road. I explained what we'd seen, and then put it to the vote. To my surprise, no one wanted to backtrack through Taupo. It turned out that they'd rather put in days of hard labour cutting a path than risk unknown danger.

After that, we sent everyone off about their duties. We were gradually falling into a routine, where every person knew what their task was in the group. Michael, Hemi, and a few of the other Waikato Iwi men organised the watch rotation amongst themselves, while Zain, Ryan, and I went down to check the cars as best we could by torchlight. By the time we got back, everyone was turning in for the night.

As soon as Michael spotted me, he finished his conversation and hurried over to greet me. "Hey there, pretty lady."

"Hey, yourself." I returned the greeting, and gave him a long look. "What are you grinning about?"

"We finally have enough people on the watch roster that we can swap people in and out," he answered, grinning even wider. "That means people can have a full night's sleep when it's their turn to have a night off."

"Oh, yeah?" I raised a brow, amused by his enthusiasm. "That's good, I guess."

"No, it's great!" Suddenly, he laughed and grabbed me by the waist to draw me into a hug. "The other guys insisted that we take the first night off."

This time, both my brows shot up. "Oh? So we get a full night's sleep? Tonight?"

"Damn straight." He planted a kiss on my lips, then pushed me back and grinned at me. "I don't know about you, but it feels like I haven't had a solid night's sleep in forever. Go get ready for bed. Long drop's over there, about five meters past that big rock."

"I feel like I should be concerned that you're so excited about getting me into bed, yet your only interest is sleep," I commented dryly.

Michael laughed and spun me around, pointing me towards the makeshift facilities. "I know! Who would have guessed? Oh well. Go pee, then come and have a cuddle."

"Yes sir, Officer Chan, sir!" I gave a mock salute, and headed off to do just that.

By the time I'd finished doing my business and returned to camp, Michael had already stripped down to his underwear, hung his clothing up to dry overnight, and snuggled down in our communal nest of blankets. I'd gotten used to the lack of privacy, and didn't even think twice about stripping down to my underwear to join him. I hung up my coat and clothes, dried myself off on a towel, and snuggled down beside him.

Michael put his arms around me and drew me in against his warmth. That, combined with Alfred sleeping at our feet like a big, fur-covered space heater, left me quite warm and comfortable despite the weather and the stone beneath the tarp. I closed my eyes, buried my face in the curve of Michael's neck, and was asleep before I had time for any other thoughts.

* * *

The dawn chorus woke me the next morning, though it was so dark that I could barely even tell that it was daybreak. Michael was sound asleep, and didn't even stir when I carefully extracted myself from his embrace. Alfred lifted his head and whined in greeting, his tail thumping happily against the ground. I held my finger to my lip playfully, as if that would keep the dog quiet. Regardless, he seemed to understand well enough. He put his head back down on Michael's foot, and went right back to sleep.

I indulged myself in a stretch, and looked around the camp. Sleeping bodies surrounded me in the early morning gloom; the only sounds were birdsong, rain, and snores. I smiled to myself as I reached up and plucked my clothing from the lines strung overhead. My pants were still damp around the ankles, but Michael had definitely been right about that coat. It did an admirable job of keeping me mostly dry from the knees up.

I'd just finished pulling on my shirt and trousers when a soft cry split the peace. I jumped and spun around, but there was only silence again. Then, the doctor's tent flicked open, and Stuart looked out. He spotted me, and beckoned me over.

"Lily's awake," he explained quietly once I was close enough to hear him without him having to wake the entire camp. I glanced past him, and saw the twins clinging together inside the tent.

I took a deep breath and nodded. "I'll talk to her."

Doctor Cross absently adjusted his new spectacles, looking relieved. "I'll go find Gavin. I think he'll want to know."

"Good plan," I agreed. I waved him off, and then I slipped into the tent to take his place. There weren't many places to sit, so I just eased myself down to sit cross-legged on the pile of blankets that had probably been Stuart's bed. Both of the girls looked up at me, and I found myself wondering how on earth I was supposed to tell them apart. They were identical in every way, except for their strength of spirit.

Suddenly, I realised that was exactly how I could tell them apart. I could see fear in Lily's eyes, but none in Jasmine's.

"Good morning, Lily," I said softly, keeping my voice as low and unthreatening as possible. "I know you're scared, so you just take as much time as you need, okay? Gavin's coming, and I'm pretty sure Melody will be here soon, too. All your friends are here, and you're safe."

The girl said nothing. Jasmine leaned down and whispered something in her ear in a language I didn't understand, then hugged her tightly. Lily nodded silently, and buried her face in her sister's shoulder. It wasn't hard to guess that she was feeling just the way I had when I'd woken up with Michael's group for the first time, so I didn't push her. I just sat back and waited.

Sure enough, less than a minute later the tent flap opened and Gavin hurried inside, with Melody hot on his heels. I just sat nearby and watched while the four of them reunited. Tears were shed, more words were whispered, and I was ignored for quite some time. It was fine, though. I completely understood. Eventually, my patience was rewarded.

"Lil, this is Sandy. She saved your life."

My attention snapped back to the present when I realised that someone was trying to introduce me. I lifted my head, smiled, and waved. It was Gavin, of course. No surprise there. He hugged the three girls one more time, and then he shoved himself back and plopped down on the bedding beside me with a long sigh of relief.

"I told you she'd be okay," I said, trying to reassure him.

"I know, I know." He gave me a lopsided smile, and shrugged sheepishly. "You'll understand once you're a parent. You always worry, even when they're all grown up, no matter how smart and capable they are. I know all of my kids can take care of themselves, but how I feel isn't always rational."

"I think I understand," I replied thoughtfully. "It's like my mum used to say: we were always going to be her babies. It's human nature. The bond between parent and child is nearly unbreakable, even if they're not technically your children."

"Yeah, that's exactly it." He nodded his agreement, watching the three girls talking softly amongst themselves. Melody shot him a dark look, but said nothing. I found myself grinning in spite of everything.

"And that's exactly the same look I used to give my mum when she said that kind of thing," I commented. This time, her glare was directed at me. I held my hands up in self-defence, struggling not to laugh. "Sorry, but it's true. Anyway – Lily, you're with my group. We're all heading south, to find safer territory down near Wellington. I need to go get everyone out of bed. Is there anything I can get you?"

Lily just stared at me with enormous eyes, as if I'd asked her to jump out of an aeroplane. Jasmine sighed and shook her head. "No, thank you. Me and Mel will take care of her."

"All right," I agreed. "I'll leave you guys to it, but if you need anything you can call any one of us, okay?"

The girls just nodded, and turned their attention back to Lily. I took that as my cue to leave. Gavin followed me out of the tent, and trailed after me as I went off to get breakfast cooking. I found Skylar already there, in the process of making rice porridge. I knelt down beside her, and began unpacking our eclectic collection of bowls and cutlery from the plastic packing crate that we carried it in.

"Morning," she said cheerfully. "You two are up early. Did I miss something exciting?"

"Lily's awake," I explained, setting the bowls down on the tarp beside me. I flipped the plastic crate upside down, and then put the bowls back on top of it to use it as a table. "She's a bit freaked out, but she's going to be fine."

"Yeah, just give her time," Skye agreed pleasantly. She grabbed a jar of sugar out of the food stores, and chipped a generous chunk off the solidified granules inside. It went into the pot of porridge, then she looked over at me again. "So, what's the plan now? You do have a plan, right?"

"I always have a plan," I replied, matching her playful tone. "I'm leaving the wounded and ill here with a couple of guards while the rest of us get our hands dirty and try to clear the path. I estimate that we're only about ten kilometres from the next town, so there can't be that much of this. In the meantime, I want you and Anahera to take the kids down to that stream we saw, and see if you can catch any fish. We're probably going to be stuck here for a couple of days, so we may as well make the most of it."

I expected her to protest about being left behind, but for once Skylar just accepted my instructions without question.

"Just promise me that you won't over-exert yourself again," she demanded, fixing me with a dark look. "If I hear about you fainting because you're pushing yourself too hard, I'm going to go up there and drag you back by the ear."

"Yes, ma'am!" I agreed, sketching a salute. Both she and Gavin laughed. I eased myself back to my feet then, and set about the arduous businesses of waking people that really didn't want to have to get out of bed. I couldn't blame them, but that didn't mean I was going to show any mercy. There was a lot of work to be done, and every day we were on the road was a day closer to winter without permanent shelter and a steady supply of food.

# Chapter Twenty-One

My estimate, as it turned out, was a bit too generous. It took us eight whole days to clear the road southwards, even with every able-bodied person on the job from dawn 'til dusk. Luckily for us, the surrounding area turned out to be rich with wild game, and we found plenty of fish, eels, and ducks to pad out the supplies we'd brought with us.

Rather than waste fuel driving the trucks forward a couple of kilometres a day and going through all the effort of having to tear our camp down and set it up again, we left our camp set up on the ridge beside the stream. Each morning, the eight people chosen to work on clearing the road climbed on the bikes in pairs, drove out to the end of the road, and spent the day hacking back brush in the incessant rain. The respite gave Elly and Rebecca time to finish recovering from their colds, and also gave everyone a much-needed break from the tedium of travel.

Clearing the road was long, filthy, and unpleasant work, so we drew up a roster to try and give everyone some time off every couple of days. Compared to labouring in the mud, watching the camp or helping to collect food was practically a holiday.

Michael and I were in the road-clearing gang on the ninth day, when we finally broke through to the other side. A shout went up from the pair sent to scout ahead and plan our path, and then a second later Hemi came rushing back with the biggest grin on his face.

"We're through!" he exclaimed, waving his arms. "Just another ten meters or so, and then it's clear sailing from here on out!" He paused to gulp down an excited breath, and then clarified his meaning. "Well, not totally clear sailing. I mean, it's just a mud track, but there's no plant life growing on it. That's an improvement."

"Amen to that," I agreed, standing up straight to stretch my back. "Grab one of the bikes and head back to the campsite. Tell them it's time to go. By the time they finish packing up, we'll be just about finished here, I reckon."

Hemi nodded and raced off, leaving the rest of us to finish clearing the path. It was almost midday by the time the convoy was ready to move, and it took another hour before the trucks caught up to us. Exhausted, sopping wet, and splattered with mud from head to toe, we stripped off our soiled outerwear and tumbled into the seats reserved for us. The people who had been on guard duty back at camp piled out and grabbed the bikes, then we were back on the road again.

Progress was slow, but steady. The mud was so deep that at times we had to get out and push one of the trucks clear. Each time that happened, I worried that we were about to lose one of our precious vehicles, but by some miracle we managed to keep going. By mid-afternoon, we were all cold, filthy, and miserable, and more than one of us was starting to show symptoms of catching the 'flu.

"We're going to need to think about stopping somewhere for a couple of days, to let everyone rest up," I commented to Michael as we huddled in the back seat of the Hilux together, with Priya contentedly napping in the front.

Anahera, in the driver's seat, made a soft sound of agreement. "I think the group is desperate for it. Even you and I are exhausted, though we've both been trying to hide it. Tempers are starting to flare up. Yesterday at lunch, your friend Ryan exchanged heated words with my son. I was genuinely afraid that it was going to come to blows."

I swore softly beneath my breath. "I'll have a word with them when we make camp. We can't have infighting; it'll tear the group apart."

"Don't worry, I already handled it," Anahera replied, a faint, amused smile dancing across her lips. "I don't think they'll be doing that again any time soon. Anyway, I believe that we will reach Tokaanu by nightfall. Tokaanu is a lovely town. It would be a good place to stop and rest for a while."

"You know the area?" I asked, my annoyance melting into curiosity.

"As a matter of fact, yes," she said. "My grandparents lived there. Tokaanu was my home away from home when I was a child. It's a geothermal area, with rich fishing. We should be quite comfortable for a while."

"Geothermal?" I sat up straight, suddenly very interested. "You mean, hot springs?"

"Oh yes," she replied, laughing. "There are many hot springs in the area, along with mud pools, geysers, and some of the most beautiful rainbow trout you'll ever lay eyes on. My people have been going there for centuries to bathe in the springs. I think you'll like it, Sandrine."

"Oh, I know I'll like it," I answered dryly. "We've been half-arsed bathing in an icy stream for the last week and some. A soak in a hot spring sounds like heaven."

"Agreed!" Michael commented playfully. "You're starting to smell like Alfred."

I knew better than to take him seriously, so I just laughed right along with him.

*** 

We travelled southwards for the rest of the day. The heavy bush on either side of the road made it hard to judge distances. The road wound around overhangs and ledges, up steep hills and down slopes. Every so often, there was a gap in the foliage that revealed a glimpse of rolling green hills in the distance, dotted with flocks of sheep clustered together for protection against the weather.

Then, suddenly, between one glance and the next, the landscape changed. Gone were the rolling hills, replaced by a broad, sparkling expanse of water that could only be Lake Taupo.

"We must be getting close," I commented, as much to myself as to anyone else.

"We are," Anahera agreed. I glanced at her, and saw a troubled look on her face. "I haven't been here since before the plague, but I recognise the lay of the land. There should be a thermal resort along this road a few more kilometres – assuming it's still there."

Sensing her disquiet, I leaned forward to rest my hand on her shoulder. "We can keep on driving, if you want. I… understand. I'm not sure I could ever go back home. Not now."

"No, our people need to rest, and this area is perfect for it." Anahera shook her head, and straightened her shoulders. "My grandparents would have wanted us to take advantage of the hospitality that Aotearoa has to offer us, even if they're not here to join us. This is our land now, and we must not be afraid of where the road takes us."

"Amen to that," I agreed quietly, settling back in my seat. We all fell into silence after that, each of us alone with our thoughts. I felt Michael's hand close over mine, but there was no need for verbal communication. The touch said enough. I leaned against his shoulder, and stared out the window at the bush on the lakeside of the road.

Eventually, the bush vanished and was replaced by a carpet of thick grass along the edge of the lake. As I watched, a flock of birds exploded out of the reeds and flew up high, startled by the noise of our engines. I watched them until I could no longer see them, then I resumed staring at the lake.

"It's beautiful, isn't it?" Michael said softly, his lips right beside my ear. "Sometimes I forget just how lovely our world really is."

"Yeah," I agreed, snuggling up against him. "When you get too focused on the details, you can miss the magnificence of the whole picture."

Michael made a noise of agreement and nodded, but he said nothing.

Priya stirred in the front seat and looked around, rubbing her eyes sleepily. She yawned, then turned and looked at me expectantly. "Mama, why?"

"Huh?" I shot a confused look at her. "Why what, honey?"

"Why the trees?" She wrinkled her nose up, and pointed at a the road ahead of us. "They not be green."

"Oh, those beech trees over there?" I found myself smiling at her inquisitiveness. "The colour is called orange."

She turned back and stared at me with those enormous eyes, the way only she could. "But why?"

"Why what?"

"Why orange!" she exclaimed, making a gesture of frustration. "Trees are green, not orange."

"Oh." I paused, and glanced back at the trees. "It's because they're deciduous, Priya. That means their leaves die in autumn, and then grow again in spring. Haven't you seen that before?"

"Oooo." She nodded slowly, making a long, drawn-out sound of understanding. "Yes, have seen, but I never knew why. I wanted to know."

"That's okay." I smiled at her, trying to reassure her. "You can ask any time you see something you don't understand. Most trees here are evergreen – their leaves don't fall off in winter time. But some are deciduous, like those ones. The leaves will grow back again in spring. If you like, I can ask Doctor Cross to teach you about it in his lesson plan."

"Yes, I want to learn," she agreed, nodding firmly.

"And he should have some time," Anahera spoke up suddenly, distracting us, "because we're here."

"We are?" I sat forward, and looked over her shoulder as she eased the Hilux off the road, into the parking lot of a low, rambling building in surprisingly good condition. Warning bells went off inside my head. "Someone's been living here, Ana. Look – that hole in the roof has been patched up, and the bushes by the front door have been cut back."

"I'm not surprised," she replied. "It's too prime a location to be completely abandoned. Still, we should check."

"I want you to stay here," I told her. "Michael, you're with me."

The pair of us jumped out of the truck with our weapons at the ready. As soon as the rest of the convoy came to a halt behind us, I gestured for Hemi, Tane, and Iorangi to join us. The five of us headed for the front door together.

Before we could get there, the door opened from within. A tiny old woman shuffled out, ancient and withered with skin like carved wood. She took one look at us, then grunted something inarticulate, made a vague gesture, and vanished back inside.

I froze, uncertain how to respond or what the gesture was supposed to mean. A few seconds later, the old woman stuck her head outside again, and bellowed at us. "Come on, then! It's bloody cold out here! Get in and close the door."

Michael and I exchanged glances. There was a slim possibility that it might have been a trap, but it seemed... unlikely, somehow. I shrugged, and decided to just go with it. Shifting my shotgun into a more casual grip, I headed for the front door and followed the old woman inside.

"And about time," she complained. "Well, this is more people than I've seen in one place for a long time – and led by a woman, to boot." She paused and looked me up and down thoughtfully, but spoke again before I could say anything. "You're that McDermott woman, aren't you?"

"I am," I answered, surprised that she recognised me. "You heard our broadcast, I take it?"

"Aye, aye." The woman made another vague gesture, then turned and shuffled over to the reception desk at the back of the lobby. "Gets a wee bit lonely around these parts, so sometimes I like to see if there's anything on the radio. Lo and behold, my favourite talkback show is gone, replaced by your broadcast. How many rooms are you going to need?"

"Rooms?" I asked in genuine confusion.

She stopped and gave me the kind of look usually reserved for particularly slow children. "Aye, rooms! This is my establishment, and I'm presuming you want to stay and ride out the storm, so you'll need some place to sleep."

"Wait, you're actually running this resort?" I glanced around the lobby, and looked back at my friends. None of them had an answer any more than I did.

"Of course." She heaved a long-suffering sigh, and pulled a thick, dusty guest book out from under the counter. "I don't get many visitors these days, but when I do, I try to be courteous. I expect the same in return. Please provide your own food, and if you make a mess, clean it up. Other than that, you can have the run of the place."

My brow furrowed in concern. "Ma'am... no offense intended, but you don't know us at all. You're just inviting us into your home? We could be thieves, murderers – anything."

"Don't call me 'ma'am', young lady." She gave me another dark look. "You may call me Mrs Swanson, Netty, or Nana, but not 'ma'am'. I'm not running a brothel, here."

"Sorry," I apologised automatically, cringing in spite of myself. I just couldn't help it. The woman had to be in her late eighties or early nineties, but she carried herself with an air of total confidence. "But my question does still stand, Mrs Swanson."

"I'm too damn old to be afraid of anything these days," Netty answered dryly. "I've been running this place for the better part of thirteen years, and no one's lifted a finger against me yet. I doubt you plan to be the first."

"Well, no," I agreed, shifting uncomfortably under her scrutiny. "But... what about the gangs? Haven't they come after you, if you're here all by yourself?"

"Why would they?" Netty shrugged, picked up a pen, and started slowly writing my name in her guest book with hands that trembled with age and infirmity. "I'm everyone's nana. They know that if they ever hurt me, they'll unleash the wrath of every other person in the area on their stupid heads. Now, it was Sandrine, wasn't it? Spell that for me, dear?"

I did as I was told, and spelled out my first name for her. Once that was done, I took a breath and shook my head slowly. "I can hardly believe that you've been on your own here for this long, without anyone taking a shot at you. But... you're right. Now that I've met you, if anyone tried to hurt you I'd kick their backsides all the way to Australia and back."

"Exactly." Netty gave me an uneven smile, and laid one frail finger beside her nose. "Now, the rules of my establishment are simple. You may use any of the facilities, but I expect you to respect my space. Room 25 is mine, so stay out of it. Please attend to your own linens and cooking – I'm your landlord, not your maid. If you want access to consumables, then you're going to need to trade for them."

"Of course," I agreed immediately. "It's been a hard trip from the north, so we were planning to stay for about a week. We were going to send people out to fish and catch game birds, and I'm happy to give some of our catch to you if you'll let us stay that long... and if we can use the hot pools."

"The hot pools are open to everyone, and the same rules apply," Netty replied. "Except, there's one more: anyone that pees in the pool has to drink from the pool."

"Ew. So noted." I wrinkled my nose up, and shook my head. "Is there anywhere dry that we can store our vehicles in the mean time?"

"Aye, there's a big storage shed in the field next door. I'll find the keys." Netty turned to leave, but I stepped forward to stop her.

"Wait," I said quietly, uncomfortable with what I needed to ask but it felt necessary. "Before we agree to stay, we need to check this place is safe. Please, don't be offended, but... we've all seen some horror stories in our time, and we've got small children with us. I can't do anything that puts them at risk. I hope you understand."

"Oh, fine." Netty heaved a long-suffering sigh, and beckoned for me to follow her. "Come along, then. But, your boys can't come into my room! It wouldn't be proper. They'll have to wait outside."

"Agreed." I gave her a smile, and set off after her with my 'boys' hot on my heels.

Inspecting the entire building took most of the time we had left before sunset, but I felt better for it. I'd seen enough horror movies to know that if someone says to keep out of a particular room, it's usually the first place you want to check in case it's full of bodies. Netty's wasn't; she was just old-fashioned, and uncomfortable with the idea of men other than her husband seeing where she slept.

As we spent time together, I grew to like her more and more. She had a harsh, no-nonsense way about her, but underneath that I sensed a kind spirit. She guided us through the passages, and let me spend as much time as I needed inspecting things to ensure my charges would be safe. Eventually, we found ourselves at the rear of the building, where a heavy, fire-stop door blocked the way.

"Through here is the kitchen," she explained. "My joints don't much care for the weather. Would you mind getting the door, dear?"

"Of course," I agreed immediately, stepping past her to put my shoulder against the door. It groaned with age, but swung open reluctantly to reveal a massive, professional-grade kitchen that was very nearly as clean and tidy as the day the world had ended.

"Wow," Hemi breathed, peering over my shoulder. "Skye's going to have a field day in here."

"Just so long as she cleans up after herself!" Netty snapped, shooting a dark look at him. Then she looked back at me, and her expression immediately softened. "I've managed to keep just about everything here in working order, so feel free to use things. If you're staying for a few days, you may want to catch some extra fish and dehydrate them; the dehydrator is right over there."

"Why did a resort have a dehydrator?" I asked curiously, glancing at the machine. "Particularly an industrial-sized one?"

"Oh, that wasn't here originally," she explained, patting my arm in a motherly fashion. "One of the groups passing through brought it to me as a gift. It was their way of thanking me for my hospitality."

"Is that how you've survived all these years by yourself?" I enquired, looking down at her with interest. "I mean, most women I know have only barely made it, usually because they've had groups to protect them."

"Yes." Netty chuckled, slipped her arm through mine, and led me back out of the room. "Gratitude, kindness, and a whole lot of luck. I let people stay here, and they offer me kindness in return. I can see in your eyes that you've already been thinking about what you're going to give me. Everyone looks at me like that."

I stiffened in surprise, but the shock didn't last for long. "You're right," I admitted, laughing. "Well, sort of. I was actually thinking about how I could convince you to leave and come with us when we go."

"Well, it's sweet of you to offer, but I would have to decline. I'm much too old to travel." Netty turned a corner and led me out into a large, open-air courtyard. Around the edge of the room, mature vegetable plants grew in large planter boxes, sheltered from the elements by the walls around them. The centre of the courtyard was dominated by a tiled pool, steaming in the cool, stormy air.

I paused and sniffed, then shot a curious look at the little old lady. "I smell sulphur. Is that a geothermal pool?"

"It is," she replied proudly. "People have been coming here for centuries to bathe in the healing waters. There are less people now, but they still come. Don't spend too long in this pool – it's quite hot, and can make you light-headed. Now, come this way, I'll show you where you can park your vehicles…"

***

Once our inspection was complete, we returned to the vehicles to find everyone waiting anxiously for us to appear. It wasn't until I'd gathered everyone together and explained the situation that they began to relax. Smiles started to appear on people's faces, and I could practically feel the tension lifting away like a palpable weight.

Netty vanished before I could introduce her to everyone, but I couldn't blame her. A crowd of that size must have been intimidating to her. Once the situation had been explained, people drifted off to choose their own rooms, and fetch their things from the convoy. The complex had enough rooms for everyone to have their own space, except for the people that actually wanted to share.

Unsurprisingly, Michael and I were amongst that group. Sometime between posting the lookouts and helping unpack the gear from the convoy, we found ourselves alone together in our room. Michael stuck his head into the attached en suite, then gasped and gave me a wide-eyed look.

"We've got a spa bath in here," he announced, sounding utterly shocked. "And a shower, and our own toilet. This place is like… like…"

"…like a luxury resort?" I finished dryly.

"Yeah!" he exclaimed, as excited as a schoolboy. "No wonder people come here and bribe Netty to let them stay. This place is amazing."

"I know." I sighed, wandering over to lean against his broad back. "It's so warm in here. I read on a pamphlet by the front desk that they've got the pipes running under the building that heat all the rooms naturally. Can you imagine? The room we're standing in right now is heated by water from the heart of a volcano."

Michael stiffened at that comment, then looked back at me with an anxious expression. "Oh, I never thought of it like that. Do you think it's safe?"

"You heard Anahera, and Netty. People have been coming here for centuries, and they're all fine." I grinned at him, and gave him a playful slap on the bottom. "Stop worrying, and go back to thinking about how much fun we're going to have in that spa bath."

His expression instantly brightened. A second later, I found myself swept right off my feet, my startled squeal muffled by enthusiastic kisses.

# Chapter Twenty-Two

When we first arrived at Tokaanu, the plan had been to spend a couple of days. Nearly two weeks later, we were still there. Every time we planned to leave, someone came down with a cold, or we decided that the weather was just too foul, or the latest batch of fish wasn't quite finished drying. Although we still set watches every day and night, nothing bad happened at all. Tokaanu became our oasis, a place to stop and rest in the middle of an arduous journey.

On the thirteenth morning, Anahera and Michael found me down by the lake front pretending to fish. I hadn't even baited the hook, but I needed time to think and it seemed like a valid excuse. I didn't realise they were even there until I felt the dock move ever-so-slightly under someone's foot. I glanced up, and found them both watching me with serious expressions on their faces.

"You heard it too, then?" I asked quietly, tugging my hood forward to keep the rain out of my eyes.

"The talk about settling permanently?" Anahera asked. "Yes, that's why we're here."

"As much as I hate to say it, we need to move on soon," Michael said, easing himself down to sit beside me. "This place is wonderful, but…"

"But we need to keep moving," I finished, turning away from him to stare down into the murky water. "I know. We're still too close to the outbreak. But the question is, do we stay here until spring and then move south, or do we risk it and try to push across the Central Plateau now?"

"We have to go now," Anahera said, her expression dark and serious. "The Plateau gets snow, and if we wait even another day then we may find ourselves trapped here with no way to travel further south. What happens if the mutants reach us while we're trapped here? How would we defend ourselves?"

"We can't." I sighed and rubbed my hand across my forehead. "We need to go south, and try to beat the snow. If we can just make it across the plateau, that'll give us a solid barrier between us and them. How are our supplies looking?"

"Excellent," Anahera replied. "We've caught and preserved enough fish and duck to keep us going for a month if we ration it. Our water reservoirs have been refilled, and Zain managed to find enough parts to convert two of the bikes and one of the trucks to propane. We found a little more usable petrol in a small community down by the lake front, which should keep us going for a while."

"And the guns?" I asked, shifting my gaze to Michael. "Are they still in working order after all this rain?"

"Yes." He nodded and smiled at me. "I've checked them all over, cleaned, and lubricated them, and I'm about ninety percent sure that they shouldn't misfire at inopportune moments."

"That's going to have to do," I decided, starting to rise to my feet. Half way up, something tugged on the line and startled me so much that I ended up falling on my bottom. "Oh damn, I think I caught something!"

"Yes, that happens when you're fishing." Anahera laughed, leaning past me to help me manage the rod. "Relax, give him a little slack, then reel him in slowly."

"But I didn't even bait it!" I protested, horrified. Thank goodness no one impressionable was watching, because my response was a wee bit embarrassing: I tried to shove the rod into her hands. "I can't do this, Ana. You do it."

"Oh no you don't," she said firmly, pushing the rod back into my hands. "Even the children can fish, Sandrine. I know how you feel about hurting animals, but you have to learn sometime. Here, I'll help you. Like this."

Despite my protests, Anahera leaned over my shoulder, and guided my hands through the motions of reeling in the fish with the strength and confidence that she applied to everything she did. Her soft, even tone calmed me down from the verge of panic. Together, we hauled in the fish and pulled the poor, thrashing thing out into the light of day.

"Oh, wow, it's so big!" I cried, feeling a strange combination of horror and pride about what I'd done. "I… please don't make me kill it. I can't. I'm not ready."

"All right, all right." Anahera laughed, grabbing my struggling catch by the line above its mouth. With an expert touch, she put it out of its misery and then held it up for me to see. "This is a beautiful fish, though. It's a rainbow trout. He'll make a delicious dinner for your family tonight."

I took a deep breath to calm my rattled nerves, and let it out as a long, drawn-out sigh. "First thing tomorrow morning, we head south. We better go tell the troops."

***

The announcement was met with an odd mixture of disappointed groans, and excitement. For some, the idea of leaving our little home-away-from-home was depressing; for others, it was just another step in an on-going adventure into the unknown. I wasn't quite sure where I stood, but I knew that it had to be done. Like it or not, we had to go south.

Netty took the announcement with silent stoicism, though I could see the sadness in her eyes. By the time I'd finished answering the inevitable onslaught of questions from my groupmates, she'd vanished from the room. As soon as I could do so politely, I extracted myself from the crowd and headed to her room in search of her.

Half way there, I spotted her shuffling along slowly, one hand on the wall and the other clutching something around her throat.

"Netty?" I called, hurrying to catch up with her. She paused and looked back at me, a haunted expression on her face. It gave me pause, and slowed my approach. Suddenly, I felt a lump in my throat the size of a baseball. "Netty, please come with us. Don't make me leave you here all alone."

"I can't, dear. You know that. At my age, the journey would kill me." The old woman gave me the faintest of smiles, then looked away. "Besides, Tokaanu is my home. I've lived here for ninety-three years. I married my husband here, and buried him here. I raised four children and twelve grandchildren here, and then I buried all of them as well. I want to stay with my family."

I started to protest, but before the words even left my mouth I realised that they were fruitless. She'd made up her mind, and even if I did manage to dissuade her, she'd always regret leaving. My shoulders slumped, and my gaze dropped to the floor. "I… I understand. Is there anything we can do to help before we go? Anything that needs fixing, anything we can leave to make you more comfortable?"

"Just one thing, dear. Take this with you." She smiled and took my hand. I felt the sensation of metal against my palm, and when I looked down at it I saw that she'd given me a locket on a chain, still warm from around her neck. I looked up at her quizzically, and her smile widened. "That trinket belonged to my grandmother, who got it from her grandmother. None of my grandchildren made it through the plague, but I would like to see the tradition continue."

"I would be honoured to take on the tradition for you," I answered, blinking back the tears that threatened my vision. "Thank you, Mrs Swanson."

"The honour is mine, Sandrine McDermott," the old woman replied. Suddenly, I felt her arms around me, and I was drawn into her embrace. "It makes me happy to know that the future of our kind is in the hands of someone like you."

With those words, she released me and shuffled away. Everything that needed saying had already been said. Suddenly, I found myself facing the overwhelming urge to cry. I managed to keep myself together long enough to find Skylar, but only just.

I came up behind her and touched her arm. "Sis, I need a few minutes. Can you get everyone moving?"

She glanced back at me, but something about my expression must have warned her off asking too many questions. She just nodded and shrugged. "Sure, okay."

I couldn't find the words to thank her. I just nodded once, then I turned and fled back to my room. Michael was already there, folding our things and packing them back into our bags. He took one look at my face, and silently held his arms out to me. I ran to him, buried my face in his chest, and wept for what felt like a very long time.

***

It was unusual for our group to do anything in a subdued fashion, but preparing for our departure from Tokaanu was one of those rare times. Even the children seemed to sense that something was not right; no laughter accompanied their play, and everyone's smiles were tinged with sadness. No one suggested that we force the old woman to come with us, even though we hated the idea of leaving her behind. It was her choice, and we had to respect it.

By nightfall, the trucks were freshly fuelled and ready to go, and the bikes were strapped beneath a tarpaulin on a trailer that we'd scavenged from one of the nearby suburbs. The rain still hadn't let up, so it seemed logical to squeeze everyone into the trucks instead. It was a tight fit, but it could be done. The territory we were approaching was rough and dangerous, and the weather would make it even more treacherous.

We ate a quiet dinner, cleaned up after ourselves, and put ourselves to bed. Crying had left me exhausted; I fell asleep quickly, but my sleep was poor and troubled by dark dreams. I woke up early as a result, feeling wrung out and exhausted, but indulging in a hot shower refreshed me. Michael was still sleeping, so I dressed quietly in the bathroom, crept out into the hallway, and closed the door behind me.

Then, I turned around and almost fell over Doctor Cross. He jumped back and peered at me, a confused, sleepy look on his face. "Oh, Ms McDermott. Have you seen my granddaughter?"

"Not since last night," I replied, glancing down the hall towards their room. "Perhaps she went to the kitchen to get a drink?"

"Oh, maybe…" He yawned and rubbed his eye. "I should go get my glasses."

"It's okay, you go back to bed," I reassured him, patting his shoulder. "I'll find her."

"If you insist," he agreed without complaint. I helped guide him back to the right doorway, then headed off towards the kitchen to check for Maddy.

There was no sign of her, or anyone else. It was well before sunrise, so everyone was still fast asleep except for the lookouts on the roof. A quick call to them on the radio confirmed that the little girl hadn't left the complex overnight. Fighting the rising concern in my gut, I headed out to check the pool, the storage rooms, and anywhere else I could think of, but there was no sign of her.

I was on my way back to raise the alarm and start arranging search parties when a strange sound caught my ear. I stopped and listened intently. Someone was crying. A child was crying. The sound was coming from Room 25. Netty's room.

Fear and concern twisted my gut. I raced to the door and tried the handle, half-expecting it to be locked. It wasn't, though. It popped open effortlessly, and the scene I saw was one that I hadn't expected. Maddy was sitting on the floor beside Netty's bed, clinging to the old woman's hand and sobbing like her little heart was breaking.

At first glance it looked like Netty was just sleeping, until I realised that she was too still. The hair on the back of my neck rose as my instincts came to grip with the fact that there was a dead thing in front of me. No, not just a dead thing. A dead person.

"Netty?" I whispered, frozen with shock. My eyes saw things, but my brain didn't want to understand what they meant. There was a prescription vial on the dressing table beside her bed, and a folded slip of paper, but that just confused me. I couldn't bring myself to understand what I was seeing. "Maddy, what... what happened?"

"She called to me," the little girl sobbed, tears rolling down her cheeks. "She called to me in my sleep. She said that she didn't want to die alone."

"No... no, no, no, she can't be dead." Tears welled up in my eyes all over again, but this time they galvanised me into action. I rushed over to the bedside, and leaned down to touch the old woman's cheek. It was still warm, but not as warm as it should have been. I knew right away that she'd been dead for nearly an hour, but that didn't stop me from crying out to her. "Netty! No, you can't do this. What about your family? W-what about—"

My voice caught in my throat, and came out as a choked sob. Maddy grabbed me while I was close to her, and clung to me as though desperate for contact with the living. I put my arms around her and picked her up, but when I tried to carry her out of the room she wailed in protest.

"No!" she cried, hitting my shoulder with her little fist. "No, no, not yet! I promised I wouldn't leave her alone!"

"You already fulfilled that promise, honey. She's already gone." I struggled to keep hold of her, but she was a growing girl and weighed more than I could comfortably lift. I gave up and set her back on her feet.

She promptly raced back over to Netty's bedside, and threw herself back down beside her. "No, she's still here. I can see her, standing by the door! I promised that I'd stay until she'd left!"

"By the... what?" I turned around, and stared at the door, but I saw nothing. If the hairs on the back of my neck hadn't already been standing up, they would have just about jumped clear off my skin at that point. "There's no one there, Maddy. She's dead. You need to go back to your granddad, I'll take care of her."

"No!" she wailed, with a vehemence that made me flinch. "She's right there, and she's talking to you! Why aren't you listening? Listen to her!"

"I can't hear anything," I cried back, frustrated and scared at the same time. "There's no one there!"

"There is!" Maddy burst into tears all over again, and pointed right past me at the doorway. "She wants you to be careful. She says that you shouldn't tell Mister Michael yet, because it would break his heart if you lost it. She wants you to promise that you're going to be careful. Promise her!"

"I don't understand," I admitted, tears rolling down my own cheeks. I shoved them away anxiously, and looked back at the door. "I just... I don't understand..."

Maddy turned and looked at me, her eyes huge and glistening with tears. "You're pregnant, Miss Sandy. You're going to have a baby."

***

The shock of that pronouncement left me speechless. I managed to whisper some kind of promise about being careful, but that was it. When the others finally came looking for us, they found Maddy and me sitting side by side on the floor, just staring in shock at the body. I faintly heard voices whispering behind us, but I couldn't make out what my friends were saying. Maddy looked at them, then stood up and went over to them.

"I'll show you where she wants to be buried," she said, then I heard footsteps retreating.

I felt a warm body come up behind me and recognised Michael's familiar scent, but I couldn't figure out what was going on. His arms closed around me, but today there was no comfort in them.

Netty was dead, and I was pregnant. How could that even happen? How? I was taking pills to prevent it, but… a baby. Oh God, I was going to have a baby? Was that why I'd been feeling ill over the last few weeks? I'd blamed the nausea on the head injury, or bad food, or car sickness, anything but… that.

And… and Netty… oh God, why?

Suddenly, I remembered the note sitting on her nightstand, beside the bottle of pills that had taken her life. My hands felt stiff and robotic as I reached for it, and I couldn't quite convince them to grip it. I felt Michael reach past me and take the note for me, but he hesitated over whether or not to give it to me.

"Are you sure, Sandy?" he whispered, his voice heavy with emotion. "It won't make it better. It might make it worse."

I just nodded dumbly, and reached for the note again. This time, he surrendered it to me willingly. I unfolded it with trembling fingers, and stared at the elegant, flowing script. The letters were beautiful and careful, with only the slightest indication that her hands had been shaking as much as mine when she wrote it. Netty had obviously laboured over her last words to the world, to make them as perfect as possible. I took a deep breath, and then read the note out loud.

"'To my visitors, and especially to Sandrine McDermott,'" I began, fighting the fresh wave of emotion that came from seeing my name in her handwriting. "'By the time you receive this, I will be dead. I ask one last favour of you at this time: please bury me beneath the old cherry tree in the back yard. Ten years ago, I lay my husband to rest there, and I would very much like to spend my eternity at his side.'"

Tears obscured my vision, and I heard a muffled sob escape my throat. I felt Michael's hand close around mine, and then his deep, husky voice took over where mine had given out. "'Do not weep for me, my new old friends. I lived a good life, a long life – far longer than an old blasphemer like me had any right to, really. My husband would have scolded me, and told me that suicide is a sin, but I feel that this is my last opportunity to put my fate in the hands of someone that I think I can trust.

"'I'm dying anyway; I can feel it in my bones. This summer would have been my last, and I wouldn't have lived through the winter. Despite that, I want to thank you. You've given me a gift far beyond a little food and companionship. You – all of you – you gave me the chance to remember what it was like to be surrounded by family again. I know I'm a grumpy old chook, but seeing those children running around again has made me happier than I've been in a long, long time.

"'Sandrine, we didn't know each other for very long, but I feel like I understand you. I don't want you to feel guilty. You've given me the chance to do something

461

beautiful one last time, and I know that I can trust you to lay me to rest, and to remember me. I give you permission to take anything you want from my supplies, if it will help you. Take your people south, build your city, and know that I'll be watching over you from beyond.

"'Well, that's it. There's no graceful way to end this note, except to say goodbye. I'm off for an adventure of my own, into the last unknown frontier. It's time to find out whether my husband's faith was right. If it was, then I guess I'll be seeing him again soon. If not, at least I won't care anymore. Goodbye and with love, Netty.'"

"And just like that, another life is snuffed out," I said bitterly, my voice hoarse with tears. "She didn't have to do that. She could have asked us to stay."

"There was no point." I heard the doctor's voice from the doorway. When I looked at him, I found him looking sad. "She... she was suffering, Ms McDermott. Cancer, I think. It's hard to tell without the proper tools, but I know that she was in pain. She had been consulting with me for a while, but... I couldn't cure her. I just wish that she'd said something, so we could have all been here with her."

I looked up at the old man, struggling to make sense of what he was telling me. "Did you... did you give her the pills, Doc?"

"No." He shook his head slowly, his expression as numb and miserable as I felt. "I don't think I could have, even if she had asked."

"Of course." I slumped down, the strength draining out of me. Michael caught me, and hugged me tight against his chest, as if he could inject some of his strength into me through physical contact. Somehow, it seemed to work. I took a deep breath, and hugged him back. "We should bury her, and then we need to go."

"Let me take care of her," Michael said softly. "I know you were close. Why don't you go find something else to do? I'll call you when everything's ready."

I wanted to protest, but I knew that he was right. I needed some time alone, to think everything over and digest it. Nodding silently, I let him help me to my feet, and once I was steady I extracted myself from his embrace.

There was always too much to do and too little time, but at that moment I really didn't feel like doing anything at all. I went out into the courtyard and plopped down at the end of the pool beneath a shade umbrella, to watch the water and let my mind wander. The sound of the rain striking the water comforted me, but it also struck me as sad. It always seemed to rain on funerals, as if nature wept right along with us.

I was still sitting there staring into space when Michael came to find me. He wrapped me up in my coat and led me out to the freshly-dug grave. I watched like a statue as my friends lay Netty's body in the hole, wrapped in her favourite blanket. One by one, people stepped forward to say goodbye, but when my turn came, I couldn't find the words.

Once it was over, Michael guided me back inside and helped me to change into my travel clothes. He and the others took care of everything – packing my bags, carrying things out to the car, organizing the group, and even the unpleasant task of going through Netty's supplies to see what we could make use of. I hated that we had to, but I was grateful that they did it for me. The thought of picking over that old woman's home like a pack of vultures made me feel even more nauseated than I already did. It was like losing my grandmother all over again, and I wasn't sure how I was going to cope with that kind of pain.

Eventually, we were ready to leave. Michael helped me into the passenger's seat of the Hilux, then he vanished for a few minutes to make sure everything was in order. When he returned, he glanced at me and gave me a weak smile.

"I left everything unlocked but closed up," he said. "With the keys on the front desk, and a note saying that anyone who needed a place to stay was welcome there, so long as they clean up after themselves – and stay out of Room 25. I don't know if anyone will respect it, but… it seems like the least we can do."

I glanced at him and nodded my approval, unable to find the words to thank him. I didn't need to, though. I could see it in his eyes. He reached out to gently squeeze my hand, and from that gesture I knew that he understood my pain, and that I needed time.

When he put the car into gear and finally led our convoy away from the township of Tokaanu, I closed my eyes and let the sound of the rain on the windshield soothe me. I was almost asleep when something sharp stabbed me in the shoulder, taking me by surprise. I flinched, but that just made Tigger dig her claws in deeper. With stalwart determination, the kitten scrambled over me and descended down my shirt front into my lap, where she promptly curled up and went to sleep.

I was stunned by the gesture. Even though I had been the first human to feed her, Madeline had practically adopted the little tabby. Tigger rarely let me pat her, let alone actually cuddle her. Half-expecting to be clawed, I lifted a hand and gently ran it along her back, feeling the softness of her fur.

Tigger didn't claw me, though. She did quite the opposite. She rolled onto her back and stretched out, purring contentedly. The sight of it was beyond adorable, and I found myself smiling in spite of everything.

How was it that the animals always knew?

# Chapter Twenty-Three

For three days, we travelled southwards, slowly but surely making our way up onto the central plateau. The region had once been a national park, dominated by three massive volcanic cones, and miles of rocky desert. Nature still stood strong, even after the laws protecting it had vanished.

I wasn't surprised to discover that the road had seen better days; there had been at least one eruption in the last ten years, and numerous earthquakes. Here, the roads had been shattered and torn apart, only to have the cracks filled in by dirt, dust, ash, and weeds. It made for an uncomfortable journey, but that combination was still better than the deep mud on either side of the remains of the highway.

The group was subdued for most of the trip. I couldn't tell whether it was Netty's death bothering them, or if it was having the three volcanoes looming over them. I couldn't even say which one bothered me more. We made it past the two smaller cones without incident, but the sight of the last one – Mount Ruapehu – sent an ominous shiver down my spine.

Her familiar, jagged outline was hidden beneath a thick layer of cloud, but I didn't need to see her crest to recognise her. That mountain had been responsible for more deaths in my country than any other. If she chose to, she could wipe out my tiny party in a single swipe, and with it destroy what little hope my species had left. I kept my mouth shut, and my fears to myself. There was no point in making the others any jumpier than they already were.

By midday on the third day, we were almost clear of the central plateau. The weather had eased over the course of the morning; for the first time in weeks, the sun came out from behind a cloud.

"Let's stop for lunch," Michael suggested from the passenger seat. "Let everyone stretch their legs, and enjoy the weather while it lasts."

"I don't know," I admitted warily, my eye following Ruapehu's outline as the clouds began to lift away from her. "I'd feel better if we pushed on for another hour or two."

"Paranoid again, honey?" he teased, leaning over to playfully pat my thigh.

I gave him a dark look, then sighed and nodded. "Okay, okay. Just for a couple of minutes."

"Ten at the most." He smiled and gave my knee a gentle squeeze. "We won't even unpack anything, promise. If anything happens, we'll be ready to run in a heartbeat."

I cringed internally and cursed myself for a fool. Of course Michael knew what I was thinking. He could read me like a book. I just muttered something inarticulate and made a vague gesture for him to make the arrangements, then I focused on finding somewhere solid to park the truck.

Within a few minutes, everyone was on their feet and lunch was being handed out. Michael took Alfred down to the bushes beside the road to address the call of nature, leaving me alone. I took the opportunity to go find Dr Cross.

I found him sitting on the back bumper of one of the trucks, eating his lunch and absently swatting at the prolific sand flies that infested the region. He glanced up when I neared, adjusting his glasses.

"Ms McDermott?" he enquired. "May I assist with something?"

"I need to talk to you for a second, Doc," I replied, nervously glancing back over my shoulder to make sure that we weren't being observed. "Can we walk for a bit?"

"Of course." He eased himself up off the bumper, and gestured for me to lead on. I did so, and took him down a rocky bank beside the road, so that we were out of sight.

As we walked, I found myself silently brooding again. There was no way to be sure, except to ask my doctor. The problem was, I didn't entirely know how I felt, so I wasn't sure what answer I was hoping to hear. On the one hand, the idea of having to lug a tiny person around inside me for nine months while struggling to lead my group to a new home and found a city was almost too much for me to bear. On the other, I could imagine the look on Michael's face when I told him the news. If I really was pregnant… that would give him a reason to go on. And perhaps, it would give me one as well.

"You seem awfully concerned about privacy, Ms McDermott," Dr Cross pointed out. I looked at him, and found him watching me with the intense frown he got when he was trying to work out a puzzle.

"Well, it's a private matter," I admitted. I took a deep breath, and glanced back over my shoulder to make sure no one had noticed our departure. No one had. I turned my full attention to the doctor. "Doc… you remember when we first met, you gave me a prescription of the contraceptive pill? And you made me promise to take one every day, at the same time, and never miss a day?"

"I issue a lot of prescriptions to a lot of people, but that does sound like something I'd say," he replied in a half-hearted attempt at humour. "What of it? Do you need some more?"

"No, it's not that." I folded my arms across my chest, and stared thoughtfully across the plains at the vast, sprawling flanks of the volcano. "I've been taking them every day, just like you told me. Every day, at the same time, and I haven't missed any days. Is there… is there any chance that the pills could fail?"

"There's always a chance," he answered. "There is with any medication, particularly when we're relying on chemicals that may be well past their use-by date." He paused, then looked at me. "Do you think you're pregnant, Ms McDermott?"

"I don't know, Doc." Suddenly, I found tears welling up in my eyes, no matter how hard I tried to stay strong. "Maddy said I was. She said that Netty knew, and now that I think about it, I have been feeling pretty odd recently. Is there… is there any chance she's right?"

"There's always a chance. No contraceptive is a hundred percent effective," he answered dryly. "How long has it been since you last menstruated?"

"About six, maybe seven weeks," I replied, fighting the urge to panic. "But you said I could expect them to be irregular for a while, so I didn't notice."

"Which is entirely possible," he agreed. "Have you experienced any dizziness or nausea?"

"Yes, both." I hugged myself a little tighter, and closed my eyes to try and steady myself. "But not just in the mornings. I've always gotten travel sickness though, and I did have a concussion. I assumed that was why."

"It very well could have been either of those things. You've also been eating food that you're not used to, which can set off nausea as well," he said. "You may also be particularly sensitive due to hormonal changes in your body, pregnant or not. I believe I have some anti-nausea medication in my kit. Remind me to prescribe you some medication for the travel sickness. Now, have you noticed any tenderness, swelling, or general discomfort in your joints? Unusual fatigue?"

"My back hurts a little," I replied, with a vague shrug. "And I feel tired all the time, but I think we all do right now."

"Well, I can't tell you for sure until we've run the appropriate tests, but it does sound like congratulations may be in order," he commented thoughtfully. "Or perhaps, commiserations? I can understand if you're not particularly comfortable with the idea, after what happened to your sister."

"Christ!" The word just exploded out of me, and I buried my face in my hands. "It's not just that, Doc. I've… I've… been pregnant before, after the… the… you know… my body couldn't support it, I was too malnourished, and… God, Doc – I'm scared. I don't know if I want this or not. I don't know how to feel. What if… what if I have it, and it's born infected?"

I felt a sympathetic hand on my back, and heard him make a few reassuring noises. "It's all right, Sandy. If you don't want this, then we can… take care of it. If you are pregnant, then it's still early enough to—"

"What?" I jerked my head up and stared at him. "Are you suggesting…"

He shrugged helplessly, and gave me a weak smile. "Only as an option. No one's going to force you to do anything that you don't want to do. We don't even know for sure that you are pregnant yet. Don't jump to conclusions. Still, if it turns out that you are and you don't want the baby, then you don't have to have it."

"No!" I cried, horrified beyond words by the mere suggestion. "No, God, no – I'm not going to kill Michael's baby! No, no, no—"

"You don't have to." He grabbed my shoulders suddenly, bracing me upright. "Believe me, the last thing I want is for you to take that option but I would be doing you a disservice as your physician if I didn't at least make it available to you. You're in control of your own destiny now. You have the right to choose. No one can make the decision for you. Not Michael, not me, not your sister, not anyone else – only you get to make the choice."

"I-I… I can't do that." I swallowed a lungful of air and squeezed my eyes closed. "I just need time to think, to accept it. Please don't tell Michael, not until I'm sure."

"It's for the best. The first trimester is a dangerous period, particularly when you're still recovering," Dr Cross explained gently. Suddenly, he froze, staring over my shoulder. "Uh… Ms McDermott, perhaps it would be best if we continued this conversation another time?"

"Huh?" I glanced back over my shoulder, and stared at the not-so-distant mountain. "Is that what I think it is?"

From the crater of the mountain, a thin tendril of white smoke swirled up into the blue sky above. It looked so small, so innocent, and yet we both instinctively knew what was about to happen. We exchanged a look, then we turned and ran back towards the convoy.

We almost made it before the first earthquake struck. Almost, but not quite. Just as I tried to scream a warning to my friends and family, the ground jerked sharply and my legs went right out from under me. Panic took over when my strength failed me; the moment that the earthquake died down, I leapt back to my feet and grabbed Doc by the elbow.

"Go! Get to the cars!" I cried, half-dragging and half-guiding him the last few meters towards the nearest truck. Around us, people were screaming. A couple of the children were on the ground not far away, cowering in terror; I grabbed them, and guided them to a vehicle.

"What's going on?" I barely heard Skye's voice over the chaos, but I felt her grab my arm.

"Ruapehu's erupting!" I yelled back, forcing my voice to pierce the noise all around us. It wasn't just human voices trying to drown me out, though; a low, deep rumble echoed through the earth all around us, making it hard to hear, and nearly impossible to think. I looked at Skylar, and then I lifted my voice as high as it could go and screamed an order. "Everyone, in the cars! Go! Don't stop unless you can't drive anymore! Go, go, go!"

I grabbed my sister without another word and shoved her towards a vehicle. She stumbled but managed to keep her feet, and she took the hint. She shouted something that I couldn't quite make out, and then she was shovelling people towards cars as fast as she could. I spun around on the spot, frantically counting heads and trying to make sure that everyone was accounted for. Unfortunately, they weren't. With a devastating twist of my gut, I realised that Michael and Alfred were nowhere to be seen.

"Michael!" I screamed at the top of my lungs. "Michael! Where are you?" There was no answer, or at least no answer that I could hear. I drew a deep lungful of air, trying desperately to project my voice a few inches further, but it did me no good.

I glanced back at the others, torn with indecision. There was no way I could abandon Michael, but the children needed me, too. Skye caught my eye and made a sharp gesture, then pointed towards the rocks leading down from the road. It took me a second to work out that she was trying to tell me where my fiancé had gone.

There was no time to thank her, I just turned and ran. The pebbles crunched and gave way underfoot, just as another tremor tore through the earth. I went down hard on my knees, bruising myself painfully, but I only stayed down until the aftershock faded. As soon as I could stand again, I was up and off down the gully, searching for him.

A footprint in the mud caught my eye, and then another. I followed them deeper into the gully, past boulders the size of small cars and razor-edged desert grasses. I spotted a pile of fresh dog droppings near the path, but no sign of Michael. A quick search revealed more tracks, this time further spaced out. Something had sent Michael running in the wrong direction.

Suddenly, I heard a shout, but I couldn't make out the words.

"Michael?" I yelled again, racing towards the sound of the voice.

"I'm here!" he yelled back. "This… this stupid dog…"

Just at that moment, I rounded another large boulder and found them both on the ground, rolling in the mud; Michael was frantically trying to hold the dog down, while Alfred was just as frantically trying to get away from him.

No, not from him, I realised suddenly. From the volcano.

"I can't…" Michael gasped, out of breath and obviously nearing panic. "I sprained my ankle chasing this stupid mutt, and I can't walk and carry him at the same time."

"You focus on walking, I've got Alfred," I instructed, flinging myself into the mud without hesitation. Between the two of us, we managed to hold him down long enough for me to get a solid grip on the old sheepdog. He was heavy, but fear lent me strength from reserves that I didn't know I had. Alfred whined and howled, but once I had him he didn't fight me. He just cowered, and tried to bury his head in my armpit.

"We need to go," Michael said urgently, levering himself up on the boulder. "I smell sulphur. That can't be good."

"It isn't. We need to get out of here before there's a gas cloud, or a lahar, or something equally awful," I answered, hefting the old dog up and bracing him against my chest. "Lean on me if you need to, but we're getting the hell out of here."

Michael tried to answer, but the noise around us was too loud for me to hear him. He didn't try again. I felt his hand on my shoulder, and then we were off. It was slow going, but at least when the next tremor hit I didn't fall again. Thank heavens for small favours; my knees already felt like they were black and blue. The three of us, gasping, stumbling, and struggling to keep our balance, retraced our steps back towards the road.

By the time we reached it, all the cars were gone except for one. I heard a voice call out to us, and then Skylar ran around from the far side. She yanked open the back door, and helped me to bundle Michael and Alfred inside. A few seconds later, she was back behind the wheel again and starting the car. I flung myself into the passenger seat and slammed the door.

"Get us out of here!" I ordered, but even inside the truck it was hard to hear one another. She shouted something back, and the car leapt forward, bouncing and juddering across the uneven ground. I turned to stare out the back window, just in time to spot a wave of something grey and ominous rolling down the side of the mountain.

"Ash!" Michael gasped, his voice still ragged. "Christ, it's coming right for us. We need to cover all the vents: it could be toxic."

"There should be blankets under the seats," I answered, reaching beneath my own in search of one. Sure enough, my fingers connected with something soft. I yanked it out, and grabbed my pocket knife out of my cargo pants. With a frantic haste, I cut the blanket into strips, and handed them out. "Here, tie this over your face!"

"What do I do?" Skye begged, her tone one of absolute panic. I glanced at her, and saw that her knuckles were white on the steering wheel, and her foot on the accelerator was almost to the floor. The truck was rocketing along at entirely too fast a pace for the condition of the road, but we really had no choice.

"Just keep us going in that direction," I cried, pointing towards the distant horizon. "This is a long, straight road. Just keep going. I'm going to tie this over your face, okay?"

"Okay," she agreed, obviously struggling to stay brave. I shot a glance at the incoming ash cloud, then immediately wished I hadn't. I turned away, and focused on getting us ready. We couldn't outrun it, so we had to prepare for the possibility that the ash was poisonous. Once I'd finished tying the cloth over Skye's face, I cut off another strip and did my own.

"It's here!" Michael cried.

His warning was unnecessary. A second later, the wall of ash hit us and our world plunged into darkness. I heard Skylar scream, and had to grab the wheel to keep her from accidentally driving us off the road. I barely had time to brace myself when she slammed on the brakes, and brought us to a sudden halt.

"I can't! I can't do it!" she sobbed, tears in her eyes. "I can't see anything. Oh, God."

"Keep it together, baby sis." I grabbed her hand, and shoved a wadded up ball of cloth into it. "Hold that over those vents there. We have to keep the ash from getting in here. Michael, get the back ones."

"Got it covered." His reply sounded like it was coming from a thousand miles away, barely audible over the roar. I shoved the rest of the torn-up blanket over the vents on my side of the car, then curled up against my sister and silently prayed for our salvation.

***

After what felt like forever, the roaring finally faded away and the ground stopped shaking. Silence descended in our dark world, aside from the sound of our coughing; we'd managed to keep most of the ash out, but not all of it. I felt my sister trembling and knew instinctively that she was crying, but it was too dark for me to see her face. The ash on the windows was too thick for us to be able to tell whether it was safe to get out or not.

"The engine probably won't start now, even if we could see where we're going." Michael's voice was disembodied in the darkness. He coughed heavily, then added, "The ash is probably made up of crushed rock, volcanic glass, and silica. We'll need to clean the engine out completely before we can start this damn thing."

"So, we're stuck here?" I asked, my voice barely more than a whisper. "I left my radio in the Hilux. Does anyone else have one?"

"No," Skye replied, sounding miserable. "I didn't think I'd need it."

"Me either," Michael replied. "Whose car was this? Maybe there's one in the glove box?"

"I think this was the one Jim was driving," I replied. "I suppose they might have left something. I'll look."

I fumbled for the torch in my pocket, and found it by touch alone. The thin beam barely illuminated the darkness, but it was still enough to make me squint. After a few seconds of searching, I sighed and shook my head. "Nothing in here but someone's afternoon snack. Well, at least we have some food, I guess."

"Pass the torch here? I'll check the back." Michael's hand appeared over my shoulder from the shadows of the back seat. I placed my torch in it, and then both vanished. I heard him moving around for a few minutes, then he heaved a sigh of obvious frustration. "Nothing here, either."

"Shh!" Skye hissed unexpectedly. "I hear something."

We both froze, listening intently. A moment later, it came again and this time we all heard it: a faint scraping sound.

"Oh, please don't let that be lava," Skye whispered, clinging to my hand.

"We'd know if it were lava," I replied. "Pretty sure we'd already be dead. Besides, lava doesn't talk." I raised my voice, and shouted at the top of my lungs, "Hey! We're in here!"

There was an alarmed cry outside the vehicle, but I couldn't make out the words. The scraping sound picked up in urgency, then suddenly light penetrated our world. Light, and a familiar face.

"Hemi!" Skylar cried, her relief so palpable that it sent a shiver down my spine. The youth called a greeting back, and thumped on the window until the last of the ash fell away.

I leaned past her, and rolled down the window just a crack so that we could speak. "Boy, am I glad to see you! We've got Michael and Alfred in the back. Is everyone else accounted for?"

"Yeah." Hemi coughed and tightened the makeshift mask covering his face, similar to our own. "You guys okay? The doc's waiting down at Waiouru, but we can go get him if you need it."

"No, please just get us out of here," I answered, shaking my head. "This truck is a write-off. We need to get the supplies out, and see if we can find another one along the way."

"Okay. Just hang in there, we'll get you out," he agreed.

True to his word, Hemi and his companions had us out of that truck and into the back of theirs within a couple of minutes. It was a squeeze to fit all of us in there along with Alfred and the supplies, but we made it – primarily because I ended up sitting on Michael's lap. Despite his ankle, it was a situation that neither of us minded very much.

I draped my arms around his shoulders and stared out the back window at the shadow of the volcano against the horizon.

"I can barely see her through the haze," I commented. "There's still too much ash hanging in the air."

"She just tried to kill us," Michael answered dryly, slipping his arms around my waist to brace me securely in lieu of a seatbelt. "Do you really want to see her?"

"She didn't *try* to do anything." I shifted back a little bit, just far enough to look into his eyes. "She's a volcano. She's just doing what volcanoes do. I would like to know if she's done, though. Do you think that's it for the eruption?"

"Hard to say." He sighed heavily, nuzzling his face into the curve of my neck. I closed my eyes and relaxed, letting the contact calm my frazzled nerves. "It could be that was the first stage of a larger event, or it could be that she just needed to let off a little steam. Ruapehu isn't the kind of volcano that spits lava a thousand feet into the air, thank goodness. If she were, we'd probably all be dead."

"Next time I decide to take a shortcut through a volcanic field, talk me out of it," I replied. Michael grunted something halfway between a snort and a laugh, but said nothing. I let the conversation trail off and just enjoyed the closeness. Michael was a snuggler by nature and sometimes that bothered me, but not today.

After our brush with death, all I could think was how lucky we were that we'd all made it through. My family was safe. My fiancé was safe.

My fiancé. My mate. Maybe even father of my child. For the first time, that thought brought a smile to my face. I felt a flush of heat run up the back of my neck, and suddenly I wanted nothing more than to find some way to express my feelings in the most romantic way I could think of. I pushed myself back away from him, and looked at him with a smile.

"You know what? Screw it. Let's just do it," I told him in no uncertain terms. "Tonight. No more waiting."

"Huh?" Michael just gave me a bewildered look. "You're doing that thing where you say stuff you've been thinking about as if I'm privy to your thoughts. Use your words, sweetheart."

"Oh, sorry." Embarrassed, I laughed at myself, and then I elaborated for him. "Let's just forget about waiting and get married. Tonight. My gut's been telling me all along that you're the one, but I've been resisting it. I'm just afraid of change and commitment, but I need to stop listening to my head and listen to my heart for a change."

"Oh." Michael went silent for a second. The silence made me worry, but I could see on his face that he was just trying to process my spontaneous change of heart.

Beside us, Skylar laughed gleefully and gave me a nudge. "Well, look at you! When did you grow a set of balls, sis?"

"I'll have you know that balls are soft and squishy, and not really all that tough at all," I replied with playful mock-haughtiness. "I'm quite happy with having a vagina, thank you! They're much tougher than balls, and can put up with a heck of a pounding." Skye stared at me, wide eyed, her mouth hanging open. Suddenly, the reality of what I'd just said struck me, and I started blushing furiously. "That… came out all wrong."

Around me, the car erupted in laughter. I barely heard Michael's reply above the sound of my friends teasing me.

He said one simple word, the one that I wanted to hear more than anything else in the world. He said, "Yes."

# Chapter Twenty-Four

News of our spontaneous nuptials spread through the group like wildfire. By the time we'd checked in with the doctor and been given mostly clean bills of health, everyone knew. As soon as I stepped outside, Skylar grabbed my arm and dragged me away from the motor lodge where we planned to stay the night.

"You can't see the bride before the wedding!" she told Michael in no uncertain terms, shoving me in front of her despite my protests. Hemi and his friends appeared as if out of nowhere, and dragged my poor, limping fiancé off without another word. Skye gave me a wicked grin, grabbed my hand, and led me off towards the township of Waiouru proper. "Come on! We need to find you something to wear."

"Why bother?" I groused, though I knew better than to really fight her when she had her mind set on something. "Michael doesn't care what I look like. I mean, he sees me dressed like this every day."

"But this isn't every day," she answered, dancing ahead of me with such enthusiasm that she almost tugged my arm out of its socket. "It's your wedding day, Sandy-pants! For one day, you get to be as much of a princess as you like. And I am going to make you the prettiest princess of them all!"

"And just how do you plan to do that, little sis?" I asked dryly. "This used to be a military town. There isn't exactly a bridal boutique here."

"Maybe not, but I spotted a sign on someone's fence offering tailoring services," she replied. "I'm betting that if anyone has dresses for us, it'll be them!"

"Wait, us?" I tried to stop, only to get almost pulled off my feet. "What us? Is someone else getting married?"

"No, dummy." Skye sighed and rolled her eyes. "For you and your bridal party, of course. I'm going to be your maid of honour, Maddy's the flower girl, and everyone else is… well, they want to look nice, too!"

"Okay, this is getting way too complicated," I admitted, suddenly feeling nervous. "I just want things to be simple."

"Oh, come on, Sandy," Skye stopped suddenly and turned to fix me with an imploring look. "For once in your life, relax and have a little fun. This is supposed to be the happiest day of your life, and I want to enjoy it with you. Besides, if you want to rebuild everything that we lost, then you need to lead by example. I've never been to a wedding before, I've only seen pictures in old magazines. They're supposed to be happy – and more importantly, normal. Don't we all deserve a chance to be normal again?"

I started to protest, but something about the look on her face made me stop and reconsider. Suddenly, I realised that she needed it even more than I did. She needed to see me happy, and to share the moment with the people that she cared about. How long had it been since any of us had been able to enjoy a wedding? For all I knew, this might have been the first one since the plague struck. That thought struck me as poignant, and important somehow. There were going to be a lot of firsts in the days to come, and who was I to stop other people from enjoying them?

"I… I'm sorry. You're right," I admitted quietly. "Sometimes it's hard to remember just how much my life has changed."

"I know." She smiled at me, an expression so vibrant that it felt like it lit up the whole world. "Don't worry, sis. You've got friends now. We're taking care of everything. All you have to do is enjoy yourself."

I took a deep breath to quell the twisting in my gut, then I smiled and nodded to her. "Lead on, then! Let's go get pretty."

Skylar let out a delighted whoop and raced off down the street with me in tow. A few minutes later, we found ourselves jogging up the front steps of an ordinary-looking house, flushed and out of breath from our run.

"This is it," she explained, panting. "Melody and the twins went ahead to look for—"

Just at that moment, the door exploded open, and the three girls raced out to meet us. Their expressions startled me even more than their sudden appearance: all three of them were grinning broadly. They'd been slowly relaxing over the weeks since they'd joined our group, but this was the first time that any of them had looked truly happy. Before I could say anything, I was grabbed and half-dragged, half-ushered into the living room.

"There are so many dresses!" Jasmine told us gleefully. "In all kinds of different sizes!"

"And there's sewing stuff," Melody added, her sun-browned face split in a wide grin. "So we can adjust things to fit, if we have to."

"We found one for Sandy already," Jasmine cut in, her excitement quite obvious. She raced over to the big mound of dresses they'd gathered in the centre of the room, and pulled out a simple, elegant gown made of soft, cornflower-blue satin. It was a tiny bit crinkled, but otherwise in perfect condition.

I was too stunned to say anything, and just stood there with my mouth hanging open while Skye raced over to grab the dress.

"Oh my gosh, yes! This is perfect!" she cried. She rounded on me, clinging to the satin as though it were the most precious thing in her life. "You need to put this on." She paused, her eyes wide. "No, wait! You're all ashy! You need to go have a shower, right now."

"Um, Skye… you're ashy, too," Lily pointed out. She was quieter than her twin, but tended to have more well thought-out comments when she did opt to speak. Now was exactly one of those times.

"Huh?" Skye shot her a wide-eyed look, then looked down at the dress in her hands. Suddenly, she dropped it as though it had burned her. "Oh, no! Is it dirty? Did I get it dirty? I'm sorry!"

Melody knelt down to inspect the dress. "No, it's fine. Nothing we can't dust off. You two go get cleaned up. There's a bathroom down that hallway there, second door on your right."

"You're first, sis," Skye instructed. She grabbed my hand and dragged me down the hallway. The indicated doorway opened into a fairly ordinary-looking bathroom, with a bath, shower, and toilet all in the same room. Skye looked around for a moment, and came back with a comb. "Sit down. Let's brush the ash out of your hair first. I don't know how you deal with that much hair all the time."

"It is kind of a pain," I admitted. "I've been thinking of cutting it off, but I grew it out to honour Mum and… I'd feel weird without it."

"No way!" she gasped, sounding genuinely horrified. "Your hair is gorgeous. I will not let you cut it. Now, sit your ass down in that bathtub, and let me comb it out."

"I can brush my own hair, thanks." Laughing, I tried to grab the comb, but she held it out of my reach.

"No! I want to brush it," she replied with playful petulance. "Like we used to when we were kids. Remember?"

I paused and stared at her. "Wow, I'd almost forgotten about that. How old were you? Three? Four?"

"Four, I think." Grinning, she guided me over to the bathtub and helped me to sit down. With gentle fingers, she undid the elastic holding my hair in its usual thick braid, and gently unwound it. "You must have been, what... fourteen? I was obsessed with your hair for ages. I don't remember why."

Suddenly, the memory came rushing back in force, and it left me laughing so much I could hardly breathe. "I remember! You kept getting nits at kindy, so Mum gave you a pixie cut. You hated it."

"Is that what it was?" Skye burst out laughing as well. "I just remember desperately wanting to have hair like yours, and being ridiculously happy when you let me brush it for you. I was such a weirdo."

"Nah, you were a little kid," I replied. My laughter faded away into thoughtful silence, as I delved back into those happy, innocent memories. "You were the sweetest little thing, Skye. Did I ever tell you how much I missed you when I thought that you were dead? I cried for you so often. I don't think I ever really recovered from the grief."

"I know." I felt her fingers in my hair like a gentle caress, and it sent a shiver all the way down my spine. I sighed heavily and drew my knees up to my chest, letting her touch relax me. After a few minutes of silence, she finally spoke again. "There is one thing I've always wondered, though. When we got separated, why didn't you and Mum come back for us?"

"Grandma insisted," I replied. A surge of grief rose up in my belly all over again, thinking about the family that I'd loved so much and lost. "She decided that it was too much of a risk, with the riots already starting. I think she was afraid that she'd already lost one granddaughter and that if we went looking for you then she might lose everyone else as well. To be honest, none of us were thinking clearly at the time, and when she made the decision we just went along with it because at least it was some kind of decision. People make stupid choices when they're in life-or-death situations." I paused, and looked back over my shoulder at her. "I'm sorry, Skye. I wish it had happened differently."

She just gave me a sad smile, and gently guided my head back around to face front. "It's okay, sis. Like you said, people make dumb choices. We both made it, and that's the most important thing. Now, sit still!"

"Yes, ma'am!" I replied, sketching a salute. Skye giggled, and went back to brushing out my hair.

When she was finally done, she tossed the comb into the sink and offered me a hand up. As soon as I was up, I realised why she'd put me in the bath; a cloud of fine dust had come out of my hair with every stroke, and the bathtub kept it from going everywhere.

"In you go!" she ordered, pointing to the shower stall. "And don't forget to wash your hair."

"But it's cold!" I protested, shooting her a mortified look. "And it'll never dry in time for the ceremony. Do you want me to get married looking like a drowned rat?"

"God, you're such a drama queen," Skye complained, rolling her eyes. "We'll make it dry in time, okay? Just wash your damn hair. Today is a special day, and requires special effort."

"But--" I started to say something else, but she cut me off mid-sentence.

"No buts! Just do it, little miss!" She planted her hands on her hips, and gave me a look that resembled our mother's scolding face so closely that I burst out laughing.

"Okay, okay!" I held up my hands in mock-self-defence. "I'm washing, I'm washing. Jesus. You're so demanding."

"And that's why you love me," she answered brightly.

She hopped into the bath and started combing out her own hair, while I stripped down without modesty, and stepped into the shower stall. The water was as cold as ice, but my body was a mess of bruises and grazes again and the cold helped to numb the discomfort. The soap was so old that it was shrunken and crusty, but there was a clean washcloth sitting on a little shelf beside the door. I made do with that, and it was good enough.

By the time I finished scrubbing my hair with lavender-scented shampoo and had let it soak under conditioner for a few minutes, I was shivering convulsively. Skye was waiting with a big, soft towel when I finally stepped out. I didn't bother to ask where she'd found it, I just took it gratefully and wrapped myself up in it. I was about to get dressed again, when I realised that my clothing was gone.

"Hey!" I complained, startled. "Where are my pants, Skye?"

"We took them back to the convoy," she replied cheerfully. "You're not going to need them tonight. Melody! She's ready!"

Melody appeared in the doorway with a wicked smile on her face. She grabbed me by the shoulders, and steered me back out to the living room dressed in nothing but that towel. I spluttered in protest, but nobody seemed to care. When I got there, I found the twins holding a small mountain of towels, and soon I was being dried off from every angle by enthusiastic helping hands.

When they finished, the twins vanished for a second and then returned holding a set of very fancy lingerie.

"What is that?" I demanded, confused and a little horrified. "Guys, you don't expect me to wear that, surely. It's… it's…"

"It's pretty," Melody supplied. "And yes, you are going to wear it. Put it on, or we'll put it on for you."

"Okay, fine, geez. Give it here," I grumbled. The twins grinned in perfect unison, and handed the frilly garments over to me. Careful not to drop the towel and flash anyone more than necessary, I pulled on the knickers and fastened the bra over my chest. "Wow, this is… almost a perfect fit. Where did you guys find this?"

"There's a whole storage room full of them off the garage," Jasmine replied. "I don't know why, but they're all pretty like that. Nothing plain or practical at all."

"Whoever owned this place was probably buying it in bulk, to supply the ladies living in town," I said, staring down at myself to consider the fit of the garments. They were pretty, and very, very feminine – something I was not used to being. "I feel a bit silly, guys. Are you sure about this?"

"It doesn't look silly," Lily said, shaking her head. She came over to me holding the dress. I stepped into it, and then three sets of hands helped me to pull it up and zipped it at the small of my back. Once it was on, Lily reached into her pocket and pulled out the tiny, antique locket that Netty had given me. "We took your clothing and your ring back to the motel, but I thought you might like to wear this."

"Oh! Yes, thank you," I said, reaching out to take the locket from her outstretched hand. I fastened it around my neck, and then straightened up and looked at the girls. "Well? How do I look?"

The three of them stood back and stared at me consideringly, their expressions ranging from pleased to uncertain.

"Should we do something about the scars?" Jasmine asked suddenly. "We could try to hide them."

"No." Melody shook her head firmly. "The scars are part of who she is, and she looks lovely despite them. He's marrying all of her, not just the parts that are still in mint condition. If he doesn't realise that, then he doesn't deserve her."

I felt myself flush at the compliment, and gave her a smile. "That was well-put. Yeah, Michael's marrying all of me, and he's already seen the scars. He doesn't care. Hell, we've both taken scars defending one another in the past, and we'd do it again in a heartbeat. That's why we're getting married."

"See?" Melody looked at the twins, and gave them a stern frown. "Real life isn't like those stupid romance novels you two insist on reading. Nobody's perfect, but the whole point of love is that the feeling is perfect, even if the people are not."

Jasmine blew a raspberry at her, and all of us laughed. By the time the levity cleared, Skye was back. The twins vanished to make use of the shower, leaving the two of us alone with Melody.

I glanced between them, then looked at the door. "Someone is on watch, right?"

"Yeah, Solomon is," Skye replied. She came over to study me, and nodded her approval. "This looks good. I think we should keep it simple. Right, Mel?"

"Right," she agreed. "This is our world now, and we can do whatever we like. I think she looks beautiful just like this. Nothing fancy, nothing over the top. Just beauty the way nature intended it."

"Good grief, when did you two become philosophers?" I asked, amused. "You're starting to sound like me."

"I'll take that as a compliment," Skye said with a grin. "Okay, what are we wearing, Mel?"

"Well, we want her to stand out, so we should wear dark colours," she replied decisively. "Blue, or as close to blue as we can find, so that our dresses compliment hers."

"Sounds good to me." Skye glanced at me, and made a shooing gesture. "You go sit down, we've got this covered."

"Yes, ma'am," I agreed dryly. I found a seat on a nearby couch, and settled in for an hour of doing nothing while the other girls played dress-up. It was something that I hadn't seen in so long that for once in my life I didn't mind the inactivity at all.

*** 

The gap in the weather held off for most of the day, though the stench of sulphur permeated everything. By the time my little wedding party was ready, the sun was starting to set and cast the world around us in long, elegant shadows.

I held my skirt up to keep it out of the dirty streets as we walked back, for fear of damaging the satin. It had survived the years unscathed because the girls had found it hanging in a dress bag; now it was mine and I felt both confused and beautiful while I was wearing it. The girls had dried my hair thoroughly and brushed it until it shone like silk. They'd found a few pretty hair pins to sweep it back behind my ears, but other than that it was all natural.

I was so focused on watching where my feet were going that I didn't notice the figures lurking in the shadows until we were almost on top of them. Suddenly, someone stepped out into our line-of-sight, and the girls shouted in alarm. I jerked my head up and stared at the person, wide-eyed in shock. She stared back, her eyes narrowed, the hands holding her rifle steady and confident.

The two of us just stared at one another for the longest time. She was straight-backed and proud, dressed in the uniform of the army. Chevrons adorned her breast, but I didn't know the ranks well enough to understand them. She was substantially older than me, but there was something in her eyes that I understood on an instinctive level. A longing, a desire to protect, and a wariness of the unexpected.

Suddenly, I realised that she was waiting for me to explain our presence in her territory. Her stance was cautious but not threatening, and her expression was one of careful neutrality. It was like looking in a mirror at the person that I had become since I met Michael and found my sister again. My shock vanished, and I found the words I needed right on the tip of my tongue.

"Sorry, we weren't expecting anyone in this area," I admitted, raising my hands slowly to show that I was unarmed. That meant dropping my skirt in the process, but the stretch of pavement I was standing on at the time seemed clean enough. "We've just stopped for the night to celebrate my wedding, and we'll move on in the morning. My name is Sandrine McDermott, and these are members of my group." I quickly introduced Skye and the others, then looked back at the soldier. "I apologise for the intrusion. We had no idea this land was claimed, Lieutenant...?"

A smile cracked the woman's neutral visage. "Sergeant, actually. Sergeant Erica Bryce, Royal New Zealand Army." She lowered her rifle, and looked me up and down with some interest. "I heard your broadcast. We've been watching the roads for days for your group, but you took so long to get here that we were starting to think you'd been wiped out. Good to see that you weren't."

"The road has been much wilder than we expected," I replied, lowering my hands. "The weather hasn't exactly been very accommodating, either."

The Sergeant barked a sharp laugh, and nodded her agreement. "That it hasn't. You seem like a smart leader, so I presume there must have been good reason to move your people at this time of year. You said something about a mutation of the virus."

"Yeah. We had no choice," I replied with a shrug. "The mutants attacked us in our old home territory up near Hamilton. We lost so many people that it was worth risking the weather to head south." I paused, and shot her a long, thoughtful look. "We're heading for Avalon, in Lower Hutt. We're going to build a new city. You and your men are welcome to come, so long as we can trust you to obey the laws."

"Perhaps," she answered noncommittally. "We're quite comfortable here for now, but we'll think it over. I would be willing to consider letting you use our radio tower to update your broadcast, if you like."

"Oh?" I stood up a little straighter, surprised and pleased by the generosity. "You have the equipment up and running?"

"Of course." She shrugged and smiled wryly. "We just don't have anything to say most of the time. Sometimes, it's safer to just stay here and protect our own resources."

"I understand." I smiled back at her, and pointed towards the motor inn where my companions waited. "Why don't you and your men come to my wedding? My groupmates kind of took over when I told them I wanted to formalize my engagement, but I'm sure there will be food – and there will definitely be good company. We can talk a bit more, and get to know one another."

Sergeant Bryce paused then, and for the first time I saw a look of some uncertainty on her face. After a few long moments, she shrugged. "We'll... we'll think about it. Maybe. We know where you are, so if we decide to come we'll let you know."

"It's fine. I completely understand." I made a broad, welcoming gesture, and then I saluted her. "You're welcome if you want to, but if not then that's your choice. I know how it feels to suddenly be confronted with a large amount of people. Take all the time you need, Sergeant."

She returned the salute and nodded. "Well, we'll let you go. I'll definitely be in touch regarding the radio, whether we come or not." She paused, then gave me a shy smile. "Congratulations on your nuptials."

"Thank you," I said with a grin. Then, suddenly, the reality of it hit me in the face like a sack full of doorknobs. "Oh my God, I'm getting married."

Behind me, Skylar and the others laughed. "You wanted this, sis. Too late to back out now."

"Are you sure?" I asked, feeling a wave of terror unlike anything I'd ever felt before. "I mean, Michael would forgive me if I ran like a coward, right?"

"No, I'm pretty sure he wouldn't." Skye grabbed me by the shoulders, and started pushing me off towards the motor inn. "Besides, you wanted this. You made the call. This is all you, sis. Now, own it!"

"Yeah… yeah, you're right." I took a deep breath to steady myself, then gave them all a sheepish look. "So that's what they mean by cold feet."

Everyone laughed at that, even the Sergeant and her soldiers. They let us leave without complaint, and made no attempt to follow us as we returned home. There, I found the entire group waiting for us. One of the look-outs shouted and pointed, and then a cheer went up from the entire group.

Skye stopped pushing me, and took my hand instead. She guided me in through the front gate, past my cheering friends, and into the courtyard of the inn. I skidded to a halt, shocked by the transformation. The courtyard had been decorated with ribbons, streamers, and more flowers than I'd seen in one place for a very long time. An assortment of folding chairs had been arranged in two groups, with a short aisle down the middle. At the far end, Anahera stood resplendent in a long, black gown, and in front of her was my fiancé.

Michael glanced at me, and I saw his eyes widen – whether it was shock or delight, I couldn't tell. He was freshly-scrubbed, and dressed in his full police uniform, right down to the hat. He looked so handsome that I could hardly believe my eyes.

"Come on, big sis," Skye whispered in my ear. "It's your time to shine."

She led me forward by the hand, and suddenly I found myself excited all over again. Butterflies danced in my stomach and left me feeling light-headed and a little ill, but it was all in a good way.

Getting married. I was getting married. To Michael.

Suddenly, tears blurred my vision, and I was fighting the urge to cry. Thankfully, Skylar understood my moment of weakness, and she was there to keep me steady. She squeezed my hand and guided me down the aisle to stand opposite my beloved, and then she and my other bridesmaids went off to find their seats in the front row.

I could feel the presence of all my friends gathering, and hear the sound of chairs scraping on concrete as they settled down to watch. There were whispers and chuckles, but they were all friendly and kind – and throughout it all, I only had eyes for Michael, and he for me.

"You look beautiful," he said softly. I felt him reach out to take my hands, and the touch sent a thrill right through me.

"T-thank you," I stumbled, my wits half-gone. I tried to say a few things, but none of them quite came out right. It didn't matter, though. Michael understood. He always understood. He just smiled at me, and squeezed my hands reassuringly.

"Dearly beloved, we are gathered here today to witness the union of our friends, Sandy and Michael." Anahera's voice rose as crisp and clear as a cool breeze on a hot summer's afternoon. A hush went over the crowd. We all looked at her. She looked back, smiled, and then continued. "Marriage has been so many things over the centuries of human evolution, but now it falls to us to set its definition. These two before us have become instrumental in guiding us to the new destiny for all humankind, so it seems fitting that their wedding be the one that sets the standard for our new culture.

"It is time for the concept of marriage to evolve once again. The two of you are warriors who would fight back to back to the bitter end to protect one another, and trailblazers who share a vision for a new world for all of us. You have faced so many trials together already, and there will probably be many more in your future, but this marriage symbolizes your desire to face them together. You will always have one another's backs, and always be there to help if one of you falls.

"Michael Chan, do you pledge yourself in love and loyalty to Sandrine for the rest of your days? Do you swear to guide her, help her, and protect her for as long as you both shall live?"

"I do," he answered without hesitation, his gaze shifting back to me. I looked up at him, wide-eyed, frozen, uncertain. And then, I heard Anahera speaking to me.

"Sandrine McDermott, do you pledge yourself in love and loyalty to Michael for the rest of your days? Do you swear to guide him, help him, and protect him for as long as you both shall live?"

"I do." The words came out of my mouth even though my brain was a chaotic jumble of conflicting emotions, but the moment that they were out I felt like a huge burden had been lifted off of me. Skye was right. I did want this, more than anything else in the world. The possibility of having a baby had nothing to do with it; I wanted this for me, and not for anyone else. After all the pain I'd been through, I had finally found the one person that I knew I could trust beyond anyone else, and now… he was going to be part of my family. It just made so much sense.

"Madeline, the rings?" Anahera called. Maddy rushed forward, dressed like a tiny, raven-haired doll in a fluffy party dress. She handed the rings to Anahera, and then rushed back to her seat. Anahera held the rings out to us, one in each hand, and we took them.

Michael's strong, gentle hands took hold of mine, and guided the ring onto my finger with a tenderness that delighted me. I watched, and then I looked up at him again and saw a smile of such happiness on his face that I almost burst into tears right on the spot. My fingers trembled as I reached for his hand, but he understood. He gently guided my hands through the motions, and then he leaned down and kissed me.

Our friends burst into wild applause all around us, cheering so loudly that I could barely make out Anahera pronouncing the marriage complete. It didn't matter, though. None of it mattered. All that mattered was Michael. My friend, my lover, and now my husband. I wrapped my arms around his neck, and kissed him back with every ounce of emotion in my body.

Eventually, our lips parted and he pulled back just a little. He started to say something to me, but the cheering, dancing mob overwhelmed us before he could. Suddenly, we were both swept up into the crowd, and carried away with the tide. After that, everything became a blur of voices and friendly, smiling faces.

"You're not going to believe what Zain managed to pull off," Skye commented gleefully, from right behind my ear. I tried to turn and look at her, but she was gone before I could locate her. Then, something happened that distracted me completely: for the first time in ten years, I heard the strains of music floating above the sea of voices.

"No way!" I gasped, stunned. Music hadn't been a part of my existence for so long, and the sound of it made me want to weep with joy. Before I could give in to my emotions, though, Michael caught me around the waist and swept me away onto the makeshift dance floor that our friends had created in our honour.

Another cheer went up from the crowd, but it was promptly hushed by other members of the crowd that wanted to savour the precious notes. The song wasn't familiar to me, but it didn't matter; I remembered the feeling, the way the music could make my imagination soar, and the way it could manipulate my emotions with such skill and subtlety that I didn't realise it was doing it.

"You're crying, Sandy," Michael whispered to me, his arms protectively tight around my waist as he guided me through the unfamiliar steps of a waltz, his footing careful due to the bandaged sprain he'd managed to hide under his uniform. Neither of us really knew how to dance anymore, but that didn't matter, either – the point was being together, and we were. Nothing could separate us now.

"I'm... happy," I whispered back, my voice husky with tears. "I... I forgot how to feel like this. I forgot so much. I j-just wish that my mother and father could be here..."

"I know." He drew me in closer with a gentle hand on the small of my back, and ran his free hand through my hair. "I wish mine could be here, too. But we have to make the best of the hand that life's dealt us, and we are." There was a moment of silence, and then he gave me a thoughtful smile. "I think that you should keep your maiden name, though. Like Anahera said, this is our world now, our choices, our traditions. I don't want the McDermott name to die out when the last two women bearing the name marry. You two are the only ones to keep the name alive, and it deserves to be remembered."

I listened as he spoke, nodding slowly. When he was done, I took a deep breath and nodded again, a bit more firmly this time. "I agree. I was thinking, we could make it a tradition that when we have kids, any daughters we have take the McDermott family name, while any sons we have take the Chan family name. Or, when they're old enough, we let them pick which last name they want to have. That way, both our names have a chance to continue into the next generation."

Michael shot me a curious look. "Oh? You've been thinking about us having kids? I thought you hated the idea?"

"I don't hate it," I said softly, breaking eye-contact. I couldn't lie to him, but it was still too early to tell him everything. "I'm afraid of it. There's a difference. But sometimes, you have to confront your fears in the name of the greater good, right?"

"Very true." Michael smiled at me, and slipped his free arm around my shoulders to draw me fully into his embrace. I snuggled up against him and rested my face on his chest. I felt other bodies around us as more people piled onto the dance floor, but I ignored them. Michael's warmth and scent enveloped me, and for a few minutes my life felt perfect.

Suddenly, a shout from one of the lookouts interrupted our peace, and Wiremu came running in from the courtyard in a panic.

"Riders!" he shouted above the sound of the music. "We have three riders coming this way on horseback!"

"Three?" I lifted my head and looked at him. He nodded. "Okay, I think I know who that might be. Don't panic, guys. I invited them."

"Who are they?" Michael asked, a look of worry crossing his face.

I shook my head and smiled at him. "There are some locals in the area that we met while we were out dress-shopping. I think they're all that's left of the army. I'm pretty sure that there were three of them. Let's go out and see."

I took Michael's hand, and helped him to limp through the crowd to where Wiremu waited in the doorway. The three of us went out onto the street front, just in time to watch the riders coming to a halt not far away. It was hard to tell in the shadows of dusk, but I was fairly certain that the lead rider was familiar.

"Sergeant Bryce?" I called, cautious but not overly concerned.

The lead rider dismounted from her horse in a single, graceful movement, then turned and saluted me. As she did so, the fractured light from the courtyard struck her face, and I recognised her. She was not a pretty woman, but she was distinctive: short and stocky, with sun-browned skin and eyes that shone with intelligence.

"Ms McDermott," she greeted me. "Or is it Mrs now?"

"I guess so, but I don't really care. I'm keeping my name, so I'll probably stick with 'Ms'," I answered with a smile. "This is my husband. Michael, meet Sergeant Erica Bryce. Sergeant, this is Michael Chan."

"A constable, I see?" Erica smiled and stepped forward, to offer Michael her hand. "Nice to meet a fellow public servant."

"Likewise." Michael took her hand and shook it. "Would you like to come and enjoy the party?"

"We would, actually," she answered. "My men and I decided that there aren't exactly many opportunities to enjoy ourselves anymore, so we may as well make the most of it. We even brought a couple of bottles of liquor out of our stores."

"Well, that'll make Jim happy," I commented with a laugh, then I beckoned for all three of them to follow me. "Come on inside. There are a lot of people that I'd like you to meet."

***

A few hours later, we'd all danced until our feet hurt, laughed more than we had in years, and eaten until our bellies wanted to pop. After dinner, Doctor Cross rounded up the little kids and took them off to bed, leaving the older ones to do what they pleased. Michael and I had both opted out of the alcohol, but we still enjoyed ourselves watching the antics of our friends, particularly when they were starting to get a little tipsy.

We found ourselves a corner of the couch that was cleaner than the rest, and sat down side by side to cuddle, talk, and watch the others from afar. Michael slid his arm around my waist, encouraging me to snuggle in against him, which I was more than happy to do. We sat together like that for ages, just talking quietly, sipping water, and enjoy our first hours of married life together.

Eventually, Gavin wandered over to visit us. He plopped down on the other end of the couch with a glass of whiskey in his hand, and heaved a long, drawn out sigh. Then, he flicked his one good eye over to us, and lifted a brow. "You two look cosy. Getting tired already?"

"A little bit," I admitted. "I'm not used to late nights anymore. Besides, I forgot how much fun people-watching is." Michael laughed, and Gavin grinned.

"True that," he said thoughtfully, sipping his drink. He was silent for almost a minute, then he shot another glance at us again. "I've been meaning to say, thank you. Not just for inviting us along, but for... doing this. All of this. Moving south. Welcoming people in. Helping us to open up and remember what it was like before fear turned us into a bunch of self-interested tortoises with our heads crammed so far up our own arses that we forgot how to have fun at all."

This time, it was my turn to laugh, but it faded into seriousness after a few seconds. I glanced out across the room at all of my companions, studying them from afar.

"I don't think I really had a choice, Gav," I answered. "Look at them. Every single one of them is a refugee from a life that none of them chose. They were okay on their own, sure, but look at the joy that bringing them together has brought. These people don't just need me – they need each other. They need friends. They need a family. They need a tribe."

"They need a name," he commented thoughtfully. "An identity to attach themselves to, along with this ideal that you've been crafting." He took a long sip of his drink, then smiled at us. "*Nga Tama o te Tumanako*. The Children of Hope." Suddenly, he stood up and headed back towards the festivities, leaving Michael and me to think over what he'd said.

"It's a good name," Michael said softly, his eyes distant. "We could call our city that. Tumanako. Hope."

"And we're the children of Hope." I smiled to myself, absently running my hand over my belly, my thoughts drifting to the tiny baby growing within. "We're all children of hope in a way, aren't we?"

"We are." I felt Michael's fingers on my cheek, and let him tilt my face up until our eyes met. "And that's what you've been saying all along, isn't it? The children are our future, and our hope for a chance to start over."

"Yes." I sighed and lay my head down on his shoulder. "We can do it, Michael. Together, we can save them all, and give all of our people the hope that they deserve."

# The Survivors

Book IV: Spring

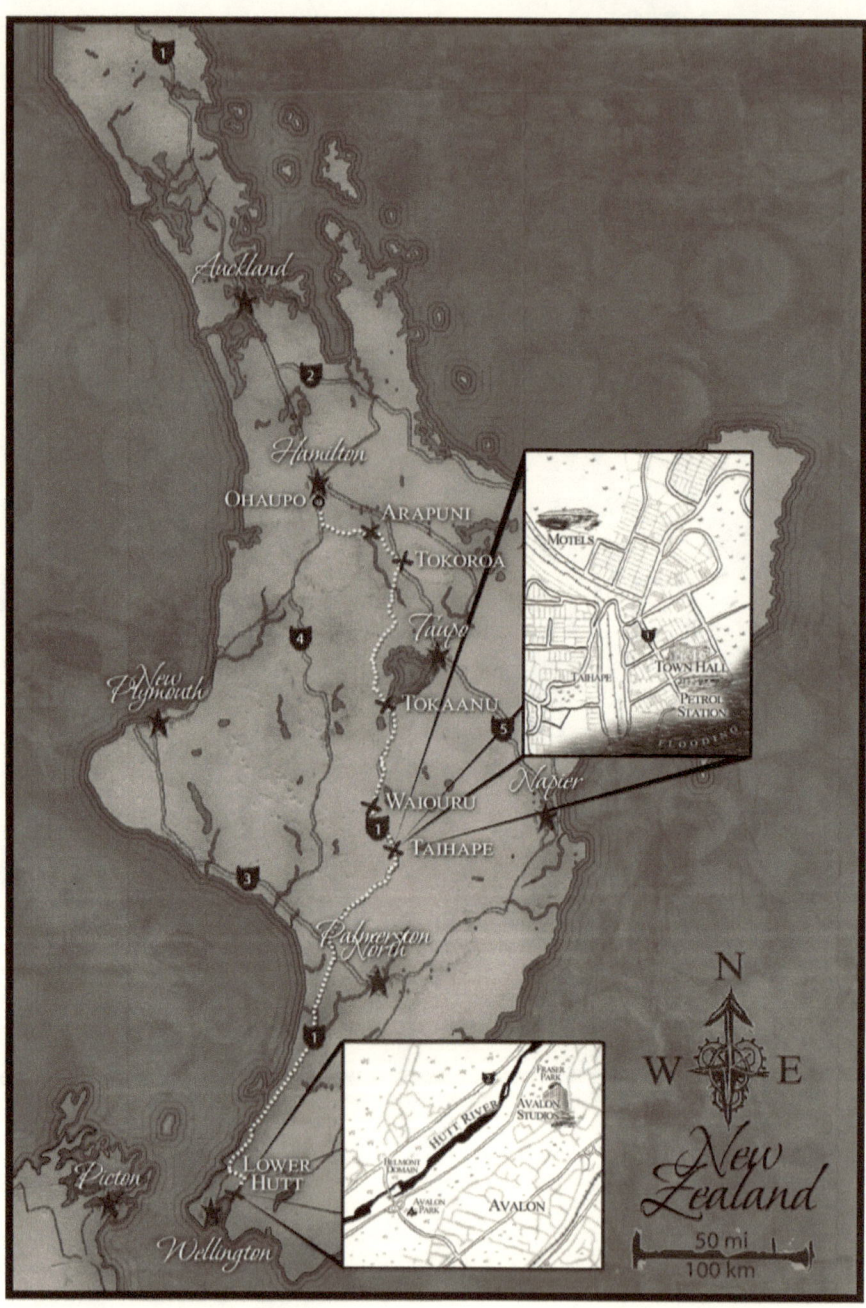

# Chapter One

"Whoa!" I cried, yanking the reins as hard as I could. The horse ignored me and took off at a trot in the wrong direction.

Sergeant Bryce laughed uproariously and shouted instructions after me, "Keep your heels down, McDermott! Lean back in the saddle, and pull gently on the reins. Gently! Stop sawing her mouth, you'll make her mad."

"Make *her* mad? She's making me mad!" I yelled back, but I followed her instructions anyway. To my surprise, the horse responded: she slowed to a walk, and then stopped.

Bryce nudged her mount forward and trotted up to my side. "That's it. Just try to remember that she's a living thing, same as you. I'm sure you wouldn't like to have someone tugging on your mouth."

"No, I suppose I wouldn't," I agreed grudgingly. I sighed and leaned forward to pat the horse's neck. "Sorry, Buttercup. My bad."

"Boudicca," Sergeant Bryce corrected. "Her name is Boudicca. I name all the horses after historical figures."

"To honour their memory?" I asked. "I like that."

"Exactly," Bryce replied. She ran her hand down her horse's mane affectionately. "This old fellow is Pericles. It seemed appropriate, somehow. He talks a lot."

I laughed, but the levity didn't last. "Are you sure you won't come with us, Erica?"

"Oh, I'm sure." She smiled at me, her sun-browned face aged far beyond its years by all the time she'd spent outdoors. "We'll follow eventually, once we're sure there are no more stragglers coming this way. Your message is bound to bring more people over the Central Plateau. We'll stay as a rear guard and direct them after you."

"That satellite phone you gave us should help us keep in touch," I replied. "At least now we can contact you when we need to, and you can update the broadcast for us. That'll save time."

"Yes. The road south of here is going to be quite tough on you, even with the horses." Bryce sighed heavily and shook her head. "We've got plenty of trucks to spare, but not nearly enough fuel."

"It's fine," I replied. I gently nudged my horse around and guided her back towards the base, with Bryce close behind me. "The horses are more useful to us right now than trucks, anyway. We've managed to convert a couple of ours to propane, but if we don't find more petrol soon then we're going to have to start abandoning the vehicles. "

"Let's hope it doesn't come to that," Bryce replied. "You're going to need all the resources you can get once you reach Avalon. In the mean time, I suggest that you keep following the highway south. It'll take you across the mountains, down onto the plains, and then along the coast. You'll have to swing eastwards at Porirua and double back a bit, but that's better than going the other way. The central route would take you across the Rimutaka Ranges, and with this cold I can guarantee the pass will be blocked by snow before you get there."

"Yeah, that's what we were planning to do," I said. "If we don't find any gas in Taihape, we may have to risk a detour through Palmerston North to search for supplies, though."

"You might get lucky," she said. "Not many people around Taihape, so there's a good chance you'll find what you need. If not... my understanding is that the riots pretty much ripped Palmerston North apart, but I haven't heard of any gang activity in the area. At least that's something."

"You keep tabs on gang activity to the south?" I asked, suddenly very interested.

She shrugged, her expression unreadable. "We do what we can to keep civilization afloat, but there are only three of us. The least we can do is attempt to keep track of danger and warn travellers."

"I'd really like to take a look at your maps before we leave, if you wouldn't mind." I glanced at her and gave her a smile. "Are you sure there isn't anything we can do for you before we go, Erica? You've helped us so much that I feel a little guilty not giving anything back."

"No, we don't need anything," she answered simply. "The base is well-stocked. We may be isolated, but we're all trained to live off the land. As soon as we realised that we were all alone out here, we planted a big garden inside the base and rounded up as many stock animals as we could find. I'm just giving you a small fraction of our surplus." She paused for a second and gave me a long look. "Though, if you really do feel indebted, there is something you can do for us."

"Anything," I replied immediately. "Well, anything within reason, of course."

The Sergeant barked a sharp laugh and gave me a smile. "Well, when I say 'us', I mean it in the broadest sense of the word. It's been, what... three days now? I've gotten a good feel for you and your little pack of misfits. What I see is a lot of people struggling to find a bond with their lost culture. I want you to help them find it."

I stared at her, confused. "You want me to help my mates to find their lost culture? How am I supposed to do that?"

Erica laughed again and shook her head. "I'll explain in a second, I promise."

She fell silent as we approached the small paddock where the rest of the horses waited, along with our friends. With the exception of the people on guard duty elsewhere, everyone was in the field talking to, playing with, and learning to ride the horses. Priya cried out a greeting and waved to me enthusiastically. Michael hurried over to open the gate for us, and then once we were safely inside he helped me dismount.

I smiled and gave him a kiss by way of greeting, ignoring the teasing hoots from all around us. Since our wedding three days earlier, my instinctive need for discretion had all but faded away and I no longer felt the desire to hide our relationship behind closed doors. It felt... good. I felt good. Despite the long journey ahead of us, I felt better than I had in a very long time.

"Hey. I'm not done with you yet, McDermott," Sergeant Bryce joked gruffly. Although it had made me a little uncomfortable at first, I'd gotten used to her rough-and-tumble sense of humour. She reminded me of Jim in many ways, except she was far more willing to open herself up and make friends.

"Sorry, sorry!" I joked right back, holding my hands up in mock self-defence. "We were talking about culture?"

"Yes, we were. Come with me." Sergeant Bryce gave Michael a long-suffering look, and added, "Yes, Mrs McDermott. You can come, too."

Michael laughed, just as he'd done every time she called him that. "You know I'm stuck with that nickname now, right? Thanks, Ricky. Much appreciated."

"You keep calling me Ricky, and I'll keep calling you Mrs McDermott. That's the arrangement," she replied, snapping her fingers playfully at him.

Michael started to chuckle again, then suddenly he froze and gave her an embarrassed look. "Wait – It just occurred to me that you might genuinely not like being called 'Ricky'. It wasn't intended as an insult or anything."

"And it wasn't taken as one." Her broad face relaxed into a smile and she made a dismissive gesture with one hand. "I like Ricky. Erica, Bryce, Ricky, Sergeant – it doesn't really bother me"

"Okay, so long as you're not actually upset," he replied, putting on that whipped puppy expression I knew so well. "I hate to admit it, but... I don't really understand. You, I mean. Not the name thing."

Erica sighed and glanced at me. "I've already had to explain it at least twice a day since you guys arrived. Explain it to your man, will you?"

"Sure," I agreed. I gestured for her to lead on, and took Michael's hand. While we were walking back towards the base that the soldiers called home, I explained the Sergeant's identity as she'd explained it to me. "Sergeant Bryce is bi-gender. That means she identifies as both male and female simultaneously." I glanced at her. "Did I get that right, Sarge?"

"Bang on, McDermott," she replied with a grin. "Good to know that you were listening."

"I'm always listening," I answered dryly. "You're just not always good at making yourself clear."

"I'm still confused," Michael admitted sheepishly. "Can I ask a question?"

"Of course, son," Sergeant Bryce responded, her expression easing back into a friendly smile. Despite the constant teasing, it was obvious that she'd developed a bit of a soft spot for him. That didn't surprise me at all, since they were birds of feather. Both of them had a wicked sense of humour, but at the core they just wanted to protect and serve. The only difference was how they'd chosen to do it.

"I'm sorry, I don't know how to ask this politely," he admitted, looking more and more sheepish by the moment. "Does that... does that mean you... have both guy *and* girl parts?"

Sergeant Bryce and I exchanged a stunned look, then we both cracked up laughing. We laughed so hard that we had to stop walking, and I started seeing stars from lack of oxygen. When my laughter finally faded, I glanced at the Sergeant to check if she was offended, but it was immediately obvious she wasn't.

I took a deep breath and looked back at Michael, struggling to keep myself under control. "No, honey. Biologically, she's a woman. I don't understand it well enough to explain it in great detail, but the simple answer is that she is who she is and we should try to respect that. She'll tell us if there's something we need to know."

"Well, that I can do," Michael agreed, his expression brightening. "Sorry if I've said anything offensive. Please don't hate me."

"I don't hate you, son," she said, her tone turning gentle again. "I don't hate anyone who's willing to learn. Learning is the most important part of life – and that's why I'm dragging you both home with me. Now, if we're done picking apart my gender identity, let's get inside before the rain comes back."

We fell into a comfortable silence as we walked the rest of the way, though once the humour was no longer distracting me I began to worry again. The rain had been nearly incessant for the last few weeks, and every droplet increased the risk of a serious flood. Still, there was some part of me that told me that we had to keep travelling. If we could just get out of the highlands and away from the Waikato, then we'd be safe.

A few minutes later, Erica shoved open a door and led us up a flight of stairs into what had obviously once been crew quarters. There were no crewmen anymore, though – just hundreds and hundreds of books. Maybe thousands. She'd managed to collect at least a dozen bookcases, but it clearly wasn't enough; books, CDs, and DVDs sat in neat piles on the floor and stacked up on the old bunk beds. In one corner, framed artwork rested beneath drop-cloths to protect it from the dust. A few small sculptures and stuffed animals sat on another small table near the door.

"Whoa," I gasped. "Is this what you meant by culture?"

"Yes. You see this? This is just a book, right?" Erica went over to one of the nearest piles and picked a book up off the top of the stack. She turned back to face us with the book in her hand, her expression intense. "Wrong. It's not just a book anymore; it's a piece of our history, our intellectual, spiritual, and cultural legacy. Someone made this, McDermott. Everything in this room was created by another person, and that's important. They're not just books anymore. Not just movies, or paintings, or albums. Not just things. These objects are a record of who we were. One day, these things may be all that's left of us. Isn't that worth protecting?"

"I never thought of it like that," I said softly. Understanding struck me like a solid wave of force, and suddenly I found tears in my eyes. I brushed them away hastily and took a deep breath. "You're right. That is worth protecting. That's the whole point of museums, isn't it? We preserve the past so that future generations can better understand their own roots. What's the point of saving lives if we can't save their identities as well?"

"Then we'll just have to figure out a way to do that, too," Michael said resolutely, all traces of humour gone from his voice and replaced by steely determination. "I have faith in us – all of us. We can do it."

"Yes." I stood up a little straighter and glanced up at him, seeking solace in his eyes. "Once we've established our new city and the weather clears up, then we'll figure out a way to transport all of this to our new city."

"Don't forget that the National Library is in Wellington," Erica said, absently trailing her fingers across the cover of the book. "The National Library is a repository of everything made by Kiwi creators over the years. Assuming that it survived the riots, we should be able to salvage a lot of material."

I nodded and took one last look around the room, then I glanced back at her. "We need to get back on the road. If we leave now, we should be able to get half way to Taihape before we run out of daylight."

Sergeant Bryce just nodded. She put the book back down and led us out of the room, back to face the mission that seemed to be taking on a life all of its own.

# Chapter Two

It took longer than anticipated to get the convoy ready to move again. Along with half-a-dozen horses, the satellite phone, and fresh supplies, Sergeant Bryce had given us a spare wagon and tracings to help us in our voyage. She accompanied us for the first few kilometres, while our people learned the art of driving a team. Skylar had insisted on taking the first shift behind the reins, for reasons that I could only guess at.

"It's a good thing you picked patient horses," I called to Sergeant Bryce. Boudicca snorted and flicked her head, not quite sure whether I was talking to her, but she calmed down when I reached out and patted the back of her neck. It had taken a while for us to get a feel for one another, but we were swiftly becoming fast friends.

"Skylar's doing just fine," Sergeant Bryce replied, her voice firm and confident. "It just takes practice."

"See? I'm doing fine!" Skye called, looking about as proud as I'd ever seen her.

I gently leaned back in the saddle and eased my mount into line beside them. "Who said anything about Skylar? I meant all of the horses, not just the team. It can't be easy for them to have to deal with a bunch of newbies like us."

"Oh, yeah." Skye laughed and shook her head. "We'll get there. Like Ricky said, it just takes practice. But hey, at least no one's fallen off yet!"

"Thank heavens for small favours," I answered dryly. I glanced up at the sky to gauge the time, then looked at Sergeant Bryce. "You're going to have to head off soon, if you want to make it back to Waiouru before dusk."

"Yes, I am." She glanced at me and gave me a tight smile. "Keep me updated on your progress southwards. I'll set your new message broadcasting tonight."

"Thank you." I hesitated for a second, then I reached over and gently touched her arm. "Not just the horses or the phone or the supplies, but… for everything. I'm glad to know there are so many people out there who share my vision."

"It's hard not to, when our other option is extinction. Safe travels, McDermott." Sergeant Bryce snapped a salute, then she turned her mount around and headed back to Waiouru.

I watched until she was out of sight, then I glanced at Skye. "Looks like we're on our own now."

"And the rain's coming back," she said, gesturing towards the horizon. A moment later I felt an icy wind strike me, and smelt the tell-tale scent of. I sighed heavily and took my radio out of its pocket.

"Button up, everyone," I advised. "Rain's going to be here any minute."

Before I'd finished speaking, I felt the first droplet land on my cheek. I hastily tucked my radio away, pulled my hood over my head, and buttoned my coat all the way up to my chin.

A moment later, the deluge began.

\*\*\*

We were all cold, wet, and miserable by the time we decided to stop for the night. We found a large farmhouse right beside the road, but it still took us until after sunset to clear the area, bed the horses down in the barn, and set the night watch. I finished grooming Boudicca by torchlight, then ducked out into the turbulent weather to make my way back to the main house.

Skylar was waiting for me at the door. She waved when she saw me, but as soon as I stepped into range of her nose, she screwed her face up and gave me a dark look. "Gross. You smell like wet horse."

"Thanks, sis. You sure know how to make a girl feel pretty," I replied. She stepped back and let me across the threshold; the moment I was inside I realised that something was amiss. "No power?"

"No power," she said with a nod. "We could set up the generator, but that means using fuel."

"Let's try to avoid that, if we can," I answered. "Do we at least have a fireplace?"

"Yeah." She nodded again, pointing through a nearby doorway. "And there's a shed with plenty of firewood up the back of the house. Plumbing seems to be working, though. That's something."

"Better than nothing," I said with a shrug. "How are we for bedding?"

"There are a few beds upstairs, but I wouldn't recommend it," she replied, wrinkling up her nose. "It's pretty gross up there. Doc's decided he wants to risk it, but I think we're better off sleeping in the living room. Kitchen's over there, if you want to grab some grub."

"Yeah, I probably should," I answered. I caught myself with a hand half-raised to rub my belly, and pretended to scratch my elbow instead. Mercifully, Skye didn't seem to notice my lapse; her expression was distracted, and I could practically see her organizing what needed to be done in her head.

Suddenly, her eyes snapped back into focus, and she looked at me. "Oh, one more thing. Doc wants to talk to you, when you have a second. He's already gone upstairs."

"Why am I not surprised? He never did like getting cosy with us," I said, chuckling. I patted her shoulder, then left her side and headed up the stairs.

I found Doctor Cross inside the first bedroom I came across, in a consultation with Michael. Michael was sitting on the edge of the bed with his foot up in Doc's lap. The room was lit only by a small gas lantern, but it was enough for Doc to see what he was doing.

"This seems to be healing nicely," Doc was saying as I walked up to the doorway, touching the bones in Michael's ankle. "It's definitely just a sprain. That's good news."

"Yeah, it's a little tender, but so long as I'm careful with my footing it's fine," Michael replied. He glanced up, and gave me a smile and a nod. "Hey, Sandy."

"Hey yourself," I returned the greeting, leaning against the doorframe with my arms folded across my chest. "So he's not dying, then? I'm too young to be a widow."

"Well, if you want to get philosophical, everyone is dying," Doc answered dryly. He lowered Michael's foot back to the floor and leaned back in his chair. "You're fine, Constable. How are the painkillers working?"

"Well enough that I've got nothing to complain about," Michael replied with his usual impish grin. He eased himself up to his feet and dusted his hands off on his jeans, then came over to stand in front of me. At first I thought he was going to lean down and kiss me, but he stopped just short, close enough that I could feel his warmth without actually touching me. His closeness sent a shiver right through me, and brought a flush to my cheeks. He always knew just the right buttons to push to make my heart race. "We've got duty tonight. You happy with the first shift?"

"Of course," I replied, reaching up to touch his chest so that my fingers could trace the line of his wedding band hidden beneath the cloth. Even after we'd formalized our marriage, we both still chose to wear our rings on necklaces around our throats rather than on our fingers. It felt like that would keep them safer while we were slogging through mud, rain, and everything else nature had to throw at us.

Michael glanced down at my hand, then looked back at me and gave me one of the subtle half-smiles that he saved just for me. "Good. I need to go organise the rest of the roster. See you downstairs afterwards?"

"Definitely," I agreed. "I'll most likely be in the kitchen."

"Then I'll see you there," he said. His hand touched my shoulder and slid down the length of my arm all the way to my hand, then he lifted it to his lips and pressed a kiss against my knuckles. A second later, he brushed past me and vanished into the hall.

Doctor Cross cleared his throat awkwardly. "Well, that was... interesting. Please close the door, Ms McDermott."

I did as I was told, then I went over to sit on the edge of the bed in the spot Michael had vacated a minute earlier.

"You got the test results, didn't you?" I asked, keeping my voice low enough that it was unlikely we'd be overheard. "Am I pregnant or not?"

Doc shot a glance at the closed door, then picked himself up and came over to sit on the bed beside me. "Yes, you are. There's no doubting it. I tested it three times, and each time was positive." He paused for a moment, and gave me a long, considering look. "You seem unusually calm about this, given that you nearly had a nervous breakdown on me a few days ago."

"I've had time to think," I admitted, absently rubbing my belly. This time, I didn't try to hide the gesture. There was no point, since he already knew. "I'm scared, Doc. I'm really, really scared. But this is also kind of what I wanted, isn't it? I mean, I didn't want to single-handedly repopulate the earth, but I want to see us flourish again. That's why I'm fighting so hard for us to make it to the south. For the kids. For the next generation. This just... makes it more personal."

"And more urgent," the doctor finished for me. I glanced at him and nodded.

"Michael and I haven't exactly had a lot of alone-time since the fire," I said. I closed my eyes for a moment and thought back, running over the figures in my mind. "I can pinpoint nearly to the day when I would have conceived. It would have been around the full moon before last. It's almost new moon again now, so I'd be about six weeks along."

"Then we should have another couple of months before you start to show," Doc said. I opened my eyes and found him studying me with a critical eye. "Possibly less, but it's hard to tell at this early stage. Most first-time mothers don't start to show until around twelve to sixteen weeks in, because it takes some time for your uterus to stretch enough to distend your abdomen. You're also quite tall, and that may help conceal it for longer."

"May, but we can't guarantee anything," I said with a sigh. "We're just going to have to play things by ear, and hope that we're worrying for nothing. I'm also going to have to be careful about what I eat and drink, but there isn't really anything we can do about the risk of the baby being born infected, is there?"

"My understanding is that a child can't be born infected," he said, frowning. "I've heard the rumours about Elira's daughter, but we can't jump to conclusions. Stillbirths happen frequently in nature, particularly when twins are involved. The baby should share your immunity until it's weaned, just like it will share your immunity to everything else that you've acquired antibodies to fight against. After that, I don't know. All we can really do is pray."

I raised a brow and shot him a curious look. "I thought you were a man of science, not religion?"

"I am, but sometimes I wonder." He shrugged sheepishly and glanced away. "I've got a granddaughter who can apparently read minds and see into the future. I think that would be enough to make anyone wonder."

"True." I stood up slowly and stretched my back. "Ugh, this horse-riding thing is hard. My back is killing me. Can you recommend anything to keep me from stiffening up like this?"

"Not really," he admitted. "It'll just take some time for your body to get used to it, I think. I can give you some painkillers, if you like?"

"Nah, it's not that bad," I replied, shaking my head. "I'll just ask Michael to give me a back rub. Thanks, though."

"Quite all right, Ms McDermott," he said. "I'll check my stores tomorrow, and see if I have any pre-natal vitamins that might give you and the baby a fighting chance."

"Thanks, Doc," I replied. I smiled at him, and touched my forehead in a rough approximation of a salute. "Have a good night."

The doctor returned the sentiment and waved me out of his room, then closed the door behind me. I fished my torch out of my pocket, and used its light to guide my way back down the stairs, into the kitchen. There, I found Anahera and Ryan washing the dishes by the light of another lantern, and talking softly to one another. I switched my torch off again to conserve its batteries, and went over to pick up a bowl of lukewarm stew that was sitting on the bench.

Anahera glanced over and gave me a stern look. "Why are you always the last one to come and have dinner? Is my cooking really that bad?"

"Your cooking is great," I hurriedly reassured her. "I just have an endless list of things to do, and never enough hours in the day. You know how it is."

"Indeed." Her frown melted into a smile, and she held a spoon out to me. I took it gratefully and settled on a stool to eat my fill. While I was eating, she turned her attention back to Ryan. "You worry far too much, my friend. Just relax and let the cards fall where they may."

"I know. It's just… it's hard," Ryan admitted, his gaze focused on the dish that he was drying. Once he was satisfied with it, he set it down and took another one out of the tray. "She's already moved on. I don't want to… you know, get in the way."

"Skylar," Anahera said to me by way of explanation, then she resumed speaking to Ryan. "I cannot presume to guess how she feels, but there's no reason for you to give up on her completely. Just try to show her that you've learned from what happened and that you really care about her. She may forgive you."

"No one makes decisions for Skye except Skye," I added, using the very same words as when I'd spoken to Hemi a few weeks earlier. "If you think you still deserve her affections, then show her that. One rule, though."

They both glanced at me, brows raised.

I grinned and waved my spoon at Ryan in mock threat. "No more fighting! Understood?"

"Yes, ma'am," Ryan answered, looking shamefaced.

Anahera just laughed and shook her head. "And on that note, I'm going to get ready for bed. All these affairs of the heart are too much for my poor, elderly psyche."

"You're only, like, ten years older than me," I pointed out.

"More like fifteen," she replied, flicking her sponge into the sink. The dishwater gurgled as it drained away, and then she rinsed her hands under the tap. "Not that it matters, I suppose. What is age but a number?"

"Exactly my point," I said, digging around in my stew for a particularly juicy-looking piece of fish. "You're a MILF and you know it, lady. You're just fishing for compliments."

Ryan froze with a dish half-dried in his hand and turned bright red. Anahera hid a chuckle behind a cough.

"Perhaps I am," she replied, amusement dancing across her tattooed lips. "Everyone likes to feel attractive. Goodnight, dear."

"Goodnight," I said simply. I scooped up the morsel I'd been hunting for and popped it into my mouth, enjoying the burst of flavour that came along with it. By the time I'd swallowed it, Anahera was gone, leaving me alone with a beet-red red-head. I looked at him, and raised a brow. "You all right, Ry?"

"Fine!" he replied, a little too enthusiastically. A second later, his shoulders slumped, and he shot a guilty look at me. "I just... never thought of her like that before. I'm not sure how to feel."

"She's not *your* mum, so you can feel any way you like," I replied with a shrug. "So, what was that I walked in on? You thinking of making another play for Skye's heart?"

"Maybe," he said. He turned away from me on the pretence of packing the dishes away, but I sensed that it was more to hide his face from me than any real desire to work. "I still love her. It's hard to see her with Hemi."

"You do realise there's no reason she has to pick just one of you, right?" I said, shovelling another spoonful into my mouth.

Ryan turned back and looked at me quizzically. "What do you mean?"

I swallowed, and gave him a grin. "This is our world, Ry. Our rules. There are a lot more men than women in this group, and I suspect that's going to be fairly standard across the board. For this generation at least, polygamous relationships may be a good idea."

"Polygamous?" he echoed, his eyes widening. "You mean... Skye could be with both me *and* Hemi? At the same time?"

"Not in bed, obviously," I said dryly, then paused to re-evaluate. "Well, unless you guys swing that way. None of my business. But, yeah, why not? Rebecca's hooking up with Tane and Iorangi, and it seems to be working out well for the three of them."

"I don't know," he admitted, looking uncertain. "I mean, maybe. I'd have to think about it. And talk to them, of course."

"Of course," I replied, shrugging again. "Your rules, kid. At least it's an option, and that way no one has to get hurt. If I remember correctly, you liked Hemi before all this happened."

"Yeah," he agreed. "I mean, I didn't know him very well, but he seemed like a cool guy."

"And do you really want to fight with a potential friend over a girl?" I said in the driest tone I could muster. That made him smile.

"I don't want to fight with anyone, really," he replied, shaking his head.

"Then don't," I said simply. I rose to my feet and went over to wash my bowl in the sink, then handed it to him to dry.

He took it, stared at it for a second, then smiled again and nodded. "Good advice, as usual. Thanks, Sandy."

"Any time, mate." I patted him on the shoulder, then dismissed myself and went off in search of Skylar.

I found her in the living room, supervising the distribution of spare blankets. We were well into our sixth week of travel, and all of us had acquired a set of blankets that we'd come to think of as our own, but with the weather getting colder and colder it was a constant struggle to stay warm. I watched for a moment, until she noticed me standing there.

"Oh, hey," she said by way of greeting. "Can you do me a favour?"

"Sure," I replied. "How can I help?"

"We're running a bit late tonight," she said, tossing a rolled-up blanket to one of the others. "Can you go round up the girls, please? I sent them upstairs to look for extra bedding, but they haven't come back down."

"I'm on it," I said, saluting her playfully. She was so busy she barely even had a chance to acknowledge me. I left her to it and headed back upstairs, flicking my torch on to guide the way. The light under Doc's door had already been extinguished, telling me that he'd decided to have an early night. I passed his door and moved deeper into the building.

The sound of whispering voices and muffled laughs drew me to a half-open doorway, lit by the faint glow of an oil lamp. I quietly pushed the door open and peeked inside: Melody, Priya, Maddy, and the twins stood huddled around an ornate vanity, playing with something I couldn't quite see. I took another step closer, straining to get a better look at what they were doing. A loose board creaked under my foot, and suddenly the girls all spun to look at me, wide-eyed, guilty-looking, their faces covered in a rainbow of multi-coloured cosmetics.

"Oh, you guys," I groaned, covering my eyes with one hand. "What have you done?"

"Well, we found this stuff," Melody said, straightening her shoulders and flicking her short, ash-blonde hair back out of her face. "So we decided to have some fun while we were up here."

"That 'stuff' will ruin your skin," I said, moving over to the vanity. I picked up one of the pallets, closed it, and squinted at the faded label. "This is twelve years old, guys. Twelve. And it's used. It's probably full of someone else's eye-gunk, and will give you a nasty infection. Go wash it off before you get sick or something."

A chorus of groans answered me, followed by complaints, whining, and then laughter as they filed out of the room and down the hall, taking the lamp with them. I heard running water, then a squeal, some splashing, and more laughter. The sound of it made me smile; there was a growing sense of camaraderie amongst the group, as people discovered similar interests with one another and friendships began to blossom. Melody had swiftly expanded her little gang to include both Priya and Madeline, while Solomon had drifted out of it and gravitated towards Matt and his younger brothers. He still never said anything, but that didn't seem to impede their budding friendship at all.

I left the girls to their own devices and set about the task that Skylar had originally given them. Gripping my torch between my teeth, I yanked the duvet and blankets off the bed near the vanity, and dragged the bedclothes out into the hallway. A musty scent came up from them and tickled my nose, but I ignored it; I didn't have to sleep in there, or even be in the room long enough to worry about mould in the walls or the bedding. We just needed a little extra warmth to ride out the chilly night.

The house was a large one, with four bedrooms in addition to the one that Doc had claimed. By the time the girls had finished disinfecting their faces, I'd stripped all the mattresses and created a fairly sizeable pile of bedding that needed to be carted downstairs. I assigned the twins to carry stuff downstairs, and put the other girls to work searching the rooms for useful objects. Melody and Priya went one way, while Madeline padded along after me.

Despite her youth, Maddy was a quick study and knew what to look for. While I was yanking open dresser drawers and digging out salvageable clothing, she went over to search the wardrobe. We worked in silence for a couple of minutes, expertly sorting what was useful from what was past its prime.

Suddenly, Madeline called my name. "Miss Sandy?"

Something about her tone of voice set me on edge, and the look on her face didn't help. The little girl wrinkled up her nose and held something out to me; by torchlight, I couldn't make out much of it besides the fact that it was a wooden case.

"We need to give this to Mister Michael," she said softly, in that odd, dreamy tone she sometimes got when her head wasn't entirely in our world.

"What is it?" I asked.

"He'll know," she said. Without asking permission, she took the case and walked out into the hall.

I hurried to catch up with her, leaving my findings to be dealt with at a later time. I'd learned to listen when Madeline got that kind of look on her face, even if she didn't make any sense. The other girls stuck their heads out as we walked past their doors, then fell into step behind us. I heard them whispering to one another, but I said nothing. Madeline's movements were stiff and robotic, like a sleepwalker; something about them had me in what felt almost felt like a trance. I was aware enough that I could have broken it if I'd wanted to, but I didn't want to.

We followed the little girl down the stairs and into the living room. She didn't even pause to look around, just walked right up to where Michael was sitting and put the case in his lap.

Michael stared at it blankly for a second, then suddenly understanding dawned in his eyes. "Is that what I think it is?"

Maddy just smiled and sat down on the ground at his feet without a word. A hushed silence fell over the group, and we all watched as Michael opened the case to reveal a violin nestled upon black velvet. He ran his hands reverently across the polished wood, and then lifted the instrument out of the case.

"I haven't held one of these since high school," he whispered, his voice barely audible. He glanced up and looked at me. I stared back at him, but I couldn't think of anything to say. Something told me to follow Madeline's lead, so I did. I heard movement around me as the others sat down, waiting. A flicker of unreadable emotion passed through Michael's eyes as he ran his fingertips softly along the length of the strings, then picked up the bow and touched it to them.

That first note sent a chill right through me and left me shivering with anticipation. His touch was tentative and uncertain as he tuned the strings, but it didn't matter. I wanted to hear the notes, I wanted it so badly that I couldn't have expressed it in words even if I'd tried. When the music began, it was the most beautiful thing I'd ever heard. It was unsteady, imperfect, even a little hesitant, but that didn't matter. My soul cried out for it, and Michael gave it to us.

I felt tears running down my cheeks and made no attempt to brush them away. Music was something we'd taken for granted before the plague, but afterwards our world had become a silent place. Hearing the notes now took my awareness into another place, a place where only my imagination and the music existed. When the piece finally ended, it left me feeling wrung out and exhausted, but satisfied beyond belief.

A hand touched my cheek, stroking away the tears that had fallen upon them. I opened my eyes and found Michael watching me with the kind of tenderness that he reserved just for me.

"Are you all right?" he asked softly, trailing his thumb across my skin. I just nodded dumbly and smiled at him, though I couldn't find the words to express how I felt.

I didn't need to, though. Michael understood me – and for once, everyone else did as well.

# Chapter Three

I awoke the next morning in pre-dawn gloom, hemmed in on all sides by sleeping bodies. Michael stirred but didn't wake as I gently extracted myself from the circle of his arms. Priya didn't even open her eyes, though she did snuggle a bit closer to Alfred for warmth. It was freezing cold despite our best efforts to keep warm overnight, but at least my clothing had managed to dry on the lines we'd strung across the kitchen.

I plucked my clothing off the line and headed into the bathroom to go through my usual morning ablutions. A thorough scrub with a washcloth was the best I was going to have in terms of bathing; it was far too cold for a full shower without the luxury of hot water. Once I was dressed, dried, and groomed, I opened the door – and almost fell over Tigger, who had chosen to ambush me by sitting right on the threshold.

She mewed at me, then hefted her tail and pranced off towards the back door, leaving no mistake about what she wanted. I rolled my eyes and followed her. Gavin was on watch by the door, wrapped in a couple of blankets. He nodded a greeting when he saw me and unlocked the door to let us outside. While Tigger was busy fussing around on the wet, frosty grass, I sat down on the stoop to put my shoes on and admire the sunrise.

"Red sky in the morning," Gavin said quietly. He stepped outside and pulled the door closed behind him. "Looks like we're in for another cracker of a day."

"If by 'cracker' you mean 'terrible', then yes," I replied with some amusement. The cold made the scar on my foot ache, but as soon as I put my shoes and socks on, it felt a bit better.

"Yep," he said, with a long, deep sigh. "It's going to be a harsh winter this year, I think. I can feel it in my bones."

"We had a long, hot summer, so I guess we're about due for it," I replied. "We just have to find ways to stay warm until spring or Avalon, whichever comes first."

Gavin chuckled softly. He leaned against one of the posts supporting the porch roof and gave me a thoughtful look. "Your group seems to be good at that."

"*Our* group, Gav," I scolded gently. "It's been over a month now, mate. You can start thinking of us as friends – or even family, if you like."

"I know," he said, his gaze drifting away to study the horizon. "I'll get there eventually. You know how I am."

"Better than most," I said, reaching up to pat his hand. Then I hesitated for a second, considering my options. I had to be careful who I told about my situation, but Gavin was one of the few people I felt I could trust to help me without giving things away before I was ready. "Gav, I need your help with something, but it has to stay just between us. Can you keep a secret?"

He glanced down at me again, his expression shifting to one of open curiosity. "Of course, Sandy. Anything."

I took a deep breath and a moment to organise my thoughts, then I looked up at him again. "I told you what happened to my sister, right? And her baby?"

He nodded silently, encouraging me to continue. I glanced away and shifted on my seat. Even though I knew it was far too small to actually feel yet, I imagined I could feel the baby inside me with every movement and it distracted me in ways I wasn't used to yet.

496

While I was still trying to figure out the right thing to say, Gavin chuckled and his voice took on a note of genuine amusement. "Oh, I know that look. My wife used to do that when she was pregnant with our daughter – sit there looking uncomfortable, hugging her belly. How far along are you?"

"About six weeks," I said, relieved that he'd guessed what I was trying to tell him. "I don't want to tell Michael just yet, not after what happened to Skye's baby."

"Your husband is a smart man," Gavin said. "He'll figure it out sooner rather than later – particularly if you keep doing that." He pointed at my hands, which were still wrapped protectively around my middle.

"I know," I said, hugging myself a little tighter. "And I'll tell him once we get to Avalon. I just can't deal with it right now. Michael's very protective, and he desperately wants a family. As soon as he finds out that I'm pregnant, he's going to try and wrap me up in cotton wool and pamper me like a princess."

"I think you're the only person I know who would put this much effort into *not* being treated like royalty," Gavin answered dryly. "Would it really be such a bad thing?"

"Under normal circumstances, it would just cramp my style," I replied. "But right now, I don't have time for it and neither does anyone else. We don't have the luxury of letting me indulging myself. There's just too much that needs to be done. I need to stay strong and put on a determined face, to keep the group together and travelling in the right direction."

"That makes sense, but... I'm not sure I'm comfortable lying to him," he said. "If I were in his position, I'd want to know. Aren't you concerned that he's going to be annoyed when he finds out?"

"A little," I admitted. "I have no intention of lying to him, though. If he asks me outright, I'll tell him the truth. But if he doesn't ask, then I'll just keep it to myself a little while longer. Just until Avalon. Just until everyone is safe and settled."

"All right," he replied, nodding slowly. "Just until Avalon. What do you need from me, then?"

"At this stage?" I glanced around, then shrugged. "Just keep an eye on Michael and let me know if you see any sign that he's on to me. He seems to like you, and we're used to you being weird and secretive. You're Mister Mysterious. That's your whole schtick. I swear, in a past life you were an international super-spy or something."

Gavin laughed at that and offered me a hand to get up. "Right, right, whatever you say, funny lady. Shouldn't you go have breakfast now that you're eating for two?"

I opened my mouth to answer him, only to be interrupted by the demanding mew of a little tabby at my feet. Tigger had one thing on her mind, and it sure as heck wasn't the contents of *my* belly.

\*\*\*

We made good time along the road towards the next stop on our voyage: the small but pretty town called Taihape, which was famous for nothing but being a waypoint along the route between Auckland and Wellington, and a statue of a giant gumboot. Melody and I rode together in the vanguard. We hadn't seen anything that resembled a threat in quite some time, so we were both starting to let our guards drop just a little, but we knew better than to relax completely. Coming up on a new town could mean anything, or it could mean nothing. Whatever happened, we were ready for it.

Just as we were closing in on the outskirts of town, a human figure jumped into view, waving frantically. Melody shouted an alert and tensed up, but I held up a hand to keep her from taking any rash action.

"Are you carrying your gun?" I asked her. She didn't bother to reply, just shot me a scathing look. Of course, she had her gun. Stupid question. I chuckled softly to myself, and pulled my walkie-talkie out from inside my coat. "Halt the convoy; we've got someone up ahead hailing us. Watch the back and sides, this may be a trap." I put my radio away and glanced at Melody. "Ask questions first, shoot second. Got it?"

She grunted and rolled her eyes. "Fine."

"Good," I said. "If they run when we get close, we'll know it's a trap. Don't follow them, just get back to the convoy as fast as you can." This time she just nodded, her natural hostility fading in the face of potential danger. Whatever else she might think of me, she knew that I'd watch her back in a fight and that I expected her to watch mine. I gave her a quick smile, then I touched my heels to Boudicca's sides and guided the horse up to a trot.

I felt a familiar tension building up inside me as we closed the gap between us and the mysterious figure, one that made me forget all about the discomfort in my back and thighs from hours in the saddle. I found myself sitting up a little straighter, stretching my muscles in anticipation. Erica's maps said that Taihape wasn't gang territory, but it never hurt to be prepared.

I needn't have worried, though. The person made no attempt to attack us. As soon as we started moving towards him he raced out to greet us, then skidded to a halt and stared up at us wide-eyed. He looked back and forth between us, then fixated on Melody.

"Are you Sandrine McDermott?" he asked, as excited as a teenager meeting his celebrity crush. He was about the right age for it, too: maybe fifteen or sixteen at the most, with skin so black that it shone like polished onyx in the rain, and a grin like lightning in contrast.

Melody snorted a laugh and shook her head, pointing at me. The boy's gaze shifted to me and his eyes widened even more. "You? You're Sandrine McDermott? Really?"

"The one and only," I answered, struggling to keep my expression serious.

The youth yelped and jumped back. "You are! You are! I recognise your voice! Wait here, I need to go get my dad." He spun around and started to dash away, only to skid to a halt again and turn back. "I mean, please wait here? Please? I won't be long, I promise."

"Go on, then," I said. I gave up on trying to keep a straight face and just grinned at him, suddenly caught by his infectious humour. The youth grinned back, then let out a whoop and ran off as fast as his legs could carry him.

As soon as he was out of sight, Melody shot me a dubious look. "Are you sure this isn't a trap? That guy was a bit weird."

"Not weird, just excited," I replied with a shrug. "My instincts say he's not a danger to any of us. What do yours say?"

Melody paused and thought it over for a minute, then she shrugged as well. "My instincts say the same. I think he's been waiting to join us."

I glanced in the direction the youth had gone, only to do a double take in surprise. "I would say you're right."

Melody followed my gaze, and then her jaw dropped. There were people coming out of the buildings nearby, watching us and whispering excitedly amongst themselves. I glanced at Melody and saw her fingering the hilt of her gun, but after a few seconds she relaxed.

"I don't see any weapons," she said quietly. "But there sure are a lot of them."

"There are," I replied, gently squeezing her arm to try and keep her calm. "There must be twenty-five people down there."

Melody gasped and pointed towards the group. "Look! That woman has a baby!"

"Well, that settles it, right?" I said. "She wouldn't bring her baby out here if they meant us any harm, would she?"

"No, she wouldn't," Melody said quietly, her tone suddenly filled with fascination and awe. "She's so tiny. I haven't seen a baby since the twins were little."

"I get the feeling you're going to see one up close very soon," I replied. Before we could discuss it any further, a tall man with ebony skin that matched the youth's pushed his way through the crowd and stepped out into the rain. He was dressed all in leather, much as I was, but his shaved head was uncovered and glistened with raindrops. He closed the distance between us with long, powerful strides, his son hot on his heels.

"Greetings, Sandrine McDermott and friend," he called, raising a hand to wave. "Welcome to Taihape!"

I returned the gesture and called a greeting back. "Hello there! And who might you be, mate?"

"My name is Johan Abrahms, and you've already met my son Dominic," he said as he came to a stop in front of us. "We came from the east when we heard your message, and picked up as many folks along the way as we could."

"By friendly means, I hope?" I asked, determined to get the uncomfortable questions out of the way before I let my guard down all the way.

Johan let out a deep, merry laugh and nodded. "Definitely. We just spread the word about what you were hoping to achieve, and all these people came with us willingly. There are some others who decided to travel on their own, but what you see here is most of the people left alive between here and Hastings."

I looked over the group of people watching us, and saw an odd mixture of expectation, hope, and fear written across every face.

"There are so many of them," I said quietly, frowning to myself. "And yet, so few at the same time. I had hoped more of us survived."

"I know what you mean," Johan said understandingly. He offered his hand to help me down from my horse; after a moment's hesitation, I accepted the help and dismounted. "We did what you told us, and brought as much as we could carry. We've been here for a few days, so we've already found a few sources of fuel that seem to be good."

"That's a relief," I admitted, letting out a long, deep sigh. "We're running low on petrol."

"Well, we're not, so you're not anymore!" Johan grinned at me, the same kind of vibrant grin that I'd seen on his son's face a minute earlier. It seemed to light up the whole world, and drew a smile from me in response. "There is one teensy problem, though."

My smile faded. "What's that?"

"Well, it's the road south," he said, looking back at me with a sheepish half-smile. "It's somewhat... underwater."

"What?" I exclaimed. "Oh no, don't tell me it's washed out?"

"Unfortunately, it is – and the water's still rising," he said. "The news gets worse from there: the water is creeping towards the petrol reservoir we found. We were just trying to work out what to do when you arrived. If it keeps rising at this rate, then we're going to lose that reservoir overnight. I've got a couple of men down there trying to seal it up right now, but they're not having much luck. The seals are just too worn."

I swore softly under my breath and pulled my radio out of my coat. "Then introductions are going to have to wait. We need to get down there and empty that reservoir before it's too late. You rally your troops, I'll rally mine. We need as many water-tight metal barrels as we can find – metal, not plastic."

"I know where we can get some," Johan answered without hesitation. "There was a bunch in a shed near one of the truck stops."

"Good," I said with a nod. "Get as many able-bodied folks as you can down there and bring them to the reservoir." I glanced over at Melody. "Mel, I'm putting you in charge of guarding the injured and children. I presume I can rely on you to take care of that for me?"

Melody nodded sharply, guided her horse around, and then took off at a gallop back towards the convoy. Once she was out of sight, I looked at Johan and Dominic again. "Dominic, can you show me where the reservoir is?"

The youth looked at his father for approval, then beckoned for me to follow him. "Yes ma'am. It's this way."

"Ma'am? What am I, your headmistress?" I said with a laugh. "Call me Sandy."

Dominic grinned broadly and nodded, then he raced off towards the township proper. I followed after him, leading Boudicca behind me. The horse followed obediently as we made our way into the pretty little township – or at least, what was left of it. I'd passed through the town of Taihape many times in my youth; it was a pit stop along the main route south, so we'd either driven through it or stopped in it every time that we'd gone south to visit my grandparents. Like every other town, it had seen better days. The brick storefronts along the main drag of the shopping centre were marred by graffiti, and many of the windows had been broken. Storm damage was very evident, and forced me to step carefully to avoid injuring myself or my horse.

"Are there many infected here?" I asked Dominic when the youth finally paused to get his bearings.

He glanced at me and shrugged. "Some, but we left them alone. They weren't hurting us."

I took a deep breath and nodded my understanding. I usually made a point of putting the infected to rest, but I knew that for many people the task was too messy, strenuous, or just plain upsetting to deal with. "We're going to need to take care of them before we leave. Don't let me forget, okay?"

"Yes ma'am," Dominic agreed good-naturedly. He paused for a second, and glanced at me with a frown. "Something's wrong."

I cocked my head, listening to the sound of the world around me. A second later, I heard what had alerted Dominic: over the whisper of the rain, I could hear voices raised in anger. I touched my finger to my lips to indicate silence, and tied Boudicca's reins to a bike stand beneath the shelter of an overhanging roof. Once my horse was secure, I slipped my shotgun off my back and carefully checked there was a cartridge loaded and ready.

Dominic's eyes went wide, and he took a few rapid steps back away from me. I held up a hand and gave him a friendly smile. "It's just in case. I'm not going to let anyone hurt either of us, okay?"

The youth stared at the gun a second longer, then he looked up at me and nodded silently. I led the way down an alley, following the sound of raised voices. As we drew closer to the source, I started to make out a few words here and there. One of the voices was an adult male, but the other sounded like a young teenager. Every time he shouted, his voice broke and squeaked awkwardly – but that didn't make the threat in his tone any less real.

"I told you to fill up the damn tank! Do it!" the youth shouted, his voice trembling with an odd mixture of anger and fear. "You think I won't do it? I will! I'll kill you both!"

"Okay, okay!" the adult voice cried back. "Look, we're filling the tank. Please, calm down."

I crept up to the end of the alleyway and held up a hand to halt Dominic, then I peeked around the corner. A hundred meters in front of me, a pudgy youth stood with an assault rifle trained on two older men in the forecourt of an abandoned petrol station. The youth had his back to me, his attention fully focused on the men. I slipped back, and beckoned Dominic in close enough that I could whisper in his ear.

"I'm going to sneak up behind him and try to disarm him," I said softly. "Stay here and keep watch. If you see anyone coming, shout and warn me."

"Yes ma'am," Dominic agreed readily. He puffed his chest up and nodded resolutely. "You can count on me."

"Good man." I gave him another smile, and then turned my attention towards defusing the hostage situation. The sound of the rain masked my footsteps as I eased myself out of cover and started creeping forward. The footpath was frequently broken up by what had been large gardens, which worked to my advantage. Every so often the youth would jump and look around, but the bushes and benches gave me enough cover to avoid being spotted.

I was tense as a bow-string and ready to snap by the time I got within a few feet of the youth's back. Just at that moment, he shouted again and very nearly made me jump out of my skin.

"Hurry up!" he yelled, his hands trembling on the assault rifle. I was close enough to see his knuckles turning white, and also close enough to see that he had no idea what he was doing with the gun. Just at that moment, one of the two adult men glanced towards us, and I saw his eyes widen. That tiny gesture was just enough to alert the youth to my presence. He spun to face me – and found himself staring down the barrel of my shotgun.

"Your safety's still on, kid," I told him gruffly, giving him a hard stare. He froze like a deer in the headlights, wide-eyed. Whatever his plan had been, he hadn't counted on any real resistance. Now that I was there and at an obvious advantage, he didn't know what to do. So, I made the decision for him.

Under any other circumstance, it probably would have been stupid to make a grab for the gun, but this time I considered it a calculated risk. I lashed out and grabbed the barrel with one hand, then I shoved as hard as I could. The boy yelped in surprise and fell over backwards, landing hard in a puddle of mud. I shoved my shotgun back over my shoulder, and trained the muzzle of the assault rifle on him instead.

"I think I'd better keep this, don't you?" I said, channelling as much power and command into my tone as I could. The youth just stared at me, his mouth gaping open like a freshly caught fish. I slipped the safety off with a dramatic click, and he jumped.

Just at that moment I heard Dominic shout a warning, followed by a female voice raised in panic. "No! No, please, don't hurt him!"

I took a step backwards and turned slowly to face the sound of running footsteps, keeping both the new arrival and the teenager in my firing line. An older woman who could only have been the youth's mother raced across the clearing towards us, her face a mask of anguish. As soon as she reached us, she threw herself down in the mud and tried to cover the boy with her own body.

"Please, don't kill my son," she begged. "He's all I have left."

"I have no intention of killing anyone," I replied without lowering the weapon. "But you'd best explain to me why your dear little boy here was trying to mug my friends."

"What? Mug?" The woman shoved herself back and stared at the boy in horror. "Bobby! Tell me you didn't?"

"I just did what Dad would have done," the youth whined, nervously scooting back away from the both of us.

The woman gasped and shook her head vigorously. "That man was *not* your father, and you know that you're not to call him that ever again. Nor are you to emulate his behaviour! He's dead, and he deserved it." The woman turned and looked at me, her hands raised in a gesture of placation. "I'm so sorry. His real father died in the plague, and we were… taken in by a group of men, who…" She took a deep breath, and even with the rain I could see the tears gathering in her eyes. It was a look that I knew well, and sympathised with better than most. I lowered the weapon and took a step closer.

"Let me guess," I said softly, understandingly. "You did what you had to do to keep your son safe."

The woman nodded and looked down at the ground. "They were bad men, all of them. They did terrible things. They hurt people. I had no choice; if I hadn't done what they told me to do, then they would have killed us."

"But you escaped?" I prompted, offering a hand to help her up. She accepted it gratefully and hauled herself up.

"No," she said, fruitlessly trying to brush the mud off her clothing. It just made the mess worse, of course. "Someone killed them. All of them. I don't know who. The lookout said there were travellers on the road, and Henry took his men out to attack them. They never came back. Bobby and I left Pukeatua the next day. There were… bodies along the road, but we never saw Henry's…" The woman took a deep breath and straightened her shoulders, obviously doing her best to put on a brave face. "It's for the best. He was a terrible man."

I felt a cold chill run down my spine, like the ghost of actions past creeping up on me. I glanced around at the others, then looked back at the woman, doing my best to keep my face expressionless. "This Henry person, was he about six-five, wore a lot of army surplus, had a tattoo on his neck about here…" I asked, pointing to a spot on my own neck.

Her eyes widened. "Yes! How did you know?"

"Because I killed him," I told her bluntly, making no attempt to sugar-coat the truth. "I was the traveller on the road, with my husband and our foster daughter. My husband is Chinese, and my foster daughter is Indian."

"Oh, no!" The woman gasped and clasped her hands to her chest. "Henry hated anyone that wasn't European, he blamed them for the plague. He… please tell me that he didn't hurt them?"

"No, they're fine." I glanced at Bobby, who was still sitting in the mud staring at me, then I looked back at the woman. "He tried to kill my family. I couldn't let that happen. I won't tell you what happened to him in front of Bobby, though. No one needs to know except me."

The woman started to say something, but Bobby cut her off before she could.

"You… you killed my dad?" he said, his voice carrying that strange mixture of fear and anger again.

"Don't call him that!" the woman cried, spinning to face her son. "Henry was not your father! Your father was a good, kind, gentle man. Your father would never have threatened this lady's child."

"He was my dad!" the stocky youth shouted back, shoving himself up to his feet. "I don't know this other person you're talking about. Henry taught me to fight and shoot and drink – he's the only dad I ever knew."

"I'm sorry, Bobby," I said, with as much sympathy as I could muster; after all, my issue was with Henry, not Bobby or his mother. "He didn't give me any choice. He attacked me, and I had to fight back."

"I don't care! I don't care what you say! You killed my dad!" Bobby screamed at me, his florid face turning red. He took a menacing step towards me, but I was no more intimidated by him than I had been by his stepfather. I raised the assault rifle and trained it on him.

"Stand down, Bobby," I told him, my voice cool and firm. "What's done is done. There's no changing that now."

"Shut up! You're a murderer, and I hate you!" the young man bellowed, then he turned on a heel and ran away from us. After a few steps, he slipped in the mud and went down hard on his knees, then picked himself up and kept running.

His mother looked at me again, her face wet with a combination of tears and rain. "I'm so sorry. Bobby… was too young, he doesn't know any better. Henry was the only man he had to look up to since his father died."

"You don't need to apologise," I said, lowering the gun. "I tell myself that I had no choice, but maybe I did. Maybe I should be held accountable for my actions." I glanced at her, and gave her a weak smile. "Amongst my group, we have a code of laws. If someone has a grievance with someone else, then they can pull the other person in front of a magistrate and a group of their peers, and have that person put to trial. If it would help Bobby to deal with his grief, then I'm willing to submit myself to a trial regarding the death of his step-father."

The woman bit her lip and looked away, watching her son slip in the mud again. She seemed to think about my offer for a second and then she was gone, running after Bobby and calling his name. Once they were out of sight, I took a deep breath to calm my frazzled nerves and turned to look at Dominic and the two strangers I'd managed to rescue.

"I really need to learn to keep my big mouth shut sometimes," I admitted, the strength draining out of me as the adrenaline started to fade. "I'm sorry you had to witness that. We need to deal with this petrol, before the flood water gets here. Let's get to it, shall we?"

# Chapter Four

By the time the others reached us, I could hear the flood-water lapping against the buildings nearby and see glimpses of it down the alleys between buildings. Bobby and his mother didn't return, but the brief encounter left me feeling wrung out and more than a little guilty. I'd tried so hard to forget what I'd done to Bobby's step-father to protect my own family, but now I had no choice but to remember it. Thankfully, the urgency of our situation helped me to keep going, even if worry still nagged at me.

Suddenly, Dominic shouted an alert. I looked up just in time to see my Hilux rounding a corner and pulling into the forecourt of the old petrol station, followed by a couple of unfamiliar vehicles. I glanced at Dominic and raised a brow. "The first truck is mine, but who are the others?"

"Those are our trucks," Dominic explained. "I see my dad driving! I bet they've got the barrels for us!"

"You have better eyesight than me, mate," I answered dryly. "Go give them an update, will you?"

"Sure!" he agreed, then he dashed off to do just that.

I smiled at the two men helping me to get the tanks ready to be drained. "He's a good kid, that one."

"Aye, seems to be," the shorter one agreed pleasantly. He was a stocky fellow named Aaron, with curly brown hair, a faint Scottish accent, and a smile that seemed to be hard-wired onto his face. The other man was tall, slender fellow named Charu. He was somewhere in his early forties but still youthful and handsome, with dark skin much like Priyanka's. That was where the similarity ended, though. Aaron had introduced him to me, but Charu hadn't said a word. He just nodded, shook his head, or shrugged when I asked him questions, and avoided eye-contact. I couldn't tell whether there was something wrong with him or if he just didn't like me, so I decided it was better to ignore his sullen attitude and just give him time to get used to me.

"I think this should be good to go," I told them, kneeling down to examine the haphazard hand-pump we'd assembled from pieces strewn around the buildings nearby. "Just keep your fingers and toes crossed that it doesn't pop loose at an inopportune moment."

Aaron laughed and nodded, but Charu just shot me a look and went back to tightening the bolts. I eased myself up to my feet again, wiped my hands on my pants, and went over to the trucks. As soon as they came to a halt, the doors of the vehicles popped open and people started piling out. Half of them were the familiar faces from my own group, but the rest I'd only glimpsed in passing at Johan's camp.

"Hey, sis!" Skylar called. "I see you found us some new friends." She ducked out of the rain and into the shelter of the forecourt. Hemi followed her a second later, with Johan and Dominic hot on her heels.

"I certainly hope so," I replied, grinning at them. Johan and Dominic both grinned back, and behind me I heard Aaron laugh again. "Anyway, as far as I can tell this petrol is still good – but it won't be for long. If that water gets anywhere near it, it'll be useless to us. We've jerry-rigged a pump, but I don't know if we're going to have enough time to get all of it. We're going to need to work fast."

"I have an idea to buy us some time," Aaron said. I glanced at him and raised an eyebrow, nodding for him to continue. He cleared his throat and stepped forward, joining the ring of people around me. "I came here as a backpacker right after I finished studying, and ended up living here for a couple of years. The outlying farmland gets flooded on a regular basis. I know they kept a supply of sandbags on hand in case of emergencies."

"Oh!" I gasped. "You're thinking that we could delay or divert the flood water long enough to get the rest of the petrol?"

"Aye," he replied, nodding. Suddenly, he grinned and pointed at a large hall just across the road from the petrol station. "And that right there is the town hall. Probably the best place to start."

"I'll agree with that," I said. "Aaron, you're with me. Johan, Hemi, I want you guys to take care of the pumping operation. Skye, you and Dominic are on watch. Show him how to use this, please." I handed the rifle that I'd confiscated from Bobby to Skye. She gave me an odd look in return.

"This isn't one of ours," she pointed out. "Where did you get this?"

"Long story," I replied. "No time to tell it now. But watch out for a kid of about fourteen who isn't part of either of our groups. He's got a grudge against me and might try to stop us."

"If you say so," she said doubtfully, then she shrugged, took the rifle, and turned her attention to Dominic. I unshouldered my shotgun and ran off towards the town hall, leaving the others to take care of their assigned tasks.

"Any idea where they would have kept these theoretical sandbags?" I called as we ran, ducking across a road marked by paint so faded it was impossible to make out what it might have once said.

"Not a clue, but I can make an educated guess," he called back. "Let's try that side door, since it's the only one at ground level. Makes sense that you wouldn't want to lug sandbags up stairs, right?"

"Right," I agreed, adjusting my course towards the door at the back of the building. When I got there, I tried the handle and found it locked from the inside. I glanced around and spotted a couple of windows a few meters farther along the wall. "Stand back and cover your eyes."

Aaron did as he was told and waited patiently while I used the butt of my shotgun to break the glass. I carefully cleared the shards out of the frame, then called him over. He cottoned on to what I was trying to do immediately, and cupped his hands on his knee to give me a boost. A second later, I was crouched inside the dark building, my shotgun at the ready.

Nothing stirred except the dust-bunnies I'd disturbed by letting in a breeze. The place smelt like a tomb, but so did everything that had been locked up for a decade. I pulled out my torch and used its thin beam of light to guide my way to the door.

Aaron joined me as soon as I unbolted the door, pulling a torch out of his own pocket. Our twin beams pushed back the darkness, illuminating a small office with nothing more than a dusty old computer on a desk against one wall, and a couple of doors leading off into other rooms. I opened one and discovered a vast, empty meeting hall. The other revealed a storage room filled with folding tables and stacked chairs.

"Nothing here," I said, disappointed. Aaron blew out a sharp breath and nodded, then he paused for a moment to think.

"Wait – there were other government buildings outside, I think," he said. He hurried past me out the door, and I followed close behind him. Our feet splashed through deep puddles as we raced down the street and across a gravel parking lot towards a low, squat grey brick building.

"The fire station?" I called after him. "You think they'll be in there?"

"Fire-fighting crews did more than just fighting fires, so it's possible," he replied, ducking into the relative shelter offered by the overhanging ledge of the building.

I joined him and took the lead again, my shotgun at the ready in case of trouble. We found the front door wide open, but this time a steady breeze did nothing to help with the stench. It was a smell that I knew all too well: decomposing flesh.

"I think there's someone in the fire engine," I said. I shouldered my shotgun, and pulled out the rag I still carried out of habit. My lifestyle might have improved, but my chances of running into something malodorous hadn't.

"Can I stay here?" Aaron asked pitifully, gagging and struggling to cover his lower face with the sleeve of his jersey. "Sweet mother Mary, that's a foul stench."

"No, we can't split up. Haven't you ever watched a horror movie?" I said dryly. Without waiting for an answer, I pulled out my taser and my torch and led the way into the reeking gloom.

My first port of call was to check the cab of the fire engine, of course; sure enough, there was a human figure sitting there, staring into space, still clad in his uniform and helmet. Not a mutant, just a regular, helpless, pathetic infected. I sighed heavily and vaulted up to the window, so that I could put the poor person out of his misery.

When I climbed back down, Aaron gave me a curious look. "Why bother? He wasn't causing any trouble."

"Three reasons," I replied as I led the way deeper into the station. "One: respect. That was a zombie fireman, who used to be a real fireman, a person who risked life and limb every day to save people. He would have done the same for any one of us. Two: mercy. God knows what those poor creatures feel, or if there's any way for their spirits to move on while their bodies linger here. I don't know, but I care. The only thing I can do for him now is to put him to rest. He deserves that much. And last but not least, three: the virus mutated. As far as we can tell, it spreads from infected to infected, so culling them is the best way to keep it from spreading."

"Oh." Aaron went quiet for a moment, then he made a noise that was somewhere between a grunt and a chuckle. "I see you've thought this through quite thoroughly."

"I've had a lot of time to think about it, yeah," I admitted. "But if it was your mum, you wouldn't want to just leave her… sitting there, rotting. Would you?"

"Hell no," Aaron agreed, his voice suddenly vehement. He went silent again for a couple of minutes while we explored the offices and storage rooms behind the fire station. There we found a few fully-loaded emergency medical kits that I wasn't about to leave behind, so the two of us set about gathering them up to take back with us. Suddenly, Aaron shot me a concerned frown. "You don't think their souls can move on until they're truly dead?"

"I have no idea," I admitted. I lifted a particularly large kit and lugged it out the door, with Aaron close behind me. "I don't know what comes next. I wish I did. I really, really wish I did. But I look at the infected and I watch them going about their business, and it makes me think. If their brains have melted, then how can they still show some of the same traits that they exhibited in life? It makes me wonder how much of what makes me who I am comes from my brain, and how much of it comes from my soul – if I have one, I don't know. I was taught to treat matters of religion with criticism, but… I just don't know anymore. What if that little bit of who they used to be comes from their soul? That means their souls must be tied to their earthly bodies, until… until they're not anymore."

"Oh Lord, that's a terrible thought," Aaron said, staring at me in horror. "I never even considered that. Do you think they're… aware?"

"I don't know," I said softly. "I don't know anything. That's the hardest part. I can only guess and follow my conscience." I shook my head, and gave him a weak smile. "Come on. We've got to find those sandbags."

Aaron nodded silently, and together we returned to the stinking darkness to search. We came up empty handed, but by the time we'd finished we had managed to find a fair supply of emergency rations as well as the medical kits.

"Well, this is shit," Aaron blurted as we were carrying our findings back to the convoy. "This stuff is nice and all, but we really need those sandbags. They must be around here somewhere!"

"Yeah," I agreed. When we reached the convoy, I yanked open the rear cab of the Hilux and piled my supplies into the back seat. Aaron did the same, then we stood back and stared around, seeking some kind of inspiration.

"If I were a sandbag, where would I be?" Aaron asked himself. The question was obviously rhetorical, but something about it twigged just the right chord to make me think.

"You'd be in a shed," I replied. "You're just a sandbag. You don't need a bathroom or food or even electricity. You just need a roof over your head that'll keep you from getting mouldy."

Aaron froze and stared at me, his mouth hanging open. Suddenly, he let out a whoop and pumped his fist in the air. "That's it! There was a big corrugated iron shed in the parking lot behind Town Hall. They must be in there! Why didn't I think of that sooner?"

"Sometimes it's hard to see something hidden in plain sight," I replied, grabbing his arm. "Come on!"

We took off at a sprint together, racing back across the road and down the gravel path behind the town hall. Sure enough, as I rounded the last corner I spotted an ugly, rusted iron shed the size of a small barn, crammed in between the equally-rusted hulks of a few abandoned minivans. I raced over to the sliding door and tried to open it, but it was held closed by a small, tarnished padlock.

"Damn!" I swore, rattling the door fruitlessly. "I don't suppose you have bolt-cutters on you, do you?"

"Aye, I've got a pair of bolt-cutters wedged down my pants, on the off chance you might happen to need them," Aaron replied sarcastically. He came up beside me and peered at the lock, then gave me a thoughtful look. "Actually, I don't think we need bolt-cutters. This is just about rusted through. Give me your gun a moment?"

"Don't waste my shells," I warned as I handed him my precious weapon.

"I wasn't planning to," he replied with a grin. He double-checked the safety was on, then turned the gun around and brought the butt down hard on the iron hoop that the padlock had been threaded through. With a few good, solid blows, the whole lock popped right off.

"Nice going," I said. He grinned again and handed me back my shotgun, then put his weight against the door. It didn't want to move at first, but he was stronger than he looked. It gave an inch, then another, then suddenly it slid all the way open. The dry, dusty interior was stacked very nearly floor to ceiling with pre-packed sandbags, ready and waiting for the moment when they'd be needed again. In the centre of the shed, half-a-dozen hand-carts waited to be filled.

Aaron looked at the sandbags, then looked at me. He flung a hand up in the air, palm towards me; the unexpected gesture just about made me jump out of my skin. I looked at his hand, then looked at him. He looked at his hand, then looked at me and wiggled his fingers. "Come on! Don't leave a brother hanging here. High five for teamwork!"

"Oh!" I cried, suddenly realising what he was trying to do. Laughing, I returned the high-five and then I led the way into the shed.

"Christ, I think the temperature's dropping," Aaron complained. We manoeuvred two of the carts around into a position where we could easily push them out the door, and then combined our strength to pack them full of as many sandbags as we could.

"I think you're right," I agreed. "It feels like we're going to have hail soon."

"No, not just hail," Aaron said. He paused and stared out the window at the dark sky, then looked at me. "Those are snow clouds."

I swore under my breath and picked up the pace. As soon as the hand-carts were full, we raced them out the door and down the road toward the petrol station. Half way there, we were met by Zain and some of the others.

"Sandy!" he cried. "Only so many of us can fill barrels at the same time, and the water's coming fast! Where are those sandbags?"

"Back there," I replied breathlessly. "In the shed behind the hall."

Zain and his group raced past us, and we hurried on. A few metres past the petrol station, I brought my hand-cart to a stop and looked around. The main road was uncomfortably wide, but I saw an opportunity to make that work to our advantage: nearly a dozen parked cars lined both sides of the road. They were rusted, filthy, and otherwise useless, but they did have one use left.

"We can use these cars to build a barricade," I shouted over the howling of the wind. "If we build it between the petrol station and that building on the other side of the road, it should buy us the time we need."

"Good idea," Aaron shouted back. He grabbed a sandbag and carried it over to the middle of the road. "Start here. We line the cars up behind this point, and then pack the sandbags in front of them."

I couldn't find the breath to reply to him, but I didn't need to. I just raced over to help him and that was answer enough. A few minutes later, Zain and the others joined us, each armed with another hand-cart full of sandbags. As soon as they arrived, I flagged them down and pointed at a couple of the cars nearby.

"Drag them over here," I cried. "Smash the windows if you have to, but get them over here. Build an arc across the road – and hurry!"

Zain shouted a wordless reply and raced off again, and this time I went with him. There was no time for finesse, but we managed to get one of the cars open, the handbrake off, and then the others helped us to man-handle the car across the road. It was long, hard, back-breaking work, but adrenaline kept us going. Twice I was forced to sit down for a second when sparkles began to dance around the edge of my vision, but nobody complained or tried to cajole me. For once in my life, for the baby's sake, I took the time my body needed to recover – but not a second longer. As soon as I could, I was back up, helping to shift cars and lug sandbags.

Every second, the water crept closer and closer. Every second, the sky got darker and darker, the rain fell heavier, and the wind got colder. I paused for a second to adjust my hood, and in that moment I glanced up at the sky – but the droplet that struck my cheek wasn't water. It was ice.

"Incoming!" I cried, ducking my head back down to avoid the downpour. Aaron swore colourfully and grabbed me by the arm, dragging me into the shadow of a nearby building. A second later, the sleet turned to a brief but violent bout of hail. We huddled together until it passed, then hurried back out to check on the others. "Everyone okay? Anyone hurt?"

"Everyone's fine," someone shouted back to me. In the chaos, I couldn't tell who it was.

Once I was sure that everyone was safe, I raced back to the barricade and threw my weight behind the last car that we needed to block the full span of the road.

"We're almost there!" I cried, as much to encourage myself as them. My feet slipped on the hailstones, but the others soon joined me and our combined strength was enough to manoeuver the car into position.

"More sandbags!" Aaron shouted over the wind. I grunted my agreement, grabbed the nearest hand-cart, and raced back towards the shed as fast as I could without risking my safety on the icy ground. The hail might have passed, but the sleet was determined to keep our world wet and dangerously slippery. I ducked into the shelter of the shed's rusted but solid roof, and paused for a second to brush a few half-formed snowflakes off my shoulders. The others arrived a moment later and took over the heavy lifting, giving me a much-needed moment to recover and catch my breath.

Did I? Of course not. I used the moment to pull out my walkie-talkie and called my husband's name. "Michael? Come in, Michael?"

After a few seconds, the radio crackled and I heard his familiar voice. "Sandy! Please tell me you're on your way back now. Waiting with the wounded is killing me."

"I know, honey, but not quite yet. It's taking longer than we expected," I replied breathlessly, lifting my voice so that I could be heard over the drone of the sleet on the roof. "I need to know, do we have power?"

"No, no power," he replied. "It's getting bloody cold, though; I think we should break out the generator and get some heaters going."

"You read my mind," I replied dryly. "We just had hail, and Aaron reckons we're going to have snow soon. We're all drenched. By the time we get back, we're going to be popsicles."

"I'll take care of it," he told me, using the deep, firm tone he used to reassure people. "Just make sure you're back before sundown. It's going to be pitch black tonight, without street lamps or stars."

"You don't have to tell me twice," I replied. I quickly said my goodbyes, tucked the radio away, and rejoined the others just as they were lugging the next load out into the weather. When we reached the barricade, I vaulted over the bonnet of one of the cars – and swore when I found my feet splashing through shallow water. "It's here! We don't have much time. Half of you get over here, the other half start throwing sandbags over. Quick!"

Everyone jumped to obey. The sleet made the work even worse, but none of us uttered a word of complaint. We worked feverishly, stacking row upon row of sandbags against the cars, until it we finally had a barricade at least waist high across the entire width of the road.

By that stage, the floodwaters had risen almost to my knees, and I was trembling from cold and exertion. I tried to vault back over to the safe side of the barrier, but my arms went as weak as cooked noodles and slid out from under me. Aaron caught me and helped me back over to where Zain waited, and together they rushed me to the shelter of the petrol station. Skylar was still standing guard, perched on the bonnet of the Hilux; as soon as she saw us coming, she jumped down and hurried over to help me.

"Not this again!" she scolded, guiding me over to sit on the front bumper of the truck. "Sandy, you know you're not supposed to—"

"I didn't," I replied, cutting her off mid-sentence. "I did what I was told, and took breaks when I needed it. I'm just cold. We all are. Let me sit down for a minute, then I'll be fine again." I glanced up at the people who'd been helping with the barricade, all of whom were in just as bad a state as me. "Take a second to recover, guys. Once we're functional again, we need to go see if there's any propane in the station itself."

"Dominic and I can do that," Skylar said, shoving a strand of sodden hair back out of her face. "You guys need to rest. Take over the watch, we'll go scout. "

"Okay," I agreed, relieved by her initiative. They ran off without another word, leaving my group to watch for trouble. We instinctively arranged ourselves so that each of us was watching a different direction. All of us had been living the survivor's life long enough that we knew what to do without being told. Once we were settled, I took a deep breath and just forced myself to relax for a couple of minutes.

Suddenly, Skye and Dominic reappeared in front of us, a whole lot wetter but with triumphant expressions on their faces.

"There are a bunch of tanks in a cage tucked around the far side," she told me excitedly. "I think they might be full, but I can't tell. Can you?"

"No," I admitted. "Zain? Can you?"

"I don't really know how anyone could survive without that knowledge," he answered dryly, his voice carrying the faintest note of humour. Zain wasn't usually one to crack jokes, but in the circumstances it was just what I needed to hear.

"Well, time for all of us to learn," I said with a laugh, levering myself back up to my feet. I waited for a second to make sure that I had my balance, then I headed towards the petrol station.

Skylar hurried into the lead, with Zain and Aaron close behind us. Sure enough, just around the corner nearest to the front door there was a steel cage painted an ugly shade of lime green, which was guarding half-a-dozen tanks. I glanced at Zain curiously.

"That's an exchange station," he explained. "It'll be a mix of full ones for customers to buy, and empties that they've returned. Should be at least one that's full, I imagine – if we can get through that padlock."

"You guys head inside and see if you can find a key, or any useful supplies," I instructed. "I'll see if I can pick this lock."

They nodded and hurried off. Before I got started, I stuck my head around the corner and called to the team that were still labouring with the petrol. "Yo, Hemi!"

"Yo, Sandy!" he called back, pausing in his work to wave to me.

"How close are we to being done?" I asked. "We're starting to lose the daylight."

"Almost there, mate," he replied, shouting to make himself heard over nature's racket. "We're nearly at the bottom of the reservoir. We should make it before dark."

"Thanks! You guys are doing a great job, keep it up!" I shot him a double-thumbs-up. He returned the gesture with a grin, then went right back to work. I turned my attention on the padlock, and was just unbuttoning my coat to fish out my lockpicks when Aaron came running back out, grinning like a mad-man.

"Don't you worry, lass; I've got this covered!" he announced gleefully, holding up a pair of huge, bright red bolt cutters.

I laughed and took a step back. "Oh, so you did have those hidden down your pants after all, huh?"

"Nope, but I do now!" he said cheerfully. With a mighty crunch of steel on steel, he cut the little padlock off the cage, then handed the bolt cutters to me so that he could start pulling the tanks out of the cage. "I could be wrong, but these seem to be in fine condition. Not a speck of rust on them."

"Well, it's under shelter on the leeward side of the building, and I guess it's never flooded this high before," I replied. "Zain, we're in!"

Zain reappeared out of the building a few seconds later, clutching a few much-needed flasks of motor oil. Aaron handed me a tank, which I passed on to Zain. He examined it for a moment, then nodded his approval and passed it back to me. "This is full. Should be fine, so long as we can keep it dry."

"On a day like today, 'dry' is going to be an issue," I said, frowning.

"No, it isn't!" Skylar interrupted, sticking her head around the corner. She gave me a huge grin and held up an enormous yellow umbrella. "Ta-da!"

"Well, I guess that'll work nicely," I said, chuckling. I set the bolt cutters down and took the umbrella instead. After a few seconds of awkward fumbling, it popped open in my hand. "Good thinking, Skye. How many are there?"

"Lots," she replied, then she started handing out gaudily-coloured umbrellas to the others.

I just laughed, hugged the tank to my chest, and made a mad dash back across the forecourt to the Hilux. The back was already full of barrels of petrol, so I opened the rear cab and set the tank on the seats instead. Aaron and Zain joined me a few seconds later; between the three of us, we had the tanks Zain had deemed to be full transferred to the trucks in no time at all.

We went back and managed to get in a couple more loads of oil and other useful supplies before the deepening gloom made it too hard to see what we were doing. Just as I was depositing my last armful in a safe place, I heard Hemi shouting. "That's it! We're done! We're done!"

I glanced at our makeshift barricade and saw that the floodwaters had already risen almost to the top, and a few ominous shadows were creeping around the sides as well.

"Then let's get out of here," I shouted back, making a broad gesture to the others. "Into the trucks, quick! The water's coming!"

There wasn't enough space left in the trucks to carry everyone. Those of us who could still function made way for supplies or people in worse condition than we were. We huddled beneath our umbrellas and waited until the trucks had headed off, then we followed on foot back to our base of operations on the far side of town.

Johan, Aaron, and Dominic appeared beside me as I trudged through the driving rain. I glanced at them and gave them a weary smile. "Well, we did it. I'm pretty sure the ground is sloping upwards, so that should help us keep above the water for the night."

"Should do, yes," Johan agreed, sounding just as tired as I felt. "I for one will be glad to find my bed tonight."

"I really hope we *can* find beds tonight," I replied, lifting my umbrella a little so that they could find some shelter beneath it. It was a token gesture at best, but Johan gave me an appreciative smile.

"Even if we can't find you an actual bed, I'm sure we can make you comfortable," he replied, his voice deep, soothing, and somehow familiar. He had the same patient, reassuring tone as Michael, and that put me at ease. "There are several motels at that end of town, and we've scouted them all. I imagine Hannah has already helped your people find the best places to set up camp for the night." He paused and shot a glance at me. "That's my wife. My new wife. We married last year. Dominic's mother died in the plague, sadly."

"Ah. I'm sorry to hear that," I said, nodding my understanding. I glanced at Dominic and gave him a smile. "It must be nice to have a mum again, huh?"

"Yeah!" Dominic agreed, nodding vigorously. "Hannah's really nice. She's a great cook, too!"

We all laughed at that. Once the levity passed, I glanced at the others and tilted my head. "I need to go get Boudicca. Who wants to keep me company?"

Aaron gave me an odd look. "I don't know how to tell you this, but I'm pretty sure Boudicca's dead. Like, a couple of thousand years ago."

"Not that Boudicca," I replied, laughing. "That's my horse's name. Don't look at me, I didn't pick the name."

Everyone chuckled again, but Aaron was the first to volunteer to come with me.

"We better move fast," he said as we peeled away from the rest of the group. "We're going to lose the light completely any minute now."

"And here comes the snow," I added, as a couple of stray snowflakes began to drift down around us. They were small, shapeless things, but they were definitely snow. We exchanged a glance, then picked up the pace.

Boudicca was exactly where I'd left her, tied to the bicycle stand and looking no worse for wear. She nickered a greeting to me and nudged me with her velvet-soft muzzle. I reached up and rubbed her nose affectionately, then I untied her reins and looped them around my wrist.

"My back hurts too much to mount up, but you can ride if you want," I said to Aaron.

He shook his head and gave me a wry smile. "After all that lifting? Nah. I haven't ridden in years, anyway."

"Me either," I said. I handed him the umbrella, so that I could focus on leading Boudicca through the mounting snow. At least the snowfall meant the rain had stopped for the time being, and I was grateful for any small favours that Mother Nature had to offer.

The conversation trailed off during the walk back to the northern end of town, so that we could focus on where we were putting our feet. The wet ground and sudden cold snap meant everything was dangerously slippery, and more than once I found my feet sliding on a patch of black ice. Boudicca seemed to have no such trouble, luckily; she was heavy enough that her hooves just broke through the fresh ice.

It was a long walk back, and by the time we got there we'd lost daylight completely. For the last kilometre or so we only had torchlight to guide us, and the distant glow from the motels where our comrades had set up camp. I found myself growing increasingly anxious the longer we were out after dark, but nothing happened that was any more dangerous than Boudicca accidentally inhaling a fluffy snowflake and then sneezing on me.

Suddenly, one of the lookouts spotted us and shouted a greeting. A minute later, Priya came racing out of the darkness and flung her arms around my waist. "Mama!"

"Priya!" I cried back, squeezing her with affectionate exuberance.

She squealed and squirmed for a second, then ducked under my arm and fell into step beside me. "Mama! Baba found a baby!"

I just about swallowed my tongue in surprise. "He what? He *found* a baby? Whose baby did he find?"

"Hannah's!" Priya replied brightly, miming the way one might hold a baby. "He hugged the baby and went 'goo-goo, gaa-gaa', made many silly noises. Why?"

"That's… something adults do around babies," I replied, forcing myself to take a deep breath to fight down the odd mixture of relief and nausea that suddenly fought to overwhelm me. So, Michael liked babies. That was no great surprise. And apparently he was feeling a bit clucky. Considering my situation, that was most likely a good thing.

My thoughts were interrupted when Priya suddenly noticed Aaron, and froze in her tracks. I just laughed and gave her a look. "Oh, don't tell me you're pretending to be shy again. Come here, munchkin."

I held my arm out to her. She raced into it and cuddled up against me, peering curiously at Aaron from the relative safety of my shadow.

He grinned and gave her a wave. "Hello there, lass. I'm Aaron. What's your name?"

Priya hid her face in my armpit, and I burst out laughing. I just couldn't help it. She always did that to me. "This is my foster daughter, Priya. Don't mind her; she plays this game sometimes when she secretly just wants a hug. Isn't that right, honey?"

Priya peeked out, looked up at me, and gave me a huge, cheesy grin. Then she detached herself from me and we all resumed walking.

"You talks funny," she said suddenly. "Why?"

"Sorry, we're still working on her English," I added. "She's asking about your accent."

"I figured as much," Aaron replied, his expression open and friendly. "I'm from another country, a faraway land called Scotland. I moved here when I was fresh out of university, a couple of years before the plague."

"You remember how we talked about how people's mamas and babas coming from different places?" I said, looking down at her. "Aaron comes from the same place as my baba."

"Oh, aye?" he asked, looking at me quizzically. "Well, I suppose I should have guessed from the 'McDermott' thing, but you don't have an accent."

"I never had the chance to visit, unfortunately," I said. "My father moved here when he was a toddler."

"That's a shame," he said thoughtfully, his eyes turning distant for a moment. "It's pretty country. Much like New Zealand, in many ways. I often wonder what it's like over there nowadays. I suppose I'll never know."

"Maybe one day we'll find out," I replied, reaching out to pat his shoulder. "In the meantime, though – Priya, where are the horses being kept?"

"Over here, Mama!" she replied, scampering off towards a field not far away. She opened a gate and led us through it, then guided us across the field to a ramshackle barn that glowed with the faint light of an oil lamp.

Inside, we found the twins hard at work, rubbing the horses down and making sure that they were fed and bedded for the night. Introductions were made, then the girls took Boudicca and led her in with the other horses.

"Do you need a hand?" I asked hesitantly, hovering near the door with the others.

"No, this is our job tonight," Jasmine replied with her usual determination.

Lily gave us a smile and nodded agreement with her twin. "We're almost done, but thank you for offering."

"Okay," I said. "Call if you need anything."

"We will," Lily replied, waving a goodbye. I waved back, then led my little party back out into the snow.

"Lots of kids with you," Aaron commented. "How did they survive?"

"Lord of the Flies-style," I answered dryly, wrapping my arm around Priya. She gave me a curious look, then snuggled in under my arm for what little warmth and shelter she could get with my coat bundled up tight around me. I briefly explained the origin stories of our various children to him as we walked back towards the glow of the motel, until someone called out and interrupted the conversation.

"Hello!" the woman called, waving frantically. "Come inside and get warm; it's freezing out here."

"Amen to that," I agreed, ushering Priya ahead of me up the short flight of stairs.

"Good evening, Hannah," Aaron greeted with his usual friendly smile. "How are things?"

"All's well, so long as you lot get in here before all the heat gets out!" Hannah replied. She chased us all inside and closed the door, then turned to offer me her hand. "Hi, I'm Hannah. I've heard so much about you!"

"Likewise," I replied, shaking the offered hand.

Hannah gasped at my touch and yanked her hand back. "Good God, you're like ice! Come with me, let's get you all warmed up before you get frostbite."

The woman grabbed my arm and all but dragged me down a long hallway flanked by doorways. Somewhere along the way, Aaron and Priya both vanished, though I didn't notice until they'd already left. Hannah paused for a second to check the doors, then opened one on the right hand side.

"Here, this is your room," she said. "Your husband already brought all your things inside, so you should be able change into something dry."

"Oh man, it's toasty in here," I said, reaching out to rest my hands over the radiator. "I take it the generator's working nicely?"

Hannah laughed and nodded. "I'm a little vague on the details, but I think they managed to use your little generator to jump start the big generator out the back. Thank goodness, because we're going to need it tonight. Now, you get that wet clothing off so I can get it in the dryer for you."

"Yes ma'am," I agreed with a playful salute. I closed the door behind me for a little privacy, then pulled my various essentials out of their pockets and set them out on a dresser nearby. My clothing was a mess: my pants were soaked to the knees, my shoes and socks were sodden, and my coat was practically dripping wet. I stared at it for a second, then just dropped it all in a pile on the floor.

A towel and a stack of clothing sat neatly folded on the end of the bed, obviously waiting for me. I recognised them from our stash of spare clothing, and suddenly I was very glad that we'd brought it with us. I changed quickly, and pulled on a pair of thick socks in lieu of my sodden shoes. When I opened the door, Hannah was waiting.

"Much better," she said approvingly. "We've got a roaring fire going down in the common room, so you go join the others and I'll take care of this. Just follow this corridor to the end, and you'll hear them before you see them."

"Thank you so much," I said, grateful to have the responsibility taken away from me for a change. Every inch of me ached, and I longed for the chance to sit down and eat something hot. I left her to take care of my clothes and padded off down the hall in the direction she'd indicated.

Sure enough, I heard them before I saw them. The buzz of human voices in conversation was a pleasantly familiar sound, and it made me smile. I opened the door, and spent a moment just relishing in the wave of heat that washed out. People were gathered around the big fireplace on the far wall, sitting on chairs or cross-legged on the floor. For once, the scent of so many bodies in close proximity didn't bother me. In fact, I didn't notice it. The moment the joy of the warmth wore off, I only had eyes for Michael.

He was sitting in an armchair, rocking a tiny bundle wrapped in a pink baby blanket. I slipped inside without being noticed and closed the door, then crept up behind him, watching with mute fascination. His big hands were so gentle, and his voice was so soft that it made my gut lurch. There was something about seeing a man being gentle with a baby that made my most primal instincts scream out in need, even if I didn't really know what to do with them.

Melody's voice interrupted my reverie. It was raised a few octaves higher than I was used to, which made it clear that she was upset and on the verge of genuine distress. "Sandy! I want to hold the baby. Make him give me the baby!"

Michael glanced up and gave me that smile he reserved just for me. "Ah, you're back." He looked at Melody and laughed. "Calm down, would you? She's trying to sleep. You can hold her, but you have to sit down and be still and quiet. You wouldn't like it if someone was running around screaming while you were trying to sleep, would you?"

"Fine, fine, I'll be good, just let me hold the baby!" Melody groaned, plopping down to sit on the floor beside his chair. Once she was settled, Michael leaned over and tenderly placed the sleeping baby in her outstretched arms.

"That's it," he said guiding her arms into the right places to keep the baby comfortable. "Like this. If she starts to wake up, just rock her gently like I was doing."

Melody barely even seemed to hear him; she just stared with rapt fascination at the tiny person in her arms. Michael and I exchanged a smile, then he held his arms out to me. I went into them as happily as any baby, snuggling up in the warmth of his lap. He kissed me, hugged me gently, and suddenly I was the happiest I'd been all day.

"I missed you," he whispered, his voice soft and tender. I could hear the frown in his voice, even if I couldn't see his face. "You're so cold. Are you okay?"

"Fine, just fine," I replied, closing my eyes to enjoy the warmth. "We got it all, and some propane as well. It should be enough to get us to Avalon with lots to spare."

"Sounds like we're going to be stuck here for a while, though," he said, his big fingers stroking a few stray tendrils of my hair away from my cheeks. "From what the others were saying, the flooding seems to be pretty bad."

"It is, but we can wait," I said. "Patience is a virtue, and we've got plenty to do in the meantime."

Michael pushed me back just far enough to see my face, and I gave him a mischievous grin in return. He just laughed and hugged me tighter.

# Chapter Five

I pressed my taser to the nape of the infected woman's neck, then leapt back out of the way as she collapsed like a decomposing water-balloon.

"Ugh, this one's over-ripe," I called to the others. "Who's on slops duty?"

"Aw, hell. I'm not sure I'll ever get used to that smell," Aaron said, reaching up as though to cover his face with his gloved hands. At the last second, he remembered that his gloves smelt just as bad and jerked them away from his face with a muttered curse.

"You think it's bad over there? Come closer and take a whiff!" I teased, tucking my taser back into my pocket. "You want some more perfume for your mask?"

"Ugh, no," he protested, waving me away. "That stuff smells even worse."

I opened my mouth to make a joke about the heightened sense of smell that came with pregnancy, but caught myself just in time. Instead, I laughed and went for sympathy. "I know, mate. I know. Seriously, though – who's on slops?"

"Charu, I think," Aaron answered. "You want me to go get him? I don't mind, anything to get out of this stink-hole."

"Nah," I replied, shaking my head. "You volunteered for this, so you don't get to escape that easily. He'll still be busy working on that last place. Looks like the infected around here were in the last stages of the virus. What a mess."

"Yeah, but like you said, better safe than sorry," Aaron said, his voice carrying a mixture of disgust and amusement. "That's the last one we had marked. You want to go do one last check around town and make sure we haven't missed any of them?"

"Sure," I agreed. We stripped off our rubber gloves and tossed them on top of the sloppy remains of the infected, then headed out into the street.

Five days had passed since our arrival in Taihape, and water still blocked the road southwards. We had nothing better to do with our time except explore this side of the flood, and gather up as much as we could carry. Combining our groups and resources had more than doubled the size of our fleet; for the first time, we had enough space to carry everyone and everything we needed, with plenty of room to spare. A few days earlier, there had been a subtle air of uncertainty amongst the group, but now it was gone. Everyone was smiling and feeling hopeful about our chances of making it to Avalon – even me.

It had taken us three days to finish stripping the resources out of that pretty little town. At that time, there had been no sign to indicate that the floodwaters were going to recede, so I'd decided we should use the time to clear away the bodies of the infected. It had taken all of my oratory skills and a wee bit of exaggerating to convince the rest of my group that the gruesome task was worthwhile, but I succeeded in the end. I'd argued that every infected we put to rest now was one that we wouldn't have to worry about catching the mutated virus in the future. Even those of us who had never encountered the mutants had heard the stories. Still, it was a victory that I occasionally regretted, what with my nose being as sensitive as it was.

"It's for the best," I said to myself. Aaron gave me a funny look, and I suddenly realised that I was doing 'that thing' again, as Michael called it. "Sorry, yabbering to myself." I paused for a second, then changed the subject. "So, what's his story anyway? Charu's, I mean?"

"Oh, that's an unpleasant tale," Aaron replied. He sighed heavily and shook his head. "Poor lad had his tongue clipped a few years back. I think it was by that big fellow you were discussing with the woman and her kid the other day, but he hasn't said." He barked a sharp laugh, and just as quickly frowned. "Though I use the term 'said' loosely, here. He can... sort of talk, but usually doesn't. He's self-conscious about it. He used to be some kind of Bollywood icon, back before the plague. A singer or an actor or something."

"That's awful," I said softly, my stomach twisting into sympathetic knots. "If he was a Bollywood star, then his voice would have been his life and a huge part of his identity. No wonder he always looks miserable. I wish I could do something to make him feel more welcome."

"I don't think he feels unwelcome," Aaron replied. "He's not the sort to just sit there and sulk if he doesn't like something. He'll find some way to let you know, even if he has to write it out on a bit of paper, wrap it around a brick, and bash you over the head with it."

I laughed and nodded my understanding. "That's good. I don't want anyone feeling uncomfortable."

We continued in silence for a couple of minutes, each keeping our own council. Just as we were emerging from another building, I realised that something was out of place. I froze in my tracks and held up a hand to stop Aaron. He glanced at me quizzically; I lifted a finger to touch my earlobe, silently indicating that he should stop and listen. The part of town we were travelling through was densely overgrown, but the birds in the trees and bushes in front of us were no longer singing. Someone was hiding just out of our line of sight.

I sighed heavily and put my hands on my hips. "I know you're there, Bobby. Why don't you just come out so we can talk?"

Aaron took a nervous step up to my side, fingering the hilt of the long hunting knife on his belt. I lifted a hand to forestall any hasty actions and just waited. Sure enough, a few seconds later there was a rustling sound, and then the youth appeared out of the bushes. I was almost surprised to see him carrying a large wood axe. Almost, but not really.

I felt Aaron tense up at the sight of the weapon, but I wasn't concerned. While a wood axe could be a lethal weapon in trained hands, my previous encounter with the youth had led me to the understanding that whatever training he'd received from the Pukeatua bandits had been rudimentary at best.

"Were you planning to put that in my back?" I asked, keeping my tone conversational rather than accusative. I took a few steps forward, my arms relaxed at my sides, nowhere near any of my weapons. "You know that's not how justice works, right?"

"My dad said that justice meant an eye for an eye," Bobby replied. "You murdered him, so now I have to kill you."

"I didn't murder anyone," I replied, fighting the urge to react in a way that would exacerbate the situation. He was just a kid, after all. A dumb, stubborn kid. I'd been the same way at his age. Everything was black and white, with no room for shades of grey. "Look, Bobby. I know that you're angry, but would killing me actually solve anything? It won't bring your step-dad back. It won't bring back any of the other innocent people your step-dad killed, either."

"I have to do something," Bobby snapped angrily. He gritted his teeth and wiped his eyes with the back of his hand, as though that would hide his tears from me. "He was my dad!"

"I know, Bobby," I said gently. I heaved another sigh, and watched my breath cloud in the frosty air. "It was a terrible situation. I wish it hadn't come to it. But the only other choice was to let him slaughter my husband and my foster-daughter. She's about your age, you know. She's a beautiful, sweet, kind girl with the soul of an angel and a smile that lights up the room. Your step-father wanted to kill her in cold blood, just because her skin is brown. She hadn't done anything to him. You have to see it wasn't right for him to kill someone just because their skin is brown. Do you think I should have just let him do it?"

Silence was my answer. Bobby shifted uncomfortably from foot to foot on the icy ground, his expression tormented and his grip on the axe increasingly awkward. Suddenly, he sniffed and wiped his eye again. "Shut up."

"We can fight if you really want to," I said gently, taking another step towards him. Rather than threaten him, I just slipped my hands into the pocket of my coat to keep them warm while I waited for him to make his choice. "You know that I'll probably still win, though. I've got ten years of experience on you, and I know how to fight. It doesn't have to be like this, though. I have no quarrel with you or your mother. I don't hurt anyone unless they try to hurt me or my family. That's my rule."

"Shut up!" he said sharply, taking a step back and shifting his axe up into an offensive position. I didn't move, didn't retreat, just looked him straight in the eye and smiled at him.

"I told your mum that I'm willing to go before a tribunal of justice, if you want me to," I explained evenly, my hands still resting comfortably in my pockets. "It was self-defence, Bobby. Everyone's allowed to defend themselves and their families from a threat. I mean, what would you do if someone attacked your mum? You'd want to protect her, right? I feel the same way about my daughter." I took another step towards him and shifted to a tone that was kind and gentle, but not condescending. "Like I said, it doesn't have to be this way. I don't know what your dad taught you, but *my* dad taught me that forgiveness is a strength, not a weakness. We're going south soon. We're going to Lower Hutt, to build a new city where everyone is welcome. I'm willing to forget this ever happened and let you come with us – if you can find the strength to forgive me, too. You deserve a chance to be happy, and so does your mum. Everyone does."

Bobby's grip on the axe faltered in his trembling hands. He lowered it until the head rested on the ground and stared at me with tears flowing down his cheeks unrestrained. Then, suddenly, he dropped the axe and fled down the street away from me as fast as his legs could take him.

I watched until he was out of sight, then turned and looked at Aaron with my eyebrows raised. "I guess that's a no?"

"You handled that so well that if you weren't already married, I'd be down on one knee right now," Aaron said solemnly. It lasted for all of two seconds, then his friendly face cracked into a smile. I smiled back, though my heart wasn't really in it. I'd barely recovered from the last encounter with Bobby, and now I was left reliving the guilt and horror about what had happened in the forest near Pukeatua all over again. No matter how many times I told myself I had no other choice, I couldn't shake the niggling feeling that I should have found another solution, somehow.

Some days, I didn't think I would ever be able to forgive myself and move on. Other days, I thought that I didn't want to, that I had to remember so I never reached the point where I could do that kind of thing without feeling sickened by it. The last thing I wanted was to become the very monster I was fighting against.

I took a deep breath to calm my roiling stomach, then looked at Aaron. "Right, let's get back to work, shall we?"

\*\*\*

It was late afternoon by the time we finished our final sweep of the town and returned to the spot we'd designated as our rendezvous. It was still raining and snowing intermittently, but we needed a way to burn the remains of the infected. The rendezvous was a large shed near the outskirts of town, which was big enough to house all those bodies but isolated enough that we could burn it down without setting the rest of the township on fire.

The volunteers handling what we'd come to refer to as 'slops duty' were the last to come back. They were wrapped from head to toe in disposable plastic suits that we'd found in a veterinarian clinic, with masks and goggles to protect their faces. For once in my life, I hadn't volunteered; my sense of smell was so sensitive that I probably wouldn't have made it through without losing my lunch. It had taken all of my willpower to hide my relief when other people had put their hands up for the gruesome task.

Charu was the last one to return, carrying two huge buckets filled with a horrible red-brown slime that I refused to believe had once been people. I took a deep breath and looked away; the sight alone was nearly enough to make me retch. Michael appeared out of nowhere and put his hands on my shoulders to reassure me. I leaned against him for a second to recover and absorb a little bit of his strength. When I looked back, Charu was emerging from the shed and stripping off his protective gear. It was too splattered with filth to try and save. Once he'd peeled it off, he tossed it into the shed and then silently walked away. I didn't need to ask to know that he was heading back to base to shower and scrub himself raw. I itched just looking at him.

"Douse the bodies with petrol," I said, pasting my mask of strength back into place. "Good thing we've got some to spare now. We need to make sure it gets hot enough to burn them to ashes. We'll bury the bones and anything left over once it cools down."

Michael gave me one last gentle squeeze, then stepped forward to do just that. He and a few of the others had spent most of the day gathering any spare firewood we weren't taking with us and stuffing it around the edge of the shed to make it burn as hot as possible. My rules were fairly simple: we could burn anything that wasn't of cultural significance. No books, artwork, musical or artistic instruments, or anything that still had value to us. Anything else was fair game.

Michael returned to my side once the work was done, leaving Hemi to do the honours. We retreated to a safe distance, where the rest of our little community had gathered to watch. The sun was setting, and it was hard to see exactly what Hemi was doing; I saw a tiny flicker of flame, then suddenly he was running towards us as fast as he could go.

"Why's he running so fast?" I wondered out loud. Before anyone could answer me, there was a small explosion, followed by a cascade of golden sparkles. My mouth fell open in surprise.

Beside me, Michael made a childlike sound that could only be described as a chortle. "Yes! Yes! It's working!"

"What's workin—" I started to ask, only to be interrupted again by another small explosion that turned into a cascade of blue sparkles. Before I could even catch my breath from the last one, a third and fourth explosion went off. Then the shed ignited with a whoosh of air, amid a dozen cascades of multi-coloured—

"Fireworks?" I gasped, my eyes wide. I wanted to turn and look at Michael, but I couldn't pry my eyes away from the impromptu display. "Where did you find those?"

"Oh, a few people had them in their garages," Michael answered breathlessly. "It was illegal to buy or sell fireworks any time except the week leading up to Guy Fawkes' Day, but lots of people used to buy extras and keep them in storage until New Year's Eve. Since the plague hit in December, they never had a chance to use them."

"No, I guess they didn't," I replied softly. I found myself clinging to him without even realising I was doing it "I didn't realise they lasted this long."

"Oh, yeah. Fireworks last forever, if you keep them clean and dry," he said. "Sophie and I used to do this every so often. We'd find some, have a little fun, get a little pyromaniacal, you know, the usual."

Just at that moment, the fire spreading up the walls of the shed reached the roof, and the first rocket shot up into the early evening sky. It exploded in a vibrant white powder-puff, and I gasped in delight. The fireworks on the ground began to fade away, but by that time we were focused on the sky instead, watching rocket after rocket shoot up above us and explode in sparkles, like the forgotten magic of a bygone era.

Which, in a way, it was.

# Chapter Six

As soon as we finished washing away the grime of an unpleasant day spent doing the necessary, we headed to bed for an early night, just as we had every night since we'd arrived in Taihape. Even though we had plenty of fuel for the generators at the moment, we were painfully aware that such resources were finite and we had a long journey ahead of us. We had no intention of wasting any more than we had to.

I awoke in the washed-out grey light of dawn, curled up in the warm alcove between Michael's body and the radiator. I stretched languidly and rolled over on my side, enjoying the warmth while I could. There was nothing that urgently needed to be done until the flood waters receded, so there was no real reason for me to get up. I decided to let myself doze for a while. My eyes drifted closed, and I fell into that pleasant space between the world of dreams and reality.

When I opened them again, the sun had crept a few inches higher. The motel curtains weren't exactly the most solid things in the world, and let in just enough light for me to pinpoint the time as somewhere near mid-morning. I glanced at Michael and saw that he was still sound asleep, so I decided I probably wasn't the only one who'd realised we had a lazy morning ahead of us. My urge to doze had been sated and now I found myself awake and alert, so I decided it was time to get up.

I slipped out of bed without disturbing him, and gently pulled the blankets up to his chin to keep him warm. He sighed softly and snuggled into the space I'd left behind, but didn't wake. The sight of it made me smile and drew my thoughts to the child growing inside me. My little secret, for now.

I'd showered before bed and it was too cold to do so again just yet, so I just grabbed my clothing off the dresser and pulled it on. My basic essentials went into their pockets, but I left my weapons and coat behind for the time being. If I decided to go outside, then I could always come back and get them. For now, I just had to worry about my daily check-up with Doc, and it was easier to do that discreetly when Michael was still asleep.

I left the room and quietly closed the door behind me, then headed down the hallway to Doc's room. His door was slightly ajar; I knocked softly, then entered when he called permission. I found him sitting with Anahera, who was holding a notebook open to a page of tidy, hand-written notes. Maddy was sitting on the floor in the corner, playing with her favourite rag dolls.

"Good morning," I said. "I'm not interrupting, am I?"

"No, we were just working on that little project you gave us," Doc replied. "Come in and close the door."

I did as I was told, and plopped down in an old armchair that Doc had acquired for reasons known only to him; my guess was that he liked having somewhere for patients to sit aside from the beds, which made sense. Anahera leaned over and handed the notebook to me. I quickly glanced over the column of figures, then shot them both a curious look.

"This looks more like a census than a training chart," I said, intrigued.

"That's because it is," Anahera answered, her smile radiant as ever. "We know that you keep a list of everyone so that no one gets left behind, but with all these new faces we decided that it would be logical to expand things a bit. Look at the next page."

I turned the page, and skimmed over the contents. "Wait, is this…"

"Yes," Doc said, looking quite pleased with himself. "That's a list of everyone's names, dates of birth if they remember it, approximate ages, religious beliefs, occupations, and unique or useful skills. We've also plotted family trees as far back as we could, which I plan to keep updating as our little group expands."

"Family trees?" I asked, glancing back at him. "Why?"

"Numerous reasons," he replied. "Genealogy is an important part of human nature, and there is no Department of Births, Deaths, and Marriages to keep track of such things anymore. It will also help us keep track of genetic anomalies, so if there's a risk of anyone developing a hereditary disease then we'll have some advance warning."

"Oh, of course," I said, nodding. "There are quite a few people with relatives that are still alive since the immunity tends to run in families, so the likelihood of hereditary stuff reoccurring is a bit higher than normal."

"Only slightly, but yes," Doc said, nodding. "It probably won't help a great deal for this generation, since so many of our citizens were too young to remember their family histories, but if we start the project now and gather as much information as we can from the people who are old enough to know and remember, then it will help in the future. As for the rest, I know that you like to respect people's choices as much as you can, so I figure that the religious data may come in handy at some stage. The career information is useful so we can keep track of who knows how to do what. "

"It is," I agreed. I skimmed the list quickly, then shot him a curious look. "Aaron's a nurse? That's interesting. He's mentioned that he studied, but he never said what. Not that I'm complaining; two nurses are always better than one."

"Definitely agreed," Doc answered dryly, adjusting his spectacles. "My understanding is that Rebecca stopped practicing a few years before the plague, so her knowledge is a little rusty. I plan to bring her and Aaron in to assist me, and to retrain them both as much as possible. With this many people, I'm going to need as much help as I can get."

"How many women and kids are with the new arrivals?" I asked, glancing back and forth between them.

"Seven women of childbearing age," Anahera answered. "There's also one woman past menopause, and sixteen men over the age of eighteen. There are five kids, aged between three months and fourteen years. Three girls, two boys. They've got a few pets and some livestock with them, too."

I drew a deep breath, and let it out slowly. "Twenty-nine new faces. I don't know how I'm going to remember all of their names."

"We already thought of that," Doc replied. He grabbed another sheet of paper, peeled something off it, and slapped it on my chest. I blinked in surprise and glanced down at it.

"Really? A name tag? This is what we've been reduced to?" I commented, laughing. "That's actually kind of brilliant."

"It is, isn't it?" Anahera grinned at me. She picked her own name tag off the sheet and stuck it to her chest. "Your sister thought of it when she found a roll of these stickers in an old stationery shop in town."

"I like it. It's good," I agreed. "Start handing them out as soon as you can."

"We already have," Doc replied. "We've also started pairing apprentices with their teachers. Hemi is due to start training with me later this morning."

"And I'm officially opening classes for the children, too," Anahera added. "We went down and checked the flooding this morning. It looks like it's going to be at least another couple of days before we can get through there safely. In the meantime, we may as well get these kids learning something."

"Sounds good, I approve," I said, not that they seemed to need my approval for anything. Still, if it helped them get things done, then I was happy to provide it. "Has anyone managed to talk to Melody's gang about what they want to do?"

"That's a bit of a funny story, actually," Anahera replied. "I asked the twins, and they both immediately told me that they wanted to join my school. Those two have a voracious thirst for knowledge, if ever I've seen it. Melody... well, that's where it gets interesting."

"Oh, let me guess," I said. "She bit your head off for even suggesting it, and now refuses to talk to you?"

Anahera laughed and shook her head. "That's what I was expecting, but no. I think all that time she's been spending around the baby has woken up her maternal instincts. She told me she wanted to apprentice to me."

I froze and stared at her in shock. "She... what?"

"I know!" Anahera laughed again and threw her hands up in mock-despair. "The sky clearly must be falling, or that girl has gone mad. She's decided that she wants to be a teacher."

"No, no, this actually makes some sense," I said, tapping a finger against my chin. "Think about it. She practically raised the twins. Not well, but she managed to keep them alive for ten years. She was only eight when she found them, and they would have been about two. She must love kids to do that. I think the problem is that we've only ever seen the protective side of her maternal instincts. She must have nurturing instincts as well, or the twins wouldn't love her so much. Not only that, but they were all literate when Gavin met them, which means she must have educated them."

"Huh." Anahera paused for a moment to think that over, then she nodded slowly. "You're right, that does make sense. I must admit, I haven't spent enough time with her to get much of a feel for her, but your logic makes her sound more promising than I first assumed. Shall I take her on, then?"

"If she wants to teach, help her learn to teach. It'll be good for her to feel like she has a reason to be here," I said. "What about Solomon? Has anyone managed to get him to talk yet?" Anahera and Doc paused, and exchanged a look. I raised a brow. "What is it? You look like you know something I don't."

"Solomon's tongue has been cut," Doc said quietly, his expression unreadable. "I found out when he was in here getting treated for a cold a few days ago. Some bastard cut out part of that poor boy's tongue."

I swore beneath my breath and squeezed my eyes closed. "The neo-nazis at Pukeatua. They did that to Charu, too. They must be the reason behind the disappearance of the Samoan gang in Tokoroa. I knew they wouldn't just let their territory markers fade like that. I'm sorry, Bobby, but the more I hear about your step-father, the more glad I am that I took him down when I had the chance."

They looked at me curiously. I quickly explained Bobby's appearance, and what had happened to us when we'd travelled through Pukeatua months earlier. "I told Bobby that I'm willing to stand trial for Henry's death if he wanted me to, but he didn't seem interested. Still, I'm not proud of what I did."

"As you said, you did what you had to do," Anahera said sympathetically. She patted my hand, smiled at me, and rose to her feet. "I should go start class, if we're going to have time to learn anything before lunch. Are you ready, Madeline?"

"Yup!" she cried happily, leaping up to her feet. Maddy scampered over and grabbed Anahera's hand, then she paused and looked at me. "Bobby's gone away, but you're going to see his mummy again soon. Her name is Isabelle. Don't worry, she's a nice lady. Sad, but nice." Suddenly, Maddy giggled and dragged Anahera off towards the door. "Come on! I want to read a big book today, with lots of words!"

Anahera shot us a look of long-suffering amusement and waved, then she was gone. I glanced back at Doc and shrugged. "Well, I guess I'm going to be seeing Bobby's mummy again or something."

"'Or something', indeed," Doc answered dryly, shaking his head. "Sometimes I just don't know what I'm going to do with that girl."

"Eh, so long as she's using her powers for good rather than evil, let her be," I said with a shrug. "She's not hurting anyone, and usually her prophecies help us in some way. I'm not complaining."

"Speaking of which," Doc rose from his chair and went over to make sure that the door was properly shut, then peered at me over his spectacles. "How are we feeling this morning?"

"We are feeling just fine, thank you," I replied, rubbing my belly pointedly.

Doc smiled and returned to his seat on the edge of the bed. "How's the morning sickness?"

"It comes and goes," I admitted. "It's not that bad, though. You were right on the mark about the sense of smell; it seems to be getting sharper every day."

"That's the one common symptom between every pregnant woman I've ever tended to," he replied, adjusting his glasses. "Did you start the notebook, like I suggested?"

"Yeah." I handed him back the census book, then reached into one of my numerous pockets and pulled out a much smaller notebook that I'd scavenged a couple of days earlier. I flicked the booklet open to the page where I'd begun to keep a running tally of the days since I'd conceived. "Today is the forty-sixth day, according to my count. Should be pretty much accurate within a day either side."

"Excellent, that's very good," Doc said approvingly. "Keep that journal up-to-date, it'll be useful for pinpointing when we can expect you to go into labour. I also want you to write down any time you feel strange, in as much detail as you can."

"Okay," I agreed. I glanced at him, suddenly nervous. "God, I didn't even think about having to go into labour. That's kind of terrifying. I'd ask if it's going to hurt, but that would pretty much be the dumbest question of all time."

Doc chuckled softly and nodded. "Somewhat, but it's an understandable terror. Just remember that once it's over you'll have a bouncing baby to add to your menagerie."

"*My* menagerie? Gosh!" I huffed in mock indignation, then shot a glance over my shoulder at the door. "Actually, it is turning into a bit of a menagerie, isn't it? You mentioned that some of the newbies brought stock animals with them?"

"Primarily chickens, but I believe they also have a pair of cows as well," Doc replied, flipping through the census notebook until he found the right page. "Ah, yes. Five more horses, two milking cows, six chickens, four dogs, and three cats."

"Cats?" I sat up straighter all of a sudden and looked at him. "I was wondering why Tigger's been skulking around looking nervous."

Doc made a thoughtful sound, but his interest clearly wasn't on the cat. A few seconds later, he glanced up and gave me a long look over the rim of his spectacles. "No matter how tempting it may be, resist the urge to drink milk from those cows."

"I wasn't planning on it," I replied, raising a brow. "I'm mildly lactose intolerant."

"Good, good." Doc sighed and took his glasses off, pinching the bridge of his nose between thumb and forefinger. "I've been reading more into the prevention and treatment of listeria poisoning. Unpasteurized milk is a particularly dangerous source of the bacteria. Stay well away from it, and anything made with it."

"Got it," I said with a nod. "You should probably speak with the kitchen crew to make sure they don't give it to anyone else who might be at risk. Maybe we can work out a way to pasteurize it ourselves."

"Maybe," he replied, making a note in his book. "Hannah's baby shouldn't be having any, and neither should the youngest children. I'll investigate the possibility of pasteurizing it, and talk to the kitchen crew in the meantime. I think I'll go do that right now, actually." He glanced up at me. "Is there anything else you wish to discuss today, Ms McDermott?"

"No, I'm fine." I took the hint and rose to my feet, stretching languidly. "I should go find some breakfast, anyway. I'll walk with you."

"Very well," Doc agreed, a faint smile touching his face. He slipped on his shoes, stood up, then together we made our way out of his room and down the hall to the common room.

There, we found Anahera in the midst of gathering the children up and seating them around the fireplace. Skylar was watching them with interest, and both Ryan and Hemi hovered near her with equally anxious expressions on their faces. Skye's back was to me, so I didn't notice the reason for their anxiety until I was almost on them: Skye was holding Hannah and Johan's infant daughter, Evelyn.

Doc didn't seem to care about how concerned Ryan and Hemi looked. He marched right up to Skye and cleared his throat. "Miss McDermott, we must speak for a moment. Will you join me in the kitchen?"

"Of course," Skye answered. "What's up?"

"We just need to discuss food safety, because of the new additions to our group." He glanced at the two young men and lifted his brows. "I believe you both help out with the cooking on a regular basis, correct?"

"Yeah?" Hemi asked, looking at him curiously. "You want us to come, too?"

"Please," he said, then he glanced around at the others. "I've already spoken to Anahera and Sandrine; who else is regularly involved in cooking?"

"Just talk to us," Skye said. "Hannah, Johan, and Elly are in the kitchen right now. One of us is always there for mealtimes, so we can disseminate the information to anyone else that needs to know." Suddenly, she turned to me and held the baby out. "Here, look after Evie for a minute."

I took the baby without thinking. Skye led the others off towards the kitchen, leaving me awkwardly clutching the poor child with no real idea what to do with her. My last experience with a baby had been eighteen years earlier, with Skye. I'd always assumed that instinct would tell me what to do, but it really didn't.

Evie squirmed in my arms and let out a disgruntled squawk; suddenly, I realised I was clutching her too tightly for fear of dropping her, and that she wasn't too happy about it. I took a deep breath and shifted my grip, struggling to find a position that was comfortable for both of us.

There was a soft chuckle behind me, then I felt familiar arms slip around me and gently guide my arms into the right places. "That's it. She's old enough that you don't have to support her head. You can sit down, if you want. There's a chair just behind you."

I felt Evie relax as my grip was adjusted, and I finally let out the breath I hadn't realised I'd been holding until that moment. If anyone knew how to take care of a baby, it was Michael.

"No, no, I think I'm okay," I said. I glanced up and caught Anahera shooting amused glances at us from the far side of the room. Suddenly embarrassed, I turned my full attention to Evie instead. If I was going to have to learn to deal with one of my own, then I needed all the practice I could get. "Hello, Evie. I'm Sandy." To my surprise, the baby gurgled and laughed in response. I blinked and glanced at Michael over my shoulder. "Does that mean she likes me?"

Michael grinned back at me. "Evie likes everyone. She's a very relaxed baby."

"That's good. It seems like I'm the only one that doesn't particularly want to babysit," I answered dryly. I looked back down at Evie and gave her a little jiggle, to which she responded with a big baby smile. I took a deep breath and turned towards Michael to ask him something, but before I could say a word Evie spotted him and let out a squeal of delight. She just about threw herself at him, her pudgy little fists making grabby motions. This time, it was my turn to laugh. "Oh, I think someone has a crush."

"She just likes me because I play with her," Michael answered, his deep voice shifting into the soft tone he used when dealing with kids. He held one finger up and wiggled it at her teasingly. "Isn't that right, Evie?"

She grabbed his finger with her little fists, and promptly pulled it into her mouth. My heart melted; she was a beautiful baby, who looked so much like my vision of what Priyanka must have looked like at that age. Her skin was a little darker than Priya's, but she had the same expressive eyes, and round, sweet face.

"Ow, my ovaries," I muttered jokingly as I watched Michael playing with the baby. It was so natural to him, so instinctive. He just… knew what she wanted and gave it to her. Kind of like how he always seemed to know what I needed. "You're such a people person, honey. How'd you get so good at that when there's no one left around?"

Michael laughed, wrapping his free arm around me. That sandwiched little Evie in between us, but she seemed perfectly happy with the arrangement. "Just empathy, I think. My parents raised me with the belief that I should always treat other people the way I'd like to be treated. I just try to take a second to stop and think about that before I do or say anything."

"That's… really quite smart," I said softly, glancing back down at the squirming baby in my arms. I felt a rush of heat up the back of my neck, and suddenly there were tears blurring my vision. I blinked them away and smiled to myself. "Good thing she doesn't have any teeth yet, she's got a heck of a bite on her."

"Yes, yes it is," Michael crooned to the baby, leaning down to until his face was right in front of hers. "But you aren't teething yet, are you? No, you're not. Not yet. Soon, though. You've got a rough bit on your gum right here in the front, don't you?"

Evie released his finger and made a two-handed grab for his nose with a delighted squeal, which she also tried to pull into her mouth. It didn't work out so well, but it left both of us laughing our heads off.

"What are you two doing to my child?" Hannah demanded from the doorway to the kitchen. I feigned innocence, but Michael just grinned shamelessly and waved at her. A second later, Evie spotted her mother and let out another joyful screech, which turned into a demanding whine.

"Uh-oh, someone's hungry," Michael said. He glanced at me and gave me a wink. "They sure look cute, but they just see us as walking, talking, snuggling food-sources. Well, her mother is. Good luck getting anything out of my nipples, kid!"

Hannah laughed and came over to us, holding her arms out to take the baby from me. I surrendered her with more reluctance than I'd anticipated, and watched as she took Evie over to an armchair to feed her.

"Speaking of feeding," Michael gave me a sideways glance and a squeeze. "Breakfast?"

"Breakfast," I agreed, nodding firmly.

# *Chapter Seven*

It took three more days for the floodwaters to recede enough for our convoy to escape from Taihape. It was early morning on the fourth day when the news finally came, and I'd just finished showing a few of the older kids how to recondition a scavenged car battery. Keeping the batteries functional was a constant problem for us, so the more hands we had to help out, the easier our voyage would be.

"Whatever you do, don't get any of the acid on yourself," I warned one last time. The teenagers nodded their understanding. A few hands came up to ask questions, but just at that moment Hemi came dashing up to us, out of breath and excited.

"Sandy!" he cried. "It's time!"

"It is?" I stared at him, scarcely able to believe my ears. It felt like we'd been trapped in that little town forever, and it took a second for the news to sink in.

"Yes!" Hemi shouted, practically jumping for joy. "We're free! We're free! Onwards, to Avalon and Tumanako!"

That brought that reality crashing home. I let out a whoop of joy and punched my fist in the air. "About time! I can't wait to get away from this snow." I paused and looked at the small group of teenagers gathered around me. "Guys, fan out and spread the news. I want everyone packed up and ready to go by mid-morning. Let's get this show back on that road!"

Everyone let out a spontaneous cheer, then they split up and ran off in different directions. I headed back towards our lodge. Along the way, I pulled my walkie-talkie out of my pocket and informed everyone else who had one about the good news. By the time I made it back to my room, the place was abuzz with excited activity. No one wanted to linger in the cold highlands any longer than we had to. Young and old, original members and new faces alike, everyone was practically chomping at the bit.

I headed to my room, grabbed our luggage from the corner by the door, and started packing everything away. Michael and I had agreed to keep our clothing and personal items separate while we travelled, to make it easier on both of us when we had to find something. I was so used to it that I had both of our bags packed before Michael even arrived on the scene. When he did, he was bright-eyed and breathless from running.

"You're such a slow-poke," I teased.

"Hey, I got roped into figuring out how to move the cows efficiently," he replied. "Do these feel like the hands of a cowboy to you?"

Right on cue, he grabbed my bottom and gave it a squeeze. I squealed in surprise and playfully slapped his hands away. Laughing, he grabbed both of our bags instead, and gestured for me to walk with him while he carried them out.

"I heard that we found a horse trailer or something?" I asked along the way.

"A small stock truck, actually," he replied. "I don't know how Zain managed to get that thing working, but he did. The man's a miracle worker when it comes to anything with an engine."

"He is," I agreed without reservation. "A stock truck, huh? There's only two cows, so that should give us some room to spare, shouldn't it?"

"Yep! Heaps of it," he replied with a grin. "We even managed to fit most of the barrels of petrol in. We are going to need to leave a few behind, though."

"That's fine," I said. "We should leave some for Erica, anyway. She's going to need it when she comes south. I'll give her a call when we stop for the night and let her know where they are. Can you make sure that the spare barrels are put somewhere obvious, but safe and out of the elements?"

"Of course." He paused for a second to deposit our bags in the back of the Hilux, then hurried off to do as I asked. I went the other direction, and headed for the barn where our growing herd of horses had been housed during our stay.

I arrived to find Lily and Jasmine hard at work saddling horses, along with a couple of the new faces from Johan's group. I waved to them, and picked my way between bodies both human and equine to find my mount. Boudicca nickered when she saw me and gave me a gentle nudge.

"Hey there, girl," I said in return, reaching up to rub her velvety nose. "Ready to get back on the road?"

The horse snorted at me and whickered again. I'd swiftly come to realise that she was far more intelligent than I'd initially given her credit for, and while she might not understand my exact words she certainly understood the tone. She stood patiently while I put on her bridle and other gear, and held still as I vaulted up into the saddle. When I was ready, I gently nudged her sides with my heels and guided her out into the brisk winter air.

The rain had finally stopped and the snow had melted a little overnight, leaving just a few inches of slippery ice-crust upon the ground. Boudicca had been born and bred in the Central Plateau highlands, though; she was far more sure-footed and agile on the ice than I could ever hope to be. I checked in with the rest of the group and discovered that they had the packing process under control, so I opted to take on the role of scout instead.

I crossed the township of Taihape at a comfortable trot. Just as I was approaching the southern edge of town, a lone figure huddled up in a ragged cardigan stepped out from between two buildings. She waved hesitantly, her fear obvious even from a distance. I reined in near her and gave her a curious look; even with her hood up, I recognised her as Isabelle, Bobby's mother.

"Hello again," I greeted, glancing around to make sure that the angry teenager wasn't sneaking up on me.

"Hello," she said warily, hugging herself against the cold. "I... I'm sorry, but... have you seen my son?"

I glanced back at her, uncertain how to respond. "Not recently. I last saw him five days ago, around midday. He approached me intent on a fight, but I talked him down. I haven't seen him since then."

"Oh." The woman's face fell, and she lowered her gaze to the frosty sidewalk. "I haven't seen him in days, either. I... I don't know what to do. I thought that he'd get sick of being alone and come back, but he hasn't."

Sympathy swelled in my breast in response to the painful emotion I could see in her eyes, and hear in her voice. I eased myself out of the saddle and went over to stand in front of her.

"Your name is Isabelle, isn't it?" I asked, holding up my hands to show her that I meant her no harm.

"Yes," she confirmed. "Isabelle Wright. I'm sorry, I know you probably don't care, but... I don't know who else to turn to. I've never been alone before. Never."

"It's okay," I said softly, reaching out to touch her shoulder. She flinched when I touched her, but swiftly seemed to realise that I was only trying to offer her a little bit of comfort through physical contact. "I'm not holding you to blame for anything Henry did, or Bobby threatened to do. I know that wasn't your fault – and I know how terrifying it is to suddenly find yourself alone."

Isabelle nodded and looked down at her feet, tears welling up in her eyes. "I'm so scared. Even after the plague, there was always Bobby. I just did what I had to do to keep him safe. I don't know how to be alone."

"I know," I said. "God, I know better than most. I was alone for the better part of ten years. It's awful. No one should have to go through that." I paused to take a deep breath, swallowing the tears that were suddenly threatening me as well. "We're leaving today, Isabelle. In the next couple of hours. You're welcome to come with us, if you want."

Isabelle glanced up at me, her face showing a mixture of warring emotions that I couldn't quite decipher. "You'd take me in? Even knowing what my son wants to do to you?"

"I'm not going to hold you responsible for something you had no control over," I replied. "I know that you were only trying to protect your son. But even if that weren't the case, you'd still be welcome. Your son is welcome, too. We're going south to build a new city, and we're going to need everyone we can get. We've all had to do terrible things to survive over the years, but if you're willing to help then we're happy to forgive." I released her shoulder, and took her hand instead. "It's up to you. Think about it. If you decide you want to come, then pack your things and meet us here in an hour. If not, we're going to Lower Hutt; you can always meet us there later."

Isabelle looked up at me for a few long seconds, then she nodded, wiped her eyes, and turned away from me. I watched until she was out of sight, my stomach twisting itself into knots. Then, suddenly, my radio chirped and I heard Michael calling for me. Thoughts of the lone woman struggling with a difficult decision vanished in the face of the arduous task of getting sixty-something people moving.

***

It took longer than anticipated to get our convoy in motion, with so many new people, vehicles, and animals to plan for. It was nearly midday by the time we were heading south, and poor Isabelle nearly frozen to the bone waiting for us. We packed her and her belongings into one of the trucks that had a working heater, and then we were on the move.

The road directly south of Taihape was in good condition, though it was framed on each side by dense bush that cast the world into perpetual shadows. After a couple of hours, the forest gave way to open plains studded with sheep and the occasional tree, but farther in the distance I caught a glimpse of white.

"What is that?" I asked, standing up in the saddle to try and get a better look. "Over there; the white?"

"That would be cliffs," Gavin said, amusement dancing across his scarred face; he and Michael had opted to ride in the vanguard with me. "Just wait until we get a bit closer, then hold on to your lunch."

"Hold onto my lunch?" I echoed, glancing back at him. Gavin just laughed. Michael shot him a dark look.

"That's not nice," he scolded. "You know she doesn't like heights."

"Oh, she doesn't?" Gavin's mirth vanished as swiftly as it had appeared. "I didn't know that, actually. It never came up."

"Wait, wait," I interrupted, holding up my free hand. "Are you guys saying we're going to have to go near those cliffs?"

"Oh dear," Gavin said, suddenly looking worried. "There's a massive canyon coming up. The road follows it for a while, then crosses a bridge over it. After that, it's all downhill to the plains."

"Ah, cripes." I took a deep breath and let it out slowly. "Think we'll get there by dark?"

Gavin glanced up at the sky, then shook his head. "At the rate we're travelling, it'll probably be tomorrow morning."

"Okay, so I've got a few hours to put my big girl panties on, that's good," I answered dryly. "But after that, nice, long, flat plains, right? Forever?"

"All the way to the sea, yeah," Gavin replied with a chuckle.

"Okay, I can do it," I said firmly, straightening my shoulders and putting on my bravest face. Did I feel it? Of course not. I really, really hated heights. But I wasn't going to let them know that, now was I?

\*\*\*

Thankfully for my pride, the bridge in question turned out to be far wider and a lot less steep than anticipated. By the time we actually reached it, I'd already constructed a terrifying image of three hundred meter drops onto solid stone in my head. What we actually crossed was barely more than a gully, packed with tall trees that made the drop seem nearly insignificant. Just as they'd promised, after that it was all downhill into broad, rolling plains that stretched as far as the eye could see.

For two weeks, we travelled south-west along the highway towards the coast. We stopped at each major town along the way to scavenge for supplies, and to clear away any of the infected that hadn't already found eternal rest. By the time we were done, the towns of Mangaweka, Hunterville, Marton, Bulls, and Sanson were safe and clear for anyone who followed after us.

Every night, I contacted Erica on the satellite phone and updated her about our progress, and she in turn updated our radio broadcast. As we moved south, we occasionally found small bands of people waiting for us. Sometimes it was a single person, wild-eyed and jumpy. Other times, it was a little family group just glad to see a friendly face.

By the time we reached the town of Levin, our group had swelled to nearly eighty souls. Some of them were shy and reluctant to join in with group activities, while others seemed positively delighted by the opportunity. I have to admit that I was one of the reluctant ones at first; although I did my best to always be there when someone needed me, I was still nervous about being around so many unfamiliar people. Michael seemed to sense my distress, and was always on hand with a reassuring arm and a kind word when I started to feel overwhelmed.

As our group grew, so did its needs. We could no longer spend the night in a single dwelling, so we split everyone into three groups and let them organise their own food and watch rosters. Although our fleet and herd grew steadily with each township, we eventually ended up with too many people and not enough seats. That meant people started having to take turns travelling on foot, which slowed our progress further still.

Despite the regular frosts and occasional sprinkling of rain or snow, we found plenty of wild produce growing along the roadside, more than enough to keep us going as we travelled. At Levin, we stopped for a week to rest, recover, and replenish our supplies by fishing in the lake that ran alongside the town. By the time we left, another ten souls had drifted in from the north-east to join us, and we had to create a fourth subdivision for the night rosters.

On the last night before we were due to leave Levin, I walked into the house my group had claimed and found a bunch of people sitting around watching the television with rapt fascination. Michael waved me over and patted a spot on the floor beside him. To my surprise, I discovered that they were all watching the evening news.

"What's got you all so interested?" I asked.

"We just switched it on and he was talking about us," Michael answered. "I don't know how, but he found out about everything. The mutants, our voyage south, Tumanako, even you."

We both fell silent after that, and focused on watching the Anchorman talking about us as if he knew us. For the first time in the ten years that I'd been watching his show, he looked excited. He'd even shaved, and somehow seemed less rumpled and miserable than he usually did. Hope shone in his vivid blue eyes.

Suddenly, I found myself with tears running down my cheeks. I rubbed them away with the back of my hand and took a deep breath to try and steady myself, but it wasn't going to happen. Simon Wentworth, the Anchorman, had been my only human contact for so long. I remembered with such clarity the feeling that he was my only friend, even though he didn't know I existed. Now, I was hearing my own name spoken from his lips. It felt unreal.

"The New Exodus is scheduled to leave Levin in the morning," he said, his voice strong and confident. "All people in the area are encouraged to join the convoy south. Survivors in the South Island are asked to head to Picton as soon as possible. Work is currently underway to refurbish a ferry, to bring you up to the North Island."

"No way!" I gasped, shocked and thrilled at the same time. "How did the South Island find out?"

"That's Simon for you," Anahera said, her eyes gleaming with tears just as much as mine were. "He always was resourceful. I guess he must have heard Erica's broadcast—"

"Shh!" Hemi said suddenly. "He's talking to Sandy!"

"Sandrine McDermott," the Anchorman said, looking straight at the camera. I froze, feeling as though he could see me somehow, even though I knew that he couldn't. "If you happen to see this broadcast, please be advised that you and your people are welcome here. We're waiting for you, and we have some very important news to share with you when you arrive. Good luck."

Then, just like that the broadcast was over. I glanced around at my friends, wide-eyed in surprise and unable to form a coherent word for nearly a minute.

"News?" I said at long last. "He's got news for us? Important news? But he can't share it on his show? What on Earth could it be?"

"There's only one thing it could be," Skylar said softly, her tone low and reverent. "The one thing that makes all of this change."

"No," I said, shaking my head. "I know what you're thinking, but it couldn't be that. That kind of news... well, we'd have heard about it by now, surely."

"Not necessarily," she said, turning to stare at me with enormous eyes. "They wouldn't want to get people's hopes up, would they?"

"What are you two talking about?" Michael asked.

I turned and stared at him, unable to say the words. Skylar felt no such compulsion, and she said them for me.

"A cure," she said, her voice barely above a whisper. "Someone's finally found a cure."

# Chapter Eight

Our slow but uneventful southward march continued for several weeks across the rolling, green plains of the Horizons Region, and down into the outskirts of the area that had once been known as Greater Wellington. The winter solstice came and went, and then the days finally started to get longer again. The fourth full moon since our departure from Ohaupo blossomed in the sky, giving us a way to mark the passage of time as our ancestors had in earlier generations.

With every day that passed, the baby within me grew. I marked the 90th day off my list while we were clearing infected out of the city of Paraparaumu. By the 93rd day, we were travelling south again. I was sitting in the passenger seat of the Hilux reading a book when I heard Priyanka frantically calling for me.

"Mama! Mama!"

I glanced up and saw her galloping back towards the convoy, her short hair blowing in the breeze. "God, would you look at her? I can't believe how much she's grown."

Michael made a sound that was somewhere between a laugh and a grunt of annoyance. "I know. I keep catching Dominic and some of the other boys peeking at her when they think we're not watching. At this rate, she's going to turn into a woman before I've figured out how to cope with that. I'm going to need a bigger stick."

"We're just going to have to trust that she's smart enough to take care of herself and know when to ask for help, which I'm pretty sure she is," I replied. By the time I finished speaking, Priya had brought her horse up beside our truck and was frantically pointing to the south-west.

"Mama, we see something!" she told me, practically vibrating with excitement. "Come and look!"

"Okay," I agreed readily. Michael didn't even bother to stop the truck; we were only moving at a snail's pace, and we'd all gotten used to climbing in and out of creeping vehicles during the voyage. Priya slipped her foot out of the stirrup and offered a hand to me. I took advantage of both, and used them to swing myself up to ride double with her.

Once I was seated, she flicked the reins and guided her horse away from the convoy again. She had things well under control, which gave me a chance to study the surrounding landscape. The hills to my left were so steep that it looked like a mountain goat would have struggled to climb them, and were shrouded in low cloud which gave everything a slightly otherworldly feel. I glanced to the right and saw very little: just thick bush at first, which eventually gave way to a few small warehouses, an overgrown parking lot, and a large restaurant advertising specials that hadn't been relevant in a very long time.

Priya rode past them without stopping. Always on the lookout for supplies, I pulled my radio out of my pocket and held down the receiver. "We've got a few buildings coming up, we should probably stop and search them. It's also time for lun—"

Just at that moment, we rounded a corner and the trees suddenly parted. My words died in my throat. I felt my mouth opening and closing like a freshly-caught fish, but no words came out. There were no words. There was only emotion.

532

"Sandy?" Michael's voice crackled through the radio, laced with concern.

"Oh God," I whispered, my thumb locked on the receiver. "Michael, we… we made it, to the coast. I can see the ocean. I-I forgot how beautiful it was." I muffled a sob behind my hand, unable to keep my emotion in check. "Stop the convoy when you get to the buildings, and bring everyone who wants to down to the beach."

I put the radio away and let Priya help me down from the horse. I barely even noticed the other scouts clustered behind me as we made our way across the gravel and down onto the sand. There was a low, crumbled sea wall not far from the edge of the ocean; I went over to it and sat down, then pulled off my shoes and socks. The feeling of sand between my toes instantly brought me back to my childhood, to all the happy memories shared with my family so long ago. Those summers had been spent on the soft golden sand of the East Coast rather than the coarse black sand of the West, but it didn't matter. The ocean was the ocean, no matter where we were.

I just sat there and watched Priya and her friends examining the shore with great interest, and I was still there when the rest of the convoy joined us. I felt Michael sit down beside me, but we didn't speak. We just watched as more and more people came down to join us. Some of them were confident and playful, but others – like me – had obviously not see the sea in half a lifetime. For many of the children, it was the first time they'd seen the ocean at all.

That didn't seem to bother them, though. Within a matter of minutes, dozens of people were stripping off their clothing and splashing around in the shallows. The water had to be freezing, but no one seemed to care. Everyone was smiling, and that made me happy.

I leaned against Michael for warmth and closed my eyes, enjoying the scent of salt water and distant storms. It was a smell that I wanted to remember forever.

*** 

We lingered by the seaside for an hour and then we moved on, following the coastline southwards towards the township of Pukerua Bay. We paused there for a few days, both to clear the town and to enjoy spending time playing in the ocean. I'd be lying if I said that the children were the only ones who enjoyed that; the adults loved it just as much, myself included. We'd all forgotten just how different salt water fish tasted. I'd been avoiding fish as much as I could because the smell bothered my nose, but even I was excited to try some. It was exotic and new, and that newness revitalised us.

When we began to move south again, we all did so with renewed energy and vigour. We were so close now that we could barely contain our excitement. The mutants were so far away that we were starting to feel safe again, though not safe enough that any of us would consider loosening our rigid safety precautions. We were still going into unknown territory, and now it felt even more vital that everyone stay safe. Our group had blossomed to over a hundred souls, and I could feel every one of them looking to me for guidance. It was a strange feeling, but wonderful at the same time. My inner council – Michael, Skylar, Anahera and the others who had been with us since the beginning – were always there to help me, and that gave me confidence.

On the second morning after we left Pukerua Bay, we reached another major milestone on our journey: we entered the outskirts of Porirua, the first place that we could rightly call a city instead of a town. At least, it had been. Skylar and I were scouting ahead of the convoy when we arrived. What we saw left our faces grim.

"What happened here?" Skye asked softly, staring at the blackened shells that had once been homes and schools and businesses.

I looked down at the ground and traced my eye towards the edge of the road, where I saw human bones hidden amongst the debris.

"A fire," I said, my voice just as low as hers. Something about the sight made us both want to whisper, even though there was no sign of life. "After the riots, I guess. There was no one left to stop it." I pointed past the ashen husks by the roadside at the hills beyond. "It must have happened years ago. Look, nature's already begun to reclaim this area. One day, this whole city will be forest again."

"Huh." Skylar guided her mount over to the edge of the road to get a better look. "You're right. It looks like there used to be a lot more buildings, but now it's all bush." She glanced at me, and a smile blossomed across her face. "Perhaps we should come back here once we're settled, and see if we can break up those concrete parts that are inhibiting the growth. Give nature a little helping hand."

"Maybe we will," I said, returning her smile. "But for now, we're going to have to try and figure out where our turn-off is in this mess. We're supposed to leave the highway now, and head up into the hills."

"I'll race you!" she shouted suddenly, putting her heels to the horse's sides. They raced off, leaving Boudicca and me in their wake. I guided my horse up to a brisk trot and followed after her, but I did so at a more sedate pace. I was comfortable in the saddle now, but there was no way in hell that I was going to put my baby's life in danger for the sake of a little fun.

***

We found the turn-off without too much difficulty, and then the convoy began its long, slow, painful climb up into the hills that the Wellington region was famous for. For those of us with horses and trucks, it wasn't so bad. For those on foot, it was a miserable and draining trek that seemed to go on forever. We packed as many people as we could into the vehicles and even broke out our quad bikes again, but we still had to stop regularly to switch out the exhausted walkers during the climb. Some parts of the road were so steep that even our four wheel drive trucks struggled with them.

By the time we made it to the top, it was almost sundown and we were all stressed and tired. Thankfully, we discovered that the fire hadn't made it far up into the hills, and we were able to find a few houses intact enough to accommodate us for the night. We turned our animals loose in their overgrown back yards, and slept soundly in our borrowed accommodation.

When morning came, we awoke to a thick sea fog clinging to the hillside around us. It didn't bother us much, though; we were the children of Aotearoa, the Land of the Long White Cloud, and we were used to living in perpetual fog. We reached the peak of the hills in good time, and once we were over the crest it was all downhill. Suburbia gave way to small farms and the occasional lifestyle block perched on the hillside. Rain came again in the afternoon, but it wasn't as cold as it had been before and it didn't hinder our progress.

For nearly a week, we followed the road eastward around the rim of the Porirua harbour, following the old green signs that directed us towards the Hutt Valley. With each passing day, excitement grew in my little group. Not only were we getting closer and closer to our goal, but we could sense the change in the seasons. We'd survived another winter and spring was getting nearer with every passing day. We passed many beds of wild daffodils, and the sight of their bright little faces sent a wave of joy through the entire group.

One day while we were breaking camp and getting ready to move off, Michael came galloping up on his favourite horse. He dismounted dramatically, and bestowed upon me three things: a bow, a goofy smile, and a single white daffodil. Before I could find the words to thank him, he'd leapt back on his horse and galloped off again, leaving me blushing furiously and holding that flower.

My sister took the flower from my hand and slipped it behind my ear. Everyone saw, of course, and a flurry of flower-giving and receiving began soon afterwards. A new tradition bloomed, with men and women of all ages presenting a single flower to the object of their affections to display their love proudly to the world.

By that evening, Skylar had one flower behind each ear. We didn't talk about it, but we didn't have to. I could see her radiant smile as while she went about her work, and I saw the way both Ryan and Hemi were looking at her. The three of them had found a balance that made all of them happy, and that was all that mattered to me.

The next morning, we began our descent into the Hutt Valley. The road was long, straight, and in perfect condition, flanked by rolling hills covered in dense bush on one side, and the sparkling expanse of the Hutt River on the other.

"There should be a bridge coming up in a couple of minutes," I said into my radio, then I put it away and glanced around. My family and several of my dearest friends rode around me: Michael, Priya, and Anahera were on my left, Skylar and Gavin on my right, and Alfred was dancing along happily between us. None of them had wanted to stay back with the convoy, and I wouldn't have tried to make them.

"This is it," Michael said quietly, his voice husky with anticipation. My heart was hammering in my chest at a mile a minute, so I could only imagine they all felt the same tension. I just nodded, swallowed hard, and guided my mount onward. The road ran parallel to the shimmering ribbon of the river, but on the far side there wasn't much to see beyond bush, trees, and the occasional flash of a building.

A few minutes later, we saw a sign guiding us to the bridge which would take us to our promised land. Miraculously, both the bridge and the sign were still intact. We guided our mounts out onto the bridge, heading towards the far side and whatever lay beyond.

"The river is so beautiful," Skylar said in a voice filled with awe. "If it looks like this now, I can only imagine what it's going to look like in summer."

"Even more beautiful, I think," I replied, struggling to keep my emotions in check.

"Look!" Gavin said suddenly, pointing at the side of the bridge. I looked and my eyes widened. There was a fallen signpost, emblazoned with a word that I'd started to think I would never see anywhere but my own imagination.

"Avalon," I said softly, reverently. "One hundred and four days on the road… and we made it. We finally made it."

Michael gave me an odd look. "You were counting?"

"Of course I was counting," I said, quickly making up an excuse to divert him from the truth behind why I'd been counting the days. He'd find out soon enough. "This is going to go down in history one day. Weren't you counting, too?"

"Oh, I didn't think of it like that," he admitted, shrugging sheepishly. "Well, I guess it's good that one of us was countin—"

"Mama, look!" Priya cried, pointing at something her sharp young eyes had managed to spot that we hadn't yet. A second later, Alfred let out a bark, but it wasn't one of warning. It was one of greeting. I looked straight ahead and saw a human figure standing on the bridge, waving frantically at us.

Anahera gasped. "That's Simon! It's been so long I barely recognised him, even after seeing him on television."

"Well, then," I said, glancing around at the group. "We better go and introduce ourselves, don't you think?"

# Chapter Nine

A few more people appeared out of the buildings on the far side of the road while we were dismounting and walking our horses the rest of the way across the bridge. They gathered in a little pack as far away from us as possible, watching us with tense, nervous expressions. Anahera obviously felt no such reservations; the moment she was close enough, she tossed her reins to Priya, raced over to Simon, and hugged him fiercely.

"It's so good to see you," she said, her voice earnest and full of emotion. "I should have come south sooner, but I had my own group and the journey was just too far for us."

"No, I understand," Simon replied, shaking his head. "It's been so hard..." He paused for a second and glanced at the rest of us. "Well, you two are obviously the McDermott sisters I've heard so much about, but I'm afraid I don't recognise the rest of you."

"I'm Sandrine, and this is Skylar," I said to clarify which of us was which, then I pointed at each of my companions in turn. "This is my husband, Michael Chan, former police officer and our security chief. That's Gavin over there, our expert in communications, and this is Priyanka, my foster daughter." I looked back at him and grinned. "You know, this is really quite eerie. I've been watching you on the telly for so long that it was starting to feel like you weren't even a real person, just a fictional character or something."

Simon laughed and nodded. "The feeling is mutual. One of the locals picked up on your radio broadcasts a few months back, and we've been following your exploits ever since. It took you so long to get here that it was starting to feel a bit like The War of the Worlds. You remember that?"

"I never heard it but I know the stories," I replied. I caught Skye and Priya looking confused, so I took a moment to explain the story to them. "The War of the Worlds was a classic novel about aliens invading Earth. In the 1930's, a company in the United States adapted it into a radio show, but they did it in a manner that made some people think it was a real news broadcast. It caused mass hysteria."

"Really?" Skye wrinkled her nose, looking doubtful. "People believed aliens were invading Earth?"

"'Mass hysteria' is a bit of an overstatement," Anahera said, her dark eyes twinkling with amusement. "Only a few people genuinely believed it was true. Most people worked out that it was fiction, even back then. They were less worldly than we are now, but they weren't stupid."

"I'm not sure anyone counts as worldly these days," I said. "I mean, when was the last time any of us communicated with a person outside New Zealand? We don't know if the United States exists anymore. It could have sunk into the sea and we'd never know. Hell, we don't even know if there's anyone alive in Australia these days." I sighed and shook my head, then I glanced at Simon. "So I guess you know why we're here, then?"

"I do, and we've already started working on it," he replied. He turned towards the group of people hovering nearby and waved at them. "Come on, you lot! Let's show Sandrine what we've been up to while we were waiting for her."

The people nodded and vanished without a word. I raised a brow. "That was weird. What's up with them?"

"Don't mind them, they're just not much on talking," he replied. "They showed up here a couple of weeks ago, and told me that they wanted to help build the city. From what I've managed to piece together, they're from some type of religious community that lived up in the hills, but beyond that I don't know much. There are a few other folks scattered around between Wellington and Upper Hutt that I see on occasion, but these guys are definitely the weirdest." He glanced in the direction they'd gone and shrugged helplessly. "Still, they're good workers and never complain. They've helped a lot so far."

"Then you'd better show us where we're at," I replied, gesturing for him to lead on.

"Follow me," he said. He turned and led us down the road, looking about the happiest I'd ever seen him. The Anchorman I'd become so familiar with over the years was generally a miserable soul, rumpled and worn with haunted blue eyes that seemed to reflect the sadness of the world all around him. Today, he was smiling, loquacious, well-dressed, and clean-shaven. My grandmother would have been so proud.

"I have no idea how you knew, but Avalon Studios is the perfect location to build our new city," he said. "The river is teeming with trout, so we've got a nearly unlimited source of food right on our doorstep, plus it's right beside the park. If we put fences up, it'll be perfect for grazing livestock. The studio itself is a huge complex that already has fences all the way around, so we can all stay inside the grounds without worrying that we're going to trip over one another. See that big tower over there?"

I looked in the direction he was pointing and nodded. "The office block with the— is that solar panels I see on the top there?"

"Yes!" he replied proudly, his smile widening. "One of the locals helped me hook those up years ago, to keep the news broadcasts going. The national grid is pretty much non-existent down here."

"That's quite brilliant, actually," I replied, studying the lay of the building in the distance. "I wonder if we can hook up enough to keep the whole city going indefinitely."

"We can," he said with absolute confidence. "I know where to find more panels, and I know how to install them now. We'd probably need a car or a wagon to bring back enough panels to light up the city, though."

"We've got trucks, no worries," I replied. I handed Boudicca's reins to Michael, then pulled my notebook out of my pocket and flicked to the back page to start making notes about what needed to be done. "Let's prioritize that fairly high. We don't want to live in the dark more than we absolutely have to, and fuel for the generators is limited. Now, you were saying something about living inside the compound?"

He nodded enthusiastically, and led us off the road into the long grass of what had obviously once been a park. "There are a bunch of really nice houses just outside the fence that we should be able to do up eventually, and also a few inside that used to be used for filming, but in the meantime we've got the tower." Simon glanced back and gave me a wry smile. "We used to call it that as a joke. It's only ten stories. I've seen stacks of pancakes taller than that."

We all laughed at that. Once the levity subsided, he continued. "The inside of the tower is divided up into a mixture of offices, film studios, sound studios, and equipment rooms. There are toilets, showers, changing rooms, and small kitchenettes on every level. Once we get a few more solar panels up, we should have no trouble powering the whole building, including the elevator."

I grinned at him, suddenly understanding. "So what you're saying is that we turn the tower into a bunch of apartments?"

"Bingo!" he said. "There's a full cafeteria on the second floor, and it's set up to feed twice as many people as this. I haven't used it in ages, but it'll be fine once we give it a good dusting and a scrub."

"Excellent." I scribbled another note and nodded to myself. "Do we have a basement? A parking garage or something?"

"No," he replied, "but there are a bunch of big buildings around that we can use for storing vehicles."

"I was thinking about stuff like our food and medical supplies," I said. "We're close enough to the river that I'm slightly concerned about flooding."

"There should be plenty of room on the second floor," Simon said reassuringly. He reached out and clapped me on the shoulder in a friendly fashion, an unexpected gesture that almost made me jump out of my skin. "Don't worry, I've got this all planned out. Didn't Ana tell you that I was studying to be a city planner before I changed my major to journalism?"

I glanced back over my shoulder at her, but she just laughed and shrugged. Who could tell if he was being serious? It didn't really matter, anyway. We'd arrived, and it was time to break ground on our new home.

*** 

"Well, I don't know about you but I like this one," Michael said, glancing around the little suite on the third floor. It was nothing more than a lobby with an office off to one side, but it was bright, airy, and the afternoon sun poured in through the west-facing windows.

"You're just saying that because this is the lowest floor we're turning into apartments and you know I don't like heights, but I appreciate the sentiment," I teased. I gave him a playful pat on the rump, then went over to stare out the wide-glass windows at all the people milling about in the parking lot. The convoy had arrived not long after we had, and now everyone was in the process of exploring the building.

"Maybe," he said with a grin, "but it is perfect for just the two of us. Priya told me she wants to bunk down in the girls' dorms, so we don't have to worry about her."

"The girls' dorms?" I asked, shooting a curious look back over my shoulder. "This is the first I'm hearing about it. Since when are we setting up dormitories?"

"It was Ana's idea," he replied, wandering up behind me. He put his arms around my waist and stared down at the parking lot over my shoulder. "It's nothing formal at this stage. She suggested that we give the older kids the chance to live in communal dormitories, so that they can socialise with one another and we know where to find them if there's an emergency. She said it'll also make it easier to organise their classes and apprenticeships."

"Huh, I had no idea," I admitted. "I guess she's taking the whole headmistress thing pretty seriously. Glad someone is. What about the younger kids?"

"They can sleep in the dorm or with their parents, whichever they prefer," he replied. "Like I said, it's nothing formal. The kids don't have to stay there if they don't want to. Ana said that the teens she's spoken to are all excited about the idea, though."

I turned within the circle of his arms and rubbed my face against his chest. "I can't say I blame them. They've been alone for so long, they're just starting to learn how wonderful it is to have friends around them."

Suddenly, a voice spoke up from the doorway. "What's really funny is that Melody just proclaimed herself 'Queen of the Girls' Dorms', and now she's prancing around the place in a plastic tiara."

I pulled away from Michael, laughing. "Oh, hey Skye. Didn't hear you sneak up."

"That's 'cause I'm a ninja," she replied without missing a beat, a giant grin on her face. She wandered into the room and looked around curiously. "So this is you guys, huh?"

"I think so, yeah," I said, glancing up at Michael. "You sure you want this one, honey? Last chance to change your mind."

"I'm not changing my mind," he replied. "Hell, I'm already thinking about how to arrange the furniture."

"What furniture?" I asked, looking around at the barren interior. "The desk, the chair, the tiny couch, the tiny armchairs, or the dead house plant?"

"Hey, it's not great furniture, but it's a start," he replied. "We'll head out into town and start collecting proper furniture once we've got the basics handled."

"Speaking of which," Skye interjected, drawing our attention back to her. "I wanted to talk to you guys about something."

"Oh?" I raised my brows and looked at her. "What's up, little sis?"

Skylar sighed heavily, and went over to sit in one of the armchairs. She immediately grimaced and shifted in her seat. "Wow, these really are tiny."

"I told you," I replied dryly. "I think they're made for kids or something."

"We'll find something better later," she said absently. "Anyway, I wanted to talk to you about my role within the group." Another sigh, and she glanced up at me thoughtfully. "Now that we're here, you don't really need me to keep the provisioning and rationing under control anymore. I just… I dunno, I don't want to go back to being useless. You've got Gavin now to handle any radio communications, so you don't need me for that. Michael handles security, Anahera handles schooling and organises the kids, and Doc's already setting up a medical bay down by the cafeteria. Everyone has their place except for me. I don't want to live my life in your shadow, just being 'the other McDermott sister', you know?"

"Aw, you'll never be that," I said. I disentangled myself from Michael and went over to sit on the couch. "We need you to keep doing what you're doing, now more than ever. We've got so many people looking up to us, and we need to make sure that we've always got enough resources to feed them, clothe them, and keep them warm and clean. Hell, now we've got to think about the acquisition of furniture for everyone, too. We need someone who knows exactly what we have and what we need, and can tell us what we need to make or find before it's too late."

"Oh." Skye paused for a long moment, then suddenly she looked at me. "Oh! I can do all of those things! I didn't even think about that. Great. So I can be the… what's the word?"

"The quartermaster?" Michael suggested.

"Yeah!" She nodded enthusiastically, her golden curls bobbing around her face. "I can be the quartermaster! Well, quartermistress, I guess. Quarterperson?"

"You can call yourself whatever you like," I said, reaching over to squeeze her hand. "The job is yours, if you want it. We want to try and avoid people helping themselves to more than we can spare, so it's best if we set you up with an office and keep the supplies under lock and key when you're not there. Can you find something suitable?"

"Just watch me!" she said, leaping up out of the armchair so fast that she almost knocked it over. Halfway out the door, she paused and glanced back at us. "Oh, Simon's looking for you. He asked me to ask you to meet him in his recording studio, which is up on Level Five."

"Will do," I agreed. She waved and ran off, then I glanced over at Michael. "Coming?"

"Absolutely," he replied. "I've got to find out what this big news is before it kills me. Give me a second, though."

I nodded my agreement and waited while he vanished into the room which had been an office, and was going to be our bedroom. A minute later, he came out with a roll of tape and a piece of paper with our names written on it. He taped the sign to the front door, tossed the tape aside, and offered me his hand.

We made our way back to the stairwell and up to Level Five. Along the way, we passed a few familiar faces who waved to us; we waved back, but kept on walking. It took a few minutes for us to find Simon's recording studio. I eventually spotted him through an open door; he was sitting at a desk surrounded by sheets of paper and assorted stationery, intensely focused on writing in a worn exercise book. He was so focused that he nearly jumped out of his skin when I cleared my throat and knocked.

"Oh, Sandrine!" he cried, almost levitating out of his chair. "I've been waiting for you. Come in, please." He glanced at Michael and nodded a greeting. "Hello again… Michael, wasn't it?"

"Yes," Michael confirmed, nodding. "Sorry, we came as soon as we heard you were looking for us."

"Well, I was just looking for her but you're welcome to come along," Simon admitted, with an embarrassed smile. "Come in, have a seat."

We went over to the indicated couch and seated ourselves. A moment later, Simon plunked down in an armchair nearby.

"We caught one of your broadcasts where you mentioned having news for us," I said. "Care to tell us what you were hinting at before we all go crazy?"

Simon laughed and nodded. "I will, don't worry. First of all, though, we must make some plans for tonight's broadcast. I need you up there with me."

"What?" I froze, staring at him. "You want me to be on the news?"

"I believe I said 'need'," he answered dryly. "I definitely need you to appear on the show. We can do a recording if you don't want to go on live, but the people have to see you. They need to see your face, and hear your voice. They need to know that you're a real person, not just a rumour."

"Oh, that makes sense," I said softly, struggling to fight down the wave of nausea that rose inside me. "I'm going to need some time to think about what I'm going to say. Do we have very long?"

"If you're happy being on the live broadcast, then you've got a couple of hours," he said. "If you're too nervous to do it live, then we'll need to get recording as soon as possible."

I took a deep breath and nodded. "We'll do it live. I need as much time as I can to work my speech out. In the meantime, tell us the other news. When you dropped that little titbit on your show, it started a whole slew of rumours that someone's found a cure for Ebola-X."

"They have," Simon said simply.

My jaw fell open in shock. "What? Really?"

A faint smile touched his lips, and his deadpan relaxed. "In a roundabout sort of way."

"Er, what?" I glanced at Michael, then looked back at him. "Explain, please."

"It's probably best if I let him explain it himself," Simon said. He pulled a remote control out of his back pocket and pointed it at a large flat-screen television hanging on the wall opposite us. "While I was out scavenging about two months ago, I found a USB flash drive taped to a door in a plastic bag. It was too weird to ignore, so I decided to open it. I think you'll find it as interesting as I did."

The screen lit up, and a moment later a video began to play. The camera shook for a second, then a scrawny young man in thick glasses and a lab coat sat down in front of the lens.

"If you've found this, I'm probably dead – but you're obviously not, so... hey there!" the young man on the video said, waving to the camera in a way that just made him look even more awkward. "It's February 23rd. We've been down here for forty-three days, trying to find a way to kill the goma ebolavirus before it kills us. We've been making slow but steady progress, but this morning there was a setback: Collins tested positive for the virus during our regular screenings. We've had to put him in the isolation ward and everyone else has come up clean, but we're all a bit shaken."

"Wait," I said, holding up a hand. Simon paused the playback and looked at me quizzically. "Is this what I think it is? I heard rumours about an underground laboratory, but we always assumed it was just that: rumours."

"I thought it was, too – until I found this," Simon answered, his voice losing all traces of humour. "I found a facility, up in the hills. I didn't feel safe exploring it by myself, but this was taped to the front door. We'll need to go back and look for more information, but for now just keep watching." He resumed playback, and we turned our full attention back to the screen.

"Yeah, so um... I'm Clyde. Clyde Russell. Dr Russell – or I would have been at the end of next year." The young man threw his arms wide and grinned at the screen. "Dr Russell, boy genius and geneticist to the stars!" He slumped and heaved a long sigh. "Okay, maybe not. I guess there probably aren't any stars left out there anymore. But we have to keep working, just in case. Maybe there's someone left alive. Maybe someone survived this mess. Well, I guess if you're hearing this then someone has, right?"

"Russell!" someone shouted from out of the view of the camera. "Where are my goddamn cultures?!"

Clyde squeaked in surprise and slapped the camera off. Simon pressed a few buttons on his remote control, then a second video began to play. The screen shook for a few seconds, then Clyde sat down in front of it again. His clothing had changed and he was looking tired and frazzled. "It's day forty-five now, and something's gone wrong. I don't know how. We're deep underground, and we're on filtered air, filtered water, sterilized food. Everything is sealed up tight, nothing's coming in from the outside at all. It should have been enough. It should have! But Dr Scott's caught the virus now, we tested her this morning. I don't know how this is happening. How is this happening? Argh!"

He made a frustrated sound and slammed his fist down on the table, then sighed and looked into the camera again. "We're all going to die. It's inevitable. There's an immunity gene, but none of us are carriers. We've been trying so hard to prevent exposure... it doesn't matter. I'm recording this because I don't want to die without my life meaning something. I think we might be onto something. Maybe. I'll update as soon as I know more."

He leaned over and switched off the camera again. Simon set a third video playing without a word. This time, the young doctor was looking tired and rumpled, his eyes bloodshot with dark circles under them. "Day fifty-three. Collins and Scott are dead. They hung themselves in the isolation rooms. We can't even go in and cut the bodies down; Professor Fa'amoe says it's too dangerous. I don't think it's going to make much of a difference, to be honest. It's too late for us, we'll be joining them soon enough – but at least we've made progress.

"We've determined that a cure is impossible," he said, absently removing his glasses and rubbing the bridge of his nose between finger and thumb. "The virus does too much damage, too quickly. Once the damage is done, it's impossible to reverse. But we think we've worked out a way to engineer a course of vaccines based off blood samples we took from people with the immunity gene before we had to go full dark. I have no idea whether it will do much good for whoever has survived, but I hope it'll help. If not… well, there isn't much else we can do. I'm sorry. We tried."

The screen went dead again, and this time it was permanent. I sat up straight and looked at Simon. "Is that all of it? What happened to him?"

"I don't know yet," he admitted. "There was more data on the flash drive, but the files were corrupted. I didn't want to risk going into that facility alone, so I've been waiting for you to arrive."

"How much good would a vaccine do us, though?" Michael asked, a deep frown on his face. "We're already immune."

"I'm not sure, but if they have it then we should try and find it," Simon said. "It might be the most important discovery of our time."

"It is," I said, hugging myself against a chill that only I could feel. "But it's not for us. It's for our children. We still don't know for certain whether or not the child of two immune parents will always be immune herself. A vaccine would eliminate the chance altogether. If they completed it, it works, and we can figure out a way to make it, then we'll never have to worry about losing a baby to Ebola X. Ever."

Neither of them had anything to say to that.

# Chapter Ten

"You ready for your television debut?" Michael asked, squeezing my shoulder in a way that somehow managed to be both teasing and reassuring. We were waiting off to one side of the stage while Simon was running through the last few smaller bits of news at the beginning of his show.

"No, not really," I admitted.

Michael laughed and shook his head. "Well, I think you'd better get ready, because it looks like you're up."

Sure enough, Simon turned and gave me a nod. I swallowed hard, straightened my shoulders, flicked my hair back over my shoulders, and glanced at Michael again. "Do I look all right?"

"…Asks the most beautiful woman on earth," he replied. "Get out there before the Anchorman has a fit."

His comment made me laugh, and gave me the boost of confidence I needed to walk out onto the stage in front of the camera that would broadcast my face to the rest of the country. I already had my entire speech planned out, along with every step, every gesture, and every facial expression. I'd practiced it a dozen times. I knew that I could do it. I came up beside Simon and turned to face the camera with just the faintest smile on my lips.

"Hello, New Zealand," I said, my words practised and even. "By now, I'm sure that you've heard my name. I am Sandrine McDermott, the leader of the group that the media—" I glanced at Simon and smiled wryly. "—or what's left of it, has taken calling the New Exodus."

I put my hands on my hips and looked straight into the camera, forcing myself to project as much strength and kindness as I possibly could. "The New Exodus is over. We've reached our destination. Now, the next step of our journey begins. Today we broke ground on Tumanako, the City of Hope, which we are building out of the ruins of what used to be Lower Hutt.

"One hundred and thirty-four souls call Tumanako home on this, the first day of our new beginning. Men and women, young and old, our citizens cover the spectrum of human society. We have doctors and nurses, veterinarians and engineers, soldiers and teachers – a cross-section of everything you could imagine. Come to us as a friend, and we will welcome you with open arms. Come to us as an enemy, and we will fight you to our last breath.

"You no longer need to live in fear, New Zealand. You no longer need to hide amongst the ruins and run from strangers. I know how that feels, because I have lived that life, and I swear to you that no citizen of Tumanako will ever have to live like that again unless they choose to.

"Come to Lower Hutt, my friends. We're waiting for you to join us. You are welcome here, and you will be safe. Contribute equally, and you will be fed and clothed as one of our own. We'll protect you and your family, and help your children grow up in a world better than the one left to us.

"Together, we will forge a new world, a world like the one we left behind but adapted to fit our ideals and our culture. This is our world now, and we will face the trials it holds together – you, me, and every other Child of Hope. Join us, and we will stand as one to face the future. Thank you."

"No, thank you," Simon said, his voice soft and almost reverent. He smiled at me and nodded his approval. "And there you have it, viewers. The magnificent Sandrine McDermott, in the flesh. Thank you, Sandrine. I can take care of things from here."

I nodded and made my way off the set. Simon's praise was unexpected, and it left my cheeks burning; I'd had a crush on the man for nearly ten years, and some parts of me apparently weren't as dead as I thought they were. The look he'd given me at the end of my speech... it was the kind of look I usually only received from Michael. A special kind of look.

I found Michael waiting for me outside the set. He fell in beside me and matched my step as we walked back towards the stairs. Eventually, I calmed down enough to take a deep breath and let it out as a long sigh. "Well, that was stressful. Let's not do that again."

"I don't think you'll have to," he said, sliding an arm around my waist. I tensed a little, suddenly afraid that he'd noticed my reaction to Simon's praise, but he hadn't. He just smiled at me and gave me a sideways hug. "Simon said something about recording the broadcast, so I assume he can just keep replaying your speech when he needs to."

"Good," I replied. I took another deep breath, but this time I let it out as a playfully grumpy sound that was a hybrid of a growl and a whine. "I am not cut out for television!"

"I beg to differ," he said, squeezing me tenderly. "If I hadn't seen you falling apart before you went on stage, I never would have guessed that you were nervous at all. You did a fantastic job."

"Flatterer," I replied without missing a beat, then I gave him a playful slap on the rump. "Come on. Let's go see what kind of state this kitchen is in. It's almost dinner time, and the natives will start getting restless if we don't feed them."

Right on cue, my stomach rumbled. Michael and I both laughed, and together we headed down the stairs towards Level Two. The majority of that level was taken up by a big cafeteria, with dozens of tables and chairs set up around the middle of the room, and couches and armchairs around the outside. Huge windows gave us a view out across the park to the river, and through them we could see the sun setting on the horizon.

"We're going to need to see about getting curtains up," I said as we walked through the room towards the door at the back that most likely led into the kitchens. "The former tenants may not have cared about all the heat they were letting out those lovely big windows, but we do. No point wasting our precious power, right?"

"Right," he agreed, nodding. "We'll need to get some people in here to clean off these tables. Looks like Simon didn't come in here much."

"Yeah, there's an inch of dust on everything," I replied. I reached the end of the counter and lifted up the little door that was designed to keep the public out, then made my way behind the display cabinets. A few seconds later, I let myself into the kitchen – and almost bowled over poor Elly.

"Oh!" she cried, leaping away from me.

"Ack!" I jumped in surprise and hopped backwards, stumbling into Michael. "Elly! God, you just about gave me a heart attack."

"Likewise," she replied. She swallowed a deep breath, and then gave us a smile. "Sorry, I was just standing here trying to figure out where to begin. They'll be bringing the food up any minute and... well, look for yourself."

I glanced around the big kitchen and cringed. "Wow, I see what you mean. Looks like the folks here left in a hurry."

"Yes, and they left all the food behind to rot," she replied. "We did have one stroke of luck, though. I don't quite know how, but somehow that cooler over there is still working."

"What? Really?" I went over to the big metal door and opened it. The smell of decomposing meat hit me immediately and sent me reeling back, gagging, but the air was still cold. Heavy with the stench of rot, but cold.

Michael reached past me and pushed the door closed, blocking out the worst of the stink. "Let's just leave that closed for now, shall we?"

"Good plan," I replied, struggling to get my gag reflex back under control. I took a couple of deep breaths, then looked at Elly and Michael. "First step is that we need to clean. Let's get as many people in here to help as possible. Many hands make light work. Honey, could you please go round up everyone you can find? We should make this top priority before it gets dark. Oh, and while you're at it, see if you can get the electricians to hook up our generator in here. We're going to need it sooner rather than later."

"I'm on it," Michael replied. He saluted me and hurried out, leaving Elly and me to work out how to handle the mess.

"Okay, you and I are going to get into the cupboards and inventory the cleaning supplies," I said. "You start here, and I'll go check out that room up the back. Sound good?"

"Sure," she agreed readily. While she set to work, I headed across the room to the far side and opened a small door. The room beyond was a storage room, lined with an array of enormous, restaurant-grade tin cans, sacks of flour and rice, and other assorted food items, most of which were way too far gone to be of any use to us. Off to one side, a second door opened into a cleaning closet.

I tried the light switch and found that it was weak and flickering, so I opted to use my torch instead; there was power in the building, but not enough for us to rely on until we had a chance to extend Simon's solar panel array. I sorted through the various bottles and jars of cleaning products, and grabbed the ones that would be most useful to us.

Just as I was bringing out the last load, the door opened and Michael led in a small army of volunteers. I exchanged a glance with Elly, then we started distributing cleaning rags and jobs to everyone.

\*\*\*

The sun set while we were working, but Jim, Zain, and Gavin appeared right on time with the generator. They managed to hook up lights for us to see what we were doing, and enough electricity to power the cooking facilities as well. As soon as the big, industrial stove had been cleaned, we started it up and got dinner going. With a hundred and thirty-six mouths to feed, we needed every second we could get.

Sure enough, the rest of our settlers drifted in looking for food soon enough. One by one we set them working, cleaning the dining room, scrubbing dishes, or whatever else needed doing. Skylar appeared out of nowhere yet again, her voice effortlessly commanding. Soon we had food ready to be served, and more than a hundred hungry mouths lined up waiting their turn to be fed.

By the time my turn came to be relieved of duty and fed, I was exhausted. I took my bowl of delicious mystery slop out into the dining room and plopped down on a couch beside Michael. Neither of us said anything while we ate. We were too busy shovelling food to communicate with anything more than inarticulate caveman grunts.

When we finished, we went our separate ways. He went off to fetch our belongings from the convoy, make sure that the trucks were safely stowed away, and assign the night watch, while I returned to the kitchen to help with the washing up. There were enough people there that we finished in record time, even without the aid of the automatic dish-sterilizer that sat in the corner of the room. I made a note in my book to get that working again as soon as possible, then mucked in beside the others.

Afterwards, I headed back up to level three and found my way into the ladies room to relieve myself and indulge in a quick cold shower by the light of my torch. A few minutes later, I switched off the shower, dried myself, then wrapped myself in my towel and opened the stall door. My new apartment was just across the way, so I planned to grab my stuff and scamper home to get ready for bed.

It didn't work out quite how I planned it, though. When I stepped out of the stall, I found myself face to face with a group of near-strangers, both male and female, standing in a semi-circle around my shower stall. They didn't say a word, just stared at me, their faces ominously cast in shadow.

"Uh... hello?" I said, taking a step back into the stall. Suddenly, I was afraid for my safety. I was all alone and I didn't like the expressions on their faces. There was someone standing between me and my belongings; the only way to get to my taser would be to somehow get past him.

"We've been waiting for you," one of the men said, stepping forward into my torchlight. I recognised him as a member of the reclusive commune which had come down from the hills, but that didn't really help my confidence. Simon's words had implied that they were fanatics, after all. Nothing good ever came from fanatics.

"Yeah, so Simon said," I replied, trying to keep my voice calm and even. I inched back a little farther and shot a quick glance around, but there was no way for me to get out of the room without passing within arm's length of at least one of them. "So, uh, you guys know this is the ladies room, right? You're not really meant to be in here."

"It was the best way to get you alone," a woman said. I didn't recognise her voice, but I understood the threat in her tone. Suddenly, I caught sight of a glint of steel in her hand. I couldn't tell whether it was a knife or something else, but I leapt back just in time to avoid being struck across the face by whatever it was. It turned out to be a metal crucifix, and pain exploded across my collarbone when its sharp edge bit into my skin. I slammed the door of the shower stall closed and threw the bolt into place; a second later, someone struck the outside of the stall with enough force to make the whole structure shake.

"Blasphemer!" the woman screamed. There was another heavy thud, and I heard the horrible sound of wood cracking and metal shrieking. I threw my weight against the door to keep it closed, but there were a half-dozen of them and only one of me.

"Michael!" I screamed at the top of my lungs, for want of a better option. "Michael! Skye! Someone help me!"

"Silence your tongue, blasphemer!" the woman screamed back at me, and I heard the sound of flesh striking the other side of the door. "New Exodus, indeed? You are not Moses, and you should be punished for your sin of presumption!"

"Wait!" I cried, struggling to keep the shattered door closed. "I wasn't— I didn't choose that name, that's just what Simon started calling us. My only intention was to help people, I swear! All people, regardless of faith, race, or gender. I only want to help our people find a home!"

"Lies! All lies!" the man accused. "We weren't certain of what you were doing until you arrived, but then we heard your people whispering about the prophet in their midst. We know what you're telling them! We know that you are spreading false belief to control them, and we will not let you continue!"

Before I could defend my innocence, there was another blow to the door and it gave in with an almighty crash. I slipped on the wet tiles and fell hard, striking my head on the way down. Stars danced around the edges of my vision and a wave of nausea rose inside me. Before I quite knew what was happening, I felt myself being grabbed by the shoulders and dragged back to my feet, but I couldn't coordinate myself enough to fight back. I was frogmarched towards the door, but then the man holding me stopped suddenly.

"Move, child!" he shouted. "This is none of your concern!"

"Actually, it is," a tiny voice replied, delicate, feminine, and yet supremely in control. I recognised it immediately: Madeline.

"This woman is a false prophet and will be punished as such," one of the women growled. She shoved me so roughly that the man holding me lost his grip, and I slid back to the ground again. When I managed to lift my head, I found Maddy standing over me.

"Miss Sandy isn't the prophet," Maddy told them calmly, her voice carrying a note of derision. "I am. And even if she had tried to claim that title – which she hasn't – violence is not the answer. Now, stop acting like fools and go back to your rooms."

The man took a menacing step towards her, but Maddy didn't even flinch. She looked him straight in the eye, her expression deathly calm. "Your name is Daniel Ferguson. That's your daughter, Mary. You lost your wife, Nicole, to the plague, along with your two little boys. Your youngest son's name was Andrew, and his favourite colour was green. He died holding his favourite toy, a green stuffed dinosaur named Poppet."

I glanced up just in time to see the man turn pale and take a step back. "How do you know that?"

"Because they told me," she hissed, in a voice that sent a shiver all the way down my spine. "They're waiting for you. Now, they're ashamed to see how far you've fallen. Is that what you want, Mister Ferguson?"

"Nicole?" he whispered, his expression changing to one of horror. "They should be in Heaven, waiting for me there. Not here on Earth."

Madeline tilted her head to one side and paused, listening to something that only she could hear. "Not yet. They're still waiting. They'll wait as long as they have to. Time passes differently where they are." Maddy looked at me and smiled. "It's okay, Miss Sandy. They're not going to hurt you anymore. Are you, Mister Ferguson?"

The big man looked down at me and slowly shook his head. He turned and walked towards the door, his movements slow and jerky as though walking in a dream. The others glanced at one another, then hurried out after him, leaving me alone with Maddy.

She looked at me and smiled. "Don't worry, he'll be here in a second."

"Who?" I asked, dazed and a little confused. Maddy just smiled.

A second later, I heard Michael's voice. "Sandy? Where are you?"

"She's in here," Maddy called before I could answer. "She's a bit dizzy, please come and help her up."

"Dizzy?" Michael stuck his head into the room, and then I saw his eyes widen. "Honey! What happened?"

"I had an encounter with a few people who…" I trailed off and shook my head. "I'm cold and I don't feel good. I just want to go home. Can we go home, please?"

"Of course," he said, his expression softening. He hurried over and scooped me up, as easily as if I were a child. My towel was almost gone, but I managed to pull it around me enough to keep from flashing everyone as he carried me back to our suite. Maddy picked up my belongings from the bench beside the shower stalls and followed after us.

A few people stared as we passed, but Michael didn't stop until we were safely home. He'd apparently managed to drag a thin mattress up to our rooms while I had been in the shower, and now he gently lay me down on the rumpled sheets. He left for a moment and I heard him talking to Maddy, then the door to our suite closed and locked.

A few seconds later, Michael came back and sat down beside me. Without a word, he gathered me in his arms and hugged me close to him, stroking my hair with gentle hands. I closed my eyes and leaned against him, letting his touch comfort me and drive away the feeling of disquiet. The bruises would heal and they hadn't done any real harm, but now I had something new to worry about – and it was something I'd never considered, and didn't know how to handle.

# Chapter Eleven

I slept fitfully that night. Every time I started to drift off, something would jerk me awake and leave me tense and nervous. Michael was there to comfort me every time. Whenever he felt me wake up, he stroked my hair and spoke softly to me in the dark until I started to relax again. Eventually, sometime in the middle of the night, I finally fell into a deeper sleep.

The next time I opened my eyes, it was sunrise. There were no curtains in our room yet, just some pathetic blinds that were so dusty we were afraid to touch them. The room was cold as a result, but not cold enough to discourage me from getting up. There was so much that needed to be done, and working would give me a chance to think over the practical ramifications of what had happened the night before. I shuffled out from beneath our blankets and slowly sat up, hyper-alert for any symptoms that would indicate I'd sustained another concussion.

Luckily, this time there were no signs of one. I could feel a bruise through my hair, but my head was steady and my eyes were no more sensitive to daylight than on any other day. Content that I was in my usual rude health, I stood up and pulled on my clothing.

Michael was still fast asleep, and I decided to leave him that way. I leaned down and pulled the blankets up to his chin, then ran one hand affectionately over the back of his head. His hair was perfectly trimmed as it always was, but in the evenings and early mornings there was a shadow of dark stubble on his chin. Those were my favourite times. As much as I loved the fact that he was always so well-groomed, those little moments of imperfection made me feel closer to him.

I sighed softly to myself, adjusted the blanket a tiny bit more, then I left him to sleep. Our bags sat waiting for us in the living room, small and pathetic but somehow enough to give me hope. With time and effort, this place would be our home. Our baby would be born here in a little under six months. I smiled and ran my hand across my belly; there was no sign of her yet, but I knew she was in there somewhere.

Our baby. My baby. Unexpectedly, I found tears in my eyes. To think, I'd been so terrified of the idea not very long ago, and now... I realised with some shock that I was looking forward to meeting my firstborn child. I glanced towards my bedroom and stared at the closed door. I'd have to tell Michael soon, once I worked out the best way to break the news. He was going to be so happy.

A knock on the door interrupted my train of thought and drew me back to the present. I went over to the door, but my hand hesitated on the lock. Was it safe out there? I wasn't so sure anymore.

"Who's there?" I called, my hand resting on the door handle.

"It's Mary. Mary Ferguson," a female voice replied. I immediately tensed up; the last time I'd heard that voice, it had been raised in anger. But now it sounded shy, and just as nervous as I felt. I took a deep breath, unlocked the door, and opened it.

Mary was alone, and her face was a mask of shame. I moved out into the corridor and pulled the door closed behind me. The moment the door was closed, she looked at me and the words tumbled out of her.

"I'm so sorry," she said earnestly. "About what we did last night. We made a terrible mistake – and a stupid mistake, at that." She took a deep breath, then looked down at her feet. "I'm here on behalf of the others. They were all going to come, but we realised that you'd probably be… afraid of us, after what we did. Dad asked me to represent us. Really, we can't apologise enough. I hope we didn't hurt you."

I stared at her while her words sank in, unsure what to make of the apology. It certainly seemed honest and heartfelt, but did that make up for what they'd almost done? If Maddy hadn't shown up when she had, then I might not have survived the night.

"Mary…" I said, a little hesitantly. "Look, I'll be honest with you. You scared the hell out of me. I thought that you and your friends were going to kill me. I'm sorry, but it's going to take time for me to get over that enough to forgive you. I hope you understand."

"I do," she said, awkwardly shuffling her feet. "We weren't… we weren't going to kill you. I don't know what we thought we were going to do. Maybe punish you, scare you enough to see that your path was wrong, but… it doesn't matter now. We see now that we were in the wrong, not you. We should have taken the time to ask, rather than just jumping to conclusions. We can leave, if you want us to—"

"No, you don't have to leave," I said quickly, shaking my head. "Everyone is welcome in Tumanako. You made a mistake, but I'm not going to hold that against you in the long term. It's just going to take some time before I can personally forgive you. But I do appreciate the effort you made in coming here. In future, if you have a problem with anyone, please talk to them first. If it's a serious problem, you can always come to me or one of the other council members and we'll help you work it out."

"I understand," she said, glancing up at me again, her eyes brimming with tears. "Thank you. We'll… we'll find some way to make this up to you, I promise. You were only trying to do the right thing for everyone." She hesitated for a moment, and took a step backwards. "I'll go and leave you be. I hope you have a good morning."

"Likewise," I replied. She curtseyed awkwardly, then turned on her heel and raced off. Behind me, the door opened and Michael stuck his head out.

"What was that about?" he asked.

"She came to apologise for last night," I replied, shaking my head. "I wish they'd thought of that before they attacked me and scared the hell out of me, but I guess the last ten years have been a bit hard on everyone. No one's thinking rationally right now. We're all learning how to be… human all over again."

Michael touched my shoulder and nodded. "We'll get there eventually. All of us. I'm sorry that I wasn't there for you last night."

"It's okay," I said, brushing his apology away with a gesture. "It wasn't your fault. We've all gotten so used to the people with us that we forget some people have conflicting beliefs, or might be offended by the little things we say without thinking. That's an important lesson for all of us to remember: everyone is different. Hopefully, we can learn how to use that to bring us together instead of tearing us apart, because these very different people are the only ones we have left to rely on."

"Very true," he replied. He put his arm around me and gave me a kiss, then smiled. "Shall we go get breakfast on?"

"Yeah," I agreed. "We've got a lot to do today, and it looks like the weather isn't going to be very agreeable. Red sky in the morning…"

Michael just laughed and nodded. Hand in hand, we headed downstairs to get ready to face the day.

***

It was nearly mid-morning before we had everyone fed, clothed, and ready for work or school. I put away the last clean dish and went out into the dining room, where I found just about every citizen of Tumanako sitting around waiting for instructions on where to begin.

That was a big task. I took a deep breath and decided to start with the smallest piece of the puzzle: the kids. Anahera was sitting on one of the couches, surrounded by a mob of adoring youngsters. I smiled to myself, remembering the day I'd first met her. I remembered wondering how anyone could get anything done with someone that beautiful for their teacher, but suddenly it made sense. Anahera wasn't just gorgeous, she was charismatic. The children wanted to pay attention to her, as did most of the men – and not a few of the women, either.

Melody was obviously one of them. She was sitting on another couch nearby with Priya and the rest of her gang, but she only had eyes for Ana.

"Yeah, I see it, too," Skye said softly, right beside my elbow.

I jumped in surprise. "Dammit, Skye! Again with the sneaking!"

"Sorry," she said brightly, clearly not meaning it at all. "But I see it, like I said. Melody's got the hots for Anahera."

I could only laugh. "Everyone's got the hots for Anahera. I've seen you looking at her like that."

"Hey, you have too!" she replied, nudging me with her elbow. "Let's just agree that she's everyone's girl crush and move on."

"Who's got a crush on a girl?" Hemi asked, appearing in the doorway nearby. Skye and I exchanged a look, then laughed and shook our heads.

"I'll let you explain the joke," I told her dryly, then I made my way out from behind the counter and over to Anahera and the kids.

She looked up as I approached, and gave me one of her heart-stopping smiles. "Good morning, Sandrine. You look very well today. You're practically glowing."

"Likewise," I replied with a smile. "I can still hardly believe that we've arrived, and yet here we are! Have you figured out where you're going to hold classes yet?"

"Not yet," she admitted. "I think for the first few days the children and I will set up shop in one of the sound studios on the other side of this level. Once the elevators are working, I'd like to move the children farther upstairs, so they can be closer to the dormitories."

"Sounds good," I said, nodding my approval. "Let me know which room or rooms you want, and we'll make sure to keep them aside." I glanced over at Melody. "I hear you're the new Queen of the Dorms. How was it last night?"

"A little uncomfortable, since we don't have any beds yet," Melody replied. I was surprised to see a smile on her usually sour face, and her eyes were bright and alive in a way that I'd never seen before. "They're up on level seven. It's a bit of a hike, but the view makes it so worth it!"

"Mama, did you see the sky when the sun came up this morning?" Priya asked. "So pretty! So much pink!"

"I did," I said, smiling at her. "I bet it looked much prettier up that high, though. Did you get any sleep at all last night, or did you spend all night awake, whispering with your friends?"

Priya giggled and hid her face behind her hands, which was all the answer I needed. I laughed and shook my head, then I looked back at the others.

"Okay, we need to get started for the day," I told them. "Anahera, Melody, can you take the kids off to one of the other rooms, so I can organise things? I'd like to see class started as soon as possible."

"I have enough books and such put aside that I should be able to find something for them to do," Anahera replied. She rose to her feet and beckoned to the youngsters around her. "Come, children! Time for school. Melody, dear, could you please go fetch the littlest ones from their parents and bring them to us, as well? We can watch them while the adults work."

Melody nodded vigorously. She grabbed Priya and the twins and ran off. Poor Solomon was left behind, looking lost and bewildered. I took pity on him, and addressed him next.

"Hey Sol, you want to work with the adults today?" I asked. He shot a confused look at me for a second, then his eyes brightened and he nodded. "Good man. We're going to need all the help we can get. Come on!"

The youth hurried after me as I went over to a nearby table, pulled out an empty chair, and vaulted up to stand on it. I waved to everyone, but they were too wrapped up in their conversations to notice.

"Hey!" I tried again, but only a few faces turned towards me. I sighed, put aside all attempts at decorum, and cupped my hands around my mouth to shout, "Hey, guys! Shut up for a second!"

The room fell deathly silent for all of three seconds. Then, right on cue, everyone started laughing. I slapped my palm against my forehead. Well, at least I had their attention. The laughter passed swiftly, and when it did they were all looking at me.

"Okay, we've got a lot to do today," I called, projecting as much volume as I could so that everyone could hear me. "I figure eventually we're all going to find our own places and know what needs to be done, but for today I'm going to get everyone started by playing drill sergeant. If any of you can think of something you should be doing that will benefit the group more than what I ask you to do, just sing out. First of all, everyone who has already been assigned guard duty for the day shift, please go stand over there with Michael so I know that you're already occupied. Anyone with technical training or experience with electrical stuff and solar power, come here please. That includes anyone apprenticed to an engineer or electrician at the moment."

A small group of people stood up and came over to me, including Gavin, Zain, and Jim.

"I want you guys to work with Simon to extend the solar grid," I told them. "Requisition whatever you need from the supplies, you have my permission. Simon said something about a stash of extra panels, so talk to him and see what he knows. I also want to get the elevators working again as soon as possible."

"We'll take care of it," Gavin said, saluting me. The rest of the group did the same, then they filtered out of the room and went off about their task.

I waited until they were gone, then looked back at the larger group. "Okay, plumbers. I think we have a plumber, right?"

"Yeah, me," a voice called from a table on the other side of the room. Someone stood up, and I immediately recognised him as Petera, a member of the Waikato Iwi. He came over to me and gave me a grin. "You want me to make sure all the loos work?"

"How'd you guess?" I replied, grinning back at him. "The loos, showers, sinks. Once you've checked them over, I'd like you to track down whatever makes the water flow and make sure that it's all in working order, right back to the source. You got an apprentice yet?"

"No, not yet," he replied. "I could use some help, though. It's going to be a big job."

I glanced up and looked around at the crowd. "It's not a pretty job, but it's one of the most important. Anyone interested in apprenticing to our plumber?"

Silence was my answer – at least, for the first few seconds. Then, I felt a tug on my sleeve. I glanced down to see Solomon looking up at me, his eyes shining with excitement.

"Really?" I asked, a little surprised. "You want to be a plumber?"

The mute boy nodded vigorously.

I raised both brows. "You do know that means dealing with everyone else's poo, right?"

Solomon just nodded harder, then stood up straight and thumped himself on the chest. He tried to say something, but I couldn't quite make out his words.

"I think he's trying to say that he knows how important it is," Petera said, looking at the boy curiously. "And it is. Making sure everyone has clean water is the most important job of all. Right, boy?"

Solomon made a noise of agreement and gave us both a thumbs-up gesture. Petera laughed and clapped the young man on the shoulder, then he looked up at me.

"Well, that answers that question," he said. "Looks like I've got myself an apprentice."

I nodded and grinned at them both. "That's great. Thank you for volunteering, Sol. It means a lot to everyone. If you two need anything, go see Skylar. She's handling all our stores."

"Will do," Petera agreed cheerfully. He waved to me, then took Solomon and left as well. I watched until they were out of sight, then looked back at the others.

"We've got plenty of food," I told them. "But I'd like to get some fresh stuff coming in as soon as possible to keep our reserves going until the gardens are reliable. I want ten of you to spend the day down at the river, fishing. Volunteers?"

This time, hands went up all over the room, and everyone laughed. I picked ten people at random, and sent them off about their business.

"Doc, Rebecca, Aaron, and Hemi," I called. The four people I'd named stood up and came over to me. "I want you guys to get the sick bay organised. Consider it a high priority. Every life here is precious, and accidents always happen at the most inconvenient moment. I believe there's a hospital nearby, so I'll arrange a trip out there over the next few days. For now, just make sure we're as prepared as we can be. Make up a list of anything that we're running low on, and I'll send it with the scavengers when they go check out the hospital."

"Of course," Doc replied, adjusting his glasses. He glanced back at his new assistants, then beckoned for them to follow him and headed out the door.

"Johan," I called. "You're a vet, right?"

"I was, yes," he replied, grinning at me.

"Cool. I want you to take care of the horses and livestock," I said. "Find somewhere safe to keep them, and make sure they'll be healthy and comfortable."

"I know just the place," he replied. "I'll need some help getting the fences back up, though. Say, five people?"

"Volunteers?" I said, looking at the others. Sure enough, hands went up all over the room. Johan picked his five people and left. I switched my attention to the next item on my agenda, and looked around for a familiar face. "Richard, where are you? Wait, I see you. I believe you were a gardener, correct?"

"Yes," he replied softly.

I gave him a smile; Richard was a shy soul, but sweet and gentle. Even though he was older than me, my instinct was to protect and nurture him. "I'd like you to be our head gardener, since you know more about plants than any of us. Would you be happy to take on that role?"

Richard gave me a rare smile in return and nodded. "I... would like that, thank you."

"Good," I said, silently pleased that he'd accepted. I'd come to like him a lot in the months that we'd known one another. "What I want you to do today is take ten people out and scout the gardens around here. There will be a lot of plants growing wild. Some of them we can pick now and eat, but there will also be some we can dig up and transplant into our gardens here."

He nodded his understanding and stood up. "We're well past the coldest part of winter now. We should try and get the garden in soon so that it can grow through spring."

"I'll leave that in your capable hands," I replied. "If you need more people, just tell me or Skye."

"Ten should be enough for today," he replied. He cast a nervous glance over his shoulders at the group, then shot me a helpless look. He didn't need to say what he was thinking: he was too shy to ask for volunteers.

"Who wants to help with the garden?" I called. Hands shot up again, and I picked ten people for him. Richard hurried out, and they followed after him. "Now, the rest of us are on 'unskilled labour' duty," I said jokingly, making air-quotes with my fingers. "That means scavenger duty right now. What we need to do is fan out and search the surrounding area. Bring back everything that's important or useful, so that we can store it safely inside the walls of Tumanako. Eventually, I want that to include things like books, movies, music, and even photographs, but for now let's focus on furniture and supplies, particularly beds. Let's break up into teams of five and six people – unless I'm forgetting something? Or someone has another idea? It kinda freaks me out when you guys are this quiet." The group laughed again, but a hand did pop up at the back of the room. I pointed to the bearer and called his name. "Yes, Nick? What's your idea, mate?"

"A chicken coop," he called back. "I was a tattoo artist before the plague, but that isn't really useful anymore so Ropata's been teaching me his carpentry voodoo. I bet we could build us a real nice coop with a little bit of effort."

"That's a brilliant idea," I replied, pleased by both the concept and the sentiment behind it. "Do you need a few people to help you?"

"Nah, we can handle it," he said. He shot a glance at Ropata and grinned. "Right, Teach?"

Ropata laughed and nodded. The two of them stood without any further prompting from me, and hurried out the door. I looked back at the rest of my people, but no one else had anything to offer.

"Well, then," I said. "Let's get to it before it starts raining, shall we?"

A spontaneous cheer went up from the remaining citizens of Tumanako, and then we divided up and went our separate ways.

***

It was nearly sundown by the time the rain finally started to close in. I'd picked the people no one else wanted for my team: Warren, Quentin, and Kurt, who were the three most standoffish lone wolves of the pack, plus the silent, eternally-sullen Charu, and poor, nervous Isabelle. Even though she'd been with us for over a month now, she was still struggling to settle in and make friends besides me. Whenever she could, she glued herself to my side and followed me like a lost puppy.

At first I'd found it a little confusing, then mildly annoying, but then I'd finally realised that she was just feeling anxious and found my presence comforting. After that, I forced myself to relax and just let her do what she needed to do. She wasn't in the way, and keeping her close meant I could watch for opportunities to help her expand her social circle. The only problem was that her constant anxiety made her a little irritating at times, and not everyone was as patient with her as I tried to be.

I was in the middle of helping the men strip a bed down to the base when she suddenly came rushing into the room, wringing her hands.

"It's raining," she told us, in the kind of voice that usually meant the sky was falling. "Oh goodness, it's getting terribly dark. I think we should go back."

"We will," I said, keeping my tone calm and reassuring. "We're okay, though. We've got lots of time. Why don't you go look in the back bedroom and see if you can find anything useful?"

"O-okay," she stammered, then she hurried off without another word. I glanced back at the others and smiled indulgently. They weren't as tolerant of her antics as I was, but they seemed content to leave it at dark looks and frowns.

"I think we can get this back before dark," I said. They didn't respond, so I shrugged and gave them orders. They'd shown time and again that they weren't interested in debating anything, but they'd follow orders. "Quentin, Warren, take the top mattress. Charu, you and Kurt take the base. Who's got the tarps?"

Quentin raised his hand, then unshouldered his backpack without a word and fished them out. I left them to it and went off in search of Isabelle.

I found her in the back bedroom, looking lost and confused. I cleared my throat, and she jumped.

"Oh, Sandy," she said, letting out a sharp breath as though I'd given her the fright of a lifetime. "Sorry. I'm just not sure where to begin. I'm not very good at this."

"It's fine, really," I reassured her. "Let's walk through this together and I'll teach you. What do you see here?"

"Well, I think it was a baby's room, or maybe a toddler's," she replied, lacing her fingers together in front of her as if to protect herself. "I mean, I guess it must be. There's a crib over there."

"You're right," I said, fighting the urge to laugh. Her obvious desire to please struck me as humorous, even though I immediately felt guilty for feeling that way. I shoved the feeling aside and focused on educating her. "So, we've got the crib, a few baby blankets, some toys, and a chest of drawers. What's in the drawers?"

"Oh, um…" She paused and shot an uncertain look at me. I nodded encouragingly towards the drawers.

"Go on," I instructed gently. "Take a look and see what's in them. They won't bite."

Isabelle nodded nervously and went over to do just that. She opened the top drawer delicately, using just her finger and thumb, then poked the clothing inside. "Just… just baby clothes, I think. Some cloth nappies." Suddenly, she let out a blood-curdling shriek and leapt backwards, almost bowling me right off my feet.

"What? What is it?" I cried, grabbing her shoulders to steady her.

She turned towards me, white as a sheet and trembling all over. "There's a spider in there! A big one!"

Just at that moment, the men appeared in the doorway, weapons in hand and ready for a fight. I heaved a sigh and waved them away.

"Everything's fine," I said. "I'll take care of it."

Charu and the others lowered their weapons and left, but not without shooting scornful looks at Isabelle – and she wasn't oblivious to it, either. By the time they were gone, she had tears in her eyes and was wringing her hands pathetically.

"I'm sorry. I just… I don't know how to do this," she admitted. "Henry took care of everything, even if he was horrible to me. I never had to survive on my own."

I took a deep breath to push down the sense of disdain that kept rising in me. I had no right to feel like that, not after what she'd been through. Ten years at the mercy of a man like Henry would have broken just about anyone's spirit, even mine.

"It's completely okay," I said with as much kindness as I could muster. "Look, I know you're really trying your best, but you've been miserable today. How about tomorrow I assign you house duties instead, something you'll enjoy. What do you like doing?"

"Enjoy?" She stared at me as though I'd just sprouted a second head. "I... have no idea. I'm just, you know, used to doing what I'm told so that he wouldn't hit me. I don't know what I like doing."

"What about before the plague? What did you like doing then?" I asked. She just shrugged. I sighed and nodded. "Okay, here's my idea. Why don't we let you try something different every day, until you learn what you enjoy doing? You can swap it around later, or learn something new – with a population this small, it's not like you're going to be married to whatever career you pick for the rest of your life, you know?"

Isabelle nodded and looked down at her feet. She was silent for a few long seconds, then gave me a shy smile. "Okay. I think I'd like that. Thank you for being so patient with me. I know I'm not like these other people, or... or like you. You're all so strong and independent. I wish I was more like you."

My heart melted more than a little. I reached out and put my hand on her shoulder, giving it a gentle squeeze. "I hope you never have to learn to be like me, Isabelle. You don't need to be. You just need to remember what it's like to be *you* again – and you will, with time. How would you like to help out at the school tomorrow? I know you like kids. Or maybe you could help Skye with the inventory?"

She thought about it for a second, then nodded. "I think I'd like to help Skye. I like Skye. She's very... outspoken."

I laughed and nodded my agreement. "She is definitely that. Come on, let's go home. I'll deal with this stuff another day. We've got all the time in the world."

Together, we headed out of the house and closed up behind us, then hurried to catch up with the rest of our group. Isabelle complained the whole way about the rain and the cold, but I took it with good grace and didn't say a word. We made it back just in time to see Charu and the others manhandling the bed into the stairwell.

"Hey, what are you guys doing?" I called. "You can just leave that down here until the elevators are working, you know. That's why all this other stuff is down here."

They ignored me, with the exception of Charu. He looked at me and tried to say something, but all that came out was garbled gibberish.

"Sorry, I can't understand you," I admitted, hurrying over to help them. As soon as I got close they waved me away.

"He said 'no'," Warren snapped, sounding disgruntled – but he always sounded disgruntled so I couldn't tell if this was a different mood to usual or not. "Leave off. We've got this."

None of them seemed inclined to tell me what they were doing, so I just held my hands up in defeat and stood back. "Fine, but I'm just saying that you don't have to do that."

"Yes, we do," Warren replied, but he offered nothing in the way of an explanation.

I decided not to press him. I understood his type better than most: if he wasn't in the mood to talk, then trying to force him to would just annoy him.

"Can I at least get the door for you?" I offered. "I feel bad standing here not doing anything to help."

"Yeah, all right," Warren said. He and Quentin shoved the mattress hard up against the wall, giving me just enough room to squeeze by. I did so, then repeated the process with Charu and Karl's bed base. It was a tight fit, but I made it. Isabelle stayed behind, watching from the bottom of the stairs.

I stayed a few steps ahead of them as the lugged the bed up, waiting silently for the instruction to open the door. They passed the first level without saying a word, and the second as well. Just as we were about to reach the third floor landing, Charu grunted something incomprehensible and jerked his chin towards me. I took the hint and shoved the heavy door open for them.

The four men lugged their burden out into the hallway of level three, and down the passage leading towards the north-western corner of the building. I followed curiously, ready to lend my aid if there was another door that needed opening, but where they stopped took me completely by surprise: they stopped right outside my quarters.

Charu jerked his chin towards my door, and this time I managed to make out what he was saying. "Open."

"But… that's my room," I protested. "Why…?"

"Open!" he repeated, a little more clearly this time. His clipped tongue made it hard to understand what he was saying most of the time, but there was no mistaking his tone. I hurried past them and opened the door.

The men lugged the bed inside without another word, and carried it into the side-room that we'd already decided to use as our bedroom. My jaw fell open as I watched them drag the thin mattress we'd slept on the night before out of the way, then they set the new bed up beneath the windows. Once they were done, they turned and left without another word, all except for Warren.

Warren lingered in the doorway a second longer, watching me with an unreadable expression. I looked at him, fighting the unreasonable urge to cry. "But why me? Any one of you deserves that bed as much as I do."

Warren shrugged and glanced away. "It was Charu's idea. You've been good to us. Better than we deserve. And it ain't right for a lady to sleep on the floor."

Then he was gone, leaving me in shock.

# Chapter Twelve

After nearly three months on the road, our new bed felt like sleeping on a cloud. We slept deeply each night, and woke up feeling refreshed and energetic. We and the other new citizens of Tumanako spent the next week getting settled in and working on the various tasks that would eventually turn an office block into a home fit to live in. There was always something to do, never a moment to be bored, and there was certainly no time to miss the freedom of travelling.

Though I'd spent the last decade living the nomad's life, I was not a traveller by nature. Having a place to settle down and call my own was a dream come true. Every day, when Michael and I retired to our beds, we'd have a few little things to add to our apartment. Some days it was something practical, like new sheets for our bed or a pillow. Other days, it was something beautiful and useless, such as a painting to hang on the wall. For the first time, we had the opportunity to really nest together. We'd tried to do it in Ohaupo, but fate had intervened. Tumanako was our second chance, our opportunity to indulge our nesting instincts, and we were both happier for it.

As the days passed, I found myself needing to give commands less and less. People began to find their own niches, and were generally content to trundle off and do their own thing without guidance from anyone. That left me and the other members of the council with more time on our hands, which we all used wisely.

On the fifth morning, I was just leaving for the day when I almost tripped over a colourful gift that someone had left in my doorway: it was a bouquet of artificial flowers, artfully arranged in a porcelain vase. There was no card or tag on the flowers, but the arrangement was beautiful. I accepted the gift for what it was, and set it on our coffee table so that it could bring a little colour to an otherwise bland room.

The next few days passed without incident. Occasionally a new face would drift in or something interesting happen, but mostly I spent my time scavenging. Around mid-morning on the seventh day after our arrival, I was leading my little group of loners back in from another mission with an armload full of small, useful things. I was still working with the same group, minus Isabelle of course, but I hadn't said anything about the bed. It felt strange, but a part of me instinctively knew that they didn't *want* me to thank them. I knew they appreciated just being understood, both by me and by each other. Slowly, my loners were becoming friends – or at least whatever passed for friends amongst people that didn't really speak unless it was vital.

I led the men down the corridor towards the cluster of rooms we'd converted into a storage facility. The door was open, and I could see Skylar talking to a strange woman with a baby in her arms and a toddler clinging to her skirt. Skye spotted me before the newcomer did and waved a greeting.

"Good morning," I said, keeping my tone as light and friendly as I could manage. Despite my best efforts to appear non-threatening, the woman fearfully clutched her children closer and edged away from the door. I sensed that the last thing she needed was more unfamiliar faces, so I stepped back out to address my scavenging party. "Hey guys, can you please just leave the stuff out here and head back out for another load? I'll catch up later."

They nodded, piled their sacks up beside the door, then headed out without a word of protest. This wasn't the first skittish survivor to arrive on our doorstep.

"Hey sis, this is Tala Navarro," Skye said, gesturing towards the petite woman. She hesitated and looked at Tala. "Sorry, what were the names of your daughters?"

"The big one is Nenita," Tala said softly, hugging her baby tightly as if she was afraid I'd try to take the child away. "The baby doesn't have a name yet. She only came a few days ago."

"You delivered her all by yourself?" I asked, suddenly understanding why she was so afraid; that had to have been a special kind of trauma. "You're very brave. I couldn't even imagine going through that on my own. You're welcome here, Tala – you and your girls. My name is Sandy."

"I know who you are," she replied. She drew a deep breath and held it for a second, then I could see her force herself to relax a little bit. "It was… hard, yes. My man vanished not so long ago. I had no choice."

"Oh, I'm so sorry," I said. I put the sack I was carrying down beside the door and took a couple of steps towards them. Tala didn't flinch this time, but Nenita did. She ducked behind her mother's leg and hid from me. I eased myself down into a crouch that put me at eye level with the little girl and waved to her. "Hi Nenita. You're a very brave little girl to travel with your mummy, aren't you? How old are you, sweetheart?"

Nenita just stared at me with huge eyes and didn't say a word.

Tala smiled and looked down at her daughter with obvious affection. "She does not talk much. Losing her father has been hard on her… on both of us. Nenita will be three years old come springtime."

"You're both very brave," I told her, shoving myself back up again. Even though my own child was still so tiny that I often forgot she was there, the hormonal changes in my body left my joints aching from the slightest exercise. I stretched my back for a second, then looked at Skye. "Have you fed them yet?"

"Not yet," she replied. "They just got here. Why don't you go feed them while I sort out a room and bedding?"

"Sure," I agreed. I looked at Tala and gave her a smile. "Would you care for some lunch? You look like you haven't had a proper meal in way too long."

"We've been doing the best we can, but it's hard," she said, her eyes dropping to the baby in her arms. "I can't leave the two little ones alone while I hunt. We were okay before, when Franco was still with us, because there was always one of us to stay with Nenita. When I got too big with the baby, then Franco could go and I'd stay with her. Except one day he didn't come home."

"What happened to him?" I asked, gently reaching out to her, both to comfort her and to guide her towards the kitchen.

"I don't know," she replied, her eyes filling with tears. "He just didn't come home. I waited, but then the baby came and… and I didn't know what else to do. I saw you on the television, so I decided to come here." She glanced back at me, studying me with eyes as deep and fathomless as the ocean. "You seemed kind."

"I try to be," I said. I paused for a second as we entered the dining room, then I asked a question as subtly as I could. "Where were you staying before this, Tala?"

"Bodhinyanarama," she replied.

I shot her a bewildered look. "Bodhinwhatawhata?"

"Oh." Tala glanced at me, her expression a little sheepish. "Sorry. Bodhinyanarama was a Buddhist monastery in Stokes Valley. Franco loved it up there…"

I saw the first tear break loose and roll down her cheek. A second later, I had my arm around her shoulders and held her while she silently wept. I led her over to one of the couches and sat down with her. "I know, honey. I know it hurts. But at least you and your babies are safe now. I won't let anything happen to them."

Tala nodded miserably and wiped her eyes. "I know. It's just… so hard."

"You don't have to do it alone anymore," I told her gently, feeling a surge of sympathy towards the woman that I wouldn't have been able to explain in words. "Wait here and rest, I'll go get your food. Is there anything that you or Nenita can't have? Any allergies?"

"No... no." Tala took a deep breath and shook her head. "We appreciate anything that you offer us."

"You're part of our family now," I said, easing myself up to my feet again. "Our food is your food. I'll be back in a minute, okay?"

Tala nodded her understanding, so I left her and her children and went into the kitchen. There, I found Elly and Isabelle puttering around starting preparations for lunch. I waved a greeting to them, but didn't stop and say hello just yet. By the time the door had swung closed behind me, I had my radio out of my pocket.

"Michael?" I said into the receiver.

A few seconds passed, then his voice came on the line. "I'm here. What's up?"

"We may have a wounded man out there in need of our help," I told him. I quickly conveyed Tala's story, and he grunted his understanding.

"You want to send out a search party," he translated without further prompting. "How many people?"

"Six," I said. "You, me, and one of the nurses. Please round up three more people, preferably the best trackers we have, and get the horses ready. I'll meet you down there in a few minutes."

"I'm on it," he replied, then he was gone. Both Elly and Isabelle were watching me, obviously waiting for instructions. They didn't have to wait for long.

"Elly, can you please prepare travel rations for six people?" I asked. "We should be back by dark, but better safe than sorry. Make it a day's worth." Elly just nodded and hurried off without bothering to reply. I looked at Isabelle, and gave her a smile. "Can you please go talk to Skylar for me? I need her to get weapons out of storage for us."

"Okay," she agreed, nervously folding her hands in front of her. She started towards the door, then hesitated and looked back at me. "Anything else...?"

"Yes, if you wouldn't mind," I replied. "Can you please visit the infirmary, and ask one of the nurses to come along? It doesn't matter which one – I'd feel better having someone with medical training on hand."

"Sure," she said, and then she was out the door.

I took a deep breath to calm my racing heart, then turned my attention towards getting Tala's babies fed. I grabbed a couple of plates off a drying rack and went into the cooler to see what was left over from dinner the night before. I found a big bowl of cold stew covered with cling wrap, and some boiled vegetables. It probably wasn't very tasty, but they looked half-starved and food was food when you were hungry. A cold, tasteless meal was better than no meal at all.

Sure enough, when I brought the food out to them, Tala and Nenita set to it without a word of complaint. I sat with them while they ate, until Elly appeared with the rations I'd asked her to prepare. I introduced them, and then I left Tala in Elly's very capable care and excused myself.

Skylar was waiting for me in the hallway, burdened with an armload of guns and bottled water. Once we'd settled in and secured the fence around Tumanako, we'd taken to only carrying weapons when on guard duty or when going outside the fence for long periods of time. I took my favourite shotgun, put it over my shoulder, and stuffed a handful of spare cartridges into my pocket.

"Do you need to go back to your room?" Skye asked. "I can take those rations downstairs with me, if you like."

"Are you sure? You barely have a spare hand," I commented dryly.

Skye just laughed and grabbed the bag out of my hand, then she was off at a rapid clip. I went the opposite direction and climbed the stairs to the third floor to go retrieve my travel gear from my room. Most of it was already on my person, but I'd fallen out of the habit of carrying my GPS unit when I was just visiting the local township.

I quickly found it, checked that it was charged, and tucked it into my pocket, then I wrapped my coat around me and put on my backpack. Michael's backpack sat nearby; I knew him well enough to pack what he needed without a second thought. As soon as I was done, I raced out the door and down the stairs to the lobby.

Michael and Skylar were waiting by the front door, talking softly. Just outside the door, I could see Tane, Iorangi, Warren, and Aaron standing by the horses. I hurried over and gave Michael his backpack, then we divided up the rations, water, and guns between us.

"Be careful," Skye said quietly. "Remember what happened when you decided to play the hero for Anahera's clan. You almost didn't come home."

"What, you still haven't forgiven me for that?" I teased.

She laughed and shook her head. "Nope, and I'm going to keep reminding you about it so that you take better care of yourself in the future. Got it?"

"Got it," I agreed. I yanked her into a hug and planted a kiss on her cheek. "Don't worry, little sis. I have a reason to live these days."

"God, you are so depressing," she answered, giving me a light shove. "Get off me, slobber-puss. You've got work to do."

I released her, then I waved and raced out the door to where Aaron was holding my horse. I put my backpack back on, took Boudicca's reins, and vaulted expertly up into the saddle; if nothing else, the weeks that we'd spent on the road had turned all of us into expert riders. Boudicca pranced and nickered, but I stilled her with a firm hand on the reins and a touch of my heel.

While the others were putting on their gear and mounting up, I pulled my GPS out of my pocket and programmed in the location. Michael drew his horse up beside me and gave me a quizzical look.

"It's a little over eight kilometres away, if we follow the roads," I said, glancing up to study the skyline. "I don't think we'll be able to cut across country. Too many hills."

"The roads are safer," he said. "And eight kilometres isn't far, without a convoy slowing us down. We should be there before midday."

"Agreed," I said, tucking my GPS unit into an easily-accessible pocket. "Everyone ready?"

Everyone called out that they were. I touched Boudicca's sides with my heels and guided her up to a trot, then a canter. If there was even the slightest chance that Franco was still alive, then seconds could prove precious. All our horses were fit and healthy, and seemed to enjoy the chance to stretch their legs.

The gates were open before we even reached them, and the guards shut them behind us before we were out of sight. I led the group down towards the river, then swung northwards and followed the old highway. A surge of excitement rose in my breast as a breeze off the river struck me. It was cold, but there was something exhilarating about it. We rarely had the opportunity to travel at speed unless lives were at stake, and this was the first time that I wasn't worried about wasting precious petrol in the process.

It took all of my willpower to fight down the urge to push Boudicca a little faster, ride her a little harder, but I knew if I did that then she'd end up exhausted before we got there. No, as fun as it was, I had to pace us for the journey ahead. A flock of birds exploded out of the long grass beside the river and up into the sky, leaving me wondering what it felt like to fly. The freedom. The absolute freedom. Riding a horse at speed was probably the closest we'd ever get to feeling like that, and it was glorious in its own way.

The highway was a long, straight road that followed the riverbank for a good four kilometres, until we eventually passed out of the densely-packed suburban jungle into an area that was populated by larger, nicer houses and wide green spaces. Everything was overgrown, but it was still beautiful; green, alive, and refreshing. I lifted a hand and pointed to the right, telling my friends that it was time to make our turn off. Our horses took the turn without breaking stride, onto another road which wound up into the hills.

Much like the area closer to Avalon, the roads here were still in excellent condition and it was an easy ride for both of us. I barely even had to look where I was going, since there was nothing in our way and Boudicca was smart enough to negotiate her own footing. I found myself staring at the hills flanking the valley, watching the dark, ominous clouds gathering above the treeline. We were in for again rain soon.

The first droplet struck my face just as we reached the final leg of the journey, and the road finally began to climb at a gradient that forced us to slow to a trot. We dodged around the rusted hulks of parked cars and one obnoxious purple bus, until we finally reached the crest of the hill. There, several long driveways led off a small cul-de-sac, vanishing into dense forest.

"Which one is it?" Aaron called.

I shielded my eyes from the rain and looked around, then pointed at a small wooden sign nestled amongst flax bushes. "The writing's worn off, but that looks like the kind of thing you'd use to mark a Buddhist monastery, don't you think?"

"If I remember correctly, this place practiced Thai Forest Tradition," Michael said thoughtfully. "It's a branch of Theravada Buddhism." I shot him a curious glance; he returned it with a shrug and a smile. "My mother was very serious about her faith, even the branches that she didn't personally adhere to."

"Makes sense, I suppose," I replied. "Curiosity and all that. Do you know anything about the layout here, or what we can expect?"

"Not specifically, but I have a general idea," he said, turning his attention back towards the shadowy gateway. He pointed to it, then made a broad, all-encompassing gesture towards the hills around us. "These hills will be full of pathways and staircases, leading up to solitary meditation retreats high up the hillside. There should be offices and a public meditation hall closer to where we are, though; the monks in places like this relied on the generosity of their guests to survive, so they needed somewhere convenient for the general public to visit."

"Let's go find out, then," I said. I dismounted and led Boudicca down the driveway. The branches hung so low that I had to push them aside to keep them out of my face, but not for long. A short way in, the bush gave way to a gravel-lined courtyard, surrounded by elegant wooden buildings crafted in a manner that was an odd hybrid of Eastern and Western styles. I paused to admire them while the others caught up with me; even after ten years, they were still solid and quite beautiful in a way that was somewhat alien to my eye.

"This'll be it," Michael said. "The public meditation hall, and probably their office as well."

"What do monks need an office for?" I enquired, genuinely curious to hear the answer.

Michael laughed and shook his head. "No one was immune to the lure of technology. They still had to pay their bills, and probably maintain a website so people knew they existed."

"Oh, good point," I said. I led my horse over to a patch of grass and tied her reins to a low branch. "Let's see if we can figure out where Tala and Franco were living, then maybe we can track Franco from there."

"I'd say in there," Warren said suddenly, speaking up for the first time since we'd left.

I followed his finger towards a smaller building off to one side. "I think you're right. I see signs of recent occupation. Let's go take a look."

Michael and Warren fell in on either side of me with their weapons at the ready, leaving the others to keep an eye on the horses. I climbed the stairs onto the porch and glanced around for a moment, then I tried the door handle. It opened easily, revealing an interior that was dark but smelled relatively clean. I tried the light switch and got no response, so I pulled out my torch instead.

It was immediately clear to all of us that someone had been living there for quite some time. There were beds in one of the rooms, a makeshift couch, and even a television set. We split up to investigate the building as swiftly as possible; I headed down a hall and found myself in a small room with a generator that had either been disabled or run out of gas. I was just about to check which when a shout caught my attention.

"I've got blood!" Warren yelled from the other end of the building. I forgot all about the generator and raced towards the sound of his voice, nearly bumping into Michael along the way. We found Warren crouched over a large puddle of congealed blood on the floor of a bathroom. He glanced up, nodded once, and stood. It only took me a second to see why he wasn't concerned.

"A placenta," I said, as much to myself as anyone else. "Odds are pretty good that it was Tala's, so this is definitely where they were living. Where would Franco have gone?"

"What did Tala say, exactly?" Michael asked.

"She said he went hunting," I replied, then I paused and glanced around. "There's nothing to hunt in these woods, though. Just possums, I guess?"

"No…" Michael paused for a second to collect his thoughts, then shook his head firmly. "Is English her native language?"

"I don't think so," I replied. "She has a strong accent, and I'd guess by her appearance that she's Filipino."

"Ah, that's it!" he said, snapping his fingers. "I don't know much Filipino, but I learned a bit from one of my friends in the Academy. The word 'hunt' has a bunch of synonyms, just like it does in English. It could also mean that they were seeking something, or scouting, or—"

"Or scavenging?" I finished for him, picking up the idea. Michael nodded and gave me a smile.

"Let's divide up into pairs and go in different directions," he suggested. "We'll have a better chance of finding any sign of him that way."

I nodded and gestured for them to follow me, then led the way back out into the courtyard where Aaron, Tane, and Iorangi were still waiting with the horses. They looked at us expectantly as we gathered in a circle.

"We need to split up to try and find this guy," I said once I'd conveyed what we'd found. "Who has a radio?" Warren and Iorangi both put their hands up. "Okay, good. Michael and I have one each, too. How's your tracking, Aaron?"

"Pretty terrible," Aaron admitted with a shrug. "Never been much of a huntsman."

"That fine," I replied. "You're our medic. Stick with Warren, he can do the tracking for both of you. If Franco's still alive, there's a chance he's conscious. He might be trapped somewhere. It seems safe enough to try calling out to him. Watch yourselves, though: we're pretty close to the bush so there's a chance there might be pigs around, and I see some signs of earthquake damage. Mind your footing."

Warren made an approving grunt and nodded. "Looks like the quake was fairly recent, too."

"How can you tell?" Michael asked curiously.

"I'll show you while we're walking," I said. "We'll leave the horses here and travel on foot. Warren, can you please take Aaron and check around the monastery for any sign he might have gone up into the hills?"

Warren nodded and headed off without waiting for further instructions, leaving Aaron scrambling to keep up with him. I watched until they were out of sight, then took a deep breath and looked back at the others.

"Michael and I will take the left side of the road heading back the way we came," I said. "You two take the right. If you see anything out of the ordinary, check it out – but keep your guns close, just in case."

Tane and Iorangi both nodded and departed, leaving me alone with Michael. I glanced at him and gave him a smile. "I wish I'd thought to bring Alfred along. We could use his nose."

"We'll figure it out," he said in that voice of pure confidence he used when he was trying to reassure me that everything was going to be fine. He reached out and took my hand, then together we walked back down towards the road to begin our search.

The cul-de-sac near the entrance of the monastery was solid tarmac, but the driveways leading to the other properties nearby were all gravel. I knelt to examine the ground, then frowned and shook my head.

"I see a lot of different tracks here," I explained, "but I can't tell how recent any of them are. It's rained a few times, and that's muddled the spoor. Let's head up to that house and see if there's anything fresher that way."

Michael nodded silently and followed my lead. We climbed the steep driveway towards an old wooden homestead set amongst heavy bush. At the top, I glanced back at him and caught him staring at a slender, hairline fracture bisecting the concrete porch.

"That's the earthquake damage," I said by way of explanation. "I'll teach you what I know. Most of it's just logic, really. I mean… look at that planter pot over there and tell me what you see. What's out of place?"

Michael glanced in the direction I was pointing, but he didn't say anything right away. Eventually, he nodded and looked back at me. "I think I get it. The outside of the pot is all green with moss or mildew or whatever that is, and so are the paving stones around it – but not the part underneath where the pot was. The pot was knocked over recently."

"Bingo," I said, pleased but not surprised by his quick uptake. He always had been a quick study. "If we look closer, we can see that there were some spiders or bugs living there and they're all gone now. The moss is also starting to grow over the clear patch under where the pot was. I'd say that it probably fell over a few weeks ago."

"Do you think Tumanako is at risk?" he asked, his voice suddenly filled with concern.

"No more than anywhere else," I replied with a shrug. "We're living on a tectonic fault line. Earthquakes are inevitable no matter where we go."

"True," he said quietly. Suddenly, he grinned. "Hey, at least we're not living in Volcano Land anymore, right?"

I laughed and nodded. "True that. We're living in Flood Plains Land instead."

"Hey, what did I tell you about being negative?" he said. "Anyway, Franco. What now?"

"No sign of him here," I replied. "Let's head down that way towards the back fence. The long grass will help us spot any fresh tracks."

Michael followed obediently as we made our way down to the edge of the yard, and descended into the wet grass. I picked my way carefully, wary of any hidden obstructions or dangers. While we didn't have to worry about snakes like our Australian cousins, my close encounter with a nail six months earlier left me cautious. Plus, now I had the baby to worry about. It was unlikely that me stepping on something would hurt her, but it was better to be safe than sorry.

For half an hour or so, we made our way through the back yards of the houses on our side of the road, looking for any sign of the missing man. While there were plenty of footprints around, some of them as recent as a few weeks old, there was nothing fresh enough to have come from Franco's latest – and possibly last – hunt. Eventually, I stopped and pulled my radio out of my coat to check in with the others.

"Nothing so far on our side," I said into the receiver. "How about you guys?"

"Nothing here," Iorangi replied, sounding as frustrated as I felt.

"Nothing here, either," Warren said. "There's a lot of spoor around, but none of it fresh."

"Yeah, that's what I'm seeing, too," I replied. "Where the hell did this guy go?"

"Hey," Michael said suddenly. "Sandy, what's that? I saw a flash of red through the trees over there."

"Hold on a second, guys," I said into the radio, "we might have something."

I looked where Michael was pointing, shading my eyes against the rain. Sure enough, I saw a brief flash of red, then it was gone. I raised my shotgun and crept towards the treeline. As I drew closer, I saw fresh tracks in the mud and a little strip of red cloth flapping in the breeze. It was firmly attached to the rough bark on the side of a tree.

"Someone came through here in a hurry," I said, easing myself down into a crouch to get a better look at the tracks. After a couple of seconds, I nodded and spoke into the radio again. "We've definitely found something. Head down towards the place with the big pohutukawa tree in the front yard and meet us here."

The others acknowledged my request, while Michael came over to crouch beside me, studying the tracks.

"That looks like a boot print," he said thoughtfully, point at a particularly clear mark left in the mud. "A man's, I think."

"Yeah, looks like it," I replied. "There's something else here, though, and it worries me."

"Why?" he asked, glancing up at me.

"Because I think it's pig tracks," I said. I glanced at him and saw all the colour drain out of his face. Even though we'd successfully killed a couple of pigs together, neither of us were eager to take on another – and neither of us wanted to imagine what might have happened to Franco if he'd been chased down by a one of the damn things.

We stood back and waited beneath the shelter of a half-collapsed patio. It didn't do a lot of good since we were already soaked and freezing, but at least I felt a little better for trying. A few minutes later, a familiar voice shouted our names.

"Sandy? Michael?"

"Back here," I called back. Iorangi stuck his head around the edge of the building and waved to us, with the others close behind him.

"Warren," I said, pointing at the tracks. "Reckon that's a pig?"

He went over to examine them more closely, then nodded. "Yep. I reckon that's a pig."

I sighed heavily and swore beneath my breath.

Aaron looked at us curiously. "A pig?"

"Zombie pigs," Michael said sympathetically. "They're a thing. A really *bad* thing. We don't want to tangle with a pig unless we absolutely have to."

"I think we might have to," I said, pointing along the length of the tracks. "It looks like he went through the fence here and I'd say the pig followed him. Let's just hope he was smart enough to go up into the hills rather than try and circle around the base. Pigs can't really climb, from what I hear."

"Zombie pigs," Aaron repeated, as if trying the words on for size.

"Yep. Really a thing," Michael and I said simultaneously, then we glanced at one another and smiled.

"Well, wherever he is, he's probably gotten himself into trouble," I said. "Keep your eyes and ears peeled, guys."

They made noises of agreement and fell in behind me as I led the way towards the rear of the yard. I stepped carefully over a few fallen fence posts and followed the trail into the thigh-high grass on the other side. Mud squelched beneath my shoes but I ignored it, focusing all my attention on the world around us. There was nothing to be heard, except the sound of the falling rain, our footsteps, and our breathing.

The tracks almost made it to the hillside before they turned sharply away and ran parallel to the edge of the forest. I muttered a low curse beneath my breath, but before I could say anything Warren's voice intervened.

"I see blood drops," he said quietly. I frowned and nodded but said nothing. At this stage, blood could have meant anything – it could have even come from the pig.

"Sandy," Michael called suddenly. "What the hell is *that*?"

I looked up and stared into the distance, but this time I didn't have an answer. "I… I don't know. Warren? What the hell is that?"

"I believe that's a crevice," he replied, his voice flat and showing no sign of the shock I felt.

In the distance, a dark shadow yawned like a wound in the skin of the very earth itself, and it looked for all the world like it was sucking in the trees and grass that grew along its edges. It took a second for me to make sense of what I was seeing: a long, slender pit, a fracture in the bedrock. The vegetation wasn't being sucked in, it was sliding in, slowly, courtesy of gravity.

"I think I know what happened to Franco," I said softly. I took a moment to steel myself, then led the way towards the crevice. "Mind your footing, everyone. We don't know how stable the ground is around here."

No one answered, but they didn't need to. We could all see the devastation that the crevice had wrought on the landscape around it. At first glance it looked like the trees around it were going to tumble in at any second, but on closer inspection I realised that many of them had been that way for a while – their trunks were twisted up towards the sun, and their roots were firmly planted in the earth. The crevice had been there for a while. Perhaps Franco had known about it, and decided to use it as a means to escape from the pig.

A dozen meters from the edge, we came to a stop and looked at one another.

"I don't suppose anyone brought rope, did they?" I asked. Everyone shook their heads, except for Aaron.

"Did I mention I used to be a Scout?" he commented dryly. He shrugged off his backpack, pulled out a short length of rope, and handed it to me. "Which one of us goes?"

"I'm the smallest, so it should be me," I said, silently dreading what I volunteering to do.

"No!" Michael protested. "I'll go. You hate heights."

"I know," I answered dryly. "But I'm not strong enough to pull you up if you slip in, and you are."

Michael opened his mouth to say something, then seemed to think better of it. His shoulders slumped, and he nodded. "Just... be careful."

"Oh believe me, I have no intention of falling into a crevice," I replied. I took off my backpack and shotgun and handed them both to Warren, then I wound the rope around my waist. My coat had belt loops on the outside for a terribly fashionable sash that I'd discarded on the first day, but now they finally had a use. I threaded the rope through them, then Michael knotted it at the small of my back.

I took a deep breath to steady myself and began to slowly walk towards the edge of the pit, still following the tracks. With each step, I paused to test the stability of the earth with my shoe before I committed my full weight to it, but it didn't give out or collapse beneath me. When I got within the last couple of meters, I eased myself down onto hands and knees and crawled the rest of the way.

Below me, the crevice vanished into darkness. I reached into my pocket and pulled out my torch, clicked it on, and pointed it downwards.

There was little to see. My tiny light did almost nothing to penetrate the darkness, except show me that the crevice went down deep. I swung the light a little farther to the left, and then I froze: six or seven meters below the lip of the crevice, I saw a flash of crimson cloth.

"Franco?" I called, straining to better make out what I was seeing. "Franco, are you alive down there? Franco!"

The cloth shifted a little, but there was no response.

I called out again. "Franco, mate, please answer me."

Suddenly, there was a bewildered-looking face peering up at me, struggling to block the light of my torch with one hand. "H-hello? Is someone there?"

"He's alive!" I cried. "Guys, head back to the houses. We need more rope, or a chain – anything we can use to get him out of there. We'll need a good ten meters or so to reach him." I looked back down into the crevice and called out to him again. "We're coming, Franco. Just hang in there a little bit longer."

"Tala?" he asked, sounding dazed and confused. Given that he'd been down there for days with no food and only rainwater to drink, I wasn't surprised.

"No, my name is Sandrine," I said to him, switching off the torch and tucking it away. "When you didn't come home, Tala panicked and came looking for us. She thinks you're dead."

"Am I dead?" the man asked, his voice disembodied in the darkness. "I don't know. Everything hurts."

"Don't move," I told him. "I think you're on a ledge. If you move, you might fall again. Just stay right there and keep talking to me. Are you injured?"

"Injured?" he echoed. There was a long moment of silence, then a distant cough. "Yes. My leg. It's broken."

"It's okay, we'll fix it," I said, trying to reassure him as best I could from afar. "What happened to the pig? We saw its tracks."

"It fell in the hole," he said, his words slurred. "I tried to jump, but I slipped. The pig fell into the deep part. I think it's dead, but I don't know."

"He sounds a bit delirious, the poor fellow," a soft voice said beside me. I glanced sideways and saw that Aaron had crept up beside me, lying on his belly. "He'll be in shock, not to mention suffering from hypothermia and probably osteomyelitis." He glanced at me, his brow furrowed in concern. "Blood poisoning."

I nodded my understanding and focused on keeping Franco as alert as I could. The last thing we needed was for him to slip and fall to his death. "We didn't see the pig anywhere, so it probably died when it fell. Don't worry about it. My friends have gone to get some rope to haul you out, so just try and stay with me, okay? Keep talking to me. Um… tell me about Tala."

"Tala?" he repeated her name, a strange wistfulness filling his voice. "Ah, my Tala. I love her. She's a good woman. Have you met her?"

"Yeah, she came to us after you fell," I repeated. "She'll be so happy to see you. The baby's come now, but she hasn't picked a name."

"The baby?" he gasped. "Is it healthy? A girl or a boy?"

"Don't move, Franco," I warned him again. "It's a little girl, and she looked pretty healthy when I saw her this morning. Tala's taking good care of her."

"She's a good mama, my Tala," he said. Even at a distance, I could hear the smile in his voice. "I thought for sure I was never going to see her again…"

"You will," I said, channelling as much confidence as I could into my voice. "Just stay awake. My friends will be here soon. Why don't you tell me about how you met Tala?"

He sighed dreamily and did just that. Aaron and I exchanged worried glances throughout his rambling dialogue, but neither of us interrupted except to prompt him with more questions to keep him talking. Franco wasn't the only one wet and miserable by the time the others returned with more rope, but no one complained.

When I heard Michael call my name to alert me to his return, my relief was so palpable it felt like a weight lifted off my stomach. He tossed one end of the rope to me, and I caught it.

"Franco?" I called, interrupting him. "We've got the rope, mate. I'm going to lower one end down to you, and I want you to tie it around your chest, underneath your arms. Can you do that for me?"

"Anything to get me out of this stupid hole," he replied; the humour in his voice gave me a flash of hope and brought a smile to my face.

"Okay, the rope's coming down," I said. "Tell me when you've got it."

I carefully guided the rope over the edge, while Michael and the others fed it out a little at a time. None of the trees nearby were sturdy enough to tie the rope to, so we were just going to have to do it by hand.

"I've got it," Franco shouted at last. There was a pause of a few seconds, then he spoke again. "Okay, I've tied it around me. This rope is pretty slippery. I hope it'll be strong enough."

"It only has to hold you for a little while," I replied. "Keep hold of it, and I'll be waiting at the top to take you home to Tala. Are you ready?"

"As ready as I'll ever be," he replied.

I glanced up and signalled to the men. They wrapped the rope around their wrists and over their shoulders, and strained with all their might. The rope went taut on the grass beside me, and then slowly it began to creep upwards. After a tense few seconds, I saw a shadow moving beneath me, and then that shadow resolved itself into a slender human figure.

"That's it," I called to everyone. "Keep pulling, just a few more meters."

"Sandrine?" Franco yelled suddenly. "Sandrine, the rope! It's slipping!"

I swore and shoved myself a few inches further forward, peering downwards into shadow. Sure enough, I could see the knot around Franco's chest coming a little bit looser with each tug of the rope. With the rain and the mud, if the knot failed completely there would be no way for him to keep his grip.

"Hang on with both hands," I advised, struggling to fight down the urge to panic. "It's just a little bit more. I can almost reach you." I glanced back again, and shouted, "Keep pulling! We're almost—"

"Sandrine!" Franco's cry was one of pure terror. I glanced back just in time to see the knot slipping the last few millimetres.

"Give me your hand!" I cried, thrusting myself as far forward as I could without falling into the pit myself. Franco screamed something inarticulate and made a grab for it. I felt his hand close around my wrist, nearly tugging my arm out of its socket, and then suddenly I was sliding forward into the gaping abyss.

I felt someone grab the rope around my waist before I had a chance to cry for help, and that saved me from tumbling into darkness: Aaron. A second later, Michael was there with him, then the others. I was briefly buried by a mound of strong male bodies, and when it cleared all seven of us were sitting in the mud. Stunned, but safe.

I looked at Franco, then I looked at the others. I started to say something, but all that came out was a hysterical laugh. They looked at me like I was crazy for all of three seconds, then something in each of them broke and laughed right along with me.

# Chapter Thirteen

By the time we'd calmed down enough to be much good for anything, the drizzle had turned into a downpour. All of us were sodden and covered in mud, but that didn't stop us from mucking in to help Franco. Michael and Tane half-helped, half-lifted him to his feet, and carried him back towards the shelter of the monastery – and more importantly, the medical kit we'd left with the horses.

When we finally made it, I was evicted from the room while the men stripped Franco of his soiled garments and Aaron tended to his wounds. I retreated to the small kitchen, stripped off my muddy outer garments, and set about preparing a light meal for Franco to eat once he was ready for it. The others eventually came out to join me, all except for Aaron. I conscripted one of the men to take the food in, then we all sat around just waiting for news. Warren vanished out the door to enjoy his own company, and the rest of us just chatted to pass the time.

Eventually, Aaron finished piecing Franco back together and came out to join us.

"How is he?" I asked, almost afraid to hear the answer.

"Better than he should be, to be honest," Aaron replied. "It's not a bad break, but I'm concerned about the risk of osteomyelitis because it went untreated for so long. We need to get him back to Tumanako as soon as possible. If we don't get him on antibiotic treatments soon, it may end up costing him that leg."

I took a deep breath and nodded. "Can we get him on a horse, or should we send for one of the trucks?"

Aaron went quiet for a moment while he considered the possibilities, then he shrugged. "If wait for a truck, then we'll lose at least an hour and this condition is time-sensitive. If we try and get him to ride double with someone, he may pass out from pain and fall, or make the injury worse. Either way, it's a risk."

"Let's stick with the safest option," I suggested. "I'll call home and get Doc up here in one of the trucks. He should make good time along that road. Can you take care of Franco until he gets here?"

Aaron nodded silently, his face an odd mixture of relief and regret. He vanished out of the room, and I stood to call Warren back inside for a group meeting.

"I need two people to head back the way we came and lead the truck up here," I said. Everyone volunteered. I picked Tane and Iorangi and sent them off, then I pulled out my radio and tuned it to the frequency we'd taken to using around home. "Come in, Tumanako. It's Sandy."

There was a few moments of silence, then the line crackled and a familiar voice came on. "Hey, sis. Any luck?"

"Yes," I replied. "We've found Franco. He's alive, but we need to get him back home for treatment and he's not well enough to ride. He's got a broken leg, and Aaron says he may be suffering from osteo-something – some kind of blood poisoning. I need Doc up here in the Hilux with antibiotics, and I need it now."

"You got it," she answered confidently. "He'll be on the road within 15 minutes, if I have to push him out the door myself. Give me the directions."

I did, then we ended the conversation. I looked at the others and gave them a weak smile. "Nothing to do now except for wait."

"Well, there is one thing," Michael said. "You mentioned Tala arrived with pretty much nothing, just the clothes on her back and her kids. They don't have a lot of stuff here. I bet we could fit it in the back of the Hilux, no problem."

I hesitated for a second, then I smiled and reached out to touch his hand. "Trust you to always know the right thing to do. Good plan. Let's get packing!"

***

It took us virtually no time at all to gather up the pieces of Tala and Franco's life, and pack them into a few bags and boxes. They'd obviously been there since before their eldest was born, but they lived simply and didn't have much. Franco watched silently from the bed while I was in their bedroom, but he said nothing. When I looked at him, he just gave me a weak smile and nodded his approval.

Within an hour, we were ready. Michael and I settled in a chair by the front door, snuggled together watching the rain. I was just beginning to doze off when a strange noise caught my ear. I sat up a little straighter and stared out the window, waiting. Sure enough, a few seconds later Tane sprinted into view, with his brother close behind him. By the time they reached the door, I was on my feet and there to meet them.

"The truck's waiting on the other side of the overgrowth," Tane shouted, pointing back towards the road. I breathed a huge sigh of relief, nodded, and hurried off to convey the news to Aaron. While he was busy getting Franco ready for transport, I pulled my muddy outerwear back on and dove in to help the others carry stuff out to the truck.

I was half way there, lugging a couple of plastic bags of children's clothing, when I spotted Hemi and Rebecca running towards me carrying a makeshift stretcher between them. I didn't bother to ask where they'd gotten the stretcher from, I just dropped one of the bags and pointed back the way I'd come.

"Turn left at the end of the driveway," I called. "You'll see an open door. Whoever's there will point you the rest of the way."

They nodded and ran on without a word. I picked up the bag and resumed my trek down the driveway, picking my footing carefully on the muddy ground. They probably could have driven up closer, but I agreed with their decision; there wasn't much gravel left on the driveway, and the last thing we needed was for the Hilux to get stuck in the mud. When I rounded the last bend, I saw Doctor Cross waiting beside the truck with a slightly sour look on his face.

"Hey, Doc," I greeted. "Thank you for coming out here. I'm sorry you had to come out in the rain, but—"

"But time is of the essence," he replied, finishing my sentence. "Your sister conveyed the message. I presume by 'osteo-something', you meant 'osteomyelitis'?"

"Yeah, that," I replied, nodding. I put my bags down again and went over to open the back canopy of the ute. "I don't know what it is, but Aaron made it sound bad."

"It is bad," Doc said simply. He came around to stand beside me, staring into the back of the ute. "Would there be enough room to lie him flat in here, do you think?"

"I don't see why not," I replied. "He's a pretty small guy. Why not just put him in the back seat, though?"

"You said his leg was broken," he said. "Until we have a chance to set the break, it's best to have him lying flat or sitting with his legs stretched out in a way that won't jostle the break too badly when we gain speed."

"Oh, of course," I said. "We've got some more clothing and bedding coming, we can use it to pad him so that he doesn't bounce around." I heard the sound of footsteps behind me, and turned to see the others hurrying towards us. Michael and Tane had the stretcher, while the others were carrying various boxes, bags, and mounds of blankets.

Doc took command of the situation before I could say a word, and guided the others through the process of creating a comfortable nest in the back of the ute. Once it was secure, they carefully lifted Franco into the remaining space, stretcher and all. I left Doc, Rebecca, and Hemi to deal with the patient himself, and took everyone else back to the monastery to grab our belongings and fetch the horses.

By the time we returned, the Hilux had already left. We mounted up and followed after it as fast as we could safely travel. The rain was coming down in buckets now, but at least it washed away the mud. I tugged my hood down low over my eyes and hunkered over Boudicca's broad back to salvage what little warmth I could from her skin.

It wasn't a pleasant trip back to Tumanako, but we'd spent all winter on the road so we were used to unpleasant trips. Every so often I sat up and glanced back to do a headcount, just to make sure that we didn't lose anyone in the weather. The Hilux managed much better speed than we did, and we soon lost track of it in the gloom. When we finally made it back to Tumanako, we found the outer gates firmly closed and locked, just as they should be.

"Hello?" I shouted, cupping my hands around my mouth to try and make myself heard. A few seconds later, a head popped up in the window of the security shed beside the gate, then one of the people on guard duty jogged out to let us in.

We waved a greeting, but rode past her without stopping to say hello. It was only when we reached the front of the office building and saw the Hilux parked there that I finally relaxed and breathed a sigh of relief. They'd made it.

"We'll take the horses back, if you and Aaron want to go on ahead," Michael volunteered.

"Thank you," I said, appreciating his intuition. "Doc will need Aaron's help, and I should speak to Tala."

"Any time," he replied. "Go, we've got this covered."

I dismounted and handed my reins up to him, then hurried into the shelter of the tower's entrance – and almost bowled Skylar right off her feet.

"Hey, watch it!" she cried, leaping back just in time to avoid being run down.

I yelped in surprise and skidded to a halt so suddenly that I nearly ended up on my ass. "Shoot, sorry! I didn't see you waiting there."

"You never do," she said, laughing and shaking her head. "Took you guys long enough to get here. Doc wants Aaron in the infirmary urgently."

"We figured he'd be needed," I replied. "Aaron was right behind m—"

I didn't hear the door open in time to get out of the way. Aaron barrelled right into me from behind, knocking me into Skye, and all three of us went down in a sodden tangle of limbs.

"Sorry! Sorry! Oh God, sorry!" Aaron cried, leaping back up to his feet with the kind of dexterity that was only born from shock. "The rain was in my eyes and I wasn't looking where I was going. Is everyone all right?"

"I'm fine," I replied. I accepted the offered hand and hauled myself up off the ground, then offered my hand to Skye in turn. She slapped it away. For a second I was worried, until I realised that she was shaking from silent hysterics. They weren't silent for long, though; suddenly, she threw her head back and laughed uproariously.

Aaron and I exchanged an amused look. We waited until she finally got herself back under control, then helped her to her feet and guided her towards the stairs. At the last second, she stopped and looked at us.

"Oh, the elevator's working now," she said. "The electrical crew got it going just after you left."

"That's fantastic," I said, surprised and pleased by the news. "Does that mean that there's enough power coming in from the solar array for the whole building now?"

"Should be, yep!" she replied. She led us over to the elevators and pushed the call button. "I haven't tested every level, but the ones I've been to all have power. Gavin said they're going to keep extending the grid until they run out of space, so there will be enough to cover any extra people who join us, but for now it should be enough for us to have light, heat, and hot water whenever we need it."

"Hallelujah!" I cried, throwing my hands up in the air. "We're civilized again!"

Skye laughed and gave me a light shove. "Civilized? Please, you wouldn't know civility if it up and bit you on the butt."

"It confuses me when you use big words like that," I replied, teasing her back. "Who are you and what did you do with my semi-literate baby sister?"

"Doc made me his pet project," she answered, her expression turning thoughtful. "He's got me up to reading classic novels. I'm reading one right now called *Pride and Prejudice*, by an old-timey author named Jane Austen."

"Oh?" I asked, looking at her in surprise. "That doesn't strike me as your type of book. Are you enjoying it?"

"I…" She hesitated to think over her answer, then she shrugged. "Yeah, actually. I am. A lot of it I don't really understand, but it's fascinating to learn about how people lived back then. And it makes me think Erica's right: we really should try and preserve as many books as possible, so that we don't forget these people. I don't know how to express it, but it feels… important, somehow."

The elevator dinged open. Our conversation halted for a second while we climbed in, then we picked up where we'd left off.

"I agree," I said. "The way Sergeant Bryce phrased it really struck me. She said, 'someone made those books, and that's important.'"

"It's not just that, though," she said, absently hugging herself against a chill that most likely came from within. "Every person is important, even the ones who didn't write a book or make a movie or an album, because those people made *us*. I want to… do something to remember them. I just don't know what yet."

I reached out and touched her shoulder gently. "Whatever you decide to do, you know I'll support you. Just say the word."

The elevator chimed again, and the doors opened to let us out onto the second level. I was just about to step out of the elevator, when I was very nearly bowled right off my feet again. Tala threw her arms around me and hugged me fiercely, then jerked back and planted a succession of kisses on my cheeks. I just froze and took it, not sure how to deal with so much gratitude in one place. Beside me, Aaron and Skylar both burst out laughing, and I could hear a few other people laughing as well.

The elevator doors started to close again, but a hand caught them and held them open. Then Anahera stepped through and grabbed Tala by the shoulders.

"Come here, little mama," she said gently, prying the tiny woman away from me. "Let Sandy breathe."

I gave her a grateful look and a smile over Tala's head. Tala was nearly hysterical and I couldn't make sense of a word she was saying, since most of it was in her native language. We guided her out of the elevator and into the dining room, where we found Melody happily babysitting her two young children. Anahera sat Tala down beside them, then a few seconds later Elly appeared out of the kitchen carrying a steaming hot mug of tea. Anahera took it and placed it in Tala's hands.

"Here we go, dear," she said, her voice soft and maternal. She sat down beside Tala, resting one hand comfortingly on her upper back. "You just sip that, and breathe. Deep breaths. Can you do that?"

Tala nodded and did as she was told. She drew a deep breath and held it for a second, then let it out slowly and took a sip of her tea. It seemed to calm her down enough for her to at least switch to English.

"Sorry," she said sheepishly, looking up at me. "I just... I thought he was dead. I never expected that you would go and find him for me." She gulped down another anxious breath, tears gathering in her eyes. "It seems... it seems like a miracle. Or a dream."

"Well, it isn't a dream, that much I know for sure," I said. "But moments like this are the fruition of *my* dream for Tumanako. This is what we – ordinary people – can achieve if we work together and share a common goal. This is why we're all here, every single one of us. Humanity is capable of creating so many miracles, if we just try hard enough."

"Speaking of which," Anahera said, suddenly fixing me with an intense look. "You and I need to have a talk."

"Oh?" I replied, raising an eyebrow. "That sounds somewhat ominous. Should I be afraid?"

"Possibly," she said. She rubbed Tala's back one last time, then rose to her feet and looked at me. "Best if we do this now, if you wouldn't mind. Elly can take care of Tala."

"Sure, okay," I agreed, shrugging. "Lead the way."

She nodded and did just that. After a few seconds, I realised that Skye was following along as well, but neither of them said anything. They just led me out the door and down the hall to the storage rooms. Skye unlocked the door, then locked it again once the three of us were inside.

"Whoa, I'm being cornered," I pointed out dryly, looking back and forth between the two of them. "What's going on, ladies?"

Anahera heaved a deep sigh and reached out to lay her hand on my arm. "You're not going to like what we have to say, but I think it's important that you hear us out before you react."

"She's right," Skye said. "There's a chair over here; I think you might want to sit down."

"Just say whatever you're going to say and get on with it," I replied. "I'm a big girl. I can take it."

Anahera and Skye exchanged a look.

"If you insist," Anahera said. "Sandrine, we've noticed a few things that make us think that we might know something that you don't."

"Don't beat around the bush, Ana," Skye scolded. Suddenly, she reached out and poked me right in the tit. "You've gained a good five kilograms, and your boobs are bulging out of your bra. We think you might be pregnant."

Anahera shot her a filthy look. "There's honesty and then there's kindness, Skylar. We discussed this."

"Okay, fine!" Skye threw her hands up in annoyance. "Ana says that you've been 'glowing' and throwing up. Same conclusion: we think that you're pregnant."

I recovered from my shock just in time to muffle an inelegant snort of laughter with my hand. Both their expressions changed to confusion.

"Damn, I was hoping to keep it secret a little while longer," I admitted. "Yeah, I'm pregnant."

Anahera's brows shot up, and Skye's mouth fell open.

"You already knew?" Skye gasped. "And you didn't tell us? You didn't tell *me*?"

"Sorry, sis," I said. "You're not good at keeping secrets, and I didn't want Michael to find out until I was ready to tell him. You know, in case anything happens to the baby. He'd be devastated if anything happened to it."

"Ohh…" she breathed, understanding dawning on her face. "Yeah, that would be pretty rough on him. But—wait, what do you mean I'm not good at keeping secrets?"

I laughed and shook my head. "You're a gossip fiend, Skye. Face it. And the whole point of gossip is sharing juicy secrets. Right now, the only people who know are Doctor Cross, Maddy, and Gavin. Maddy knows because she's the one who told me, Doc knows because, well, I needed his help to make sure I get through this okay, and Gavin knows because I asked him to keep an eye on Michael in case he figures out something's going on." I paused and gave the two of them the hairy eyeball. "I guess I should have asked him to keep an eye on you two, as well."

"I don't think Michael suspects anything at this stage," Anahera said, her expression shifting from surprised to thoughtful. "But you won't be able to hide it from him for much longer. It's still early enough that a stranger wouldn't notice any changes, but we both know you intimately – as does he. His knowledge of female biology is somewhat lacking so he probably assumes the weight gain and missed periods are just because you were so malnourished when you met, but eventually he's going to start to wonder."

"Yeah, especially if you start lactating blood!" Skye said with a salacious gesture.

I shot her a horrified look. "You lactated *blood*? That's not normal!"

"It is fairly normal, actually," Anahera said, a smile dancing across her lips. "Not pleasant, but normal. Don't worry about it too much."

"And this is the other reason I didn't tell you, Skye," I said, fighting a sudden wave of irrational annoyance. "You know how nervous I am about this. The last thing I need is to be told horror stories about bleeding nipples!"

"Hey!" She scowled at me, planting her hands on her hips. "It's not my fault that happened! Don't make me pull the 'pity me, I lost my baby' card again."

"Girls, stop," Anahera said, holding her hands up in a placating gesture. "Skylar, your sister is very anxious about this, and with good reason. Don't forget, she had to *watch* you lose your baby. That's almost as traumatizing as what you had to go through. You both need to calm down and try to see things from one another's perspectives. You're sisters, after all. What do sisters do?"

"They stand together, no matter what," Skye said grudgingly. She heaved a sigh, then looked at me. "Sorry. I didn't think."

I nodded and gave her a weak smile. "I know. My problem is that I think too much, and work myself into anxious knots. After what happened to you, and then hearing about what happened to Elly's baby… I've been trying not to think about it too much."

"What happened to Elly's baby?" Skye asked.

"Javed told me that Ommie originally had a twin sister," I explained, "but she was born infected. Doc says that isn't possible, but… I don't know, I still worry."

"Elly and I have spoken about it," Anahera said, touching my arm reassuringly. "The female twin was definitely not born infected. There was a complication with the birth, and only Ommie survived. The other baby lived for a few minutes, but there was something wrong with her lungs and she couldn't breathe. Neither Elly nor Zain had the tools or knowledge to save her."

"Oh, God," I whispered, an oddly mismatched flood of relief and distress pouring through me. "That's why she didn't cry? It was Javed's comment about her not crying that made me worry most. But if she didn't cry because she couldn't, because of her lungs... that's different. Poor Elly."

"The good doctor and I have discussed the topic at length," Anahera said, her expression turning thoughtful again. "I was worried, too. Tumanako cannot grow if we don't have children, after all. He's reassured me that the child is not at risk while she's being breastfed, only once she starts to wean."

I heaved a deep sigh and nodded. "At least that gives us a bit of leeway, but it makes finding that vaccine even more important. Most of the kids are old enough to be past the danger point, but we still have Evie and Tala's baby to worry about. Evie's got to be pushing six months old now. She's going to start weaning eventually, and after that it's up to us to protect her." I stood up straight and looked each of them in the eye in turn. "Tomorrow morning, we're going to go find the vaccine. One way or another."

# Chapter Fourteen

Going after the vaccine felt like a big decision, but I still slept soundly after making it. That might have had something to do with the electric blanket that we'd found two days earlier, though. I'd forgotten the sheer bliss of climbing into a warm bed at the end of a long day, and sliding my legs between sheets that were almost – but not quite – hot enough to burn. It was wonderful, and it put me into such a coma that I slept late again.

Michael eventually woke up and started nibbling on my neck, and there was no way I could sleep through that. Not that I minded in the least; there were far worse ways to be woken up than by a handsome man in a playful mood. I rolled around in the circle of his arms, and swiftly discovered that his mood wasn't exactly *playful*, per se. It was something else entirely – and that something matched my mood exactly.

We made love languidly in the early morning gloom, enjoying the closeness shared only by two. When we were both satisfied, we lay back and stretched, talking quietly about nothing in particular until it was time to get up.

Michael was on the team I planned to take with me, of course. We'd been together for more than half a year now, and in that time he'd become absolutely integral to my world. He wasn't just my husband, but my best friend, my partner, my protector, my confidant, and my soul-mate. I don't know how I knew it, but I just did. Michael was the one that made me understand what the phrase 'The One' meant.

I glanced up in the middle of getting dressed and watched him opening the curtains we'd installed to keep our bedroom warm and private. Despite how I felt about him, I was still lying to him by omission about the one thing that had the potential to bring us closer together: our baby. I may have had a good reason in the beginning, but I was running out of excuses to avoid confronting the inevitable. I took a deep breath and let it out slowly, then looked back down at my gear. There was too much to be done to worry about it today. Once we had the vaccine, then I'd tell him.

"That was a big sigh," he pointed out. I felt his arms creep around my waist from behind, and his breath warm across the side of my neck. "What's the matter, sour-puss?"

"Nothing," I said, turning within the circle of his arms to give him a smile. "Everything's just perfect. That was a happy sigh."

"Really?" he said dryly, raising one eyebrow.

I just laughed and gave him a light shove. "Yes, really. Put your clothes on, nudist; we've got work to do."

"God, you're always complaining when I'm naked," he replied, throwing his hands up in mock despair. "Anyone would think you didn't like it. You don't see me complaining when *you're* naked, do you?"

"You're usually too busy to complain," I replied. I pulled away and gave him a slap on the bum. "Just for the record, I only complain about it when we're going out. Can't have you traumatising the children, now can we?"

"All right, all right, I'm getting dressed," he replied, grinning. He went over to the stack of clean clothing on the floor and fished out his gear, then plopped down on the edge of the bed. "I found a wardrobe in one of the houses that I want to lug up here. It'd be nice to get our stuff up off the floor."

"Sounds good," I said, sitting down beside him to pull on my socks and shoes. "I was thinking that it might be nice to drag a few of those big industrial-grade washing machines and dryers into the tower now that we've got power. I don't know about you, but I'm so sick of everything being damp."

"Oh yeah, it's making me crazy," he replied. "Add it to the to-do list, right?"

"You're starting to sound like me," I said. "Careful, or you'll turn into a sour-puss, too."

"You're not actually a sour-puss," he said, his tone and expression softening. "I was just teasing."

"I know, and I'm teasing back," I replied with a laugh and a nudge. "I thought you would have figured out my deadpan sense of humour by now."

"I don't think I'll ever figure out your deadpan sense of humour, honey," he replied, leaning down to plant a kiss on the top of my head. I grinned and hugged him, then we both turned our attention towards getting ready to leave.

*** 

Within the hour, our chosen team was fed, ready, and sitting around a table in the dining room, talking quietly about what we had to do.

"It was up around here," Simon said, touching a point on the map spread out in front of us. "I'm not a hundred percent sure of the exact location on the map, but I can find it again once we're in the area. There's an unmarked building, surrounded by chain-link fences and barbed wire. I can't be sure, but it had the feel of a government facility about it."

"What makes you think that?" I asked.

"It was big," he replied. "Really big. Like, it went all the way back into the hills. But there were no signposts, no branding, no logos. If it had been a corporate facility, they would've had signs posted, right? But like I said, I didn't go inside so I don't know for sure. The flash drive was taped to the door in a plastic bag, with a piece of paper that had a short message written on it. It said 'Don't give up hope.' I picked the bag up and was looking at it when I spotted movement inside. I think it was just an infected, but... I was alone and pretty freaked out by that stage. I shoved the bag in my pocket and ran my ass back home as fast as I could."

"Well, now I'm not creeped out at all," I said dryly. "Thanks, Simon."

"You're so very welcome," he replied, grinning. "In retrospect, I think I made the right choice."

"You did."

The voice came from behind us, and by this stage of our journey I almost expected to hear it. Madeline came up to the table with a very serious look on her face, and climbed into my lap without being invited.

"What do you mean, Maddy?" I asked. I'd learned not to question the accuracy of her instincts, even if she wasn't always clear about her meaning.

"Mister Simon made the right choice by waiting," she replied, snuggling comfortably up against me. "He couldn't open the door. Not without me. That's why I'm here."

"You've lost me, kiddo," I admitted, putting my arms around her and giving her a hug. "Talk us through it from the beginning."

"I'm not sure," she admitted. "Sometimes the things I see don't always make sense. But I know that I have to be there or you won't be able to find the vaccine. You need to take me with you."

I shot a startled look at the others over top of her head. "Uh... have you told your granddaddy that you want to go yet? He's not going to like that."

"He doesn't have a choice," she replied, in a voice that sounded entirely too old to be coming out of such a small child. "We need that vaccine, and you need me to get it." She glanced up, and gave me an endearing smile. "Don't worry, Miss Sandy. I'll be fine. I'd know if something bad was going to happen to me."

"That's true," I agreed grudgingly. "Okay. Go tell your granddad. He's the one you need to convince, not me."

"Okay!" she agreed cheerfully. She gave me a quick hug, then wriggled out of my lap and ran off, leaving the rest of us staring after her with an assortment of different looks on our faces. Aaron was the first one to voice his concerns.

"That wee lass can't be more than six," he said. "Are we really going to take her with us?"

"She's almost eight, she's just a bit small for her age," I corrected him. "And... if she says that she needs to go with us, then we're better off just taking her with us than arguing about it. Maddy has a gift, and she hasn't been wrong yet."

"I've heard the stories, but I don't know what to believe," he admitted, absently rubbing his chin. "I just... I don't know. She's so young."

"When it comes to Madeline Cross, age is just a number," Michael said. "That little girl has saved us numerous times. If she says that she *needs* to come, then we're just wasting our time if we go without her. We'll end up having to come back and get her later on."

"If you say so," Aaron said doubtfully. "Okay, so we've got me in case anyone gets hurt, Simon to guide us, Sandrine for smarts, Michael for muscle, and Gavin because he knows a little bit about everything. Do we need anyone else?"

"You don't need us, but we'd like to come if you'd have us," said a voice from the doorway. I glanced back over my shoulder and saw Mary Ferguson, her father, and several other members of their group standing in the doorway.

I raised a brow and gave her a curious look. "You're not still trying to earn my forgiveness, are you? Because I already forgive you. You guys can stop leaving flowers on my doorstep now."

Mary laughed and shook her head. "Sorry, that was entirely my doing. I do still feel bad, but that wasn't why I left the flowers. I try to do something nice for one person every day, and these rooms are so bland and boring. They need a little colour to bring them to life."

I smiled in spite of what had happened a week earlier. That was a sentiment I understood. "Well, thank you anyway. They certainly have livened up the place. But, why do you guys want to come?"

Daniel stepped forward and rested a hand on his daughter's shoulder. "Word's gotten around about what you're going to look for, and one of these days I'm going to have grandkids to worry about. It's only right that we offer our assistance any way that we can."

Mary shot her father a dark look at the comment about grandkids, then she looked back at me and her expression relaxed again. "We also feel like it's our duty to help protect the Child Prophet. We were listening when she was here, and if she needs to go then we do, too. You've already forgiven us and we appreciate that, but we still feel like we have to earn God's forgiveness as well. Not just for what we almost did to you, but for... everything. Humanity's sins. We believe that the plague was His way of punishing us all for humanity's arrogance, but if there truly is a vaccine then we'll know that we've finally earned His forgiveness." She paused, and gave me a tiny smile. "It's important to us. Please let us come."

"Well, if it means that much to you..." I hesitated and glanced at the others. Michael nodded and smiled to me, while the others seemed fairly ambivalent on the matter. I looked back at Mary and Daniel, and nodded my approval. "Sure. Go get your travel clothes on and grab some rations from the kitchen. We'll be returning here by evening, so pack light. No need to bring overnight gear. If you need some wet weather gear, go see Skylar in the Quartermaster's office and she'll get you kitted out."

They nodded and departed. I turned back to the others, only to find Aaron obviously struggling to keep silent. I smiled at him and made a friendly gesture. "Out with it, then?"

He sighed and rolled his eyes heavenwards. "Look, I consider myself as open-minded as they come... but that bunch weird me out. Do we have to bring them with us, too?"

"Aren't you Irish Catholic?" I asked, equal parts amused and concerned by his protests.

"Officially, yeah," he said. "But you don't see me ambushing ladies in the women's room, now do you? There's something very peculiar about that lot, and I don't much care for it. I cannot fathom why you let them stay here after what they did."

"Everyone makes mistakes," I replied. "What they did was a genuine misunderstanding. They thought they were doing what was best for everyone by protecting you from a false prophet. There was no real malice or hatred behind it. It wouldn't be right for me to evict them for their beliefs."

Michael lay a hand on my shoulder, picking up the thought where I left off. "Tumanako was always supposed to be a place of acceptance, where everyone is welcome regardless of race or creed. That's what Sandy preached to us in the beginning, and that's what we want to live by now. We know it isn't always easy for different people to live in harmony – there have been enough wars to prove that – but there are so few of us now that we have to try."

"He's right," Gavin said. "You remember what it was like before the plague? All the fear and hatred directed towards anyone who had different bodies or beliefs? Catholics and Protestants, Muslims, Jews, atheists... it didn't matter how innocent you were, there was always someone who hated you. Well, you're Christian, I'm atheist, Michael's a Buddhist, and guess what? We're all good people. The Yousefi family are Muslim, and contrary to what pre-plague society would have believed, they aren't terrorists. Hell, they're some of the best people I know. You heard the story about how they came to join us, right?"

"I haven't," Simon said, looking back and forth between us curiously. "What happened?"

"They gave Skye and Doc concussions and set our house on fire," Michael said, grinning. "We nearly lost everything!"

Aaron's eyes bulged, and Simon's jaw fell open. Before either of them could say anything, I jumped in to finish the story.

"But the point is, we gave them a chance to explain themselves," I said. "It turned out that they were starving, had four kids to feed, and there was a misunderstanding. Everything that happened was an accident."

Gavin nodded and picked up his thought where he'd left off. "If they'd chased the Yousefi family away, not only would there be six more dead people in the world, but we'd have missed out on the opportunity to learn what good friends they can be. My point being, we shouldn't judge people based on what we *think* we know about them without giving them a chance to show us the truth."

I gave Gavin a quizzical look and a grin. "You've been thinking about this a lot."

"I have," he admitted. "I've been spending a lot of time with the engineering crew, including Zain. He told me the story, and how guilty he felt about it in retrospect. It made me realise why you've been trying so hard to be forgiving, even when I know that your first instinct is to push people away to protect yourself from getting hurt. You're trying to lead by example."

I felt a rush of heat in my cheeks and glanced down, suddenly embarrassed. "Everyone deserves a second chance. That's the other thing Tumanako was meant to be: a second chance for all of us. I wish that I could say I lived without regrets, but that would be a lie. I've had to take lives, or have lives taken to protect my own, and I still think about them all the time. I don't want anyone else to have to live with that kind of darkness weighing on their soul."

Michael squeezed my hand, and everyone else fell silent around the table. Everyone except Simon, who looked at me.

"You know, you should write it down," he said.

"Write what down?" I asked, raising a brow. "The darkness weighing on my soul?"

"No, just... your story," he replied, shaking his head. "Everyone should, if they can. One day, people are going to look back on what we're doing here as history. Wouldn't it be better to tell them your story in your own words, rather than have it passed down by goodness knows however many generations of storytellers around the campfire?"

I had to stop and think about that, turning the idea over in my head until I could make sense of it. Suddenly, the pieces clicked into place, and I sat back in my chair.

"You're right," I said. "I mean, what if some kid is looking back on this day in a thousand years, and trying to write a report about us for school? Everyone's voice is a thread in the tapestry that made this happen, and the best way for our voices to be remembered is through our own words. What better way for us to immortalize our families, and those who were lost to the plague? Simon, that's a brilliant idea. Why didn't I think of that?"

"Disseminating information is kind of my business," he answered dryly. "I'll do it if you do it."

"You're on," I agreed, then I looked at Michael and the others. "What about you guys? Michael? Gavin? Aaron?"

"Sure, why not?" Aaron said with a shrug. "If I can find the time, I'll write something."

Michael nodded thoughtfully. "Our stories are pretty closely intertwined since Hamilton, but it's always good to have two different perspectives on the same events."

"I'll... think about it," said Gavin. I glanced at Gavin, but he wouldn't meet my eye. "There are some parts I'd rather not remember."

"I know," I replied, reaching out to touch his scarred hand. "I know better than anyone. Think about it, and take as much time as you need."

Gavin started to reply, but before he could we were interrupted by a commotion out in the hall. The door burst open and Skylar dashed inside, her face alight with excitement.

"Sandy!" she cried when she saw me. "Oh thank goodness, you haven't left yet. I was just talking to Mary and she had the *best* idea. You're going to love it!"

"Wait, back up," I replied, holding my hands up to stall her. "The best idea for what?"

"For a memorial to all the people who died in the plague," she replied. She grabbed my hand and pulled me out of my chair, dragging me over to the big, whitewashed wall that ran along one side of the room. "A photo mural, right here. There are photographs everywhere, right? You see them all the time. Magazines, newspapers, even albums in people's houses. So we gather them all up, and we cover this whole wall with them. The whole wall!"

"With pictures of random strangers?" I asked, bewildered. "What good would that do?"

"But they're not just random strangers," she said enthusiastically, struggling to illustrate the idea with broad gestures. "They're *people.* They're our history. Our ancestors. We collect and preserve the photographs, so that we can remember what the world looked like back then. Mary just told me that historians used to look back on Ancient Greece and make guesses about what things looked like based off their art, but if we collect photos then people in the future won't have to make any guesses because they'll just be able to look at the pictures."

"That… actually, that makes a lot of sense," I replied. "Clever. Okay, you're in charge of the project, so organise it as you see fit. We were also just talking about having people write down their personal stories for pretty much the same reason. Can you get hold of a bunch of notebooks and writing instruments?"

"Will do," she said. "There's a big stationery cupboard that we haven't even started to inventory yet, or failing that I'm sure there's a supply store nearby. I'll take care of everything." She paused and glanced around the table, then grinned. "You guys just focus on the vaccine."

"You got it," I replied. I glanced out the window, then looked back at my group. "We better go find Maddy and see what's going on. Looks like the rain's only going to get heavier the longer we wait."

The others nodded and rose. We gathered up our backpacks and left the cafeteria. Michael took the rest of the group downstairs to get our transport ready, while I went off in search of Doc. I found him in his office, a small room off the infirmary, hunched over a book. He didn't notice me at first, which gave me the chance to get close enough to spy on what he was reading.

"Herbal medicine, Doc?" I asked, surprised. "Are our medical supplies running that low?"

He almost jumped out of his skin, then shot a glare over his shoulder at me. "Yes, we are – as your current condition illustrates. I need to work out an alternative, and soon. I can make some things from scratch but not everything. Speaking of which – you need to tell Michael soon. You're beginning to show."

"I'm well aware, don't worry," I replied, glancing back over my shoulder. Tala and Franco were sleeping side by side in the infirmary, but none of the nurses were around. "Skye and Anahera cornered me last night and tried to give me 'the talk', so now they know. I'm planning to tell him tonight, once we get home."

"Not a moment too soon," he replied. "I'm getting tired of tiptoeing around the subject."

"*You're* getting tired of it?" I echoed, laughing. "How do you think I feel? I have to suck my tummy in whenever he's around. At this rate, my baby bump's going to pop out of my back!"

To my surprise, Doc laughed right along with me. "Now, that would be something I don't know how to fix, so you'd best stop sucking it in. However, I do think you made the right choice by not to telling him until you were past the danger zone. I'm surprised you've gotten this far, all things considered."

"What can I say?" I shrugged and grinned at him. "I'm stubborn. Michael's stubborn. Stubbornness is an inherited trait, apparently. I predict tantrums aplenty in this stubborn baby's future. Oh, and speaking of stubborn – did Maddy come and talk to you?"

"Yes, she did," he replied, his smile fading. "I expect you to take care of her, Ms McDermott. She's the only family I've got left."

I lifted my eyebrows, surprised. "You gave her permission to come along?"

"I did," he said quietly. "I don't like it, but… I've come to accept that Madeline's gift is outside my field of expertise. If she needs to go, then she needs to go. I know that I can trust you and Michael to protect her as if she were your own daughter. I sent her off to get her raincoat and boots. She should be back any minute."

Right on cue, the door opened and Maddy scampered in, all wrapped up in her favourite pink raincoat. She skidded to a stop and grinned up at me. "Hi! Granddaddy said I can go, so let's go."

"Did you go and get some lunch?" I asked.

She nodded enthusiastically. "Yup! I'm ready."

"One more thing," Doc said, reaching out to touch my arm. "Once you've told Michael, please bring him by to see me. I'd like to compile as much information on potential problems as possible. Plus, I need to weigh you again to make sure you're gaining enough weight. I'm somewhat concerned that you're still underweight, but we'll find out."

"Will do, Doc," I replied, sketching a salute. Then I offered my hand to Maddy, and led the little girl out into the hall.

"Mister Michael is going to be happy," she whispered as she skipped along beside me. "He wants a baby very much."

"I know," I replied. "Every time I see him cuddling Evelyn and casting furtive glances at me, I want to tell him. I can't hide it much longer."

"It's okay," Maddy said, suddenly turning solemn. "It's almost time to tell him. You'll know when." We rounded a corner into the little alley leading to the elevators, and her seriousness vanished in a flash of youthful exuberance. "Oh! Oh! Can I push the button? Please?"

I couldn't help but laugh at how swiftly she went from stone-faced adult to bouncy child. "Sure, hon. Push the button."

"Yay!" she cheered, and raced over to do just that.

A few minutes later, we headed out the door, and found the rest of the group waiting for us. I bundled Madeline into the back of the Hilux, then I took Boudicca's reins from Michael and vaulted up into the saddle.

"Everyone ready?" I asked, glancing at him.

He nodded and smiled. "We were just waiting on you two, now we're good to go whenever you are."

"Good," I said. I paused to do a quick mental headcount, then I nodded and led the way out into the gloomy streets.

# Chapter Fifteen

We travelled east as far as we could go, then turned south and followed the old train tracks through the outer suburbs of Lower Hutt. Even after ten years, even in the middle of a spring rainstorm, it was beautiful country. The houses were run down and overgrown, but they still looked cosy and warm. I found myself looking at them with sadness and longing. Perhaps one day I could have a real home for my family. Maybe we'd be able to raise our baby there.

It was a pointless dream for the moment, though. Until we knew we were safe from the mutated infected, we couldn't leave the safety of Tumanako's walls. But at least now I could hope and dream, and there was a chance that the dream might come true.

A few kilometres before we would have reached the northern shoreline of Wellington Harbour we swung east again, into the industrial zone that lined the inside of the hills. Pretty houses and wild gardens gave way to huge, sprawling factories and the rusted hulks of cars and trucks.

Suddenly, the radio in my pocket crackled to life and I head Simon calling my name. I unbuttoned my coat and pulled the walkie-talkie out. "I'm here. Which way?"

"Left at this roundabout, then keep an eye out to your right," he replied. "You'll see a long driveway going up into the hills."

"Gotcha," I said. I clicked the radio off again and tucked it away.

"One of these days, we really need to teach him to ride," Michael commented dryly.

I laughed and nodded. "Sometimes I think he doesn't want to learn, so he doesn't have to get wet."

"Damn!" Michael swore. "Why didn't I think of that?"

"Because you knew I wouldn't let you get away with it," I replied. I was about to make another joke when we rounded a corner, and I spotted our destination. "There! That must be the driveway he was talking about."

"Huh. That's an awfully big fence," Michael said, studying the edge of the property. The fence line was hemmed by a thick layer of bushes and small trees, but beyond it we could see the moss-covered rooflines of a sprawling complex of buildings outlined against the darker green of the hills.

"Hm. No signs, just like he said," I commented. I pulled out my GPS and checked it, then glanced at him. "The maps say it was an industrial research facility, but it's also flagged as permanently closed. Which means it was closed *before* the plague."

"Suspicious and fascinating at the same time," he said.

I nodded my agreement and led the way up the driveway towards those distant buildings. The gate still hung open from Simon's previous visit, but there was no sign of life aside from the birds singing in the trees all around us. I ducked beneath a low-hanging branch and brought my horse to a stop outside the front door.

"This is pretty creepy," I admitted. "No wonder Simon ran off when he was here by himself. I would have, too."

"Says the lady who risked a mutant-infested hospital at midnight because her foot hurt," he said dryly.

I shot him a dark look. "I didn't have a choice. Besides, if I hadn't done that you wouldn't have a wife."

"Touché," he said, and let the topic drop.

We both dismounted and tied our horses to a rusted bike stand in front of the building, then waited while the other riders did likewise and Simon parked the Hilux. Once we were all assembled in front of the building, I took a long look around. "It really does look like a government facility, doesn't it? I don't see a single sign except for that fire exit over there. Weird. Why would they build something way out here?"

"It makes sense, when you think about it," Gavin said. "We're fairly close to Wellington, but it's also far enough away from the capital that it wouldn't be a target if we were attacked by a foreign power. It's within driving distance of the suburbs so the workers could go home at night, but also far enough out of town that you wouldn't have civvies walking past all day."

"He says it's bigger on the inside," Madeline said dreamily. "The facility goes way back into the hills, and deep underground." She paused and glanced at me quizzically. "What's a facility?"

I stumbled over the answer, still struggling to make sense of her words. "It's just a general word for a place or tool that serves a purpose. Who is 'he', Maddy?"

"The big boy," she said, looking at me like I was crazy. "He went inside. He says we'll need his key, so we should follow him."

"The... big boy?" I echoed. I tried to keep my voice casual, but suddenly I found all the hairs on the back of my neck were standing up. "I don't see anything so I'm going to have to trust you on that, kiddo. Can you show us where the big boy went?"

"Of course," she replied. She took my hand and led me into the building. The others fell in behind us, weapons at the ready. The interior of the building was dark, and when I tried a light switch I discovered that the power was off.

"We should have brought a portable generator with us," I said over my shoulder.

"We can always go back and get one," Michael replied. "It's not that far."

"No need," Maddy said in that same dreamy voice. She was very nearly in a trance, I realised suddenly. Her movements were jerky, and her eyes weren't entirely focused. She raised a hand and pointed down a long corridor. "There's a backup generator down there somewhere. He's never been there, but he saw the signs."

"I'll go take a look," Gavin volunteered. "It would help if we could see properly."

"Good," I replied. "Take David, Simon, and Mary with you for backup."

Gavin pulled out a torch, and they vanished into the gloom. The rest of us pulled out our torches and resumed following Madeline. At the first junction, she turned right and led us down another long corridor without even stopping to orientate herself. This one was faintly lit by the odd cracked, filthy skylight, but it wasn't bright enough for me to put my torch away.

Each doorway that we passed was a dark, hollow recess, like a missing tooth in the grim smile of whitewashed concrete walls. I swung my torch into each one as we passed by, and saw offices, laboratories, and even a break room or two. We travelled for nearly five minutes, working our way deeper and deeper into the facility. Eventually I realised that there were no more skylights above us, and we were probably under the hills.

"In there," Maddy whispered, her voice disembodied in the gloom. I swung my torch towards her and saw her pointing to an office coming up on our right.

I took a deep breath, nodded, and released her hand. "Stay here, honey. I'll go in. Where am I looking?"

"It's around his neck," she whispered. Suddenly, she turned and looked up at me, squinting against the glare of my torch. "Don't kill him, though. If you kill him, he'll will go away. We still need him."

My gorge rose, and I had to force myself to swallow hard to keep my lunch down. "He's infected?"

"Yes, and he's in there," she said, pointing at the doorway again. "We need his key—"

"I know. I'm going," I replied, steeling myself to what I had to do. I shifted my shotgun off my shoulder into a position where I could grab it if I needed it, and walked up to the doorway. A metallic sign glinted in the beam of my torch, which told me that the office had belonged to someone named C. Russell. Someone had taped a bright yellow Post-It note beside the plaque, with a smiley face and the letters 'PhD' written in pencil. I could smell the infected before I opened the door; the stench of decay was one that I was all too familiar with. With one last deep breath of the relatively clean air outside the office, I shoved the door open and stepped inside.

The skinny geneticist's body was familiar even in undeath. He was still wearing the same lab coat that had been a permanent fixture of his videos, though now his glasses were missing. I found them quite by accident, when I heard something crunch under my foot. I glanced down and flinched. "Damn. Sorry, Clyde."

There was no response. Clyde's infected body was just sitting in its chair, randomly poking at the blood-splattered keyboard of a computer that hadn't functioned in years. I cringed when I realised that it had quite literally worked its fingers to the bone, presumably typing away at a dissertation that no longer mattered. It was a heart-wrenching, miserable sight, but Maddy had been clear about what I needed to do. I inched closer and reached out to grab the lanyard around Clyde's neck. On the end of it was a small plastic card, which I assumed had to be the key Maddy had mentioned.

The infected didn't move, didn't look at me, didn't notice me at all. A second later, I was back out in the hallway, clutching my rancid prize and struggling not to throw up. I must have been pale as a ghost, because Michael took one look at me, then he grabbed the lanyard out of my hand, tossed it to Aaron, and pulled me into a hug. I clung to him and buried my face in his chest, drawing long, deep breaths of his scent to get the stink of death out of my nostrils.

After a few seconds, I pulled back and nodded my appreciation. "It's okay. I'm all right. It's just, he's…" I hesitated, uncertain how to express my feelings. In the end, I gave up and shook my head. "We'll be back, to put him to rest once we have what we need."

"It's okay, Miss Sandy," Maddy said, taking my hand again. "He can't feel pain anymore. He says that he's tethered to his body, but it doesn't hurt."

I shuddered and squeezed the little girl's hand. "I always wondered whether the infected could move on, or if they were stuck here. How many… how many people do you see trapped like that, Maddy?"

She glanced around then looked back at me and shrugged. "Only a few in here, but outside there are lots."

"Do they all talk to you?" I asked, fighting a rising wave of horror. What she was describing was my worst fear for the victims of the plague: that they wouldn't be able to rest while their bodies still walked the earth.

"No," she said, shaking her head. "Most of them aren't really there. They're sort of going away on their own, but it's taking a long time. But when you kill them, then they're free. They go away really fast. Not like, whoosh!" She made a gesture to illustrate her noise. "But quieter. They slowly turn see-through. What's the word?"

"Fade?" I suggested.

"Yes!" she exclaimed. "They fade until they're all gone. But they look happier."

"What about Clyde?" I asked. "I mean, I understand why you saw Netty's ghost, she'd only just died. But why is Clyde still here?"

Maddy glanced away, and tilted her head as though listening to a voice that only she could hear. "He says... he says that he's tried to go away, but something stopped him. Every time he started to go, he was pulled back. He says that he had to wait for us to get here. He doesn't know what pulled him back, he just knows that he's not allowed to leave until we're finished."

I took a second to digest what she was telling me, then I nodded. "So what do we do next?"

"We should go find the others," Maddy told me. "We need power to make the elevator work."

"Okay," I agreed, nodding. "Let's go get the power working, then."

We made it halfway back to the junction where we'd gone our separate ways when our radios crackled.

"We've got it," Gavin said. "We found the generator, and it's just powering up. We should start seeing electricity in a few seconds."

The fluorescent bulbs on the ceiling above us began to flicker to life. I turned to the others and started to say something, but whatever I'd been thinking was forgotten when a bulb a couple of meters in front of us exploded. I yelped and jumped back, pulling Maddy up against me to shield her from the falling glass. Once the socket shorted itself out, I looked at the others. "Everyone okay? Anyone hurt?"

"Aside from a minor heart attack?" Michael asked dryly. "Yeah, just peachy. But hey, at least we can see now."

"What, you weren't enjoying wandering around a pitch black research lab full of zombies?" Aaron quipped. "I'm pretty sure I used to play this game when I was a teenager, but those zombies were a lot more... bitey."

We all laughed, though the laughter was a little strained. We hurried the rest of the way back to the intersection and waited until Gavin's group returned, then took a moment to catch our breath and relay the events of the last few minutes to one another. Once we were done, we all looked at Maddy for further instructions.

"We need to go down," she said matter-of-factly. "Follow me, I know where to go. This way!"

We exchanged glances, but before any of us could say anything Madeline marched off, heading back into the heart of the hills. We all fell in behind and beside her, silently following her through the passageways.

Suddenly, she stopped and pointed. "There, that's it."

"That's a strange-looking elevator," Simon said, frowning. "It almost looks like a freight elevator."

"It was supposed to keep the virus out," Maddy told us solemnly. "But it didn't work."

"Is it safe for us to be going in there?" I asked, suddenly but justifiably nervous. The plague had robbed all of us of our families, so we were entitled to be wary of disease.

"Of course," she said. "We're immune, silly."

"Well, that makes sense," I replied. "Stupid question, I guess."

"It's okay, Miss Sandy." She smiled at me, then she went over to the elevator and pressed the call button. A few seconds later, the doors slid open and she led us inside. Once we were all in, I glanced at the control panel and saw that there was only one choice aside from the floor we were on, but beside it was a security lock and a keypad.

"We have a problem," I said. "Looks like we need a number as well as the key card."

"I know the number," Maddy said. "I'll unlock it, so we can go up and down without the card or the number. He said he'd show me how."

She took the key card, swiped it through the security lock, then punched in a long string of numbers. I glanced at the others, uncertain what to make of Maddy's assertion, but as usual she proved to know far more than she should have. The doors swept shut, and we felt the telltale sensation of descending into the earth.

Aaron made a surprised sound and looked at me. "I'm starting to feel like a fool for doubting her."

I just nodded and said nothing. A few seconds later, the doors swished open with a gust of stale, malodorous air. I shifted my shotgun around into the offensive position, and carefully led the way out into the room beyond. The lights were dim and flickering, and I saw broken glass from other bulbs that hadn't survived the shock of being re-ignited when the generator came back on, but there was enough light that I wasn't forced to rely on my torch.

The lobby we arrived in had obviously been used as a decontamination area, with a heavy door on the other side that probably would have been air-tight if it hadn't been hanging wide open. Biohazard suits hung on hooks on the walls, beside high-pressure showers and coiled hoses that had clearly done no good.

"He was the last one alive," Maddy said softly. "When he got sick, he decided that he wasn't going to die alone in the dark, so he put all his videos onto a... memory thing, and taped it to the door. Then he went outside to enjoy the sun while he could."

I shuddered and swallowed a lungful of stagnant air, trying to ignore the familiar stench of decomposition. "Ugh, it smells rancid in here. From what I saw in the video, they were down here for weeks. Surely there must have been some kind of ventilation system, right?"

"There is one," Gavin said, pointing upwards. I followed his finger and saw a small air vent on the ceiling above our heads. "it's definitely working, I can feel a breeze. It would have gone off when the power died, so it'll probably just take a little while to get going."

"Why is there a vent in the decontamination room?" Simon asked. "They wouldn't have had time to build this just to deal with Ebola X, so it must have been built as a general-purpose facility. Why weren't they thinking about airborne pathogens?"

"They were," Aaron said. "If they went to the effort to build a facility like this for biological research, then there will be at least two separate filtration and recycling systems, probably more. One for out here, a second for inside the facility, and one for each isolated ward. You don't spare any expense on that kind of thing."

"So how did the pathogen get to them?" I asked, glancing back and forth between them. "That door is an airlock, and Clyde said that they were on recycled air and water, and the food was all sterilized. How did they die?"

Without quite meaning to, I looked at Maddy for an answer. She looked back at me, but something about her expression was... wrong. I knew before she spoke that something had changed, and it had all the hairs on the back of my neck standing on end again.

"I never did find out," she said. "Someone must have dropped a culture dish, or not quite sterilized something enough. It's too late to find out now, and I guess it doesn't really matter anymore. Not for us, anyway."

By the time she finished speaking, everyone was staring at her with wide eyes. The voice wasn't Madeline's. Well, it was but it wasn't at the same time. I couldn't explain how I knew, but I just knew. I could feel it in my bones.

"Clyde?" I whispered.

Maddy gave me a lopsided smile and nodded. "She thought it would be easier if we could talk directly. I gotta tell you, it feels pretty weird. I'm not sure how long I'll be able to stay in here."

I glanced at the others, and saw each one of them looking as disturbed as I felt. A couple of the more religiously-orientated members crossed themselves or made other signs to ward off evil. Maddy – Clyde – Madelyde ignored them. She turned and walked away, beckoning for us to follow her.

"I guess my message made it, then?" she asked, pausing in the doorway to make sure that I was following her. I hesitated for a second, then hurried to catch up with her. Behind me, I heard Michael setting a watch near the entrance in case anything happened to us, and I was silently grateful to him for it. The others waited with him to be given instructions, with the exception of Simon; he was way too curious by nature to wait behind when there was an answer to his questions close at hand.

"Sort of," I replied. "We got part of the message, but half of it was too degraded for us to open. The last thing we got was something about him – I mean, you – giving up on finding a cure and focusing on a vaccine made from the blood of the immune."

"Yeah!" she exclaimed. "Pretty awesome, right? I know, I'm just that good. Man, it would have made such a great topic for my dissertation, if not for... well, you know."

"Yeah, we know," I said. "How does it work, then?"

"Well, the main reason that Ebola X was so devastating is because it causes irreparable damage before our bodies have a chance to learn how to fight it," she replied, folding her hands behind her back as she walked. "The only reason that you're immune and I'm not is because your body can produce antibodies straight away. Why? We don't know, it just sort of happened. Evolution, I guess."

"Then why the zombies?" I asked. It was a question that had been bothering me for ten years, and now was the first opportunity I'd had to ask from someone that might actually know the answer.

"Oh, that's a weird one," he replied. "The virus targets the cerebellum – the upper brain, if you like. That's responsible for thought, speech, dreams, the senses, you name it. All the higher brain function. The brainstem is responsible for movement, and the virus pretty much ignores it. I guess it's too... I don't know, chewy or something. Om nom nom, tasty soft higher brain meat, icky brain stem meat."

"Ugh, Clyde, you're in a seven-year-old's body," I protested. "I didn't need that visual."

"Yeah, I know, it's weird being this close to the floor," he replied with entirely too much cheer for a dead person possessing a child's body. "Anyway, you've heard the term 'brain death', I presume. Cerebral death and brain stem death are two totally different things. Under normal circumstances, a person with a dead cerebellum goes into something called a permanent vegetative state. You know, when the lights are on but nobody's home?"

"Yeah, but these people aren't vegetables," Simon pointed out. "They're zombies."

"Well, that's about as far as my research went, so I can't tell you exactly what's going on," she admitted with a shrug. "I went into a persistent zombietative state about sixty days after the outbreak. How long has it been?"

"Uh, ten years," I replied, suddenly fighting the unreasonable urge to laugh. The kid had a sense of humour that I could appreciate, even if it was a little morbid. "Closer to eleven now, I guess."

"Oh wow," she gasped. "And you're only just finding my research now? Damn. That does change things." She paused for a second, and seemed to be listening to a voice that only she could hear. "The power's been off? Okay. My samples of the vaccine are not going to be viable anymore, so you'll need to create your own. I'll give you all my research. If you can find someone that knows anything about pharmacology, they should be able to replicate the vaccine from that."

I breathed a sigh of relief and nodded. "We have a trained pharmacist, I'm glad to say. However, we don't have access to a lot of chemicals."

"That's fine, he or she should be able to get a little creative with the ingredients and it'll still work," she replied. "Like I was saying before we got distracted, the biggest problem with Ebola X is that it does permanent damage before our immune systems can figure out how to produce antibodies to fight it off. So, we do this as a two-step process. The first thing we do is something called immunoglobulin therapy. That's where we take your plasma – that's the clear goop that your red and white blood cells float in – and inject it into the non-immune person. That gives them a boost of your antibodies to protect them while you move on to the second phase. Then while the live antibodies are still circulating, we inject them with a vaccine made from the dead virus. What that does is expose their immune system to the virus without actually infecting them, so their body has a chance to figure the virus out. Their body should learn to produce the antibodies on their own."

"Should?" I repeated, shooting a nervous glance at her. "These are our kids we're talking about. 'Should' isn't really good enough."

"There's no way to be sure until we've had a chance to test it," she replied. "No science is ever a hundred percent guaranteed. Nothing is perfect. But we're only going to use dead viruses, so at least the subject can't get infected from that. The worst that can happen is that their immune system won't kick in, in which case you give them a booster shot of the immunoglobulin and keep trying."

The look on my face must have been pretty intense; I felt Simon touch my arm to comfort me. I took a deep breath and nodded, burying my fear through sheer force of will. Even if there was a small chance that my baby might not be born immune, this still gave us a way to save her. She might have to be on regular injections for the rest of her life, that was still a life. That was more of a chance than so many of us had before.

Madelyde rounded a corner, and entered a small laboratory, one of the many in the sprawling underground labyrinth. She looked around for a second, then went over to a desk and sat down – or tried to, but she wasn't quite tall enough to reach the chair.

"Man, I used to be six-four. Now I feel short," she said, shooting a look at me. "Lift me up?"

I obliged. Once she was settled, she pushed the power button on the computer, and we waited several painful minutes to see if it would boot. While we were waiting, Gavin stuck his head through the doorway.

"It's not going to start," he said. "The CMOS battery will be long dead." He looked at me and raised an eyebrow. "Did I teach you nothing, young padawan?"

I laughed and shrugged. "We never talked about computers, old man. You just taught me important survival stuff, remember?"

"Oh, right." He grinned at me and winked, though it looked a little odd with his milky-white eye. "Anyway, I can take care of this. Unplug the machine and we'll take it back with us."

"Sounds good," I agreed, then I looked at Madelyde. "Is there anything else we should take?"

"Um…" she looked around thoughtfully, then pointed at a small stack of notebooks on a bookshelf nearby. "Those. You probably won't need them, but take them anyway. Those are all my hand-written lab notes. And you should probably take the network server, too. It'll have backups of everyone else's research on it."

I nodded and gestured to her. "Okay. I'm feeling a bit light-headed and need to sit down for a minute. Can you please show Gavin where it is?"

"Sure," Madelyde agreed. She jumped out of her chair and scampered off, with Gavin right behind her.

Once they were gone, I took another long, deep breath and sat down in the chair that she'd just vacated. Whether it was the hormones, the excitement, or just the unfamiliar chill of air conditioning, I wasn't feeling my best. Simon put his hand on my shoulder, and looked at me in obvious concern.

"You okay, Sandrine?" he asked gently. "Can I get you some water or something?"

"No, no, I'm fine," I said, shaking my head. "I just need to sit for a second."

He nodded understandingly, then he pulled another chair over and sat down beside me. "Well, I've been wanting a second to talk to you alone, anyway. No time like the present, I guess."

"Oh?" I looked at him and raised a brow. "Is something wrong?"

"No, not wrong," he said, smiling. He reached over and took my hand, then looked me in the eye. "There's something I've been wanting to say to you since the moment we met, but I wasn't sure if you felt the same way. I think I've finally figured it out."

I just looked at him, bewildered.

"I've been alone for so long," he admitted, running his thumb across the back of my hand. It was a gesture that was tender and intimate, and it immediately set off warning bells in the back of my head – but not soon enough. Before I quite realised what was happening, he leaned in and kissed me.

I froze, shocked by the totally unexpected gesture of affection. Sure, I'd had a crush on him for years, but I'd never, ever imagined that the attraction would be mutual. I was stunned, so stunned that it took a few seconds before the part of me that was totally in love with Michael screeched like a horrified banshee. All of a sudden my body was back under my control, and it was not impressed. I shoved Simon away and leapt to my feet, glaring at him. "What the hell?! I'm a married woman, Simon!"

His eyes flew wide, and a look of absolute horror crossed his face. "But... I thought you were flirting with me! You've been giving me all of the signals! I thought you wanted a threesome relationship, like your sister has. I—"

"No!" I cried, covering my face with my hands. "No, no, no! I wasn't flirting, I was just being nice! I'm nice to everyone!"

"Oh, God, I'm so sorry!" he gasped, slumping forward and burying his face in his hands. "I misunderstood. I thought—"

Suddenly, Aaron raced into the room. "Sandy! What's going on?"

I nearly jumped out of my skin. "What? Nothing! Nothing's going on!"

"Well, something must be going on," he replied, "because Michael went off looking for you a minute ago, then he came tearing back through the lobby looking bloody furious. I've never seen him that angry. He went right up the elevator without a word to any of us. Did you two have a fight or something?"

"Oh, no," I gasped. "He must have seen... Oh no, no, no."

I didn't even try to explain. I just brushed past Aaron and ran off, racing back towards the elevator. There, I found the rest of our party standing around looking bewildered. Mary waved and called out to me, but I couldn't hear her. The only thing on my mind was Michael... and saving my short-lived marriage from a misunderstanding of epic proportions. The elevator pinged open a second later; Maddy had left it unlocked, just as she'd promised. I pushed the button for the ground floor, and then slammed my hand against the button to close the doors and kept pushing it frantically as if that would somehow make it work better. It didn't, but at least it gave me something to do with my hands.

Thirty seconds later, I was back on the ground floor of the research facility, my heart hammering in my chest.

"Michael!" I cried, cupping my hands around my mouth. "Please, it's not what it looked like!"

There was no answer. Tears gathered in my eyes, blurring my vision. I could survive a plague, fight a mutant, and wrestle a goddamn undead pig if I needed to, but the thought of living without Michael was more than I could bear. I took off running, with no idea where I was going or how I'd find him. The logical guess was that he was running away from what he'd seen, which meant that he was probably heading back towards the horses.

My head swam and tears ran down my cheeks, making it harder and harder to see where I was going. I rounded a corner too fast, slipped, and slid into a wall, only to bounce back off again and keep running without falling. By the time I burst out of the front door, I was a mess. I felt it, and I really must have looked it.

All the horses were exactly where we'd left them. I was still staring at them, struggling to make sense of what I was seeing, when a voice spoke from the shadows of the eaves a few meters to my left.

"I trusted you," Michael said softly. I jumped in surprise and looked at him; he was sitting on the ground with his back against the wall, arms wrapped around his legs, his face set in an unreadable mask.

"Michael," I whispered. I hurried to his side and knelt down beside him, but when I tried to take his hand he pulled it away.

"I don't even know how to be mad at you," he said in a tone that wasn't angry so much as bewildered. "I never thought that I'd have to be. Why would you do this?"

"I didn't, honey," I replied, shaking my head. "I swear to you, I'd never betray you. You're the only man I've ever truly loved. I'd never throw that love away."

"I saw you kissing Simon," he replied, his tone harsh and accusative for the span of the sentence, and then it turned soft again. "How is that not what it looks like?"

"Because that was a stupid misunderstanding," I replied, reaching for his hand again. This time, he let me take it. I pressed a kiss to his knuckles, then looked him in the eye. "Simon thought that I'd been flirting with him, and that I wanted to have a three-way relationship with him and you."

A flicker of understanding passed through his dark eyes. "He... what? You've told me again and again that you're afraid of that kind of relationship."

"I am," I replied with a shrug. "But I guess we're not close enough for him to know that. I've never deliberately flirted with him or anyone else, except for you – and you know how bad I am at flirting."

"You're not that bad," he replied, a faint smile tugging the corner of his lips. "Is he going to be sporting a hell of a shiner tomorrow?"

"Nah, I reserve my love-taps for you," I replied, as light-heartedly as I could in the moment. "But... seriously though, he caught me completely by surprise. I just froze. I've gotten out of the habit of automatically punching anyone who tries to touch me, you know? And I do like Simon, just... not like that. I couldn't be like that with anyone but you. You're the only one to earn the privilege."

Michael took a deep breath, and I could see him visibly relaxing. "I should have known better than to assume the worst."

"I can't blame you for doing so," I replied. "I mean, it must have looked pretty bad. But... honey, there's something I need to tell you. I've been putting it off for a while now because I wanted to make sure that it wasn't going to break your heart. I was going to tell you tonight, but I think if I tell you now it'll help you understand how I feel about you."

"Break my heart?" he echoed, confusion crossing his face. "What are you talking about, Sandy?"

"I'm talking about this, you big doofus," I replied, guiding his hand to rest on my stomach. He glanced down at it, and I saw a plethora of emotions cross his face in the span of a few seconds.

"Wait, what?" he asked, looking bewildered. "Are you saying...?"

"I'm saying that we're going to have a baby," I replied. "She's due in about five months. I didn't want to tell you until I made it through the first trimester, in case I lost her. You lost Sophie not even a year ago, and then we both had to watch Skye lose her baby. I knew how much you wanted a child, and I knew it would kill you if I miscarried. Doc said there was a good chance I could lose this one in the first trimester, not just because of the malnutrition thing but because..." I glanced away and swallowed hard. "I've had miscarriages before... after... you know."

"Oh, Sandy," he whispered. I felt his arms close around me, and suddenly I was being hugged. "You should have told me, but I understand why you didn't."

I sniffed and rubbed my eye, brushing away a few tears that were trying to break free. "I know. I just didn't want to make you suffer. You've already lost enough. It's been hard enough watching you grieve for Sophie; I'm not sure I could bear watching you grieve for our baby, too."

"You won't have to," he said, his voice suddenly taking on that tone of total determination I knew so well. "We're going to get through this together, you and me. Nothing is going to happen to the baby on my watch." I heard him laugh, then suddenly his grip around me tightened to the point that I could barely breathe. A few seconds later, he leaned back and looked at me, grinning like a madman. "A baby! I can't believe it! You know I'm going to have to tease you mercilessly for not telling me straight away, right?"

"Oh, I fully expect you to," I answered dryly. "And I deserve it, so it's all good. A few other people already know, but not many. Maddy was the one who told me, and Doc's confirmed the diagnosis. Gavin knows because I asked him to make sure you were okay, and Skye and Anahera know because they figured it out last night. Apparently I've been gaining weight or something."

"You have," Michael replied, giving me a playful tickle. "I just assumed you were eating more than usual to make yourself extra cuddly for me. I didn't know you were eating for two."

I squeaked and shoved his hand away. "Hey, no tickling! Bladder is weak right now!"

"Sorry, I just can't help i—" he started to say, then suddenly he went stiff in my arms. "Wait... if you've known about the baby for months, is that the only reason you wanted to marry me?"

"Oh, hell no," I replied, with an appropriately sassy gesture. "I married you because I want to claim ownership over you 'til death do us part'. I couldn't care less if our baby was born out of wedlock. I wanted to marry you because you're my Officer Sexy, and I love you." I gave him a cheeky grin, and draped my arms around his neck. "Well, that and the fact I wanted to see you in uniform again."

Michael laughed and I felt him relax again. "Well, if that's what you wanted, all you had to do was ask."

# Chapter Sixteen

The building's eaves offered little protection from the elements, so we were both sopping wet by the time we finally finished making peace and returned to the facility, but the look on Michael's face more than made up for the discomfort. His couldn't stop grinning, and I was so relieved to have the burden of secrecy off my chest that I found myself laughing over the most ridiculous things – like the looks on people's faces when the elevator doors opened, and we stepped out. I took one look at the worried faces of my friends, then dissolved into a fit of childlike giggles.

Michael grinned even wider and held his hands up to get everyone's attention. "Don't worry, guys! Everything is fine! We had a misunderstanding but it's all sorted now, and we have some really awesome news." He glanced at me and raised an eyebrow. "Do you want to tell them, or shall I?"

"You do it," I said, still struggling to get my laughter back under control.

Gavin looked at me and raised an eyebrow, but he didn't say anything. Michael wrapped an arm around me and pulled me up against his side, then gently rested a hand on my belly. "Everyone, I am thrilled to announce that we are officially pregnant!"

A ripple of surprise passed through the gathered people, then Mary nudged her father in the side and cheered for us. Soon, everyone else joined in – everyone except Simon, who just looked even more embarrassed.

"And about bloody time," Gavin said, breathing a huge sigh of relief. He looked at me again, and gave me a very pointed scowl. "I'm not spying for you again, little miss. That was way too stressful."

"Speaking of which, you and I are going to have words about this later," Michael told him, in a tone of mock anger. "Come on, man! What happened to the bro-code?"

"I'm pretty sure that's not actually a thing," Gavin answered dryly. "And have words with your wife, it was her doing."

Michael laughed and gave me a squeeze. "Oh don't worry, we're going to be having plenty of words. Though now that I think about it, I *was* wondering why you were following me around like a lost puppy."

"I was not!" Gavin scoffed. "I just made excuses every now and then to strike up a conversation. Besides, I think that was secretly her plan all along. She wanted us to spend more time together so that your sense of humour would rub off on me."

"Guilty as charged," I said brightly. Then, I suddenly realised someone was missing and my amusement faded. "Hey, where's Simon? He was here a second ago."

The group glanced around, then exchanged looks and shrugs. I sighed and nodded.

"Honey, I need to go talk to him," I said to Michael. "He's still our friend, after all. He made a dumb mistake, but we can work through it and save our friendship. Can you and the others work with Madelyde to finish gathering up everything we need to take back home?"

"Sure, you just worry about Simon," he started to reply, then paused and looked at me quizzically. "Wait... when did we start calling her Madelyde?"

"Oh, uh, we didn't," I replied, embarrassed. "I've been calling her that inside my head since she got possessed, and it just kinda... came out."

"Ahh." Michael nodded understandingly and gave me a silly grin. "Just your inner monologue showing again. Gotcha. Off you go, talk to Simon. We'll be here when you get back."

He gave me a gentle shove in the direction of the airlock, just enough to get me moving. I caught myself easily and jogged past my friends, who reached out to pat me on the back and offer congratulations as I passed. By the time I was safely around the corner, I could feel myself blushing.

I wasn't sure how to feel about everyone knowing that I was knocked up. In some ways, it was kind of cool. In others, it was embarrassing as hell. I was doing my duty as one of the last women alive by propagating my species, but I still had conflicting feelings about that duty. It was all up to me and the thirty-two other women who had made their home in Tumanako. It was our duty to bear the next generation. It was an honour, but also a burden. In some ways it felt like my right to choose had vanished along with civilization, but in other ways I felt like I would have made the choice – or sacrifice, depending on how I looked at it – willingly in the end.

Without the miracles of modern medicine, carrying a child had become a huge risk again, just as it had been for our ancestors. But I was a Kiwi woman, the latest in a long line of pioneering women. Barely more than a hundred years before the plague, New Zealand had been a wilderness. Now she was a wilderness again, and I was going to help create a whole new type of pioneer.

I laughed and shook my head. Anahera's whole goddess earth mama vibe was starting to rub off on me, just like I'd hoped it would.

A few seconds later, I heard the sound of footsteps. I crept up to the corner and peered around it. Sure enough, there was Simon pacing back and forth, his expression so miserable that I immediately felt sorry for him. I took a deep breath to steel myself, then I stepped into his line of sight and waved. "Uh, hey."

"Oh, hey," he replied. He turned his back to me and hung his head. "I'm sorry. I feel like such an idiot. I guess I've completely lost my knack for reading people."

"It's okay, mate," I said, touching his shoulder. "It was an honest mistake, and an innocent one. Under different circumstances, I might have been flattered, or even reciprocated your interest. I had a celebrity crush on you for ages, you know?"

He glanced at me and smiled weakly. "You did?"

"Yeah, totally," I replied, smiling back at him. "If I weren't married, then you'd be my first choice." My smile faded and I glanced away. "Unfortunately, some things happened to me, Simon. Nasty things. Really nasty. I'm not as relaxed around men as my sister is. That's not your fault, either. You're a good person, and you deserve to be happy."

His shoulders sagged and he heaved a deep sigh. "Sometimes I wonder. I did everything I could think of to help, both in the past and now, but maybe it wasn't enough. Maybe I do deserve to be alone for the rest of my life."

I frowned and squeezed his shoulder. "Aw, hey, don't say that. You've given us more over the years than any of us had a right to ask. Keeping the news going gave us some kind of hope that maybe we could find civilization again. You kept me company when no one else did, even though you didn't know I existed. I guarantee that you won't be alone for long."

"You think so?" he asked, shooting a shy, uncertain glance at me.

"I know so." I winked and grinned. "I've caught more than one of the new girls giving you the eye, and I'll bet once the South Islanders get here you'll be fighting the ladies off with a stick. You're a good-looking man, Simon Wentworth – even if you do forget to shave a lot."

Simon smiled and rubbed a hand across his stubbly chin. "Yeah, I'm pretty forgetful. Scatter-brained. I always have been, to be honest. My producer said I was never going to amount to much. I could never remember my lines."

"Well, I guess you proved him wrong," I replied. "Because now you're the only celebrity we've got left."

"I'd disagree with that," he said dryly. "I may be a familiar face from the telly, but the only celebrity these people have – or need, for that matter – is you. You're the rock star here, not me."

"You're sweet," I said, then I gave him a light punch on the arm. "Now stop flirting with me. You keep that sugar for the single girls, you hear me?"

"I wasn't flirting, I was just being nice," he protested, though there was a twinkle of humour in his eyes.

I laughed and threaded my arm through his, then led him back to the rest of the group.

The others were waiting by the time we reached the elevator, in huddle around a stack of old computers, equipment, and filing cabinets. I released Simon's arm and gave him a pat on the shoulder, then went over to admire the stack of information we needed to lug back with us.

"This is going to keep you and Doc busy for days, Gav," I commented.

He glanced at me and heaved a sigh. "More like weeks, maybe even months."

"Take as much time as you need," I replied. "This project takes priority over everything else except food, water, and shelter, and we've got all of those things covered. We need that vaccine ready by the time Evie starts to wean."

He nodded and started gathering up equipment. The others pitched in to help him, all except for me and Madelyde. We had something else to discuss.

I guided Madelyde off to one side so that we weren't in the way, then I knelt down and put my hands on her shoulders. "Clyde, we're going to have to go soon. That means we need to figure out what to do about you and Madeline."

"I know," she said matter-of-factly. "Maddy and I have been discussing it at length, and we both think it's best if I stick around until the vaccine is ready – you know, in case you need anything."

I raised an eyebrow and gave her a long look. "And how is that going to work? You can't keep possessing Maddy forever. Aside from the fact that it would be weird and upset her grandfather a lot... well, what would you do when it's time to go to the bathroom?"

Madelyde gave me the kind of look that told me exactly what Clyde thought of that idea. "Don't be disgusting, I'm not going to stay in her body. This was just a temporary arrangement, and she could have booted me out at any time. Maddy says that the key card you took from my body has been close enough to me for long enough that it should be able to act as a focus, so that she can call me to her when you need to ask me questions. There's just one catch, though: it means you can't kill my body yet, and if my body falls apart on its own... well, we don't know exactly what will happen."

I shuddered at the thought, but nodded. "Whatever you two think is best. This is your show. But are you sure you want to linger here for that long? It can't be fun."

"It's not that bad," Madelyde replied with a faint smile. "I mean, it's not like I'm sitting around getting poked by a little devil with a pitchfork or something. There are still a lot of things to see and do. The Patupaiarehe are starting to come back now that most of the people are gone, and they sometimes roam down into these parts when there are no humans around. They don't like people, but they're friendly enough to rogue spirits."

"The Patuparawhats?" I repeated, confused. Madelyde just laughed and shook her head.

"Don't worry, you'll never see them," she said. "Not unless they want you to. Maddy might, but she'll tell you if they're going to be a problem. Anyway, I'd best let Maddy have her body back. As a matter of fact, she needs to go to the loo pretty badly right now. Lavatories are at the top of the elevator, two doors down on the right."

"Oh, well... goodbye, then," I said, shooting a glance at the others nearby.

Maddy blinked a few times, then shook her head as if to wake herself up. "Oh, he's gone. That was weird."

"Maddy?" I asked, touching the girl's cheek. "How do you feel, honey? Are you okay?"

"I'm fine, Miss Sandy," she replied, then she gave me a smile that was very much her own. "But... I really need to pee."

I laughed and nodded, easing myself back up to my feet. "Me too. Come on, let's go home."

***

It didn't take long to find the lavatories, then we loaded the Hilux up and we were back on the road. It was nearly sundown by the time we reached the outskirts of Tumanako. Just as we were nearing the front gate, someone shouted and waved frantically; it took a second before I realised it was Ryan. I glanced at the others, then put my heels to Boudicca's sides and urged her forward at a trot.

"What's wrong?" I demanded as soon as I was close enough to do so without shouting.

"We had an... arrival while you were out," he said, hurrying to open the gate for me. "I've been ordered to take you straight up as soon as you get here."

I raised an eyebrow, then dismounted and handed my reins to Michael without a word. I didn't need to say anything; Ryan's demeanour told us all that something was wrong. Very, very wrong.

Ryan led me in and waited with me for the elevator, but as soon as we were inside he pushed the button to close the doors and held it down so that they wouldn't open again until he was ready.

"Whatever happens in the next few minutes, I want you to know that I'm on your side," he said, his voice almost a whisper.

My heart leapt into my throat. "Ry? What is it?"

"You'll understand soon," he said cryptically. He took his finger off the button, and we rode the elevator up to the second floor in silence.

As soon as the doors slid open, I could hear the commotion coming from the dining room. People were shouting at one another, though I couldn't make out what they were saying. I glanced at Ryan again, suddenly afraid. The voices sounded angry. Were they angry at me?

Ryan took my arm and led me down the hall, into the dining room. As soon as the doors opened, people turned to look at me, their familiar faces so twisted by anger that I barely recognised them. I couldn't tell whether the anger was directed at me or not. I'd never seen so much rage in one place and I didn't know how to react to it, so I just froze.

Skylar appeared out of the crowd, shouting at those around her to calm down. She took one look at my face, then grabbed me and hugged me tight.

I clung to her, bewildered and confused. "What's going on? Why is everyone yelling at me?"

"You remember Bobby Wright, I presume?" she said. "Isabelle's son? Well, he showed up at the gates right after you left this morning, demanding that you be held accountable for the death of his stepfather. I've been trying to tell them that it was self-defence, but they're demanding a trial. It's the only way people will trust you again."

"Well, then," I said, struggling to keep myself rational despite the wave of animal panic that sought to overwhelm me. "Let's give the people what they want."

# Chapter Seventeen

As soon as the crowd heard that I'd agreed to a trial it began to calm down, with the exception of a handful of unfamiliar people that seemed to be Bobby's friends. While Skye was busy trying to negotiate with them, I was bundled out of the room and confined to my apartment with guards outside the door.

Still in shock, I sat down on the couch and just waited. Michael would be back soon enough, and then I'd have someone to talk to – or a shoulder to cry on, if I needed it. With my current hormone levels, tears were pretty much inevitable.

Sure enough, within a few minutes there was a fuss outside the door. I cringed at the sound of raised voices, but it took a second before I realised that the person shouting wasn't Michael, it was a young female. The door was flung open and Melody stormed in, followed closely by Priyanka and the twins. Priya rushed over and flung her arms around me, her eyes full of tears.

"You'll be all right, Mama," she told me. "We'll stand up for you. All of us. I'll be a—what's the word?"

"A witness," Melody supplied.

"Yes," she agreed, hugging me tight. "I'll be a witness. I saw what happened. You saved my life, and Baba's!"

"I know, honey," I whispered, hugging her back. "We did what we had to do. And now we're doing what we have to do again, for Bobby's sake."

"That stupid brat needs a swift kick in the teeth," Melody snapped, her demeanour tense and angry. "Just give me five minutes alone with him..."

"As satisfying as that would be, we don't want to stoop to that level," I said. "We need to do this, not just for Bobby's sake but for everyone's. People need to know that everyone will be held accountable for their actions, even me. Don't worry, we'll make it through this – and hopefully we'll give Bobby some closure in the process."

The conversation stalled when another ruckus started up outside the door, then Michael stormed in looking about as angry as I'd ever seen him. He took in the people gathered around me at a glance, then planted himself beside me and wrapped his arms around both me and Priya.

"I cannot believe this kid," he said, his voice almost a snarl. "He's down there right now, trying to rile people up. Last I heard was your sister threatening to lock him in a cupboard until he calmed down. It's like he's trying to cause a riot or something."

"I think he is," I said softly, snuggling up against his warm bulk for comfort. "Those people he's with, they're gangers. I'm guessing he found them on his way south and convinced them to come here and 'defend' him. I'll bet if we don't keep a really close eye on them, half our supplies will be gone by morning."

Michael swore under his breath, then shot a plaintive look at the twins. "Girls, can you please run a message for me? I need you to tell Tane and Iorangi to keep a close eye on these new folks, and not to let them anywhere near our supplies." He glanced at me and lowered his voice. "Or the women and children."

Jasmine and Lily nodded in perfect synchronization and dashed off, almost bumping into Anahera as she was making her way inside. She watched the twins go with raised eyebrows, then looked back at me and smiled.

"No wonder your guards are looking frustrated," she commented. "It seems that you've got a steady stream of visitors."

"I think they've given up on even locking the door," I answered dryly. "Not that they really need to. Where would I go? I've invested way too much in Tumanako to just run away."

"You won't have to, anyway," Anahera said with a smile. "This boy, Bobby – he knows he doesn't stand a chance, but he's making trouble because he can. Sometimes people do that. He and his friends have managed to convince a few of the newer members of our community that you are worthy of suspicion, but once they hear what actually happened, they'll understand."

"And if they don't," Melody said, her face set in an angry mask, "then they can leave any time they like!"

I laughed softly and shook my head. "There's your example of people making trouble, in the flesh!"

Everyone laughed right along with me, except for Melody. She just gave me a dark look, then turned away – but not quite fast enough to hide the smile breaking through her stony expression. It was fine, though. We'd gotten to know one another well enough over the last few months that I knew she wasn't offended by my teasing, even if she pretended to be. Still, I didn't want to risk alienating the people I needed most in the coming days, so I looked back at Anahera and changed the subject.

"I told Michael," I admitted. "It didn't quite go how I was planning, but the cat's out of the bag."

"Finally," Anahera said dryly. "At least now I can officially congratulate you both."

"Wait, what'd I miss?" Melody demanded.

"Well, as it so happens, Michael and I are expecting a baby," I told her shyly. "She's due around mid-summer."

"What?" Melody echoed, staring at me blankly. It took a good ten seconds before the news sunk in. Suddenly, her eyes lit up and she leapt on us with a squeal of delight. "Oh my God, you're having a baby?! You're so lucky!"

I yelped in surprise when I suddenly found myself in the middle of a people-sandwich, with Michael on one side, and Priya and Melody on the other.

"Well, it's not really luck," I gasped when I could finally catch a breath, then I paused and looked at her. "Wait – you guys do know where babies come from, right?"

"Of course we do," Melody replied, giving me an annoyed look. "The twins are obsessed with romance novels, remember? We figured it out." She heaved a long sigh, and her expression softened. "I really want to have a baby, but... I don't like boys."

"Well, if you really want to have a baby you could just borrow one for a night," I replied. "It's not like you have to get married."

"No, no, not like that." She shook her head vigorously and gave me a frown. "I don't like boys at all. I mean, I like them fine as people, but I don't want to have sex with them. It's gross. I like girls." Suddenly looking nervous, she shot a glance back and forth between me and Anahera. "Is that weird?"

Anahera smiled and shook her head. "Not at all, dear. There are many different types of people in the world. I like men and women equally. My soul mate just happened to be in a man's body."

The revelation of Anahera's bisexuality didn't faze me in the least. I'd suspected it from the moment I met her. She wasn't the sort to let gender boundaries hold her back. I just gave her a smile, then looked back at Melody. "Yeah, what she said. It's totally normal. Jim and Richard prefer men, and I'm pretty sure Iorangi is bi. You are the way nature made you, no big deal. If you want to have a baby, the doctor can help you."

"He can?" she asked, shooting a look of earnest curiosity at me. "How?"

"Artificial insemination," I replied. "Basically, you pick a guy you like enough to father the child, and if he agrees then the doctor can inject his sperm into you, without you having to have sex with him. You'll still have to have something going up there, of course, but it might be less uncomfortable for you. If you're serious, ask him. It's your choice."

Melody made a thoughtful sound and fell silent. Anahera looked at me again and gave me one of her delightfully radiant smiles. "Speaking of Jim and Richard – did you hear that they're engaged?"

"What?" I gasped. "No! When did that happen?"

"Last night," she replied. "Richard couldn't wait to tell me this morning. I've never seen him looking so happy.

"Oh, that's fantastic," I said, pleased beyond all reason by the news. I elbowed Michael and gave him a grin. "Who's a busybody now, huh?"

"Still you, honey," he replied without missing a beat. "But you mean well, and this time it worked out for the best."

Anahera looked at me with raised eyebrows, and suddenly I found myself muffling a girlish giggle. "I may have sent them on a few missions together, secretly hoping that they'd hit it off."

"You sneaky thing," she replied, a slow smile creeping across her face. "Well, they seem very happy and that's the important thing."

"Then my work here is done," I said brightly, sketching a bow as best I could under the circumstances. "Next project: find Simon a girlfriend."

"Why Simon?" she asked curiously. "He seems perfectly happy as he is."

I cleared my throat and shot a glance at Michael. "That's what I thought, until he tried to kiss me today."

"He did *what*?!" Melody gasped. Priya gaped at me, and even Anahera looked shocked.

"Yep," I said, nodding. "He thought that I was flirting with him, and that I was interested in a three-way relationship. I set him straight but now I kind of feel bad for him, you know?"

Anahera glanced down at her hands, a thoughtful expression crossing her face. "Perhaps I should go talk to him. We dated for a while, before I met my husband. There was a spark between us once. Maybe it's still there."

This time, it was my turn to look at her in shock. "I thought you weren't going to get involved with anyone after you lost your husband?"

"So I swore, but…" She let out a long, deep sigh and shrugged. "When I made that vow, I still had a young son to fill my life with laughter and love. Now, he's grown up and found a woman of his own, and my home is empty. It is the way of nature for little ones to leave the nest, and build nests of their own, but I still find myself feeling lonely."

"Aw, Ana." I reached for her, and gently touched her hand. "Then talk to him. Your husband would understand. He'd want you to be happy. It's been ten years – that's more than any reasonable person would ask their spouse to mourn for them. Go, talk to him right now. He's going to be feeling really sad tonight, after what happened. I'll be fine."

She nodded thoughtfully and glanced at the door. "I think I will. I'll be there for the trial, though, no matter what."

"Good. It wouldn't be any fun without you," I replied dryly, making a shooing motion at her. "Go on, off with you. The rest of us should head to bed, anyway."

"Have you eaten?" she asked, giving me one of those motherly looks that I'd gotten so used to.

"Not yet, but I've got some rations in my bag," I replied. "That'll do until breakfast. No point poking the hive, you know?"

"If you say so," she said. Melody hopped up and went over to her without being prompted, but Priya lingered beside me. Anahera smiled indulgently and held out a hand to her. "Come, little one. Let Mama and Baba sleep."

"I'm not little!" Priya protested. She still wriggled out of my arms and bounced over to stand in front of Anahera. "I had a growth spurt. See?"

"In more ways than one," Anahera said dryly. "We're going to need to get you a training bra soon, my dear."

I glanced at Michael, just in time to see him turn bright red and suddenly look very interested in a spot on the ceiling. The rest of us just exchanged a glance, then burst out laughing.

*** 

I woke early the next morning, dragged out of the warm, pleasant haze of sleep by the sound of shouting outside our door. Michael snorted awake and vaulted out of bed before I'd even had a chance to figure out what was going on. He rushed out of our bedroom while I was still struggling to get my clothes on, and I heard his voice join in the shouting. I was just pulling on my shoes and socks when he returned, grim-faced and angry.

"Trouble?" I asked softly, struggling to keep my wits about me and stay strong even though I was terrified.

Michael nodded, glaring over his shoulder at the door. "Bobby. He wants the trial to begin now, and he's angry the guards wouldn't let him drag you out of bed." He looked back at me and his expression softened. "I'm glad I assigned guards who are on your side. This is turning into a witch hunt."

"I knew this was going to get bad the second I met him," I admitted, reaching out to touch Michael's hand. "They may not be related by blood, but that kid is a lot like his stepfather."

"Unfortunately for him," Michael replied, hugging me tenderly. "You're being really patient about all of this. I have to admit, I'm surprised. I half expected you to be out there kicking his ass."

"I need to lead by example now, and I have more to worry about than just myself," I said, resting a hand over my belly. "I can't go rushing off half-cocked anymore. I have to think about her. I should probably stop going on missions outside Tumanako soon – well, assuming I don't get assassinated on the way to my trial today."

"Don't say that," Michael protested, laying his hands over mine. "There are only five of them, and Bobby's the only one actively trying to cause trouble. The majority of the people here consider you their friend and ally, and if it comes to it then we'll fight to protect you."

I smiled and nodded, though I wasn't really as reassured as I pretended to be. "We should go get this over with, but I really need to pee first. This baby thing is hard."

"I'd apologise for that, but I'm not sorry at all," he said dryly, helping me to my feet. He kept his arm around me as he led me to the door, carefully shielding me with his body just in case. I could hear voices speaking outside even before the door opened, but at least they weren't shouting any more. Michael knocked on the door, and waited for the guards to unlock it. When it opened, the first thing I saw was Skylar standing not far from the doorway, speaking calmly and rationally to a mixed group of faces both new and old. On either side of her stood Ryan and Hemi, weapons in their hands and expressions of steely determination on their faces.

"…with us in a second," she said, making a placating gesture. "Just give her time. She made the rules, and if there's one thing I know about my sister it's that she's a stickler for leading by example."

"Skye," I whispered, reaching out to touch her shoulder. She glanced back at me and gave me a reassuring smile.

"See, there she is, just like she promised," she said to the crowd. "Head down to the dining room, everyone. We'll be announcing the adjudicator in a few minutes."

"When did Skylar become such a good bailiff?" I whispered to Michael. She overheard me and shot me a glance, but her expression was unreadable.

"She needs the 'loo before we begin," Michael said, his face revealing no trace of his usual sense of humour.

Skye nodded to the guards, who stepped forward and made a path for us through the wall of bodies. As soon as we were free of the crowd, Michael picked up the pace. By the time we reached the bathroom, we were almost running.

Anahera was waiting there, flanked by every single one of my closest female friends. They took over guard duty from Michael, and protected me while I raced through my early-morning ablutions. Once I was ready, they surrounded me in a wall of protective bodies and led me down to the dining room. The tables had all been pushed back against the walls and the chairs arranged into a makeshift courtroom, with a handful on one side of the room and the rest in rows so that people could observe the proceedings. The seats were already packed, and as I was led inside all eyes turned towards me.

"How are we going to pick the adjudicator?" I asked Anahera nervously.

She squeezed my arm and gave me a reassuring smile. "We drew up a list of eligible candidates last night and held a vote on it. They're just counting up the votes now."

Michael and Priya were both waiting for me up the front. The makeshift courtroom had been set up with a low platform in the middle for the adjudicator and the witness stand, and groups of chairs on each side for the prosecution and the defence. Anahera guided me into a seat between my husband and foster daughter, then stood back to wait.

I glanced at the prosecution and saw Bobby glaring at me from amidst his friends. The boy had grown a couple of inches since I'd last seen him, and gained a rather prominent tattoo on the side of his neck. That set off alarm bells in my head: I recognised the symbol as belonging to one of the gangs that I'd so carefully avoided over the years. The people with him were male, heavily scarred, covered in tattoos, and practically reeking of danger. I glanced at the crowd, and checked faces against the ever-increasing list of citizens I kept in my head.

As if sensing my concern, Anahera leaned forward and touched my shoulder. "Everyone is safe and accounted for, don't worry. Elly and Rebecca are looking after the younger children downstairs and the people on guard duty are all loyal to you. They have walkie-talkies on them, so if anything happens we'll know about it."

I nodded and took a deep breath, willing myself to relax. It wasn't going to happen, though. As positive as I was that I'd only done what I needed to do to protect my family, Henry's death had always bothered me. I felt guilty about it, and that feeling coloured my thoughts.

The kitchen door opened and Skylar emerged, again flanked by Ryan and Hemi. A step behind her was a tall, dark-haired man I didn't recognise. Although he had the same tattoo on his neck as the other gangers Bobby had brought with him, he carried himself differently, with authority and a confidence that reeked of intelligence rather than violence.

Skye stood in front of the gathered crowd and addressed them without further ado. "We've counted your votes, and Johan has been selected to act as the adjudicator. Johan, please come forward."

All eyes turned to the veterinarian. He stood and came to the front, his expression unreadable. While he was settling into the adjudicator's chair, Skylar addressed the crowd again.

"I will be acting as Sandy's defence," she said, then she gestured to the tall man following her. "This is Owen Gordon. He'll be speaking on behalf of the prosecution. Whenever you're ready, Owen."

"Thank you, Miss McDermott," Owen replied. His voice was smooth and practiced, and something about it sent a shiver down my spine. It didn't take a rocket scientist to guess that he'd probably been a lawyer before the plague. "My client accuses the defendant of murder, for taking the life of Henry Barrett in cold blood four months ago. Sandrine McDermott, the prosecution calls you to bear witness."

I took another deep breath and stood up, making my way up onto the makeshift stage to sit in the witness chair. Suddenly I felt very alone and exposed, looking out across the sea of faces. I swallowed hard and looked at Owen.

"Ms McDermott," he said, "please tell us in your own words what happened that day."

I started in surprise and looked at Skye. "Just like that? Aren't you supposed to swear me in or something?"

"What, you want me to make you swear on a Bible?" she said dryly. "Last time I checked, you were an atheist obsessed with telling the truth anyway. Just tell us what happened."

"Okay, okay." I backed down and closed my eyes, focusing on the story I had to tell. It was a story I'd replayed a thousand times in my head but it still seemed somehow unreal, as if it had happened to someone else or occurred in a dream I only half remembered. "It started when we were living in Ohaupo – 'we' being Michael, Skylar, Doctor Cross, Madeline, and myself. We'd received a plea for help by radio, from Jim and Rebecca at the Arapuni Power Station. We agreed to help them. Michael and I originally set off in our car, but it broke down near Te Awamutu and forced us to travel the rest of the way on foot. Along the way, we met Priyanka and decided to bring her with us.

"While we were passing through the township of Pukeatua, Henry Barrett ambushed us. He came up behind us and grabbed Priyanka by the throat before I knew he was there. He said that I could leave if I wanted, but he was going to kill Michael and Priyanka..." I paused for a second, glancing towards the prosecution, "...because he said he believed anyone who wasn't fair-skinned and of European descent was responsible for the plague."

A stir passed through the crowd at that. While many of us matched that description, myself included, more than half of the people in the room did not.

Owen glanced at the crowd, then looked back at me. "I bet that made you angry, didn't it?"

"I married a Chinese man and adopted an Indian girl as my daughter," I answered dryly. "You better believe that it made me mad."

"Did you try to talk to him?" Owen asked. "Or did you just decide that was enough to warrant his death?"

I shot him a scathing look and a deep frown. "Of course I tried to talk him down. We both did. He wouldn't let us reason with him, and he had a machete against Priyanka's throat. As soon as I saw an opportunity, I took it."

"So, you admit that you attacked him first?" Owen asked, raising his eyebrows.

"No, he'd already attacked us," I argued. "He'd grabbed Priya and was holding a bloody great machete against her throat. He'd left bruises on her and told us twice that he was going to kill her and Michael."

"But you said that he was willing to let you go," Owen said. "Why didn't you just leave?"

"He said he was willing to let *me* go, as in just me," I repeated. "He wasn't going to let Michael or Priya go."

"Doesn't that make it their problem, then?" Owen said cryptically. "Your argument is that it was self-defence, but *you* were in no direct danger."

"But the people I love were!" I argued back, stunned and furious by the implication of his words. "Would you leave your wife and child to die? Of course not! It was my duty to defend them."

"But you weren't married at the time, and you didn't have a formal adoption," Owen said, his expression one of practiced intensity. "So you're telling us that you killed someone because he said threatening things to the man you were sleeping with and a girl you'd just met?"

"I didn't kill him," I snapped, anger clouding my mind. I knew that every word I said was being measured and judged, but for a second I was just too furious to care. "I haven't finished telling everyone what happened yet! Would you just shut up and let me tell the story?"

Someone in the crowd laughed at my outburst, and a few others whooped and whistled. Owen glared at them until they fell silent, then finally nodded to me.

I nodded curtly in return and resumed my narrative. "Henry had Priya pinned, with one hand around her throat, and in the other hand he was holding this massive machete. He got himself so angry while he was ranting and raving that his guard dropped for a second. I could tell by that stage the only way I was going to save Priya was to go on the offensive, so I did. I hit him in the face with the butt of my shotgun to distract him, then I yanked Priya out of his grip."

"So, your foster daughter was safe?" Owen extrapolated. "But you continued the fight?"

"No, I did not," I replied, giving him another scathing look to shut him up. "I stayed on the defensive. He attacked me. I had a shotgun, but I did not at any point shoot him with it. I was trying really hard not to kill him or even do any permanent harm. I can't say he felt the same way." To illustrate my point, I lifted the hem of my shirt up to reveal a deep scar across my ribs from where the machete had cut me. "This is what he did to me. Can you imagine what he would have done to Priya?"

Another ripple passed through the crowd. I glanced over and caught them exchanging looks and whispers, and I could see uncertainty on more than one face. I lowered my shirt and looked back at Owen.

"It's important to note that Henry was a very big man," I said, raising my voice a little more, so that there could be no doubt that everyone could hear me. "He must have been six-five, built like a bodybuilder, outfitted in full battledress and carrying a sidearm in a holster. I mean, Michael's big and even I'm on the tall side, but this guy could have torn Priya in half if he wanted. She was terrified – hell, I was terrified. Any sane person would be when there's a wall of muscle coming at you swinging a machete. I managed to flatten him with a well-placed kick to the groin, but not for long. We grabbed Priya and ran for our lives."

"You ran?" Owen echoed. For the first time, he looked a little uncertain of himself.

"Yes, we ran," I replied. "He had other men with him, all of them armed. I managed to knock one over before he could shoot us, then we all ran into the bush. While we were running, we heard him shouting orders to the other men. He ordered them to kill us. We were travelling on foot and we were heavily outnumbered. I had to do something… something I didn't want to do."

"What did you do?" Owen asked, and this time there was no guile in his voice, just honest curiosity.

I sat up a little straighter and steeled myself. "Priya, honey, I want you to cover your ears."

"Yes, Mama," she replied obediently. I didn't have to look to know that she'd done as instructed. She was still a good girl like that, even with Melody's rebellious influence.

"While we were running, I heard the sound of pigs in the bush nearby," I said, forcing myself to lift my voice high enough to be heard even though I dreaded saying the words. "There were two of them, a boar and a sow. Both infected, of course. I sent Michael and Priya off towards Arapuni, and then I shot the pigs to goad them into chasing me. That was the only time I fired my weapon. Then I turned and ran back towards Henry and his men with the pigs hot on my tail."

There were gasps all around the room, and the whispering increased in volume. I swallowed hard and looked Owen right in the eye. "At the time, I didn't think it was going to work. It felt suicidal. I've fought pigs off before, but never by myself. I made the choice, even if it cost me my life, because it might just buy my loved ones the time to escape. I could still hear Henry shouting for his men to kill us, so I ran towards the sound of his voice. He grabbed me and we scuffled for a second, but I managed to get away and hide just in time. He didn't see the pigs coming. They knocked him to the ground, and they… they killed him."

Tears welled up in my eyes, and I suddenly found myself unable to maintain eye-contact any longer. "I didn't mean for any of it to happen. We were trying to do the right thing, to help the people at Arapuni keep the power going. We didn't know anyone lived in Pukeatua, and there were no warning signs. We had no way to know about Bobby and Isabelle, and by the time we'd fought off the rest of Henry's men we were too exhausted to even think about the possibility that they might have had captives. I've regretted what happened for every moment since, and I don't think I'll ever stop regretting it, but even now I can't think of anything else I could have done."

I finally worked up the courage to look up and found Owen watching me thoughtfully. After a few long seconds, he looked at Johan. "I have no more questions."

Johan nodded and looked at Skylar. "Do you have any questions for her?"

"Nope," Skye said dryly. "As usual, my sister has managed to express herself quite eloquently. I would, however, like to call a few new witnesses to the stand. Some new information has come to light in relation to the nature of the deceased."

"Oh?" Johan raised his eyebrows and looked at her curiously. "That's fine, but who did you have in mind?"

"Solomon and Charu," she said, her expression one of stern resolution. She turned to face the crowd, and beckoned to the young man in question. "Solo, are you still happy to come up here and tell us what Henry Barrett did to your family?"

Solomon leapt to his feet, nodding vigorously. He said something that none of us could understand thanks to his missing tongue – none of us, except for Melody.

"He says that he will, for Sandy's sake," Melody translated. "He says that it's a painful memory for him, but Sandy's always been kind to him so he'll do it for her."

"All right, come on up here," Johan said. He glanced at me and gave me a smile. "You can go back to your seat, Sandrine."

I relinquished the witness chair and rushed back to my place with Michael and Priya. They both hugged me, and then we all turned our attention to Solomon. Melody came up to the stand with him, to act as a interpreter. Solomon looked at me for a second, then looked back at Skylar and began to speak. It was the first time I'd heard more than two words out of his mouth, and listening to him struggle over his syllables hurt more than I'd ever imagined it could. He was so determined to get his story across, though. I'd never seen that kind of look on his face, and it made me proud.

"Solomon's grandfather was the leader of the Samoan gang in Tokoroa," Melody translated as the young man spoke. "They were happy there, and hurt no one. Occasionally people came to trade with them. That's how Henry Barrett got inside their compound. He said that he was there to trade, but once his men were inside the walls they started shooting…"

# Chapter Eighteen

By the time Solomon finished telling the gruesome tale of his torture and mutilation, there were tears running down my cheeks and I had my hands clamped firmly over Priya's ears. She had been through enough; I didn't want her to have to think about that kind of pain. It made me sick to my stomach, and if I'd eaten breakfast then I might have lost it. Even Owen looked a little green around the gills.

Skye didn't stop there, though. She called Charu to the stand next, and he came willingly for the same reason as Solomon. Part of me was grateful that they were so willing to help me, but a bigger part was just horrified by what they'd gone through. The emotional onslaught didn't stop with Charu, though. Once he was done, Skye called Isabelle to the stand.

Like the others, Isabelle came willingly, but she was obviously feeling miserable. The only person she'd look at was me, as if looking at me and thinking about how she was helping me kept her focused on what she wanted to do. Hearing her story was too much for me, it struck too close to the bone. I pleaded for a momentary respite to collect myself, and Johan permitted it. Anahera took me by the shoulders and led me out, just as Skye was calling Michael to the stand.

We managed to make it to the ladies room before I broke down and wept as if my heart was breaking. Anahera just hugged me and held me silently, letting me vent my grief on her shoulder like the mother I'd lost ten years ago. That was all I could ask from anyone, even when I didn't have the words to express how much I needed it.

Eventually, my tears ran dry. Anahera helped me over to the sink so that I could wash my face, then she led me back to the dining room where the trial had continued without us. Michael's testimony was over and he'd been released back to his seat. Skylar called Priya's name. She promptly panicked and looked around for me. It wasn't until she saw that I was on my way back that she relaxed again. I gave her a quick, reassuring hug and sent her up to give her testimony.

I barely heard a word she said. I was feeling so drained, both physically and emotionally, that I planted my face in the side of Michael's neck and stayed there. Owen barely had any questions for her, and now when he asked them he was subdued. No more doublespeak, no more trying to catch us in lies or twist our words to make us sound guilty. The time for that was long past; now, he looked as exhausted as I felt. The only person who seemed to have any energy left was Bobby, who was still glaring at me in spite of everything.

Once Priya had been sent back to her seat, Johan looked at Owen and Skylar. "It seems like we're just about done here, unless any of you have any other witnesses you'd like to call?"

"Nope, I think we've made our case," Skye said. Everyone looked at Owen, but he just shook his head.

"All right, well I think the verdict is fairly obvious," Johan said. He glanced around for a second and shrugged sheepishly. "I feel like I should bang a gavel or something, but I don't have one. It's obvious to me that Sandrine was just doing what she had to do to protect the people she cares about, and that she made every reasonable attempt to salvage the situation. I find her not guilty of the charge of murder. If anyone believes I have made the wrong decision, please raise your hand."

We all looked at the gathered crowd expectantly. Not a single hand rose. I let out a deep breath I hadn't even realised I'd been holding until that moment, and managed a weak smile.

Before I could say anything, Bobby rocketed out of his chair, red-faced and shouting. "What?! That's it? She killed him, and you're just going to let her get away with it? That's bullshit! You bitch! I'll kill you, you stupid bitch!"

Gasps of shock and horror echoed through the crowd as Bobby vaulted right over the table and rushed at me, slipping through the fingers of his gang-mates when they tried to hold him back. Ryan grabbed me and pulled me away, while Michael and the guards on duty rushed in to try and subdue him.

He was strong, though. That growth spurt had packed muscle on him, and I could see the other men struggling to hold him back. Ryan tugged my arm and pulled me towards the door, but I resisted him. Too many people I loved were in that room for me to just run away. I wanted to help. I wanted to fight! There were so many bodies everywhere that I could barely make out what was happening – but I definitely heard the scream.

"Look out! He's got a gun! *He's got a gun!*"

The world seemed to slow down in that instant, and everything came into perfect focus. I saw Michael lose his balance and fall to the ground, giving Bobby the moment of opportunity he needed to lift that gun and point it straight at me.

A body flew into me just at the moment the gunshot rang out, bowling me right off my feet. I hit the ground so hard that it left me momentarily stunned. By the time I'd regained my wits enough to shove myself up, Bobby had vanished beneath a mound of angry bodies.

Unfortunately, his single shot was enough to turn my world upside-down.

"Ryan!" Skylar gasped, rushing past me. "No, no, no, oh God, hold on!"

She dropped to her knees beside him, frantically trying to staunch the blood pumping from his chest. Doctor Cross flung himself down beside her a second later and joined in the efforts, but the wound was too deep. I could see the blood around the wound frothing and bubbling as air escaped from his lungs with every breath.

"Skye?" he whispered, groping for her hand. His skin was already turning pale from shock, paler than I'd ever seen it before.

"I'm here, Ryan," she said, grabbing his hand in both of hers and holding it to her chest. "Just stay with me. Doc will take care of you."

He tried to answer, but all that came out was a sick gurgling. Skye leaned in close to listen, but I couldn't make out what he was saying from afar. I could see her nodding as she listened to him struggling to speak. People gathered around me, whispering and staring, and I shared the sense of disbelief running through the mob.

"This wasn't supposed to happen," Owen said. I hadn't noticed him come up beside me, and part of me was too deeply in shock to understand what he was saying. I glanced at him and saw the same kind of utter stupefaction on his face. "No one was supposed to get hurt. We just wanted to see what was going on here, and get Bobby justice. This... this wasn't supposed to happen."

"Well, it did," I replied, my words coming out much harsher than I intended. The sound of my own hoarse voice stirred me out of my daze. There was nothing I could do for Ryan now, and he was in the most capable hands we had. In the meantime, there was a situation that needed to be addressed. "Where's Bobby?"

"Unconscious, I think," Owen replied. I looked around, but all I could see was a crowd of faces watching on with concern. At the back of the crowd, I spotted Rebecca and Aaron trying to get through; Bobby was forgotten for the moment, in favour of getting Ryan the medical care that he needed.

"Make way!" I shouted, putting as much force behind my words as I could. "Let them through! Make a hole, people!"

Whether it was my tone of voice or the expression on my face, people moved enough for the two nurses to get through. By the time they reached him, Ryan had lapsed into unconsciousness. Skylar knelt on the floor, just staring into space while the doctor and nurses picked Ryan up and raced him off to the infirmary.

I went to my sister's side and put my arms around her. It was the only thing I could do for her now. Skye hugged me and buried her face in the side of my neck, silent and shivering. Everyone around us fell silent, and when I glanced up I could see them exchanging uncertain looks.

Suddenly, someone shoved through from the back of the crowd, and I heard a familiar deep, husky voice ordering people out of the way. A few seconds later, Michael burst through, his expression frantic. He rushed over to us and wrapped both of us up in a hug. Skye barely seemed to notice, but I was grateful for it.

"What happened to Bobby?" I asked him over my sister's head. "Owen said he was unconscious?"

"He got knocked out in the scramble," Michael replied. "I had my boys move him to one of the spare rooms and lock him up. We can deal with him later. Ryan...?"

"They took him to the infirmary," I said quietly. "We don't know yet, but..."

"It's an unsurvivable wound," Skye said, her voice laced with a mixture of bitterness and regret. "If he's not dead yet, then he will be soon." She laughed, but there was no humour in it. "He knew it. He was trying to say goodbye, but he couldn't speak properly."

I sighed heavily and tightened my grip on her. "I'm so sorry, Skye. After everything you two have been through together... it just isn't fair."

"Life isn't fair," she replied. This time, her voice lost its bitter edge and just sounded exhausted, far more exhausted than any eighteen-year-old had a right to be. "He made a choice, and he chose to save you."

"He didn't just save me, though," I said. "He saved my baby, too. He saved my family. He must have known the risk, but he made that choice anyway." I glanced up and made eye contact with Michael. "At least now we know what to name the baby."

"Actually, I might have to fight you for that," Skylar said. "I think I'm pregnant again. I'm late. Just a few days, but... if I am, it might be his, or it might be Hemi's. I guess I won't know until after it's born."

I felt tears gather in my eyes, and this time I made no attempt to hide them. "Dammit, little sis. When I said that we needed to repopulate the earth, I didn't mean that we had to do it personally."

Skye managed another humourless laugh and wriggled out of our three-way embrace. "I want to wait with him. Even if he's not awake. I need to say goodbye."

"Do you want me to come with you?" I asked.

She shook her head. "No. I just need some space, please. I know where you are if I need you."

Part of me screamed in protest about leaving her alone at a time like this, but she'd proven time and again that she was mature enough to cope with far more than I knew how to give her credit for. I was learning, though. I was learning not just how to be there for her when she needed me, but how to take a step back and not pressure her when she needed space. That was a hard lesson for me when all of my instincts told me to wrap her up in cotton wool and protect her from the world.

"Can we at least walk you to the infirmary?" I asked, reaching out to touch her hand. Skye just nodded and threaded her fingers through mine, letting me offer her what comfort I could from physical contact.

The crowd parted in front of us as we walked out of the dining hall, with Michael a step behind us. The infirmary was so close that it was a symbolic gesture more than anything else, but Skye seemed to appreciate it. When we got there, we found Hemi waiting outside the door. He took Skylar's elbow and guided her inside, leaving the rest of us out in the hall.

I looked at Michael, but he had no advice or guidance for me today. None of us had known Ryan for more than a year except for Skye, but he'd touched so many of our lives. I took Michael's hand and sat down on the floor. The least we could do was sit out the death watch in his honour.

# Chapter Nineteen

People came and went over the course of the next few hours, but Michael and I stayed. Maddy came to join us, carrying Tigger in her arms. The kitten – now a young-adult – pranced back and forth across our laps, then curled up and went to sleep on my thigh. I stroked her for a while, but there were no words to make my churning gut feel any better today.

Slowly but surely, other people came to join the watch. Priya brought Alfred up, though the old sheepdog had no idea what was going on. He lay down beside Michael and went straight back to sleep, while Priya sat down in front of us and stared into space. Elly, Zain, and their older boys sat on the floor not far away, and Richard and Jim sat across from them. Anahera and the rest of the Waikato Iwi arrived one by one, and then other citizens started to join us as well. Eventually, the hall was packed with people.

I couldn't look at them. Seeing so many people gathered around just made it all seem more real, and I couldn't bring myself to accept the reality of his impending death just yet. I knew that the doctor would do everything in his power to save Ryan's life, but we weren't equipped to treat gunshot wounds, let alone collapsed lungs. My gut told me his death was inevitable, and that was so tragic that it made my mind scream and thrash in rebellion. Too many young people had died. Far too many. Sophie, Dog, Kylie, and now Ryan – they'd barely had a chance to live. It wasn't fair for them to have to die. Netty had broken my heart, but at least she'd lived a full life and gone to her grave on her own terms.

Another friend, gone forever in the blink of an eye.

"This is the last one," I said softly, as much to myself as anyone else. "We can't lose anyone else before their time. We just can't. It's wrong. He's the last one. For his sake, this cannot happen again."

Michael touched my shoulder, a simple gesture that told me he understood, then he rose to his feet. "I'll be back in a minute. I'm going to go get something."

I nodded dumbly, my head a million miles away and busy replaying the collection of moments that Ryan and I had shared together. Our joy over their baby, then despair. The moments when we'd sighed together over Skye's stubborn nature and swapped loving jokes at her expense. In a few minutes, those memories were going to be the only thing I had left of my friend.

I was still brooding when Michael returned and sat beside me, carrying his violin in its case.

"My parents taught me that the dying can still hear, and sometimes music can ease their passing," he explained as he set the case on the ground at his feet.

I just nodded again, closed my eyes, and leaned back against the wall to listen. While I might not share his beliefs, I accepted them for what they were and was happy to let him do what he wanted to do. If there was even the slightest chance that it would help, then it was worth it. More people joined us as Michael played, squeezing into whatever gap they could find in that narrow hallway. It was hard to judge the passage of time without watches or windows, but it didn't really matter anyway. We would wait as long as it took, for the sake of our friend.

Just as I was thinking that, Madeline reached out and touched my hand, then Michael's. The violin fell silent.

"We need to go in now," she said. "It's time."

"Time for what?" I whispered.

"Time to say goodbye," she replied simply. The little girl rose and beckoned for us to follow her, then led the way into the infirmary. Nobody seemed surprised by our arrival, not anymore. Madeline's gift had seen to that. Skye was sitting beside Ryan's bed, her face drawn and red, but no tears shone in her eyes. Doctor Cross and the nurses were covered in his blood from their efforts to save him, but now they'd given up and just stood in a huddle nearby, their expressions utterly devoid of hope.

I went straight to Skylar's side and put my arms around her without being asked. She looked up at me, her face unreadable.

"I can't cry," she told me. "I should, but... I feel like I've already said goodbye to him. I don't know how to do it again. Ever since he told me that he tried to kill himself, I knew we were living on borrowed time. I knew it wouldn't be long until we were saying goodbye for the last time. The man who came back after Kylie's death was never *my* Ryan, the happy-go-lucky kid with the ready laugh and the shy eyes. I buried my Ryan when I buried our daughter. I still love him, and I'll always love him, but... now all I feel is relief. Every minute of our lives is pain and struggle. He's played his part, and now he doesn't have to suffer any longer. He's finally free of the misery, the fear, and the dread, and who knows? Maybe he's gone to be with Kylie and our parents. He's at peace. It's the rest of us I'm worried about."

I looked at Ryan, struggling to process her words but I couldn't. I just stared and stared, and all I could think was that I'd never seen his freckles stand out so much. The rosy glow of life was already fading away, leaving his skin pale and translucent. It was a miserable thing to see. He was far, far too young to die. I felt a small hand touch my back, and then I heard Madeline's voice.

"He wants me to tell you not to worry about him, Miss Sandy," she said, her voice soft and serious. "He always knew he'd give his life to save a McDermott someday, and you've been a good friend to him. He says to make the most of it, and to remember every day as his last gift."

A shiver ran down my spine, much as it did every time she spoke for the dead and dying. I closed my eyes and nodded. "Thank you. Please tell him that I appreciate it. My baby appreciates it. We'll never forget him."

"He says that he already knows that," she replied, then she looked at Michael. "He wants you to know that he's not angry at you. He knows why you treated him the way you did, and he gets it. He says that he's always respected you, and he wishes fate had given him the time to earn your friendship back. He wants you to promise to take care of his girls for him."

Michael drew a deep breath and nodded sharply. "I promise, and... thank you. Please tell him that I forgive him. I made a mistake by treating him the way I did, because I didn't understand his choices until it was too late. But when it came time to make the most important choice of all, he made exactly the same one that I hope I would have been strong enough to make. I'll remember him as a brother and a friend."

"That made him happy," Maddy said with a smile and a nod, then she turned to Skylar at last. "Miss Skye... he wants me to tell you that you made his life worth living, and that you were his first and only love. You were his hopes and dreams, and he'll be waiting for you when it's your time – which he hopes will not be for a long time."

I looked up just in time to see a smile cross Skylar's face. Finally, tears welled up in her eyes. She reached out and took Ryan's pale hand, pressing it to her cheek.

"You silly boy," she whispered. "I'll miss you so much. I'm so glad you came back and I'll always be grateful for the time we had together. You better be waiting for me when I get there. If you aren't, I'll hunt you down."

I hugged her tighter, and felt Michael's arms closing around both of us again. A few seconds later, I heard Maddy sigh. "He's gone."

"May he rest in peace," I said softly. Around me, I heard the stir of people in distress, followed by a wave of grief and confusion. Though few had been as close to him as we were, everyone had known him in some way. Now, for the first time, Tumanako had to grieve as a community.

***

We buried Ryan just before sunset, in the park overlooking the river. Just like the graves in Hamilton, we picked a beautiful green place with old trees and wildflowers scattered amidst the long grass. It rained again, just like it always seemed to, but that didn't deter anyone from attending the funeral. Even Owen and his comrades joined us; they stood off to one side with their heads bowed respectfully while I read a short eulogy and shared a few stories from our time together. By the time I was done, everyone was dripping wet, shivering, and red-faced from crying.

One by one, the others drifted away to find dry clothes and warm up, until only a few of my most trusted friends and family remained. I looked around at the ring of faces and heaved a long sigh. "We need to figure out what to do about Bobby."

"If he were a few years older, then the answer would be obvious," Doc said, his expression troubled. "But he's just a child. We cannot execute a child, and exiling him would inevitably come back to haunt us. Imprisoning him seems like the logical option, but we aren't equipped for a long-term prisoner."

"No, we aren't," I agreed. "We don't need to hold a trial to determine whether he's guilty or not this time. We all saw him do it. But... Skye, you're the next of kin. What do you want us to do?"

"He's just a kid," she said, her expression sad but thoughtful. "Ryan wouldn't want him to die, and if we exile him then you know Isabelle would go with him and she doesn't deserve to be punished. There must be another option."

"Give him to me," Gavin said. All eyes turned to him.

"What do you mean?" I asked.

"I mean, let me take custody of him for the duration of his punishment," he replied, absently flexing his hands. "You're right that execution is out of the picture, exile is a bad idea, and imprisonment is impractical. That just leaves rehabilitation. Taming rotten youngsters is kind of my field of expertise, isn't it? With enough time, patience, and a firm, guiding hand, I bet I can turn him into a productive member of our community."

I looked at Skylar and raised my eyebrows. "If anyone can, it's Gavin. What do you think?"

"I..." Skye hesitated, uncertainty flickering across her face. "If you think you can do that, then I agree. It's what Ryan would want. He was really listening to what you've been saying these last few months, Sandy. About lives being precious, and that we can't be too quick to kill or we risk becoming the very monsters we're fighting against. We talked about it a lot, and I'm starting to believe it, too."

I nodded and reached out to touch her arm, then I looked at Gavin. "You know it's not going to be easy. He's going to fight you every step of the way."

"Of course he is," Gavin replied, a faint smile crossing his scarred face. "Nothing in life is easy. It's not meant to be. It wouldn't feel like an achievement if it were. Still, I'm willing to do it if you're willing to let me."

"Then I'm officially putting you in charge of his rehabilitation," I replied. "Just ask for any resources or assistance you need, and I want a progress report every few days. I'll leave it in your hands."

"You make the public announcement, and I'll take care of Isabelle?" he suggested.

"I better tell her," I said. "As much as I'd love to not have to deal with that conversation, Isabelle trusts me. If it's going to come from anyone, it should come from me. Take Michael and Skye with you, and tell the others what's going to happen."

We started to head back towards Tumanako, but before we'd made it more than a few hundred meters we spotted a handful of figures standing in the gloom beneath a nearby tree. I held up a hand to halt the others, and went forward to meet Owen on my own.

Less than a year ago, I wouldn't have dreamed of confronting a gang on my own, but so much had changed since then. I was a different person now: stronger, more self-assured, and backed by a group of people that I trusted with my life. I came to a stop a few meters away from them and gave Owen a curious look.

"I thought you lot had gone home," I said, carefully modulating my tone so it was neither mocking nor accusative, but merely interested.

"We're about to leave, but we wanted to talk to you first," Owen replied. He hesitated for a second, then stepped out of the tree's shadow and came over to me. "We wanted to apologise for everything that happened. We knew the kid was a bit unbalanced, but we didn't know how imbalanced. He found us about a month ago, all full of fire and brimstone, shouting something about justice for his dad. If my father had still been in charge he'd probably have sent the kid packing, but I made the mistake of believing him. Dad just died a few months ago, and something about his situation struck a chord with me. I should have known better."

"Okay, fair enough," I said. "I don't blame you for what Bobby did. He's the only one responsible for his own actions. You're free to go any time you want."

"Actually, that's just it," he said, absently scratching his neck. "The lads and I… we don't particularly want to go. We've got nothing to go back to. There are people here – real people, normal people, good people. Underneath the leather and tattoos, we're just like everyone else. We crave normality. We dream about having a home again. We're not bad people, either. I know some of the gangs think nothing of using violence to get what they want, but Dad never let us turn into that. He was a biker, but he was a good man. If you're willing to have us, then we'd like to help you build a home for all of us right here."

In spite of the day's tragedy, a smile crept across my face. "Well, all right. But no stealing from us, okay?"

"If we stole from you, then we'd be stealing from ourselves," he answered. "We never wanted to steal to begin with. Hell, I was a prosecutor for the crown. My job was making sure murderers and child-molesters saw justice. Necessity makes criminals of us all."

"That is very true, unfortunately," I replied. "Okay, let's go see which rooms are available."

"Can I do that?" Skylar asked, coming up behind me. "I'd rather keep myself busy with work than have to listen to Gavin explaining the Bobby deal again."

I sighed and nodded my understanding. "If it'll make you feel better, then go ahead. Assign them rooms and bedding, and then bring them down to Doctor Cross for a physical examination and a workup of their personal histories."

"I know what to do," she answered dryly, then she gestured to Owen and his friends. "This way, guys. Let's get inside before it gets dark."

I watched her gather up the newest members of our community and lead them away, then I looked back over my shoulder to see who was left. Everyone had vanished, except for the last three remaining members of our original group: Michael, Doctor Cross, and Madeline. Michael took my hand and I fell into step beside him.

"We're probably not going to have much time to talk over the next few days, Doc," I said. "Maybe you should ask whatever it was you wanted to ask us now."

Doc sighed and hiked his glasses back up the bridge of his nose. "It wasn't much, really. I just wanted to ask you both a few questions regarding the medical histories of your families so that I can work out what we should be able to expect when your due date comes."

Michael laughed suddenly. "You know, in all this excitement I nearly forgot about the baby."

"You're such a bad liar, honey," I told him, squeezing his hand. "It's okay to show your excitement, it's not going to freak me out or anything. Hell, knowing how much this baby would mean to you was what got me through the first few months."

He glanced at me and gave me one of his silly, sheepish grins, then he grabbed me and hugged me tight. "Am I that transparent?"

"Like glass," I replied, laughing. Almost as suddenly as it had started, my laughter faded away. "Damn, it feels so wrong to be smiling right after a funeral."

"I think that your sister is right in more ways than she realises," Doc said, absently adjusting his glasses again. With a sudden grunt of annoyance, he took them off and started wiping the raindrops off the lenses. "Ryan would want us to carry on. We were never what you would call close, but I knew that much about him."

"You're right, of course," I replied. "Like she said, he's at peace now. After everything we've been through, death is almost a blessing." I shook my head and snuggled in against Michael's warmth. "Not that I plan to embrace it any time soon. Anyway, what did you want to ask?"

"Ah, yes," Doc said. "I want you both to think as far back as you can when you answer, and also consider any extended family you know of. I need to know if there's any history of congenital defects, genetic conditions, or even a history of multiple births in either of your families."

"Multiple births?!" I exclaimed. "Oh, hell no. That is *not* what I signed up for!"

Doctor Cross gave me a dark look. "I'm just asking, Ms McDermott."

"Right… just asking," I echoed, glowering right back at him. "Nothing on my side, as far as I'm aware. I don't really know my extended family, though. Mum used to tell me that both Skylar and I were born a little early, but we were both healthy regardless."

"Sometimes a baby is just more anxious than most to get out into the world," Doc replied, a faint smile crossing his lips. "We'll keep that in mind towards the end. And what about you, Constable? Anything we should know about?"

"Not as far as I'm aware of," he replied with a shrug. "No twins or triplets, heart defects or anything like that."

"Good, good," Doc said, nodding thoughtfully. "Of course, that doesn't rule out difficulties, but it does mean less to worry about."

I grunted and shook my head. "I think the plague is enough to worry about."

"Very true," he agreed. "On a more positive note, I believe we've managed to save Franco's leg. It will be a while until he's up and about unassisted, but he should heal cleanly. It's a very good thing you found him when you did – another hour and he might have lost that leg, or even died from exposure."

"Thank goodness," I said, letting out a long sigh of relief. "You're right, that's a good thing. Do whatever you need to take care of him. You know you have my permission to draw on any of the resources you need."

"I do, and I shall," he said. The conversation halted as we stepped across the threshold, and spotted a small figured huddled up in the shadows waiting for us. As soon as she saw us, she jumped up and rushed towards us.

"You guys go on without me," I said softly. "Isabelle and I have to have a talk…"

# Chapter Twenty

Isabelle took the news of her son's rehabilitation about as well as I thought she would, which is to say that she was so grateful, it took me weeks to make her understand that she didn't owe me anything. Eventually, I managed to convince her that it was all Gavin's idea, and then her gratitude transferred to him. Every so often, I'd spot her running after him with some gift that she'd made clutched to her breast, which always left him looking flustered.

As the days passed, Tumanako settled into a comfortable routine. New faces emerged from the wilds to join our community on a daily basis, and every morning the sun shone a little bit brighter. Winter was over and most of us had survived. Most, but not all.

Ryan's death hit Skylar hard, and I'd be lying if I said it hadn't affected me almost as much. I often found myself retiring to the dark places where grief lingered, thinking about another friend lost before his time. Just as I'd been there for him in the wake of Sophie's death, Michael was there for me. He always seemed to know when I needed the space, but never let me mope for long.

We spent as much time together as we could justify, and even when we couldn't be together he found ways to make me feel loved. Some days I'd come home to a bouquet of freshly-picked wildflowers in a vase, or a piece of furniture for our apartment, a new book, or even something for the baby. Somehow, he managed to dote on me without making me feel put-upon. It was a remarkable feat of ingenuity, really. I was secretly impressed – but I didn't tell him, of course. I didn't have to. It was Michael. He just knew.

Still, there were some days when I was in a dark place and the only person I wanted to talk to was Skye. This time, she let me in. Neither of us had to grieve alone. We'd grown close enough over the course of our journey south that she really was my sister again, not just in name but in every way. If we wanted to sit together in silence and cry, we could. No judgement, no awkwardness, just understanding. Something about that was comforting. Together, we both began to slowly recover.

One morning about six weeks after the shooting, I trudged inside after a few hours of pulling weeds in the garden and found Skylar sitting in the dining hall with a petite, dark-haired woman whose name I didn't know. Both of them were hunched over a table, talking quietly.

"Whatcha doing, little sis?" I asked curiously, walking up behind her.

Skylar jumped and shot me a dark look. "Damn it, don't sneak up on me!"

"Honey, I'm a three hundred kilogram placenta-filled water-balloon right now," I said dryly. "'Waddling' and 'sneaking' are two different things. If I scared you, that's your fault."

"Oh my god, you're so over dramatic," Skye replied, rolling her eyes. "You're barely even showing yet. If you think this is waddling, just give it another three months."

"Don't remind me. I'm already getting stretch marks," I said. I invited myself to sit down at the table opposite them, and leaned over to look at the sketchpad sitting open on the table in front of the new arrival. "Hey, what's this?"

"It's going to be Ryan," Skye said, suddenly looking very pleased with herself. She picked the sketchpad up and turned it around so that I could get a better look at the picture. "Isn't it wonderful? Aicel was an illustrator before the plague. I convinced her to draw Ryan for the memory wall."

Aicel smiled shyly and tucked a strand of hair back behind her ear. "You're too kind. It's just a doodle at this stage. Once I complete the painting, it will look much better."

"Oh, you're going to paint it?" I asked, surprised and pleased. "That would be a wonderful tribute to him. Once it's done, would you consider doing some others?"

"We're already planning to," Skye replied, looking happy for the first time in weeks. "This is just the start. Aicel's going to help me with the photographs, and we're going to try to paint everyone we can remember into a huge mural – not just down here, but anywhere there's space. I think we should do Kylie, Sophie, Dog, and Netty first, then move on to our families. It's going to take us years, but once we're done we're going to have a memorial to every person we loved and lost. It's going to be magnificent."

"Wow," I breathed, impressed by both the scope of the idea and the emotion behind it. "Do we... do we have the resources to make that happen?"

"We'll find the resources," Skylar said, her voice firm and resolute. "Aicel says that artist's paints last just about forever, and I know a few stores in town that we can raid. If that isn't enough, then I'm sure there are plenty down in Wellington."

"Another brilliant idea," I said, nodding my approval. "Add it to the list. It seems like every time we start a project, we have another dozen good ideas to distract us."

Skye laughed and nodded. "Yeah, we've got way too many ideas and not enough time, but we'll get there. Speaking of which, I forgot to tell you – I got the notebooks and stuff you wanted. I'll start handing them out over dinner tonight."

"Thank you," I said. I rose to my feet and stretched my aching back. "I have to go do some stuff. Let me know if you need me, okay?"

"You're going to need to start taking it easy soon, missy," Skye said, wagging a finger at me. "Don't make me give you the same lecture you gave me last summer."

"Oh, I won't," I said dryly, running a hand across my growing belly. "I have no intention of doing anything that might put the baby at risk, even accidentally. It's going to be hard when those tomatoes start ripening, but I'm even going to resist eating anything fresh out of the ground until it's been thoroughly washed."

"Good," she said. "I guess we'll see you later, then."

"Absolutely," I agreed. "Nice to meet you, Aicel."

The woman waved a shy farewell. I waved back, and then trudged out of the room and down the hall towards the elevator. A few minutes later, I was making my way towards the suite of rooms we'd put aside for our communications equipment and research facilities when a door opened and Gavin stepped out. He froze in his tracks, blinking in surprise, then he grinned.

"Well, I suppose that saves me coming to look for you," he said. "We just had a call from Sergeant Bryce."

I raised an eyebrow. "Oh? Is everything all right?"

"Yeah, everything's fine," he said, beckoning for me to follow him. I did, and he led me into the room he'd just come from. Through a doorway, I could see Doctor Cross hunkered over his latest set of experiments. Bobby was sitting at a small table in a corner, intensely focused on a book that lay open on the table in front of him. He didn't even glance up when I came in.

Gavin and I hadn't really talked about the details of his rehabilitation regime, but whatever he was doing seemed to be working. I hadn't seen Bobby much, just at meals and occasionally in the garden, but whenever I did he just nodded politely and kept walking. There had been no further attempts on my life, and no sign that he was planning anything untoward. It was entirely possible that he'd just learned his lesson, but I thought it more likely that Gavin was just enough like his former stepfather for Bobby to respect him and be willing to follow his lead. Fortunately, Gavin was a much more responsible father-figure than Henry had been.

Gavin led me through another doorway, into a small room where he kept the various bits of radio and long-range communications equipment he'd scavenged from the area. I settled in a random chair without being prompted, happy to be off my feet even for a moment.

"Sergeant Bryce wanted me to tell you that no one's come through Waiouru in more than two weeks," he said, sitting down in the chair opposite me. "No sign of the mutants, either. She's decided it's time for her to come south, and she's bringing the library."

"Does she need us to send her any aid?" I asked.

"No," he said, shaking his head. "She said that she and her men already have things well in order. She's going to follow the same route we did, and estimates she should be here in under a month."

"That's good," I replied, then I sighed and admitted the truth to him. "I am concerned, though. New Zealand isn't that big. The mutants are going to keep spreading in the north, and eventually they're going to start roaming south. What if we haven't gone far enough?"

"Michael and I have been working on a plan for that," he said. "We've worked out that the mutants aren't a short-term problem anymore. They're a long-term problem. We need to stop thinking about what we can do about them today and tomorrow, and start working on how we can deal with them over the next decade."

I gave him a curious look and said nothing. He smiled sheepishly, but took that as his cue to keep talking.

"Right now, there just aren't enough of us to deal with them in an efficient manner," he explained. "So what we're going to do instead is create a firebreak between us and them. You know what a firebreak is, right?"

I nodded. "It's a strip of land where all the trees and brush have been cleared out, to prevent forest fires from spreading by restricting their potential fuel."

"Exactly," he said with a smile. "So the plan is that we treat the mutated infected like a natural disaster, and build a break around us. The regular infected don't move around much, so we're going to start taking teams out and clearing them from the area surrounding Lower Hutt and Wellington. Once this region is totally clear, we'll start moving north. Obviously we can't take anyone vital to the day-to-day running of Tumanako, so it's going to take a long time for us to even finish the Wellington region."

"But we'll get there eventually," I finished for him. "Just by taking it one day at a time. That's as good a plan as any I've heard."

"Obviously, the mutated infected themselves can cross the break," he added, "but at least this will prevent those plague-bearer things from having any effect on us. Can't spread a plague where there's nothing to receive it, right? Eventually, once we have enough people, we can move up the North Island and clear out the old cities—"

Just at that moment, our conversation was interrupted when the door burst open and Priya raced inside. She glanced around frantically, then as soon as she saw me she scampered over and grabbed my hand.

"Mama!" she cried. "Mama, come quick, must see!"

"Whoa, what is it honey?" I asked, rising to my feet. She just squealed something inarticulate and dragged me out of the room. Gavin leapt up, shouted something to Doc, and hurried after us. The four of us raced down the corridor towards the north-west corner of the building. We completely forgot about Bobby in all the excitement, but he soon caught up with us of his own free will. Priya threw open the door to the corner suite and pulled me over to the window overlooking the front gates.

Outside the gate was a massive crowd of people.

"Good Lord, there must be two hundred people down there," Doc cried. "Where did they all come from?"

I glanced at Gavin, but he had no answer for me.

"I don't know," I started to say, but suddenly realisation struck me. "Wait! Yes, I do. We all do. It's the South Islanders! Remember, they were camped out in Picton, trying to get the ferry working again? They must have done it, and now they're here! The South Islanders are here! Come on!"

This time, it was me dragging Priya along, with Doc, Gavin, and Bobby hot on our heels. The elevator was too busy to be of any use to us, so we took the stairs instead. By the time we reached ground level, the entire population of Tumanako was gathered outside. The chatter of excited voices and the bright-eyed looks on every face sent a thrill of excitement right through me.

I lost my grip on Priya's hand as I was trying to wriggle my way to the front of the crowd, but it didn't matter. We were surrounded by friends and family, no one would hurt her. Someone shouted my name, and then suddenly I found the way open before me and helpful hands guiding me through. On the far side, Michael and Skye were waiting for me, along with Anahera, Simon, and a few of the other more prominent members of the council.

"Sandy!" Michael cried as soon as he spotted me. "You're not going to believe this."

"Oh, yes I would," I replied.

I grabbed my advisors and led them towards the gates. The gates were still closed, but the people on the other side looked just as excited as my people. There wasn't the slightest hint of a threat in either their voices or on their faces. Someone I didn't know spotted me and shouted my name, then a spontaneous cheer went up from the crowd. By the time we reached them, they were chanting my name like a mantra. I came to a stop on the far side of the gates and held up my hands, but it still took a minute for the chant to die down.

Once it was finally quiet enough for me to be heard, I addressed them all. "I think I can already guess, but where are you guys from?"

"Nelson!" a woman at the front of the crowd shouted.

"Dunedin!" someone else cried.

"Picton!" called a third voice, then the noise level rose to impossible again as everyone announced their home cities. By the time they were done, there was a tear in every eye. Everyone fell silent, looking at me expectantly.

"To be honest with you all, I wasn't sure that you were going to make it," I admitted. "But, you have no idea how glad I am that you did. Welcome, everyone! Welcome to Tumanako! Your new home!"

A cheer exploded from the crowd, both inside the gate and out. I beckoned to the guards to unlock the gate and let the people in, and they did. A few moments later, we were caught up in a flood of happy, crying, excited people, strangers exchanging handshakes and hugs as if they were old friends.

For the first time in my life, I wasn't scared of being surrounded by strangers. I was excited. Truly, unbearably, ridiculously excited. These strangers were not a scary mob of potential danger, they were the living embodiment of the one thing that humanity needed more than anything else in the world: hope.

# Chapter Twenty-One

The arrival of our Southern brethren more than doubled the population of Tumanako overnight. Even more critical to the survival of the human species, we discovered that there was a much higher percentage of adult women amongst the South Island survivors than the North. I could only guess that the thinner population in the South Island had given the women a better chance of making it through the years after the plague. Half of them were already married, but the other half… well, let's just say that there was a lot of friendly competition amongst the men of Tumanako to try and win the hands of the new arrivals.

It took us weeks to record everyone's biographical information, but as we worked our way through them we were delighted to discover that we'd gained a number of useful professionals. Once we'd finally completed the monumental project, Doctor Cross called a meeting of the council to update us on what our newest citizens were capable of.

"I am thrilled to advise that I am no longer the only doctor here," he told us as soon as we'd all seated ourselves. We all laughed at his obvious relief, and he glared at us. "Oh yes, laugh your little heads off. You weren't the one faced with the prospect of having to tend the needs of four hundred and seven people!"

"Sorry, Doc," I replied. "We were just laughing at the look on your face. We're thrilled there's someone else to help out. Tell us about the new doctor."

"Oh, yes." He relaxed a little and adjusted his glasses. "Her name is Ngaire Madurrit, and she was a professor of obstetrics at Otago University before the plague. She managed to keep a small group of students from the school together, including a couple who were involved in the medical sciences." Doc paused and gave me a significant look. "One was studying immunology. I've already commandeered her services."

I grinned at him and nodded my approval. "She's all yours. And, is obstetrics what I think it is?"

"Yes, yes it is," he replied dryly. "I've set her up with an office in the other spare room off the infirmary, and I expect you both to check in with her as soon as possible. You'll be spending a lot of time together."

Skylar shot me a quizzical look. "Does he mean us?"

"Yes," I said, laughing. "She specialises in pregnancy and childbirth. Thank goodness she survived – we're going to need her services a lot in the years to come."

Michael perked up and gave me a half-excited, half-terrified look. "We are?"

"That was a general statement about the community, honey," I replied, patting his knee comfortingly. "Don't worry, we've got to get through this pregnancy before we think about having any more kids. We're probably going to get divorced about ten minutes after I go into labour."

Everyone laughed again. Once the levity faded, Doc picked up his list and checked it. "We've also got a handful of builders and engineers who were in Christchurch helping with the rebuild, another plumber, a psychologist, a potter, a tailor, two teachers, three artists, and a bunch of farmers. Oh, and we've got four soldiers from Burnham Military Camp, and two officers from the Air Force base in Blenheim."

I sat up straight and looked at him with interest. "Are they pilots?"

Doc consulted his list for a moment, then nodded. "One is an engineer, but the other was a helicopter pilot."

I glanced around the circle of faces and raised an eyebrow. "You guys thinking what I'm thinking?"

"Fuel is limited, but a helicopter could be useful in a pinch," Michael said thoughtfully. "We need to head down to Wellington to raid the National Library anyway, so we could check out the airport while we're there."

"Maybe," I said, holding up a hand. "Long-term plans. Right now, I want everyone focusing on getting Tumanako self-sufficient. We'll head down to check out the library once Erica gets here; she'll never forgive me if we go without her. How far away is she, Gav?"

"She checked in this morning, said she's three days out," Gavin replied. "She should be here by new moon."

"Hang on a sec, what do you mean 'we'," Skye interjected, giving me a dark look. "You are not thinking about going down to Wellington in your condition."

"Just to watch," I replied. "It should only be a day trip, and I plan to take good care of myself. I won't help with the lifting or anything, I just want to be part of the mission. Promise."

Skye folded her arms across her chest and glared at me. "You better not. If I hear about you fainting again, I'll kick your butt."

"I don't doubt it," I answered dryly, then I turned my attention back to the rest of the group. "We need to send a scouting party down to check whether there are any books worth saving. No point going if the place is a smouldering ruin."

"I'll take care of it," Michael said, rising to his feet.

"And I'll go organise their supplies," Skye chipped in.

"Wow, I don't need to do anything these days," I said with a laugh. "Thanks, guys."

"You just go see that obstetrician lady and check on our baby," Michael replied, his tone light and playful. "Don't make me nag you, woman."

"All right, all right," I said, easing myself up to my feet. Michael hurried over to help me, but I didn't really need the assistance. I might not have been used to lugging around the extra weight, but I was still an athletic person by nature and pregnancy had done nothing to change that.

Still, he liked to help me and I was happy to let him do it if it made him feel better. We headed down to the second level together, then he kissed me goodbye and hurried off to organise the scouting party. I let myself into the infirmary, where I found Franco and Tala talking to Rebecca. Tala's face lit up with a smile as soon as she saw me, and she waved shyly.

I waved back and returned the smile. "Hey, guys. How's the leg, Franco?"

"Good," he replied. "The doctor says I'll probably have a limp forever, but I'm just grateful to be alive and walking. Things could have turned out much, much worse for me."

"I'm glad to hear you're recovering nicely," I told him. "I'm always impressed when I see you whizzing around on your crutches. You've really got that motion down to an art. I never could get the hang of it."

Franco laughed and nodded. "Practice makes perfect, eh? Life is good here. I'm glad we came." He put his arm around Tala's slender shoulders and kissed her cheek. "I just wish we'd come a little sooner."

"You can't change the past, and regrets won't fix what happened to you," I replied. "The important thing is that you're all okay, and you've been given a second chance at life. Anyway, I shouldn't interrupt your consultation. Is the Professor around?"

"She's in her office, reviewing our patient files," Rebecca replied, pointing me towards one of the doors at the back of the room.

"Thank you," I said, then I went over and knocked on the door.

A few seconds later, the door swung open and I found myself face to face with a tall, slender woman with dark skin, intelligent eyes, and short brown hair frosted with grey. She took one look at me, then smiled and beckoned me inside.

"Sandrine," she said by way of greeting. "I was wondering when you were going to avail yourself of my services."

"Doctor Cross only just got around to telling me what your speciality is," I replied. "I've seen you around, but I had no idea that you were an obstetrician until five minutes ago. I can't tell you how glad we are to have you here. And by 'we', I mean every woman of childbearing age in Tumanako."

Professor Madurrit laughed and reached out to touch my elbow, gently guiding me into a chair beside her desk. "I can imagine. Stewart just about had kittens when I told him, and I can understand why. Obstetrics is an intimidating field, where even the slightest miscalculation can cost more than one life if you're not sure what you're doing. Now, hold still a moment while I give you a check-up. Where did I put your file…?"

I waited patiently while she dug through the mound of paperwork on her desk, then she came back over and ran me through a series of quick tests. Though most of them were the same as what Doctor Cross did, there was something reassuring about being examined by a professional who knew what was best for both me and my baby. When she was done, she sat down at her desk again and made some notes in my file, then turned back to me with a smile.

"I'm pleased to advise that both of you seem to be in excellent health," she said. "I would like you to come back for an ultrasound once the scavengers manage to find a machine in working order, but I doubt there's anything to worry about at this stage. Have you made plans for the birthing yet?"

"Plans for the birthing?" I echoed, giving her a confused look. "What do you mean? It's just point and shoot, isn't it? Oh, and scream. Scream a lot."

She laughed again and shook her head. "Don't worry, most first-time mothers think that's how it is. No, there are an assortment of different options for you to choose from in terms of where and how your delivery takes place. I've got a few books here that we can look over, and then we can start making plans together…"

***

By the time I finally left the infirmary, my head was spinning from all the new information. I'd made my choices, though, and I felt better for having a clearer understanding of what my body was going through. Yeah, I was still fairly terrified by the whole process, but the professor had a way of making it all seem normal.

Which it is, I reminded myself. Women have been having babies for thousands of years. They got through it, so I can get through it, too.

I took a deep breath, nodded firmly to reassure myself, then I headed for the kitchen to make myself a nice cup of tea. On my way through the dining room, I spotted Skylar talking to Aicel and a couple of other people I only knew in passing. She waved a greeting, finished up her conversation, and raced over to catch up with me.

"Hey! How did the obstinate lady go?" she asked.

"You mean the obstetrician?" I replied dryly. "Good. She gave me a list of exercises to do to keep my girly-parts in peak baby-pushing condition, and yet another lecture on nutrition."

Skylar laughed and nodded. "Gotta keep them girly-parts working nicely if you want to repopulate the earth, sis."

"I keep telling you, we're not doing that single-handedly," I teased her, which just made her laugh even more. It was a pleasant sound to hear, and one that I decided I was going to squeeze out of her more often because it meant that she was finally recovering from Ryan's death. Once she stopped laughing, I gave her a nudge. "Hey, weren't you supposed to be getting supplies ready for the scouts?"

"I was on my way there when I got distracted," she admitted. "Did you see how well the mural is coming along? I requisitioned all the artists from the South Island group, and some other folks who are willing to learn. You wouldn't think it to look at her, but Melody is really good with a brush."

"I'd believe it," I said, glancing at the mural. With every passing day, it was spreading across the blank stone wall, filling it with colour and faces both familiar and new. Suddenly, I realised that there was something out of place and shot a quizzical glance at my sister. "I thought there were three new artists? I only see two over there."

"The third one is a sculptor," she explained. "I've got him working on another project. It's going to take a while, but I think you'll like it when it's done."

"Oh?" I asked, genuinely curious. Skye wasn't usually the sort to keep secrets.

This time, she just shook her head and smiled mysteriously. "Come on, we've got a lot to do before Erica gets here."

***

The next couple of days flew by. Word spread about the impending arrival of Erica and her books, and I found myself with no shortage of volunteers eager to help me transform a large chunk of one of the spare levels into a vast library. Of course, the rain may have also had something to do with it; the weather closed in on the day we sent the scouts south, and it was still drizzling when Sergeant Bryce finally arrived.

I was hard at work in the kitchen getting get lunch ready when the radio I still carried out of habit crackled to life. "Sandy, you there?"

"I'm here," I replied. I wandered over to the big windows that looked down on the courtyard, and immediately spotted the reason the guards were calling me: there was a slow-moving but determined convoy heading towards our front gates. "Oh, I see it. That's Sergeant Bryce. Let her in, and I'll be down in a second."

By the time I'd washed my hands and fought my way through the crowds to the ground level, Erica had already dismounted and was deep in conversation with Johan. I got there just in time to catch the tail end of a conversation about horse husbandry that went way over my head.

"Don't worry, we've got plenty of space here for the rest of the herd," Johan reassured her, then he spotted me and grinned. "Ah, there she is. I was just telling your friend that the mares are going to start coming into heat any day now, so we should start thinking about expanding our herd. No reason not to, since we've got the space and the numbers to warrant it."

"Sounds good to me," I agreed. I glanced at the herd milling around the courtyard and grinned. "Wow, it looks like you managed to bring the whole lot of them with you, Sergeant. How did you manage to pull that off?"

"It's easier than it looks," Erica replied. "Horses are herd beasts by nature, and tend to follow a single dominant mare. I just rode the dominant mare, and the others were happy to follow. I'll admit, I've never done it over such a long distance, but I'm very happy to say that I didn't lose any of them along the way. Quite a feat, really!"

"Well, I'm glad you managed to pull it off," I replied. "So, those trucks are the books?"

"Yes ma'am," she said, glancing back at the pair of trucks just coming to a stop behind the herd. "We had to leave a few things behind, but we've got the important stuff. Now that we know the way is open and fairly easy, I'm betting we could make the trip back in half the time if we need to."

"I doubt we'll need to," I told her. "We have enough resources here in the south not to worry about it. I think you'll be very pleased once you've had a chance to look around and meet people. It's actually starting to get a little cramped up there, if you can believe it. We're going to need to start moving people out of the main tower and into the houses inside the fence soon."

"There are houses inside the perimeter?" Erica asked, looking both surprised and pleased. "Well, this really was an ideal spot to build your new town, isn't it?"

"It is," I agreed. "This used to be a film studio. We've checked the fence for holes and patched up any weak points, so it's all secure. There's enough space to graze the animals, grow crops, and even expand our living space, all without leaving the security of the complex. We've even been working on a plan to turn that big warehouse over there into a giant greenhouse to keep us in fresh fruit and vegetables come winter. It was being used for sound stages, so the walls are removable and it's got built-in heating to keep it warm all year round."

"Sounds brilliant," Erica said, then she grinned. "I, for one, will just be glad to sleep in a proper bed tonight. I hope you can arrange that for us?"

I laughed and nodded. "Yep, and hot showers for everyone. Let the volunteers take care of the horses and unload the trucks. I've got a lot to show you."

# Chapter Twenty-Two

I awoke the next morning to the sound of activity out in the hall. Michael was up and halfway through getting dressed, which meant we were already late. I muttered a low curse and rolled out of bed – or I tried to, but I overshot the edge and ended up in a heap on the floor with sheets and duvets all around me.

Michael took one look at me, then cracked up laughing and raced over to help me up. "Dammit, Sandy. Do I need to keep reminding you that you're not as agile as you used to be?"

"Apparently," I answered dryly. "Well, nothing injured but my pride. How late are we?"

"Not late enough to matter," he replied. He gave me an affectionate smile, then leaned down to press a kiss to my lips. "We're back in that happy no-man's land where time doesn't really matter all that much, honey. Relax. We have a lovely home, we're going to have a family together, and we're safe." I opened my mouth to protest, but he just grinned and pressed a finger to my lips. "Hush. No one's going to leave us behind. Now, go do your stretches before the professor scolds you like a naughty school girl."

Whatever I'd been planning to say vanished in laughter at the mental image he conjured up. I just nodded obediently and headed out into the living room to do the exercises Professor Madurrit had assigned me, while Michael packed a day bag for us to share.

"Think we should toss in a change of clothes, just in case?" he called from the other room.

"Better safe than sorry," I replied. "The scouts reported the building's in pretty bad shape, so it might take us a bit longer than we planned to clear everything out. Ugh, man, when did it get so hard to do squats?"

Michael stuck his head out the door and watched with a cheeky grin on his face. "I'll take the blame for that. You need a hand?"

"Only if I get stuck," I replied.

He laughed and ducked back into our bedroom. "I'll pack a change, just in case. I mean, it's the National Library. It's gotta be pretty big, right?"

"Yeah," I agreed. I paused between reps to catch my breath and stretch my back. "This place is supposed to be a repository of all the literature ever written in or about New Zealand. Assuming it's not burned out, that should be a fairly large amount of information."

Michael came out of the bedroom with my backpack over his shoulder, and wandered over to kiss my cheek. "After all this preparation, it better not be burned out. I'm going to grab some breakfast. Want me to get your usual?"

"Since when do I have a usual?" I asked, surprised.

He laughed and gently prodded my swollen belly. "Since her. I do listen, you know. It's always fried tomatoes this, fried tomatoes that. With parsley. Always with parsley."

I blinked owlishly and felt myself turning red. "Wow, I didn't realise I was that predictable."

"You're not," he replied, his tone softening. "I just know you better than anyone else, remember? So, omelette and fried tomatoes, my love?"

I couldn't help but laugh and nod. "Okay, okay. But don't forget the parsley!"

"I wouldn't dream of it," he replied, then he gave me another quick kiss and left the room.

I spent a few minutes finishing my prescribed stretches, then I headed off to indulge in a long, hot shower. By the time I was done, I was surprised to find myself feeling much better. Whatever else she had going for her, the professor definitely knew what my body needed.

When I finished bathing, I changed into my travel gear – or at least the pieces that still fitted – and made my way down to the dining room. Before I even made it through the doorway, I heard the sound of whoops and laughter, but there were too many bodies gathered around for me to see what was going on.

"Lower!" a voice demanded. It took me a second to recognise it as Professor Madurrit. A few seconds passed, then she grunted in what sounded like mock annoyance. "I said lower, young man! You know what 'lower' means, or she wouldn't have ended up in this condition to begin with."

The people around them hooted and jeered so loudly that I could barely hear the deep, male voice apologise to her. "Sorry, Professor."

"Michael?" I called, struggling not to laugh. "Is that you in there? What's she doing to you?"

"Mama!" Priya's voice greeted me. A few seconds later, she wriggled her way out of the crowd and threw her arms around me. "You're missing the funnies."

"Oh, am I just?" I glanced up, just as the crowd peeled back to reveal the last thing I'd expected to see: Hemi was sitting backwards in a chair with his chin on the top rung while Michael massaged his back, with Anahera and Professor Madurrit watching like a pair of hawks. Michael shot a guilty look over his shoulder. I raised my eyebrows questioningly. "Well? What's this, then? And where are my fried tomatoes with parsley?"

"Skye's making them," he replied apologetically. "As soon as I got down here, the ladies jumped me and insisted I learn the basics of haputanga massage before we leave."

I looked at the ladies in question. "Oh? What is haputanga massage, and should I be afraid?"

"Afraid? No, dear heart." Anahera laughed and came over to me. She put her arm around my shoulders and guided me to the centre of the circle. "Haputanga is an important part of my culture, and one that I think we could all benefit from sharing. While I am not qualified to teach it, Ngaire is. 'Haputanga' is the Maori phrase for pregnancy and pre-natal care. We believe that it is important for both mother and baby to be relaxed, and that the father's help is instrumental in making sure that happens."

"And why is he practicing on Hemi?" I asked dryly. "Last time I checked, he wasn't a pregnant woman."

Everyone laughed at that, including Hemi himself. Anahera shook her head and grinned at me. "Well, if I am to be a grandmother, either by blood or adoption, it seems logical to teach them both at the same time. They're not the only ones, either. Many of our citizens will become parents in the days to come, so we'll be teaching the art of haputanga to anyone who wants to learn."

"Well, if it'll keep my back from playing up, then I'm all for it," I announced, then I marched over to the chair, shoved Hemi out of it, and plopped down in his place.

Again, the people around us whooped with laughter and cheered, and for once I wasn't embarrassed at all.

***

A few hours later, we were fed, dressed, and on the road with all the trucks that were still in working order. Between a hefty dose of fried tomatoes and a good massage, I was feeling sleepy and relaxed. I napped most of the way to Wellington, and woke just as Michael was guiding the Hilux along the last stretch of motorway leading into our country's former capital.

Michael grabbed the walkie-talkie off the dashboard and spoke into it. "I'm seeing a lot of rubble up ahead. Are you sure it's safe to take the trucks this way?"

There was a momentary silence, then one of the scouts replied. "Yeah, the Molesworth Street overpass is down. You should see an off-ramp on your left just before it. Take that, it's still good."

"There," I said, pointing to an overgrown concrete ramp not far from in front of us. Michael nodded and handed the radio to me, then focused on driving.

We crept up the off-ramp carefully, with a few people walking on either side to make sure that the concrete wasn't going to crumble beneath us, but it supported our weight just fine. At the top, we spotted a group of people on horses waving to us; from there, the way was easier. The streets were narrow, winding, and choked with the rusted hulks of old cars, but the scouts had made the most of the last few days and cleared a path for us. A few of the buildings had been reduced to rubble, but I was pleasantly surprised to see just how many were still intact.

"Wellington was always prone to earthquakes, so most of the buildings here were built to a high standard," Michael commented thoughtfully. "Looks like they did a good job of it, huh?"

"Looks like," I agreed. "Shame there are still so many bones, though."

"We're going to bury them," he told me. "As part of the project to put to rest the infected, we're going to bury the bones as well."

I shot him a startled look. "What? You're going to bury the remains of four million people? There's barely even four hundred of us!"

"I didn't say it was going to be easy," he replied, "and I didn't say it was going to be quick – but it is the right thing to do. Hell, it may come down to our kids and grandkids to finish what we start, but you taught me that we need to think about the future. I don't want my daughter tripping over the bones of the dead while she's learning to walk. Do you?"

"No," I admitted. "I'm just having trouble wrapping my head around the scope of what you and Gavin want to do. I never said that I disapprove, it's just... massive."

"It is, but it's the right thing to do," he said firmly. "Not just for the sake of hygiene, but also for respect. Like you always remind us, those bones were people once, people just like us. They deserve to rest in peace. If it were my bones lying on the pavement over there, I would hope that someone would take the time to bury them one day. If I have to work every day of the rest of my life to make this world a better place for the next generation and to let the last generation rest in peace, then I will."

The determination in his voice made me smile. I let the conversation drop and focused on the road instead. After a few minutes of negotiating the clogged streets, I spotted a sign etched into the side of a building.

"There!" I cried. "That weird-looking one, with the angled front. That's it!"

The scouts guided our trucks up into the tiled arcade that ran alongside the library. I glanced at Michael and started to say something, only to stop when I saw the look on his face. "Whoa... honey, what's wrong?"

"It just..." He hesitated for a second, shaking his head. "It looks so much like the place where Sophie died. It was always the books with her. She loved going to the library."

"I'm so sorry, Michael," I said, reaching out to touch his hand.

He wrapped his fingers around mine and drew them up to his lips, then smiled sadly at me. "It's hard to believe it's been nearly ten months since I saw her smiling face. Sometimes, it feels like just yesterday…"

"Do you want to go home?" I asked. "We can leave the guys to take care of this, if you want. We don't really have to be here, they're perfectly capable of doing it."

"No," he said, shaking his head. "I can handle it. It just gave me a shock, is all. I'll be okay."

I frowned and nodded. "If you're sure…"

"I'm sure," he replied. He put the truck in park, then climbed out and hurried around to help me out. Though it usually bugged me when people pampered me because of my condition, this time I just let it go without saying a word. If it gave him something to think about besides Sophie's grisly death, then that was fine by me.

Within a few minutes, all of us had disembarked and gathered in front of the building, standing in a ring around the scouts. Warren stepped forward to address the group on their behalf, his face tense and alert.

"We haven't been able to breach the interior of the building yet," he explained. "The doors are all locked, and we haven't been able to unlock them by conventional means. We decided to wait until you got here before we tried anything more drastic. You bought sledgehammers, right?"

"We've got them, just like you asked," I replied. "You want us to try and break the glass?"

"We can try that, I doubt it'll work," he said, shaking his head. "If the rioters weren't able to break in, then I doubt we can do much unless we resort to explosives. No, we found a weak point in the wall around the back. I'm pretty sure that we can bust through it without too much effort."

"Assuming it's not a load-bearing wall," I commented dryly. "Show us anyway. We brought one of the engineers along, he should be able to tell us whether it's safe or not. Eugene?"

A tall, painfully thin man with short, black hair and thick glasses stepped forward and nodded to us. "Show me the weak point, please."

Warren grunted inarticulately and gestured for us to follow him. We picked our way across the crumbling flagstones, down a short flight of steps, and into an alley that ran behind the library. Warren stopped beside a fire door and pointed at the wall just beside it.

"Here," he said, running his finger over the concrete. "If you look closely, there are some fine, hairline cracks running all the way through it. What do you think?"

"Mmm." Eugene leaned in close to get a better look at the cracks – but his inspection was interrupted by a metallic shriek as the fire door swung open unexpectedly.

I barely leapt out of the way in time to avoid being struck. Before I could even think of reaching for a weapon, I found myself staring down the barrel of a pair of rifles.

"Get away from there and go back to wherever you came from," the woman behind one of the guns demanded, her tone cool and professional. She was a few years older than me, with the same intense, wild-eyed look that I'd seen in the mirror every morning up until recently. The man beside her was the complete opposite – small, nervous, and mousy – but while his hands did tremble on the hilt of the gun, there was determination in his eyes that made me think twice about crossing him.

"Whoa, we don't mean any harm," I said, holding my hands up as if that might placate them. "We were coming to rescue the books, that's all. We didn't know there was anyone here."

The woman raised an eyebrow and took a step towards me, though she didn't lower her weapon. "Rescue the books from what, exactly? And where were you planning to take them?"

"From…" I hesitated, then shrugged and told her the truth. "I don't know, anything. We've founded a new city just north of here, in the Hutt Valley, and we're trying to collect anything we can find to remember and preserve the old world. Since we live so close to Wellington, it seemed logical to come here and try to save whatever we could before it was lost to fire, or the ocean, or just time."

She hesitated for a second, then slowly lowered her gun. "You're not going to try and destroy anything?"

I blinked in surprise and shock. "What? Why would we want to destroy our cultural history?"

"People do strange things," she answered dryly. "We've been locked down in here for four days while your men were nosing around outside, so you'll forgive me for being a little suspicious. We've protected this library for ten years and we have no intention of giving it up without a fight."

"You're… protecting it?" I echoed, then I looked at Erica and smiled. "All this worrying for nothing."

Sergeant Bryce grunted inarticulately and nodded. "We should have known we weren't the only ones around who gave a damn about the books."

Michael laughed and reached out to rub my shoulder reassuringly, then he glanced past me at the woman. "You know, I can't help but feel like I know you from somewhere."

"I was just thinking the same thing, actually," she replied. "Did we go to school together? Or to Police College? I graduated about a year before the plague."

"Oh, that's it!" he said, snapping his fingers. "I knew your face was familiar. I don't think we ever spoke, but I remember seeing your face in my classes. I'm Michael, and this is my wife, Sandrine."

"Valerie, but you can call me Val," she replied. "This is Xander. Don't mind him, he's not much of a people person. He just really loves his books."

Xander shot her a dirty look, then muttered something and vanished back into the bowels of the building. Val rolled her eyes and gave us a long-suffering look. "Story of my life. He practically lived here before the plague, and nothing much changed when everyone died. He just lets me and the kids stay here because I'm bigger than him and because it means he doesn't have to find his own food."

"The kids?" I echoed. "You have children?"

"I have one," she replied, her expression suddenly turning dark. "My son, Dennis. He's four. Don't ask about his father. The others are foundlings. I couldn't very well leave them to starve after their parents died, so I adopted them."

I grimaced at the implications of the situation regarding her son's paternity, because it was one all too familiar to me. I just nodded my understanding.

"Yeah, we've got quite a few foundlings with us, too," I said, deliberately changing the subject to safer territory. "Like you said, it wouldn't be right to leave them to starve. We founded Tumanako – our little city – in hopes that no child would ever have to grow up alone. You're welcome to come and visit, if you want."

A flicker passed through Valerie's eyes, then she glanced away. "Are there many people there?"

"More than four hundred now," I said softly, gently. "All people like you and me. People who have been alone for way too long, and just want to be surrounded by friendly faces again. Men, women, children – we even have some pets running around. It's not exactly like the old days, but we're doing our best to build something worthwhile."

Valerie sighed and nodded. "I guess it can't hurt to look. Maybe we could think about transferring some of the books there. Are you sure it's secure? Doesn't Lower Hutt get flooding?"

"Sometimes," I replied. "But we've got a multi-level building, and we've dedicated the top floor to the preservation of cultural artefacts. The plan was that if we fill up the top floor, we'll gradually move the people out of the apartments on the next floor down and make room for books there. We're not sure how many people are left alive around here, but if it's more than a thousand I'll be surprised. Still, we've got plenty of good buildings near our main base, and builders to help us make more as we need them. We just need to find a way to contact the people who didn't see our television broadcast or hear our radio transmission, like you."

"I never was one for TV," she admitted with a shrug. "Well, come on then. I suppose I better introduce you to the others, then you can show me what you've got."

***

I sent the majority of my group off to check out the airport, while Michael, Erica, and I stayed behind to talk to Val and Xander. Once they'd relaxed and gotten used to us, they started opening up to us. Xander and Erica were drawn to one another almost immediately by their mutual intense love of books, and soon vanished out of sight. Val stuck with me and Michael. After the initial wariness wore off, she was perfectly happy to chatter away about whatever was on her mind, which mostly seemed to revolve around two things: the books, and her son.

No matter how he'd come to be, she obviously loved Dennis with an intensity that almost hurt to see. Every so often, I'd catch her looking at me and Michael with longing, but just as regularly she'd shut up shop and shy away from us as if suddenly remembering something painful. I understood, and made no attempt to pressure her into opening up before she was ready.

Unsurprisingly, Dennis and the younger kids gravitated towards Michael, and he to them. Val and I watched on from the relative safety of a couple of plush armchairs while Michael and the kids dashed frantically up and down the long aisles between bookshelves. Their laughter and shrieks of glee filled the library, driving back any shadows of doubt that either of us might have had about meeting one another.

"You know, I've lost track of who's chasing whom," I admitted as they tore past us again.

"Yeah, I have no idea," she replied. "I'm tired just watching them." She glanced back over her shoulder, then gave me a wink and a secretive smile. "You know, Xander's taken quite a shine to your army friend. I don't think I've ever seen him open up that fast to someone. When I first met him, it took me a week to convince him to even tell me his name."

"Well, they have a common obsession," I said. "I'm not sure what's going on with them, but I'm happy to see it. Erica's a brave woman, and she deserves a friend. She volunteered to stay behind while we came south to establish the city, and I was worried she was going to have difficulty getting used to being surrounded by people again. I know I did."

"She's a soldier," Val replied simply. "Adapt and survive. That's what soldiers are trained to do. Police officers, too. I'm not surprised that she thrived all these years, and I'm not surprised Michael did either. We have the training to help us. I am, however, surprised that you did. You can't have been more than, what... sixteen when the plague hit?"

"Eighteen," I corrected her. "But yeah, you're right. I'm not entirely sure how I survived, either. A lot of it was just trial and error, a lot of it was luck, some of it was reading, and the rest I put down to a few good teachers over the years. My mum and dad taught me a lot of valuable lessons before the plague, and then afterwards I met an ex-soldier named Gavin who's a lot like you, minus the love of books. Smart, quick to learn and slow to forget, and knows a lot about keeping himself alive."

Val laughed and nodded. "No, I get it. There was a lot of luck involved. A lot of luck. I was twenty-two, but I had my training to fall back on. I was assigned to Wellington after Police College, and this was one of the first places that got badly hit by the riots. They wanted us to protect parliament, but we soon figured out that the prime minister and the rest of cabinet had already fled. Why risk our lives to protect something that didn't matter anymore? So we just went home."

"I guess it's safe to say that your parents didn't make it?" I asked as gently as I could, watching her face for any sign that I was crossing a line.

She just shrugged and glanced away. "My dad died of a stroke when I was a teenager, and my mum just sort of... wasted away after that. She died a week after I was accepted into Police College. I think she was just waiting to see me on the road to a good career before she went to join Dad, you know?"

"Yeah, I know." I reached over to touch the back of her hand. She didn't pull away. "Some people are just meant to be together, in life and in death. My parents were like that. It's a long, not-nice story, but they died during the plague. So, is that why you came to protect the books?"

"Pretty much," she said with a shrug. "I went back to the flat I was living in at the time, but it was on fire and there was no sign of the fire service coming to deal with it. I figured out pretty quickly that the whole city was going to go that way if we didn't do something to stop it, so I grabbed the riot gear out of my car and came back into town, looking for some way to stop what was happening.

"I made it to the downtown area, then I was cornered by a group of rioters. They pulled me out of my car, and I thought for sure that my number was up – until someone laid into them from behind and managed to chase them off."

In spite of the fact that she'd obviously survived the encounter, I found myself sitting forward in my seat, anxious to hear the rest. "Who was it?"

"It was my partner," she replied softly. "Him, and a few of the other officers that he'd managed to round up. I found out afterwards that they'd barricaded themselves inside the library because it was the safest place they could find in a pinch, but when they saw me get pulled from my car they'd rallied out to save me. I was bruised up pretty badly, but they carried me back inside the library and took care of me."

"They didn't go home, either?" I asked.

She shook her head and looked down at the floor. "They'd tried. I don't know about the others, but my partner's wife was dead. He couldn't say the words, but I could see it in his eyes. He never told me what happened. It's probably for the best." She closed her eyes and took a deep breath to steady her shaking voice. "Most of the others died over the course of the next few weeks from the plague, until it was just me, Xander, and Dennis."

I blinked in surprise. "Wait, but Dennis is only four..."

Val cringed, then she sighed heavily. "Dennis senior was my partner. He was immune, like us. There was an accident, a few years ago... I don't want to talk about it."

"Then don't talk about it," I said, grabbing her hand in both of mine to offer her some kind of support. "It's okay, you don't have to say anything at all. I'm sorry. I didn't mean to bring up bad memories."

"It's not your fault," she replied, staring down at my hands as if they were some kind of alien life-form that had latched onto her. She swallowed hard, then put her free hand over top of mine and gave it a gentle squeeze. "Every day is hard. Every day, I wonder how I'm going to get through it all alone. I mean, I have Xander and the kids but they're always looking up to me, whether it's for food or protection or even just to play with. I'm not sure how much longer I can put up with this."

"Then come home with me, Val," I said gently. "You can leave the kids here if you want. Xander can watch them for one night. Come and see Tumanako. It's not just a city, it's an idea. The name means 'hope'. People like you are exactly why we founded it. You need something to hope for as much as anyone – and you deserve it."

"Sometimes I don't feel like I deserve it," she admitted, her voice husky. "Sometimes I wonder if those of us who survived did something horrible in a past life to deserve this fate. Like maybe we're suffering because we were mass murderers or something."

"I used to feel that way, too," I admitted. "When I was all alone, with no one to help me, I used to cry myself to sleep every night, wondering what I'd done to deserve my fate. But, you know what? We haven't done anything to deserve this. We all deserve better. The problem is that the people who used to make things better for us are all gone now, so we have to make things better for ourselves. Come with us, Val. Just for one night. No contracts, no obligations. If you don't want to stay, then you don't have to. If you don't want to see us again, you don't have to. But if you do, then you'll be welcome to stay. You won't have to live in a library anymore. You won't have to do everything. Dennis can go to school with the other kids and make new friends. You can make new friends, too. I bet you don't remember what it's like to have friends anymore, do you?"

"Well, I guess Xander counts as a friend, but only because there's no one else," she said hesitantly, then she bit her lip and fell silent. I just waited, watching her, letting her think through the decision without pushing her any more.

Sure enough, less than a minute later, she looked up at me and nodded.

# Chapter Twenty-Three

Once we took Val home, we couldn't have convinced her to leave even if we'd wanted to. She lasted about ten minutes before she burst into tears, and had to sit down for a while to recover. Maddy appeared out of nowhere, just as she had that first day I'd awoken in the Hamilton bunker, and her tiny, unthreatening presence helped Val through the shock.

By midday, she'd seen everything we had to see and was thoroughly convinced that she wanted to be part of it. She insisted that we go fetch her son and bring him to Tumanako, and it took all of my wiles to convince her that she'd need to go with us or Xander was unlikely to let him go. She saw sense in the end, but heavy emotion left her a little irrational. She demanded that I come with her, and cried on my shoulder most of the way back to Wellington. Once she got there, the sight of her son's face seemed to steady her. She packed up their belongings, chased Xander and her foundlings into the trucks, and took them all back to Tumanako that very evening.

Val and the kids settled in quickly, but Xander was another story. If not for Valerie and Erica, then he might well have slipped off in the night and never come back. But with their help, he eventually decided to give us an honest chance – and although he wasn't as vocal about it as Val, it swiftly became clear that he liked what he saw.

Val metamorphosed into 'one of us' in no time flat. Within a couple of days, she became the perfect representation of my vision for the people of Tumanako: a lonely, frightened flower that bloomed within the greenhouse of safety and social acceptance into a happy, healthy, smiling rose. Every time I saw her, she was laughing and joking around with her new friends, and something about her unabashed joy was infectious. Even my little group of loners smiled when she was around. I saw her teasing stoic Warren on more than one occasion, and I could have sworn that he actually liked it.

The new kids went through a similar transformation over the course of the first week. At first, they were shy and standoffish, until they met Melody. With that special kind of magic only she was capable of, she took the new kids under her wing and taught them how to be children again. Soon, they were all part of her little pack of wild, fun-loving raggamuffins. There wasn't a morning that went by in silence with her there to lead them. They filled the corridors with happy noise, until it was time for class.

On one such morning not quite two weeks after their arrival, I was sitting in the dining room staring out the window and fiddling with a pen when I heard someone pull out the chair across from me. I glanced over, and was surprised to discover Johan sitting down with a bundle of purring tabby fluff in his arms.

"Wow, I can't believe Tigger's letting you carry her around," I commented, amused.

Johan laughed and nodded. "I have secret vet voodoo, didn't you hear? It's the first thing they teach you when you start studying."

I chuckled, setting put my pen down. "I can't believe how big she's getting. She must be almost a year old by now, but she's still all fluff."

"You're not all fluff anymore, are you?" he asked the cat, stroking her fur. She didn't answer, of course. She just purred and wound herself around his hands, rubbing herself against him. He smiled and glanced up at me. "Did you know she's pregnant, too?"

"What?" I gasped. "Who impregnated my kitten? I'll kill him!"

Johan just laughed again, not fazed by my horror. "It's a natural thing, Sandrine. Life comes, life goes. She seems to be quite happy with her condition, so it's nothing to get upset about. I just wanted to check if you'd like me to spay her after she's had the kittens. She's due in the next few weeks."

"Natural... right." I took a deep breath and closed my eyes for a second to calm myself down, then I shook my head. "Not just yet. There aren't a lot of domestic cats left around here, and we could use them to keep the pests out of the crops. Plus, they kind of help keep people sane. She certainly did that for me."

"Why don't you write about that, then?" he suggested, gesturing towards the blank page in front of me. "You seem to be at a loss for where to start."

"I am," I admitted, absently tracing my fingers over the smooth paper. "There's just so much to tell, you know? Ten years. More, if you count before the plague. Where do I even begin?"

"Start with how you met Tigger," he replied. He placed the kitten – now a cat – on the table beside me and rose to his feet. "See her back home when you're done with her?"

"Of course." I watched until he left the room, then I looked down at the fluffy tabby face staring up at me. I reached out to her and ran my hand across her back, marvelling at her softness.

As I did so, a memory surfaced of a time not so long ago, a time when I'd needed that softness to keep me sane. Ohaupo. It felt like a lifetime ago, even though it wasn't quite a year yet. How much things had changed – and so much for the better. One year earlier, I'd been a shaken, traumatised loner without a friend in the world except for this little feline. Now, I had a home, a husband, a baby on the way, friends and family all around me. I had a life. I had hope. It was a beautiful thing.

Tears welled up in my eyes as I picked up the pen, and began to transcribe the tale to paper for the very first time.

***

Knowing the library was water-tight and secure took the pressure off us and relieved the urgency we felt. We could take our time moving the contents back to Tumanako, and lock the place up when we weren't there. It was a slow, laborious process, but now we could pick and choose the days we went down there. Whenever the weather was fine, we'd send a group down with the best trucks and horse-drawn wagons we had and they'd come back full to the brim with cultural treasures.

As our library expanded, so did my waistline, until it got to the point I could barely waddle from bed to the toilet and back again without significant effort. One of our teams brought back an ultrasound machine, and I was its first victim. After a few minutes of cursing and scowling, and a fair amount of uncomfortable prodding, Professor Madurrit finally smiled and told us that our baby was very healthy.

I was a different story. As the weeks progressed, I started to feel less and less healthy. I could sense the change in the seasons, but summer's impending arrival did nothing to improve my mood. Eventually, I gave up on toughing it out in silence and went to see the doctor and the professor. Again, I was poked and prodded, examined from all angles, had tests run on me, blood drawn, and then they left the room to consult with one another in private.

A few minutes later, they came back in and both of them were smiling.

"You're a little bit vitamin D deficient, but not enough to be worried about," Professor Madurrit told me. "The baby's fine. You just haven't been getting as much sun as you're used to recently, and that's why you're feeling off-colour. Try sitting in the sun for fifteen minutes every day, and you'll feel right as rain in no time."

"No pun intended," Doctor Cross added, giving her a dark look. "And while we have you here, we should mention that we're almost ready to begin trials of the vaccine. Evie isn't showing any signs of wanting to wean yet, so we should be ready with plenty of time to spare."

"Good," I said, nodding my approval. I hauled myself up to my feet and stretched my back with a deep groan. "Are you sure it isn't twins? It feels like twins."

"It's definitely not twins," Professor Madurrit said with a laugh, slipping her arm around me to help. "Nor is it triplets, quadruplets, or an elephant calf. Come, dear. Let's go see if there's any trout left in the kitchen. It's not as good as salmon for vitamin D content, but it'll help."

"Oh, I've been avoiding the fish," I admitted, suddenly feeling guilty. "It made my morning sickness really bad in the first trimester, so I started staying away from it."

"And there's the culprit," Professor Madurrit said, her voice a mixture of teasing and gentle understanding. "It was probably the smell bothering you. I'm sure you noticed that your nose was particularly sensitive in the early days, too."

"It's still pretty sensitive," I replied. "Not as bad, though."

"Good," she said. "Between the fish and a bit of sunbathing, you'll feel better in no time."

She was right. I was back to my normal chirpy, sarcastic self within a couple of days. I made peace with my fishy friends and spent a little time sitting in the sun every day. My skin broke out in a rash of freckles, but I didn't care anymore. I remembered being horribly embarrassed by them when I was younger, but I'd outgrown that phase of my life. I was just happy to have friendly faces all around me, and many of those faces were just as freckled as mine.

As my due date grew closer and closer, I finally managed to convince myself that it was okay for me to sit around and gestate quietly. There were more than enough capable hands to help with the construction now, and people knew what needed to be done well enough that my leadership was only really needed in a spiritual sense. So, I forced myself to just relax, and divided my time between napping, working on my memoir, and organizing our ever-growing library.

Jim and Richard decided to officially get married and I was asked to officiate, which I did with great pleasure. When it came time to exchange the rings, they hit us all with a surprise: instead of physical rings, they announced that they wanted to have matching designs tattooed on their ring fingers.

"Nikora?" Richard asked, his face alive with new-found confidence. "My old friend, I know you studied *ta moko* in the old days, and I've seen you practicing it from time to time. Will you do the honours for us?"

"I'd be honoured to," Nick replied, grinning broadly.

After the reception, I stole a moment to approach the happy couple.

"Hey, guys," I said. "When you get those tattoos done, could I maybe watch?"

They both looked surprised for a second, then they laughed and nodded.

"Of course," Jim said. "Thinking of having it done yourself?"

"Maybe," I admitted. "It's a good idea, and I think Michael will like it."

"You can't do it until after the baby's born," a voice behind me said. I turned around, and found Nikora and Michael walking towards us. I raised my eyebrows at my husband, but he just shrugged and grinned at me. "I always wanted to get a tattoo, so I figured it couldn't hurt to ask. Nick says we can't get yours done until after the baby, but if you want to, I'm game."

This time, it was my turn to laugh. He really did know me too well. By the end of the evening, plans had been made for the two of us to get inked after the baby was born, and we both felt a strange sense of relief. As much as we loved the idea of our rings, the reality was something that we'd both struggled with. The tattoos gave as an alternative, one that I suspected would spread in popularity just as the flowers had.

One afternoon a few days later, Tigger vanished. When we eventually found her secret hidey-hole, there were four tiny kittens suckling on her belly. She'd never looked happier. The human citizens of Tumanako immediately started fighting over who was going to get to adopt the kittens when they were old enough, until Madeline put her foot down and scolded us all like naughty children.

Priya stuck to me like glue all the way through the last weeks of my pregnancy, and since she was Melody's favourite that meant that I was usually surrounded by a friendly mob of teens and pre-teens. Once I got used to it, it was pretty useful. Michael always looked like he was afraid to coddle me for fear of annoying me, but having the kids around meant that I had someone to help me at all times. That freed him up to be useful in other ways – ways that he was strangely closed-lipped about. I knew there was a surprise coming long before anyone said anything directly, from the stealthy glances and whispered conversations whenever I was around. I didn't know exactly what they were planning, but I knew it was going to be interesting.

Two weeks before my official due date, I was sitting in the library working on my memoirs again when Priya and Melody suddenly came rushing up out of nowhere, with the rest of the gang hot on their heels. I'd gotten used to their sudden appearances and disappearances by now, so I just looked up at them and raised an eyebrow.

Priya looked at Melody, then she giggled and shoved a bundle of cloth into my hand. "Put this on, Mama. We have a surprise for you!"

"That's not how it works," Melody said, her voice halfway between amusement and annoyance. She took the cloth back and held it up to show me that it was a makeshift blindfold. "No peeking, okay? You don't want to ruin the surprise!"

I just laughed and nodded. "Okay, okay. No peeking."

Once she'd tied the blindfold securely, the girls helped me to my feet and led me down the hallway to the elevator. I lost track of exactly where we were after that. I felt the ground change in texture beneath my feet from carpet to concrete, then I felt a breeze on my face. I could make an educated guess that I was outside, but that was about it.

Just as I was starting to wonder what was going on, I heard Michael's familiar voice. "Over here."

The girls led me a few steps closer, then Michael's big hands took over the process of guiding me. He turned me around and removed the blindfold.

I blinked a few times as my eyes adjusted to the bright sunlight – then I gasped in surprise.

"Michael? What is this?" I demanded, fixing my husband with the hairy eyeball.

"Well, I figured our apartment was a bit small to have kids running around in," he replied, giving me an embarrassed look that was so obviously faked I had to laugh.

"Did you deliberately add a white picket fence? I'm pretty sure this place didn't have one before." I paused and gave the little cottage a long, considering look. "Though, I guess it is quite pretty. It must have taken forever to tame the gardens."

"The fence isn't for you," he answered, putting on a haughty, defensive look. "The fence is for *me*. There's something else for you."

"Oh, is there just?" I replied, still laughing. "Should I be afraid?"

"No, you should just open the damn door, woman!" he instructed, folding his arms across his chest.

"Okay, fine. I will then." I stuck my tongue out at him, then I walked up to the door and opened it. It took a second for my eyes to adjust again, but when they did my heart just about melted. "Oh, Michael, it's beautiful. Look at this furniture."

"I thought you'd like that," he replied. I felt his arms slide around me from behind and his lips brushed my cheek. "Everyone helped me to salvage the best antique furniture we could find, and we picked a house outside the floodplain so you never have to worry about losing it. This is for you, honey. You, me, Priya, and our baby. Oh, and Alfred, too."

The dog's ears pricked up at the sound of his name, then he let out a happy yelp. Behind us, the girls giggled.

"There's something else, too," Priya said.

"Yup!" Melody agreed, nodding. "There used to be a tradition back in the old days, and we thought it was a good one to continue. It's called a…"

"Surprise party!" Several dozen voices yelled the words all at once. Right on cue, people sprang out from behind furniture and poured in from other rooms. I almost jumped out of my skin, but Michael was right there to keep me from falling over and hurting myself. He hugged me protectively while the others all cheered and threw flower petals over us. Bouquets of fresh-cut flowers appeared like magic, along with platters of food and bottles of homemade wine and juice. Before I could recover, Michael and the girls swept me into the crowd, and I found myself the recipient of more hugs than I'd ever had in my life.

Eventually, I was guided into a big, plush armchair, and people brought out gifts wrapped in shining paper. The sight of it brought tears to my eyes.

"Oh my God, you guys," I gasped, struggling not to cry. "You didn't have to do this…"

"No, we didn't have to," Anahera said gently, pressing a soft package wrapped in sparkly silver paper into my hands. "We wanted to. There's a difference."

"You've given us so much, Sandy," Gavin said, resting a hand on my shoulder. "And you've given it completely selflessly. You deserve every ounce of happiness that we can bring into your life, because you've brought so much joy into ours."

I sniffed and wiped my eyes, unable to think of any way to reply that would adequately express how I felt. Michael knelt down on the floor in front of me and took my hands in his, then together we carefully peeled the tape off the paper and opened the gift. Inside was a set of tiny baby clothes, little rompers that would stretch as our baby grew.

I picked them up and ran my figures over the fabric, marvelling at its softness. Finally, I looked up at Anahera and the others and gave them a tear-filled smile. "Thank you. Thank you all so much."

"Oh, we're only just beginning," Skye said. She threw her head back and let out the evilest cackle I'd ever heard in my life. We all froze and stared at her, then burst out laughing.

*** 

We spent the next few hours doing nothing but eating, drinking, laughing, and unwrapping presents, but it felt like food for the soul. Still, despite the relaxed atmosphere there was some part of us that was still conscious of our situation. Nothing went to waste, except for the tape on the presents. Even the paper was carefully salvaged, folded up, and put away to be reused. It used to be that survival turned us into the ultimate recyclers; now, planning for the future had the same result. Once the presents had been opened and everyone had come through to congratulate us and eat their fill, Skylar twined her arm around mine and gave me a wicked little smile.

"We're still not done yet," she told me. "This was all just a distraction while we finished off the last piece of your present."

"There's more?" I asked. "What more could there possibly be?"

"Come and see," she replied mysteriously. She helped me to my feet and led me back out into the sunshine. My new home was close to the Tumanako tower, but far enough away to ensure our privacy. The walk back took a couple of minutes, and I spent the entire time wondering just what she had in store for me. By the time we were approaching the corner that would bring us back to the front of the tower, I'd turned every possibility over in my head, but what I actually saw still took me completely by surprise.

"A statue?" I asked, confused. It took a second before I grasped exactly what I was seeing. "Wait, is that *me*? But… how?"

"Remember the sculptor who came up with the South Island guys?" Skye replied. "He's been working on this in secret for months. We moved it out here while you were at the baby shower. The base isn't quite finished, but he wanted to polish that off when it was in its final location."

"I can't believe this," I whispered. I moved closer and ran my fingertips over the smooth stone. My long hair was unmistakable, and even without me acting as a model the sculptor had managed to carve a striking resemblance of my face. I was carved much larger than life, kneeling on the ground with my head bowed. Opposite me, a smaller female figure was posed in the same way. It took me a second to realise that it was Maddy. We both had our hands cupped around something tiny and fragile. I looked closer, and saw that it was a stylized representation of New Zealand, sculpted to look like a delicate seedling.

"We call it 'The Prophet and the Hero'," Skye explained. "Once the base is finished, we're going to add a plaque with your names on it, so that future generations will remember the spirit that founded Tumanako."

"Everyone was important to the founding of Tumanako," I protested, suddenly upset. "Not just me and Maddy. Every single soul here deserves to be recognised for their contribution."

"And they are," she replied. "This statue has your face on it, but it represents all of us, the founding family of the new New Zealand. You represent our strength, our creativity, our drive, and our stubborn determination, while Maddy's image represents our heart, our soul, our spirituality, and our hope for the future."

"Well, I like it," Maddy said. I hadn't heard her arrive, so her sudden appearance made me jump. She just smiled and reached up to take my hand. "Are you ready, Miss Sandy?"

"Ready for what?" I asked, suddenly perplexed.

Maddy just smiled a little wider. A second later, a terrible pain shot through me, and sent me reeling.

"Ow! Jesus! What was that?" I demanded, clutching my swollen belly. "Ow! Ow, ow, ow!"

"Sandy!" Skye cried, rushing over to grab me and help keep me upright. "What's wrong? What is it?"

"It… it hurts…" I gasped, struggling to articulate my pain.

Maddy let out a girlish giggle and did a little pirouette beside us. "Don't worry, Granddaddy's already on his way. The baby's coming!"

# Chapter Twenty-Four

"What?" I cried, horrified. "But it's too early! The baby isn't due for another two weeks!"

Suddenly, Michael was beside me, and both Professor Madurrit and Doctor Cross were shoving their way to the front of the crowd.

"Doc!" I called. "It's too soon! Isn't it too soon?"

"Calm down, Ms McDermott," Doc instructed calmly. "Some babies are just in a hurry to be born. Let's get you upstairs and take a look. And remember – breathe."

"That's easy for you to say!" I complained. "It's taken me a while to accept that I'm going to be a mum, but by God I will kill someone if this baby is not okay."

Michael snatched me off my feet and carried me up to the infirmary without another word, with just about the entire population of Tumanako following along behind us. Once we reached the infirmary, Doc kicked them all out except for the Professor, the nurses, Michael, Skye, and Anahera, who was to act as my labour coach – but even with just them the room felt crowded.

Rebecca and Professor Madurrit stripped me and dressed me in a light robe, then they lifted me up onto one of the infirmary beds. After a few minutes of tests and examinations, Doc smiled reassuringly and patted my shoulder. "Everything's fine, Ms McDermott."

"Thank goodness," I gasped, leaning back against the pillows. Then realisation struck, and I shot him a horrified look. "Wait – does this mean I'm actually in labour? Now? But I'm not ready yet!"

"Ready or not, it looks like your baby is in quite a hurry," Professor Madurrit told me. "I just had a look, and you're already at four centimetres. Nothing's actually going to happen for a while yet, so just lie back and try to relax. We'll tell you when it's time for you to get into the birthing position. You still want to squat, right?"

I tried to answer, but my voice didn't want to respond to me so I just nodded vigorously. If gravity would help the pain be over quicker, then so be it. I'd cursed my way through all those exercises for a reason, now it was time to use the muscles I'd toned up preparing for this day.

Professor Madurrit beckoned Anahera over, and she fell into place beside me. She held my hand gently and guided me through the breathing exercises just like we'd practised. I heard other voices around me as the medical staff organised things, but I just ignored them and, focused on Anahera. There was no chance of an epidural, and even if there had been I would have refused it. Once the initial shock wore off, my natural stubbornness surfaced. If I had to become a mother then I was determined to do it as naturally as possible, unless there was a good reason not to. The health and well-being of my baby was my first concern, even above my own.

"Don't worry, dear," Anahera whispered, brushing my hair back away from my forehead with a gentle, maternal hand. "You can do this. I know you can. Just think, once this is over you'll have a beautiful bouncing baby of your very own."

"I'm not sure I'm ready," I admitted, my voice a harsh whisper. Another contraction clenched my midsection and made me growl like a wild animal, but I pushed past the pain to focus on Anahera. "I've been trying to tell myself I'm ready, but I'm not sure."

"You're never ready to be a mother," she replied. "Everyone is terrified, confused, and anxious the first time, but experience will teach you everything you need to know. Don't forget, you're going to be surrounded by many mothers the whole way through, both new mums like yourself and experienced ones like me. We'll take care of you and help you take care of your baby."

I nodded and tried to answer, but the pain stole my breath away again. Anahera helped me into a sitting position and put her arms around me.

"You'll do fine," she whispered reassuringly. "We've got some time before your baby is ready to actually come out. Sometimes moving helps relieve the pain. Would you like to walk around? Or perhaps take a warm shower?"

The contraction faded again, and I finally found the breath to reply. "Yeah… I think a shower would be nice." I finally looked up and saw Michael hovering nearby looking anxious, while Skye was busy helping the nurses with whatever they were doing.

"Do you want me to help you?" Michael asked nervously. "You're not going to punch me again, are you?"

"I might, but not yet," I replied dryly. To answer his question about whether or not I wanted his help, I just held a hand out to him and gave him a tiny smile. He returned the smile with obvious relief, and hurried over to put his arm around me. He and Anahera did the robe up around my middle to preserve what little dignity I had left, then they marched me off to the bathrooms.

I was surprised to discover that the hallway outside was packed with people, just like after Ryan had been shot, but the atmosphere was completely different now. Everyone was smiling. They looked excited, anxious, and even a little bit nervous, but all of them looked happy.

"They're on birth watch," Michael said suddenly, looking almost as surprised as I felt. "Like the death watch, except the other way around. This is the first baby to officially be born in Tumanako, and they already love her as much as they love you."

The thought made me smile, despite the pain of another contraction. Everyone had a kind word for me as we walked past them, and helping hands were everywhere if I needed them. Michael and Anahera helped me through a quick, hot shower, and then we spent the next few hours just keeping me busy while nature took its course.

Eventually, the contractions started to come closer and closer together. I was ushered back onto the table so the doctors could check on our progress, but by that stage the pain was so intense that I couldn't keep track of what was going on. I heard Professor Madurrit tell me that it was time, then I was ushered over to squat on a birthing stool that they'd salvaged a few weeks earlier. Anahera knelt in front of me, her hands on my shoulders to brace me and help me keep my balance.

"It's time, darling," she told me firmly. "Time to meet your baby. Breathe deep, and push!"

I did as I was told. The pain was intense, worse than anything else I'd ever been through in my life, but Anahera's words rang in my mind and gave me the strength I needed to make it through. I heard myself yelling until my throat was raw, swearing up a storm, and even threatening poor Michael, but all of that stopped mattering when I heard one thing: the sound of a baby's cry. I burst into tears and barely heard Anahera say, "It's a girl!"

I lost track of the baby while Michael and Anahera helped me back into bed, but only for a few seconds. Skye came over as soon as I was settled and placed the squirming newborn in my arms.

"Oh my god," I gasped, staring down at her little face. "I… I made this. I made a people! A tiny people!"

"No, *we* made a tiny people," Michael replied, laughing. "I helped, too!"

"Oh sure," I answered, unable to keep the smile off my face despite the pain and exhaustion. "I just lugged her around inside my body for the last eight and a half months, then tore myself in half squeezing her out, but by all means, take all the credit."

Michael just laughed even harder. He wrapped his arms around me and planted a kiss on my cheek. "I don't want all the credit. Just some. And lots of hugs. You know, daddy privileges."

"Oh, well I guess you can have that," I replied. I gave him a quick kiss, then looked back down at our baby again. She was red, wrinkled, and wriggling like an eel, but to my eyes she was the most beautiful thing in the world. She wasn't just my firstborn child, she was something more. A symbol. A step towards the future. She represented the end of one chapter of my life, and the beginning of something new and wonderful.

I couldn't wait to get started.

***

With Skylar's blessing, we named the baby Ryana. In the days and weeks following her birth, I often found myself struggling to cope with balancing my newfound responsibilities as a mother with my duties as the leader of Tumanako, but everyone was patient with me. To no one's great surprise, Michael look on far more than his fair share of the tasks required to keep our baby content and healthy. I'd never seen him happier than when he was changing her nappy or rocking her to sleep.

Occasionally I found myself struggling to produce enough milk to feed her, but when that happened the rest of the community came to my rescue. Hannah or Tala or any of the other new mothers were always there to help, either by acting as a wet nurse or by bottling their spare milk for us. Their willingness to help left me feeling warm inside, because it was exactly the kind of community spirit that I'd hoped to create when we founded Tumanako. Just as Anahera had promised, the community was there to help us learn to care for our baby, and to teach us how to be the best parents we could possibly be.

It took weeks for my body to recover from the traumatic act of giving birth, but it did. Thanks to the excellent medical care I received from my friends and the exercises that Professor Madurrit had insisted I do every day, I bounced back in good time. By the middle of summer, I was fit enough that I could work in the garden, or even help with the construction projects around the village. Michael and I had our tattoos done, and took our rings off permanently. They meant too much for us to throw away, of course, so we mounted them on the wall above our bed, strung together on a single chain to symbolize our unity.

Our community grew right along with our new baby. Every day, stragglers drifted in from the countryside and new faces joined our community. By the end of summer, Tumanako was home to nearly six hundred souls. Just as we'd hoped, we outgrew the tower and began to spread out into the grounds around Tumanako. Couples began to settle down and start families.

Skylar came to term and gave birth to a healthy baby boy with a shock of red hair. Though it was obvious who the biological father was, Hemi adopted the baby as his own without question, and it was a delight to see them both so happy.

Shortly after Skylar gave birth, Bobby approached us both and did the unthinkable: he apologised to us, honestly and sincerely, with tears in his eyes. We were stunned, but once the shock wore off we both accepted his apology without reservation. Matt Yousefi took a liking to him, and the two of them struck up a tentative friendship. With Matt's help, Bobby finally began to integrate into our society. Watching him learn to smile again was one of the most rewarding things I'd ever seen.

Isabelle began to outgrow her nervousness and come into her own, thanks to the friendship she developed with Gavin. I gave in to curiosity one day and asked if there was anything between them, only to be told that Isabelle had finally discovered what she liked best was her own freedom. Whenever I saw her, she was learning something new. One day I saw her working on the mural with our resident artists, and the next she was training with one of the self-defence classes. The combat classes gave her a confidence I'd never seen before, and watching her squeal and jump for joy whenever she won a sparring match brought me great pleasure.

The community became so focused on what was happening inside it that we almost forgot there was a world outside the walls. We kept reminding one another to be aware and watchful, but no one could have predicted the momentous event that would force us to start thinking of ourselves as part of a wider world again.

That event came in early autumn, as the leaves were just starting to think about changing colour. I'd led a short scavenging trip to Wellington to look for anything we could use; winter was coming again, and although we felt secure in our new home we wanted to be prepared. We were half way through loading the truck with salvaged blankets and duvets when one of the scouts came running up to me, frantically flailing his arms.

"There's a boat!" he cried breathlessly. "There's a boat in the harbour!"

I shot him a curious look. "There are always boats in the harbour. They don't go anywhere."

"No!" he gasped, shaking his head. "No, there's a new boat – a frigate! It's just arrived!"

"What?" I froze, staring at him. "Are you serious?"

"Yes, I'm serious," the scout replied. He grabbed my arm and half-led, half-dragged me through the winding streets towards the waterfront. The rest of our party dropped whatever they were doing and raced after us.

By the time we reached the waterfront, the frigate had dropped anchor in the harbour. "Binoculars!" I demanded.

Someone put a pair into my hand. I lifted them up and stared through them, trying to make out the details of what we were seeing.

"There are people moving about on the deck," I told the people around me. "I can't tell how many. I think they're preparing a boat to come ashore. Wait – there's a flag! It's… it's the New Zealand flag? No– no it's not, there are too many stars. Oh my God! It's the Australian flag! The Australians are here!" Gasps of shock rang out all around me. I lowered the binoculars and looked around, just as stunned as the others sounded. "What are they doing here? *How* are they here?"

"If they're coming ashore, then I guess we're going to find out in a couple of minutes," Gavin said, his expression painfully neutral but I could see the concern in his eye. If this was an invasion, then we were sitting ducks. A ship like that would need almost a third of Tumanako's entire population to man it, which meant that we were seriously outnumbered – not to mention outgunned.

Gavin put his hand on my shoulder and gave it a squeeze, a gesture of silent solidarity that spoke far more than words. We all waited together as the frigate lowered a smaller craft into the water. The inflatable swung around and crept towards shore at what felt like a snail's pace, even though we could see from its wake that it was travelling at a good speed. By the time it was close enough that we could see the faces of the people on board, I was feeling sick with anxiety and anticipation, but there was nothing we could do except wait.

Finally, the boat came to a rest against the edge of the dock not even a few meters away from us, and a single, uniformed man stood up. He gave us a long look, and for a second we all held our breath – then, suddenly, he saluted us.

"Permission to come ashore?" he called, in a voice that carried an accent I hadn't heard in a very long time.

Tears sprang unbidden into my eyes. I pulled away from the group and walked over to offer him a hand up onto the dock. "Permission granted."

Once he was on dry ground, he straightened his uniform and looked at the little group of faces huddled behind me.

"You have no idea how glad I am to see someone alive down here," he said, his voice thick with emotion. "I'm sorry it took us so long to get here, but it took a lot of doing to assemble and train a crew."

"You came to check on us?" I asked, struggling to blink back the tears that very much wanted to roll down my cheeks. "It's been a decade."

"I know," he said. "We never forgot about you. There aren't many of us left, but there are some. We had to find a way to check on our little sister nation somehow. It wasn't easy, but I guess you know that better than most."

"Yes, I do," I replied, suddenly fighting the urge to laugh. "We were so afraid... we thought we might have been the only humans left on Earth, and everyone else was gone forever. I can't believe you're standing here."

"We thought the same thing for a while," the sailor replied, "but we've managed to make contact with little pockets of survivors all over the world. The Royal Family may be dead for all we know, but the spirit of the Commonwealth lives on in us."

Something about that sentence struck just the right chord with me. I burst into tears and threw my arms around the stranger's neck in a hug. We embraced for nearly a minute, then I shoved him back and gave him a watery smile.

"Bring your crew ashore," I suggested. "Let us show you the city we've built for ourselves. It isn't perfect, but it doesn't have to be. It's home."

# Epilogue

"...And they lived happily ever after. The end!" The little girl slammed the book closed, and looked expectantly at her teacher. "Can we go now?"

"Sophie!" Kylie exclaimed, struggling to hide her amusement behind a mask of horror. "That isn't even close to the end of their story. Don't you want to know what happens next?"

"We already know what happens next, Mum," Sophie complained, rolling her eyes and folding her arms across her chest. "We read this last year. We don't want to read it again!"

The rest of the class laughed. Kylie hid a chuckle behind a cough, then shook her head. "Come on, kids. This is your great-grandparents we're talking about. Without them, we wouldn't have a home, we wouldn't have the vaccine – most of us wouldn't even be alive. Just one more chapter?"

"No!" Sophie cried, covering her face with her hands. "It's Founder's Day! We want to go to the feasting before the grown-ups eat everything. Please, Mum? Please?"

"Please, miss?" another child asked, and then they all joined in. "Please? Pleeeease?"

Kylie finally gave in and laughed. "Oh, fine. It's Founder's Day. I suppose the best way you can honour their memory is by enjoying it. Go on, then – but I want you back here bright and early tomorrow morning! Don't forget you've got a maths test."

A chorus of cheers and groans went up from around the class, but it was swiftly drowned out by the screech of chairs and the pounding of footsteps as the entire class raced out of the room. Kylie heaved a sigh, then she stood up and walked around the room collecting the copies of the collected memoirs of Tumanako's founders from the desks. Just as she was returning the last copy to its place on the shelves, there was a light tap on the door. She glanced back over her shoulder, and found a familiar face loitering in the doorway.

"Hello, Mr Cross," she greeted with mock formality. The young man laughed and came over to kiss her cheek.

"Hello, Ms McDermott," he replied. "Did you let your class out early, too?"

"Yeah," she said, absently touching the locket around her throat, passed down to her by her foster aunt, Priyanka; her cousins were all boys, and her aunt had wanted the keepsake to stay on the female side of the family. It could have gone to her mother, Ryana, but they'd decided to pass it straight down to her. Kylie sighed in memory, then shook her head and smiled at her husband. "You know how the kids get on Founder's Day. They don't want to sit around reading books when they could be running around, playing, and stuffing food down their gullets."

"I know," he said, putting his arm around her shoulders. "Just remember, to them these people may as well be characters from a novel. They're not as real to the kids as they are to you and me. They were our grandparents, our aunts and uncles. We knew them. Sophie was only a baby when we buried them. Speaking of which – Nana will want us at the memorial, and you know how much your mum hates it when we're late. We should probably get a move on."

Kylie nodded and went to fetch her coat. Founder's Day fell in early spring, and that meant that the weather was fickle at best. It could go from brilliant sunshine to pouring with rain in a heartbeat. Tumanako was her home, though, and she knew the weather better than her own moods.

Tama linked his arm through hers, and together they left the school building and went out into the city streets. People were everywhere, a swarming mass of smiling humanity out enjoying the holiday regardless of the weather. Kylie smiled and waved to her friends, but she didn't stop to chat. There would be time for that later. Now was the time for remembrance.

The walk to the family crypt was long but ultimately pleasant. She still remembered the day they'd decided to build it. The entire community had gotten together both to collectively mourn the loss of their heroes, and to thank them for a lifetime of service. Beautiful flowers grew in well-tended beds on either side of the path, and the sweeping boughs of trees protected them from sun and rain alike.

Where once the grave of Ryan Knowles had stood alone, they'd built a crypt to honour the memory of every person who had dedicated their life in the name of an idealistic dream all those years ago. A plaque adorned the entrance, carved with dozens of names that were so familiar to her – and in front of the plaque stood a wizened old woman with long hair that had once been raven black, and was now steel-grey with age.

"Nana?" Tama called. It was unnecessary, of course. No one could ever sneak up on his grandmother. Even as a child, he'd never been able to get away with anything when she was around. Somehow, she always knew.

The woman turned and smiled at them both. "Hello, dear. Hello, Kylie – ah, I see you've been reading the stories again. Trying to remember?"

"Every year," Kylie said softly. She walked up beside the old woman and reached out to touch the names of her grandparents, carved at the very top of the list of founders. "I miss them sometimes. I wish that Sophie could have gotten to know them better."

A smile crinkled the old woman's lips. "At least your Sophie will have the chance to grow up safe and healthy. That's the most important thing."

"I know." Kylie sighed and closed her eyes, running her fingers across the cold metal as if that could help the twisting of grief in her gut. "The children don't understand, though. I try to teach them, try to keep the memory alive, but the founders are just stories to them."

"Not stories, my dear," Madeline Cross said, turning to face her fully. "Legends. The founders have passed from our world into the world of legends. That means they'll *never* be forgotten."

"Let me guess," Kylie said, a shy smile dancing across her face. "You know because you've foreseen it?"

Madeline laughed and shook her head. "I don't need to foresee it to know it'll happen, dear. It already has."

THE END

# Kiwiana Language Guide

| | |
|---|---|
| *Aotearoa* | Maori, New Zealand. Literally "The Land Of The Long White Cloud". |
| *Arapuni* | Location; a town in the central Waikato, home to the Arapuni Power Station. |
| *Bush* | Specifically, "native bush". Refers to an area of native forest, which is characterised by a particularly thick shrub layer dominated by indigenous ferns and bushes. Native bush is often very thick and dark, and can be very difficult to travel through as a result. |
| *Central Plateau* | Colloquial, the Tongariro National Park. It is an area of major cultural significance to the various peoples of New Zealand, and contains numerous Maori sacred sites. Above ground, it is a massive rock desert that covers approximately 795.98 kilometres and is home to the volcanic cones Tongariro, Ruapehu, and Ngauruhoe. Below ground, it is the centre of a massive geothermal field that spreads across most of the North Island. It is one of the few North Island areas that regularly sees snowfall. |
| *G'day* | Colloquial version of "Good day". |
| *Hamilton* | Location; A medium-sized city in the Waikato |
| *Horizons Region* | The Horizons Region is an agricultural region in the lower half of the North Island. The official name of the area is the Manawatu-Wanganui region. |
| *Hutt Valley* | An area in the Greater Wellington Region that contains the cities of Upper and Lower Hutt, and the fertile Hutt River. |
| *Kia Ora* | Maori, "Hello". |
| *Maori* | Relating to the original peoples of New Zealand. May be used to refer to their cultural traits (*e.g. "she tried to live by the traditional Maori ways."*), language (*e.g. "he spoke Maori."*) or ethnicity (*e.g. "my grandmother was Maori"*). The Maori culture evolved from Polynesian migrants that arrived in New Zealand around 1,000 years ago. |
| *Mate* | Colloquial, a contextually sensitive word that is usually used in place of the word "friend". Can be used sarcastically or in threat just as readily as being used in a friendly fashion, *e.g. "You're going to regret that, mate."* |
| *Ngauruhoe* | Geography; the central volcano in Tongariro National Park. Ngauruhoe is an active stratovolcano. |
| *Ohaupo* | Location; a small town in the Waikato region, 17 kilometres south of Hamilton. |

| | |
|---|---|
| *Porirua* | A coastal city in the Wellington Region. |
| *Ruapehu* | Geography; the southernmost volcano in Tongariro National Park. Ruapehu is one of the most active stratovolcanoes in the world. |
| *Taihape* | A small town in the central North Island. |
| *Tā Moko* | Maori Culture; traditional Maori face and body tattoos. |
| *Te Awamutu* | Location; a medium-sized township in the central Waikato. In the *Survivors* world, this town was razed by a large earthquake several years after the plague. |
| *Tokaanu* | Location; a small township on the southern shore of Lake Taupo. |
| *Tokoroa* | Location; a medium-sized town located in the central Waikato, half way between Hamilton and Taupo. |
| *Tumanako* | Maori, "Hope". |
| *Waikato* | A large agricultural region in the central North Island. |
| *Waiouru* | Location; a small town in the Manawatu-Wanganui region, located approximately 25 kilometres south of Mount Ruapehu. It is home to the Waiouru Army Camp and Airfield. |
| *Wellington* | Location; capital of New Zealand, and southernmost city in the North Island. |

# Afterword

When I started this project in December 2012, I honestly didn't believe that I was going to see the end of it. I never could have guessed just how popular *The Survivors* would become. Now, just over two years later, I've written the final book in the series and you've just finished reading it.

Is this the end for *The Survivors*? Doubtful. This is the end of the first arc, yes, but I've already got a few ideas for future novels. There are still so many adventures to be had, and so many concepts to explore. I don't know when it'll happen, but I have no doubt that it will.

While you're waiting for that day to come, why not check out my other series, *The Immortelle*? It's a raunchy, action-packed science fiction series with a side of humour, and writing it helped keep me sane through the darker moments of *The Survivors*. There are sample chapters available free of charge on my website.

If you enjoyed this book as much as I enjoyed bringing it to you, please consider leaving a review. Reviews are the life-blood of all independent authors, and are vital to our success. Plus, I love hearing that people enjoyed my story! Reviews may drive my sales, but it's you – the reader – that keeps *me* going through all the ups and downs.

Please feel free to contact me via any of the following with your questions, comments, or feedback:

| | |
|---|---|
| Website: | http://www.vldreyer.com |
| Email: | info@vldreyer.com |
| Amazon: | http://amazon.com/author/vldreyer |
| Facebook: | http://www.facebook.com/VictoriaLDreyer |
| Twitter: | @VL_Dreyer |
| Patreon: | http://www.patreon.com/vldreyer |

It has been my pleasure and my honour to write this series for all of you, and I thank each and every one of you for joining me on this journey. Where will the future take us? I don't know yet, but like Sandy said… I can't wait to find out!

*V. L. Dreyer*

# About The Author

Born in Auckland, New Zealand, Victoria Dreyer began her career in the most peculiar of ways: as the writer and illustrator of graphic novels. Although her ultimate dream was always to become a novelist, she spent many years exploring other mediums before finally returning to the one she felt most comfortable with, the written word.

Ms Dreyer is a voracious reader, and in addition to the post-apocalyptic genre she also enjoys reading and writing science fiction, modern fantasy, and the paranormal romance genres.

She currently resides in the Waikato with a large collection of books and several very spoiled cats.

HTTP://WWW.VLDREYER.COM